"To all the readers who discovered The Fountainhead *and asked me many questions about the wider application of its ideas, I want to say that I am answering these questions in the present novel, and that* The Fountainhead *was only an overture to* Atlas Shrugged. *I trust that no one will tell me that men such as I write about don't exist. That this book has been written—and published—is my proof that they do."*
—*Ayn Rand*

AYN RAND's first novel, *We the Living*, was published in 1936, followed by *Anthem*. With the publication of *The Fountainhead* in 1943, she achieved a spectacular and enduring success. Rand's unique philosophy, Objectivism, has gained a worldwide audience. The fundamentals of her philosophy are set forth in such books as *Introduction to Objectivist Epistemology, The Virtue of Selfishness, Capitalism: The Unknown Ideal,* and *The Romantic Manifesto. Journals of Ayn Rand*, a selection from her notebooks, is available in a Plume edition. Ayn Rand died in 1982.

LEONARD PEIKOFF, universally recognized as the world's premier Ayn Rand scholar, worked closely with Rand for thirty years and was designated by her as heir to her estate. He has taught philosophy at Hunter College and New York University. His books include *The Ominous Parallels* and *Objectivism: The Philosophy of Ayn Rand,* and he is the co-editor of *The Ayn Rand Reader*, which is available in a Plume edition. For further information, go to his website, alshow.com.

THE WRITINGS OF AYN RAND

FICTION

Atlas Shrugged
The Fountainhead
We the Living
Anthem
The Early Ayn Rand
Night of January 16th

PHILOSOPHY

General
Objectivism: The Philosophy of Ayn Rand
by Dr. Leonard Peikoff
The Ayn Rand Lexicon
The Ayn Rand Reader
Philosophy: Who Needs It?
The Voice of Reason
For the New Intellectual
The Ominous Parallels by Dr. Leonard Peikoff
The Virtue of Selfishness

Epistemology
An Introduction to Objectivist Epistemology

Politics/Economics
Capitalism: The Unknown Ideal
Return of the Primitive

Art, Literature, and Letters
The Romantic Manifesto
The Art of Fiction
The Art of Nonfiction
Journals of Ayn Rand
Letters of Ayn Rand

ATLAS

SHRUGGED

AYN RAND

A PLUME BOOK

PLUME
Published by Penguin Group
Penguin Group (USA) Inc., 375 Hudson Street, New York, New York 10014, USA
Penguin Group (Canada), 10 Alcorn Avenue, Toronto, Ontario M4V 3B2, Canada (a division of Pearson Penguin Canada Inc.)
Penguin Books Ltd., 80 Strand, London WC2R 0RL, England
Penguin Ireland, 25 St. Stephen's Green, Dublin 2, Ireland (a division of Penguin Books Ltd.)
Penguin Group (Australia), 250 Camberwell Road, Camberwell, Victoria 3124, Australia (a division of Pearson Australia Group Pty. Ltd.)
Penguin Books India Pvt. Ltd., 11 Community Centre, Panchsheel Park, New Delhi - 110 017, India
Penguin Group (NZ), Cnr Airborne and Rosedale Roads, Albany, Auckland 1310, New Zealand (a division of Pearson New Zealand Ltd.)
Penguin Books (South Africa) (Pty.) Ltd., 24 Sturdee Avenue, Rosebank, Johannesburg 2196, South Africa

Penguin Books Ltd., Registered Offices: 80 Strand, London WC2R 0RL, England

Published by Plume, a member of Penguin Group (USA) Inc. Previously published in a Dutton edition.

First Plume Printing, August 1999
First Plume Printing (Centennial Edition), January 2005
20 19 18 17 16 15 14 13 12 11

℗ REGISTERED TRADEMARK—MARCA REGISTRADA

The Library of Congress has catalogued the Dutton edition as follows:
Rand, Ayn.
  Atlas shrugged / Ayn Rand.
  With a new introduction
    p. cm.
  ISBN 0-525-93418-9
  ISBN 0-452-01187-6 (pbk.)
  ISBN 0-452-28636-0 (centennial ed.)
  I. Title.
PS3535.A547A94   1992
813'.52—dc20   91-36842
                                          CIP

Printed in the United States of America

PUBLISHER'S NOTE
This is a work of fiction. Names, characters, places, and incidents either are the product of the author's imagination or are used fictitiously, and any resemblance to actual persons, living or dead, business establishments, events, or locales is entirely coincidental.

TO FRANK O'CONNOR

CONTENTS

PART

III

A IS A

INTRODUCTION TO
THE 35th ANNIVERSARY EDITION

Ayn Rand held that art is a "re-creation of reality according to an artist's metaphysical value-judgments." By its nature, therefore, a novel (like a statue or a symphony) does not require or tolerate an explanatory preface; it is a self-contained universe, aloof from commentary, beckoning the reader to enter, perceive, respond.

Ayn Rand would never have approved of a didactic (or laudatory) introduction to her book, and I have no intention of flouting her wishes. Instead, I am going to give her the floor. I am going to let you in on some of the thinking she did as she was preparing to write *Atlas Shrugged*.

Before starting a novel, Ayn Rand wrote voluminously in her journals about its theme, plot, and characters. She wrote not for any audience, but strictly for herself—that is, for the clarity of her own understanding. The journals dealing with *Atlas Shrugged* are powerful examples of her mind in action, confident even when groping, purposeful even when stymied, luminously eloquent even though wholly unedited. These journals are also a fascinating record of the step-by-step birth of an immortal work of art.

In due course, all of Ayn Rand's writings will be published. For this 35th anniversary edition of *Atlas Shrugged*, however, I have selected, as a kind of advance bonus for her fans, four typical journal entries. Let me warn new readers that the passages reveal the plot and will spoil the book for anyone who reads them before knowing the story.

As I recall, "Atlas Shrugged" did not become the novel's title until Miss Rand's husband made the suggestion in 1956. The working title throughout the writing was "The Strike."

The earliest of Miss Rand's notes for "The Strike" are dated January 1, 1945, about a year after the publication of *The Fountainhead*. Naturally enough, the subject on her mind was how to differentiate the present novel from its predecessor.

Theme: What happens to the world when the Prime Movers go on strike.

This means—a picture of the world with its motor cut off. Show: what, how, why. The specific steps and incidents—in terms of persons, their spirits, motives, psychology and actions—and, secondarily, proceeding from persons, in terms of history, society and the world.

The theme requires: to show who are the prime movers and why, how they function. Who are their enemies and why, what are the motives behind the hatred for and the enslavement of the prime movers; the nature of the obstacles placed in their way, and the reasons for it.

This last paragraph is contained entirely in *The Fountainhead*. Roark and Toohey are the complete statement of it. Therefore, this is not the direct theme of *The Strike*—but it is part of the theme and must be kept in mind, stated again (though briefly) to have the theme clear and complete.

First question to decide is on whom the emphasis must be placed—on the prime movers, the parasites or the world. The answer is: *The world*. The story must be primarily a picture of the whole.

In this sense, *The Strike* is to be much more a "social" novel than *The Fountainhead*. *The Fountainhead* was about "individualism and collectivism within man's soul"; it showed the nature and function of the creator and the second-hander. The primary concern there was with Roark and Toohey—showing *what they are*. The rest of the characters were variations of the theme of the relation of the ego to others—mixtures of the two extremes, the two poles: Roark and Toohey. The primary concern of the story was the characters, the people as such—their *natures*. Their relations to each other—which is society, men in relation to men—were secondary, an unavoidable, direct consequence of Roark set against Toohey. But it was not the theme.

Now, it is this *relation* that must be the theme. Therefore, the personal becomes secondary. That is, the personal is necessary only to the extent needed to make the relationships clear. In *The Fountainhead* I showed that Roark moves the world—that the Keatings feed upon him and hate him for it, while the Tooheys are out consciously to destroy him. But the theme was Roark—not Roark's relation to the world. Now it will be the relation.

In other words, I must show in what concrete, specific way the world is moved by the creators. Exactly *how* do the second-handers live on the creators. Both in *spiritual* matters—*and* (most particularly) in concrete physical events. (Concentrate on the concrete, physical events—but don't forget to keep in mind at all times how the physical proceeds from the spiritual.) . . .

However, for the purpose of this story, I do not start by showing *how* the second-handers live on the prime movers in actual, everyday reality—nor do I start by showing a normal world. (That comes in only in necessary retrospect, or flashback, or by implication in the events themselves.) I start with *the fantastic premise of the prime movers going on strike*. This is the actual heart and center of the novel. A distinction carefully to be observed here: I do not set out to glorify the prime mover (*that* was *The Fountainhead*). I set out to show how desperately the world needs prime movers, and how viciously it treats them. And I show it on a hypothetical case—*what happens to the world without them*.

In *The Fountainhead* I did not show how desperately the world needed Roark—except by implication. I did show how viciously the world treated him, and why. I showed *mainly what he is*. It was Roark's story. *This* must be the world's story—in relation to its prime movers. (Almost—the story of a body in relation to its heart—a body dying of anemia.)

I don't show directly what the prime movers *do*—that's shown only by implication. *I show what happens when they don't do it.* (Through that, you see the picture of what they do, their place and their role.) (*This* is an important guide for the construction of the story.)

In order to work out the story, Ayn Rand had to understand fully why the prime movers *allowed* the second handers to live on them—why the creators had not gone on strike throughout history—what errors even the best of them made that kept them in thrall to the worst. Part of the answer is dramatized in the character of Dagny Taggart, the railroad heiress who declares war on the strikers. Here is a note on her psychology, dated April 18, 1946:

Her error—and the cause of her refusal to join the strike—is over-optimism and over-confidence (particularly this last).

Over-optimism—in that she thinks men are better than they are, she doesn't really understand them and is generous about it.

Over-confidence—in that she thinks she can do more than an individual actually can. She thinks she can run a railroad (or the world) single-handed, she can make people do what she wants or needs, what is right, by the sheer force of her own talent; not by *forcing* them, of course, not by enslaving them and giving orders—but by the sheer over-abundance of her own energy; she will show them how, she can teach them and persuade them, she is so able that they'll catch it from her. (This is still faith in their rationality, in the omnipotence of reason. The mistake? Reason is not automatic. Those who deny it cannot be conquered by it. Do not count on them. Leave them alone.)

On these two points, Dagny is committing an important (but excusable and understandable) error in thinking, the kind of error individualists and creators often make. It is an error proceeding from the best in their nature and from a proper principle, but this principle is misapplied. . . .

The error is this: it is proper for a creator to be optimistic, in the deepest, most basic sense, since the creator believes in a benevolent universe and functions on that premise. But it is an error to extend that optimism to other *specific* men. First, it's not necessary, the creator's life and the nature of the universe do not require it, his life does not depend on others. Second, man is a being with free will; therefore, each man is potentially good or evil, and it's up to him and only to him (through his reasoning mind) to decide which he wants to be. The decision will affect only him; it is not (and cannot and should not be) the primary concern of any other human being.

Therefore, while a creator does and must worship *Man* (which means his own highest potentiality; which is his natural self-reverence), he must not make the mistake of thinking that this means the necessity to worship *Mankind* (as a collective). These are two entirely different conceptions, with entirely— (immensely and diametrically opposed)—different consequences.

Man, at his highest potentiality, is realized and fulfilled within each creator himself. . . . Whether the creator is alone, or finds only a handful of others like him, or is among the majority of mankind, is of no importance or consequence whatever; numbers have nothing to do with it. He alone or he and a few others like him *are* mankind, in the proper sense of being the proof of what man actually is, man at his best, the essential man, man at his highest possibility. (The *rational* being, who acts according to his nature.)

It should not matter to a creator whether anyone or a million or *all* the men around him fall short of the ideal of Man; let him live up to that ideal himself; this is all the "optimism" about Man that he needs. But this is a hard and subtle thing to realize—and it would be natural for Dagny always to make the mistake of believing others are better than they really are (or will become better, or she will teach them to become better or, actually, she so desperately *wants* them to be better)—and to be tied to the world by that hope.

It is proper for a creator to have an unlimited confidence in himself and his ability, to feel certain that he can get anything he wishes out of life, that he can accomplish anything he decides to accomplish, and that it's up to him to do it. (He feels it because he is a man of reason . . .) [But] here is what he must keep clearly in mind: it is true that a creator can accomplish anything he wishes— if he functions according to the nature of man, the universe and his own proper morality, that is, if he does not place his wish primarily within others and does not attempt or desire anything that is of a collective nature, anything that concerns others primarily or requires *primarily* the exercise of the will of others. (This would be an *immoral* desire or attempt, contrary to his nature as a creator.) If he attempts that, he is out of a creator's province and in that of the collectivist and the second-hander.

Therefore, he must never feel confident that he can do anything whatever to, by or through others. (He can't—and he shouldn't even wish to try it—and the mere attempt is improper.) He must not think that he can . . . somehow transfer his energy and his intelligence to them and make them fit for his purposes in that way. He must face other men as they are, recognizing them as essentially independent entities, by nature, and beyond his *primary* influence; [he must] deal with them only on his own, independent terms, deal with such as he judges can fit his purpose or live up to his standards (by themselves and of their own will, independently of him)—and expect nothing from the others. . . .

Now, in Dagny's case, her desperate desire is to run Taggart Transcontinental. She sees that there are no men suited to her purpose around her, no men of ability, independence and competence. She thinks she can run it with others, with the incompetent and the parasites, either by training them or merely by treating them as robots who will take her orders and function without personal initiative or responsibility; *with herself, in effect, being the spark of initiative, the bearer of responsibility for a whole collective.* This can't be done. This is her crucial error. This is where she fails.

Ayn Rand's basic purpose as a novelist was to present not villains or even heroes with errors, but the ideal man—the consistent, the fully integrated, the perfect. In *Atlas Shrugged,* this is John Galt, the towering figure who moves the world and the novel, yet does not appear onstage until Part III. By his nature (and that of the story) Galt is necessarily central to the lives of all the characters. In one note, "Galt's relation to the others," dated June 27, 1946, Miss Rand defines succinctly what Galt represents to each of them:

For Dagny—the ideal. The answer to her two quests: the man of genius and the man she loves. The first quest is expressed in her search for the inventor of the engine. The second—her growing conviction that she will never be in love . . .

For Rearden—the friend. The kind of understanding and appreciation he has always wanted and did not know he wanted (or he thought he had it—he tried to find it in those around him, to get it from his wife, his mother, brother and sister).

For Francisco d'Anconia—the aristocrat. The only man who represents a challenge and a stimulant—almost the "proper kind" of audience, worthy of stunning for the sheer joy and color of life.

For Danneskjöld—the anchor. The only man who represents land and roots to a restless, reckless wanderer, like the goal of a struggle, the port at the end of a fierce sea-voyage—the only man he can respect.

For the Composer—the inspiration and the perfect audience.

For the Philosopher—the embodiment of his abstractions.

For Father Amadeus—the source of his conflict. The uneasy realization that Galt is the end of his endeavors, the man of virtue, the perfect man—and that his means do not fit this end (and that he is destroying this, his ideal, for the sake of those who are evil).

To James Taggart—the eternal threat. The secret dread. The reproach. The guilt (his own guilt). He has no specific tie-in with Galt—but he has that constant, causeless, unnamed, hysterical fear. And he recognizes it when he hears Galt's broadcast and when he sees Galt in person for the first time.

To the Professor—his conscience. The reproach and reminder. The ghost that haunts him through everything he does, without a moment's peace. The thing that says: *"No"* to his whole life.

Some notes on the above: Rearden's sister, Stacy, was a minor character later cut from the novel.

"Francisco" was spelled "Francesco" in these early years, while Danneskjöld's first name at this point was Ivar, presumably after Ivar Kreuger, the Swedish "match king," who was the real-life model of Bjorn Faulkner in *Night of January 16th.*

Father Amadeus was Taggart's priest, to whom he confessed his sins. The priest was supposed to be a positive character, honestly devoted to the good but practicing consistently the morality of mercy. Miss Rand dropped him, she told me, when she found that it was impossible to make such a character convincing.

The Professor is Robert Stadler.

This brings me to a final excerpt. Because of her passion for ideas, Miss Rand was often asked whether she was primarily a philosopher or a novelist. In later years, she was impatient with this question, but she gave her own answer, to and for herself, in a note dated May 4, 1946. The broader context was a discussion of the nature of creativity.

I seem to be both a theoretical philosopher and a fiction writer. But it is the last that interests me most; the first is only the means to the last; the absolutely necessary means, but only the means; the fiction story is the end. Without an understanding and statement of the right philosophical principle, I cannot create the right story; but the discovery of the principle interests me only as the discovery of the proper knowledge to be used for my life purpose; and my life purpose is the creation of the kind of world (people and events) that I like—that is, that represents human perfection.

Philosophical knowledge is necessary in order to define human perfection. But I do not care to stop at the definition. I want to *use* it, to apply it—in my work; (in my personal life, too—but the core, center and purpose of my personal life, of my *whole* life, is my work).

This is why, I think, the idea of writing a philosophical non-fiction book bored me. In such a book, the purpose would actually be to teach others, to present my idea to *them*. In a book of fiction the purpose is to create, for myself, the kind of world I want and to live in it while I am creating it; then, as a secondary consequence, to let others enjoy this world, if, and to the extent that, they can.

It may be said that the first purpose of a philosophical book is the clarification or statement of your new knowledge to and for yourself; and then, as a secondary step, the offering of your knowledge to others. But here is the difference, as far as I am concerned: I have to acquire and state to myself the new philosophical knowledge or principle I used in order to write a fiction story as its embodiment and illustration; I do not care to write a story on a theme or thesis of old knowledge, knowledge stated or discovered by someone else, that is, someone else's philosophy (because those philosophies are wrong). To this extent, I am an abstract philosopher (I want to present the perfect man and his perfect life—and I must also discover my own philosophical statement and definition of this perfection).

But when and if I have discovered such new knowledge, I am not interested in stating it in its abstract, general form, that is, as knowledge. I am interested in using it, in applying it—that is, in stating it in the concrete form of men and events, in the form of a fiction story. *This last* is my final purpose, my end; the philosophical knowledge or discovery is only the means to it. For *my* purpose, the non-fiction form of abstract knowledge doesn't interest me; the final, applied form of fiction, of story, does. (I state the knowledge to myself, anyway; but I choose the final form of it, the expression, in the completed cycle that leads back to man.)

I wonder to what extent I represent a peculiar phenomenon in this respect. I think I represent the proper integration of a complete human being. Anyway, *this* should be my lead for the character of John Galt. *He,* too, is a combination of an abstract philosopher and a practical inventor; the thinker and the man of action together . . .

In learning, we draw an abstraction from concrete objects and events. In creating, we make our own concrete objects and events out of the abstraction; we bring the abstraction down and back to its specific meaning, to the concrete;

but the abstraction has helped us to make the *kind of concrete we want the concrete to be.* It has helped us to create—to re-shape the world as we wish it to be for our purposes.

I cannot resist quoting one further paragraph. It comes a few pages later in the same discussion.

Incidentally, as a sideline observation: if creative fiction writing is a process of translating an abstraction into the concrete, there are three possible grades of such writing: translating an old (known) abstraction (theme or thesis) through the medium of old fiction means, (that is, characters, events or situations used before for that same purpose, that same translation)—this is most of the popular trash; translating an old abstraction through new, original fiction means—this is most of the good literature; creating a new, original abstraction and translating it through new, original means. This, as far as I know, is only *me*—my kind of fiction writing. May God forgive me (Metaphor!) if this is mistaken conceit! As near as I can now see it, it isn't. (A fourth possibility—translating a new abstraction through old means—is impossible, by definition: if the abstraction is new, there can be no means used by anybody else before to translate it.)

Is her conclusion "mistaken conceit"? It is now forty-five years since she wrote this note, and you are holding Ayn Rand's masterwork in your hands. You decide.

—Leonard Peikoff
September 1991

NON-CONTRADICTION

I

THE THEME

"Who is John Galt?"

The light was ebbing, and Eddie Willers could not distinguish the bum's face. The bum had said it simply, without expression. But from the sunset far at the end of the street, yellow glints caught his eyes, and the eyes looked straight at Eddie Willers, mocking and still—as if the question had been addressed to the causeless uneasiness within him.

"Why did you say that?" asked Eddie Willers, his voice tense.

The bum leaned against the side of the doorway; a wedge of broken glass behind him reflected the metal yellow of the sky.

"Why does it bother you?" he asked.

"It doesn't," snapped Eddie Willers.

He reached hastily into his pocket. The bum had stopped him and asked for a dime, then had gone on talking, as if to kill that moment and postpone the problem of the next. Pleas for dimes were so frequent in the streets these days that it was not necessary to listen to explanations, and he had no desire to hear the details of this bum's particular despair.

"Go get your cup of coffee," he said, handing the dime to the shadow that had no face.

"Thank you, sir," said the voice, without interest, and the face leaned forward for a moment. The face was wind-browned, cut by lines of weariness and cynical resignation; the eyes were intelligent.

Eddie Willers walked on, wondering why he always felt it at this time of day, this sense of dread without reason. No, he thought, not dread, there's nothing to fear: just an immense, diffused apprehension, with no source or object. He had become accustomed to the feeling, but he could find no explanation for it; yet the bum had spoken as if he knew that Eddie felt it, as if he thought that one should feel it, and more: as if he knew the reason.

Eddie Willers pulled his shoulders straight, in conscientious self-discipline. He had to stop this, he thought; he was beginning to imagine things. Had he always felt it? He was thirty-two years old. He tried to think back. No, he hadn't; but he could not remember when it had started. The feeling came to him suddenly, at random intervals, and now it was coming more often than ever. It's the twilight, he thought; I hate the twilight.

The clouds and the shafts of skyscrapers against them were turning brown, like an old painting in oil, the color of a fading masterpiece. Long streaks of grime ran from under the pinnacles down the slender, soot-eaten walls. High on the side of a tower there was a crack in the shape of a motionless lightning, the length of ten stories. A jagged object cut the sky above the roofs; it was half a spire, still holding the glow of the sunset; the gold leaf had long since peeled off the other half. The glow was red and still, like the reflection of a fire: not an active fire, but a dying one which it is too late to stop.

No, thought Eddie Willers, there was nothing disturbing in the sight of the city. It looked as it had always looked.

He walked on, reminding himself that he was late in returning to the office. He did not like the task which he had to perform on his return, but it had to be done. So he did not attempt to delay it, but made himself walk faster.

He turned a corner. In the narrow space between the dark silhouettes of two buildings, as in the crack of a door, he saw the page of a gigantic calendar suspended in the sky.

It was the calendar that the mayor of New York had erected last year on the top of a building, so that citizens might tell the day of the month as they told the hours of the day, by glancing up at a public tower. A white rectangle hung over the city, imparting the date to the men in the streets below. In the rusty light of this evening's sunset, the rectangle said: September 2.

Eddie Willers looked away. He had never liked the sight of that calendar. It disturbed him, in a manner he could not explain or define. The feeling seemed to blend with his sense of uneasiness; it had the same quality.

He thought suddenly that there was some phrase, a kind of quotation, that expressed what the calendar seemed to suggest. But he could not recall it. He walked, groping for a sentence that hung in his mind as an empty shape. He could neither fill it nor dismiss it. He glanced back. The white rectangle stood above the roofs, saying in immovable finality: September 2.

Eddie Willers shifted his glance down to the street, to a vegetable pushcart at the stoop of a brownstone house. He saw a pile of bright gold carrots and the fresh green of onions. He saw a clean white curtain blowing at an open window. He saw a bus turning a corner, expertly steered. He wondered why he felt reassured—and then, why he felt the sudden, inexplicable wish that these things were not left in the open, unprotected against the empty space above.

When he came to Fifth Avenue, he kept his eyes on the windows of the stores he passed. There was nothing he needed or wished to buy; but he liked to see the display of goods, any goods, objects made by men, to be used by men. He enjoyed the sight of a prosperous street; not more than every fourth one of the stores was out of business, its windows dark and empty.

He did not know why he suddenly thought of the oak tree. Nothing had recalled it. But he thought of it and of his childhood summers on the Taggart estate. He had spent most of his childhood with the Taggart children, and now he worked for them, as his father and grandfather had worked for their father and grandfather.

The great oak tree had stood on a hill over the Hudson, in a lonely spot of the Taggart estate. Eddie Willers, aged seven, liked to come and look at that tree. It had stood there for hundreds of years, and he thought it would always stand there. Its roots clutched the hill like a fist with fingers sunk into the soil, and he thought that if a giant were to seize it by the top, he would not be able to uproot it, but would swing the hill and the whole of the earth with it, like a ball at the end of a string. He felt safe in the oak tree's presence; it was a thing that nothing could change or threaten; it was his greatest symbol of strength.

One night, lightning struck the oak tree. Eddie saw it the next morning. It lay broken in half, and he looked into its trunk as into the mouth of a black tunnel. The trunk was only an empty shell; its heart had rotted away long ago; there was nothing inside—just a thin gray dust that was being dispersed by the whim of the faintest wind. The living power had gone, and the shape it left had not been able to stand without it.

Years later, he heard it said that children should be protected from shock, from their first knowledge of death, pain or fear. But these had never scarred him; his shock came when he stood very quietly, looking into the black hole of the trunk. It was an immense betrayal—the more terrible because he could not grasp what it was that had been betrayed. It was not himself, he knew, nor his trust; it was something else. He stood there for a while, making no sound, then he walked back to the house. He never spoke about it to anyone, then or since.

Eddie Willers shook his head, as the screech of a rusty mechanism changing a traffic light stopped him on the edge of a curb. He felt anger at himself. There was no reason that he had to remember the oak tree tonight. It meant nothing to him any longer, only a faint tinge of sadness—and somewhere within him, a drop of pain moving briefly and vanishing, like a raindrop on the glass of a window, its course in the shape of a question mark.

He wanted no sadness attached to his childhood; he loved its memories: any day of it he remembered now seemed flooded by a still, brilliant sunlight. It seemed to him as if a few rays from it reached into his present: not rays, more like pinpoint spotlights that gave an occasional moment's glitter to his job, to his lonely apartment, to the quiet, scrupulous progression of his existence.

He thought of a summer day when he was ten years old. That day, in a clearing of the woods, the one precious companion of his childhood told him what they would do when they grew up. The words were harsh and glowing, like the sunlight. He listened in admiration and in wonder. When he was asked what he would want to do, he answered at once, "Whatever is right," and added, "You ought to do something great . . . I mean, the two of us together." "What?" she asked. He said, "I don't know. That's what we ought to find out. Not just what you said. Not just business and earning a living. Things like winning battles, or saving people out of fires, or climbing mountains." "What for?" she asked. He said, "The minister said last Sunday that we must always reach for the best within us. What do you suppose is the best within us?" "I don't know." "We'll have to find out." She did not answer; she was looking away, up the railroad track.

Eddie Willers smiled. He had said, "Whatever is right," twenty-two years ago. He had kept that statement unchallenged ever since; the other questions had faded in his mind; he had been too busy to ask them. But he still thought it self-evident that one had to do what was right; he had never learned how people could want to do otherwise; he had learned only that they did. It still seemed simple and incomprehensible to him: simple that things should be right, and incomprehensible that they weren't. He knew that they weren't. He thought of that, as he turned a corner and came to the great building of Taggart Transcontinental.

The building stood over the street as its tallest and proudest structure. Eddie Willers always smiled at his first sight of it. Its long bands of windows were unbroken, in contrast to those of its neighbors. Its rising lines cut the sky, with no crumbling corners or worn edges. It seemed to stand above the years, untouched. It would always stand there, thought Eddie Willers.

Whenever he entered the Taggart Building, he felt relief and a sense of security. This was a place of competence and power. The floors of its hallways were mirrors made of marble. The frosted rectangles of its electric fixtures were chips of solid light. Behind sheets of glass, rows of girls sat at typewriters, the clicking of their keys like the sound of speeding train wheels. And like an answering echo, a faint shudder went through the walls at times, rising from under the building, from the tunnels of the great terminal where trains started out to cross a continent and stopped after crossing it again, as they had started and stopped for generation after generation. Taggart Transcontinental, thought Eddie Willers, From Ocean to Ocean—the proud slogan of his childhood, so much more shining and holy than any commandment of the Bible. From Ocean to Ocean, forever—thought Eddie Willers, in the manner of a rededication, as he walked through the spotless halls into the heart of the building, into the office of James Taggart, President of Taggart Transcontinental.

James Taggart sat at his desk. He looked like a man approaching fifty, who had crossed into age from adolescence, without the intermediate stage of youth. He had a small, petulant mouth, and thin hair clinging to a bald forehead. His posture had a limp, decentralized sloppiness, as if in defiance of his tall, slender body, a body with an elegance of line intended for the confident poise of an aristocrat, but transformed into the gawkiness of a lout. The flesh of his face was pale and soft. His eyes were pale and veiled, with a glance that moved slowly, never quite stopping, gliding off and past things in eternal resentment of their existence. He looked obstinate and drained. He was thirty-nine years old.

He lifted his head with irritation, at the sound of the opening door.

"Don't bother me, don't bother me, don't bother me," said James Taggart.

Eddie Willers walked toward the desk.

"It's important, Jim," he said, not raising his voice.

"All right, all right, what is it?"

Eddie Willers looked at a map on the wall of the office. The map's colors had faded under the glass—he wondered dimly how many Taggart presidents had sat before it and for how many years. The Taggart Transcontinental Railroad, the network of red lines slashing the faded body of the country from New York to San Francisco, looked like a system of blood vessels. It looked as if once, long ago, the blood had shot down the main artery and, under the pressure of its own overabundance, had branched out at random points, running all over the country. One red streak twisted its way from Cheyenne, Wyoming, down to El Paso, Texas—the Rio Norte Line of Taggart Transcontinental. New tracing had been added recently and the red streak had been extended south beyond El Paso—but Eddie Willers turned away hastily when his eyes reached that point.

He looked at James Taggart and said, "It's the Rio Norte Line." He noticed Taggart's glance moving down to a corner of the desk. "We've had another wreck."

"Railroad accidents happen every day. Did you have to bother me about that?"

"You know what I'm saying, Jim. The Rio Norte is done for. That track is shot. Down the whole line."

"We are getting a new track."

Eddie Willers continued as if there had been no answer: "That track is shot. It's no use trying to run trains down there. People are giving up trying to use them."

"There is not a railroad in the country, it seems to me, that doesn't have a few branches running at a deficit. We're not the only ones. It's a national condition—a temporary national condition."

Eddie stood looking at him silently. What Taggart disliked about Eddie Willers was this habit of looking straight into people's eyes.

Eddie's eyes were blue, wide and questioning; he had blond hair and a square face, unremarkable except for that look of scrupulous attentiveness and open, puzzled wonder.

"What do you want?" snapped Taggart.

"I just came to tell you something you had to know, because somebody had to tell you."

"That we've had another accident?"

"That we can't give up the Rio Norte Line."

James Taggart seldom raised his head; when he looked at people, he did so by lifting his heavy eyelids and staring upward from under the expanse of his bald forehead.

"Who's thinking of giving up the Rio Norte Line?" he asked. "There's never been any question of giving it up. I resent your saying it. I resent it very much."

"But we haven't met a schedule for the last six months. We haven't completed a run without some sort of breakdown, major or minor. We're losing all our shippers, one after another. How long can we last?"

"You're a pessimist, Eddie. You lack faith. That's what undermines the morale of an organization."

"You mean that nothing's going to be done about the Rio Norte Line?"

"I haven't said that at all. Just as soon as we get the new track—"

"Jim, there isn't going to be any new track." He watched Taggart's eyelids move up slowly. "I've just come back from the office of Associated Steel. I've spoken to Orren Boyle."

"What did he say?"

"He spoke for an hour and a half and did not give me a single straight answer."

"What did you bother him for? I believe the first order of rail wasn't due for delivery until next month."

"And before that, it was due for delivery three months ago."

"Unforeseen circumstances. Absolutely beyond Orren's control."

"And before that, it was due six months earlier. Jim, we have waited for Associated Steel to deliver that rail for thirteen months."

"What do you want me to do? I can't run Orren Boyle's business."

"I want you to understand that we can't wait."

Taggart asked slowly, his voice half-mocking, half-cautious, "What did my sister say?"

"She won't be back until tomorrow."

"Well, what do you want me to do?"

"That's for you to decide."

"Well, whatever else you say, there's one thing you're not going to mention next—and that's Rearden Steel."

Eddie did not answer at once, then said quietly, "All right, Jim. I won't mention it."

"Orren is my friend." He heard no answer. "I resent your attitude.

Orren Boyle will deliver that rail just as soon as it's humanly possible. So long as he can't deliver it, nobody can blame us."

"Jim! What are you talking about? Don't you understand that the Rio Norte Line is breaking up—whether anybody blames us or not?"

"People would put up with it—they'd have to—if it weren't for the Phoenix-Durango." He saw Eddie's face tighten. "Nobody ever complained about the Rio Norte Line, until the Phoenix-Durango came on the scene."

"The Phoenix-Durango is doing a brilliant job."

"Imagine a thing called the Phoenix-Durango competing with Taggart Transcontinental! It was nothing but a local milk line ten years ago."

"It's got most of the freight traffic of Arizona, New Mexico and Colorado now." Taggart did not answer. "Jim, we can't lose Colorado. It's our last hope. It's everybody's last hope. If we don't pull ourselves together, we'll lose every big shipper in the state to the Phoenix-Durango. We've lost the Wyatt oil fields."

"I don't see why everybody keeps talking about the Wyatt oil fields."

"Because Ellis Wyatt is a prodigy who—"

"Damn Ellis Wyatt!"

Those oil wells, Eddie thought suddenly, didn't they have something in common with the blood vessels on the map? Wasn't that the way the red stream of Taggart Transcontinental had shot across the country, years ago, a feat that seemed incredible now? He thought of the oil wells spouting a black stream that ran over a continent almost faster than the trains of the Phoenix-Durango could carry it. That oil field had been only a rocky patch in the mountains of Colorado, given up as exhausted long ago. Ellis Wyatt's father had managed to squeeze an obscure living to the end of his days, out of the dying oil wells. Now it was as if somebody had given a shot of adrenalin to the heart of the mountain, the heart had started pumping, the black blood had burst through the rocks—of course it's blood, thought Eddie Willers, because blood is supposed to feed, to give life, and that is what Wyatt Oil had done. It had shocked empty slopes of ground into sudden existence, it had brought new towns, new power plants, new factories to a region nobody had ever noticed on any map. New factories, thought Eddie Willers, at a time when the freight revenues from all the great old industries were dropping slowly year by year; a rich new oil field, at a time when the pumps were stopping in one famous field after another; a new industrial state where nobody had expected anything but cattle and beets. One man had done it, and he had done it in eight years; this, thought Eddie Willers, was like the stories he had read in school books and never quite believed, the stories of men who had lived in the days of the country's youth. He wished he could meet Ellis Wyatt. There was a great deal of talk about him, but few had ever met him; he seldom came to New York. They said he was thirty-three years old and had a violent temper. He had discovered some way to revive exhausted oil wells and he had proceeded to revive them.

"Ellis Wyatt is a greedy bastard who's after nothing but money," said James Taggart. "It seems to me that there are more important things in life than making money."

"What are you talking about, Jim? What has that got to do with—"

"Besides, he's double-crossed us. We served the Wyatt oil fields for years, most adequately. In the days of old man Wyatt, we ran a tank train a week."

"These are not the days of old man Wyatt, Jim. The Phoenix-Durango runs two tank trains a day down there—and it runs them on schedule."

"If he had given us time to grow along with him—"

"He has no time to waste."

"What does he expect? That we drop all our other shippers, sacrifice the interests of the whole country and give him all our trains?"

"Why, no. He doesn't expect anything. He just deals with the Phoenix-Durango."

"I think he's a destructive, unscrupulous ruffian. I think he's an irresponsible upstart who's been grossly overrated." It was astonishing to hear a sudden emotion in James Taggart's lifeless voice. "I'm not so sure that his oil fields are such a beneficial achievement. It seems to me that he's dislocated the economy of the whole country. Nobody expected Colorado to become an industrial state. How can we have any security or plan anything if everything changes all the time?"

"Good God, Jim! He's—"

"Yes, I know, I know, he's making money. But that is not the standard, it seems to me, by which one gauges a man's value to society. And as for his oil, he'd come crawling to us, and he'd wait his turn along with all the other shippers, and he wouldn't demand more than his fair share of transportation—if it weren't for the Phoenix-Durango. We can't help it if we're up against destructive competition of that kind. Nobody can blame us."

The pressure in his chest and temples, thought Eddie Willers, was the strain of the effort he was making; he had decided to make the issue clear for once, and the issue was so clear, he thought, that nothing could bar it from Taggart's understanding, unless it was the failure of his own presentation. So he had tried hard, but he was failing, just as he had always failed in all of their discussions; no matter what he said, they never seemed to be talking about the same subject.

"Jim, what are you saying? Does it matter that nobody blames us—when the road is falling apart?"

James Taggart smiled; it was a thin smile, amused and cold. "It's touching, Eddie," he said. "It's touching—your devotion to Taggart

Transcontinental. If you don't look out, you'll turn into one of those real feudal serfs."

"That's what I am, Jim."

"But may I ask whether it is your job to discuss these matters with me?"

"No, it isn't."

"Then why don't you learn that we have departments to take care of things? Why don't you report all this to whoever's concerned? Why don't you cry on my dear sister's shoulder?"

"Look Jim, I know it's not my place to talk to you. But I can't understand what's going on. I don't know what it is that your proper advisers tell you, or why they can't make you understand. So I thought I'd try to tell you myself."

"I appreciate our childhood friendship, Eddie, but do you think that that should entitle you to walk in here unannounced whenever you wish? Considering your own rank, shouldn't you remember that I am president of Taggart Transcontinental?"

This was wasted. Eddie Willers looked at him as usual, not hurt, merely puzzled, and asked, "Then you don't intend to do anything about the Rio Norte Line?"

"I haven't said that. I haven't said that at all." Taggart was looking at the map, at the red streak south of El Paso. "Just as soon as the San Sebastián Mines get going and our Mexican branch begins to pay off—"

"Don't let's talk about that, Jim."

Taggart turned, startled by the unprecedented phenomenon of an implacable anger in Eddie's voice. "What's the matter?"

"You know what's the matter. Your sister said—"

"Damn my sister!" said James Taggart.

Eddie Willers did not move. He did not answer. He stood looking straight ahead. But he did not see James Taggart or anything in the office.

After a moment, he bowed and walked out.

In the anteroom, the clerks of James Taggart's personal staff were switching off the lights, getting ready to leave for the day. But Pop Harper, chief clerk, still sat at his desk, twisting the levers of a half-dismembered typewriter. Everybody in the company had the impression that Pop Harper was born in that particular corner at that particular desk and never intended to leave it. He had been chief clerk for James Taggart's father.

Pop Harper glanced up at Eddie Willers as he came out of the president's office. It was a wise, slow glance; it seemed to say that he knew that Eddie's visit to their part of the building meant trouble on the line, knew that nothing had come of the visit, and was completely indifferent to the knowledge. It was the cynical indifference which Eddie Willers had seen in the eyes of the bum on the street corner.

"Say, Eddie, know where I could get some woolen undershirts?"
he asked. "Tried all over town, but nobody's got 'em."

"I don't know," said Eddie, stopping. "Why do you ask me?"

"I just ask everybody. Maybe somebody'll tell me."

Eddie looked uneasily at the blank, emaciated face and white hair.

"It's cold in this joint," said Pop Harper. "It's going to be colder this
winter."

"What are you doing?" Eddie asked, pointing at the pieces of typewriter.

"The damn thing's busted again. No use sending it out, took them
three months to fix it the last time. Thought I'd patch it up myself. Not
for long, I guess." He let his fist drop down on the keys. "You're ready
for the junk pile, old pal. Your days are numbered."

Eddie started. That was the sentence he had tried to remember:
Your days are numbered. But he had forgotten in what connection he
had tried to remember it.

"It's no use, Eddie," said Pop Harper.

"What's no use?"

"Nothing. Anything."

"What's the matter, Pop?"

"I'm not going to requisition a new typewriter. The new ones are
made of tin. When the old ones go, that will be the end of type-
writing. There was an accident in the subway this morning, their brakes
wouldn't work. You ought to go home, Eddie, turn on the radio and
listen to a good dance band. Forget it, boy. Trouble with you is you
never had a hobby. Somebody stole the electric light bulbs again, from
off the staircase, down where I live. I've got a pain in my chest. Couldn't
get any cough drops this morning, the drugstore on our corner went
bankrupt last week. The Texas-Western Railroad went bankrupt last
month. They closed the Queensborough Bridge yesterday for temporary repairs. Oh well, what's the use? Who is John Galt?"

* * *

She sat at the window of the train, her head thrown back, one leg
stretched across to the empty seat before her. The window frame
trembled with the speed of the motion, the pane hung over empty darkness, and dots of light slashed across the glass as luminous streaks, once
in a while.

Her leg, sculptured by the tight sheen of the stocking, its long line running straight, over an arched instep, to the tip of a foot in a high-heeled
pump, had a feminine elegance that seemed out of place in the dusty
train car and oddly incongruous with the rest of her. She wore a battered camel's hair coat that had been expensive, wrapped shapelessly
about her slender, nervous body. The coat collar was raised to the
slanting brim of her hat. A sweep of brown hair fell back, almost touching the line of her shoulders. Her face was made of angular planes,

the shape of her mouth clear-cut, a sensual mouth held closed with inflexible precision. She kept her hands in the coat pockets, her posture taut, as if she resented immobility, and unfeminine, as if she were unconscious of her own body and that it was a woman's body.

She sat listening to the music. It was a symphony of triumph. The notes flowed up, they spoke of rising and they were the rising itself, they were the essence and the form of upward motion, they seemed to embody every human act and thought that had ascent as its motive. It was a sunburst of sound, breaking out of hiding and spreading open. It had the freedom of release and the tension of purpose. It swept space clean, and left nothing but the joy of an unobstructed effort. Only a faint echo within the sounds spoke of that from which the music had escaped, but spoke in laughing astonishment at the discovery that there was no ugliness or pain, and there never had had to be. It was the song of an immense deliverance.

She thought: For just a few moments—while this lasts—it is all right to surrender completely—to forget everything and just permit yourself to feel. She thought: Let go—drop the controls—this is it.

Somewhere on the edge of her mind, under the music, she heard the sound of train wheels. They knocked in an even rhythm, every fourth knock accented, as if stressing a conscious purpose. She could relax, because she heard the wheels. She listened to the symphony, thinking: This is why the wheels have to be kept going, and this is where they're going.

She had never heard that symphony before, but she knew that it was written by Richard Halley. She recognized the violence and the magnificent intensity. She recognized the style of the theme; it was a clear, complex melody—at a time when no one wrote melody any longer. . . . She sat looking up at the ceiling of the car, but she did not see it and she had forgotten where she was. She did not know whether she was hearing a full symphony orchestra or only the theme; perhaps she was hearing the orchestration in her own mind.

She thought dimly that there had been premonitory echoes of this theme in all of Richard Halley's work, through all the years of his long struggle, to the day, in his middle-age, when fame struck him suddenly and knocked him out. This—she thought, listening to the symphony— had been the goal of his struggle. She remembered half-hinted attempts in his music, phrases that promised it, broken bits of melody that started but never quite reached it; when Richard Halley wrote this, he . . . She sat up straight. *When* did Richard Halley write this?

In the same instant, she realized where she was and wondered for the first time where that music came from.

A few steps away, at the end of the car, a brakeman was adjusting the controls of the air-conditioner. He was blond and young. He was whistling the theme of the symphony. She realized that he had been whistling it for some time and that this was all she had heard.

She watched him incredulously for a while, before she raised her voice to ask, "Tell me please, what are you whistling?"

The boy turned to her. She met a direct glance and saw an open, eager smile, as if he were sharing a confidence with a friend. She liked his face—its lines were tight and firm, it did not have that look of loose muscles evading the responsibility of a shape, which she had learned to expect in people's faces.

"It's the Halley Concerto," he answered, smiling.

"Which one?"

"The Fifth."

She let a moment pass, before she said slowly and very carefully, "Richard Halley wrote only four concertos."

The boy's smile vanished. It was as if he were jolted back to reality, just as she had been a few moments ago. It was as if a shutter were slammed down, and what remained was a face without expression, impersonal, indifferent and empty.

"Yes, of course," he said. "I'm wrong. I made a mistake."

"Then what was it?"

"Something I heard somewhere."

"What?"

"I don't know."

"Where did you hear it?"

"I don't remember."

She paused helplessly; he was turning away from her without further interest.

"It sounded like a Halley theme," she said. "But I know every note he's ever written and he never wrote that."

There was still no expression, only a faint look of attentiveness on the boy's face, as he turned back to her and asked, "You like the music of Richard Halley?"

"Yes," she said, "I like it very much."

He considered her for a moment, as if hesitating, then he turned away. She watched the expert efficiency of his movements as he went on working. He worked in silence.

She had not slept for two nights, but she could not permit herself to sleep; she had too many problems to consider and not much time: the train was due in New York early in the morning. She needed the time, yet she wished the train would go faster; but it was the Taggart Comet, the fastest train in the country.

She tried to think; but the music remained on the edge of her mind and she kept hearing it, in full chords, like the implacable steps of something that could not be stopped. . . . She shook her head angrily, jerked her hat off and lighted a cigarette.

She would not sleep, she thought; she could last until tomorrow night. . . . The train wheels clicked in accented rhythm. She was so used to them that she did not hear them consciously, but the sound became a sense of peace within her. . . . When she extinguished her cigarette, she knew that she needed another one, but thought that she would give herself a minute, just a few minutes, before she would light it. . . .

She had fallen asleep and she awakened with a jolt, knowing that something was wrong, before she knew what it was: the wheels had stopped. The car stood soundless and dim in the blue glow of the night lamps. She glanced at her watch: there was no reason for stopping. She looked out the window: the train stood still in the middle of empty fields.

She heard someone moving in a seat across the aisle, and asked, "How long have we been standing?"

A man's voice answered indifferently, "About an hour."

The man looked after her, sleepily astonished, because she leaped to her feet and rushed to the door.

There was a cold wind outside, and an empty stretch of land under an empty sky. She heard weeds rustling in the darkness. Far ahead, she saw the figures of men standing by the engine—and above them, hanging detached in the sky, the red light of a signal.

She walked rapidly toward them, past the motionless line of wheels. No one paid attention to her when she approached. The train crew and a few passengers stood clustered under the red light. They had stopped talking, they seemed to be waiting in placid indifference.

"What's the matter?" she asked.

The engineer turned, astonished. Her question had sounded like an order, not like the amateur curiosity of a passenger. She stood, hands in pockets, coat collar raised, the wind beating her hair in strands across her face.

"Red light, lady," he said, pointing up with his thumb.

"How long has it been on?"

"An hour."

"We're off the main track, aren't we?"

"That's right."

"Why?"

"I don't know."

The conductor spoke up. "I don't think we had any business being sent off on a siding, that switch wasn't working right, and this thing's not working at all." He jerked his head up at the red light. "I don't think the signal's going to change. I think it's busted."

"Then what are you doing?"

"Waiting for it to change."

In her pause of startled anger, the fireman chuckled. "Last week, the crack special of the Atlantic Southern got left on a siding for two hours— just somebody's mistake."

"This is the Taggart Comet," she said. "The Comet has never been late."

"She's the only one in the country that hasn't," said the engineer.

"There's always a first time," said the fireman.

"You don't know about railroads, lady," said a passenger. "There's not a signal system or a dispatcher in the country that's worth a damn."

She did not turn or notice him, but spoke to the engineer. "If you know that the signal is broken, what do you intend to do?"

He did not like her tone of authority, and he could not understand why she assumed it so naturally. She looked like a young girl; only her mouth and eyes showed that she was a woman in her thirties. The dark gray eyes were direct and disturbing, as if they cut through things, throwing the inconsequential out of the way. The face seemed faintly familiar to him, but he could not recall where he had seen it.

"Lady, I don't intend to stick my neck out," he said.

"He means," said the fireman, "that our job's to wait for orders."

"Your job is to run this train."

"Not against a red light. If the light says stop, we stop."

"A red light means danger, lady," said the passenger.

"We're not taking any chances," said the engineer. "Whoever's responsible for it, he'll switch the blame to us if we move. So we're not moving till somebody tells us to."

"And if nobody does?"

"Somebody will turn up sooner or later."

"How long do you propose to wait?"

The engineer shrugged. "Who is John Galt?"

"He means," said the fireman, "don't ask questions nobody can answer."

She looked at the red light and at the rail that went off into the black, untouched distance.

She said, "Proceed with caution to the next signal. If it's in order, proceed to the main track. Then stop at the first open office."

"Yeah? Who says so?"

"I do."

"Who are you?"

It was only the briefest pause, a moment of astonishment at a question she had not expected, but the engineer looked more closely at her face, and in time with her answer he gasped, "Good God!"

She answered, not offensively, merely like a person who does not hear the question often:

"Dagny Taggart."

"Well, I'll be—" said the fireman, and then they all remained silent.

She went on, in the same tone of unstressed authority. "Proceed to the main track and hold the train for me at the first open office."

"Yes, Miss Taggart."

"You'll have to make up time. You've got the rest of the night to do it. Get the Comet in on schedule."

"Yes, Miss Taggart."

She was turning to go, when the engineer asked, "If there's any trouble, are you taking the responsibility for it, Miss Taggart?"

"I am."

The conductor followed her as she walked back to her car. He was saying, bewildered, "But . . . just a seat in a day coach, Miss Taggart? But how come? But why didn't you let us know?"

She smiled easily. "Had no time to be formal. Had my own car attached to Number 22 out of Chicago, but got off at Cleveland—and Number 22 was running late, so I let the car go. The Comet came next and I took it. There was no sleeping-car space left."

The conductor shook his head. "Your brother—he wouldn't have taken a coach."

She laughed. "No, he wouldn't have."

The men by the engine watched her walking away. The young brakeman was among them. He asked, pointing after her, "Who is that?"

"*That's* who runs Taggart Transcontinental," said the engineer; the respect in his voice was genuine. "That's the Vice-President in Charge of Operation."

When the train jolted forward, the blast of its whistle dying over the fields, she sat by the window, lighting another cigarette. She thought: It's cracking to pieces, like this, all over the country, you can expect it anywhere, at any moment. But she felt no anger or anxiety; she had no time to feel.

This would be just one more issue, to be settled along with the others. She knew that the superintendent of the Ohio Division was no good and that he was a friend of James Taggart. She had not insisted on throwing him out long ago only because she had no better man to put in his place. Good men were so strangely hard to find. But she would have to get rid of him, she thought, and she would give his post to Owen Kellogg, the young engineer who was doing a brilliant job as one of the assistants to the manager of the Taggart Terminal in New York; it was Owen Kellogg who ran the Terminal. She had watched his work for some time; she had always looked for sparks of competence, like a diamond prospector in an unpromising wasteland. Kellogg was still too young to be made superintendent of a division; she had wanted to give him another year, but there was no time to wait. She would have to speak to him as soon as she returned.

The strip of earth, faintly visible outside the window, was running faster now, blending into a gray stream. Through the dry phrases of calculations in her mind, she noticed that she did have time to feel something: it was the hard, exhilarating pleasure of action.

*   *   *

With the first whistling rush of air, as the Comet plunged into the tunnels of the Taggart Terminal under the city of New York, Dagny

Taggart sat up straight. She always felt it when the train went underground—this sense of eagerness, of hope and of secret excitement. It was as if normal existence were a photograph of shapeless things in badly printed colors, but this was a sketch done in a few sharp strokes that made things seem clean, important—and worth doing.

She watched the tunnels as they flowed past: bare walls of concrete, a net of pipes and wires, a web of rails that went off into black holes where green and red lights hung as distant drops of color. There was nothing else, nothing to dilute it, so that one could admire naked purpose and the ingenuity that had achieved it. She thought of the Taggart Building standing above her head at this moment, growing straight to the sky, and she thought: These are the roots of the building, hollow roots twisting under the ground, feeding the city.

When the train stopped, when she got off and heard the concrete of the platform under her heels, she felt light, lifted, impelled to action. She started off, walking fast, as if the speed of her steps could give form to the things she felt. It was a few moments before she realized that she was whistling a piece of music—and that it was the theme of Halley's Fifth Concerto.

She felt someone looking at her and turned. The young brakeman stood watching her tensely.

* * *

She sat on the arm of the big chair facing James Taggart's desk, her coat thrown open over a wrinkled traveling suit. Eddie Willers sat across the room, making notes once in a while. His title was that of Special Assistant to the Vice-President in Charge of Operation, and his main duty was to be her bodyguard against any waste of time. She asked him to be present at interviews of this nature, because then she never had to explain anything to him afterwards. James Taggart sat at his desk, his head drawn into his shoulders.

"The Rio Norte Line is a pile of junk from one end to the other," she said. "It's much worse than I thought. But we're going to save it."

"Of course," said James Taggart.

"Some of the rail can be salvaged. Not much and not for long. We'll start laying new rail in the mountain sections, Colorado first. We'll get the new rail in two months."

"Oh, did Orren Boyle say he'll—"

"I've ordered the rail from Rearden Steel."

The slight, choked sound from Eddie Willers was his suppressed desire to cheer.

James Taggart did not answer at once. "Dagny, why don't you sit in the chair as one is supposed to?" he said at last; his voice was petulant. "Nobody holds business conferences this way."

"I do."

She waited. He asked, his eyes avoiding hers, "Did you say that you *have* ordered the rail from Rearden?"

"Yesterday evening. I phoned him from Cleveland."

"But the Board hasn't authorized it. I haven't authorized it. You haven't consulted me."

She reached over, picked up the receiver of a telephone on his desk and handed it to him.

"Call Rearden and cancel it," she said.

James Taggart moved back in his chair. "I haven't said that," he answered angrily. "I haven't said that at all."

"Then it stands?"

"I haven't said that, either."

She turned. "Eddie, have them draw up the contract with Rearden Steel. Jim will sign it." She took a crumpled piece of notepaper from her pocket and tossed it to Eddie. "There's the figures and terms."

Taggart said, "But the Board hasn't—"

"The Board hasn't anything to do with it. They authorized you to buy the rail thirteen months ago. Where you buy it is up to you."

"I don't think it's proper to make such a decision without giving the Board a chance to express an opinion. And I don't see why I should be made to take the responsibility."

"I am taking it."

"What about the expenditure which—"

"Rearden is charging less than Orren Boyle's Associated Steel."

"Yes, and what about Orren Boyle?"

"I've cancelled the contract. We had the right to cancel it six months ago."

"When did you do that?"

"Yesterday."

"But he hasn't called to have me confirm it."

"He won't."

Taggart sat looking down at his desk. She wondered why he resented the necessity of dealing with Rearden, and why his resentment had such an odd, evasive quality. Rearden Steel had been the chief supplier of Taggart Transcontinental for ten years, ever since the first Rearden furnace was fired, in the days when their father was president of the railroad. For ten years, most of their rail had come from Rearden Steel. There were not many firms in the country who delivered what was ordered, when and as ordered. Rearden Steel was one of them. If she were insane, thought Dagny, she would conclude that her brother hated to deal with Rearden because Rearden did his job with superlative efficiency; but she would not conclude it, because she thought that such a feeling was not within the humanly possible.

"It isn't fair," said James Taggart.

"What isn't?"

"That we always give all our business to Rearden. It seems to me we should give somebody else a chance, too. Rearden doesn't need us; he's plenty big enough. We ought to help the smaller fellows to develop. Otherwise, we're just encouraging a monopoly."

"Don't talk tripe, Jim."

"Why do we always have to get things from Rearden?"

"Because we always get them."

"I don't like Henry Rearden."

"I do. But what does that matter, one way or the other? We need rails and he's the only one who can give them to us."

"The human element is very important. You have no sense of the human element at all."

"We're talking about saving a railroad, Jim."

"Yes, of course, of course, but still, you haven't any sense of the human element."

"No. I haven't."

"If we give Rearden such a large order for steel rails—"

"They're not going to be steel. They're Rearden Metal."

She had always avoided personal reactions, but she was forced to break her rule when she saw the expression on Taggart's face. She burst out laughing.

Rearden Metal was a new alloy, produced by Rearden after ten years of experiments. He had placed it on the market recently. He had received no orders and had found no customers.

Taggart could not understand the transition from the laughter to the sudden tone of Dagny's voice; the voice was cold and harsh: "Drop it, Jim. I know everything you're going to say. Nobody's ever used it before. Nobody approves of Rearden Metal. Nobody's interested in it. Nobody wants it. Still, our rails are going to be made of Rearden Metal."

"But . . ." said Taggart, "but . . . but nobody's ever used it before!"

He observed, with satisfaction, that she was silenced by anger. He liked to observe emotions; they were like red lanterns strung along the dark unknown of another's personality, marking vulnerable points. But how one could feel a personal emotion about a metal alloy, and what such an emotion indicated, was incomprehensible to him; so he could make no use of his discovery.

"The consensus of the best metallurgical authorities," he said, "seems to be highly skeptical about Rearden Metal, contending—"

"Drop it, Jim."

"Well, whose opinion did you take?"

"I don't ask for opinions."

"What do you go by?"

"Judgment."

"Well, whose judgment did you take?"

"Mine."

"But whom did you consult about it?"

"Nobody."

"Then what on earth do you know about Rearden Metal?"

"That it's the greatest thing ever put on the market."

"Why?"

"Because it's tougher than steel, cheaper than steel and will outlast any hunk of metal in existence."

"But who says so?"

"Jim, I studied engineering in college. When I see things, I see them."

"What did you see?"

"Rearden's formula and the tests he showed me."

"Well, if it were any good, somebody would have used it, and nobody has." He saw the flash of anger, and went on nervously: "How can you *know* it's good? How can you be sure? How can you decide?"

"Somebody decides such things, Jim. Who?"

"Well, I don't see why we have to be the first ones. I don't see it at all."

"Do you want to save the Rio Norte Line or not?" He did not answer. "If the road could afford it, I would scrap every piece of rail over the whole system and replace it with Rearden Metal. All of it needs replacing. None of it will last much longer. But we can't afford it. We have to get out of a bad hole, first. Do you want us to pull through or not?"

"We're still the best railroad in the country. The others are doing much worse."

"Then do you want us to remain in the hole?"

"I haven't said that! Why do you always oversimplify things that way? And if you're worried about money, I don't see why you want to waste it on the Rio Norte Line, when the Phoenix-Durango has robbed us of all our business down there. Why spend money when we have no protection against a competitor who'll destroy our investment?"

"Because the Phoenix-Durango is an excellent railroad, but I intend to make the Rio Norte Line better than that. Because I'm going to beat the Phoenix-Durango, if necessary—only it won't be necessary, because there will be room for two or three railroads to make fortunes in Colorado. Because I'd mortgage the system to build a branch to any district around Ellis Wyatt."

"I'm sick of hearing about Ellis Wyatt."

He did not like the way her eyes moved to look at him and remained still, looking, for a moment.

"I don't see any need for immediate action," he said; he sounded offended. "Just what do you consider so alarming in the present situation of Taggart Transcontinental?"

"The consequences of your policies, Jim."

"Which policies?"

"That thirteen months' experiment with Associated Steel, for one. Your Mexican catastrophe, for another."

"The Board approved the Associated Steel contract," he said hastily. "The Board voted to build the San Sebastián Line. Besides, I don't see why you call it a catastrophe."

"Because the Mexican government is going to nationalize your line any day now."

"That's a lie!" His voice was almost a scream. "That's nothing but vicious rumors! I have it on very good inside authority that—"

"Don't show that you're scared, Jim," she said contemptuously.

He did not answer.

"It's no use getting panicky about it now," she said. "All we can do is try to cushion the blow. It's going to be a bad blow. Forty million dollars is a loss from which we won't recover easily. But Taggart Transcontinental has withstood many bad shocks in the past. I'll see to it that it withstands this one."

"I refuse to consider, I absolutely refuse to consider the possibility of the San Sebastián Line being nationalized!"

"All right. Don't consider it."

She remained silent. He said defensively, "I don't see why you're so eager to give a chance to Ellis Wyatt, yet you think it's wrong to take part in developing an underprivileged country that never had a chance."

"Ellis Wyatt is not asking anybody to give him a chance. And I'm not in business to give chances. I'm running a railroad."

"That's an extremely narrow view, it seems to me. I don't see why we should want to help one man instead of a whole nation."

"I'm not interested in helping anybody. I want to make money."

"That's an impractical attitude. Selfish greed for profit is a thing of the past. It has been generally conceded that the interests of society as a whole must always be placed first in any business undertaking which—"

"How long do you intend to talk in order to evade the issue, Jim?"

"What issue?"

"The order for Rearden Metal."

He did not answer. He sat studying her silently. Her slender body, about to slump from exhaustion, was held erect by the straight line of the shoulders, and the shoulders were held by a conscious effort of will. Few people liked her face: the face was too cold, the eyes too intense; nothing could ever lend her the charm of a soft focus. The beautiful legs, slanting down from the chair's arm in the center of his vision, annoyed him; they spoiled the rest of his estimate.

She remained silent; he was forced to ask, "Did you decide to order it just like that, on the spur of the moment, over a telephone?"

"I decided it six months ago. I was waiting for Hank Rearden to get ready to go into production."

"Don't call him *Hank* Rearden. It's vulgar."

"That's what everybody calls him. Don't change the subject."

"Why did you have to telephone him last night?"

"Couldn't reach him sooner."

"Why didn't you wait until you got back to New York and—"

"Because I had seen the Rio Norte Line."

"Well, I need time to consider it, to place the matter before the Board, to consult the best—"

"There is no time."

"You haven't given me a chance to form an opinion."

"I don't give a damn about your opinion. I am not going to argue with you, with your Board or with your professors. You have a choice to make and you're going to make it now. Just say yes or no."

"That's a preposterous, high-handed, arbitrary way of—"

"Yes or no?"

"That's the trouble with you. You always make it 'Yes' or 'No.' Things are never absolute like that. Nothing is absolute."

"Metal rails are. Whether we get them or not, is."

She waited. He did not answer.

"Well?" she asked.

"Are you taking the responsibility for it?"

"I am."

"Go ahead," he said, and added, "but at your own risk. I won't cancel it, but I won't commit myself as to what I'll say to the Board."

"Say anything you wish."

She rose to go. He leaned forward across the desk, reluctant to end the interview and to end it so decisively.

"You realize, of course, that a lengthy procedure will be necessary to put this through," he said; the words sounded almost hopeful. "It isn't as simple as that."

"Oh sure," she said. "I'll send you a detailed report, which Eddie will prepare and which you won't read. Eddie will help you put it through the works. I'm going to Philadelphia tonight to see Rearden. He and I have a lot of work to do." She added, "It's as simple as that, Jim."

She had turned to go, when he spoke again—and what he said seemed bewilderingly irrelevant. "That's all right for you, because you're lucky. Others can't do it."

"Do what?"

"Other people are human. They're sensitive. They can't devote their whole life to metals and engines. You're lucky—you've never had any feelings. You've never felt anything at all."

As she looked at him, her dark gray eyes went slowly from astonishment to stillness, then to a strange expression that resembled a look of weariness, except that it seemed to reflect much more than the endurance of this one moment.

"No, Jim," she said quietly, "I guess I've never felt anything at all."

Eddie Willers followed her to her office. Whenever she returned, he felt as if the world became clear, simple, easy to face—and he forgot his moments of shapeless apprehension. He was the only person who found it completely natural that she should be the Operating Vice-President of a great railroad, even though she was a woman. She had told him, when he was ten years old, that she would run the railroad some day. It did not astonish him now, just as it had not astonished him that day in a clearing of the woods.

When they entered her office, when he saw her sit down at the desk and glance at the memos he had left for her—he felt as he did in his car when the motor caught on and the wheels could move forward.

He was about to leave her office, when he remembered a matter he had not reported. "Owen Kellogg of the Terminal Division has asked me for an appointment to see you," he said.

She looked up, astonished. "That's funny. I was going to send for him. Have him come up. I want to see him. . . . Eddie," she added suddenly, "before I start, tell them to get me Ayers of the Ayers Music Publishing Company on the phone."

"The Music Publishing Company?" he repeated incredulously.

"Yes. There's something I want to ask him."

When the voice of Mr. Ayers, courteously eager, inquired of what service he could be to her, she asked, "Can you tell me whether Richard Halley has written a new piano concerto, the Fifth?"

"A *fifth* concerto, Miss Taggart? Why, no, of course he hasn't."

"Are you sure?"

"Quite sure, Miss Taggart. He has not written anything for eight years."

"Is he still alive?"

"Why, yes—that is, I can't say for certain, he has dropped out of public life entirely—but I'm sure we would have heard of it if he had died."

"If he wrote anything, would you know about it?"

"Of course. We would be the first to know. We publish all of his work. But he has stopped writing."

"I see. Thank you."

When Owen Kellogg entered her office, she looked at him with satisfaction. She was glad to see that she had been right in her vague recollection of his appearance—his face had the same quality as that of the young brakeman on the train, the face of the kind of man with whom she could deal.

"Sit down, Mr. Kellogg," she said, but he remained standing in front of her desk.

"You had asked me once to let you know if I ever decided to change my employment, Miss Taggart," he said. "So I came to tell you that I am quitting."

She had expected anything but that; it took her a moment before she asked quietly, "Why?"

"For a personal reason."

"Were you dissatisfied here?"

"No."

"Have you received a better offer?"

"No."

"What railroad are you going to?"

"I'm not going to any railroad, Miss Taggart."

"Then what job are you taking?"

"I have not decided that yet."

She studied him, feeling slightly uneasy. There was no hostility in his face; he looked straight at her, he answered simply, directly; he spoke like one who has nothing to hide, or to show; the face was polite and empty.

"Then why should you wish to quit?"

"It's a personal matter."

"Are you ill? Is it a question of your health?"

"No."

"Are you leaving the city?"

"No."

"Have you inherited money that permits you to retire?"

"No."

"Do you intend to continue working for a living?"

"Yes."

"But you do not wish to work for Taggart Transcontinental?"

"No."

"In that case, something must have happened here to cause your decision. What?"

"Nothing, Miss Taggart."

"I wish you'd tell me. I have a reason for wanting to know."

"Would you take my word for it, Miss Taggart?"

"Yes."

"No person, matter or event connected with my job here had any bearing upon my decision."

"You have no specific complaint against Taggart Transcontinental?"

"None."

"Then I think you might reconsider when you hear what I have to offer you."

"I'm sorry, Miss Taggart. I can't."

"May I tell you what I have in mind?"

"Yes, if you wish."

"Would you take my word for it that I decided to offer you the post I'm going to offer, before you asked to see me? I want you to know that."

"I will always take your word, Miss Taggart."

"It's the post of Superintendent of the Ohio Division. It's yours, if you want it."

His face showed no reaction, as if the words had no more significance for him than for a savage who had never heard of railroads.

"I don't want it, Miss Taggart," he answered.

After a moment, she said, her voice tight, "Write your own ticket, Kellogg. Name your price. I want you to stay. I can match anything any other railroad offers you."

"I am not going to work for any other railroad."

"I thought you loved your work."

This was the first sign of emotion in him, just a slight widening of his eyes and an oddly quiet emphasis in his voice when he answered, "I do."

"Then tell me what it is that I should say in order to hold you!"

It had been involuntary and so obviously frank that he looked at her as if it had reached him.

"Perhaps I am being unfair by coming here to tell you that I'm quitting, Miss Taggart. I know that you asked me to tell you because you wanted to have a chance to make me a counter-offer. So if I came, it looks as if I'm open to a deal. But I'm not. I came only because I . . . I wanted to keep my word to you."

That one break in his voice was like a sudden flash that told her how much her interest and her request had meant to him; and that his decision had not been an easy one to make.

"Kellogg, is there nothing I can offer you?" she asked.

"Nothing, Miss Taggart. Nothing on earth."

He turned to go. For the first time in her life, she felt helpless and beaten.

"Why?" she asked, not addressing him.

He stopped. He shrugged and smiled—he was alive for a moment and it was the strangest smile she had ever seen: it held secret amusement, and heartbreak, and an infinite bitterness. He answered:

"Who is John Galt?"

II

THE CHAIN

It began with a few lights. As a train of the Taggart line rolled toward Philadelphia, a few brilliant, scattered lights appeared in the darkness; they seemed purposeless in the empty plain, yet too powerful to have no purpose. The passengers watched them idly, without interest.

The black shape of a structure came next, barely visible against the sky, then a big building, close to the tracks; the building was dark, and the reflections of the train lights streaked across the solid glass of its walls.

An oncoming freight train hid the view, filling the windows with a rushing smear of noise. In a sudden break above the flat cars, the passengers saw distant structures under a faint, reddish glow in the sky; the glow moved in irregular spasms, as if the structures were breathing.

When the freight train vanished, they saw angular buildings wrapped in coils of steam. The rays of a few strong lights cut straight sheafs through the coils. The steam was red as the sky.

The thing that came next did not look like a building, but like a shell of checkered glass enclosing girders, cranes and trusses in a solid, blinding, orange spread of flame.

The passengers could not grasp the complexity of what seemed to be a city stretched for miles, active without sign of human presence. They saw towers that looked like contorted skyscrapers, bridges hanging in mid-air, and sudden wounds spurting fire from out of solid walls. They saw a line of glowing cylinders moving through the night; the cylinders were red-hot metal.

An office building appeared, close to the tracks. The big neon sign on its roof lighted the interiors of the coaches as they went by. It said: REARDEN STEEL.

A passenger, who was a professor of economics, remarked to his companion: "Of what importance is an individual in the titanic collective achievements of our industrial age?" Another, who was a journalist, made a note for future use in his column: "Hank Rearden is the kind of man who sticks his name on everything he touches. You may, from this, form your own opinion about the character of Hank Rearden."

The train was speeding on into the darkness when a red gasp shot to

"That's the trouble I've always had with you." She was not looking at him, but reciting words into space. "It's no use trying to do things for you, you don't appreciate it. I could never make you eat properly."

"Henry, you work too hard," said Philip. "It's not good for you."

Rearden laughed. "I like it."

"That's what you tell yourself. It's a form of neurosis, you know. When a man drowns himself in work, it's because he's trying to escape from something. You ought to have a hobby."

"Oh, Phil, for Christ's sake!" he said, and regretted the irritation in his voice.

Philip had always been in precarious health, though doctors had found no specific defect in his loose, gangling body. He was thirty-eight, but his chronic weariness made people think at times that he was older than his brother.

"You ought to learn to have some fun," said Philip. "Otherwise, you'll become dull and narrow. Single-tracked, you know. You ought to get out of your little private shell and take a look at the world. You don't want to miss life, the way you're doing."

Fighting anger, Rearden told himself that this was Philip's form of solicitude. He told himself that it would be unjust to feel resentment: they were all trying to show their concern for him—and he wished these were not the things they had chosen for concern.

"I had a pretty good time today, Phil," he answered, smiling—and wondered why Philip did not ask him what it was.

He wished one of them would ask him. He was finding it hard to concentrate. The sight of the running metal was still burned into his mind, filling his consciousness, leaving no room for anything else.

"You might have apologized, only I ought to know better than to expect it." It was his mother's voice; he turned: she was looking at him with that injured look which proclaims the long-bearing patience of the defenseless.

"Mrs. Beecham was here for dinner," she said reproachfully.

"What?"

"Mrs. Beecham. My friend Mrs. Beecham."

"Yes?"

"I told you about her, I told you many times, but you never remember anything I say. Mrs. Beecham was so anxious to meet you, but she had to leave after dinner, she couldn't wait, Mrs. Beecham is a very busy person. She wanted so much to tell you about the wonderful work we're doing in our parish school, and about the classes in metal craftsmanship, and about the beautiful wrought-iron doorknobs that the little slum children are making all by themselves."

It took the whole of his sense of consideration to force himself to answer evenly, "I'm sorry if I disappointed you, Mother."

"You're not sorry. You could've been here if you'd made the effort. But when did you ever make an effort for anybody but yourself? You're not interested in any of us or in anything we do. You think that if you pay the bills, that's enough, don't you? Money! That's all you know. And all you give us is money. Have you ever given us any time?"

If this meant that she missed him, he thought, then it meant affection, and if it meant affection, then he was unjust to experience a heavy, murky feeling which kept him silent lest his voice betray that the feeling was disgust.

"You don't care," her voice went half-spitting, half-begging on. "Lillian needed you today for a very important problem, but I told her it was no use waiting to discuss it with you."

"Oh, Mother, it's not important!" said Lillian. "Not to Henry."

He turne 1 to her. He stood in the middle of the room, with his trenchcoat still on, as if he were trapped in an unreality that would not become real to him.

"It's not important at all," said Lillian gaily; he could not tell whether her voice was apologetic or boastful. "It's not business. It's purely non-commercial."

"What is it?"

"Just a party I'm planning to give."

"A party?"

"Oh, don't look frightened, it's not for tomorrow night. I know that you're so very busy, but it's for three months from now and I want it to be a very big, very special affair, so would you promise me to be here that night and not in Minnesota or Colorado or California?"

She was looking at him in an odd manner, speaking too lightly and too purposefully at once, her smile overstressing an air of innocence and suggesting something like a hidden trump card.

"Three months from now?" he said. "But you know that I can't tell what urgent business might come up to call me out of town."

"Oh, I know! But couldn't I make a formal appointment with you, way in advance, just like any railroad executive, automobile manufacturer or junk—I mean, scrap—dealer? They say you never miss an appointment. Of course, I'd let you pick the date to suit your convenience." She was looking up at him, her glance acquiring some special quality of feminine appeal by being sent from under her lowered forehead up toward his full height; she asked, a little too casually and too cautiously, "The date I had in mind was December tenth, but would you prefer the ninth or the eleventh?"

"It makes no difference to me."

She said gently, "December tenth is our wedding anniversary, Henry."

They were all watching his face; if they expected a look of guilt, what they saw, instead, was a faint smile of amusement. She could not have intended this as a trap, he thought, because he could escape it so easily, by refusing to accept any blame for his forgetfulness and by leaving her spurned; she knew that his feeling for her was her only weapon. Her motive, he thought, was a proudly indirect attempt to test his feeling and to confess her own. A party was not his form of celebration, but it was hers. It meant nothing in his terms; in hers, it meant the best tribute she could offer to him and to their marriage. He had to respect her intention, he thought, even if he did not share her standards, even if he did not know whether he still cared for any tribute from her. He had to let her win, he thought, because she had thrown herself upon his mercy.

He smiled, an open, unresentful smile in acknowledgment of her victory. "All right, Lillian," he said quietly, "I promise to be here on the night of December tenth."

"Thank you, dear." Her smile had a closed, mysterious quality; he wondered why he had a moment's impression that his attitude had disappointed them all.

If she trusted him, he thought, if her feeling for him was still alive, then he would match her trust. He had to say it; words were a lens to focus one's mind, and he could not use words for anything else tonight. "I'm sorry I'm late, Lillian, but today at the mills we poured the first heat of Rearden Metal."

There was a moment of silence. Then Philip said, "Well, that's nice."

The others said nothing.

He put his hand in his pocket. When he touched it, the reality of the bracelet swept out everything else; he felt as he had felt when the liquid metal had poured through space before him.

"I brought you a present, Lillian."

He did not know that he stood straight and that the gesture of his arm was that of a returning crusader offering his trophy to his love, when he dropped a small chain of metal into her lap.

Lillian Rearden picked it up, hooked on the tips of two straight fingers, and raised it to the light. The links were heavy, crudely made, the shining metal had an odd tinge, it was greenish-blue.

"What's that?" she asked.

"The first thing made from the first heat of the first order of Rearden Metal."

"You mean," she said, "it's fully as valuable as a piece of railroad rails?"

He looked at her blankly.

She jingled the bracelet, making it sparkle under the light. "Henry, it's perfectly wonderful! What originality! I shall be the sensation of New York, wearing jewelry made of the same stuff as bridge girders, truck motors, kitchen stoves, typewriters, and—what was it you were saying about it the other day, darling?—soup kettles?"

"God, Henry, but you're conceited!" said Philip.

Lillian laughed. "He's a sentimentalist. All men are. But, darling, I do appreciate it. It isn't the gift, it's the intention, I know."

"The intention's plain selfishness, if you ask me," said Rearden's mother. "Another man would bring a diamond bracelet, if he wanted to give his wife a present, because it's *her* pleasure he'd think of, not his own. But Henry thinks that just because he's made a new kind of tin, why, it's got to be more precious than diamonds to everybody, just because it's he that's made it. That's the way he's been since he was five years old—the most conceited brat you ever saw—and I knew he'd grow up to be the most selfish creature on God's earth."

"No, it's sweet," said Lillian. "It's charming." She dropped the bracelet down on the table. She got up, put her hands on Rearden's shoulders, and raising herself on tiptoe, kissed him on the cheek, saying, "Thank you, dear."

He did not move, did not bend his head down to her.

After a while, he turned, took off his coat and sat down by the fire, apart from the others. He felt nothing but an immense exhaustion.

He did not listen to their talk. He heard dimly that Lillian was arguing, defending him against his mother.

"I know him better than you do," his mother was saying. "Hank Rearden's not interested in man, beast or weed unless it's tied in some way to himself and his work. That's all he cares about. I've tried my best to teach him some humility, I've tried all my life, but I've failed."

He had offered his mother unlimited means to live as and where she pleased; he wondered why she had insisted that she wanted to live with him. His success, he had thought, meant something to her, and if it did, then it was a bond between them, the only kind of bond he recognized; if she wanted a place in the home of her successful son, he would not deny it to her.

"It's no use hoping to make a saint out of Henry, Mother," said Philip. "He wasn't meant to be one."

"Oh but, Philip, you're wrong!" said Lillian. "You're so wrong! Henry has all the makings of a saint. That's the trouble."

What did they seek from him?—thought Rearden—what were they after? He had never asked anything of them; it was they who wished to hold him, they who pressed a claim on him—and the claim seemed to have the form of affection, but it was a form which he found harder to endure than any sort of hatred. He despised causeless affection, just as he despised unearned wealth. They professed to love him for some unknown reason and they ignored all the things for which he could wish to be loved. He wondered what response they could hope to obtain from him in such manner—if his response was what they wanted. And it was, he thought; else why those constant complaints, those unceasing accusations about his indifference? Why that chronic air of suspicion, as if they were waiting to be hurt? He had never had a desire to hurt them, but he had always felt their defensive, reproachful expectation; they seemed wounded by anything he said, it was not a matter of his words or actions, it was almost . . . almost as if they were wounded by the mere fact of his being. Don't start imagining the insane

—he told himself severely, struggling to face the riddle with the strictest of his ruthless sense of justice. He could not condemn them without understanding; and he could not understand.

Did he like them? No, he thought; he had wanted to like them, which was not the same. He had wanted it in the name of some unstated potentiality which he had once expected to see in any human being. He felt nothing for them now, nothing but the merciless zero of indifference, not even the regret of a loss. Did he need any person as part of his life? Did he miss the feeling he had wanted to feel? No, he thought. Had he ever missed it? Yes, he thought, in his youth; not any longer.

His sense of exhaustion was growing; he realized that it was boredom. He owed them the courtesy of hiding it, he thought—and sat motionless, fighting a desire for sleep that was turning into physical pain.

His eyes were closing, when he felt two soft, moist fingers touching his hand: Paul Larkin had pulled a chair to his side and was leaning over for a private conversation.

"I don't care what the industry says about it, Hank, you've got a great product in Rearden Metal, a great product, it will make a fortune, like everything you touch."

"Yes," said Rearden, "it will."

"I just . . . I just hope you don't run into trouble."

"What trouble?"

"Oh, I don't know . . . the way things are nowadays . . . there's people, who . . . but how can we tell? . . . anything can happen. . . ."

"What trouble?"

Larkin sat hunched, looking up with his gentle, pleading eyes. His short, plumpish figure always seemed unprotected and incomplete, as if he needed a shell to shrink into at the slightest touch. His wistful eyes, his lost, helpless, appealing smile served as substitute for the shell. The smile was disarming, like that of a boy who throws himself at the mercy of an incomprehensible universe. He was fifty-three years old.

"Your public relations aren't any too good, Hank," he said. "You've always had a bad press."

"So what?"

"You're not popular, Hank."

"I haven't heard any complaints from my customers."

"That's not what I mean. You ought to hire yourself a good press agent to sell *you* to the public."

"What for? It's steel that I'm selling."

"But you don't want to have the public against you. Public opinion, you know—it can mean a lot."

"I don't think the public's against me. And I don't think that it means a damn, one way or another."

"The newspapers are against you."

"They have time to waste. I haven't."

"I don't like it, Hank. It's not good."

"What?"

"What they write about you."

"What do they write about me?"

"Well, you know the stuff. That you're intractable. That you're ruthless. That you won't allow anyone any voice in the running of your mills. That your only goal is to make steel and to make money."

"But that *is* my only goal."

"But you shouldn't say it."

"Why not? What is it I'm supposed to say?"

"Oh, I don't know . . . But your mills—"

"They're *my* mills, aren't they?"

"Yes, but—but you shouldn't remind people of that too loudly. . . . You know how it is nowadays. . . . They think that your attitude is anti-social."

"I don't give a damn what they think."

Paul Larkin sighed.

"What's the matter, Paul? What are you driving at?"

"Nothing . . . nothing in particular. Only one never knows what can happen in times like these. . . . One has to be so careful . . ."

Rearden chuckled. "You're not trying to worry about me, are you?"

"It's just that I'm your friend, Hank. I'm your friend. You know how much I admire you."

Paul Larkin had always been unlucky. Nothing he touched ever came off quite well, nothing ever quite failed or succeeded. He was a businessman, but he could not manage to remain for long in any one line of business. At the moment, he was struggling with a modest plant that manufactured mining equipment.

He had clung to Rearden for years, in awed admiration. He came for advice, he asked for loans at times, but not often; the loans were modest and were always repaid, though not always on time. His motive in the relationship seemed to resemble the need of an anemic person who receives a kind of living transfusion from the mere sight of a savagely overabundant vitality.

Watching Larkin's efforts, Rearden felt what he did when he watched an ant struggling under the load of a matchstick. It's so hard for him, thought Rearden, and so easy for me. So he gave advice, attention and a tactful, patient interest, whenever he could.

"I'm your friend, Hank."

Rearden looked at him inquiringly.

Larkin glanced away, as if debating something in his mind. After a while, he asked cautiously, "How is your man in Washington?"

"Okay, I guess."

"You ought to be sure of it. It's important." He looked up at Rearden, and repeated with a kind of stressed insistence, as if discharging a painful moral duty, "Hank, it's very important."

"I suppose so."

"In fact, that's what I came here to tell you."

"For any special reason?"

Larkin considered it and decided that the duty was discharged. "No," he said.

Rearden disliked the subject. He knew that it was necessary to have a man to protect him from the legislature; all industrialists had to employ such men. But he had never given much attention to this aspect of his business; he could not quite convince himself that it was necessary. An inexplicable kind of distaste, part fastidiousness, part boredom, stopped him whenever he tried to consider it.

"Trouble is, Paul," he said, thinking aloud, "that the men one has to pick for that job are such a crummy lot."

Larkin looked away. "That's life," he said.

"Damned if I see why. Can you tell me that? What's wrong with the world?"

Larkin shrugged sadly. "Why ask useless questions? How deep is the ocean? How high is the sky? Who is John Galt?"

Rearden sat up straight. "No," he said sharply. "No. There's no reason to feel that way."

He got up. His exhaustion had gone while he talked about his business. He felt a sudden spurt of rebellion, a need to recapture and defiantly to reassert his own view of existence, that sense of it which he had held while walking home tonight and which now seemed threatened in some nameless manner.

He paced the room, his energy returning. He looked at his family. They were bewildered, unhappy children—he thought—all of them, even his mother, and he was foolish to resent their ineptitude; it came from their helplessness, not from malice. It was he who had to make himself learn to understand them, since he had so much to give, since they could never share his sense of joyous, boundless power.

He glanced at them from across the room. His mother and Philip were engaged in some eager discussion; but he noted that they were not really eager, they were nervous. Philip sat in a low chair, his stomach forward, his weight on his shoulder blades, as if the miserable discomfort of his position were intended to punish the onlookers.

"What's the matter, Phil?" Rearden asked, approaching him. "You look done in."

"I've had a hard day," said Philip sullenly.

"You're not the only one who works hard," said his mother. "Others have problems, too—even if they're not billion-dollar, trans-super-continental problems like yours."

"Why, that's good. I always thought that Phil should find some interest of his own."

"Good? You mean you like to see your brother sweating his health away? It amuses you, doesn't it? I always thought it did."

"Why, no, Mother. I'd like to help."

"You don't have to help. You don't have to feel anything for any of us."

Rearden had never known what his brother was doing or wished to do. He had sent Philip through college, but Philip had not been able to decide on any specific ambition. There was something wrong, by Rearden's standards, with a man who did not seek any gainful employment, but he would not impose his standards on Philip; he could afford to support his brother and never notice the expense. Let him take it easy, Rearden had thought for years, let him have a chance to choose his career without the strain of struggling for a livelihood.

"What were you doing today, Phil?" he asked patiently.

"It wouldn't interest you."

"It does interest me. That's why I'm asking."

"I had to see twenty different people all over the place, from here to Redding to Wilmington."

"What did you have to see them about?"

"I am trying to raise money for Friends of Global Progress."

Rearden had never been able to keep track of the many organizations to which Philip belonged, nor to get a clear idea of their activities. He had heard Philip talking vaguely about this one for the last six months. It seemed to be devoted to some sort of free lectures on psychology, folk music and co-operative farming. Rearden felt contempt for groups of that kind and saw no reason for a closer inquiry into their nature.

He remained silent. Philip added without being prompted, "We need ten thousand dollars for a vital program, but it's a martyr's task, trying to raise money. There's not a speck of social conscience left in people. When I think of the kind of bloated money-bags I saw today—why, they spend more than that on any whim, but I couldn't squeeze just a hundred bucks a piece out of them, which was all I asked. They have no sense of moral duty, no . . . What are you laughing at?" he asked sharply. Rearden stood before him, grinning.

It was so childishly blatant, thought Rearden, so helplessly crude: the hint and the insult, offered together. It would be so easy to squash Philip by returning the insult, he thought—by returning an insult which would be deadly because it would be true—that he could not bring himself to utter it. Surely, he thought, the poor fool knows he's at my mercy, knows he's opened himself to be hurt, so I don't have to do it, and my not doing it is my best answer, which he won't be able to miss. What sort of misery does he really live in, to get himself twisted quite so badly?

And then Rearden thought suddenly that he could break through Philip's chronic wretchedness for once, give him a shock of pleasure, the unexpected gratification of a hopeless desire. He thought: What do I care about the nature of his desire?—it's his, just as Rearden Metal was mine—it must mean to him what that meant to me—let's see him happy just once, it might teach him something—didn't I say that happiness is the agent of purification?—I'm celebrating tonight, so let him share in it—it will be so much for him, and so little for me.

"Philip," he said, smiling, "call Miss Ives at my office tomorrow. She'll have a check for you for ten thousand dollars."

Philip stared at him blankly; it was neither shock nor pleasure; it was just the empty stare of eyes that looked glassy.

"Oh," said Philip, then added, "We'll appreciate it very much." There was no emotion in his voice, not even the simple one of greed.

Rearden could not understand his own feeling: it was as if something leaden and empty were collapsing within him, he felt both the weight and the emptiness, together. He knew it was disappointment, but he wondered why it was so gray and ugly.

"It's very nice of you, Henry," Philip said dryly. "I'm surprised. I didn't expect it of you."

"Don't you understand it, Phil?" said Lillian, her voice peculiarly clear and lilting. "Henry's poured his metal today." She turned to Rearden. "Shall we declare it a national holiday, darling?"

"You're a good man, Henry," said his mother, and added, "but not often enough."

Rearden stood looking at Philip, as if waiting.

Philip looked away, then raised his eyes and held Rearden's glance, as if engaged in a scrutiny of his own.

"You don't really care about helping the underprivileged, do you?" Philip asked—and Rearden heard, unable to believe it, that the tone of his voice was reproachful.

"No, Phil, I don't care about it at all. I only wanted you to be happy."

"But that money is not for me. I am not collecting it for any personal motive. I have no selfish interest in the matter whatever." His voice was cold, with a note of self-conscious virtue.

Rearden turned away. He felt a sudden loathing: not because the words were hypocrisy, but because they were true; Philip meant them.

"By the way, Henry," Philip added, "do you mind if I ask you to have Miss Ives give me the money in cash?" Rearden turned back to him, puzzled. "You see, Friends of Global Progress are a very progressive group and they have always maintained that you represent the blackest element of social retrogression in the country, so it would embarrass us, you know, to have your name on our list of contributors, because somebody might accuse us of being in the pay of Hank Rearden."

He wanted to slap Philip's face. But an almost unendurable contempt made him close his eyes, instead.

available on schedule. But who gets the benefit of it? Nobody except its owner. Would you say that that's fair?"

"No," said Taggart, "it isn't fair."

"Most of us don't own iron mines. How can we compete with a man who's got a corner on God's natural resources? Is it any wonder that he can always deliver steel, while we have to struggle and wait and lose our customers and go out of business? Is it in the public interest to let one man destroy an entire industry?"

"No," said Taggart, "it isn't."

"It seems to me that the national policy ought to be aimed at the objective of giving everybody a chance at his fair share of iron ore, with a view toward the preservation of the industry as a whole. Don't you think so?"

"I think so."

Boyle sighed. Then he said cautiously, "But I guess there aren't many people in Washington capable of understanding a progressive social policy."

Taggart said slowly, "There are. No, not many and not easy to approach, but there are. I might speak to them."

Boyle picked up his drink and swallowed it in one gulp, as if he had heard all he had wanted to hear.

"Speaking of progressive policies, Orren," said Taggart, "you might ask yourself whether at a time of transportation shortages, when so many railroads are going bankrupt and large areas are left without rail service, whether it is in the public interest to tolerate wasteful duplication of services and the destructive, dog-eat-dog competition of newcomers in territories where established companies have historical priority."

"Well, now," said Boyle pleasantly, "that seems to be an interesting question to consider. I might discuss it with a few friends in the National Alliance of Railroads."

"Friendships," said Taggart in the tone of an idle abstraction, "are more valuable than gold." Unexpectedly, he turned to Larkin. "Don't you think so, Paul?"

"Why . . . yes," said Larkin, astonished. "Yes, of course."

"I am counting on yours."

"Huh?"

"I am counting on your many friendships."

They all seemed to know why Larkin did not answer at once; his shoulders seemed to shrink down, closer to the table. "If everybody could pull for a common purpose, then nobody would have to be hurt!" he cried suddenly, in a tone of incongruous despair; he saw Taggart watching him and added, pleading, "I wish we didn't have to hurt anybody."

"That is an anti-social attitude," drawled Taggart. "People who are afraid to sacrifice somebody have no business talking about a common purpose."

"But I'm a student of history," said Larkin hastily. "I recognize historical necessity."

"Good," said Taggart.

"I can't be expected to buck the trend of the whole world, can I?" Larkin seemed to plead, but the plea was not addressed to anyone. "Can I?"

"You can't, Mr. Larkin," said Wesley Mouch. "You and I are not to be blamed, if we—"

Larkin jerked his head away; it was almost a shudder; he could not bear to look at Mouch.

"Did you have a good time in Mexico, Orren?" asked Taggart, his voice suddenly loud and casual. All of them seemed to know that the purpose of their meeting was accomplished and whatever they had come here to understand was understood.

"Wonderful place, Mexico," Boyle answered cheerfully. "Very stimulating and thought-provoking. Their food rations are something awful, though. I got sick. But they're working mighty hard to put their country on its feet."

"How are things going down there?"

"Pretty splendid, it seems to me, pretty splendid. Right at the moment, however, they're . . . But then, what they're aiming at is the future. The People's State of Mexico has a great future. They'll beat us all in a few years."

"Did you go down to the San Sebastián Mines?"

The four figures at the table sat up straighter and tighter; all of them had invested heavily in the stock of the San Sebastián Mines.

Boyle did not answer at once, so that his voice seemed unexpected and unnaturally loud when it burst forth: "Oh, sure, certainly, that's what I wanted to see most."

"And?"

"And what?"

"How are things going?"

"Great. Great. They must certainly have the biggest deposits of copper on earth, down inside that mountain!"

"Did they seem to be busy?"

"Never saw such a busy place in my life."

"What were they busy doing?"

"Well, you know, with the kind of Spic superintendent they have down there, I couldn't understand half of what he was talking about, but they're certainly busy."

"Any . . . trouble of any kind?"

"Trouble? Not at San Sebastián. It's private property, the last piece of it left in Mexico, and that does seem to make a difference."

"Orren," Taggart asked cautiously, "what about those rumors that they're planning to nationalize the San Sebastián Mines?"

"Slander," said Boyle angrily, "plain, vicious slander. I know it for certain. I had dinner with the Minister of Culture and lunches with all the rest of the boys."

"There ought to be a law against irresponsible gossip," said Taggart sullenly. "Let's have another drink."

He waved irritably at a waiter. There was a small bar in a dark corner of the room, where an old, wizened bartender stood for long stretches of time without moving. When called upon, he moved with contemptuous slowness. His job was that of servant to men's relaxation and pleasure, but his manner was that of an embittered quack ministering to some guilty disease.

The four men sat in silence until the waiter returned with their drinks. The glasses he placed on the table were four spots of faint blue glitter in the semi-darkness, like four feeble jets of gas flame. Taggart reached for his glass and smiled suddenly.

"Let's drink to the sacrifices to historical necessity," he said, looking at Larkin.

There was a moment's pause; in a lighted room, it would have been the contest of two men holding each other's eyes; here, they were merely looking at each other's eye sockets. Then Larkin picked up his glass.

"It's my party, boys," said Taggart, as they drank.

Nobody found anything else to say, until Boyle spoke up with indifferent curiosity. "Say, Jim, I meant to ask you, what in hell's the matter with your train service down on the San Sebastián Line?"

"Why, what do you mean? What is the matter with it?"

"Well, I don't know, but running just one passenger train a day is—"

"*One* train?"

"—is pretty measly service, it seems to me, and what a train! You must have inherited those coaches from your great-grandfather, and he must have used them pretty hard. And where on earth did you get that wood-burning locomotive?"

"*Wood*-burning?"

"That's what I said, wood-burning. I never saw one before, except in photographs. What museum did you drag it out of? Now don't act as if you didn't know it, just tell me what's the gag?"

"Yes, of course I knew it," said Taggart hastily. "It was just . . . You just happened to choose the one week when we had a little trouble with our motive power—our new engines are on order, but there's been a slight delay—you know what a problem we're having with the manufacturers of locomotives—but it's only temporary."

"Of course," said Boyle. "Delays can't be helped. It's the strangest train I ever rode on, though. Nearly shook my guts out."

Within a few minutes, they noticed that Taggart had become silent. He seemed preoccupied with a problem of his own. When he rose abruptly, without apology, they rose, too, accepting it as a command.

Larkin muttered, smiling too strenuously, "It was a pleasure, Jim. A pleasure. That's how great projects are born—over a drink with friends."

"Social reforms are slow," said Taggart coldly. "It is advisable to be patient and cautious." For the first time, he turned to Wesley Mouch. "What I like about you, Mouch, is that you don't talk too much."

Wesley Mouch was Rearden's Washington man.

There was still a remnant of sunset light in the sky, when Taggart and Boyle emerged together into the street below. The transition was faintly shocking to them—the enclosed barroom led one to expect midnight darkness. A tall building stood outlined against the sky, sharp and straight like a raised sword. In the distance beyond it, there hung the calendar.

Taggart fumbled irritably with his coat collar, buttoning it against the chill of the streets. He had not intended to go back to the office tonight, but he had to go back. He had to see his sister.

". . . a difficult undertaking ahead of us, Jim," Boyle was saying, "a difficult undertaking, with so many dangers and complications and so much at stake . . ."

"It all depends," James Taggart answered slowly, "on knowing the people who make it possible. . . . That's what has to be known—who makes it possible."

* * *

Dagny Taggart was nine years old when she decided that she would run the Taggart Transcontinental Railroad some day. She stated it to herself when she stood alone between the rails, looking at the two straight lines of steel that went off into the distance and met in a single point. What she felt was an arrogant pleasure at the way the track cut through the woods: it did not belong in the midst of ancient trees, among green branches that hung down to meet green brush and the lonely spears of wild flowers—but there it was. The two steel lines were brilliant in the sun, and the black ties were like the rungs of a ladder which she had to climb.

It was not a sudden decision, but only the final seal of words upon something she had known long ago. In unspoken understanding, as if bound by a vow it had never been necessary to take, she and Eddie Willers had given themselves to the railroad from the first conscious days of their childhood.

She felt a bored indifference toward the immediate world around her, toward other children and adults alike. She took it as a regrettable accident, to be borne patiently for a while, that she happened to be imprisoned among people who were dull. She had caught a glimpse of another world and she knew that it existed somewhere, the world that had created trains, bridges, telegraph wires and signal lights winking in the night. She had to wait, she thought, and grow up to that world.

She never tried to explain why she liked the railroad. Whatever it was that others felt, she knew that this was one emotion for which they had no equivalent and no response. She felt the same emotion in school, in classes of mathematics, the only lessons she liked. She felt the excitement of solving problems, the insolent delight of taking up a challenge and disposing of it without effort, the eagerness to meet another, harder test. She felt, at the same time, a growing respect for the adversary, for a science that was so clean, so strict, so luminously rational. Studying mathematics, she felt, quite simply and at once: "How great that men have done this" and "How wonderful that I'm so good at it." It was the joy of admiration and of one's own ability, growing together. Her feeling for the railroad was the same: worship of the skill that had gone to make it, of the ingenuity of someone's clean, reasoning mind, worship with a secret smile that said she would know how to make it better some day. She hung around the tracks and the roundhouses like a humble student, but the humility had a touch of future pride, a pride to be earned.

"You're unbearably conceited," was one of the two sentences she heard throughout her childhood, even though she never spoke of her own ability. The other sentence was: "You're selfish." She asked what was meant, but never received an answer. She looked at the adults, wondering how they could imagine that she would feel guilt from an undefined accusation.

She was twelve years old when she told Eddie Willers that she would run the railroad when they grew up. She was fifteen when it occurred to her for the first time that women did not run railroads and that people might object. To hell with that, she thought—and never worried about it again.

She went to work for Taggart Transcontinental at the age of sixteen. Her father permitted it: he was amused and a little curious. She started as night operator at a small country station. She had to work nights for the first few years, while attending a college of engineering.

James Taggart began his career on the railroad at the same time; he was twenty-one. He started in the Department of Public Relations.

Dagny's rise among the men who operated Taggart Transcontinental was swift and uncontested. She took positions of responsibility because there was no one else to take them. There were a few rare men of talent around her, but they were becoming rarer every year. Her superiors, who held the authority, seemed afraid to exercise it, they spent their time avoiding decisions, so she told people what to do and they did it. At every step of her rise, she did the work long before she was granted the title. It was like advancing through empty rooms. Nobody opposed her, yet nobody approved of her progress.

Her father seemed astonished and proud of her, but he said nothing and there was sadness in his eyes when he looked at her in the office. She was twenty-nine years old when he died. "There has always been a Taggart to run the railroad," was the last thing he said to her. He looked at her with an odd glance: it had the quality of a salute and of compassion, together.

The controlling stock of Taggart Transcontinental was left to James Taggart. He was thirty-four when he became President of the railroad. Dagny had expected the Board of Directors to elect him, but she had never been able to understand why they did it so eagerly. They talked about tradition, the president had always been the eldest son of the Taggart family; they elected James Taggart in the same manner as they refused to walk under a ladder, to propitiate the same kind of fear. They talked about his gift of "making railroads popular," his "good press," his "Washington ability." He seemed unusually skillful at obtaining favors from the Legislature.

Dagny knew nothing about the field of "Washington ability" or what such an ability implied. But it seemed to be necessary, so she dismissed it with the thought that there were many kinds of work which were offensive, yet necessary, such as cleaning sewers; somebody had to do it, and Jim seemed to like it.

She had never aspired to the presidency; the Operating Department was her only concern. When she went out on the line, old railroad men, who hated Jim, said, "There will always be a Taggart to run the railroad," looking at her as her father had looked. She was armed against Jim by the conviction that he was not smart enough to harm the railroad too much and that she would always be able to correct whatever damage he caused.

At sixteen, sitting at her operator's desk, watching the lighted windows of Taggart trains roll past, she had thought that she had entered her kind of world. In the years since, she learned that she hadn't. The adversary she found herself forced to fight was not worth matching or beating; it was not a superior ability which she would have found honor in challenging; it was ineptitude—a gray spread of cotton that seemed soft and shapeless, that could offer no resistance to anything or anybody, yet managed to be a barrier in her way. She stood, disarmed, before the riddle of what made this possible. She could find no answer.

It was only in the first few years that she felt herself screaming silently, at times, for a glimpse of human ability, a single glimpse of clean, hard, radiant competence. She had fits of tortured longing for a friend or an enemy with a mind better than her own. But the longing passed. She had a job to do. She did not have time to feel pain; not often.

The first step of the policy that James Taggart brought to the railroad was the construction of the San Sebastián Line. Many men were responsible for it; but to Dagny, one name stood written across that venture, a name that wiped out all others wherever she saw it. It stood across five years of struggle, across miles of wasted track, across sheets of figures that recorded the losses of Taggart Transcontinental like a red trickle from a wound which would not heal—as it stood on the ticker tape of every stock exchange left in the world—as it stood on smoke-stacks in the red glare of furnaces melting copper—as it stood in scandalous headlines—as it stood on parchment pages recording the nobility of the centuries—as it stood on cards attached to flowers in the boudoirs of women scattered through three continents.

The name was Francisco d'Anconia.

At the age of twenty-three, when he inherited his fortune, Francisco d'Anconia had been famous as the copper king of the world. Now, at thirty-six, he was famous as the richest man and the most spectacularly worthless playboy on earth. He was the last descendant of one of the noblest families of Argentina. He owned cattle ranches, coffee planta-tions and most of the copper mines of Chile. He owned half of South America and sundry mines scattered through the United States as small change.

When Francisco d'Anconia suddenly bought miles of bare mountains in Mexico, news leaked out that he had discovered vast deposits of copper. He made no effort to sell stock in his venture; the stock was begged out of his hands, and he merely chose those whom he wished to favor from among the applicants. His financial talent was called phenomenal; no one had ever beaten him in any transaction—he added to his incredible fortune with every deal he touched and every step he made, when he took the trouble to make it. Those who censured him most were first to seize the chance of riding on his talent, toward a share of his new wealth. James Taggart, Orren Boyle and their friends were among the heaviest stockholders of the project which Francisco d'Anconia had named the San Sebastián Mines.

Dagny was never able to discover what influences prompted James Taggart to build a railroad branch from Texas into the wilderness of San Sebastián. It seemed likely that he did not know it himself: like a field without a windbreak, he seemed open to any current, and the final sum was made by chance. A few among the Directors of Taggart Transcontinental objected to the project. The company needed all its resources to rebuild the Rio Norte Line; it could not do both. But James Taggart was the road's new president. It was the first year of his administration. He won.

The People's State of Mexico was eager to co-operate, and signed a contract guaranteeing for two hundred years the property right of Tag-gart Transcontinental to its railroad line in a country where no property rights existed. Francisco d'Anconia had obtained the same guaranty for his mines.

Dagny fought against the building of the San Sebastián Line. She fought by means of whoever would listen to her; but she was only an assistant in the Operating Department, too young, without authority, and nobody listened.

She was unable, then or since, to understand the motives of those who decided to build the line. Sitting as a helpless spectator, a minority member, at one of the Board meetings, she felt a strange evasiveness in the air of the room, in every speech, in every argument, as if the real reason of their decision were never stated, but clear to everyone except herself.

They spoke about the future importance of the trade with Mexico, about a rich stream of freight, about the large revenues assured to the exclusive carrier of an inexhaustible supply of copper. They proved it by citing Francisco d'Anconia's past achievements. They did not mention any mineralogical facts about the San Sebastián Mines. Few facts were available; the information which d'Anconia had released was not very specific; but they did not seem to need facts.

They spoke at great length about the poverty of the Mexicans and their desperate need of railroads. "They've never had a chance." "It is our duty to help an underprivileged nation to develop. A country, it seems to me, is its neighbors' keeper."

She sat, listening, and she thought of the many branch lines which Taggart Transcontinental had had to abandon; the revenues of the great railroad had been falling slowly for many years. She thought of the ominous need of repairs, ominously neglected over the entire system. Their policy on the problem of maintenance was not a policy but a game they seemed to be playing with a piece of rubber that could be stretched a little, then a little more.

"The Mexicans, it seems to me, are a very diligent people, crushed by their primitive economy. How can they become industrialized if nobody lends them a hand?" "When considering an investment, we should, in my opinion, take a chance on human beings, rather than on purely material factors."

She thought of an engine that lay in a ditch beside the Rio Norte Line, because a splice bar had cracked. She thought of the five days when all traffic was stopped on the Rio Norte Line, because a retaining wall had collapsed, pouring tons of rock across the track.

"Since a man must think of the good of his brothers before he thinks of his own, it seems to me that a nation must think of its neighbors before it thinks of itself."

She thought of a newcomer called Ellis Wyatt whom people were beginning to watch, because his activity was the first trickle of a torrent of goods about to burst from the dying stretches of Colorado. The Rio Norte Line was being allowed to run its way to a final collapse, just when its fullest efficiency was about to be needed and used.

"Material greed isn't everything. There are non-material ideals to consider." "I confess to a feeling of shame when I think that we own a huge network of railways, while the Mexican people have nothing but one or two inadequate lines." "The old theory of economic self-sufficiency has been exploded long ago. It is impossible for one country to prosper in the midst of a starving world."

She thought that to make Taggart Transcontinental what it had been once, long before her time, every available rail, spike and dollar was needed—and how desperately little of it was available.

They spoke also, at the same session, in the same speeches, about the efficiency of the Mexican government that held complete control of everything. Mexico had a great future, they said, and would become a dangerous competitor in a few years. "Mexico's got discipline," the men of the Board kept saying, with a note of envy in their voices.

James Taggart let it be understood—in unfinished sentences and undefined hints—that his friends in Washington, whom he never named, wished to see a railroad line built in Mexico, that such a line would be of great help in matters of international diplomacy, that the good will of the public opinion of the world would more than repay Taggart Transcontinental for its investment.

They voted to build the San Sebastián Line at a cost of thirty million dollars.

When Dagny left the Board room and walked through the clean, cold air of the streets, she heard two words repeated clearly, insistently in the numbed emptiness of her mind: Get out . . . Get out . . . Get out.

She listened, aghast. The thought of leaving Taggart Transcontinental did not belong among the things she could hold as conceivable. She felt terror, not at the thought, but at the question of what had made her think it. She shook her head angrily; she told herself that Taggart Transcontinental would now need her more than ever.

Two of the Directors resigned; so did the Vice-President in Charge of Operation. He was replaced by a friend of James Taggart.

Steel rail was laid across the Mexican desert—while orders were issued to reduce the speed of trains on the Rio Norte Line, because the track was shot. A depot of reinforced concrete, with marble columns and mirrors, was built amidst the dust of an unpaved square in a Mexican village—while a train of tank cars carrying oil went hurtling down an embankment and into a blazing junk pile, because a rail had split on the Rio Norte Line. Ellis Wyatt did not wait for the court to decide whether the accident was an act of God, as James Taggart claimed. He transferred the shipping of his oil to the Phoenix-Durango, an obscure railroad which was small and struggling, but struggling well. This was the rocket that sent the Phoenix-Durango on its way. From then on, it grew, as Wyatt Oil grew, as factories grew in nearby valleys —as a band of rails and ties grew, at the rate of two miles a month, across the scraggly fields of Mexican corn.

Dagny was thirty-two years old, when she told James Taggart that she would resign. She had run the Operating Department for the past three years, without title, credit or authority. She was defeated by loathing for the hours, the days, the nights she had to waste circumventing the interference of Jim's friend who bore the title of Vice-President in Charge of Operation. The man had no policy, and any decision he made was always hers, but he made it only after he had made every effort to make it impossible. What she delivered to her brother was an ultimatum. He gasped, "But, Dagny, you're a woman! A woman as Operating Vice-President? It's unheard of! The Board won't consider it!" "Then I'm through," she answered.

She did not think of what she would do with the rest of her life. To face leaving Taggart Transcontinental was like waiting to have her legs amputated; she thought she would let it happen, then take up the load of whatever was left.

She never understood why the Board of Directors voted unanimously to make her Vice-President in Charge of Operation.

It was she who finally gave them their San Sebastián Line. When she took over, the construction had been under way for three years; one third of its track was laid; the cost to date was beyond the authorized total. She fired Jim's friends and found a contractor who completed the job in one year.

The San Sebastián Line was now in operation. No surge of trade had come across the border, nor any trains loaded with copper. A few carloads came clattering down the mountains from San Sebastián, at long intervals. The mines, said Francisco d'Anconia, were still in the process of development. The drain on Taggart Transcontinental had not stopped.

Now she sat at the desk in her office, as she had sat for many evenings, trying to work out the problem of what branches could save the system and in how many years.

The Rio Norte Line, when rebuilt, would redeem the rest. As she looked at the sheets of figures announcing losses and more losses, she did not think of the long, senseless agony of the Mexican venture. She thought of a telephone call. "Hank, can you save us? Can you give us rail on the shortest notice and the longest credit possible?" A quiet, steady voice had answered, "Sure."

The thought was a point of support. She leaned over the sheets of paper on her desk, finding it suddenly easier to concentrate. There was one thing, at least, that could be counted upon not to crumble when needed.

James Taggart crossed the anteroom of Dagny's office, still holding the kind of confidence he had felt among his companions at the barroom half an hour ago. When he opened her door, the confidence vanished. He crossed the room to her desk like a child being dragged to punishment, storing the resentment for all his future years.

He saw a head bent over sheets of paper, the light of the desk lamp glistening on strands of disheveled hair, a white shirt clinging to her shoulders, its loose folds suggesting the thinness of her body.

"What is it, Jim?"

"What are you trying to pull on the San Sebastián Line?"

She raised her head. "Pull? Why?"

"What sort of schedule are we running down there and what kind of trains?"

She laughed; the sound was gay and a little weary. "You really ought to read the reports sent to the president's office, Jim, once in a while."

"What do you mean?"

"We've been running that schedule and those trains on the San Sebastián for the last three months."

"*One* passenger train a day?"

"—in the morning. And one freight train every other night."

"Good God! On an important branch like that?"

"The important branch can't pay even for those two trains."

"But the Mexican people expect real service from us!"

"I'm sure they do."

"They need trains!"

"For what?"

"For . . . To help them develop local industries. How do you expect them to develop if we don't give them transportation?"

"I don't expect them to develop."

"That's just your personal opinion. I don't see what right you had to take it upon yourself to cut our schedules. Why, the copper traffic alone will pay for everything."

"When?"

He looked at her; his face assumed the satisfaction of a person about to utter something that has the power to hurt. "You don't doubt the success of those copper mines, do you?—when it's Francisco d'Anconia who's running them?" He stressed the name, watching her.

She said, "He may be your friend, but—"

"*My* friend? I thought he was *yours.*"

She said steadily, "Not for the last ten years."

"That's too bad, isn't it? Still, he's one of the smartest operators on earth. He's never failed in a venture—I mean, a *business* venture—and he's sunk millions of his own money into those mines, so we can rely on his judgment."

"When will you realize that Francisco d'Anconia has turned into a worthless bum?"

He chuckled. "I always thought that that's what he was—as far as his personal character is concerned. But you didn't share my opinion. Yours was opposite. Oh my, how opposite! Surely you remember our quarrels on the subject? Shall I quote some of the things you *said* about him? I can only surmise as to some of the things you *did.*"

"Do you wish to discuss Francisco d'Anconia? Is that what you came here for?"

His face showed the anger of failure—because hers showed nothing. "You know damn well what I came here for!" he snapped. "I've heard some incredible things about our trains in Mexico."

"What things?"

"What sort of rolling stock are you using down there?"

"The worst I could find."

"You admit that?"

"I've stated it on paper in the reports I sent you."

"Is it true that you're using wood-burning locomotives?"

"Eddie found them for me in somebody's abandoned roundhouse down in Louisiana. He couldn't even learn the name of the railroad."

"And that's what you're running as Taggart trains?"

"Yes."

"What in hell's the big idea? What's going on? I want to know what's going on!"

She spoke evenly, looking straight at him. "If you want to know, I have left nothing but junk on the San Sebastián Line, and as little of that as possible. I have moved everything that could be moved—switch engines, shop tools, even typewriters and mirrors—out of Mexico."

"Why in blazes?"

"So that the looters won't have too much to loot when they nationalize the line."

He leaped to his feet. "You won't get away with that! This is one time you won't get away with it! To have the nerve to pull such a low, unspeakable . . . just because of some vicious rumors, when we have a contract for two hundred years and . . ."

"Jim," she said slowly, "there's not a car, engine or ton of coal that we can spare anywhere on the system."

"I won't permit it, I absolutely won't permit such an outrageous policy toward a friendly people who need our help. Material greed isn't everything. After all, there are non-material considerations, even though you wouldn't understand them!"

She pulled a pad forward and picked up a pencil. "All right, Jim. How many trains do you wish me to run on the San Sebastián Line?"

"Huh?"

"Which runs do you wish me to cut and on which of our lines—in order to get the Diesels and the steel coaches?"

"I don't want you to cut any runs!"

"Then where do I get the equipment for Mexico?"

"That's for you to figure out. It's *your* job."

"I am not able to do it. You will have to decide."

"That's your usual rotten trick—switching the responsibility to me!"

"I'm waiting for orders, Jim."

"I'm not going to let you trap me like that!"

She dropped the pencil. "Then the San Sebastián schedule will remain as it is."

"Just wait till the Board meeting next month. I'll demand a decision, once and for all, on how far the Operating Department is to be permitted to exceed its authority. You're going to have to answer for this."

"I'll answer for it."

She was back at her work before the door had closed on James Taggart.

When she finished, pushed the papers aside and glanced up, the sky was black beyond the window, and the city had become a glowing spread of lighted glass without masonry. She rose reluctantly. She resented the small defeat of being tired, but she knew that she was, tonight.

The outer office was dark and empty; her staff had gone. Only Eddie Willers was still there, at his desk in his glass-partitioned enclosure that looked like a cube of light in a corner of the large room. She waved to him on her way out.

She did not take the elevator to the lobby of the building, but to the concourse of the Taggart Terminal. She liked to walk through it on her way home.

She had always felt that the concourse looked like a temple. Glancing up at the distant ceiling, she saw dim vaults supported by giant granite columns, and the tops of vast windows glazed by darkness. The vaulting held the solemn peace of a cathedral, spread in protection high above the rushing activity of men.

Dominating the concourse, but ignored by the travelers as a habitual sight, stood a statue of Nathaniel Taggart, the founder of the railroad. Dagny was the only one who remained aware of it and had never been able to take it for granted. To look at that statue whenever she crossed the concourse, was the only form of prayer she knew.

Nathaniel Taggart had been a penniless adventurer who had come from somewhere in New England and built a railroad across a continent, in the days of the first steel rails. His railroad still stood; his battle to build it had dissolved into a legend, because people preferred not to understand it or to believe it possible.

He was a man who had never accepted the creed that others had the right to stop him. He set his goal and moved toward it, his way as straight as one of his rails. He never sought any loans, bonds, subsidies, land grants or legislative favors from the government. He obtained money from the men who owned it, going from door to door— from the mahogany doors of bankers to the clapboard doors of lonely farmhouses. He never talked about the public good. He merely told people that they would make big profits on his railroad, he told them why he expected the profits and he gave his reasons. He had good reasons. Through all the generations that followed, Taggart Transcontinental was one of the few railroads that never went bankrupt and the only one whose controlling stock remained in the hands of the founder's descendants.

In his lifetime, the name "Nat Taggart" was not famous, but notorious; it was repeated, not in homage, but in resentful curiosity; and if anyone admired him, it was as one admires a successful bandit. Yet no penny of his wealth had been obtained by force or fraud; he was guilty of nothing, except that he earned his own fortune and never forgot that it was his.

Many stories were whispered about him. It was said that in the wilderness of the Middle West, he murdered a state legislator who attempted to revoke a charter granted to him, to revoke it when his rail was laid halfway across the state; some legislators had planned to make a fortune on Taggart stock—by selling it short. Nat Taggart was indicted for the murder, but the charge could never be proved. He had no trouble with legislators from then on.

It was said that Nat Taggart had staked his life on his railroad many times; but once, he staked more than his life. Desperate for funds, with the construction of his line suspended, he threw down three flights of stairs a distinguished gentleman who offered him a loan from the government. Then he pledged his wife as security for a loan from a millionaire who hated him and admired her beauty. He repaid the loan on time and did not have to surrender his pledge. The deal had been made with his wife's consent. She was a great beauty from the noblest family of a southern state, and she had been disinherited by her family because she eloped with Nat Taggart when he was only a ragged young adventurer.

Dagny regretted at times that Nat Taggart was her ancestor. What she felt for him did not belong in the category of unchosen family affections. She did not want her feeling to be the thing one was supposed to owe an uncle or a grandfather. She was incapable of love for any object not of her own choice and she resented anyone's demand for it. But had it been possible to choose an ancestor, she would have chosen Nat Taggart, in voluntary homage and with all of her gratitude.

Nat Taggart's statue was copied from an artist's sketch of him, the only record ever made of his appearance. He had lived far into old age, but one could never think of him except as he was on that sketch —as a young man. In her childhood, his statue had been Dagny's first concept of the exalted. When she was sent to church or to school, and heard people using that word, she thought that she knew what they meant: she thought of the statue.

The statue was of a young man with a tall, gaunt body and an angular face. He held his head as if he faced a challenge and found joy in his capacity to meet it. All that Dagny wanted of life was contained in the desire to hold her head as he did.

Tonight, she looked at the statue when she walked across the concourse. It was a moment's rest; it was as if a burden she could not name were lightened and as if a faint current of air were touching her forehead.

In a corner of the concourse, by the main entrance, there was a small newsstand. The owner, a quiet, courteous old man with an air of breeding, had stood behind his counter for twenty years. He had owned a cigarette factory once, but it had gone bankrupt, and he had resigned himself to the lonely obscurity of his little stand in the midst of an eternal whirlpool of strangers. He had no family or friends left alive. He had a hobby which was his only pleasure: he gathered cigarettes from all over the world for his private collection; he knew every brand made or that had ever been made.

Dagny liked to stop at his newsstand on her way out. He seemed to be part of the Taggart Terminal, like an old watchdog too feeble to protect it, but reassuring by the loyalty of his presence. He liked to see her coming, because it amused him to think that he alone knew the importance of the young woman in a sports coat and a slanting hat, who came hurrying anonymously through the crowd.

She stopped tonight, as usual, to buy a package of cigarettes. "How is the collection?" she asked him. "Any new specimens?"

He smiled sadly, shaking his head. "No, Miss Taggart. There aren't any new brands made anywhere in the world. Even the old ones are going, one after another. There's only five or six kinds left selling now. There used to be dozens. People aren't making anything new any more."

"They will. That's only temporary."

He glanced at her and did not answer. Then he said, "I like cigarettes, Miss Taggart. I like to think of fire held in a man's hand. Fire, a dangerous force, tamed at his fingertips. I often wonder about the hours when a man sits alone, watching the smoke of a cigarette, thinking. I wonder what great things have come from such hours. When a man thinks, there is a spot of fire alive in his mind—and it is proper that he should have the burning point of a cigarette as his one expression."

"Do they ever think?" she asked involuntarily, and stopped; the question was her one personal torture and she did not want to discuss it.

The old man looked as if he had noticed the sudden stop and understood it; but he did not start discussing it; he said, instead, "I don't like the thing that's happening to people, Miss Taggart."

"What?"

"I don't know. But I've watched them here for twenty years and I've seen the change. They used to rush through here, and it was wonderful to watch, it was the hurry of men who knew where they were going and were eager to get there. Now they're hurrying because they are afraid. It's not a purpose that drives them, it's fear. They're not going anywhere, they're escaping. And I don't think they know what it is that they want to escape. They don't look at one another. They jerk when brushed against. They smile too much, but it's an ugly kind of smiling: it's not joy, it's pleading. I don't know what it is that's happening to the world." He shrugged. "Oh well, who is John Galt?"

"He's just a meaningless phrase!"

She was startled by the sharpness of her own voice, and she added in apology, "I don't like that empty piece of slang. What does it mean? Where did it come from?"

"Nobody knows," he answered slowly.

"Why do people keep saying it? Nobody seems able to explain just what it stands for, yet they all use it as if they knew the meaning."

"Why does it disturb you?" he asked.

"I don't like what they seem to mean when they say it."

"I don't, either, Miss Taggart."

* * *

Eddie Willers ate his dinners in the employees' cafeteria of the Taggart Terminal. There was a restaurant in the building, patronized by Taggart executives, but he did not like it. The cafeteria seemed part of the railroad, and he felt more at home.

The cafeteria lay underground. It was a large room with walls of white tile that glittered in the reflections of electric lights and looked like silver brocade. It had a high ceiling, sparkling counters of glass and chromium, a sense of space and light.

There was a railroad worker whom Eddie Willers met at times in the cafeteria. Eddie liked his face. They had been drawn into a chance conversation once, and then it became their habit to dine together whenever they happened to meet.

Eddie had forgotten whether he had ever asked the worker's name or the nature of his job; he supposed that the job wasn't much, because the man's clothes were rough and grease-stained. The man was not a person to him, but only a silent presence with an enormous intensity of interest in the one thing which was the meaning of his own life: in Taggart Transcontinental.

Tonight, coming down late, Eddie saw the worker at a table in a corner of the half-deserted room. Eddie smiled happily, waving to him, and carried his tray of food to the worker's table.

In the privacy of their corner, Eddie felt at ease, relaxing after the long strain of the day. He could talk as he did not talk anywhere else, admitting things he would not confess to anyone, thinking aloud, looking into the attentive eyes of the worker across the table.

"The Rio Norte Line is our last hope," said Eddie Willers. "But it will save us. We'll have at least one branch in good condition, where it's needed most, and that will help to save the rest. . . . It's funny—isn't it?—to speak about a last hope for Taggart Transcontinental. Do you take it seriously if somebody tells you that a meteor is going to destroy the earth? . . . I don't, either. . . . 'From Ocean to Ocean, forever'—that's what we heard all through our childhood, she and I. No, they didn't say 'forever,' but that's what it meant. . . . You know, I'm not any kind of a great man. I couldn't have built that railroad. If it goes, I won't be able to bring it back. I'll have to go with it. . . . Don't pay any attention to me. I don't know why I should want to say things like that. Guess I'm just a little tired tonight. . . . Yes, I worked late. She didn't ask me to stay, but there was a light under her door, long after all the others had gone . . . Yes, she's gone home now. . . . Trouble? Oh, there's always trouble in the office. But she's not worried. She knows she can pull us through. . . . Of course, it's bad. We're having many more accidents than you hear about. We lost two Diesels again, last week. One—just from old age, the other—in a head-on collision. . . . Yes, we have Diesels on order, at the United Locomotive Works, but we've waited for them for two years. I don't know whether we'll ever get them or not. . . . God, do we need them! Motive power —you can't imagine how important that is. That's the heart of everything. . . . What are you smiling at? . . . Well, as I was saying, it's bad. But at least the Rio Norte Line is set. The first shipment of rail will get to the site in a few weeks. In a year, we'll run the first train on the new track. Nothing's going to stop us, this time. . . . Sure, I know who's going to lay the rail. McNamara, of Cleveland. He's the contractor who finished the San Sebastián Line for us. There, at least, is one man who knows his job. So we're safe. We can count on him. There aren't many good contractors left. . . . We're rushed as hell, but I like it. I've been coming to the office an hour earlier than usual, but she beats me to it. She's always there first. . . . What? . . . I don't know what she does at night. Nothing much, I guess. . . . No, she never goes out with anyone. She sits at home, mostly, and listens to music. She plays records. . . . What do you care, which records? Richard Halley. She loves the music of Richard Halley. Outside the railroad, that's the only thing she loves."

THE IMMOVABLE MOVERS

Motive power—thought Dagny, looking up at the Taggart Building in the twilight—was its first need; motive power, to keep that building standing; movement, to keep it immovable. It did not rest on piles driven into granite; it rested on the engines that rolled across a continent.

She felt a dim touch of anxiety. She was back from a trip to the plant of the United Locomotive Works in New Jersey, where she had gone to see the president of the company in person. She had learned nothing: neither the reason for the delays nor any indication of the date when the Diesel engines would be produced. The president of the company had talked to her for two hours. But none of his answers had connected to any of her questions. His manner had conveyed a peculiar note of condescending reproach whenever she attempted to make the conversation specific, as if she were giving proof of ill-breeding by breaking some unwritten code known to everyone else.

On her way through the plant, she had seen an enormous piece of machinery left abandoned in a corner of the yard. It had been a precision machine tool once, long ago, of a kind that could not be bought anywhere now. It had not been worn out; it had been rotted by neglect, eaten by rust and the black drippings of a dirty oil. She had turned her face away from it. A sight of that nature always blinded her for an instant by the burst of too violent an anger. She did not know why; she could not define her own feeling; she knew only that there was, in her feeling, a scream of protest against injustice, and that it was a response to something much beyond an old piece of machinery.

The rest of her staff had gone, when she entered the anteroom of her office, but Eddie Willers was still there, waiting for her. She knew at once that something had happened, by the way he looked and the way he followed her silently into her office.

"What's the matter, Eddie?"

"McNamara quit."

She looked at him blankly. "What do you mean, quit?"

"Left. Retired. Went out of business."

"McNamara, our contractor?"

"Yes."

"But that's impossible!"

"I know it."

"What happened? Why?"

"Nobody knows."

Taking her time deliberately, she unbuttoned her coat, sat down at her desk, started to pull off her gloves. Then she said, "Begin at the beginning, Eddie. Sit down."

He spoke quietly, but he remained standing. "I talked to his chief engineer, long distance. The chief engineer called from Cleveland, to tell us. That's all he said. He knew nothing else."

"What did he say?"

"That McNamara has closed his business and gone."

"Where?"

"He doesn't know. Nobody knows."

She noticed that she was holding with one hand two empty fingers of the glove of the other, the glove half-removed and forgotten. She pulled it off and dropped it on the desk.

Eddie said, "He's walked out on a pile of contracts that are worth a fortune. He had a waiting list of clients for the next three years. . . ." She said nothing. He added, his voice low, "I wouldn't be frightened if I could understand it. . . . But a thing that can't have any possible reason . . ." She remained silent. "He was the best contractor in the country."

They looked at each other. What she wanted to say was, "Oh God, Eddie!" Instead, her voice even, she said, "Don't worry. We'll find another contractor for the Rio Norte Line."

It was late when she left her office. Outside, on the sidewalk at the door of the building, she paused, looking at the streets. She felt suddenly empty of energy, of purpose, of desire, as if a motor had crackled and stopped.

A faint glow streamed from behind the buildings into the sky, the reflection of thousands of unknown lights, the electric breath of the city. She wanted to rest. To rest, she thought, and to find enjoyment somewhere.

Her work was all she had or wanted. But there were times, like tonight, when she felt that sudden, peculiar emptiness, which was not emptiness, but silence, not despair, but immobility, as if nothing within her were destroyed, but everything stood still. Then she felt the wish to find a moment's joy outside, the wish to be held as a passive spectator by some work or sight of greatness. Not to make it, she thought, but to accept; not to begin, but to respond; not to create, but to admire. I need it to let me go on, she thought, because joy is one's fuel.

She had always been—she closed her eyes with a faint smile of amusement and pain—the motive power of her own happiness. For once, she wanted to feel herself carried by the power of someone else's achievement. As men on a dark prairie liked to see the lighted windows of a train going past, her achievement, the sight of power and purpose that gave them reassurance in the midst of empty miles and night —so she wanted to feel it for a moment, a brief greeting, a single glimpse, just to wave her arm and say: Someone is going somewhere. . . .

She started walking slowly, her hands in the pockets of her coat, the shadow of her slanting hat brim across her face. The buildings around her rose to such heights that her glance could not find the sky. She thought: It has taken so much to build this city, it should have so much to offer.

Above the door of a shop, the black hole of a radio loudspeaker was hurling sounds at the streets. They were the sounds of a symphony concert being given somewhere in the city. They were a long screech without shape, as of cloth and flesh being torn at random. They scattered with no melody, no harmony, no rhythm to hold them. If music was emotion and emotion came from thought, then this was the scream of chaos, of the irrational, of the helpless, of man's self-abdication.

She walked on. She stopped at the window of a bookstore. The window displayed a pyramid of slabs in brownish-purple jackets, inscribed: *The Vulture Is Molting.* "The novel of our century," said a placard. "The penetrating study of a businessman's greed. A fearless revelation of man's depravity."

She walked past a movie theater. Its lights wiped out half a block, leaving only a huge photograph and some letters suspended in blazing mid-air. The photograph was of a smiling young woman; looking at her face, one felt the weariness of having seen it for years, even while seeing it for the first time. The letters said: ". . . in a momentous drama giving the answer to the great problem: Should a woman tell?"

She walked past the door of a night club. A couple came staggering out to a taxicab. The girl had blurred eyes, a perspiring face, an ermine cape and a beautiful evening gown that had slipped off one shoulder like a slovenly housewife's bathrobe, revealing too much of her breast, not in a manner of daring, but in the manner of a drudge's indifference. Her escort steered her, gripping her naked arm; his face did not have the expression of a man anticipating a romantic adventure, but the sly look of a boy out to write obscenities on fences.

What had she hoped to find?—she thought, walking on. These were the things men lived by, the forms of their spirit, of their culture, of their enjoyment. She had seen nothing else anywhere, not for many years.

At the corner of the street where she lived, she bought a newspaper and went home.

Her apartment was two rooms on the top floor of a skyscraper. The sheets of glass in the corner window of her living room made it look like the prow of a ship in motion, and the lights of the city were like phosphorescent sparks on the black waves of steel and stone. When she turned on a lamp, long triangles of shadow cut the bare walls, in a geometrical pattern of light rays broken by a few angular pieces of furniture.

She stood in the middle of the room, alone between sky and city. There was only one thing that could give her the feeling she wanted to experience tonight; it was the only form of enjoyment she had found. She turned to a phonograph and put on a record of the music of Richard Halley.

It was his Fourth Concerto, the last work he had written. The crash of its opening chords swept the sights of the streets away from her mind. The Concerto was a great cry of rebellion. It was a "No" flung at some vast process of torture, a denial of suffering, a denial that held the agony of the struggle to break free. The sounds were like a voice saying: There is no necessity for pain—why, then, is the worst pain reserved for those who will not accept its necessity?—we who hold the love and the secret of joy, to what punishment have we been sentenced for it, and by whom? . . . The sounds of torture became defiance, the statement of agony became a hymn to a distant vision for whose sake anything was worth enduring, even this. It was the song of rebellion—and of a desperate quest.

She sat still, her eyes closed, listening.

No one knew what had happened to Richard Halley, or why. The story of his life had been like a summary written to damn greatness by showing the price one pays for it. It had been a procession of years spent in garrets and basements, years that had taken the gray tinge of the walls imprisoning a man whose music overflowed with violent color. It had been the gray of a struggle against long flights of unlighted tenement stairs, against frozen plumbing, against the price of a sandwich in an ill-smelling delicatessen store, against the faces of men who listened to music, their eyes empty. It had been a struggle without the relief of violence, without the recognition of finding a conscious enemy, with only a deaf wall to batter, a wall of the most effective soundproofing: indifference, that swallowed blows, chords and screams—a battle of silence, for a man who could give to sounds a greater eloquence than they had ever carried—the silence of obscurity, of loneliness, of the nights when some rare orchestra played one of his works and he looked at the darkness, knowing that his soul went in trembling, widening circles from a radio tower through the air of the city, but there were no receivers tuned to hear it.

"The music of Richard Halley has a quality of the heroic. Our age has outgrown that stuff," said one critic. "The music of Richard Halley is out of key with our times. It has a tone of ecstasy. Who cares for ecstasy nowadays?" said another.

His life had been a summary of the lives of all the men whose reward is a monument in a public park a hundred years after the time when a reward can matter—except that Richard Halley did not die soon enough. He lived to see the night which, by the accepted laws of history, he was not supposed to see. He was forty-three years old and it was the opening night of *Phaëthon,* an opera he had written at the age of twenty-four. He had changed the ancient Greek myth to his own purpose and meaning: Phaëthon, the young son of Helios, who stole his father's chariot and, in ambitious audacity, attempted to drive the sun across the sky, did not perish, as he perished in the myth; in Halley's opera, Phaëthon succeeded. The opera had been performed then, nineteen years ago, and had closed after one performance, to the sound of booing and catcalls. That night, Richard Halley had walked the streets of the city till dawn, trying to find an answer to a question, which he did not find.

On the night when the opera was presented again, nineteen years later, the last sounds of the music crashed into the sounds of the greatest ovation the opera house had ever heard. The ancient walls could not contain it, the sounds of cheering burst through to the lobbies, to the stairs, to the streets, to the boy who had walked those streets nineteen years ago.

Dagny was in the audience on the night of the ovation. She was one of the few who had known the music of Richard Halley much earlier; but she had never seen him. She saw him being pushed out on the stage, saw him facing the enormous spread of waving arms and cheering heads. He stood without moving, a tall, emaciated man with graying hair. He did not bow, did not smile; he just stood there, looking at the crowd. His face had the quiet, earnest look of a man staring at a question.

"The music of Richard Halley," wrote a critic next morning, "belongs to mankind. It is the product and the expression of the greatness of the people." "There is an inspiring lesson," said a minister, "in the life of Richard Halley. He has had a terrible struggle, but what does that matter? It is proper, it is noble that he should have endured suffering, injustice, abuse at the hands of his brothers—in order to enrich their lives and teach them to appreciate the beauty of great music."

On the day after the opening, Richard Halley retired.

He gave no explanation. He merely told his publishers that his career was over. He sold them the rights to his works for a modest sum, even though he knew that his royalties would now bring him a fortune. He went away, leaving no address. It was eight years ago; no one had seen him since.

Dagny listened to the Fourth Concerto, her head thrown back, her eyes closed. She lay half-stretched across the corner of a couch, her body relaxed and still; but tension stressed the shape of her mouth on her motionless face, a sensual shape drawn in lines of longing.

After a while, she opened her eyes. She noticed the newspaper she had thrown down on the couch. She reached for it absently, to turn the vapid headlines out of sight. The paper fell open. She saw the photograph of a face she knew, and the heading of a story. She slammed the pages shut and flung them aside.

It was the face of Francisco d'Anconia. The heading said that he had arrived in New York. What of it?—she thought. She would not have to see him. She had not seen him for years.

She sat looking down at the newspaper on the floor. Don't read it, she thought; don't look at it. But the face, she thought, had not changed. How could a face remain the same when everything else was gone? She wished they had not caught a picture of him when he smiled. That kind of smile did not belong in the pages of a newspaper. It was the smile of a man who is able to see, to know and to create the glory of existence. It was the mocking, challenging smile of a brilliant intelligence. Don't read it, she thought; not now—not to that music—oh, not to that music!

She reached for the paper and opened it.

The story said that Señor Francisco d'Anconia had granted an interview to the press in his suite at the Wayne-Falkland Hotel. He said that he had come to New York for two important reasons: a hat-check girl at the Cub Club, and the liverwurst at Moe's Delicatessen on Third Avenue. He had nothing to say about the coming divorce trial of Mr. and Mrs. Gilbert Vail. Mrs. Vail, a lady of noble breeding and unusual loveliness, had taken a shot at her distinguished young husband, some months ago, publicly declaring that she wished to get rid of him for the sake of her lover, Francisco d'Anconia. She had given to the press a detailed account of her secret romance, including a description of the night of last New Year's Eve which she had spent at d'Anconia's villa in the Andes. Her husband had survived the shot and had sued for divorce. She had countered with a suit for half of her husband's millions, and with a recital of his private life which, she said, made hers look innocent. All of that had been splashed over the newspapers for weeks. But Señor d'Anconia had nothing to say about it, when the reporters questioned him. Would he deny Mrs. Vail's story, they asked. "I never deny anything," he answered. The reporters had been astonished by his sudden arrival in town; they had thought that he would not wish to be there just when the worst of the scandal was about to explode on the front pages. But they had been wrong. Francisco d'Anconia added one more comment to the reasons for his arrival. "I wanted to witness the farce," he said.

Dagny let the paper slip to the floor. She sat, bent over, her head on her arms. She did not move, but the strands of hair, hanging down to her knees, trembled in sudden jolts once in a while.

The great chords of Halley's music went on, filling the room, piercing the glass of the windows, streaming out over the city. She was hearing the music. It was *her* quest, her cry.

* * *

James Taggart glanced about the living room of his apartment, wondering what time it was; he did not feel like moving to find his watch. He sat in an armchair, dressed in wrinkled pajamas, barefooted; it was too much trouble to look for his slippers. The light of the gray sky in the windows hurt his eyes, still sticky with sleep. He felt, inside his skull, the nasty heaviness which is about to become a headache. He wondered angrily why he had stumbled out into the living room. Oh yes, he remembered, to look for the time.

He slumped sidewise over the arm of the chair and caught sight of a clock on a distant building: it was twenty minutes past noon.

Through the open door of the bedroom, he heard Betty Pope washing her teeth in the bathroom beyond. Her girdle lay on the floor, by the side of a chair with the rest of her clothes; the girdle was a faded pink, with broken strands of rubber.

"Hurry up, will you?" he called irritably. "I've got to dress."

She did not answer. She had left the door of the bathroom open; he could hear the sound of gargling.

Why do I do those things?—he thought, remembering last night. But it was too much trouble to look for an answer.

Betty Pope came into the living room, dragging the folds of a satin negligee harlequin-checkered in orange and purple. She looked awful in a negligee, thought Taggart; she was ever so much better in a riding habit, in the photographs on the society pages of the newspapers. She was a lanky girl, all bones and loose joints that did not move smoothly. She had a homely face, a bad complexion and a look of impertinent condescension derived from the fact that she belonged to one of the very best families.

"Aw, hell!" she said at nothing in particular, stretching herself to limber up. "Jim, where are your nail clippers? I've got to trim my toenails."

"I don't know. I have a headache. Do it at home."

"You look unappetizing in the morning," she said indifferently. "You look like a snail."

"Why don't you shut up?"

She wandered aimlessly about the room. "I don't want to go home," she said with no particular feeling. "I hate morning. Here's another day and nothing to do. I've got a tea session on for this afternoon, at Liz Blane's. Oh well, it might be fun, because Liz is a bitch." She picked up a glass and swallowed the stale remnant of a drink. "Why don't you have them repair your air-conditioner? This place smells."

"Are you through in the bathroom?" he asked. "I have to dress. I have an important engagement today."

"Go right in. I don't mind. I'll share the bathroom with you. I hate to be rushed."

While he shaved, he saw her dressing in front of the open bathroom door. She took a long time twisting herself into her girdle, hooking garters to her stockings, pulling on an ungainly, expensive tweed suit. The harlequin negligee, picked from an advertisement in the smartest fashion magazine, was like a uniform which she knew to be expected on certain occasions, which she had worn dutifully for a specified purpose and then discarded.

The nature of their relationship had the same quality. There was no passion in it, no desire, no actual pleasure, not even a sense of shame. To them, the act of sex was neither joy nor sin. It meant nothing. They had heard that men and women were supposed to sleep together, so they did.

"Jim, why don't you take me to the Armenian restaurant tonight?" she asked. "I love shish-kebab."

"I can't," he answered angrily through the soap lather on his face. "I've got a busy day ahead."

"Why don't you cancel it?"

"What?"

"Whatever it is."

"It is very important, my dear. It is a meeting of our Board of Directors."

"Oh, don't be stuffy about your damn railroad. It's boring. I hate businessmen. They're dull."

He did not answer.

She glanced at him slyly, and her voice acquired a livelier note when she drawled, "Jock Benson said that you have a soft snap on that railroad anyway, because it's your sister who runs the whole works."

"Oh, he did, did he?"

"I think that your sister is awful. I think it's disgusting—a woman acting like a grease-monkey and posing around like a big executive. It's so unfeminine. Who does she think she is, anyway?"

Taggart stepped out to the threshold. He leaned against the doorjamb, studying Betty Pope. There was a faint smile on his face, sarcastic and confident. They had, he thought, a bond in common.

"It might interest you to know, my dear," he said, "that I'm putting the skids under my sister this afternoon."

"No?" she said, interested. "Really?"

"And that is why this Board meeting is so important."

"Are you really going to kick her out?"

"No. That's not necessary or advisable. I shall merely put her in her place. It's the chance I've been waiting for."

"You got something on her? Some scandal?"

"No, no. You wouldn't understand. It's merely that she's gone too far, for once, and she's going to get slapped down. She's pulled an inexcusable sort of stunt, without consulting anybody. It's a serious offense against our Mexican neighbors. When the Board hears about it, they'll pass a couple of new rulings on the Operating Department, which will make my sister a little easier to manage."

"You're smart, Jim," she said.

"I'd better get dressed." He sounded pleased. He turned back to the washbowl, adding cheerfully, "Maybe I *will* take you out tonight and buy you some shish-kebab."

The telephone rang.

He lifted the receiver. The operator announced a long-distance call from Mexico City.

The hysterical voice that came on the wire was that of his political man in Mexico.

"I couldn't help it, Jim!" it gulped. "I couldn't help it! . . . We had no warning, I swear to God, nobody suspected, nobody saw it coming, I've done my best, you can't blame me, Jim, it was a bolt out of the blue! The decree came out this morning, just five minutes ago, they sprang it on us like that, without any notice! The government of the People's State of Mexico has nationalized the San Sebastián Mines and the San Sebastián Railroad."

* * *

". . . and, therefore, I can assure the gentlemen of the Board that there is no occasion for panic. The event of this morning is a regrettable development, but I have full confidence—based on my knowledge of the inner processes shaping our foreign policy in Washington—that our government will negotiate an equitable settlement with the government of the People's State of Mexico, and that we will receive full and just compensation for our property."

James Taggart stood at the long table, addressing the Board of Directors. His voice was precise and monotonous; it connoted safety.

"I am glad to report, however, that I foresaw the possibility of such a turn of events and took every precaution to protect the interests of Taggart Transcontinental. Some months ago, I instructed our Operating Department to cut the schedule on the San Sebastián Line down to a single train a day, and to remove from it our best motive power and rolling stock, as well as every piece of equipment that could be moved. The Mexican government was able to seize nothing but a few wooden cars and one superannuated locomotive. My decision has saved the company many millions of dollars—I shall have the exact figures computed and submit them to you. I do feel, however, that our stockholders will be justified in expecting that those who bore the major responsibility for this venture should now bear the consequences of their negligence. I would suggest, therefore, that we request the resignation of Mr. Clarence Eddington, our economic consultant, who recommended the construction of the San Sebastián Line, and of Mr. Jules Mott, our representative in Mexico City."

The men sat around the long table, listening. They did not think of what they would have to do, but of what they would have to say to the men they represented. Taggart's speech gave them what they needed.

* * *

Orren Boyle was waiting for him, when Taggart returned to his office. Once they were alone, Taggart's manner changed. He leaned against the desk, sagging, his face loose and white.

"Well?" he asked.

Boyle spread his hands out helplessly. "I've checked, Jim," he said. "It's straight all right: d'Anconia's lost fifteen million dollars of his own money in those mines. No, there wasn't anything phony about that, he didn't pull any sort of trick, he put up his own cash and now he's lost it."

"Well, what's he going to do about it?"

"That—I don't know. Nobody does."

"He's not going to let himself be robbed, is he? He's too smart for that. He must have something up his sleeve."

"I sure hope so."

"He's outwitted some of the slickest combinations of money-grubbers on earth. Is he going to be taken by a bunch of Greaser politicians with a decree? He must have something on them, and he'll get the last word, and we must be sure to be in on it, too!"

"That's up to you, Jim. You're his friend."

"Friend be damned! I hate his guts."

He pressed a button for his secretary. The secretary entered uncertainly, looking unhappy; he was a young man, no longer too young, with a bloodless face and the well-bred manner of genteel poverty.

"Did you get me an appointment with Francisco d'Anconia?" snapped Taggart.

"No, sir."

"But, God damn it, I told you to call the—"

"I wasn't able to, sir. I have tried."

"Well, try again."

"I mean I wasn't able to obtain the appointment, Mr. Taggart."

"Why not?"

"He declined it."

"You mean he refused to see me?"

"Yes, sir, that is what I mean."

"He *wouldn't* see me?"

"No, sir, he wouldn't."

"Did you speak to him in person?"

"No, sir, I spoke to his secretary."

"What did he tell you? Just what did he say?" The young man hesitated and looked more unhappy. "What did he say?"

"He said that Señor d'Anconia said that you bore him, Mr. Taggart."

* * *

The proposal which they passed was known as the "Anti-dog-eat-dog Rule." When they voted for it, the members of the National Alliance of Railroads sat in a large hall in the deepening twilight of a late autumn evening and did not look at one another.

The National Alliance of Railroads was an organization formed, it was claimed, to protect the welfare of the railroad industry. This was to be achieved by developing methods of co-operation for a common purpose; this was to be achieved by the pledge of every member to subordinate his own interests to those of the industry as a whole; the interests of the industry as a whole were to be determined by a majority vote, and every member was committed to abide by any decision the majority chose to make.

"Members of the same profession or of the same industry should stick together," the organizers of the Alliance had said. "We all have the same problems, the same interests, the same enemies. We waste our energy fighting one another, instead of presenting a common front to the world. We can all grow and prosper together, if we pool our efforts." "Against whom is this Alliance being organized?" a skeptic had asked. The answer had been: "Why, it's not 'against' anybody. But if you want to put it that way, why, it's against shippers or supply manufacturers or anyone who might try to take advantage of us. Against whom is any union organized?" "That's what I wonder about," the skeptic had said.

When the Anti-dog-eat-dog Rule was offered to the vote of the full membership of the National Alliance of Railroads at its annual meeting, it was the first mention of this Rule in public. But all the members had heard of it; it had been discussed privately for a long time, and more insistently in the last few months. The men who sat in the large hall of the meeting were the presidents of the railroads. They did not like the Anti-dog-eat-dog Rule; they had hoped it would never be brought up. But when it was brought up, they voted for it.

No railroad was mentioned by name in the speeches that preceded the voting. The speeches dealt only with the public welfare. It was said that while the public welfare was threatened by shortages of transportation, railroads were destroying one another through vicious competition, on "the brutal policy of dog-eat-dog." While there existed blighted areas where rail service had been discontinued, there existed at the same time large regions where two or more railroads were competing for a traffic barely sufficient for one. It was said that there were great opportunities for younger railroads in the blighted areas. While it was true that such areas offered little economic incentive at present, a public-spirited railroad, it was said, would undertake to provide transportation for the struggling inhabitants, since the prime purpose of a railroad was public service, not profit.

Then it was said that large, established railroad systems were essential to the public welfare; and that the collapse of one of them would be a national catastrophe; and that if one such system had happened to sustain a crushing loss in a public-spirited attempt to contribute to international good will, it was entitled to public support to help it survive the blow.

No railroad was mentioned by name. But when the chairman of the meeting raised his hand, as a solemn signal that they were about to vote, everybody looked at Dan Conway, president of the Phoenix-Durango.

There were only five dissenters who voted against it. Yet when the chairman announced that the measure had passed, there was no cheering, no sounds of approval, no movement, nothing but a heavy silence. To the last minute, every one of them had hoped that someone would save them from it.

The Anti-dog-eat-dog Rule was described as a measure of "voluntary self-regulation" intended "the better to enforce" the laws long since passed by the country's Legislature. The Rule provided that the members of the National Alliance of Railroads were forbidden to engage in practices defined as "destructive competition"; that in regions declared to be restricted, no more than one railroad would be permitted to operate; that in such regions, seniority belonged to the oldest railroad now operating there, and that the newcomers, who had encroached unfairly upon its territory, would suspend operations within nine months after being so ordered; that the Executive Board of the National Alliance of Railroads was empowered to decide, at its sole discretion, which regions were to be restricted.

When the meeting adjourned, the men hastened to leave. There were no private discussions, no friendly loitering. The great hall became deserted in an unusually short time. Nobody spoke to or looked at Dan Conway.

In the lobby of the building, James Taggart met Orren Boyle. They had made no appointment to meet, but Taggart saw a bulky figure outlined against a marble wall and knew who it was before he saw the face. They approached each other, and Boyle said, his smile less soothing than usual, "I've delivered. Your turn now, Jimmie." "You didn't have to come here. Why did you?" said Taggart sullenly. "Oh, just for the fun of it," said Boyle.

Dan Conway sat alone among rows of empty seats. He was still there when the charwoman came to clean the hall. When she hailed him, he rose obediently and shuffled to the door. Passing her in the aisle, he fumbled in his pocket and handed her a five dollar bill, silently, meekly, not looking at her face. He did not seem to know what he was doing; he acted as if he thought that he was in some place where generosity demanded that he give a tip before leaving.

Dagny was still at her desk when the door of her office flew open and James Taggart rushed in. It was the first time he had ever entered in such manner. His face looked feverish.

She had not seen him since the nationalization of the San Sebastián

Line. He had not sought to discuss it with her, and she had said nothing about it. She had been proved right so eloquently, she had thought, that comments were unnecessary. A feeling which was part courtesy, part mercy had stopped her from stating to him the conclusion to be drawn from the events. In all reason and justice, there was but one conclusion he could draw. She had heard about his speech to the Board of Directors. She had shrugged, contemptuously amused; if it served his purpose, whatever that was, to appropriate her achievements, then, for his own advantage, if for no other reason, he would leave her free to achieve, from now on.

"So you think you're the only one who's doing anything for this railroad?"

She looked at him, bewildered. His voice was shrill; he stood in front of her desk, tense with excitement.

"So you think that I've ruined the company, don't you?" he yelled. "And now you're the only one who can save us? Think I have no way to make up for the Mexican loss?"

She asked slowly, "What do you want?"

"I want to tell you some news. Do you remember the Anti-dog-eat-dog proposal of the Railroad Alliance that I told you about months ago? You didn't like the idea. You didn't like it at all."

"I remember. What about it?"

"It has been passed."

"What has been passed?"

"The Anti-dog-eat-dog Rule. Just a few minutes ago. At the meeting. Nine months from now, there's not going to be any Phoenix-Durango Railroad in Colorado!"

A glass ashtray crashed to the floor off the desk, as she leaped to her feet.

"You rotten bastards!"

He stood motionless. He was smiling.

She knew that she was shaking, open to him, without defense, and that this was the sight he enjoyed, but it did not matter to her. Then she saw his smile—and suddenly the blinding anger vanished. She felt nothing. She studied that smile with a cold, impersonal curiosity.

They stood facing each other. He looked as if, for the first time, he was not afraid of her. He was gloating. The event meant something to him much beyond the destruction of a competitor. It was not a victory over Dan Conway, but over her. She did not know why or in what manner, but she felt certain that he knew.

For the flash of one instant, she thought that here, before her, in James Taggart and in that which made him smile, was a secret she had never suspected, and it was crucially important that she learn to understand it. But the thought flashed and vanished.

She whirled to the door of a closet and seized her coat.

"Where are you going?" Taggart's voice had dropped; it sounded disappointed and faintly worried.

She did not answer. She rushed out of the office.

* * *

"Dan, you have to fight them. I'll help you. I'll fight for you with everything I've got."

Dan Conway shook his head.

He sat at his desk, the empty expanse of a faded blotter before him, one feeble lamp lighted in a corner of the room. Dagny had rushed straight to the city office of the Phoenix-Durango. Conway was there, and he still sat as she had found him. He had smiled at her entrance and said, "Funny, I thought you would come," his voice gentle, lifeless. They did not know each other well, but they had met a few times in Colorado.

"No," he said, "it's no use."

"Do you mean because of that Alliance agreement that you signed? It won't hold. This is plain expropriation. No court will uphold it. And if Jim tries to hide behind the usual looters' slogan of 'public welfare,' I'll go on the stand and swear that Taggart Transcontinental can't handle the whole traffic of Colorado. And if any court rules against you, you can appeal and keep on appealing for the next ten years."

"Yes," he said, "I could . . . I'm not sure I'd win, but I could try and I could hang onto the railroad for a few years longer, but . . . No, it's not the legal points that I'm thinking about, one way or the other. It's not that."

"What, then?"

"I don't want to fight it, Dagny."

She looked at him incredulously. It was the one sentence which, she felt sure, he had never uttered before; a man could not reverse himself so late in life.

Dan Conway was approaching fifty. He had the square, stolid, stubborn face of a tough freight engineer, rather than a company president; the face of a fighter, with a young, tanned skin and graying hair. He had taken over a shaky little railroad in Arizona, a road whose net revenue was less than that of a successful grocery store, and he had built it into the best railroad of the Southwest. He spoke little, seldom read books, had never gone to college. The whole sphere of human endeavors, with one exception, left him blankly indifferent; he had no touch of that which people called culture. But he knew railroads.

"Why don't you want to fight?"

"Because they had the right to do it."

"Dan," she asked, "have you lost your mind?"

"I've never gone back on my word in my life," he said tonelessly. "I don't care what the courts decide. I promised to obey the majority. I have to obey."

"Did you expect the majority to do this to you?"

"No." There was a kind of faint convulsion in the stolid face. He spoke softly, not looking at her, the helpless astonishment still raw within him. "No, I didn't expect it. I heard them talking about it for over a year, but I didn't believe it. Even when they were voting, I didn't believe it."

"What did you expect?"

"I thought . . . They said all of us were to stand for the common good. I thought what I had done down there in Colorado was good. Good for everybody."

"Oh, you damn fool! Don't you see that that's what you're being punished for—because it was good?"

He shook his head. "I don't understand it," he said. "But I see no way out."

"Did you promise them to agree to destroy yourself?"

"There doesn't seem to be any choice for any of us."

"What do you mean?"

"Dagny, the whole world's in a terrible state right now. I don't know what's wrong with it, but something's very wrong. Men have to get together and find a way out. But who's to decide which way to take, unless it's the majority? I guess that's the only fair method of deciding, I don't see any other. I suppose somebody's got to be sacrificed. If it turned out to be me, I have no right to complain. The right's on their side. Men have to get together."

She made an effort to speak calmly; she was trembling with anger. "If that's the price of getting together, then I'll be damned if I want to live on the same earth with any human beings! If the rest of them can survive only by destroying us, then why should we wish them to survive? Nothing can make self-immolation proper. Nothing can give them the right to turn men into sacrificial animals. Nothing can make it moral to destroy the best. One can't be punished for being good. One can't be penalized for ability. If that is right, then we'd better start slaughtering one another, because there isn't any right at all in the world!"

He did not answer. He looked at her helplessly.

"If it's that kind of world, how can we live in it?" she asked.

"I don't know . . ." he whispered.

"Dan, do you really think it's right? In all truth, deep down, do you think it's right?"

He closed his eyes. "No," he said. Then he looked at her and she saw a look of torture for the first time. "That's what I've been sitting here trying to understand. I know that I ought to think it's right—but I can't. It's as if my tongue wouldn't turn to say it. I keep seeing every tie of the track down there, every signal light, every bridge, every night that I spent when . . ." His head dropped down on his arms. "Oh God, it's so damn unjust!"

"Dan," she said through her teeth, "fight it."

He raised his head. His eyes were empty. "No," he said. "It would be wrong. I'm just selfish."

"Oh, damn that rotten tripe! You know better than that!"

"I don't know . . ." His voice was very tired. "I've been sitting here, trying to think about it . . . I don't know what is right any more. . . ." He added, "I don't think I care."

She knew suddenly that all further words were useless and that Dan Conway would never be a man of action again. She did not know what made her certain of it. She said, wondering, "You've never given up in the face of a battle before."

"No, I guess I haven't. . . ." He spoke with a quiet, indifferent astonishment. "I've fought storms and floods and rock slides and rail fissure. . . . I knew how to do it, and I liked doing it. . . . But this kind of battle—it's one I can't fight."

"Why?"

"I don't know. Who knows why the world is what it is? Oh, who is John Galt?"

She winced. "Then what are you going to do?"

"I don't know . . ."

"I mean—" She stopped.

He knew what she meant. "Oh, there's always something to do. . . ." He spoke without conviction. "I guess it's only Colorado and New Mexico that they're going to declare restricted. I'll still have the line in Arizona to run." He added, "As it was twenty years ago . . . Well, it will keep me busy. I'm getting tired, Dagny. I didn't take time to notice it, but I guess I am."

She could say nothing.

"I'm not going to build a line through one of their blighted areas," he said in the same indifferent voice. "That's what they tried to hand me for a consolation prize, but I think it's just talk. You can't build a railroad where there's nothing for hundreds of miles but a couple of farmers who're not growing enough to feed themselves. You can't build a road and make it pay. If you don't make it pay, who's going to? It doesn't make sense to me. They just didn't know what they were saying."

"Oh, to hell with their blighted areas! It's you I'm thinking about." She had to name it. "What will you do with yourself?"

"I don't know . . . Well, there's a lot of things I haven't had time to do. Fishing, for instance. I've always liked fishing. Maybe I'll start reading books, always meant to. Guess I'll take it easy now. Guess I'll go fishing. There's some nice places down in Arizona, where it's peaceful and quiet and you don't have to see a human being for miles. . . ." He glanced up at her and added, "Forget it. Why should you worry about me?"

"It's not about you, it's . . . Dan," she said suddenly, "I hope you know it's not for your sake that I wanted to help you fight."

He smiled; it was a faint, friendly smile. "I know," he said.

"It's not out of pity or charity or any ugly reason like that. Look, I intended to give you the battle of your life, down there in Colorado. I intended to cut into your business and squeeze you to the wall and drive you out, if necessary."

He chuckled faintly; it was appreciation. "You would have made a pretty good try at it, too," he said.

"Only I didn't think it would be necessary. I thought there was enough room there for both of us."

"Yes," he said. "There was."

"Still, if I found that there wasn't, I would have fought you, and if I could make my road better than yours, I'd have broken you and not given a damn about what happened to you. But this . . . Dan, I don't think I want to look at our Rio Norte Line now. I . . . Oh God, Dan, I don't want to be a looter!"

He looked at her silently for a moment. It was an odd look, as if from a great distance. He said softly, "You should have been born about a hundred years earlier, kid. Then you would have had a chance."

"To hell with that. I intend to make my own chance."

"That's what I intended at your age."

"You succeeded."

"Have I?"

She sat still, suddenly unable to move.

He sat up straight and said sharply, almost as if he were issuing orders, "You'd better look at that Rio Norte Line of yours, and you'd better do it fast. Get it ready before I move out, because if you don't, that will be the end of Ellis Wyatt and all the rest of them down there, and they're the best people left in the country. You can't let that happen. It's all on your shoulders now. It would be no use trying to explain to your brother that it's going to be much tougher for you down there without me to compete with. But you and I know it. So go to it. Whatever you do, you won't be a looter. No looter could run a railroad in that part of the country and last at it. Whatever you make down there, you will have earned it. Lice like your brother don't count, anyway. It's up to you now."

She sat looking at him, wondering what it was that had defeated a man of this kind; she knew that it was not James Taggart.

She saw him looking at her, as if he were struggling with a question mark of his own. Then he smiled, and she saw, incredulously, that the smile held sadness and pity.

"You'd better not feel sorry for me," he said. "I think, of the two of us, it's you who have the harder time ahead. And I think you're going to get it worse than I did."

* * *

She had telephoned the mills and made an appointment to see Hank Rearden that afternoon. She had just hung up the receiver and was bending over the maps of the Rio Norte Line spread on her desk, when the door opened. Dagny looked up, startled; she did not expect the door of her office to open without announcement.

The man who entered was a stranger. He was young, tall, and something about him suggested violence, though she could not say what it was, because the first trait one grasped about him was a quality of self-control that seemed almost arrogant. He had dark eyes, disheveled hair, and his clothes were expensive, but worn as if he did not care or notice what he wore.

"Ellis Wyatt," he said in self-introduction.

She leaped to her feet, involuntarily. She understood why nobody had or could have stopped him in the outer office.

"Sit down, Mr. Wyatt," she said, smiling.

"It won't be necessary." He did not smile. "I don't hold long conferences."

Slowly, taking her time by conscious intention, she sat down and leaned back, looking at him.

"Well?" she asked.

"I came to see you because I understand you're the only one who's got any brains in this rotten outfit."

"What can I do for you?"

"You can listen to an ultimatum." He spoke distinctly, giving an unusual clarity to every syllable. "I expect Taggart Transcontinental, nine months from now, to run trains in Colorado as my business requires them to be run. If the snide stunt you people perpetrated on the Phoenix-Durango was done for the purpose of saving yourself from the necessity of effort, this is to give you notice that you will not get away with it. I made no demands on you when you could not give me the kind of service I needed. I found someone who could. Now you wish to force me to deal with you. You expect to dictate terms by leaving me no choice. You expect me to hold my business down to the level of your incompetence. This is to tell you that you have miscalculated."

She said slowly, with effort, "Shall I tell you what I intend to do about our service in Colorado?"

"No. I have no interest in discussions and intentions. I expect transportation. What you do to furnish it and how you do it, is your problem, not mine. I am merely giving you a warning. Those who wish to deal with me, must do so on my terms or not at all. I do not make terms with incompetence. If you expect to earn money by carrying the oil I produce, you must be as good at your business as I am at mine. I wish this to be understood."

She said quietly, "I understand."

"I shan't waste time proving to you why you'd better take my ultimatum seriously. If you have the intelligence to keep this corrupt organization functioning at all, you have the intelligence to judge this for yourself. We both know that if Taggart Transcontinental runs trains in Colorado the way it did five years ago, it will ruin me. I know that that is what you people intend to do. You expect to feed off me while you can and to find another carcass to pick dry after you have finished mine. That is the policy of most of mankind today. So here is my ultimatum: it is now in your power to destroy me; I may have to go; but if I go, I'll make sure that I take all the rest of you along with me."

Somewhere within her, under the numbness that held her still to receive the lashing, she felt a small point of pain, hot like the pain of scalding. She wanted to tell him of the years she had spent looking for men such as he to work with; she wanted to tell him that his enemies were hers, that she was fighting the same battle; she wanted to cry to him: I'm not one of them! But she knew that she could not do it. She bore the responsibility for Taggart Transcontinental and for everything done in its name; she had no right to justify herself now.

Sitting straight, her glance as steady and open as his, she answered evenly, "You will get the transportation you need, Mr. Wyatt."

She saw a faint hint of astonishment in his face; this was not the manner or the answer he had expected; perhaps it was what she had not said that astonished him most: that she offered no defense, no excuses. He took a moment to study her silently. Then he said, his voice less sharp:

"All right. Thank you. Good day."

She inclined her head. He bowed and left the office.

*　*　*

"That's the story, Hank. I had worked out an almost impossible schedule to complete the Rio Norte Line in twelve months. Now I'll have to do it in nine. You were to give us the rail over a period of one year. Can you give it to us within nine months? If there's any human way to do it, do it. If not, I'll have to find some other means to finish it."

Rearden sat behind his desk. His cold, blue eyes made two horizontal cuts across the gaunt planes of his face; they remained horizontal, impassively half-closed; he said evenly, without emphasis:

"I'll do it."

Dagny leaned back in her chair. The short sentence was a shock. It was not merely relief: it was the sudden realization that nothing else was necessary to guarantee that it would be done; she needed no proofs, no questions, no explanations; a complex problem could rest safely on three syllables pronounced by a man who knew what he was saying.

"Don't show that you're relieved." His voice was mocking. "Not too obviously." His narrowed eyes were watching her with an unrevealing smile. "I might think that I hold Taggart Transcontinental in my power."

"You know that, anyway."

"I do. And I intend to make you pay for it."

"I expect to. How much?"

"Twenty dollars extra per ton on the balance of the order delivered after today."

"Pretty steep, Hank. Is that the best price you can give me?"

"No. But that's the one I'm going to get. I could ask twice that and you'd pay it."

"Yes, I would. And you could. But you won't."

"Why won't I?"

"Because you need to have the Rio Norte Line built. It's your first showcase for Rearden Metal."

He chuckled. "That's right. I like to deal with somebody who has no illusions about getting favors."

"Do you know what made me feel relieved, when you decided to take advantage of it?"

"What?"

"That I was dealing, for once, with somebody who doesn't pretend to give favors."

His smile had a discernible quality now: it was enjoyment. "You always play it open, don't you?" he asked.

"I've never noticed you doing otherwise."

"I thought I was the only one who could afford to."

"I'm not broke, in that sense, Hank."

"I think I'm going to break you some day—in that sense."

"Why?"

"I've always wanted to."

"Don't you have enough cowards around you?"

"That's why I'd enjoy trying it—because you're the only exception. So you think it's right that I should squeeze every penny of profit I can, out of your emergency?"

"Certainly. I'm not a fool. I don't think you're in business for my convenience."

"Don't you wish I were?"

"I'm not a moocher, Hank."

"Aren't you going to find it hard to pay?"

"That's my problem, not yours. I want that rail."

"At twenty dollars extra per ton?"

"Okay, Hank."

"Fine. You'll get the rail. I may get my exorbitant profit—or Taggart Transcontinental may crash before I collect it."

She said, without smiling, "If I don't get that line built in nine months, Taggart Transcontinental *will* crash."

"It won't, so long as you run it."

When he did not smile, his face looked inanimate, only his eyes remained alive, active with a cold, brilliant clarity of perception. But what he was made to feel by the things he perceived, no one would be permitted to know, she thought, perhaps not even himself.

"They've done their best to make it harder for you, haven't they?" he said.

"Yes. I was counting on Colorado to save the Taggart system. Now it's up to me to save Colorado. Nine months from now, Dan Conway will close his road. If mine isn't ready, it won't be any use finishing it. You can't leave those men without transportation for a single day, let alone a week or a month. At the rate they've been growing, you can't stop them dead and then expect them to continue. It's like slamming brakes on an engine going two hundred miles an hour."

"I know."

"I can run a good railroad. I can't run it across a continent of share-croppers who're not good enough to grow turnips successfully. I've got to have men like Ellis Wyatt to produce something to fill the trains I run. So I've got to give him a train and a track nine months from now, if I have to blast all the rest of us into hell to do it!"

He smiled, amused. "You feel very strongly about it, don't you?"

"Don't *you?*"

He would not answer, but merely held the smile.

"Aren't you concerned about it?" she asked, almost angrily.

"No."

"Then you don't realize what it means?"

"I realize that I'm going to get the rail rolled and you're going to get the track laid in nine months."

She smiled, relaxing, wearily and a little guiltily. "Yes. I know we will. I know it's useless—getting angry at people like Jim and his friends. We haven't any time for it. First, I have to undo what they've done. Then afterwards"—she stopped, wondering, shook her head and shrugged—"afterwards, they won't matter."

"That's right. They won't. When I heard about that Anti-dog-eat-dog business, it made me sick. But don't worry about the goddamn bastards." The two words sounded shockingly violent, because his face and voice remained calm. "You and I will always be there to save the country from the consequences of their actions." He got up; he said, pacing the office, "Colorado isn't going to be stopped. You'll pull it through. Then Dan Conway will be back, and others. All that lunacy is temporary. It can't last. It's demented, so it has to defeat itself. You and I will just have to work a little harder for a while, that's all."

She watched his tall figure moving across the office. The office suited him; it contained nothing but the few pieces of furniture he needed, all of them harshly simplified down to their essential purpose, all of them exorbitantly expensive in the quality of materials and the skill of design. The room looked like a motor—a motor held within the glass case of broad windows. But she noticed one astonishing detail: a vase of jade that stood on top of a filing cabinet. The vase was a solid, dark green stone carved into plain surfaces; the texture of its smooth curves provoked an irresistible desire to touch it. It seemed startling in that office, incongruous with the sternness of the rest: it was a touch of sensuality.

"Colorado is a great place," he said. "It's going to be the greatest in the country. You're not sure that I'm concerned about it? That state's becoming one of my best customers, as you ought to know if you take time to read the reports on your freight traffic."

"I know. I read them."

"I've been thinking of building a plant there in a few years. To save them your transportation charges." He glanced at her. "You'll lose an awful lot of steel freight, if I do."

"Go ahead. I'll be satisfied with carrying your supplies, and the groceries for your workers, and the freight of the factories that will follow you there—and perhaps I won't have time to notice that I've lost your steel. . . . What are you laughing at?"

"It's wonderful."

"What?"

"The way you don't react as everybody else does nowadays."

"Still, I must admit that for the time being you're the most important single shipper of Taggart Transcontinental."

"Don't you suppose I know it?"

"So I can't understand why Jim—" She stopped.

"—tries his best to harm my business? Because your brother Jim is a fool."

"He is. But it's more than that. There's something worse than stupidity about it."

"Don't waste time trying to figure him out. Let him spit. He's no danger to anyone. People like Jim Taggart just clutter up the world."

"I suppose so."

"Incidentally, what would you have done if I'd said I couldn't deliver your rails sooner?"

"I would have torn up sidings or closed some branch line, any branch line, and I would have used the rail to finish the Rio Norte track on time."

He chuckled. "That's why I'm not worried about Taggart Transcontinental. But you won't have to start getting rail out of old sidings. Not so long as I'm in business."

She thought suddenly that she was wrong about his lack of emotion: the hidden undertone of his manner was enjoyment. She realized that she had always felt a sense of light-hearted relaxation in his presence and known that he shared it. He was the only man she knew to whom she could speak without strain or effort. This, she thought, was a mind she respected, an adversary worth matching. Yet there had always been an odd sense of distance between them, the sense of a closed door; there was an impersonal quality in his manner, something within him that could not be reached.

He had stopped at the window. He stood for a moment, looking out. "Do you know that the first load of rail is being delivered to you today?" he asked.

"Of course I know it."

"Come here."

She approached him. He pointed silently. Far in the distance, beyond the mill structures, she saw a string of gondolas waiting on a siding. The bridge of an overhead crane cut the sky above them. The crane was moving. Its huge magnet held a load of rails glued to a disk by the sole power of contact. There was no trace of sun in the gray spread of clouds, yet the rails glistened, as if the metal caught light out of space. The metal was a greenish-blue. The great chain stopped over a car, descended, jerked in a brief spasm and left the rails in the car. The crane moved back in majestic indifference; it looked like the giant drawing of a geometrical theorem moving above the men and the earth.

They stood at the window, watching silently, intently. She did not speak, until another load of green-blue metal came moving across the sky. Then the first words she said were not about rail, track or an order completed on time. She said, as if greeting a new phenomenon of nature:

"Rearden Metal . . ."

He noticed that, but said nothing. He glanced at her, then turned back to the window.

"Hank, this is great."

"Yes."

He said it simply, openly. There was no flattered pleasure in his voice, and no modesty. This, she knew, was a tribute to her, the rarest one person could pay another: the tribute of feeling free to acknowledge one's own greatness, knowing that it is understood.

She said, "When I think of what that metal can do, what it will make possible . . . Hank, this is the most important thing happening in the world today, and none of them know it."

"We know it."

They did not look at each other. They stood watching the crane. On the front of the locomotive in the distance, she could distinguish the letters TT. She could distinguish the rails of the busiest industrial siding of the Taggart system.

"As soon as I can find a plant able to do it," she said, "I'm going to order Diesels made of Rearden Metal."

"You'll need them. How fast do you run your trains on the Rio Norte track?"

"Now? We're lucky if we manage to make twenty miles an hour."

He pointed at the cars. "When that rail is laid, you'll be able to run trains at two hundred and fifty, if you wish."

"I will, in a few years, when we'll have cars of Rearden Metal, which will be half the weight of steel and twice as safe."

"You'll have to look out for the air lines. We're working on a plane of Rearden Metal. It will weigh practically nothing and lift anything. You'll see the day of long-haul, heavy-freight air traffic."

"I've been thinking of what that metal will do for motors, any motors, and what sort of thing one can design now."

"Have you thought of what it will do for chicken wire? Just plain chicken-wire fences, made of Rearden Metal, that will cost a few pennies a mile and last two hundred years. And kitchenware that will be bought at the dime store and passed on from generation to generation. And ocean liners that one won't be able to dent with a torpedo."

"Did I tell you that I'm having tests made of communications wire of Rearden Metal?"

"I'm making so many tests that I'll never get through showing people what can be done with it and how to do it."

They spoke of the metal and of the possibilities which they could not exhaust. It was as if they were standing on a mountain top, seeing a limitless plain below and roads open in all directions. But they merely spoke of mathematical figures, of weights, pressures, resistances, costs.

She had forgotten her brother and his National Alliance. She had forgotten every problem, person and event behind her; they had always been clouded in her sight, to be hurried past, to be brushed aside, never final, never quite real. *This* was reality, she thought, this sense of clear outlines, of purpose, of lightness, of hope. This was the way she had expected to live—she had wanted to spend no hour and take no action that would mean less than this.

She looked at him in the exact moment when he turned to look at her. They stood very close to each other. She saw, in his eyes, that he felt as she did. If joy is the aim and the core of existence, she thought, and if that which has the power to give one joy is always guarded as one's deepest secret, then they had seen each other naked in that moment.

He made a step back and said in a strange tone of dispassionate wonder, "We're a couple of blackguards, aren't we?"

"Why?"

"We haven't any spiritual goals or qualities. All we're after is material things. That's all we care for."

She looked at him, unable to understand. But he was looking past her, straight ahead, at the crane in the distance. She wished he had not said it. The accusation did not trouble her, she never thought of herself in such terms and she was completely incapable of experiencing a feeling of fundamental guilt. But she felt a vague apprehension which she could not define, the suggestion that there was something of grave consequence in whatever had made him say it, something dangerous to him. He had not said it casually. But there had been no feeling in his voice, neither plea nor shame. He had said it indifferently, as a statement of fact.

Then, as she watched him, the apprehension vanished He was looking at his mills beyond the window; there was no guilt in his face, no doubt, nothing but the calm of an inviolate self-confidence.

"Dagny" he said, "whatever we are, it's we who move the world and it's we who'll pull it through."

THE CLIMAX OF THE D'ANCONIAS

The newspaper was the first thing she noticed. It was clutched tightly in Eddie's hand, as he entered her office. She glanced up at his face: it was tense and bewildered.

"Dagny, are you very busy?"

"Why?"

"I know that you don't like to talk about him. But there's something here I think you ought to see."

She extended her hand silently for the newspaper.

The story on the front page announced that upon taking over the San Sebastián Mines, the government of the People's State of Mexico had discovered that they were worthless—blatantly, totally, hopelessly worthless. There was nothing to justify the five years of work and the millions spent; nothing but empty excavations, laboriously cut. The few traces of copper were not worth the effort of extracting them. No great deposits of metal existed or could be expected to exist there, and there were no indications that could have permitted anyone to be deluded. The government of the People's State of Mexico was holding emergency sessions about their discovery, in an uproar of indignation; they felt that they had been cheated.

Watching her, Eddie knew that Dagny sat looking at the newspaper long after she had finished reading. He knew that he had been right to feel a hint of fear, even though he could not tell what frightened him about that story.

He waited. She raised her head. She did not look at him. Her eyes were fixed, intent in concentration, as if trying to discern something at a great distance.

He said, his voice low, "Francisco is not a fool. Whatever else he may be, no matter what depravity he's sunk to—and I've given up trying to figure out why—he is not a fool. He couldn't have made a mistake of this kind. It is not possible. I don't understand it."

"I'm beginning to."

She sat up, jolted upright by a sudden movement that ran through her body like a shudder. She said:

"Phone him at the Wayne-Falkland and tell the bastard that I want to see him."

"Dagny," he said sadly, reproachfully, "it's Frisco d'Anconia."

"It was."

*   *   *

She walked through the early twilight of the city streets to the Wayne-Falkland Hotel. "He says, any time you wish," Eddie had told her. The first lights appeared in a few windows high under the clouds. The skyscrapers looked like abandoned lighthouses sending feeble, dying signals out into an empty sea where no ships moved any longer. A few snowflakes came down, past the dark windows of empty stores, to melt in the mud of the sidewalks. A string of red lanterns cut the street, going off into the murky distance.

She wondered why she felt that she wanted to run, that she should be running; no, not down this street; down a green hillside in the blazing sun to the road on the edge of the Hudson, at the foot of the Taggart estate. That was the way she always ran when Eddie yelled, "It's Frisco d'Anconia!" and they both flew down the hill to the car approaching on the road below.

He was the only guest whose arrival was an event in their childhood, their biggest event. The running to meet him had become part of a contest among the three of them. There was a birch tree on the hillside, halfway between the road and the house; Dagny and Eddie tried to get past the tree, before Francisco could race up the hill to meet them. On all the many days of his arrivals, in all the many summers, they never reached the birch tree; Francisco reached it first and stopped them when he was way past it. Francisco always won, as he always won everything.

His parents were old friends of the Taggart family. He was an only son and he was being brought up all over the world; his father, it was said, wanted him to consider the world as his future domain. Dagny and Eddie could never be certain of where he would spend his winter; but once a year, every summer, a stern South American tutor brought him for a month to the Taggart estate.

Francisco found it natural that the Taggart children should be chosen as his companions: they were the crown heirs of Taggart Transcontinental, as he was of d'Anconia Copper. "We are the only aristocracy left in the world—the aristocracy of money," he said to Dagny once, when he was fourteen. "It's the only real aristocracy, if people understood what it means, which they don't."

He had a caste system of his own: to him, the Taggart children were not Jim and Dagny, but Dagny and Eddie. He seldom volunteered to notice Jim's existence. Eddie asked him once, "Francisco, you're some kind of very high nobility, aren't you?" He answered, "Not yet. The reason my family has lasted for such a long time is that none of us has ever been permitted to think he is born a d'Anconia. We are expected to become one." He pronounced his name as if he wished his listeners to be struck in the face and knighted by the sound of it.

Sebastián d'Anconia, his ancestor, had left Spain many centuries ago, at a time when Spain was the most powerful country on earth and his was one of Spain's proudest figures. He left, because the lord of the Inquisition did not approve of his manner of thinking and suggested, at a court banquet, that he change it. Sebastián d'Anconia threw the contents of his wine glass at the face of the lord of the Inquisition, and escaped before he could be seized. He left behind him his fortune, his estate, his marble palace and the girl he loved—and he sailed to a new world.

His first estate in Argentina was a wooden shack in the foothills of the Andes. The sun blazed like a beacon on the silver coat-of-arms of the d'Anconias, nailed over the door of the shack, while Sebastián d'Anconia dug for the copper of his first mine. He spent years, pickax in hand, breaking rock from sunrise till darkness, with the help of a few stray derelicts: deserters from the armies of his countrymen, escaped convicts, starving Indians.

Fifteen years after he left Spain, Sebastián d'Anconia sent for the girl he loved; she had waited for him. When she arrived, she found the silver coat-of-arms above the entrance of a marble palace, the gardens of a great estate, and mountains slashed by pits of red ore in the distance. He carried her in his arms across the threshold of his home. He looked younger than when she had seen him last.

"My ancestor and yours," Francisco told Dagny, "would have liked each other."

Through the years of her childhood, Dagny lived in the future—in the world she expected to find, where she would not have to feel contempt or boredom. But for one month each year, she was free. For one month, she could live in the present. When she raced down the hill to meet Francisco d'Anconia, it was a release from prison.

"Hi, Slug!"

"Hi, Frisco!"

They had both resented the nicknames, at first. She had asked him angrily, "What do you think you mean?" He had answered, "In case you don't know it, 'Slug' means a great fire in a locomotive firebox." "Where did you pick that up?" "From the gentlemen along the Taggart iron." He spoke five languages, and he spoke English without a trace of accent, a precise, cultured English deliberately mixed with slang. She had retaliated by calling him Frisco. He had laughed, amused and annoyed. "If you barbarians had to degrade the name of a great city of yours, you could at least refrain from doing it to me." But they had grown to like the nicknames.

It had started in the days of their second summer together, when he was twelve years old and she was ten. That summer, Francisco began vanishing every morning for some purpose nobody could discover. He went off on his bicycle before dawn, and returned in time to appear at the white and crystal table set for lunch on the terrace, his manner courteously punctual and a little too innocent. He laughed, refusing to answer, when Dagny and Eddie questioned him. They tried to follow him once, through the cold, pre-morning darkness, but they gave it up; no one could track him when he did not want to be tracked.

After a while, Mrs. Taggart began to worry and decided to investigate. She never learned how he had managed to by-pass all the child-labor laws, but she found Francisco working—by an unofficial deal with the dispatcher—as a call boy for Taggart Transcontinental, at a division point ten miles away. The dispatcher was stupefied by her personal visit; he had no idea that his call boy was a house guest of the Taggarts. The boy was known to the local railroad crews as Frankie, and Mrs. Taggart preferred not to enlighten them about his full name. She merely explained that he was working without his parents' permission and had to quit at once. The dispatcher was sorry to lose him; Frankie, he said, was the best call boy they had ever had. "I'd sure like to keep him on. Maybe we could make a deal with his parents?" he suggested. "I'm afraid not," said Mrs. Taggart faintly.

"Francisco," she asked, when she brought him home, "what would your father say about this, if he knew?"

"My father would ask whether I was good at the job or not. That's all he'd want to know."

"Come now, I'm serious."

Francisco was looking at her politely, his courteous manner suggesting centuries of breeding and drawing rooms; but something in his eyes made her feel uncertain about the politeness. "Last winter," he answered, "I shipped out as cabin boy on a cargo steamer that carried d'Anconia copper. My father looked for me for three months, but that's all he asked me when I came back."

"So that's how you spend your winters?" said Jim Taggart. Jim's smile had a touch of triumph, the triumph of finding cause to feel contempt.

"That was last winter," Francisco answered pleasantly, with no change in the innocent, casual tone of his voice. "The winter before last I spent in Madrid, at the home of the Duke of Alba."

"Why did you want to work on a railroad?" asked Dagny.

They stood looking at each other: hers was a glance of admiration, his of mockery; but it was not the mockery of malice—it was the laughter of a salute.

"To learn what it's like, Slug," he answered, "and to tell you that I've had a job with Taggart Transcontinental before you did."

Dagny and Eddie spent their winters trying to master some new skill, in order to astonish Francisco and beat him, for once. They never succeeded. When they showed him how to hit a ball with a bat, a game he had never played before, he watched them for a few minutes, then said, "I think I get the idea. Let me try." He took the bat and sent the ball flying over a line of oak trees far at the end of the field.

When Jim was given a motorboat for his birthday, they all stood on the river landing, watching the lesson, while an instructor showed Jim how to run it. None of them had ever driven a motorboat before. The sparkling white craft, shaped like a bullet, kept staggering clumsily across the water, its wake a long record of shivering, its motor choking with hiccoughs, while the instructor, seated beside him, kept seizing the wheel out of Jim's hands. For no apparent reason, Jim raised his head suddenly and yelled at Francisco, "Do you think you can do it any better?" "I can do it." "Try it!"

When the boat came back and its two occupants stepped out, Francisco slipped behind the wheel. "Wait a moment," he said to the instructor, who remained on the landing. "Let me take a look at this." Then, before the instructor had time to move, the boat shot out to the middle of the river, as if fired from a gun. It was streaking away before they grasped what they were seeing. As it went shrinking into the distance and sunlight, Dagny's picture of it was three straight lines: its wake, the long shriek of its motor, and the aim of the driver at its wheel.

She noticed the strange expression of her father's face as he looked at the vanishing speedboat. He said nothing; he just stood looking. She remembered that she had seen him look that way once before. It was when he inspected a complex system of pulleys which Francisco, aged twelve, had erected to make an elevator to the top of a rock; he was teaching Dagny and Eddie to dive from the rock into the Hudson. Francisco's notes of calculation were still scattered about on the ground; her father picked them up, looked at them, then asked, "Francisco, how many years of algebra have you had?" "Two years." "Who taught you to do this?" "Oh, that's just something I figured out." She did not know that what her father held on the crumpled sheets of paper was the crude version of a differential equation.

The heirs of Sebastián d'Anconia had been an unbroken line of first sons, who knew how to bear his name. It was a tradition of the family that the man to disgrace them would be the heir who died, leaving the d'Anconia fortune no greater than he had received it. Throughout the generations, that disgrace had not come. An Argentinian legend said that the hand of a d'Anconia had the miraculous power of the saints— only it was not the power to heal, but the power to produce.

The d'Anconia heirs had been men of unusual ability, but none of them could match what Francisco d'Anconia promised to become. It was as if the centuries had sifted the family's qualities through a fine mesh, had discarded the irrelevant, the inconsequential, the weak, and had let nothing through except pure talent; as if chance, for once, had achieved an entity devoid of the accidental.

Francisco could do anything he undertook, he could do it better than anyone else, and he did it without effort. There was no boasting in his manner and consciousness, no thought of comparison. His attitude was not: "I can do it better than you," but simply: "I can do it." What he meant by doing was doing superlatively.

No matter what discipline was required of him by his father's exacting plan for his education, no matter what subject he was ordered to study, Francisco mastered it with effortless amusement. His father adored him, but concealed it carefully, as he concealed the pride of knowing that he was bringing up the most brilliant phenomenon of a brilliant family line. Francisco, it was said, was to be the climax of the d'Anconias.

"I don't know what sort of motto the d'Anconias have on their family crest," Mrs. Taggart said once, "but I'm sure that Francisco will change it to 'What for?' " It was the first question he asked about any activity proposed to him—and nothing would make him act, if he found no valid answer. He flew through the days of his summer month like a rocket, but if one stopped him in mid-flight, he could always name the purpose of his every random moment. Two things were impossible to him: to stand still or to move aimlessly.

"Let's find out" was the motive he gave to Dagny and Eddie for anything he undertook, or "Let's make it." These were his only forms of enjoyment.

"I can do it," he said, when he was building his elevator, clinging to the side of a cliff, driving metal wedges into rock, his arms moving with an expert's rhythm, drops of blood slipping, unnoticed, from under a bandage on his wrist. "No, we can't take turns, Eddie, you're not big enough yet to handle a hammer. Just cart the weeds off and keep the way clear for me, I'll do the rest. . . . What blood? Oh, that's nothing, just a cut I got yesterday. Dagny, run to the house and bring me a clean bandage."

Jim watched them. They left him alone, but they often saw him standing in the distance, watching Francisco with a peculiar kind of intensity.

He seldom spoke in Francisco's presence. But he would corner Dagny and he would smile derisively, saying, "All those airs you put on, pretending that you're an iron woman with a mind of her own! You're a spineless dishrag, that's all you are. It's disgusting, the way you let that conceited punk order you about. He can twist you around his little finger. You haven't any pride at all. The way you run when he whistles and wait on him! Why don't you shine his shoes?" "Because he hasn't told me to," she answered.

Francisco could win any game in any local contest. He never entered contests. He could have ruled the junior country club. He never came within sight of their clubhouse, ignoring their eager attempts to enroll the most famous heir in the world. Dagny and Eddie were his only friends. They could not tell whether they owned him or were owned by him completely; it made no difference: either concept made them happy.

The three of them set out every morning on adventures of their own kind. Once, an elderly professor of literature, Mrs. Taggart's friend, saw them on top of a pile in a junk yard, dismantling the carcass of an automobile. He stopped, shook his head and said to Francisco, "A young man of your position ought to spend his time in libraries, absorbing the culture of the world." "What do you think I'm doing?" asked Francisco.

There were no factories in the neighborhood, but Francisco taught Dagny and Eddie to steal rides on Taggart trains to distant towns, where they climbed fences into mill yards or hung on window sills, watching machinery as other children watched movies. "When I run Taggart Transcontinental . . ." Dagny would say at times. "When I run d'Anconia Copper . . ." said Francisco. They never had to explain the rest to each other; they knew each other's goal and motive.

Railroad conductors caught them, once in a while. Then a stationmaster a hundred miles away would telephone Mrs. Taggart: "We've got three young tramps here who say that they are—" "Yes," Mrs. Taggart would sigh, "they are. Please send them back."

"Francisco," Eddie asked him once, as they stood by the tracks of the Taggart station, "you've been just about everywhere in the world. What's the most important thing on earth?" "This," answered Francisco, pointing to the emblem TT on the front of an engine. He added, "I wish I could have met Nat Taggart."

He noticed Dagny's glance at him. He said nothing else. But minutes later, when they went on through the woods, down a narrow path of damp earth, ferns and sunlight, he said, "Dagny, I'll always bow to a coat-of-arms. I'll always worship the symbols of nobility. Am I not supposed to be an aristocrat? Only I don't give a damn for moth-eaten turrets and tenth-hand unicorns. The coats-of-arms of our day are to be found on billboards and in the ads of popular magazines." "What do you mean?" asked Eddie. "Industrial trademarks, Eddie," he answered.

Francisco was fifteen years old, that summer.

"When I run d'Anconia Copper . . ." "I'm studying mining and mineralogy, because I must be ready for the time when I run d'Anconia Copper. . . ." "I'm studying electrical engineering, because power companies are the best customers of d'Anconia Copper. . . ." "I'm going to study philosophy, because I'll need it to protect d'Anconia Copper. . . ."

"Don't you ever think of anything but d'Anconia Copper?" Jim asked him once.

"No."

"It seems to me that there are other things in the world."

"Let others think about them."

"Isn't that a very selfish attitude?"

"It is."

"What are you after?"

"Money."

"Don't you have enough?"

"In his lifetime, every one of my ancestors raised the production of d'Anconia Copper by about ten per cent. I intend to raise it by one hundred."

"What for?" Jim asked, in sarcastic imitation of Francisco's voice.

"When I die, I hope to go to heaven—whatever the hell that is—and I want to be able to afford the price of admission."

"Virtue is the price of admission," Jim said haughtily.

"That's what I mean, James. So I want to be prepared to claim the greatest virtue of all—that I was a man who made money."

"Any grafter can make money."

"James, you ought to discover some day that words have an exact meaning."

Francisco smiled; it was a smile of radiant mockery. Watching them, Dagny thought suddenly of the difference between Francisco and her brother Jim. Both of them smiled derisively. But Francisco seemed to laugh at things because he saw something much greater. Jim laughed as if he wanted to let nothing remain great.

She noticed the particular quality of Francisco's smile again, one night, when she sat with him and Eddie at a bonfire they had built in the woods. The glow of the fire enclosed them within a fence of broken, moving strips that held pieces of tree trunks, branches and distant stars. She felt as if there were nothing beyond that fence, nothing but black emptiness, with the hint of some breath-stopping, frightening promise . . . like the future. But the future, she thought, would be like Francisco's smile, *there* was the key to it, the advance warning of its nature —in his face in the firelight under the pine branches—and suddenly she felt an unbearable happiness, unbearable because it was too full and she had no way to express it. She glanced at Eddie. He was looking at Francisco. In some quiet way of his own, Eddie felt as she did.

"Why do you like Francisco?" she asked him weeks later, when Francisco was gone.

Eddie looked astonished; it had never occurred to him that the feeling could be questioned. He said, "He makes me feel safe."

She said, "He makes me expect excitement and danger."

Francisco was sixteen, next summer, the day when she stood alone with him on the summit of a cliff by the river, their shorts and shirts torn in their climb to the top. They stood looking down the Hudson; they had heard that on clear days one could see New York in the distance. But they saw only a haze made of three different kinds of light merging together: the river, the sky and the sun.

She knelt on a rock, leaning forward, trying to catch some hint of the city, the wind blowing her hair across her eyes. She glanced back over her shoulder—and saw that Francisco was not looking at the distance:

he stood looking at her. It was an odd glance, intent and unsmiling. She remained still for a moment, her hands spread flat on the rock, her arms tensed to support the weight of her body; inexplicably, his glance made her aware of her pose, of her shoulder showing through the torn shirt, of her long, scratched, sunburned legs slanting from the rock to the ground. She stood up angrily and backed away from him. And while throwing her head up, resentment in her eyes to meet the sternness in his, while feeling certain that his was a glance of condemnation and hostility, she heard herself asking him, a tone of smiling defiance in her voice:

"What do you like about me?"

He laughed; she wondered, aghast, what had made her say it. He answered, "There's what I like about you," pointing to the glittering rails of the Taggart station in the distance.

"It's not mine," she said, disappointed.

"What I like is that it's going to be."

She smiled, conceding his victory by being openly delighted. She did not know why he had looked at her so strangely; but she felt that he had seen some connection, which she could not grasp, between her body and something within her that would give her the strength to rule those rails some day.

He said brusquely, "Let's see if we can see New York," and jerked her by the arm to the edge of the cliff. She thought that he did not notice that he twisted her arm in a peculiar way, holding it down along the length of his side; it made her stand pressed against him, and she felt the warmth of the sun in the skin of his legs against hers. They looked far out into the distance, but they saw nothing ahead except a haze of light.

When Francisco left, that summer, she thought that his departure was like the crossing of a frontier which ended his childhood: he was to start college, that fall. Her turn would come next. She felt an eager impatience touched by the excitement of fear, as if he had leaped into an unknown danger. It was like the moment, years ago, when she had seen him dive first from a rock into the Hudson, had seen him vanish under the black water and had stood, knowing that he would reappear in an instant and that it would then be her turn to follow.

She dismissed the fear; dangers, to Francisco, were merely opportunities for another brilliant performance; there were no battles he could lose, no enemies to beat him. And then she thought of a remark she had heard a few years earlier. It was a strange remark—and it was strange that the words had remained in her mind, even though she had thought them senseless at the time. The man who said it was an old professor of mathematics, a friend of her father, who came to their country house for just that one visit. She liked his face, and she could still see the peculiar sadness in his eyes when he said to her father one evening, sitting on the terrace in the fading light, pointing to Francisco's figure in the garden, "That boy is vulnerable. He has too great a capacity for joy.

What will he do with it in a world where there's so little occasion for it?"

Francisco went to a great American school, which his father had chosen for him long ago. It was the most distinguished institution of learning left in the world, the Patrick Henry University of Cleveland. He did not come to visit her in New York, that winter, even though he was only a night's journey away. They did not write to each other, they had never done it. But she knew that he would come back to the country for one summer month.

There were a few times, that winter, when she felt an undefined apprehension: the professor's words kept returning to her mind, as a warning which she could not explain. She dismissed them. When she thought of Francisco, she felt the steadying assurance that she would have another month as an advance against the future, as a proof that the world she saw ahead was real, even though it was not the world of those around her.

"Hi, Slug!"

"Hi, Frisco!"

Standing on the hillside, in the first moment of seeing him again, she grasped suddenly the nature of that world which they, together, held against all others. It was only an instant's pause, she felt her cotton skirt beating in the wind against her knees, felt the sun on her eyelids, and the upward thrust of such an immense relief that she ground her feet into the grass under her sandals, because she thought she would rise, weightless, through the wind.

It was a sudden sense of freedom and safety—because she realized that she knew nothing about the events of his life, had never known and would never need to know. The world of chance—of families, meals, schools, people, of aimless people dragging the load of some unknown guilt—was not theirs, could not change him, could not matter. He and she had never spoken of the things that happened to them, but only of what they thought and of what they would do. . . . She looked at him silently, as if a voice within her were saying: Not the things that are, but the things we'll make . . . We are not to be stopped, you and I . . . Forgive me the fear, if I thought I could lose you to them—forgive me the doubt, they'll never reach you—I'll never be afraid for you again. . . .

He, too, stood looking at her for a moment—and it seemed to her that it was not a look of greeting after an absence, but the look of someone who had thought of her every day of that year. She could not be certain, it was only an instant, so brief that just as she caught it, he was turning to point at the birch tree behind him and saying in the tone of their childhood game:

"I wish you'd learn to run faster. I'll always have to wait for you."

"Will you wait for me?" she asked gaily.

He answered, without smiling, "Always."

As they went up the hill to the house, he spoke to Eddie, while she walked silently by his side. She felt that there was a new reticence between them which, strangely, was a new kind of intimacy.

She did not question him about the university. Days later, she asked him only whether he liked it.

"They're teaching a lot of drivel nowadays," he answered, "but there are a few courses I like."

"Have you made any friends there?"

"Two."

He told her nothing else.

Jim was approaching his senior year in a college in New York. His studies had given him a manner of odd, quavering belligerence, as if he had found a new weapon. He addressed Francisco once, without provocation, stopping him in the middle of the lawn to say in a tone of aggressive self-righteousness:

"I think that now that you've reached college age, you ought to learn something about ideals. It's time to forget your selfish greed and give some thought to your social responsibilities, because I think that all those millions you're going to inherit are not for your personal pleasure, they are a trust for the benefit of the underprivileged and the poor, because I think that the person who doesn't realize this is the most depraved type of human being."

Francisco answered courteously, "It is not advisable, James, to venture unsolicited opinions. You should spare yourself the embarrassing discovery of their exact value to your listener."

Dagny asked him, as they walked away, "Are there many men like Jim in the world?"

Francisco laughed. "A great many."

"Don't you mind it?"

"No. I don't have to deal with them. Why do you ask that?"

"Because I think they're dangerous in some way . . . I don't know how . . ."

"Good God, Dagny! Do you expect me to be afraid of an object like James?"

It was days later, when they were alone, walking through the woods on the shore of the river, that she asked:

"Francisco, what's the most depraved type of human being?"

"The man without a purpose."

She was looking at the straight shafts of the trees that stood against the great, sudden, shining spread of space beyond. The forest was dim and cool, but the outer branches caught the hot, silver sunrays from the water. She wondered why she enjoyed the sight, when she had never taken any notice of the country around her, why she was so aware of her enjoyment, of her movements, of her body in the process of walking. She did not want to look at Francisco. She felt that his presence seemed more intensely real when she kept her eyes away from him, almost as if the stressed awareness of herself came from him, like the sunlight from the water.

"You think you're good, don't you?" he asked.

"I always did," she answered defiantly, without turning.

"Well, let me see you prove it. Let me see how far you'll rise with Taggart Transcontinental. No matter how good you are, I'll expect you to wring everything you've got, trying to be still better. And when you've worn yourself out to reach a goal, I'll expect you to start for another."

"Why do you think that I care to prove anything to you?" she asked.

"Want me to answer?"

"No," she whispered, her eyes fixed upon the other shore of the river in the distance.

She heard him chuckling, and after a while he said, "Dagny, there's nothing of any importance in life—except how well you do your work. Nothing. Only that. Whatever else you are, will come from that. It's the only measure of human value. All the codes of ethics they'll try to ram down your throat are just so much paper money put out by swindlers to fleece people of their virtues. The code of competence is the only system of morality that's on a gold standard. When you grow up, you'll know what I mean."

"I know it now. But . . . Francisco, why are you and I the only ones who seem to know it?"

"Why should you care about the others?"

"Because I like to understand things, and there's something about people that I can't understand."

"What?"

"Well, I've always been unpopular in school and it didn't bother me, but now I've discovered the reason. It's an impossible kind of reason. They dislike me, not because I do things badly, but because I do them well. They dislike me because I've always had the best grades in the class. I don't even have to study. I always get A's. Do you suppose I should try to get D's for a change and become the most popular girl in school?"

Francisco stopped, looked at her and slapped her face.

What she felt was contained in a single instant, while the ground rocked under her feet, in a single blast of emotion within her. She knew that she would have killed any other person who struck her; she felt the violent fury which would have given her the strength for it—and as violent a pleasure that Francisco had done it. She felt pleasure from the dull, hot pain in her cheek and from the taste of blood in the corner of her mouth. She felt pleasure in what she suddenly grasped about him, about herself and about his motive.

She braced her feet to stop the dizziness, she held her head straight and stood facing him in the consciousness of a new power, feeling herself his equal for the first time, looking at him with a mocking smile of triumph.

"Did I hurt you as much as that?" she asked.

He looked astonished; the question and the smile were not those of a child. He answered, "Yes—if it pleases you."

"It does."

"Don't ever do that again. Don't crack jokes of that kind."

"Don't be a fool. Whatever made you think that I cared about being popular?"

"When you grow up, you'll understand what sort of unspeakable thing you said."

"I understand it now."

He turned abruptly, took out his handkerchief and dipped it in the water of the river. "Come here," he ordered.

She laughed, stepping back. "Oh no. I want to keep it as it is. I hope it swells terribly. I like it."

He looked at her for a long moment. He said slowly, very earnestly, "Dagny, you're wonderful."

"I thought that you always thought so," she answered, her voice insolently casual.

When she came home, she told her mother that she had cut her lip by falling against a rock. It was the only lie she ever told. She did not do it to protect Francisco; she did it because she felt, for some reason which she could not define, that the incident was a secret too precious to share.

Next summer, when Francisco came, she was sixteen. She started running down the hill to meet him, but stopped abruptly. He saw it, stopped, and they stood for a moment, looking at each other across the distance of a long, green slope. It was he who walked up toward her, walked very slowly, while she stood waiting.

When he approached, she smiled innocently, as if unconscious of any contest intended or won.

"You might like to know," she said, "that I have a job on the railroad. Night operator at Rockdale."

He laughed. "All right, Taggart Transcontinental, now it's a race. Let's see who'll do greater honor, you—to Nat Taggart, or I—to Sebastián d'Anconia."

That winter, she stripped her life down to the bright simplicity of a geometrical drawing: a few straight lines—to and from the engineering college in the city each day, to and from her job at Rockdale Station each night—and the closed circle of her room, a room littered with diagrams of motors, blueprints of steel structures, and railroad timetables.

Mrs. Taggart watched her daughter in unhappy bewilderment. She could have forgiven all the omissions, but one: Dagny showed no sign of interest in men, no romantic inclination whatever. Mrs. Taggart did not approve of extremes; she had been prepared to contend with an extreme of the opposite kind, if necessary; she found herself thinking that this was worse. She felt embarrassed when she had to admit that hei daughter, at seventeen, did not have a single admirer.

"Dagny and Francisco d'Anconia?" she said, smiling ruefully, in answer to the curiosity of her friends. "Oh no, it's not a romance. It's an international industrial cartel of some kind. That's all they seem to care about."

Mrs. Taggart heard James say one evening, in the presence of guests, a peculiar tone of satisfaction in his voice, "Dagny, even though you were named after her, you really look more like Nat Taggart than like that first Dagny Taggart, the famous beauty who was his wife." Mrs. Taggart did not know which offended her most: that James said it or that Dagny accepted it happily as a compliment.

She would never have a chance, thought Mrs. Taggart, to form some conception of her own daughter. Dagny was only a figure hurrying in and out of the apartment, a slim figure in a leather jacket, with a raised collar, a short skirt and long show-girl legs. She walked, cutting across a room, with a masculine, straight-line abruptness, but she had a peculiar grace of motion that was swift, tense and oddly, challengingly feminine.

At times, catching a glimpse of Dagny's face, Mrs. Taggart caught an expression which she could not quite define: it was much more than gaiety, it was the look of such an untouched purity of enjoyment that she found it abnormal, too: no young girl could be so insensitive as to have discovered no sadness in life. Her daughter, she concluded, was incapable of emotion.

"Dagny," she asked once, "don't you ever want to have a good time?" Dagny looked at her incredulously and answered, "What do you think I'm having?"

The decision to give her daughter a formal debut cost Mrs. Taggart a great deal of anxious thought. She did not know whether she was introducing to New York society Miss Dagny Taggart of the Social Register or the night operator of Rockdale Station; she was inclined to believe it was more truly this last; and she felt certain that Dagny would reject the idea of such an occasion. She was astonished when Dagny accepted it with inexplicable eagerness, for once like a child.

She was astonished again, when she saw Dagny dressed for the party. It was the first feminine dress she had ever worn—a gown of white chiffon with a huge skirt that floated like a cloud. Mrs. Taggart had expected her to look like a preposterous contrast. Dagny looked like a beauty. She seemed both older and more radiantly innocent than usual; standing in front of a mirror, she held her head as Nat Taggart's wife would have held it.

"Dagny," Mrs. Taggart said gently, reproachfully, "do you see how beautiful you can be when you want to?"

"Yes," said Dagny, without any astonishment.

The ballroom of the Wayne-Falkland Hotel had been decorated under Mrs. Taggart's direction; she had an artist's taste, and the setting of that evening was her masterpiece. "Dagny, there are things I would like you to learn to notice," she said, "lights, colors, flowers, music. They are not as negligible as you might think." "I've never thought they're negligible," Dagny answered happily. For once, Mrs. Taggart felt a bond between them; Dagny was looking at her with a child's grateful trust. "They're the things that make life beautiful," said Mrs. Taggart. "I want this evening to be very beautiful for you, Dagny. The first ball is the most romantic event of one's life."

To Mrs. Taggart, the greatest surprise was the moment when she saw Dagny standing under the lights, looking at the ballroom. This was not a child, not a girl, but a woman of such confident, dangerous power that Mrs. Taggart stared at her with shocked admiration. In an age of casual, cynical, indifferent routine, among people who held themselves as if they were not flesh, but meat—Dagny's bearing seemed almost indecent, because this was the way a woman would have faced a ballroom centuries ago, when the act of displaying one's half-naked body for the admiration of men was an act of daring, when it had meaning, and but one meaning, acknowledged by all as a high adventure. And this—thought Mrs. Taggart, smiling—was the girl she had believed to be devoid of sexual capacity. She felt an immense relief, and a touch of amusement at the thought that a discovery of this kind should make her feel relieved.

The relief lasted only for a few hours. At the end of the evening, she saw Dagny in a corner of the ballroom, sitting on a balustrade as if it were a fence rail, her legs dangling under the chiffon skirt as if she were dressed in slacks. She was talking to a couple of helpless young men, her face contemptuously empty.

Neither Dagny nor Mrs. Taggart said a word when they rode home together. But hours later, on a sudden impulse, Mrs. Taggart went to her daughter's room. Dagny stood by the window, still wearing the white evening gown; it looked like a cloud supporting a body that now seemed too thin for it, a small body with sagging shoulders. Beyond the window, the clouds were gray in the first light of morning.

When Dagny turned, Mrs. Taggart saw only puzzled helplessness in her face; the face was calm, but something about it made Mrs. Taggart wish she had not wished that her daughter should discover sadness.

"Mother, do they think it's exactly in reverse?" she asked.

"What?" asked Mrs. Taggart, bewildered.

"The things you were talking about. The lights and the flowers. Do they expect those things to make them romantic, not the other way around?"

"Darling, what do you mean?"

"There wasn't a person there who enjoyed it," she said, her voice lifeless, "or who thought or felt anything at all. They moved about, and they said the same dull things they say anywhere. I suppose they thought the lights would make it brilliant."

"Darling, you take everything too seriously. One is not supposed to be intellectual at a ball. One is simply supposed to be gay."

"How? By being stupid?"

"I mean, for instance, didn't you enjoy meeting the young men?"

"What men? There wasn't a man there I couldn't squash ten of."

Days later, sitting at her desk at Rockdale Station, feeling light-heartedly at home, Dagny thought of the party and shrugged in contemptuous reproach at her own disappointment. She looked up: it was spring and there were leaves on the tree branches in the darkness outside; the air was still and warm. She asked herself what she had expected from that party. She did not know. But she felt it again, here, now, as she sat slouched over a battered desk, looking out into the darkness: a sense of expectation without object, rising through her body, slowly, like a warm liquid. She slumped forward across the desk, lazily, feeling neither exhaustion nor desire to work.

When Francisco came, that summer, she told him about the party and about her disappointment. He listened silently, looking at her for the first time with that glance of unmoving mockery which he reserved for others, a glance that seemed to see too much. She felt as if he heard, in her words, more than she knew she told him.

She saw the same glance in his eyes on the evening when she left him too early. They were alone, sitting on the shore of the river. She had another hour before she was due at Rockdale. There were long, thin strips of fire in the sky, and red sparks floating lazily on the water. He had been silent for a long time, when she rose abruptly and told him that she had to go. He did not try to stop her; he leaned back, his elbows in the grass, and looked at her without moving; his glance seemed to say that he knew her motive. Hurrying angrily up the slope to the house, she wondered what had made her leave; she did not know; it had been a sudden restlessness that came from a feeling she did not identify till now: a feeling of expectation.

Each night, she drove the five miles from the country house to Rockdale. She came back at dawn, slept a few hours and got up with the rest of the household. She felt no desire to sleep. Undressing for bed in the first rays of the sun, she felt a tense, joyous, causeless impatience to face the day that was starting.

She saw Francisco's mocking glance again, across the net of a tennis court. She did not remember the beginning of that game; they had often played tennis together and he had always won. She did not know at what moment she decided that she would win, this time. When she became aware of it, it was no longer a decision or a wish, but a quiet fury rising within her. She did not know why she had to win; she did not know why it seemed so crucially, urgently necessary; she knew only that she had to and that she would.

It seemed easy to play; it was as if her will had vanished and someone's power were playing for her. She watched Francisco's figure —a tall, swift figure, the suntan of his arms stressed by his short white shirt sleeves. She felt an arrogant pleasure in seeing the skill of his movements, because *this* was the thing which she would beat, so that his every expert gesture became her victory, and the brilliant competence of his body became the triumph of hers.

She felt the rising pain of exhaustion—not knowing that it was pain, feeling it only in sudden stabs that made her aware of some part of her body for an instant, to be forgotten in the next: her arm socket— her shoulder blades—her hips, with the white shorts sticking to her skin —the muscles of her legs, when she leaped to meet the ball, but did not remember whether she came down to touch the ground again—her eyelids, when the sky went dark red and the ball came at her through the darkness like a whirling white flame—the thin, hot wire that shot from her ankle, up her back, and went on shooting straight across the air, driving the ball at Francisco's figure. . . . She felt an exultant pleasure—because every stab of pain begun in her body had to end in his, because he was being exhausted as she was—what she did to herself, she was doing it also to him—this was what he felt—this was what she drove him to—it was not her pain that she felt or her body, but his.

In the moments when she saw his face, she saw that he was laughing. He was looking at her as if he understood. He was playing, not to win, but to make it harder for her—sending his shots wild to make her run —losing points to see her twist her body in an agonizing backhand— standing still, letting her think he would miss, only to let his arm shoot out casually at the last moment and send the ball back with such force that she knew she would miss it. She felt as if she could not move again, not ever—and it was strange to find herself landing suddenly at the other side of the court, smashing the ball in time, smashing it as if she wished it to burst to pieces, as if she wished it were Francisco's face.

Just once more, she thought, even if the next one would crack the bones of her arm . . . Just once more, even if the air which she forced down in gasps past her tight, swollen throat, would be stopped altogether . . . Then she felt nothing, no pain, no muscles, only the thought that she had to beat him, to see him exhausted, to see him collapse, and then she would be free to die in the next moment.

She won. Perhaps it was his laughing that made him lose, for once. He walked to the net, while she stood still, and threw his racket across, at her feet, as if knowing that this was what she wanted. He walked out of the court and fell down on the grass of the lawn, collapsing, his head on his arm.

She approached him slowly. She stood over him, looking down at his body stretched at her feet, looking at his sweat-drenched shirt and the strands of his hair spilled across his arm. He raised his head. His glance moved slowly up the line of her legs, to her shorts, to her blouse, to her eyes. It was a mocking glance that seemed to see straight through her clothes and through her mind. And it seemed to say that he had won.

She sat at her desk at Rockdale, that night, alone in the old station building, looking at the sky in the window. It was the hour she liked best, when the top panes of the window grew lighter, and the rails of the track outside became threads of blurred silver across the lower panes. She turned off her lamp and watched the vast, soundless motion of light over a motionless earth. Things stood still, not a leaf trembled on the branches, while the sky slowly lost its color and became an expanse that looked like a spread of glowing water.

Her telephone was silent at this hour, almost as if movement had stopped everywhere along the system. She heard steps approaching outside, suddenly, close to the door. Francisco came in. He had never come here before, but she was not astonished to see him.

"What are you doing up at this hour?" she asked.

"I didn't feel like sleeping."

"How did you get here? I didn't hear your car."

"I walked."

Moments passed before she realized that she had not asked him why he came and that she did not want to ask it.

He wandered through the room, looking at the clusters of waybills that hung on the walls, at the calendar with a picture of the Taggart Comet caught in a proud surge of motion toward the onlooker. He seemed casually at home, as if he felt that the place belonged to them, as they always felt wherever they went together. But he did not seem to want to talk. He asked a few questions about her job, then kept silent.

As the light grew outside, movement grew down on the line and the telephone started ringing in the silence. She turned to her work. He sat in a corner, one leg thrown over the arm of his chair, waiting.

She worked swiftly, feeling inordinately clear-headed. She found pleasure in the rapid precision of her hands. She concentrated on the sharp, bright sound of the phone, on the figures of train numbers, car numbers, order numbers. She was conscious of nothing else.

But when a thin sheet of paper fluttered down to the floor and she bent to pick it up, she was suddenly as intently conscious of that particular moment, of herself and her own movement. She noticed her gray linen skirt, the rolled sleeve of her gray blouse and her naked arm reaching down for the paper. She felt her heart stop causelessly in the kind of gasp one feels in moments of anticipation. She picked up the paper and turned back to her desk.

It was almost full daylight. A train went past the station, without stopping. In the purity of the morning light, the long line of car roofs melted into a silver string, and the train seemed suspended above the ground, not quite touching it, going past through the air. The floor of the station trembled, and glass rattled in the windows. She watched the train's flight with a smile of excitement. She glanced at Francisco: he was looking at her, with the same smile.

When the day operator arrived, she turned the station over to him, and they walked out into the morning air. The sun had not yet risen and the air seemed radiant in its stead. She felt no exhaustion. She felt as if she were just getting up.

She started toward her car, but Francisco said, "Let's walk home. We'll come for the car later."

"All right."

She was not astonished and she did not mind the prospect of walking five miles. It seemed natural; natural to the moment's peculiar reality that was sharply clear, but cut off from everything, immediate, but disconnected, like a bright island in a wall of fog, the heightened, unquestioning reality one feels when one is drunk.

The road led through the woods. They left the highway for an old trail that went twisting among the trees across miles of untouched country. There were no traces of human existence around them. Old ruts, overgrown with grass, made human presence seem more distant, adding the distance of years to the distance of miles. A haze of twilight remained over the ground, but in the breaks between the tree trunks there were leaves that hung in patches of shining green and seemed to light the forest. The leaves hung still. They walked, alone to move through a motionless world. She noticed suddenly that they had not said a word for a long time.

They came to a clearing. It was a small hollow at the bottom of a shaft made of straight rock hillsides. A stream cut across the grass, and tree branches flowed low to the ground, like a curtain of green fluid. The sound of the water stressed the silence. The distant cut of open sky made the place seem more hidden. Far above, on the crest of a hill, one tree caught the first rays of sunlight.

They stopped and looked at each other. She knew, only when he did it, that she had known he would. He seized her, she felt her lips in his mouth, felt her arms grasping him in violent answer, and knew for the first time how much she had wanted him to do it.

She felt a moment's rebellion and a hint of fear. He held her, pressing the length of his body against hers with a tense, purposeful insistence, his hand moving over her breasts as if he were learning a proprietor's intimacy with her body, a shocking intimacy that needed no consent from her, no permission. She tried to pull herself away, but she only leaned back against his arms long enough to see his face and his smile, the smile that told her she had given him permission long ago. She thought that she must escape; instead, it was she who pulled his head down to find his mouth again.

She knew that fear was useless, that he would do what he wished, that the decision was his, that he left nothing possible to her except the thing she wanted most—to submit. She had no conscious realization of his purpose, her vague knowledge of it was wiped out, she had no power to believe it clearly, in this moment, to believe it about herself, she knew only that she was afraid—yet what she felt was as if she were crying to him: Don't ask me for it—oh, don't ask me—do it!

She braced her feet for an instant, to resist, but his mouth was pressed to hers and they went down to the ground together, never breaking their lips apart. She lay still—as the motionless, then the quivering object of an act which he did simply, unhesitatingly, as of right, the right of the unendurable pleasure it gave them.

He named what it meant to both of them in the first words he spoke afterwards. He said, "We had to learn it from each other." She looked at his long figure stretched on the grass beside her, he wore black slacks and a black shirt, her eyes stopped on the belt pulled tight across his slender waistline, and she felt the stab of an emotion that was like a gasp of pride, pride in her ownership of his body. She lay on her back, looking up at the sky, feeling no desire to move or think or know that there was any time beyond this moment.

When she came home, when she lay in bed, naked because her body had become an unfamiliar possession, too precious for the touch of a nightgown, because it gave her pleasure to feel naked and to feel as if the white sheets of her bed were touched by Francisco's body—when she thought that she would not sleep, because she did not want to rest and lose the most wonderful exhaustion she had ever known—her last thought was of the times when she had wanted to express, but found no way to do it, an instant's knowledge of a feeling greater than happiness, the feeling of one's blessing upon the whole of the earth, the feeling of being in love with the fact that one exists and in this kind of world; she thought that the act she had learned was the way one expressed it. If this was a thought of the gravest importance, she did not know it; nothing could be grave in a universe from which the concept of pain had been wiped out; she was not there to weigh her conclusion; she was asleep, a faint smile on her face, in a silent, luminous room filled with the light of morning.

That summer, she met him in the woods, in hidden corners by the river, on the floor of an abandoned shack, in the cellar of the house. These were the only times when she learned to feel a sense of beauty— by looking up at old wooden rafters or at the steel plate of an air-conditioning machine that whirred tensely, rhythmically above their heads. She wore slacks or cotton summer dresses, yet she was never so feminine as when she stood beside him, sagging in his arms, abandoning herself to anything he wished, in open acknowledgment of his power to reduce her to helplessness by the pleasure he had the power to give her. He taught her every manner of sensuality he could invent. "Isn't it wonderful that our bodies can give us so much pleasure?" he said to her once, quite simply. They were happy and radiantly innocent. They were both incapable of the conception that joy is sin.

They kept their secret from the knowledge of others, not as a shameful guilt, but as a thing that was immaculately theirs, beyond anyone's right of debate or appraisal. She knew the general doctrine on sex, held by people in one form or another, the doctrine that sex was an ugly weakness of man's lower nature, to be condoned regretfully. She experienced an emotion of chastity that made her shrink, not from the desires of her body, but from any contact with the minds who held this doctrine.

That winter, Francisco came to see her in New York, at unpredictable intervals. He would fly down from Cleveland, without warning, twice a week, or he would vanish for months. She would sit on the floor of her room, surrounded by charts and blueprints, she would hear a knock at her door and snap, "I'm busy!" then hear a mocking voice ask, "Are you?" and leap to her feet to throw the door open, to find him standing there. They would go to an apartment he had rented in the city, a small apartment in a quiet neighborhood. "Francisco," she asked him once, in sudden astonishment, "I'm your mistress, am I not?" He laughed. "That's what you are." She felt the pride a woman is supposed to experience at being granted the title of wife.

In the many months of his absence, she never wondered whether he was true to her or not; she knew he was. She knew, even though she was too young to know the reason, that indiscriminate desire and unselective indulgence were possible only to those who regarded sex and themselves as evil.

She knew little about Francisco's life. It was his last year in college; he seldom spoke of it, and she never questioned him. She suspected that he was working too hard, because she saw, at times, the unnaturally bright look of his face, the look of exhilaration that comes from driving one's energy beyond its limit. She laughed at him once, boasting that she was an old employee of Taggart Transcontinental, while he had not started to work for a living. He said, "My father refuses to let me work for d'Anconia Copper until I graduate." "When did you learn to be obedient?" "I must respect his wishes. He is the owner of d'Anconia Copper. . . . He is not, however, the owner of all the copper companies in the world." There was a hint of secret amusement in his smile.

She did not learn the story until the next fall, when he had graduated and returned to New York after a visit to his father in Buenos Aires. Then he told her that he had taken two courses of education during the last four years: one at the Patrick Henry University, the other in a copper foundry on the outskirts of Cleveland. "I like to learn things for myself," he said. He had started working at the foundry as furnace boy, when he was sixteen—and now, at twenty, he owned it. He acquired his first title of property, with the aid of some inaccuracy about his age, on the day when he received his university diploma, and he sent them both to his father.

He showed her a photograph of the foundry. It was a small, grimy place, disreputable with age, battered by years of a losing struggle; above its entrance gate, like a new flag on the mast of a derelict, hung the sign: d'Anconia Copper.

The public relations man of his father's office in New York had moaned, outraged, "But, Don Francisco, you can't do that! What will the public think? *That* name on a dump of this kind?" "It's my name," Francisco had answered.

When he entered his father's office in Buenos Aires, a large room, severe and modern as a laboratory, with photographs of the properties of d'Anconia Copper as sole ornament on its walls—photographs of the greatest mines, ore docks and foundries in the world—he saw, in the place of honor, facing his father's desk, a photograph of the Cleveland foundry with the new sign above its gate.

His father's eyes moved from the photograph to Francisco's face as he stood in front of the desk.

"Isn't it a little too soon?" his father asked.

"I couldn't have stood four years of nothing but lectures."

"Where did you get the money for your first payment on that property?"

"By playing the New York stock market."

"*What?* Who taught you to do that?"

"It is not difficult to judge which industrial ventures will succeed and which won't."

"Where did you get the money to play with?"

"From the allowance you sent me, sir, and from my wages."

"When did you have time to watch the stock market?"

"While I was writing a thesis on the influence—upon subsequent metaphysical systems—of Aristotle's theory of the Immovable Mover."

Francisco's stay in New York was brief, that fall. His father was sending him to Montana as assistant superintendent of a d'Anconia mine. "Oh well," he said to Dagny, smiling, "my father does not think it advisable to let me rise too fast. I would not ask him to take me on faith. If he wants a factual demonstration, I shall comply." In the spring, Francisco came back—as head of the New York office of d'Anconia Copper.

She did not see him often in the next two years. She never knew where he was, in what city or on what continent, the day after she had seen him. He always came to her unexpectedly—and she liked it, because it made him a continuous presence in her life, like the ray of a hidden light that could hit her at any moment.

Whenever she saw him in his office, she thought of his hands as she had seen them on the wheel of a motorboat: he drove his business with the same smooth, dangerous, confidently mastered speed. But one small incident remained in her mind as a shock: it did not fit him. She saw him standing at the window of his office, one evening, looking at the brown winter twilight of the city. He did not move for a long time. His face was hard and tight; it had the look of an emotion she had never believed possible to him: of bitter, helpless anger. He said, "There's something wrong in the world. There's always been. Something no one has ever named or explained." He would not tell her what it was.

When she saw him again, no trace of that incident remained in his manner. It was spring and they stood together on the roof terrace of a restaurant, the light silk of her evening gown blowing in the wind against his tall figure in formal black clothes. They looked at the city. In the dining room behind them, the sounds of the music were a concert étude by Richard Halley; Halley's name was not known to many, but they had discovered it and they loved his music. Francisco said, "We don't have to look for skyscrapers in the distance, do we? We've reached them." She smiled and said, "I think we're going past them. . . . I'm almost afraid . . . we're on a speeding elevator of some kind." "Sure. Afraid of what? Let it speed. Why should there be a limit?"

He was twenty-three when his father died and he went to Buenos Aires to take over the d'Anconia estate, now his. She did not see him for three years.

He wrote to her, at first, at random intervals. He wrote about d'Anconia Copper, about the world market, about issues affecting the interests of Taggart Transcontinental. His letters were brief, written by hand, usually at night.

She was not unhappy in his absence. She, too, was making her first steps toward the control of a future kingdom. Among the leaders of industry, her father's friends, she heard it said that one had better watch the young d'Anconia heir; if that copper company had been great before, it would sweep the world now, under what his management promised to become. She smiled, without astonishment. There were moments when she felt a sudden, violent longing for him, but it was only impatience, not pain. She dismissed it, in the confident knowledge that they were both working toward a future that would bring them everything they wanted, including each other. Then his letters stopped.

She was twenty-four on that day of spring when the telephone rang on her desk, in an office of the Taggart Building. "Dagny," said a voice she recognized at once, "I'm at the Wayne-Falkland. Come to have dinner with me tonight. At seven." He said it without greeting, as if they had parted the day before. Because it took her a moment to regain the art of breathing, she realized for the first time how much that voice meant to her. "All right . . . Francisco," she answered. They needed to say nothing else. She thought, replacing the receiver, that his return was natural and as she had always expected it to happen, except that she had not expected her sudden need to pronounce his name or the stab of happiness she felt while pronouncing it.

When she entered his hotel room, that evening, she stopped short. He stood in the middle of the room, looking at her—and she saw a smile that came slowly, involuntarily, as if he had lost the ability to smile and were astonished that he should regain it. He looked at her incredulously, not quite believing what she was or what he felt. His glance was like a plea, like the cry for help of a man who could never cry. At her entrance, he had started their old salute, he had started to say, "Hi—" but he did not finish it. Instead, after a moment, he said, "You're beautiful, Dagny." He said it as if it hurt him.

"Francisco, I—"

He shook his head, not to let her pronounce the words they had never said to each other—even though they knew that both had said and heard them in that moment.

He approached, he took her in his arms, he kissed her mouth and held her for a long time. When she looked up at his face, he was smiling down at her confidently, derisively. It was a smile that told her he was in control of himself, of her, of everything, and ordered her to forget what she had seen in that first moment. "Hi, Slug," he said.

Feeling certain of nothing except that she must not ask questions, she smiled and said, "Hi, Frisco."

She could have understood any change, but not the things she saw. There was no sparkle of life in his face, no hint of amusement; the face had become implacable. The plea of his first smile had not been a plea of weakness; he had acquired an air of determination that seemed merciless. He acted like a man who stood straight, under the weight of an unendurable burden. She saw what she could not have believed possible: that there were lines of bitterness in his face and that he looked tortured.

"Dagny, don't be astonished by anything I do," he said, "or by anything I may ever do in the future."

That was the only explanation he granted her, then proceeded to act as if there were nothing to explain.

She could feel no more than a faint anxiety; it was impossible to feel fear for his fate or in his presence. When he laughed, she thought they were back in the woods by the Hudson: he had not changed and never would.

The dinner was served in his room. She found it amusing to face him across a table laid out with the icy formality pertaining to excessive cost, in a hotel room designed as a European palace.

The Wayne-Falkland was the most distinguished hotel left on any continent. Its style of indolent luxury, of velvet drapes, sculptured panels and candlelight, seemed a deliberate contrast to its function: no one could afford its hospitality except men who came to New York on business, to settle transactions involving the world. She noticed that the manner of the waiters who served their dinner suggested a special deference to this particular guest of the hotel, and that Francisco did not notice it. He was indifferently at home. He had long since become accustomed to the fact that he was Señor d'Anconia of d'Anconia Copper.

But she thought it strange that he did not speak about his work. She had expected it to be his only interest, the first thing he would share with her. He did not mention it. He led her to talk, instead, about her job, her progress, and what she felt for Taggart Transcontinental. She spoke of it as she had always spoken to him, in the knowledge that he was the only one who could understand her passionate devotion. He made no comment, but he listened intently.

A waiter had turned on the radio for dinner music; they had paid no attention to it. But suddenly, a crash of sound jarred the room, almost as if a subterranean blast had struck the walls and made them tremble. The shock came, not from the loudness, but from the quality of the sounds. It was Halley's new Concerto, recently written, the Fourth.

They sat in silence, listening to the statement of rebellion—the anthem of the triumph of the great victims who would refuse to accept pain. Francisco listened, looking out at the city.

Without transition or warning, he asked, his voice oddly unstressed, "Dagny, what would you say if I asked you to leave Taggart Transcontinental and let it go to hell, as it will when your brother takes over?"

"What would I say if you asked me to consider the idea of committing suicide?" she answered angrily.

He remained silent.

"Why did you say that?" she snapped. "I didn't think you'd joke about it. It's not like you."

There was no touch of humor in his face. He answered quietly, gravely, "No. Of course. I shouldn't."

She brought herself to question him about his work. He answered the questions; he volunteered nothing. She repeated to him the comments of the industrialists about the brilliant prospects of d'Anconia Copper under his management. "That's true," he said, his voice lifeless.

In sudden anxiety, not knowing what prompted her, she asked, "Francisco, why did you come to New York?"

He answered slowly, "To see a friend who called for me."

"Business?"

Looking past her, as if answering a thought of his own, a faint smile of bitter amusement on his face, but his voice strangely soft and sad, he answered:

"Yes."

It was long past midnight when she awakened in bed by his side.

No sounds came from the city below. The stillness of the room made life seem suspended for a while. Relaxed in happiness and in complete exhaustion, she turned lazily to glance at him. He lay on his back, half-propped by a pillow. She saw his profile against the foggy glow of the night sky in the window. He was awake, his eyes were open. He held his mouth closed like a man lying in resignation in unbearable pain, bearing it, making no attempt to hide it.

She was too frightened to move. He felt her glance and turned to her. He shuddered suddenly, he threw off the blanket, he looked at her naked body, then he fell forward and buried his face between her breasts. He held her shoulders, hanging onto her convulsively. She heard the words, muffled, his mouth pressed to her skin:

"I can't give it up! I can't!"

"What?" she whispered.

"You."

"Why should—"

"And everything."

"Why should you give it up?"

"Dagny! Help me to remain. To refuse. Even though he's right!"

She asked evenly, "To refuse what, Francisco?"

He did not answer, only pressed his face harder against her.

She lay very still, conscious of nothing but a supreme need of caution. His head on her breast, her hand caressing his hair gently, steadily, she lay looking up at the ceiling of the room, at the sculptured garlands faintly visible in the darkness, and she waited, numb with terror.

He moaned, "It's right, but it's so hard to do! Oh God, it's so hard!"

After a while, he raised his head. He sat up. He had stopped trembling.

"What is it, Francisco?"

"I can't tell you." His voice was simple, open, without attempt to disguise suffering, but it was a voice that obeyed him now. "You're not ready to hear it."

"I want to help you."

"You can't."

"You said, to help you refuse."

"I can't refuse."

"Then let me share it with you."

He shook his head.

He sat looking down at her, as if weighing a question. Then he shook his head again, in answer to himself.

"If I'm not sure I can stand it," he said, and the strange new note in his voice was tenderness, "how could you?"

She said slowly, with effort, trying to keep herself from screaming, "Francisco, I have to know."

"Will you forgive me? I know you're frightened, and it's cruel. But will you do this for me—will you let it go, just let it go, and don't ask me anything?"

"I—"

"That's all you can do for me. Will you?"

"Yes, Francisco."

"Don't be afraid for me. It was just this once. It won't happen to me again. It will become much easier . . . later."

"If I could—"

"No. Go to sleep, dearest."

It was the first time he had ever used that word.

In the morning, he faced her openly, not avoiding her anxious glance, but saying nothing about it. She saw both serenity and suffering in the calm of his face, an expression like a smile of pain, though he was not smiling. Strangely, it made him look younger. He did not look like a man bearing torture now, but like a man who sees that which makes the torture worth bearing.

She did not question him. Before leaving, she asked only, "When will I see you again?"

He answered, "I don't know. Don't wait for me, Dagny. Next time we meet, you will not want to see me. I will have a reason for the things I'll do. But I can't tell you the reason and you will be right to damn me. I am not committing the contemptible act of asking you to take me on faith. You have to live by your own knowledge and judgment. You will damn me. You will be hurt. Try not to let it hurt you too much. Remember that I told you this and that it was all I could tell you."

She heard nothing from him or about him for a year. When she began to hear gossip and to read newspaper stories, she did not believe, at first, that they referred to Francisco d'Anconia. After a while, she had to believe it.

She read the story of the party he gave on his yacht, in the harbor of Valparaiso; the guests wore bathing suits, and an artificial rain of champagne and flower petals kept falling upon the decks throughout the night.

She read the story of the party he gave at an Algerian desert resort; he built a pavilion of thin sheets of ice and presented every woman guest with an ermine wrap, as a gift to be worn for the occasion, on condition that they remove their wraps, then their evening gowns, then all the rest, in tempo with the melting of the walls.

She read the accounts of the business ventures he undertook at lengthy intervals; the ventures were spectacularly successful and ruined his competitors, but he indulged in them as in an occasional sport, staging a sudden raid, then vanishing from the industrial scene for a year or two, leaving d'Anconia Copper to the management of his employees.

She read the interview where he said, "Why should I wish to make money? I have enough to permit three generations of descendants to have as good a time as I'm having."

She saw him once, at a reception given by an ambassador in New York. He bowed to her courteously, he smiled, and he looked at her with a glance in which no past existed. She drew him aside. She said only, "Francisco, why?" "Why—what?" he asked. She turned away. "I warned you," he said. She did not try to see him again.

She survived it. She was able to survive it, because she did not believe in suffering. She faced with astonished indignation the ugly fact of feeling pain, and refused to let it matter. Suffering was a senseless accident, it was not part of life as she saw it. She would not allow pain to become important. She had no name for the kind of resistance she offered, for the emotion from which the resistance came; but the words that stood as its equivalent in her mind were: It does not count —it is not to be taken seriously. She knew these were the words, even in the moments when there was nothing left within her but screaming and she wished she could lose the faculty of consciousness so that it would not tell her that what could not be true was true. Not to be taken seriously—an immovable certainty within her kept repeating— pain and ugliness are never to be taken seriously.

She fought it. She recovered. Years helped her to reach the day when she could face her memories indifferently, then the day when she felt no necessity to face them. It was finished and of no concern to her any longer.

There had been no other men in her life. She did not know whether this had made her unhappy. She had had no time to know. She found the clean, brilliant sense of life as she wanted it—in her work. Once, Francisco had given her the same sense, a feeling that belonged with her work and in her world. The men she had met since were like the men she met at her first ball.

She had won the battle against her memories. But one form of torture remained, untouched by the years, the torture of the word "why?"

Whatever the tragedy he met, why had Francisco taken the ugliest way of escape, as ignoble as the way of some cheap alcoholic? The boy she had known could not have become a useless coward. An incomparable mind could not turn its ingenuity to the invention of melting ballrooms. Yet he had and did, and there was no explanation to make it conceivable and to let her forget him in peace. She could not doubt the fact of what he had been; she could not doubt the fact of what he had become; yet one made the other impossible. At times, she almost doubted her own rationality or the existence of any rationality anywhere; but this was a doubt which she did not permit to anyone. Yet there was no explanation, no reason, no clue to any conceivable reason —and in all the days of ten years she had found no hint of an answer.

No, she thought—as she walked through the gray twilight, past the windows of abandoned shops, to the Wayne-Falkland Hotel—no, there could be no answer. She would not seek it. It did not matter now.

The remnant of violence, the emotion rising as a thin trembling within her, was not for the man she was going to see; it was a cry of protest against a sacrilege—against the destruction of what had been greatness.

In a break between buildings, she saw the towers of the Wayne-Falkland. She felt a slight jolt, in her lungs and legs, that stopped her for an instant. Then she walked on evenly.

By the time she walked through the marble lobby, to the elevator, then down the wide, velvet-carpeted, soundless corridors of the Wayne-Falkland, she felt nothing but a cold anger that grew colder with every step.

She was certain of the anger when she knocked at his door. She heard his voice, answering, "Come in." She jerked the door open and entered.

Francisco Domingo Carlos Andres Sebastián d'Anconia sat on the floor, playing marbles.

Nobody ever wondered whether Francisco d'Anconia was good-looking or not; it seemed irrelevant; when he entered a room, it was impossible to look at anyone else. His tall, slender figure had an air of distinction, too authentic to be modern, and he moved as if he had a cape floating behind him in the wind. People explained him by saying that he had the vitality of a healthy animal, but they knew dimly that that was not correct. He had the vitality of a healthy human being, a thing so rare that no one could identify it. He had the power of certainty.

Nobody described his appearance as Latin, yet the word applied to him, not in its present, but in its original sense, not pertaining to Spain, but to ancient Rome. His body seemed designed as an exercise in consistency of style, a style made of gauntness, of tight flesh, long legs and swift movements. His features had the fine precision of sculpture. His hair was black and straight, swept back. The suntan of his skin intensified the startling color of his eyes: they were a pure, clear blue. His face was open, its rapid changes of expression reflecting whatever he felt, as if he had nothing to hide. The blue eyes were still and changeless, never giving a hint of what he thought.

He sat on the floor of his drawing room, dressed in sleeping pajamas of thin black silk. The marbles spread on the carpet around him were made of the semi-precious stones of his native country: carnelian and rock crystal. He did not rise when Dagny entered. He sat looking up at her, and a crystal marble fell like a teardrop out of his hand. He smiled, the unchanged, insolent, brilliant smile of his childhood.

"Hi, Slug!"

She heard herself answering, irresistibly, helplessly, happily:

"Hi, Frisco!"

She was looking at his face; it was the face she had known. It bore no mark of the kind of life he had led, nor of what she had seen on their last night together. There was no sign of tragedy, no bitterness, no tension—only the radiant mockery, matured and stressed, the look of dangerously unpredictable amusement, and the great, guiltless serenity of spirit. But this, she thought, was impossible; this was more shocking than all the rest.

His eyes were studying her: the battered coat thrown open, half-slipping off her shoulders, and the slender body in a gray suit that looked like an office uniform.

"If you came here dressed like this in order not to let me notice how lovely you are," he said, "you miscalculated. You're lovely. I wish I could tell you what a relief it is to see a face that's intelligent though a woman's. But you don't want to hear it. That's not what you came here for."

The words were improper in so many ways, yet were said so lightly that they brought her back to reality, to anger and to the purpose of her visit. She remained standing, looking down at him, her face blank, refusing him any recognition of the personal, even of its power to offend her. She said, "I came here to ask you a question."

"Go ahead."

"When you told those reporters that you came to New York to witness the farce, which farce did you mean?"

He laughed aloud, like a man who seldom finds a chance to enjoy the unexpected.

"That's what I like about you, Dagny. There are seven million people in the city of New York, at present. Out of seven million people, you are the only one to whom it could have occurred that I wasn't talking about the Vail divorce scandal."

"What were you talking about?"

"What alternative occurred to you?"

"The San Sebastián disaster."

"That's much more amusing than the Vail divorce scandal, isn't it?"

She said in the solemn, merciless tone of a prosecutor, "You did it consciously, cold-bloodedly and with full intention."

"Don't you think it would be better if you took your coat off and sat down?"

She knew she had made a mistake by betraying too much intensity. She turned coldly, removed her coat and threw it aside. He did not rise to help her. She sat down in an armchair. He remained on the floor, at some distance, but it seemed as if he were sitting at her feet.

"What was it I did with full intention?" he asked.

"The entire San Sebastián swindle."

"What was my *full* intention?"

"That is what I want to know."

He chuckled, as if she had asked him to explain in conversation a complex science requiring a lifetime of study.

"You knew that the San Sebastián mines were worthless," she said. "You knew it before you began the whole wretched business."

"Then why did I begin it?"

"Don't start telling me that you gained nothing. I know it. I know you lost fifteen million dollars of your own money. Yet it was done on purpose."

"Can you think of a motive that would prompt me to do it?"

"No. It's inconceivable."

"Is it? You assume that I have a great mind, a great knowledge and a great productive ability, so that anything I undertake must necessarily be successful. And then you claim that I had no desire to put out my best effort for the People's State of Mexico. Inconceivable, isn't it?"

"You knew, before you bought that property, that Mexico was in the hands of a looters' government. You didn't have to start a mining project for them."

"No, I didn't have to."

"You didn't give a damn about that Mexican government, one way or another, because—"

"You're wrong about that."

"—because you knew they'd seize those mines sooner or later. What you were after is your American stockholders."

"That's true." He was looking straight at her, he was not smiling, his face was earnest. He added, "That's part of the truth."

"What's the rest?"

"It was not all I was after."

"What else?"

"That's for you to figure out."

"I came here because I wanted you to know that I am beginning to understand your purpose."

He smiled. "If you did, you wouldn't have come here."

"That's true. I *don't* understand and probably never shall. I am merely beginning to see part of it."

"Which part?"

"You had exhausted every other form of depravity and sought a new thrill by swindling people like Jim and his friends, in order to watch them squirm. I don't know what sort of corruption could make anyone enjoy that, but that's what you came to New York to see, at the right time."

"They certainly provided a spectacle of squirming on the grand scale. Your brother James in particular."

"They're rotten fools, but in this case their only crime was that they trusted you. They trusted your name and your honor."

Again, she saw the look of earnestness and again knew with certainty that it was genuine, when he said, "Yes. They did. I know it."

"And do you find it amusing?"

"No. I don't find it amusing at all."

He had continued playing with his marbles, absently, indifferently, taking a shot once in a while. She noticed suddenly the faultless accuracy of his aim, the skill of his hands. He merely flicked his wrist and sent a drop of stone shooting across the carpet to click sharply against another drop. She thought of his childhood and of the predictions that anything he did would be done superlatively.

"No," he said, "I don't find it amusing. Your brother James and his friends knew nothing about the copper-mining industry. They knew nothing about making money. They did not think it necessary to learn. They considered knowledge superfluous and judgment inessential. They observed that there I was in the world and that I made it my honor to know. They thought they could trust my honor. One does not betray a trust of this kind, does one?"

"Then you did betray it intentionally?"

"That's for you to decide. It was you who spoke about their trust and my honor. I don't think in such terms any longer. . . ." He shrugged, adding, "I don't give a damn about your brother James and his friends. Their theory was not new, it has worked for centuries. But it wasn't foolproof. There is just one point that they overlooked. They thought it was safe to ride on my brain, because they assumed that the goal of my journey was wealth. All their calculations rested on the premise that I wanted to make money. What if I didn't?"

"If you didn't, what did you want?"

"They never asked me that. Not to inquire about my aims, motives or desires is an essential part of their theory."

"If you didn't want to make money, what possible motive could you have had?"

"Any number of them. For instance, to spend it."

"To spend money on a certain, total failure?"

"How was I to know that those mines were a certain, total failure?"

"How could you help knowing it?"

"Quite simply. By giving it no thought."

"You started that project without giving it any thought?"

"No, not exactly. But suppose I slipped up? I'm only human. I made a mistake. I failed. I made a bad job of it." He flicked his wrist; a crystal marble shot, sparkling, across the floor and cracked violently against a brown one at the other end of the room.

"I don't believe it," she said.

"No? But haven't I the right to be what is now accepted as human? Should I pay for everybody's mistakes and never be permitted one of my own?"

"That's not like you."

"No?" He stretched himself full-length on the carpet, lazily, relaxing. "Did you intend me to notice that if you think I did it on purpose, then you still give me credit for having a purpose? You're still unable to accept me as a bum?"

She closed her eyes. She heard him laughing; it was the gayest sound in the world. She opened her eyes hastily; but there was no hint of cruelty in his face, only pure laughter.

"My motive, Dagny? You don't think that it's the simplest one of all—the spur of the moment?"

No, she thought, no, that's not true; not if he laughed like that, not if he looked as he did. The capacity for unclouded enjoyment, she thought, does not belong to irresponsible fools; an inviolate peace of spirit is not the achievement of a drifter; to be able to laugh like that is the end result of the most profound, most solemn thinking.

Almost dispassionately, looking at his figure stretched on the carpet at her feet, she observed what memory it brought back to her: the black pajamas stressed the long lines of his body, the open collar showed a smooth, young, sunburned skin—and she thought of the figure in black slacks and shirt stretched beside her on the grass at sunrise. She had felt pride then, the pride of knowing that she owned his body; she still felt it. She remembered suddenly, specifically, the excessive acts of their intimacy; the memory should have been offensive to her now, but wasn't. It was still pride, without regret or hope, an emotion that had no power to reach her and that she had no power to destroy.

Unaccountably, by an association of feeling that astonished her, she remembered what had conveyed to her recently the same sense of consummate joy as his.

"Francisco," she heard herself saying softly, "we both loved the music of Richard Halley. . . ."

"I still love it."

"Have you ever met him?"

"Yes. Why?"

"Do you happen to know whether he has written a Fifth Concerto?"

He remained perfectly still. She had thought him impervious to shock; he wasn't. But she could not attempt to guess why of all the things she had said, this should be the first to reach him. It was only an instant; then he asked evenly, "What makes you think he has?"

"Well, has he?"

"You know that there are only four Halley Concertos."

"Yes. But I wondered whether he had written another one."

"He has stopped writing."

"I know."

"Then what made you ask that?"

"Just an idle thought. What is he doing now? Where is he?"

"I don't know. I haven't seen him for a long time. What made you think that there was a Fifth Concerto?"

"I didn't say there was. I merely wondered about it."

"Why did you think of Richard Halley just now?"

"Because"—she felt her control cracking a little—"because my mind can't make the leap from Richard Halley's music to . . . to Mrs. Gilbert Vail."

He laughed, relieved. "Oh, that? . . . Incidentally, if you've been following my publicity, have you noticed a funny little discrepancy in the story of Mrs. Gilbert Vail?"

"I don't read the stuff."

"You should. She gave such a beautiful description of last New Year's Eve, which we spent together in my villa in the Andes. The moonlight on the mountain peaks, and the blood-red flowers hanging on vines in the open windows. See anything wrong in the picture?"

She said quietly, "It's I who should ask you that, and I'm not going to."

"Oh, I see nothing wrong—except that last New Year's Eve I was in El Paso, Texas, presiding at the opening of the San Sebastián Line of Taggart Transcontinental, as you should remember, even if you didn't choose to be present on the occasion. I had my picture taken with my arms around your brother James and the Señor Orren Boyle."

She gasped, remembering that this was true, remembering also that she had seen Mrs. Vail's story in the newspapers.

"Francisco, what . . . what does that mean?"

He chuckled. "Draw your own conclusions. . . . Dagny"—his face was serious—"why did you think of Halley writing a Fifth Concerto? Why not a new symphony or opera? Why specifically a concerto?"

"Why does that disturb you?"

"It doesn't." He added softly, "I still love his music, Dagny." Then he spoke lightly again. "But it belonged to another age. Our age provides a different kind of entertainment."

He rolled over on his back and lay with his hands crossed under his head, looking up as if he were watching the scenes of a movie farce unrolling on the ceiling.

"Dagny, didn't you enjoy the spectacle of the behavior of the People's State of Mexico in regard to the San Sebastián Mines? Did you read their government's speeches and the editorials in their newspapers? They're saying that I am an unscrupulous cheat who has defrauded them. They expected to have a successful mining concern to seize. I had no right to disappoint them like that. Did you read about the scabby little bureaucrat who wanted them to sue me?"

He laughed, lying flat on his back; his arms were thrown wide on the carpet, forming a cross with his body; he seemed disarmed, relaxed and young.

"It was worth whatever it's cost me. I could afford the price of that show. If I had staged it intentionally, I would have beaten the record of the Emperor Nero. What's burning a city—compared to tearing the lid off hell and letting men see it?"

He raised himself, picked up a few marbles and sat shaking them absently in his hand; they clicked with the soft, clear sound of good stone. She realized suddenly that playing with those marbles was not a deliberate affectation on his part; it was restlessness; he could not remain inactive for long.

"The government of the People's State of Mexico has issued a proclamation," he said, "asking the people to be patient and put up with hardships just a little longer. It seems that the copper fortune of the San Sebastián Mines was part of the plans of the central planning council. It was to raise everybody's standard of living and provide a roast of pork every Sunday for every man, woman, child and abortion in the People's State of Mexico. Now the planners are asking their people not to blame the government, but to blame the depravity of the rich, because I turned out to be an irresponsible playboy, instead of the greedy capitalist I was expected to be. How were they to know, they're asking, that I would let them down? Well, true enough. How were they to know it?"

She noticed the way he fingered the marbles in his hand. He was not conscious of it, he was looking off into some grim distance, but she felt certain that the action was a relief to him, perhaps as a contrast. His fingers were moving slowly, feeling the texture of the stones with sensual enjoyment. Instead of finding it crude, she found it strangely attractive— as if, she thought suddenly, as if sensuality were not physical at all, but came from a fine discrimination of the spirit.

"And that's not all they didn't know," he said. "They're in for some more knowledge. There's that housing settlement for the workers of San Sebastián. It cost eight million dollars. Steel-frame houses, with plumbing, electricity and refrigeration. Also a school, a church, a hospital and a movie theater. A settlement built for people who had lived in hovels made of driftwood and stray tin cans. My reward for building it was to be the privilege of escaping with my skin, a special concession due to the accident of my not being a native of the People's State of Mexico. That workers' settlement was also part of their plans. A model example of progressive State housing. Well, those steel-frame houses are mainly cardboard, with a coating of good imitation shellac. They won't stand another year. The plumbing pipes—as well as most of our mining equipment—were purchased from the dealers whose main source of supply are the city dumps of Buenos Aires and Rio de Janeiro. I'd give those pipes another five months, and the electric system about six. The wonderful roads we graded up four thousand feet of rock for the People's State of Mexico, will not last beyond a couple of winters: they're cheap cement without foundation, and the bracing at the bad turns is just painted clapboard. Wait for one good mountain slide. The church, I think, will stand. They'll need it."

"Francisco," she whispered, "did you do it on purpose?"

He raised his head; she was startled to see that his face had a look of infinite weariness. "Whether I did it on purpose," he said, "or through neglect, or through stupidity, don't you understand that that doesn't make any difference? The same element was missing."

She was trembling. Against all her decisions and control, she cried, "Francisco! If you see what's happening in the world, if you understand all the things you said, you can't laugh about it! You, of all men, *you* should fight them!"

"Whom?"

"The looters, and those who make world-looting possible. The Mexican planners and their kind."

His smile had a dangerous edge. "No, my dear. It's you that I have to fight."

She looked at him blankly. "What are you trying to say?"

"I am saying that the workers' settlement of San Sebastián cost eight million dollars," he answered with slow emphasis, his voice hard. "The price paid for those cardboard houses was the price that could have bought steel structures. So was the price paid for every other item. That money went to men who grow rich by such methods. Such men do not remain rich for long. The money will go into channels which will carry it, not to the most productive, but to the most corrupt. By the standards of our time, the man who has the least to offer is the man who wins. That money will vanish in projects such as the San Sebastián Mines."

She asked with effort, "Is that what you're after?"

"Yes."

"Is that what you find amusing?"

"Yes."

"I am thinking of your name," she said, while another part of her mind was crying to her that reproaches were useless. "It was a tradition of your family that a d'Anconia always left a fortune greater than the one he received."

"Oh yes, my ancestors had a remarkable ability for doing the right thing at the right time—and for making the right investments. Of course, 'investment' is a relative term. It depends on what you wish to accomplish. For instance, look at San Sebastián. It cost me fifteen million dollars, but these fifteen million wiped out forty million belonging to Taggart Transcontinental, thirty-five million belonging to stockholders such as James Taggart and Orren Boyle, and hundreds of millions which will be lost in secondary consequences. That's not a bad return on an investment, is it, Dagny?"

She was sitting straight. "Do you realize what you're saying?"

"Oh, fully! Shall I beat you to it and name the consequences you were going to reproach me for? First, I don't think that Taggart Transcontinental will recover from its loss on that preposterous San Sebastián Line. You think it will, but it won't. Second, the San Sebastián helped your brother James to destroy the Phoenix-Durango, which was about the only good railroad left anywhere."

"You realize all that?"

"And a great deal more."

"Do you"—she did not know why she had to say it, except that the memory of the face with the dark, violent eyes seemed to stare at her—"do you know Ellis Wyatt?"

"Sure."

"Do you know what this might do to him?"

"Yes. He's the one who's going to be wiped out next."

"Do you . . . find that . . . amusing?"

"Much more amusing than the ruin of the Mexican planners."

She stood up. She had called him corrupt for years; she had feared it, she had thought about it, she had tried to forget it and never think of it again; but she had never suspected how far the corruption had gone.

She was not looking at him; she did not know that she was saying it aloud, quoting his words of the past: ". . . who'll do greater honor, you—to Nat Taggart, or I—to Sebastián d'Anconia . . ."

"But didn't you realize that I named those mines in honor of my great ancestor? I think it was a tribute which he would have liked."

It took her a moment to recover her eyesight; she had never known what was meant by blasphemy or what one felt on encountering it; she knew it now.

He had risen and stood courteously, smiling down at her; it was a cold smile, impersonal and unrevealing.

She was trembling, but it did not matter. She did not care what he saw or guessed or laughed at.

"I came here because I wanted to know the reason for what you've done with your life," she said tonelessly, without anger.

"I have told you the reason," he answered gravely, "but you don't want to believe it."

"I kept seeing you as you were. I couldn't forget it. And that you should have become what you are—*that* does not belong in a rational universe."

"No? And the world as you see it around you, does?"

"You were not the kind of man who gets broken by any kind of world."

"True."

"Then—why?"

He shrugged. "Who is John Galt?"

"Oh, don't use gutter language!"

He glanced at her. His lips held the hint of a smile, but his eyes were still, earnest and, for an instant, disturbingly perceptive.

"Why?" she repeated.

He answered, as he had answered in the night, in this hotel, ten years ago, "You're not ready to hear it."

He did not follow her to the door. She had put her hand on the doorknob when she turned—and stopped. He stood across the room, looking at her; it was a glance directed at her whole person; she knew its meaning and it held her motionless.

"I still want to sleep with you," he said. "But I am not a man who is happy enough to do it."

"Not happy enough?" she repeated in complete bewilderment.

He laughed. "Is it proper that that should be the first thing you'd answer?" He waited, but she remained silent. "You want it, too, don't you?"

She was about to answer "No," but realized that the truth was worse than that. "Yes," she answered coldly, "but it doesn't matter to me that I want it."

He smiled, in open appreciation, acknowledging the strength she had needed to say it.

But he was not smiling when he said, as she opened the door to leave, "You have a great deal of courage, Dagny. Some day, you'll have enough of it."

"Of what? Courage?"

But he did not answer.

VI

THE NON-COMMERCIAL

Rearden pressed his forehead to the mirror and tried not to think.

That was the only way he could go through with it, he told himself. He concentrated on the relief of the mirror's cooling touch, wondering how one went about forcing one's mind into blankness, particularly after a lifetime lived on the axiom that the constant, clearest, most ruthless function of his rational faculty was his foremost duty. He wondered why no effort had ever seemed beyond his capacity, yet now he could not scrape up the strength to stick a few black pearl studs into his starched white shirt front.

This was his wedding anniversary and he had known for three months that the party would take place tonight, as Lillian wished. He had promised it to her, safe in the knowledge that the party was a long way off and that he would attend to it, when the time came, as he attended to every duty on his overloaded schedule. Then, during three months of eighteen-hour workdays, he had forgotten it happily—until half an hour ago, when, long past dinner time, his secretary had entered his office and said firmly, "Your party, Mr. Rearden." He had cried, "Good God!" leaping to his feet; he had hurried home, rushed up the stairs, started tearing his clothes off and gone through the routine of dressing, conscious only of the need to hurry, not of the purpose. When the full realization of the purpose struck him like a sudden blow, he stopped.

"You don't care for anything but business." He had heard it all his life, pronounced as a verdict of damnation. He had always known that business was regarded as some sort of secret, shameful cult, which one did not impose on innocent laymen, that people thought of it as of an ugly necessity, to be performed but never mentioned, that to talk shop was an offense against higher sensibilities, that just as one washed machine grease off one's hands before coming home, so one was supposed to wash the stain of business off one's mind before entering a drawing room. He had never held that creed, but he had accepted it as natural that his family should hold it. He took it for granted—wordlessly, in the manner of a feeling absorbed in childhood, left unquestioned and unnamed—that he had dedicated himself, like the martyr of some dark religion, to the service of a faith which was his passionate love, but which made him an outcast among men, whose sympathy he was not to expect.

He had accepted the tenet that it was his duty to give his wife some form of existence unrelated to business. But he had never found the capacity to do it or even to experience a sense of guilt. He could neither force himself to change nor blame her if she chose to condemn him.

He had given Lillian none of his time for months—no, he thought, for years; for the eight years of their marriage. He had no interest to spare for her interests, not even enough to learn just what they were. She had a large circle of friends, and he had heard it said that their names represented the heart of the country's culture, but he had never had time to meet them or even to acknowledge their fame by knowing what achievements had earned it. He knew only that he often saw their names on the magazine covers on newsstands. If Lillian resented his attitude, he thought, she was right. If her manner toward him was objectionable, he deserved it. If his family called him heartless, it was true.

He had never spared himself in any issue. When a problem came up at the mills, his first concern was to discover what error he had made; he did not search for anyone's fault but his own; it was of himself that he demanded perfection. He would grant himself no mercy now; he took the blame. But at the mills, it prompted him to action in an immediate impulse to correct the error; now, it had no effect. . . . Just a few more minutes, he thought, standing against the mirror, his eyes closed.

He could not stop the thing in his mind that went on throwing words at him; it was like trying to plug a broken hydrant with his bare hands. Stinging jets, part words, part pictures, kept shooting at his brain. . . . Hours of it, he thought, hours to spend watching the eyes of the guests getting heavy with boredom if they were sober or glazing into an imbecile stare if they weren't, and pretend that he noticed neither, and strain to think of something to say to them, when he had nothing to say —while he needed hours of inquiry to find a successor for the superintendent of his rolling mills who had resigned suddenly, without explanation—he had to do it at once—men of that sort were so hard to find—and if anything happened to break the flow of the rolling mills—it was the Taggart rail that was being rolled. . . . He remembered the silent reproach, the look of accusation, long-bearing patience and scorn, which he always saw in the eyes of his family when they caught some evidence of his passion for his business—and the futility of his silence, of his hope that they would not think Rearden Steel meant as much to him as it did—like a drunkard pretending indifference to liquor, among people who watch him with the scornful amusement of their full knowledge of his shameful weakness. . . . "I heard you last night coming home at two in the morning, where were you?" his mother saying to him at the dinner table, and Lillian answering, "Why, at the mills, of course," as another wife would say, "At the corner saloon." . . . Or

Lillian asking him, the hint of a wise half-smile on her face, "What were you doing in New York yesterday?" "It was a banquet with the boys." "Business?" "Yes." *"Of course"*—and Lillian turning away, nothing more, except the shameful realization that he had almost hoped she would think he had attended some sort of obscene stag party. . . . An ore carrier had gone down in a storm on Lake Michigan, with thousands of tons of Rearden ore—those boats were falling apart—if he didn't take it upon himself to help them obtain the replacements they needed, the owners of the line would go bankrupt, and there was no other line left in operation on Lake Michigan. . . . "That nook?" said Lillian, pointing to an arrangement of settees and coffee tables in their drawing room. "Why, no, Henry, it's not new, but I suppose I should feel flattered that three weeks is all it took you to notice it. It's my own adaptation of the morning room of a famous French palace —but things like that can't possibly interest you, darling, there's no stock market quotation on them, none whatever." . . . The order for copper, which he had placed six months ago, had not been delivered, the promised date had been postponed three times—"We can't help it, Mr. Rearden"—he had to find another company to deal with, the supply of copper was becoming increasingly uncertain. . . . Philip did not smile, when he looked up in the midst of a speech he was making to some friend of their mother's, about some organization he had joined, but there was something that suggested a smile of superiority in the loose muscles of his face when he said, "No, you wouldn't care for this, it's not business, Henry, not business at all, it's a strictly non-commercial endeavor." . . . That contractor in Detroit, with the job of rebuilding a large factory, was considering structural shapes of Rearden Metal —he should fly to Detroit and speak to him in person—he should have done it a week ago—he could have done it tonight. . . . "You're not listening," said his mother at the breakfast table, when his mind wandered to the current coal price index, while she was telling him about the dream she'd had last night. "You've never listened to a living soul. You're not interested in anything but yourself. You don't give a damn about people, not about a single human creature on God's earth." . . . The typed pages lying on the desk in his office were a report on the tests of an airplane motor made of Rearden Metal—perhaps of all things on earth, the one he wanted most at this moment was to read it— it had lain on his desk, untouched, for three days, he had had no time for it—why didn't he do it now and—

He shook his head violently, opening his eyes, stepping back from the mirror.

He tried to reach for the shirt studs. He saw his hand reaching, instead, for the pile of mail on his dresser. It was mail picked as urgent, it had to be read tonight, but he had had no time to read it in the office. His secretary had stuffed it into his pocket on his way out. He had thrown it there while undressing.

A newspaper clipping fluttered down to the floor. It was an editorial which his secretary had marked with an angry slash in red pencil. It was entitled "Equalization of Opportunity." He had to read it: there had been too much talk about this issue in the last three months, ominously too much.

He read it, with the sound of voices and forced laughter coming from downstairs, reminding him that the guests were arriving, that the party had started and that he would face the bitter, reproachful glances of his family when he came down.

The editorial said that at a time of dwindling production, shrinking markets and vanishing opportunities to make a living, it was unfair to let one man hoard several business enterprises, while others had none; it was destructive to let a few corner all the resources, leaving others no chance; competition was essential to society, and it was society's duty to see that no competitor ever rose beyond the range of anybody who wanted to compete with him. The editorial predicted the passage of a bill which had been proposed, a bill forbidding any person or corporation to own more than one business concern.

Wesley Mouch, his Washington man, had told Rearden not to worry; the fight would be stiff, he had said, but the bill would be defeated. Rearden understood nothing about that kind of fight. He left it to Mouch and his staff. He could barely find time to skim through their reports from Washington and to sign the checks which Mouch requested for the battle.

Rearden did not believe that the bill would pass. He was incapable of believing it. Having dealt with the clean reality of metals, technology, production all his life, he had acquired the conviction that one had to concern oneself with the rational, not the insane—that one had to seek that which was right, because the right answer always won—that the senseless, the wrong, the monstrously unjust could not work, could not succeed, could do nothing but defeat itself. A battle against a thing such as that bill seemed preposterous and faintly embarrassing to him, as if he were suddenly asked to compete with a man who calculated steel mixtures by the formulas of numerology.

He had told himself that the issue was dangerous. But the loudest screaming of the most hysterical editorial roused no emotion in him—while a variation of a decimal point in a laboratory report on a test of Rearden Metal made him leap to his feet in eagerness or apprehension. He had no energy to spare for anything else.

He crumpled the editorial and threw it into the wastebasket. He felt the leaden approach of that exhaustion which he never felt at his job, the exhaustion that seemed to wait for him and catch him the moment he turned to other concerns. He felt as if he were incapable of any desire except a desperate longing for sleep.

He told himself that he had to attend the party—that his family had the right to demand it of him—that he had to learn to like their kind of pleasure, for their sake, not his own.

He wondered why this was a motive that had no power to impel him. Throughout his life, whenever he became convinced that a course of action was right, the desire to follow it had come automatically. What was happening to him?—he wondered. The impossible conflict of feeling reluctance to do that which was right—wasn't it the basic formula of moral corruption? To recognize one's guilt, yet feel nothing but the coldest, most profound indifference—wasn't it a betrayal of that which had been the motor of his life-course and of his pride?

He gave himself no time to seek an answer. He finished dressing, quickly, pitilessly.

Holding himself erect, his tall figure moving with the unstressed, unhurried confidence of habitual authority, the white of a fine handkerchief in the breast pocket of his black dinner jacket, he walked slowly down the stairs to the drawing room, looking—to the satisfaction of the dowagers who watched him—like the perfect figure of a great industrialist.

He saw Lillian at the foot of the stairs. The patrician lines of a lemon-yellow Empire evening gown stressed her graceful body, and she stood like a person proudly in control of her proper background. He smiled; he liked to see her happy; it gave some reasonable justification to the party.

He approached her—and stopped. She had always shown good taste in her use of jewelry, never wearing too much of it. But tonight she wore an ostentatious display: a diamond necklace, earrings, rings and brooches. Her arms looked conspicuously bare by contrast. On her right wrist, as sole ornament, she wore the bracelet of Rearden Metal. The glittering gems made it look like an ugly piece of dime-store jewelry.

When he moved his glance from her wrist to her face, he found her looking at him. Her eyes were narrowed and he could not define their expression; it was a look that seemed both veiled and purposeful, the look of something hidden that flaunted its security from detection.

He wanted to tear the bracelet off her wrist. Instead, in obedience to her voice gaily pronouncing an introduction, he bowed to the dowager who stood beside her, his face expressionless.

"Man? What is man? He's just a collection of chemicals with delusions of grandeur," said Dr. Pritchett to a group of guests across the room.

Dr. Pritchett picked a canapé off a crystal dish, held it speared between two straight fingers and deposited it whole into his mouth.

"Man's metaphysical pretensions," he said, "are preposterous. A miserable bit of protoplasm, full of ugly little concepts and mean little emotions—and it imagines itself important! Really, you know, that is the root of all the troubles in the world."

"But which concepts are not ugly or mean, Professor?" asked an earnest matron whose husband owned an automobile factory.

"None," said Dr. Pritchett. "None within the range of man's capacity."

A young man asked hesitantly, "But if we haven't any good concepts, how do we know that the ones we've got are ugly? I mean, by what standard?"

"There aren't any standards."

This silenced his audience.

"The philosophers of the past were superficial," Dr. Pritchett went on. "It remained for our century to redefine the purpose of philosophy. The purpose of philosophy is not to help men find the meaning of life, but to prove to them that there isn't any."

An attractive young woman, whose father owned a coal mine, asked indignantly, "Who can tell us that?"

"I am trying to," said Dr. Pritchett. For the last three years, he had been head of the Department of Philosophy at the Patrick Henry University.

Lillian Rearden approached, her jewels glittering under the lights. The expression on her face was held to the soft hint of a smile, set and faintly suggested, like the waves of her hair.

"It is this insistence of man upon meaning that makes him so difficult," said Dr. Pritchett. "Once he realizes that he is of no importance whatever in the vast scheme of the universe, that no possible significance can be attached to his activities, that it does not matter whether he lives or dies, he will become much more . . . tractable."

He shrugged and reached for another canapé. A businessman said uneasily, "What I asked you about, Professor, was what you thought about the Equalization of Opportunity Bill."

"Oh, that?" said Dr. Pritchett. "But I believe I made it clear that I am in favor of it, because I am in favor of a free economy. A free economy cannot exist without competition. Therefore, men must be forced to compete. Therefore, we must control men in order to force them to be free."

"But, look . . . isn't that sort of a contradiction?"

"Not in the higher philosophical sense. You must learn to see beyond the static definitions of old-fashioned thinking. Nothing is static in the universe. Everything is fluid."

"But it stands to reason that if—"

"Reason, my dear fellow, is the most naïve of all superstitions. That, at least, has been generally conceded in our age."

"But I don't quite understand how we can—"

"You suffer from the popular delusion of believing that things can be understood. You do not grasp the fact that the universe is a solid contradiction."

"A contradiction of what?" asked the matron.

"Of itself."

"How . . . how's that?"

"My dear madam, the duty of thinkers is not to explain, but to demonstrate that nothing can be explained."

"Yes, of course . . . only . . ."

"The purpose of philosophy is not to seek knowledge, but to prove that knowledge is impossible to man."

"But when we prove it," asked the young woman, "what's going to be left?"

"Instinct," said Dr. Pritchett reverently.

At the other end of the room, a group was listening to Balph Eubank. He sat upright on the edge of an armchair, in order to counteract the appearance of his face and figure, which had a tendency to spread if relaxed.

"The literature of the past," said Balph Eubank, "was a shallow fraud. It whitewashed life in order to please the money tycoons whom it served. Morality, free will, achievement, happy endings, and man as some sort of heroic being—all that stuff is laughable to us. Our age has given depth to literature for the first time, by exposing the real essence of life."

A very young girl in a white evening gown asked timidly, "What is the real essence of life, Mr. Eubank?"

"Suffering," said Balph Eubank. "Defeat and suffering."

"But . . . but why? People are happy . . . sometimes . . . aren't they?"

"That is a delusion of those whose emotions are superficial."

The girl blushed. A wealthy woman who had inherited an oil refinery, asked guiltily, "What should we do to raise the people's literary taste, Mr. Eubank?"

"That is a great social problem," said Balph Eubank. He was described as the literary leader of the age, but had never written a book that sold more than three thousand copies. "Personally, I believe that an Equalization of Opportunity Bill applying to literature would be the solution."

"Oh, do you approve of that Bill for industry? I'm not sure I know what to think of it."

"Certainly, I approve of it. Our culture has sunk into a bog of materialism. Men have lost all spiritual values in their pursuit of material production and technological trickery. They're too comfortable. They will return to a nobler life if we teach them to bear privations. So we ought to place a limit upon their material greed."

"I hadn't thought of it that way," said the woman apologetically.

"But how are you going to work an Equalization of Opportunity Bill for literature, Ralph?" asked Mort Liddy. "That's a new one on me."

"My name is Balph," said Eubank angrily. "And it's a new one on you because it's my own idea."

"Okay, okay, I'm not quarreling, am I? I'm just asking." Mort Liddy smiled. He spent most of his time smiling nervously. He was a composer who wrote old-fashioned scores for motion pictures, and modern symphonies for sparse audiences.

"It would work very simply," said Balph Eubank. "There should be a law limiting the sale of any book to ten thousand copies. This would throw the literary market open to new talent, fresh ideas and non-commercial writing. If people were forbidden to buy a million copies of the same piece of trash, they would be forced to buy better books."

"You've got something there," said Mort Liddy. "But wouldn't it be kinda tough on the writers' bank accounts?"

"So much the better. Only those whose motive is not money-making should be allowed to write."

"But, Mr. Eubank," asked the young girl in the white dress, "what if more than ten thousand people want to buy a certain book?"

"Ten thousand readers is enough for any book."

"That's not what I mean. I mean, what if they *want* it?"

"That is irrelevant."

"But if a book has a good story which—"

"Plot is a primitive vulgarity in literature," said Balph Eubank contemptuously.

Dr. Pritchett, on his way across the room to the bar, stopped to say, "Quite so. Just as logic is a primitive vulgarity in philosophy."

"Just as melody is a primitive vulgarity in music," said Mort Liddy.

"What's all this noise?" asked Lillian Rearden, glittering to a stop beside them.

"Lillian, my angel," Balph Eubank drawled, "did I tell you that I'm dedicating my new novel to you?"

"Why, thank you, darling."

"What is the name of your new novel?" asked the wealthy woman.

"The Heart Is a Milkman."

"What is it about?"

"Frustration."

"But, Mr. Eubank," asked the young girl in the white dress, blushing desperately, "if everything is frustration, what is there to live for?"

"Brother-love," said Balph Eubank grimly.

Bertram Scudder stood slouched against the bar. His long, thin face looked as if it had shrunk inward, with the exception of his mouth and eyeballs, which were left to protrude as three soft globes. He was the editor of a magazine called *The Future* and he had written an article on Hank Rearden, entitled "The Octopus."

Bertram Scudder picked up his empty glass and shoved it silently toward the bartender, to be refilled. He took a gulp from his fresh drink, noticed the empty glass in front of Philip Rearden, who stood beside him, and jerked his thumb in a silent command to the bartender. He ignored the empty glass in front of Betty Pope, who stood at Philip's other side.

"Look, bud," said Bertram Scudder, his eyeballs focused approximately in the direction of Philip, "whether you like it or not, the Equalization of Opportunity Bill represents a great step forward."

"What made you think that I did not like it, Mr. Scudder?" Philip asked humbly.

"Well, it's going to pinch, isn't it? The long arm of society is going to trim a little off the hors d'oeuvres bill around here." He waved his hand at the bar.

"Why do you assume that I object to that?"

"You don't?" Bertram Scudder asked without curiosity.

"I don't!" said Philip hotly. "I have always placed the public good above any personal consideration. I have contributed my time and money to Friends of Global Progress in their crusade for the Equalization of Opportunity Bill. I think it is perfectly unfair that one man should get all the breaks and leave none to others."

Bertram Scudder considered him speculatively, but without particular interest. "Well, that's quite unusually nice of you," he said.

"Some people do take moral issues seriously, Mr. Scudder," said Philip, with a gentle stress of pride in his voice.

"What's he talking about, Philip?" asked Betty Pope. "We don't know anybody who owns more than one business, do we?"

"Oh, pipe down!" said Bertram Scudder, his voice bored.

"I don't see why there's so much fuss about that Equalization of Opportunity Bill," said Betty Pope aggressively, in the tone of an expert on economics. "I don't see why businessmen object to it. It's to their own advantage. If everybody else is poor, they won't have any market for their goods. But if they stop being selfish and share the goods they've hoarded—they'll have a chance to work hard and produce some more."

"I do not see why industrialists should be considered at all," said Scudder. "When the masses are destitute and yet there are goods available, it's idiotic to expect people to be stopped by some scrap of paper called a property deed. Property rights are a superstition. One holds property only by the courtesy of those who do not seize it. The people can seize it at any moment. If they can, why shouldn't they?"

"They should," said Claude Slagenhop. "They need it. Need is the only consideration. If people are in need, we've got to seize things first and talk about it afterwards."

Claude Slagenhop had approached and managed to squeeze himself between Philip and Scudder, shoving Scudder aside imperceptibly. Slagenhop was not tall or heavy, but he had a square, compact bulk, and a broken nose. He was the president of Friends of Global Progress.

"Hunger won't wait," said Claude Slagenhop. "Ideas are just hot air. An empty belly is a solid fact. I've said in all my speeches that it's not necessary to talk too much. Society is suffering for lack of business opportunities at the moment, so we've got the right to seize such opportunities as exist. Right is whatever's good for society."

"He didn't dig that ore single-handed, did he?" cried Philip suddenly, his voice shrill. "He had to employ hundreds of workers. They did it. Why does he think he's so good?"

The two men looked at him, Scudder lifting an eyebrow, Slagenhop without expression.

"Oh, dear me!" said Betty Pope, remembering.

Hank Rearden stood at a window in a dim recess at the end of the drawing room. He hoped no one would notice him for a few minutes. He had just escaped from a middle-aged woman who had been telling him about her psychic experiences. He stood, looking out. Far in the distance, the red glow of Rearden Steel moved in the sky. He watched it for a moment's relief.

He turned to look at the drawing room. He had never liked his house; it had been Lillian's choice. But tonight, the shifting colors of the evening dresses drowned out the appearance of the room and gave it an air of brilliant gaiety. He liked to see people being gay, even though he did not understand this particular manner of enjoyment.

He looked at the flowers, at the sparks of light on the crystal glasses, at the naked arms and shoulders of women. There was a cold wind outside, sweeping empty stretches of land. He saw the thin branches of a tree being twisted, like arms waving in an appeal for help. The tree stood against the glow of the mills.

He could not name his sudden emotion. He had no words to state its cause, its quality, its meaning. Some part of it was joy, but it was solemn like the act of baring one's head—he did not know to whom.

When he stepped back into the crowd, he was smiling. But the smile vanished abruptly; he saw the entrance of a new guest: it was Dagny Taggart.

Lillian moved forward to meet her, studying her with curiosity. They had met before, on infrequent occasions, and she found it strange to see Dagny Taggart wearing an evening gown. It was a black dress with a bodice that fell as a cape over one arm and shoulder, leaving the other bare; the naked shoulder was the gown's only ornament. Seeing her in the suits she wore, one never thought of Dagny Taggart's body. The black dress seemed excessively revealing—because it was astonishing to discover that the lines of her shoulder were fragile and beautiful, and that the diamond band on the wrist of her naked arm gave her the most feminine of all aspects: the look of being chained.

"Miss Taggart, it is such a wonderful surprise to see you here," said Lillian Rearden, the muscles of her face performing the motions of a smile. "I had not really dared to hope that an invitation from me would take you away from your ever so much weightier concerns. Do permit me to feel flattered."

James Taggart had entered with his sister. Lillian smiled at him, in the manner of a hasty postscript, as if noticing him for the first time.

"Hello, James. That's your penalty for being popular—one tends to lose sight of you in the surprise of seeing your sister."

"No one can match you in popularity, Lillian," he answered, smiling thinly, "nor ever lose sight of you."

"Me? Oh, but I am quite resigned to taking second place in the shadow of my husband. I am humbly aware that the wife of a great man has to be contented with reflected glory—don't you think so, Miss Taggart?"

"No," said Dagny, "I don't."

"Is this a compliment or a reproach, Miss Taggart? But do forgive me if I confess I'm helpless. Whom may I present to you? I'm afraid I have nothing but writers and artists to offer, and they wouldn't interest you, I'm sure."

"I'd like to find Hank and say hello to him."

"But of course. James, do you remember you said you wanted to meet Balph Eubank?—oh yes, he's here—I'll tell him that I heard you rave about his last novel at Mrs. Whitcomb's dinner!"

Walking across the room, Dagny wondered why she had said that she wanted to find Hank Rearden, what had prevented her from admitting that she had seen him the moment she entered.

Rearden stood at the other end of the long room, looking at her. He watched her as she approached, but he did not step forward to meet her.

"Hello, Hank."

"Good evening."

He bowed, courteously, impersonally, the movement of his body matching the distinguished formality of his clothes. He did not smile.

"Thank you for inviting me tonight," she said gaily.

"I cannot claim that I knew you were coming."

"Oh? Then I'm glad that Mrs. Rearden thought of me. I wanted to make an exception."

"An exception?"

"I don't go to parties very often."

"I am pleased that you chose this occasion as the exception." He did not add "Miss Taggart," but it sounded as if he had.

The formality of his manner was so unexpected that she was unable to adjust to it. "I wanted to celebrate," she said.

"To celebrate my wedding anniversary?"

"Oh, is it your wedding anniversary? I didn't know. My congratulations, Hank."

"What did you wish to celebrate?"

"I thought I'd permit myself a rest. A celebration of my own—in your honor and mine."

"For what reason?"

She was thinking of the new track on the rocky grades of the Colorado mountains, growing slowly toward the distant goal of the Wyatt oil fields. She was seeing the greenish-blue glow of the rails on the frozen ground, among the dried weeds, the naked boulders, the rotting shanties of half-starved settlements.

"In honor of the first sixty miles of Rearden Metal track," she answered.

"I appreciate it." The tone of his voice was the one that would have been proper if he had said, "I've never heard of it."

She found nothing else to say. She felt as if she were speaking to a stranger.

"Why, Miss Taggart!" a cheerful voice broke their silence. "Now *this* is what I mean when I say that Hank Rearden can achieve any miracle!"

A businessman whom they knew had approached, smiling at her in delighted astonishment. The three of them had often held emergency conferences about freight rates and steel deliveries. Now he looked at her, his face an open comment on the change in her appearance, the change, she thought, which Rearden had not noticed.

She laughed, answering the man's greeting, giving herself no time to recognize the unexpected stab of disappointment, the unadmitted thought that she wished she had seen this look on Rearden's face, instead. She exchanged a few sentences with the man. When she glanced around, Rearden was gone.

"So that is your famous sister?" said Balph Eubank to James Taggart, looking at Dagny across the room.

"I was not aware that my sister was famous," said Taggart, a faint bite in his voice.

"But, my good man, she's an unusual phenomenon in the field of economics, so you must expect people to talk about her. Your sister is a symptom of the illness of our century. A decadent product of the machine age. Machines have destroyed man's humanity, taken him away from the soil, robbed him of his natural arts, killed his soul and turned him into an insensitive robot. There's an example of it—a woman who runs a railroad, instead of practicing the beautiful craft of the handloom and bearing children."

Rearden moved among the guests, trying not to be trapped into conversation. He looked at the room; he saw no one he wished to approach.

"Say, Hank Rearden, you're not such a bad fellow at all when seen close up in the lion's own den. You ought to give us a press conference once in a while, you'd win us over."

Rearden turned and looked at the speaker incredulously. It was a young newspaperman of the seedier sort, who worked on a radical tabloid. The offensive familiarity of his manner seemed to imply that he chose to be rude to Rearden because he knew that Rearden should never have permitted himself to associate with a man of his kind.

Rearden would not have allowed him inside the mills; but the man was Lillian's guest; he controlled himself; he asked dryly, "What do you want?"

"You're not so bad. You've got talent. Technological talent. But, of course, I don't agree with you about Rearden Metal."

"I haven't asked you to agree."

"Well, Bertram Scudder said that your policy—" the man started belligerently, pointing toward the bar, but stopped, as if he had slid farther than he intended.

Rearden looked at the untidy figure slouched against the bar. Lillian had introduced them, but he had paid no attention to the name. He turned sharply and walked off, in a manner that forbade the young bum to tag him.

Lillian glanced up at his face, when Rearden approached her in the midst of a group, and, without a word, stepped aside where they could not be heard.

"Is that Scudder of *The Future?*" he asked, pointing.

"Why, yes."

He looked at her silently, unable to begin to believe it, unable to find the lead of a thought with which to begin to understand. Her eyes were watching him.

"How could you invite him here?" he asked.

"Now, Henry, don't let's be ridiculous. You don't want to be narrow-minded, do you? You must learn to tolerate the opinions of others and respect their right of free speech."

"In my house?"

"Oh, don't be stuffy!"

He did not speak, because his consciousness was held, not by coherent statements, but by two pictures that seemed to glare at him insistently. He saw the article, "The Octopus," by Bertram Scudder, which was not an expression of ideas, but a bucket of slime emptied in public—an article that did not contain a single fact, not even an invented one, but poured a stream of sneers and adjectives in which nothing was clear except the filthy malice of denouncing without considering proof necessary. And he saw the lines of Lillian's profile, the proud purity which he had sought in marrying her.

When he noticed her again, he realized that the vision of her profile was in his own mind, because she was turned to him full-face, watching him. In the sudden instant of returning to reality, he thought that what he saw in her eyes was enjoyment. But in the next instant he reminded himself that he was sane and that this was not possible.

"It's the first time you've invited that . . ." he used an obscene word with unemotional precision, "to my house. It's the last."

"How dare you use such—"

"Don't argue, Lillian. If you do, I'll throw him out right now."

He gave her a moment to answer, to object, to scream at him if she wished. She remained silent, not looking at him, only her smooth cheeks seemed faintly drawn inward, as if deflated.

Moving blindly away through the coils of lights, voices and perfume, he felt a cold touch of dread. He knew that he should think of Lillian and find the answer to the riddle of her character, because this was a revelation which he could not ignore; but he did not think of her—and he felt the dread because he knew that the answer had ceased to matter to him long ago.

The flood of weariness was starting to rise again. He felt as if he could almost see it in thickening waves; it was not within him, but outside, spreading through the room. For an instant, he felt as if he were alone, lost in a gray desert, needing help and knowing that no help would come.

He stopped short. In the lighted doorway, the length of the room between them, he saw the tall, arrogant figure of a man who had paused for a moment before entering. He had never met the man, but of all the notorious faces that cluttered the pages of newspapers, this was the one he despised. It was Francisco d'Anconia.

Rearden had never given much thought to men like Bertram Scudder. But with every hour of his life, with the strain and the pride of every moment when his muscles or his mind had ached from effort, with every step he had taken to rise out of the mines of Minnesota and to turn his effort into gold, with all of his profound respect for money and for its meaning, he despised the squanderer who did not know how to deserve the great gift of inherited wealth. There, he thought, was the most contemptible representative of the species.

He saw Francisco d'Anconia enter, bow to Lillian, then walk into the crowd as if he owned the room which he had never entered before. Heads turned to watch him, as if he pulled them on strings in his wake.

Approaching Lillian once more, Rearden said without anger, the contempt becoming amusement in his voice, "I didn't know you knew that one."

"I've met him at a few parties."

"Is he one of your friends, too?"

"Certainly not!" The sharp resentment was genuine.

"Then why did you invite him?"

"Well, you can't give a party—not a party that counts—while he's in this country, without inviting him. It's a nuisance if he comes, and a social black mark if he doesn't."

Rearden laughed. She was off guard; she did not usually admit things of this kind. "Look," he said wearily, "I don't want to spoil your party. But keep that man away from me. Don't come around with introductions. I don't want to meet him. I don't know how you'll work that, but you're an expert hostess, so work it."

Dagny stood still when she saw Francisco approaching. He bowed to her as he passed by. He did not stop, but she knew that he had stopped the moment in his mind. She saw him smile faintly in deliberate emphasis of what he understood and did not choose to acknowledge. She turned away. She hoped to avoid him for the rest of the evening.

Balph Eubank had joined the group around Dr. Pritchett, and was saying sullenly, ". . . no, you cannot expect people to understand the higher reaches of philosophy. Culture should be taken out of the hands of the dollar-chasers. We need a national subsidy for literature. It is disgraceful that artists are treated like peddlers and that art works have to be sold like soap."

"You mean, your complaint is that they *don't* sell like soap?" asked Francisco d'Anconia.

They had not noticed him approach; the conversation stopped, as if slashed off; most of them had never met him, but they all recognized him at once.

"I meant—" Balph Eubank started angrily and closed his mouth; he saw the eager interest on the faces of his audience, but it was not interest in philosophy any longer.

"Why, hello, Professor!" said Francisco, bowing to Dr. Pritchett.

There was no pleasure in Dr. Pritchett's face when he answered the greeting and performed a few introductions.

"We were just discussing a most interesting subject," said the earnest matron. "Dr. Pritchett was telling us that nothing is anything."

"He should, undoubtedly, know more than anyone else about that," Francisco answered gravely.

"I wouldn't have supposed that you knew Dr. Pritchett so well, Señor d'Anconia," she said, and wondered why the professor looked displeased by her remark.

"I am an alumnus of the great school that employs Dr. Pritchett at present, the Patrick Henry University. But I studied under one of his predecessors—Hugh Akston."

"Hugh Akston!" the attractive young woman gasped. "But you couldn't have, Señor d'Anconia! You're not old enough. I thought he was one of those great names of . . . of the last century."

"Perhaps in spirit, madame. Not in fact."

"But I thought he died years ago."

"Why, no. He is still alive."

"Then why don't we ever hear about him any more?"

"He retired, nine years ago."

"Isn't it odd? When a politician or a movie star retires, we read front page stories about it. But when a philosopher retires, people do not even notice it."

"They do, eventually."

A young man said, astonished, "I thought Hugh Akston was one of those classics that nobody studied any more, except in histories of philosophy. I read an article recently which referred to him as the last of the great advocates of reason."

"Just what did Hugh Akston teach?" asked the earnest matron.

Francisco answered, "He taught that everything is something."

"Your loyalty to your teacher is laudable, Señor d'Anconia," said Dr. Pritchett dryly. "May we take it that you are an example of the practical results of his teaching?"

"I am."

James Taggart had approached the group and was waiting to be noticed.

"Hello, Francisco."

"Good evening, James."

"What a wonderful coincidence, seeing you here! I've been very anxious to speak to you."

"That's new. You haven't always been."

"Now you're joking, just like in the old days." Taggart was moving slowly, as if casually, away from the group, hoping to draw Francisco after him. "You know that there's not a person in this room who wouldn't love to talk to you."

"Really? I'd be inclined to suspect the opposite." Francisco had followed obediently, but stopped within hearing distance of the others.

"I have tried in every possible way to get in touch with you," said Taggart, "but . . . but circumstances didn't permit me to succeed."

"Are you trying to hide from me the fact that I refused to see you?"

"Well . . . that is . . . I mean, why did you refuse?"

"I couldn't imagine what you wanted to speak to me about."

"The San Sebastián Mines, of course!" Taggart's voice rose a little.

"Why, what about them?"

"But . . . Now, look, Francisco, this is serious. It's a disaster, an unprecedented disaster—and nobody can make any sense out of it. I don't know what to think. I don't understand it at all. I have a right to know."

"A right? Aren't you being old-fashioned, James? But what is it you want to know?"

"Well, first of all, that nationalization—what are you going to do about it?"

"Nothing."

"Nothing?!"

"But surely you don't want me to do anything about it. My mines and your railroad were seized by the will of the people. You wouldn't want me to oppose the will of the people, would you?"

"Francisco, this is not a laughing matter!"

"I never thought it was."

"I'm entitled to an explanation! You owe your stockholders an account of the whole disgraceful affair! Why did you pick a worthless mine? Why did you waste all those millions? What sort of rotten swindle was it?"

Francisco stood looking at him in polite astonishment. "Why, James," he said, "I thought you would approve of it."

"Approve?!"

"I thought you would consider the San Sebastián Mines as the practical realization of an ideal of the highest moral order. Remembering that you and I have disagreed so often in the past, I thought you would be gratified to see me acting in accordance with your principles."

"What are you talking about?"

Francisco shook his head regretfully. "I don't know why you should call my behavior rotten. I thought you would recognize it as an honest effort to practice what the whole world is preaching. Doesn't everyone believe that it is evil to be selfish? I was totally selfless in regard to the San Sebastián project. Isn't it evil to pursue a personal interest? I had no personal interest in it whatever. Isn't it evil to work for profit? I did not work for profit—I took a loss. Doesn't everyone agree that the purpose and justification of an industrial enterprise are not production, but the livelihood of its employees? The San Sebastián Mines were the most eminently successful venture in industrial history: they produced no copper, but they provided a livelihood for thousands of men who could not have achieved, in a lifetime, the equivalent of what they got for one day's work, which they could not do. Isn't it generally agreed that an owner is a parasite and an exploiter, that it is the employees who do all the work and make the product possible? I did not exploit anyone. I did not burden the San Sebastián Mines with my useless presence; I left them in the hands of the men who count. I did not pass judgment on the value of that property. I turned it over to a mining specialist. He was not a very good specialist, but he needed the job very badly. Isn't it generally conceded that when you hire a man for a job, it is his need that counts, not his ability? Doesn't everyone believe that in order to get the goods, all you have to do is need them? I have carried out every moral precept of our age. I expected gratitude and a citation of honor. I do not understand why I am being damned."

In the silence of those who had listened, the sole comment was the shrill, sudden giggle of Betty Pope: she had understood nothing, but she saw the look of helpless fury on James Taggart's face.

People were looking at Taggart, expecting an answer. They were indifferent to the issue, they were merely amused by the spectacle of someone's embarrassment. Taggart achieved a patronizing smile.

"You don't expect me to take this seriously?" he asked.

"There was a time," Francisco answered, "when I did not believe that anyone could take it seriously. I was wrong."

"This is outrageous!" Taggart's voice started to rise. "It's perfectly outrageous to treat your public responsibilities with such thoughtless levity!" He turned to hurry away.

Francisco shrugged, spreading his hands. "You see? I didn't think you wanted to speak to me."

Rearden stood alone, far at the other end of the room. Philip noticed him, approached and waved to Lillian, calling her over.

"Lillian, I don't think that Henry is having a good time," he said, smiling; one could not tell whether the mockery of his smile was directed at Lillian or at Rearden. "Can't we do something about it?"

"Oh, nonsense!" said Rearden.

"I wish I knew what to do about it, Philip," said Lillian. "I've always wished Henry would learn to relax. He's so grimly serious about everything. He's such a rigid Puritan. I've always wanted to see him drunk, just once. But I've given up. What would you suggest?"

"Oh, I don't know! But he shouldn't be standing around all by himself."

"Drop it," said Rearden. While thinking dimly that he did not want to hurt their feelings, he could not prevent himself from adding, "You don't know how hard I've tried to be left standing all by myself."

"There—you see?" Lillian smiled at Philip. "To enjoy life and people is not so simple as pouring a ton of steel. Intellectual pursuits are not learned in the market place."

Philip chuckled. "It's not intellectual pursuits I'm worried about. How sure are you about that Puritan stuff, Lillian? If I were you, I wouldn't leave him free to look around. There are too many beautiful women here tonight."

"Henry entertaining thoughts of infidelity? You flatter him, Philip. You overestimate his courage." She smiled at Rearden, coldly, for a brief, stressed moment, then moved away.

Rearden looked at his brother. "What in hell do you think you're doing?"

"Oh, stop playing the Puritan! Can't you take a joke?"

Moving aimlessly through the crowd, Dagny wondered why she had accepted the invitation to this party. The answer astonished her: it was because she had wanted to see Hank Rearden. Watching him in the crowd, she realized the contrast for the first time. The faces of the others looked like aggregates of interchangeable features, every face oozing to blend into the anonymity of resembling all, and all looking as if they were melting. Rearden's face, with the sharp planes, the pale blue eyes, the ash-blond hair, had the firmness of ice; the uncompromising clarity of its lines made it look, among the others, as if he were moving through a fog, hit by a ray of light.

Her eyes kept returning to him involuntarily. She never caught him glancing in her direction. She could not believe that he was avoiding her intentionally; there could be no possible reason for it; yet she felt certain that he was. She wanted to approach him and convince herself that she was mistaken. Something stopped her; she could not understand her own reluctance.

Rearden bore patiently a conversation with his mother and two ladies whom she wished him to entertain with stories of his youth and his struggle. He complied, telling himself that she was proud of him in her own way. But he felt as if something in her manner kept suggesting that she had nursed him through his struggle and that she was the source of his success. He was glad when she let him go. Then he escaped once more to the recess of the window.

He stood there for a while, leaning on a sense of privacy as if it were a physical support.

"Mr. Rearden," said a strangely quiet voice beside him, "permit me to introduce myself. My name is d'Anconia."

Rearden turned, startled; d'Anconia's manner and voice had a quality he had seldom encountered before: a tone of authentic respect.

"How do you do," he answered. His voice was brusque and dry; but he had answered.

"I have observed that Mrs. Rearden has been trying to avoid the necessity of presenting me to you, and I can guess the reason. Would you prefer that I leave your house?"

The action of naming an issue instead of evading it, was so unlike the usual behavior of all the men he knew, it was such a sudden, startling relief, that Rearden remained silent for a moment, studying d'Anconia's face. Francisco had said it very simply, neither as a reproach nor a plea, but in a manner which, strangely, acknowledged Rearden's dignity and his own.

"No," said Rearden, "whatever else you guessed, I did not say that."

"Thank you. In that case, you will allow me to speak to you."

"Why should you wish to speak to me?"

"My motives cannot interest you at present."

"Mine is not the sort of conversation that could interest you at all."

"You are mistaken about one of us, Mr. Rearden, or both. I came to this party solely in order to meet you."

There had been a faint tone of amusement in Rearden's voice; now it hardened into a hint of contempt. "You started by playing it straight. Stick to it."

"I am."

"What did you want to meet me for? In order to make me lose money?"

Francisco looked straight at him. "Yes—eventually."

"What is it, this time? A gold mine?"

Francisco shook his head slowly; the conscious deliberation of the movement gave it an air that was almost sadness. "No," he said, "I don't want to sell you anything. As a matter of fact, I did not attempt to sell the copper mine to James Taggart, either. He came to me for it. You won't."

Rearden chuckled. "If you understand that much, we have at least a sensible basis for conversation. Proceed on that. If you don't have some fancy investment in mind, what did you want to meet me for?"

"In order to become acquainted with you."

"That's not an answer. It's just another way of saying the same thing."

"Not quite, Mr. Rearden."

"Unless you mean—in order to gain my confidence?"

"No. I don't like people who speak or think in terms of gaining anybody's confidence. If one's actions are honest, one does not need the predated confidence of others, only their rational perception. The person who craves a moral blank check of that kind, has dishonest intentions, whether he admits it to himself or not."

Rearden's startled glance at him was like the involuntary thrust of a hand grasping for support in a desperate need. The glance betrayed how much he wanted to find the sort of man he thought he was seeing. Then Rearden lowered his eyes, almost closing them, slowly, shutting out the vision and the need. His face was hard; it had an expression of severity, an inner severity directed at himself; it looked austere and lonely.

"All right," he said tonelessly. "What do you want, if it's not my confidence?"

"I want to learn to understand you."

"What for?"

"For a reason of my own which need not concern you at present."

"What do you want to understand about me?"

Francisco looked silently out at the darkness. The fire of the mills was dying down. There was only a faint tinge of red left on the edge of the earth, just enough to outline the scraps of clouds ripped by the tortured battle of the storm in the sky. Dim shapes kept sweeping through space and vanishing, shapes which were branches, but looked as if they were the fury of the wind made visible.

"It's a terrible night for any animal caught unprotected on that plain," said Francisco d'Anconia. "This is when one should appreciate the meaning of being a man."

Rearden did not answer for a moment; then he said, as if in answer to himself, a tone of wonder in his voice, "Funny . . ."

"What?"

"You told me what I was thinking just a while ago . . ."

"You were?"

". . . only I didn't have the words for it."

"Shall I tell you the rest of the words?"

"Go ahead."

"You stood here and watched the storm with the greatest pride one can ever feel—because you are able to have summer flowers and half-naked women in your house on a night like this, in demonstration of your victory over that storm. And if it weren't for you, most of those who are here would be left helpless at the mercy of that wind in the middle of some such plain."

"How did you know that?"

In time with his question, Rearden realized that it was not his thoughts this man had named, but his most hidden, most personal emotion; and that he, who would never confess his emotions to anyone, had confessed it in his question. He saw the faintest flicker in Francisco's eyes, as of a smile or a check mark.

"What would *you* know about a pride of that kind?" Rearden asked sharply, as if the contempt of the second question could erase the confidence of the first.

"That is what I felt once, when I was young."

Rearden looked at him. There was neither mockery nor self-pity in Francisco's face; the fine, sculptured planes and the clear, blue eyes held a quiet composure, the face was open, offered to any blow, unflinching.

"Why do you want to talk about it?" Rearden asked, prompted by a moment's reluctant compassion.

"Let us say—by way of gratitude, Mr. Rearden."

"Gratitude to me?"

"If you will accept it."

Rearden's voice hardened. "I haven't asked for gratitude. I don't need it."

"I have not said you needed it. But of all those whom you are saving from the storm tonight, I am the only one who will offer it."

After a moment's silence, Rearden asked, his voice low with a sound which was almost a threat, "What are you trying to do?"

"I am calling your attention to the nature of those for whom you are working."

"It would take a man who's never done an honest day's work in his life, to think or say that." The contempt in Rearden's voice had a note of relief; he had been disarmed by a doubt of his judgment on the character of his adversary; now he felt certain once more. "You wouldn't understand it if I told you that the man who works, works for himself, even if he does carry the whole wretched bunch of you along. Now *I'll* guess what you're thinking: go ahead, say that it's evil, that I'm selfish, conceited, heartless, cruel. I am. I don't want any part of that tripe about working for others. I'm not."

For the first time, he saw the look of a personal reaction in Francisco's eyes, the look of something eager and young. "The only thing that's wrong in what you said," Francisco answered, "is that you permit anyone to call it evil." In Rearden's pause of incredulous silence, he pointed at the crowd in the drawing room. "Why are you willing to carry them?"

"Because they're a bunch of miserable children who struggle to remain alive, desperately and very badly, while I—I don't even notice the burden."

"Why don't you tell them that?"

"What?"

"That you're working for your own sake, not theirs."

"They know it."

"Oh yes, they know it. Every single one of them here knows it. But they don't think you do. And the aim of all their efforts is to keep you from knowing it."

"Why should I care what they think?"

"Because it's a battle in which one must make one's stand clear."

"A battle? What battle? I hold the whip hand. I don't fight the disarmed."

"Are they? They have a weapon against you. It's their only weapon, but it's a terrible one. Ask yourself what it is, some time."

"Where do you see any evidence of it?"

"In the unforgivable fact that you're as unhappy as you are."

Rearden could accept any form of reproach, abuse, damnation anyone chose to throw at him; the only human reaction which he would not accept was pity. The stab of a coldly rebellious anger brought him back to the full context of the moment. He spoke, fighting not to acknowledge the nature of the emotion rising within him. "What sort of effrontery are you indulging in? What's your motive?"

"Let us say—to give you the words you need, for the time when you'll need them."

"Why should you want to speak to me on such a subject?"

"In the hope that you will remember it."

What he felt, thought Rearden, was anger at the incomprehensible fact that he had allowed himself to enjoy this conversation. He felt a dim sense of betrayal, the hint of an unknown danger. "Do you expect me to forget what you are?" he asked, knowing that this was what he had forgotten.

"I do not expect you to think of me at all."

Under his anger, the emotion which Rearden would not acknowledge remained unstated and unthought; he knew it only as a hint of pain. Had he faced it, he would have known that he still heard Francisco's voice saying, "I am the only one who will offer it . . . if you will accept it. . . ." He heard the words and the strangely solemn inflection of the quiet voice and an inexplicable answer of his own, something within him that wanted to cry yes, to accept, to tell this man that he accepted, that he needed it—though there was no name for what he needed, it was not gratitude, and he knew that it was not gratitude this man had meant.

Aloud, he said, "I didn't seek to talk to you. But you've asked for it and you're going to hear it. To me, there's only one form of human depravity—the man without a purpose."

"That is true."

"I can forgive all those others, they're not vicious, they're merely helpless. But you—you're the kind who can't be forgiven."

"It is against the sin of forgiveness that I wanted to warn you."

"You had the greatest chance in life. What have you done with it? If you have the mind to understand all the things you said, how can you speak to me at all? How can you face anyone after the sort of irresponsible destruction you've perpetrated in that Mexican business?"

"It is your right to condemn me for it, if you wish."

Dagny stood by the corner of the window recess, listening. They did not notice her. She had seen them together and she had approached, drawn by an impulse she could not explain or resist; it seemed crucially important that she know what these two men said to each other.

She had heard their last few sentences. She had never thought it possible that she would see Francisco taking a beating. He could smash any adversary in any form of encounter. Yet he stood, offering no defense. She knew that it was not indifference; she knew his face well enough to see the effort his calm cost him—she saw the faint line of a muscle pulled tight across his cheek.

"Of all those who live by the ability of others," said Rearden, "you're the one real parasite."

"I have given you grounds to think so."

"Then what right have you to talk about the meaning of being a man? You're the one who has betrayed it."

"I am sorry if I have offended you by what you may rightly consider as a presumption."

Francisco bowed and turned to go. Rearden said involuntarily, not knowing that the question negated his anger, that it was a plea to stop this man and hold him, "What did you want to learn to understand about me?"

Francisco turned. The expression of his face had not changed; it was still a look of gravely courteous respect. "I have learned it," he answered.

Rearden stood watching him as he walked off into the crowd. The figures of a butler, with a crystal dish, and of Dr. Pritchett, stooping to choose another canapé, hid Francisco from sight. Rearden glanced out at the darkness; nothing could be seen there but the wind.

Dagny stepped forward, when he came out of the recess; she smiled, openly inviting conversation. He stopped. It seemed to her that he had stopped reluctantly. She spoke hastily, to break the silence. "Hank, why do you have so many intellectuals of the looter persuasion here? I wouldn't have them in my house."

This was not what she had wanted to say to him. But she did not know what she wanted to say; never before had she felt herself left wordless in his presence.

She saw his eyes narrowing, like a door being closed. "I see no reason why one should not invite them to a party," he answered coldly.

"Oh, I didn't mean to criticize your choice of guests. But . . . Well, I've been trying not to learn which one of them is Bertram Scudder. If I do, I'll slap his face." She tried to sound casual. "I don't want to create a scene, but I'm not sure I'll be able to control myself. I couldn't believe it when somebody told me that Mrs. Rearden had invited him."

"*I* invited him."

"But . . ." Then her voice dropped. "Why?"

"I don't attach any importance to occasions of this kind."

"I'm sorry, Hank. I didn't know you were so tolerant. I'm not."

He said nothing.

"I know you don't like parties. Neither do I. But sometimes I wonder . . . perhaps we're the only ones who were meant to be able to enjoy them."

"I am afraid I have no talent for it."

"Not for this. But do you think any of these people are enjoying it? They're just straining to be more senseless and aimless than usual. To be light and unimportant . . . You know, I think that only if one feels immensely important can one feel truly light."

"I wouldn't know."

"It's just a thought that disturbs me once in a while. . . . I thought it about my first ball. . . . I keep thinking that parties are intended to be celebrations, and celebrations should be only for those who have something to celebrate."

"I have never thought of it."

She could not adapt her words to the rigid formality of his manner; she could not quite believe it. They had always been at ease together, in his office. Now he was like a man in a strait jacket.

"Hank, look at it. If you didn't know any of these people, wouldn't it seem beautiful? The lights and the clothes and all the imagination that went to make it possible . . ." She was looking at the room. She did not notice that he had not followed her glance. He was looking down at the shadows on her naked shoulder, the soft, blue shadows made by the light that fell through the strands of her hair. "Why have we left it all to fools? It should have been ours."

"In what manner?"

"I don't know . . . I've always expected parties to be exciting and brilliant, like some rare drink." She laughed; there was a note of sadness in it. "But I don't drink, either. That's just another symbol that doesn't mean what it was intended to mean." He was silent. She added, "Perhaps there's something that we have missed."

"I am not aware of it."

In a flash of sudden, desolate emptiness, she was glad that he had not understood or responded, feeling dimly that she had revealed too much, yet not knowing what she had revealed. She shrugged, the movement running through the curve of her shoulder like a faint convulsion. "It's just an old illusion of mine," she said indifferently. "Just a mood that comes once every year or two. Let me see the latest steel price index and I'll forget all about it."

She did not know that his eyes were following her, as she walked away from him.

She moved slowly through the room, looking at no one. She noticed a small group huddled by the unlighted fireplace. The room was not cold, but they sat as if they drew comfort from the thought of a non-existent fire.

"I do not know why, but I am growing to be afraid of the dark. No, not now, only when I am alone. What frightens me is night. Night as such."

The speaker was an elderly spinster with an air of breeding and hopelessness. The three women and two men of the group were well dressed, the skin of their faces was smoothly well tended, but they had a manner of anxious caution that kept their voices one tone lower than normal and blurred the differences of their ages, giving them all the same gray look of being spent. It was the look one saw in groups of respectable people everywhere. Dagny stopped and listened.

"But, my dear," one of them asked, "why should it frighten you?"

"I don't know," said the spinster. "I am not afraid of prowlers or robberies or anything of the sort. But I stay awake all night. I fall asleep only when I see the sky turning pale. It is very odd. Every evening, when it grows dark, I get the feeling that this time it is final, that daylight will not return."

"My cousin who lives on the coast of Maine wrote me the same thing," said one of the women.

"Last night," said the spinster, "I stayed awake because of the shooting. There were guns going off all night, way out at sea. There were no flashes. There was nothing. Just those detonations, at long intervals, somewhere in the fog over the Atlantic."

"I read something about it in the paper this morning. Coast Guard target practice."

"Why, no," the spinster said indifferently. "Everybody down on the shore knows what it was. It was Ragnar Danneskjöld. It was the Coast Guard trying to catch him."

"Ragnar Danneskjöld in Delaware Bay?" a woman gasped.

"Oh, yes. They say it is not the first time."

"Did they catch him?"

"No."

"Nobody can catch him," said one of the men.

"The People's State of Norway has offered a million-dollar reward for his head."

"That's an awful lot of money to pay for a pirate's head."

"But how are we going to have any order or security or planning in the world, with a pirate running loose all over the seven seas?"

"Do you know what it was that he seized last night?" said the spinster.

"The big ship with the relief supplies we were sending to the People's State of France."

"How does he dispose of the goods he seizes?"

"Ah, that—nobody knows."

"I met a sailor once, from a ship he'd attacked, who'd seen him in person. He said that Ragnar Danneskjöld has the purest gold hair and the most frightening face on earth, a face with no sign of any feeling. If there ever was a man born without a heart, he's it—the sailor said."

"A nephew of mine saw Ragnar Danneskjöld's ship one night, off the coast of Scotland. He wrote me that he couldn't believe his eyes. It was a better ship than any in the navy of the People's State of England."

"They say he hides in one of those Norwegian fjords where neither God nor man will ever find him. That's where the Vikings used to hide in the Middle Ages."

"There's a reward on his head offered by the People's State of Portugal, too. And by the People's State of Turkey."

"They say it's a national scandal in Norway. He comes from one of their best families. The family lost its money generations ago, but the name is of the noblest. The ruins of their castle are still in existence. His father is a bishop. His father has disowned him and excommunicated him. But it had no effect."

"Did you know that Ragnar Danneskjöld went to school in this country? Sure. The Patrick Henry University."

"Not really?"

"Oh yes. You can look it up."

"What bothers me is . . . You know, I don't like it. I don't like it that he's now appearing right here, in our own waters. I thought things like that could happen only in the wastelands. Only in Europe. But a big-scale outlaw of that kind operating in Delaware in our day and age!"

"He's been seen off Nantucket, too. And at Bar Harbor. The newspapers have been asked not to write about it."

"Why?"

"They don't want people to know that the navy can't cope with him."

"I don't like it. It feels funny. It's like something out of the Dark Ages."

Dagny glanced up. She saw Francisco d'Anconia standing a few steps away. He was looking at her with a kind of stressed curiosity; his eyes were mocking.

"It's a strange world we're living in," said the spinster, her voice low.

"I read an article," said one of the women tonelessly. "It said that times of trouble are good for us. It is good that people are growing poorer. To accept privations is a moral virtue."

"I suppose so," said another, without conviction.

"We must not worry. I heard a speech that said it is useless to worry or to blame anyone. Nobody can help what he does, that is the way things made him. There is nothing we can do about anything. We must learn to bear it."

"What's the use anyway? What is man's fate? Hasn't it always been to hope, but never to achieve? The wise man is the one who does not attempt to hope."

"That is the right attitude to take."

"I don't know . . . I don't know what is right any more . . . How can we ever know?"

"Oh well, who is John Galt?"

Dagny turned brusquely and started away from them. One of the women followed her.

"But I do know it," said the woman, in the soft, mysterious tone of sharing a secret.

"You know what?"

"I know who is John Galt."

"Who?" Dagny asked tensely, stopping.

"I know a man who knew John Galt in person. This man is an old friend of a great-aunt of mine. He was there and he saw it happen. Do you know the legend of Atlantis, Miss Taggart?"

"What?"

"Atlantis."

"Why . . . vaguely."

"The Isles of the Blessed. That is what the Greeks called it, thousands of years ago. They said Atlantis was a place where hero-spirits lived in a happiness unknown to the rest of the earth. A place which only the spirits of heroes could enter, and they reached it without dying, because they carried the secret of life within them. Atlantis was lost to mankind, even then. But the Greeks knew that it had existed. They tried to find it. Some of them said it was underground, hidden in the heart of the earth. But most of them said it was an island. A radiant island in the Western Ocean. Perhaps what they were thinking of was America. They never found it. For centuries afterward, men said it was only a legend. They did not believe it, but they never stopped looking for it, because they knew that that was what they had to find."

"Well, what about John Galt?"

"He found it."

Dagny's interest was gone. "Who was he?"

"John Galt was a millionaire, a man of inestimable wealth. He was sailing his yacht one night, in mid-Atlantic, fighting the worst storm ever wreaked upon the world, when he found it. He saw it in the depth, where it had sunk to escape the reach of men. He saw the towers of Atlantis shining on the bottom of the ocean. It was a sight of such kind that when one had seen it, one could no longer wish to look at the rest of the earth. John Galt sank his ship and went down with his entire crew. They all chose to do it. My friend was the only one who survived."

"How interesting."

"My friend saw it with his own eyes," said the woman, offended. "It happened many years ago. But John Galt's family hushed up the story."

"And what happened to his fortune? I don't recall ever hearing of a Galt fortune."

"It went down with him." She added belligerently, "You don't have to believe it."

"Miss Taggart doesn't," said Francisco d'Anconia. "I do."

They turned. He had followed them and he stood looking at them with the insolence of exaggerated earnestness.

"Have you ever had faith in anything, Señor d'Anconia?" the woman asked angrily.

"No, madame."

He chuckled at her brusque departure. Dagny asked coldly, "What's the joke?"

"The joke's on that fool woman. She doesn't know that she was telling you the truth."

"Do you expect me to believe that?"

"No."

"Then what do you find so amusing?"

"Oh, a great many things here. Don't you?"

"No."

"Well, *that's* one of the things I find amusing."

"Francisco, will you leave me alone?"

"But I have. Didn't you notice that you were first to speak to me tonight?"

"Why do you keep watching me?"

"Curiosity."

"About what?"

"Your reaction to the things which you don't find amusing."

"Why should you care about my reaction to anything?"

"That is my own way of having a good time, which, incidentally, you are not having, are you, Dagny? Besides, you're the only woman worth watching here."

She stood defiantly still, because the way he looked at her demanded an angry escape. She stood as she always did, straight and taut, her head lifted impatiently. It was the unfeminine pose of an executive. But her naked shoulder betrayed the fragility of the body under the black dress, and the pose made her most truly a woman. The proud strength became a challenge to someone's superior strength, and the fragility a reminder that the challenge could be broken. She was not conscious of it. She had met no one able to see it.

He said, looking down at her body, "Dagny, what a magnificent waste!"

She had to turn and escape. She felt herself blushing, for the first time in years: blushing because she knew suddenly that the sentence named what she had felt all evening.

She ran, trying not to think. The music stopped her. It was a sudden blast from the radio. She noticed Mort Liddy, who had turned it on, waving his arms to a group of friends, yelling, "That's it! That's it! I want you to hear it!"

The great burst of sound was the opening chords of Halley's Fourth Concerto. It rose in tortured triumph, speaking its denial of pain, its hymn to a distant vision. Then the notes broke. It was as if a handful of mud and pebbles had been flung at the music, and what followed was the sound of the rolling and the dripping. It was Halley's Concerto swung into a popular tune. It was Halley's melody torn apart, its holes stuffed with hiccoughs. The great statement of joy had become the giggling of a barroom. Yet it was still the remnant of Halley's melody that gave it form; it was the melody that supported it like a spinal cord.

"Pretty good?" Mort Liddy was smiling at his friends, boastfully and nervously. "Pretty good, eh? Best movie score of the year. Got me a prize. Got me a long-term contract. Yeah, this was my score for *Heaven's in Your Backyard*."

Dagny stood, staring at the room, as if one sense could replace another, as if sight could wipe out sound. She moved her head in a slow circle, trying to find an anchor somewhere. She saw Francisco leaning against a column, his arms crossed; he was looking straight at her; he was laughing.

Don't shake like this, she thought. Get out of here. This was the approach of an anger she could not control. She thought: Say nothing. Walk steadily. Get out.

She had started walking, cautiously, very slowly. She heard Lillian's words and stopped. Lillian had said it many times this evening, in answer to the same question, but it was the first time that Dagny heard it.

"This?" Lillian was saying, extending her arm with the metal bracelet for the inspection of two smartly groomed women. "Why, no, it's not from a hardware store, it's a very special gift from my husband. Oh, yes, of course it's hideous. But don't you see? It's supposed to be priceless. Of course, I'd exchange it for a common diamond bracelet any time, but somehow nobody will offer me one for it, even though it is so very, very valuable. Why? My dear, it's the first thing ever made of Rearden Metal."

Dagny did not see the room. She did not hear the music. She felt the pressure of dead stillness against her eardrums. She did not know the moment that preceded, or the moments that were to follow. She did not know those involved, neither herself, nor Lillian, nor Rearden, nor the meaning of her own action. It was a single instant, blasted out of context. She had heard. She was looking at the bracelet of green-blue metal.

She felt the movement of something being torn off her wrist, and she heard her own voice saying in the great stillness, very calmly, a voice cold as a skeleton, naked of emotion, "If you are not the coward that I think you are, you will exchange it."

On the palm of her hand, she was extending her diamond bracelet to Lillian.

"You're not serious, Miss Taggart?" said a woman's voice.

It was not Lillian's voice. Lillian's eyes were looking straight at her. She saw them. Lillian knew that she was serious.

"Give me that bracelet," said Dagny, lifting her palm higher, the diamond band glittering across it.

"This is horrible!" cried some woman. It was strange that the cry stood out so sharply. Then Dagny realized that there were people standing around them and that they all stood in silence. She was hearing sounds now, even the music; it was Halley's mangled Concerto, somewhere far away.

She saw Rearden's face. It looked as if something within him were mangled, like the music; she did not know by what. He was watching them.

Lillian's mouth moved into an upturned crescent. It resembled a smile. She snapped the metal bracelet open, dropped it on Dagny's palm and took the diamond band.

"Thank you, Miss Taggart," she said.

Dagny's fingers closed about the metal. She felt that; she felt nothing else.

Lillian turned, because Rearden had approached her. He took the diamond bracelet from her hand. He clasped it on her wrist, raised her hand to his lips and kissed it.

He did not look at Dagny.

Lillian laughed, gaily, easily, attractively, bringing the room back to its normal mood.

"You may have it back, Miss Taggart, when you change your mind," she said.

Dagny had turned away. She felt calm and free. The pressure was gone. The need to get out had vanished.

She clasped the metal bracelet on her wrist. She liked the feel of its weight against her skin. Inexplicably, she felt a touch of feminine vanity, the kind she had never experienced before: the desire to be seen wearing this particular ornament.

From a distance, she heard snatches of indignant voices: "The most offensive gesture I've ever seen. . . . It was vicious. . . . I'm glad Lillian took her up on it. . . . Serves her right, if she feels like throwing a few thousand dollars away. . . ."

For the rest of the evening, Rearden remained by the side of his wife. He shared her conversations, he laughed with her friends, he was suddenly the devoted, attentive, admiring husband.

He was crossing the room, carrying a tray with drinks requested by someone in Lillian's group—an unbecoming act of informality which nobody had ever seen him perform—when Dagny approached him. She stopped and looked up at him, as if they were alone in his office. She stood like an executive, her head lifted. He looked down at her. In the line of his glance, from the fingertips of her one hand to her face, her body was naked but for his metal bracelet.

"I'm sorry, Hank," she said, "but I had to do it."

His eyes remained expressionless. Yet she was suddenly certain that she knew what he felt: he wanted to slap her face.

"It was not necessary," he answered coldly, and walked on.

*　*　*

It was very late when Rearden entered his wife's bedroom. She was still awake. A lamp burned on her bedside table.

She lay in bed, propped up on pillows of pale green linen. Her bed-jacket was pale green satin, worn with the untouched perfection of a window model; its lustrous folds looked as if the crinkle of tissue paper still lingered among them. The light, shaded to a tone of apple blossoms, fell on a table that held a book, a glass of fruit juice, and toilet accessories of silver glittering like instruments in a surgeon's case. Her arms had a tinge of porcelain. There was a touch of pale pink lipstick on her mouth. She showed no sign of exhaustion after the party—no sign of life to be exhausted. The place was a decorator's display of a lady groomed for sleep, not to be disturbed.

He still wore his dress clothes; his tie was loose, and a strand of hair hung over his face. She glanced at him without astonishment, as if she knew what the last hour in his room had done to him.

He looked at her silently. He had not entered her room for a long time. He stood, wishing he had not entered it now.

"Isn't it customary to talk, Henry?"

"If you wish."

"I wish you'd send one of your brilliant experts from the mills to take a look at our furnace. Do you know that it went out during the party and Simons had a terrible time getting it started again? . . . Mrs. Weston says that our best achievement is our cook—she loved the hors d'oeuvres. . . . Balph Eubank said a very funny thing about you, he said you're a crusader with a factory's chimney smoke for a plume. . . . I'm glad you don't like Francisco d'Anconia. I can't stand him."

He did not care to explain his presence, or to disguise defeat, or to admit it by leaving. Suddenly, it did not matter to him what she guessed or felt. He walked to the window and stood, looking out.

Why had she married him?—he thought. It was a question he had not asked himself on their wedding day, eight years ago. Since then, in tortured loneliness, he had asked it many times. He had found no answer.

It was not for position, he thought, or for money. She came from an old family that had both. Her family's name was not among the most distinguished and their fortune was modest, but both were sufficient to let her be included in the top circles of New York's society, where he had met her. Nine years ago, he had appeared in New York like an explosion, in the glare of the success of Rearden Steel, a success that had been thought impossible by the city's experts. It was his indifference that made him spectacular. He did not know that he was expected to attempt to buy his way into society and that they anticipated the pleasure of rejecting him. He had no time to notice their disappointment.

He attended, reluctantly, a few social occasions to which he was invited by men who sought his favor. He did not know, but they knew, that his courteous politeness was condescension toward the people who had expected to snub him, the people who had said that the age of achievement was past.

It was Lillian's austerity that attracted him—the conflict between her austerity and her behavior. He had never liked anyone or expected to be liked. He found himself held by the spectacle of a woman who was obviously pursuing him but with obvious reluctance, as if against her own will, as if fighting a desire she resented. It was she who planned that they should meet, then faced him coldly, as if not caring that he knew it. She spoke little; she had an air of mystery that seemed to tell him he would never break through her proud detachment, and an air of amusement, mocking her own desire and his.

He had not known many women. He had moved toward his goal, sweeping aside everything that did not pertain to it in the world and in himself. His dedication to his work was like one of the fires he dealt with, a fire that burned every lesser element, every impurity out of the white stream of a single metal. He was incapable of halfway concerns. But there were times when he felt a sudden access of desire, so violent that it could not be given to a casual encounter. He had surrendered to it, on a few rare occasions through the years, with women he had thought he liked. He had been left feeling an angry emptiness—because he had sought an act of triumph, though he had not known of what nature, but the response he received was only a woman's acceptance of a casual pleasure, and he knew too clearly that what he had won had no meaning. He was left, not with a sense of attainment, but with a sense of his own degradation. He grew to hate his desire. He fought it. He came to believe the doctrine that this desire was wholly physical, a desire, not of consciousness, but of matter, and he rebelled against the thought that his flesh could be free to choose and that its choice was impervious to the will of his mind. He had spent his life in mines and mills, shaping matter to his wishes by the power of his brain—and he found it intolerable that he should be unable to control the matter of his own body. He fought it. He had won his every battle against inanimate nature; but this was a battle he lost.

It was the difficulty of the conquest that made him want Lillian. She seemed to be a woman who expected and deserved a pedestal; this made him want to drag her down to his bed. To drag her down, were the words in his mind; they gave him a dark pleasure, the sense of a victory worth winning.

He could not understand why—he thought it was an obscene conflict, the sign of some secret depravity within him—why he felt, at the same time, a profound pride at the thought of granting to a woman the title of his wife. The feeling was solemn and shining; it was almost as if he felt that he wished to honor a woman by the act of possessing her. Lillian seemed to fit the image he had not known he held, had not known he wished to find; he saw the grace, the pride, the purity; the rest was in himself; he did not know that he was looking at a reflection.

He remembered the day when Lillian came from New York to his office, of her own sudden choice, and asked him to take her through his mills. He heard a soft, low, breathless tone—the tone of admiration—growing in her voice, as she questioned him about his work and looked at the place around her. He looked at her graceful figure moving against the bursts of furnace flame, and at the light, swift steps of her high heels stumbling through drifts of slag, as she walked resolutely by his side. The look in her eyes, when she watched a heat of steel being poured, was like his own feeling for it made visible to him. When her eyes moved up to his face, he saw the same look, but intensified to a degree that seemed to make her helpless and silent. It was at dinner, that evening, that he asked her to marry him.

It took him some time after his marriage before he admitted to himself that this was torture. He still remembered the night when he admitted it, when he told himself—the veins of his wrists pulled tight as he stood by the bed, looking down at Lillian—that he deserved the torture and that he would endure it. Lillian was not looking at him; she was adjusting her hair. "May I go to sleep now?" she asked.

She had never objected; she had never refused him anything; she submitted whenever he wished. She submitted in the manner of complying with the rule that it was, at times, her duty to become an inanimate object turned over to her husband's use.

She did not censure him. She made it clear that she took it for granted that men had degrading instincts which constituted the secret, ugly part of marriage. She was condescendingly tolerant. She smiled, in amused distaste, at the intensity of what he experienced. "It's the most undignified pastime I know of," she said to him once, "but I have never entertained the illusion that men are superior to animals."

His desire for her had died in the first week of their marriage. What remained was only a need which he was unable to destroy. He had never entered a whorehouse; he thought, at times, that the self-loathing he would experience there could be no worse than what he felt when he was driven to enter his wife's bedroom.

He would often find her reading a book. She would put it aside, with a white ribbon to mark the pages. When he lay exhausted, his eyes closed, still breathing in gasps, she would turn on the light, pick up the book and continue her reading.

He told himself that he deserved the torture, because he had wished never to touch her again and was unable to maintain his decision. He despised himself for that. He despised a need which now held no shred of joy or meaning, which had become the mere need of a woman's body, an anonymous body that belonged to a woman whom he had to forget while he held it. He became convinced that the need was depravity.

He did not condemn Lillian. He felt a dreary, indifferent respect for her. His hatred of his own desire had made him accept the doctrine that women were pure and that a pure woman was one incapable of physical pleasure.

Through the quiet agony of the years of his marriage, there had been one thought which he would not permit himself to consider: the thought of infidelity. He had given his word. He intended to keep it. It was not loyalty to Lillian; it was not the person of Lillian that he wished to protect from dishonor—but the person of his wife.

He thought of that now, standing at the window. He had not wanted to enter her room. He had fought against it. He had fought, more fiercely, against knowing the particular reason why he would not be able to withstand it tonight. Then, seeing her, he had known suddenly that he would not touch her. The reason which had driven him here tonight was the reason which made it impossible for him.

He stood still, feeling free of desire, feeling the bleak relief of indifference to his body, to this room, even to his presence here. He had turned away from her, not to see her lacquered chastity. What he thought he should feel was respect; what he felt was revulsion.

". . . but Dr. Pritchett said that our culture is dying because our universities have to depend on the alms of the meat packers, the steel puddlers and the purveyors of breakfast cereals."

Why had she married him?—he thought. That bright, crisp voice was not talking at random. She knew why he had come here. She knew what it would do to him to see her pick up a silver buffer and go on talking gaily, polishing her fingernails. She was talking about the party. But she did not mention Bertram Scudder—or Dagny Taggart.

What had she sought in marrying him? He felt the presence of some cold, driving purpose within her—but found nothing to condemn. She had never tried to use him. She made no demands on him. She found no satisfaction in the prestige of industrial power—she spurned it—she preferred her own circle of friends. She was not after money—she spent little—she was indifferent to the kind of extravagance he could have afforded. He had no right to accuse her, he thought, or ever to break the bond. She was a woman of honor in their marriage. She wanted nothing material from him.

He turned and looked at her wearily.

"Next time you give a party," he said, "stick to your own crowd. Don't invite what you think are my friends. I don't care to meet them socially."

She laughed, startled and pleased. "I don't blame you, darling," she said.

He walked out, adding nothing else.

What did she want from him?—he thought. What was she after? In the universe as he knew it, there was no answer.

THE EXPLOITERS AND THE EXPLOITED

The rails rose through the rocks to the oil derricks and the oil derricks rose to the sky. Dagny stood on the bridge, looking up at the crest of the hill where the sun hit a spot of metal on the top of the highest rigging. It looked like a white torch lighted over the snow on the ridges of Wyatt Oil.

By spring, she thought, the track would meet the line growing toward it from Cheyenne. She let her eyes follow the green-blue rails that started from the derricks, came down, went across the bridge and past her. She turned her head to follow them through the miles of clear air, as they went on in great curves hung on the sides of the mountains, far to the end of the new track, where a locomotive crane, like an arm of naked bones and nerves, moved tensely against the sky.

A tractor went past her, loaded with green-blue bolts. The sound of drills came as a steady shudder from far below, where men swung on metal cables, cutting the straight stone drop of the canyon wall to reinforce the abutments of the bridge. Down the track, she could see men working, their arms stiff with the tension of their muscles as they gripped the handles of electric tie tampers.

"Muscles, Miss Taggart," Ben Nealy, the contractor, had said to her, "muscles—that's all it takes to build anything in the world."

No contractor equal to McNamara seemed to exist anywhere. She had taken the best she could find. No engineer on the Taggart staff could be trusted to supervise the job; all of them were skeptical about the new metal. "Frankly, Miss Taggart," her chief engineer had said, "since it is an experiment that nobody has ever attempted before, I do not think it's fair that it should be my responsibility." "It's mine," she had answered. He was a man in his forties, who still preserved the breezy manner of the college from which he had graduated. Once, Taggart Transcontinental had had a chief engineer, a silent, gray-haired, self-educated man, who could not be matched on any railroad. He had resigned, five years ago.

She glanced down over the bridge. She was standing on a slender beam of steel above a gorge that had cracked the mountains to a depth of fifteen hundred feet. Far at the bottom, she could distinguish the dim outlines of a dry river bed, of piled boulders, of trees contorted by centuries. She wondered whether boulders, tree trunks and muscles could ever bridge that canyon. She wondered why she found herself thinking suddenly that cave-dwellers had lived naked on the bottom of that canyon for ages.

She looked up at the Wyatt oil fields. The track broke into sidings among the wells. She saw the small disks of switches dotted against the snow. They were metal switches, of the kind that were scattered in thousands, unnoticed, throughout the country—but these were sparkling in the sun and the sparks were greenish-blue. What they meant to her was hour upon hour of speaking quietly, evenly, patiently, trying to hit the centerless target that was the person of Mr. Mowen, president of the Amalgamated Switch and Signal Company, Inc., of Connecticut. "But, Miss Taggart, my dear Miss Taggart! My company has served your company for generations, why, your grandfather was the first customer of my grandfather, so you cannot doubt our eagerness to do anything you ask, but—did you say switches made of Rearden Metal?"

"Yes."

"But, Miss Taggart! Consider what it would mean, having to work with that metal. Do you know that the stuff won't melt under less than four thousand degrees? . . . Great? Well, maybe that's great for motor manufacturers, but what I'm thinking of is that it means a new type of furnace, a new process entirely, men to be trained, schedules upset, work rules shot, everything balled up and then God only knows whether it will come out right or not! . . . How do you know, Miss Taggart? How can you know, when it's never been done before? . . . Well, I can't say that that metal is good and I can't say that it isn't. . . . Well, no, I can't tell whether it's a product of genius, as you say, or just another fraud as a great many people are saying, Miss Taggart, a great many. . . . Well, no, I can't say that it does matter one way or the other, because who am I to take a chance on a job of this kind?"

She had doubled the price of her order. Rearden had sent two metallurgists to train Mowen's men, to teach, to show, to explain every step of the process, and had paid the salaries of Mowen's men while they were being trained.

She looked at the spikes in the rail at her feet. They meant the night when she had heard that Summit Casting of Illinois, the only company willing to make spikes of Rearden Metal, had gone bankrupt, with half of her order undelivered. She had flown to Chicago, that night, she had got three lawyers, a judge and a state legislator out of bed, she had bribed two of them and threatened the others, she had obtained a paper that was an emergency permit of a legality no one would ever be able to untangle, she had had the padlocked doors of the Summit Casting plant unlocked and a random, half-dressed crew working at the smelters before the windows had turned gray with daylight. The crews had remained at work, under a Taggart engineer and a Rearden metallurgist. The rebuilding of the Rio Norte Line was not held up.

She listened to the sound of the drills. The work had been held up once, when the drilling for the bridge abutments was stopped. "I couldn't help it, Miss Taggart," Ben Nealy had said, offended. "You know how fast drill heads wear out. I had them on order, but Incorporated Tool ran into a little trouble, they couldn't help it either, Associated Steel was delayed in delivering the steel to them, so there's nothing we can do but wait. It's no use getting upset, Miss Taggart. I'm doing my best."

"I've hired you to do a job, not to do your best—whatever that is."

"That's a funny thing to say. That's an unpopular attitude, Miss Taggart, mighty unpopular."

"Forget Incorporated Tool. Forget the steel. Order the drill heads made of Rearden Metal."

"Not me. I've had enough trouble with the damn stuff in that rail of yours. I'm not going to mess up my own equipment."

"A drill head of Rearden Metal will outlast three of steel."

"Maybe."

"I said order them made."

"Who's going to pay for it?"

"I am."

"Who's going to find somebody to make them?"

She had telephoned Rearden. He had found an abandoned tool plant, long since out of business. Within an hour, he had purchased it from the relatives of its last owner. Within a day, the plant had been reopened. Within a week, drill heads of Rearden Metal had been delivered to the bridge in Colorado.

She looked at the bridge. It represented a problem badly solved, but she had had to accept it. The bridge, twelve hundred feet of steel across the black gap, was built in the days of Nat Taggart's son. It was long past the stage of safety; it had been patched with stringers of steel, then of iron, then of wood; it was barely worth the patching. She had thought of a new bridge of Rearden Metal. She had asked her chief engineer to submit a design and an estimate of the cost. The design he had submitted was the scheme of a steel bridge badly scaled down to the greater strength of the new metal; the cost made the project impossible to consider.

"I beg your pardon, Miss Taggart," he had said, offended. "I don't know what you mean when you say that I haven't made use of the metal. This design is an adaptation of the best bridges on record. What else did you expect?"

"A new method of construction."

"What do you mean, a new method?"

"I mean that when men got structural steel, they did not use it to build steel copies of wooden bridges." She had added wearily, "Get me an estimate on what we'll need to make our old bridge last for another five years."

"Yes, Miss Taggart," he had said cheerfully. "If we reinforce it with steel—"

"We'll reinforce it with Rearden Metal."

"Yes, Miss Taggart," he had said coldly.

She looked at the snow-covered mountains. Her job had seemed hard at times, in New York. She had stopped for blank moments in the middle of her office, paralyzed by despair at the rigidity of time which she could not stretch any further—on a day when urgent appointments had succeeded one another, when she had discussed worn Diesels, rotting freight cars, failing signal systems, falling revenues, while thinking of the latest emergency on the Rio Norte construction; when she had talked, with the vision of two streaks of green-blue metal cutting across her mind; when she had interrupted the discussions, realizing suddenly why a certain news item had disturbed her, and seized the telephone receiver to call long-distance, to call her contractor, to say, "Where do you get the food from, for your men? . . . I thought so. Well, Barton and Jones of Denver went bankrupt yesterday. Better find another supplier at once, if you don't want to have a famine on your hands." She had been building the line from her desk in New York. It had seemed hard. But now she was looking at the track. It was growing. It would be done on time.

She heard sharp, hurried footsteps, and turned. A man was coming up the track. He was tall and young, his head of black hair was hatless in the cold wind, he wore a workman's leather jacket, but he did not look like a workman, there was too imperious an assurance in the way he walked. She could not recognize the face until he came closer. It was Ellis Wyatt. She had not seen him since that one interview in her office.

He approached, stopped, looked at her and smiled.

"Hello, Dagny," he said.

In a single shock of emotion, she knew everything the two words were intended to tell her. It was forgiveness, understanding, acknowledgment. It was a salute.

She laughed, like a child, in happiness that things should be as right as that.

"Hello," she said, extending her hand.

His hand held hers an instant longer than a greeting required. It was their signature under a score settled and understood.

"Tell Nealy to put up new snow fences for a mile and a half on Granada Pass," he said. "The old ones are rotted. They won't stand through another storm. Send him a rotary plow. What he's got is a piece of junk that wouldn't sweep a back yard. The big snows are coming any day now."

She considered him for a moment. "How often have you been doing this?" she asked.

"What?"

"Coming to watch the work."

"Every now and then. When I have the time. Why?"

"Were you here the night when they had the rock slide?"

"Yes."

"I was surprised how quickly and well they cleared the track, when I got the reports about it. It made me think that Nealy was a better man than I had thought."

"He isn't."

"Was it you who organized the system of moving his day's supplies down to the line?"

"Sure. His men used to spend half their time hunting for things. Tell him to watch his water tanks. They'll freeze on him one of these nights. See if you can get him a new ditcher. I don't like the looks of the one he's got. Check on his wiring system."

She looked at him for a moment. "Thanks, Ellis," she said.

He smiled and walked on. She watched him as he walked across the bridge, as he started up the long rise toward his derricks.

"He thinks he owns the place, doesn't he?"

She turned, startled. Ben Nealy had approached her; his thumb was pointing at Ellis Wyatt.

"What place?"

"The railroad, Miss Taggart. Your railroad. Or the whole world maybe. That's what he thinks."

Ben Nealy was a bulky man with a soft, sullen face. His eyes were stubborn and blank. In the bluish light of the snow, his skin had the tinge of butter.

"What does he keep hanging around here for?" he said. "As if nobody knew their business but him. The snooty show-off. Who does he think he is?"

"God damn you," said Dagny evenly, not raising her voice.

Nealy could never know what had made her say it. But some part of him, in some way of his own, knew it: the shocking thing to her was that he was not shocked. He said nothing.

"Let's go to your quarters," she said wearily, pointing to an old railway coach on a spur in the distance. "Have somebody there to take notes."

"Now about those crossties, Miss Taggart," he said hastily as they started. "Mr. Coleman of your office okayed them. He didn't say anything about too much bark. I don't see why you think they're—"

"I said you're going to replace them."

When she came out of the coach, exhausted by two hours of effort to be patient, to instruct, to explain—she saw an automobile parked on the torn dirt road below, a black two-seater, sparkling and new. A new car was an astonishing sight anywhere; one did not see them often.

She glanced around and gasped at the sight of the tall figure standing at the foot of the bridge. It was Hank Rearden; she had not expected to find him in Colorado. He seemed absorbed in calculations, pencil and notebook in hand. His clothes attracted attention, like his car and for the same reason; he wore a simple trenchcoat and a hat with a slanting brim, but they were of such good quality, so flagrantly expensive that they appeared ostentatious among the seedy garments of the crowds everywhere, the more ostentatious because worn so naturally.

She noticed suddenly that she was running toward him; she had lost all trace of exhaustion. Then she remembered that she had not seen him since the party. She stopped.

He saw her, he waved to her in a gesture of pleased, astonished greeting, and he walked forward to meet her. He was smiling.

"Hello," he said. "Your first trip to the job?"

"My fifth, in three months."

"I didn't know you were here. Nobody told me."

"I thought you'd break down some day."

"Break down?"

"Enough to come and see this. There's your Metal. How do you like it?"

He glanced around. "If you ever decide to quit the railroad business, let me know."

"You'd give me a job?"

"Any time."

She looked at him for a moment. "You're only half-kidding, Hank. I think you'd like it—having me ask you for a job. Having me for an employee instead of a customer. Giving me orders to obey."

"Yes. I would."

She said, her face hard, "Don't quit the steel business. I won't promise you a job on the railroad."

He laughed. "Don't try it."

"What?"

"To win any battle when I set the terms."

She did not answer. She was struck by what the words made her feel; it was not an emotion, but a physical sensation of pleasure, which she could not name or understand.

"Incidentally," he said, "this is not my first trip. I was here yesterday."

"You were? Why?"

"Oh, I came to Colorado on some business of my own, so I thought I'd take a look at this."

"What are you after?"

"Why do you assume that I'm after anything?"

"You wouldn't waste time coming here just to look. Not twice."

He laughed. "True." He pointed at the bridge. "I'm after that."

"What about it?"

"It's ready for the scrap heap."

"Do you suppose that I don't know it?"

"I saw the specifications of your order for Rearden Metal members for that bridge. You're wasting your money. The difference between what you're planning to spend on a makeshift that will last a couple of years, and the cost of a new Rearden Metal bridge, is comparatively so little that I don't see why you want to bother preserving this museum piece."

"I've thought of a new Rearden Metal bridge. I've had my engineers give me an estimate."

"What did they tell you?"

"Two million dollars."

"Good God!"

"What would you say?"

"Eight hundred thousand."

She looked at him. She knew that he never spoke idly. She asked, trying to sound calm, "How?"

"Like this."

He showed her his notebook. She saw the disjoined notations he had made, a great many figures, a few rough sketches. She understood his scheme before he had finished explaining it. She did not notice that they had sat down, that they were sitting on a pile of frozen lumber, that her legs were pressed to the rough planks and she could feel the cold through her thin stockings. They were bent together over a few scraps of paper which could make it possible for thousands of tons of freight to cross a cut of empty space. His voice sounded sharp and clear, while he explained thrusts, pulls, loads, wind pressures. The bridge was to be a single twelve-hundred-foot truss span. He had devised a new type of truss. It had never been made before and could not be made except with members that had the strength and the lightness of Rearden Metal.

"Hank," she asked, "did you invent this in two days?"

"Hell, no. I 'invented' it long before I had Rearden Metal. I figured it out while making steel for bridges. I wanted a metal with which one would be able to do this, among other things. I came here just to see your particular problem for myself."

He chuckled, when he saw the slow movement of her hand across her eyes and the line of bitterness in the set of her mouth, as if she were trying to wipe out the things against which she had fought such an exhausting, cheerless battle.

"This is only a rough scheme," he said, "but I believe you see what can be done?"

"I can't tell you all that I see, Hank."

"Don't bother. I know it."

"You're saving Taggart Transcontinental for the second time."

"You used to be a better psychologist than that."

"What do you mean?"

"Why should I give a damn about saving Taggart Transcontinental? Don't you know that I want to have a bridge of Rearden Metal to show the country?"

"Yes, Hank. I know it."

"There are too many people yelping that rails of Rearden Metal are unsafe. So I thought I'd give them something real to yelp about. Let them see a bridge of Rearden Metal."

She looked at him and laughed aloud in simple delight.

"Now what's that?" he asked.

"Hank, I don't know anyone, not anyone in the world, who'd think of such an answer to people, in such circumstances—except you."

"What about you? Would you want to make the answer with me and face the same screaming?"

"You knew I would."

"Yes. I knew it."

He glanced at her, his eyes narrowed; he did not laugh as she had, but the glance was an equivalent.

She remembered suddenly their last meeting, at the party. The memory seemed incredible. Their ease with each other—the strange, light-headed feeling, which included the knowledge that it was the only sense of ease either of them found anywhere—made the thought of hostility impossible. Yet she knew that the party had taken place; he acted as if it had not.

They walked to the edge of the canyon. Together, they looked at the dark drop, at the rise of rock beyond it, at the sun high on the derricks of Wyatt Oil. She stood, her feet apart on the frozen stones, braced firmly against the wind. She could feel, without touching it, the line of his chest behind her shoulder. The wind beat her coat against his legs.

"Hank, do you think we can build it in time? There are only six months left."

"Sure. It will take less time and labor than any other type of bridge. Let me have my engineers work out the basic scheme and submit it to you. No obligation on your part. Just take a look at it and see for yourself whether you'll be able to afford it. You will. Then you can let your college boys work out the details."

"What about the Metal?"

"I'll get the Metal rolled if I have to throw every other order out of the mills."

"You'll get it rolled on so short a notice?"

"Have I ever held you up on an order?"

"No. But the way things are going nowadays, you might not be able to help it."

"Who do you think you're talking to—Orren Boyle?"

She laughed. "All right. Let me have the drawings as soon as possible. I'll take a look and let you know within forty-eight hours. As to my college boys, they—" She stopped, frowning. "Hank, why is it so hard to find good men for any job nowadays?"

"I don't know . . ."

He looked at the lines of the mountains cut across the sky. A thin jet of smoke was rising from a distant valley.

"Have you seen the new towns of Colorado and the factories?" he asked.

"Yes."

"It's great, isn't it?—to see the kind of men they've gathered here from every corner of the country. All of them young, all of them starting on a shoestring and moving mountains."

"What mountain have *you* decided to move?"

"Why?"

"What are you doing in Colorado?"

He smiled. "Looking at a mining property."

"What sort?"

"Copper."

"Good God, don't you have enough to do?"

"I know it's a complicated job. But the supply of copper is becoming completely unreliable. There doesn't seem to be a single first-rate company left in the business in this country—and I don't want to deal with d'Anconia Copper. I don't trust that playboy."

"I don't blame you," she said, looking away.

"So if there's no competent person left to do it, I'll have to mine my own copper, as I mine my own iron ore. I can't take any chances on being held up by all those failures and shortages. I need a great deal of copper for Rearden Metal."

"Have you bought the mine?"

"Not yet. There are a few problems to solve. Getting the men, the equipment, the transportation."

"Oh . . . !" She chuckled. "Going to speak to me about building a branch line?"

"Might. There's no limit to what's possible in this state. Do you know that they have every kind of natural resource here, waiting, untouched? And the way their factories are growing! I feel ten years younger when I come here."

"I don't." She was looking east, past the mountains. "I think of the contrast, all over the rest of the Taggart system. There's less to carry, less tonnage produced each year. It's as if . . . Hank, what's wrong with the country?"

"I don't know."

"I keep thinking of what they told us in school about the sun losing energy, growing colder each year. I remember wondering, then, what it would be like in the last days of the world. I think it would be . . . like this. Growing colder and things stopping."

"I never believed that story. I thought by the time the sun was exhausted, men would find a substitute."

"You did? Funny. I thought that, too."

He pointed at the column of smoke. "There's your new sunrise. It's going to feed the rest."

"If it's not stopped."

"Do you think it can be stopped?"

She looked at the rail under her feet. "No," she said.

He smiled. He looked down at the rail, then let his eyes move along the track, up the sides of the mountains, to the distant crane. She saw two things, as if, for a moment, the two stood alone in her field of vision: the lines of his profile and the green-blue cord coiling through space.

"We've done it, haven't we?" he said.

In payment for every effort, for every sleepless night, for every silent thrust against despair, this moment was all she wanted. "Yes. We have."

She looked away, noticed an old crane on a siding, and thought that its cables were worn and would need replacing: This was the great clarity of being beyond emotion, after the reward of having felt everything one could feel. Their achievement, she thought, and one moment of acknowledging it, of possessing it together—what greater intimacy could one share? Now she was free for the simplest, most commonplace concerns of the moment, because nothing could be meaningless within her sight.

She wondered what made her certain that he felt as she did. He turned abruptly and started toward his car. She followed. They did not look at each other.

"I'm due to leave for the East in an hour," he said.

She pointed at the car. "Where did you get that?"

"Here. It's a Hammond. Hammond of Colorado—they're the only people who're still making a good car. I just bought it, on this trip."

"Wonderful job."

"Yes, isn't it?"

"Going to drive it back to New York?"

"No. I'm having it shipped. I flew my plane down here."

"Oh, you did? I drove down from Cheyenne—I had to see the line —but I'm anxious to get home as fast as possible. Would you take me along? Can I fly back with you?"

He did not answer at once. She noticed the empty moment of a pause. "I'm sorry," he said; she wondered whether she imagined the note of abruptness in his voice. "I'm not flying back to New York. I'm going to Minnesota."

"Oh well, then I'll try to get on an air liner, if I can find one today."

She watched his car vanish down the winding road. She drove to the airport an hour later. The place was a small field at the bottom of a break in the desolate chain of mountains. There were patches of snow on the hard, pitted earth. The pole of a beacon stood at one side, trailing wires to the ground; the other poles had been knocked down by a storm.

A lonely attendant came to meet her. "No, Miss Taggart," he said regretfully, "no planes till day after tomorrow. There's only one transcontinental liner every two days, you know, and the one that was due today has been grounded, down in Arizona. Engine trouble, as usual." He added, "It's a pity you didn't get here a bit sooner. Mr. Rearden took off for New York, in his private plane, just a little while ago."

"He wasn't flying to New York, was he?"

"Why, yes. He said so."

"Are you sure?"

"He said he had an appointment there tonight."

She looked at the sky to the east, blankly, without moving. She had no clue to any reason, nothing to give her a foothold, nothing with which to weigh this or fight it or understand.

* * *

"Damn these streets!" said James Taggart. "We're going to be late."

Dagny glanced ahead, past the back of the chauffeur. Through the circle made by a windshield wiper on the sleet-streaked glass, she saw black, worn, glistening car tops strung in a motionless line. Far ahead, the smear of a red lantern, low over the ground, marked a street excavation.

"There's something wrong on every other street," said Taggart irritably. "Why doesn't somebody fix them?"

She leaned back against the seat, tightening the collar of her wrap. She felt exhausted at the end of a day she had started at her desk, in her office, at seven A.M.; a day she had broken off, uncompleted, to rush home and dress, because she had promised Jim to speak at the dinner of the New York Business Council. "They want us to give them a talk about Rearden Metal," he had said. "You can do it so much better than I. It's very important that we present a good case. There's such a controversy about Rearden Metal."

Sitting beside him in his car, she regretted that she had agreed. She looked at the streets of New York and thought of the race between metal and time, between the rails of the Rio Norte Line and the passing days. She felt as if her nerves were being pulled tight by the stillness of the car, by the guilt of wasting an evening when she could not afford to waste an hour.

"With all those attacks on Rearden that one hears everywhere," said Taggart, "he might need a few friends."

She glanced at him incredulously. "You mean you want to stand by him?"

He did not answer at once; he asked, his voice bleak, "That report of the special committee of the National Council of Metal Industries—what do you think of it?"

"You know what I think of it."

"They said Rearden Metal is a threat to public safety. They said its chemical composition is unsound, it's brittle, it's decomposing molecularly, and it will crack suddenly, without warning . . ." He stopped, as if begging for an answer. She did not answer. He asked anxiously, "You haven't changed your mind about it, have you?"

"About what?"

"About that metal."

"No, Jim, I have not changed my mind."

"They're experts, though . . . the men on that committee. . . . Top experts . . . Chief metallurgists for the biggest corporations, with a string of degrees from universities all over the country . . ." He said it unhappily, as if he were begging her to make him doubt these men and their verdict.

She watched him, puzzled; this was not like him.

The car jerked forward. It moved slowly through a gap in a plank barrier, past the hole of a broken water main. She saw the new pipe stacked by the excavation; the pipe bore a trademark: Stockton Foundry, Colorado. She looked away; she wished she were not reminded of Colorado.

"I can't understand it . . ." said Taggart miserably. "The top experts of the National Council of Metal Industries . . ."

"Who's the president of the National Council of Metal Industries, Jim? Orren Boyle, isn't it?"

Taggart did not turn to her, but his jaw snapped open. "If that fat slob thinks he can—" he started, but stopped and did not finish.

She looked up at a street lamp on the corner. It was a globe of glass filled with light. It hung, secure from storm, lighting boarded windows and cracked sidewalks, as their only guardian. At the end of the street, across the river, against the glow of a factory, she saw the thin tracing of a power station. A truck went by, hiding her view. It was the kind of truck that fed the power station—a tank truck, its bright new paint impervious to sleet, green with white letters: Wyatt Oil, Colorado.

"Dagny, have you heard about that discussion at the structural steel workers' union meeting in Detroit?"

"No. What discussion?"

"It was in all the newspapers. They debated whether their members should or should not be permitted to work with Rearden Metal. They didn't reach a decision, but that was enough for the contractor who was going to take a chance on Rearden Metal. He cancelled his order, but fast! . . . What if . . . what if everybody decides against it?"

"Let them."

A dot of light was rising in a straight line to the top of an invisible tower. It was the elevator of a great hotel. The car went past the building's alley. Men were moving a heavy, crated piece of equipment from a truck into the basement. She saw the name on the crate: Nielsen Motors, Colorado.

"I don't like that resolution passed by the convention of the grade school teachers of New Mexico," said Taggart.

"What resolution?"

"They resolved that it was their opinion that children should not be permitted to ride on the new Rio Norte Line of Taggart Transcontinental when it's completed, because it is unsafe. . . . They said it specifically, the new line of *Taggart Transcontinental*. It was in all the newspapers. It's terrible publicity for us. . . . Dagny, what do you think we should do to answer them?"

"Run the first train on the new Rio Norte Line."

He remained silent for a long time. He looked strangely dejected. She could not understand it: he did not gloat, he did not use the opinions of his favorite authorities against her, he seemed to be pleading for reassurance.

A car flashed past them; she had a moment's glimpse of power—a smooth, confident motion and a shining body. She knew the make of the car: Hammond, Colorado.

"Dagny, are we . . . are we going to have that line built . . . on time?"

It was strange to hear a note of plain emotion in his voice, the uncomplicated sound of animal fear.

"God help this city, if we don't!" she answered.

The car turned a corner. Above the black roofs of the city, she saw the page of the calendar, hit by the white glare of a spotlight. It said: January 29.

"Dan Conway is a bastard!"

The words broke out suddenly, as if he could not hold them any longer.

She looked at him, bewildered. "Why?"

"He refused to sell us the Colorado track of the Phoenix-Durango."

"You didn't—" She had to stop. She started again, keeping her voice flat in order not to scream. "You haven't approached him about it?"

"Of course I have!"

"You didn't expect him . . . to sell it . . . to *you?*"

"Why not?" His hysterically belligerent manner was back. "I offered him more than anybody else did. We wouldn't have had the expense of tearing it up and carting it off, we could have used it as is. And it would have been wonderful publicity for us—that we're giving up the Rearden Metal track in deference to public opinion. It would have been worth every penny of it in good will! But the son of a bitch refused. He's actually declared that not a foot of rail would be sold to Taggart Transcontinental. He's selling it piecemeal to any stray comer, to one-horse railroads in Arkansas or North Dakota, selling it at a loss, way under what I offered him, the bastard! Doesn't even want to take a profit! And you should see those vultures flocking to him! They know they'd never have a chance to get rail anywhere else!"

She sat, her head bowed. She could not bear to look at him.

"I think it's contrary to the intent of the Anti-dog-eat-dog Rule," he said angrily. "I think it was the intent and purpose of the National Alliance of Railroads to protect the essential systems, not the jerkwaters of North Dakota. But I can't get the Alliance to vote on it now, because they're all down there, outbidding one another for that rail!"

She said slowly, as if she wished it were possible to wear gloves to handle the words, "I see why you want me to defend Rearden Metal."

"I don't know what you're—"

"Shut up, Jim," she said quietly.

He remained silent for a moment. Then he drew his head back and drawled defiantly, "You'd better do a good job of defending Rearden Metal, because Bertram Scudder can get pretty sarcastic."

"Bertram Scudder?"

"He's going to be one of the speakers tonight."

"One of the . . . You didn't tell me there were to be other speakers."

"Well . . . I . . . What difference does that make? You're not afraid of him, are you?"

"The New York *Business* Council . . . and you invite Bertram Scudder?"

"Why not? Don't you think it's smart? He doesn't have any hard feelings toward businessmen, not really. He's accepted the invitation. We want to be broad-minded and hear all sides and maybe win him over. . . . Well, what are you staring at? You'll be able to beat him, won't you?"

". . . to beat him?"

"On the air. It's going to be a radio broadcast. You're going to debate with him the question: 'Is Rearden Metal a lethal product of greed?' "

She leaned forward. She pulled open the glass partition of the front seat, ordering, "Stop the car!"

She did not hear what Taggart was saying. She noticed dimly that his voice rose to screams: "They're waiting! . . . Five hundred people at the dinner, and a national hook-up! . . . You can't do this to me!" He seized her arm, screaming, "But why?"

"You goddamn fool, do you think I consider their question debatable?"

The car stopped, she leaped out and ran.

The first thing she noticed after a while, was her slippers. She was walking slowly, normally, and it was strange to feel iced stone under the thin soles of black satin sandals. She pushed her hair back, off her forehead, and felt drops of sleet melting on her palm.

She was quiet now; the blinding anger was gone; she felt nothing but a gray weariness. Her head ached a little, she realized that she was hungry and remembered that she was to have had dinner at the Business Council. She walked on. She did not want to eat. She thought she would get a cup of coffee somewhere, then take a cab home.

She glanced around her. There were no cabs in sight. She did not know the neighborhood. It did not seem to be a good one. She saw an empty stretch of space across the street, an abandoned park encircled by a jagged line that began as distant skyscrapers and came down to factory chimneys; she saw a few lights in the windows of dilapidated houses, a few small, grimy shops closed for the night, and the fog of the East River two blocks away.

She started back toward the center of the city. The black shape of a ruin rose before her. It had been an office building, long ago; she saw the sky through the naked steel skeleton and the angular remnants of the bricks that had crumbled. In the shadow of the ruin, like a blade of grass fighting to live at the roots of a dead giant, there stood a small diner. Its windows were a bright band of glass and light. She went in.

There was a clean counter inside, with a shining strip of chromium at the edges. There was a bright metal boiler and the odor of coffee. A few derelicts sat at the counter, a husky, elderly man stood behind it, the sleeves of his clean white shirt rolled at the elbows. The warm air made her realize, in simple gratitude, that she had been cold. She pulled her black velvet cape tight about her and sat down at the counter.

"A cup of coffee, please," she said.

The men looked at her without curiosity. They did not seem astonished to see a woman in evening clothes enter a slum diner; nothing astonished anyone, these days. The owner turned impassively to fill her order; there was, in his stolid indifference, the kind of mercifulness that asks no questions.

She could not tell whether the four at the counter were beggars or working men; neither clothes nor manner showed the difference, these days. The owner placed a mug of coffee before her. She closed both hands about it, finding enjoyment in its warmth.

She glanced around her and thought, in habitual professional calculation, how wonderful it was that one could buy so much for a dime. Her eyes moved from the stainless steel cylinder of the coffee boiler to the cast-iron griddle, to the glass shelves, to the enameled sink, to the chromium blades of a mixer. The owner was making toast. She found pleasure in watching the ingenuity of an open belt that moved slowly, carrying slices of bread past glowing electric coils. Then she saw the name stamped on the toaster: Marsh, Colorado.

Her head fell down on her arm on the counter.

"It's no use, lady," said the old bum beside her.

She had to raise her head. She had to smile in amusement, at him and at herself.

"It isn't?" she asked.

"No. Forget it. You're only fooling yourself."

"About what?"

"About anything being worth a damn. It's dust, lady, all of it, dust and blood. Don't believe the dreams they pump you full of, and you won't get hurt."

"What dreams?"

"The stories they tell you when you're young—about the human spirit. There isn't any human spirit. Man is just a low-grade animal, without intellect, without soul, without virtues or moral values. An animal with only two capacities: to eat and to reproduce."

His gaunt face, with staring eyes and shrunken features that had been delicate, still retained a trace of distinction. He looked like the hulk of an evangelist or a professor of esthetics who had spent years in contemplation in obscure museums. She wondered what had destroyed him, what error on the way could bring a man to this.

"You go through life looking for beauty, for greatness, for some sublime achievement," he said. "And what do you find? A lot of trick machinery for making upholstered cars or inner-spring mattresses."

"What's wrong with inner-spring mattresses?" said a man who looked like a truck driver. "Don't mind him, lady. He likes to hear himself talk. He don't mean no harm."

"Man's only talent is an ignoble cunning for satisfying the needs of his body," said the old bum. "No intelligence is required for that. Don't believe the stories about man's mind, his spirit, his ideals, his sense of unlimited ambition."

"I don't," said a young boy who sat at the end of the counter. He wore a coat ripped across one shoulder; his square-shaped mouth seemed formed by the bitterness of a lifetime.

"Spirit?" said the old bum. "There's no spirit involved in manufacturing or in sex. Yet these are man's only concerns. Matter—that's all men know or care about. As witness our great industries—the only accomplishment of our alleged civilization—built by vulgar materialists with the aims, the interests and the moral sense of hogs. It doesn't take any morality to turn out a ten-ton truck on an assembly line."

"What is morality?" she asked.

"Judgment to distinguish right and wrong, vision to see the truth, courage to act upon it, dedication to that which is good, integrity to stand by the good at any price. But where does one find it?"

The young boy made a sound that was half-chuckle, half-sneer: "Who is John Galt?"

She drank the coffee, concerned with nothing but the pleasure of feeling as if the hot liquid were reviving the arteries of her body.

"I can tell you," said a small, shriveled tramp who wore a cap pulled low over his eyes. "I know."

Nobody heard him or paid any attention. The young boy was watching Dagny with a kind of fierce, purposeless intensity.

"You're not afraid," he said to her suddenly, without explanation, a flat statement in a brusque, lifeless voice that had a note of wonder.

She looked at him. "No," she said, "I'm not."

"I know who is John Galt," said the tramp. "It's a secret, but I know it."

"Who?" she asked without interest.

"An explorer," said the tramp. "The greatest explorer that ever lived. The man who found the fountain of youth."

"Give me another cup. Black," said the old bum, pushing his cup across the counter.

"John Galt spent years looking for it. He crossed oceans, and he crossed deserts, and he went down into forgotten mines, miles under the earth. But he found it on the top of a mountain. It took him ten years to climb that mountain. It broke every bone in his body, it tore the skin off his hands, it made him lose his home, his name, his love. But he climbed it. He found the fountain of youth, which he wanted to bring down to men. Only he never came back."

"Why didn't he?" she asked.

"Because he found that it couldn't be brought down."

* * *

The man who sat in front of Rearden's desk had vague features and a manner devoid of all emphasis, so that one could form no specific image of his face nor detect the driving motive of his person. His only mark of distinction seemed to be a bulbous nose, a bit too large for the rest of him; his manner was meek, but it conveyed a preposterous hint, the hint of a threat deliberately kept furtive, yet intended to be recognized. Rearden could not understand the purpose of his visit. He was Dr. Potter, who held some undefined position with the State Science Institute.

"What do you want?" Rearden asked for the third time.

"It is the social aspect that I am asking you to consider, Mr. Rearden," the man said softly. "I urge you to take note of the age we're living in. Our economy is not ready for it."

"For what?"

"Our economy is in a state of extremely precarious equilibrium. We all have to pool our efforts to save it from collapse."

"Well, what is it you want me to do?"

"These are the considerations which I was asked to call to your attention. I am from the State Science Institute, Mr. Rearden."

"You've said so before. But what did you wish to see me about?"

"The State Science Institute does not hold a favorable opinion of Rearden Metal."

"You've said that, too."

"Isn't that a factor which you must take into consideration?"

"No."

The light was growing dim in the broad windows of the office. The days were short. Rearden saw the irregular shadow of the nose on the man's cheek, and the pale eyes watching him; the glance was vague, but its direction purposeful.

"The State Science Institute represents the best brains of the country, Mr. Rearden."

"So I'm told."

"Surely you do not want to pit your own judgment against theirs?"

"I do."

The man looked at Rearden as if pleading for help, as if Rearden had broken an unwritten code which demanded that he should have understood long ago. Rearden offered no help.

"Is this all you wanted to know?" he asked.

"It's only a question of time, Mr. Rearden," the man said placatingly. "Just a temporary delay. Just to give our economy a chance to get stabilized. If you'd only wait for a couple of years—"

Rearden chuckled, gaily, contemptuously. "So that's what you're after? Want me to take Rearden Metal off the market? Why?"

"Only for a few years, Mr. Rearden. Only until—"

"Look," said Rearden. "Now I'll ask you a question: did your scientists decide that Rearden Metal is not what I claim it is?"

"We have not committed ourselves as to that."

"Did they decide it's no good?"

"It is the social impact of a product that must be considered. We are thinking in terms of the country as a whole, we are concerned with the public welfare and the terrible crisis of the present moment, which—"

"Is Rearden Metal good or not?"

"If we view the picture from the angle of the alarming growth of unemployment, which at present—"

"Is Rearden Metal good?"

"At a time of desperate steel shortage, we cannot afford to permit the expansion of a steel company which produces too much, because it might throw out of business the companies which produce too little, thus creating an unbalanced economy which—"

"Are you going to answer my question?"

The man shrugged. "Questions of value are relative. If Rearden Metal is not good, it's a physical danger to the public. If it *is* good—it's a social danger."

"If you have anything to say to me about the physical danger of Rearden Metal, say it. Drop the rest of it. Fast. I don't speak that language."

"But surely questions of social welfare—"

"Drop it."

The man looked bewildered and lost, as if the ground had been cut from under his feet. In a moment, he asked helplessly, "But what, then, is your chief concern?"

"The market."

"How do you mean?"

"There's a market for Rearden Metal and I intend to take full advantage of it."

"Isn't the market somewhat hypothetical? The public response to your metal has not been encouraging. Except for the order from Taggart Transcontinental, you haven't obtained any major—"

"Well, then, if you think the public won't go for it, what are you worrying about?"

"If the public doesn't go for it, you will take a heavy loss, Mr. Rearden."

"That's my worry, not yours."

"Whereas, if you adopt a more co-operative attitude and agree to wait for a few years—"

"Why should I wait?"

"But I believe I have made it clear that the State Science Institute does not approve of the appearance of Rearden Metal on the metallurgical scene at the present time."

"Why should I give a damn about that?"

The man sighed. "You are a very difficult man, Mr. Rearden."

The sky of the late afternoon was growing heavy, as if thickening against the glass of the windowpanes. The outlines of the man's figure seemed to dissolve into a blob among the sharp, straight planes of the furniture.

"I gave you this appointment," said Rearden, "because you told me that you wished to discuss something of extreme importance. If this is all you had to say, you will please excuse me now. I am very busy."

The man settled back in his chair. "I believe you have spent ten years of research on Rearden Metal," he said. "How much has it cost you?"

Rearden glanced up: he could not understand the drift of the question, yet there was an undisguised purposefulness in the man's voice; the voice had hardened.

"One and a half million dollars," said Rearden.

"How much will you take for it?"

Rearden had to let a moment pass. He could not believe it. "For what?" he asked, his voice low.

"For all rights to Rearden Metal."

"I think you had better get out of here," said Rearden.

"There is no call for such an attitude. You are a businessman. I am offering you a business proposition. You may name your own price."

"The *rights* to Rearden Metal are not for sale."

"I am in a position to speak of large sums of money. *Government* money."

Rearden sat without moving, the muscles of his cheeks pulled tight; but his glance was indifferent, focused only by the faint pull of morbid curiosity.

"You are a businessman, Mr. Rearden. This is a proposition which you cannot afford to ignore. On the one hand, you are gambling against great odds, you are bucking an unfavorable public opinion, you run a good chance of losing every penny you put into Rearden Metal. On the other hand, we can relieve you of the risk and the responsibility, at an impressive profit, an immediate profit, much larger than you could hope to realize from the sale of the metal for the next twenty years."

"The State Science Institute is a scientific establishment, not a commercial one," said Rearden. "What is it that they're so afraid of?"

"You are using ugly, unnecessary words, Mr. Rearden. I am endeavoring to suggest that we keep the discussion on a friendly plane. The matter is serious."

"I am beginning to see that."

"We are offering you a blank check on what is, as you realize, an unlimited account. What else can you want? Name your price."

"The sale of the rights to Rearden Metal is not open to discussion. If you have anything else to say, please say it and leave."

The man leaned back, looked at Rearden incredulously and asked, "What are you after?"

"I? What do you mean?"

"You're in business to make money, aren't you?"

"I am."

"You want to make as big a profit as possible, don't you?"

"I do."

"Then why do you want to struggle for years, squeezing out your gains in the form of pennies per ton—rather than accept a fortune for Rearden Metal? Why?"

"Because it's *mine*. Do you understand the word?"

The man sighed and rose to his feet. "I hope you will not have cause to regret your decision, Mr. Rearden," he said; the tone of his voice was suggesting the opposite.

"Good day," said Rearden.

"I think I must tell you that the State Science Institute may issue an official statement condemning Rearden Metal."

"That is their privilege."

"Such a statement would make things more difficult for you."

"Undoubtedly."

"As to further consequences . . ." The man shrugged. "This is not the day for people who refuse to co-operate. In this age, one needs friends. You are not a popular man, Mr. Rearden."

"What are you trying to say?"

"Surely, you understand."

"I don't."

"Society is a complex structure. There are so many different issues awaiting decision, hanging by a thin thread. We can never tell when one such issue may be decided and what may be the decisive factor in a delicate balance. Do I make myself clear?"

"No."

The red flame of poured steel shot through the twilight. An orange glow, the color of deep gold, hit the wall behind Rearden's desk. The glow moved gently across his forehead. His face had an unmoving serenity.

"The State Science Institute is a *government* organization, Mr. Rearden. There are certain bills pending in the Legislature, which may be passed at any moment. Businessmen are peculiarly vulnerable these days. I am sure you understand me."

Rearden rose to his feet. He was smiling. He looked as if all tension had left him.

"No, Dr. Potter," he said, "I don't understand. If I did, I'd have to kill you."

The man walked to the door, then stopped and looked at Rearden in a way which, for once, was simple human curiosity. Rearden stood motionless against the moving glow on the wall; he stood casually, his hands in his pockets.

"Would you tell me," the man asked, "just between us, it's only my personal curiosity—why are you doing this?"

Rearden answered quietly, "I'll tell you. You won't understand. You see, it's because Rearden Metal is *good.*"

* * *

Dagny could not understand Mr. Mowen's motive. The Amalgamated Switch and Signal Company had suddenly given notice that they would not complete her order. Nothing had happened, she could find no cause for it and they would give no explanation.

She had hurried to Connecticut, to see Mr. Mowen in person, but the sole result of the interview was a heavier, grayer weight of bewilderment in her mind. Mr. Mowen stated that he would not continue to make switches of Rearden Metal. For sole explanation, he said, avoiding her eyes, "Too many people don't like it."

"What? Rearden Metal or your making the switches?"

"Both, I guess . . . People don't like it . . . I don't want any trouble."

"What kind of trouble?"

"Any kind."

"Have you heard a single thing against Rearden Metal that's true?"

"Aw, who knows what's true? . . . That resolution of the National Council of Metal Industries said—"

"Look, you've worked with metals all your life. For the last four months, you've worked with Rearden Metal. Don't you know that it's the greatest thing you've ever handled?" He did not answer. "Don't you know it?" He looked away. "Don't you know what's true?"

"Hell, Miss Taggart, I'm in business. I'm only a little guy. I just want to make money."

"How do you think one makes it?"

But she knew that it was useless. Looking at Mr. Mowen's face, at the eyes which she could not catch, she felt as she had felt once on a lonely section of track, when a storm blew down the telephone wires: that communications were cut and that words had become sounds which transmitted nothing.

It was useless to argue, she thought, and to wonder about people who would neither refute an argument nor accept it. Sitting restlessly in the train, on her way back to New York, she told herself that Mr. Mowen did not matter, that nothing mattered now, except finding somebody else to manufacture the switches. She was wrestling with a list of names in her mind wondering who would be easiest to convince, to beg or to bribe.

She knew, the moment she entered the anteroom of her office, that something had happened. She saw the unnatural stillness, with the faces of her staff turned to her as if her entrance were the moment they had all waited for, hoped for and dreaded.

Eddie Willers rose to his feet and started toward the door of her office, as if knowing that she would understand and follow. She had seen his face. No matter what it was, she thought, she wished it had not hurt him quite so badly.

"The State Science Institute," he said quietly, when they were alone in her office, "has issued a statement warning people against the use of Rearden Metal." He added, "It was on the radio. It's in the afternoon papers."

"What did they say?"

"Dagny, they didn't say it! . . . They haven't really said it, yet it's there—and it isn't. That's what's monstrous about it."

His effort was focused on keeping his voice quiet; he could not control his words. The words were forced out of him by the unbelieving, bewildered indignation of a child screaming in denial at his first encounter with evil.

"What did they say, Eddie?"

"They . . . You'd have to read it." He pointed to the newspaper he had left on her desk. "They haven't said that Rearden Metal is bad. They haven't said that it's unsafe. What they've done is . . ." His hands spread and dropped in a gesture of futility.

She saw at a glance what they had done. She saw the sentences: "It may be possible that after a period of heavy usage, a sudden fissure may appear, though the length of this period cannot be predicted. . . . The possibility of a molecular reaction, at present unknown, cannot be entirely discounted. . . . Although the tensile strength of the metal is obviously demonstrable, certain questions in regard to its behavior under unusual stress are not to be ruled out. . . . Although there is no evidence to support the contention that the use of the metal should be prohibited, a further study of its properties would be of value."

"We can't fight it. It can't be answered," Eddie was saying slowly. "We can't demand a retraction. We can't show them our tests or prove anything. They've said nothing. They haven't said a thing that could be refuted and embarrass them professionally. It's the job of a coward. You'd expect it from some con-man or blackmailer. But, Dagny! It's the State Science Institute!"

She nodded silently. She stood, her eyes fixed on some point beyond the window. At the end of a dark street, the bulbs of an electric sign kept going on and off, as if winking at her maliciously.

Eddie gathered his strength and said in the tone of a military report, "Taggart stock has crashed. Ben Nealy quit. The National Brotherhood of Road and Track Workers has forbidden its members to work on the Rio Norte Line. Jim has left town."

She took her hat and coat off, walked across the room and slowly, very deliberately sat down at her desk.

She noticed a large brown envelope lying before her; it bore the letterhead of Rearden Steel.

"That came by special messenger, right after you left," said Eddie.

She put her hand on the envelope, but did not open it. She knew what it was: the drawings of the bridge.

After a while, she asked, "Who issued that statement?"

Eddie glanced at her and smiled briefly, bitterly, shaking his head. "No," he said. "I thought of that, too. I called the Institute long-distance and asked them. No, it was issued by the office of Dr. Floyd Ferris, their co-ordinator."

She said nothing.

"But still! Dr. Stadler is the head of that Institute. He *is* the Institute. He must have known about it. He permitted it. If it's done, it's done in his name . . . Dr. Robert Stadler . . . Do you remember

. . . when we were in college . . . how we used to talk about the great names in the world . . . the men of pure intellect . . . and we always chose his name as one of them, and—" He stopped. "I'm sorry, Dagny. I know it's no use saying anything. Only—"

She sat, her hand pressed to the brown envelope.

"Dagny," he asked, his voice low, "what is happening to people? Why did that statement succeed? It's such an obvious smear-job, so obvious and so rotten. You'd think a decent person would throw it in the gutter. How could"—his voice was breaking in gentle, desperate, rebellious anger—"how could they accept it? Didn't they read it? Didn't they see? Don't they think? Dagny! What is it in people that lets them do this—and how can we live with it?"

"Quiet, Eddie," she said, "quiet. Don't be afraid."

* * *

The building of the State Science Institute stood over a river of New Hampshire, on a lonely hillside, halfway between the river and the sky. From a distance, it looked like a solitary monument in a virgin forest. The trees were carefully planted, the roads were laid out as a park, the roof tops of a small town could be seen in a valley some miles away. But nothing had been allowed to come too close and detract from the building's austerity.

The white marble of the walls gave it a classical grandeur; the composition of its rectangular masses gave it the cleanliness and beauty of a modern plant. It was an inspired structure. From across the river, people looked at it with reverence and thought of it as a monument to a living man whose character had the nobility of the building's lines. Over the entrance, a dedication was cut into the marble: "To the fearless mind. To the inviolate truth." In a quiet aisle, in a bare corridor, a small brass plate, such as dozens of other name plates on other doors, said: Dr. Robert Stadler.

At the age of twenty-seven, Dr. Robert Stadler had written a treatise on cosmic rays, which demolished most of the theories held by the scientists who preceded him. Those who followed, found his achievement somewhere at the base of any line of inquiry they undertook. At the age of thirty, he was recognized as the greatest physicist of his time. At thirty-two, he became head of the Department of Physics of the Patrick Henry University, in the days when the great University still deserved its glory. It was of Dr. Robert Stadler that a writer had said: "Perhaps, among the phenomena of the universe which he is studying, none is so miraculous as the brain of Dr. Robert Stadler himself." It was Dr. Robert Stadler who had once corrected a student: "Free scientific inquiry? The first adjective is redundant."

At the age of forty, Dr. Robert Stadler addressed the nation, endorsing the establishment of a State Science Institute. "Set science free of the rule of the dollar," he pleaded. The issue had hung in the balance; an obscure group of scientists had quietly forced a bill through its long way to the floor of the Legislature; there had been some public hesitation about the bill, some doubt, an uneasiness no one could define. The name of Dr. Robert Stadler acted upon the country like the cosmic rays he studied: it pierced any barrier. The nation built the white marble edifice as a personal present to one of its greatest men.

Dr. Stadler's office at the Institute was a small room that looked like the office of the bookkeeper of an unsuccessful firm. There was a cheap desk of ugly yellow oak, a filing cabinet, two chairs, and a blackboard chalked with mathematical formulas. Sitting on one of the chairs against a blank wall, Dagny thought that the office had an air of ostentation and elegance, together: ostentation, because it seemed intended to suggest that the owner was great enough to permit himself such a setting; elegance, because he truly needed nothing else.

She had met Dr. Stadler on a few occasions, at banquets given by leading businessmen or great engineering societies, in honor of some solemn cause or another. She had attended the occasions as reluctantly as he did, and had found that he liked to talk to her. "Miss Taggart," he had said to her once, "I never expect to encounter intelligence. That I should find it here is such an astonishing relief!" She had come to his office, remembering that sentence. She sat, watching him in the manner of a scientist: assuming nothing, discarding emotion, seeking only to observe and to understand.

"Miss Taggart," he said gaily, "I'm curious about you. I'm curious whenever anything upsets a precedent. As a rule, visitors are a painful duty to me. I'm frankly astonished that I should feel such a simple pleasure in seeing you here. Do you know what it's like to feel suddenly that one can talk without the strain of trying to force some sort of understanding out of a vacuum?"

He sat on the edge of his desk, his manner gaily informal. He was not tall, and his slenderness gave him an air of youthful energy, almost of boyish zest. His thin face was ageless; it was a homely face, but the great forehead and the large gray eyes held such an arresting intelligence that one could notice nothing else. There were wrinkles of humor in the corners of the eyes, and faint lines of bitterness in the corners of the mouth. He did not look like a man in his early fifties; the slightly graying hair was his only sign of age.

"Tell me more about yourself," he said. "I always meant to ask you what you're doing in such an unlikely career as heavy industry and how you can stand those people."

"I cannot take too much of your time, Dr. Stadler." She spoke with polite, impersonal precision. "And the matter I came to discuss is extremely important."

He laughed. *"There's* a sign of the businessman—wanting to come to the point at once. Well, by all means. But don't worry about my time—it's yours. Now, what was it you said you wanted to discuss? Oh yes. Rearden Metal. Not exactly one of the subjects on which I'm best informed, but if there's anything I can do for you—" His hand moved in a gesture of invitation.

"Do you know the statement issued by this Institute in regard to Rearden Metal?"

He frowned slightly. "Yes, I've heard about it."

"Have you read it?"

"No."

"It was intended to prevent the use of Rearden Metal."

"Yes, yes, I gathered that much."

"Could you tell me why?"

He spread his hands; they were attractive hands—long and bony, beautiful in their suggestion of nervous energy and strength. "I really wouldn't know. That is the province of Dr. Ferris. I'm sure he had his reasons. Would you like to speak to Dr. Ferris?"

"No. Are you familiar with the metallurgical nature of Rearden Metal, Dr. Stadler?"

"Why, yes, a little. But tell me, why are you concerned about it?"

A flicker of astonishment rose and died in her eyes; she answered without change in the impersonal tone of her voice, "I am building a branch line with rails of Rearden Metal, which—"

"Oh, but of course! I did hear something about it. You must forgive me, I don't read the newspapers as regularly as I should. It's *your* railroad that's building that new branch, isn't it?"

"The existence of my railroad depends upon the completion of that branch—and, I think, eventually, the existence of this country will depend on it as well."

The wrinkles of amusement deepened about his eyes. "Can you make such a statement with positive assurance, Miss Taggart? I couldn't."

"In this case?"

"In any case. Nobody can tell what the course of a country's future may be. It is not a matter of calculable trends, but a chaos subject to the rule of the moment, in which anything is possible."

"Do you think that production is necessary to the existence of a country, Dr. Stadler?"

"Why, yes, yes, of course."

"The building of our branch line has been stopped by the statement of this Institute."

He did not smile and he did not answer.

"Does that statement represent your conclusion about the nature of Rearden Metal?" she asked.

"I have said that I have not read it." There was an edge of sharpness in his voice.

She opened her bag, took out a newspaper clipping and extended it to him. "Would you read it and tell me whether this is a language which science may properly speak?"

He glanced through the clipping, smiled contemptuously and tossed it aside with a gesture of distaste. "Disgusting, isn't it?" he said. "But what can you do when you deal with people?"

She looked at him, not understanding. "You do not approve of that statement?"

He shrugged. "My approval or disapproval would be irrelevant."

"Have you formed a conclusion of your own about Rearden Metal?"

"Well, metallurgy is not exactly—what shall we say?—my specialty."

"Have you examined any data on Rearden Metal?"

"Miss Taggart, I don't see the point of your questions." His voice sounded faintly impatient.

"I would like to know your personal verdict on Rearden Metal."

"For what purpose?"

"So that I may give it to the press."

He got up. "That is quite impossible."

She said, her voice strained with the effort of trying to force understanding, "I will submit to you all the information necessary to form a conclusive judgment."

"I cannot issue any public statements about it."

"Why not?"

"The situation is much too complex to explain in a casual discussion."

"But if you should find that Rearden Metal is, in fact, an extremely valuable product which—"

"That is beside the point."

"The value of Rearden Metal is beside the point?"

"There are other issues involved, besides questions of fact."

She asked, not quite believing that she had heard him right, "What other issues is science concerned with, besides questions of fact?"

The bitter lines of his mouth sharpened into the suggestion of a smile. "Miss Taggart, you do not understand the problems of scientists."

She said slowly, as if she were seeing it suddenly in time with her words, "I believe that you do know what Rearden Metal really is."

He shrugged. "Yes. I know. From such information as I've seen, it appears to be a remarkable thing. Quite a brilliant achievement—as far as technology is concerned." He was pacing impatiently across the office. "In fact, I should like, some day, to order a special laboratory motor that would stand just such high temperatures as Rearden Metal can take. It would be very valuable in connection with certain phenomena I should like to observe. I have found that when particles are accelerated to a speed approaching the speed of light, they—"

"Dr. Stadler," she asked slowly, "you know the truth, yet you will not state it publicly?"

"Miss Taggart, you are using an abstract term, when we are dealing with a matter of practical reality."

"We are dealing with a matter of science."

"Science? Aren't you confusing the standards involved? It is only in the realm of pure science that truth is an absolute criterion. When we deal with applied science, with technology—we deal with people. And when we deal with people, considerations other than truth enter the question."

"What considerations?"

"I am not a technologist, Miss Taggart. I have no talent or taste for dealing with people. I cannot become involved in so-called practical matters."

"That statement was issued in your name."

"I had nothing to do with it!"

"The name of this Institute is your responsibility."

"That's a perfectly unwarranted assumption."

"People think that the honor of your name is the guarantee behind any action of this Institute."

"I can't help what people think—if they think at all!"

"They accepted your statement. It was a lie."

"How can one deal in truth when one deals with the public?"

"I don't understand you," she said very quietly.

"Questions of truth do not enter into social issues. No principles have ever had any effect on society."

"What, then, directs men's actions?"

He shrugged. "The expediency of the moment."

"Dr. Stadler," she said, "I think I must tell you the meaning and the consequences of the fact that the construction of my branch line is being stopped. I am stopped, in the name of public safety, because I am using the best rail ever produced. In six months, if I do not complete that line, the best industrial section of the country will be left without transportation. It will be destroyed, because it was the best and there were men who thought it expedient to seize a share of its wealth."

"Well, that may be vicious, unjust, calamitous—but such is life in society. Somebody is always sacrificed, as a rule unjustly; there is no other way to live among men. What can any one person do?"

"You can state the truth about Rearden Metal."

He did not answer.

"I could beg you to do it in order to save me. I could beg you to do it in order to avert a national disaster. But I won't. These may not be valid reasons. There is only one reason: you must say it, because it is true."

"I was not consulted about that statement!" The cry broke out involuntarily. "I wouldn't have allowed it! I don't like it any better than you do! But I can't issue a public denial!"

"You were not consulted? Then shouldn't you want to find out the reasons behind that statement?"

"I can't destroy the Institute now!"

"Shouldn't you want to find out the reasons?"

"I know the reasons! They won't tell me, but I know. And I can't say that I blame them, either."

"Would you tell me?"

"I'll tell you, if you wish. It's the truth that you want, isn't it? Dr. Ferris cannot help it, if the morons who vote the funds for this Institute insist on what they call results. They are incapable of conceiving of such a thing as abstract science. They can judge it only in terms of the latest gadget it has produced for them. I do not know how Dr. Ferris has managed to keep this Institute in existence, I can only marvel at his practical ability. I don't believe he ever was a first-rate scientist—but what a priceless valet of science! I know that he has been facing a grave problem lately. He's kept me out of it, he spares me all that, but I do hear rumors. People have been criticizing the Institute, because, they say, we have not produced enough. The public has been demanding economy. In times like these, when their fat little comforts are threatened, you may be sure that science is the first thing men will sacrifice. This is the only establishment left. There are practically no private research foundations any longer. Look at the greedy ruffians who run our industries. You cannot expect them to support science."

"Who is supporting you now?" she asked, her voice low.

He shrugged. "Society."

She said, with effort, "You were going to tell me the reasons behind that statement."

"I wouldn't think you'd find them hard to deduce. If you consider that for thirteen years this Institute has had a department of metallurgical research, which has cost over twenty million dollars and has produced nothing but a new silver polish and a new anti-corrosive preparation, which, I believe, is not so good as the old ones—you can imagine what the public reaction will be if some private individual comes out with a product that revolutionizes the entire science of metallurgy and proves to be sensationally successful!"

Her head dropped. She said nothing.

"I don't blame our metallurgical department!" he said angrily. "I know that results of this kind are not a matter of any predictable time. But the public won't understand it. What, then, should we sacrifice? An excellent piece of smelting—or the last center of science left on earth, and the whole future of human knowledge? That is the alternative."

She sat, her head down. After a while, she said, "All right, Dr. Stadler. I won't argue."

He saw her groping for her bag, as if she were trying to remember the automatic motions necessary to get up.

"Miss Taggart," he said quietly. It was almost a plea. She looked up. Her face was composed and empty.

He came closer; he leaned with one hand against the wall above her head, almost as if he wished to hold her in the circle of his arm. "Miss Taggart," he said, a tone of gentle, bitter persuasiveness in his voice, "I am older than you. Believe me, there is no other way to live on earth. Men are not open to truth or reason. They cannot be reached by a rational argument. The mind is powerless against them. Yet we have to deal with them. If we want to accomplish anything, we have to deceive them into letting us accomplish it. Or force them. They understand nothing else. We cannot expect their support for any endeavor of the intellect, for any goal of the spirit. They are nothing but vicious animals. They are greedy, self-indulgent, predatory dollar-chasers who—"

"I am one of the dollar-chasers, Dr. Stadler," she said, her voice low.

"You are an unusual, brilliant child who has not seen enough of life to grasp the full measure of human stupidity. I've fought it all my life. I'm very tired. . . ." The sincerity of his voice was genuine. He walked slowly away from her. "There was a time when I looked at the tragic mess they've made of this earth, and I wanted to cry out, to beg them to listen—I could teach them to live so much better than they did—but there was nobody to hear me, they had nothing to hear me with. . . . Intelligence? It is such a rare, precarious spark that flashes for a moment somewhere among men, and vanishes. One cannot tell its nature, or its future . . . or its death. . . ."

She made a movement to rise.

"Don't go, Miss Taggart. I'd like you to understand."

She raised her face to him, in obedient indifference. Her face was not pale, but its planes stood out with strangely naked precision, as if its skin had lost the shadings of color.

"You're young," he said. "At your age, I had the same faith in the unlimited power of reason. The same brilliant vision of man as a rational being. I have seen so much, since. I have been disillusioned so often. . . . I'd like to tell you just one story."

He stood at the window of his office. It had grown dark outside. The darkness seemed to rise from the black cut of the river, far below. A few lights trembled in the water, from among the hills of the other shore. The sky was still the intense blue of evening. A lonely star, low over the earth, seemed unnaturally large and made the sky look darker.

"When I was at the Patrick Henry University," he said, "I had three pupils. I have had many bright students in the past, but these three were the kind of reward a teacher prays for. If ever you could wish to receive the gift of the human mind at its best, young and delivered into your hands for guidance, they were this gift. Theirs was the kind of intelligence one expects to see, in the future, changing the course of the world. They came from very different backgrounds, but they were inseparable friends. They made a strange choice of studies. They majored in two subjects—mine and Hugh Akston's. Physics and philosophy. It is not a combination of interests one encounters nowadays. Hugh Akston was a distinguished man, a great mind . . . unlike the incredible creature whom that University has now put in his place. . . . Akston and I were a little jealous of each other over these three students. It was a kind of contest between us, a friendly contest, because we understood each other. I heard Akston saying one day that he regarded them as his sons. I resented it a little . . . because I thought of them as mine. . . ."

He turned and looked at her. The bitter lines of age were visible now, cutting across his cheeks. He said, "When I endorsed the establishment of this Institute, one of these three damned me. I have not seen him since. It used to disturb me, in the first few years. I wondered, once in a while, whether he had been right. . . . It has ceased to disturb me, long ago."

He smiled. There was nothing but bitterness now, in his smile and his face.

"These three men, these three who held all the hope which the gift of intelligence ever proffered, these three from whom we expected such a magnificent future—one of them was Francisco d'Anconia, who became a depraved playboy. Another was Ragnar Danneskjöld, who became a plain bandit. So much for the promise of the human mind."

"Who was the third one?" she asked.

He shrugged. "The third one did not achieve even that sort of notorious distinction. He vanished without a trace—into the great unknown of mediocrity. He is probably a second assistant bookkeeper somewhere."

* * *

"It's a lie! I didn't run away!" cried James Taggart. "I came here because I happened to be sick. Ask Dr. Wilson. It's a form of flu. He'll prove it. And how did you know that I was here?"

Dagny stood in the middle of the room; there were melting snowflakes on her coat collar, on the brim of her hat. She glanced around, feeling an emotion that would have been sadness, had she had time to acknowledge it.

It was a room in the house of the old Taggart estate on the Hudson. Jim had inherited the place, but he seldom came here. In their childhood, this had been their father's study. Now it had the desolate air of a room which is used, yet uninhabited. There were slipcovers on all but two chairs, a cold fireplace and the dismal warmth of an electric heater with a cord twisting across the floor, a desk, its glass surface empty.

Jim lay on the couch, with a towel wrapped for a scarf around his neck. She saw a stale, filled ashtray on a chair beside him, a bottle of whisky, a wilted paper cup, and two-day-old newspapers scattered about the floor. A portrait of their grandfather hung over the fireplace, full figure, with a railroad bridge in the fading background.

"I have no time for arguments, Jim."

"It was your idea! I hope you'll admit to the Board that it was your idea. That's what your goddamn Rearden Metal has done to us! If we had waited for Orren Boyle . . ." His unshaved face was pulled by a twisted scramble of emotions: panic, hatred, a touch of triumph, the relief of screaming at a victim—and the faint, cautious, begging look that sees a hope of help.

He had stopped tentatively, but she did not answer. She stood watching him, her hands in the pockets of her coat.

"There's nothing we can do now!" he moaned. "I tried to call Washington, to get them to seize the Phoenix-Durango and turn it over to us, on the ground of emergency, but they won't even discuss it! Too many people objecting, they say, afraid of some fool precedent or another! . . . I got the National Alliance of Railroads to suspend the deadline and permit Dan Conway to operate his road for another year —that would have given us time—but he's refused to do it! I tried to get Ellis Wyatt and his bunch of friends in Colorado to demand that Washington order Conway to continue operations—but all of them, Wyatt and all the rest of those bastards, refused! It's *their* skin, worse than ours, they're sure to go down the drain—but they've refused!"

She smiled briefly, but made no comment.

"Now there's nothing left for us to do! We're caught. We can't give up that branch and we can't complete it. We can't stop or go on. We have no money. Nobody will touch us with a ten-foot pole! What have we got left without the Rio Norte Line? But we can't finish it. We'd be boycotted. We'd be blacklisted. That union of track workers would sue us. They would, there's a law about it. We can't complete that Line! Christ! What are we going to do?"

She waited. "Through, Jim?" she asked coldly. "If you are, I'll tell you what we're going to do."

He kept silent, looking up at her from under his heavy eyelids.

"This is not a proposal, Jim. It's an ultimatum. Just listen and accept. I am going to complete the construction of the Rio Norte Line. I personally, not Taggart Transcontinental. I will take a leave of absence from the job of Vice-President. I will form a company in my own name. Your Board will turn the Rio Norte Line over to me. I will act as my own contractor. I will get my own financing. I will take full charge and sole responsibility. I will complete the Line on time. After you have seen how the Rearden Metal rails can take it, I will transfer the Line back to Taggart Transcontinental and I'll return to my job. That is all."

He was looking at her silently, dangling a bedroom slipper on the tip of his foot. She had never supposed that hope could look ugly in a man's face, but it did: it was mixed with cunning. She turned her eyes away from him, wondering how it was possible that a man's first thought in such a moment could be a search for something to put over on her.

Then, preposterously, the first thing he said, his voice anxious, was, "But who will run Taggart Transcontinental in the meantime?"

She chuckled; the sound astonished her, it seemed old in its bitterness. She said, "Eddie Willers."

"Oh no! He couldn't!"

She laughed, in the same brusque, mirthless way. "I thought you were smarter than I about things of this kind. Eddie will assume the title of Acting Vice-President. He will occupy my office and sit at my desk. But who do you suppose will run Taggart Transcontinental?"

"But I don't see how—"

"I will commute by plane between Eddie's office and Colorado. Also, there are long-distance phones available. I will do just what I have been doing. Nothing will change, except the kind of show you will put on for your friends . . . and the fact that it will be a little harder for me."

"What show?"

"You understand me, Jim. I have no idea what sort of games you're tangled in, you and your Board of Directors. I don't know how many ends you're all playing against the middle and against one another, or how many pretenses you have to keep up in how many opposite directions. I don't know or care. You can all hide behind me. If you're all afraid, because you've made deals with friends who're threatened by Rearden Metal—well, here's your chance to go through the motions of assuring them that you're not involved, that you're not doing this—*I* am. You can help them to curse me and denounce me. You can all stay home, take no risks and make no enemies. Just keep out of my way."

"Well . . ." he said slowly, "of course, the problems involved in the policy of a great railroad system are complex . . . while a small, independent company, in the name of one person, could afford to—"

"Yes, Jim, yes, I know all that. The moment you announce that you're turning the Rio Norte Line over to me, the Taggart stock will rise. The bedbugs will stop crawling from out of unlikely corners, since they won't have the incentive of a big company to bite. Before they decide what to do about me, I will have the Line finished. And as for me, I don't want to have you and your Board to account to, to argue with, to beg permissions from. There isn't any time for that, if I am to do the kind of job that has to be done. So I'm going to do it alone."

"And . . . if you fail?"

"If I fail, I'll go down alone."

"You understand that in such case Taggart Transcontinental will not be able to help you in any way?"

"I understand."

"You will not count on us?"

"No."

"You will cut all official connection with us, so that your activities will not reflect upon our reputation?"

"Yes."

"I think we should agree that in case of failure or public scandal . . . your leave of absence will become permanent . . . that is, you will not expect to return to the post of Vice-President."

She closed her eyes for a moment. "All right, Jim. In such case, I will not return."

"Before we transfer the Rio Norte Line to you, we must have a written agreement that you will transfer it back to us, along with your controlling interest at cost, in case the Line becomes successful. Otherwise you might try to squeeze us for a windfall profit, since we need that Line."

There was only a brief stab of shock in her eyes, then she said indifferently, the words sounding as if she were tossing alms, "By all means, Jim. Have that stated in writing."

"Now as to your temporary successor . . ."

"Yes?"

"You don't really want it to be Eddie Willers, do you?"

"Yes. I do."

"But he couldn't even *act* like a vice-president! He doesn't have the presence, the manner, the—"

"He knows his work and mine. He knows what I want. I trust him. I'll be able to work with him."

"Don't you think it would be better to pick one of our more distinguished young men, somebody from a good family, with more social poise and—"

"It's going to be Eddie Willers, Jim."

He sighed. "All right. Only . . . only we must be careful about it. . . . We don't want people to suspect that it's you who're still running Taggart Transcontinental. Nobody must know it."

"Everybody will know it, Jim. But since nobody will admit it openly, everybody will be satisfied."

"But we must preserve appearances."

"Oh, certainly! You don't have to recognize me on the street, if you don't want to. You can say you've never seen me before and I'll say I've never heard of Taggart Transcontinental."

He remained silent, trying to think, staring down at the floor.

She turned to look at the grounds beyond the window. The sky had the even, gray-white pallor of winter. Far below, on the shore of the Hudson, she saw the road she used to watch for Francisco's car—she saw the cliff over the river, where they climbed to look for the towers of New York—and somewhere beyond the woods were the trails that led to Rockdale Station. The earth was snow-covered now, and what remained was like the skeleton of the countryside she remembered—a thin design of bare branches rising from the snow to the sky. It was gray and white, like a photograph, a dead photograph which one keeps hopefully for remembrance, but which has no power to bring back anything.

"What are you going to call it?"

She turned, startled. "What?"

"What are you going to call your company?"

"Oh . . . Why, the Dagny Taggart Line, I guess."

"But . . . Do you think that's wise? It might be misunderstood. The *Taggart* might be taken as—"

"Well, what do you want me to call it?" she snapped, worn down to anger. "The Miss Nobody? The Madam X? The John Galt?" She stopped. She smiled suddenly, a cold, bright, dangerous smile. "That's what I'm going to call it: the John Galt Line."

"Good God, no!"

"Yes."

"But it's . . . it's just a cheap piece of slang!"

"Yes."

"You can't make a joke out of such a serious project! . . . You can't be so vulgar and . . . and undignified!"

"Can't I?"

"But for God's sake, why?"

"Because it's going to shock all the rest of them just as it shocked you."

"I've never seen you playing for effects."

"I am, this time."

"But . . ." His voice dropped to an almost superstitious sound: "Look, Dagny, you know, it's . . . it's bad luck. . . . What it stands for is . . ." He stopped.

"What does it stand for?"

"I don't know . . . But the way people use it, they always seem to say it out of—"

"Fear? Despair? Futility?"

"Yes . . . yes, that's what it is."

"That's what I want to throw in their faces!"

The bright, sparkling anger in her eyes, her first look of enjoyment, made him understand that he had to keep still.

"Draw up all the papers and all the red tape in the name of the John Galt Line," she said.

He sighed. "Well, it's *your* Line."

"You bet it is!"

He glanced at her, astonished. She had dropped the manners and style of a vice-president; she seemed to be relaxing happily to the level of yard crews and construction gangs.

"As to the papers and the legal side of it," he said, "there might be some difficulties. We would have to apply for the permission of—"

She whirled to face him. Something of the bright, violent look still remained in her face. But it was not gay and she was not smiling. The look now had an odd, primitive quality. When he saw it, he hoped he would never have to see it again.

"Listen, Jim," she said; he had never heard that tone in any human voice. "There is one thing you can do as your part of the deal and you'd better do it: keep your Washington boys off. See to it that they give me all the permissions, authorizations, charters and other waste paper that their laws require. Don't let them try to stop me. If they try . . . Jim, people say that our ancestor, Nat Taggart, killed a politician who tried to refuse him a permission he should never have had to ask. I don't know whether Nat Taggart did it or not. But I'll tell you this: I know how he felt, if he did. If he didn't—I might do the job for him, to complete the family legend. I mean it, Jim."

* * *

Francisco d'Anconia sat in front of her desk. His face was blank. It had remained blank while Dagny explained to him, in the clear, impersonal tone of a business interview, the formation and purpose of her own railroad company. He had listened. He had not pronounced a word.

She had never seen his face wear that look of drained passivity. There was no mockery, no amusement, no antagonism; it was as if he did not belong in these particular moments of existence and could not be reached. Yet his eyes looked at her attentively; they seemed to see more than she could suspect; they made her think of one-way glass: they let all light rays in, but none out.

"Francisco, I asked you to come here, because I wanted you to see me in my office. You've never seen it. It would have meant something to you, once."

His eyes moved slowly to look at the office. Its walls were bare, except for three things: a map of Taggart Transcontinental—the original drawing of Nat Taggart, that had served as model for his statue —and a large railroad calendar, in cheerfully crude colors, the kind that was distributed each year, with a change of its picture, to every station along the Taggart track, the kind that had hung once in her first work place at Rockdale.

He got up. He said quietly, "Dagny, for your own sake, and"—it was a barely perceptible hesitation—"and in the name of any pity you might feel for me, don't request what you're going to request. Don't. Let me go now."

This was not like him and like nothing she could ever have expected to hear from him. After a moment, she asked, "Why?"

"I can't answer you. I can't answer any questions. That is one of the reasons why it's best not to discuss it."

"You know what I am going to request?"

"Yes." The way she looked at him was such an eloquent, desperate question, that he had to add, "I know that I am going to refuse."

"Why?"

He smiled mirthlessly, spreading his hands out, as if to show her that this was what he had predicted and had wanted to avoid.

She said quietly, "I have to try, Francisco. I have to make the request. That's my part. What you'll do about it is yours. But I'll know that I've tried everything."

He remained standing, but he inclined his head a little, in assent, and said, "I will listen, if that will help you."

"I need fifteen million dollars to complete the Rio Norte Line. I have obtained seven million against the Taggart stock I own free and clear. I can raise nothing else. I will issue bonds in the name of my new company, in the amount of eight million dollars. I called you here to ask you to buy these bonds."

He did not answer.

"I am simply a beggar, Francisco, and I am begging you for money. I had always thought that one did not beg in business. I thought that one stood on the merit of what one had to offer, and gave value for value. This is not so any more, though I don't understand how we can act on any other rule and continue to exist. Judging by every objective fact, the Rio Norte Line is to be the best railroad in the country. Judging by every known standard, it is the best investment possible. And that is what damns me. I cannot raise money by offering people a good business venture: the fact that it's good, makes people reject it. There is no bank that would buy the bonds of my company. So I can't plead merit. I can only plead."

Her voice was pronouncing the words with impersonal precision. She stopped, waiting for his answer. He remained silent.

"I know that I have nothing to offer you," she said. "I can't speak to you in terms of investment. You don't care to make money. Industrial projects have ceased to concern you long ago. So I won't pretend that it's a fair exchange. It's just begging." She drew her breath and said, "Give me that money as alms, because it means nothing to you."

"Don't," he said, his voice low. She could not tell whether the strange sound of it was pain or anger; his eyes were lowered.

"Will you do it, Francisco?"

"No."

After a moment, she said, "I called you, not because I thought you would agree, but because you were the only one who could understand what I am saying. So I had to try it." Her voice was dropping lower, as if she hoped it would make emotion harder to detect. "You see, I can't believe that you're really gone . . . because I know that you're still able to hear me. The way you live is depraved. But the way you act is not. Even the way you speak of it, is not. . . . I had to try . . . But I can't struggle to understand you any longer."

"I'll give you a hint. Contradictions do not exist. Whenever you think that you are facing a contradiction, check your premises. You will find that one of them is wrong."

"Francisco," she whispered, "why don't you tell me what it was that happened to you?"

"Because, at this moment, the answer would hurt you more than the doubt."

"Is it as terrible as that?"

"It is an answer which you must reach by yourself."

She shook her head. "I don't know what to offer you. I don't know what is of value to you any longer. Don't you see that even a beggar has to give value in return, has to offer some reason why you might want to help him? . . . Well, I thought . . . at one time, it meant a great deal to you—success. Industrial success. Remember how we used to talk about it? You were very severe. You expected a lot from me. You told me I'd better live up to it. I have. You wondered how far I'd rise with Taggart Transcontinental." She moved her hand, pointing at the office. "This is how far I've risen. . . . So I thought . . . if the memory of what had been your values still has some meaning for you, if only as amusement, or a moment's sadness, or just like . . . like putting flowers on a grave . . . you might want to give me the money . . . in the name of that."

"No."

She said, with effort, "That money would mean nothing to you— you've wasted that much on senseless parties—you've wasted much more on the San Sebastián Mines—"

He glanced up. He looked straight at her and she saw the first spark of a living response in his eyes, a look that was bright, pitiless and, incredibly, proud: as if this were an accusation that gave him strength.

"Oh, yes," she said slowly, as if answering his thought, "I realize that. I've damned you for those mines, I've denounced you, I've thrown my contempt at you in every way possible, and now I come back to you—for money. Like Jim, like any moocher you've ever met. I know it's a triumph for you, I know that you can laugh at me and despise me with full justice. Well—perhaps I can offer you that. If it's amusement that you want, if you enjoyed seeing Jim and the Mexican planners crawl—wouldn't it amuse you to break me? Wouldn't it give you pleasure? Don't you want to hear me acknowledge that I'm beaten by you? Don't you want to see me crawling before you? Tell me what form of it you'd like and I'll submit."

He moved so swiftly that she could not notice how he started; it only seemed to her that his first movement was a shudder. He came around the desk, he took her hand and raised it to his lips. It began as a gesture of the gravest respect, as if its purpose were to give her strength; but as he held his lips, then his face, pressed to her hand, she knew that he was seeking strength from it himself.

He dropped her hand, he looked down at her face, at the frightened stillness of her eyes, he smiled, not trying to hide that his smile held suffering, anger and tenderness.

"Dagny, you want to crawl? You don't know what the word means and never will. One doesn't crawl by acknowledging it as honestly as that. Don't you suppose I know that your begging me was the bravest thing you could do? But . . . Don't ask me, Dagny."

"In the name of anything I ever meant to you . . ." she whispered, "anything left within you . . ."

In the moment when she thought that she had seen this look before, that this was the way he had looked against the night glow of the city, when he lay in bed by her side for the last time—she heard his cry, the kind of cry she had never torn from him before:

"My love, I can't!"

Then, as they looked at each other, both shocked into silence by astonishment, she saw the change in his face. It was as crudely abrupt as if he had thrown a switch. He laughed, he moved away from her and said, his voice jarringly offensive by being completely casual:

"Please excuse the mixture in styles of expression. I've been supposed to say that to so many women, but on somewhat different occasions."

Her head dropped, she sat huddled tight together, not caring that he saw it.

When she raised her head, she looked at him indifferently. "All right, Francisco. It was a good act. I did believe it. If that was your own way of having the kind of fun I was offering you, you succeeded. I won't ask you for anything."

"I warned you."

"I didn't know which side you belonged on. It didn't seem possible —but it's the side of Orren Boyle and Bertram Scudder and your old teacher."

"My old teacher?" he asked sharply.

"Dr. Robert Stadler."

He chuckled, relieved. "Oh, that one? He's the looter who thinks that his end justifies his seizure of my means." He added, "You know, Dagny, I'd like you to remember which side you said I'm on. Some day, I'll remind you of it and ask you whether you'll want to repeat it."

"You won't have to remind me."

He turned to go. He tossed his hand in a casual salute and said, "If it could be built, I'd wish good luck to the Rio Norte Line."

"It's going to be built. And it's going to be called the John Galt Line."

"*What?!*"

It was an actual scream; she chuckled derisively. "The John Galt Line."

"Dagny, in heaven's name, why?"

"Don't you like it?"

"How did you happen to choose that?"

"It sounds better than Mr. Nemo or Mr. Zero, doesn't it?"

"Dagny, why that?"

"Because it frightens you."

"What do you think it stands for?"

"The impossible. The unattainable. And you're all afraid of my Line just as you're afraid of that name."

He started laughing. He laughed, not looking at her, and she felt strangely certain that he had forgotten her, that he was far away, that he was laughing—in furious gaiety and bitterness—at something in which she had no part.

When he turned to her, he said earnestly, "Dagny, I wouldn't, if I were you."

She shrugged. "Jim didn't like it, either."

"What do you like about it?"

"I hate it! I hate the doom you're all waiting for, the giving up, and that senseless question that always sounds like a cry for help. I'm sick of hearing pleas for John Galt. I'm going to fight him."

He said quietly, "You are."

"I'm going to build a railroad line for him. Let him come and claim it!"

He smiled sadly and nodded: "He will."

* * *

The glow of poured steel streamed across the ceiling and broke against one wall. Rearden sat at his desk, in the light of a single lamp. Beyond its circle, the darkness of the office blended with the darkness outside. He felt as if it were empty space where the rays of the furnaces moved at will; as if the desk were a raft hanging in mid-air, holding two persons imprisoned in privacy. Dagny sat in front of his desk.

She had thrown her coat off, and she sat outlined against it, a slim, tense body in a gray suit, leaning diagonally across the wide armchair. Only her hand lay in the light, on the edge of the desk; beyond it, he saw the pale suggestion of her face, the white of a blouse, the triangle of an open collar.

"All right, Hank," she said, "we're going ahead with a new Rearden Metal bridge. This is the official order of the official owner of the John Galt Line."

He smiled, looking down at the drawings of the bridge spread in the light on his desk. "Have you had a chance to examine the scheme we submitted?"

"Yes. You don't need my comments or compliments. The order says it."

"Very well. Thank you. I'll start rolling the Metal."

"Don't you want to ask whether the John Galt Line is in a position to place orders or to function?"

"I don't need to. Your coming here says it."

She smiled. "True. It's all set, Hank. I came to tell you that and to discuss the details of the bridge in person."

"All right, I *am* curious: who are the bondholders of the John Galt Line?"

"I don't think any of them could afford it. All of them have growing enterprises. All of them needed their money for their own concerns. But they needed the Line and they did not ask anyone for help." She took a paper out of her bag. "Here's John Galt, Inc.," she said, handing it across the desk.

He knew most of the names on the list: "Ellis. Wyatt, Wyatt Oil, Colorado. Ted Nielsen, Nielsen Motors, Colorado. Lawrence Hammond, Hammond Cars, Colorado. Andrew Stockton, Stockton Foundry, Colorado." There were a few from other states; he noticed the name: "Kenneth Danagger, Danagger Coal, Pennsylvania." The amounts of their subscriptions varied, from sums in five figures to six.

He reached for his fountain pen, wrote at the bottom of the list "Henry Rearden, Rearden Steel, Pennsylvania—$1,000,000" and tossed the list back to her.

"Hank," she said quietly, "I didn't want you in on this. You've invested so much in Rearden Metal that it's worse for you than for any of us. You can't afford another risk."

"I never accept favors," he answered coldly.

"What do you mean?"

"I don't ask people to take greater chances on my ventures than I take myself. If it's a gamble, I'll match anybody's gambling. Didn't you say that that track was my first showcase?"

She inclined her head and said gravely, "All right. Thank you."

"Incidentally, I don't expect to lose this money. I am aware of the conditions under which these bonds can be converted into stock at my option. I therefore expect to make an inordinate profit—and you're going to earn it for me."

She laughed. "God, Hank, I've spoken to so many yellow fools that they've almost infected me into thinking of the Line as of a hopeless loss! Thanks for reminding me. Yes, I think I'll earn your inordinate profit for you."

"If it weren't for the yellow fools, there wouldn't be any risk in it at all. But we have to beat them. We will." He reached for two telegrams from among the papers on his desk. "There are still a few men in existence." He extended the telegrams. "I think you'd like to see these."

One of them read: "I had intended to undertake it in two years, but the statement of the State Science Institute compels me to proceed at once. Consider this a commitment for the construction of a 12-inch pipe line of Rearden Metal, 600 miles, Colorado to Kansas City. Details follow. Ellis Wyatt."

The other read: "Re our discussion of my order. Go ahead. Ken Danagger."

He added, in explanation, "He wasn't prepared to proceed at once, either. It's eight thousand tons of Rearden Metal. Structural metal. For coal mines."

They glanced at each other and smiled. They needed no further comment.

He glanced down, as she handed the telegrams back to him. The skin of her hand looked transparent in the light, on the edge of his desk, a young girl's hand with long, thin fingers, relaxed for a moment, defenseless.

"The Stockton Foundry in Colorado," she said, "is going to finish that order for me—the one that the Amalgamated Switch and Signal Company ran out on. They're going to get in touch with you about the Metal."

"They have already. What have you done about the construction crews?"

"Nealy's engineers are staying on, the best ones, those I need. And most of the foremen, too. It won't be too hard to keep them going. Nealy wasn't of much use, anyway."

"What about labor?"

"More applicants than I can hire. I don't think the union is going to interfere. Most of the applicants are giving phony names. They're union members. They need the work desperately. I'll have a few guards on the Line, but I don't expect any trouble."

"What about your brother Jim's Board of Directors?"

"They're all scrambling to get statements into the newspapers to the effect that they have no connection whatever with the John Galt Line and how reprehensible an undertaking they think it is. They agreed to everything I asked."

The line of her shoulders looked taut, yet thrown back easily, as if poised for flight. Tension seemed natural to her, not a sign of anxiety, but a sign of enjoyment; the tension of her whole body, under the gray suit, half-visible in the darkness.

"Eddie Willers has taken over the office of Operating Vice-President," she said. "If you need anything, get in touch with him. I'm leaving for Colorado tonight."

"Tonight?"

"Yes. We have to make up time. We've lost a week."

"Flying your own plane?"

"Yes. I'll be back in about ten days. I intend to be in New York once or twice a month."

"Where will you live out there?"

"On the site. In my own railway car—that is, Eddie's car, which I'm borrowing."

"Will you be safe?"

"Safe from what?" Then she laughed, startled. "Why, Hank, it's the first time you've ever thought that I wasn't a man. Of course I'll be safe."

He was not looking at her; he was looking at a sheet of figures on his desk. "I've had my engineers prepare a breakdown of the cost of the bridge," he said, "and an approximate schedule of the construction time required. That is what I wanted to discuss with you." He extended the papers. She settled back to read them.

A wedge of light fell across her face. He saw the firm, sensual mouth in sharp outline. Then she leaned back a little, and he saw only a suggestion of its shape and the dark lines of her lowered lashes.

Haven't I?—he thought. Haven't I thought of it since the first time I saw you? Haven't I thought of nothing else for two years? . . . He sat motionless, looking at her. He heard the words he had never allowed himself to form, the words he had felt, known, yet had not faced, had hoped to destroy by never letting them be said within his own mind. Now it was as sudden and shocking as if he were saying it to her. . . . Since the first time I saw you . . . Nothing but your body, that mouth of yours, and the way your eyes would look at me, if . . . Through every sentence I ever said to you, through every conference you thought so safe, through the importance of all the issues we discussed . . . You trusted me, didn't you? To recognize your greatness? To think of you as you deserved—as if you were a man? . . . Don't you suppose I know how much I've betrayed? The only bright encounter of my life—the only person I respected—the best businessman I know—my ally—my partner in a desperate battle . . . The lowest of all desires—as my answer to the highest I've met . . . Do you know what I am? I thought of it, because it should have been unthinkable. For that degrading need, which should never touch you, I have never wanted anyone but you . . . I hadn't known what it was like, to want it, until I saw you for the first time. I had thought: Not I, I couldn't be broken by it . . . Since then . . . for two years . . . with not a moment's respite . . . Do you know what it's like, to want it? Would you wish to hear what I thought when I looked at you . . . when I lay awake at night . . . when I heard your voice over a telephone wire . . . when I worked, but could not drive it away? . . . To bring you down to things you can't conceive—and to know that it's I who have done it. To reduce you to a body, to teach you an animal's pleasure, to see you need it, to see you asking me for it, to see your wonderful spirit dependent upon the obscenity of your need. To watch you as you are, as you face the world with your clean, proud strength—then to see you, in my bed, submitting to any infamous whim I may devise, to any act which I'll perform for the sole purpose of watching your dishonor and to which you'll submit for the sake of an unspeakable sensation . . . I want you—and may I be damned for it! . . .

She was reading the papers, leaning back in the darkness—he saw the reflection of the fire touching her hair, moving to her shoulder, down her arm, to the naked skin of her wrist.

. . . Do you know what I'm thinking now, in this moment? . . . Your gray suit and your open collar . . . you look so young, so austere, so sure of yourself . . . What would you be like if I knocked your head back, if I threw you down in that formal suit of yours, if I raised your skirt—

She glanced up at him. He looked down at the papers on his desk. In a moment, he said, "The actual cost of the bridge is less than our original estimate. You will note that the strength of the bridge allows for the eventual addition of a second track, which, I think, that section of the country will justify in a very few years. If you spread the cost over a period of—"

He spoke, and she looked at his face in the lamplight, against the black emptiness of the office. The lamp was outside her field of vision, and she felt as if it were his face that illuminated the papers on the desk. His face, she thought, and the cold, radiant clarity of his voice, of his mind, of his drive to a single purpose. The face was like his words—as if the line of a single theme ran from the steady glance of the eyes, through the gaunt muscles of the cheeks, to the faintly scornful, downward curve of the mouth—the line of a ruthless asceticism.

* * *

The day began with the news of a disaster: a freight train of the Atlantic Southern had crashed head-on into a passenger train, in New Mexico, on a sharp curve in the mountains, scattering freight cars all over the slopes. The cars carried five thousand tons of copper, bound from a mine in Arizona to the Rearden mills.

Rearden telephoned the general manager of the Atlantic Southern, but the answer he received was: "Oh God, Mr. Rearden, how can we tell? How can anybody tell how long it will take to clear that wreck? One of the worst we've ever had . . . I don't know, Mr. Rearden. There are no other lines anywhere in that section. The track is torn for twelve hundred feet. There's been a rockslide. Our wrecking train can't get through. I don't know how we'll ever get those freight cars back on rails, or when. Can't expect it sooner than two weeks . . . *Three days?* Impossible, Mr. Rearden! . . . But we can't help it!

. . . But surely you can tell your customers that it's an act of God! What if you do hold them up? Nobody can blame you in a case of this kind!"

In the next two hours, with the assistance of his secretary, two young engineers from his shipping department, a road map, and the long-distance telephone, Rearden arranged for a fleet of trucks to proceed to the scene of the wreck, and for a chain of hopper cars to meet them at the nearest station of the Atlantic Southern. The hopper cars had been borrowed from Taggart Transcontinental. The trucks had been recruited from all over New Mexico, Arizona and Colorado. Rearden's engineers had hunted by telephone for private truck owners and had offered payments that cut all arguments short.

It was the third of three shipments of copper that Rearden had expected; two orders had not been delivered: one company had gone out of business, the other was still pleading delays that it could not help.

He had attended to the matter without breaking his chain of appointments, without raising his voice, without sign of strain, uncertainty or apprehension; he had acted with the swift precision of a military commander under sudden fire—and Gwen Ives, his secretary, had acted as his calmest lieutenant. She was a girl in her late twenties, whose quietly harmonious, impenetrable face had a quality matching the best-designed office equipment; she was one of his most ruthlessly competent employees; her manner of performing her duties suggested the kind of rational cleanliness that would consider any element of emotion, while at work, as an unpardonable immorality.

When the emergency was over, her sole comment was, "Mr. Rearden, I think we should ask all our suppliers to ship via Taggart Transcontinental." "I'm thinking that, too," he answered; then added, "Wire Fleming in Colorado. Tell him I'm taking an option on that copper mine property."

He was back at his desk, speaking to his superintendent on one phone and to his purchasing manager on another, checking every date and ton of ore on hand—he could not leave to chance or to another person the possibility of a single hour's delay in the flow of a furnace: it was the last of the rail for the John Galt Line that was being poured—when the buzzer rang and Miss Ives' voice announced that his mother was outside, demanding to see him.

He had asked his family never to come to the mills without appointment. He had been glad that they hated the place and seldom appeared in his office. What he now felt was a violent impulse to order his mother off the premises. Instead, with a greater effort than the problem of the train wreck had required of him, he said quietly, "All right. Ask her to come in."

His mother came in with an air of belligerent defensiveness. She looked at his office as if she knew what it meant to him and as if she were declaring her resentment against anything being of greater importance to him than her own person. She took a long time settling down in an armchair, arranging and rearranging her bag, her gloves, the folds of her dress, while droning, "It's a fine thing when a mother has to wait in an anteroom and ask permission of a stenographer before she's allowed to see her own son who—"

"Mother, is it anything important? I am very rushed today."

"You're not the only one who's got problems. Of course, it's important. Do you think I'd go to the trouble of driving way out here, if it wasn't important?"

"What is it?"

"It's about Philip."

"Yes?"

"Philip is unhappy."

"Well?"

"He feels it's not right that he should have to depend on your charity and live on handouts and never be able to count on a single dollar of his own."

"Well!" he said with a startled smile. "I've been waiting for him to realize that."

"It isn't right for a sensitive man to be in such a position."

"It certainly isn't."

"I'm glad you agree with me. So what you have to do is give him a job."

"A . . . what?"

"You must give him a job, here, at the mills—but a nice, clean job, of course, with a desk and an office and a decent salary, where he wouldn't have to be among your day laborers and your smelly furnaces."

He knew that he was hearing it; he could not make himself believe it. "Mother, you're not serious."

"I certainly am. I happen to know that that's what he wants, only he's too proud to ask you for it. But if you offer it to him and make it look like it's you who're asking him a favor—why, I know he'd be happy to take it. That's why I had to come here to talk to you—so he wouldn't guess that I put you up to it."

It was not in the nature of his consciousness to understand the nature of the things he was hearing. A single thought cut through his mind like a spotlight, making him unable to conceive how any eyes could miss it. The thought broke out of him as a cry of bewilderment: "But he knows nothing about the steel business!"

"What has that got to do with it? He needs a job."

"But he couldn't do the work."

"He needs to gain self-confidence and to feel important."

"But he wouldn't be any good whatever."

"He needs to feel that he's wanted."

"Here? What could I want him for?"

"You hire plenty of strangers."

"I hire men who produce. What has he got to offer?"

"He's your brother, isn't he?"

"What has that got to do with it?"

She stared incredulously, in turn, silenced by shock. For a moment, they sat looking at each other, as if across an interplanetary distance.

"He's your brother," she said, her voice like a phonograph record repeating a magic formula she could not permit herself to doubt. "He needs a position in the world. He needs a salary, so that he'd feel that he's got money coming to him as his due, not as alms."

"As his due? But he wouldn't be worth a nickel to me."

"Is that what you think of first? Your profit? I'm asking you to help your brother, and you're figuring how to make a nickel on him, and you won't help him unless there's money in it for *you*—is that it?" She saw the expression of his eyes, and she looked away, but spoke hastily, her voice rising. "Yes, sure, you're helping him—like you'd help any stray beggar. *Material* help—that's all you know or understand. Have you thought about his *spiritual* needs and what his position is doing to his self-respect? He doesn't want to live like a beggar. He wants to be independent of you."

"By means of getting from me a salary he can't earn for work he can't do?"

"You'd never miss it. You've got enough people here who're making money for you."

"Are you asking me to help him stage a fraud of that kind?"

"You don't have to put it that way."

"Is it a fraud—or isn't it?"

"That's why I can't talk to you—because you're not human. You have no pity, no feeling for your brother, no compassion for his feelings."

"Is it a fraud or not?"

"You have no mercy for anybody."

"Do you think that a fraud of this kind would be just?"

"You're the most immoral man living—you think of nothing but justice! You don't feel any love at all!"

He got up, his movement abrupt and stressed, the movement of ending an interview and ordering a visitor out of his office. "Mother, I'm running a steel plant—not a whorehouse."

"Henry!" The gasp of indignation was at his choice of language, nothing more.

"Don't ever speak to me again about a job for Philip. I would not give him the job of a cinder sweeper. I would not allow him inside my mills. I want you to understand that, once and for all. You may try to help him in any way you wish, but don't ever let me see you thinking of my mills as a means to that end."

The wrinkles of her soft chin trickled into a shape resembling a sneer. "What are they, your mills—a holy temple of some kind?"

"Why . . . yes," he said softly, astonished at the thought.

"Don't you ever think of people and of your moral duties?"

"I don't know what it is that you choose to call morality. No, I don't think of people—except that if I gave a job to Philip, I wouldn't be able to face any competent man who needed work and deserved it."

She got up. Her head was drawn into her shoulders, and the righteous bitterness of her voice seemed to push the words upward at his tall, straight figure: *"That's* your cruelty, that's what's mean and selfish about you. If you loved your brother, you'd give him a job he didn't deserve, precisely because he didn't deserve it—*that* would be true love and kindness and brotherhood. Else what's love for? If a man *deserves* a job, there's no virtue in giving it to him. Virtue is the giving of the undeserved."

He was looking at her like a child at an unfamiliar nightmare, incredulity preventing it from becoming horror. "Mother," he said slowly, "you don't know what you're saying. I'm not able ever to despise you enough to believe that you mean it."

The look on her face astonished him more than all the rest: it was a look of defeat and yet of an odd, sly, cynical cunning, as if, for a moment, she held some worldly wisdom that mocked his innocence.

The memory of that look remained in his mind, like a warning signal telling him that he had glimpsed an issue which he had to understand. But he could not grapple with it, he could not force his mind to accept it as worthy of thought, he could find no clue except his dim uneasiness and his revulsion—and he had no time to give it, he could not think of it now, he was facing his next caller seated in front of his desk—he was listening to a man who pleaded for his life.

The man did not state it in such terms, but Rearden knew that that was the essence of the case. What the man put into words was only a plea for five hundred tons of steel.

He was Mr. Ward, of the Ward Harvester Company of Minnesota. It was an unpretentious company with an unblemished reputation, the kind of business concern that seldom grows large, but never fails. Mr. Ward represented the fourth generation of a family that had owned the plant and had given it the conscientious best of such ability as they possessed.

He was a man in his fifties, with a square, stolid face. Looking at him, one knew that he would consider it as indecent to let his face show suffering as to remove his clothes in public. He spoke in a dry, businesslike manner. He explained that he had always dealt, as his father had, with one of the small steel companies now taken over by Orren Boyle's Associated Steel. He had waited for his last order of steel for a year. He had spent the last month struggling to obtain a personal interview with Rearden.

"I know that your mills are running at capacity, Mr. Rearden," he said, "and I know that you are not in a position to take care of new orders, what with your biggest, oldest customers having to wait their turn, you being the only decent—I mean, reliable—steel manufacturer left in the country. I don't know what reason to offer you as to why you should want to make an exception in my case. But there was nothing else for me to do, except close the doors of my plant for good, and I"— there was a slight break in his voice—"I can't quite see my way to closing the doors . . . as yet . . . so I thought I'd speak to you, even if I didn't have much chance . . . still, I had to try everything possible."

This was language that Rearden could understand. "I wish I could help you out," he said, "but this is the worst possible time for me, because of a very large, very special order that has to take precedence over everything."

"I know. But would you just give me a hearing, Mr. Rearden?"

"Sure."

"If it's a question of money, I'll pay anything you ask. If I could make it worth your while that way, why, charge me any extra you please, charge me double the regular price, only let me have the steel. I wouldn't care if I had to sell the harvester at a loss this year, just so I could keep the doors open. I've got enough, personally, to run at a loss for a couple of years, if necessary, just to hold out—because, I figure, things can't go on this way much longer, conditions are bound to improve, they've got to or else we'll—" He did not finish. He said firmly, "They've got to."

"They will," said Rearden.

The thought of the John Galt Line ran through his mind like a harmony under the confident sound of his words. The John Galt Line was moving forward. The attacks on his Metal had ceased. He felt as if, miles apart across the country, he and Dagny Taggart now stood in empty space, their way cleared, free to finish the job. They'll leave us alone to do it, he thought. The words were like a battle hymn in his mind: They'll leave us alone.

"Our plant capacity is one thousand harvesters per year," said Mr. Ward. "Last year, we put out three hundred. I scraped the steel together from bankruptcy sales, and begging a few tons here and there from big companies, and just going around like a scavenger to all sorts of unlikely places—well, I won't bore you with that, only I never thought I'd live to see the time when I'd have to do business that way. And all the while Mr. Orren Boyle was swearing to me that he was going to deliver the steel next week. But whatever he managed to pour, it went to new customers of his, for some reason nobody would mention, only I heard it whispered that they were men with some sort of political pull. And now I can't even get to Mr. Boyle at all.

He's in Washington, been there for over a month. And all his office tells me is just that they can't help it, because they can't get the ore."

"Don't waste your time on them," said Rearden. "You'll never get anything from that outfit."

"You know, Mr. Rearden," he said in the tone of a discovery which he could not quite bring himself to believe, "I think there's something phony about the way Mr. Boyle runs his business. I can't understand what he's after. They've got half their furnaces idle, but last month there were all those big stories about Associated Steel in all the newspapers. About their output? Why, no—about the wonderful housing project that Mr. Boyle's just built for his workers. Last week, it was colored movies that Mr. Boyle sent to all the high schools, showing how steel is made and what great service it performs for everybody. Now Mr. Boyle's got a radio program, they give talks about the importance of the steel industry to the country and they keep saying that we must preserve the steel industry as a whole. I don't understand what he means by 'as a whole.' "

"I do. Forget it. He won't get away with it."

"You know, Mr. Rearden, I don't like people who talk too much about how everything they do is just for the sake of others. It's not true, and I don't think it would be right if it ever were true. So I'll say that what I need the steel for is to save my own business. Because it's mine. Because if I had to close it . . . oh well, nobody understands that nowadays."

"I do."

"Yes . . . Yes, I think you would. . . . So, you see, that's my first concern. But still, there are my customers, too. They've dealt with me for years. They're counting on me. It's just about impossible to get any sort of machinery anywhere. Do you know what it's getting to be like, out in Minnesota, when the farmers can't get tools, when machines break down in the middle of the harvest season and there are no parts, no replacements . . . nothing but Mr. Orren Boyle's colored movies about . . . Oh well . . . And then there are my workers, too. Some of them have been with us since my father's time. They've got no other place to go. Not now."

It was impossible, thought Rearden, to squeeze more steel out of mills where every furnace, every hour and every ton were scheduled in advance for urgent orders, for the next six months. But . . . The John Galt Line, he thought. If he could do that, he could do anything. . . . He felt as if he wished to undertake ten new problems at once. He felt as if this were a world where nothing was impossible to him.

"Look," he said, reaching for the telephone, "let me check with my superintendent and see just what we're pouring in the next few weeks. Maybe I'll find a way to borrow a few tons from some of the orders and—"

Mr. Ward looked quickly away from him, but Rearden had caught a glimpse of his face. It's so much for him, thought Rearden, and so little for me!

He lifted the telephone receiver, but he had to drop it, because the door of his office flew open and Gwen Ives rushed in.

It seemed impossible that Miss Ives should permit herself a breach of that kind, or that the calm of her face should look like an unnatural distortion, or that her eyes should seem blinded, or that her steps should sound a shred of discipline away from staggering. She said, "Excuse me for interrupting, Mr. Rearden," but he knew that she did not see the office, did not see Mr. Ward, saw nothing but him. "I thought I must tell you that the Legislature has just passed the Equalization of Opportunity Bill."

It was the stolid Mr. Ward who screamed, "Oh God, no! Oh, no!"—staring at Rearden.

Rearden had leaped to his feet. He stood unnaturally bent, one shoulder drooping forward. It was only an instant. Then he looked around him, as if regaining eyesight, said, "Excuse me," his glance including both Miss Ives and Mr. Ward, and sat down again.

"We were not informed that the Bill had been brought to the floor, were we?" he asked, his voice controlled and dry.

"No, Mr. Rearden. Apparently, it was a surprise move and it took them just forty-five minutes."

"Have you heard from Mouch?"

"No, Mr. Rearden." She stressed the no. "It was the office boy from the fifth floor who came running in to tell me that he'd just heard it on the radio. I called the newspapers to verify it. I tried to reach Mr. Mouch in Washington. His office does not answer."

"When did we hear from him last?"

"Ten days ago, Mr. Rearden."

"All right. Thank you, Gwen. Keep trying to get his office."

"Yes, Mr. Rearden."

She walked out. Mr. Ward was on his feet, hat in hand. He muttered, "I guess I'd better—"

"Sit down!" Rearden snapped fiercely.

Mr. Ward obeyed, staring at him.

"We had business to transact, didn't we?" said Rearden. Mr. Ward could not define the emotion that contorted Rearden's mouth as he spoke. "Mr. Ward, what is it that the foulest bastards on earth denounce us for, among other things? Oh yes, for our motto of 'Business as usual.' Well—business as usual, Mr. Ward!"

He picked up the telephone receiver and asked for his superintendent. "Say, Pete . . . What? . . . Yes, I've heard. Can it. We'll talk about that later. What I want to know is, could you let me have five hundred tons of steel, extra, above schedule, in the next few weeks? . . . Yes, I know . . . I know it's tough. . . . Give me the dates and the figures." He listened, rapidly jotting notes down on a sheet of paper. Then he said, "Right. Thank you," and hung up.

He studied the figures for a few moments, marking some brief calculations on the margin of the sheet. Then he raised his head.

"All right, Mr. Ward," he said. "You will have your steel in ten days."

When Mr. Ward had gone, Rearden came out into the anteroom. He said to Miss Ives, his voice normal, "Wire Fleming in Colorado. He'll know why I have to cancel that option." She inclined her head, in the manner of a nod signifying obedience. She did not look at him.

He turned to his next caller and said, with a gesture of invitation toward his office, "How do you do. Come in."

He would think of it later, he thought; one moves step by step and one must keep moving. For the moment, with an unnatural clarity, with a brutal simplification that made it almost easy, his consciousness contained nothing but one thought: It must not stop me. The sentence hung alone, with no past and no future. He did not think of what it was that must not stop him, or why this sentence was such a crucial absolute. It held him and he obeyed. He went step by step. He completed his schedule of appointments, as scheduled.

It was late when his last caller departed and he came out of his office. The rest of his staff had gone home. Miss Ives sat alone at her desk in an empty room. She sat straight and stiff, her hands clasped tightly together in her lap. Her head was not lowered, but held rigidly level, and her face seemed frozen. Tears were running down her cheeks, with no sound, with no facial movement, against her resistance, beyond control.

She saw him and said dryly, guiltily, in apology, "I'm sorry, Mr. Rearden," not attempting the futile pretense of hiding her face.

He approached her. "Thank you," he said gently.

She looked up at him, astonished.

He smiled. "But don't you think you're underestimating me, Gwen? Isn't it too soon to cry over me?"

"I could have taken the rest of it," she whispered, "but they"—she pointed at the newspapers on her desk—"they're calling it a victory for anti-greed."

He laughed aloud. "I can see where such a distortion of the English language would make you furious," he said. "But what else?"

As she looked at him, her mouth relaxed a little. The victim whom she could not protect was her only point of reassurance in a world dissolving around her.

He moved his hand gently across her forehead; it was an unusual break of formality for him, and a silent acknowledgment of the things at which he had not laughed. "Go home, Gwen. I won't need you tonight. I'm going home myself in just a little while. No, I don't want you to wait."

It was past midnight, when, still sitting at his desk, bent over blue-prints of the bridge for the John Galt Line, he stopped his work abruptly, because emotion reached him in a sudden stab, not to be escaped any longer, as if a curtain of anesthesia had broken.

He slumped down, halfway, still holding onto some shred of resistance, and sat, his chest pressed to the edge of the desk to stop him, his head hanging down, as if the only achievement still possible to him was not to let his head drop down on the desk. He sat that way for a few moments, conscious of nothing but pain, a screaming pain without content or limit—he sat, not knowing whether it was in his mind or his body, reduced to the terrible ugliness of pain that stopped thought.

In a few moments, it was over. He raised his head and sat up straight, quietly, leaning back against his chair. Now he saw that in postponing this moment for hours, he had not been guilty of evasion: he had not thought of it, because there was nothing to think.

Thought—he told himself quietly—is a weapon one uses in order to act. No action was possible. Thought is the tool by which one makes a choice. No choice was left to him. Thought sets one's purpose and the way to reach it. In the matter of his life being torn piece by piece out of him, he was to have no voice, no purpose, no way, no defense.

He thought of this in astonishment. He saw for the first time that he had never known fear because, against any disaster, he had held the omnipotent cure of being able to act. No, he thought, not an assurance of victory—who can ever have that?—only the chance to act, which is all one needs. Now he was contemplating, impersonally and for the first time, the real heart of terror: being delivered to destruction with one's hands tied behind one's back.

Well, then, go on with your hands tied, he thought. Go on in chains. Go on. It must not stop you. . . . But another voice was telling him things he did not want to hear, while he fought back, crying through and against it: There's no point in thinking of that . . . there's no use . . . what for? . . . leave it alone!

He could not choke it off. He sat still, over the drawings of the bridge for the John Galt Line, and heard the things released by a voice that was part-sound, part-sight: They decided it without him. . . . They did not call for him, they did not ask, they did not let him speak. . . . They were not bound even by the duty to let him know—to let him know that they had slashed part of his life away and that he had to be ready to walk on as a cripple. . . . Of all those concerned, whoever they were, for whichever reason, for whatever need, *he* was the one they had not had to consider.

The sign at the end of a long road said: Rearden Ore. It hung over black tiers of metal . . . and over years and nights . . . over a clock ticking drops of his blood away . . . the blood he had given gladly, exultantly in payment for a distant day and a sign over a road . . . paid for with his effort, his strength, his mind, his hope . . . Destroyed at the whim of some men who sat and voted . . . Who knows by what minds? . . . Who knows whose will had placed them in power?—what motive moved them?—what was their knowledge?—which one of them, unaided, could bring a chunk of ore out of the earth? . . . Destroyed at the whim of men whom he had never seen and who had never seen those tiers of metal . . . Destroyed, because they so decided. By what right?

He shook his head. There are things one must not contemplate, he thought. There is an obscenity of evil which contaminates the observer. There is a limit to what it is proper for a man to see. He must not think of this, or look within it, or try to learn the nature of its roots.

Feeling quiet and empty, he told himself that he would be all right tomorrow. He would forgive himself the weakness of this night, it was like the tears one is permitted at a funeral, and then one learns how to live with an open wound or with a crippled factory.

He got up and walked to the window. The mills seemed deserted and still; he saw feeble snatches of red above black funnels, long coils of steam, the webbed diagonals of cranes and bridges.

He felt a desolate loneliness, of a kind he had never known before. He thought that Gwen Ives and Mr. Ward could look to him for hope, for relief, for renewal of courage. To whom could *he* look for it? He, too, needed it, for once. He wished he had a friend who could be permitted to see him suffer, without pretense or protection, on whom he could lean for a moment, just to say, "I'm very tired," and find a moment's rest. Of all the men he knew, was there one he wished he had beside him now? He heard the answer in his mind, immediate and shocking: Francisco d'Anconia.

His chuckle of anger brought him back. The absurdity of the longing jolted him into calm. That's what you get, he thought, when you indulge yourself in weakness.

He stood at the window, trying not to think. But he kept hearing words in his mind: Rearden Ore . . . Rearden Coal . . . Rearden Steel . . . Rearden Metal . . . What was the use? Why had he done it? Why should he ever want to do anything again? . . .

His first day on the ledges of the ore mines . . . The day when he stood in the wind, looking down at the ruins of a steel plant . . . The day when he stood here, in this office, at this window, and thought that a bridge could be made to carry incredible loads on just a few bars of metal, if one combined a truss with an arch, if one built diagonal bracing with the top members curved to—

He stopped and stood still. He *had not* thought of combining a truss with an arch, that day.

In the next moment, he was at his desk, bending over it, with one knee on the seat of the chair, with no time to think of sitting down, he was drawing lines, curves, triangles, columns of calculations, indiscriminately on the blueprints, on the desk blotter, on somebody's letters.

And an hour later, he was calling for a long-distance line, he was waiting for a phone to ring by a bed in a railway car on a siding, he was saying, "Dagny! That bridge of ours—throw in the ash can all the drawings I sent you, because . . . What? . . . Oh, that? To hell with that! Never mind the looters and their laws! Forget it! Dagny, what do we care! Listen, you know the contraption you called the Rearden Truss, that you admired so much? It's not worth a damn. I've figured out a truss that will beat anything ever built! Your bridge will carry four trains at once, stand three hundred years and cost you less than your cheapest culvert. I'll send you the drawings in two days, but I wanted to tell you about it right now. You see, it's a matter of combining a truss with an arch. If we take diagonal bracing and . . . What? . . . I can't hear you. Have you caught a cold? . . . What are you thanking me for, as yet? Wait till I explain it to you."

The worker smiled, looking at Eddie Willers across the table.

"I feel like a fugitive," said Eddie Willers. "I guess you know why I haven't been here for months?" He pointed at the underground cafeteria. "I'm supposed to be a vice-president now. The Vice-President in Charge of Operation. For God's sake, don't take it seriously. I stood it as long as I could, and then I had to escape, if only for one evening. . . . The first time I came down here for dinner, after my alleged promotion, they all stared at me so much, I didn't dare come back. Well, let them stare. You don't. I'm glad that it doesn't make any difference to you. . . . No, I haven't seen her for two weeks. But I speak to her on the phone every day, sometimes twice a day. . . . Yes, I know how she feels: she loves it. What is it we hear over the telephone—sound vibrations, isn't it? Well, her voice sounds as if it were turning into light vibrations—if you know what I mean. She enjoys running that horrible battle single-handed and winning. . . . Oh yes, she's winning! Do you know why you haven't read anything about the John Galt Line in the newspapers for some time? Because it's going so well . . . Only . . . that Rearden Metal rail will be the greatest track ever built, but what will be the use, if we don't have any engines powerful enough to take advantage of it? Look at the kind of patched coal-burners we've got left—they can barely manage to drag themselves fast enough for old trolley-car rails. . . . Still, there's hope. The United Locomotive Works went bankrupt. That's the best break we've had in the last few weeks, because their plant has been bought by Dwight Sanders. He's a brilliant young engineer who's got the only good aircraft plant in the country. He had to sell the aircraft plant to his brother, in order to take over United Locomotive. That's on account of the Equalization of Opportunity Bill. Sure, it's just a setup between them, but can you blame him? Anyway, we'll see Diesels coming out of the United Locomotive Works now. Dwight Sanders will start things going. . . . Yes, she's counting on him. Why do you ask that? . . . Yes, he's crucially important to us right now. We've just signed a contract with him, for the first ten Diesel engines he'll build. When I phoned her that the contract was signed, she laughed and said, 'You see? Is there ever any reason to be afraid?' . . . She said that, because she knows—I've never told her, but she knows—that I'm afraid. . . . Yes, I am. . . . I don't know . . . I wouldn't be afraid if I knew of what, I could do something about it. But this . . . Tell me, don't you really despise me for being Operating Vice-President? . . . But don't you see that it's vicious? . . . What honor? I don't know what it is that I really am: a clown, a ghost, an understudy or just a rotten stooge. When I sit in her office, in her chair, at her desk, I feel worse than that: I feel like a murderer. . . . Sure, I know that I'm supposed to be a stooge for *her*—and that would be an honor—but . . . but I feel as if in some horrible way which I can't quite grasp, I'm a stooge for Jim Taggart. Why should it be necessary for her to have a stooge? Why does she have to hide? Why did they throw her out of the building? Do you know that she had to move out into a dinky hole in the back alley, across from our Express and Baggage Entrance? You ought to take a look at it some time, that's the office of John Galt, Inc. Yet everybody knows that it's she who's still running Taggart Transcontinental. Why does she have to hide the magnificent job she's doing? Why are they giving her no credit? Why are they robbing her of her achievement—with me as the receiver of stolen goods? Why are they doing everything in their power to make it impossible for her to succeed, when she's all they've got standing between them and destruction? Why are they torturing her in return for saving their lives? . . . What's the matter with you? Why do you look at me like that? . . . Yes, I guess you understand. . . . There's something about it all that I can't define, and it's something evil. That's why I'm afraid. . . . I don't think one can get away with it. . . . You know, it's strange, but I think they know it, too, Jim and his crowd and all of them in the building. There's something guilty and sneaky about the whole place. Guilty and sneaky and dead. Taggart Transcontinental is now like a man who's lost his soul . . . who's *betrayed* his soul. . . . No, she doesn't care. Last time she was in New York, she came in unexpectedly—I was in my office, in *her* office—and suddenly the door opened and there she was. She came in, saying, 'Mr. Willers, I'm looking for a job as a station operator, would you give me a chance?' I wanted to damn them all, but I had to laugh, I was so glad to see her and she was laughing so happily. She had come straight from the airport—she wore slacks and a flying jacket—she looked wonderful—she'd got windburned, it looked like a suntan, just as if she'd returned from a vacation. She made me remain where I was, in her chair, and she sat on the desk and talked about the new bridge of the John Galt Line. . . . No. No, I never asked her why she chose that name. . . . I don't know what it means to her. A sort of challenge, I guess . . . I don't know to whom . . . Oh, it doesn't matter, it doesn't mean a thing, there isn't any John Galt, but I wish she hadn't used it. I don't like it, do you? . . . You do? You don't sound very happy saying it."

*   *   *

The windows of the offices of the John Galt Line faced a dark alley. Looking up from her desk, Dagny could not see the sky, only the wall of a building rising past her range of vision. It was the side wall of the great skyscraper of Taggart Transcontinental.

Her new headquarters were two rooms on the ground floor of a half-collapsed structure. The structure still stood, but its upper stories were boarded off as unsafe for occupancy. Such tenants as it sheltered were half-bankrupt, existing, as it did, on the inertia of the momentum of the past.

She liked her new place: it saved money. The rooms contained no superfluous furniture or people. The furniture had come from junk shops. The people were the choice best she could find. On her rare visits to New York, she had no time to notice the room where she worked; she noticed only that it served its purpose.

She did not know what made her stop tonight and look at the thin streaks of rain on the glass of the window, at the wall of the building across the alley.

It was past midnight. Her small staff had gone. She was due at the airport at three A.M., to fly her plane back to Colorado. She had little left to do, only a few of Eddie's reports to read. With the sudden break of the tension of hurrying, she stopped, unable to go on. The reports seemed to require an effort beyond her power. It was too late to go home and sleep, too early to go to the airport. She thought: You're tired—and watched her own mood with severe, contemptuous detachment, knowing that it would pass.

She had flown to New York unexpectedly, at a moment's notice, leaping to the controls of her plane within twenty minutes after hearing a brief item in a news broadcast. The radio voice had said that Dwight Sanders had retired from business, suddenly, without reason or explanation. She had hurried to New York, hoping to find him and stop him. But she had felt, while flying across the continent, that there would be no trace of him to find.

The spring rain hung motionless in the air beyond the window, like a thin mist. She sat, looking across at the open cavern of the Express and Baggage Entrance of the Taggart Terminal. There were naked lights inside, among the steel girders of the ceiling, and a few piles of luggage on the worn concrete of the floor. The place looked abandoned and dead.

She glanced at a jagged crack on the wall of her office. She heard no sound. She knew she was alone in the ruins of a building. It seemed as if she were alone in the city. She felt an emotion held back for years: a loneliness much beyond this moment, beyond the silence of the room and the wet, glistening emptiness of the street; the loneliness of a gray wasteland where nothing was worth reaching; the loneliness of her childhood.

She rose and walked to the window. By pressing her face to the pane, she could see the whole of the Taggart Building, its lines converging abruptly to its distant pinnacle in the sky. She looked up at the dark window of the room that had been her office. She felt as if she were in exile, never to return, as if she were separated from the building by much more than a sheet of glass, a curtain of rain and the span of a few months.

She stood, in a room of crumbling plaster, pressed to the window-pane, looking up at the unattainable form of everything she loved. She did not know the nature of her loneliness. The only words that named it were: This is not the world I expected.

Once, when she was sixteen, looking at a long stretch of Taggart track, at the rails that converged—like the lines of a skyscraper—to a single point in the distance, she had told Eddie Willers that she had always felt as if the rails were held in the hand of a man beyond the horizon—no, not her father or any of the men in the office—and some day she would meet him.

She shook her head and turned away from the window.

She went back to her desk. She tried to reach for the reports. But suddenly she was slumped across the desk, her head on her arm. Don't, she thought; but she did not move to rise, it made no difference, there was no one to see her.

This was a longing she had never permitted herself to acknowledge. She faced it now. She thought: If emotion is one's response to the things the world has to offer, if she loved the rails, the building, and more: if she loved her love for them—there was still one response, the greatest, that she had missed. She thought: To find a feeling that would hold, as their sum, as their final expression, the purpose of all the things she loved on earth . . . To find a consciousness like her own, who would be the meaning of her world, as she would be of his . . . No, not Francisco d'Anconia, not Hank Rearden, not any man she had ever met or admired . . . A man who existed only in her knowledge of her capacity for an emotion she had never felt, but would have given her life to experience . . . She twisted herself in a slow, faint movement, her breasts pressed to the desk; she felt the longing in her muscles, in the nerves of her body.

Is that what you want? Is it as simple as that?—she thought, but knew that it was not simple. There was some unbreakable link between her love for her work and the desire of her body; as if one gave her the right to the other, the right and the meaning; as if one were the comple-tion of the other—and the desire would never be satisfied, except by a being of equal greatness.

Her face pressed to her arm, she moved her head, shaking it slowly in negation. She would never find it. Her own thought of what life could be like, was all she would ever have of the world she had wanted. Only the thought of it—and a few rare moments, like a few lights reflected from it on her way—to know, to hold, to follow to the end . . .

She raised her head.

On the pavement of the alley, outside her window, she saw the shadow of a man who stood at the door of her office.

The door was some steps away; she could not see him, or the street light beyond, only his shadow on the stones of the pavement. He stood perfectly still.

He was so close to the door, like a man about to enter, that she waited to hear him knock. Instead, she saw the shadow jerk abruptly, as if he were jolted backward, then he turned and walked away. There was only the outline of his hat brim and shoulders left on the ground, when he stopped. The shadow lay still for a moment, wavered, and grew longer again as he came back.

She felt no fear. She sat at her desk, motionless, watching in blank wonder. He stopped at the door, then backed away from it; he stood somewhere in the middle of the alley, then paced restlessly and stopped again. His shadow swung like an irregular pendulum across the pavement, describing the course of a soundless battle: it was a man fighting himself to enter that door or to escape.

She looked on, with peculiar detachment. She had no power to react, only to observe. She wondered numbly, distantly: Who was he? Had he been watching her from somewhere in the darkness? Had he seen her slumped across her desk, in the lighted, naked window? Had he watched her desolate loneliness as she was now watching his? She felt nothing. They were alone in the silence of a dead city—it seemed to her that he was miles away, a reflection of suffering without identity, a fellow survivor whose problem was as distant to her as hers would be to him. He paced, moving out of her sight, coming back again. She sat, watching—on the glistening pavement of a dark alley—the shadow of an unknown torment.

The shadow moved away once more. She waited. It did not return. Then she leaped to her feet. She had wanted to see the outcome of the battle; now that he had won it—or lost—she was struck by the sudden, urgent need to know his identity and motive. She ran through the dark anteroom, she threw the door open and looked out.

The alley was empty. The pavement went tapering off into the distance, like a band of wet mirror under a few spaced lights. There was no one in sight. She saw the dark hole of a broken window in an abandoned shop. Beyond it, there were the doors of a few rooming houses. Across the alley, streaks of rain glittered under a light that hung over the black gap of an open door leading down to the underground tunnels of Taggart Transcontinental.

* * *

Rearden signed the papers, pushed them across the desk and looked away, thinking that he would never have to think of them again, wishing he were carried to the time when this moment would be far behind him.

Paul Larkin reached for the papers hesitantly; he looked ingratiatingly helpless. "It's only a legal technicality, Hank," he said. "You know that I'll always consider these ore mines as yours."

Rearden shook his head slowly; it was just a movement of his neck muscles; his face looked immovable, as if he were speaking to a stranger. "No," he said. "Either I own a property or I don't."

"But . . . but you know that you can trust me. You don't have to worry about your supply of ore. We've made an agreement. You know that you can count on me."

"I don't know it. I hope I can."

"But I've given you my word."

"I have never been at the mercy of anyone's word before."

"Why . . . why do you say that? We're friends. I'll do anything you wish. You'll get my entire output. The mines are still yours—just as good as yours. You have nothing to fear. I'll . . . Hank, what's the matter?"

"Don't talk."

"But . . . but what's the matter?"

"I don't like assurances. I don't want any pretense about how safe I am. I'm not. We have made an agreement which I can't enforce. I want you to know that I understand my position fully. If you intend to keep your word, don't talk about it, just *do* it."

"Why do you look at me as if it were my fault? You know how badly I feel about it. I bought the mines only because I thought it would help you out—I mean, I thought you'd rather sell them to a friend than to some total stranger. It's not my fault. I don't like that miserable Equalization Bill, I don't know who's behind it, I never dreamed they'd pass it, it was such a shock to me when they—"

"Never mind."

"But I only—"

"Why do you insist on talking about it?"

"I . . ." Larkin's voice was pleading. "I gave you the best price, Hank. The law said 'reasonable compensation.' My bid was higher than anyone else's."

Rearden looked at the papers still lying across the desk. He thought of the payment these papers gave him for his ore mines. Two-thirds of the sum was money which Larkin had obtained as a loan from the government; the new law made provisions for such loans "in order to give a fair opportunity to the new owners who have never had a chance." Two-thirds of the rest was a loan he himself had granted to Larkin, a mortgage he had accepted on his own mines. . . . And the government money, he thought suddenly, the money now given to him as payment for his property, where had that come from? Whose work had provided it?

"You don't have to worry, Hank," said Larkin, with that incomprehensible, insistent note of pleading in his voice. "It's just a paper formality."

Rearden wondered dimly what it was that Larkin wanted from him. He felt that the man was waiting for something beyond the physical fact of the sale, some words which he, Rearden, was supposed to pronounce, some action pertaining to mercy which he was expected to grant. Larkin's eyes, in this moment of his best fortune, had the sickening look of a beggar.

"Why should you be angry, Hank? It's only a new form of legal red tape. Just a new historical condition. Nobody can help it, if it's a historical condition. Nobody can be blamed for it. But there's always a way to get along. Look at all the others. They don't mind. They're—"

"They're setting up stooges whom they control, to run the properties extorted from them. I—"

"Now why do you want to use such words?"

"I might as well tell you—and I think you know it—that I am not good at games of that kind. I have neither the time nor the stomach to devise some form of blackmail in order to tie you up and own my mines through you. Ownership is a thing I don't share. And I don't wish to hold it by the grace of your cowardice—by means of a constant struggle to outwit you and keep some threat over your head. I don't do business that way and I don't deal with cowards. The mines are yours. If you wish to give me first call on all the ore produced, you will do so. If you wish to double-cross me, it's in your power."

Larkin looked hurt. "That's very unfair of you," he said; there was a dry little note of righteous reproach in his voice. "I have never given you cause to distrust me." He picked up the papers with a hasty movement.

Rearden saw the papers disappear into Larkin's inside coat pocket. He saw the flare of the open coat, the wrinkles of a vest pulled tight over flabby bulges, and a stain of perspiration in the armpit of the shirt.

Unsummoned, the picture of a face seen twenty-seven years ago rose suddenly in his mind. It was the face of a preacher on a street corner he had passed, in a town he could not remember any longer. Only the dark walls of the slums remained in his memory, the rain of an autumn evening, and the righteous malice of the man's mouth, a small mouth stretched to yell into the darkness: ". . . the noblest ideal—that man live for the sake of his brothers, that the strong work for the weak, that he who has ability serve him who hasn't . . ."

Then he saw the boy who had been Hank Rearden at eighteen. He saw the tension of the face, the speed of the walk, the drunken exhilaration of the body, drunk on the energy of sleepless nights, the proud lift of the head, the clear, steady, ruthless eyes, the eyes of a man who drove himself without pity toward that which he wanted. And he saw what Paul Larkin must have been at that time—a youth with an aged baby's face, smiling ingratiatingly, joylessly, begging to be spared, pleading with the universe to give him a chance. If someone had shown that youth to the Hank Rearden of that time and told him that this was to be the goal of his steps, the collector of the energy of his aching tendons, what would he have—

It was not a thought, it was like the punch of a fist inside his skull. Then, when he could think again, Rearden knew what the boy he had been would have felt: a desire to step on the obscene thing which was Larkin and grind every wet bit of it out of existence.

He had never experienced an emotion of this kind. It took him a few moments to realize that this was what men called hatred.

He noticed that rising to leave and muttering some sort of good-byes, Larkin had a wounded, reproachful, mouth-pinched look, as if he, Larkin, were the injured party.

When he sold his coal mines to Ken Danagger, who owned the largest coal company in Pennsylvania, Rearden wondered why he felt as if it were almost painless. He felt no hatred. Ken Danagger was a man in his fifties, with a hard, closed face; he had started in life as a miner.

When Rearden handed to him the deed to his new property, Danagger said impassively, "I don't believe I've mentioned that any coal you buy from me, you'll get it at cost."

Rearden glanced at him, astonished. "It's against the law," he said.

"Who's going to find out what sort of cash I hand to you in your own living room?"

"You're talking about a rebate."

"I am."

"That's against two dozen laws. They'll sock you worse than me, if they catch you at it."

"Sure. That's your protection—so you won't be left at the mercy of my good will."

Rearden smiled; it was a happy smile, but he closed his eyes as under a blow. Then he shook his head. "Thanks," he said. "But I'm not one of them. I don't expect anybody to work for me at cost."

"I'm not one of them, either," said Danagger angrily. "Look here, Rearden, don't you suppose I know what I'm getting, unearned? The money doesn't pay you for it. Not nowadays."

"You didn't volunteer to bid to buy my property. I asked you to buy it. I wish there had been somebody like you in the ore business, to take over my mines. There wasn't. If you want to do me a favor, don't offer me rebates. Give me a chance to pay you higher prices, higher than anyone else will offer, sock me anything you wish, just so I'll be first to get the coal. I'll manage my end of it. Only let me have the coal."

"You'll have it."

Rearden wondered, for a while, why he heard no word from Wesley Mouch. His calls to Washington remained unanswered. Then he received a letter consisting of a single sentence which informed him that

Mr. Mouch was resigning from his employ. Two weeks later, he read in the newspapers that Wesley Mouch had been appointed Assistant Co-ordinator of the Bureau of Economic Planning and National Resources.

Don't dwell on any of it—thought Rearden, through the silence of many evenings, fighting the sudden access of that new emotion which he did not want to feel—there is an unspeakable evil in the world, you know it, and it's no use dwelling on the details of it. You must work a little harder. Just a little harder. Don't let it win.

The beams and girders of the Rearden Metal bridge were coming daily out of the rolling mills, and were being shipped to the site of the John Galt Line, where the first shapes of green-blue metal, swung into space to span the canyon, glittered in the first rays of the spring sun. He had no time for pain, no energy for anger. Within a few weeks, it was over; the blinding stabs of hatred ceased and did not return.

He was back in confident self-control on the evening when he tele-phoned Eddie Willers. "Eddie, I'm in New York, at the Wayne-Falk-land. Come to have breakfast with me tomorrow morning. There's some-thing I'd like to discuss with you."

Eddie Willers went to the appointment with a heavy feeling of guilt. He had not recovered from the shock of the Equalization of Opportunity Bill; it had left a dull ache within him, like the black-and-blue mark of a blow. He disliked the sight of the city: it now looked as if it hid the threat of some malicious unknown. He dreaded facing one of the Bill's victims: he felt almost as if he, Eddie Willers, shared the responsibility for it in some terrible way which he could not define.

When he saw Rearden, the feeling vanished. There was no hint sug-gesting a victim, in Rearden's bearing. Beyond the windows of the hotel room, the spring sunlight of early morning sparkled on the windows of the city, the sky was a very pale blue that seemed young, the offices were still closed, and the city did not look as if it held malice, but as if it were joyously, hopefully ready to swing into action—in the same man-ner as Rearden. He looked refreshed by an untroubled sleep, he wore a dressing gown, he seemed impatient of the necessity to dress, unwilling to delay the exciting game of his business duties.

"Good morning, Eddie. Sorry if I got you out so early. It's the only time I had. Have to go back to Philadelphia right after breakfast. We can talk while we're eating."

The dressing gown he wore was of dark blue flannel, with the white initials "H R" on the breast pocket. He looked young, relaxed, at home in this room and in the world.

Eddie watched a waiter wheel the breakfast table into the room with a swift efficiency that made him feel braced. He found himself enjoying the stiff freshness of the white tablecloth and the sunlight sparkling on the silver, on the two bowls of crushed ice holding glasses of orange juice; he had not known that such things could give him an invigorating pleasure.

"I didn't want to phone Dagny long distance about this particular matter," said Rearden. "She has enough to do. We can settle it in a few minutes, you and I."

"If I have the authority to do it."

Rearden smiled. "You have." He leaned forward across the table. "Eddie, what's the financial state of Taggart Transcontinental at the moment? Desperate?"

"Worse than that, Mr. Rearden."

"Are you able to meet pay rolls?"

"Not quite. We've kept it out of the newspapers, but I think everybody knows it. We're in arrears all over the system and Jim is running out of excuses."

"Do you know that your first payment for the Rearden Metal rail is due next week?"

"Yes, I know it."

"Well, let's agree on a moratorium. I'm going to give you an extension—you won't have to pay me anything until six months after the opening of the John Galt Line."

Eddie Willers put down his cup of coffee with a sharp thud. He could not say a word.

Rearden chuckled. "What's the matter? You do have the authority to accept, don't you?"

"Mr. Rearden . . . I don't know . . . what to say to you."

"Why, just 'okay' is all that's necessary."

"Okay, Mr. Rearden." Eddie's voice was barely audible.

"I'll draw up the papers and send them to you. You can tell Jim about it and have him sign them."

"Yes, Mr. Rearden."

"I don't like to deal with Jim. He'd waste two hours trying to make himself believe that he's made me believe that he's doing me a favor by accepting."

Eddie sat without moving, looking down at his plate.

"What's the matter?"

"Mr. Rearden, I'd like . . . to say thank you . . . but there isn't any form of it big enough to—"

"Look, Eddie. You've got the makings of a good businessman, so you'd better get a few things straight. There aren't any thank-you's in situations of this kind. I'm not doing it for Taggart Transcontinental. It's a simple, practical, selfish matter on my part. Why should I collect my money from you now, when it might prove to be the death blow to your company? If your company were no good, I'd collect, and fast. I don't engage in charity and I don't gamble on incompetents. But you're still the best railroad in the country. When the John Galt Line is completed, you'll be the soundest one financially. So I have good reason to wait. Besides, you're in trouble on account of my rail. I intend to see you win."

"I still owe you thanks, Mr. Rearden . . . for something much greater than charity."

"No. Don't you see? I have just received a great deal of money . . . which I didn't want. I can't invest it. It's of no use to me whatever. . . . So, in a way, it pleases me that I can turn that money against the same people in the same battle. They made it possible for me to give you an extension to help you fight them."

He saw Eddie wincing, as if he had hit a wound. "That's what's horrible about it!"

"What?"

"What they've done to you—and what you're doing in return. I mean—" He stopped. "Forgive me, Mr. Rearden. I know this is no way to talk business."

Rearden smiled. "Thanks, Eddie. I know what you mean. But forget it. To hell with them."

"Yes. Only . . . Mr. Rearden, may I say something to you? I know it's completely improper and I'm not speaking as a vice-president."

"Go ahead."

"I don't have to tell you what your offer means to Dagny, to me, to every decent person on Taggart Transcontinental. You know it. And you know you can count on us. But . . . but I think it's horrible that Jim Taggart should benefit, too—that you should be the one to save him and people like him, after they—"

Rearden laughed. "Eddie, what do we care about people like him? We're driving an express, and they're riding on the roof, making a lot of noise about being leaders. Why should we care? We have enough power to carry them along—haven't we?"

*　*　*

"It won't stand."

The summer sun made blotches of fire on the windows of the city, and glittering sparks in the dust of the streets. Columns of heat shimmered through the air, rising from the roofs to the white page of the calendar. The calendar's motor ran on, marking off the last days of June.

"It won't stand," people said. "When they run the first train on the John Galt Line, the rail will split. They'll never get to the bridge. If they do, the bridge will collapse under the engine."

From the slopes of Colorado, freight trains rolled down the track of the Phoenix-Durango, north to Wyoming and the main line of Taggart Transcontinental, south to New Mexico and the main line of the Atlantic Southern. Strings of tank cars went radiating in all directions from the Wyatt oil fields to industries in distant states. No one spoke about them. To the knowledge of the public, the tank trains moved as silently as rays and, as rays, they were noticed only when they became the light of electric lamps, the heat of furnaces, the movement of motors; but as such, they were not noticed, they were taken for granted.

The Phoenix-Durango Railroad was to end operations on July 25.

"Hank Rearden is a greedy monster," people said. "Look at the fortune he's made. Has he ever given anything in return? Has he ever shown any sign of social conscience? Money, that's all he's after. He'll do anything for money. What does he care if people lose their lives when his bridge collapses?"

"The Taggarts have been a band of vultures for generations," people said. "It's in their blood. Just remember that the founder of that family was Nat Taggart, the most notoriously anti-social scoundrel that ever lived, who bled the country white to squeeze a fortune for himself. You can be sure that a Taggart won't hesitate to risk people's lives in order to make a profit. They bought inferior rail, because it's cheaper than steel—what do they care about catastrophes and mangled human bodies, after they've collected the fares?"

People said it because other people said it. They did not know why it was being said and heard everywhere. They did not give or ask for reasons. "Reason," Dr. Pritchett had told them, "is the most naïve of all superstitions."

"The source of public opinion?" said Claude Slagenhop in a radio speech. "There is no source of public opinion. It is spontaneously general. It is a reflex of the collective instinct of the collective mind."

Orren Boyle gave an interview to *Globe,* the news magazine with the largest circulation. The interview was devoted to the subject of the grave social responsibility of metallurgists, stressing the fact that metal performed so many crucial tasks where human lives depended on its quality. "One should not, it seems to me, use human beings as guinea pigs in the launching of a new product," he said. He mentioned no names.

"Why, no, I don't say that that bridge will collapse," said the chief metallurgist of Associated Steel, on a television program. "I don't say it at all. I just say that if I had any children, I wouldn't let them ride on the first train that's going to cross that bridge. But it's only a personal preference, nothing more, just because I'm overly fond of children."

"I don't claim that the Rearden-Taggart contraption will collapse," wrote Bertram Scudder in *The Future.* "Maybe it will and maybe it won't. That's not the important issue. The important issue is: what protection does society have against the arrogance, selfishness and greed of two unbridled individualists, whose records are conspicuously devoid of any public-spirited actions? These two, apparently, are willing to stake the lives of their fellow men on their own conceited notions about their powers of judgment, against the overwhelming majority opinion of recognized experts. Should society permit it? If that thing does collapse, won't it be too late to take precautionary measures? Won't it be like locking the barn after the horse has escaped? It has always been the belief of this column that certain kinds of horses should be kept bridled and locked, on general social principles."

A group that called itself "Committee of Disinterested Citizens" collected signatures on a petition demanding a year's study of the John Galt Line by government experts before the first train were allowed to run. The petition stated that its signers had no motive other than "a sense of civic duty." The first signatures were those of Balph Eubank and Mort Liddy. The petition was given a great deal of space and comment in all the newspapers. The consideration it received was respectful, because it came from people who were disinterested.

No space was given by the newspapers to the progress of the construction of the John Galt Line. No reporter was sent to look at the scene. The general policy of the press had been stated by a famous editor five years ago. "There are no objective facts," he had said. "Every report on facts is only somebody's opinion. It is, therefore, useless to write about facts."

A few businessmen thought that one should think about the possibility that there might be commercial value in Rearden Metal. They undertook a survey of the question. They did not hire metallurgists to examine samples, nor engineers to visit the site of construction. They took a public poll. Ten thousand people, guaranteed to represent every existing kind of brain, were asked the question: "Would you ride on the John Galt Line?" The answer, overwhelmingly, was: "No, sir-ree!"

No voices were heard in public in defense of Rearden Metal. And nobody attached significance to the fact that the stock of Taggart Transcontinental was rising on the market, very slowly, almost furtively. There were men who watched and played safe. Mr. Mowen bought Taggart stock in the name of his sister. Ben Nealy bought it in the name of a cousin. Paul Larkin bought it under an alias. "I don't believe in raising controversial issues," said one of these men.

"Oh yes, of course, the construction is moving on schedule," said James Taggart, shrugging, to his Board of Directors. "Oh yes, you may feel full confidence. My dear sister does not happen to be a human being, but just an internal combustion engine, so one must not wonder at her success."

When James Taggart heard a rumor that some bridge girders had split and crashed, killing three workmen, he leaped to his feet and ran to his secretary's office, ordering him to call Colorado. He waited, pressed against the secretary's desk, as if seeking protection; his eyes had the unfocused look of panic. Yet his mouth moved suddenly into almost a smile and he said, "I'd give anything to see Henry Rearden's face right now." When he heard that the rumor was false, he said, "Thank God!" But his voice had a note of disappointment.

"Oh well!" said Philip Rearden to his friends, hearing the same rumor. "Maybe he can fail, too, once in a while. Maybe my great brother isn't as great as he thinks."

"Darling," said Lillian Rearden to her husband, "I fought for you yesterday, at a tea where the women were saying that Dagny Taggart is your mistress. . . . Oh, for heaven's sake, don't look at me like that!

I know it's preposterous and I gave them hell for it. It's just that those silly bitches can't imagine any other reason why a woman would take such a stand against everybody for the sake of your Metal. Of course, I know better than that. I know that the Taggart woman is perfectly sexless and doesn't give a damn about you—and, darling, I know that if you ever had the courage for anything of the sort, which you haven't, you wouldn't go for an adding machine in tailored suits, you'd go for some blond, feminine chorus girl who—oh, but Henry, I'm only joking! —don't look at me like that!"

"Dagny," James Taggart said miserably, "what's going to happen to us? Taggart Transcontinental has become so unpopular!"

Dagny laughed, in enjoyment of the moment, any moment, as if the undercurrent of enjoyment was constant within her and little was needed to tap it. She laughed easily, her mouth relaxed and open. Her teeth were very white against her sun-scorched face. Her eyes had the look, acquired in open country, of being set for great distances. On her last few visits to New York, he had noticed that she looked at him as if she did not see him.

"What are we going to do? The public is so overwhelmingly against us!"

"Jim, do you remember the story they tell about Nat Taggart? He said that he envied only one of his competitors, the one who said 'The public be damned!' He wished he had said it."

In the summer days and in the heavy stillness of the evenings of the city, there were moments when a lonely man or woman—on a park bench, on a street corner, at an open window—would see in a newspaper a brief mention of the progress of the John Galt Line, and would look at the city with a sudden stab of hope. They were the very young, who felt that it was the kind of event they longed to see happening in the world—or the very old, who had seen a world in which such events did happen. They did not care about railroads, they knew nothing about business, they knew only that someone was fighting against great odds and winning. They did not admire the fighters' purpose, they believed the voices of public opinion—and yet, when they read that the Line was growing, they felt a moment's sparkle and wondered why it made their own problems seem easier.

Silently, unknown to everyone except to the freight yard of Taggart Transcontinental in Cheyenne and the office of the John Galt Line in the dark alley, freight was rolling in and orders for cars were piling up— for the first train to run on the John Galt Line. Dagny Taggart had announced that the first train would be, not a passenger express loaded with celebrities and politicians, as was the custom, but a freight special.

The freight came from farms, from lumber yards, from mines all over the country, from distant places whose last means of survival were the new factories of Colorado. No one wrote about these shippers, because they were men who were not disinterested.

The Phoenix-Durango Railroad was to close on July 25. The first train of the John Galt Line was to run on July 22.

"Well, it's like this, Miss Taggart," said the delegate of the Union of Locomotive Engineers. "I don't think we're going to allow you to run that train."

Dagny sat at her battered desk, against the blotched wall of her office. She said, without moving, "Get out of here."

It was a sentence the man had never heard in the polished offices of railroad executives. He looked bewildered. "I came to tell you—"

"If you have anything to say to me, start over again."

"What?"

"Don't tell me what you're going to allow me to do."

"Well, I meant we're not going to allow our men to run your train."

"That's different."

"Well, that's what we've decided."

"Who's decided it?"

"The committee. What you're doing is a violation of human rights. You can't force men to go out to get killed—when that bridge collapses —just to make money for you."

She reached for a sheet of blank paper and handed it to him. "Put it down in writing," she said, "and we'll sign a contract to that effect."

"What contract?"

"That no member of your union will ever be employed to run an engine on the John Galt Line."

"Why . . . wait a minute . . . I haven't said—"

"You don't want to sign such a contract?"

"No, I—"

"Why not, since you know that the bridge is going to collapse?"

"I only want—"

"I know what you want. You want a stranglehold on your men by means of the jobs which *I* give them—and on me, by means of your men. You want me to provide the jobs, and you want to make it impossible for me to have any jobs to provide. Now I'll give you a choice. That train is going to be run. You have no choice about that. But you can choose whether it's going to be run by one of your men or not. If you choose not to let them, the train will still run, if I have to drive the engine myself. Then, if the bridge collapses, there won't be any railroad left in existence, anyway. But if it doesn't collapse, no member of your union will ever get a job on the John Galt Line. If you think that I need your men more than they need me, choose accordingly. If you know that I can run an engine, but they can't build a railroad, choose according to that. Now are you going to forbid your men to run that train?"

"I didn't say we'd forbid it. I haven't said anything about forbidding. But . . . but you can't force men to risk their lives on something nobody's ever tried before."

"I'm not going to force anyone to take that run."

"What are you going to do?"

"I'm going to ask for a volunteer."

"And if none of them volunteers?"

"Then it will be my problem, not yours."

"Well, let me tell you that I'm going to advise them to refuse."

"Go ahead. Advise them anything you wish. Tell them whatever you like. But leave the choice to them. Don't try to forbid it."

The notice that appeared in every roundhouse of the Taggart system was signed "Edwin Willers, Vice-President in Charge of Operation." It asked engineers, who were willing to drive the first train on the John Galt Line, so to inform the office of Mr. Willers, not later than eleven A.M. of July 15.

It was a quarter of eleven, on the morning of the fifteenth, when the telephone rang in her office. It was Eddie, calling from high up in the Taggart Building outside her window. "Dagny, I think you'd better come over." His voice sounded queer.

She hurried across the street, then down the marble-floored halls, to the door that still carried the name "Dagny Taggart" on its glass panel. She pulled the door open.

The anteroom of the office was full. Men stood jammed among the desks, against the walls. As she entered, they took their hats off in sudden silence. She saw the graying heads, the muscular shoulders, she saw the smiling faces of her staff at their desks and the face of Eddie Willers at the end of the room. Everybody knew that nothing had to be said.

Eddie stood by the open door of her office. The crowd parted to let her approach him. He moved his hand, pointing at the room, then at a pile of letters and telegrams.

"Dagny, every one of them," he said. "Every engineer on Taggart Transcontinental. Those who could, came here, some from as far as the Chicago Division." He pointed at the mail. "There's the rest of them. To be exact, there's only three I haven't heard from: one's on a vacation in the north woods, one's in a hospital, and one's in jail for reckless driving—of his automobile."

She looked at the men. She saw the suppressed grins on the solemn faces. She inclined her head, in acknowledgment. She stood for a moment, head bowed, as if she were accepting a verdict, knowing that the verdict applied to her, to every man in the room and to the world beyond the walls of the building.

"Thank you," she said.

Most of the men had seen her many times. Looking at her, as she raised her head, many of them thought—in astonishment and for the first time—that the face of their Operating Vice-President was the face of a woman and that it was beautiful.

Someone in the back of the crowd cried suddenly, cheerfully, "To hell with Jim Taggart!"

An explosion answered him. The men laughed, they cheered, they broke into applause. The response was out of all proportion to the sentence. But the sentence had given them the excuse they needed. They seemed to be applauding the speaker, in insolent defiance of authority. But everyone in the room knew who it was that they were cheering.

She raised her hand. "We're too early," she said, laughing. "Wait till a week from today. That's when we ought to celebrate. And believe me, we will!"

They drew lots for the run. She picked a folded slip of paper from among a pile containing all their names. The winner was not in the room, but he was one of the best men on the system, Pat Logan, engineer of the Taggart Comet on the Nebraska Division.

"Wire Pat and tell him he's been demoted to a freight," she said to Eddie. She added casually, as if it were a last-moment decision, but it fooled no one, "Oh yes, tell him that I'm going to ride with him in the cab of the engine on that run."

An old engineer beside her grinned and said, "I thought you would, Miss Taggart."

* * *

Rearden was in New York on the day when Dagny telephoned him from her office. "Hank, I'm going to have a press conference tomorrow."

He laughed aloud. "No!"

"Yes." Her voice sounded earnest, but, dangerously, a bit too earnest. "The newspapers have suddenly discovered me and are asking questions. I'm going to answer them."

"Have a good time."

"I will. Are you going to be in town tomorrow? I'd like to have you in on it."

"Okay. I wouldn't want to miss it."

The reporters who came to the press conference in the office of the John Galt Line were young men who had been trained to think that their job consisted of concealing from the world the nature of its events. It was their daily duty to serve as audience for some public figure who made utterances about the public good, in phrases carefully chosen to convey no meaning. It was their daily job to sling words together in any combination they pleased, so long as the words did not fall into a sequence saying something specific. They could not understand the interview now being given to them.

Dagny Taggart sat behind her desk in an office that looked like a slum basement. She wore a dark blue suit with a white blouse, beautifully tailored, suggesting an air of formal, almost military elegance. She sat straight, and her manner was severely dignified, just a shade too dignified.

Rearden sat in a corner of the room, sprawled across a broken armchair, his long legs thrown over one of its arms, his body leaning against the other. His manner was pleasantly informal, just a bit too informal.

In the clear, monotonous voice of a military report, consulting no papers, looking straight at the men, Dagny recited the technological facts about the John Galt Line, giving exact figures on the nature of the rail, the capacity of the bridge, the method of construction, the costs. Then, in the dry tone of a banker, she explained the financial prospects of the Line and named the large profits she expected to make. "That is all," she said.

"All?" said one of the reporters. "Aren't you going to give us a message for the public?"

"That was my message."

"But hell—I mean, aren't you going to defend yourself?"

"Against what?"

"Don't you want to tell us something to justify your Line?"

"I have."

A man with a mouth shaped as a permanent sneer asked, "Well, what I want to know, as Bertram Scudder stated, is what protection do we have against your Line being no good?"

"Don't ride on it."

Another asked, "Aren't you going to tell us your motive for building that Line?"

"I have told you: the profit which I expect to make."

"Oh, Miss Taggart, don't say that!" cried a young boy. He was new, he was still honest about his job, and he felt that he liked Dagny Taggart, without knowing why. "That's the wrong thing to say. That's what they're all saying about you."

"Are they?"

"I'm sure you didn't mean it the way it sounds and . . . and I'm sure you'll want to clarify it."

"Why, yes, if you wish me to. The average profit of railroads has been two per cent of the capital invested. An industry that does so much and keeps so little, should consider itself immoral. As I have explained, the cost of the John Galt Line in relation to the traffic which it will carry makes me expect a profit of not less than fifteen per cent on our investment. Of course, any industrial profit above four per cent is considered usury nowadays. I shall, nevertheless, do my best to make the John Galt Line earn a profit of twenty per cent for me, if possible. That was my motive for building the Line. Have I made myself clear now?"

The boy was looking at her helplessly. "You don't mean, to earn a profit for *you*, Miss Taggart? You mean, for the small stockholders, of course?" he prompted hopefully.

"Why, no. I happen to be one of the largest stockholders of Taggart Transcontinental, so my share of the profits will be one of the largest. Now, Mr. Rearden is in a much more fortunate position, because he has no stockholders to share with—or would you rather make your own statement, Mr. Rearden?"

"Yes, gladly," said Rearden. "Inasmuch as the formula of Rearden Metal is my own personal secret, and in view of the fact that the Metal costs much less to produce than you boys can imagine, I expect to skin the public to the tune of a profit of twenty-five per cent in the next few years."

"What do you mean, skin the public, Mr. Rearden?" asked the boy. "If it's true, as I've read in your ads, that your Metal will last three times longer than any other and at half the price, wouldn't the public be getting a bargain?"

"Oh, have you noticed that?" said Rearden.

"Do the two of you realize you're talking for publication?" asked the man with the sneer.

"But, Mr. Hopkins," said Dagny, in polite astonishment, "is there any reason why we would talk to you, if it weren't for publication?"

"Do you want us to quote all the things you said?"

"I hope I may trust you to be sure and quote them. Would you oblige me by taking this down verbatim?" She paused to see their pencils ready, then dictated: "Miss Taggart says—quote—I expect to make a pile of money on the John Galt Line. I will have earned it. Close quote. Thank you so much."

"Any questions, gentlemen?" asked Rearden.

There were no questions.

"Now I must tell you about the opening of the John Galt Line," said Dagny. "The first train will depart from the station of Taggart Transcontinental in Cheyenne, Wyoming, at four P.M. on July twenty-second. It will be a freight special, consisting of eighty cars. It will be driven by an eight-thousand-horsepower, four-unit Diesel locomotive—which I'm leasing from Taggart Transcontinental for the occasion. It will run non-stop to Wyatt Junction, Colorado, traveling at an average speed of one hundred miles per hour. I beg your pardon?" she asked, hearing the long, low sound of a whistle.

"What did you say, Miss Taggart?"

"I said, one hundred miles per hour—grades, curves and all."

"But shouldn't you cut the speed below normal rather than . . . Miss Taggart, don't you have any consideration whatever for public opinion?"

"But I *do*. If it weren't for public opinion, an average speed of sixty-five miles per hour would have been quite sufficient."

"Who's going to run that train?"

"I had quite a bit of trouble about that. All the Taggart engineers volunteered to do it. So did the firemen, the brakemen and the conductors. We had to draw lots for every job on the train's crew. The engineer will be Pat Logan, of the Taggart Comet, the fireman—Ray McKim. I shall ride in the cab of the engine with them."

"Not really!"

"Please do attend the opening. It's on July twenty-second. The press is most eagerly invited. Contrary to my usual policy, I have become a publicity hound. Really. I should like to have spotlights, radio micro-phones and television cameras. I suggest that you plant a few cameras around the bridge. The collapse of the bridge would give you some interesting shots."

"Miss Taggart," asked Rearden, "why didn't you mention that I'm going to ride in that engine, too?"

She looked at him across the room, and for a moment they were alone, holding each other's glance.

"Yes, of course, Mr. Rearden," she answered.

*   *   *

She did not see him again until they looked at each other across the platform of the Taggart station in Cheyenne, on July 22.

She did not look for anyone when she stepped out on the platform: she felt as if her senses had merged, so that she could not distinguish the sky, the sun or the sounds of an enormous crowd, but perceived only a sensation of shock and light.

Yet he was the first person she saw, and she could not tell for how long a time he was also the only one. He stood by the engine of the John Galt train, talking to somebody outside the field of her consciousness. He was dressed in gray slacks and shirt, he looked like an expert me-chanic, but he was stared at by the faces around him, because he was Hank Rearden of Rearden Steel. High above him, she saw the letters TT on the silver front of the engine. The lines of the engine slanted back, aimed at space.

There was distance and a crowd between them, but his eyes moved to her the moment she came out. They looked at each other and she knew that he felt as she did. This was not to be a solemn venture upon which their future depended, but simply their day of enjoyment. Their work was done. For the moment, there was no future. They had earned the present.

Only if one feels immensely important, she had told him, can one feel truly light. Whatever the train's run would mean to others, for the two of them their own persons were this day's sole meaning. Whatever it was that others sought in life, their right to what they now felt was all the two of them wished to find. It was as if, across the platform, they said it to each other.

Then she turned away from him.

She noticed that she, too, was being stared at, that there were people around her, that she was laughing and answering questions.

She had not expected such a large crowd. They filled the platform, the tracks, the square beyond the station; they were on the roofs of the box-cars on the sidings, at the windows of every house in sight. Something had drawn them here, something in the air which, at the last moment, had made James Taggart want to attend the opening of the John Galt Line. She had forbidden it. "If you come, Jim," she had said, "I'll have you thrown out of your own Taggart station. This is one event you're not going to see." Then she had chosen Eddie Willers to represent Taggart Transcontinental at the opening.

She looked at the crowd and she felt, simultaneously, astonishment that they should stare at her, when this event was so personally her own that no communication about it was possible, and a sense of fitness that they should be here, that they should want to see it, because the sight of an achievement was the greatest gift a human being could offer to others.

She felt no anger toward anyone on earth. The things she had endured had now receded into some outer fog, like pain that still exists, but has no power to hurt. Those things could not stand in the face of this moment's reality, the meaning of this day was as brilliantly, violently clear as the splashes of sun on the silver of the engine, all men had to perceive it now, no one could doubt it and she had no one to hate.

Eddie Willers was watching her. He stood on the platform, surrounded by Taggart executives, division heads, civic leaders, and the various local officials who had been outargued, bribed or threatened, to obtain permits to run a train through town zones at a hundred miles an hour. For once, for this day and event, his title of Vice-President was real to him and he carried it well. But while he spoke to those around him, his eyes kept following Dagny through the crowd. She was dressed in blue slacks and shirt, she was unconscious of official duties, she had left them to him, the train was now her sole concern, as if she were only a member of its crew.

She saw him, she approached, and she shook his hand; her smile was like a summation of all the things they did not have to say. "Well, Eddie, you're Taggart Transcontinental now."

"Yes," he said solemnly, his voice low.

There were reporters asking questions, and they dragged her away from him. They were asking him questions, too. "Mr. Willers, what is the policy of Taggart Transcontinental in regard to this line?" "So Taggart Transcontinental is just a disinterested observer, is it, Mr. Willers?" He answered as best he could. He was looking at the sun on a Diesel engine. But what he was seeing was the sun in a clearing of the woods and a twelve-year-old girl telling him that he would help her run the railroad some day.

He watched from a distance while the train's crew was lined up in front of the engine, to face a firing squad of cameras. Dagny and Rearden were smiling, as if posing for snapshots of a summer vacation. Pat Logan, the engineer, a short, sinewy man with graying hair and a contemptuously inscrutable face, posed in a manner of amused indifference. Ray McKim, the fireman, a husky young giant, grinned with an air of embarrassment and superiority together. The rest of the crew looked as if they were about to wink at the cameras. A photographer said, laughing, "Can't you people look doomed, please? I know that's what the editor wants."

Dagny and Rearden were answering questions for the press. There was no mockery in their answers now, no bitterness. They were enjoying it. They spoke as if the questions were asked in good faith. Irresistibly, at some point which no one noticed, this became true.

"What do you expect to happen on this run?" a reporter asked one of the brakemen. "Do you think you'll get there?"

"I think we'll get there," said the brakeman, "and so do you, brother."

"Mr. Logan, do you have any children? Did you take out any extra insurance? I'm just thinking of the bridge, you know."

"Don't cross that bridge till I come to it," Pat Logan answered con- temptuously.

"Mr. Rearden, how do you know that your rail will hold?"

"The man who taught people to make a printing press," said Rearden, "how did *he* know it?"

"Tell me, Miss Taggart, what's going to support a seven-thousand-ton train on a three-thousand-ton bridge?"

"My judgment," she answered.

The men of the press, who despised their own profession, did not know why they were enjoying it today. One of them, a young man with years of notorious success behind him and a cynical look of twice his age, said suddenly, "I know what I'd like to be: I wish I could be a man who covers *news!*"

The hands of the clock on the station building stood at 3:45. The crew started off toward the caboose at the distant end of the train. The movement and noise of the crowd were subsiding. Without conscious intention, people were beginning to stand still.

The dispatcher had received word from every local operator along the line of rail that wound through the mountains to the Wyatt oil fields three hundred miles away. He came out of the station building and, looking at Dagny, gave the signal for clear track ahead. Standing by the engine, Dagny raised her hand, repeating his gesture in sign of an order received and understood.

The long line of boxcars stretched off into the distance, in spaced, rectangular links, like a spinal cord. When the conductor's arm swept through the air, far at the end, she moved her arm in answering signal.

Rearden, Logan and McKim stood silently, as if at attention, letting her be first to get aboard. As she started up the rungs on the side of the engine, a reporter thought of a question he had not asked.

"Miss Taggart," he called after her, "who is John Galt?"

She turned, hanging onto a metal bar with one hand, suspended for an instant above the heads of the crowd.

"We are!" she answered.

Logan followed her into the cab, then McKim; Rearden went last, then the door of the engine was shut, with the tight finality of sealed metal.

The lights, hanging on a signal bridge against the sky, were green. There were green lights between the tracks, low over the ground, dropping off into the distance where the rails turned and a green light stood at the curve, against leaves of a summer green that looked as if they, too, were lights.

Two men held a white silk ribbon stretched across the track in front of the engine. They were the superintendent of the Colorado Division and Nealy's chief engineer, who had remained on the job. Eddie Willers was to cut the ribbon they held and thus to open the new line.

The photographers posed him carefully, scissors in hand, his back to the engine. He would repeat the ceremony two or three times, they explained, to give them a choice of shots; they had a fresh bolt of ribbon ready. He was about to comply, then stopped. "No," he said suddenly. "It's not going to be a phony."

In a voice of quiet authority, the voice of a vice-president, he ordered, pointing at the cameras, "Stand back—way back. Take one shot when I cut it, then get out of the way, fast."

They obeyed, moving hastily farther down the track. There was only one minute left. Eddie turned his back to the cameras and stood between the rails, facing the engine. He held the scissors ready over the white ribbon. He took his hat off and tossed it aside. He was looking up at the engine. A faint wind stirred his blond hair. The engine was a great silver shield bearing the emblem of Nat Taggart.

Eddie Willers raised his hand as the hand of the station clock reached the instant of four.

"Open her up, Pat!" he called.

In the moment when the engine started forward, he cut the white ribbon and leaped out of the way.

From the side track, he saw the window of the cab go by and Dagny waving to him in an answering salute. Then the engine was gone, and he stood looking across at the crowded platform that kept appearing and vanishing as the freight cars clicked past him.

*　*　*

The green-blue rails ran to meet them, like two jets shot out of a single point beyond the curve of the earth. The crossties melted, as they approached, into a smooth stream rolling down under the wheels. A blurred streak clung to the side of the engine, low over the ground. Trees and telegraph poles sprang into sight abruptly and went by as if jerked back. The green plains stretched past, in a leisurely flow. At the edge of the sky, a long wave of mountains reversed the movement and seemed to follow the train.

She felt no wheels under the floor. The motion was a smooth flight on a sustained impulse, as if the engine hung above the rails, riding a current. She felt no speed. It seemed strange that the green lights of the signals kept coming at them and past, every few seconds. She knew that the signal lights were spaced two miles apart.

The needle on the speedometer in front of Pat Logan stood at one hundred.

She sat in the fireman's chair and glanced across at Logan once in a while. He sat slumped forward a little, relaxed, one hand resting lightly on the throttle as if by chance; but his eyes were fixed on the track ahead. He had the ease of an expert, so confident that it seemed casual, but it was the ease of a tremendous concentration, the concentration on one's task that has the ruthlessness of an absolute. Ray McKim sat on a bench behind them. Rearden stood in the middle of the cab.

He stood, hands in pockets, feet apart, braced against the motion, looking ahead. There was nothing he could now care to see by the side of the track: he was looking at the rail.

Ownership—she thought, glancing back at him—weren't there those who knew nothing of its nature and doubted its reality? No, it was not made of papers, seals, grants and permissions. There it was—in his eyes.

The sound filling the cab seemed part of the space they were crossing. It held the low drone of the motors—the sharper clicking of the many parts that rang in varied cries of metal—and the high, thin chimes of trembling glass panes.

Things streaked past—a water tank, a tree, a shanty, a grain silo. They had a windshield-wiper motion: they were rising, describing a curve and dropping back. The telegraph wires ran a race with the train, rising and falling from pole to pole, in an even rhythm, like the cardiograph record of a steady heartbeat written across the sky.

She looked ahead, at the haze that melted rail and distance, a haze that could rip apart at any moment to some shape of disaster. She wondered why she felt safer than she had ever felt in a car behind the engine, safer here, where it seemed as if, should an obstacle rise, her breast and the glass shield would be first to smash against it. She smiled, grasping the answer: it was the security of being first, with full sight and full knowledge of one's course—not the blind sense of being pulled into the unknown by some unknown power ahead. It was the greatest sensation of existence: not to trust, but to know.

The glass sheets of the cab's windows made the spread of the fields seem vaster: the earth looked as open to movement as it was to sight. Yet nothing was distant and nothing was out of reach. She had barely grasped the sparkle of a lake ahead—and in the next instant she was beside it, then past.

It was a strange foreshortening between sight and touch, she thought, between wish and fulfillment, between—the words clicked sharply in her mind after a startled stop—between spirit and body. First, the vision—then the physical shape to express it. First, the thought—then the purposeful motion down the straight line of a single track to a chosen goal. Could one have any meaning without the other? Wasn't it evil to wish without moving—or to move without aim? Whose malevolence was it that crept through the world, struggling to break the two apart and set them against each other?

She shook her head. She did not want to think or to wonder why the world behind her was as it was. She did not care. She was flying away from it, at the rate of a hundred miles an hour. She leaned to the open window by her side, and felt the wind of the speed blowing her hair off her forehead. She lay back, conscious of nothing but the pleasure it gave her.

Yet her mind kept racing. Broken bits of thought flew past her attention, like the telegraph poles by the track. Physical pleasure?—she thought. This is a train made of steel . . . running on rails of Rearden Metal . . . moved by the energy of burning oil and electric generators . . . it's a physical sensation of physical movement through space . . . but is that the cause and the meaning of what I now feel? . . . Do they call it a low, animal joy—this feeling that I would not care if the rail did break to bits under us now—it won't—but I wouldn't care, because I have experienced this? A low, physical, material, degrading pleasure of the body?

She smiled, her eyes closed, the wind streaming through her hair.

She opened her eyes and saw that Rearden stood looking down at her. It was the same glance with which he had looked at the rail. She felt her power of volition knocked out by some single, dull blow that made her unable to move. She held his eyes, lying back in her chair, the wind pressing the thin cloth of her shirt to her body.

He looked away, and she turned again to the sight of the earth tearing open before them.

She did not want to think, but the sound of thought went on, like the drone of the motors under the sounds of the engine. She looked at the cab around her. The fine steel mesh of the ceiling, she thought, and the row of rivets in the corner holding sheets of steel sealed together—who made them? The brute force of men's muscles? Who made it possible for four dials and three levers in front of Pat Logan to hold the incredible power of the sixteen motors behind them and deliver it to the effortless control of one man's hand?

These things and the capacity from which they came—was this the pursuit men regarded as evil? Was this what they called an ignoble concern with the physical world? Was this the state of being enslaved by matter? Was this the surrender of man's spirit to his body?

She shook her head, as if she wished she could toss the subject out of the window and let it get shattered somewhere along the track. She looked at the sun on the summer fields. She did not have to think, because these questions were only details of a truth she knew and had always known. Let them go past like the telegraph poles. The thing she knew was like the wires flying above in an unbroken line. The words for it, and for this journey, and for her feeling, and for the whole of man's earth, were: It's so simple and so right!

She looked out at the country. She had been aware for some time of the human figures that flashed with an odd regularity at the side of the track. But they went by so fast that she could not grasp their meaning until, like the squares of a movie film, brief flashes blended into a whole and she understood it. She had had the track guarded since its completion, but she had not hired the human chain she saw strung out along the right-of-way. A solitary figure stood at every mile post. Some were young schoolboys, others were so old that the silhouettes of their bodies looked bent against the sky. All of them were armed, with anything they had found, from costly rifles to ancient muskets. All of them wore railroad caps. They were the sons of Taggart employees, and old railroad men who had retired after a full lifetime of Taggart service. They had come, unsummoned, to guard this train. As the engine went past him, every man in his turn stood erect, at attention, and raised his gun in a military salute.

When she grasped it, she burst out laughing, suddenly, with the abruptness of a cry. She laughed, shaking, like a child; it sounded like sobs of deliverance. Pat Logan nodded to her with a faint smile; he had noted the guard of honor long ago. She leaned to the open window, and her arm swept in wide curves of triumph, waving to the men by the track.

On the crest of a distant hill, she saw a crowd of people, their arms swinging against the sky. The gray houses of a village were scattered through a valley below, as if dropped there once and forgotten; the roof lines slanted, sagging, and the years had washed away the color of the walls. Perhaps generations had lived there, with nothing to mark the passage of their days but the movement of the sun from east to west. Now, these men had climbed the hill to see a silver-headed comet cut through their plains like the sound of a bugle through a long weight of silence.

As houses began to come more frequently, closer to the track, she saw people at the windows, on the porches, on distant roofs. She saw crowds blocking the roads at grade crossings. The roads went sweeping past like the spokes of a fan, and she could not distinguish human figures, only their arms greeting the train like branches waving in the wind of its speed. They stood under the swinging red lights of warning signals, under the signs saying: "Stop. Look. Listen."

The station past which they flew, as they went through a town at a hundred miles an hour, was a swaying sculpture of people from platform to roof. She caught the flicker of waving arms, of hats tossed in the air, of something flung against the side of the engine, which was a bunch of flowers.

As the miles clicked past them, the towns went by, with the stations at which they did not stop, with the crowds of people who had come only to see, to cheer and to hope. She saw garlands of flowers under the sooted eaves of old station buildings, and bunting of red-white-and-blue on the time-eaten walls. It was like the pictures she had seen—and envied—in schoolbook histories of railroads, from the era when people gathered to greet the first run of a train. It was like the age when Nat Taggart moved across the country, and the stops along his way were marked by men eager for the sight of achievement. That age, she had thought, was gone; generations had passed, with no event to greet anywhere, with nothing to see but the cracks lengthening year by year on the walls built by Nat Taggart. Yet men came again, as they had come in his time, drawn by the same response.

She glanced at Rearden. He stood against the wall, unaware of the crowds, indifferent to admiration. He was watching the performance of track and train with an expert's intensity of professional interest; his bearing suggested that he would kick aside, as irrelevant, any thought such as "They like it," when the thought ringing in his mind was "It works!"

His tall figure in the single gray of slacks and shirt looked as if his body were stripped for action. The slacks stressed the long lines of his legs, the light, firm posture of standing without effort or being ready to swing forward at an instant's notice; the short sleeves stressed the gaunt strength of his arms; the open shirt bared the tight skin of his chest.

She turned away, realizing suddenly that she had been glancing back at him too often. But this day had no ties to past or future—her thoughts were cut off from implications—she saw no further meaning, only the immediate intensity of the feeling that she was imprisoned with him, sealed together in the same cube of air, the closeness of his presence underscoring her awareness of this day, as his rails underscored the flight of the train.

She turned deliberately and glanced back. He was looking at her. He did not turn away, but held her glance, coldly and with full intention. She smiled defiantly, not letting herself know the full meaning of her smile, knowing only that it was the sharpest blow she could strike at his inflexible face. She felt a sudden desire to see him trembling, to tear a cry out of him. She turned her head away, slowly, feeling a reckless amusement, wondering why she found it difficult to breathe.

She sat leaning back in her chair, looking ahead, knowing that he was as aware of her as she was of him. She found pleasure in the special self-consciousness it gave her. When she crossed her legs, when she leaned on her arm against the window sill, when she brushed her hair off her forehead—every movement of her body was underscored by a feeling the unadmitted words for which were: Is he seeing it?

The towns had been left behind. The track was rising through a country growing more grimly reluctant to permit approach. The rails kept vanishing behind curves, and the ridges of hills kept moving closer, as if the plains were being folded into pleats. The flat stone shelves of Colorado were advancing to the edge of the track—and the distant reaches of the sky were shrinking into waves of bluish mountains.

Far ahead, they saw a mist of smoke over factory chimneys—then the web of a power station and the lone needle of a steel structure. They were approaching Denver.

She glanced at Pat Logan. He was leaning forward a little farther; she saw a slight tightening in the fingers of his hand and in his eyes. He knew, as she did, the danger of crossing a city at the speed they were traveling.

It was a succession of minutes, but it hit them as a single whole. First, they saw the lone shapes, which were factories, rolling across their windowpanes—then the shapes fused into the blur of streets—then a delta of rails spread out before them, like the mouth of a funnel sucking them into the Taggart station, with nothing to protect them but the small green beads of lights scattered over the ground—from the height of the cab, they saw boxcars on sidings streak past as flat ribbons of roof tops —the black hole of the train-shed flew at their faces—they hurtled through an explosion of sound, the beating of wheels against the glass panes of a vault, and the screams of cheering from a mass that swayed like a liquid in the darkness among steel columns—they flew toward a glowing arch and the green lights hanging in the open sky beyond, the green lights that were like the doorknobs of space, throwing door after door open before them. Then, vanishing behind them, went the streets clotted with traffic, the open windows bulging with human figures, the screaming sirens, and—from the top of a distant skyscraper—a cloud of paper snowflakes shimmering on the air, flung by someone who saw the passage of a silver bullet across a city stopped still to watch it.

Then they were out again, on a rocky grade—and with shocking suddenness, the mountains were before them, as if the city had flung them straight at a granite wall, and a thin ledge had caught them in time. They were clinging to the side of a vertical cliff, with the earth rolling down, dropping away, and giant tiers of twisted boulders streaming up and shutting out the sun, leaving them to speed through a bluish twilight, with no sight of soil or sky.

The curves of rail became coiling circles among walls that advanced to grind them off their sides. But the track cut through at times and the mountains parted, flaring open like two wings at the tip of the rail—one wing green, made of vertical needles, with whole pines serving as the pile of a solid carpet—the other reddish-brown, made of naked rock.

She looked down through the open window and saw the silver side of the engine hanging over empty space. Far below, the thin thread of a stream went falling from ledge to ledge, and the ferns that drooped to the water were the shimmering tops of birch trees. She saw the engine's tail of boxcars winding along the face of a granite drop—and miles of contorted stone below, she saw the coils of green-blue rail unwinding behind the train.

A wall of rock shot upward in their path, filling the windshield, darkening the cab, so close that it seemed as if the remnant of time could not let them escape it. But she heard the screech of wheels on curve, the light came bursting back—and she saw an open stretch of rail on a narrow shelf. The shelf ended in space. The nose of the engine was aimed straight at the sky. There was nothing to stop them but two strips of green-blue metal strung in a curve along the shelf.

To take the pounding violence of sixteen motors, she thought, the thrust of seven thousand tons of steel and freight, to withstand it, grip it and swing it around a curve, was the impossible feat performed by two strips of metal no wider than her arm. What made it possible? What power had given to an unseen arrangement of molecules the power on which their lives depended and the lives of all the men who waited for the eighty boxcars? She saw a man's face and hands in the glow of a laboratory oven, over the white liquid of a sample of metal.

She felt the sweep of an emotion which she could not contain, as of something bursting upward. She turned to the door of the motor units, she threw it open to a screaming jet of sound and escaped into the pounding of the engine's heart.

For a moment, it was as if she were reduced to a single sense, the sense of hearing, and what remained of her hearing was only a long, rising, falling, rising scream. She stood in a swaying, sealed chamber of metal, looking at the giant generators. She had wanted to see them, because the sense of triumph within her was bound to them, to her love for them, to the reason of the life-work she had chosen. In the abnormal clarity of a violent emotion, she felt as if she were about to grasp something she had never known and had to know. She laughed aloud, but heard no sound of it; nothing could be heard through the continuous explosion. "The John Galt Line!" she shouted, for the amusement of feeling her voice swept away from her lips.

She moved slowly along the length of the motor units, down a narrow passage between the engines and the wall. She felt the immodesty of an intruder, as if she had slipped inside a living creature, under its silver skin, and were watching its life beating in gray metal cylinders, in twisted coils, in sealed tubes, in the convulsive whirl of blades in wire cages. The enormous complexity of the shape above her was drained by invisible channels, and the violence raging within it was led to fragile needles on glass dials, to green and red beads winking on panels, to tall, thin cabinets stenciled "High Voltage."

Why had she always felt that joyous sense of confidence when looking at machines?—she thought. In these giant shapes, two aspects pertaining to the inhuman were radiantly absent: the causeless and the purposeless. Every part of the motors was an embodied answer to "Why?" and "What for?"—like the steps of a life-course chosen by the sort of mind she worshipped. The motors were a moral code cast in steel.

They *are* alive, she thought, because they are the physical shape of the action of a living power—of the mind that had been able to grasp the whole of this complexity, to set its purpose, to give it form. For an instant, it seemed to her that the motors were transparent and she was seeing the net of their nervous system. It was a net of connections, more intricate, more crucial than all of their wires and circuits: the rational connections made by that human mind which had fashioned any one part of them for the first time.

They *are* alive, she thought, but their soul operates them by remote control. Their soul is in every man who has the capacity to equal this achievement. Should the soul vanish from the earth, the motors would stop, because *that* is the power which keeps them going—not the oil under the floor under her feet, the oil that would then become primeval ooze again—not the steel cylinders that would become stains of rust on the walls of the caves of shivering savages—the power of a living mind —the power of thought and choice and purpose.

She was making her way back toward the cab, feeling that she wanted to laugh, to kneel or to lift her arms, wishing she were able to release the thing she felt, knowing that it had no form of expression.

She stopped She saw Rearden standing by the steps of the door to the cab. He was looking at her as if he knew why she had escaped and what she felt. They stood still, their bodies becoming a glance that met across a narrow passage. The beating within her was one with the beating of the motors—and she felt as if both came from him; the pounding rhythm wiped out her will. They went back to the cab, silently, knowing that there had been a moment which was not to be mentioned between them.

The cliffs ahead were a bright, liquid gold. Strips of shadow were lengthening in the valleys below. The sun was descending to the peaks in the west. They were going west and up, toward the sun.

The sky had deepened to the greenish-blue of the rails, when they saw smokestacks in a distant valley. It was one of Colorado's new towns, the towns that had grown like a radiation from the Wyatt oil fields. She saw the angular lines of modern houses, flat roofs, great sheets of windows. It was too far to distinguish people. In the moment when she thought that they would not be watching the train at that distance, a rocket shot out from among the buildings, rose high above the town and broke as a fountain of gold stars against the darkening sky. Men whom she could not see, were seeing the streak of the train on the side of the mountain, and were sending a salute, a lonely plume of fire in the dusk, the symbol of celebration or of a call for help.

Beyond the next turn, in a sudden view of distance, she saw two dots of electric light, white and red, low in the sky. They were not airplanes —she saw the cones of metal girders supporting them—and in the moment when she knew that they were the derricks of Wyatt Oil, she saw that the track was sweeping downward, that the earth flared open, as if the mountains were flung apart—and at the bottom, at the foot of the Wyatt hill, across the dark crack of a canyon, she saw the bridge of Rearden Metal.

They were flying down, she forgot the careful grading, the great curves of the gradual descent, she felt as if the train were plunging downward, head first, she watched the bridge growing to meet them—a small, square tunnel of metal lace work, a few beams criss-crossed through the air, green-blue and glowing, struck by a long ray of sunset light from some crack in the barrier of mountains. There were people by the bridge, the dark splash of a crowd, but they rolled off the edge of her consciousness. She heard the rising, accelerating sound of the wheels—and some theme of music, heard to the rhythm of wheels, kept tugging at her mind, growing louder—it burst suddenly within the cab, but she knew that it was only in her mind: the Fifth Concerto by Richard Halley—she thought: did he write it for this? had he known a feeling such as this?— they were going faster, they had left the ground, she thought, flung off by the mountains as by a springboard, they were now sailing through space—it's not a fair test, she thought, we're not going to touch that bridge—she saw Rearden's face above her, she held his eyes and her head leaned back, so that her face lay still on the air under his face— they heard a ringing blast of metal, they heard a drum roll under their feet, the diagonals of the bridge went smearing across the windows with the sound of a metal rod being run along the pickets of a fence—then the windows were too suddenly clear, the sweep of their downward plunge was carrying them up a hill, the derricks of Wyatt Oil were reeling before them—Pat Logan turned, glancing up at Rearden with the hint of a smile—and Rearden said, "That's that."

The sign on the edge of a roof read: Wyatt Junction. She stared, feeling that there was something odd about it, until she grasped what it was: the sign did not move. The sharpest jolt of the journey was the realization that the engine stood still.

She heard voices somewhere, she looked down and saw that there were people on the platform. Then the door of the cab was flung open, she knew that she had to be first to descend, and she stepped to the edge. For the flash of an instant, she felt the slenderness of her own body, the lightness of standing full-figure in a current of open air. She gripped the metal bars and started down the ladder. She was halfway down when she felt the palms of a man's hands slam tight against her ribs and waist-line, she was torn off the steps, swung through the air and deposited on the ground. She could not believe that the young boy laughing in her face was Ellis Wyatt. The tense, scornful face she remembered, now had the purity, the eagerness, the joyous benevolence of a child in the kind of world for which he had been intended.

She was leaning against his shoulder, feeling unsteady on the motionless ground, with his arm about her, she was laughing, she was listening to the things he said, she was answering, "But didn't you know we would?"

In a moment, she saw the faces around them. They were the bondholders of the John Galt Line, the men who were Nielsen Motors, Hammond Cars, Stockton Foundry and all the others. She shook their hands, and there were no speeches; she stood against Ellis Wyatt, sagging a little, brushing her hair away from her eyes, leaving smudges of soot on her forehead. She shook the hands of the men of the train's crew, without words, with the seal of the grins on their faces. There were flash bulbs exploding around them, and men waving to them from the riggings of the oil wells on the slopes of the mountains. Above her head, above the heads of the crowd, the letters TT on a silver shield were hit by the last ray of a sinking sun.

Ellis Wyatt had taken charge. He was leading her somewhere, the sweep of his arm cutting a path for them through the crowd, when one of the men with the cameras broke through to her side. "Miss Taggart," he called, "will you give us a message for the public?" Ellis Wyatt pointed at the long string of freight cars. "She has."

Then she was sitting in the back seat of an open car, driving up the curves of a mountain road. The man beside her was Rearden, the driver was Ellis Wyatt.

They stopped at a house that stood on the edge of a cliff, with no other habitation anywhere in sight, with the whole of the oil fields spread on the slopes below.

"Why, of course you're staying at my house overnight, both of you," said Ellis Wyatt, as they went in. "Where did you expect to stay?"

She laughed. "I don't know. I hadn't thought of it at all."

"The nearest town is an hour's drive away. That's where your crew has gone: your boys at the division point are giving a party in their honor. So is the whole town. But I told Ted Nielsen and the others that we'd have no banquets for you and no oratory. Unless you'd like it?"

"God, no!" she said. "Thanks, Ellis."

It was dark when they sat at the dinner table in a room that had large windows and a few pieces of costly furniture. The dinner was served by a silent figure in a white jacket, the only other inhabitant of the house, an elderly Indian with a stony face and a courteous manner. A few points of fire were scattered through the room, running over and out beyond the windows: the candles on the table, the lights on the derricks, and the stars.

"Do you think that you have your hands full now?" Ellis Wyatt was saying. "Just give me a year and I'll give you something to keep you busy. Two tank trains a day, Dagny? It's going to be four or six or as many as you wish me to fill." His hand swept over the lights on the mountains. "This? It's nothing, compared to what I've got coming." He pointed west. "The Buena Esperanza Pass. Five miles from here. Everybody's wondering what I'm doing with it. Oil shale. How many years ago was it that they gave up trying to get oil from shale, because it was too expensive? Well, wait till you see the process I've developed. It will be the cheapest oil ever to splash in their faces, and an unlimited supply of it, an untapped supply that will make the biggest oil pool look like a mud puddle. Did I order a pipe line? Hank, you and I will have to build pipe lines in all directions to . . . Oh, I beg your pardon. I don't believe I introduced myself when I spoke to you at the station. I haven't even told you my name."

Rearden grinned. "I've guessed it by now."

"I'm sorry, I don't like to be careless, but I was too excited."

"What were you excited about?" asked Dagny, her eyes narrowed in mockery.

Wyatt held her glance for a moment; his answer had a tone of solemn intensity strangely conveyed by a smiling voice. "About the most beautiful slap in the face I ever got and deserved."

"Do you mean, for our first meeting?"

"I mean, for our first meeting."

"Don't. You were right."

"I was. About everything but you. Dagny, to find an exception after years of . . . Oh, to hell with them! Do you want me to turn on the radio and hear what they're saying about the two of you tonight?"

"No."

"Good. I don't want to hear them. Let them swallow their own speeches. They're all climbing on the band wagon now. *We're* the band." He glanced at Rearden. "What are you smiling at?"

"I've always been curious to see what you're like."

"I've never had a chance to be what I'm like—except tonight."

"Do you live here alone, like this, miles away from everything?"

Wyatt pointed at the window. "I'm a couple of steps away from—everything."

"What about people?"

"I have guest rooms for the kind of people who come to see me on business. I want as many miles as possible between myself and all the other kinds." He leaned forward to refill their wine glasses. "Hank, why don't you move to Colorado? To hell with New York and the Eastern Seaboard! This is the capital of the Renaissance. The Second Renaissance—not of oil paintings and cathedrals—but of oil derricks, power plants, and motors made of Rearden Metal. They had the Stone Age and the Iron Age and now they're going to call it the Rearden Metal Age—because there's no limit to what your Metal has made possible."

"I'm going to buy a few square miles of Pennsylvania," said Rearden. "The ones around my mills. It would have been cheaper to build a branch here, as I wanted, but you know why I can't, and to hell with them! I'll beat them anyway. I'm going to expand the mills—and if she can give me three-day freight service to Colorado, I'll give you a race for who's going to be the capital of the Renaissance!"

"Give me a year," said Dagny, "of running trains on the John Galt Line, give me time to pull the Taggart system together—and I'll give you three-day freight service across the continent, on a Rearden Metal track from ocean to ocean!"

"Who was it that said he needed a fulcrum?" said Ellis Wyatt. "Give me an unobstructed right-of-way and I'll show them how to move the earth!"

She wondered what it was that she liked about the sound of Wyatt's laughter. Their voices, even her own, had a tone she had never heard before. When they rose from the table, she was astonished to notice that the candles were the only illumination of the room: she had felt as if she were sitting in a violent light.

Ellis Wyatt picked up his glass, looked at their faces and said, "To the world as it seems to be right now!"

He emptied the glass with a single movement.

She heard the crash of the glass against the wall in the same instant that she saw a circling current—from the curve of his body to the sweep of his arm to the terrible violence of his hand that flung the glass across the room. It was not the conventional gesture meant as celebration, it was the gesture of a rebellious anger, the vicious gesture which is movement substituted for a scream of pain.

"Ellis," she whispered, "what's the matter?"

He turned to look at her. With the same violent suddenness, his eyes were clear, his face was calm; what frightened her was seeing him smile gently. "I'm sorry," he said. "Never mind. We'll try to think that it will last."

The earth below was streaked with moonlight, when Wyatt led them up an outside stairway to the second floor of the house, to the open gallery at the doors of the guest rooms. He wished them good night and they heard his steps descending the stairs. The moonlight seemed to drain sound as it drained color. The steps rolled into a distant past, and when they died, the silence had the quality of a solitude that had lasted for a long time, as if no person were left anywhere in reach.

She did not turn to the door of her room. He did not move. At the level of their feet, there was nothing but a thin railing and a spread of space. Angular tiers descended below, with shadows repeating the steel tracery of derricks, criss-crossing sharp, black lines on patches of glowing rock. A few lights, white and red, trembled in the clear air, like drops of rain caught on the edges of steel girders. Far in the distance, three small drops were green, strung in a line along the Taggart track. Beyond them, at the end of space, at the foot of a white curve, hung a webbed rectangle which was the bridge.

She felt a rhythm without sound or movement, a sense of beating tension, as if the wheels of the John Galt Line were still speeding on. Slowly, in answer and in resistance to an unspoken summons, she turned and looked at him.

The look she saw on his face made her know for the first time that she had known this would be the end of the journey. That look was not as men are taught to represent it, it was not a matter of loose muscles, hanging lips and mindless hunger. The lines of his face were pulled tight, giving it a peculiar purity, a sharp precision of form, making it clean and young. His mouth was taut, the lips faintly drawn inward, stressing the outline of its shape. Only his eyes were blurred, their lower lids swollen and raised, their glance intent with that which resembled hatred and pain.

The shock became numbness spreading through her body—she felt a tight pressure in her throat and her stomach—she was conscious of nothing but a silent convulsion that made her unable to breathe. But what she felt, without words for it, was: Yes, Hank, yes—now—because it is part of the same battle, in some way that I can't name . . . because it is our being, against theirs . . . our great capacity, for which they torture us, the capacity of happiness . . . Now, like this, without words or questions . . . because we want it. . . .

It was like an act of hatred, like the cutting blow of a lash encircling her body: she felt his arms around her, she felt her legs pulled forward against him and her chest bent back under the pressure of his, his mouth on hers.

Her hand moved from his shoulders to his waist to his legs, releasing the unconfessed desire of her every meeting with him. When she tore her mouth away from him, she was laughing soundlessly, in triumph, as if saying: Hank Rearden—the austere, unapproachable Hank Rearden of the monklike office, the business conferences, the harsh bargains—do you remember them now?—I'm thinking of it, for the pleasure of knowing that I've brought you to this. He was not smiling, his face was tight, it was the face of an enemy, he jerked her head and caught her mouth again, as if he were inflicting a wound.

She felt him trembling and she thought that this was the kind of cry she had wanted to tear from him—this surrender through the shreds of his tortured resistance. Yet she knew, at the same time, that the triumph was his, that her laughter was her tribute to him, that her defiance was submission, that the purpose of all of her violent strength was only to make his victory the greater—he was holding her body against his, as if stressing his wish to let her know that she was now only a tool for the satisfaction of his desire—and his victory, she knew, was her wish to let him reduce her to that. Whatever I am, she thought, whatever pride of person I may hold, the pride of my courage, of my work, of my mind and my freedom—*that* is what I offer you for the pleasure of your body, *that* is what I want you to use in your service—and that you want it to serve you is the greatest reward I can have.

There were lights burning in the two rooms behind them. He took her wrist and threw her inside his room, making the gesture tell her that he needed no sign of consent or resistance. He locked the door, watching her face. Standing straight, holding his glance, she extended her arm to the lamp on the table and turned out the light. He approached. He turned the light on again, with a single, contemptuous jerk of his wrist. She saw him smile for the first time, a slow, mocking, sensual smile that stressed the purpose of his action.

He was holding her half-stretched across the bed, he was tearing her clothes off, while her face was pressed against him, her mouth moving down the line of his neck, down his shoulder. She knew that every gesture of her desire for him struck him like a blow, that there was some shudder of incredulous anger within him—yet that no gesture would satisfy his greed for every evidence of her desire.

He stood looking down at her naked body, he leaned over, she heard his voice—it was more a statement of contemptuous triumph than a question: "You want it?" Her answer was more a gasp than a word, her eyes closed, her mouth open: "Yes."

She knew that what she felt with the skin of her arms was the cloth of his shirt, she knew that the lips she felt on her mouth were his, but in the rest of her there was no distinction between his being and her own, as there was no division between body and spirit. Through all the steps of the years behind them, the steps down a course chosen in the courage of a single loyalty: their love of existence—chosen in the knowledge that nothing will be given, that one must make one's own desire and every shape of its fulfillment—through the steps of shaping metal, rails and motors—they had moved by the power of the thought that one remakes the earth for one's enjoyment, that man's spirit gives meaning to insentient matter by molding it to serve one's chosen goal. The course led them to the moment when, in answer to the highest of one's values, in an admiration not to be expressed by any other form of tribute, one's spirit makes one's body become the tribute, recasting it—as proof, as sanction, as reward—into a single sensation of such intensity of joy that no other sanction of one's existence is necessary. He heard the moan of her breath, she felt the shudder of his body, in the same instant.

CHAPTER IX

THE SACRED AND THE PROFANE

She looked at the glowing bands on the skin of her arm, spaced like bracelets from her wrist to her shoulder. They were strips of sunlight from the Venetian blinds on the window of an unfamiliar room. She saw a bruise above her elbow, with dark beads that had been blood. Her arm lay on the blanket that covered her body. She was aware of her legs and hips, but the rest of her body was only a sense of lightness, as if it were stretched restfully across the air in a place that looked like a cage made of sunrays.

Turning to look at him, she thought: From his aloofness, from his manner of glass-enclosed formality, from his pride in never being made to feel anything—to this, to Hank Rearden in bed beside her, after hours of a violence which they could not name now, not in words or in daylight—but which was in their eyes, as they looked at each other, which they wanted to name, to stress, to throw at each other's face.

He saw the face of a young girl, her lips suggesting a smile, as if her natural state of relaxation were a state of radiance, a lock of hair falling across her cheek to the curve of a naked shoulder, her eyes looking at him as if she were ready to accept anything he might wish to say, as she had been ready to accept anything he had wished to do.

He reached over and moved the lock of hair from her cheek, cautiously, as if it were fragile. He held it back with his fingertips and looked at her face. Then his fingers closed suddenly in her hair and he raised the lock to his lips. The way he pressed his mouth to it was tenderness, but the way his fingers held it was despair.

He dropped back on the pillow and lay still, his eyes closed. His face seemed young, at peace. Seeing it for a moment without the reins of tension, she realized suddenly the extent of the unhappiness he had borne; but it's past now, she thought, it's over.

He got up, not looking at her. His face was blank and closed again. He picked up his clothes from the floor and proceeded to dress, standing in the middle of the room, half-turned away from her. He acted, not as if she wasn't present, but as if it did not matter that she was. His movements, as he buttoned his shirt, as he buckled the belt of his slacks, had the rapid precision of performing a duty.

She lay back on the pillow, watching him, enjoying the sight of his figure in motion. She liked the gray slacks and shirt—the expert mechanic of the John Galt Line, she thought, in the stripes of sunlight and shadow, like a convict behind bars. But they were not bars any longer, they were the cracks of a wall which the John Galt Line had broken, the advance notice of what awaited them outside, beyond the Venetian blinds—she thought of the trip back, on the new rail, with the first train from Wyatt Junction—the trip back to her office in the Taggart Building and to all the things now open for her to win—but she was free to let it wait, she did not want to think of it, she was thinking of the first touch of his mouth on hers—she was free to feel it, to hold a moment when nothing else was of any concern—she smiled defiantly at the strips of sky beyond the blinds.

"I want you to know this."

He stood by the bed, dressed, looking down at her. His voice had pronounced it evenly, with great clarity and no inflection. She looked up at him obediently. He said:

"What I feel for you is contempt. But it's nothing, compared to the contempt I feel for myself. I don't love you. I've never loved anyone. I wanted you from the first moment I saw you. I wanted you as one wants a whore—for the same reason and purpose. I spent two years damning myself, because I thought you were above a desire of this kind. You're not. You're as vile an animal as I am. I should loathe my discovering it. I don't. Yesterday, I would have killed anyone who'd tell me that you were capable of doing what I've had you do. Today, I would give my life not to let it be otherwise, not to have you be anything but the bitch you are. All the greatness that I saw in you—I would not take it in exchange for the obscenity of your talent at an animal's sensation of pleasure. We were two great beings, you and I, proud of our strength, weren't we? Well, this is all that's left of us—and I want no self-deception about it."

He spoke slowly, as if lashing himself with his words. There was no sound of emotion in his voice, only the lifeless pull of effort; it was not the tone of a man's willingness to speak, but the ugly, tortured sound of duty.

"I held it as my honor that I would never need anyone. I need you. It had been my pride that I had always acted on my convictions. I've given in to a desire which I despise. It is a desire that has reduced my mind, my will, my being, my power to exist into an abject dependence upon you—not even upon the Dagny Taggart whom I admired—but upon your body, your hands, your mouth and the few seconds of a convulsion of your muscles. I had never broken my word. Now I've broken an oath I gave for life. I had never committed an act that had to be hidden. Now I am to lie, to sneak, to hide. Whatever I wanted, I was free to proclaim it aloud and achieve it in the sight of the whole world. Now my only desire is one I loathe to name even to myself. But it is my only desire. I'm going to have you—I'd give up everything I own for it, the mills, the Metal, the achievement of my whole life. I'm going to have you at the price of more than myself: at the price of my self-esteem—and I want you to know it. I want no pretense, no evasion, no silent indulgence, with the nature of our actions left unnamed. I want no pretense about love, value, loyalty or respect. I want no shred of honor left to us, to hide behind. I've never begged for mercy. I've chosen to do this—and I'll take all the consequences, including the full recognition of my choice. It's depravity—and I accept it as such—and there is no height of virtue that I wouldn't give up for it. Now if you wish to slap my face, go ahead. I wish you would."

She had listened, sitting up straight, holding the blanket clutched at her throat to cover her body. At first, he had seen her eyes growing dark with incredulous shock. Then it seemed to him that she was listening with greater attentiveness, but seeing more than his face, even though her eyes were fixed on his. She looked as if she were studying intently some revelation that had never confronted her before. He felt as if some ray of light were growing stronger on his face, because he saw its reflection on hers, as she watched him—he saw the shock vanishing, then the wonder—he saw her face being smoothed into a strange serenity that seemed quiet and glittering at once.

When he stopped, she burst out laughing.

The shock to him was that he heard no anger in her laughter. She laughed simply, easily, in joyous amusement, in release, not as one laughs at the solution of a problem, but at the discovery that no problem had ever existed.

She threw the blanket off with a stressed, deliberate sweep of her arm. She stood up. She saw her clothes on the floor and kicked them aside. She stood facing him, naked. She said:

"I want you, Hank. I'm much more of an animal than you think. I wanted you from the first moment I saw you—and the only thing I'm ashamed of is that I did not know it. I did not know why, for two years, the brightest moments I found were the ones in your office, where I could lift my head to look up at you. I did not know the nature of what I felt in your presence, nor the reason. I know it now. That is all I want, Hank. I want you in my bed—and you are free of me for all the rest of your time. There's nothing you'll have to pretend—don't think of me, don't feel, don't care—I do not want your mind, your will, your being or your soul, so long as it's to me that you will come for that lowest one of your desires. I am an animal who wants nothing but that sensation of pleasure which you despise—but I want it from you. You'd give up any height of virtue for it, while I—I haven't any to give up. There's none I seek or wish to reach. I am so low that I would exchange the greatest sight of beauty in the world for the sight of your figure in the cab of a railroad engine. And seeing it, I would not be able to see it indifferently. You don't have to fear that you're now dependent upon me. It's I who will depend on any whim of yours. You'll have me any time you wish, anywhere, on any terms. Did you call it the obscenity of my talent? It's such that it gives you a safer hold on me than on any other property you own. You may dispose of me as you please—I'm not afraid to admit it—I have nothing to protect from you and nothing to reserve. You think that this is a threat to your achievement, but it is not to mine. I will sit at my desk, and work, and when the things around me get hard to bear, I will think that for my reward I will be in your bed that night. Did you call it depravity? I am much more depraved than you are: you hold it as your guilt, and I—as my pride. I'm more proud of it than of anything I've done, more proud than of building the Line. If I'm asked to name my proudest attainment, I will say: I have slept with Hank Rearden. I had earned it."

When he threw her down on the bed, their bodies met like the two sounds that broke against each other in the air of the room: the sound of his tortured moan and of her laughter.

* * *

The rain was invisible in the darkness of the streets, but it hung like the sparkling fringe of a lampshade under the corner light. Fumbling in his pockets, James Taggart discovered that he had lost his handkerchief. He swore half-aloud, with resentful malice, as if the loss, the rain and his head cold were someone's personal conspiracy against him.

There was a thin gruel of mud on the pavements; he felt a gluey suction under his shoe soles and a chill slipping down past his collar. He did not want to walk or to stop. He had no place to go.

Leaving his office, after the meeting of the Board of Directors, he had realized suddenly that there were no other appointments, that he had a long evening ahead and no one to help him kill it. The front pages of the newspapers were screaming of the triumph of the John Galt Line, as the radios had screamed it yesterday and all through the night. The name of Taggart Transcontinental was stretched in headlines across the continent, like its track, and he had smiled in answer to the congratulations. He had smiled, seated at the head of the long table, at the Board meeting, while the Directors spoke about the soaring rise of the Taggart stock on the Exchange, while they cautiously asked to see his written agreement with his sister—just in case, they said—and commented that it was fine, it was holeproof, there was no doubt but that she would have to turn the Line over to Taggart Transcontinental at once, they spoke about their brilliant future and the debt of gratitude which the company owed to James Taggart.

He had sat through the meeting, wishing it were over with, so that he could go home. Then he had stepped out into the street and realized that home was the one place where he dared not go tonight. He could not be alone, not in the next few hours, yet there was nobody to call. He did not want to see people. He kept seeing the eyes of the men of the Board when they spoke about his greatness: a sly, filmy look that held contempt for him and, more terrifyingly, for themselves.

He walked, head down, a needle of rain pricking the skin of his neck once in a while. He looked away whenever he passed a newsstand. The papers seemed to shriek at him the name of the John Galt Line, and another name which he did not want to hear: Ragnar Danneskjöld. A ship bound for the People's State of Norway with an Emergency Gift cargo of machine tools had been seized by Ragnar Danneskjöld last night. That story disturbed him in some personal manner which he could not explain. The feeling seemed to have some quality in common with the things he felt about the John Galt Line.

It's because he had a cold, he thought; he wouldn't feel this way if he didn't have a cold; a man couldn't be expected to be in top form when he had a cold—he couldn't help it—what did they expect him to do tonight, sing and dance?—he snapped the question angrily at the unknown judges of his unwitnessed mood. He fumbled for his handkerchief again, cursed and decided that he'd better stop somewhere to buy some paper tissues.

Across the square of what had once been a busy neighborhood, he saw the lighted windows of a dime store, still open hopefully at this late hour. There's another one that will go out of business pretty soon, he thought as he crossed the square; the thought gave him pleasure.

There were glaring lights inside, a few tired salesgirls among a spread of deserted counters, and the screaming of a phonograph record being played for a lone, listless customer in a corner. The music swallowed the sharp edges of Taggart's voice: he asked for paper tissues in a tone which implied that the salesgirl was responsible for his cold. The girl turned to the counter behind her, but turned back once to glance swiftly at his face. She took a packet, but stopped, hesitating, studying him with peculiar curiosity.

"Are you James Taggart?" she asked.

"Yes!" he snapped. "Why?"

"Oh!"

She gasped like a child at a burst of firecrackers; she was looking at him with a glance which he had thought to be reserved only for movie stars.

"I saw your picture in the paper this morning, Mr. Taggart," she said very rapidly, a faint flush appearing on her face and vanishing. "It said what a great achievement it was and how it was really you who had done it all, only you didn't want it to be known."

"Oh," said Taggart. He was smiling.

"You look just like your picture," she said in immense astonishment, and added, "Imagine you walking in here like this, in person!"

"Shouldn't I?" His tone was amused.

"I mean, everybody's talking about it, the whole country, and you're the man who did it—and here you are! I've never seen an important person before. I've never been so close to anything important, I mean to any newspaper news."

He had never had the experience of seeing his presence give color to a place he entered: the girl looked as if she was not tired any longer, as if the dime store had become a scene of drama and wonder.

"Mr. Taggart, is it true, what they said about you in the paper?"

"What did they say?"

"About your secret."

"What secret?"

"Well, they said that when everybody was fighting about your bridge, whether it would stand or not, you didn't argue with them, you just went ahead, because you knew it would stand, when nobody else was sure of it—so the Line was a Taggart project and you were the guiding spirit behind the scenes, but you kept it secret, because you didn't care whether you got credit for it or not."

He had seen the mimeographed release of his Public Relations Department. "Yes," he said, "it's true." The way she looked at him made him feel as if it were.

"It was wonderful of you, Mr. Taggart."

"Do you always remember what you read in the newspapers, so well, in such detail?"

"Why, yes, I guess so—all the interesting things. The big things. I like to read about them. Nothing big ever happens to me."

She said it gaily, without self-pity. There was a young, determined brusqueness in her voice and movements. She had a head of reddish-brown curls, wide-set eyes, a few freckles on the bridge of an upturned nose. He thought that one would call her face attractive if one ever noticed it, but there was no particular reason to notice it. It was a common little face, except for a look of alertness, of eager interest, a look that expected the world to contain an exciting secret behind every corner.

"Mr. Taggart, how does it feel to be a great man?"

"How does it feel to be a little girl?"

She laughed. "Why, wonderful."

"Then you're better off than I am."

"Oh, how can you say such a—"

"Maybe you're lucky if you don't have anything to do with the big events in the newspapers. Big. What do you call big, anyway?"

"Why . . . important."

"What's important?"

"You're the one who ought to tell me that, Mr. Taggart."

"Nothing's important."

She looked at him incredulously. "You, of all people, saying that to-night of all nights!"

"I don't feel wonderful at all, if that's what you want to know. I've never felt less wonderful in my life."

He was astonished to see her studying his face with a look of concern such as no one had ever granted him. "You're worn out, Mr. Taggart," she said earnestly. "Tell them to go to hell."

"Whom?"

"Whoever's getting you down. It isn't right."

"What isn't?"

"That you should feel this way. You've had a tough time, but you've licked them all, so you ought to enjoy yourself now. You've earned it."

"And how do you propose that I enjoy myself?"

"Oh, I don't know. But I thought you'd be having a celebration to-night, a party with all the big shots, and champagne, and things given to you, like keys to cities, a real swank party like that—instead of walking around all by yourself, shopping for paper handkerchiefs, of all fool things!"

"You give me those handkerchiefs, before you forget them alto-gether," he said, handing her a dime. "And as to the swank party, did it occur to you that I might not want to see anybody tonight?"

She considered it earnestly. "No," she said, "I hadn't thought of it. But I can see why you wouldn't."

"Why?" It was a question to which he had no answer.

"Nobody's really good enough for you, Mr. Taggart," she answered very simply, not as flattery, but as a matter of fact.

"Is that what you think?"

"I don't think I like people very much, Mr. Taggart. Not most of them."

"I don't either. Not any of them."

"I thought a man like you—you wouldn't know how mean they can be and how they try to step on you and ride on your back, if you let them. I thought the big men in the world could get away from them and not have to be flea-bait all of the time, but maybe I was wrong."

"What do you mean, flea-bait?"

"Oh, it's just something I tell myself when things get tough—that I've got to beat my way out to where I won't feel like I'm flea-bitten all the time by all kinds of lousiness—but maybe it's the same anywhere, only the fleas get bigger."

"Much bigger."

She remained silent, as if considering something. "It's funny," she said sadly to some thought of her own.

"What's funny?"

"I read a book once where it said that great men are always unhappy, and the greater—the unhappier. It didn't make sense to me. But maybe it's true."

"It's much truer than you think."

She looked away, her face disturbed.

"Why do you worry so much about the great men?" he asked. "What are you, a hero worshipper of some kind?"

She turned to look at him and he saw the light of an inner smile, while her face remained solemnly grave; it was the most eloquently personal glance he had ever seen directed at himself, while she answered in a quiet, impersonal voice, "Mr. Taggart, what else is there to look up to?"

A screeching sound, neither quite bell nor buzzer, rang out suddenly and went on ringing with nerve-grating insistence.

She jerked her head, as if awakening at the scream of an alarm clock, then sighed. "That's closing time, Mr. Taggart," she said regretfully.

"Go get your hat—I'll wait for you outside," he said.

She stared at him, as if among all of life's possibilities this was one she had never held as conceivable.

"No kidding?" she whispered.

"No kidding."

She whirled around and ran like a streak to the door of the employees' quarters, forgetting her counter, her duties and all feminine concern about never showing eagerness in accepting a man's invitation.

He stood looking after her for a moment, his eyes narrowed. He did not name to himself the nature of his own feeling—never to identify his emotions was the only steadfast rule of his life; he merely felt it—and this particular feeling was pleasurable, which was the only identification he cared to know. But the feeling was the product of a thought he would not utter. He had often met girls of the lower classes, who had put on a brash little act, pretending to look up to him, spilling crude flattery for an obvious purpose; he had neither liked nor resented them; he had found a bored amusement in their company and he had granted them the status of his equals in a game he considered natural to both players involved. This girl was different. The unuttered words in his mind were: The damn little fool means it.

That he waited for her impatiently, when he stood in the rain on the sidewalk, that she was the one person he needed tonight, did not disturb him or strike him as a contradiction. He did not name the nature of his need. The unnamed and the unuttered could not clash into a contradiction.

When she came out, he noted the peculiar combination of her shyness and of her head held high. She wore an ugly raincoat, made worse by a gob of cheap jewelry on the lapel, and a small hat of plush flowers planted defiantly among her curls. Strangely, the lift of her head made the apparel seem attractive; it stressed how well she wore even the things she wore.

"Want to come to my place and have a drink with me?" he asked.

She nodded silently, solemnly, as if not trusting herself to find the right words of acceptance. Then she said, not looking at him, as if stating it to herself, "You didn't want to see anybody tonight, but you want to see *me*. . . ." He had never heard so solemn a tone of pride in anyone's voice.

She was silent, when she sat beside him in the taxicab. She looked up at the skyscrapers they passed. After a while, she said, "I heard that things like this happened in New York, but I never thought they'd happen to me."

"Where do you come from?"

"Buffalo."

"Got any family?"

She hesitated. "I guess so. In Buffalo."

"What do you mean, you guess so?"

"I walked out on them."

"Why?"

"I thought that if I ever was to amount to anything, I had to get away from them, clean away."

"Why? What happened?"

"Nothing happened. And nothing was ever going to happen. That's what I couldn't stand."

"What do you mean?"

"Well, they . . . well, I guess I ought to tell you the truth, Mr. Taggart. My old man's never been any good, and Ma didn't care whether he was or not, and I got sick of it always turning out that I was the only one of the seven of us that kept a job, and the rest of them always being out of luck, one way or another. I thought if I didn't get out, it would get me—I'd rot all the way through, like the rest of them. So I bought a railroad ticket one day and left. Didn't say good-bye. They didn't even know I was going." She gave a soft, startled little laugh at a sudden thought. "Mr. Taggart," she said, "it was a Taggart train."

"When did you come here?"

"Six months ago."

"And you're all alone?"

"Yes," she said happily.

"What was it you wanted to do?"

"Well, you know—make something of myself, get somewhere."

"Where?"

"Oh, I don't know, but . . . but people do things in the world. I saw pictures of New York and I thought"—she pointed at the giant buildings beyond the streaks of rain on the cab window—"I thought, somebody built those buildings—he didn't just sit and whine that the kitchen was filthy and the roof leaking and the plumbing clogged and it's a goddamn world and . . . Mr. Taggart"—she jerked her head in a shudder and looked straight at him—"we were stinking poor and not giving a damn about it. That's what I couldn't take—that they didn't really give a damn. Not enough to lift a finger. Not enough to empty the garbage pail. And the woman next door saying it was my duty to help them, saying it made no difference what became of me or of her or of any of us, because what could anybody do anyway!" Beyond the bright look of her eyes, he saw something within her that was hurt and hard.

"I don't want to talk about them," she said. "Not with you. This—my meeting you, I mean—that's what they couldn't have. That's what I'm not going to share with them. It's mine, not theirs."

"How old are you?" he asked.

"Nineteen."

When he looked at her in the lights of his living room, he thought that she'd have a good figure if she'd eat a few meals; she seemed too thin for the height and structure of her bones. She wore a tight, shabby little black dress, which she had tried to camouflage by the gaudy plastic bracelets tinkling on her wrist. She stood looking at his room as if it were a museum where she must touch nothing and reverently memorize everything.

"What's your name?" he asked.

"Cherryl Brooks."

"Well, sit down."

He mixed the drinks in silence, while she waited obediently, sitting on the edge of an armchair. When he handed her a glass, she swallowed dutifully a few times, then held the glass clutched in her hand. He knew that she did not taste what she was drinking, did not notice it, had no time to care.

He took a gulp of his drink and put the glass down with irritation: he did not feel like drinking, either. He paced the room sullenly, knowing that her eyes followed him, enjoying the knowledge, enjoying the sense of tremendous significance which his movements, his cuff links, his shoe-laces, his lampshades and ashtrays acquired in that gentle, unquestioning glance.

"Mr. Taggart, what is it that makes you so unhappy?"

"Why should you care whether I am or not?"

"Because . . . well, if you haven't the right to be happy and proud, who has?"

"That's what I want to know—who has?" He turned to her abruptly, the words exploding as if a safety fuse had blown. "He didn't invent iron ore and blast furnaces, did he?"

"Who?"

"Rearden. He didn't invent smelting and chemistry and air compression. He couldn't have invented his Metal but for thousands and thousands of other people. *His* Metal! Why does he think it's his? Why does he think it's his invention? Everybody uses the work of everybody else. Nobody ever invents anything."

She said, puzzled, "But the iron ore and all those other things were there all the time. Why didn't anybody else make that Metal, but Mr. Rearden did?"

"He didn't do it for any noble purpose, he did it just for his own profit, he's never done anything for any other reason."

"What's wrong with that, Mr. Taggart?" Then she laughed softly, as if at the sudden solution of a riddle. "That's nonsense, Mr. Taggart. You don't mean it. You know that Mr. Rearden has *earned* all his profits, and so have you. You're saying those things just to be modest, when everybody knows what a great job you people have done—you and Mr. Rearden and your sister, who must be such a wonderful person!"

"Yeah? That's what *you* think. She's a hard, insensitive woman who spends her life building tracks and bridges, not for any great ideal, but only because that's what she enjoys doing. If she enjoys it, what is there to admire about her doing it? I'm not so sure it was great—building that Line for all those prosperous industrialists in Colorado, when there are so many poor people in blighted areas who need transportation."

"But, Mr. Taggart, it was you who fought to build that Line."

"Yes, because it was my duty—to the company and the stockholders and our employees. But don't expect me to enjoy it. I'm not so sure it was great—inventing this complex new Metal, when so many nations are in need of plain iron—why, do you know that the People's State of China hasn't even got enough nails to put wooden roofs over people's heads?"

"But . . . but I don't see that that's your fault."

"Somebody should attend to it. Somebody with the vision to see beyond his own pocketbook. No sensitive person these days—when there's so much suffering around us—would devote ten years of his life to splashing about with a lot of trick metals. You think it's great? Well, it's not any kind of superior ability, but just a hide that you couldn't pierce if you poured a ton of his own steel over his head! There are many people of much greater ability in the world, but you don't read about them in the headlines and you don't run to gape at them at grade crossings—because they can't invent non-collapsible bridges at a time when the suffering of mankind weighs on their spirit!"

She was looking at him silently, respectfully, her joyous eagerness toned down, her eyes subdued. He felt better.

He picked up his drink, took a gulp, and chuckled abruptly at a sudden recollection.

"It was funny, though," he said, his tone easier, livelier, the tone of a confidence to a pal. "You should have seen Orren Boyle yesterday, when the first flash came through on the radio from Wyatt Junction! He turned green—but I mean, *green,* the color of a fish that's been lying around too long! Do you know what he did last night, by way of taking the bad news? Hired himself a suite at the Valhalla Hotel—and you know what *that* is—and the last I heard, he was still there today, drinking himself under the table and the beds, with a few choice friends of his and half the female population of upper Amsterdam Avenue!"

"Who is Mr. Boyle?" she asked, stupefied.

"Oh, a fat slob that's inclined to overreach himself. A smart guy who gets too smart at times. You should have seen his face yesterday! I got a kick out of that. That—and Dr. Floyd Ferris. That smoothy didn't like it a bit, oh not a bit!—the elegant Dr. Ferris of the State Science Institute, the servant of the people, with the patent-leather vocabulary—but he carried it off pretty well, I must say, only you could see him squirming in every paragraph—I mean, that interview he gave out this morning, where he said, 'The country gave Rearden that Metal, now we expect him to give the country something in return.' That was pretty nifty, considering who's been riding on the gravy train and . . . well, considering. That was better than Bertram Scudder—Mr. Scudder couldn't think of anything but 'No comment,' when his fellow gentlemen of the press asked him to voice his sentiments. 'No comment'—from Bertram Scudder who's never been known to shut his trap from the day he was born, about anything you ask him or don't ask, Abyssinian poetry or the state of the ladies' rest rooms in the textile industry! And Dr. Pritchett, the old fool, is going around saying that he knows for certain that Rearden didn't invent that Metal—because he was told, by an unnamed reliable source, that Rearden stole the formula from a penniless inventor whom he murdered!"

He was chuckling happily. She was listening as to a lecture on higher mathematics, grasping nothing, not even the style of the language, a style which made the mystery greater, because she was certain that it did not mean—coming from him—what it would have meant anywhere else.

He refilled his glass and drained it, but his gaiety vanished abruptly. He slumped into an armchair, facing her, looking up at her from under his bald forehead, his eyes blurred.

"She's coming back tomorrow," he said, with a sound like a chuckle devoid of amusement.

"Who?"

"My sister. My dear sister. Oh, she'll think she's great, won't she?"

"You dislike your sister, Mr. Taggart?" He made the same sound; its meaning was so eloquent that she needed no other answer. "Why?" she asked.

"Because she thinks she's so good. What right has she to think it? What right has anybody to think he's good? Nobody's any good."

"You don't mean it, Mr. Taggart."

"I mean, we're only human beings—and what's a human being? A weak, ugly, sinful creature, born that way, rotten in his bones—so humility is the one virtue he ought to practice. He ought to spend his life on his knees, begging to be forgiven for his dirty existence. When a man thinks he's good—*that's* when he's rotten. Pride is the worst of all sins, no matter what he's done."

"But if a man knows that what he's done is good?"

"Then he ought to apologize for it."

"To whom?"

"To those who haven't done it."

"I . . . I don't understand."

"Of course you don't. It takes years and years of study in the higher reaches of the intellect. Have you ever heard of *The Metaphysical Contradictions of the Universe,* by Dr. Simon Pritchett?" She shook her head, frightened. "How do you know what's good, anyway? Who knows what's good? Who can ever know? There are no absolutes—as Dr. Pritchett has proved irrefutably. Nothing is absolute. Everything is a matter of opinion. How do you know that bridge hasn't collapsed? You only *think* it hasn't. How do you know that there's any bridge at all? You think that a system of philosophy—such as Dr. Pritchett's—is just something academic, remote, impractical? But it isn't. Oh, boy, how it isn't!"

"But, Mr. Taggart, the Line you built—"

"Oh, what's that Line, anyway? It's only a material achievement. Is that of any importance? Is there any greatness in anything material? Only a low animal can gape at that bridge—when there are so many higher things in life. But do the higher things ever get recognition? Oh no! Look at people. All that hue and cry and front pages about some trick arrangement of some scraps of matter. Do they care about any nobler issue? Do they ever give front pages to a phenomenon of the spirit? Do they notice or appreciate a person of finer sensibility? And you wonder whether it's true that a great man is doomed to unhappiness in this depraved world!" He leaned forward, staring at her intently. "I'll tell you . . . I'll tell you something . . . unhappiness is the hallmark of virtue. If a man is unhappy, really, truly unhappy, it means that he is a superior sort of person."

He saw the puzzled, anxious look of her face. "But, Mr. Taggart, you got everything you wanted. Now you have the best railroad in the country, the newspapers call you the greatest business executive of the age, they say the stock of your company made a fortune for you overnight, you got everything you could ask for—aren't you glad of it?"

In the brief space of his answer, she felt frightened, sensing a sudden fear within him. He answered, "No."

She didn't know why her voice dropped to a whisper. "You'd rather the bridge had collapsed?"

"I haven't said that!" he snapped sharply. Then he shrugged and waved his hand in a gesture of contempt. "You don't understand."

"I'm sorry . . . Oh, I know that I have such an awful lot to learn!"

"I am talking about a hunger for something much beyond that bridge. A hunger that nothing material will ever satisfy."

"What, Mr. Taggart? What is it you want?"

"Oh, there you go! The moment you ask, 'What is it?' you're back in the crude, material world where everything's got to be tagged and measured. I'm speaking of things that can't be named in materialistic words . . . the higher realms of the spirit, which man can never reach. . . . What's any human achievement, anyway? The earth is only an atom whirling in the universe—of what importance is that bridge to the solar system?"

A sudden, happy look of understanding cleared her eyes. "It's great of you, Mr. Taggart, to think that your own achievement isn't good enough for you. I guess no matter how far you've gone, you want to go still farther. You're ambitious. That's what I admire most: ambition. I mean, doing things, not stopping and giving up, but doing. I understand, Mr. Taggart . . . even if I don't understand all the big thoughts."

"You'll learn."

"Oh, I'll work very hard to learn!"

Her glance of admiration had not changed. He walked across the room, moving in that glance as in a gentle spotlight. He went to refill his glass. A mirror hung in the niche behind the portable bar. He caught a glimpse of his own figure: the tall body distorted by a sloppy, sagging posture, as if in deliberate negation of human grace, the thinning hair, the soft, sullen mouth. It struck him suddenly that she did not see him at all: what she saw was the heroic figure of a builder, with proudly straight shoulders and wind-blown hair. He chuckled aloud, feeling that this was a good joke on her, feeling dimly a satisfaction that resembled a sense of victory: the superiority of having put something over on her.

Sipping his drink, he glanced at the door of his bedroom and thought of the usual ending for an adventure of this kind. He thought that it would be easy: the girl was too awed to resist. He saw the reddish-bronze sparkle of her hair—as she sat, head bent, under a light—and a wedge of smooth, glowing skin on her shoulder. He looked away. Why bother? —he thought.

The hint of desire that he felt, was no more than a sense of physical discomfort. The sharpest impulse in his mind, nagging him to action, was not the thought of the girl, but of all the men who would not pass up an opportunity of this kind. He admitted to himself that she was a much better person than Betty Pope, perhaps the best person ever offered to him. The admission left him indifferent. He felt no more than he had felt for Betty Pope. He felt nothing. The prospect of experiencing pleasure was not worth the effort; he had no desire to experience pleasure.

"It's getting late," he said. "Where do you live? Let me give you another drink and then I'll take you home."

When he said good-bye to her at the door of a miserable rooming house in a slum neighborhood, she hesitated, fighting not to ask a question which she desperately wished to ask him.

"Will I . . ." she began, and stopped.

"What?"

"No, nothing, nothing!"

He knew that the question was: "Will I see you again?" It gave him pleasure not to answer, even though he knew that she would.

She glanced up at him once more, as if it were perhaps for the last time, then said earnestly, her voice low, "Mr. Taggart, I'm very grateful to you, because you . . . I mean, any other man would have tried to . . . I mean, that's all he'd want, but you're so much better than that, oh, so much better!"

He leaned closer to her with a faint, interested smile. "Would you have?" he asked.

She drew back from him, in sudden terror at her own words. "Oh, I didn't mean it that way!" she gasped. "Oh God, I wasn't hinting or . . . or . . ." She blushed furiously, whirled around and ran, vanishing up the long, steep stairs of the rooming house.

He stood on the sidewalk, feeling an odd, heavy, foggy sense of satisfaction: feeling as if he had committed an act of virtue—and as if he had taken his revenge upon every person who had stood cheering along the three-hundred-mile track of the John Galt Line.

* * *

When their train reached Philadelphia, Rearden left her without a word, as if the nights of their return journey deserved no acknowledgment in the daylight reality of crowded station platforms and moving engines, the reality he respected. She went on to New York, alone. But late that evening, the doorbell of her apartment rang and Dagny knew that she had expected it.

He said nothing when he entered, he looked at her, making his silent presence more intimate a greeting than words. There was the faint suggestion of a contemptuous smile in his face, at once admitting and mocking his knowledge of her hours of impatience and his own. He stood in the middle of her living room, looking slowly around him; this was her apartment, the one place in the city that had been the focus of two years of his torment, as the place he could not think about and did, the place he could not enter—and was now entering with the casual, unannounced right of an owner. He sat down in an armchair, stretching his legs forward—and she stood before him, almost as if she needed his permission to sit down and it gave her pleasure to wait.

"Shall I tell you that you did a magnificent job, building that Line?" he asked. She glanced at him in astonishment; he had never paid her open compliments of that kind; the admiration in his voice was genuine, but the hint of mockery remained in his face, and she felt as if he were speaking to some purpose which she could not guess. "I've spent all day answering questions about you—and about the Line, the Metal and the future. That, and counting the orders for the Metal. They're coming in at the rate of thousands of tons an hour. When was it, nine months ago?—I couldn't get a single answer anywhere. Today, I had to cut off my phone, not to listen to all the people who wanted to speak to me personally about their urgent need of Rearden Metal. What did you do today?"

"I don't know. Tried to listen to Eddie's reports—tried to get away from people—tried to find the rolling stock to put more trains on the John Galt Line, because the schedule I'd planned won't be enough for the business that's piled up in just three days."

"A great many people wanted to see you today, didn't they?"

"Why, yes."

"They'd have given anything just for a word with you, wouldn't they?"

"I . . . I suppose so."

"The reporters kept asking me what you were like. A young boy from a local sheet kept saying that you were a great woman. He said he'd be afraid to speak to you, if he ever had the chance. He's right. That future that they're all talking and trembling about—it will be as *you* made it, because you had the courage none of them could conceive of. All the roads to wealth that they're scrambling for now, it's your strength that broke them open. The strength to stand against everyone. The strength to recognize no will but your own."

She caught the sinking gasp of her breath: she knew his purpose. She stood straight, her arms at her sides, her face austere, as if in unflinching endurance; she stood under the praise as under a lashing of insults.

"They kept asking you questions, too, didn't they?" He spoke intently, leaning forward. "And they looked at you with admiration. They looked, as if you stood on a mountain peak and they could only take their hats off to you across the great distance. Didn't they?"

"Yes," she whispered.

"They looked as if they knew that one may not approach you or speak in your presence or touch a fold of your dress. They knew it and it's true. They looked at you with respect, didn't they? They looked up to you?"

He seized her arm, threw her down on her knees, twisting her body against his legs, and bent down to kiss her mouth. She laughed soundlessly, her laughter mocking, but her eyes half-closed, veiled with pleasure.

Hours later, when they lay in bed together, his hand moving over her body, he asked suddenly, throwing her back against the curve of his arm, bending over her—and she knew, by the intensity of his face, by the sound of a gasp somewhere in the quality of his voice, even though his voice was low and steady, that the question broke out of him as if it were worn by the hours of torture he had spent with it:

"Who were the other men that had you?"

He looked at her as if the question were a sight visualized in every detail, a sight he loathed, but would not abandon; she heard the contempt in his voice, the hatred, the suffering—and an odd eagerness that did not pertain to torture; he had asked the question, holding her body tight against him.

She answered evenly, but he saw a dangerous flicker in her eyes, as of a warning that she understood him too well. "There was only one other, Hank."

"When?"

"When I was seventeen."

"Did it last?"

"For some years."

"Who was he?"

She drew back, lying against his arm; he leaned closer, his face taut; she held his eyes. "I won't answer you."

"Did you love him?"

"I won't answer."

"Did you like sleeping with him?"

"Yes!"

The laughter in her eyes made it sound like a slap across his face, the laughter of her knowledge that this was the answer he dreaded and wanted.

He twisted her arms behind her, holding her helpless, her breasts pressed against him; she felt the pain ripping through her shoulders, she heard the anger in his words and the huskiness of pleasure in his voice: "Who was he?"

She did not answer, she looked at him, her eyes dark and oddly brilliant, and he saw that the shape of her mouth, distorted by pain, was the shape of a mocking smile.

He felt it change to a shape of surrender, under the touch of his lips. He held her body as if the violence and the despair of the way he took her could wipe his unknown rival out of existence, out of her past, and more: as if it could transform any part of her, even the rival, into an instrument of his pleasure. He knew, by the eagerness of her movement as her arms seized him, that this was the way she wanted to be taken.

* * *

The silhouette of a conveyor belt moved against the strips of fire in the sky, raising coal to the top of a distant tower, as if an inexhaustible number of small black buckets rode out of the earth in a diagonal line across the sunset. The harsh, distant clatter kept going through the rattle of the chains which a young man in blue overalls was fastening over the machinery, securing it to the flatcars lined on the siding of the Quinn Ball Bearing Company of Connecticut.

Mr. Mowen, of the Amalgamated Switch and Signal Company across the street, stood by, watching. He had stopped to watch, on his way home from his own plant. He wore a light overcoat stretched over his short, paunchy figure, and a derby hat over his graying, blondish head. There was a first touch of September chill in the air. All the gates of the Quinn plant buildings stood wide open, while men and cranes moved the machinery out; like taking the vital organs and leaving a carcass, thought Mr. Mowen.

"Another one?" asked Mr. Mowen, jerking his thumb at the plant, even though he knew the answer.

"Huh?" asked the young man, who had not noticed him standing there.

"Another company moving to Colorado?"

"Uh-huh."

"It's the third one from Connecticut in the last two weeks," said Mr. Mowen. "And when you look at what's happening in New Jersey, Rhode Island, Massachusetts and all along the Atlantic coast . . ." The young man was not looking and did not seem to listen. "It's like a leaking faucet," said Mr. Mowen, "and all the water's running out to Colorado. All the money." The young man flung the chain across and followed it deftly, climbing over the big shape covered with canvas. "You'd think people would have some feeling for their native state, some loyalty . . . But they're running away. I don't know what's happening to people."

"It's the Bill," said the young man.

"What Bill?"

"The Equalization of Opportunity Bill."

"How do you mean?"

"I hear Mr. Quinn was making plans a year ago to open a branch in Colorado. The Bill knocked that out cold. So now he's made up his mind to move there, lock, stock and barrel."

"I don't see where that makes it right. The Bill was necessary. It's a rotten shame—old firms that have been here for generations . . . There ought to be a law . . ."

The young man worked swiftly, competently, as if he enjoyed it. Behind him, the conveyor belt kept rising and clattering against the sky. Four distant smokestacks stood like flagpoles, with coils of smoke weaving slowly about them, like long banners at half-mast in the reddish glow of the evening.

Mr. Mowen had lived with every smokestack of that skyline since the days of his father and grandfather. He had seen the conveyor belt from his office window for thirty years. That the Quinn Ball Bearing Company should vanish from across the street had seemed inconceivable; he had known about Quinn's decision and had not believed it; or rather, he had believed it as he believed any words he heard or spoke: as sounds that bore no fixed relation to physical reality. Now he knew that it was real. He stood by the flatcars on the siding as if he still had a chance to stop them.

"It isn't right," he said; he was speaking to the skyline at large, but the young man above was the only part of it that could hear him. "That's not the way it was in my father's time. I'm not a big shot. I don't want to fight anybody. What's the matter with the world?" There was no answer. "Now you, for instance—are they taking you along to Colorado?"

"Me? No. I don't work here. I'm just transient labor. Just picked up this job helping to lug the stuff out."

"Well, where are you going to go when they move away?"

"Haven't any idea."

"What are you going to do, if more of them move out?"

"Wait and see."

Mr. Mowen glanced up dubiously: he could not tell whether the answer was intended to apply to him or to the young man. But the young man's attention was fixed on his task; he was not looking down. He moved on to the shrouded shapes on the next flatcar, and Mr. Mowen followed, looking up at him, pleading with something up in space: "I've got rights, haven't I? I was born here. I expected the old companies to be here when I grew up. I expected to run the plant like my father did. A man is part of his community, he's got a right to count on it, hasn't he? . . . Something ought to be done about it."

"About what?"

"Oh, I know, you think it's great, don't you?—that Taggart boom and Rearden Metal and the gold rush to Colorado and the drunken spree out there, with Wyatt and his bunch expanding their production like kettles boiling over! Everybody thinks it's great—that's all you hear anywhere you go—people are slap-happy, making plans like six-year-olds on a vacation—you'd think it was a national honeymoon of some kind or a permanent Fourth of July!"

The young man said nothing.

"Well, I don't think so," said Mr. Mowen. He lowered his voice. "The newspapers don't say so, either—mind you that—the newspapers aren't saying anything."

Mr. Mowen heard no answer, only the clanking of the chains.

"Why are they all running to Colorado?" he asked. "What have they got down there that we haven't got?"

The young man grinned. "Maybe it's something you've got that they haven't got."

"What?" The young man did not answer. "I don't see it. It's a backward, primitive, unenlightened place. They don't even have a modern government. It's the worst government in any state. The laziest. It does nothing—outside of keeping law courts and a police department. It doesn't do anything for the people. It doesn't help anybody. I don't see why all our best companies want to run there."

The young man glanced down at him, but did not answer.

Mr. Mowen sighed. "Things aren't right," he said. "The Equalization of Opportunity Bill was a sound idea. There's got to be a chance for everybody. It's a rotten shame if people like Quinn take unfair advantage of it. Why didn't he let somebody else start manufacturing ball bearings in Colorado? . . . I wish the Colorado people would leave us alone. That Stockton Foundry out there had no right going into the switch and signal business. That's been my business for years, I have the right of seniority, it isn't fair, it's dog-eat-dog competition, new-comers shouldn't be allowed to muscle in. Where am I going to sell switches and signals? There were two big railroads out in Colorado. Now the Phoenix-Durango's gone, so there's just Taggart Transcontinental left. It isn't fair—their forcing Dan Conway out. There's got to be room for competition. . . . And I've been waiting six months for an order of steel from Orren Boyle—and now he says he can't promise me anything, because Rearden Metal has shot his market to hell, there's a run on that Metal, Boyle has to retrench. It isn't fair—Rearden being allowed to ruin other people's markets that way. . . . And I want to get some Rearden Metal, too, I need it—but try and get it! He has a waiting line that would stretch across three states—nobody can get a scrap of it, except his old friends, people like Wyatt and Danagger and such. It isn't fair. It's discrimination. I'm just as good as the next fellow. I'm entitled to my share of that Metal."

The young man looked up. "I was in Pennsylvania last week," he said. "I saw the Rearden mills. *There's* a place that's busy! They're building four new open-hearth furnaces, and they've got six more coming. . . . New furnaces," he said, looking off to the south. "Nobody's built a new furnace on the Atlantic coast for the last five years. . . ." He stood against the sky, on the top of a shrouded motor, looking off at the dusk with a faint smile of eagerness and longing, as one looks at the distant vision of one's love. "They're busy. . . ." he said.

Then his smile vanished abruptly; the way he jerked the chain was the first break in the smooth competence of his movements: it looked like a jolt of anger.

Mr. Mowen looked at the skyline, at the belts, the wheels, the smoke—the smoke that settled heavily, peacefully across the evening air, stretching in a long haze all the way to the city of New York somewhere beyond the sunset—and he felt reassured by the thought of New York in its ring of sacred fires, the ring of smokestacks, gas tanks, cranes and high tension lines. He felt a current of power flowing through every grimy structure of his familiar street; he liked the figure of the young man above him, there was something reassuring in the way he worked, something that blended with the skyline. . . . Yet Mr. Mowen wondered why he felt that a crack was growing somewhere, eating through the solid, the eternal walls.

"Something ought to be done," said Mr. Mowen. "A friend of mine went out of business last week—the oil business—had a couple of wells down in Oklahoma—couldn't compete with Ellis Wyatt. It isn't fair. They ought to leave the little people a chance. They ought to place a limit on Wyatt's output. He shouldn't be allowed to produce so much that he'll swamp everybody else off the market. . . . I got stuck in New York yesterday, had to leave my car there and come home on a damn commuters' local, couldn't get any gas for the car, they said there's a shortage of oil in the city. . . . Things aren't right. Something ought to be done about it. . . ."

Looking at the skyline, Mr. Mowen wondered what was the nameless threat to it and who was its destroyer.

"What do you want to do about it?" asked the young man.

"Who, me?" said Mr. Mowen. "I wouldn't know. I'm not a big shot. I can't solve national problems. I just want to make a living. All I know is, somebody ought to do something about it. . . . Things aren't right. . . . Listen—what's your name?"

"Owen Kellogg."

"Listen, Kellogg, what do you think is going to happen to the world?"

"You wouldn't care to know."

A whistle blew on a distant tower, the night-shift whistle, and Mr. Mowen realized that it was getting late. He sighed, buttoning his coat, turning to go.

"Well, things are being done," he said. "Steps are being taken. Constructive steps. The Legislature has passed a Bill giving wider powers to the Bureau of Economic Planning and National Resources. They've appointed a very able man as Top Co-ordinator. Can't say I've heard of him before, but the newspapers said he's a man to be watched. His name is Wesley Mouch."

* * *

Dagny stood at the window of her living room, looking at the city. It was late and the lights were like the last sparks left glittering on the black remnants of a bonfire.

She felt at peace, and she wished she could hold her mind still to let her own emotions catch up with her, to look at every moment of the month that had rushed past her. She had had no time to feel that she was back in her own office at Taggart Transcontinental; there had been so much to do that she forgot it was a return from exile. She had not noticed what Jim had said on her return or whether he had said anything. There had been only one person whose reaction she had wanted to know; she had telephoned the Wayne-Falkland Hotel; but Señor Francisco d'Anconia, she was told, had gone back to Buenos Aires.

She remembered the moment when she signed her name at the bottom of a long legal page; it was the moment that ended the John Galt Line. Now it was the Rio Norte Line of Taggart Transcontinental again—except that the men of the train crews refused to give up its name. She, too, found it hard to give up; she forced herself not to call it "the John Galt," and wondered why that required an effort, and why she felt a faint wrench of sadness.

One evening, on a sudden impulse, she had turned the corner of the Taggart Building, for a last look at the office of John Galt, Inc., in the alley; she did not know what she wanted—just to see it, she thought. A plank barrier had been raised along the sidewalk: the old building was being demolished; it had given up, at last. She had climbed over the planks and, by the light of the street lamp that had once thrown a stranger's shadow across the pavement, she had looked in through the window of her former office. Nothing was left of the ground floor; the partitions had been torn down, there were broken pipes hanging from the ceiling and a pile of rubble on the floor. There was nothing to see.

She had asked Rearden whether he had come there one night last spring and stood outside her window, fighting his desire to enter. But she had known, even before he answered, that he had not. She did not tell him why she asked it. She did not know why that memory still disturbed her at times.

Beyond the window of her living room, the lighted rectangle of the calendar hung like a small shipping tag in the black sky. It read: September 2. She smiled defiantly, remembering the race she had run against its changing pages: there were no deadlines now, she thought, no barriers, no threats, no limits.

She heard a key turning in the door of her apartment; this was the sound she had waited for, had wanted to hear tonight.

Rearden came in, as he had come many times, using the key she had given him, as sole announcement. He threw his hat and coat down on a chair with a gesture that had become familiar; he wore the formal black of dinner clothes.

"Hello," she said.

"I'm still waiting for the evening when I won't find you in," he answered.

"Then you'll have to phone the offices of Taggart Transcontinental."

"Any evening? Nowhere else?"

"Jealous, Hank?"

"No. Curious what it would feel like, to be."

He stood looking at her across the room, refusing to let himself approach her, deliberately prolonging the pleasure of knowing that he could do it whenever he wished. She wore the tight gray skirt of an office suit and a blouse of transparent white cloth tailored like a man's shirt; the blouse flared out above her waistline, stressing the trim flatness of her hips; against the glow of a lamp behind her, he could see the slender silhouette of her body within the flaring circle of the blouse.

"How was the banquet?" she asked.

"Fine. I escaped as soon as I could. Why didn't you come? You were invited."

"I didn't want to see you in public."

He glanced at her, as if stressing that he noted the full meaning of her answer; then the lines of his face moved to the hint of an amused smile. "You missed a lot. The National Council of Metal Industries won't put itself again through the ordeal of having me for guest of honor. Not if they can help it."

"What happened?"

"Nothing. Just a lot of speeches."

"Was it an ordeal for you?"

"No . . . Yes, in a way . . . I had really wanted to enjoy it."

"Shall I get you a drink?"

"Yes, will you?"

She turned to go. He stopped her, grasping her shoulders from behind; he bent her head back and kissed her mouth. When he raised his head, she pulled it down again with a demanding gesture of ownership, as if stressing her right to do it. Then she stepped away from him.

"Never mind the drink," he said, "I didn't really want it—except for seeing you wait on me."

"Well, then, let me wait on you."

"No."

He smiled, stretching himself out on the couch, his hands crossed under his head. He felt at home; it was the first home he had ever found.

"You know, the worst part of the banquet was that the only wish of every person present was to get it over with," he said. "What I can't understand is why they wanted to do it at all. They didn't have to. Certainly not for my sake."

She picked up a cigarette box, extended it to him, then held the flame of a lighter to the tip of his cigarette, in the deliberate manner of waiting on him. She smiled in answer to his chuckle, then sat down on the arm of a chair across the room.

"Why did you accept their invitation, Hank?" she asked. "You've always refused to join them."

"I didn't want to refuse a peace offer—when I've beaten them and they know it. I'll never join them, but an invitation to appear as a guest of honor—well, I thought they were good losers. I thought it was generous of them."

"Of *them?*"

"Are you going to say: of *me?*"

"Hank! After all the things they've done to stop you—"

"I won, didn't I? So I thought . . . You know, I didn't hold it against them that they couldn't see the value of the Metal sooner—so long as they saw it at last. Every man learns in his own way and time. Sure, I knew there was a lot of cowardice there, and envy and hypocrisy, but I thought that that was only the surface—*now,* when I've proved my case, when I've proved it so loudly!—I thought their real motive for inviting me was their appreciation of the Metal, and—"

She smiled in the brief space of his pause; she knew the sentence he had stopped himself from uttering: " —and for that, I would forgive anyone anything."

"But it wasn't," he said. "And I couldn't figure out what their motive was. Dagny, I don't think they had any motive at all. They didn't give that banquet to please me, or to gain something from me, or to save face with the public. There was no purpose of any kind about it, no meaning. They didn't really care when they denounced the Metal—and they don't care now. They're not really afraid that I'll drive them all off the market—they don't care enough even about that. Do you know what that banquet was like? It's as if they'd heard that there are values one is supposed to honor and this is what one does to honor them—so they went through the motions, like ghosts pulled by some sort of distant echoes from a better age. I . . . I couldn't stand it."

She said, her face tight, "And you don't think you're generous!"

He glanced up at her; his eyes brightened to a look of amusement. "Why do they make you so angry?"

She said, her voice low to hide the sound of tenderness, "You wanted to enjoy it . . ."

"It probably serves me right. I shouldn't have expected anything. I don't know what it was that I wanted."

"I do."

"I've never liked occasions of that sort. I don't see why I expected it to be different, this time. . . . You know, I went there feeling almost as if the Metal had changed everything, even people."

"Oh yes, Hank, I know!"

"Well, it was the wrong place to seek anything. . . . Do you remember? You said once that celebrations should be only for those who have something to celebrate."

The dot of her lighted cigarette stopped in mid-air; she sat still. She had never spoken to him of that party or of anything related to his home. In a moment, she answered quietly, "I remember."

"I know what you meant . . . I knew it then, too."

He was looking straight at her. She lowered her eyes.

He remained silent; when he spoke again, his voice was gay. "The worst thing about people is not the insults they hand out, but the compliments. I couldn't bear the kind they spouted tonight, particularly when they kept saying how much everybody needs me—they, the city, the country and the whole world, I guess. Apparently, their idea of the height of glory is to deal with people who need them. I can't stand people who need me." He glanced at her. "Do you need me?"

She answered, her voice earnest, "Desperately."

He laughed. "No. Not the way I meant. You didn't say it the way they do."

"How did I say it?"

"Like a trader—who pays for what he wants. They say it like beggars who use a tin cup as a claim check."

"I . . . pay for it, Hank?"

"Don't look innocent. You know exactly what I mean."

"Yes," she whispered; she was smiling.

"Oh, to hell with them!" he said happily, stretching his legs, shifting the position of his body on the couch, stressing the luxury of relaxation. "I'm no good as a public figure. Anyway, it doesn't matter now. We don't have to care what they see or don't see. They'll leave us alone. It's clear track ahead. What's the next undertaking, Mr. Vice-President?"

"A transcontinental track of Rearden Metal."

"How soon do you want it?"

"Tomorrow morning. Three years from now is when I'll get it."

"Think you can do it in three years?"

"If the John Galt . . . if the Rio Norte Line does as well as it's doing now."

"It's going to do better. That's only the beginning."

"I have an installment plan made out. As the money comes in, I'm going to start tearing up the main track, one division at a time, and replacing it with Rearden Metal rail."

"Okay. Any time you wish to start."

"I'll keep moving the old rail to the branch lines—they won't last much longer, if I don't. In three years, you'll ride on your own Metal into San Francisco, if somebody wants to give you a banquet there."

"In three years, I'll have mills pouring Rearden Metal in Colorado, in Michigan and in Idaho. That's *my* installment plan."

"Your own mills? Branches?"

"Uh-huh."

"What about the Equalization of Opportunity Bill?"

"You don't think it's going to exist three years from now, do you? We've given them such a demonstration that all that rot is going to be swept away. The whole country is with us. Who'll want to stop things now? Who'll listen to the bilge? There's a lobby of the better kind of men working in Washington right this moment. They're going to get the Equalization Bill scrapped at the next session."

"I . . . I hope so."

"I've had a terrible time, these last few weeks, getting the new furnaces started, but it's all set now, they're being built, I can sit back and take it easy. I can sit at my desk, rake in the money, loaf like a bum, watch the orders for the Metal pouring in and play favorites all over the place. . . . Say, what's the first train you've got for Philadelphia tomorrow morning?"

"Oh, I don't know."

"You don't? What's the use of an Operating Vice-President? I have to be at the mills by seven tomorrow. Got anything running around six?"

"Five-thirty A.M. is the first one, I think."

"Will you wake me up in time to make it or would you rather order the train held for me?"

"I'll wake you up."

She sat, watching him as he remained silent. He had looked tired when he came in; the lines of exhaustion were gone from his face now.

"Dagny," he asked suddenly; his tone had changed, there was some hidden, earnest note in his voice, "why didn't you want to see me in public?"

"I don't want to be part of your . . . official life."

He did not answer; in a moment, he asked casually, "When did you take a vacation last?"

"I think it was two . . . no, three years ago."

"What did you do?"

"Went to the Adirondacks for a month. Came back in a week."

"I did that five years ago. Only it was Oregon." He lay flat on his back, looking at the ceiling. "Dagny, let's take a vacation together. Let's take my car and drive away for a few weeks, anywhere, just drive, down the back roads, where no one knows us. We'll leave no address, we won't look at a newspaper, we won't touch a phone—we won't have any official life at all."

She got up. She approached him, she stood by the side of the couch, looking down at him, the light of the lamp behind her; she did not want him to see her face and the effort she was making not to smile.

"You can take a few weeks off, can't you?" he said. "Things are set and going now. It's safe. We won't have another chance in the next three years."

"All right, Hank," she said, forcing her voice to sound calmly toneless.

"Will you?"

"When do you want to start?"

"Monday morning."

"All right."

She turned to step away. He seized her wrist, pulled her down, swung her body to lie stretched full-length on top of him, he held her still, uncomfortably, as she had fallen, his one hand in her hair, pressing her mouth to his, his other hand moving from the shoulder blades under her thin blouse to her waist, to her legs. She whispered, "And you say I don't need you . . . !"

She pulled herself away from him, and stood up, brushing her hair off her face. He lay still, looking up at her, his eyes narrowed, the bright flicker of some particular interest in his eyes, intent and faintly mocking. She glanced down: a strap of her slip had broken, the slip hung diagonally from her one shoulder to her side, and he was looking at her breast under the transparent film of the blouse. She raised her hand to adjust the strap. He slapped her hand down. She smiled, in understanding, in answering mockery. She walked slowly, deliberately across the room and leaned against a table, facing him, her hands holding the table's edge, her shoulders thrown back. It was the contrast he liked—the severity of her clothes and the half-naked body, the railroad executive who was a woman he owned.

He sat up; he sat leaning comfortably across the couch, his legs crossed and stretched forward, his hands in his pockets, looking at her with the glance of a property appraisal.

"Did you say you wanted a transcontinental track of Rearden Metal, Mr. Vice-President?" he asked. "What if I don't give it to you? I can choose my customers now and demand any price I please. If this were a year ago, I would have demanded that you sleep with me in exchange."

"I wish you had."

"Would you have done it?"

"Of course."

"As a matter of business? As a sale?"

"If you were the buyer. You would have liked that, wouldn't you?"

"Would you?"

"Yes . . ." she whispered.

He approached her, he grasped her shoulders and pressed his mouth to her breast through the thin cloth.

Then, holding her, he looked at her silently for a long moment. "What did you do with that bracelet?" he asked.

They had never referred to it; she had to let a moment pass to regain the steadiness of her voice. "I have it," she answered.

"I want you to wear it."

"If anyone guesses, it will be worse for you than for me."

"Wear it."

She brought out the bracelet of Rearden Metal. She extended it to him without a word, looking straight at him, the green-blue chain glittering across her palm. Holding her glance, he clasped the bracelet on her wrist. In the moment when the clasp clicked shut under his fingers, she bent her head down to them and kissed his hand.

* * *

The earth went flowing under the hood of the car. Uncoiling from among the curves of Wisconsin's hills, the highway was the only evidence of human labor, a precarious bridge stretched across a sea of brush, weeds and trees. The sea rolled softly, in sprays of yellow and orange, with a few red jets shooting up on the hillsides, with pools of remnant green in the hollows, under a pure blue sky. Among the colors of a picture post card, the car's hood looked like the work of a jeweler, with the sun sparkling on its chromium steel, and its black enamel reflecting the sky.

Dagny leaned against the corner of the side window, her legs stretched forward; she liked the wide, comfortable space of the car's seat and the warmth of the sun on her shoulders; she thought that the countryside was beautiful.

"What I'd like to see," said Rearden, "is a billboard."

She laughed: he had answered her silent thought. "Selling what and to whom? We haven't seen a car or a house for an hour."

"That's what I don't like about it." He bent forward a little, his hands on the wheel; he was frowning. "Look at that road."

The long strip of concrete was bleached to the powdery gray of bones left on a desert, as if sun and snows had eaten away the traces of tires, oil and carbon, the lustrous polish of motion. Green weeds rose from the angular cracks of the concrete. No one had used the road or repaired it for many years; but the cracks were few.

"It's a good road," said Rearden. "It was built to last. The man who built it must have had a good reason for expecting it to carry a heavy traffic in the years ahead."

"Yes . . ."

"I don't like the looks of this."

"I don't either." Then she smiled. "But think how often we've heard people complain that billboards ruin the appearance of the countryside. Well, there's the unruined countryside for them to admire." She added, "They're the people I hate."

She did not want to feel the uneasiness which she felt like a thin crack under her enjoyment of this day. She had felt that uneasiness at times, in the last three weeks, at the sight of the country streaming past the wedge of the car's hood. She smiled: it was the hood that had been the immovable point in her field of vision, while the earth had gone by, it was the hood that had been the center, the focus, the security in a blurred, dissolving world . . . the hood before her and Rearden's hands on the wheel by her side . . . she smiled, thinking that she was satisfied to let this be the shape of her world.

After the first week of their wandering, when they had driven at random, at the mercy of unknown crossroads, he had said to her one morning as they started out, "Dagny, does resting have to be purposeless?" She had laughed, answering, "No. What factory do you want to see?" He had smiled—at the guilt he did not have to assume, at the explanations he did not have to give—and he had answered, "It's an abandoned ore mine around Saginaw Bay, that I've heard about. They say it's exhausted."

They had driven across Michigan to the ore mine. They had walked through the ledges of an empty pit, with the remnants of a crane like a skeleton bending above them against the sky, and someone's rusted lunchbox clattering away from under their feet. She had felt a stab of uneasiness, sharper than sadness—but Rearden had said cheerfully, "Exhausted, hell! I'll show them how many tons and dollars I can draw out of this place!" On their way back to the car, he had said, "If I could find the right man, I'd buy that mine for him tomorrow morning and set him up to work it."

The next day, when they were driving west and south, toward the

plains of Illinois, he had said suddenly, after a long silence, "No, I'll
have to wait till they junk the Bill. The man who could work that mine,
wouldn't need me to teach him. The man who'd need me, wouldn't be
worth a damn."

They could speak of their work, as they always had, with full confidence in being understood. But they never spoke of each other. He
acted as if their passionate intimacy were a nameless physical fact, not
to be identified in the communication between two minds. Each night,
it was as if she lay in the arms of a stranger who let her see every
shudder of sensation that ran through his body, but would never permit
her to know whether the shocks reached any answering tremor within
him. She lay naked at his side, but on her wrist there was the bracelet of
Rearden Metal.

She knew that he hated the ordeal of signing the "Mr. and Mrs.
Smith" on the registers of squalid roadside hotels. There were evenings
when she noticed the faint contraction of anger in the tightness of his
mouth, as he signed the expected names of the expected fraud, anger
at those who made fraud necessary. She noticed, indifferently, the air
of knowing slyness in the manner of the hotel clerks, which seemed to
suggest that guests and clerks alike were accomplices in a shameful
guilt: the guilt of seeking pleasure. But she knew that it did not matter
to him when they were alone, when he held her against him for a moment and she saw his eyes look alive and guiltless.

They drove through small towns, through obscure side roads, through
the kind of places they had not seen for years. She felt uneasiness at the
sight of the towns. Days passed before she realized what it was that she
missed most: a glimpse of fresh paint. The houses stood like men in
unpressed suits, who had lost the desire to stand straight: the cornices
were like sagging shoulders, the crooked porch steps like torn hem lines,
the broken windows like patches, mended with clapboard. The people
in the streets stared at the new car, not as one stares at a rare sight, but
as if the glittering black shape were an impossible vision from another
world. There were few vehicles in the streets and too many of them
were horse-drawn. She had forgotten the literal shape and usage of
horsepower; she did not like to see its return.

She did not laugh, that day at the grade crossing, when Rearden
chuckled, pointing, and she saw the train of a small local railroad come
tottering from behind a hill, drawn by an ancient locomotive that
coughed black smoke through a tall stack.

"Oh God, Hank, it's not funny!"

"I know," he said.

They were seventy miles and an hour away from it, when she said,
"Hank, do you see the Taggart Comet being pulled across the continent
by a coal-burner of that kind?"

"What's the matter with you? Pull yourself together."

"I'm sorry . . . It's just that I keep thinking it won't be any use, all my new track and all your new furnaces, if we don't find someone able to produce Diesel engines. If we don't find him fast."

"Ted Nielsen of Colorado is your man."

"Yes, if he finds a way to open his new plant. He's sunk more money than he should into the bonds of the John Galt Line."

"That's turned out to be a pretty profitable investment, hasn't it?"

"Yes, but it's held him up. Now he's ready to go ahead, but he can't find the tools. There are no machine tools to buy, not anywhere, not at any price. He's getting nothing but promises and delays. He's combing the country, looking for old junk to reclaim from closed factories. If he doesn't start soon—"

"He will. Who's going to stop him now?"

"Hank," she said suddenly, "could we go to a place I'd like to see?"

"Sure. Anywhere. Which place?"

"It's in Wisconsin. There used to be a great motor company there, in my father's time. We had a branch line serving it, but we closed the line—about seven years ago—when they closed the factory. I think it's one of those blighted areas now. Maybe there's still some machinery left there that Ted Nielsen could use. It might have been overlooked—the place is forgotten and there's no transportation to it at all."

"I'll find it. What was the name of the factory?"

"The Twentieth Century Motor Company."

"Oh, of course! That was one of the best motor firms in my youth, perhaps the best. I seem to remember that there was something odd about the way it went out of business . . . can't recall what it was."

It took them three days of inquiries, but they found the bleached, abandoned road—and now they were driving through the yellow leaves that glittered like a sea of gold coins, to the Twentieth Century Motor Company.

"Hank, what if anything happens to Ted Nielsen?" she asked suddenly, as they drove in silence.

"Why should anything happen to him?"

"I don't know, but . . . well, there was Dwight Sanders. He vanished. United Locomotives is done for now. And the other plants are in no condition to produce Diesels. I've stopped listening to promises. And . . . and of what use is a railroad without motive power?"

"Of what use is anything, for that matter, without it?"

The leaves sparkled, swaying in the wind. They spread for miles, from grass to brush to trees, with the motion and all the colors of fire; they seemed to celebrate an accomplished purpose, burning in unchecked, untouched abundance.

Rearden smiled. "There's something to be said for the wilderness. I'm beginning to like it. New country that nobody's discovered." She nodded gaily. "It's good soil—look at the way things grow. I'd clear that brush and I'd build a—"

And then they stopped smiling. The corpse they saw in the weeds by the roadside was a rusty cylinder with bits of glass—the remnant of a gas-station pump.

It was the only thing left visible. The few charred posts, the slab of concrete and the sparkle of glass dust—which had been a gas station—were swallowed in the brush, not to be noticed except by a careful glance, not to be seen at all in another year.

They looked away. They drove on, not wanting to know what else lay hidden under the miles of weeds. They felt the same wonder like a weight in the silence between them: wonder as to how much the weeds had swallowed and how fast.

The road ended abruptly behind the turn of a hill. What remained was a few chunks of concrete sticking out of a long, pitted stretch of tar and mud. The concrete had been smashed by someone and carted away; even weeds could not grow in the strip of earth left behind. On the crest of a distant hill, a single telegraph pole stood slanted against the sky, like a cross over a vast grave.

It took them three hours and a punctured tire to crawl in low gear through trackless soil, through gullies, then down ruts left by cart wheels—to reach the settlement that lay in the valley beyond the hill with the telegraph pole.

A few houses still stood within the skeleton of what had once been an industrial town. Everything that could move, had moved away; but some human beings had remained. The empty structures were vertical rubble; they had been eaten, not by time, but by men: boards torn out at random, missing patches of roofs, holes left in gutted cellars. It looked as if blind hands had seized whatever fitted the need of the moment, with no concept of remaining in existence the next morning. The inhabited houses were scattered at random among the ruins; the smoke of their chimneys was the only movement visible in town. A shell of concrete, which had been a schoolhouse, stood on the outskirts; it looked like a skull, with the empty sockets of glassless windows, with a few strands of hair still clinging to it, in the shape of broken wires.

Beyond the town, on a distant hill, stood the factory of the Twentieth Century Motor Company. Its walls, roof lines and smokestacks looked trim, impregnable like a fortress. It would have seemed intact but for a silver water tank: the water tank was tipped sidewise.

They saw no trace of a road to the factory in the tangled miles of trees and hillsides. They drove to the door of the first house in sight that showed a feeble signal of rising smoke. The door was open. An old woman came shuffling out at the sound of the motor. She was bent and swollen, barefooted, dressed in a garment of flour sacking. She looked at the car without astonishment, without curiosity; it was the blank stare of a being who had lost the capacity to feel anything but exhaustion.

"Can you tell me the way to the factory?" asked Rearden.

The woman did not answer at once; she looked as if she would be unable to speak English. "What factory?" she asked.

Rearden pointed. "That one."

"It's closed."

"I know it's closed. But is there any way to get there?"

"I don't know."

"Is there any sort of road?"

"There's roads in the woods."

"Any for a car to drive through?"

"Maybe."

"Well, which would be the best road to take?"

"I don't know."

Through the open door, they could see the interior of her house. There was a useless gas stove, its oven stuffed with rags, serving as a chest of drawers. There was a stove built of stones in a corner, with a few logs burning under an old kettle, and long streaks of soot rising up the wall. A white object lay propped against the legs of a table: it was a porcelain washbowl, torn from the wall of some bathroom, filled with wilted cabbages. A tallow candle stood in a bottle on the table. There was no paint left on the floor; its boards were scrubbed to a soggy gray that looked like the visual expression of the pain in the bones of the person who had bent and scrubbed and lost the battle against the grime now soaked into the grain of the boards.

A brood of ragged children had gathered at the door behind the woman, silently, one by one. They stared at the car, not with the bright curiosity of children, but with the tension of savages ready to vanish at the first sign of danger.

"How many miles is it to the factory?" asked Rearden.

"Ten miles," said the woman, and added, "Maybe five."

"How far is the next town?"

"There ain't any next town."

"There are other towns somewhere. I mean, how far?"

"Yeah. Somewhere."

In the vacant space by the side of the house, they saw faded rags hanging on a clothesline, which was a piece of telegraph wire. Three chickens pecked among the beds of a scraggly vegetable garden; a fourth sat roosting on a bar which was a length of plumber's pipe. Two pigs waddled in a stretch of mud and refuse; the stepping stones laid across the muck were pieces of the highway's concrete.

They heard a screeching sound in the distance and saw a man drawing water from a public well by means of a rope pulley. They watched him as he came slowly down the street. He carried two buckets that seemed too heavy for his thin arms. One could not tell his age. He approached and stopped, looking at the car. His eyes darted at the strangers, then away, suspicious and furtive.

Rearden took out a ten-dollar bill and extended it to him, asking, "Would you please tell us the way to the factory?"

The man stared at the money with sullen indifference, not moving, not lifting a hand for it, still clutching the two buckets. If one were ever to see a man devoid of greed, thought Dagny, there he was.

"We don't need no money around here," he said.

"Don't you work for a living?"

"Yeah."

"Well, what do you use for money?"

The man put the buckets down, as if it had just occurred to him that he did not have to stand straining under their weight. "We don't use no money," he said. "We just trade things amongst us."

"How do you trade with people from other towns?"

"We don't go to no other towns."

"You don't seem to have it easy here."

"What's that to you?"

"Nothing. Just curiosity. Why do you people stay here?"

"My old man used to have a grocery store here. Only the factory closed."

"Why didn't you move?"

"Where to?"

"Anywhere."

"What for?"

Dagny was staring at the two buckets: they were square tins with rope handles; they had been oil cans.

"Listen," said Rearden, "can you tell us whether there's a road to the factory?"

"There's plenty of roads."

"Is there one that a car can take?"

"I guess so."

"Which one?"

The man weighed the problem earnestly for some moments. "Well, now, if you turn to the left by the schoolhouse," he said, "and go on till you come to the crooked oak, there's a road up there that's fine when it don't rain for a couple of weeks."

"When did it rain last?"

"Yesterday."

"Is there another road?"

"Well, you could go through Hanson's pasture and across the woods and then there's a good, solid road there, all the way down to the creek."

"Is there a bridge across the creek?"

"No."

"What are the other roads?"

"Well, if it's a car road that you want, there's one the other side of

Miller's patch, it's paved, it's the best road for a car, you just turn to the right by the schoolhouse and—"

"But that road doesn't go to the factory, does it?"

"No, not to the factory."

"All right," said Rearden. "Guess we'll find our own way."

He had pressed the starter, when a rock came smashing into the windshield. The glass was shatterproof, but a sunburst of cracks spread across it. They saw a ragged little hoodlum vanishing behind a corner with a scream of laughter, and they heard the shrill laughter of children answering him from behind some windows or crevices.

Rearden suppressed a swear word. The man looked vapidly across the street, frowning a little. The old woman looked on, without reaction. She had stood there silently, watching, without interest or purpose, like a chemical compound on a photographic plate, absorbing visual shapes because they were there to be absorbed, but unable ever to form any estimate of the objects of her vision.

Dagny had been studying her for some minutes. The swollen shapelessness of the woman's body did not look like the product of age and neglect: it looked as if she was pregnant. This seemed impossible, but glancing closer Dagny saw that her dust-colored hair was not gray and that there were few wrinkles on her face; it was only the vacant eyes, the stooped shoulders, the shuffling movements that gave her the stamp of senility.

Dagny leaned out and asked, "How old are you?"

The woman looked at her, not in resentment, but merely as one looks at a pointless question. "Thirty-seven," she answered.

They had driven five former blocks away, when Dagny spoke.

"Hank," she said in terror, "that woman is only two years older than I!"

"Yes."

"God, how did they ever come to such a state?"

He shrugged. "Who is John Galt?"

The last thing they saw, as they left the town, was a billboard. A design was still visible on its peeling strips, imprinted in the dead gray that had once been color. It advertised a washing machine.

In a distant field, beyond the town, they saw the figure of a man moving slowly, contorted by the ugliness of a physical effort beyond the proper use of a human body: he was pushing a plow by hand.

They reached the factory of the Twentieth Century Motor Company two miles and two hours later. They knew, as they climbed the hill, that their quest was useless. A rusted padlock hung on the door of the main entrance, but the huge windows were shattered and the place was open to anyone, to the woodchucks, the rabbits and the dried leaves that lay in drifts inside.

The factory had been gutted long ago. The great pieces of machinery had been moved out by some civilized means—the neat holes of their bases still remained in the concrete of the floor. The rest had gone to random looters. There was nothing left, except refuse which the neediest tramp had found worthless, piles of twisted, rusted scraps, of boards, plaster and glass splinters—and the steel stairways, built to last and lasting, rising in trim spirals to the roof.

They stopped in the great hall where a ray of light fell diagonally from a gap in the ceiling, and the echoes of their steps rang around them, dying far away in rows of empty rooms. A bird darted from among the steel rafters and went in a hissing streak of wings out into the sky.

"We'd better look through it, just in case," said Dagny. "You take the shops and I'll take the annexes. Let's do it as fast as possible."

"I don't like to let you wander around alone. I don't know how safe they are, any of those floors or stairways."

"Oh, nonsense! I can find my way around a factory—or in a wrecking crew. Let's get it over with. I want to get out of here."

When she walked through the silent yards—where steel bridges still hung overhead, tracing lines of geometrical perfection across the sky —her only wish was not to see any of it, but she forced herself to look. It was like having to perform an autopsy on the body of one's love. She moved her glance as an automatic searchlight, her teeth clamped tight together. She walked rapidly—there was no necessity to pause anywhere.

It was in a room of what had been the laboratory that she stopped. It was a coil of wire that made her stop. The coil protruded from a pile of junk. She had never seen that particular arrangement of wires, yet it seemed familiar, as if it touched the hint of some memory, faint and very distant. She reached for the coil, but could not move it: it seemed to be part of some object buried in the pile.

The room looked as if it had been an experimental laboratory—if she was right in judging the purpose of the torn remnants she saw on the walls: a great many electrical outlets, bits of heavy cable, lead conduits, glass tubing, built-in cabinets without shelves or doors. There was a great deal of glass, rubber, plastic and metal in the junk pile, and dark gray splinters of slate that had been a blackboard. Scraps of paper rustled dryly all over the floor. There were also remnants of things which had not been brought here by the owner of that room: popcorn wrappers, a whiskey bottle, a confession magazine.

She attempted to extricate the coil from the scrap pile. It would not move; it was part of some large object. She knelt and began to dig through the junk.

She had cut her hands, she was covered with dust by the time she stood up to look at the object she had cleared. It was the broken remnant of the model of a motor. Most of its parts were missing, but enough was left to convey some idea of its former shape and purpose.

She had never seen a motor of this kind or anything resembling it.

She could not understand the peculiar design of its parts or the functions they were intended to perform.

She examined the tarnished tubes and odd-shaped connections. She tried to guess their purpose, her mind going over every type of motor she knew and every possible kind of work its parts could perform. None fitted the model. It looked like an electric motor, but she could not tell what fuel it was intended to burn. It was not designed for steam, or oil, or anything she could name.

Her sudden gasp was not a sound, but a jolt that threw her at the junk pile. She was on her hands and knees, crawling over the wreckage, seizing every piece of paper in sight, flinging it away, searching further. Her hands were shaking.

She found part of what she hoped had remained in existence. It was a thin sheaf of typewritten pages clamped together—the remnant of a manuscript. Its beginning and end were gone; the bits of paper left under the clamp showed the thick number of pages it had once contained. The paper was yellowed and dry. The manuscript had been a description of the motor.

From the empty enclosure of the plant's powerhouse, Rearden heard her voice screaming, "Hank!" It sounded like a scream of terror.

He ran in the direction of the voice. He found her standing in the middle of a room, her hands bleeding, her stockings torn, her suit smeared with dust, a bunch of papers clutched in her hand.

"Hank, what does this look like?" she asked, pointing at an odd piece of wreckage at her feet; her voice had the intense, obsessed tone of a person stunned by a shock, cut off from reality. "What does it look like?"

"Are you hurt? What happened?"

"No! . . . Oh, never mind, don't look at me! I'm all right. Look at this. Do you know what that is?"

"What did you do to yourself?"

"I had to dig it out of there. I'm all right."

"You're shaking."

"You will, too, in a moment. Hank! Look at it. Just look and tell me what you think it is."

He glanced down, then looked attentively—then he was sitting on the floor, studying the object intently. "It's a queer way to put a motor together," he said, frowning.

"Read this," she said, extending the pages.

He read, looked up and said, "Good God!"

She was sitting on the floor beside him, and for a moment they could say nothing else.

"It was the coil," she said. She felt as if her mind were racing, she could not keep up with all the things which a sudden blast had opened to her vision, and her words came hurtling against one another. "It was the coil that I noticed first—because I had seen drawings like it, not quite, but something like it, years ago, when I was in school—it was in an old book, it was given up as impossible long, long ago—but I liked to read everything I could find about railroad motors. That book said that there was a time when men were thinking of it—they worked on it, they spent years on experiments, but they couldn't solve it and they gave it up. It was forgotten for generations. I didn't think that any living scientist ever thought of it now. But someone did. Someone has solved it, now, today! . . . Hank, do you understand? Those men, long ago, tried to invent a motor that would draw static electricity from the atmosphere, convert it and create its own power as it went along. They couldn't do it. They gave it up." She pointed at the broken shape. "But there it is."

He nodded. He was not smiling. He sat looking at the remnant, intent on some thought of his own; it did not seem to be a happy thought.

"Hank! Don't you understand what this means? It's the greatest revolution in power motors since the internal-combustion engine—greater than that! It wipes everything out—and makes everything possible. To hell with Dwight Sanders and all of them! Who'll want to look at a Diesel? Who'll want to worry about oil, coal or refueling stations? Do you see what I see? A brand-new locomotive half the size of a single Diesel unit, and with ten times the power. A self-generator, working on a few drops of fuel, with no limits to its energy. The cleanest, swiftest, cheapest means of motion ever devised. Do you see what this will do to our transportation systems and to the country—in about one year?"

There was no spark of excitement in his face. He said slowly, "Who designed it? Why was it left here?"

"We'll find out."

He weighed the pages in his hand reflectively. "Dagny," he asked, "if you don't find the man who made it, will you be able to reconstruct that motor from what is left?"

She took a long moment, then the word fell with a sinking sound: "No."

"Nobody will. He had it all right. It worked—judging by what he writes here. It is the greatest thing I've ever laid eyes on. It was. We can't make it work again. To supply what's missing would take a mind as great as his."

"I'll find him—if I have to drop every other thing I'm doing."

"—and if he's still alive."

She heard the unstated guess in the tone of his voice. "Why do you say it like that?"

"I don't think he is. If he were, would he leave an invention of this kind to rot on a junk pile? Would he abandon an achievement of this size? If he were still alive, you would have had the locomotives with the self-generators years ago. And you wouldn't have had to look for him, because the whole world would know his name by now."

"I don't think this model was made so very long ago."

He looked at the paper of the manuscript and at the rusty tarnish of the motor. "About ten years ago, I'd guess. Maybe a little longer."

"We've got to find him or somebody who knew him. This is more important—"

"—than anything owned or manufactured by anyone today. I don't think we'll find him. And if we don't, nobody will be able to repeat his performance. Nobody will rebuild his motor. There's not enough of it left. It's only a lead, an invaluable lead, but it would take the sort of mind that's born once in a century, to complete it. Do you see our present-day motor designers attempting it?"

"No."

"There's not a first-rate designer left. There hasn't been a new idea in motors for years. That's one profession that seems to be dying—or dead."

"Hank, do you know what that motor would have meant, if built?"

He chuckled briefly. "I'd say: about ten years added to the life of every person in this country—if you consider how many things it would have made easier and cheaper to produce, how many hours of human labor it would have released for other work, and how much more anyone's work would have brought him. Locomotives? What about automobiles and ships and airplanes with a motor of this kind? And tractors. And power plants. All hooked to an unlimited supply of energy, with no fuel to pay for, except a few pennies' worth to keep the converter going. That motor could have set the whole country in motion and on fire. It would have brought an electric light bulb into every hole, even into the homes of those people we saw down in the valley."

"It would have? It will. I'm going to find the man who made it."

"We'll try."

He rose abruptly, but stopped to glance down at the broken remnant and said, with a chuckle that was not gay, *"There* was the motor for the John Galt Line."

Then he spoke in the brusque manner of an executive. "First, we'll try to see if we can find their personnel office here. We'll look for their records, if there's any left. We want the names of their research staff and their engineers. I don't know who owns this place now, and I suspect that the owners will be hard to find, or they wouldn't have let it come to this. Then we'll go over every room in the laboratory. Later, we'll get a few engineers to fly here and comb the rest of the place."

They started out, but she stopped for a moment on the threshold. "Hank, that motor was the most valuable thing inside this factory," she said, her voice low. "It was more valuable than the whole factory and everything it ever contained. Yet it was passed up and left in the refuse. It was the one thing nobody found worth the trouble of taking."

"That's what frightens me about this," he answered.

The personnel office did not take them long. They found it by the sign which was left on the door, but it was the only thing left. There was no furniture inside, no papers, nothing but the splinters of smashed windows.

They went back to the room of the motor. Crawling on hands and knees, they examined every scrap of the junk that littered the floor. There was little to find. They put aside the papers that seemed to contain laboratory notes, but none referred to the motor, and there were no pages of the manuscript among them. The popcorn wrappers and the whiskey bottle testified to the kind of invading hordes that had rolled through the room, like waves washing the remnants of destruction away to unknown bottoms.

They put aside a few bits of metal that could have belonged to the motor, but these were too small to be of value. The motor looked as if parts of it had been ripped off, perhaps by someone who thought he could put them to some customary use. What had remained was too unfamiliar to interest anybody.

On aching knees, her palms spread flat upon the gritty floor, she felt the anger trembling within her, the hurting, helpless anger that answers the sight of desecration. She wondered whether someone's diapers hung on a clothesline made of the motor's missing wires—whether its wheels had become a rope pulley over a communal well—whether its cylinder was now a pot containing geraniums on the window sill of the sweetheart of the man with the whiskey bottle.

There was a remnant of light on the hill, but a blue haze was moving in upon the valleys, and the red and gold of the leaves was spreading to the sky in strips of sunset.

It was dark when they finished. She rose and leaned against the empty frame of the window for a touch of cool air on her forehead. The sky was dark blue. "It could have set the whole country in motion and on fire." She looked down at the motor. She looked out at the country. She moaned suddenly, hit by a single long shudder, and dropped her head on her arm, standing pressed to the frame of the window.

"What's the matter?" he asked.

She did not answer.

He looked out. Far below, in the valley, in the gathering night, there trembled a few pale smears which were the lights of tallow candles.

CHAPTER X

WYATT'S TORCH

"God have mercy on us, ma'am!" said the clerk of the Hall of Records. "Nobody knows who owns that factory now. I guess nobody will ever know it."

The clerk sat at a desk in a ground-floor office, where dust lay undisturbed on the files and few visitors ever called. He looked at the shining automobile parked outside his window, in the muddy square that had once been the center of a prosperous county seat; he looked with a faint, wistful wonder at his two unknown visitors.

"Why?" asked Dagny.

He pointed helplessly at the mass of papers he had taken out of the files. "The court will have to decide who owns it, which I don't think any court can do. If a court ever gets to it. I don't think it will."

"Why? What happened?"

"Well, it was sold out—the Twentieth Century, I mean. The Twentieth Century Motor Company. It was sold twice, at the same time and to two different sets of owners. That was sort of a big scandal at the time, two years ago, and now it's just"—he pointed—"just a bunch of paper lying around, waiting for a court hearing. I don't see how any judge will be able to untangle any property rights out of it—or any right at all."

"Would you tell me please just what happened?"

"Well, the last legal owner of the factory was The People's Mortgage Company, of Rome, Wisconsin. That's the town the other side of the factory, thirty miles north. That Mortgage Company was a sort of noisy outfit that did a lot of advertising about easy credit. Mark Yonts was the head of it. Nobody knew where he came from and nobody knows where he's gone to now, but what they discovered, the morning after The People's Mortgage Company collapsed, was that Mark Yonts had sold the Twentieth Century Motor factory to a bunch of suckers from South Dakota, and that he'd also given it as collateral for a loan from a bank in Illinois. And when they took a look at the factory, they discovered that he'd moved all the machinery out and sold it piecemeal, God only knows where and to whom. So it seems like everybody owns the place—and nobody. That's how it stands now—the South

Dakotans and the bank and the attorney for the creditors of The People's Mortgage Company all suing one another, all claiming this factory, and nobody having the right to move a wheel in it, except that there's no wheels left to move."

"Did Mark Yonts operate the factory before he sold it?"

"Lord, no, ma'am! He wasn't the kind that ever operates anything. He didn't want to *make* money, only to *get* it. Guess he got it, too—more than anyone could have made out of that factory."

He wondered why the blond, hard-faced man, who sat with the woman in front of his desk, looked grimly out the window at their car, at a large object wrapped in canvas, roped tightly under the raised cover of the car's luggage compartment.

"What happened to the factory records?"

"Which do you mean, ma'am?"

"Their production records. Their work records. Their . . . personnel files."

"Oh, there's nothing left of that now. There's been a lot of looting going on. All the mixed owners grabbed what furniture or things they could haul out of there, even if the sheriff did put a padlock on the door. The papers and stuff like that—I guess it was all taken by the scavengers from Starnesville, that's the place down in the valley, where they're having it pretty tough these days. They burned the stuff for kindling, most likely."

"Is there anyone left here who used to work in the factory?" asked Rearden.

"No, sir. Not around here. They all lived down in Starnesville."

"All of them?" whispered Dagny; she was thinking of the ruins. "The . . . engineers, too?"

"Yes, ma'am. That was the factory town. They've all gone, long ago."

"Do you happen to remember the names of any men who worked there?"

"No, ma'am."

"What owner was the last to operate the factory?" asked Rearden.

"I couldn't say, sir. There's been so much trouble up there and the place has changed hands so many times, since old Jed Starnes died. He's the man who built the factory. He made this whole part of the country, I guess. He died twelve years ago."

"Can you give us the names of all the owners since?"

"No, sir. We had a fire in the old courthouse, about three years ago, and all the old records are gone. I don't know where you could trace them now."

"You don't know how this Mark Yonts happened to acquire the factory?"

"Yes, I know that. He bought it from Mayor Bascom of Rome. How Mayor Bascom happened to own it, I don't know."

"Where is Mayor Bascom now?"

"Still there, in Rome."

"Thank you very much," said Rearden, rising. "We'll call on him."

They were at the door when the clerk asked, "What is it you're looking for, sir?"

"We're looking for a friend of ours," said Rearden. "A friend we've lost, who used to work in that factory."

* * *

Mayor Bascom of Rome, Wisconsin, leaned back in his chair; his chest and stomach formed a pear-shaped outline under his soiled shirt. The air was a mixture of sun and dust, pressing heavily upon the porch of his house. He waved his arm, the ring on his finger flashing a large topaz of poor quality.

"No use, no use, lady, absolutely no use," he said. "Would be just a waste of your time, trying to question the folks around here. There's no factory people left, and nobody that would remember much about them. So many families have moved away that what's left here is plain no good, if I do say so myself, plain no good, just being Mayor of a bunch of trash."

He had offered chairs to his two visitors, but he did not mind it if the lady preferred to stand at the porch railing. He leaned back, studying her long-lined figure; high-class merchandise, he thought; but then, the man with her was obviously rich.

Dagny stood looking at the streets of Rome. There were houses, sidewalks, lampposts, even a sign advertising soft drinks; but they looked as if it were now only a matter of inches and hours before the town would reach the stage of Starnesville.

"Naw, there's no factory records left," said Mayor Bascom. "If that's what you want to find, lady, give it up. It's like chasing leaves in a storm now. Just like leaves in a storm. Who cares about papers? At a time like this, what people save is good, solid, material objects. One's got to be practical."

Through the dusty windowpanes, they could see the living room of his house: there were Persian rugs on a buckled wooden floor, a portable bar with chromium strips against a wall stained by the seepage of last year's rains, an expensive radio with an old kerosene lamp placed on top of it.

"Sure, it's me that sold the factory to Mark Yonts. Mark was a nice fellow, a nice, lively, energetic fellow. Sure, he did trim a few corners, but who doesn't? Of course, he went a bit too far. That, I didn't expect. I thought he was smart enough to stay within the law—whatever's left of it nowadays."

Mayor Bascom smiled, looking at them in a manner of placid frankness. His eyes were shrewd without intelligence, his smile good-natured without kindness.

"I don't think you folks are detectives," he said, "but even if you were, it wouldn't matter to me. I didn't get any rake-off from Mark, he didn't let me in on any of his deals, I haven't any idea where he's gone to now." He sighed. "I liked that fellow. Wish he'd stayed around. Never mind the Sunday sermons. He had to live, didn't he? He was no worse than anybody, only smarter. Some get caught at it and some don't—that's the only difference. . . . Nope, I didn't know what he was going to do with it, when he bought that factory. Sure, he paid me quite a bit more than the old booby trap was worth. Sure, he was doing me a favor when he bought it. Nope, I didn't put any pressure on him to make him buy it. Wasn't necessary. I'd done him a few favors before. There's plenty of laws that's sort of made of rubber, and a mayor's in a position to stretch them a bit for a friend. Well, what the hell? That's the only way anybody ever gets rich in this world"—he glanced at the luxurious black car—"as you ought to know."

"You were telling us about the factory," said Rearden, trying to control himself.

"What I can't stand," said Mayor Bascom, "is people who talk about principles. No principle ever filled anybody's milk bottle. The only thing that counts in life is solid, material assets. It's no time for theories, when everything is falling to pieces around us. Well, me—I don't aim to go under. Let them keep their ideas and I'll take the factory. I don't want ideas, I just want my three square meals a day."

"Why did you buy that factory?"

"Why does anybody buy any business? To squeeze whatever can be squeezed out of it. I know a good chance when I see it. It was a bankruptcy sale and nobody much who'd want to bid on the old mess. So I got the place for peanuts. Didn't have to hold it long, either—Mark took it off my hands in two-three months. Sure, it was a smart deal, if I say so myself. No big business tycoon could have done any better with it."

"Was the factory operating when you took it over?"

"Naw. It was shut down."

"Did you attempt to reopen it?"

"Not me. I'm a practical person."

"Can you recall the names of any men who worked there?"

"No. Never met 'em."

"Did you move anything out of the factory?"

"Well, I'll tell you. I took a look around—and what I liked was old Jed's desk. Old Jed Starnes. He was a real big shot in his time. Wonderful desk, solid mahogany. So I carted it home. And some executive, don't know who he was, had a stall shower in his bathroom, the like of which I never saw. A glass door with a mermaid cut in the glass, real art work, and hot stuff, too, hotter than any oil painting. So I had that shower lifted and moved here. What the hell, I owned it, didn't I? I was entitled to get something valuable out of that factory."

"Whose bankruptcy sale was it, when you bought the factory?"

"Oh, that was the big crash of the Community National Bank in Madison. Boy, was that a crash! It just about finished the whole state of Wisconsin—sure finished this part of it. Some say it was this motor factory that broke the bank, but others say it was only the last drop in a leaking bucket, because the Community National had bum investments all over three or four states. Eugene Lawson was the head of it. The banker with a heart, they called him. He was quite famous in these parts two-three years ago."

"Did Lawson operate the factory?"

"No. He merely lent an awful lot of money on it, more than he could ever hope to get back out of the old dump. When the factory busted, that was the last straw for Gene Lawson. The bank busted three months later." He sighed. "It hit the folks pretty hard around here. They all had their life savings in the Community National."

Mayor Bascom looked regretfully past his porch railing at his town. He jerked his thumb at a figure across the street: it was a white-haired charwoman, moving painfully on her knees, scrubbing the steps of a house.

"See that woman, for instance? They used to be solid, respectable folks. Her husband owned the dry-goods store. He worked all his life to provide for her in her old age, and he did, too, by the time he died— only the money was in the Community National Bank."

"Who operated the factory when it failed?"

"Oh, that was some quicky corporation called Amalgamated Service, Inc. Just a puff-ball. Came up out of nothing and went back to it."

"Where are its members?"

"Where are the pieces of a puff-ball when it bursts? Try and trace them all over the United States. Try it."

"Where is Eugene Lawson?"

"Oh, him? He's done all right. He's got a job in Washington—in the Bureau of Economic Planning and National Resources."

Rearden rose too fast, thrown to his feet by a jolt of anger, then said, controlling himself, "Thank you for the information."

"You're welcome, friend, you're welcome," said Mayor Bascom placidly. "I don't know what it is you're after, but take my word for it, give it up. There's nothing more to be had out of that factory."

"I told you that we are looking for a friend of ours."

"Well, have it your way. Must be a pretty good friend, if you'll go to so much trouble to find him, you and the charming lady who is not your wife."

Dagny saw Rearden's face go white, so that even his lips became a sculptured feature, indistinguishable against his skin. "Keep your dirty —" he began, but she stepped between them.

"Why do you think that I am not his wife?" she asked calmly.

Mayor Bascom looked astonished by Rearden's reaction; he had made the remark without malice, merely like a fellow cheat displaying his shrewdness to his partners in guilt.

"Lady, I've seen a lot in my lifetime," he said good-naturedly. "Married people don't look as if they have a bedroom on their minds when they look at each other. In this world, either you're virtuous or you enjoy yourself. Not both, lady, not both."

"I've asked him a question," she said to Rearden in time to silence him. "He's given me an instructive explanation."

"If you want a tip, lady," said Mayor Bascom, "get yourself a wedding ring from the dime store and wear it. It's not sure fire, but it helps."

"Thank you," she said. "Good-bye."

The stern, stressed calm of her manner was a command that made Rearden follow her back to their car in silence.

They were miles beyond the town when he said, not looking at her, his voice desperate and low, "Dagny, Dagny, Dagny . . . I'm sorry!"

"I'm not."

Moments later, when she saw the look of control returning to his face, she said, "Don't ever get angry at a man for stating the truth."

"That particular truth was none of his business."

"His particular estimate of it was none of your concern or mine."

He said through his teeth, not as an answer, but as if the single thought battering his brain turned into sounds against his will, "I couldn't protect you from that unspeakable little—"

"I didn't need protection."

He remained silent, not looking at her.

"Hank, when you're able to keep down the anger, tomorrow or next week, give some thought to that man's explanation and see if you recognize any part of it."

He jerked his head to glance at her, but said nothing.

When he spoke, a long time later, it was only to say in a tired, even voice, "We can't call New York and have our engineers come here to search the factory. We can't meet them here. We can't let it be known that we found the motor together. . . . I had forgotten all that . . . up there . . . in the laboratory."

"Let me call Eddie, when we find a telephone. I'll have him send two engineers from the Taggart staff. I'm here alone, on my vacation, for all they'll know or have to know."

They drove two hundred miles before they found a long-distance telephone line. When she called Eddie Willers, he gasped, hearing her voice.

"Dagny! For God's sake, where are you?"

"In Wisconsin. Why?"

"I didn't know where to reach you. You'd better come back at once. As fast as you can."

"What happened?"

"Nothing—yet. But there are things going on, which . . . You'd better stop them now, if you can. If anybody can."

"What things?"

"Haven't you been reading the newspapers?"

"No."

"I can't tell you over the phone. I can't give you all the details. Dagny, you'll think I'm insane, but I think they're planning to kill Colorado."

"I'll come back at once," she said.

* * *

Cut into the granite of Manhattan, under the Taggart Terminal, there were tunnels which had once been used as sidings, at a time when traffic ran in clicking currents through every artery of the Terminal every hour of the day. The need for space had shrunk through the years, with the shrinking of the traffic, and the side tunnels had been abandoned, like dry river beds; a few lights remained as blue patches on the granite over rails left to rust on the ground.

Dagny placed the remnant of the motor into a vault in one of the tunnels; the vault had once contained an emergency electric generator, which had been removed long ago. She did not trust the useless young men of the Taggart research staff; there were only two engineers of talent among them, who could appreciate her discovery. She had shared her secret with the two and sent them to search the factory in Wisconsin. Then she had hidden the motor where no one else would know of its existence.

When her workers carried the motor down to the vault and departed, she was about to follow them and lock the steel door, but she stopped, key in hand, as if the silence and solitude had suddenly thrown her at the problem she had been facing for days, as if this were the moment to make her decision.

Her office car was waiting for her at one of the Terminal platforms, attached to the end of a train due to leave for Washington in a few minutes. She had made an appointment to see Eugene Lawson, but she had told herself that she would cancel it and postpone her quest—if she could think of some action to take against the things she had found on her return to New York, the things Eddie begged her to fight.

She had tried to think, but she could see no way of fighting, no rules of battle, no weapons. Helplessness was a strange experience, new to her; she had never found it hard to face things and make decisions; but she was not dealing with things—this was a fog without shapes or definitions, in which something kept forming and shifting before it could be seen, like semi-clots in a not-quite-liquid—it was as if her eyes were reduced to side-vision and she were sensing blurs of disaster coiling toward her, but she could not move her glance, she had no glance to move and focus.

The Union of Locomotive Engineers was demanding that the maximum speed of all trains on the John Galt Line be reduced to sixty miles an hour. The Union of Railway Conductors and Brakemen was demanding that the length of all freight trains on the John Galt Line be reduced to sixty cars.

The states of Wyoming, New Mexico, Utah and Arizona were demanding that the number of trains run in Colorado not exceed the number of trains run in each of these neighboring states.

A group headed by Orren Boyle was demanding the passage of a Preservation of Livelihood Law, which would limit the production of Rearden Metal to an amount equal to the output of any other steel mill of equal plant capacity.

A group headed by Mr. Mowen was demanding the passage of a Fair Share Law to give every customer who wanted it an equal supply of Rearden Metal.

A group headed by Bertram Scudder was demanding the passage of a Public Stability Law, forbidding Eastern business firms to move out of their states.

Wesley Mouch, Top Co-ordinator of the Bureau of Economic Planning and National Resources, was issuing a great many statements, the content and purpose of which could not be defined, except that the words "emergency powers" and "unbalanced economy" kept appearing in the text every few lines.

"Dagny, by what right?" Eddie Willers had asked her, his voice quiet, but the words sounding like a cry. "By what right are they all doing it? By what right?"

She had confronted James Taggart in his office and said, "Jim, this is your battle. I've fought mine. You're supposed to be an expert at dealing with the looters. Stop them."

Taggart had said, not looking at her, "You can't expect to run the national economy to suit your own convenience."

"I don't want to run the national economy! I want your national economy runners to leave me alone! I have a railroad to run—and I know what's going to happen to your national economy if my railroad collapses!"

"I see no necessity for panic."

"Jim, do I have to explain to you that the income from our Rio Norte Line is all we've got, to save us from collapsing? That we need every penny of it, every fare, every carload of freight—as fast as we can get it?" He had not answered. "When we have to use every bit of power in every one of our broken-down Diesels, when we don't have enough of them to give Colorado the service it needs—what's going to happen if we reduce the speed and the length of trains?"

"Well, there's something to be said for the unions' viewpoint, too. With so many railroads closing and so many railroad men out of work, they feel that those extra speeds you've established on the Rio Norte

Line are unfair—they feel that there should be more trains, instead, so that the work would be divided around—they feel that it's not fair for us to get all the benefit of that new rail, they want a share of it, too."

"Who wants a share of it? In payment for what?" He had not answered. "Who'll bear the cost of two trains doing the work of one?" He had not answered. "Where are you going to get the cars and the engines?" He had not answered. "What are those men going to do after they've put Taggart Transcontinental out of existence?"

"I fully intend to protect the interests of Taggart Transcontinental."

"How?" He had not answered. "How—if you kill Colorado?"

"It seems to me that before we worry about giving some people a chance to expand, we ought to give some consideration to the people who need a chance of bare survival."

"If you kill Colorado, what is there going to be left for your damn looters to survive on?"

"You have always been opposed to every progressive social measure. I seem to remember that you predicted disaster when we passed the Anti-dog-eat-dog Rule—but the disaster has not come."

"Because *I* saved you, you rotten fools! I won't be able to save you this time!" He had shrugged, not looking at her. "And if I don't, who will?" He had not answered.

It did not seem real to her, here, under the ground. Thinking of it here, she knew she could have no part in Jim's battle. There was no action she could take against the men of undefined thought, of unnamed motives, of unstated purposes, of unspecified morality. There was nothing she could say to them—nothing would be heard or answered. What were the weapons, she thought, in a realm where reason was not a weapon any longer? It was a realm she could not enter. She had to leave it to Jim and count on his self-interest. Dimly, she felt the chill of a thought telling her that self-interest was not Jim's motive.

She looked at the object before her, a glass case containing the remnant of the motor. The man who made the motor—she thought suddenly, the thought coming like a cry of despair. She felt a moment's helpless longing to find him, to lean against him and let him tell her what to do. A mind like his would know the way to win this battle.

She looked around her. In the clean, rational world of the underground tunnels, nothing was of so urgent an importance as the task of finding the man who made the motor. She thought: Could she delay it in order to argue with Orren Boyle?—to reason with Mr. Mowen?—to plead with Bertram Scudder? She saw the motor, completed, built into an engine that pulled a train of two hundred cars down a track of Rearden Metal at two hundred miles an hour. When the vision was within her reach, within the possible, was she to give it up and spend her time bargaining about sixty miles and sixty cars? She could not descend to an existence where her brain would explode under the pressure of forcing itself not to outdistance incompetence. She could not function to the rule of: Pipe down—keep down—slow down—don't do your best, it is not wanted!

She turned resolutely and left the vault, to take the train for Washington.

It seemed to her, as she locked the steel door, that she heard a faint echo of steps. She glanced up and down the dark curve of the tunnel. There was no one in sight; there was nothing but a string of blue lights glistening on walls of damp granite.

* * *

Rearden could not fight the gangs who demanded the laws. The choice was to fight them or to keep his mills open. He had lost his supply of iron ore. He had to fight one battle or the other. There was no time for both.

He had found, on his return, that a scheduled shipment of ore had not been delivered. No word or explanation had been heard from Larkin. When summoned to Rearden's office, Larkin appeared three days later than the appointment made, offering no apology. He said, not looking at Rearden, his mouth drawn tightly into an expression of rancorous dignity:

"After all, you can't order people to come running to your office any time you please."

Rearden spoke slowly and carefully. "Why wasn't the ore delivered?"

"I won't take abuse, I simply won't take any abuse for something I couldn't help. I can run a mine just as well as you ran it, every bit as well, I did everything you did—I don't know why something keeps going wrong unexpectedly all the time. I can't be blamed for the unexpected."

"To whom did you ship your ore last month?"

"I intended to ship you your share of it, I fully intended it, but I couldn't help it if we lost ten days of production last month on account of the rainstorm in the whole of north Minnesota—I intended to ship you the ore, so you can't blame me, because my intention was completely honest."

"If one of my blast furnaces goes down, will I be able to keep it going by feeding your intention into it?"

"That's why nobody can deal with you or talk to you—because you're inhuman."

"I have just learned that for the last three months, you have not been shipping your ore by the lake boats, you have been shipping it by rail. Why?"

"Well, after all, I have a right to run my business as I see fit."

"Why are you willing to pay the extra cost?"

"What do you care? I'm not charging it to you."

"What will you do when you find that you can't afford the rail rates and that you have destroyed the lake shipping?"

"I am sure you wouldn't understand any consideration other than dollars and cents, but some people do consider their social and patriotic responsibilities."

"What responsibilities?"

"Well, I think that a railroad like Taggart Transcontinental is essential to the national welfare and it is one's public duty to support Jim's Minnesota branch line, which is running at a deficit."

Rearden leaned forward across the desk; he was beginning to see the links of a sequence he had never understood. "To whom did you ship your ore last month?" he asked evenly.

"Well, after all, that is my private business which—"

"To Orren Boyle, wasn't it?"

"You can't expect people to sacrifice the entire steel industry of the nation to your selfish interests and—"

"Get out of here," said Rearden. He said it calmly. The sequence was clear to him now.

"Don't misunderstand me, I didn't mean—"

"Get out."

Larkin got out.

Then there followed the days and nights of searching a continent by phone, by wire, by plane—of looking at abandoned mines and at mines ready to be abandoned—of tense, rushed conferences held at tables in the unlighted corners of disreputable restaurants. Looking across the table, Rearden had to decide how much he could risk to invest upon the sole evidence of a man's face, manner and tone of voice, hating the state of having to hope for honesty as for a favor, but risking it, pouring money into unknown hands in exchange for unsupported promises, into unsigned, unrecorded loans to dummy owners of failing mines— money handed and taken furtively, as an exchange between criminals, in anonymous cash; money poured into unenforceable contracts—both parties knowing that in case of fraud, the defrauded was to be punished, not the defrauder—but poured that a stream of ore might continue flowing into furnaces, that the furnaces might continue to pour a stream of white metal.

"Mr. Rearden," asked the purchasing manager of his mills, "if you keep that up, where will be your profit?"

"We'll make it up on tonnage," said Rearden wearily. "We have an unlimited market for Rearden Metal."

The purchasing manager was an elderly man with graying hair, a lean, dry face, and a heart which, people said, was given exclusively to the task of squeezing every last ounce of value out of a penny. He stood in front of Rearden's desk, saying nothing else, merely looking straight at Rearden, his cold eyes narrowed and grim. It was a look of the most profound sympathy that Rearden had ever seen.

There's no other course open, thought Rearden, as he had thought through days and nights. He knew no weapons but to pay for what he wanted, to give value for value, to ask nothing of nature without trading his effort in return, to ask nothing of men without trading the product of his effort. What were the weapons, he thought, if values were not a weapon any longer?

"An unlimited market, Mr. Rearden?" the purchasing manager asked dryly.

Rearden glanced up at him. "I guess I'm not smart enough to make the sort of deals needed nowadays," he said, in answer to the unspoken thoughts that hung across his desk.

The purchasing manager shook his head. "No, Mr. Rearden, it's one or the other. The same kind of brain can't do both. Either you're good at running the mills or you're good at running to Washington."

"Maybe I ought to learn their method."

"You couldn't learn it and it wouldn't do you any good. You wouldn't win in any of those deals. Don't you understand? You're the one who's got something to be looted."

When he was left alone, Rearden felt a jolt of blinding anger, as it had come to him before, painful, single and sudden like an electric shock—the anger bursting out of the knowledge that one cannot deal with pure evil, with the naked, full-conscious evil that neither has nor seeks justification. But when he felt the wish to fight and kill in the rightful cause of self-defense—he saw the fat, grinning face of Mayor Bascom and heard the drawling voice saying, ". . . you and the charming lady who is not your wife."

Then no rightful cause was left, and the pain of anger was turning into the shameful pain of submission. He had no right to condemn anyone—he thought—to denounce anything, to fight and die joyously, claiming the sanction of virtue. The broken promises, the unconfessed desires, the betrayal, the deceit, the lies, the fraud—he was guilty of them all. What form of corruption could he scorn? Degrees do not matter, he thought; one does not bargain about inches of evil.

He did not know—as he sat slumped at his desk, thinking of the honesty he could claim no longer, of the sense of justice he had lost—that it was his rigid honesty and ruthless sense of justice that were now knocking his only weapon out of his hands. He would fight the looters, but the wrath and fire were gone. He would fight, but only as one guilty wretch against the others. He did not pronounce the words, but the pain was their equivalent, the ugly pain saying: Who am I to cast the first stone?

He let his body fall across the desk. . . . Dagny, he thought, Dagny, if this is the price I have to pay, I'll pay it. . . . He was still the trader who knew no code except that of full payment for his desires.

It was late when he came home and hurried soundlessly up the stairs to his bedroom. He hated himself for being reduced to sneaking, but he had done it on most of his evenings for months. The sight of his family had become unbearable to him; he could not tell why. Don't hate them for your own guilt, he had told himself, but knew dimly that this was not the root of his hatred.

He closed the door of his bedroom like a fugitive winning a moment's reprieve. He moved cautiously, undressing for bed: he wanted no sound to betray his presence to his family, he wanted no contact with them, not even in their own minds.

He had put on his pajamas and stopped to light a cigarette, when the door of his bedroom opened. The only person who could properly enter his room without knocking had never volunteered to enter it, so he stared blankly for a moment before he was able to believe that it was Lillian who came in.

She wore an Empire garment of pale chartreuse, its pleated skirt streaming gracefully from its high waistline; one could not tell at first glance whether it was an evening gown or a negligee; it was a negligee. She paused in the doorway, the lines of her body flowing into an attractive silhouette against the light.

"I know I shouldn't introduce myself to a stranger," she said softly, "but I'll have to: my name is Mrs. Rearden." He could not tell whether it was sarcasm or a plea.

She entered and threw the door closed with a casual, imperious gesture, the gesture of an owner.

"What is it, Lillian?" he asked quietly.

"My dear, you mustn't confess so much so bluntly"—she moved in a leisurely manner across the room, past his bed, and sat down in an armchair—"and so unflatteringly. It's an admission that I need to show special cause for taking your time. Should I make an appointment through your secretary?"

He stood in the middle of the room, holding the cigarette at his lips, looking at her, volunteering no answer.

She laughed. "My reason is so unusual that I know it will never occur to you: loneliness, darling. Do you mind throwing a few crumbs of your expensive attention to a beggar? Do you mind if I stay here without any formal reason at all?"

"No," he said quietly, "not if you wish to."

"I have nothing weighty to discuss—no million-dollar orders, no transcontinental deals, no rails, no bridges. Not even the political situation. I just want to chatter like a woman about perfectly unimportant things."

"Go ahead."

"Henry, there's no better way to stop me, is there?" She had an air of helpless, appealing sincerity. "What can I say after that? Suppose I wanted to tell you about the new novel which Balph Eubank is writing—he is dedicating it to me—would that interest you?"

"If it's the truth that you want—not in the least."

She laughed. "And if it's not the truth that I want?"

"Then I wouldn't know what to say," he answered—and felt a rush of blood to his brain, tight as a slap, realizing suddenly the double infamy of a lie uttered in protestation of honesty; he had said it sincerely, but it implied a boast to which he had no right any longer. "Why would you want it, if it's not the truth?" he asked. "What for?"

"Now you see, *that's* the cruelty of conscientious people. You wouldn't understand it—would you?—if I answered that real devotion consists of being willing to lie, cheat and fake in order to make another person happy—to create for him the reality he wants, if he doesn't like the one that exists."

"No," he said slowly, "I wouldn't understand it."

"It's really very simple. If you tell a beautiful woman that she is beautiful, what have you given her? It's no more than a fact and it has cost you nothing. But if you tell an ugly woman that she is beautiful, you offer her the great homage of corrupting the concept of beauty. To love a woman for her virtues is meaningless. She's earned it, it's a payment, not a gift. But to love her for her vices is a real gift, unearned and undeserved. To love her for her vices is to defile all virtue for her sake—and *that* is a real tribute of love, because you sacrifice your conscience, your reason, your integrity and your invaluable self-esteem."

He looked at her blankly. It sounded like some sort of monstrous corruption that precluded the possibility of wondering whether anyone could mean it; he wondered only what was the point of uttering it.

"What's love, darling, if it's not self-sacrifice?" she went on lightly, in the tone of a drawing-room discussion. "What's self-sacrifice, unless one sacrifices that which is one's most precious and most important? But I don't expect you to understand it. Not a stainless-steel Puritan like you. That's the immense selfishness of the Puritan. You'd let the whole world perish rather than soil that immaculate self of yours with a single spot of which you'd have to be ashamed."

He said slowly, his voice oddly strained and solemn, "I have never claimed to be immaculate."

She laughed. "And what is it you're being right now? You're giving me an honest answer, aren't you?" She shrugged her naked shoulders. "Oh, darling, don't take me seriously! I'm just talking."

He ground his cigarette into an ashtray; he did not answer.

"Darling," she said, "I actually came here only because I kept thinking that I had a husband and I wanted to find out what he looked like."

She studied him as he stood across the room, the tall, straight, taut lines of his body emphasized by the single color of the dark blue pajamas.

"You're very attractive," she said. "You look so much better—these last few months. Younger. Should I say happier? You look less tense. Oh, I know you're rushed more than ever and you act like a commander in an air raid, but that's only the surface. You're less tense—inside."

He looked at her, astonished. It was true; he had not known it, had not admitted it to himself. He wondered at her power of observation. She had seen little of him in these last few months. He had not entered her bedroom since his return from Colorado. He had thought that she would welcome their isolation from each other. Now he wondered what motive could have made her so sensitive to a change in him—unless it was a feeling much greater than he had ever suspected her of experiencing.

"I was not aware of it," he said.

"It's quite becoming, dear—and astonishing, since you've been having such a terribly difficult time."

He wondered whether this was intended as a question. She paused, as if waiting for an answer, but she did not press it and went on gaily:

"I know you're having all sorts of trouble at the mills—and then the political situation is getting to be ominous, isn't it? If they pass those laws they're talking about, it will hit you pretty hard, won't it?"

"Yes. It will. But that is a subject which is of no interest to *you*, Lillian, is it?"

"Oh, but it is!" She raised her head and looked straight at him; her eyes had the blank, veiled look he had seen before, a look of deliberate mystery and of confidence in his inability to solve it. "It is of great interest to me . . . though not because of any possible financial losses," she added softly.

He wondered, for the first time, whether her spite, her sarcasm, the cowardly manner of delivering insults under the protection of a smile, were not the opposite of what he had always taken them to be—not a method of torture, but a twisted form of despair, not a desire to make him suffer, but a confession of her own pain, a defense for the pride of an unloved wife, a secret plea—so that the subtle, the hinted, the evasive in her manner, the thing begging to be understood, was not the open malice, but the hidden love. He thought of it, aghast. It made his guilt greater than he had ever contemplated.

"If we're talking politics, Henry, I had an amusing thought. The side you represent—what is that slogan you all use so much, the motto you're supposed to stand for? 'The sanctity of contract'—is that it?"

She saw his swift glance, the intentness of his eyes, the first response of something she had struck, and she laughed aloud.

"Go on," he said; his voice was low; it had the sound of a threat.

"Darling, what for?—since you understood me quite well."

"What was it you intended to say?" His voice was harshly precise and without any color of feeling.

"Do you really wish to bring me to the humiliation of complaining? It's so trite and such a common complaint—although I did think I had a husband who prides himself on being different from lesser men. Do you want me to remind you that you once swore to make my happiness the aim of your life? And that you can't really say in all honesty whether I'm happy or unhappy, because you haven't even inquired whether I exist?"

He felt them as a physical pain—all the things that came tearing at him impossibly together. Her words were a plea, he thought—and he felt the dark, hot flow of guilt. He felt pity—the cold ugliness of pity without affection. He felt a dim anger, like a voice he tried to choke, a voice crying in revulsion: Why should I deal with her rotten, twisted lying?—why should I accept torture for the sake of pity?—why is it I who should have to take the hopeless burden of trying to spare a feeling she won't admit, a feeling I can't know or understand or try to guess? —if she loves me, why doesn't the damn coward say so and let us both face it in the open? He heard another, louder voice, saying evenly: Don't switch the blame to her, that's the oldest trick of all cowards— *you're* guilty—no matter what she does, it's nothing compared to your guilt—she's right—it makes you sick, doesn't it, to know it's she who's right?—let it make you sick, you damn adulterer—it's she who's right!

"What would make you happy, Lillian?" he asked. His voice was toneless.

She smiled, leaning back in her chair, relaxing; she had been watching his face intently.

"Oh, dear!" she said, as in bored amusement. "That's the shyster question. The loophole. The escape clause."

She got up, letting her arms fall with a shrug, stretching her body in a limp, graceful gesture of helplessness.

"What would make me happy, Henry? That is what *you* ought to tell me. That is what you should have discovered for me. I don't know. You were to create it and offer it to me. That was your trust, your obligation, your responsibility. But you won't be the first man to default on that promise. It's the easiest of all debts to repudiate. Oh, you'd never welsh on a payment for a load of iron ore delivered to you. Only on a life."

She was moving casually across the room, the green-yellow folds of her skirt coiling in long waves about her.

"I know that claims of this kind are impractical," she said. "I have no mortgage on you, no collateral, no guns, no chains. I have no hold on you at all, Henry—nothing but your honor."

He stood looking at her as if it took all of his effort to keep his eyes directed at her face, to keep seeing her, to endure the sight. "What do you want?" he asked.

"Darling, there are so many things you could guess by yourself, if you really wished to know what I want. For instance, if you have been avoiding me so blatantly for months, wouldn't I want to know the reason?"

"I have been very busy."

She shrugged. "A wife expects to be the first concern of her husband's existence. I didn't know that when you swore to forsake all others, it didn't include blast furnaces."

She came closer and, with an amused smile that seemed to mock them both, she slipped her arms around him.

It was the swift, instinctive, ferocious gesture of a young bridegroom at the unrequested contact of a whore—the gesture with which he tore her arms off his body and threw her aside.

He stood, paralyzed, shocked by the brutality of his own reaction. She was staring at him, her face naked in bewilderment, with no mystery, no pretense or protection; whatever calculations she had made, this was a thing she had not expected.

"I'm sorry, Lillian . . ." he said, his voice low, a voice of sincerity and of suffering.

She did not answer.

"I'm sorry . . . It's just that I'm very tired," he added, his voice lifeless; he was broken by the triple lie, one part of which was a disloyalty he could not bear to face; it was not the disloyalty to Lillian.

She gave a brief chuckle. "Well, if that's the effect your work has on you, I may come to approve of it. Do forgive me, I was merely trying to do my duty. I thought that you were a sensualist who'd never rise above the instincts of an animal in the gutter. I'm not one of those bitches who belong in it." She was snapping the words dryly, absently, without thinking. Her mind was on a question mark, racing over every possible answer.

It was her last sentence that made him face her suddenly, face her simply, directly, not as one on the defensive any longer. "Lillian, what purpose do you live for?" he asked.

"What a crude question! No enlightened person would ever ask it."

"Well, what is it that enlightened people do with their lives?"

"Perhaps they do not attempt to do anything. *That* is their enlightenment."

"What do they do with their time?"

"They certainly don't spend it on manufacturing plumbing pipes."

"Tell me, why do you keep making those cracks? I know that you feel contempt for the plumbing pipes. You've made that clear long ago. Your contempt means nothing to me. Why keep repeating it?"

He wondered why this hit her; he did not know in what manner, but he knew that it did. He wondered why he felt with absolute certainty that *that* had been the right thing to say.

She asked, her voice dry, "What's the purpose of the sudden questionnaire?"

He answered simply, "I'd like to know whether there's anything that you really want. If there is, I'd like to give it to you, if I can."

"You'd like to *buy* it? That's all you know—*paying* for things. You get off easily, don't you? No, it's not as simple as that. What I want is non-material."

"What is it?"

"You."

"How do you mean that, Lillian? You don't mean it in the gutter sense."

"No, not in the gutter sense."

"How, then?"

She was at the door, she turned, she raised her head to look at him and smiled coldly.

"You wouldn't understand it," she said and walked out.

The torture remaining to him was the knowledge that she would never want to leave him and he would never have the right to leave—the thought that he owed her at least the feeble recognition of sympathy, of respect for a feeling he could neither understand nor return—the knowledge that he could summon nothing for her, except contempt, a strange, total, unreasoning contempt, impervious to pity, to reproach, to his own pleas for justice—and, hardest to bear, the proud revulsion against his own verdict, against his demand that he consider himself lower than this woman he despised.

Then it did not matter to him any longer, it all receded into some outer distance, leaving only the thought that he was willing to bear anything—leaving him in a state which was both tension and peace—because he lay in bed, his face pressed to the pillow, thinking of Dagny, of her slender, sensitive body stretched beside him, trembling under the touch of his fingers. He wished she were back in New York. If she were, he would have gone there, now, at once, in the middle of the night.

* * *

Eugene Lawson sat at his desk as if it were the control panel of a bomber plane commanding a continent below. But he forgot it, at times, and slouched down, his muscles going slack inside his suit, as if he were pouting at the world. His mouth was the one part of him which he could not pull tight at any time; it was uncomfortably prominent in his lean face, attracting the eyes of any listener: when he spoke, the movement ran through his lower lip, twisting its moist flesh into extraneous contortions of its own.

"I am not ashamed of it," said Eugene Lawson. "Miss Taggart, I want you to know that I am not ashamed of my past career as president of the Community National Bank of Madison."

"I haven't made any reference to shame," said Dagny coldly.

"No moral guilt can be attached to me, inasmuch as I lost everything I possessed in the crash of that bank. It seems to me that I would have the right to feel proud of such a sacrifice."

"I merely wanted to ask you some questions about the Twentieth Century Motor Company which—"

"I shall be glad to answer any questions. I have nothing to hide. My conscience is clear. If you thought that the subject was embarrassing to me, you were mistaken."

"I wanted to inquire about the men who owned the factory at the time when you made a loan to—"

"They were perfectly good men. They were a perfectly sound risk—though, of course, I am speaking in human terms, not in the terms of cold cash, which you are accustomed to expect from bankers. I granted them the loan for the purchase of that factory, because they needed the money. If people needed money, that was enough for me. Need was my standard, Miss Taggart. Need, not greed. My father and grandfather built up the Community National Bank just to amass a fortune for themselves. I placed their fortune in the service of a higher ideal. I did not sit on piles of money and demand collateral from poor people who needed loans. The heart was my collateral. Of course, I do not expect anyone in this materialistic country to understand me. The rewards I got were not of a kind that people of *your* class, Miss Taggart, would appreciate. The people who used to sit in front of my desk at the bank, did not sit as you do, Miss Taggart. They were humble, uncertain, worn with care, afraid to speak. My rewards were the tears of gratitude in their eyes, the trembling voices, the blessings, the woman who kissed my hand when I granted her a loan she had begged for in vain everywhere else."

"Will you please tell me the names of the men who owned the motor factory?"

"That factory was essential to the region, absolutely essential. I was perfectly justified in granting that loan. It provided employment for thousands of workers who had no other means of livelihood."

"Did you know any of the people who worked in the factory?"

"Certainly. I knew them all. It was men that interested me, not machines. I was concerned with the human side of industry, not the cash-register side."

She leaned eagerly across the desk. "Did you know any of the engineers who worked there?"

"The engineers? No, no. I was much more democratic than that. It's the real workers that interested me. The common men. They all knew me by sight. I used to come into the shops and they would wave and shout, 'Hello, Gene.' That's what they called me—Gene. But I'm sure this is of no interest to you. It's past history. Now if you really came to Washington in order to talk to me about your railroad"—he straightened up briskly, the bomber-plane pose returning—"I don't know whether I can promise you any special consideration, inasmuch as I must hold the national welfare above any private privileges or interests which—"

"I didn't come to talk to you about my railroad," she said, looking at him in bewilderment. "I have no desire to talk to you about my railroad."

"No?" He sounded disappointed.

"No. I came for information about the motor factory. Could you possibly recall the names of any of the engineers who worked there?"

"I don't believe I ever inquired about their names. I wasn't concerned with the parasites of office and laboratory. I was concerned with the real workers—the men of calloused hands who keep a factory going. They were my friends."

"Can you give me a few of their names? Any names, of anyone who worked there?"

"My dear Miss Taggart, it was so long ago, there were thousands of them, how can I remember?"

"Can't you recall one, any one?"

"I certainly cannot. So many people have always filled my life that I can't be expected to recall individual drops in the ocean."

"Were you familiar with the production of that factory? With the kind of work they were doing—or planning?"

"Certainly. I took a personal interest in all my investments. I went to inspect that factory very often. They were doing exceedingly well. They were accomplishing wonders. The workers' housing conditions were the best in the country. I saw lace curtains at every window and flowers on the window sills. Every home had a plot of ground for a garden. They had built a new schoolhouse for the children."

"Did you know anything about the work of the factory's research laboratory?"

"Yes, yes, they had a wonderful research laboratory, very advanced, very dynamic, with forward vision and great plans."

"Do you . . . remember hearing anything about . . . any plans to produce a new type of motor?"

"Motor? What motor, Miss Taggart? I had no time for details. My objective was social progress, universal prosperity, human brotherhood and love. Love, Miss Taggart. That is the key to everything. If men learned to love one another, it would solve all their problems."

She turned away, not to see the damp movements of his mouth.

A chunk of stone with Egyptian hieroglyphs lay on a pedestal in a corner of the office—the statue of a Hindu goddess with six spider arms stood in a niche—and a huge graph of bewildering mathematical detail, like the sales chart of a mail-order house, hung on the wall.

"Therefore, if you're thinking of your railroad, Miss Taggart—as, of course, you are, in view of certain possible developments—I must point out to you that although the welfare of the country is my first consideration, to which I would not hesitate to sacrifice anyone's profits, still, I have never closed my ears to a plea for mercy and—"

She looked at him and understood what it was that he wanted from her, what sort of motive kept him going.

"I don't wish to discuss my railroad," she said, fighting to keep her voice monotonously flat, while she wanted to scream in revulsion. "Anything you have to say on the subject, you will please say it to my brother, Mr. James Taggart."

"I'd think that at a time like this you wouldn't want to pass up a rare opportunity to plead your case before—"

"Have you preserved any records pertaining to the motor factory?" She sat straight, her hands clasped tight together.

"What records? I believe I told you that I lost everything I owned when the bank collapsed." His body had gone slack once more, his interest had vanished. "But I do not mind it. What I lost was mere material wealth. I am not the first man in history to suffer for an ideal. I was defeated by the selfish greed of those around me. I couldn't establish a system of brotherhood and love in just one small state, amidst a nation of profit-seekers and dollar-grubbers. It was not my fault. But I won't let them beat me. I am not to be stopped. I am fighting—on a wider scale—for the privilege of serving my fellow men. Records, Miss Taggart? The record I left, when I departed from Madison, is inscribed in the hearts of the poor, who had never had a chance before."

She did not want to utter a single unnecessary word; but she could not stop herself: she kept seeing the figure of the old charwoman scrubbing the steps. "Have you seen that section of the country since?" she asked.

"It's not my fault!" he yelled. "It's the fault of the rich who still had money, but wouldn't sacrifice it to save my bank and the people of Wisconsin! You can't blame me! I lost everything!"

"Mr. Lawson," she said with effort, "do you perhaps recall the name of the man who headed the corporation that owned the factory? The corporation to which you lent the money. It was called Amalgamated Service, wasn't it? Who was its president?"

"Oh, him? Yes, I remember him. His name was Lee Hunsacker. A very worthwhile young man, who's taken a terrible beating."

"Where is he now? Do you know his address?"

"Why—I believe he's somewhere in Oregon. Grangeville, Oregon. My secretary can give you his address. But I don't see of what interest . . . Miss Taggart, if what you have in mind is to try to see Mr. Wesley Mouch, let me tell you that Mr. Mouch attaches a great deal of weight to my opinion in matters affecting such issues as railroads and other—"

"I have no desire to see Mr. Mouch," she said, rising.

"But then, I can't understand . . . What, really, was your purpose in coming here?"

"I am trying to find a certain man who used to work for the Twentieth Century Motor Company."

"Why do you wish to find him?"

"I want him to work for my railroad."

He spread his arms wide, looking incredulous and slightly indignant. "At such a moment, when crucial issues hang in the balance, you choose to waste your time on looking for some *one* employee? Believe me, the fate of your railroad depends on Mr. Mouch much more than on any employee you ever find."

"Good day," she said.

She had turned to go, when he said, his voice jerky and high, "You haven't any right to despise me."

She stopped to look at him. "I have expressed no opinion."

"I am perfectly innocent, since I lost my money, since I lost all of my own money for a good cause. My motives were pure. I wanted nothing for myself. I've never sought anything for myself. Miss Taggart, I can proudly say that in all of my life I have *never* made a profit!"

Her voice was quiet, steady and solemn:

"Mr. Lawson, I think I should let you know that of all the statements a man can make, *that* is the one I consider most despicable."

* * *

"I never had a chance!" said Lee Hunsacker.

He sat in the middle of the kitchen, at a table cluttered with papers. He needed a shave; his shirt needed laundering. It was hard to judge his age: the swollen flesh of his face looked smooth and blank, untouched by experience; the graying hair and filmy eyes looked worn by exhaustion; he was forty-two.

"Nobody ever gave me a chance. I hope they're satisfied with what they've made of me. But don't think that I don't know it. I know I was cheated out of my birthright. Don't let them put on any airs about how kind they are. They're a stinking bunch of hypocrites."

"Who?" asked Dagny.

"Everybody," said Lee Hunsacker. "People are bastards at heart and it's no use pretending otherwise. Justice? Huh! Look at it!" His arm swept around him. "A man like me reduced to this!"

Beyond the window, the light of noon looked like grayish dusk among the bleak roofs and naked trees of a place that was not country and could never quite become a town. Dusk and dampness seemed soaked into the walls of the kitchen. A pile of breakfast dishes lay in the sink; a pot of stew simmered on the stove, emitting steam with the greasy odor of cheap meat; a dusty typewriter stood among the papers on the table.

"The Twentieth Century Motor Company," said Lee Hunsacker, "was one of the most illustrious names in the history of American industry. *I* was the president of that company. I owned that factory. But they wouldn't give me a chance."

"You were not the president of the Twentieth Century Motor Company, were you? I believe you headed a corporation called Amalgamated Service?"

"Yes, yes, but it's the same thing. We took over their factory. We were going to do just as well as they did. Better. We were just as important. Who the hell was Jed Starnes anyway? Nothing but a backwoods garage mechanic—did you know that that's how he started?—without any background at all. My family once belonged to the New York Four Hundred. My grandfather was a member of the national legislature. It's not my fault that my father couldn't afford to give me a car of my own, when he sent me to school. All the other boys had cars. My family name was just as good as any of theirs. When I went to college—" He broke off abruptly. "What newspaper did you say you're from?"

She had given him her name; she did not know why she now felt glad that he had not recognized it and why she preferred not to enlighten him. "I did not say I was from a newspaper," she answered. "I need some information on that motor factory for a private purpose of my own, not for publication."

"Oh." He looked disappointed. He went on sullenly, as if she were guilty of a deliberate offense against him. "I thought maybe you came for an advance interview because I'm writing my autobiography." He pointed to the papers on the table. "And what I intend to tell is plenty. I intend—Oh, hell!" he said suddenly, remembering something.

He rushed to the stove, lifted the lid off the pot and went through the motions of stirring the stew, hatefully, paying no attention to his performance. He flung the wet spoon down on the stove, letting the grease drip into the gas burners, and came back to the table.

"Yeah, I'll write my autobiography *if* anybody ever gives me a chance," he said. "How can I concentrate on serious work when this is the sort of thing I have to do?" He jerked his head at the stove. "Friends, huh! Those people think that just because they took me in, they can exploit me like a Chinese coolie! Just because I had no other place to go. They have it easy, those good old friends of mine. He never lifts a finger around the house, just sits in his store all day; a lousy little two-bit stationery store—can it compare in importance with the book I'm writing? And she goes out shopping and asks me to watch her damn stew for her. She knows that a writer needs peace and concentration, but does she care about that? Do you know what she did today?" He leaned confidentially across the table, pointing at the dishes in the sink. "She went to the market and left all the breakfast dishes there and said she'd do them later. I know what she wanted. She expected me to do them. Well, I'll fool her. I'll leave them just where they are."

"Would you allow me to ask you a few questions about the motor factory?"

"Don't imagine that that motor factory was the only thing in my life. I'd held many important positions before. I was prominently connected, at various times, with enterprises manufacturing surgical appliances, paper containers, men's hats and vacuum cleaners. Of course, that sort of stuff didn't give me much scope. But the motor factory—*that* was my big chance. That was what I'd been waiting for."

"How did you happen to acquire it?"

"It was meant for me. It was my dream come true. The factory was shut down—bankrupt. The heirs of Jed Starnes had run it into the ground pretty fast. I don't know exactly what it was, but there had been something goofy going on up there, so the company went broke. The railroad people closed their branch line. Nobody wanted the place, nobody would bid on it. But there it was, this great factory, with all the equipment, all the machinery, all the things that had made millions for Jed Starnes. That was the kind of setup I wanted, the kind of opportunity I was entitled to. So I got a few friends together and we formed the Amalgamated Service Corporation and we scraped up a little money. But we didn't have enough, we needed a loan to help us out and give us a start. It was a perfectly safe bet, we were young men embarking on great careers, full of eagerness and hope for the future. But do you think anybody gave us any encouragement? They did not. Not those greedy, entrenched vultures of privilege! How were we to succeed in life if nobody would give us a factory? We couldn't compete against the little snots who inherit whole chains of factories, could we? Weren't we entitled to the same break? Aw, don't let me hear anything about justice! I worked like a dog, trying to get somebody to lend us the money. But that bastard Midas Mulligan put me through the wringer."

She sat up straight. "Midas Mulligan?"

"Yeah—the banker who looked like a truck driver and acted it, too!"

"Did you know Midas Mulligan?"

"Did I know him? I'm the only man who ever beat him—not that it did me any good!"

At odd moments, with a sudden sense of uneasiness, she had wondered—as she wondered about the stories of deserted ships found floating at sea or of sourceless lights flashing in the sky—about the disappearance of Midas Mulligan. There was no reason why she felt that she had to solve these riddles, except that they were mysteries which had no business being mysteries: they could not be causeless, yet no known cause could explain them.

Midas Mulligan had once been the richest and, consequently, the most denounced man in the country. He had never taken a loss on any investment he made; everything he touched turned into gold. "It's because I know what to touch," he said. Nobody could grasp the pattern of his investments: he rejected deals that were considered flawlessly safe, and he put enormous amounts into ventures that no other banker would handle. Through the years, he had been the trigger that had sent unexpected, spectacular bullets of industrial success shooting over the country. It was he who had invested in Rearden Steel at its start, thus helping Rearden to complete the purchase of the abandoned steel mills in Pennsylvania. When an economist referred to him once as an audacious gambler, Mulligan said, "The reason why you'll never get rich is because you think that what I do is gambling."

It was rumored that one had to observe a certain unwritten rule when dealing with Midas Mulligan: if an applicant for a loan ever mentioned his personal need or any personal feeling whatever, the interview ended and he was never given another chance to speak to Mr. Mulligan.

"Why yes, I can," said Midas Mulligan, when he was asked whether he could name a person more evil than the man with a heart closed to pity. "The man who uses another's pity for him as a weapon."

In his long career, he had ignored all the public attacks on him, except one. His first name had been Michael; when a newspaper columnist of the humanitarian clique nicknamed him Midas Mulligan and the tag stuck to him as an insult, Mulligan appeared in court and petitioned for a legal change of his first name to "Midas." The petition was granted.

In the eyes of his contemporaries, he was a man who had committed the one unforgivable sin: he was proud of his wealth.

These were the things Dagny had heard about Midas Mulligan; she had never met him. Seven years ago, Midas Mulligan had vanished. He left his home one morning and was never heard from again. On the next day, the depositors of the Mulligan Bank in Chicago received notices requesting that they withdraw their funds, because the bank was closing. In the investigations that followed, it was learned that Mulligan had planned the closing in advance and in minute detail; his employees were merely carrying out his instructions. It was the most orderly run on a bank that the country ever witnessed. Every depositor received his money down to the last fraction of interest due. All of the bank's assets had been sold piecemeal to various financial institutions. When the books were balanced, it was found that they balanced perfectly, to the penny; nothing was left over; the Mulligan Bank had been wiped out.

No clue was ever found to Mulligan's motive, to his personal fate or to the many millions of his personal fortune. The man and the fortune vanished as if they had never existed. No one had had any warning about his decision, and no events could be traced to explain it. If he had wished to retire—people wondered—why hadn't he sold his establishment at a huge profit, as he could have done, instead of destroying it? There was nobody to give an answer. He had no family, no friends. His servants knew nothing: he had left his home that morning as usual and did not come back; that was all.

There was—Dagny had thought uneasily for years—a quality of the impossible about Mulligan's disappearance; it was as if a New York skyscraper had vanished one night, leaving nothing behind but a vacant lot on a street corner. A man like Mulligan, and a fortune such as he had taken along with him, could not stay hidden anywhere; a skyscraper could not get lost, it would be seen rising above any plain or forest chosen for its hiding place; were it destroyed, even its pile of rubble could not remain unnoticed. But Mulligan had gone—and in the seven years since, in the mass of rumors, guesses, theories, Sunday supplement stories, and eyewitnesses who claimed to have seen him in every part of the world, no clue to a plausible explanation had ever been discovered.

Among the stories, there was one so preposterously out of character that Dagny believed it to be true: nothing in Mulligan's nature could have given anyone ground to invent it. It was said that the last person to see him, on the spring morning of his disappearance, was an old woman who sold flowers on a Chicago street corner by the Mulligan Bank. She related that he stopped and bought a bunch of the year's first bluebells. His face was the happiest face she had ever seen; he had the look of a youth starting out into a great, unobstructed vision of life lying open before him; the marks of pain and tension, the sediment of years upon a human face, had been wiped off, and what remained was only joyous eagerness and peace. He picked up the flowers as if on a sudden impulse, and he winked at the old woman, as if he had some shining joke to share with her. He said, "Do you know how much I've always loved it—being alive?" She stared at him, bewildered, and he walked away, tossing the flowers like a ball in his hand—a broad, straight figure in a sedate, expensive, businessman's overcoat, going off into the distance against the straight cliffs of office buildings with the spring sun sparkling on their windows.

"Midas Mulligan was a vicious bastard with a dollar sign stamped on his heart," said Lee Hunsacker, in the fumes of the acrid stew. "My whole future depended upon a miserable half-million dollars, which was just small change to him, but when I applied for a loan, he turned me down flat—for no better reason than that I had no collateral to offer. How could I have accumulated any collateral, when nobody had ever given me a chance at anything big? Why did he lend money to others, but not to me? It was plain discrimination. He didn't even care about my feelings—he said that my past record of failures disqualified me for ownership of a vegetable pushcart, let alone a motor factory. What failures? I couldn't help it if a lot of ignorant grocers refused to co-operate with me about the paper containers. By what right did he pass judgment on my ability? Why did my plans for my own future have to depend upon the arbitrary opinion of a selfish monopolist? I wasn't going to stand for that. I wasn't going to take it lying down. I brought suit against him."

"You did *what?*"

"Oh yes," he said proudly, "I brought suit. I'm sure it would seem strange in some of your hidebound Eastern states, but the state of Illinois had a very humane, very progressive law under which I could sue him. I must say it was the first case of its kind, but I had a very smart, liberal lawyer who saw a way for us to do it. It was an economic emergency law which said that people were forbidden to discriminate for any reason whatever against any person in any matter involving his livelihood. It was used to protect day laborers and such, but it applied to me and my partners as well, didn't it? So we went to court, and we testified about the bad breaks we'd all had in the past, and I quoted Mulligan saying that I couldn't even own a vegetable pushcart, and we proved that all the members of the Amalgamated Service corporation had no prestige, no credit, no way to make a living —and, therefore, the purchase of the motor factory was our only chance of livelihood—and, therefore, Midas Mulligan had no right to discriminate against us—and, therefore, we were entitled to demand a loan from him under the law. Oh, we had a perfect case all right, but the man who presided at the trial was Judge Narragansett, one of those old-fashioned monks of the bench who thinks like a mathematician and never feels the human side of anything. He just sat there all through the trial like a marble statue—like one of those blindfolded marble statues. At the end, he instructed the jury to bring in a verdict in favor of Midas Mulligan—and he said some very harsh things about me and my partners. But we appealed to a higher court—and the higher court reversed the verdict and ordered Mulligan to give us the loan on our terms. He had three months in which to comply, but before the three months were up, something happened that nobody can figure out and he vanished into thin air, he and his bank. There wasn't an extra penny left of that bank, to collect our lawful claim. We wasted a lot of money on detectives, trying to find him—as who didn't?—but we gave it up."

No—thought Dagny—no, apart from the sickening feeling it gave her, this case was not much worse than any of the other things that Midas Mulligan had borne for years. He had taken many losses under laws of a similar justice, under rules and edicts that had cost him much larger sums of money; he had borne them and fought and worked the harder; it was not likely that this case had broken him.

"What happened to Judge Narragansett?" she asked involuntarily, and wondered what subconscious connection had made her ask it. She knew little about Judge Narragansett, but she had heard and remembered his name, because it was a name that belonged so exclusively to the North American continent. Now she realized suddenly that she had heard nothing about him for years.

"Oh, he retired," said Lee Hunsacker.

"He did?" The question was almost a gasp.

"Yeah."

"When?"

"Oh, about six months later."

"What did he do after he retired?"

"I don't know. I don't think anybody's heard from him since."

He wondered why she looked frightened. Part of the fear she felt, was that she could not name its reason, either. "Please tell me about the motor factory," she said with effort.

"Well, Eugene Lawson of the Community National Bank in Madison finally gave us a loan to buy the factory—but he was just a messy cheapskate, he didn't have enough money to see us through, he couldn't help us when we went bankrupt. It was not our fault. We had everything against us from the start. How could we run a factory when we had no railroad? Weren't we entitled to a railroad? I tried to get them to reopen their branch line, but those damn people at Taggart Trans—" He stopped. "Say, are you by any chance one of *those* Taggarts?"

"I am the Operating Vice-President of Taggart Transcontinental."

For a moment, he stared at her in blank stupor; she saw the struggle of fear, obsequiousness and hatred in his filmy eyes. The result was a sudden snarl: "I don't need any of you big shots! Don't think I'm going to be afraid of you. Don't expect me to beg for a job. I'm not asking favors of anybody. I bet you're not used to hear people talk to you this way, are you?"

"Mr. Hunsacker, I will appreciate it very much if you will give me the information I need about the factory."

"You're a little late getting interested. What's the matter? Your conscience bothering you? You people let Jed Starnes grow filthy rich on that factory, but you wouldn't give us a break. It was the same factory. We did everything he did. We started right in manufacturing the particular type of motor that had been his biggest money-maker for years. And then some newcomer nobody ever heard of opened a two-bit factory down in Colorado, by the name of Nielsen Motors, and put out a new motor of the same class as the Starnes model, at half the price! We couldn't help that, could we? It was all right for Jed Starnes, no destructive competitor happened to come up in his time, but what were we to do? How could we fight this Nielsen, when nobody had given us a motor to compete with his?"

"Did you take over the Starnes research laboratory?"

"Yes, yes, it was there. Everything was there."

"His staff, too?"

"Oh, some of them. A lot of them had gone while the factory was closed."

"His research staff?"

"They were gone."

"Did you hire any research men of your own?"

"Yes, yes, some—but let me tell you, I didn't have much money to spend on such things as laboratories, when I never had enough funds to give me a breathing spell. I couldn't even pay the bills I owed for the absolutely essential modernizing and redecorating which I'd had to do —that factory was disgracefully old-fashioned from the standpoint of human efficiency. The executive offices had bare plaster walls and a dinky little washroom. Any modern psychologist will tell you that nobody could do his best in such depressing surroundings. I had to have a brighter color scheme in my office, and a decent modern bathroom with a stall shower. Furthermore, I spent a lot of money on a new cafeteria and a playroom and rest room for the workers. We had to have morale, didn't we? Any enlightened person knows that man is made by the material factors of his background, and that a man's mind is shaped by his tools of production. But people wouldn't wait for the laws of economic determinism to operate upon us. We never had a motor factory before. We had to let the tools condition our minds, didn't we? But nobody gave us time."

"Can you tell me about the work of your research staff?"

"Oh, I had a group of very promising young men, all of them guaranteed by diplomas from the best universities. But it didn't do me any good. I don't know what they were doing. I think they were just sitting around, eating up their salaries."

"Who was in charge of your laboratory?"

"Hell, how can I remember that now?"

"Do you remember any of the names of your research staff?"

"Do you think I had time to meet every hireling in person?"

"Did any of them ever mention to you any experiments with a . . . with an entirely new kind of motor?"

"What motor? Let me tell you that an executive of my position does not hang around laboratories. I spent most of my time in New York and Chicago, trying to raise money to keep us going."

"Who was the general manager of the factory?"

"A very able fellow by the name of Roy Cunningham. He died last year in an auto accident. Drunk driving, they said."

"Can you give me the names and addresses of any of your associates? Anyone you remember?"

"I don't know what's become of them. I wasn't in a mood to keep track of that."

"Have you preserved any of the factory records?"

"I certainly have."

She sat up eagerly. "Would you let me see them?"

"You bet!"

He seemed eager to comply; he rose at once and hurried out of the room. What he put down before her, when he returned, was a thick album of clippings: it contained his newspaper interviews and his press agent's releases.

"I was one of the big industrialists, too," he said proudly. "I was a national figure, as you can see. My life will make a book of deep, human significance. I'd have written it long ago, if I had the proper tools of production." He banged angrily upon his typewriter. "I can't work on this damn thing. It skips spaces. How can I get any inspiration and write a best seller with a typewriter that skips spaces?"

"Thank you, Mr. Hunsacker," she said. "I believe this is all you can tell me." She rose. "You don't happen to know what became of the Starnes heirs?"

"Oh, they ran for cover after they'd wrecked the factory. There were three of them, two sons and a daughter. Last I heard, they were hiding their faces out in Durance, Louisiana."

The last sight she caught of Lee Hunsacker, as she turned to go, was his sudden leap to the stove; he seized the lid off the pot and dropped it to the floor, scorching his fingers and cursing: the stew was burned.

* * *

Little was left of the Starnes fortune and less of the Starnes heirs.

"You won't like having to see them, Miss Taggart," said the chief of police of Durance, Louisiana; he was an elderly man with a slow, firm manner and a look of bitterness acquired not in blind resentment, but in fidelity to clear-cut standards. "There's all sorts of human beings to see in the world, there's murderers and criminal maniacs—but, somehow, I think these Starnes persons are what decent people shouldn't have to see. They're a bad sort, Miss Taggart. Clammy and bad . . . Yes, they're still here in town—two of them, that is. The third one is dead. Suicide. That was four years ago. It's an ugly story. He was the youngest of the three, Eric Starnes. He was one of those chronic young men who go around whining about their sensitive feelings, when they're well past forty. He needed love, was his line. He was being kept by older women, when he could find them. Then he started running after a girl of sixteen, a nice girl who wouldn't have anything to do with him. She married a boy she was engaged to. Eric Starnes got into their house on the wedding day, and when they came back from church after the ceremony, they found him in their bedroom, dead, messy dead, his wrists slashed. . . . Now I say there might be forgiveness for a man who kills himself quietly. Who can pass judgment on another man's suffering and on the limit of what he can bear? But the man who kills himself, making a show of his death in order to hurt somebody, the man who gives his life for malice—there's no forgiveness for him, no excuse, he's rotten clear through, and what he deserves is that people spit at his memory, instead of feeling sorry for him and hurt, as he wanted them to be. . . . Well, that was Eric Starnes. I can tell you where to find the other two, if you wish."

She found Gerald Starnes in the ward of a flophouse. He lay half-twisted on a cot. His hair was still black, but the white stubble of his chin was like a mist of dead weeds over a vacant face. He was soggy drunk. A pointless chuckle kept breaking his voice when he spoke, the sound of a static, unfocused malevolence.

"It went bust, the great factory. That's what happened to it. Just went up and bust. Does that bother you, madam? The factory was rotten. Everybody is rotten. I'm supposed to beg somebody's pardon, but I won't. I don't give a damn. People get fits trying to keep up the show, when it's all rot, black rot, the automobiles, the buildings and the souls, and it doesn't make any difference, one way or another. You should've seen the kind of literati who turned flip-flops when I whistled, when I had the dough. The professors, the poets, the intellectuals, the world-savers and the brother-lovers. Any way I whistled. I had lots of fun. I wanted to do good, but now I don't. There isn't any good. Not any goddamn good in the whole goddamn universe. I don't propose to take a bath if I don't feel like it, and that's that. If you want to know anything about the factory, ask my sister. My sweet sister who had a trust fund they couldn't touch, so she got out of it safe, even if she's in the hamburger class now, not the filet mignon à la Sauce Béarnaise, but would she give a penny of it to her brother? The noble plan that busted was her idea as much as mine, but will she give me a penny? Hah! Go take a look at the duchess, take a look. What do I care about the factory? It was just a pile of greasy machinery. I'll sell you all my rights, claims and title to it—for a drink. I'm the last of the Starnes name. It used to be a great name—Starnes. I'll sell it to you. You think I'm a stinking bum, but that goes for all the rest of them and for rich ladies like you, too. I wanted to do good for humanity. Hah! I wish they'd all boil in oil. Be lots of fun. I wish they'd choke. What does it matter? What does anything matter?"

On the next cot, a white-haired, shriveled little tramp turned in his sleep, moaning; a nickel clattered to the floor out of his rags. Gerald Starnes picked it up and slipped it into his own pocket. He glanced at Dagny. The creases of his face were a malignant smile.

"Want to wake him up and start trouble?" he asked. "If you do, I'll say that you're lying."

The ill-smelling bungalow, where she found Ivy Starnes, stood on the edge of town, by the shore of the Mississippi. Hanging strands of moss and clots of waxy foliage made the thick vegetation look as if it were drooling; the too many draperies, hanging in the stagnant air of a small room, had the same look. The smell came from undusted corners and from incense burning in silver jars at the feet of contorted Oriental deities. Ivy Starnes sat on a pillow like a baggy Buddha. Her mouth was a tight little crescent, the petulant mouth of a child demanding adulation—on the spreading, pallid face of a woman past fifty. Her eyes were two lifeless puddles of water. Her voice had the even, dripping monotone of rain:

"I can't answer the kind of questions you're asking, my girl. The research laboratory? The engineers? Why should I remember anything about them? It was my father who was concerned with such matters, not I. My father was an evil man who cared for nothing but business. He had no time for love, only for money. My brothers and I lived on a different plane. Our aim was not to produce gadgets, but to do good. We brought a great, new plan into the factory. It was eleven years ago. We were defeated by the greed, the selfishness and the base, animal nature of men. It was the eternal conflict between spirit and matter, between soul and body. They would not renounce their bodies, which was all we asked of them. I do not remember any of those men. I do not care to remember. . . . The engineers? I believe it was they who started the hemophilia. . . . Yes, that is what I said: the hemophilia—the slow leak—the loss of blood that cannot be stopped. They ran first. They deserted us, one after another . . . Our plan? We put into practice that noble historical precept: From each according to his ability, to each according to his need. Everybody in the factory, from charwomen to president, received the same salary—the barest minimum necessary. Twice a year, we all gathered in a mass meeting, where every person presented his claim for what he believed to be his needs. We voted on every claim, and the will of the majority established every person's need and every person's ability. The income of the factory was distributed accordingly. Rewards were based on need, and penalties on ability. Those whose needs were voted to be the greatest, received the most. Those who had not produced as much as the vote said they could, were fined and had to pay the fines by working overtime without pay. That was our plan. It was based on the principle of selflessness. It required men to be motivated, not by personal gain, but by love for their brothers."

Dagny heard a cold, implacable voice saying somewhere within her: Remember it—remember it well—it is not often that one can see pure evil—look at it—remember—and some day you'll find the words to name its essence. . . . She heard it through the screaming of other voices that cried in helpless violence: It's nothing—I've heard it before—I'm hearing it everywhere—it's nothing but the same old tripe—why can't I stand it?—I can't stand it—I can't stand it!

"What's the matter with you, my girl? Why did you jump up like that? Why are you shaking? . . . What? Do speak louder, I can't hear you. . . . How did the plan work out? I do not care to discuss it. Things became very ugly indeed and went fouler every year. It has cost me my faith in human nature. In four years, a plan conceived, not by the cold calculations of the mind, but by the pure love of the heart, was brought to an end in the sordid mess of policemen, lawyers and bankruptcy proceedings. But I have seen my error and I am free of it. I am through with the world of machines, manufacturers and money, the world enslaved by matter. I am learning the emancipation of the spirit, as revealed in the great secrets of India, the release from bondage to flesh, the victory over physical nature, the triumph of the spirit over matter."

Through the blinding white glare of anger, Dagny was seeing a long strip of concrete that had been a road, with weeds rising from its cracks, and the figure of a man contorted by a hand plow.

"But, my girl, I said that I do not remember. . . . But I do not know their names, I do not know any names, I do not know what sort of adventurers my father may have had in that laboratory! . . .

Don't you hear me? . . . I am not accustomed to being questioned in such manner and . . . Don't keep repeating it. Don't you know any words but 'engineer'? . . . Don't you hear me at all? . . . What's the matter with you? I—I don't like your face, you're . . . Leave me alone. I don't know who you are, I've never hurt you, I'm an old woman, don't look at me like that, I . . . Stand back! Don't come near me or I'll call for help! I'll . . . Oh, yes, yes, I know that one! The chief engineer. Yes. He was the head of the laboratory. Yes. William Hastings. That was his name—William Hastings. I remember. He went off to Brandon, Wyoming. He quit the day after we introduced the plan. He was the second man to quit us. . . . No. No, I don't remember who was the first. He wasn't anybody important."

* * *

The woman who opened the door had graying hair and a poised, distinguished look of grooming; it took Dagny a few seconds to realize that her garment was only a simple cotton housedress.

"May I see Mr. William Hastings?" asked Dagny.

The woman looked at her for the briefest instant of a pause; it was an odd glance, inquiring and grave. "May I ask your name?"

"I am Dagny Taggart, of Taggart Transcontinental."

"Oh. Please come in, Miss Taggart. I am Mrs. William Hastings." The measured tone of gravity went through every syllable of her voice, like a warning. Her manner was courteous, but she did not smile.

It was a modest home in the suburbs of an industrial town. Bare tree branches cut across the bright, cold blue of the sky, on the top of the rise that led to the house. The walls of the living room were silver-gray; sunlight hit the crystal stand of a lamp with a white shade; beyond an open door, a breakfast nook was papered in red-dotted white.

"Were you acquainted with my husband in business, Miss Taggart?"

"No. I have never met Mr. Hastings. But I should like to speak to him on a matter of business of crucial importance."

"My husband died five years ago, Miss Taggart."

Dagny closed her eyes; the dull, sinking shock contained the conclusions she did not have to make in words: This, then, had been the man she was seeking, and Rearden had been right; this was why the motor had been left unclaimed on a junk pile.

"I'm sorry," she said, both to Mrs. Hastings and to herself.

The suggestion of a smile on Mrs. Hastings' face held sadness, but the face had no imprint of tragedy, only a grave look of firmness, acceptance and quiet serenity.

"Mrs. Hastings, would you permit me to ask you a few questions?"

"Certainly. Please sit down."

"Did you have some knowledge of your husband's scientific work?"

"Very little. None, really. He never discussed it at home."

"He was, at one time, chief engineer of the Twentieth Century Motor Company?"

"Yes. He had been employed by them for eighteen years."

"I wanted to ask Mr. Hastings about his work there and the reason why he gave it up. If you can tell me, I would like to know what happened in that factory."

The smile of sadness and humor appeared fully on Mrs. Hastings' face. "That is what I would like to know myself," she said. "But I'm afraid I shall never learn it now. I know why he left the factory. It was because of an outrageous scheme which the heirs of Jed Starnes established there. He would not work on such terms or for such people. But there was something else. I've always felt that something happened at Twentieth Century Motors, which he would not tell me."

"I'm extremely anxious to know any clue you may care to give me."

"I have no clue to it. I've tried to guess and given up. I cannot understand or explain it. But I know that something happened. When my husband left Twentieth Century, we came here and he took a job as head of the engineering department of Acme Motors. It was a growing, successful concern at the time. It gave my husband the kind of work he liked. He was not a person prone to inner conflicts, he had always been sure of his actions and at peace with himself. But for a whole year after we left Wisconsin, he acted as if he were tortured by something, as if he were struggling with a personal problem he could not solve. At the end of that year, he came to me one morning and told me that he had resigned from Acme Motors, that he was retiring and would not work anywhere else. He loved his work; it was his whole life. Yet he looked calm, self-confident and happy, for the first time since we'd come here. He asked me not to question him about the reason of his decision. I didn't question him and I didn't object. We had this house, we had our savings, we had enough to live on modestly for the rest of our days. I never learned his reason. We went on living here, quietly and very happily. He seemed to feel a profound contentment. He had an odd serenity of spirit that I had never seen in him before. There was nothing strange in his behavior or activity—except that at times, very rarely, he went out without telling me where he went or whom he saw. In the last two years of his life, he went away for one month, each summer; he did not tell me where. Otherwise, he lived as he always had. He studied a great deal and he spent his time on engineering research of his own, working in the basement of our house. I don't know what he did with his notes and experimental models. I found no trace of them in the basement, after his death. He died five years ago, of a heart ailment from which he had suffered for some time."

Dagny asked hopelessly, "Did you know the nature of his experiments?"

"No. I know very little about engineering."

"Did you know any of his professional friends or co-workers, who might have been acquainted with his research?"

"No. When he was at Twentieth Century Motors, he worked such long hours that we had very little time for ourselves and we spent it together. We had no social life at all. He never brought his associates to the house."

"When he was at Twentieth Century, did he ever mention to you a motor he had designed, an entirely new type of motor that could have changed the course of all industry?"

"A motor? Yes. Yes, he spoke of it several times. He said it was an invention of incalculable importance. But it was not he who had designed it. It was the invention of a young assistant of his."

She saw the expression on Dagny's face, and added slowly, quizzically, without reproach, merely in sad amusement, "I see."

"Oh, I'm sorry!" said Dagny, realizing that her emotion had shot to her face and become a smile as obvious as a cry of relief.

"It's quite all right. I understand. It's the inventor of that motor that you're interested in. I don't know whether he is still alive, but at least I have no reason to think that he isn't."

"I'd give half my life to know that he is—and to find him. It's as important as that, Mrs. Hastings. Who is he?"

"I don't know. I don't know his name or anything about him. I never knew any of the men on my husband's staff. He told me only that he had a young engineer who, some day, would up-turn the world. My husband did not care for anything in people except ability. I think this was the only man he ever loved. He didn't say so, but I could tell it, just by the way he spoke of this young assistant. I remember—the day he told me that the motor was completed—how his voice sounded when he said, 'And he's only twenty-six!' This was about a month before the death of Jed Starnes. He never mentioned the motor or the young engineer, after that."

"You don't know what became of the young engineer?"

"No."

"You can't suggest any way to find him?"

"No."

"You have no clue, no lead to help me learn his name?"

"None. Tell me, was that motor extremely valuable?"

"More valuable than any estimate I could give you."

"It's strange, because, you see, I thought of it once, some years after we'd left Wisconsin, and I asked my husband what had become of that invention he'd said was so great, what would be done with it. He looked at me very oddly and answered, 'Nothing.' "

"Why?"

"He wouldn't tell me."

"Can you remember anyone at all who worked at Twentieth Century? Anyone who knew that young engineer? Any friend of his?"

"No, I . . . Wait! Wait, I think I can give you a lead. I can tell you where to find one friend of his. I don't even know that friend's name, either, but I know his address. It's an odd story. I'd better explain how it happened. One evening—about two years after we'd come here—my husband was going out and I needed our car that night, so he asked me to pick him up after dinner at the restaurant of the railroad station. He did not tell me with whom he was having dinner. When I drove up to the station, I saw him standing outside the restaurant with two men. One of them was young and tall. The other was elderly; he looked very distinguished. I would still recognize those men anywhere; they had the kind of faces one doesn't forget. My husband saw me and left them. They walked away toward the station platform; there was a train coming. My husband pointed after the young man and said, 'Did you see him? That's the boy I told you about.' 'The one who's the great maker of motors?' 'The one who was.'"

"And he told you nothing else?"

"Nothing else. This was nine years ago. Last spring, I went to visit my brother who lives in Cheyenne. One afternoon, he took the family out for a long drive. We went up into pretty wild country, high in the Rockies, and we stopped at a roadside diner. There was a distinguished, gray-haired man behind the counter. I kept staring at him while he fixed our sandwiches and coffee, because I knew that I had seen his face before, but could not remember where. We drove on, we were miles away from the diner, when I remembered. You'd better go there. It's on Route 86, in the mountains, west of Cheyenne, near a small industrial settlement by the Lennox Copper Foundry. It seems strange, but I'm certain of it: the cook in that diner is the man I saw at the railroad station with my husband's young idol."

* * *

The diner stood on the summit of a long, hard climb. Its glass walls spread a coat of polish over the view of rocks and pines descending in broken ledges to the sunset. It was dark below, but an even, glowing light still remained in the diner, as in a small pool left behind by a receding tide.

Dagny sat at the end of the counter, eating a hamburger sandwich. It was the best-cooked food she had ever tasted, the product of simple ingredients and of an unusual skill. Two workers were finishing their dinner; she was waiting for them to depart.

She studied the man behind the counter. He was slender and tall; he had an air of distinction that belonged in an ancient castle or in the inner office of a bank; but his peculiar quality came from the fact that he made the distinction seem appropriate here, behind the counter of a diner. He wore a cook's white jacket as if it were a full-dress suit. There was an expert competence in his manner of working; his movements were easy, intelligently economical. He had a lean face and gray hair that blended in tone with the cold blue of his eyes; somewhere beyond his look of courteous sternness, there was a note of humor, so faint that it vanished if one tried to discern it.

The two workers finished, paid and departed, each leaving a dime for a tip. She watched the man as he removed their dishes, put the dimes into the pocket of his white jacket, wiped the counter, working with swift precision. Then he turned and looked at her. It was an impersonal glance, not intended to invite conversation; but she felt certain that he had long since noted her New York suit, her high-heeled pumps, her air of being a woman who did not waste her time; his cold, observant eyes seemed to tell her that he knew she did not belong here and that he was waiting to discover her purpose.

"How is business?" she asked.

"Pretty bad. They're going to close the Lennox Foundry next week, so I'll have to close soon, too, and move on." His voice was clear, impersonally cordial.

"Where to?"

"I haven't decided."

"What sort of thing do you have in mind?"

"I don't know. I'm thinking of opening a garage, if I can find the right spot in some town."

"Oh no! You're too good at your job to change it. You shouldn't want to be anything but a cook."

A strange, fine smile moved the curve of his mouth. "No?" he asked courteously.

"No! How would you like a job in New York?" He looked at her, astonished. "I'm serious. I can give you a job on a big railroad, in charge of the dining-car department."

"May I ask why you should want to?"

She raised the hamburger sandwich in its white paper napkin. "There's one of the reasons."

"Thank you. What are the others?"

"I don't suppose you've lived in a big city, or you'd know how miserably difficult it is to find any competent men for any job whatever."

"I know a little about that."

"Well? How about it, then? Would you like a job in New York at ten thousand dollars a year?"

"No."

She had been carried away by the joy of discovering and rewarding ability. She looked at him silently, shocked. "I don't think you understood me," she said.

"I did."

"You're refusing an opportunity of this kind?"

"Yes."

"But why?"

"That is a personal matter."

"Why should you work like this, when you can have a better job?"

"I am not looking for a better job."

"You don't want a chance to rise and make money?"

"No. Why do you insist?"

"Because I hate to see ability being wasted!"

He said slowly, intently, "So do I."

Something in the way he said it made her feel the bond of some profound emotion which they held in common; it broke the discipline that forbade her ever to call for help. "I'm so sick of them!" Her voice startled her: it was an involuntary cry. "I'm so hungry for any sight of anyone who's able to do whatever it is he's doing!"

She pressed the back of her hand to her eyes, trying to dam the outbreak of a despair she had not permitted herself to acknowledge; she had not known the extent of it, nor how little of her endurance the quest had left her.

"I'm sorry," he said, his voice low. It sounded, not as an apology, but as a statement of compassion.

She glanced up at him. He smiled, and she knew that the smile was intended to break the bond which he, too, had felt: the smile had a trace of courteous mockery. He said, "But I don't believe that you came all the way from New York just to hunt for railroad cooks in the Rockies."

"No. I came for something else." She leaned forward, both forearms braced firmly against the counter, feeling calm and in tight control again, sensing a dangerous adversary. "Did you know, about ten years ago, a young engineer who worked for the Twentieth Century Motor Company?"

She counted the seconds of a pause; she could not define the nature of the way he looked at her, except that it was the look of some special attentiveness.

"Yes, I did," he answered.

"Could you give me his name and address?"

"What for?"

"It's crucially important that I find him."

"That man? Of what importance is he?"

"He is the most important man in the world."

"Really? Why?"

"Did you know anything about his work?"

"Yes."

"Did you know that he hit upon an idea of the most tremendous consequence?"

He let a moment pass. "May I ask who you are?"

"Dagny Taggart. I'm the Vice-Pres—"

"Yes, Miss Taggart. I know who you are."

He said it with impersonal deference. But he looked as if he had found the answer to some special question in his mind and was not astonished any longer.

"Then you know that my interest is not idle," she said. "I'm in a position to give him the chance he needs and I'm prepared to pay anything he asks."

"May I ask what has aroused your interest in him?"

"His motor."

"How did you happen to know about his motor?"

"I found a broken remnant of it in the ruins of the Twentieth Century factory. Not enough to reconstruct it or to learn how it worked. But enough to know that it did work and that it's an invention which can save my railroad, the country and the economy of the whole world. Don't ask me to tell you now what trail I've followed, trying to trace that motor and to find its inventor. That's not of any importance, even my life and work are not of any importance to me right now, nothing is of any importance, except that I must find him. Don't ask me how I happened to come to you. You're the end of the trail. Tell me his name."

He had listened without moving, looking straight at her; the attentiveness of his eyes seemed to take hold of every word and store it carefully away, giving her no clue to his purpose. He did not move for a long time. Then he said, "Give it up, Miss Taggart. You won't find him."

"What is his name?"

"I can tell you nothing about him."

"Is he still alive?"

"I can tell you nothing."

"What is *your* name?"

"Hugh Akston."

Through the blank seconds of recapturing her mind, she kept telling herself: You're hysterical . . . don't be preposterous . . . it's just a coincidence of names—while she knew, in certainty and numb, inexplicable terror, that this was *the* Hugh Akston.

"Hugh Akston?" she stammered. "The philosopher? . . . The last of the advocates of reason?"

"Why, yes," he answered pleasantly. "Or the first of their return."

He did not seem startled by her shock, but he seemed to find it unnecessary. His manner was simple, almost friendly, as if he felt no need to hide his identity and no resentment at its being discovered.

"I didn't think that any young person would recognize my name or attach any significance to it, nowadays," he said.

"But . . . but what are you doing here?" Her arm swept at the room. "This doesn't make sense!"

"Are you sure?"

"What is it? A stunt? An experiment? A secret mission? Are you studying something for some special purpose?"

"No, Miss Taggart. I'm earning my living." The words and the voice had the genuine simplicity of truth.

"Dr. Akston, I . . . it's inconceivable, it's . . . You're . . . you're a philosopher . . . the greatest philosopher living . . . an immortal name . . . why would *you* do *this?*"

"Because I am a philosopher, Miss Taggart."

She knew with certainty—even though she felt as if her capacity for certainty and for understanding were gone—that she would obtain no help from him, that questions were useless, that he would give her no explanation, neither of the inventor's fate nor of his own.

"Give it up, Miss Taggart," he said quietly, as if giving proof that he could guess her thoughts, as she had known he would. "It is a hopeless quest, the more hopeless because you have no inkling of what an impossible task you have chosen to undertake. I would like to spare you the strain of trying to devise some argument, trick or plea that would make me give you the information you are seeking. Take my word for it: it can't be done. You said I'm the end of your trail. It's a blind alley, Miss Taggart. Do not attempt to waste your money and effort on other, more conventional methods of inquiry: do not hire detectives. They will learn nothing. You may choose to ignore my warning, but I think that you are a person of high intelligence, able to know that I know what I am saying. Give it up. The secret you are trying to solve involves something greater—much greater—than the invention of a motor run by atmospheric electricity. There is only one helpful suggestion that I can give you: By the essence and nature of existence, contradictions cannot exist. If you find it inconceivable that an invention of genius should be abandoned among ruins, and that a philosopher should wish to work as a cook in a diner—check your premises. You will find that one of them is wrong."

She started: she remembered that she had heard this before and that it was Francisco who had said it. And then she remembered that this man had been one of Francisco's teachers.

"As you wish, Dr. Akston," she said. "I won't attempt to question you about it. But would you permit me to ask you a question on an entirely different subject?"

"Certainly."

"Dr. Robert Stadler once told me that when you were at the Patrick Henry University, you had three students who were your favorites and his, three brilliant minds from whom you expected a great future. One of them was Francisco d'Anconia."

"Yes. Another was Ragnar Danneskjöld."

"Incidentally—this is not my question—who was the third?"

"His name would mean nothing to you. He is not famous."

"Dr. Stadler said that you and he were rivals over these three students, because you both regarded them as your sons."

"Rivals? *He* lost them."

"Tell me, are you proud of the way these three have turned out?"

He looked off, into the distance, at the dying fire of the sunset on the farthest rocks; his face had the look of a father who watches his sons bleeding on a battlefield. He answered:

"More proud than I had ever hoped to be."

It was almost dark. He turned sharply, took a package of cigarettes from his pocket, pulled out one cigarette, but stopped, remembering her presence, as if he had forgotten it for a moment, and extended the package to her. She took a cigarette and he struck the brief flare of a match, then shook it out, leaving only two small points of fire in the darkness of a glass room and of miles of mountains beyond it.

She rose, paid her bill, and said, "Thank you, Dr. Akston. I will not molest you with tricks or pleas. I will not hire detectives. But I think I should tell you that I will not give up. I must find the inventor of that motor. I will find him."

"Not until the day when he chooses to find *you*—as he will."

When she walked to her car, he switched on the lights in the diner, she saw the mailbox by the side of the road and noted the incredible fact that the name "Hugh Akston" stood written openly across it.

She had driven far down the winding road, and the lights of the diner were long since out of sight, when she noticed that she was enjoying the taste of the cigarette he had given her: it was different from any she had ever smoked before. She held the small remnant to the light of the dashboard, looking for the name of the brand. There was no name, only a trademark. Stamped in gold on the thin, white paper there stood the sign of the dollar.

She examined it curiously: she had never heard of that brand before. Then she remembered the old man at the cigar stand of the Taggart Terminal, and smiled, thinking that this was a specimen for his collection. She stamped out the fire and dropped the butt into her handbag.

Train Number 57 was lined along the track, ready to leave for Wyatt Junction, when she reached Cheyenne, left her car at the garage where she had rented it, and walked out on the platform of the Taggart station. She had half an hour to wait for the eastbound main liner to New York. She walked to the end of the platform and leaned wearily against a lamppost; she did not want to be seen and recognized by the station employees, she did not want to talk to anyone, she needed rest. A few people stood in clusters on the half-deserted platform; animated conversations seemed to be going on, and newspapers were more prominently in evidence than usual.

She looked at the lighted windows of Train Number 57—for a moment's relief in the sight of a victorious achievement. Train Number 57 was about to start down the track of the John Galt Line, through the towns, through the curves of the mountains, past the green signals where people had stood cheering and the valleys where rockets had risen to the summer sky. Twisted remnants of leaves now hung on the branches beyond the train's roof line, and the passengers wore furs and mufflers, as they climbed aboard. They moved with the casual manner of a daily event, with the security of expecting a performance long since taken for granted. . . . We've done it—she thought—this much, at least, is done.

It was the chance conversation of two men somewhere behind her that came beating suddenly against her closed attention.

"But laws shouldn't be passed that way, so quickly."

"They're not laws, they're directives."

"Then it's illegal."

"It's not illegal, because the Legislature passed a law last month giving him the power to issue directives."

"I don't think directives should be sprung on people that way, out of the blue, like a punch in the nose."

"Well, there's no time to palaver when it's a national emergency."

"But I don't think it's right and it doesn't jibe. How is Rearden going to do it, when it says here—"

"Why should you worry about Rearden? He's rich enough. He can find a way to do anything."

Then she leaped to the first newsstand in sight and seized a copy of the evening paper.

It was on the front page. Wesley Mouch, Top Co-ordinator of the Bureau of Economic Planning and National Resources, "in a surprise move," said the paper, "and in the name of the national emergency," had issued a set of directives, which were strung in a column down the page:

The railroads of the country were ordered to reduce the maximum speed of all trains to sixty miles per hour—to reduce the maximum length of all trains to sixty cars—and to run the same number of trains in every state of a zone composed of five neighboring states, the country being divided into such zones for the purpose.

The steel mills of the country were ordered to limit the maximum production of any metal alloy to an amount equal to the production of other metal alloys by other mills placed in the same classification of plant capacity—and to supply a fair share of any metal alloy to all consumers who might desire to obtain it.

All the manufacturing establishments of the country, of any size and nature, were forbidden to move from their present locations, except when granted a special permission to do so by the Bureau of Economic Planning and National Resources.

To compensate the railroads of the country for the extra costs involved and "to cushion the process of readjustment," a moratorium on payments of interest and principal on all railroad bonds—secured and unsecured, convertible and non-convertible—was declared for a period of five years.

To provide the funds for the personnel to enforce these directives, a special tax was imposed on the state of Colorado, "as the state best able to assist the needier states to bear the brunt of the national emergency," such tax to consist of five per cent of the gross sales of Colorado's industrial concerns.

The cry she uttered was one she had never permitted herself before, because she made it her pride always to answer it herself—but she saw a man standing a few steps away, she did not see that he was a ragged bum, and she uttered the cry because it was the plea of reason and he was a human figure:

"What are we going to do?"

The bum grinned mirthlessly and shrugged:

"Who is John Galt?"

It was not Taggart Transcontinental that stood as the focus of terror in her mind, it was not the thought of Hank Rearden tied to a rack pulled in opposite directions—it was Ellis Wyatt. Wiping out the rest, filling her consciousness, leaving no room for words, no time for wonder, as a glaring answer to the questions she had not begun to ask, stood two pictures: Ellis Wyatt's implacable figure in front of her desk, saying, "It is now in your power to destroy me; I may have to go; but if I go, I'll make sure that I take all the rest of you along with me"— and the circling violence of Ellis Wyatt's body when he flung a glass to shatter against the wall.

The only consciousness the pictures left her was the feeling of the approach of some unthinkable disaster, and the feeling that she had to outrun it. She had to reach Ellis Wyatt and stop him. She did not know what it was that she had to prevent. She knew only that she had to stop him.

And because, were she lying crushed under the ruins of a building, were she torn by the bomb of an air raid, so long as she was still in existence she would know that action is man's foremost obligation, regardless of anything he feels—she was able to run down the platform and to see the face of the stationmaster when she found him—she was able to order: "Hold Number 57 for me!"—then to run to the privacy of a telephone booth in the darkness beyond the end of the platform, and to give the long-distance operator the number of Ellis Wyatt's house.

She stood, propped up by the walls of the booth, her eyes closed, and listened to the dead whirl of metal which was the sound of a bell ringing somewhere. It brought no answer. The bell kept coming in sudden spasms, like a drill going through her ear, through her body. She clutched the receiver as if, unheeded, it were still a form of contact. She wished the bell were louder. She forgot that the sound she heard was not the one ringing in his house. She did not know that she was screaming, "Ellis, don't! Don't! Don't!"—until she heard the cold, re-proving voice of the operator say, "Your party does not answer."

She sat at the window of a coach of Train Number 57, and listened to the clicking of the wheels on the rails of Rearden Metal. She sat, unresisting, swaying with the motion of the train. The black luster of the window hid the countryside she did not want to see. It was her second run on the John Galt Line, and she tried not to think of the first.

The bondholders, she thought, the bondholders of the John Galt Line—it was to her honor that they had entrusted their money, the saving and achievement of years, it was on her ability that they had staked it, it was on her work that they had relied and on their own—and she had been made to betray them into a looters' trap: there would be no trains and no life-blood of freight, the John Galt Line had been only a drainpipe that had permitted Jim Taggart to make a deal and to drain their wealth, unearned, into his pocket, in exchange for letting others drain his railroad—the bonds of the John Galt Line, which, this morning, had been the proud guardians of their owners' security and future, had become in the space of an hour, scraps of paper that no one would buy, with no value, no future, no power, save the power to close the doors and stop the wheels of the last hope of the country—and Taggart Transcontinental was not a living plant, fed by blood it had worked to produce, but a cannibal of the moment, devouring the un-born children of greatness.

The tax on Colorado, she thought, the tax collected from Ellis Wyatt to pay for the livelihood of those whose job was to tie him and make him unable to live, those who would stand on guard to see that he got no trains, no tank cars, no pipeline of Rearden Metal—Ellis Wyatt, stripped of the right of self-defense, left without voice, without weapons, and worse: made to be the tool of his own destruction, the supporter of his own destroyers, the provider of their food and of their weapons—Ellis Wyatt being choked, with his own bright energy turned against him as the noose—Ellis Wyatt, who had wanted to tap an un-limited source of shale oil and who spoke of a Second Renaissance. . . .

She sat bent over, her head on her arms, slumped at the ledge of the window—while the great curves of the green-blue rail, the mountains, the valleys, the new towns of Colorado went by in the darkness, un-seen.

The sudden jolt of brakes on wheels threw her upright. It was an unscheduled stop, and the platform of the small station was crowded with people, all looking off in the same direction. The passengers around her were pressing to the windows, staring. She leaped to her feet, she ran down the aisle, down the steps, into the cold wind sweeping the platform.

In the instant before she saw it and her scream cut the voices of the crowd, she knew that she had known that which she was to see. In a break between mountains, lighting the sky, throwing a glow that swayed on the roofs and walls of the station, the hill of Wyatt Oil was a solid sheet of flame.

Later, when they told her that Ellis Wyatt had vanished, leaving nothing behind but a board he had nailed to a post at the foot of the hill, when she looked at his handwriting on the board, she felt as if she had almost known that these would be the words:

"I am leaving it as I found it. Take over. It's yours."

THE MAN WHO BELONGED ON EARTH

Dr. Robert Stadler paced his office, wishing he would not feel the cold.

Spring had been late in coming. Beyond the window, the dead gray of the hills looked like the smeared transition from the soiled white of the sky to the leaden black of the river. Once in a while, a distant patch of hillside flared into a silver-yellow that was almost green, then vanished. The clouds kept cracking for the width of a single sunray, then oozing closed again. It was not cold in the office, thought Dr. Stadler, it was that view that froze the place.

It was not cold today, the chill was in his bones—he thought—the stored accumulation of the winter months, when he had had to be distracted from his work by an awareness of such a matter as inadequate heating and people had talked about conserving fuel. It was preposterous, he thought, this growing intrusion of the accidents of nature into the affairs of men: it had never mattered before, if a winter happened to be unusually severe; if a flood washed out a section of railroad track, one did not spend two weeks eating canned vegetables; if an electric storm struck some power station, an establishment such as the State Science Institute was not left without electricity for five days. Five days of stillness this winter, he thought, with the great laboratory motors stopped and irretrievable hours wiped out, when his staff had been working on problems that involved the heart of the universe. He turned angrily away from the window—but stopped and turned back to it again. He did not want to see the book that lay on his desk.

He wished Dr. Ferris would come. He glanced at his watch: Dr. Ferris was late—an astonishing matter—late for an appointment with *him*—Dr. Floyd Ferris, the valet of science, who had always faced him in a manner that suggested an apology for having but one hat to take off.

This was outrageous weather for the month of May, he thought, looking down at the river; it was certainly the weather that made him feel as he did, not the book. He had placed the book in plain view on his desk, when he had noted that his reluctance to see it was more than mere revulsion, that it contained the element of an emotion never to be admitted. He told himself that he had risen from his desk, not because the book lay there, but merely because he had wanted to move, feeling cold. He paced the room, trapped between the desk and the window. He would throw that book in the ash can where it belonged, he thought, just as soon as he had spoken to Dr. Ferris.

He watched the patch of green and sunlight on the distant hill, the promise of spring in a world that looked as if no grass or bud would ever function again. He smiled eagerly—and when the patch vanished, he felt a stab of humiliation, at his own eagerness, at the desperate way he had wanted to hold it. It reminded him of that interview with the eminent novelist, last winter. The novelist had come from Europe to write an article about him—and he, who had once despised interviews, had talked eagerly, lengthily, too lengthily, seeing a promise of intelligence in the novelist's face, feeling a causeless, desperate need to be understood. The article had come out as a collection of sentences that gave him exorbitant praise and garbled every thought he had expressed. Closing the magazine, he had felt what he was feeling now at the desertion of a sunray.

All right—he thought, turning away from the window—he would concede that attacks of loneliness had begun to strike him at times; but it was a loneliness to which he was entitled, it was hunger for the response of some living, thinking mind. He was so tired of all those people, he thought in contemptuous bitterness; he dealt with cosmic rays, while they were unable to deal with an electric storm.

He felt the sudden contraction of his mouth, like a slap denying him the right to pursue this course of thought. He was looking at the book on his desk. Its glossy jacket was glaring and new; it had been published two weeks ago. But I had nothing to do with it!—he screamed to himself; the scream seemed wasted on a merciless silence; nothing answered it, no echo of forgiveness. The title on the book's jacket was *Why Do You Think You Think?*

There was no sound in that courtroom silence within him, no pity, no voice of defense—nothing but the paragraphs which his great memory had reprinted on his brain:

"Thought is a primitive superstition. Reason is an irrational idea. The childish notion that we are able to think has been mankind's costliest error."

"What you think you think is an illusion created by your glands, your emotions and, in the last analysis, by the content of your stomach."

"That gray matter you're so proud of is like a mirror in an amusement park which transmits to you nothing but distorted signals from a reality forever beyond your grasp."

"The more certain you feel of your rational conclusions, the more certain you are to be wrong. Your brain being an instrument of distortion, the more active the brain the greater the distortion."

"The giants of the intellect, whom you admire so much, once taught you that the earth was flat and that the atom was the smallest particle of matter. The entire history of science is a progression of exploded fallacies, not of achievements."

"The more we know, the more we learn that we know nothing."

"Only the crassest ignoramus can still hold to the old-fashioned notion that seeing is believing. That which you see is the first thing to disbelieve."

"A scientist knows that a stone is not a stone at all. It is, in fact, identical with a feather pillow. Both are only a cloud formation of the same invisible, whirling particles. But, you say, you can't use a stone for a pillow? Well, that merely proves your helplessness in the face of actual reality."

"The latest scientific discoveries—such as the tremendous achievements of Dr. Robert Stadler—have demonstrated conclusively that our reason is incapable of dealing with the nature of the universe. These discoveries have led scientists to contradictions which are impossible, according to the human mind, but which exist in reality nonetheless. If you have not yet heard it, my dear old-fashioned friends, it has now been proved that the rational is the insane."

"Do not expect consistency. Everything is a contradiction of everything else. Nothing exists but contradictions."

"Do not look for 'common sense.' To demand 'sense' is the hallmark of nonsense. Nature does not make sense. Nothing makes sense. The only crusaders for 'sense' are the studious type of adolescent old maid who can't find a boy friend, and the old-fashioned shopkeeper who thinks that the universe is as simple as his neat little inventory and beloved cash register."

"Let us break the chains of the prejudice called Logic. Are we going to be stopped by a syllogism?"

"So you think you're sure of your opinions? You cannot be sure of anything. Are you going to endanger the harmony of your community, your fellowship with your neighbors, your standing, reputation, good name and financial security—for the sake of an illusion? For the sake of the mirage of thinking that you think? Are you going to run risks and court disasters—at a precarious time like ours—by opposing the existing social order in the name of those imaginary notions of yours which you call your convictions? You say that you're sure you're right? Nobody is right, or ever can be. You feel that the world around you is wrong? You have no means to know it. Everything is wrong in human eyes—so why fight it? Don't argue. Accept. Adjust yourself. Obey."

The book was written by Dr. Floyd Ferris and published by the State Science Institute.

"I had nothing to do with it!" said Dr. Robert Stadler. He stood still by the side of his desk, with the uncomfortable feeling of having missed some beat of time, of not knowing how long the preceding moment had lasted. He had pronounced the words aloud, in a tone of rancorous sarcasm directed at whoever had made him say it.

He shrugged. Resting on the belief that self-mockery is an act of virtue, the shrug was the emotional equivalent of the sentence: You're Robert Stadler, don't act like a high-school neurotic. He sat down at his desk and pushed the book aside with the back of his hand.

Dr. Floyd Ferris arrived half an hour late. "Sorry," he said, "but my car broke down again on the way from Washington and I had a hell of a time trying to find somebody to fix it—there's getting to be so damn few cars out on the road that half the service stations are closed."

There was more annoyance than apology in his voice. He sat down without waiting for an invitation to do so.

Dr. Floyd Ferris would not have been noticed as particularly handsome in any other profession, but in the one he had chosen he was always described as "that good-looking scientist." He was six feet tall and forty-five years old, but he managed to look taller and younger. He had an air of immaculate grooming and a ballroom grace of motion, but his clothes were severe, his suits being usually black or midnight blue. He had a finely traced mustache, and his smooth black hair made the Institute office boys say that he used the same shoe polish on both ends of him. He did not mind repeating, in the tone of a joke on himself, that a movie producer once said he would cast him for the part of a titled European gigolo. He had begun his career as a biologist, but that was forgotten long ago; he was famous as the Top Co-ordinator of the State Science Institute.

Dr. Stadler glanced at him with astonishment—the lack of apology was unprecedented—and said dryly, "It seems to me that you are spending a great deal of your time in Washington."

"But, Dr. Stadler, wasn't it you who once paid me the compliment of calling me the watchdog of this Institute?" said Dr. Ferris pleasantly. "Isn't that my most essential duty?"

"A few of your duties seem to be accumulating right around this place. Before I forget it, would you mind telling me what's going on here about that oil shortage mess?"

He could not understand why Dr. Ferris' face tightened into an injured look. "You will permit me to say that this is unexpected and unwarranted," said Dr. Ferris in that tone of formality which conceals pain and reveals martyrdom. "None of the authorities involved have found cause for criticism. We have just submitted a detailed report on the progress of the work to date to the Bureau of Economic Planning and National Resources, and Mr. Wesley Mouch has expressed himself as satisfied. We have done our best on that project. We have heard no one else describe it as a mess. Considering the difficulties of the terrain, the hazards of the fire and the fact that it has been only six months since we—"

"What are you talking about?" asked Dr. Stadler.

"The Wyatt Reclamation Project. Isn't that what you asked me?"

"No," said Dr. Stadler, "no, I . . . Wait a moment. Let me get this straight. I seem to recall something about this Institute taking charge of a reclamation project. What is it that you're reclaiming?"

"Oil," said Dr. Ferris. "The Wyatt oil fields."

"That was a fire, wasn't it? In Colorado? That was . . . wait a moment . . . that was the man who set fire to his own oil wells."

"I'm inclined to believe that that's a rumor created by public hysteria," said Dr. Ferris dryly. "A rumor with some undesirable, unpatriotic implications. I wouldn't put too much faith in those newspaper stories. Personally, I believe that it was an accident and that Ellis Wyatt perished in the fire."

"Well, who owns those fields now?"

"Nobody—at the moment. There being no will or heirs, the government has taken charge of operating the fields—as a measure of public necessity—for seven years. If Ellis Wyatt does not return within that time, he will be considered officially dead."

"Well, why did they come to you—to us, for such an unlikely assignment as oil pumping?"

"Because it is a problem of great technological difficulty, requiring the services of the best scientific talent available. You see, it is a matter of reconstructing the special method of oil extraction that Wyatt had employed. His equipment is still there, though in a dreadful condition; some of his processes are known, but somehow there is no full record of the complete operation or the basic principle involved. That is what we have to rediscover."

"And how is it going?"

"The progress is most gratifying. We have just been granted a new and larger appropriation. Mr. Wesley Mouch is pleased with our work. So are Mr. Balch of the Emergency Commission, Mr. Anderson of Crucial Supplies and Mr. Pettibone of Consumers' Protection. I do not see what more could be expected of us. The project is fully successful."

"Have you produced any oil?"

"No, but we have succeeded in forcing a flow from one of the wells, to the extent of six and a half gallons. This, of course, is merely of experimental significance, but you must take into consideration the fact that we had to spend three full months just to put out the fire, which has now been totally—almost totally—extinguished. We have a much tougher problem than Wyatt ever had, because he started from scratch while we have to deal with the disfigured wreckage of an act of vicious, anti-social sabotage which . . . I mean to say, it is a difficult problem, but there is no doubt that we will be able to solve it."

"Well, what I really asked you about was the oil shortage here, in the Institute. The level of temperature maintained in this building all winter was outrageous. They told me that they had to conserve oil.

Surely you could have seen to it that the matter of keeping this place adequately supplied with such things as oil was handled more efficiently."

"Oh, is that what you had in mind, Dr. Stadler? Oh, but I am so sorry!" The words came with a bright smile of relief on Dr. Ferris' face; his solicitous manner returned. "Do you mean that the temperature was low enough to cause you discomfort?"

"I mean that I nearly froze to death."

"But that is unforgivable! Why didn't they tell me? Please accept my personal apology, Dr. Stadler, and rest assured that you will never be inconvenienced again. The only excuse I can offer for our maintenance department is that the shortage of fuel was not due to their negligence, it was—oh, I realize that you would not know about it and such matters should not take up your invaluable attention—but, you see, the oil shortage last winter was a nation-wide crisis."

"Why? For heaven's sake, don't tell me that those Wyatt fields were the only source of oil in the country!"

"No, no, but the sudden disappearance of a major supply wrought havoc in the entire oil market. So the government had to assume control and impose oil rationing on the country, in order to protect the essential enterprises. I did obtain an unusually large quota for the Institute—and only by the special favor of some very special connections—but I feel abjectly guilty if this proved insufficient. Rest assured that it will not happen again. It is only a temporary emergency. By next winter, we shall have the Wyatt fields back in production, and conditions will return to normal. Besides, as far as this Institute is concerned, I made all the arrangements to convert our furnaces to coal, and it was to be done next month, only the Stockton Foundry in Colorado closed down suddenly, without notice—they were casting parts for our furnaces, but Andrew Stockton retired, quite unexpectedly, and now we have to wait till his nephew reopens the plant."

"I see. Well, I trust that you will take care of it among all your other activities." Dr. Stadler shrugged with annoyance. "It is becoming a little ridiculous—the number of technological ventures that an institution of science has to handle for the government."

"But, Dr. Stadler—"

"I know, I know, it can't be avoided. By the way, what is Project X?"

Dr. Ferris' eyes shot to him swiftly—an odd, bright glance of alertness, that seemed startled, but not frightened. "Where did you hear about Project X, Dr. Stadler?"

"Oh, I heard a couple of your younger boys saying something about it with an air of mystery you'd expect from amateur detectives. They told me it was something very secret."

"That's right, Dr. Stadler. It is an extremely secret research project which the government has entrusted to us. And it is of utmost importance that the newspapers get no word about it."

"What's the X?"

"Xylophone. Project Xylophone. That is a code name, of course. The work has to do with sound. But I am sure that it would not interest you. It is a purely technological undertaking."

"Yes, do spare me the story. I have no time for your technological undertakings."

"May I suggest that it would be advisable to refrain from mentioning the words 'Project X' to anyone, Dr. Stadler?"

"Oh, all right, all right. I must say I do not enjoy discussions of that kind."

"But of course! And I wouldn't forgive myself if I allowed your time to be taken up by such concerns. Please feel certain that you may safely leave it to me." He made a movement to rise. "Now if this was the reason you wanted to see me, please believe that I—"

"No," said Dr. Stadler slowly. "This was not the reason I wanted to see you."

Dr. Ferris volunteered no questions, no eager offers of service; he remained seated, merely waiting.

Dr. Stadler reached over and made the book slide from the corner to the center of his desk, with a contemptuous flick of one hand. "Will you tell me, please," he asked, "what is this piece of indecency?"

Dr. Ferris did not glance at the book, but kept his eyes fixed on Stadler's for an inexplicable moment; then he leaned back and said with an odd smile, "I feel honored that you chose to make such an exception for my sake as reading a popular book. This little piece has sold twenty thousand copies in two weeks."

"I have read it."

"And?"

"I expect an explanation."

"Did you find the text confusing?"

Dr. Stadler looked at him in bewilderment. "Do you realize what theme you chose to treat and in what manner? The style alone, the style, the gutter kind of attitude—for a subject of this nature!"

"Do you think, then, that the content deserved a more dignified form of presentation?" The voice was so innocently smooth that Dr. Stadler could not decide whether this was mockery.

"Do you realize what you're preaching in this book?"

"Since you do not seem to approve of it, Dr. Stadler, I'd rather have you think that I wrote it innocently."

This was it, thought Dr. Stadler, this was the incomprehensible element in Ferris' manner: he had supposed that an indication of his disapproval would be sufficient, but Ferris seemed to remain untouched by it.

"If a drunken lout could find the power to express himself on paper," said Dr. Stadler, "if he could give voice to his essence—the eternal savage, leering his hatred of the mind—this is the sort of book I would expect him to write. But to see it come from a scientist, under the imprint of this Institute!"

"But, Dr. Stadler, this book was not intended to be read by scientists. It was written for that drunken lout."

"What do you mean?"

"For the general public."

"But, good God! The feeblest imbecile should be able to see the glaring contradictions in every one of your statements."

"Let us put it this way, Dr. Stadler: the man who doesn't see that, deserves to believe all my statements."

"But you've given the prestige of science to that unspeakable stuff! It was all right for a disreputable mediocrity like Simon Pritchett to drool it as some sort of woozy mysticism—nobody listened to him. But you've made them think it's science. *Science!* You've taken the achievements of the mind to destroy the mind. By what right did you use *my* work to make an unwarranted, preposterous switch into another field, pull an inapplicable metaphor and draw a monstrous generalization out of what is merely a mathematical problem? By what right did you make it sound as if I—*I!*—gave my sanction to that book?"

Dr. Ferris did nothing, he merely looked at Dr. Stadler calmly; but the calm gave him an air that was almost patronizing. "Now, you see, Dr. Stadler, you're speaking as if this book were addressed to a thinking audience. If it were, one would have to be concerned with such matters as accuracy, validity, logic and the prestige of science. But it isn't. It's addressed to the public. And you have always been first to believe that the public does not think." He paused, but Dr. Stadler said nothing. "This book may have no philosophical value whatever, but it has a great psychological value."

"Just what is that?"

"You see, Dr. Stadler, people don't want to think. And the deeper they get into trouble, the less they want to think. But by some sort of instinct, they feel that they ought to and it makes them feel guilty. So they'll bless and follow anyone who gives them a justification for not thinking. Anyone who makes a virtue—a highly intellectual virtue—out of what they know to be their sin, their weakness and their guilt."

"And you propose to pander to that?"

"That is the road to popularity."

"Why should you seek popularity?"

Dr. Ferris' eyes moved casually to Dr. Stadler's face, as if by pure accident. "We are a public institution," he answered evenly, "supported by public funds."

"So you tell people that science is a futile fraud which ought to be abolished!"

"That is a conclusion which could be drawn, in logic, from my book. But that is not the conclusion they will draw."

"And what about the disgrace to the Institute in the eyes of the men of intelligence, wherever such may be left?"

"Why should we worry about them?"

Dr. Stadler could have regarded the sentence as conceivable, had it been uttered with hatred, envy or malice; but the absence of any such emotion, the casual ease of the voice, an ease suggesting a chuckle, hit him like a moment's glimpse of a realm that could not be taken as part of reality; the thing spreading down to his stomach was cold terror.

"Did you observe the reactions to my book, Dr. Stadler? It was received with considerable favor."

"Yes—and *that* is what I find impossible to believe." He had to speak, he had to speak as if this were a civilized discussion, he could not allow himself time to know what it was he had felt for a moment. "I am unable to understand the attention you received in all the reputable academic magazines and how they could permit themselves to discuss your book seriously. If Hugh Akston were around, no academic publication would have dared to treat this as a work admissible into the realm of philosophy."

"He is not around."

Dr. Stadler felt that there were words which he was now called upon to pronounce—and he wished he could end this conversation before he discovered what they were.

"On the other hand," said Dr. Ferris, "the ads for my book—oh, I'm sure you wouldn't notice such things as ads—quote a letter of high praise which I received from Mr. Wesley Mouch."

"Who the hell is Mr. Wesley Mouch?"

Dr. Ferris smiled. "In another year, even you won't ask that question, Dr. Stadler. Let us put it this way: Mr. Mouch is the man who is rationing oil—for the time being."

"Then I suggest that you stick to your job. Deal with Mr. Mouch and leave him the realm of oil furnaces, but leave the realm of ideas to me."

"It would be curious to try to formulate the line of demarcation," said Dr. Ferris, in the tone of an idle academic remark. "But if we're talking about my book, why, then we're talking about the realm of public relations." He turned to point solicitously at the mathematical formulas chalked on the blackboard. "Dr. Stadler, it would be disastrous if you allowed the realm of public relations to distract you from the work which you alone on earth are capable of doing."

It was said with obsequious deference, and Dr. Stadler could not tell what made him hear in it the sentence: "Stick to your blackboard!" He felt a biting irritation and he switched it against himself, thinking angrily that he had to get rid of these suspicions.

"Public relations?" he said contemptuously. "I don't see any practical purpose in your book. I don't see what it's intended to accomplish."

"Don't you?" Dr. Ferris' eyes flickered briefly to his face; the sparkle of insolence was too swift to be identified with certainty.

"I cannot permit myself to consider certain things as possible in a civilized society," Dr. Stadler said sternly.

"That is admirably exact," said Dr. Ferris cheerfully. "You cannot permit yourself."

Dr. Ferris rose, being first to indicate that the interview was ended. "Please call for me whenever anything occurs in this Institute to cause you discomfort, Dr. Stadler," he said. "It is my privilege always to be at your service."

Knowing that he had to assert his authority, smothering the shameful realization of the sort of substitute he was choosing, Dr. Stadler said imperiously, in a tone of sarcastic rudeness, "The next time I call for you, you'd better do something about that car of yours."

"Yes, Dr. Stadler. I shall make certain never to be late again, and I beg you to forgive me." Dr. Ferris responded as if playing a part on cue; as if he were pleased that Dr. Stadler had learned, at last, the modern method of communication. "My car has been causing me a great deal of trouble, it's falling to pieces, and I had ordered a new one sometime ago, the best one on the market, a Hammond convertible— but Lawrence Hammond went out of business last week, without reason or warning, so now I'm stuck. Those bastards seem to be vanishing somewhere. Something will have to be done about it."

When Ferris had gone, Dr. Stadler sat at his desk, his shoulders shrinking together, conscious only of a desperate wish not to be seen by anyone. In the fog of the pain which he would not define, there was also the desperate feeling that no one—no one of those he valued— would ever wish to see him again.

He knew the words which he had not uttered. He had not said that he would denounce the book in public and repudiate it in the name of the Institute. He had not said it, because he had been afraid to discover that the threat would leave Ferris unmoved, that Ferris was safe, that the word of Dr. Robert Stadler had no power any longer. And while he told himself that he would consider later the question of making a public protest, he knew that he would not make it.

He picked up the book and let it drop into the wastebasket.

A face came to his mind, suddenly and clearly, as if he were seeing the purity of its every line, a young face he had not permitted himself to recall for years. He thought: No, he has not read this book, he won't see it, he's dead, he must have died long ago. . . . The sharp pain was the shock of discovering simultaneously that this was the man he longed to see more than any other being in the world—and that he had to hope that this man was dead.

He did not know why—when the telephone rang and his secretary told him that Miss Dagny Taggart was on the line—why he seized the receiver with eagerness and noticed that his hand was trembling. She would never want to see him again, he had thought for over a year. He heard her clear, impersonal voice asking for an appointment to see him. "Yes, Miss Taggart, certainly, yes, indeed. . . . Monday morning? Yes—look, Miss Taggart, I have an engagement in New York today, I could drop in at your office this afternoon, if you wish. . . . No, no —no trouble at all, I'll be delighted. . . . This afternoon, Miss Taggart, about two—I mean, about four o'clock."

He had no engagement in New York. He did not give himself time to know what had prompted him to do it. He was smiling eagerly, looking at a patch of sunlight on a distant hill.

* * *

Dagny drew a black line across Train Number 93 on the schedule, and felt a moment's desolate satisfaction in noting that she did it calmly. It was an action which she had had to perform many times in the last six months. It had been hard, at first; it was becoming easier. The day would come, she thought, when she would be able to deliver that death stroke even without the small salute of an effort. Train Number 93 was a freight that had earned its living by carrying supplies to Hammondsville, Colorado.

She knew what steps would come next: first, the death of the special freights—then the shrinking in the number of boxcars for Hammondsville, attached, like poor relatives, to the rear end of freights bound for other towns—then the gradual cutting of the stops at Hammondsville Station from the schedules of the passenger trains—then the day when she would strike Hammondsville, Colorado, off the map. That had been the progression of Wyatt Junction and of the town called Stockton.

She knew—once word was received that Lawrence Hammond had retired—that it was useless to wait, to hope and to wonder whether his cousin, his lawyer or a committee of local citizens would reopen the plant. She knew it was time to start cutting the schedules.

It had lasted less than six months after Ellis Wyatt had gone—that period which a columnist had gleefully called "the field day of the little fellow." Every oil operator in the country, who owned three wells and whined that Ellis Wyatt left him no chance of livelihood, had rushed to fill the hole which Wyatt had left wide open. They formed leagues, co-operatives, associations; they pooled their resources and their letterheads. "The little fellow's day in the sun," the columnist had said. Their sun had been the flames that twisted through the derricks of Wyatt Oil. In its glare, they made the kind of fortunes they had dreamed about, fortunes requiring no competence or effort. Then their biggest customers, such as power companies, who drank oil by the trainful and would make no allowances for human frailty, began to convert to coal —and the smaller customers, who were more tolerant, began to go out of business—the boys in Washington imposed rationing on oil and an emergency tax on employers to support the unemployed oil field workers—then a few of the big oil companies closed down—then the little fellows in the sun discovered that a drilling bit which had cost a hundred dollars, now cost them five hundred, there being no market for oil field equipment, and the suppliers having to earn on one drill what they had earned on five, or perish—then the pipe lines began to close, there being no one able to pay for their upkeep—then the railroads were granted permission to raise their freight rates, there being little oil to carry and the cost of running tank trains having crushed two small lines out of existence—and when the sun went down, they saw that the operating costs, which had once permitted them to exist on their sixty-acre fields, had been made possible by the miles of Wyatt's hillside and had gone in the same coils of smoke. Not until their fortunes had vanished and their pumps had stopped, did the little fellows realize that no business in the country could afford to buy oil at the price it would now take them to produce it. Then the boys in Washington granted subsidies to the oil operators, but not all of the oil operators had friends in Washington, and there followed a situation which no one cared to examine too closely or to discuss.

Andrew Stockton had been in the sort of position which most of the businessmen envied. The rush to convert to coal had descended upon his shoulders like a weight of gold: he had kept his plant working around the clock, running a race with next winter's blizzards, casting parts for coal-burning stoves and furnaces. There were not many dependable foundries left; he had become one of the main pillars supporting the cellars and kitchens of the country. The pillar collapsed without warning. Andrew Stockton announced that he was retiring, closed his plant and vanished. He left no word on what he wished to be done with the plant or whether his relatives had the right to reopen it.

There still were cars on the roads of the country, but they moved like travelers in the desert, who ride past the warning skeletons of horses bleached by the sun: they moved past the skeletons of cars that had collapsed on duty and had been left in the ditches by the side of the road. People were not buying cars any longer, and the automobile factories were closing. But there were men still able to get oil, by means of friendships that nobody cared to question. These men bought cars at any price demanded. Lights flooded the mountains of Colorado from the great windows of the plant, where the assembly belts of Lawrence Hammond poured trucks and cars to the sidings of Taggart Transcontinental. The word that Lawrence Hammond had retired came when least expected, brief and sudden like the single stroke of a bell in a heavy stillness. A committee of local citizens was now broadcasting appeals on the radio, begging Lawrence Hammond, wherever he was, to give them permission to reopen his plant. There was no answer.

She had screamed when Ellis Wyatt went; she had gasped when Andrew Stockton retired; when she heard that Lawrence Hammond had quit, she asked impassively, "Who's next?"

"No, Miss Taggart, I can't explain it," the sister of Andrew Stockton had told her on her last trip to Colorado, two months ago. "He never said a word to me and I don't even know whether he's dead or living, same as Ellis Wyatt. No, nothing special had happened the day before he quit. I remember only that some man came to see him on that last evening. A stranger I'd never seen before. They talked late into the night—when I went to sleep, the light was still burning in Andrew's study."

People were silent in the towns of Colorado. Dagny had seen the way they walked in the streets, past their small drugstores, hardware stores and grocery markets: as if they hoped that the motions of their jobs would save them from looking ahead at the future. She, too, had walked through those streets, trying not to lift her head, not to see the ledges of sooted rock and twisted steel, which had been the Wyatt oil fields. They could be seen from many of the towns; when she had looked ahead, she had seen them in the distance.

One well, on the crest of the hill, was still burning. Nobody had been able to extinguish it. She had seen it from the streets: a spurt of fire twisting convulsively against the sky, as if trying to tear loose. She had seen it at night, across the distance of a hundred clear, black miles, from the window of a train: a small, violent flame, waving in the wind. People called it Wyatt's Torch.

The longest train on the John Galt Line had forty cars; the fastest ran at fifty miles an hour. The engines had to be spared: they were coal-burning engines, long past their age of retirement. Jim obtained the oil for the Diesels that pulled the Comet and a few of their transcontinental freights. The only source of fuel she could count on and deal with was Ken Danagger of Danagger Coal in Pennsylvania.

Empty trains clattered through the four states that were tied, as neighbors, to the throat of Colorado. They carried a few carloads of sheep, some corn, some melons and an occasional farmer with an over-dressed family, who had friends in Washington. Jim had obtained a subsidy from Washington for every train that was run, not as a profit-making carrier, but as a service of "public equality."

It took every scrap of her energy to keep trains running through the sections where they were still needed, in the areas that were still producing. But on the balance sheets of Taggart Transcontinental, the checks of Jim's subsidies for empty trains bore larger figures than the profit brought by the best freight train of the busiest industrial division.

Jim boasted that this had been the most prosperous six months in Taggart history. Listed as profit, on the glossy pages of his report to the stockholders, was the money he had not earned—the subsidies for empty trains; and the money he did not own—the sums that should have gone to pay the interest and the retirement of Taggart bonds, the debt which, by the will of Wesley Mouch, he had been permitted not to pay. He boasted about the greater volume of freight carried by Taggart trains in Arizona—where Dan Conway had closed the last of the Phoenix-Durango and retired; and in Minnesota—where Paul Larkin was shipping iron ore by rail, and the last of the ore boats on the Great Lakes had gone out of existence.

"You have always considered money-making as such an important virtue," Jim had said to her with an odd half-smile. "Well, it seems to me that I'm better at it than you are."

Nobody professed to understand the question of the frozen railroad bonds; perhaps, because everybody understood it too well. At first, there had been signs of a panic among the bondholders and of a dangerous indignation among the public. Then, Wesley Mouch had issued another directive, which ruled that people could get their bonds "defrozen" upon a plea of "essential need": the government would purchase the bonds, if it found the proof of the need satisfactory. There were three questions that no one answered or asked: "What constituted proof?" "What constituted need?" "Essential—to whom?"

Then it became bad manners to discuss why one man received the grant defreezing his money, while another had been refused. People turned away in mouth-pinched silence, if anybody asked a "why?" One was supposed to describe, not to explain, to catalogue facts, not to evaluate them: Mr. Smith had been defrozen, Mr. Jones had not; that was all. And when Mr. Jones committed suicide, people said, "Well, I don't know, if he'd really needed his money, the government would have given it to him, but some men are just greedy."

One was not supposed to speak about the men who, having been refused, sold their bonds for one-third of the value to other men who possessed needs which, miraculously, made thirty-three frozen cents melt into a whole dollar; or about a new profession practiced by bright young boys just out of college, who called themselves "defreezers" and offered their services "to help you draft your application in the proper modern terms." The boys had friends in Washington.

Looking at the Taggart rail from the platform of some country station, she had found herself feeling, not the brilliant pride she had once felt, but a foggy, guilty shame, as if some foul kind of rust had grown on the metal, and worse: as if the rust had a tinge of blood. But then, in the concourse of the Terminal, she looked at the statue of Nat Taggart and thought: It was *your* rail, you made it, you fought for it, you were not stopped by fear or by loathing—I won't surrender it to the men of blood and rust—and I'm the only one left to guard it.

She had not given up her quest for the man who invented the motor. It was the only part of her work that made her able to bear the rest. It was the only goal in sight that gave meaning to her struggle. There were times when she wondered why she wanted to rebuild that motor. What for?—some voice seemed to ask her. Because I'm still alive, she answered. But her quest had remained futile. Her two engineers had found nothing in Wisconsin. She had sent them to search through the country for men who had worked for Twentieth Century, to learn the name of the inventor. They had learned nothing. She had sent them to search through the files of the Patent Office; no patent for the motor had ever been registered.

The only remnant of her personal quest was the stub of the cigarette with the dollar sign. She had forgotten it, until a recent evening, when she had found it in a drawer of her desk and given it to her friend at the cigar counter of the concourse. The old man had been very astonished, as he examined the stub, holding it cautiously between two fingers; he had never heard of such a brand and wondered how he could have missed it. "Was it of good quality, Miss Taggart?" "The best I've ever smoked." He had shaken his head, puzzled. He had promised to discover where those cigarettes were made and to get her a carton.

She had tried to find a scientist able to attempt the reconstruction of the motor. She had interviewed the men recommended to her as the best in their field. The first one, after studying the remnants of the motor and of the manuscript, had declared, in the tone of a drill sergeant, that the thing could not work, had never worked and he would prove that no such motor could ever be made to work. The second one had drawled, in the tone of an answer to a boring imposition, that he did not know whether it could be done or not and did not care to find out. The third had said, his voice belligerently insolent, that he would attempt the task on a ten-year contract at twenty-five thousand dollars a year—"After all, Miss Taggart, if you expect to make huge profits on that motor, it's you who should pay for the gamble of my time." The fourth, who was the youngest, had looked at her silently for a moment and the lines of his face had slithered from blankness into a suggestion of contempt. "You know, Miss Taggart, I don't think that such a motor should ever be made, even if somebody did learn how to make it. It would be so superior to anything we've got that it would be unfair to lesser scientists, because it would leave no field for their achievements and abilities. I don't think that the strong should have the right to wound the self-esteem of the weak." She had ordered him out of her office, and had sat in incredulous horror before the fact that the most vicious statement she had ever heard had been uttered in a tone of moral righteousness.

The decision to speak to Dr. Robert Stadler had been her last recourse.

She had forced herself to call him, against the resistance of some immovable point within her that felt like brakes slammed tight. She had argued against herself. She had thought: I deal with men like Jim and Orren Boyle—his guilt is less than theirs—why can't I speak to him? She had found no answer, only a stubborn sense of reluctance, only the feeling that of all the men on earth, Dr. Robert Stadler was the one she must not call.

As she sat at her desk, over the schedules of the John Galt Line, waiting for Dr. Stadler to come, she wondered why no first-rate talent had risen in the field of science for years. She was unable to look for an answer. She was looking at the black line which was the corpse of Train Number 93 on the schedule before her.

A train has the two great attributes of life, she thought, motion and purpose; this had been like a living entity, but now it was only a number of dead freight cars and engines. Don't give yourself time to feel, she thought, dismember the carcass as fast as possible, the engines are needed all over the system, Ken Danagger in Pennsylvania needs trains, more trains, if only—

"Dr. Robert Stadler," said the voice of the interoffice communicator on her desk.

He came in, smiling; the smile seemed to underscore his words: "Miss Taggart, would you care to believe how helplessly glad I am to see you again?"

She did not smile, she looked gravely courteous as she answered, "It was very kind of you to come here." She bowed, her slender figure standing tautly straight but for the slow, formal movement of her head.

"What if I confessed that all I needed was some plausible excuse in order to come? Would it astonish you?"

"I would try not to overtax your courtesy." She did not smile. "Please sit down, Dr. Stadler."

He looked brightly around him. "I've never seen the office of a railroad executive. I didn't know it would be so . . . so solemn a place. Is that in the nature of the job?"

"The matter on which I'd like to ask your advice is far removed from the field of your interests, Dr. Stadler. You may think it odd that I should call on you. Please allow me to explain my reason."

"The fact that you wished to call on me is a fully sufficient reason. If I can be of any service to you, any service whatever, I don't know what would please me more at this moment." His smile had an attractive quality, the smile of a man of the world who used it, not to cover his words, but to stress the audacity of expressing a sincere emotion.

"My problem is a matter of technology," she said, in the clear, expressionless tone of a young mechanic discussing a difficult assignment. "I fully realize your contempt for that branch of science. I do not expect you to solve my problem—it is not the kind of work which you do or care about. I should like only to submit the problem to you, and then I'll have just two questions to ask you. I had to call on you, because it is a matter that involves someone's mind, a very great mind, and"—she spoke impersonally, in the manner of rendering exact justice—"and you are the only great mind left in this field."

She could not tell why her words hit him as they did. She saw the stillness of his face, the sudden earnestness of the eyes, a strange earnestness that seemed eager and almost pleading, then she heard his voice come gravely, as if from under the pressure of some emotion that made it sound simple and humble:

"What is your problem, Miss Taggart?"

She told him about the motor and the place where she had found it; she told him that it had proved impossible to learn the name of the inventor; she did not mention the details of her quest. She handed him photographs of the motor and the remnant of the manuscript.

She watched him as he read. She saw the professional assurance in the swift, scanning motion of his eyes, at first, then the pause, then the growing intentness, then a movement of his lips which, from another man, would have been a whistle or a gasp. She saw him stop for long minutes and look off, as if his mind were racing over countless sudden trails, trying to follow them all—she saw him leaf back through the pages, then stop, then force himself to read on, as if he were torn between his eagerness to continue and his eagerness to seize all the possibilities breaking open before his vision. She saw his silent excitement, she knew that he had forgotten her office, her existence, everything but the sight of an achievement—and in tribute to his being capable of such reaction, she wished it were possible for her to like Dr. Robert Stadler.

They had been silent for over an hour, when he finished and looked up at her. "But this is extraordinary!" he said in the joyous, astonished tone of announcing some news she had not expected.

She wished she could smile in answer and grant him the comradeship of a joy celebrated together, but she merely nodded and said coldly, "Yes."

"But, Miss Taggart, this is tremendous!"

"Yes."

"Did you say it's a matter of technology? It's more, much, much more than that. The pages where he writes about his converter—you can see what premise he's speaking from. He arrived at some new concept of energy. He discarded all our standard assumptions, according to which his motor would have been impossible. He formulated a new premise of his own and he solved the secret of converting static energy into kinetic power. Do you know what *that* means? Do you realize what a feat of pure, abstract science he had to perform before he could make his motor?"

"Who?" she asked quietly.

"I beg your pardon?"

"That was the first of the two questions I wanted to ask you, Dr. Stadler: can you think of any young scientist you might have known ten years ago, who would have been able to do this?"

He paused, astonished; he had not had time to wonder about that question. "No," he said slowly, frowning, "no, I can't think of anyone. . . . And that's odd . . . because an ability of this kind couldn't have passed unnoticed anywhere . . . somebody would have called him to my attention . . . they always sent promising young physicists to me. . . . Did you say you found this in the research laboratory of a plain, commercial motor factory?"

"Yes."

"That's odd. What was he doing in such a place?"

"Designing a motor."

"That's what I mean. A man with the genius of a great scientist, who chose to be a commercial inventor? I find it outrageous. He wanted a motor, and he quietly performed a major revolution in the science of energy, just as a means to an end, and he didn't bother to publish his findings, but went right on making his motor. Why did he want to waste his mind on practical appliances?"

"Perhaps because he liked living on this earth," she said involuntarily.

"I beg your pardon?"

"No, I . . . I'm sorry, Dr. Stadler. I did not intend to discuss any . . . irrelevant subject."

He was looking off, pursuing his own course of thought. "Why didn't he come to me? Why wasn't he in some great scientific establishment where he belonged? If he had the brains to achieve this, surely he had the brains to know the importance of what he had done. Why didn't he publish a paper on his definition of energy? I can see the general direction he'd taken, but God damn him!—the most important pages are missing, the statement isn't here! Surely somebody around him should have known enough to announce his work to the whole world of science. Why didn't they? How could they abandon, just abandon, a thing of this kind?"

"These are the questions to which I found no answers."

"And besides, from the purely practical aspect, why was that motor left in a junk pile? You'd think any greedy fool of an industrialist would have grabbed it in order to make a fortune. No intelligence was needed to see its commercial value."

She smiled for the first time—a smile ugly with bitterness; she said nothing.

"You found it impossible to trace the inventor?" he asked.

"Completely impossible—so far."

"Do you think that he is still alive?"

"I have reason to think that he is. But I can't be sure."

"Suppose I tried to advertise for him?"

"No. Don't."

"But if I were to place ads in scientific publications and have Dr. Ferris"—he stopped; he saw her glance at him as swiftly as he glanced at her; she said nothing, but she held his glance; he looked away and finished the sentence coldly and firmly—"and have Dr. Ferris broadcast on the radio that *I* wish to see him, would he refuse to come?"

"Yes, Dr. Stadler, I think he would refuse."

He was not looking at her. She saw the faint tightening of his facial muscles and, simultaneously, the look of something going slack in the lines of his face; she could not tell what sort of light was dying within him nor what made her think of the death of a light.

He tossed the manuscript down on the desk with a casual, contemptuous movement of his wrist. "Those men who do not mind being practical enough to sell their brains for money, ought to acquire a little knowledge of the conditions of practical reality."

He looked at her with a touch of defiance, as if waiting for an angry answer. But her answer was worse than anger: her face remained expressionless, as if the truth or falsehood of his convictions were of no concern to her any longer. She said politely, "The second question I wanted to ask you was whether you would be kind enough to tell me the name of any physicist you know who, in your judgment, would possess the ability to attempt the reconstruction of this motor."

He looked at her and chuckled; it was a sound of pain. "Have you been tortured by it, too, Miss Taggart? By the impossibility of finding any sort of intelligence anywhere?"

"I have interviewed some physicists who were highly recommended to me and I have found them to be hopeless."

He leaned forward eagerly. "Miss Taggart," he asked, "did you call on me because you trusted the integrity of my scientific judgment?" The question was a naked plea.

"Yes," she answered evenly, "I trusted the integrity of your scientific judgment."

He leaned back; he looked as if some hidden smile were smoothing the tension away from his face. "I wish I could help you," he said, as to a comrade. "I most selfishly wish I could help you, because, you see, this has been my hardest problem—trying to find men of talent for my own staff. Talent, hell! I'd be satisfied with just a semblance of promise —but the men they send me couldn't be honestly said to possess the potentiality of developing into decent garage mechanics. I don't know whether I am getting older and more demanding, or whether the human race is degenerating, but the world didn't seem to be so barren of intelligence in my youth. Today, if you saw the kind of men I've had to interview, you'd—"

He stopped abruptly, as if at a sudden recollection. He remained silent; he seemed to be considering something he knew, but did not wish to tell her; she became certain of it, when he concluded brusquely, in that tone of resentment which conceals an evasion, "No, I don't know anyone I'd care to recommend to you."

"This was all I wanted to ask you, Dr. Stadler," she said. "Thank you for giving me your time."

He sat silently still for a moment, as if he could not bring himself to leave.

"Miss Taggart," he asked, "could you show me the actual motor itself?"

She looked at him, astonished. "Why, yes . . . if you wish. But it's in an underground vault, down in our Terminal tunnels."

"I don't mind, if you wouldn't mind taking me down there. I have no special motive. It's only my personal curiosity. I would like to see it—that's all."

When they stood in the granite vault, over a glass case containing a shape of broken metal, he took off his hat with a slow, absent movement—and she could not tell whether it was the routine gesture of remembering that he was in a room with a lady, or the gesture of baring one's head over a coffin.

They stood in silence, in the glare of a single light refracted from the glass surface to their faces. Train wheels were clicking in the distance, and it seemed at times as if a sudden, sharper jolt of vibration were about to awaken an answer from the corpse in the glass case.

"It's so wonderful," said Dr. Stadler, his voice low. "It's so wonderful to see a great, new, crucial idea which is not mine!"

She looked at him, wishing she could believe that she understood him correctly. He spoke, in passionate sincerity, discarding convention, discarding concern for whether it was proper to let her hear the confession of his pain, seeing nothing but the face of a woman who was able to understand:

"Miss Taggart, do you know the hallmark of the second-rater? It's resentment of another man's achievement. Those touchy mediocrities who sit trembling lest someone's work prove greater than their own—they have no inkling of the loneliness that comes when you reach the top. The loneliness for an equal—for a mind to respect and an achievement to admire. They bare their teeth at you from out of their rat holes, thinking that you take pleasure in letting your brilliance dim them—while you'd give a year of your life to see a flicker of talent anywhere among them. They envy achievement, and their dream of greatness is a world where all men have become their acknowledged inferiors. They don't know that that dream is the infallible proof of mediocrity, because that sort of world is what the man of achievement would not be able to bear. They have no way of knowing what he feels when surrounded by inferiors—hatred? no, not hatred, but boredom—the terrible, hopeless, draining, paralyzing boredom. Of what account are praise and adulation from men whom you don't respect? Have you ever felt the longing for someone you could admire? For something, not to look down at, but up to?"

"I've felt it all my life," she said. It was an answer she could not refuse him.

"I know," he said—and there was beauty in the impersonal gentleness of his voice. "I knew it the first time I spoke to you. That was why I came today—" He stopped for the briefest instant, but she did not answer the appeal and he finished with the same quiet gentleness, "Well, that was why I wanted to see the motor."

"I understand," she said softly; the tone of her voice was the only form of acknowledgment she could grant him.

"Miss Taggart," he said, his eyes lowered, looking at the glass case, "I know a man who might be able to undertake the reconstruction of that motor. He would not work for me—so he is probably the kind of man you want."

But by the time he raised his head—and before he saw the look of admiration in her eyes, the open look he had begged for, the look of forgiveness—he destroyed his single moment's atonement by adding in a voice of drawing-room sarcasm, "Apparently, the young man had no desire to work for the good of society or the welfare of science. He told me that he would not take a government job. I presume he wanted the bigger salary he could hope to obtain from a private employer."

He turned away, not to see the look that was fading from her face, not to let himself know its meaning. "Yes," she said, her voice hard, "he is probably the kind of man I want."

"He's a young physicist from the Utah Institute of Technology," he said dryly. "His name is Quentin Daniels. A friend of mine sent him to me a few months ago. He came to see me, but he would not take the job I offered. I wanted him on my staff. He had the mind of a scientist. I don't know whether he can succeed with your motor, but at least he has the ability to attempt it. I believe you can still reach him at the Utah Institute of Technology. I don't know what he's doing there now—they closed the Institute a year ago."

"Thank you, Dr. Stadler. I shall get in touch with him."

"If . . . if you want me to, I'll be glad to help him with the theoretical part of it. I'm going to do some work myself, starting from the leads of that manuscript. I'd like to find the cardinal secret of energy that its author had found. It's his basic principle that we must discover. If we succeed, Mr. Daniels may finish the job, as far as your motor is concerned."

"I will appreciate any help you may care to give me, Dr. Stadler."

They walked silently through the dead tunnels of the Terminal, down the ties of a rusted track under a string of blue lights, to the distant glow of the platforms.

At the mouth of the tunnel, they saw a man kneeling on the track, hammering at a switch with the unrhythmical exasperation of uncertainty. Another man stood watching him impatiently.

"Well, what's the matter with the damn thing?" asked the watcher.

"Don't know."

"You've been at it for an hour."

"Yeah."

"How long is it going to take?"

"Who is John Galt?"

Dr. Stadler winced. They had gone past the men, when he said, "I don't like that expression."

"I don't, either," she answered.

"Where did it come from?"

"Nobody knows."

They were silent, then he said, "I knew a John Galt once. Only he died long ago."

"Who was he?"

"I used to think that he was still alive. But now I'm certain that he must have died. He had such a mind that, had he lived, the whole world would have been talking of him by now."

"But the whole world *is* talking of him."

He stopped still. "Yes . . ." he said slowly, staring at a thought that had never struck him before, "yes . . . Why?" The word was heavy with the sound of terror.

"Who was he, Dr. Stadler?"

"Why are they talking of him?"

"Who was he?"

He shook his head with a shudder and said sharply, "It's just a coincidence. The name is not uncommon at all. It's a meaningless coincidence. It has no connection with the man I knew. That man is dead."

He did not permit himself to know the full meaning of the words he added:

"He has to be dead."

* * *

The order that lay on his desk was marked "Confidential . . . Emergency . . . Priority . . . Essential need certified by office of Top Co-ordinator . . . for the account of Project X"—and demanded that he sell ten thousand tons of Rearden Metal to the State Science Institute.

Rearden read it and glanced up at the superintendent of his mills who stood before him without moving. The superintendent had come in and put the order down on his desk without a word.

"I thought you'd want to see it," he said, in answer to Rearden's glance.

Rearden pressed a button, summoning Miss Ives. He handed the order to her and said, "Send this back to wherever it came from. Tell them that I will not sell any Rearden Metal to the State Science Institute."

Gwen Ives and the superintendent looked at him, at each other and back at him again; what he saw in their eyes was congratulation.

"Yes, Mr. Rearden," Gwen Ives said formally, taking the slip as if it were any other kind of business paper. She bowed and left the room. The superintendent followed.

Rearden smiled faintly, in greeting to what they felt. He felt nothing about that paper or its possible consequences.

By a sort of inner convulsion—which had been like tearing a plug out to cut off the current of his emotions—he had told himself six months ago: Act first, keep the mills going, feel later. It had made him able to watch dispassionately the working of the Fair Share Law.

Nobody had known how that law was to be observed. First, he had been told that he could not produce Rearden Metal in an amount greater than the tonnage of the best special alloy, other than steel, produced by Orren Boyle. But Orren Boyle's best special alloy was some cracking mixture that no one cared to buy. Then he had been told that he could produce Rearden Metal in the amount that Orren Boyle *could have* produced, if he could have produced it. Nobody had known how this was to be determined. Somebody in Washington had announced a figure, naming a number of tons per year, giving no reasons. Everybody had let it go at that.

He had not known how to give every consumer who demanded it an equal share of Rearden Metal. The waiting list of orders could not be filled in three years, even had he been permitted to work at full capacity. New orders were coming in daily. They were not orders any longer, in the old, honorable sense of trade; they were demands. The law provided that he could be sued by any consumer who failed to receive his fair share of Rearden Metal.

Nobody had known how to determine what constituted a fair share of what amount. Then a bright young boy just out of college had been sent to him from Washington, as Deputy Director of Distribution. After many telephone conferences with the capital, the boy announced that customers would get five hundred tons of the Metal each, in the order of the dates of their applications. Nobody had argued against his figure. There was no way to form an argument; the figure could have been one pound or one million tons, with the same validity. The boy had established an office at the Rearden mills, where four girls took applications for shares of Rearden Metal. At the present rate of the mills' production, the applications extended well into the next century.

Five hundred tons of Rearden Metal could not provide three miles of rail for Taggart Transcontinental; it could not provide the bracing for one of Ken Danagger's coal mines. The largest industries, Rearden's best customers, were denied the use of his Metal. But golf clubs made of Rearden Metal were suddenly appearing on the market, as well as coffee pots, garden tools and bathroom faucets. Ken Danagger, who had seen the value of the Metal and had dared to order it against a fury of public opinion, was not permitted to obtain it; his order had been left unfilled, cut off without warning by the new laws. Mr. Mowen, who had betrayed Taggart Transcontinental in its most dangerous hour, was now making switches of Rearden Metal and selling them to the Atlantic Southern. Rearden looked on, his emotions plugged out.

He turned away, without a word, when anybody mentioned to him what everybody knew: the quick fortunes that were being made on

Rearden Metal. "Well, no," people said in drawing rooms, "you musn't call it a black market, because it isn't, really. Nobody is selling the *Metal* illegally. They're just selling their *right* to it. Not selling really, just pooling their shares." He did not want to know the insect intricacy of the deals through which the "shares" were sold and pooled—nor how a manufacturer in Virginia had produced, in two months, five thousand tons of castings made of Rearden Metal—nor what man in Washington was that manufacturer's unlisted partner. He knew that their profit on a ton of Rearden Metal was five times larger than his own. He said nothing. Everybody had a right to the Metal, except himself.

The young boy from Washington—whom the steel workers had nick-named the Wet Nurse—hung around Rearden with a primitive, astonished curiosity which, incredibly, was a form of admiration. Rearden watched him with disgusted amusement. The boy had no inkling of any concept of morality; it had been bred out of him by his college; this had left him an odd frankness, naïve and cynical at once, like the innocence of a savage.

"You despise me, Mr. Rearden," he had declared once, suddenly and without any resentment. "That's impractical."

"Why is it impractical?" Rearden had asked.

The boy had looked puzzled and had found no answer. He never had an answer to any "why?" He spoke in flat assertions. He would say about people, "He's old-fashioned," "He's unreconstructed," "He's unadjusted," without hesitation or explanation; he would also say, while being a graduate in metallurgy, "Iron smelting, I think, seems to require a high temperature." He uttered nothing but uncertain opinions about physical nature—and nothing but categorical imperatives about men.

"Mr. Rearden," he had said once, "if you feel you'd like to hand out more of the Metal to friends of yours—I mean, in bigger hauls—it could be arranged, you know. Why don't we apply for a special permission on the ground of essential need? I've got a few friends in Washington. Your friends are pretty important people, big businessmen, so it wouldn't be difficult to get away with the essential need dodge. Of course, there would be a few expenses. For things in Washington. You know how it is, things always occasion expenses."

"What things?"

"You understand what I mean."

"No," Rearden had said, "I don't. Why don't you explain it to me?"

The boy had looked at him uncertainly, weighed it in his mind, then come out with: "It's bad psychology."

"What is?"

"You know, Mr. Rearden, it's not necessary to use such words as that."

"As what?"

"Words are relative. They're only symbols. If we don't use ugly symbols, we won't have any ugliness. Why do you want me to say things one way, when I've already said them another?"

"Which way do I want you to say them?"

"Why do you want me to?"

"For the same reason that you don't."

The boy had remained silent for a moment, then had said, "You know, Mr. Rearden, there are no absolute standards. We can't go by rigid principles, we've got to be flexible, we've got to adjust to the reality of the day and act on the expediency of the moment."

"Run along, punk. Go and try to pour a ton of steel without rigid principles, on the expediency of the moment."

A strange sense, which was almost a sense of style, made Rearden feel contempt for the boy, but no resentment. The boy seemed to fit the spirit of the events around them. It was as if they were being carried back across a long span of centuries to the age where the boy had belonged, but he, Rearden, had not. Instead of building new furnaces, thought Rearden, he was now running a losing race to keep the old ones going; instead of starting new ventures, new research, new experiments in the use of Rearden Metal, he was spending the whole of his energy on a quest for sources of iron ore: like the men at the dawn of the Iron Age—he thought—but with less hope.

He tried to avoid these thoughts. He had to stand on guard against his own feeling—as if some part of him had become a stranger that had to be kept numb, and his will had to be its constant, watchful anesthetic. That part was an unknown of which he knew only that he must never see its root and never give it voice. He had lived through one dangerous moment which he could not allow to return.

It was the moment when—alone in his office, on a winter evening, held paralyzed by a newspaper spread on his desk with a long column of directives on the front page—he had heard on the radio the news of Ellis Wyatt's flaming oil fields. Then, his first reaction—before any thought of the future, any sense of disaster, any shock, terror or protest—had been to burst out laughing. He had laughed in triumph, in deliverance, in a spurting, living exultation—and the words which he had not pronounced, but felt, were: God bless you, Ellis, whatever you're doing!

When he had grasped the implications of his laughter, he had known that he was now condemned to constant vigilance against himself. Like the survivor of a heart attack, he knew that he had had a warning and that he carried within him a danger that could strike him at any moment.

He had held it off, since then. He had kept an even, cautious, severely controlled pace in his inner steps. But it had come close to him for a moment, once again. When he had looked at the order of the State Science Institute on his desk, it had seemed to him that the glow moving over the paper did not come from the furnaces outside, but from the flames of a burning oil field.

"Mr. Rearden," said the Wet Nurse, when he heard about the rejected order, "you shouldn't have done that."

"Why not?"

"There's going to be trouble."

"What kind of trouble?"

"It's a government order. You can't reject a government order."

"Why can't I?"

"It's an Essential Need project, and secret, too. It's very important."

"What kind of a project is it?"

"I don't know. It's secret."

"Then how do you know it's important?"

"It said so."

"Who said so?"

"You can't doubt such a thing as that, Mr. Rearden!"

"Why can't I?"

"But you can't."

"If I can't, then that would make it an absolute and you said there aren't any absolutes."

"That's different."

"How is it different?"

"It's the government."

"You mean, there aren't any absolutes except the government?"

"I mean, if they say it's important, then it is."

"Why?"

"I don't want you to get in trouble, Mr. Rearden, and you're going to, sure as hell. You ask too many why's. Now why do you do that?"

Rearden glanced at him and chuckled. The boy noticed his own words and grinned sheepishly, but he looked unhappy.

The man who came to see Rearden a week later was youngish and slenderish, but neither as young nor as slender as he tried to make himself appear. He wore civilian clothes and the leather leggings of a traffic cop. Rearden could not quite get it clear whether he came from the State Science Institute or from Washington.

"I understand that you refused to sell metal to the State Science Institute, Mr. Rearden," he said in a soft, confidential tone of voice.

"That's right," said Rearden.

"But wouldn't that constitute a willful disobedience of the law?"

"It's for you to interpret."

"May I ask your reason?"

"My reason is of no interest to you."

"Oh, but of course it is! We are not your enemies, Mr. Rearden. We want to be fair to you. You mustn't be afraid of the fact that you are a big industrialist. We won't hold it against you. We actually want to be as fair to you as to the lowest day laborer. We would like to know your reason."

"Print my refusal in the newspapers, and any reader will tell you my reason. It appeared in all the newspapers a little over a year ago."

"Oh, no, no, no! Why talk of newspapers? Can't we settle this as a friendly, private matter?"

"That's up to you."

"We don't want this in the newspapers."

"No?"

"No. We wouldn't want to hurt you."

Rearden glanced at him and asked, "Why does the State Science Institute need ten thousand tons of metal? What is Project X?"

"Oh, that? It's a very important project of scientific research, an undertaking of great social value that may prove of inestimable public benefit, but, unfortunately, the regulations of top policy do not permit me to tell you its nature in fuller detail."

"You know," said Rearden, "I could tell you—as my reason—that I do not wish to sell my Metal to those whose purpose is kept secret from me. I created that Metal. It is my moral responsibility to know for what purpose I permit it to be used."

"Oh, but you don't have to worry about that, Mr. Rearden! We relieve you of the responsibility."

"Suppose I don't wish to be relieved of it?"

"But . . . but that is an old-fashioned and . . . and purely theoretical attitude."

"I said I could name it as my reason. But I won't—because, in this case, I have another, inclusive reason. I would not sell any Rearden Metal to the State Science Institute for any purpose whatever, good or bad, secret or open."

"But why?"

"Listen," said Rearden slowly, "there might be some sort of justification for the savage societies in which a man had to expect that enemies could murder him at any moment and had to defend himself as best he could. But there can be no justification for a society in which a man is expected to manufacture the weapons for his own murderers."

"I don't think it's advisable to use such words, Mr. Rearden. I don't think it's practical to think in such terms. After all, the government cannot—in the pursuit of wide, national policies—take cognizance of your personal grudge against some one particular institution."

"Then don't take cognizance of it."

"What do you mean?"

"Don't come asking my reason."

"But, Mr. Rearden, we cannot let a refusal to obey the law pass unnoticed. What do you expect us to do?"

"Whatever you wish."

"But this is totally unprecedented. Nobody has ever refused to sell an essential commodity to the government. As a matter of fact, the law does not permit you to refuse to sell your Metal to *any* consumer, let alone the government."

"Well, why don't you arrest me, then?"

"Mr. Rearden, this is an amicable discussion. Why speak of such things as arrests?"

"Isn't that your ultimate argument against me?"

"Why bring it up?"

"Isn't it implied in every sentence of this discussion?"

"Why name it?"

"Why not?" There was no answer. "Are you trying to hide from me the fact that if it weren't for that trump card of yours, I wouldn't have allowed you to enter this office?"

"But I'm not speaking of arrests."

"I am."

"I don't understand you, Mr. Rearden."

"I am not helping you to pretend that this is any sort of amicable discussion. It isn't. Now do what you please about it."

There was a strange look on the man's face: bewilderment, as if he had no conception of the issue confronting him, and fear, as if he had always had full knowledge of it and had lived in dread of exposure.

Rearden felt a strange excitement; he felt as if he were about to grasp something he had never understood, as if he were on the trail of some discovery still too distant to know, except that it had the most immense importance he had ever glimpsed.

"Mr. Rearden," said the man, "the government needs your Metal. You have to sell it to us, because surely you realize that the government's plans cannot be held up by the matter of your consent."

"A sale," said Rearden slowly, "requires the seller's consent." He got up and walked to the window. "I'll tell you what you can do." He pointed to the siding where ingots of Rearden Metal were being loaded onto freight cars. "There's Rearden Metal. Drive down there with your trucks—like any other looter, but without his risk, because I won't shoot you, as you know I can't—take as much of the Metal as you wish and go. Don't try to send me payment. I won't accept it. Don't print out a check to me. It won't be cashed. If you want that Metal, you have the guns to seize it. Go ahead."

"Good God, Mr. Rearden, what would the public think!"

It was an instinctive, involuntary cry. The muscles of Rearden's face moved briefly in a soundless laughter. Both of them had understood the implications of that cry. Rearden said evenly, in the grave, unstrained tone of finality, "You need my help to make it look like a sale—like a safe, just, moral transaction. I will not help you."

The man did not argue. He rose to leave. He said only, "You will regret the stand you've taken, Mr. Rearden."

"I don't think so," said Rearden.

He knew that the incident was not ended. He knew also that the secrecy of Project X was not the main reason why these people feared to make the issue public. He knew that he felt an odd, joyous, light-hearted self-confidence. He knew that these were the right steps down the trail he had glimpsed.

* * *

Dagny lay stretched in an armchair of her living room, her eyes closed. This day had been hard, but she knew that she would see Hank Rearden tonight. The thought of it was like a lever lifting the weight of hours of senseless ugliness away from her.

She lay still, content to rest with the single purpose of waiting quietly for the sound of the key in the lock. He had not telephoned her, but she had heard that he was in New York today for a conference with producers of copper, and he never left the city till next morning, nor spent a night in New York that was not hers. She liked to wait for him. She needed a span of time as a bridge between her days and his nights.

The hours ahead, like all her nights with him, would be added, she thought, to that savings account of one's life where moments of time are stored in the pride of having been lived. The only pride of her workday was not that it had been lived, but that it had been survived. It was wrong, she thought, it was viciously wrong that one should ever be forced to say that about any hour of one's life. But she could not think of it now. She was thinking of him, of the struggle she had watched through the months behind them, his struggle for deliverance; she had known that she could help him win, but must help him in every way except in words.

She thought of the evening last winter when he came in, took a small package from his pocket and held it out to her, saying, "I want you to have it." She opened it and stared in incredulous bewilderment at a pendant made of a single pear-shaped ruby that spurted a violent fire on the white satin of the jeweler's box. It was a famous stone, which only a dozen men in the world could properly afford to purchase; he was not one of them.

"Hank . . . why?"

"No special reason. I just wanted to see you wear it."

"Oh, no, not a thing of this kind! Why waste it? I go so rarely to occasions where one has to dress. When would I ever wear it?"

He looked at her, his glance moving slowly from her legs to her face. "I'll show you," he said.

He led her to the bedroom, he took off her clothes, without a word, in the manner of an owner undressing a person whose consent is not required. He clasped the pendant on her shoulders. She stood naked, the stone between her breasts, like a sparkling drop of blood.

"Do you think a man should give jewelry to his mistress for any purpose but his own pleasure?" he asked. "This is the way I want you to wear it. Only for me. I like to look at it. It's beautiful."

She laughed; it was a soft, low, breathless sound. She could not speak or move, only nod silently in acceptance and obedience; she nodded several times, her hair swaying with the wide, circular movement of her head, then hanging still as she kept her head bowed to him.

She dropped down on the bed. She lay stretched lazily, her head thrown back, her arms at her sides, palms pressed to the rough texture of the bedspread, one leg bent, the long line of the other extended across the dark blue linen of the spread, the stone glowing like a wound in the semi-darkness, throwing a star of rays against her skin.

Her eyes were half-closed in the mocking, conscious triumph of being admired, but her mouth was half-open in helpless, begging expectation. He stood across the room, looking at her, at her flat stomach drawn in, as her breath was drawn, at the sensitive body of a sensitive consciousness. He said, his voice low, intent and oddly quiet:

"Dagny, if some artist painted you as you are now, men would come to look at the painting to experience a moment that nothing could give them in their own lives. They would call it great art. They would not know the nature of what they felt, but the painting would show them everything—even that you're not some classical Venus, but the Vice-President of a railroad, because that's part of it—even what I am, because that's part of it, too. Dagny, they'd feel it and go away and sleep with the first barmaid in sight—and they'd never try to reach what they had felt. *I* wouldn't want to seek it from a painting. I'd want it real. I'd take no pride in any hopeless longing. I wouldn't hold a stillborn aspiration. I'd want to have it, to make it, to live it. Do you understand?"

"Oh yes, Hank, *I* understand!" she said. Do *you*, my darling?—do you understand it fully?—she thought, but did not say it aloud.

On the evening of a blizzard, she came home to find an enormous spread of tropical flowers standing in her living room against the dark glass of windows battered by snowflakes. They were stems of Hawaiian Torch Ginger, three feet tall; their large heads were cones of petals that had the sensual texture of soft leather and the color of blood. "I saw them in a florist's window," he told her when he came, that night. "I liked seeing them through a blizzard. But there's nothing as wasted as an object in a public window."

She began to find flowers in her apartment at unpredictable times, flowers sent without a card, but with the signature of the sender in their fantastic shapes, in the violent colors, in the extravagant cost. He brought her a gold necklace made of small hinged squares that formed a spread of solid gold to cover her neck and shoulders, like the collar of a knight's armor—"Wear it with a black dress," he ordered. He brought her a set of glasses that were tall, slender blocks of square-cut crystal, made by a famous jeweler. She watched the way he held one of the glasses when she served him a drink—as if the touch of the texture under his fingers, the taste of the drink and the sight of her face were the single form of an indivisible moment of enjoyment. "I used to see things I liked," he said, "but I never bought them. There didn't seem to be much meaning in it. There is, now."

He telephoned her at the office, one winter morning, and said, not in the tone of an invitation, but in the tone of an executive's order, "We're going to have dinner together tonight. I want you to dress. Do you have any sort of blue evening gown? Wear it."

The dress she wore was a slender tunic of dusty blue that gave her a look of unprotected simplicity, the look of a statue in the blue shadows of a garden under the summer sun. What he brought and put over her shoulders was a cape of blue fox that swallowed her from the curve of her chin to the tips of her sandals. "Hank, that's preposterous"—she laughed—"it's not my kind of thing!" "No?" he asked, drawing her to a mirror.

The huge blanket of fur made her look like a child bundled for a snowstorm; the luxurious texture transformed the innocence of the awkward bundle into the elegance of a perversely intentional contrast: into a look of stressed sensuality. The fur was a soft brown, dimmed by an aura of blue that could not be seen, only felt like an enveloping mist, like a suggestion of color grasped not by one's eyes but by one's hands, as if one felt, without contact, the sensation of sinking one's palms into the fur's softness. The cape left nothing to be seen of her, except the brown of her hair, the blue-gray of her eyes, the shape of her mouth.

She turned to him, her smile startled and helpless. "I . . . I didn't know it would look like that."

"I did."

She sat beside him in his car as he drove through the dark streets of the city. A sparkling net of snow flashed into sight once in a while, when they went past the lights on the corners. She did not ask where they were going. She sat low in the seat, leaning back, looking up at the snowflakes. The fur cape was wrapped tightly about her; within it, her dress felt as light as a nightgown and the feel of the cape was like an embrace.

She looked at the angular tiers of lights rising through the snowy curtain, and—glancing at him, at the grip of his gloved hands on the wheel, at the austere, fastidious elegance of the figure in black overcoat and white muffler—she thought that he belonged in a great city, among polished sidewalks and sculptured stone.

The car went down into a tunnel, streaked through an echoing tube of tile under the river and rose to the coils of an elevated highway under an open black sky. The lights were below them now, spread in flat miles of bluish windows, of smokestacks, slanting cranes, red gusts of fire, and long, dim rays silhouetting the contorted shapes of an industrial district. She thought that she had seen him once, at his mills, with smudges of soot on his forehead, dressed in acid-eaten overalls; he had worn them as naturally well as he wore his formal clothes. He belonged here, too—she thought, looking down at the flats of New Jersey—among the cranes, the fires and the grinding clatter of gears.

When they sped down a dark road through an empty countryside, with the strands of snow glittering across their headlights—she remembered how he had looked in the summer of their vacation, dressed in slacks, stretched on the ground of a lonely ravine, with the grass under his body and the sun on his bare arms. He belonged in the countryside, she thought—he belonged everywhere—he was a man who belonged on earth—and then she thought of the words which were more exact: he was a man to whom the earth belonged, the man at home on earth and in control. Why, then—she wondered—should he have had to carry a burden of tragedy which, in silent endurance, he had accepted so completely that he had barely known he carried it? She knew part of the answer; she felt as if the whole answer were close and she would grasp it on some approaching day. But she did not want to think of it now, because they were moving away from the burdens, because within the space of a speeding car they held the stillness of full happiness. She moved her head imperceptibly to let it touch his shoulder for a moment.

The car left the highway and turned toward the lighted squares of distant windows, that hung above the snow beyond a grillwork of bare branches. Then, in a soft, dim light, they sat at a table by a window facing darkness and trees. The inn stood on a knoll in the woods; it had the luxury of high cost and privacy, and an air of beautiful taste suggesting that it had not been discovered by those who sought high cost and notice. She was barely aware of the dining room; it blended away into a sense of superlative comfort, and the only ornament that caught her attention was the glitter of iced branches beyond the glass of the window.

She sat, looking out, the blue fur half-slipping off her naked arms and shoulders. He watched her through narrowed eyes, with the satisfaction of a man studying his own workmanship.

"I like giving things to you," he said, "because you don't need them."

"No?"

"And it's not that I want you to have them. I want you to have them *from me.*"

"That is the way I do need them, Hank. From you."

"Do you understand that it's nothing but vicious self-indulgence on my part? I'm not doing it for your pleasure, but for mine."

"Hank!" The cry was involuntary; it held amusement, despair, indignation and pity. "If you'd given me those things just for *my* pleasure, not yours, I would have thrown them in your face."

"Yes . . . Yes, then you would—and should."

"Did you call it your vicious self-indulgence?"

"That's what they call it."

"Oh, yes! That's what they call it. What do *you* call it, Hank?"

"I don't know," he said indifferently, and went on intently. "I know only that if it's vicious, then let me be damned for it, but that's what I want to do more than anything else on earth."

She did not answer; she sat looking straight at him with a faint smile, as if asking him to listen to the meaning of his own words.

"I've always wanted to enjoy my wealth," he said. "I didn't know how to do it. I didn't even have time to know how much I wanted to. But I knew that all the steel I poured came back to me as liquid gold, and the gold was meant to harden into any shape I wished, and it was I who had to enjoy it. Only I couldn't. I couldn't find any purpose for it. I've found it, now. It's I who've produced that wealth and it's I who am going to let it buy for me every kind of pleasure I want—including the pleasure of seeing how much I'm able to pay for—including the preposterous feat of turning *you* into a luxury object."

"But I'm a luxury object that you've paid for long ago," she said; she was not smiling.

"How?"

"By means of the same values with which you paid for your mills."

She did not know whether he understood it with that full, luminous finality which is a thought named in words; but she knew that what he felt in that moment was understanding. She saw the relaxation of an invisible smile in his eyes.

"I've never despised luxury," he said, "yet I've always despised those who enjoyed it. I looked at what they called their pleasures and it seemed so miserably senseless to me—after what I felt at the mills. I used to watch steel being poured, tons of liquid steel running as I wanted it to, where I wanted it. And then I'd go to a banquet and I'd see people who sat trembling in awe before their own gold dishes and lace tablecloths, as if their dining room were the master and they were just objects serving it, objects created by their diamond shirt studs and necklaces, not the other way around. Then I'd run to the sight of the first slag heap I could find—and they'd say that I didn't know how to enjoy life, because I cared for nothing but business."

He looked at the dim, sculptured beauty of the room and at the people who sat at the tables. They sat in a manner of self-conscious display, as if the enormous cost of their clothes and the enormous care of their grooming should have fused into splendor, but didn't. Their faces had a look of rancorous anxiety.

"Dagny, look at those people. They're supposed to be the playboys of life, the amusement-seekers and luxury-lovers. They sit there, waiting for this place to give them meaning, not the other way around. But they're always shown to us as the enjoyers of material pleasures —and then we're taught that enjoyment of material pleasures is evil. Enjoyment? Are they enjoying it? Isn't there some sort of perversion in what we're taught, some error that's vicious and very important?"

"Yes, Hank—very vicious and very, very important."

"They are the playboys, while we're just tradesmen, you and I. Do you realize that we're much more capable of enjoying this place than they can ever hope to be?"

"Yes."

He said slowly, in the tone of a quotation, "Why have we left it all to fools? It should have been ours." She looked at him, startled. He smiled. "I remember every word you said to me at that party. I didn't answer you then, because the only answer I had, the only thing your words meant to me, was an answer that you would hate me for, I thought; it was that I wanted you." He looked at her. "Dagny, you didn't intend it then, but what you were saying was that you wanted to sleep with me, wasn't it?"

"Yes, Hank. Of course."

He held her eyes, then looked away. They were silent for a long time. He glanced at the soft twilight around them, then at the sparkle of two wine glasses on their table. "Dagny, in my youth, when I was working in the ore mines in Minnesota, I thought that I wanted to reach an evening like this. No, that was not what I was working for, and I didn't think of it often. But once in a while, on a winter night, when the stars were out and it was very cold, when I was tired, because I had worked two shifts, and wanted nothing on earth except to lie down and fall asleep right there, on the mine ledge—I thought that some day I would sit in a place like this, where one drink of wine would cost more than my day's wages, and I would have earned the price of every minute of it and of every drop and of every flower on the table, and I would sit there for no purpose but my own amusement."

She asked, smiling, "With your mistress?"

She saw the shot of pain in his eyes and wished desperately that she had not said it.

"With . . . a woman," he answered. She knew the word he had not pronounced. He went on, his voice soft and steady: "When I became rich and saw what the rich did for their amusement, I thought that the place I had imagined, did not exist. I had not even imagined it too clearly. I did not know what it would be like, only what I would feel. I gave up expecting it years ago. But I feel it tonight."

He raised his glass, looking at her.

"Hank, I . . . I'd give up anything I've ever had in my life, except my being a . . . a luxury object of your amusement."

He saw her hand trembling as she held her glass. He said evenly, "I know it, dearest."

She sat shocked and still: he had never used that word before. He threw his head back and smiled the most brilliantly gay smile she had ever seen on his face.

"Your first moment of weakness, Dagny," he said.

She laughed and shook her head. He stretched his arm across the table and closed his hand over her naked shoulder, as if giving her an instant's support. Laughing softly, and as if by accident, she let her mouth brush against his fingers; it kept her face down for the one moment when he could have seen that the brilliance of her eyes was tears.

When she looked up at him, her smile matched his—and the rest of the evening was their celebration—for all his years since the nights on the mine ledges—for all her years since the night of her first ball when, in desolate longing for an uncaptured vision of gaiety, she had wondered about the people who expected the lights and the flowers to make them brilliant.

"Isn't there . . . in what we're taught . . . some error that's vicious and very important?"—she thought of his words, as she lay in an armchair of her living room, on a dismal evening of spring, waiting for him to come. . . . Just a little farther, my darling—she thought—look a little farther and you'll be free of that error and of all the wasted pain you never should have had to carry. . . . But she felt that she, too, had not seen the whole of the distance, and she wondered what were the steps left for her to discover. . . .

Walking through the darkness of the streets, on his way to her apartment, Rearden kept his hands in his coat pockets and his arms pressed to his sides, because he felt that he did not want to touch anything or brush against anyone. He had never experienced it before—this sense of revulsion that was not aroused by any particular object, but seemed to flood everything around him, making the city seem sodden. He could understand disgust for any one thing, and he could fight that thing with the healthy indignation of knowing that it did not belong in the world; but this was new to him—this feeling that the world was a loathsome place where he did not want to belong.

He had held a conference with the producers of copper, who had just been garroted by a set of directives that would put them out of existence in another year. He had had no advice to give them, no solution to offer; his ingenuity, which had made him famous as the man who would always find a way to keep production going, had not been able to discover a way to save them. But they had all known that there was no way; ingenuity was a virtue of the mind—and in the issue confronting them, the mind had been discarded as irrelevant long ago. "It's a deal between the boys in Washington and the importers of copper," one of the men had said, "mainly d'Anconia Copper."

This was only a small, extraneous stab of pain, he thought, a feeling of disappointment in an expectation he had never had the right to expect; he should have known that this was just what a man like Francisco d'Anconia would do—and he wondered angrily why he felt as if a bright, brief flame had died somewhere in a lightless world.

He did not know whether the impossibility of acting had given him this sense of loathing, or whether the loathing had made him lose the desire to act. It's both, he thought; a desire presupposes the possibility of action to achieve it; action presupposes a goal which is worth achieving. If the only goal possible was to wheedle a precarious moment's favor from men who held guns, then neither action nor desire could exist any longer.

Then could life?—he asked himself indifferently. Life, he thought, had been defined as motion; man's life was purposeful motion; what was the state of a being to whom purpose and motion were denied, a being held in chains but left to breathe and to see all the magnificence of the possibilities he could have reached, left to scream "Why?" and to be shown the muzzle of a gun as sole explanation? He shrugged, walking on; he did not care even to find an answer.

He observed, indifferently, the devastation wrought by his own indifference. No matter how hard a struggle he had lived through in the past, he had never reached the ultimate ugliness of abandoning the will to act. In moments of suffering, he had never let pain win its one permanent victory: he had never allowed it to make him lose the desire for joy. He had never doubted the nature of the world or man's greatness as its motive power and its core. Years ago, he had wondered with contemptuous incredulity about the fanatical sects that appeared among men in the dark corners of history, the sects who believed that man was trapped in a malevolent universe ruled by evil for the sole purpose of his torture. Tonight, he knew what their vision of the world and their feel of it had been. If what he now saw around him was the world in which he lived, then he did not want to touch any part of it, he did not want to fight it, he was an outsider with nothing at stake and no concern for remaining alive much longer.

Dagny and his wish to see her were the only exception left to him. The wish remained. But in a sudden shock, he realized that he felt no desire to sleep with her tonight. That desire—which had never given him a moment's rest, which had been growing, feeding on its own satisfaction—was wiped out. It was an odd impotence, neither of his mind nor of his body. He felt, as passionately as he had ever felt it, that she was the most desirable woman on earth; but what came from it was only a desire to desire her, a wish to feel, not a feeling. The sense of numbness seemed impersonal, as if its root were neither in him nor in her; as if it were the act of sex that now belonged to a realm which he had left.

"Don't get up—stay there—it's so obvious that you've been waiting for me that I want to look at it longer."

He said it, from the doorway of her apartment, seeing her stretched in an armchair, seeing the eager little jolt that threw her shoulders forward as she was about to rise; he was smiling.

He noted—as if some part of him were watching his reactions with detached curiosity—that his smile and his sudden sense of gaiety were real. He grasped a feeling that he had always experienced, but never identified because it had always been absolute and immediate: a feeling that forbade him ever to face her in pain. It was much more than the pride of wishing to conceal his suffering: it was the feeling that suffering must not be granted recognition in her presence, that no form of claim between them should ever be motivated by pain and aimed at pity. It was not pity that he brought here or came here to find.

"Do you still need proof that I'm always waiting for you?" she asked, leaning obediently back in her chair; her voice was neither tender nor pleading, but bright and mocking.

"Dagny, why is it that most women would never admit that, but you do?"

"Because they're never sure that they ought to be wanted. I am."

"I do admire self-confidence."

"Self-confidence was only one part of what I said, Hank."

"What's the whole?"

"Confidence of my value—and yours." He glanced at her as if catching the spark of a sudden thought, and she laughed, adding, "I wouldn't be sure of holding a man like Orren Boyle, for instance. He wouldn't want me at all. You would."

"Are you saying," he asked slowly, "that I rose in your estimation when you found that I wanted you?"

"Of course."

"That's not the reaction of most people to being wanted."

"It isn't."

"Most people feel that they rise in their own eyes, if others want them."

"I feel that others live up to me, if they want me. And that is the way you feel, too, Hank, about yourself—whether you admit it or not."

That's not what I said to you then, on that first morning—he thought, looking down at her. She lay stretched out lazily, her face blank, but her eyes bright with amusement. He knew that she was thinking of it and that she knew he was. He smiled, but said nothing else.

As he sat half-stretched on the couch, watching her across the room, he felt at peace—as if some temporary wall had risen between him and the things he had felt on his way here. He told her about his encounter with the man from the State Science Institute, because, even though he knew that the event held danger, an odd, glowing sense of satisfaction still remained from it in his mind.

He chuckled at her look of indignation. "Don't bother being angry at them," he said. "It's no worse than all the rest of what they're doing every day."

"Hank, do you want me to speak to Dr. Stadler about it?"

"Certainly not!"

"He ought to stop it. He could at least do that much."

"I'd rather go to jail. Dr. Stadler? You're not having anything to do with him, are you?"

"I saw him a few days ago."

"Why?"

"In regard to the motor."

"The motor . . . ?" He said it slowly, in a strange way, as if the thought of the motor had suddenly brought back to him a realm he had forgotten. "Dagny . . . the man who invented that motor . . . he did exist, didn't he?"

"Why . . . of course. What do you mean?"

"I mean only that . . . that it's a pleasant thought, isn't it? Even if he's dead now, he was alive once . . . so alive that he designed that motor. . . ."

"What's the matter, Hank?"

"Nothing. Tell me about the motor."

She told him about her meeting with Dr. Stadler. She got up and paced the room, while speaking; she could not lie still, she always felt a surge of hope and of eagerness for action when she dealt with the subject of the motor.

The first thing he noticed were the lights of the city beyond the window: he felt as if they were being turned on, one by one, forming the great skyline he loved; he felt it, even though he knew that the lights had been there all the time. Then he understood that the thing which was returning was within him: the shape coming back drop by drop was his love for the city. Then he knew that it had come back because he was looking at the city past the taut, slender figure of a woman whose head was lifted eagerly as at a sight of distance, whose steps were a restless substitute for flight. He was looking at her as at a stranger, he was barely aware that she was a woman, but the sight was flowing into a feeling the words for which were: *This* is the world and the core of it, this is what made the city—they go together, the angular shapes of the buildings and the angular lines of a face stripped of everything but purpose—the rising steps of steel and the steps of a being intent upon his goal—this is what they had been, all the men who had lived to invent the lights, the steel, the furnaces, the motors—*they* were the world, *they,* not the men who crouched in dark corners, half-begging, half-threatening, boastfully displaying their open sores as their only claim on life and virtue—so long as he knew that there existed one man with the bright courage of a new thought, could he give up the world to those others?—so long as he could find a single sight to give him a life-restoring shot of admiration, could he believe that the world belonged to the sores, the moans and the guns?—the men who invented motors did exist, he would never doubt their reality, it was his vision of them that had made the contrast unbearable, so that even the loathing was the tribute of his loyalty to them and to that world which was theirs and his.

"Darling . . ." he said, "darling . . ." like a man awakening suddenly, when he noticed that she had stopped speaking.

"What's the matter, Hank?" she asked softly.

"Nothing . . . Except that you shouldn't have called Stadler." His face was bright with confidence, his voice sounded amused, protective and gentle; she could discover nothing else, he looked as he had always looked, it was only the note of gentleness that seemed strange and new.

"I kept feeling that I shouldn't have," she said, "but I didn't know why."

"I'll tell you why." He leaned forward. "What he wanted from you was a recognition that he was still the Dr. Robert Stadler he should have been, but wasn't and knew he wasn't. He wanted you to grant him your respect, in spite of and in contradiction to his actions. He wanted you to juggle reality for him, so that his greatness would remain, but the State Science Institute would be wiped out, as if it had never existed—and you're the only one who could do it for him."

"Why I?"

"Because you're the victim."

She looked at him, startled. He spoke intently; he felt a sudden, violent clarity of perception, as if a surge of energy were rushing into the activity of sight, fusing the half-seen and half-grasped into a single shape and direction.

"Dagny, they're doing something that we've never understood. They know something which we don't, but should discover. I can't see it fully yet, but I'm beginning to see parts of it. That looter from the State Science Institute was scared when I refused to help him pretend that he was just an honest buyer of my Metal. He was scared way deep. Of what? I don't know—public opinion was just his name for it, but it's not the full name. Why should he have been scared? He has the guns, the jails, the laws—he could have seized the whole of my mills, if he wished, and nobody would have risen to defend me, and he knew it—so why should he have cared what I thought? But he did. It was I who had to tell him that he wasn't a looter, but my customer and friend. That's what he needed from me. And that's what Dr. Stadler needed from you—it was you who had to act as if he were a great man who had never tried to destroy your rail and my Metal. I don't know what it is that they think they accomplish—but they want us to pretend that we see the world as they pretend they see it. They need some sort of sanction from us. I don't know the nature of that sanction—but, Dagny, I know that if we value our lives, we must not give it to them. If they put you on a torture rack, don't give it to them. Let them destroy your railroad and my mills, but don't give it to them. Because I know this much: I know that that's our only chance."

She had remained standing still before him, looking attentively at the faint outline of some shape she, too, had tried to grasp.

"Yes . . ." she said, "yes, I know what you've seen in them. . . . I've felt it, too—but it's only like something brushing past that's gone before I know I've seen it, like a touch of cold air, and what's left is always the feeling that I should have stopped it. . . . I know that you're right. I can't understand their game, but this much is right: We must not see the world as they want us to see it. It's some sort of fraud, very ancient and very vast—and the key to break it is: to check every premise they teach us, to question every precept, to—"

She whirled to him at a sudden thought, but she cut the motion and the words in the same instant: the next words would have been the ones she did not want to say to him. She stood looking at him with a slow, bright smile of curiosity.

Somewhere within him, he knew the thought she would not name, but he knew it only in that prenatal shape which has to find its words in the future. He did not pause to grasp it now—because in the flooding brightness of what he felt, another thought, which was its predecessor, had become clear to him and had been holding him for many minutes past. He rose, approached her and took her in his arms.

He held the length of her body pressed to his, as if their bodies were two currents rising upward together, each to a single point, each carrying the whole of their consciousness to the meeting of their lips.

What she felt in that moment contained, as one nameless part of it, the knowledge of the beauty in the posture of his body as he held her, as they stood in the middle of a room high above the lights of the city.

What he knew, what he had discovered tonight, was that his recaptured love of existence had not been given back to him by the return of his desire for her—but that the desire had returned after he had regained his world, the love, the value and the sense of his world—and that the desire was not an answer to her body, but a celebration of himself and of his will to live.

He did not know it, he did not think of it, he was past the need of words, but in the moment when he felt the response of her body to his, he felt also the unadmitted knowledge that that which he had called her depravity was her highest virtue—this capacity of hers to feel the joy of being, as he felt it.

THE ARISTOCRACY OF PULL

The calendar in the sky beyond the window of her office said: September 2. Dagny leaned wearily across her desk. The first light to snap on at the approach of dusk was always the ray that hit the calendar; when the white-glowing page appeared above the roofs, it blurred the city, hastening the darkness.

She had looked at that distant page every evening of the months behind her. Your days are numbered, it had seemed to say—as if it were marking a progression toward something it knew, but she didn't. Once, it had clocked her race to build the John Galt Line; now it was clocking her race against an unknown destroyer.

One by one, the men who had built new towns in Colorado, had departed into some silent unknown, from which no voice or person had yet returned. The towns they had left were dying. Some of the factories they built had remained ownerless and locked; others had been seized by the local authorities; the machines in both stood still.

She had felt as if a dark map of Colorado were spread before her like a traffic control panel, with a few lights scattered through its mountains. One after another, the lights had gone out. One after another, the men had vanished. There had been a pattern about it, which she felt, but could not define; she had become able to predict, almost with certainty, who would go next and when; she was unable to grasp the "why?"

Of the men who had once greeted her descent from the cab of an engine on the platform of Wyatt Junction, only Ted Nielsen was left, still running the plant of Nielsen Motors. "Ted, you won't be the next one to go?" she had asked him, on his recent visit to New York; she had asked it, trying to smile. He had answered grimly, "I hope not." "What do you mean, you hope?—aren't you sure?" He had said slowly, heavily, "Dagny, I've always thought that I'd rather die than stop working. But so did the men who're gone. It seems impossible to me that I could ever want to quit. But a year ago, it seemed impossible that they ever could. Those men were my friends. They knew what their going would do to us, the survivors. They would not have gone like that, without a word, leaving to us the added terror of the inexplicable—unless they had some reason of supreme importance. A month ago, Roger Marsh, of Marsh Electric, told me that he'd have himself chained to his desk, so that he wouldn't be able to leave it, no matter what ghastly temptation struck him. He was furious with anger at the men who'd left. He swore to me that he'd never do it. 'And if it's something that I can't resist,' he said, 'I swear that I'll keep enough of my mind to leave you a letter and give you some hint of what it is, so that you won't have to rack your brain in the kind of dread we're both feeling now.' That's what he swore. Two weeks ago, he went. He left me no letter. . . . Dagny, I can't tell what I'll do when I see it—whatever it was that they saw when they went."

It seemed to her that some destroyer was moving soundlessly through the country and the lights were dying at his touch—someone, she thought bitterly, who had reversed the principle of the Twentieth Century motor and was now turning kinetic energy into static.

That was the enemy—she thought, as she sat at her desk in the gathering twilight—with whom she was running a race. The monthly report from Quentin Daniels lay on her desk. She could not be certain, as yet, that Daniels would solve the secret of the motor; but the destroyer, she thought, was moving swiftly, surely, at an ever accelerating tempo; she wondered whether, by the time she rebuilt the motor, there would be any world left to use it.

She had liked Quentin Daniels from the moment he entered her office on their first interview. He was a lanky man in his early thirties, with a homely, angular face and an attractive smile. A hint of the smile remained in his features at all times, particularly when he listened; it was a look of good-natured amusement, as if he were swiftly and patiently discarding the irrelevant in the words he heard and going straight to the point a moment ahead of the speaker.

"Why did you refuse to work for Dr. Stadler?" she asked.

The hint of his smile grew harder and more stressed; this was as near as he came to showing an emotion; the emotion was anger. But he answered in his even, unhurried drawl, "You know, Dr. Stadler once said that the first word of 'Free, scientific inquiry' was redundant. He seems to have forgotten it. Well, I'll just say that 'Governmental scientific inquiry' is a contradiction in terms."

She asked him what position he held at the Utah Institute of Technology. "Night watchman," he answered. *"What?"* she gasped. "Night watchman," he repeated politely, as if she had not caught the words, as if there were no cause for astonishment.

Under her questioning, he explained that he did not like any of the scientific foundations left in existence, that he would have liked a job in the research laboratory of some big industrial concern—"But which one of them can afford to undertake any long-range work nowadays, and why should they?"—so when the Utah Institute of Technology was closed for lack of funds, he had remained there as night watchman and sole inhabitant of the place; the salary was sufficient to pay for his needs—and the Institute's laboratory was there, intact, for his own private, undisturbed use.

"So you're doing research work of your own?"

"That's right."

"For what purpose?"

"For my own pleasure."

"What do you intend to do, if you discover something of scientific importance or commercial value? Do you intend to put it to some public use?"

"I don't know. I don't think so."

"Haven't you any desire to be of service to humanity?"

"I don't talk that kind of language, Miss Taggart. I don't think you do, either."

She laughed. "I think we'll get along together, you and I."

"We will."

When she had told him the story of the motor, when he had studied the manuscript, he made no comment, but merely said that he would take the job on any terms she named.

She asked him to choose his own terms. She protested, in astonishment, against the low monthly salary he quoted. "Miss Taggart," he said, "if there's something that I won't take, it's something for nothing. I don't know how long you might have to pay me, or whether you'll get anything at all in return. I'll gamble on my own mind. I won't let anybody else do it. I don't collect for an intention. But I sure do intend to collect for goods delivered. If I succeed, that's when I'll skin you alive, because what I want then is a percentage, and it's going to be high, but it's going to be worth your while."

When he named the percentage he wanted, she laughed. "That *is* skinning me alive and it *will* be worth my while. Okay."

They agreed that it was to be her private project and that he was to be her private employee; neither of them wanted to have to deal with the interference of the Taggart Research Department. He asked to remain in Utah, in his post of watchman, where he had all the laboratory equipment and all the privacy he needed. The project was to remain confidential between them, until and unless he succeeded.

"Miss Taggart," he said in conclusion, "I don't know how many years it will take me to solve this, if ever. But I know that if I spend the rest of my life on it and succeed, I will die satisfied." He added, "There's only one thing that I want more than to solve it: it's to meet the man who has."

Once a month, since his return to Utah, she had sent him a check and he had sent her a report on his work. It was too early to hope, but his reports were the only bright points in the stagnant fog of her days in the office.

She raised her head, as she finished reading his pages. The calendar in the distance said: September 2. The lights of the city had grown beneath it, spreading and glittering. She thought of Rearden. She wished he were in the city; she wished she would see him tonight.

Then, noticing the date, she remembered suddenly that she had to rush home to dress, because she had to attend Jim's wedding tonight. She had not seen Jim, outside the office, for over a year. She had not met his fiancée, but she had read enough about the engagement in the newspapers. She rose from her desk in wearily distasteful resignation: it seemed easier to attend the wedding than to bother explaining her absence afterwards.

She was hurrying across the concourse of the Terminal when she heard a voice calling, "Miss Taggart!" with a strange note of urgency and reluctance, together. It stopped her abruptly; she took a few seconds to realize that it was the old man at the cigar stand who had called.

"I've been waiting to catch sight of you for days, Miss Taggart. I've been extremely anxious to speak to you." There was an odd expression on his face, the look of an effort not to look frightened.

"I'm sorry," she said, smiling, "I've been rushing in and out of the building all week and didn't have time to stop."

He did not smile. "Miss Taggart, that cigarette with the dollar sign that you gave me some months ago—where did you get it?"

She stood still for a moment. "I'm afraid that's a long, complicated story," she answered.

"Have you any way of getting in touch with the person who gave it to you?"

"I suppose so—though I'm not too sure. Why?"

"Would he tell you where he got it?"

"I don't know. What makes you suspect that he wouldn't?"

He hesitated, then asked, "Miss Taggart, what do you do when you have to tell someone something which you know to be impossible?"

She chuckled. "The man who gave me the cigarette said that in such a case one must check one's premises."

"He did? About the cigarette?"

"Well, no, not exactly. But why? What is it you have to tell me?"

"Miss Taggart, I have inquired all over the world. I have checked every source of information in and about the tobacco industry. I have had that cigarette stub put through a chemical analysis. There is no plant that manufactures that kind of paper. The flavoring elements in that tobacco have never been used in any smoking mixture I could find. That cigarette was machine-made, but it was not made in any factory I know—and I know them all. Miss Taggart, to the best of my knowledge, that cigarette was not made anywhere on earth."

* * *

Rearden stood by, watching absently, while the waiter wheeled the dinner table out of his hotel room. Ken Danagger had left. The room was half-dark; by an unspoken agreement, they had kept the lights low during their dinner, so that Danagger's face would not be noticed and, perhaps, recognized by the waiters.

They had had to meet furtively, like criminals who could not be seen together. They could not meet in their offices or in their homes, only in the crowded anonymity of a city, in his suite at the Wayne-Falkland Hotel. There could be a fine of $10,000 and ten years of imprisonment for each of them, if it became known that he had agreed to deliver to Danagger four thousand tons of structural shapes of Rearden Metal.

They had not discussed that law, at their dinner together, or their motives or the risk they were taking. They had merely talked business. Speaking clearly and dryly, as he always spoke at any conference, Danagger had explained that half of his original order would be sufficient to brace such tunnels as would cave in, if he delayed the bracing much longer, and to recondition the mines of the Confederated Coal Company, gone bankrupt, which he had purchased three weeks ago— "It's an excellent property, but in rotten condition; they had a nasty accident there last month, cave-in and gas explosion, forty men killed." He had added, in the monotone of reciting some impersonal, statistical report, "The newspapers are yelling that coal is now the most crucial commodity in the country. They are also yelling that the coal operators are profiteering on the oil shortage. One gang in Washington is yelling that I am expanding too much and something should be done to stop me, because I am becoming a monopoly. Another gang in Washington is yelling that I am not expanding enough and something should be done to let the government seize my mines, because I am greedy for profits and unwilling to satisfy the public's need of fuel. At my present rate of profit, this Confederated Coal property will bring back the money I spent on it—in forty-seven years. I have no children. I bought it, because there's one customer I don't dare leave without coal —and that's Taggart Transcontinental. I keep thinking of what would happen if the railroads collapsed." He had stopped, then added, "I don't know why I still care about that, but I do. Those people in Washington don't seem to have a clear picture of what that would be like. I have." Rearden had said, "I'll deliver the Metal. When you need the other half of your order, let me know. I'll deliver that, too."

At the end of the dinner, Danagger had said in the same precise, impassive tone, the tone of a man who knows the exact meaning of his words, "If any employee of yours or mine discovers this and attempts private blackmail, I will pay it, within reason. But I will not pay, if he has friends in Washington. If any of those come around, then I go to jail." "Then we go together," Rearden had said.

Standing alone in his half-darkened room, Rearden noted that the prospect of going to jail left him blankly indifferent. He remembered the time when, aged fourteen, faint with hunger, he would not steal fruit from a sidewalk stand. Now, the possibility of being sent to jail—if this dinner was a felony—meant no more to him than the possibility of being run over by a truck: an ugly physical accident without any moral significance.

He thought that he had been made to hide, as a guilty secret, the only business transaction he had enjoyed in a year's work—and that he was hiding, as a guilty secret, his nights with Dagny, the only hours that kept him alive. He felt that there was some connection between the two secrets, some essential connection which he had to discover. He could not grasp it, he could not find the words to name it, but he felt that the day when he would find them, he would answer every question of his life.

He stood against the wall, his head thrown back, his eyes closed, and thought of Dagny, and then he felt that no questions could matter to him any longer. He thought that he would see her tonight, almost hating it, because tomorrow morning seemed so close and then he would have to leave her—he wondered whether he could remain in town tomorrow, or whether he should leave now, without seeing her, so that he could wait, so that he could always have it ahead of him: the moment of closing his hands over her shoulders and looking down at her face. You're going insane, he thought—but he knew that if she were beside him through every hour of his days, it would still be the same, he would never have enough of it, he would have to invent some senseless form of torture for himself in order to bear it—he knew he would see her tonight, and the thought of leaving without it made the pleasure greater, a moment's torture to underscore his certainty of the hours ahead. He would leave the light on in her living room, he thought, and hold her across the bed, and see nothing but the curve of the strip of light running from her waist to her ankle, a single line drawing the whole shape of her long, slim body in the darkness, then he would pull her head into the light, to see her face, to see it falling back, unresisting, her hair over his arm, her eyes closed, the face drawn as in a look of pain, her mouth open to him.

He stood at the wall, waiting, to let all the events of the day drop away from him, to feel free, to know that the next span of time was his.

When the door of his room flew open without warning, he did not quite hear or believe it, at first. He saw the silhouette of a woman, then of a bellboy who put down a suitcase and vanished. The voice he heard was Lillian's: "Why, Henry! All alone and in the dark?"

She pressed a light switch by the door. She stood there, fastidiously groomed, wearing a pale beige traveling suit that looked as if she had traveled under glass; she was smiling and pulling her gloves off with the air of having reached home.

"Are you in for the evening, dear?" she asked. "Or were you going out?"

He did not know how long a time passed before he answered, "What are you doing here?"

"Why, don't you remember that Jim Taggart invited us to his wedding? It's tonight."

"I didn't intend to go to his wedding."

"Oh, but I did!"

"Why didn't you tell me this morning, before I left?"

"To surprise you, darling." She laughed gaily. "It's practically impossible to drag you to any social function, but I thought you might do it like this, on the spur of the moment, just to go out and have a good time, as married couples are supposed to. I thought you wouldn't mind it—you've been staying overnight in New York so often!"

He saw the casual glance thrown at him from under the brim of her fashionably tilted hat. He said nothing.

"Of course, I was running a risk," she said. "You might have been taking somebody out to dinner." He said nothing. "Or were you, perhaps, intending to return home tonight?"

"No."

"Did you have an engagement for this evening?"

"No."

"Fine." She pointed at her suitcase. "I brought my evening clothes. Will you bet me a corsage of orchids that I can get dressed faster than you can?"

He thought that Dagny would be at her brother's wedding tonight; the evening did not matter to him any longer. "I'll take you out, if you wish," he said, "but not to that wedding."

"Oh, but that's where I want to go! It's the most preposterous event of the season, and everybody's been looking forward to it for weeks, all my friends. I wouldn't miss it for the world. There isn't any better show in town—nor better publicized. It's a perfectly ridiculous marriage, but just about what you'd expect from Jim Taggart."

She was moving casually through the room, glancing around, as if getting acquainted with an unfamiliar place. "I haven't been in New York for years," she said. "Not with you, that is. Not on any formal occasion."

He noticed the pause in the aimless wandering of her eyes, a glance that stopped briefly on a filled ashtray and moved on. He felt a stab of revulsion.

She saw it in his face and laughed gaily. "Oh but, darling, I'm not relieved! I'm disappointed. I did hope I'd find a few cigarette butts smeared with lipstick."

He gave her credit for the admission of the spying, even if under cover of a joke. But something in the stressed frankness of her manner made him wonder whether she was joking; for the flash of an instant, he felt that she had told him the truth. He dismissed the impression, because he could not conceive of it as possible.

"I'm afraid that you'll never be human," she said. "So I'm sure that I have no rival. And if I have—which I doubt, darling—I don't think I'll worry about it, because if it's a person who's always available on call, without appointment—well, everybody knows what sort of a person *that* is."

He thought that he would have to be careful; he had been about to slap her face. "Lillian, I think you know," he said, "that humor of this kind is more than I can stand."

"Oh, you're so serious!" she laughed. "I keep forgetting it. You're so serious about everything—particularly yourself."

Then she whirled to him suddenly, her smile gone. She had the strange, pleading look which he had seen in her face at times, a look that seemed made of sincerity and courage:

"You prefer to be serious, Henry? All right. How long do you wish me to exist somewhere in the basement of your life? How lonely do you want me to become? I've asked nothing of you. I've let you live your life as you pleased. Can't you give me one evening? Oh, I know you hate parties and you'll be bored. But it means a great deal to me. Call it empty, social vanity—I want to appear, for once, with my husband. I suppose you never think of it in such terms, but you're an important man, you're envied, hated, respected and feared, you're a man whom any woman would be proud to show off as her husband. You may say it's a low form of feminine ostentation, but that's the form of any woman's happiness. You don't live by such standards, but I do. Can't you give me this much, at the price of a few hours of boredom? Can't you be strong enough to fulfill your obligation and to perform a husband's duty? Can't you go there, not for your own sake, but mine, not because *you* want to go, but only because *I* want it?"

Dagny—he thought desperately—Dagny, who had never said a word about his life at home, who had never made a claim, uttered a reproach or asked a question—he could not appear before her with his wife, he could not let her see him as the husband being proudly shown off—he wished he could die now, in this moment, before he committed this action—because he knew that he would commit it.

Because he had accepted his secret as guilt and promised himself to take its consequences—because he had granted that the right was with Lillian, and he was able to bear any form of damnation, but not able to deny the right when it was claimed of him—because he knew that the reason for his refusal to go, was the reason that gave him no right to refuse—because he heard the pleading cry in his mind: "Oh God, Lillian, anything but that party!" and he did not allow himself to beg for mercy—

—he said evenly, his voice lifeless and firm:

"All right, Lillian. I'll go."

* * *

The wedding veil of rose-point lace caught on the splintered floor of her tenement bedroom. Cherryl Brooks lifted it cautiously, stepping to look at herself in a crooked mirror that hung on the wall. She had been photographed here all day, as she had been many times in the past two months. She still smiled with incredulous gratitude when newspaper people wanted to take her picture, but she wished they would not do it so often.

An aging sob sister, who had a drippy love column in print and the bitter wisdom of a policewoman in person, had taken Cherryl under her protection weeks ago, when the girl had first been thrown into press interviews as into a meat grinder. Today, the sob sister had chased the reporters out, had snapped, "All right, all right, beat it!" at the neighbors, had slammed Cherryl's door in their faces and had helped her to dress. She was to drive Cherryl to the wedding; she had discovered that there was no one else to do it.

The wedding veil, the white satin gown, the delicate slippers and the strand of pearls at her throat, had cost five hundred times the price of the entire contents of Cherryl's room. A bed took most of the room's space, and the rest was taken by a chest of drawers, one chair, and her few dresses hanging behind a faded curtain. The huge hoop skirt of the wedding gown brushed against the walls when she moved, her slender figure swaying above the skirt in the dramatic contrast of a tight, severe, long-sleeved bodice; the gown had been made by the best designer in the city.

"You see, when I got the job in the dime store, I could have moved to a better room," she said to the sob sister, in apology, "but I don't think it matters much where you sleep at night, so I saved my money, because I'll need it for something important in the future—" She stopped and smiled, shaking her head dazedly. "I *thought* I'd need it," she said.

"You look fine," said the sob sister. "You can't see much in that alleged mirror, but you're okay."

"The way all this happened, I . . . I haven't had time to catch up with myself. But you see, Jim is wonderful. He doesn't mind it, that I'm only a salesgirl from a dime store, living in a place like this. He doesn't hold it against me."

"Uh-huh," said the sob sister; her face looked grim.

Cherryl remembered the wonder of the first time Jim Taggart had come here. He had come one evening, without warning, a month after their first meeting, when she had given up hope of ever seeing him again. She had been miserably embarrassed, she had felt as if she were trying to hold a sunrise within the space of a mud puddle—but Jim had smiled, sitting on her only chair, looking at her flushed face and at her room. Then he had told her to put on her coat, and he had taken her to dinner at the most expensive restaurant in the city. He had smiled at her uncertainty, at her awkwardness, at her terror of picking the wrong fork, and at the look of enchantment in her eyes. She had not known what he thought. But he had known that she was stunned, not by the place, but by his bringing her there, that she barely touched the costly food, that she took the dinner, not as booty from a rich sucker—as all the girls he knew would have taken it—but as some shining award she had never expected to deserve.

He had come back to her two weeks later, and then their dates had grown progressively more frequent. He would drive up to the dime store at the closing hour, and she would see her fellow salesgirls gaping at her, at his limousine, at the uniformed chauffeur who opened the door for her. He would take her to the best night clubs, and when he introduced her to his friends, he would say, "Miss Brooks works in the dime store in Madison Square." She would see the strange expressions on their faces and Jim watching them with a hint of mockery in his eyes. He wanted to spare her the need of pretense or embarrassment, she thought with gratitude. He had the strength to be honest and not to care whether others approved of him or not, she thought with admiration. But she felt an odd, burning pain, new to her, the night she heard some woman, who worked for a highbrow political magazine, say to her companion at the next table, "How generous of Jim!"

Had he wished, she would have given him the only kind of payment she could offer in return. She was grateful that he did not seek it. But she felt as if their relationship was an immense debt and she had nothing to pay it with, except her silent worship. He did not need her worship, she thought.

There were evenings when he came to take her out, but remained in her room, instead, and talked to her, while she listened in silence. It always happened unexpectedly, with a kind of peculiar abruptness, as if he had not intended doing it, but something burst within him and he had to speak. Then he sat slumped on her bed, unaware of his surroundings and of her presence, yet his eyes jerked to her face once in a while, as if he had to be certain that a living being heard him.

". . . it wasn't for myself, it wasn't for myself at all—why won't they believe me, those people? I had to grant the unions' demands to cut down the trains—and the moratorium on bonds was the only way I could do it, so that's why Wesley gave it to me, for the workers, not for myself. All the newspapers said that I was a great example for all businessmen to follow—a businessman with a sense of social responsibility. That's what they said. It's true, isn't it? . . . Isn't it? . . .

What was wrong about that moratorium? What if we did skip a few technicalities? It was for a good purpose. Everyone agrees that anything you do is good, so long as it's not for yourself. . . . But she won't give me credit for a good purpose. She doesn't think anybody's any good except herself. My sister is a ruthless, conceited bitch, who won't take anyone's ideas but her own. . . . Why do they keep looking at me that way—she and Rearden and all those people? Why are they so sure they're right? . . . If I acknowledge their superiority in the material realm, why don't they acknowledge mine in the spiritual? They have the brain, but I have the heart. They have the capacity to produce wealth, but I have the capacity to love. Isn't mine the greater capacity? Hasn't it been recognized as the greatest through all the centuries of human history? Why won't *they* recognize it? . . . Why are they so sure they're great? . . . And if they're great and I'm not —isn't that exactly why they should bow to me, because I'm not? Wouldn't that be an act of true humanity? It takes no kindness to respect a man who deserves respect—it's only a payment which he's earned. To give an unearned respect is the supreme gesture of charity. . . . But they're incapable of charity. They're not human. They feel no concern for anyone's need . . . or weakness. No concern . . . and no pity . . ."

She could understand little of it, but she understood that he was unhappy and that somebody had hurt him. He saw the pain of tenderness in her face, the pain of indignation against his enemies, and he saw the glance intended for heroes—given to him by a person able to experience the emotion behind that glance.

She did not know why she felt certain that she was the only one to whom he could confess his torture. She took it as a special honor, as one more gift.

The only way to be worthy of him, she thought, was never to ask him for anything. He offered her money once, and she refused it, with such a bright, painful flare of anger in her eyes that he did not attempt it again. The anger was at herself: she wondered whether she had done something to make him think she was that kind of person. But she did not want to be ungrateful for his concern, or to embarrass him by her ugly poverty; she wanted to show him her eagerness to rise and justify his favor; so she told him that he could help her, if he wished, by helping her to find a better job. He did not answer. In the weeks that followed, she waited, but he never mentioned the subject. She blamed herself: she thought that she had offended him, that he had taken it as an attempt to use him.

When he gave her an emerald bracelet, she was too shocked to understand. Trying desperately not to hurt him, she pleaded that she could not accept it. "Why not?" he asked. "It isn't as if you were a bad woman paying the usual price for it. Are you afraid that I'll start making demands? Don't you trust me?" He laughed aloud at her

stammering embarrassment. He smiled, with an odd kind of enjoyment, all through the evening when they went to a night club and she
wore the bracelet with her shabby black dress.

He made her wear that bracelet again, on the night when he took
her to a party, a great reception given by Mrs. Cornelius Pope. If he
considered her good enough to bring into the home of his friends, she
thought—the illustrious friends whose names she had seen on the inaccessible mountain peaks that were the society columns of the newspapers—she could not embarrass him by wearing her old dress. She
spent her year's savings on an evening gown of bright green chiffon with
a low neckline, a belt of yellow roses and a rhinestone buckle. When
she entered the stern residence, with the cold, brilliant lights and a terrace suspended over the roofs of skyscrapers, she knew that her dress
was wrong for the occasion, though she could not tell why. But she
kept her posture proudly straight and she smiled with the courageous
trust of a kitten when it sees a hand extended to play: people gathered
to have a good time would not hurt anyone, she thought.

At the end of an hour, her attempt to smile had become a helpless,
bewildered plea. Then the smile went, as she watched the people
around her. She saw that the trim, confident girls had a nasty insolence
of manner when they spoke to Jim, as if they did not respect him
and never had. One of them in particular, a Betty Pope, the daughter
of the hostess, kept making remarks to him which Cherryl could not
understand, because she could not believe that she understood them
correctly.

No one had paid any attention to her, at first, except for a few
astonished glances at her gown. After a while, she saw them looking at
her. She heard an elderly woman ask Jim, in the anxious tone of re-
ferring to some distinguished family she had missed knowing, "Did you
say Miss Brooks of Madison Square?" She saw an odd smile on Jim's
face, when he answered, making his voice sound peculiarly clear, "Yes
—the cosmetics counter of Raleigh's Five and Ten." Then she saw some
people becoming too polite to her, and others moving away in a
pointed manner, and most of them being senselessly awkward in simple
bewilderment, and Jim watching silently with that odd smile.

She tried to get out of the way, out of their notice. As she slipped
by, along the edge of the room, she heard some man say, with a shrug,
"Well, Jim Taggart is one of the most powerful men in Washington at
the moment." He did not say it respectfully.

Out on the terrace, where it was darker, she heard two men talking
and wondered why she felt certain that they were talking about her.
One of them said, "Taggart can afford to do it, if he pleases," and the
other said something about the horse of some Roman emperor named
Caligula.

She looked at the lone straight shaft of the Taggart Building rising
in the distance—and then she thought that she understood: these peo-

ple hated Jim because they envied him. Whatever they were, she thought, whatever their names and their money, none of them had an achievement comparable to his, none of them had defied the whole country to build a railroad everybody thought impossible. For the first time, she saw that she did have something to offer Jim: these people were as mean and small as the people from whom she had escaped in Buffalo; he was as lonely as she had always been, and the sincerity of her feeling was the only recognition he had found.

Then she walked back into the ballroom, cutting straight through the crowd, and the only thing left of the tears she had tried to hold back in the darkness of the terrace, was the fiercely luminous sparkle of her eyes. If he wished to stand by her openly, even though she was only a shopgirl, if he wished to flaunt it, if he had brought her here to face the indignation of his friends—then it was the gesture of a courageous man defying their opinion, and she was willing to match his courage by serving as the scarecrow of the occasion.

But she was glad when it was over, when she sat beside him in his car, driving home through the darkness. She felt a bleak kind of relief. Her battling defiance ebbed into a strange, desolate feeling; she tried not to give way to it. Jim said little; he sat looking sullenly out the car window; she wondered whether she had disappointed him in some manner.

On the stoop of her rooming house, she said to him forlornly, "I'm sorry if I let you down . . ."

He did not answer for a moment, and then he asked, "What would you say if I asked you to marry me?"

She looked at him, she looked around them—there was a filthy mattress hanging on somebody's window sill, a pawnshop across the street, a garbage pail at the stoop beside them—one did not ask such a question in such a place, she did not know what it meant, and she answered, "I guess I . . . I haven't any sense of humor."

"This is a proposal, my dear."

Then this was the way they reached their first kiss—with tears running down her face, tears unshed at the party, tears of shock, of happiness, of thinking that this should be happiness, and of a low, desolate voice telling her that this was not the way she would have wanted it to happen.

She had not thought about the newspapers, until the day when Jim told her to come to his apartment and she found it crowded with people who had notebooks, cameras and flash bulbs. When she saw her picture in the papers for the first time—a picture of them together, Jim's arm around her—she giggled with delight and wondered proudly whether every person in the city had seen it. After a while, the delight vanished.

They kept photographing her at the dime-store counter, in the subway, on the stoop of the tenement house, in her miserable room. She would have taken money from Jim now and run to hide in some obscure hotel for the weeks of their engagement—but he did not offer it. He seemed to want her to remain where she was. They printed pictures of Jim at his desk, in the concourse of the Taggart Terminal, by the steps of his private railway car, at a formal banquet in Washington. The huge spreads of full newspaper pages, the articles in magazines, the radio voices, the newsreels, all were a single, long, sustained scream—about the "Cinderella Girl" and the "Democratic Businessman."

She told herself not to be suspicious, when she felt uneasy; she told herself not to be ungrateful, when she felt hurt. She felt it only in a few rare moments, when she awakened in the middle of the night and lay in the silence of her room, unable to sleep. She knew that it would take her years to recover, to believe, to understand. She was reeling through her days like a person with a sunstroke, seeing nothing but the figure of Jim Taggart as she had seen him first on the night of his great triumph.

"Listen, kid," the sob sister said to her, when she stood in her room for the last time, the lace of the wedding veil streaming like crystal foam from her hair to the blotched planks of the floor. "You think that if one gets hurt in life, it's through one's own sins—and that's true, in the long run. But there are people who'll try to hurt you through the good they see in you—knowing that it's the good, needing it and punishing you for it. Don't let it break you when you discover that."

"I don't think I'm afraid," she said, looking intently straight before her, the radiance of her smile melting the earnestness of her glance. "I have no right to be afraid of anything. I'm too happy. You see, I always thought that there wasn't any sense in people saying that all you can do in life is suffer. I wasn't going to knuckle down to that and give up. I thought that things could happen which were beautiful and very great. I didn't expect it to happen to me—not so much and so soon. But I'll try to live up to it."

* * *

"Money is the root of all evil," said James Taggart. "Money can't buy happiness. Love will conquer any barrier and any social distance. That may be a bromide, boys, but that's how I feel."

He stood under the lights of the ballroom of the Wayne-Falkland Hotel, in a circle of reporters who had closed about him the moment the wedding ceremony ended. He heard the crowd of guests beating like a tide beyond the circle. Cherryl stood beside him, her white-gloved hand on the black of his sleeve. She was still trying to hear the words of the ceremony, not quite believing that she had heard them.

"How do you feel, *Mrs. Taggart?*"

She heard the question from somewhere in the circle of reporters. It was like the jolt of returning to consciousness: two words suddenly made everything real to her. She smiled and whispered, choking, "I . . . I'm very happy . . ."

At opposite ends of the ballroom, Orren Boyle, who seemed too stout for his full-dress clothes, and Bertram Scudder, who seemed too meager for his, surveyed the crowd of guests with the same thought, though neither of them admitted that he was thinking it. Orren Boyle half-told himself that he was looking for the faces of friends, and Bertram Scudder suggested to himself that he was gathering material for an article. But both, unknown to each other, were drawing a mental chart of the faces they saw, classifying them under two headings which, if named, would have read: "Favor" and "Fear." There were men whose presence signified a special protection extended to James Taggart, and men whose presence confessed a desire to avoid his hostility—those who represented a hand lowered to pull him up, and those who represented a back bent to let him climb. By the unwritten code of the day, nobody received or accepted an invitation from a man of public prominence except in token of one or the other of these motives. Those in the first group were, for the most part, youthful; they had come from Washington. Those in the second group were older; they were businessmen.

Orren Boyle and Bertram Scudder were men who used words as a public instrument, to be avoided in the privacy of one's own mind. Words were a commitment, carrying implications which they did not wish to face. They needed no words for their chart; the classification was done by physical means: a respectful movement of their eyebrows, equivalent to the emotion of the word "So!" for the first group—and a sarcastic movement of their lips, equivalent to the emotion of "Well, well!" for the second. One face blew up the smooth working of their calculating mechanisms for a moment: when they saw the cold blue eyes and blond hair of Hank Rearden, their muscles tore at the register of the second group in the equivalent of "Oh, boy!" The sum of the chart was an estimate of James Taggart's power. It added up to an impressive total.

They knew that James Taggart was fully aware of it, when they saw him moving among his guests. He walked briskly, in a Morse code pattern of short dashes and brief stops, with a manner of faint irritation, as if conscious of the number of people whom his displeasure might worry. The hint of a smile on his face had a flavor of gloating— as if he knew that the act of coming to honor him was an act that disgraced the men who had come; as if he knew and enjoyed it.

A tail of figures kept trailing and shifting behind him, as if their function were to give him the pleasure of ignoring them. Mr. Mowen flickered briefly among the tail, and Dr. Pritchett, and Balph Eubank.

The most persistent one was Paul Larkin. He kept describing circles around Taggart, as if trying to acquire a suntan by means of an occasional ray, his wistful smile pleading to be noticed.

Taggart's eyes swept over the crowd once in a while, swiftly and furtively, in the manner of a prowler's flashlight; this, in the muscular shorthand legible to Orren Boyle, meant that Taggart was looking for someone and did not want anyone to know it. The search ended when Eugene Lawson came to shake Taggart's hand and to say, his wet lower lip twisting like a cushion to soften the blow, "Mr. Mouch couldn't come, Jim, Mr. Mouch is so sorry, he had a special plane chartered, but at the last minute things came up, crucial national problems, you know." Taggart stood still, did not answer and frowned.

Orren Boyle burst out laughing. Taggart turned to him so sharply that the others melted away without waiting for a command to vanish.

"What do you think you're doing?" snapped Taggart.

"Having a good time, Jimmy, just having a good time," said Boyle. "Wesley is *your* boy, *wasn't* he?"

"I know somebody who's my boy and he'd better not forget it."

"Who? Larkin? Well, no, I don't think you're talking about Larkin. And if it's not Larkin that you're talking about, why then I think you ought to be careful in your use of the possessive pronouns. I don't mind the age classification, I know I look young for my years, but I'm just allergic to pronouns."

"That's very smart, but you're going to get too smart one of these days."

"If I do, you just go ahead and make the most of it, Jimmy. *If.*"

"The trouble with people who overreach themselves is that they have short memories. You'd better remember who got Rearden Metal choked off the market for you "

"Why, I remember who promised to. That was the party who then pulled every string he could lay his hands on to try to prevent that particular directive from being issued, because he figured he might need rail of Rearden Metal in the future."

"Because *you* spent ten thousand dollars pouring liquor into people you hoped would prevent the directive about the bond moratorium!"

"That's right. So I did. I had friends who had railroad bonds. And besides, I have friends in Washington, too, Jimmy. Well, your friends beat mine on that moratorium business, but mine beat yours on Rearden Metal—and I'm not forgetting it. But what the hell!—it's all right with me, that's the way to share things around, only don't you try to fool *me*, Jimmy. Save the act for the suckers."

"If you don't believe that I've always tried to do my best for you—"

"Sure, you have. The best that could be expected, all things considered. And you'll continue to do it, too, so long as I've got somebody you need—and not a minute longer. So I just wanted to remind you that I've got my own friends in Washington. Friends that money can't buy—just like yours, Jimmy."

"What do you think you mean?"

"Just what you're thinking. The ones you buy aren't really worth a damn, because somebody can always offer them more, so the field's wide open to anybody and it's just like old-fashioned competition again. But if you get the goods on a man, then you've got him, then there's no higher bidder and you can count on his friendship. Well, you have friends, and so have I. You have friends I can use, and vice versa. That's all right with me—what the hell!—one's got to trade something. If we don't trade money—and the age of money is past—then we trade men."

"What is it you're driving at?"

"Why, I'm just telling you a few things that you ought to remember. Now take Wesley, for instance. You promised him the assistant's job in the Bureau of National Planning—for double-crossing Rearden, at the time of the Equalization of Opportunity Bill. You had the connections to do it, and that's what I asked you to do—in exchange for the Anti-dog-eat-dog Rule, where I had the connections. So Wesley did his part, and you saw to it that you got it all on paper—oh sure, I know that you've got written proof of the kind of deals he pulled to help pass that bill, while he was taking Rearden's money to defeat it and keeping Rearden off guard. They were pretty ugly deals. It would be pretty messy for Mr. Mouch, if it all came out in public. So you kept your promise and you got the job for him, because you thought you had him. And so you did. And he paid off pretty handsomely, didn't he? But it works only just so long. After a while, Mr. Wesley Mouch might get to be so powerful and the scandal so old, that nobody will care how he got his start or whom he double-crossed. Nothing lasts forever. Wesley was Rearden's man, and then he was your man, and he might be somebody else's man tomorrow "

"Are you giving me a hint?"

"Why no, I'm giving you a friendly warning. We're old friends, Jimmy, and I think that that's what we ought to remain. I think we can be very useful to each other, you and I, if you don't start getting the wrong ideas about friendship. Me—I believe in a balance of power."

"Did *you* prevent Mouch from coming here tonight?"

"Well, maybe I did and maybe I didn't. I'll let you worry about it. That's good for me, if I did—and still better, if I didn't."

Cherryl's eyes followed James Taggart through the crowd. The faces that kept shifting and gathering around her seemed so friendly and their voices were so eagerly warm that she felt certain there was no malice anywhere in the room. She wondered why some of them talked to her about Washington, in a hopeful, confidential manner of half-sentences, half-hints, as if they were seeking her help for something secret she was supposed to understand. She did not know what to say, but she smiled and answered whatever she pleased. She could not disgrace the person of "Mrs. Taggart" by any touch of fear.

Then she saw the enemy. It was a tall, slender figure in a gray evening gown, who was now her sister-in-law.

The pressure of anger in Cherryl's mind was the stored accumulation of the sounds of Jim's tortured voice. She felt the nagging pull of a duty left undone. Her eyes kept returning to the enemy and studying her intently. The pictures of Dagny Taggart in the newspapers had shown a figure dressed in slacks, or a face with a slanting hat brim and a raised coat collar. Now she wore a gray evening gown that seemed indecent, because it looked austerely modest, so modest that it vanished from one's awareness and left one too aware of the slender body it pretended to cover. There was a tone of blue in the gray cloth that went with the gun-metal gray of her eyes. She wore no jewelry, only a bracelet on her wrist, a chain of heavy metal links with a green-blue cast.

Cherryl waited, until she saw Dagny standing alone, then tore forward, cutting resolutely across the room. She looked at close range into the gun-metal eyes that seemed cold and intense at once, the eyes that looked at her directly with a polite, impersonal curiosity.

"There's something I want you to know," said Cherryl, her voice taut and harsh, "so that there won't be any pretending about it. I'm not going to put on the sweet relative act. I know what you've done to Jim and how you've made him miserable all his life. I'm going to protect him against you. I'll put you in your place. *I'm* Mrs. Taggart. I'm the woman in this family now."

"That's quite all right," said Dagny. "I'm the man."

Cherryl watched her walk away, and thought that Jim had been right: this sister of his was a creature of cold evil who had given her no response, no acknowledgment, no emotion of any kind except a touch of something that looked like an astonished, indifferent amusement.

Rearden stood by Lillian's side and followed her when she moved. She wished to be seen with her husband; he was complying. He did not know whether anyone looked at him or not; he was aware of no one around them, except the person whom he could not permit himself to see.

The image still holding his consciousness was the moment when he had entered this room with Lillian and had seen Dagny looking at them. He had looked straight at her, prepared to accept any blow her eyes would choose to give him. Whatever the consequences to Lillian, he would have confessed his adultery publicly, there and in that moment, rather than commit the unspeakable act of evading Dagny's eyes, of closing his face into a coward's blankness, of pretending to her that he did not know the nature of his action.

But there had been no blow. He knew every shade of sensation ever reflected in Dagny's face; he had known that she had felt no shock; he had seen nothing but an untouched serenity. Her eyes had moved to his, as if acknowledging the full meaning of this encounter, but looking at him as she would have looked anywhere, as she looked at him in his office or in her bedroom. It had seemed to him that she had stood before them both, at the distance of a few steps, revealed to them as simply and openly as the gray dress revealed her body.

She had bowed to them, the courteous movement of her head including them both. He had answered, he had seen Lillian's brief nod, and then he had seen Lillian moving away and realized that he had stood with his head bowed for a long moment.

He did not know what Lillian's friends were saying to him or what he was answering. As a man goes step by step, trying not to think of the length of a hopeless road, so he went moment by moment, keeping no imprint of anything in his mind. He heard snatches of Lillian's pleased laughter and a tone of satisfaction in her voice.

After a while, he noticed the women around him; they all seemed to resemble Lillian, with the same look of static grooming, with thin eyebrows plucked to a static lift and eyes frozen in static amusement. He noticed that they were trying to flirt with him, and that Lillian watched it as if she were enjoying the hopelessness of their attempts. This, then —he thought—was the happiness of feminine vanity which she had begged him to give her, these were the standards which he did not live by, but had to consider. He turned for escape to a group of men.

He could not find a single straight statement in the conversation of the men; whatever subject they seemed to be talking about never seemed to be the subject they were actually discussing. He listened like a foreigner who recognized some of the words, but could not connect them into sentences. A young man, with a look of alcoholic insolence, staggered past the group and snapped, chuckling, "Learned your lesson, Rearden?" He did not know what the young rat had meant; everybody else seemed to know it; they looked shocked and secretly pleased.

Lillian drifted away from him, as if letting him understand that she did not insist upon his literal attendance. He retreated to a corner of the room where no one would see him or notice the direction of his eyes. Then he permitted himself to look at Dagny.

He watched the gray dress, the shifting movement of the soft cloth when she walked, the momentary pauses sculptured by the cloth, the shadows and the light. He saw it as a bluish-gray smoke held shaped for an instant into a long curve that slanted forward to her knee and back to the tip of her sandal. He knew every facet the light would shape if the smoke were ripped away.

He felt a murky, twisting pain: it was jealousy of every man who spoke to her. He had never felt it before; but he felt it here, where everyone had the right to approach her, except himself.

Then, as if a single, sudden blow to his brain blasted a moment's shift of perspective, he felt an immense astonishment at what he was doing here and why. He lost, for that moment, all the days and dogmas of his past; his concepts, his problems, his pain were wiped out; he knew only—as from a great, clear distance—that man exists for the achievement of his desires, and he wondered why he stood here, he wondered who had the right to demand that he waste a single irreplaceable hour of his life, when his only desire was to seize the slender figure in gray and hold her through the length of whatever time there was left for him to exist.

In the next moment, he felt the shudder of recapturing his mind. He felt the tight, contemptuous movement of his lips pressed together in token of the words he cried to himself: You made a contract once, now stick to it. And then he thought suddenly that in business transactions the courts of law did not recognize a contract wherein no valuable consideration had been given by one party to the other. He wondered what made him think of it. The thought seemed irrelevant. He did not pursue it.

James Taggart saw Lillian Rearden drift casually toward him at the one moment when he chanced to be alone in the dim corner between a potted palm and a window. He stopped and waited to let her approach. He could not guess her purpose, but this was the manner which, in the çode he understood, meant that he had better hear her.

"How do you like my wedding gift, Jim?" she asked, and laughed at his look of embarrassment. "No, no, don't try to go over the list of things in your apartment, wondering which one the hell it was. It's not in your apartment, it's right here, and it's a non-material gift, darling."

He saw the half-hint of a smile on her face, the look understood among his friends as an invitation to share a secret victory; it was the look, not of having outthought, but of having outsmarted somebody. He answered cautiously, with a safely pleasant smile, "Your presence is the best gift you could give me."

"*My* presence, Jim?"

The lines of his face were shock-bound for a moment. He knew what she meant, but he had not expected her to mean it.

She smiled openly. "We both know whose presence is the most valuable one for you tonight—and the unexpected one. Didn't you really think of giving me credit for it? I'm surprised at you. I thought you had a genius for recognizing potential friends."

He would not commit himself; he kept his voice carefully neutral. "Have I failed to appreciate your friendship, Lillian?"

"Now, now, darling, you know what I'm talking about. You didn't expect *him* to come here, you didn't really think that *he* is afraid of you, did you? But to have the others think he is—that's quite an inestimable advantage, isn't it?"

"I'm . . . surprised, Lillian."

"Shouldn't you say 'impressed'? Your guests are quite impressed. I can practically hear them thinking all over the room. Most of them are thinking: 'If *he* has to seek terms with Jim Taggart, we'd better toe the line.' And a few are thinking: 'If *he's* afraid, we'll get away with much more.' This is as you want it, of course—and I wouldn't think of spoiling your triumph—but you and I are the only ones who know that you didn't achieve it single-handed."

He did not smile; he asked, his face blank, his voice smooth, but with a carefully measured hint of harshness, "What's your angle?"

She laughed. "Essentially—the same as yours, Jim. But speaking practically—none at all. It's just a favor I've done you, and I need no favor in return. Don't worry, I'm not lobbying for any special interests, I'm not after squeezing some particular directive out of Mr. Mouch, I'm not even after a diamond tiara from you. Unless, of course, it's a tiara of a non-material order, such as your appreciation."

He looked straight at her for the first time, his eyes narrowed, his face relaxed to the same half-smile as hers, suggesting the expression which, for both of them, meant that they felt at home with each other: an expression of contempt. "You know that I have always admired you, Lillian, as one of the truly superior women."

"I'm aware of it." There was the faintest coating of mockery spread, like shellac, over the smooth notes of her voice.

He was studying her insolently. "You must forgive me if I think that some curiosity is permissible between friends," he said, with no tone of apology. "I'm wondering from what angle you contemplate the possibility of certain financial burdens—or losses—which affect your own personal interests."

She shrugged. "From the angle of a horsewoman, darling. If you had the most powerful horse in the world, you would keep it bridled down to the gait required to carry you in comfort, even though this meant the sacrifice of its full capacity, even though its top speed would never be seen and its great power would be wasted. You would do it—because if you let the horse go full blast, it would throw you off in no time. . . . However, financial aspects are not my chief concern —nor yours, Jim."

"I did underestimate you," he said slowly.

"Oh, well, that's an error I'm willing to help you correct. I know the sort of problem *he* presents to you. I know why you're afraid of him, as you have good reason to be. But . . . well, you're in business and in politics, so I'll try to say it in your language. A businessman says that he can deliver the goods, and a ward heeler says that he can deliver the vote, is that right? Well, what I wanted you to know is that I can deliver *him,* any time I choose. You may act accordingly."

In the code of his friends, to reveal any part of one's self was to give a weapon to an enemy—but he signed her confession and matched it, when he said, "I wish I were as smart about my sister."

She looked at him without astonishment; she did not find the words irrelevant. "Yes, *there's* a tough one," she said. "No vulnerable point? No weaknesses?"

"None."

"No love affairs?"

"God, no!"

She shrugged, in sign of changing the subject; Dagny Taggart was a person on whom she did not care to dwell. "I think I'll let you run along, so that you can chat a little with Balph Eubank," she said. "He looks worried, because you haven't looked at him all evening and he's wondering whether literature will be left without a friend at court."

"Lillian, you're wonderful!" he said quite spontaneously.

She laughed. "That, my dear, is the non-material tiara I wanted!"

The remnant of a smile stayed on her face as she moved through the crowd, a fluid smile that ran softly into the look of tension and boredom worn by all the faces around her. She moved at random, enjoying the sense of being seen, her eggshell satin gown shimmering like heavy cream with the motion of her tall figure.

It was the green-blue spark that caught her attention: it flashed for an instant under the lights, on the wrist of a thin, naked arm. Then she saw the slender body, the gray dress, the fragile, naked shoulders. She stopped. She looked at the bracelet, frowning.

Dagny turned at her approach. Among the many things that Lillian resented, the impersonal politeness of Dagny's face was the one she resented most.

"What do you think of your brother's marriage, Miss Taggart?" she asked casually, smiling.

"I have no opinion about it."

"Do you mean to say that you don't find it worthy of any thought?"

"If you wish to be exact—yes, that's what I mean."

"Oh, but don't you see any human significance in it?"

"No."

"Don't you think that a person such as your brother's bride does deserve some interest?"

"Why, no."

"I envy you, Miss Taggart. I envy your Olympian detachment. It is, I think, the secret of why lesser mortals can never hope to equal your success in the field of business. They allow their attention to be divided—at least to the extent of acknowledging achievements in other fields."

"What achievements are we talking about?"

"Don't you grant any recognition at all to the women who attain unusual heights of conquest, not in the industrial, but in the human realm?"

"I don't think that there is such a word as 'conquest'—in the human realm."

"Oh, but consider, for instance, how hard other women would have had to work—if work were the only means available to them—to achieve what this girl has achieved through the person of your brother."

"I don't think she knows the exact nature of what she has achieved."

Rearden saw them together. He approached. He felt that he had to hear it, no matter what the consequences. He stopped silently beside them. He did not know whether Lillian was aware of his presence; he knew that Dagny was.

"Do show a little generosity toward her, Miss Taggart," said Lillian. "At least, the generosity of attention. You must not despise the women who do not possess your brilliant talent, but who exercise their own particular endowments. Nature always balances her gifts and offers compensations—don't you think so?"

"I'm not sure I understand you."

"Oh, I'm sure you don't want to hear me become more explicit!"

"Why, yes, I do."

Lillian shrugged angrily; among the women who were her friends, she would have been understood and stopped long ago; but this was an adversary new to her—a woman who refused to be hurt. She did not care to speak more clearly, but she saw Rearden looking at her. She smiled and said, "Well, consider your sister-in-law, Miss Taggart. What chance did she have to rise in the world? None—by your exacting standards. She could not have made a successful career in business. She does not possess your unusual mind. Besides, men would have made it impossible for her. They would have found her too attractive. So she took advantage of the fact that men have standards which, unfortunately, are not as high as yours. She resorted to talents which, I'm sure, you despise. You have never cared to compete with us lesser women in the sole field of our ambition—in the achievement of power over men."

"If you call it power, Mrs. Rearden—then, no, I haven't."

She turned to go, but Lillian's voice stopped her: "I would like to believe that you're fully consistent, Miss Taggart, and fully devoid of human frailties. I would like to believe that you've never felt the desire to flatter—or to offend—anyone. But I see that you expected both Henry and me to be here tonight."

"Why, no, I can't say that I did, I had not seen my brother's guest list."

"Then why are you wearing that bracelet?"

Dagny's eyes moved deliberately straight to hers. "I always wear it."

"Don't you think that that's carrying a joke too far?"

"It was never a joke, Mrs. Rearden."

"Then you'll understand me if I say that I'd like you to give that bracelet back to me."

"I understand you. But I will not give it back."

Lillian let a moment pass, as if to let them both acknowledge the meaning of their silence. For once, she held Dagny's glance without smiling. "What do you expect me to think, Miss Taggart?"

"Anything you wish."

"What is your motive?"

"You knew my motive when you gave me the bracelet."

Lillian glanced at Rearden. His face was expressionless; she saw no reaction, no hint of intention to help her or stop her, nothing but an attentiveness that made her feel as if she were standing in a spotlight.

Her smile came back, as a protective shield, an amused, patronizing smile, intended to convert the subject into a drawing-room issue again. "I'm sure, Miss Taggart, that you realize how enormously improper this is."

"No."

"But surely you know that you are taking a dangerous and ugly risk."

"No."

"You do not take into consideration the possibility of being . . . misunderstood?"

"No."

Lillian shook her head in smiling reproach. "Miss Taggart, don't you think that this is a case where one cannot afford to indulge in abstract theory, but must consider practical reality?"

Dagny would not smile. "I have never understood what is meant by a statement of that kind."

"I mean that your attitude may be highly idealistic—as I am sure it is—but, unfortunately, most people do not share your lofty frame of mind and will misinterpret your action in the one manner which would be most abhorrent to you."

"Then the responsibility and the risk will be theirs, not mine."

"I admire your . . . no, I must not say 'innocence,' but shall I say 'purity?' You have never thought of it, I'm sure, but life is not as straight and logical as . . . as a railroad track. It is regrettable, but possible, that your high intentions may lead people to suspect things which . . . well, which I'm sure you know to be of a sordid and scandalous nature."

Dagny was looking straight at her. "I don't."

"But you cannot ignore that possibility."

"I do." Dagny turned to go.

"Oh, but should you wish to evade a discussion if you have nothing to hide?" Dagny stopped. "And if your brilliant—and reckless—courage permits you to gamble with your reputation, should you ignore the danger to Mr. Rearden?"

Dagny asked slowly, "What is the danger to Mr. Rearden?"

"I'm sure you understand me."

"I don't."

"Oh, but surely it isn't necessary to be more explicit."

"It is—if you wish to continue this discussion."

Lillian's eyes went to Rearden's face, searching for some sign to help her decide whether to continue or to stop. He would not help her.

"Miss Taggart," she said, "I am not your equal in philosophical altitude. I am only an average wife. Please give me that bracelet—if you do not wish me to think what I might think and what you wouldn't want me to name."

"Mrs. Rearden, is this the manner and place in which you choose to suggest that I am sleeping with your husband?"

"Certainly not!" The cry was immediate; it had a sound of panic and the quality of an automatic reflex, like the jerk of withdrawal of a pickpocket's hand caught in action. She added, with an angry, nervous chuckle, in a tone of sarcasm and sincerity that confessed a reluctant admission of her actual opinion, "That would be the possibility farthest from my mind."

"Then you will please apologize to Miss Taggart," said Rearden.

Dagny caught her breath, cutting off all but the faint echo of a gasp. They both whirled to him. Lillian saw nothing in his face; Dagny saw torture.

"It isn't necessary, Hank," she said.

"It is—for me," he answered coldly, not looking at her; he was looking at Lillian in the manner of a command that could not be disobeyed.

Lillian studied his face with mild astonishment, but without anxiety or anger, like a person confronted by a puzzle of no significance. "But of course," she said complaisantly, her voice smooth and confident again. "Please accept my apology, Miss Taggart, if I gave you the impression that I suspected the existence of a relationship which I would consider improbable for you and—from my knowledge of his inclinations—impossible for my husband."

She turned and walked away indifferently, leaving them together, as if in deliberate proof of her words.

Dagny stood still, her eyes closed; she was thinking of the night when Lillian had given her the bracelet. He had taken his wife's side, then; he had taken hers, now. Of the three of them, she was the only one who understood fully what this meant.

"Whatever is the worst you may wish to say to me, you will be right."

She heard him and opened her eyes. He was looking at her coldly, his face harsh, allowing no sign of pain or apology to suggest a hope of forgiveness.

"Dearest, don't torture yourself like that," she said. "I knew that you're married. I've never tried to evade that knowledge. I'm not hurt by it tonight."

Her first word was the most violent of the several blows he felt: she had never used that word before. She had never let him hear that particular tone of tenderness. She had never spoken of his marriage in the privacy of their meetings—yet she spoke of it here with effortless simplicity.

She saw the anger in his face—the rebellion against pity—the look of saying to her contemptuously that he had betrayed no torture and needed no help—then the look of the realization that she knew his face as thoroughly as he knew hers—he closed his eyes, he inclined his head a little, and he said very quietly, "Thank you."

She smiled and turned away from him.

James Taggart held an empty champagne glass in his hand and noticed the haste with which Balph Eubank waved at a passing waiter, as if the waiter were guilty of an unpardonable lapse. Then Eubank completed his sentence:

"—but *you*, Mr. Taggart, would know that a man who lives on a higher plane cannot be understood or appreciated. It's a hopeless struggle—trying to obtain support for literature from a world ruled by businessmen. They are nothing but stuffy, middle-class vulgarians or else predatory savages like Rearden."

"Jim," said Bertram Scudder, slapping his shoulder, "the best compliment I can pay you is that you're *not* a real businessman!"

"You're a man of culture, Jim," said Dr. Pritchett, "you're not an ex-ore-digger like Rearden. I don't have to explain to you the crucial need of Washington assistance to higher education."

"You really liked my last novel, Mr. Taggart?" Balph Eubank kept asking. "You *really* liked it?"

Orren Boyle glanced at the group, on his way across the room, but did not stop. The glance was sufficient to give him an estimate of the nature of the group's concerns. Fair enough, he thought, one's got to trade something. He knew, but did not care to name just what was being traded.

"We are at the dawn of a new age," said James Taggart, from above the rim of his champagne glass. "We are breaking up the vicious tyranny of economic power. We will set men free of the rule of the dollar. We will release our spiritual aims from dependence on the owners of material means. We will liberate our culture from the stranglehold of the profit-chasers. We will build a society dedicated to higher ideals, and we will replace the aristocracy of money by—"

"—the aristocracy of pull," said a voice beyond the group.

They whirled around. The man who stood facing them was Francisco d'Anconia.

His face looked tanned by a summer sun, and his eyes were the exact color of the sky on the kind of day when he had acquired his tan. His smile suggested a summer morning. The way he wore his formal clothes made the rest of the crowd look as if they were masquerading in borrowed costumes.

"What's the matter?" he asked in the midst of their silence. "Did I say something that somebody here didn't know?"

"How did *you* get here?" was the first thing James Taggart found himself able to utter.

"By plane to Newark, by taxi from there, then by elevator from my suite fifty-three floors above you."

"I didn't mean . . . that is, what I meant was—"

"Don't look so startled, James. If I land in New York and hear that there's a party going on, I wouldn't miss it, would I? You've always said that I'm just a party hound."

The group was watching them.

"I'm delighted to see you, of course," Taggart said cautiously, then added belligerently, to balance it, "But if you think you're going to—"

Francisco would not pick up the threat; he let Taggart's sentence slide into mid-air and stop, then asked politely, "If I think what?"

"You understand me very well."

"Yes. I do. Shall I tell you what I think?"

"This is hardly the moment for any—"

"I think you should present me to your bride, James. Your manners have never been glued to you too solidly—you always lose them in an emergency, and that's the time when one needs them most."

Turning to escort him toward Cherryl, Taggart caught the faint sound that came from Bertram Scudder; it was an unborn chuckle. Taggart knew that the men who had crawled at his feet a moment ago, whose hatred for Francisco d'Anconia was, perhaps, greater than his own, were enjoying the spectacle none the less. The implications of this knowledge were among the things he did not care to name.

Francisco bowed to Cherryl and offered his best wishes, as if she were the bride of a royal heir. Watching nervously, Taggart felt relief—and a touch of nameless resentment, which, if named, would have told him he wished the occasion deserved the grandeur that Francisco's manner gave it for a moment.

He was afraid to remain by Francisco's side and afraid to let him loose among the guests. He backed a few tentative steps away, but Francisco followed him, smiling.

"You didn't think I'd want to miss your wedding, James—when you're my childhood friend and best stockholder?"

"What?" gasped Taggart, and regretted it: the sound was a confession of panic.

Francisco did not seem to take note of it; he said, his voice gaily innocent, "Oh, but of course I know it. I know the stooge behind the stooge behind every name on the list of the stockholders of d'Anconia Copper. It's surprising how many men by the name of Smith and Gomez are rich enough to own big chunks of the richest corporation in the world—so you can't blame me if I was curious to learn what distinguished persons I actually have among my minority stockholders. I seem to be popular with an astonishing collection of public figures from all over the world—from People's States where you wouldn't think there's any money left at all."

Taggart said dryly, frowning, "There are many reasons—business reasons—why it is sometimes advisable not to make one's investments directly."

"One reason is that a man doesn't want people to know he's rich. Another is that he doesn't want them to learn how he got that way."

"I don't know what you mean or why you should object."

"Oh, I don't object at all. I appreciate it. A great many investors —the old-fashioned sort—dropped me after the San Sebastián Mines. It scared them away. But the modern ones had more faith in me and acted as they always do—on faith. I can't tell you how thoroughly I appreciate it."

Taggart wished Francisco would not talk so loudly; he wished people would not gather around them. "You have been doing extremely well," he said, in the safe tone of a business compliment.

"Yes, haven't I? It's wonderful how the stock of d'Anconia Copper has risen within the last year. But I don't think I should be too conceited about it—there's not much competition left in the world, there's no place to invest one's money, if one happens to get rich quickly, and here's d'Anconia Copper, the oldest company on earth, the one that's been the safest bet for centuries. Just think of what it managed to survive through the ages. So if you people have decided that it's the best place for your hidden money, that it can't be beaten, that it would take a most unusual kind of man to destroy d'Anconia Copper—you were right."

"Well, I hear it said that you've begun to take your responsibilities seriously and that you've settled down to business at last. They say you've been working very hard."

"Oh, has anybody noticed that? It was the old-fashioned investors who made it a point to watch what the president of a company was doing. The modern investors don't find knowledge necessary. I don't think they ever look into my activities."

Taggart smiled. "They look at the ticker tape of the stock exchange. That tells the whole story, doesn't it?"

"Yes. Yes, it does—in the long run."

"I must say I'm glad that you haven't been much of a party hound this past year. The results show in your work."

"Do they? Well, no, not quite yet."

"I suppose," said Taggart, in the cautious tone of an indirect question, "that I should feel flattered you chose to come to this party."

"Oh, but I had to come. I thought you were expecting me."

"Why, no, I wasn't . . . that is, I mean—"

"You should have expected me, James. This is the great, formal, nose-counting event, where the victims come in order to show how safe it is to destroy them, and the destroyers form pacts of eternal friendship, which lasts for three months. I don't know exactly which group I belong to, but I had to come and be counted, didn't I?"

"What in hell do you think you're saying?" Taggart cried furiously, seeing the tension on the faces around them.

"Be careful, James. If you try to pretend that you don't understand me, I'm going to make it much clearer."

"If you think it's proper to utter such—"

"I think it's funny. There was a time when men were afraid that somebody would reveal some secret of theirs that was unknown to their fellows. Nowadays, they're afraid that somebody will name what everybody knows. Have you practical people ever thought that that's all it would take to blast your whole, big, complex structure, with all your laws and guns—just somebody naming the exact nature of what you're doing?"

"If you think it's proper to come to a celebration such as a wedding, in order to insult the host—"

"Why, James, I came here to thank you."

"To thank me?"

"Of course. You've done me a great favor—you and your boys in Washington and the boys in Santiago. Only I wonder why none of you took the trouble to inform me about it. Those directives that somebody issued here a few months ago are choking off the entire copper industry of this country. And the result is that this country suddenly has to import much larger amounts of copper. And where in the world is there any copper left—unless it's d'Anconia copper? So you see that I have good reason to be grateful."

"I assure you I had nothing to do with it," Taggart said hastily, "and besides, the vital economic policies of this country are not determined by any considerations such as you're intimating or—"

"I know how they're determined, James. I know that the deal started with the boys in Santiago, because they've been on the d'Anconia pay roll for centuries—well, no, 'pay roll' is an honorable word, it would be more exact to say that d'Anconia Copper has been paying them protection money for centuries—isn't that what your gangsters call it? Our boys in Santiago call it taxes. They've been getting their cut on every ton of d'Anconia copper sold. So they have a vested interest to see me sell as many tons as possible. But with the world turning into People's States, this is the only country left where men are not yet reduced to digging for roots in forests for their sustenance—so this is the only market left on earth. The boys in Santiago wanted to corner this market. I don't know what they offered to the boys in Washington, or who traded what and to whom—but I know that you came in on it somewhere, because you do hold a sizable chunk of d'Anconia Copper stock. And it surely didn't displease you—that morning, four months ago, the day after the directives were issued—to see the kind of soaring leap that d'Anconia Copper performed on the Stock Exchange. Why, it practically leaped off the ticker tape and into your face."

"Who gave you any grounds to invent an outrageous story of this kind?"

"Nobody. I knew nothing about it. I just saw the leap on the ticker tape that morning. That told the whole story, didn't it? Besides, the boys in Santiago slapped a new tax on copper the following week—and they told me that I shouldn't mind it, not with that sudden rise of my stock. They were working for my best interests, they said. They said, why should I care—taking the two events together, I was richer than I had been before. True enough. I was."

"Why do you wish to tell me this?"

"Why don't you wish to take any credit for it, James? That's out of character and out of the policy at which you're such an expert. In an age when men exist, not by right, but by favor, one does not reject a grateful person, one tries to trap into gratitude as many people as possible. Don't you want to have me as one of your men under obligation?"

"I don't know what you're talking about."

"Think what a favor I received without any effort on my part. I wasn't consulted, I wasn't informed, I wasn't thought about, everything was arranged without me—and all I have to do now is produce the copper. That was a great favor, James—and you may be sure that I will repay it."

Francisco turned abruptly, not waiting for an answer, and started away. Taggart did not follow; he stood, feeling that anything was preferable to one more minute of their conversation.

Francisco stopped when he came to Dagny. He looked at her for a silent instant, without greeting, his smile acknowledging that she had been the first person he saw and the first one to see him at his entrance into the ballroom.

Against every doubt and warning in her mind, she felt nothing but a joyous confidence; inexplicably, she felt as if his figure in that crowd was a point of indestructible security. But in the moment when the beginning of a smile told him how glad she was to see him, he asked, "Don't you want to tell me what a brilliant achievement the John Galt Line turned out to be?"

She felt her lips trembling and tightening at once, as she answered, "I'm sorry if I show that I'm still open to be hurt. It shouldn't shock me that you've come to the stage where you despise achievement."

"Yes, don't I? I despised that Line so much that I didn't want to see it reach the kind of end it has reached."

He saw her look of sudden attentiveness, the look of thought rushing into a breach torn open upon a new direction. He watched her for a moment, as if he knew every step she would find along that road, then chuckled and said, "Don't you want to ask me now: Who is John Galt?"

"Why should I want to, and why now?"

"Don't you remember that you dared him to come and claim your Line? Well, he has."

He walked on, not waiting to see the look in her eyes—a look that held anger, bewilderment and the first faint gleam of a question mark.

It was the muscles of his own face that made Rearden realize the nature of his reaction to Francisco's arrival: he noticed suddenly that he was smiling and that his face had been relaxed into the dim well-being of a smile for some minutes past, as he watched Francisco d'Anconia in the crowd.

He acknowledged to himself, for the first time, all the half-grasped, half-rejected moments when he had thought of Francisco d'Anconia and thrust the thought aside before it became the knowledge of how much he wanted to see him again. In moments of sudden exhaustion—at his desk, with the fires of the furnaces going down in the twilight—in the darkness of the lonely walk through the empty countryside to his house—in the silence of sleepless nights—he had found himself thinking of the only man who had once seemed to be his spokesman. He had pushed the memory aside, telling himself: But that one is worse than all the others!—while feeling certain that this was not true, yet being unable to name the reason of his certainty. He had caught himself glancing through the newspapers to see whether Francisco d'Anconia had returned to New York—and he had thrown the newspapers aside, asking himself angrily: What if he did return?—would you go chasing him through night clubs and cocktail parties?—what is it that you want from him?

This was what he had wanted—he thought, when he caught himself smiling at the sight of Francisco in the crowd—this strange feeling of expectation that held curiosity, amusement and hope.

Francisco did not seem to have noticed him. Rearden waited, fighting a desire to approach; not after the kind of conversation we had, he thought—what for?—what would I say to him? And then, with the same smiling, light-hearted feeling, the feeling of being certain that it was right, he found himself walking across the ballroom, toward the group that surrounded Francisco d'Anconia.

He wondered, looking at them, why these people were drawn to Francisco, why they chose to hold him imprisoned in a clinging circle, when their resentment of him was obvious under their smiles. Their faces had the hint of a look peculiar, not to fear, but to cowardice: a look of guilty anger. Francisco stood cornered against the side edge of a marble stairway, half-leaning, half-sitting on the steps; the informality of his posture, combined with the strict formality of his clothes, gave him an air of superlative elegance. His was the only face that had the carefree look and the brilliant smile proper to the enjoyment of a party; but his eyes seemed intentionally expressionless, holding no trace of gaiety, showing—like a warning signal—nothing but the activity of a heightened perceptiveness.

Standing unnoticed on the edge of the group, Rearden heard a woman, who had large diamond earrings and a flabby, nervous face, ask tensely, "Señor d'Anconia, what do you think is going to happen to the world?"

"Just exactly what it deserves."

"Oh, how cruel!"

"Don't you believe in the operation of the moral law, madame?" Francisco asked gravely. "I do."

Rearden heard Bertram Scudder, outside the group, say to a girl who made some sound of indignation, "Don't let him disturb you. You know, money is the root of all evil—and he's the typical product of money."

Rearden did not think that Francisco could have heard it, but he saw Francisco turning to them with a gravely courteous smile.

"So you think that money is the root of all evil?" said Francisco d'Anconia. "Have you ever asked what is the root of money? Money is a tool of exchange, which can't exist unless there are goods produced and men able to produce them. Money is the material shape of the principle that men who wish to deal with one another must deal by trade and give value for value. Money is not the tool of the moochers, who claim your product by tears, or of the looters, who take it from you by force. Money is made possible only by the men who produce. Is this what you consider evil?

"When you accept money in payment for your effort, you do so only on the conviction that you will exchange it for the product of the effort of others. It is not the moochers or the looters who give value to money. Not an ocean of tears nor all the guns in the world can transform those pieces of paper in your wallet into the bread you will need to survive tomorrow. Those pieces of paper, which should have been gold, are a token of honor—your claim upon the energy of the men who produce. Your wallet is your statement of hope that somewhere in the world around you there are men who will not default on that moral principle which is the root of money. Is this what you consider evil?

"Have you ever looked for the root of production? Take a look at an electric generator and dare tell yourself that it was created by the muscular effort of unthinking brutes. Try to grow a seed of wheat without the knowledge left to you by men who had to discover it for the first time. Try to obtain your food by means of nothing but physical motions—and you'll learn that man's mind is the root of all the goods produced and of all the wealth that has ever existed on earth.

"But you say that money is made by the strong at the expense of the weak? What strength do you mean? It is not the strength of guns or muscles. Wealth is the product of man's capacity to think. Then is money made by the man who invents a motor at the expense of those who did not invent it? Is money made by the intelligent at the expense of the fools? By the able at the expense of the incompetent? By the ambitious at the expense of the lazy? Money is *made*—before it can be looted or mooched—made by the effort of every honest man, each to the extent of his ability. An honest man is one who knows that he can't consume more than he has produced.

"To trade by means of money is the code of the men of good will. Money rests on the axiom that every man is the owner of his mind and his effort. Money allows no power to prescribe the value of your effort except the voluntary choice of the man who is willing to trade you his effort in return. Money permits you to obtain for your goods and your labor that which they are worth to the men who buy them, but no more. Money permits no deals except those to mutual benefit by the unforced judgment of the traders. Money demands of you the recognition that men must work for their own benefit, not for their own injury, for their gain, not their loss—the recognition that they are not beasts of burden, born to carry the weight of your misery—that you must offer them values, not wounds—that the common bond among men is not the exchange of suffering, but the exchange of *goods*. Money demands that you sell, not your weakness to men's stupidity, but your talent to their reason; it demands that you buy, not the shoddiest they offer, but the best that your money can find. And when men live by trade—with reason, not force, as their final arbiter—it is the best product that wins, the best performance, the man of best judgment and highest ability—and the degree of a man's productiveness is the degree of his reward. This is the code of existence whose tool and symbol is money. Is this what you consider evil?

"But money is only a tool. It will take you wherever you wish, but it will not replace you as the driver. It will give you the means for the satisfaction of your desires, but it will not provide you with desires. Money is the scourge of the men who attempt to reverse the law of causality—the men who seek to replace the mind by seizing the products of the mind.

"Money will not purchase happiness for the man who has no concept of what he wants: money will not give him a code of values, if he's evaded the knowledge of what to value, and it will not provide him with a purpose, if he's evaded the choice of what to seek. Money will not buy intelligence for the fool, or admiration for the coward, or respect for the incompetent. The man who attempts to purchase the brains of his superiors to serve him, with his money replacing his judgment, ends up by becoming the victim of his inferiors. The men of intelligence desert him, but the cheats and the frauds come flocking to him, drawn by a law which he has not discovered: that no man may be smaller than his money. Is this the reason why you call it evil?

"Only the man who does not need it, is fit to inherit wealth—the man who would make his own fortune no matter where he started. If an heir is equal to his money, it serves him; if not, it destroys him. But you look on and you cry that money corrupted him. Did it? Or did he corrupt his money? Do not envy a worthless heir; his wealth is not yours and you would have done no better with it. Do not think that it should have been distributed among you; loading the world with fifty parasites instead of one, would not bring back the dead virtue which was the fortune. Money is a living power that dies without its root. Money will not serve the mind that cannot match it. Is this the reason why you call it evil?

"Money is your means of survival. The verdict you pronounce upon the source of your livelihood is the verdict you pronounce upon your life. If the source is corrupt, you have damned your own existence. Did you get your money by fraud? By pandering to men's vices or men's stupidity? By catering to fools, in the hope of getting more than your ability deserves? By lowering your standards? By doing work you despise for purchasers you scorn? If so, then your money will not give you a moment's or a penny's worth of joy. Then all the things you buy will become, not a tribute to you, but a reproach; not an achievement, but a reminder of shame. Then you'll scream that money is evil. Evil, because it would not pinch-hit for your self-respect? Evil, because it would not let you enjoy your depravity? Is this the root of your hatred of money?

"Money will always remain an effect and refuse to replace you as the cause. Money is the product of virtue, but it will not give you virtue and it will not redeem your vices. Money will not give you the unearned, neither in matter nor in spirit. Is this the root of your hatred of money?

"Or did you say it's the *love* of money that's the root of all evil? To love a thing is to know and love its nature. To love money is to know and love the fact that money is the creation of the best power within you, and your passkey to trade your effort for the effort of the best among men. It's the person who would sell his soul for a nickel, who is loudest in proclaiming his hatred of money—and he has good reason to hate it. The lovers of money are willing to work for it. They know they are able to deserve it.

"Let me give you a tip on a clue to men's characters: the man who damns money has obtained it dishonorably; the man who respects it has earned it.

"Run for your life from any man who tells you that money is evil. That sentence is the leper's bell of an approaching looter. So long as men live together on earth and need means to deal with one another—their only substitute, if they abandon money, is the muzzle of a gun.

"But money demands of you the highest virtues, if you wish to make it or to keep it. Men who have no courage, pride or self-esteem, men who have no moral sense of their right to their money and are not willing to defend it as they defend their life, men who apologize for being rich—will not remain rich for long. They are the natural bait for the swarms of looters that stay under rocks for centuries, but come crawling out at the first smell of a man who begs to be forgiven for the guilt of owning wealth. They will hasten to relieve him of the guilt—and of his life, as he deserves.

"Then you will see the rise of the men of the double standard—the men who live by force, yet count on those who live by trade to create the value of their looted money—the men who are the hitchhikers of virtue. In a moral society, these are the criminals, and the statutes are written to protect you against them. But when a society establishes criminals-by-right and looters-by-law—men who use force to seize the wealth of *disarmed* victims—then money becomes its creators' avenger. Such looters believe it safe to rob defenseless men, once they've passed a law to disarm them. But their loot becomes the magnet for other looters, who get it from them as they got it. Then the race goes, not to the ablest at production, but to those most ruthless at brutality. When force is the standard, the murderer wins over the pickpocket. And then that society vanishes, in a spread of ruins and slaughter.

"Do you wish to know whether that day is coming? Watch money. Money is the barometer of a society's virtue. When you see that trading is done, not by consent, but by compulsion—when you see that in order to produce, you need to obtain permission from men who produce nothing—when you see that money is flowing to those who deal, not in goods, but in favors—when you see that men get richer by graft and by pull than by work, and your laws don't protect you against them, but protect them against you—when you see corruption being rewarded and honesty becoming a self-sacrifice—you may know that your society is doomed. Money is so noble a medium that it does not compete with guns and it does not make terms with brutality. It will not permit a country to survive as half-property, half-loot.

"Whenever destroyers appear among men, they start by destroying money, for money is men's protection and the base of a moral existence. Destroyers seize gold and leave to its owners a counterfeit pile of paper. This kills all objective standards and delivers men into the arbitrary power of an arbitrary setter of values. Gold was an objective value, an equivalent of wealth produced. Paper is a mortgage on wealth that does not exist, backed by a gun aimed at those who are expected to produce it. Paper is a check drawn by legal looters upon an account which is not theirs: upon the virtue of the victims. Watch for the day when it bounces, marked: 'Account overdrawn.'

"When you have made evil the means of survival, do not expect men to remain good. Do not expect them to stay moral and lose their lives for the purpose of becoming the fodder of the immoral. Do not expect them to produce, when production is punished and looting rewarded. Do not ask, 'Who is destroying the world?' You are.

"You stand in the midst of the greatest achievements of the greatest productive civilization and you wonder why it's crumbling around you, while you're damning its life-blood—money. You look upon money as the savages did before you, and you wonder why the jungle is creeping back to the edge of your cities. Throughout men's history, money was always seized by looters of one brand or another, whose names changed, but whose method remained the same: to seize wealth by force and to keep the producers bound, demeaned, defamed, deprived of honor. That phrase about the evil of money, which you mouth with such righteous recklessness, comes from a time when wealth was produced by the labor of slaves—slaves who repeated the motions once discovered by somebody's mind and left unimproved for centuries. So long as production was ruled by force, and wealth was obtained by conquest, there was little to conquer. Yet through all the centuries of stagnation and starvation, men exalted the looters, as aristocrats of the sword, as aristocrats of birth, as aristocrats of the bureau, and despised the producers, as slaves, as traders, as shopkeepers—as industrialists.

"To the glory of mankind, there was, for the first and only time in history, a *country of money*—and I have no higher, more reverent tribute to pay to America, for this means: a country of reason, justice, freedom, production, achievement. For the first time, man's mind and money were set free, and there were no fortunes-by-conquest, but only fortunes-by-work, and instead of swordsmen and slaves, there appeared the real maker of wealth, the greatest worker, the highest type of human being—the self-made man—the American industrialist.

"If you ask me to name the proudest distinction of Americans, I would choose—because it contains all the others—the fact that they were the people who created the phrase 'to *make* money.' No other language or nation had ever used these words before; men had always thought of wealth as a static quantity—to be seized, begged, inherited, shared, looted or obtained as a favor. Americans were the first to understand that wealth has to be created. The words 'to make money' hold the essence of human morality.

"Yet these were the words for which Americans were denounced by the rotted cultures of the looters' continents. Now the looters' credo has brought you to regard your proudest achievements as a hallmark of shame, your prosperity as guilt, your greatest men, the industrialists, as blackguards, and your magnificent factories as the product and property of muscular labor, the labor of whip-driven slaves, like the pyramids of Egypt. The rotter who simpers that he sees no difference between the power of the dollar and the power of the whip, ought to learn the difference on his own hide—as, I think, he will.

"Until and unless you discover that money is the root of all good, you ask for your own destruction. When money ceases to be the tool by which men deal with one another, then men become the tools of men. Blood, whips and guns—or dollars. Take your choice—there is no other—and your time is running out."

Francisco had not glanced at Rearden once while speaking; but the moment he finished, his eyes went straight to Rearden's face. Rearden stood motionless, seeing nothing but Francisco d'Anconia across the moving figures and angry voices between them.

There were people who had listened, but now hurried away, and people who said, "It's horrible!"—"It's not true!"—"How vicious and selfish!"—saying it loudly and guardedly at once, as if wishing that their neighbors would hear them, but hoping that Francisco would not.

"Señor d'Anconia," declared the woman with the earrings, "I don't agree with you!"

"If you can refute a single sentence I uttered, madame, I shall hear it gratefully."

"Oh, I can't answer you. I don't have any answers, my mind doesn't work that way, but I don't *feel* that you're right, so I know that you're wrong."

"How do you know it?"

"I *feel* it. I don't go by my head, but by my heart. You might be good at logic, but you're heartless."

"Madame, when we'll see men dying of starvation around us, your heart won't be of any earthly use to save them. And I'm heartless enough to say that when you'll scream, 'But I didn't know it!'—you will not be forgiven."

The woman turned away, a shudder running through the flesh of her cheeks and through the angry tremor of her voice: "Well, it's certainly a funny way to talk at a party!"

A portly man with evasive eyes said loudly, his tone of forced cheerfulness suggesting that his sole concern in any issue was not to let it become unpleasant, "If this is the way you feel about money, señor, I think I'm darn glad that I've got a goodly piece of d'Anconia Copper stock."

Francisco said gravely, "I suggest that you think twice, sir."

Rearden started toward him—and Francisco, who had not seemed to look in his direction, moved to meet him at once, as if the others had never existed.

"Hello," said Rearden simply, easily, as to a childhood friend; he was smiling.

He saw his own smile reflected in Francisco's face. "Hello."

"I want to speak to you."

"To whom do you think I've been speaking for the last quarter of an hour?"

Rearden chuckled, in the manner of acknowledging an opponent's round. "I didn't think you had noticed me."

"I noticed, when I came in, that you were one of the only two persons in this room who were glad to see me."

"Aren't you being presumptuous?"

"No—grateful."

"Who was the other person glad to see you?"

Francisco shrugged and said lightly, "A woman."

Rearden noticed that Francisco had led him aside, away from the group, in so skillfully natural a manner that neither he nor the others had known it was being done intentionally.

"I didn't expect to find you here," said Francisco. "You shouldn't have come to this party."

"Why not?"

"May I ask what made you come?"

"My wife was anxious to accept the invitation."

"Forgive me if I put it in such form, but it would have been more proper and less dangerous if she had asked you to take her on a tour of whorehouses."

"What danger are you talking about?"

"Mr. Rearden, you do not know these people's way of doing business or how they interpret your presence here. In your code, but not in theirs, accepting a man's hospitality is a token of good will, a declaration that you and your host stand on terms of a civilized relationship. Don't give them that kind of sanction."

"Then why did *you* come here?"

Francisco shrugged gaily. "Oh, I—it doesn't matter what I do. I'm only a party hound."

"What are you doing at this party?"

"Just looking for conquests."

"Found any?"

His face suddenly earnest, Francisco answered gravely, almost solemnly, "Yes—what I think is going to be my best and greatest."

Rearden's anger was involuntary, the cry, not of reproach, but of despair: "How can you waste yourself that way?"

The faint suggestion of a smile, like the rise of a distant light, came into Francisco's eyes as he asked, "Do you care to admit that you care about it?"

"You're going to hear a few more admissions, if that's what you're after. Before I met you, I used to wonder how you could waste a fortune such as yours. Now it's worse, because I can't despise you as I did, as I'd like to, yet the question is much more terrible: How can you waste a mind such as yours?"

"I don't think I'm wasting it right now."

"I don't know whether there's ever been anything that meant a damn to you—but I'm going to tell you what I've never said to anyone before. When I met you, do you remember that you said you wanted to offer me your gratitude?"

There was no trace of amusement left in Francisco's eyes; Rearden had never faced so solemn a look of respect. "Yes, Mr. Rearden," he answered quietly.

"I told you that I didn't need it and I insulted you for it. All right, you've won. That speech you made tonight—that was what you were offering me, wasn't it?"

"Yes, Mr. Rearden."

"It was more than gratitude, and I needed the gratitude; it was more than admiration, and I needed that, too; it was much more than any word I can find, it will take me days to think of all that it's given me—but one thing I do know: I needed it. I've never made an admission of this kind, because I've never cried for anyone's help. If it amused you to guess that I was glad to see you, you have something real to laugh about now, if you wish."

"It might take me a few years, but I will prove to you that these are the things I do not laugh about."

"Prove it now—by answering one question: Why don't you practice what you preach?"

"Are you sure that I don't?"

"If the things you said are true, if you have the greatness to know it, you should have been the leading industrialist of the world by now."

Francisco said gravely, as he had said to the portly man, but with an odd note of gentleness in his voice, "I suggest that you think twice, Mr. Rearden."

"I've thought about you more than I care to admit. I have found no answer."

"Let me give you a hint: If the things I said are true, who is the guiltiest man in this room tonight?"

"I suppose—James Taggart?"

"No, Mr. Rearden, it is not James Taggart. But you must define the guilt and choose the man yourself."

"A few years ago, I would have said that it's you. I still think that that's what I ought to say. But I'm almost in the position of that fool woman who spoke to you: every reason I know tells me that you're guilty—and yet I can't feel it."

"You *are* making the same mistake as that woman, Mr. Rearden, though in a nobler form."

"What do you mean?"

"I mean much more than just your judgment of me. That woman and all those like her keep evading the thoughts which they know to be good. You keep pushing out of your mind the thoughts which you believe to be evil. They do it, because they want to avoid effort. You do it, because you won't permit yourself to consider anything that would spare you. They indulge their emotions at any cost. You sacrifice your emotions as the first cost of any problem. They are willing to bear nothing. You are willing to bear anything. They keep evading responsibility. You keep assuming it. But don't you see that the essential error is the same? Any refusal to recognize reality, for any reason whatever, has disastrous consequences. There are no evil thoughts except one: the refusal to think. Don't ignore your own desires, Mr. Rearden. Don't sacrifice them. Examine their cause. There is a limit to how much you should have to bear."

"How did you know this about me?"

"I made the same mistake, once. But not for long."

"I wish—" Rearden began and stopped abruptly.

Francisco smiled. "Afraid to wish, Mr. Rearden?"

"I wish I could permit myself to like you as much as I do."

"I'd give—" Francisco stopped; inexplicably, Rearden saw the look of an emotion which he could not define, yet felt certain to be pain; he saw Francisco's first moment of hesitation. "Mr. Rearden, do you own any d'Anconia Copper stock?"

Rearden looked at him, bewildered. "No."

"Some day, you'll know what treason I'm committing right now, but . . . Don't ever buy any d'Anconia Copper stock. Don't ever deal with d'Anconia Copper in any way."

"Why?"

"When you'll learn the full reason, you'll know whether there's ever been anything—or anyone—that meant a damn to me, and . . . and how much he did mean."

Rearden frowned: he had remembered something. "I wouldn't deal with your company. Didn't you call them the men of the double standard? Aren't you one of the looters who is growing rich right now by means of directives?"

Inexplicably, the words did not hit Francisco as an insult, but cleared his face back into his look of assurance. "Did you think that it was I who wheedled those directives out of the robber-planners?"

"If not, then who did it?"

"My hitchhikers."

"Without your consent?"

"Without my knowledge."

"I'd hate to admit how much I want to believe you—but there's no way for you to prove it now."

"No? I'll prove it to you within the next fifteen minutes."

"How? The fact remains that you've profited the most from those directives."

"That's true. I've profited more than Mr. Mouch and his gang could ever imagine. After my years of work, they gave me just the chance I needed."

"Are you boasting?"

"You bet I am!" Rearden saw incredulously that Francisco's eyes had a hard, bright look, the look, not of a party hound, but of a man of action. "Mr. Rearden, do you know where most of those new aristocrats keep their hidden money? Do you know where most of the fairshare vultures have invested their profits from Rearden Metal?"

"No, but—"

"In d'Anconia Copper stock. Safely out of the way and out of the country. D'Anconia Copper—an old, invulnerable company, so rich that it would last for three more generations of looting. A company managed by a decadent playboy who doesn't give a damn, who'll let them use his property in any way they please and just continue to make money for them—automatically, as did his ancestors. Wasn't that a perfect setup for the looters, Mr. Rearden? Only—what one single point did they miss?"

Rearden was staring at him. "What are you driving at?"

Francisco laughed suddenly. "It's too bad about those profiteers on Rearden Metal. You wouldn't want them to lose the money you made for them, would you, Mr. Rearden? But accidents do happen in the world—you know what they say, man is only a helpless plaything at the mercy of nature's disasters. For instance, there was a fire at the d'Anconia ore docks in Valparaiso tomorrow morning, a fire that razed them to the ground along with half of the port structures. What time is it, Mr. Rearden? Oh, did I mix my tenses? Tomorrow afternoon, there will be a rock slide in the d'Anconia mines at Oráno—no lives lost, no casualties, except the mines themselves. It will be found that the mines are done for, because they had been worked in the wrong places for months—what can you expect from a playboy's management? The great deposits of copper will be buried under tons of mountain where a Sebastián d'Anconia would not be able to reclaim them in less than three years, and a People's State will never reclaim them at all. When the stockholders begin to look into things, they will find that the mines at Campos, at San Félix, at Las Heras have been worked in exactly the same manner and have been running at a loss for over a year, only the playboy juggled the books and kept it out of the newspapers. Shall I tell you what they will discover about the management of the d'Anconia foundries? Or of the d'Anconia ore fleet? But all these discoveries won't do the stockholders any good anyway, because the stock of d'Anconia Copper will have crashed tomorrow morning, crashed like an electric bulb against concrete, crashed like an express elevator, spattering pieces of hitchhikers all over the gutters!"

The triumphant rise of Francisco's voice merged with a matching sound: Rearden burst out laughing.

Rearden did not know how long that moment lasted or what he had felt, it had been like a blow hurling him into another kind of consciousness, then a second blow returning him to his own—all that was left, as at the awakening from a narcotic, was the feeling that he had known some immense kind of freedom, never to be matched in reality. This was like the Wyatt fire again, he thought, this was his secret danger.

He found himself backing away from Francisco d'Anconia. Francisco stood watching him intently, and looked as if he had been watching him all through that unknown length of time.

"There are no evil thoughts, Mr. Rearden," Francisco said softly, "except one: the refusal to think."

"No," said Rearden; it was almost a whisper, he had to keep his voice down, he was afraid that he would hear himself scream it, "no . . . if this is the key to you, no, don't expect me to cheer you . . . you didn't have the strength to fight them . . . you chose the easiest, most vicious way . . . deliberate destruction . . . the destruction of an achievement you hadn't produced and couldn't match. . . ."

"That's not what you'll read in the newspapers tomorrow. There won't be any evidence of deliberate destruction. Everything happened in the normal, explicable, justifiable course of plain incompetence. Incompetence isn't supposed to be punished nowadays, is it? The boys in Buenos Aires and the boys in Santiago will probably want to hand me a subsidy, by way of consolation and reward. There's still a great part of the d'Anconia Copper Company left, though a great part of it is gone for good. Nobody will say that I've done it intentionally. You may think what you wish."

"I think you're the guiltiest man in this room," said Rearden quietly, wearily; even the fire of his anger was gone; he felt nothing but the emptiness left by the death of a great hope. "I think you're worse than anything I had supposed. . . ."

Francisco looked at him with a strange half-smile of serenity, the serenity of a victory over pain, and did not answer.

It was their silence that let them hear the voices of the two men who stood a few steps away, and they turned to look at the speakers.

The stocky, elderly man was obviously a businessman of the conscientious, unspectacular kind. His formal dress suit was of good quality, but of a cut fashionable twenty years before, with the faintest tinge of green at the seams; he had had few occasions to wear it. His shirt studs were ostentatiously too large, but it was the pathetic ostentation of an heirloom, intricate pieces of old-fashioned workmanship, that had probably come to him through four generations, like his business. His face had the expression which, these days, was the mark of an honest man: an expression of bewilderment. He was looking at his companion, trying hard—conscientiously, helplessly, hopelessly—to understand.

His companion was younger and shorter, a small man with lumpy flesh, with a chest thrust forward and the thin points of a mustache thrust up. He was saying, in a tone of patronizing boredom, "Well, I don't know. All of you are crying about rising costs, it seems to be the stock complaint nowadays, it's the usual whine of people whose profits are squeezed a little. I don't know, we'll have to see, we'll have to decide whether we'll permit you to make any profits or not."

Rearden glanced at Francisco—and saw a face that went beyond his conception of what the purity of a single purpose could do to a human countenance: it was the most merciless face one could ever be permitted to see. He had thought of himself as ruthless, but he knew that he could not match this level, naked, implacable look, dead to all feeling but justice. Whatever the rest of him—thought Rearden—the man who could experience this was a giant.

It was only a moment. Francisco turned to him, his face normal, and said very quietly, "I've changed my mind, Mr. Rearden. I'm glad that you came to this party. I want you to see this."

Then, raising his voice, Francisco said suddenly, in the gay, loose, piercing tone of a man of complete irresponsibility, "You won't grant me that loan, Mr. Rearden? It puts me on a terrible spot. I must get the money—I must raise it tonight—I must raise it before the Stock Exchange opens in the morning, because otherwise—"

He did not have to continue, because the little man with the mustache was clutching at his arm.

Rearden had never believed that a human body could change dimensions within one's sight, but he saw the man shrinking in weight, in posture, in form, as if the air were let out of his lumps, and what had been an arrogant ruler was suddenly a piece of scrap that could not be a threat to anyone.

"Is . . . is there something wrong, Señor d'Anconia? I mean, on . . . on the Stock Exchange?"

Francisco jerked his finger to his lips, with a frightened glance. "Keep quiet," he whispered. "For God's sake, keep quiet!"

The man was shaking. "Something's . . . wrong?"

"You don't happen to own any d'Anconia Copper stock, do you?" The man nodded, unable to speak. "Oh my, that's too bad! Well, listen, I'll tell you, if you give me your word of honor that you won't repeat it to anyone. You don't want to start a panic."

"Word of honor . . ." gasped the man.

"What you'd better do is run to your stockbroker and sell as fast as you can—because things haven't been going too well for d'Anconia Copper, I'm trying to raise some money, but if I don't succeed, you'll be lucky if you'll have ten cents on your dollar tomorrow morning—oh my! I forgot that you can't reach your stockbroker before tomorrow morning—well, it's too bad, but—"

The man was running across the room, pushing people out of his way, like a torpedo shot into the crowd.

"Watch," said Francisco austerely, turning to Rearden.

The man was lost in the crowd, they could not see him, they could not tell to whom he was selling his secret or whether he had enough of his cunning left to make it a trade with those who held favors—but they saw the wake of his passage spreading through the room, the sudden cuts splitting the crowd, like the first few cracks, then like the accelerating branching that runs through a wall about to crumble, the streaks of emptiness slashed, not by a human touch, but by the impersonal breath of terror.

There were the voices abruptly choked off, the pools of silence, then sounds of a different nature: the rising, hysterical inflections of uselessly repeated questions, the unnatural whispers, a woman's scream, the few spaced, forced giggles of those still trying to pretend that nothing was happening.

There were spots of immobility in the motion of the crowd, like spreading blotches of paralysis; there was a sudden stillness, as if a motor had been cut off; then came the frantic, jerking, purposeless, rudderless movement of objects bumping down a hill by the blind mercy of gravitation and of every rock they hit on the way. People were running out, running to telephones, running to one another, clutching or pushing the bodies around them at random. These men, the most powerful men in the country, those who held, unanswerable to any power, the power over every man's food and every man's enjoyment of his span of years on earth—these men had become a pile of rubble, clattering in the wind of panic, the rubble left of a structure when its key pillar has been cut.

James Taggart, his face indecent in its exposure of emotions which centuries had taught men to keep hidden, rushed up to Francisco and screamed, "Is it true?"

"Why, James," said Francisco, smiling, "what's the matter? Why do you seem to be upset? Money is the root of all evil—so I just got tired of being evil."

Taggart ran toward the main exit, yelling something to Orren Boyle on the way. Boyle nodded and kept on nodding, with the eagerness and humility of an inefficient servant, then darted off in another direction. Cherryl, her wedding veil coiling like a crystal cloud upon the air, as she ran after him, caught Taggart at the door. "Jim, what's the matter?" He pushed her aside and she fell against the stomach of Paul Larkin, as Taggart rushed out.

Three persons stood immovably still, like three pillars spaced through the room, the lines of their sight cutting across the spread of the wreckage: Dagny, looking at Francisco—Francisco and Rearden, looking at each other.

III

WHITE BLACKMAIL

"What time is it?"

It's running out, thought Rearden—but he answered, "I don't know. Not yet midnight," and remembering his wrist watch, added, "Twenty of."

"I'm going to take a train home," said Lillian.

He heard the sentence, but it had to wait its turn to enter the crowded passages to his consciousness. He stood looking absently at the living room of his suite, a few minutes' elevator ride away from the party. In a moment, he answered automatically, "At this hour?"

"It's still early. There are plenty of trains running."

"You're welcome to stay here, of course."

"No, I think I prefer to go home." He did not argue. "What about you, Henry? Do you intend going home tonight?"

"No." He added, "I have business appointments here tomorrow."

"As you wish."

She shrugged her evening wrap off her shoulders, caught it on her arm and started toward the door of his bedroom, but stopped.

"I hate Francisco d'Anconia," she said tensely. "Why did he have to come to that party? And didn't he know enough to keep his mouth shut, at least till tomorrow morning?" He did not answer. "It's monstrous—what he's allowed to happen to his company. Of course, he's nothing but a rotten playboy—still, a fortune of that size is a responsibility, there's a limit to the negligence a man can permit himself!" He glanced at her face: it was oddly tense, the features sharpened, making her look older. "He owed a certain duty to his stockholders, didn't he? . . . Didn't he, Henry?"

"Do you mind if we don't discuss it?"

She made a tightening, sidewise movement with her lips, the equivalent of a shrug, and walked into the bedroom.

He stood at the window, looking down at the streaming roofs of automobiles, letting his eyes rest on something while his faculty of sight was disconnected. His mind was still focused on the crowd in the ballroom downstairs and on two figures in that crowd. But as his living room remained on the edge of his vision, so the sense of some action he had to perform remained on the edge of his consciousness. He grasped it for a moment—it was the fact that he had to remove his evening clothes—but farther beyond the edge there was the feeling of reluctance to undress in the presence of a strange woman in his bedroom, and he forgot it again in the next moment.

Lillian came out, as trimly groomed as she had arrived, the beige traveling suit outlining her figure with efficient tightness, the hat tilted over half a head of hair set in waves. She carried her suitcase, swinging it a little, as if in demonstration of her ability to carry it.

He reached over mechanically and took the suitcase out of her hand.

"What are you doing?" she asked.

"I'm going to take you to the station."

"Like this? You haven't changed your clothes."

"It doesn't matter."

"You don't have to escort me. I'm quite able to find my own way. If you have business appointments tomorrow, you'd better go to bed."

He did not answer, but walked to the door, held it open for her and followed her to the elevator.

They remained silent when they rode in a taxicab to the station. At such moments as he remembered her presence, he noticed that she sat efficiently straight, almost flaunting the perfection of her poise; she seemed alertly awake and contented, as if she were starting out on a purposeful journey of early morning.

The cab stopped at the entrance to the Taggart Terminal. The bright lights flooding the great glass doorway transformed the lateness of the hour into a sense of active, timeless security. Lillian jumped lightly out of the cab, saying, "No, no, you don't have to get out, drive on back. Will you be home for dinner tomorrow—or next month?"

"I'll telephone you," he said.

She waved her gloved hand at him and disappeared into the lights of the entrance. As the cab started forward, he gave the driver the address of Dagny's apartment.

The apartment was dark when he entered, but the door to her bedroom was half-open and he heard her voice saying, "Hello, Hank."

He walked in, asking, "Were you asleep?"

"No."

He switched on the light. She lay in bed, her head propped by the pillow, her hair falling smoothly to her shoulders, as if she had not moved for a long time; but her face was untroubled. She looked like a schoolgirl, with the tailored collar of a pale blue nightgown lying severely high at the base of her throat; the nightgown's front was a deliberate contrast to the severity, a spread of pale blue embroidery that looked luxuriously adult and feminine.

He sat down on the edge of the bed—and she smiled, noticing that the stern formality of his full dress clothes made his action so simply, naturally intimate. He smiled in answer. He had come, prepared to reject the forgiveness she had granted him at the party, as one rejects a favor from too generous an adversary. Instead, he reached out suddenly and moved his hand over her forehead, down the line of her hair, in a gesture of protective tenderness, in the sudden feeling of how delicately childlike she was, this adversary who had borne the constant challenge of his strength, but who should have had his protection.

"You're carrying so much," he said, "and it's I who make it harder for you . . ."

"No, Hank, you don't and you know it."

"I know that you have the strength not to let it hurt you, but it's a strength I have no right to call upon. Yet I do, and I have no solution, no atonement to offer. I can only admit that I know it and that there's no way I can ask you to forgive me."

"There's nothing to forgive."

"I had no right to bring her into your presence."

"It did not hurt me. Only . . ."

"Yes?"

". . . only seeing the way you suffered . . . was hard to see."

"I don't think that suffering makes up for anything, but whatever I felt, I didn't suffer enough. If there's one thing I loathe, it's to speak of my own suffering—*that* should be no one's concern but mine. But if you want to know, since you know it already—yes, it was hell for me. And I wish it were worse. At least, I'm not letting myself get away with it."

He said it sternly, without emotion, as an impersonal verdict upon himself. She smiled, in amused sadness, she took his hand and pressed it to her lips, and shook her head in rejection of the verdict, holding her face hidden against his hand.

"What do you mean?" he asked softly.

"Nothing . . ." Then she raised her head and said firmly, "Hank, I knew you were married. I knew what I was doing. I chose to do it. There's nothing that you owe me, no duty that you have to consider."

He shook his head slowly, in protest.

"Hank, I want nothing from you except what you wish to give me. Do you remember that you called me a trader once? I want you to come to me seeking nothing but your own enjoyment. So long as you wish to remain married, whatever your reason, I have no right to resent it. My way of trading is to know that the joy you give me is paid for by the joy you get from me—not by your suffering or mine. I don't accept sacrifices and I don't make them. If you asked me for more than you meant to me, I would refuse. If you asked me to give up the railroad, I'd leave you. If ever the pleasure of one has to be bought by the pain of the other, there better be no trade at all. A trade by which one gains and the other loses is a fraud. You don't do it in business, Hank. Don't do it in your own life."

Like a dim sound track under her words, he was hearing the words said to him by Lillian; he was seeing the distance between the two, the difference in what they sought from him and from life.

"Dagny, what do you think of my marriage?"

"I have no right to think of it."

"You must have wondered about it."

"I did . . . before I came to Ellis Wyatt's house. Not since."

"You've never asked me a question about it."

"And won't."

He was silent for a moment, then said, looking straight at her, underscoring his first rejection of the privacy she had always granted him, "There's one thing I want you to know: I have not touched her since . . . Ellis Wyatt's house."

"I'm glad."

"Did you think I could?"

"I've never permitted myself to wonder about that."

"Dagny, do you mean that if I had, you . . . you'd accept that, too?"

"Yes."

"You wouldn't hate it?"

"I'd hate it more than I can tell you. But if that were your choice, I would accept it. I want you, Hank."

He took her hand and raised it to his lips, she felt the moment's struggle in his body, in the sudden movement with which he came down, half-collapsing, and let his mouth cling to her shoulder. Then he pulled her forward, he pulled the length of her body in the pale blue nightgown to lie stretched across his knees, he held it with an unsmiling violence, as if in hatred for her words and as if they were the words he had most wanted to hear.

He bent his face down to hers and she heard the question that had come again and again in the nights of the year behind them, always torn out of him involuntarily, always as a sudden break that betrayed his constant, secret torture: "Who was your first man?"

She strained back, trying to draw away from him, but he held her. "No, Hank," she said, her face hard.

The brief, taut movement of his lips was a smile. "I know that you won't answer it, but I won't stop asking—because *that* is what I'll never accept."

"Ask yourself why you won't accept it."

He answered, his hand moving slowly from her breasts to her knees, as if stressing his ownership and hating it, "Because . . . the things you've permitted me to do . . . I didn't think you could, not ever, not even for me . . . but to find that you did, and more: that you had permitted another man, had wanted him to, had—"

"Do you understand what you're saying? That you've never accepted my wanting you, either—you've never accepted that I *should* want you, just as I should have wanted him, once."

He said, his voice low, "That's true."

She tore herself away from him with a brusque, twisting movement, she stood up, but she stood looking down at him with a faint smile, and she said softly, "Do you know your only real guilt? With the greatest capacity for it, you've never learned to enjoy yourself. You've always rejected your own pleasure too easily. You've been willing to bear too much."

"He said that, too."

"Who?"

"Francisco d'Anconia."

He wondered why he had the impression that the name shocked her and that she answered an instant too late, "He said that to you?"

"We were talking about quite a different subject."

In a moment, she said calmly, "I saw you talking to him. Which one of you was insulting the other, this time?"

"We weren't. Dagny, what do you think of him?"

"I think that he's done it intentionally—that smash-up we're in for, tomorrow."

"I know he has. Still, what do you think of him as a person?"

"I don't know. I ought to think that he's the most depraved person I've ever met."

"You ought to? But you don't?"

"No. I can't quite make myself feel certain of it."

He smiled. "That's what's strange about him. I know that he's a liar, a loafer, a cheap playboy, the most viciously irresponsible waste of a human being I ever imagined possible. Yet, when I look at him, I feel that if ever there was a man to whom I would entrust my life, he's the one."

She gasped. "Hank, are you saying that you like him?"

"I'm saying that I didn't know what it meant, to like a man, I didn't know how much I missed it—until I met him."

"Good God, Hank, you've fallen for him!"

"Yes—I think I have." He smiled. "Why does it frighten you?"

"Because . . . because I think he's going to hurt you in some terrible way . . . and the more you see in him, the harder it will be to bear . . . and it will take you a long time to get over it, if ever. . . . I feel that I ought to warn you against him, but I can't—because I'm certain of nothing about him, not even whether he's the greatest or the lowest man on earth."

"I'm certain of nothing about him—except that I like him."

"But think of what he's done. It's not Jim and Boyle that he's hurt, it's you and me and Ken Danagger and the rest of us, because Jim's gang will merely take it out on us—and it's going to be another disaster, like the Wyatt fire."

"Yes . . . yes, like the Wyatt fire. But, you know, I don't think I care too much about that. What's one more disaster? Everything's going anyway, it's only a question of a little faster or a little slower, all that's left for us ahead is to keep the ship afloat as long as we can and then go down with it."

"Is that his excuse for himself? Is that what he's made you feel?"

"No. Oh no! That's the feeling I lose when I speak to him. The strange thing is what he does make me feel."

"What?"

"Hope."

She nodded, in helpless wonder, knowing that she had felt it, too.

"I don't know why," he said. "But I look at people and they seem to be made of nothing but pain. He's not. You're not. That terrible hopelessness that's all around us, I lose it only in his presence. And here. Nowhere else."

She came back to him and slipped down to sit at his feet, pressing her face to his knees. "Hank, we still have so much ahead of us . . . and so much right now. . . ."

He looked at the shape of pale blue silk huddled against the black of his clothes—he bent down to her—he said, his voice low, "Dagny . . . the things I said to you that morning in Ellis Wyatt's house . . . I think I was lying to myself."

"I know it."

* * *

Through a gray drizzle of rain, the calendar above the roofs said: September 3, and a clock on another tower said: 10:40, as Rearden rode back to the Wayne-Falkland Hotel. The cab's radio was spitting out shrilly the sounds of a panic-tinged voice announcing the crash of d'Anconia Copper.

Rearden leaned wearily against the seat: the disaster seemed to be no more than a stale news story read long ago. He felt nothing, except an uncomfortable sense of impropriety at finding himself out in the morning streets, dressed in evening clothes. He felt no desire to return from the world he had left to the world he saw drizzling past the windows of the taxi.

He turned the key in the door of his hotel suite, hoping to get back to a desk as fast as possible and have to see nothing around him.

They hit his consciousness together: the breakfast table—the door to his bedroom, open upon the sight of a bed that had been slept in—and Lillian's voice saying, "Good morning, Henry."

She sat in an armchair, wearing the suit she had worn yesterday, without the jacket or hat; her white blouse looked smugly crisp. There were remnants of a breakfast on the table. She was smoking a cigarette, with the air and pose of a long, patient vigil.

As he stood still, she took the time to cross her legs and settle down more comfortably, then asked, "Aren't you going to say anything, Henry?"

He stood like a man in military uniform at some official proceedings where emotions could not be permitted to exist. "It is for you to speak."

"Aren't you going to try to justify yourself?"

"No."

"Aren't you going to start begging my forgiveness?"

"There is no reason why you should forgive me. There is nothing for me to add. You know the truth. Now it is up to you."

She chuckled, stretching, rubbing her shoulder blades against the chair's back. "Didn't you expect to be caught, sooner or later?" she asked. "If a man like you stays pure as a monk for over a year, didn't you think that I might begin to suspect the reason? It's funny, though, that that famous brain of yours didn't prevent you from getting caught as simply as this." She waved at the room, at the breakfast table. "I felt certain that you weren't going to return here, last night. And it wasn't difficult or expensive at all to find out from a hotel employee, this morning, that you haven't spent a night in these rooms in the past year."

He said nothing.

"The man of stainless steel!" She laughed. "The man of achievement and honor who's so much better than the rest of us! Does she dance in the chorus or is she a manicurist in an exclusive barber shop patronized by millionaires?"

He remained silent.

"Who is she, Henry?"

"I won't answer that."

"I want to know."

"You're not going to."

"Don't you think it's ridiculous, your playing the part of a gentleman who's protecting the lady's name—or of any sort of gentleman, from now on? Who is she?"

"I said I won't answer."

She shrugged. "I suppose it makes no difference. There's only one standard type for the one standard purpose. I've always known that under that ascetic look of yours you were a plain, crude sensualist who sought nothing from a woman except an animal satisfaction which I pride myself on not having given you. I knew that your vaunted sense of honor would collapse some day and you would be drawn to the lowest, cheapest type of female, just like any other cheating husband." She chuckled. "That great admirer of yours, Miss Dagny Taggart, was furious at me for the mere hint of a suggestion that her hero wasn't as pure as his stainless, non-corrosive rail. And she was naïve enough to imagine that I could suspect her of being the type men find attractive for a relationship in which what they seek is most notoriously *not* brains. I knew your real nature and inclinations. Didn't I?" He said nothing. "Do you know what I think of you now?"

"You have the right to condemn me in any way you wish."

She laughed. "The great man who was so contemptuous—in business—of weaklings who trimmed corners or fell by the wayside, because they couldn't match his strength of character and steadfastness of purpose! How do you feel about it now?"

"My feelings need not concern you. You have the right to decide what you wish me to do. I will agree to any demand you make, except one: don't ask me to give it up."

"Oh, I wouldn't ask you to give it up! I wouldn't expect you to change your nature. This is your true level—under all that self-made grandeur of a knight of industry who rose by sheer genius from the ore mine gutters to finger bowls and white tie! It fits you well, that white tie, to come home in at eleven o'clock in the morning! You never rose out of the ore mines, that's where you belong—all of you self-made princes of the cash register—in the corner saloon on Saturday night, with the traveling salesmen and the dance-hall girls!"

"Do you wish to divorce me?"

"Oh, wouldn't you like that! Wouldn't that be a smart trade to pull! Don't you suppose I know that you've wanted to divorce me since the first month of our marriage?"

"If that is what you thought, why did you stay with me?"

She answered severely, "It's a question you have lost the right to ask."

"That's true," he said, thinking that only one conceivable reason, her love for him, could justify her answer.

"No, I'm not going to divorce you. Do you suppose that I will allow your romance with a floozie to deprive me of my home, my name, my social position? I shall preserve such pieces of my life as I can, whatever does not rest on so shoddy a foundation as your fidelity. Make no mistake about it: I shall never give you a divorce. Whether you like it or not, you're married and you'll stay married."

"I will, if that is what you wish."

"And furthermore, I will not consider—incidentally, why don't you sit down?"

He remained standing. "Please say what you have to say."

"I will not consider any unofficial divorce, such as a separation. You may continue your love idyll in the subways and basements where it belongs, but in the eyes of the world I will expect you to remember that I am Mrs. Henry Rearden. You have always proclaimed such an exaggerated devotion to honesty—now let me see you be condemned to the life of the hypocrite that you really are. I will expect you to maintain your residence at the home which is officially yours, but will now be mine."

"If you wish."

She leaned back loosely, in a manner of untidy relaxation, her legs spread apart, her arms resting in two strict parallels on the arms of the chair—like a judge who could permit himself to be sloppy.

"Divorce?" she said, chuckling coldly. "Did you think you'd get off as easily as that? Did you think you'd get by at the price of a few of your millions tossed off as alimony? You're so used to purchasing whatever you wish by the simple means of your dollars, that you cannot conceive of things that are non-commercial, non-negotiable, non-subject to any kind of trade. You're unable to believe that there may exist a person who feels no concern for money. You cannot imagine what *that* means. Well, I think you're going to learn. Oh yes, of course you'll agree to any demand I make, from now on. I want you to sit in that office of which you're so proud, in those precious mills of yours, and play the hero who works eighteen hours a day, the giant of industry who keeps the whole country going, the genius who is above the common herd of whining, lying, chiseling humanity. Then I want you to come home and face the only person who knows you for what you really are, who knows the actual value of your word, of your honor, of your integrity, of your vaunted self-esteem. I want you to face, in your own home, the one person who despises you and has the right to do so. I want you to look at me whenever you build another furnace, or pour another record-breaking load of steel, or hear applause and admiration, whenever you feel proud of yourself, whenever you feel clean, whenever you feel drunk on the sense of your own greatness. I want you to look at me whenever you hear of some act of depravity, or feel anger at human corruption, or feel contempt for someone's knavery, or are the victim of a new governmental extortion—to look and to know that you're no better, that you're superior to no one, that there's nothing you have the right to condemn. I want you to look at me and to learn the fate of the man who tried to build a tower to the sky, or the man who wanted to reach the sun on wings made of wax—or you, the man who wanted to hold himself as perfect!"

Somewhere outside of him and apart, as if he were reading it in a brain not his own, he observed the thought that there was some flaw in the scheme of the punishment she wanted him to bear, something wrong by its own terms, aside from its propriety or justice, some practical miscalculation that would demolish it all if discovered. He did not attempt to discover it. The thought went by as a moment's notation, made in cold curiosity, to be brought back in some distant future. There was nothing within him now with which to feel interest or to respond.

His own brain was numb with the effort to hold the last of his sense of justice against so overwhelming a tide of revulsion that it swamped Lillian out of human form, past all his pleas to himself that he had no right to feel it. If she was loathsome, he thought, it was he who had brought her to it; this was her way of taking pain—no one could prescribe the form of a human being's attempt to bear suffering—no one could blame—above all, not he, who had caused it. But he saw no evidence of pain in her manner. Then perhaps the ugliness was the only means she could summon to hide it, he thought. Then he thought of nothing except of withstanding the revulsion for the length of the next moment and of the next.

When she stopped speaking, he asked, "Have you finished?"

"Yes, I believe so."

"Then you had better take the train home now."

When he undertook the motions necessary to remove his evening clothes, he discovered that his muscles felt as if he were at the end of a long day of physical labor. His starched shirt was limp with sweat. There was neither thought nor feeling left in him, nothing but a sense that merged the remnants of both, the sense of congratulation upon the greatest victory he had ever demanded of himself: that Lillian had walked out of the hotel suite alive.

*   *   *

Entering Rearden's office, Dr. Floyd Ferris wore the expression of a man so certain of the success of his quest that he could afford a benevolent smile. He spoke with a smooth, cheerful assurance; Rearden had the impression that it was the assurance of a cardsharp who has spent a prodigious effort in memorizing every possible variation of the pattern, and is now safe in the knowledge that every card in the deck is marked.

"Well, Mr. Rearden," he said, by way of greeting, "I didn't know that even a hardened hound of public functions and shaker of famous hands, like myself, could still get a thrill out of meeting an eminent man, but that's what I feel right now, believe it or not."

"How do you do," said Rearden.

Dr. Ferris sat down and made a few remarks about the colors of the leaves in the month of October, as he had observed them by the roadside on his long drive from Washington, undertaken specifically for the purpose of meeting Mr. Rearden in person. Rearden said nothing. Dr. Ferris looked out the window and commented on the inspiring sight of the Rearden mills which, he said, were one of the most valuable productive enterprises in the country.

"That is not what you thought of my product a year and a half ago," said Rearden.

Dr. Ferris gave a brief frown, as if a dot of the pattern had slipped and almost cost him the game, then chuckled, as if he had recaptured it. "That was a year and a half ago, Mr. Rearden," he said easily. "Times change, and people change with the times—the wise ones do. Wisdom lies in knowing when to remember and when to forget. Consistency is not a habit of mind which it is wise to practice or to expect of the human race."

He then proceeded to discourse upon the foolishness of consistency in a world where nothing was absolute except the principle of compromise. He talked earnestly, but in a casual manner, as if they both understood that this was not the main subject of their interview; yet, oddly, he spoke not in the tone of a foreword, but in the tone of a post-script, as if the main subject had been settled long ago.

Rearden waited for the first "Don't you think so?" and answered, "Please state the urgent matter for which you requested this appointment."

Dr. Ferris looked astonished and blank for a moment, then said brightly, as if remembering an unimportant subject which could be disposed of without effort, "Oh, that? That was in regard to the dates·of delivery of Rearden Metal to the State Science Institute. We should like to have five thousand tons by the first of December, and then we'll be quite agreeable to waiting for the balance of the order until after the first of the year."

Rearden sat looking at him silently for a long time; each passing moment had the effect of making the gay intonations of Dr. Ferris' voice, still hanging in the air of the room, seem more foolish. When Dr. Ferris had begun to dread that he would not answer at all, Rearden answered, "Hasn't the traffic cop with the leather leggings, whom you sent here, given you a report on his conversation with me?"

"Why, yes, Mr. Rearden, but—"

"What else do you want to hear?"

"But that was five months ago, Mr. Rearden. A certain event has taken place since, which makes me quite sure that you have changed your mind and that you will make no trouble for us at all, just as we will make no trouble for you."

"What event?"

"An event of which you have far greater knowledge than I—but, you see, I do have knowledge of it, even though you would much prefer me to have none."

"What event?"

"Since it is your secret, Mr. Rearden, why not let it remain a secret? Who doesn't have secrets nowadays? For instance, Project X is a secret. You realize, of course, that we could obtain your Metal simply by having it purchased in smaller quantities by various government offices who would then transfer it to us—and you would not be able to prevent it. But this would necessitate our letting a lot of lousy bureaucrats"—Dr. Ferris smiled with disarming frankness—"oh yes, we are as unpopular with one another as we are with you private citizens—it would necessitate our letting a lot of other bureaucrats in on the secret of Project X, which would be highly undesirable at this time. And so would any newspaper publicity about the Project—if we put you on trial for refusal to comply with a government order. But if you had to stand trial on another, much more serious charge, where Project X and the State Science Institute were not involved, and where you could not raise any issue of principle or arouse any public sympathy—why, that would not inconvenience us at all, but it would cost you more than you would care to contemplate. Therefore, the only practical thing for you to do is to help us keep our secret and get us to help you keep yours—and, as I'm sure you realize, we are fully able to keep any of the bureaucrats safely off your trail for as long as we wish."

"What event, what secret and what trail?"

"Oh, come, Mr. Rearden, don't be childish! The four thousand tons of Rearden Metal which you delivered to Ken Danagger, of course," said Dr. Ferris lightly.

Rearden did not answer.

"Issues of principle are such a nuisance," said Dr. Ferris, smiling, "and such a waste of time for all concerned. Now would you care to be a martyr for an issue of principle, only in circumstances where nobody will know that that's what you are—nobody but you and me—where you won't get a chance to breathe a word about the issue or the principle—where you won't be a hero, the creator of a spectacular new metal, making a stand against enemies whose actions might appear somewhat shabby in the eyes of the public—where you won't be a hero, but a common criminal, a greedy industrialist who's cheated the law for a plain motive of profit, a racketeer of the black market who's broken the national regulations designed to protect the public welfare—a hero without glory and without public, who'll accomplish no more than about half a column of newsprint somewhere on page five—now would you still care to be that kind of martyr? Because that's just what the issue amounts to now: either you let us have the Metal or you go to jail for ten years and take your friend Danagger along, too."

As a biologist, Dr. Ferris had always been fascinated by the theory that animals had the capacity to smell fear; he had tried to develop a similar capacity in himself. Watching Rearden, he concluded that the man had long since decided to give in—because he caught no trace of any fear.

"Who was your informer?" asked Rearden.

"One of your friends, Mr. Rearden. The owner of a copper mine in Arizona, who reported to us that you had purchased an extra amount of copper last month, above the regular tonnage required for the monthly quota of Rearden Metal which the law permits you to produce. Copper is one of the ingredients of Rearden Metal, isn't it? That was all the information we needed. The rest was easy to trace. You mustn't blame that mine owner too much. The copper producers, as you know, are being squeezed so badly right now that the man had to offer something of value in order to obtain a favor, an 'emergency need' ruling which suspended a few of the directives in his case and gave him a little breathing spell. The person to whom he traded his information knew where it would have the highest value, so he traded it to me, in return for certain favors *he* needed. So all the necessary evidence, as well as the next ten years of your life, are now in my possession—and I am offering you a trade. I'm sure you won't object, since trade is your specialty. The form may be a little different from what it was in your youth—but you're a smart trader, you've always known how to take advantage of changing conditions, and these are the conditions of our day, so it should not be difficult for you to see where your interests lie and to act accordingly."

Rearden said calmly, "In my youth, this was called blackmail."

Dr. Ferris grinned. "That's what it is, Mr. Rearden. We've entered a much more realistic age."

But there was a peculiar difference, thought Rearden, between the manner of a plain blackmailer and that of Dr. Ferris. A blackmailer would show signs of gloating over his victim's sin and of acknowledging its evil, he would suggest a threat to the victim and a sense of danger to them both. Dr. Ferris conveyed none of it. His manner was that of dealing with the normal and the natural, it suggested a sense of safety, it held no tone of condemnation, but a hint of comradeship, a comradeship based—for both of them—on self-contempt. The sudden feeling that made Rearden lean forward in a posture of eager attentiveness, was the feeling that he was about to discover another step along his half-glimpsed trail.

Seeing Rearden's look of interest, Dr. Ferris smiled and congratulated himself on having caught the right key. The game was clear to him now, the markings of the pattern were falling in the right order; some men, thought Dr. Ferris, would do anything so long as it was left unnamed, but this man wanted frankness, this was the tough realist he had expected to find.

"You're a practical man, Mr. Rearden," said Dr. Ferris amiably. "I can't understand why you should want to stay behind the times. Why don't you adjust yourself and play it right? You're smarter than most of them. You're a valuable person, we've wanted you for a long time, and when I heard that you were trying to string along with Jim Taggart, I knew you could be had. Don't bother with Jim Taggart, he's nothing, he's just flea-bait. Get into the big game. We can use you and you can use us. Want us to step on Orren Boyle for you? He's given you an awful beating, want us to trim him down a little? It can be done. Or want us to keep Ken Danagger in line? Look how impractical you've been about that. I know why you sold him the Metal—it's because you need him to get coal from. So you take a chance on going to jail and paying huge fines, just to keep on the good side of Ken Danagger. Do you call that good business? Now, make a deal with us and just let Mr. Danagger understand that if he doesn't toe the line, *he'll* go to jail, but *you* won't, because you've got friends he hasn't got—and you'll never have to worry about your coal supply from then on. Now *that's* the modern way of doing business. Ask yourself which way is more practical. And whatever anyone's said about you, nobody's ever denied that you're a great businessman and a hard-headed realist."

"That's what I am," said Rearden.

"That's what I thought," said Dr. Ferris. "You rose to riches in an age when most men were going bankrupt, you've always managed to blast obstacles, to keep your mills going and to make money—that's your reputation—so you wouldn't want to be impractical now, would you? What for? What do you care, so long as you make money? Leave the theories to people like Bertram Scudder and the ideals to people like Balph Eubank—and be yourself. Come down to earth. You're not the man who'd let sentiment interfere with business."

"No," said Rearden slowly, "I wouldn't. Not any kind of sentiment."

Dr. Ferris smiled. "Don't you suppose we knew it?" he said, his tone suggesting that he was letting his patent-leather hair down to impress a fellow criminal by a display of superior cunning. "We've waited a long time to get something on you. You honest men are such a problem and such a headache. But we knew you'd slip sooner or later—and this is just what we wanted."

"You seem to be pleased about it."

"Don't I have good reason to be?"

"But, after all, I did break one of your laws."

"Well, what do you think they're for?"

Dr. Ferris did not notice the sudden look on Rearden's face, the look of a man hit by the first vision of that which he had sought to see. Dr. Ferris was past the stage of seeing; he was intent upon delivering the last blows to an animal caught in a trap.

"Did you really think that we want those laws to be observed?" said Dr. Ferris. "We *want* them broken. You'd better get it straight that it's not a bunch of boy scouts you're up against—then you'll know that this is not the age for beautiful gestures. We're after power and we mean it. You fellows were pikers, but we know the real trick, and you'd better get wise to it. There's no way to rule innocent men. The only power any government has is the power to crack down on criminals. Well, when there aren't enough criminals, one *makes* them. One declares so many things to be a crime that it becomes impossible for men to live without breaking laws. Who wants a nation of law-abiding citizens? What's there in that for anyone? But just pass the kind of laws that can neither be observed nor enforced nor objectively interpreted—and you create a nation of law-breakers—and then you cash in on guilt. Now that's the system, Mr. Rearden, that's the game, and once you understand it, you'll be much easier to deal with."

Watching Dr. Ferris watch him, Rearden saw the sudden twitch of anxiety, the look that precedes panic, as if a clean card had fallen on the table from a deck Dr. Ferris had never seen before.

What Dr. Ferris was seeing in Rearden's face was the look of luminous serenity that comes from the sudden answer to an old, dark problem, a look of relaxation and eagerness together; there was a youthful clarity in Rearden's eyes and the faintest touch of contempt in the line of his mouth. Whatever this meant—and Dr. Ferris could not decipher it —he was certain of one thing: the face held no sign of guilt.

"There's a flaw in your system, Dr. Ferris," Rearden said quietly, almost lightly, "a practical flaw which you will discover when you put me on trial for selling four thousand tons of Rearden Metal to Ken Danagger."

It took twenty seconds—Rearden could feel them moving past slowly—at the end of which Dr. Ferris became convinced that he had heard Rearden's final decision.

"Do you think we're bluffing?" snapped Dr. Ferris; his voice suddenly had the quality of the animals he had spent so much time studying: it sounded as if he were baring his teeth.

"I don't know," said Rearden. "I don't care, one way or the other."

"Are you going to be as impractical as that?"

"The evaluation of an action as 'practical,' Dr. Ferris, depends on what it is that one wishes to practice."

"Haven't you always placed your self-interest above all else?"

"That is what I am doing right now."

"If you think we'll let you get away with a—"

"You will now please get out of here."

"Whom do you think you're fooling?" Dr. Ferris' voice had risen close to the edge of a scream. "The day of the barons of industry is done! You've got the goods, but we've got the goods on *you*, and you're going to play it our way or you'll—"

Rearden had pressed a button; Miss Ives entered the office.

"Dr. Ferris has become confused and has lost his way, Miss Ives," said Rearden. "Will you escort him out please?" He turned to Ferris. "Miss Ives is a woman, she weighs about a hundred pounds, and she has no practical qualifications at all, only a superlative intellectual efficiency. She would never do for a bouncer in a saloon, only in an impractical place, such as a factory."

Miss Ives looked as if she was performing a duty of no greater emotional significance than taking dictation about a list of shipping invoices. Standing straight in a disciplined manner of icy formality, she held the door open, let Dr. Ferris cross the room, then walked out first; Dr. Ferris followed.

She came back a few minutes later, laughing in uncontrollable exultation.

"Mr. Rearden," she asked, laughing at her fear for him, at their danger, at everything but the triumph of the moment, "what is it you're doing?"

He sat in a pose he had never permitted himself before, a pose he had resented as the most vulgar symbol of the businessman—he sat leaning back in his chair, with his feet on his desk—and it seemed to her that the posture had an air of peculiar nobility, that it was not the pose of a stuffy executive, but of a young crusader.

"I think I'm discovering a new continent, Gwen," he answered cheerfully. "A continent that should have been discovered along with America, but wasn't."

* * *

"I have to speak of it to *you*," said Eddie Willers, looking at the worker across the table. "I don't know why it helps me, but it does—just to know that you're hearing me."

It was late and the lights of the underground cafeteria were low, but Eddie Willers could see the worker's eyes looking at him intently.

"I feel as if . . . as if there's no people and no human language left," said Eddie Willers. "I feel that if I were to scream in the middle of the streets, there would be no one to hear it. . . . No, that's not quite what I feel, it's this: I feel that someone *is* screaming in the middle of the streets, but people are passing by and no sound can reach them —and it's not Hank Rearden or Ken Danagger or I who's screaming, and yet it seems as if it's all three of us. . . . Don't you see that somebody should have risen to defend them, but nobody has or will? Rearden and Danagger were indicted this morning—for an illegal sale of Rearden Metal. They'll go on trial next month. I was there, in the courtroom in Philadelphia, when they read the indictment. Rearden was very calm—I kept feeling that he was smiling, but he wasn't. Danagger was worse than calm. He didn't say a word, he just stood there, as if the room were empty. . . . The newspapers are saying that both of them should be thrown in jail. . . . No . . . no, I'm not shaking, I'm all right, I'll be all right in a moment. . . . That's why I haven't said a word to her, I was afraid I'd explode and I didn't want to make it harder for her, I know how she feels. . . . Oh yes, *she* spoke to me about it, and she didn't shake, but it was worse— you know, the kind of rigidity when a person acts as if she didn't feel anything at all, and . . . Listen, did I ever tell you that I like you? I like you very much—for the way you look right now. You hear us. You understand . . . What did she say? It was strange: it's not Hank Rearden that she's afraid for, it's Ken Danagger. She said that Rearden will have the strength to take it, but Danagger won't. Not that he'll lack the strength, but he'll refuse to take it. She . . . she feels certain that Ken Danagger will be the next one to go. To go like Ellis Wyatt and all those others. To give up and vanish . . . Why? Well, she thinks that there's something like a shift of stress involved— economic and personal stress. As soon as all the weight of the moment shifts to the shoulders of some one man—*he's* the one who vanishes, like a pillar slashed off. A year ago, nothing worse could have happened to the country than to lose Ellis Wyatt. He's the one we lost. Since then, she says, it's been as if the center of gravity were swinging wildly—like in a sinking cargo ship out of control—shifting from industry to industry, from man to man. When we lose one, another becomes that much more desperately needed—and he's the one we lose next. Well, what could be a greater disaster now than to have the country's coal supply left in the hands of men like Boyle or Larkin? And there's no one left in the coal industry who amounts to much, except Ken Danagger. So she says that she feels almost as if he's a marked man, as if he's hit by a spotlight right now, waiting to be cut down. . . . What are you laughing at? It might sound preposterous, but I think it's true. . . . What? . . . Oh yes, you bet she's a smart woman! . . . And then there's another thing involved, she says. A man has to come to a certain mental stage—not anger or despair, but something much, much more than both—before he can be cut down. She can't tell what it is, but she knew, long before the fire, that Ellis Wyatt had reached that stage and something would happen to him. When she saw Ken Danagger in the courtroom today, she said that he was ready for the destroyer. . . . Yes, that's the words she used: he was ready for the destroyer. You see, she doesn't think it's happening by chance or accident. She thinks there's a system behind it, an intention, a man. There's a destroyer loose in the country, who's cutting down the buttresses one after another to let the structure collapse upon our heads. Some ruthless creature moved by some inconceivable purpose . . . She says that she won't let him get Ken Danagger. She keeps repeating that she must stop Danagger—she wants to speak to him, to beg, to plead, to revive whatever it is that he's losing, to arm him against the destroyer, before the destroyer comes. She's desperately anxious to reach Danagger first. He has refused to see anyone. He's gone back to Pittsburgh, to his mines. But she got him on the phone, late today, and she's made an appointment to see him tomorrow afternoon. . . . Yes, she'll go to Pittsburgh tomorrow. . . . Yes, she's afraid for Danagger, terribly afraid. . . . No. She knows nothing about the destroyer. She has no clue to his identity, no evidence of his existence—except the trail of destruction. But she feels certain that he exists. . . . No, she cannot guess his purpose. She says that nothing on earth could justify him. There are times when she feels that she'd like to find him more than any other man in the world, more than the inventor of the motor. She says that if she found the destroyer, she'd shoot him on sight—she'd be willing to give her life if she could take his first and by her own hand . . . because he's the most evil creature that's ever existed, the man who's draining the brains of the world. . . . I guess it's getting to be too much for her, at times—even for her. I don't think she allows herself to know how tired she is. The other morning, I came to work very early and I found her asleep on the couch in her office, with the light still burning on her desk. She'd been there all night. I just stood and looked at her. I wouldn't have awakened her if the whole goddamn railroad collapsed. . . . When she was asleep? Why, she looked like a young girl. She looked as if she felt certain that she would awaken in a world where no one would harm her, as if she had nothing to hide or to fear. That's what was terrible—that guiltless purity of her face, with her body twisted by exhaustion, still lying there as she had collapsed. She looked—say, why should you ask me what she looks like when she's asleep? . . . Yes, you're right, why do *I* talk about it? I shouldn't. I don't know what made me think of it. . . . Don't pay any attention to me. I'll be all right tomorrow. I guess it's just that I'm sort of shell-shocked by that courtroom. I keep thinking: if men like Rearden and Danagger are to be sent to jail, then what kind of world are we working in and what for? Isn't there any justice left on earth? I was foolish enough to say that to a reporter when we were leaving the courtroom—and he just laughed and said, 'Who is John Galt?' . . . Tell me, what's happening to us? Isn't there a single man of justice left? Isn't there anyone to defend them? Oh, do you hear me? Isn't there anyone to defend them?"

* * *

"Mr. Danagger will be free in a moment, Miss Taggart. He has a visitor in his office. Will you excuse it, please?" said the secretary.

Through the two hours of her flight to Pittsburgh, Dagny had been tensely unable to justify her anxiety or to dismiss it; there was no reason to count minutes, yet she had felt a blind desire to hurry. The anxiety vanished when she entered the anteroom of Ken Danagger's office: she had reached him, nothing had happened to prevent it, she felt safety, confidence and an enormous sense of relief.

The words of the secretary demolished it. You're becoming a coward—thought Dagny, feeling a causeless jolt of dread at the words, out of all proportion to their meaning.

"I am so sorry, Miss Taggart." She heard the secretary's respectful, solicitous voice and realized that she had stood there without answering. "Mr. Danagger will be with you in just a moment. Won't you sit down?" The voice conveyed an anxious concern over the impropriety of keeping her waiting.

Dagny smiled. "Oh, that's quite all right."

She sat down in a wooden armchair, facing the secretary's railing. She reached for a cigarette and stopped, wondering whether she would have time to finish it, hoping that she would not, then lighted it brusquely.

It was an old-fashioned frame building, this headquarters of the great Danagger Coal Company. Somewhere in the hills beyond the window were the pits where Ken Danagger had once worked as a miner. He had never moved his office away from the coal fields.

She could see the mine entrances cut into the hillsides, small frames of metal girders, that led to an immense underground kingdom. They seemed precariously modest, lost in the violent orange and red of the hills. . . . Under a harsh blue sky, in the sunlight of late October, the sea of leaves looked like a sea of fire . . . like waves rolling to swallow the fragile posts of the mine doorways. She shuddered and looked away: she thought of the flaming leaves spread over the hills of Wisconsin, on the road to Starnesville.

She noticed that there was only a stub left of the cigarette between her fingers. She lighted another.

When she glanced at the clock on the wall of the anteroom, she caught the secretary glancing at it at the same time. Her appointment was for three o'clock; the white dial said: 3:12.

"Please forgive it, Miss Taggart," said the secretary. "Mr. Danagger will be through, any moment now. Mr. Danagger is extremely punctual about his appointments. Please believe me that this is unprecedented."

"I know it." She knew that Ken Danagger was as rigidly exact about his schedule as a railroad timetable and that he had been known to cancel an interview if a caller permitted himself to arrive five minutes late.

The secretary was an elderly spinster with a forbidding manner: a manner of even-toned courtesy impervious to any shock, just as her spotless white blouse was impervious to an atmosphere filled with coal dust. Dagny thought it strange that a hardened, well-trained woman of this type should appear to be nervous: she volunteered no conversation, she sat still, bent over some pages of paper on her desk. Half of Dagny's cigarette had gone in smoke, while the woman still sat looking at the same page.

When she raised her head to glance at the clock, the dial said: 3:30. "I know that this is inexcusable, Miss Taggart." The note of apprehension was obvious in her voice now. "I am unable to understand it."

"Would you mind telling Mr. Danagger that I'm here?"

"I can't!" It was almost a cry; she saw Dagny's astonished glance and felt obliged to explain: "Mr. Danagger called me, on the interoffice communicator, and told me that he was not to be interrupted under any circumstances or for any reason whatever."

"When did he do that?"

The moment's pause was like a small air cushion for the answer: "Two hours ago."

Dagny looked at the closed door of Danagger's office. She could hear the sound of a voice beyond the door, but so faintly that she could not tell whether it was the voice of one man or the conversation of two; she could not distinguish the words or the emotional quality of the tone: it was only a low, even progression of sounds that seemed normal and did not convey the pitch of raised voices.

"How long has Mr. Danagger been in conference?" she asked.

"Since one o'clock," said the secretary grimly, then added in apology, "It was an unscheduled caller, or Mr. Danagger would never have permitted this to happen."

The door was not locked, thought Dagny; she felt an unreasoning desire to tear it open and walk in—it was only a few wooden boards with a brass knob, it would require only a small muscular contraction of her arm—but she looked away, knowing that the power of a civilized order and of Ken Danagger's right was more impregnable a barrier than any lock.

She found herself staring at the stubs of her cigarettes in the ash-tray stand beside her, and wondered why it gave her a sharper feeling of apprehension. Then she realized that she was thinking of Hugh Akston: she had written to him, at his diner in Wyoming, asking him to tell her where he had obtained the cigarette with the dollar sign; her letter had come back, with a postal inscription to inform her that he had moved away, leaving no forwarding address.

She told herself angrily that this had no connection with the present moment and that she had to control her nerves. But her hand jerked to press the button of the ashtray and make the cigarette stubs vanish inside the stand.

As she looked up, her eyes met the glance of the secretary watching her. "I am sorry, Miss Taggart. I don't know what to do about it." It was an openly desperate plea. "I don't dare interrupt."

Dagny asked slowly, as a demand, in defiance of office etiquette, "Who is with Mr. Danagger?"

"I don't know, Miss Taggart. I have never seen the gentleman before." She noticed the sudden, fixed stillness of Dagny's eyes and added, "I think it's a childhood friend of Mr. Danagger."

"Oh!" said Dagny, relieved.

"He came in unannounced and asked to see Mr. Danagger and said that this was an appointment which Mr. Danagger had made with him forty years ago."

"How old is Mr. Danagger?"

"Fifty-two," said the secretary. She added reflectively, in the tone of a casual remark, "Mr. Danagger started working at the age of twelve." After another silence, she added, "The strange thing is that the visitor does not look as if he's even forty years old. He seems to be a man in his thirties."

"Did he give his name?"

"No."

"What does he look like?"

The secretary smiled with sudden animation, as if she were about to utter an enthusiastic compliment, but the smile vanished abruptly. "I don't know," she answered uneasily. "He's hard to describe. He has a strange face."

They had been silent for a long time, and the hands of the dial were approaching 3:50 when the buzzer rang on the secretary's desk— the bell from Danagger's office, the signal of permission to enter.

They both leaped to their feet, and the secretary rushed forward, smiling with relief, hastening to open the door.

As she entered Danagger's office, Dagny saw the private exit door closing after the caller who had preceded her. She heard the knock of the door against the jamb and the faint tinkle of the glass panel.

She saw the man who had left, by his reflection on Ken Danagger's face. It was not the face she had seen in the courtroom, it was not the face she had known for years as a countenance of unchanging, unfeeling rigidity—it was a face which a young man of twenty should hope for, but could not achieve, a face from which every sign of strain had been wiped out, so that the lined cheeks, the creased forehead, the graying hair—like elements rearranged by a new theme—were made to form a composition of hope, eagerness and guiltless serenity: the theme was deliverance.

He did not rise when she entered—he looked as if he had not quite returned to the reality of the moment and had forgotten the proper routine—but he smiled at her with such simple benevolence that she found herself smiling in answer. She caught herself thinking that this was the way every human being should greet another—and she lost her anxiety, feeling suddenly certain that all was well and that nothing to be feared could exist.

"How do you do, Miss Taggart," he said. "Forgive me, I think that I have kept you waiting. Please sit down." He pointed to the chair in front of his desk.

"I didn't mind waiting," she said. "I'm grateful that you gave me this appointment. I was extremely anxious to speak to you on a matter of urgent importance."

He leaned forward across the desk, with a look of attentive concentration, as he always did at the mention of an important business matter, but she was not speaking to the man she knew, this was a stranger, and she stopped, uncertain about the arguments she had been prepared to use.

He looked at her in silence, and then he said, "Miss Taggart, this is such a beautiful day—probably the last, this year. There's a thing I've always wanted to do, but never had time for it. Let's go back to New York together and take one of those excursion boat trips around the island of Manhattan. Let's take a last look at the greatest city in the world."

She sat still, trying to hold her eyes fixed in order to stop the office from swaying. This was the Ken Danagger who had never had a personal friend, had never married, had never attended a play or a movie, had never permitted anyone the impertinence of taking his time for any concern but business.

"Mr. Danagger, I came here to speak to you about a matter of crucial importance to the future of your business and mine. I came to speak to you about your indictment."

"Oh, that? Don't worry about that. It doesn't matter. I'm going to retire."

She sat still, feeling nothing, wondering numbly whether this was how it felt to hear a death sentence one had dreaded, but had never quite believed possible.

Her first movement was a sudden jerk of her head toward the exit door; she asked, her voice low, her mouth distorted by hatred, "Who was he?"

Danagger laughed. "If you've guessed that much, you should have guessed that it's a question I won't answer."

"Oh God, Ken Danagger!" she moaned; his words made her realize that the barrier of hopelessness, of silence, of unanswered questions was already erected between them; the hatred had been only a thin wire that had held her for a moment and she broke with its breaking. "Oh God!"

"You're wrong, kid," he said gently. "I know how you feel, but you're wrong," then added more formally, as if remembering the proper manner, as if still trying to balance himself between two kinds of reality, "I'm sorry, Miss Taggart, that you had to come here so soon after."

"I came too late," she said. "That's what I came here to prevent. I knew it would happen."

"Why?"

"I felt certain that he'd get you next, whoever he is."

"You did? That's funny. I didn't."

"I wanted to warn you, to . . . to arm you against him."

He smiled. "Take my word for it, Miss Taggart, so that you won't torture yourself with regrets about the timing: *that* could not have been done."

She felt that with every passing minute he was moving away into some great distance where she would not be able to reach him, but there was still some thin bridge left between them and she had to hurry. She leaned forward, she said very quietly, the intensity of emotion taking form in the exaggerated steadiness of her voice, "Do you remember what you thought and felt, what you *were,* three hours ago? Do you remember what your mines meant to you? Do you remember Taggart Transcontinental or Rearden Steel? In the name of that, will you answer me? Will you help me to understand?"

"I will answer whatever I may."

"You have decided to retire? To give up your business?"

"Yes."

"Does it mean nothing to you now?"

"It means more to me now than it ever did before."

"But you're going to abandon it?"

"Yes."

"Why?"

"That, I won't answer."

"You, who loved your work, who respected nothing but work, who despised every kind of aimlessness, passivity and renunciation—have you renounced the kind of life you loved?"

"No. I have just discovered how much I do love it."

"But you intend to exist without work or purpose?"

"What makes you think that?"

"Are you going into the coal-mining business somewhere else?"

"No, not into the coal-mining business."

"Then what are you going to do?"

"I haven't decided that yet."

"Where are you going?"

"I won't answer."

She gave herself a moment's pause, to gather her strength, to tell herself: Don't feel, don't show him that you feel anything, don't let it cloud and break the bridge—then she said, in the same quiet, even voice, "Do you realize what your retirement will do to Hank Rearden, to me, to all the rest of us, whoever is left?"

"Yes. I realize it more fully than you do at present."

"And it means nothing to you?"

"It means more than you will care to believe."

"Then why are you deserting us?"

"You will not believe it and I will not explain, but I am not deserting you."

"We're being left to carry a greater burden, and you're indifferent to the knowledge that you'll see us destroyed by the looters."

"Don't be too sure of that."

"Of which? Your indifference or our destruction?"

"Of either."

"But you know, you knew it this morning, that it's a battle to the death, and it's we—you were one of us—against the looters."

"If I answer that *I* know it, but *you* don't—you'll think that I attach no meaning to my words. So take it as you wish, but *that* is my answer."

"Will you tell me the meaning?"

"No. It's for you to discover."

"You're willing to give up the world to the looters. We aren't."

"Don't be too sure of either."

She remained helplessly silent. The strangeness of his manner was its simplicity: he spoke as if he were being completely natural and—in the midst of unanswered questions and of a tragic mystery—he conveyed the impression that there were no secrets any longer, and no mystery need ever have existed.

But as she watched him, she saw the first break in his joyous calm: she saw him struggling against some thought; he hesitated, then said, with effort, "About Hank Rearden . . . Will you do me a favor?"

"Of course."

"Will you tell him that I . . . You see, I've never cared for people, yet he was always the man I respected, but I didn't know until today that what I felt was . . . . that he was the only man I ever loved. . . . Just tell him this and that I wish I could—no, I guess that's all I can tell him. . . . He'll probably damn me for leaving . . . still, maybe he won't."

"I'll tell him."

Hearing the dulled, hidden sound of pain in his voice, she felt so close to him that it seemed impossible he would deliver the blow he was delivering—and she made one last effort.

"Mr. Danagger, if I were to plead on my knees, if I were to find some sort of words that I haven't found—would there be . . . *is* there a chance to stop you?"

"There isn't."

After a moment, she asked tonelessly, "When are you quitting?"

"Tonight."

"What will you do with"—she pointed at the hills beyond the window—"the Danagger Coal Company? To whom are you leaving it?"

"I don't know—or care. To nobody or everybody. To whoever wants to take it."

"You're not going to dispose of it or appoint a successor?"

"No. What for?"

"To leave it in good hands. Couldn't you at least name an heir of your own choice?"

"I haven't any choice. It doesn't make any difference to me. Want me to leave it all to you?" He reached for a sheet of paper. "I'll write a letter naming you sole heiress right now, if you want me to."

She shook her head in an involuntary recoil of horror. "I'm not a looter!"

He chuckled, pushing the paper aside. "You see? You gave the right answer, whether you knew it or not. Don't worry about Danagger Coal. It won't make any difference, whether I appoint the best successor in the world, or the worst, or none. No matter who takes it over now, whether men or weeds, it won't make any difference."

"But to walk off and abandon . . . just abandon . . . an industrial enterprise, as if we were in the age of landless nomads or of savages wandering in the jungle!"

"Aren't we?" He was smiling at her, half in mockery, half in compassion. "Why should I leave a deed or a will? I don't want to help the looters to pretend that private property still exists. I am complying with the system which they have established. They do not need me, they say, they only need my coal. Let them take it."

"Then you're accepting their system?"

"Am I?"

She moaned, looking at the exit door, "What has he done to you?"

"He told me that I had the right to exist."

"I didn't believe it possible that in three hours one could make a man turn against fifty-two years of his life!"

"If that's what you think he's done, or if you think that he's told me some inconceivable revelation, then I can see how bewildering it would appear to you. But that's not what he's done. He merely named what I had lived by, what every man lives by—at and to the extent of such time as he doesn't spend destroying himself."

She knew that questions were futile and that there was nothing she could say to him.

He looked at her bowed head and said gently, "You're a brave person, Miss Taggart. I know what you're doing right now and what it's costing you. Don't torture yourself. Let me go."

She rose to her feet. She was about to speak—but suddenly he saw her stare down, leap forward and seize the ashtray that stood on the edge of the desk.

The ashtray contained a cigarette butt stamped with the sign of the dollar.

"What's the matter, Miss Taggart?"

"Did *he* . . . did he smoke this?"

"Who?"

"Your caller—did he smoke this cigarette?"

"Why, I don't know . . . I guess so . . . yes, I think I did see him smoking a cigarette once . . . let me see . . . no, that's not my brand, so it must be his."

"Were there any other visitors in this office today?"

"No. But why, Miss Taggart? What's the matter?"

"May I take this?"

"What? The cigarette butt?" He stared at her in bewilderment.

"Yes."

"Why, sure—but what for?"

She was looking down at the butt in the palm of her hand as if it were a jewel. "I don't know . . . I don't know what good it will do me, except that it's a clue to"—she smiled bitterly—"to a secret of my own."

She stood, reluctant to leave, looking at Ken Danagger in the manner of a last look at one departing for the realm of no return.

He guessed it, smiled and extended his hand. "I won't say good-bye," he said, "because I'll see you again in the not too distant future."

"Oh," she said eagerly, holding his hand clasped across the desk, "are you going to return?"

"No. You're going to join me."

* * *

There was only a faint red breath above the structures in the darkness, as if the mills were asleep but alive, with the even breathing of the furnaces and the distant heartbeats of the conveyor belts to show it.

Rearden stood at the window of his office, his hand pressed to the pane; in the perspective of distance, his hand covered half a mile of structures, as if he were trying to hold them.

He was looking at a long wall of vertical strips, which was the battery of coke ovens. A narrow door slid open with a brief gasp of flame, and a sheet of red-glowing coke came sliding out smoothly, like a slice of bread from the side of a giant toaster. It held still for an instant, then an angular crack shot through the slice and it crumbled into a gondola waiting on the rails below.

Danagger coal, he thought. These were the only words in his mind. The rest was a feeling of loneliness, so vast that even its own pain seemed swallowed in an enormous void.

Yesterday, Dagny had told him the story of her futile attempt and given him Danagger's message. This morning, he had heard the news that Danagger had disappeared. Through his sleepless night, then through the taut concentration on the duties of the day, his answer to the message had kept beating in his mind, the answer he would never have a chance to utter.

"The only man I ever loved." It came from Ken Danagger, who had never expressed anything more personal than "Look here, Rearden." He thought: Why had we let it go? Why had we both been condemned —in the hours away from our desks—to an exile among dreary strangers who had made us give up all desire for rest, for friendship, for the sound of human voices? Could I now reclaim a single hour spent listening to my brother Philip and give it to Ken Danagger? Who made it our duty to accept, as the only reward for our work, the gray torture of pretending love for those who roused us to nothing but contempt? We who were able to melt rock and metal for our purpose, why had we never sought that which we wanted from men?

He tried to choke the words in his mind, knowing that it was useless to think of them now. But the words were there and they were like words addressed to the dead: No, I don't damn you for leaving—if that is the question and the pain which you took away with you. Why didn't you give me a chance to tell you . . . what? that I approve? . . . no, but that I can neither blame you nor follow you.

Closing his eyes, he permitted himself to experience for a moment the immense relief he would feel if he, too, were to walk off, abandoning everything. Under the shock of his loss, he felt a thin thread of envy. Why didn't they come for me, too, whoever they are, and give me that irresistible reason which would make me go? But in the next moment, his shudder of anger told him that he would murder the man who'd attempt to approach him, he would murder before he could hear the words of the secret that would take him away from his mills.

It was late, his staff had gone, but he dreaded the road to his house and the emptiness of the evening ahead. He felt as if the enemy who had wiped out Ken Danagger, were waiting for him in the darkness beyond the glow of the mills. He was not invulnerable any longer, but whatever it was, he thought, wherever it came from, he was safe from it here, as in a circle of fires drawn about him to ward off evil.

He looked at the glittering white splashes on the dark windows of a structure in the distance; they were like motionless ripples of sunlight on water. It was the reflection of the neon sign that burned on the roof of the building above his head, saying: Rearden Steel. He thought of the night when he had wished to light a sign above his past, saying: Rearden Life. Why had he wished it? For whose eyes to see?

He thought—in bitter astonishment and for the first time—that the joyous pride he had once felt, had come from his respect for men, for the value of their admiration and their judgment. He did not feel it any longer. There were no men, he thought, to whose sight he could wish to offer that sign.

He turned brusquely away from the window. He seized his overcoat with the harsh sweep of a gesture intended to jolt him back into the discipline of action. He slammed the two folds of the overcoat about his body, he jerked the belt tight, then hastened to turn off the lights with rapid snaps of his hand on his way out of the office.

He threw the door open—and stopped. A single lamp was burning in a corner of the dimmed anteroom. The man who sat on the edge of a desk, in a pose of casual, patient waiting, was Francisco d'Anconia.

Rearden stood still and caught a brief instant when Francisco, not moving, looked at him with the hint of an amused smile that was like a wink between conspirators at a secret they both understood, but would not acknowledge. It was only an instant, almost too brief to grasp, because it seemed to him that Francisco rose at once at his entrance, with a movement of courteous deference. The movement suggested a strict formality, the denial of any attempt at presumption—but it stressed the intimacy of the fact that he uttered no word of greeting or explanation.

Rearden asked, his voice hard, "What are you doing here?"

"I thought that you would want to see me tonight, Mr. Rearden."

"Why?"

"For the same reason that has kept you so late in your office. You were not working."

"How long have you been sitting here?"

"An hour or two."

"Why didn't you knock at my door?"

"Would you have allowed me to come in?"

"You're late in asking that question."

"Shall I leave, Mr. Rearden?"

Rearden pointed to the door of his office. "Come in."

Turning the lights on in the office, moving with unhurried control, Rearden thought that he must not allow himself to feel anything, but felt the color of life returning to him in the tensely quiet eagerness of an emotion which he would not identify. What he told himself consciously was: Be careful.

He sat down on the edge of his desk, crossed his arms, looked at Francisco, who remained standing respectfully before him, and asked with the cold hint of a smile, "Why did you come here?"

"You don't want me to answer, Mr. Rearden. You wouldn't admit to me or to yourself how desperately lonely you are tonight. If you don't question me, you won't feel obliged to deny it. Just accept what you do know, anyway: that I know it."

Taut like a string pulled by anger against the impertinence at one end and by admiration for the frankness at the other, Rearden answered, "I'll admit it, if you wish. What should it matter to me, that you know it?"

"That I know and care, Mr. Rearden. I'm the only man around you who does."

"Why should you care? And why should I need your help tonight?"

"Because it's not easy to have to damn the man who meant most to you."

"I wouldn't damn you if you'd only stay away from me."

Francisco's eyes widened a little, then he grinned and said, "I was speaking of Mr. Danagger."

For an instant, Rearden looked as if he wanted to slap his own face, then he laughed softly and said, "All right. Sit down."

He waited to see what advantage Francisco would take of it now, but Francisco obeyed him in silence, with a smile that had an oddly boyish quality: a look of triumph and gratitude, together.

"I don't damn Ken Danagger," said Rearden.

"You don't?" The two words seemed to fall with a singular emphasis; they were pronounced very quietly, almost cautiously, with no remnant of a smile on Francisco's face.

"No. I don't try to prescribe how much a man should have to bear. If he broke, it's not for me to judge him."

"If he broke . . . ?"

"Well, didn't he?"

Francisco leaned back; his smile returned, but it was not a happy smile. "What will his disappearance do to you?"

"I will just have to work a little harder."

Francisco looked at a steel bridge traced in black strokes against red steam beyond the window, and said, pointing, "Every one of those girders has a limit to the load it can carry. What's yours?"

Rearden laughed. "Is *that* what you're afraid of? Is that why you came here? Were you afraid I'd break? Did you want to save me, as Dagny Taggart wanted to save Ken Danagger? She tried to reach him in time, but couldn't."

"She did? I didn't know it. Miss Taggart and I disagree about many things."

"Don't worry. I'm not going to vanish. Let them all give up and stop working. I won't. I don't know my limit and don't care. All I have to know is that I can't be stopped."

"Any man can be stopped, Mr. Rearden."

"How?"

"It's only a matter of knowing man's motive power."

"What is it?"

"You ought to know, Mr. Rearden. You're one of the last moral men left to the world."

Rearden chuckled in bitter amusement. "I've been called just about everything but that. And you're wrong. You have no idea how wrong."

"Are you sure?"

"I ought to know. Moral? What on earth made you say it?"

Francisco pointed to the mills beyond the window. "This."

For a long moment, Rearden looked at him without moving, then asked only, "What do you mean?"

"If you want to see an abstract principle, such as moral action, in material form—there it is. Look at it, Mr. Rearden. Every girder of it, every pipe, wire and valve was put there by a choice in answer to the question: right or wrong? You had to choose right and you had to choose the best within your knowledge—the best for your purpose, which was to make steel—and then move on and extend the knowledge, and do better, and still better, with your purpose as your standard of value. You had to act on your own judgment, you had to have the capacity to judge, the courage to stand on the verdict of your mind, and the purest, the most ruthless consecration to the rule of doing right, of doing the best, the utmost best possible to you. Nothing could have made you act against your judgment, and you would have rejected as wrong—as evil—any man who attempted to tell you that the best way to heat a furnace was to fill it with ice. Millions of men, an entire nation, were not able to deter you from producing Rearden Metal—because you had the knowledge of its superlative value and the power which such knowledge gives. But what I wonder about, Mr. Rearden, is why you live by one code of principles when you deal with nature and by another when you deal with men?"

Rearden's eyes were fixed on him so intently that the question came slowly, as if the effort to pronounce it were a distraction: "What do you mean?"

"Why don't you hold to the purpose of your life as clearly and rigidly as you hold to the purpose of your mills?"

"What do you mean?"

"You have judged every brick within this place by its value to the goal of making steel. Have you been as strict about the goal which your work and your steel are serving? What do you wish to achieve by giving your life to the making of steel? By what standard of value do you judge your days? For instance, why did you spend ten years of exacting effort to produce Rearden Metal?"

Rearden looked away, the slight, slumping movement of his shoulders like a sigh of release and disappointment. "If you have to ask that, then you wouldn't understand."

"If I told you that I understand it, but you don't—would you throw me out of here?"

"I should have thrown you out of here anyway—so go ahead, tell me what you mean."

"Are you proud of the rail of the John Galt Line?"

"Yes."

"Why?"

"Because it's the best rail ever made."

"Why did you make it?"

"In order to make money."

"There were many easier ways to make money. Why did you choose the hardest?"

"You said it in your speech at Taggart's wedding: in order to exchange my best effort for the best effort of others."

"If that was your purpose, have you achieved it?"

A beat of time vanished in a heavy drop of silence. "No," said Rearden.

"Have you made any money?"

"No."

"When you strain your energy to its utmost in order to produce the best, do you expect to be rewarded for it or punished?" Rearden did not answer. "By every standard of decency, of honor, of justice known to you—are you convinced that you should have been rewarded for it?"

"Yes," said Rearden, his voice low.

"Then if you were punished, instead—what sort of code have you accepted?"

Rearden did not answer.

"It is generally assumed," said Francisco, "that living in a human society makes one's life much easier and safer than if one were left alone to struggle against nature on a desert island. Now wherever there is a man who needs or uses metal in any way—Rearden Metal has made his life easier for him. Has it made yours easier for you?"

"No," said Rearden, his voice low.

"Has it left your life as it was before you produced the Metal?"

"No—" said Rearden, the word breaking off as if he had cut short the thought that followed.

Francisco's voice lashed at him suddenly, as a command: "Say it!"

"It has made it harder," said Rearden tonelessly.

"When you felt proud of the rail of the John Galt Line," said Francisco, the measured rhythm of his voice giving a ruthless clarity to his words, "what sort of men did you think of? Did you want to see that Line used by your equals—by giants of productive energy, such as Ellis Wyatt, whom it would help to reach higher and still higher achievements of their own?"

"Yes," said Rearden eagerly.

"Did you want to see it used by men who could not equal the power of your mind, but who would equal your moral integrity—men such as Eddie Willers—who could never invent your Metal, but who would do their best, work as hard as you did, live by their own effort, and—riding on your rail—give a moment's silent thanks to the man who gave them more than they could give him?"

"Yes," said Rearden gently.

"Did you want to see it used by whining rotters who never rouse themselves to any effort, who do not possess the ability of a filing clerk, but demand the income of a company president, who drift from failure to failure and expect you to pay their bills, who hold their wishing as an equivalent of your work and their need as a higher claim to reward than your effort, who demand that you serve them, who demand that it be the aim of your life to serve them, who demand that your strength be the voiceless, rightless, unpaid, unrewarded slave of their impotence, who proclaim that you are born to serfdom by reason of your genius, while they are born to rule by the grace of incompetence, that yours is only to give, but theirs only to take, that yours is to produce, but theirs to consume, that you are not to be paid, neither in matter nor in spirit, neither by wealth nor by recognition nor by respect nor by gratitude—so that they would ride on your rail and sneer at you and curse you, since they owe you nothing, not even the effort of taking off their hats which you paid for? Would this be what you wanted? Would you feel proud of it?"

"I'd blast that rail first," said Rearden, his lips white.

"Then why don't you do it, Mr. Rearden? Of the three kinds of men I described—which men are being destroyed and which are using your Line today?"

They heard the distant metal heartbeats of the mills through the long thread of silence.

"What I described last," said Francisco, "is any man who proclaims his right to a single penny of another man's effort."

Rearden did not answer; he was looking at the reflection of a neon sign on dark windows in the distance.

"You take pride in setting no limit to your endurance, Mr. Rearden, because you think that you are doing right. What if you aren't? What if you're placing your virtue in the service of evil and letting it become a tool for the destruction of everything you love, respect and admire?

Why don't you uphold your own code of values among men as you do among iron smelters? You who won't allow one per cent of impurity into an alloy of metal—what have you allowed into your moral code?"

Rearden sat very still; the words in his mind were like the beat of steps down the trail he had been seeking; the words were: the sanction of the victim.

"You, who would not submit to the hardships of nature, but set out to conquer it and placed it in the service of your joy and your comfort—to what have you submitted at the hands of men? You, who know from your work that one bears punishment only for being wrong —what have you been willing to bear and for what reason? All your life, you have heard yourself denounced, not for your faults, but for your greatest virtues. You have been hated, not for your mistakes, but for your achievements. You have been scorned for all those qualities of character which are your highest pride. You have been called selfish for the courage of acting on your own judgment and bearing sole responsibility for your own life. You have been called arrogant for your independent mind. You have been called cruel for your unyielding integrity. You have been called anti-social for the vision that made you venture upon undiscovered roads. You have been called ruthless for the strength and self-discipline of your drive to your purpose. You have been called greedy for the magnificence of your power to create wealth. You, who've expended an inconceivable flow of energy, have been called a parasite. You, who've created abundance where there had been nothing but wastelands and helpless, starving men before you, have been called a robber. You, who've kept them all alive, have been called an exploiter. You, the purest and most moral man among them, have been sneered at as a 'vulgar materialist.' Have you stopped to ask them: by what right?—by what code?—by what standard? No, you have borne it all and kept silent. You bowed to their code and you never upheld your own. You knew what exacting morality was needed to produce a single metal nail, but you let them brand you as immoral. You knew that man needs the strictest code of values to deal with nature, but you thought that you needed no such code to deal with men. You left the deadliest weapon in the hands of your enemies, a weapon you never suspected or understood. Their moral code is their weapon. Ask yourself how deeply and in how many terrible ways you have accepted it. Ask yourself what it is that a code of moral values does to a man's life, and why he can't exist without it, and what happens to him if he accepts the wrong standard, by which the evil is the good. Shall I tell you why you're drawn to me, even though you think you ought to damn me? It's because I'm the first man who has given you what the whole world owes you and what you should have demanded of all men before you dealt with them: a moral sanction."

Rearden whirled to him, then remained still, with a stillness like a gasp. Francisco leaned forward, as if he were reaching the landing of a dangerous flight, and his eyes were steady, but their glance seemed to tremble with intensity.

"You're guilty of a great sin, Mr. Rearden, much guiltier than they tell you, but not in the way they preach. The worst guilt is to accept an undeserved guilt—and that is what you have been doing all your life. You have been paying blackmail, not for your vices, but for your virtues. You have been willing to carry the load of an unearned punishment—and to let it grow the heavier the greater the virtues you practiced. But your virtues were those which keep men alive. Your own moral code—the one you lived by, but never stated, acknowledged or defended—was the code that preserves man's existence. If you were punished for it, what was the nature of those who punished you? Yours was the code of life. What, then, is theirs? What standard of value lies at its root? What is its ultimate purpose? Do you think that what you're facing is merely a conspiracy to seize your wealth? You, who know the source of wealth, should know it's much more and much worse than that. Did you ask me to name man's motive power? Man's motive power is his moral code. Ask yourself where their code is leading you and what it offers you as your final goal. A viler evil than to murder a man, is to sell him suicide as an act of virtue. A viler evil than to throw a man into a sacrificial furnace, is to demand that he leap in, of his own will, and that he build the furnace, besides. By their own statement, it is *they* who need you and have nothing to offer you in return. By their own statement, you must support them because they cannot survive without you. Consider the obscenity of offering their impotence and their need—their need of *you*—as a justification for your torture. Are you willing to accept it? Do you care to purchase—at the price of your great endurance, at the price of your agony—the satisfaction of the needs of your own destroyers?"

"No!"

"Mr. Rearden," said Francisco, his voice solemnly calm, "if you saw Atlas, the giant who holds the world on his shoulders, if you saw that he stood, blood running down his chest, his knees buckling, his arms trembling but still trying to hold the world aloft with the last of his strength, and the greater his effort the heavier the world bore down upon his shoulders—what would you tell him to do?"

"I . . . don't know. What . . . could he do? What would *you* tell him?"

"To shrug."

The clatter of the metal came in a flow of irregular sounds without discernible rhythm, not like the action of a mechanism, but as if some conscious impulse were behind every sudden, tearing rise that went up and crashed, scattering into the faint moan of gears. The glass of the windows tinkled once in a while.

Francisco's eyes were watching Rearden as if he were examining the course of bullets on a battered target. The course was hard to trace:

the gaunt figure on the edge of the desk was erect, the cold blue eyes showed nothing but the intensity of a glance fixed upon a great distance, only the inflexible mouth betrayed a line drawn by pain.

"Go on," said Rearden with effort, "continue. You haven't finished, have you?"

"I have barely begun." Francisco's voice was hard.

"What . . . are you driving at?"

"You'll know it before I'm through. But first, I want you to answer a question: if you understand the nature of your burden, how can you . . ."

The scream of an alarm siren shattered the space beyond the window and shot like a rocket in a long, thin line to the sky. It held for an instant, then fell, then went on in rising, falling spirals of sound, as if fighting for breath against terror to scream louder. It was the shriek of agony, the call for help, the voice of the mills as of a wounded body crying to hold its soul.

Rearden thought that he leaped for the door the instant the scream hit his consciousness, but he saw that he was an instant late, because Francisco had preceded him. Flung by the blast of the same response as his own, Francisco was flying down the hall, pressing the button of the elevator and, not waiting, racing on down the stairs. Rearden followed him and, watching the dial of the elevator on the stair landings, they met it halfway down the height of the building. Before the steel cage had ceased trembling at the sill of the ground floor, Francisco was out, racing to meet the sound of the call for help. Rearden had thought himself a good runner, but he could not keep up with the swift figure streaking off through stretches of red glare and darkness, the figure of a useless playboy he had hated himself for admiring.

The stream, gushing from a hole low on the side of a blast furnace, did not have the red glow of fire, but the white radiance of sunlight. It poured along the ground, branching off at random in sudden streaks; it cut through a dank fog of steam with a bright suggestion of morning. It was liquid iron, and what the scream of the alarm proclaimed was a break-out.

The charge of the furnace had been hung up and, breaking, had blown the tap-hole open. The furnace foreman lay knocked unconscious, the white flow spurted, slowly tearing the hole wider, and men were struggling with sand, hose and fire clay to stop the glowing streaks that spread in a heavy, gliding motion, eating everything on their way into jets of acrid smoke.

In the few moments which Rearden needed to grasp the sight and nature of the disaster, he saw a man's figure rising suddenly at the foot of the furnace, a figure outlined by the red glare almost as if it stood in the path of the torrent, he saw the swing of a white shirt-sleeved arm that rose and flung a black object into the source of the spurting metal. It was Francisco d'Anconia, and his action belonged to an art which Rearden had not believed any man to be trained to perform any longer.

Years before, Rearden had worked in an obscure steel plant in Minnesota, where it had been his job, after a blast furnace was tapped, to close the hole by hand—by throwing bullets of fire clay to dam the flow of the metal. It was a dangerous job that had taken many lives; it had been abolished years earlier by the invention of the hydraulic gun; but there had been struggling, failing mills which, on their way down, had attempted to use the outworn equipment and methods of a distant past. Rearden had done the job; but in the years since, he had met no other man able to do it. In the midst of shooting jets of live steam, in the face of a crumbling blast furnace, he was now seeing the tall, slim figure of the playboy performing the task with the skill of an expert.

It took an instant for Rearden to tear off his coat, seize a pair of goggles from the first man in sight and join Francisco at the mouth of the furnace. There was no time to speak, to feel or to wonder. Francisco glanced at him once—and what Rearden saw was a smudged face, black goggles and a wide grin.

They stood on a slippery bank of baked mud, at the edge of the white stream, with the raging hole under their feet, flinging clay into the glare where the twisting tongues that looked like gas were boiling metal. Rearden's consciousness became a progression of bending, raising the weight, aiming and sending it down and, before it had reached its unseen destination, bending for the next one again, a consciousness drawn tight upon watching the aim of his arm, to save the furnace, and the precarious posture of his feet, to save himself. He was aware of nothing else—except that the sum of it was the exultant feeling of action, of his own capacity, of his body's precision, of its response to his will. And, with no time to know it, but knowing it, seizing it with his senses past the censorship of his mind, he was seeing a black silhouette with red rays shooting from behind its shoulders, its elbows, its angular curves, the red rays circling through steam like the long needles of spotlights, following the movements of a swift, expert, confident being whom he had never seen before except in evening clothes under the lights of ballrooms.

There was no time to form words, to think, to explain, but he knew that *this* was the real Francisco d'Anconia, this was what he had seen from the first and loved—the word did not shock him, because there was no word in his mind, there was only a joyous feeling that seemed like a flow of energy added to his own.

To the rhythm of his body, with the scorching heat on his face and the winter night on his shoulder blades, he was seeing suddenly that this was the simple essence of his universe: the instantaneous refusal to submit to disaster, the irresistible drive to fight it, the triumphant feeling of his own ability to win. He was certain that Francisco felt it, too, that he had been moved by the same impulse, that it was right to feel it, right for both of them to be what they were—he caught glimpses of a sweat-streaked face intent upon action, and it was the most joyous face he had ever seen.

The furnace stood above them, a black bulk wrapped in coils of tubes and steam; she seemed to pant, shooting red gasps that hung on the air above the mills—and they fought not to let her bleed to death. Sparks hung about their feet and burst in sudden sheafs out of the metal, dying unnoticed against their clothes, against the skin of their hands. The stream was coming slower, in broken spurts through the dam rising beyond their sight.

It happened so fast that Rearden knew it fully only after it was over. He knew that there were two moments: the first was when he saw the violent swing of Francisco's body in a forward thrust that sent the bullet to continue the line in space, then he saw the sudden, unrhythmic jerk backward that did not succeed, the convulsive beating against a forward pull, the extended arms of the silhouette losing its balance, he thought that a leap across the distance between them on the slippery, crumbling ridge would mean the death of both of them—and the second moment was when he landed at Francisco's side, held him in his arms, hung swaying together between space and ridge, over the white pit, then gained his footing and pulled him back, and, for an instant, still held the length of Francisco's body against the length of his own, as he would have held the body of an only son. His love, his terror, his relief were in a single sentence:

"Be careful, you goddamn fool!"

Francisco reached for a chunk of clay and went on.

When the job was done and the gap was closed, Rearden noticed that there was a twisting pain in the muscles of his arms and legs, that his body had no strength left to move—yet that he felt as if he were entering his office in the morning, eager for ten new problems to solve. He looked at Francisco and noticed for the first time that their clothes had black-ringed holes, that their hands were bleeding, that there was a patch of skin torn on Francisco's temple and a red thread winding down his cheekbone. Francisco pushed the goggles back off his eyes and grinned at him: it was a smile of morning.

A young man with a look of chronic hurt and impertinence together, rushed up to him, crying, "I couldn't help it, Mr. Rearden!" and launched into a speech of explanation. Rearden turned his back on him without a word. It was the assistant in charge of the pressure gauge of the furnace, a young man out of college.

Somewhere on the outer edge of Rearden's consciousness, there was the thought that accidents of this nature were happening more frequently now, caused by the kind of ore he was using, but he had to use whatever ore he could find. There was the thought that his old workers had always been able to avert disaster; any of them would have seen the indications of a hang-up and known how to prevent it; but there were not many of them left, and he had to employ whatever men he could find. Through the swirling coils of steam around him, he observed that it was the older men who had rushed from all over the mills to fight the break-out and now stood in line, being given first aid by the medical staff. He wondered what was happening to the young men of the country. But the wonder was swallowed by the sight of the college boy's face, which he could not bear to see, by a wave of contempt, by the wordless thought that if *this* was the enemy, there was nothing to fear. All these things came to him and vanished in the outer darkness; the sight blotting them out was Francisco d'Anconia.

He saw Francisco giving orders to the men around him. They did not know who he was or where he came from, but they listened: they knew he was a man who knew his job. Francisco broke off in the middle of a sentence, seeing Rearden approach and listen, and said, laughing, "Oh, I beg your pardon!" Rearden said, "Go right ahead. It's all correct, so far."

They said nothing to each other when they walked together through the darkness, on their way back to the office. Rearden felt an exultant laughter swelling within him, he felt that he wanted, in his turn, to wink at Francisco like a fellow conspirator who had learned a secret Francisco would not acknowledge. He glanced at his face once in a while, but Francisco would not look at him.

After a while, Francisco said, "You saved my life." The "thank you" was in the way he said it.

Rearden chuckled. "You saved my furnace."

They went on in silence. Rearden felt himself growing lighter with every step. Raising his face to the cold air, he saw the peaceful darkness of the sky and a single star above a smokestack with the vertical lettering: Rearden Steel. He felt how glad he was to be alive.

He did not expect the change he saw in Francisco's face when he looked at it in the light of his office. The things he had seen by the glare of the furnace were gone. He had expected a look of triumph, of mockery at all the insults Francisco had heard from him, a look demanding the apology he was joyously eager to offer. Instead, he saw a face made lifeless by an odd dejection.

"Are you hurt?"

"No . . . no, not at all."

"Come here," ordered Rearden, opening the door of his bathroom. "Look at yourself."

"Never mind. You come here."

For the first time, Rearden felt that he was the older man; he felt the pleasure of taking Francisco in charge; he felt a confident, amused, paternal protectiveness. He washed the grime off Francisco's face, he put disinfectants and adhesive bandages on his temple, his hands, his scorched elbows. Francisco obeyed him in silence.

Rearden asked, in the tone of the most eloquent salute he could offer, "Where did you learn to work like that?"

Francisco shrugged. "I was brought up around smelters of every kind," he answered indifferently.

Rearden could not decipher the expression of his face: it was only a look of peculiar stillness, as if his eyes were fixed on some secret vision of his own that drew his mouth into a line of desolate, bitter, hurting self-mockery.

They did not speak until they were back in the office.

"You know," said Rearden, "everything you said here was true. But that was only part of the story. The other part is what we've done tonight. Don't you see? We're able to act. They're not. So it's we who'll win in the long run, no matter what they do to us."

Francisco did not answer.

"Listen," said Rearden, "I know what's been the trouble with you. You've never cared to do a real day's work in your life. I thought you were conceited enough, but I see that you have no idea of what you've got in you. Forget that fortune of yours for a while and come to work for me. I'll start you as furnace foreman any time. You don't know what it will do for you. In a few years, you'll be ready to appreciate and to run d'Anconia Copper."

He expected a burst of laughter and he was prepared to argue; instead, he saw Francisco shaking his head slowly, as if he could not trust his voice, as if he feared that were he to speak, he would accept. In a moment, he said, "Mr. Rearden . . . I think I would give the rest of my life for one year as your furnace foreman. But I can't."

"Why not?"

"Don't ask me. It's . . . a personal matter."

The vision of Francisco in Rearden's mind, which he had resented and found irresistibly attractive, had been the figure of a man radiantly incapable of suffering. What he saw now in Francisco's eyes was the look of a quiet, tightly controlled, patiently borne torture.

Francisco reached silently for his overcoat.

"You're not leaving, are you?" asked Rearden.

"Yes."

"Aren't you going to finish what you had to tell me?"

"Not tonight."

"You wanted me to answer a question. What was it?"

Francisco shook his head.

"You started asking me how can I . . . How can I—what?"

Francisco's smile was like a moan of pain, the only moan he would permit himself. "I won't ask it, Mr. Rearden. I *know* it."

IV

THE SANCTION OF THE VICTIM

The roast turkey had cost $30. The champagne had cost $25. The lace tablecloth, a cobweb of grapes and vine leaves iridescent in the candlelight, had cost $2,000. The dinner service, with an artist's design burned in blue and gold into a translucent white china, had cost $2,500. The silverware, which bore the initials LR in Empire wreaths of laurels, had cost $3,000. But it was held to be unspiritual to think of money and of what that money represented.

A peasant's wooden shoe, gilded, stood in the center of the table, filled with marigolds, grapes and carrots. The candles were stuck into pumpkins that were cut as open-mouthed faces drooling raisins, nuts and candy upon the tablecloth.

It was Thanksgiving dinner, and the three who faced Rearden about the table were his wife, his mother and his brother.

"This is the night to thank the Lord for our blessings," said Rearden's mother. "God has been kind to us. There are people all over the country who haven't got any food in the house tonight, and some that haven't even got a house, and more of them going jobless every day. Gives me the creeps to look around in the city. Why, only last week, who do you suppose I ran into but Lucie Judson—Henry, do you remember Lucie Judson? Used to live next door to us, up in Minnesota, when you were ten-twelve years old. Had a boy about your age. I lost track of Lucie when they moved to New York, must have been all of twenty years ago. Well, it gave me the creeps to see what she's come to—just a toothless old hag, wrapped in a man's overcoat, panhandling on a street corner. And I thought: That could've been me, but for the grace of God."

"Well, if thanks are in order," said Lillian gaily, "I think that we shouldn't forget Gertrude, the new cook. She's an artist."

"Me, I'm just going to be old-fashioned," said Philip. "I'm just going to thank the sweetest mother in the world."

"Well, for the matter of that," said Rearden's mother, "we ought to thank Lillian for this dinner and for all the trouble she took to make it so pretty. She spent hours fixing the table. It's real quaint and different."

"It's the wooden shoe that does it," said Philip, bending his head sidewise to study it in a manner of critical appreciation. "That's the real touch. Anybody can have candles, silverware and junk, that doesn't take anything but money—but this shoe, that took thought."

Rearden said nothing. The candlelight moved over his motionless face as over a portrait; the portrait bore an expression of impersonal courtesy.

"You haven't touched your wine," said his mother, looking at him. "What I think is you ought to drink a toast in gratitude to the people of this country who have given you so much."

"Henry is not in the mood for it, Mother," said Lillian. "I'm afraid Thanksgiving is a holiday only for those who have a clear conscience." She raised her wine glass, but stopped it halfway to her lips and asked, "You're not going to make some sort of stand at your trial tomorrow, are you, Henry?"

"I am."

She put the glass down. "What are you going to do?"

"You'll see it tomorrow."

"You don't really imagine that you can get away with it!"

"I don't know what you have in mind as the object I'm to get away with."

"Do you realize that the charge against you is extremely serious?"

"I do."

"You've admitted that you sold the Metal to Ken Danagger."

"I have."

"They might send you to jail for ten years."

"I don't think they will, but it's possible."

"Have you been reading the newspapers, Henry?" asked Philip, with an odd kind of smile.

"No."

"Oh, you should!"

"Should I? Why?"

"You ought to see the names they call you!"

"That's interesting," said Rearden; he said it about the fact that Philip's smile was one of pleasure.

"I don't understand it," said his mother. "Jail? Did you say jail, Lillian? Henry, are you going to be sent to jail?"

"I might be."

"But that's ridiculous! Do something about it."

"What?"

"I don't know. I don't understand any of it. Respectable people don't go to jail. Do something. You've always known what to do about business."

"Not this kind of business."

"I don't believe it." Her voice had the tone of a frightened, spoiled child. "You're saying it just to be mean."

"He's playing the hero, Mother," said Lillian. She smiled coldly, turning to Rearden. "Don't you think that your attitude is perfectly futile?"

"No."

"You know that cases of this kind are not . . . intended ever to come to trial. There are ways to avoid it, to get things settled amicably —if one knows the right people."

"I don't know the right people."

"Look at Orren Boyle. He's done much more and much worse than your little fling at the black market, but he's smart enough to keep himself out of courtrooms."

"Then I'm not smart enough."

"Don't you think it's time you made an effort to adjust yourself to the conditions of our age?"

"No."

"Well, then I don't see how you can pretend that you're some sort of victim. If you go to jail, it will be your own fault."

"What pretense are you talking about, Lillian?"

"Oh, I know that you think you're fighting for some sort of principle —but actually it's only a matter of your incredible conceit. You're doing it for no better reason than because you think you're right."

"Do you think they're right?"

She shrugged. "That's the conceit I'm talking about—the idea that it matters who's right or wrong. It's the most insufferable form of vanity, this insistence on always doing right. How do you know what's right? How can anyone ever know it? It's nothing but a delusion to flatter your own ego and to hurt other people by flaunting your superiority over them."

He was looking at her with attentive interest. "Why should it hurt other people, if it's nothing but a delusion?"

"Is it necessary for me to point out that in *your* case it's nothing but hypocrisy? That is why I find your attitude preposterous. Questions of right have no bearing on human existence. And you're certainly nothing but human—aren't you, Henry? You're no better than any of the men you're going to face tomorrow. I think you should remember that it's not for you to make a stand on any sort of principle. Maybe you're a victim in this particular mess, maybe they're pulling a rotten trick on you, but what of it? They're doing it because they're weak; they couldn't resist the temptation to grab your Metal and to muscle in on your profits, because they had no other way of ever getting rich. Why should you blame them? It's only a question of different strains, but it's the same shoddy human fabric that gives way just as quickly. You wouldn't be tempted by money, because it's so easy for you to make it. But you wouldn't withstand other pressures and you'd fall just as ignominiously. Wouldn't you? So you have no right to any righteous indignation against them. You have no moral superiority to assert or to defend. And if you haven't, then what is the point of fighting a battle that you can't win? I suppose that one might find some satisfaction in being a martyr, if one is above reproach. But you—who are you to cast the first stone?"

She paused to observe the effect. There was none, except that his look of attentive interest seemed intensified; he listened as if he were held by some impersonal, scientific curiosity. It was not the response she had expected.

"I believe you understand me," she said.

"No," he answered quietly, "I don't."

"I think you should abandon the illusion of your own perfection, which you know full well to be an illusion. I think you should learn to get along with other people. The day of the hero is past. This is the day of humanity, in a much deeper sense than you imagine. Human beings are no longer expected to be saints nor to be punished for their sins. Nobody is right or wrong, we're all in it together, we're all human—and the human is the imperfect. You'll gain nothing tomorrow by proving that they're wrong. You ought to give in with good grace, simply because it's the practical thing to do. You ought to keep silent, *precisely* because they're wrong. They'll appreciate it. Make concessions for others and they'll make concessions for you. Live and let live. Give and take. Give in and take in. That's the policy of our age—and it's time you accepted it. Don't tell me you're too good for it. You know that you're not. You know that I know it."

The look of his eyes, held raptly still upon some point in space, was not in answer to her words; it was in answer to a man's voice saying to him, "Do you think that what you're facing is merely a conspiracy to seize your wealth? You, who know the source of wealth, should know it's much more and much worse than that."

He turned to look at Lillian. He was seeing the full extent of her failure—in the immensity of his own indifference. The droning stream of her insults was like the sound of a distant riveting machine, a long, impotent pressure that reached nothing within him. He had heard her studied reminders of his guilt on every evening he had spent at home in the past three months. But guilt had been the one emotion he had found himself unable to feel. The punishment she had wanted to inflict on him was the torture of shame; what she had inflicted was the torture of boredom.

He remembered his brief glimpse—on that morning in the Wayne-Falkland Hotel—of a flaw in her scheme of punishment, which he had not examined. Now he stated it to himself for the first time. She wanted to force upon him the suffering of dishonor—but his own sense of honor was her only weapon of enforcement. She wanted to wrest from him an acknowledgment of his moral depravity—but only his own moral rectitude could attach significance to such a verdict. She wanted to injure him by her contempt—but he could not be injured, unless he respected her judgment. She wanted to punish him for the pain he had caused her and she held her pain as a gun aimed at him, as if she wished to extort his agony at the point of his pity. But her only tool was his own benevolence, his concern for her, his compassion. Her only power was the power of his own virtues. What if he chose to withdraw it?

An issue of guilt, he thought, had to rest on his own acceptance of the code of justice that pronounced him guilty. He did not accept it; he never had. His virtues, all the virtues she needed to achieve his punishment, came from another code and lived by another standard. He felt no guilt, no shame, no regret, no dishonor. He felt no concern for any verdict she chose to pass upon him: he had lost respect for her judgment long ago. And the sole chain still holding him was only a last remnant of pity.

But what was the code on which she acted? What sort of code permitted the concept of a punishment that required the victim's own virtue as the fuel to make it work? A code—he thought—which would destroy only those who tried to observe it; a punishment, from which only the honest would suffer, while the dishonest would escape unhurt. Could one conceive of an infamy lower than to equate virtue with pain, to make virtue, not vice, the source and motive power of suffering? If he were the kind of rotter she was struggling to make him believe he was, then no issue of his honor and his moral worth would matter to him. If he wasn't, then what was the nature of her attempt?

To count upon his virtue and use it as an instrument of torture, to practice blackmail with the victim's generosity as sole means of extortion, to accept the gift of a man's good will and turn it into a tool for the giver's destruction . . . he sat very still, contemplating the formula of so monstrous an evil that he was able to name it, but not to believe it possible.

He sat very still, held by the hammering of a single question: Did Lillian know the exact nature of her scheme?—was it a conscious policy, devised with full awareness of its meaning? He shuddered; he did not hate her enough to believe it.

He looked at her. She was absorbed, at the moment, in the task of cutting a plum pudding that stood as a mount of blue flame on a silver platter before her, its glow dancing over her face and her laughing mouth—she was plunging a silver knife into the flame, with a practiced, graceful curve of her arm. She had metallic leaves in the red, gold and brown colors of autumn scattered over one shoulder of her black velvet gown; they glittered in the candlelight.

He could not get rid of the impression, which he had kept receiving and rejecting for three months, that her vengeance was not a form of despair, as he had supposed—the impression, which he regarded as inconceivable, that she was enjoying it. He could find no trace of pain in her manner. She had an air of confidence new to her. She seemed to be at home in her house for the first time. Even though everything within the house was of her own choice and taste, she had always seemed to act as the bright, efficient, resentful manager of a high-class hotel, who keeps smiling in bitter amusement at her position of inferiority to the owners. The amusement remained, but the bitterness was gone. She had not gained weight, but her features had lost their delicate sharpness in a blurring, softening look of satisfaction; even her voice sounded as if it had grown plump.

He did not hear what she was saying; she was laughing in the last flicker of the blue flames, while he sat weighing the question: Did she know? He felt certain that he had discovered a secret much greater than the problem of his marriage, that he had grasped the formula of a policy practiced more widely throughout the world than he dared to contemplate at the moment. But to convict a human being of that practice was a verdict of irrevocable damnation, and he knew that he would not believe it of anyone, so long as the possibility of a doubt remained.

No—he thought, looking at Lillian, with the last effort of his generosity—he would not believe it of her. In the name of whatever grace and pride she possessed—in the name of such moments when he had seen a smile of joy on her face, the smile of a living being—in the name of the brief shadow of love he had once felt for her—he would not pronounce upon her a verdict of total evil.

The butler slipped a plate of plum pudding in front of him, and he heard Lillian's voice: "Where have you been for the last five minutes, Henry—or is it for the last century? You haven't answered me. You haven't heard a word I said."

"I heard it," he answered quietly. "I don't know what you're trying to accomplish."

"What a question!" said his mother. "Isn't that just like a man? She's trying to save you from going to jail—that's what she's trying to accomplish."

That could be true, he thought; perhaps, by the reasoning of some crude, childish cowardice, the motive of their malice was a desire to protect him, to break him down into the safety of a compromise. It's possible, he thought—but knew that he did not believe it.

"You've always been unpopular," said Lillian, "and it's more than a matter of any one particular issue. It's that unyielding, intractable attitude of yours. The men who're going to try you, know what you're thinking. That's why they'll crack down on you, while they'd let another man off."

"Why, no. I don't think they know what I'm thinking. That's what I have to let them know tomorrow."

"Unless you show them that you're willing to give in and co-operate, you won't have a chance. You've been too hard to deal with."

"No. I've been too easy."

"But if they put you in jail," said his mother, "what's going to happen to your family? Have you thought of that?"

"No. I haven't."

"Have you thought of the disgrace you'll bring upon us?"

"Mother, do you understand the issue in this case?"

"No, I don't and I don't want to understand. It's all dirty business and dirty politics. All business is just dirty politics and all politics is just dirty business. I never did want to understand any of it. I don't care who's right or wrong, but what I think a man ought to think of first is his family. Don't you know what this will do to us?"

"No, Mother, I don't know or care."

His mother looked at him, aghast.

"Well, I think you have a very provincial attitude, all of you," said Philip suddenly. "Nobody here seems to be concerned with the wider, social aspects of the case. I don't agree with you, Lillian. I don't see why you say that they're pulling some sort of rotten trick on Henry and that he's in the right. I think he's guilty as hell. Mother, I can explain the issue to you very simply. There's nothing unusual about it, the courts are full of cases of this kind. Businessmen are taking advantage of the national emergency in order to make money. They break the regulations which protect the common welfare of all—for the sake of their own personal gain. They're profiteers of the black market who grow rich by defrauding the poor of their rightful share, at a time of desperate shortage. They pursue a ruthless, grasping, grabbing, antisocial policy, based on nothing but plain, selfish greed. It's no use pretending about it, we all know it—and I think it's contemptible."

He spoke in a careless, offhand manner, as if explaining the obvious to a group of adolescents; his tone conveyed the assurance of a man who knows that the moral ground of his stand is not open to question.

Rearden sat looking at him, as if studying an object seen for the first time. Somewhere deep in Rearden's mind, as a steady, gentle, inexorable beat, was a man's voice, saying: By what right?—by what code?—by what standard?

"Philip," he said, not raising his voice, "say any of that again and you will find yourself out in the street, right now, with the suit you've got on your back, with whatever change you've got in your pocket and with nothing else."

He heard no answer, no sound, no movement. He noted that the stillness of the three before him had no element of astonishment. The look of shock on their faces was not the shock of people at the sudden explosion of a bomb, but the shock of people who had known that they were playing with a lighted fuse. There were no outcries, no protests, no questions; they knew that he meant it and they knew everything it meant. A dim, sickening feeling told him that they had known it long before he did.

"You . . . you wouldn't throw your own brother out on the street, would you?" his mother said at last; it was not a demand, but a plea.

"I would."

"But he's your brother . . . Doesn't that mean anything to you?"

"No."

"Maybe he goes a bit too far at times, but it's just loose talk, it's just that modern jabber, he doesn't know what he's saying."

"Then let him learn."

"Don't be hard on him . . . he's younger than you and . . . and weaker. He . . . Henry, don't look at me that way! I've never seen you look like that. . . . You shouldn't frighten him. You know that he needs you."

"Does he know it?"

"You can't be hard on a man who needs you, it will prey on your conscience for the rest of your life."

"It won't."

"You've got to be kind, Henry."

"I'm not."

"You've got to have some pity."

"I haven't."

"A good man knows how to forgive."

"I don't."

"You wouldn't want me to think that you're selfish."

"I am."

Philip's eyes were darting from one to the other. He looked like a man who had felt certain that he stood on solid granite and had suddenly discovered that it was thin ice, now cracking open all around him.

"But I . . ." he tried, and stopped; his voice sounded like steps testing the ice. "But don't I have any freedom of speech?"

"In your own house. Not in mine."

"Don't I have a right to my own ideas?"

"At your own expense. Not at mine."

"Don't you tolerate any differences of opinion?"

"Not when I'm paying the bills."

"Isn't there anything involved but money?"

"Yes. The fact that it's *my* money."

"Don't you want to consider any hi . . ."—he was going to say "higher," but changed his mind—"any other aspects?"

"No."

"But I'm not your slave."

"Am I yours?"

"I don't know what you—" He stopped; he knew what was meant.

"No," said Rearden, "you're not my slave. You're free to walk out of here any time you choose."

"I . . . I'm not speaking of that."

"I am."

"I don't understand it . . ."

"Don't you?"

"You've always known my . . . my political views. You've never objected before."

"That's true," said Rearden gravely. "Perhaps I owe you an explanation, if I have misled you. I've tried never to remind you that you're living on my charity. I thought that it was your place to remember it. I thought that any human being who accepts the help of another, knows that good will is the giver's only motive and that good will is the payment he owes in return. But I see that I was wrong. You were getting your food unearned and you concluded that affection did not have to be earned, either. You concluded that I was the safest person in the world for you to spit on, precisely because I held you by the throat. You concluded that I wouldn't want to remind you of it and that I would be tied by the fear of hurting your feelings. All right, let's get it straight: you're an object of charity who's exhausted his credit long ago. Whatever affection I might have felt for you once, is gone. I haven't the slightest interest in you, your fate or your future. I haven't any reason whatever for wishing to feed you. If you leave my house, it won't make any difference to me whether you starve or not. Now *that* is your position here and I will expect you to remember it, if you wish to stay. If not, then get out."

But for the movement of drawing his head a little into his shoulders, Philip showed no reaction. "Don't imagine that I enjoy living here," he said; his voice was lifeless and shrill. "If you think I'm happy, you're mistaken. I'd give anything to get away." The words pertained to defiance, but the voice had a curiously cautious quality. "If that is how you feel about it, it would be best for me to leave." The words were a statement, but the voice put a question mark at the end of it and waited; there was no answer. "You needn't worry about my future. I don't have to ask favors of anybody. I can take care of myself all right." The words were addressed to Rearden, but the eyes were looking at his mother; she did not speak; she was afraid to move. "I've always wanted to be on my own. I've always wanted to live in New York, near all my friends." The voice slowed down and added in an impersonal, reflective manner, as if the words were not addressed to anyone, "Of course, I'd have the problem of maintaining a certain social position . . . it's not my fault if I'll be embarrassed by a family name associated with a millionaire. . . . I would need enough money for a year or two . . . to establish myself in a manner suitable to my—"

"You won't get it from me."

"I wasn't asking you for it, was I? Don't imagine that I couldn't get it somewhere else, if I wanted to! Don't imagine that I couldn't leave! I'd go in a minute, if I had only myself to think about. But Mother needs me, and if I deserted her—"

"Don't explain."

"And besides, you misunderstood me, Henry. I haven't said anything to insult you. I wasn't speaking in any personal way. I was only discussing the general political picture from an abstract sociological viewpoint which—"

"Don't explain," said Rearden. He was looking at Philip's face. It was half-lowered, its eyes looking up at him. The eyes were lifeless, as if they had witnessed nothing; they held no spark of excitement, no personal sensation, neither of defiance nor of regret, neither of shame nor of suffering; they were filmy ovals that held no response to reality, no attempt to understand it, to weigh it, to reach some verdict of justice —ovals that held nothing but a dull, still, mindless hatred. "Don't explain. Just keep your mouth shut."

The revulsion that made Rearden turn his face away contained a spasm of pity. There was an instant when he wanted to seize his brother's shoulders, to shake him, to cry: How could you do this to yourself? How did you come to a stage where this is all that's left of you? Why did you let the wonderful fact of your own existence go by? . . . He looked away. He knew it was useless.

He noted, in weary contempt, that the three at the table remained silent. Through all the years past, his consideration for them had brought him nothing but their maliciously righteous reproaches. Where was their righteousness now? Now was the time to stand on their code of justice—if justice had been any part of their code. Why didn't they throw at him all those accusations of cruelty and selfishness, which he had come to accept as the eternal chorus to his life? What had permitted them to do it for years? He knew that the words he heard in his mind were the key to the answer: The sanction of the victim.

"Don't let's quarrel," said his mother, her voice cheerless and vague. "It's Thanksgiving Day."

When he looked at Lillian, he caught a glance that made him certain she had watched him for a long time: its quality was panic.

He got up. "You will please excuse me now," he said to the table at large.

"Where are you going?" asked Lillian sharply.

He stood looking at her for a deliberate moment, as if to confirm the meaning she would read in his answer: "To New York."

She jumped to her feet. "Tonight?"

"Now."

"You can't go to New York tonight!" Her voice was not loud, but it had the imperious helplessness of a shriek. "This is not the time when you can afford it. When you can afford to desert your family, I mean. You ought to think about the matter of clean hands. You're not in a position to permit yourself anything which you know to be depravity."

By what code?—thought Rearden—by what standard?

"Why do you wish to go to New York tonight?"

"I think, Lillian, for the same reason that makes you wish to stop me."

"Tomorrow is your trial."

"That is what I mean."

He made a movement to turn, and she raised her voice: "I don't want you to go!" He smiled. It was the first time he had smiled at her in the past three months; it was not the kind of smile she could care to see. "I forbid you to leave us tonight!"

He turned and left the room.

Sitting at the wheel of his car, with the glassy, frozen road flying at his face and down under the wheels at sixty miles an hour, he let the thought of his family drop away from him—and the vision of their faces went rolling back into the abyss of speed that swallowed the bare trees and lonely structures of the roadside. There was little traffic, and few lights in the distant clusters of the towns he passed; the emptiness of inactivity was the only sign of a holiday. A hazy glow, rusted by frost, flashed above the roof of a factory once in a rare while, and a cold wind shrieked through the joints of his car, beating the canvas top against the metal frame.

By some dim sense of contrast, which he did not define, the thought of his family was replaced by the thought of his encounter with the Wet Nurse, the Washington boy of his mills.

At the time of his indictment, he had discovered that the boy had known about his deal with Danagger, yet had not reported it to anyone. "Why didn't you inform your friends about me?" he had asked.

The boy had answered brusquely, not looking at him, "Didn't want to."

"It was part of your job to watch precisely for things of that kind, wasn't it?"

"Yeah."

"Besides, your friends would have been delighted to hear it."

"I know."

"Didn't you know what a valuable piece of information it was and what a stupendous trade you could have pulled with those friends of yours in Washington whom you offered to me once—remember?—the friends who always 'occasion expenses'?" The boy had not answered. "It could have made your career at the very top level. Don't tell me that you didn't know it."

"I knew it."

"Then why didn't you make use of it?"

"I didn't want to."

"Why not?"

"Don't know."

The boy had stood, glumly avoiding Rearden's eyes, as if trying to avoid something incomprehensible within himself. Rearden had laughed.

"Listen, Non-Absolute, you're playing with fire. Better go and murder somebody fast, before you let it get you—that reason that stopped you from turning informer—or else it will blast your career to hell."

The boy had not answered.

This morning, Rearden had gone to his office as usual, even though the rest of the office building was closed. At lunch time, he had stopped at the rolling mills and had been astonished to find the Wet Nurse standing there, alone in a corner, ignored by everybody, watching the work with an air of childish enjoyment.

"What are you doing here today?" Rearden had asked. "Don't you know it's a holiday?"

"Oh, I let the girls off, but I just came in to finish some business."

"What business?"

"Oh, letters and . . . Oh, hell, I signed three letters and sharpened my pencils, I know I didn't have to do it today, but I had nothing to do at home and . . . I get lonesome away from this place."

"Don't you have any family?"

"No . . . not to speak of. What about you, Mr. Rearden? Don't you have any?"

"I guess—not to speak of."

"I like this place. I like to hang around. . . . You know, Mr. Rearden, what I studied to be was a metallurgist."

Walking away, Rearden had turned to glance back and had caught the Wet Nurse looking after him as a boy would look at the hero of his childhood's favorite adventure story. God help the poor little bastard! —he had thought.

God help them all—he thought, driving through the dark streets of a small town, borrowing, in contemptuous pity, the words of their belief which he had never shared. He saw newspapers displayed on metal stands, with the black letters of headlines screaming to empty corners: "Railroad Disaster." He had heard the news on the radio, that afternoon: there had been a wreck on the main line of Taggart Transcontinental, near Rockland, Wyoming; a split rail had sent a freight train crashing over the edge of a canyon. Wrecks on the Taggart main line were becoming more frequent—the track was wearing out—the track which, less than eighteen months ago, Dagny was planning to rebuild, promising him a journey from coast to coast on his own Metal.

She had spent a year, picking worn rail from abandoned branches to patch the rail of the main line. She had spent months fighting the men of Jim's Board of Directors, who said that the national emergency was only temporary and a track that had lasted for ten years could well last for another winter, until spring, when conditions would improve, as Mr. Wesley Mouch had promised. Three weeks ago, she had made them authorize the purchase of sixty thousand tons of new rail; it could do no more than make a few patches across the continent in the worst divisions, but it was all she had been able to obtain from them.

She had had to wrench the money out of men deaf with panic: the freight revenues were falling at such a rate that the men of the Board had begun to tremble, staring at Jim's idea of the most prosperous year in Taggart history. She had had to order steel rail, there was no hope of obtaining an "emergency need" permission to buy Rearden Metal and no time to beg for it.

Rearden looked away from the headlines to the glow at the edge of the sky, which was the city of New York far ahead; his hands tightened on the wheel a little.

It was half past nine when he reached the city. Dagny's apartment was dark, when he let himself in with his key. He picked up the telephone and called her office. Her own voice answered: "Taggart Transcontinental."

"Don't you know it's a holiday?" he asked.

"Hello, Hank. Railroads have no holidays. Where are you calling from?"

"Your place."

"I'll be through in another half-hour."

"It's all right. Stay there. I'll come for you."

The anteroom of her office was dark, when he entered, except for the lighted glass cubbyhole of Eddie Willers. Eddie was closing his desk, getting ready to leave. He looked at Rearden, in puzzled astonishment.

"Good evening, Eddie. What is it that keeps you people so busy—the Rockland wreck?"

Eddie sighed. "Yes, Mr. Rearden."

"That's what I want to see Dagny about—about your rail."

"She's still here."

He started toward her door, when Eddie called after him hesitantly, "Mr. Rearden . . ."

He stopped. "Yes?"

"I wanted to say . . . because tomorrow is your trial . . . and whatever they do to you is supposed to be in the name of all the people . . . I just wanted to say that I . . . that it won't be in *my* name . . . even if there's nothing I can do about it, except to tell you . . . even if I know that that doesn't mean anything."

"It means much more than you suspect. Perhaps more than any of us suspect. Thanks, Eddie."

Dagny glanced up from her desk, when Rearden entered her office; he saw her watching him as he approached and he saw the look of weariness disappearing from her eyes. He sat down on the edge of the desk. She leaned back, brushing a strand of hair off her face, her shoulders relaxing under her thin white blouse.

"Dagny, there's something I want to tell you about the rail that you ordered. I want you to know this tonight."

She was watching him attentively; the expression of his face pulled hers into the same look of quietly solemn tension.

"I am supposed to deliver to Taggart Transcontinental, on February fifteenth, sixty thousand tons of rail, which is to give you three hundred miles of track. You will receive—for the same sum of money—eighty thousand tons of rail, which will give you five hundred miles of track. You know what material is cheaper and lighter than steel. Your rail will not be steel, it will be Rearden Metal. Don't argue, object or agree. I am not asking for your consent. You are not supposed to consent or to know anything about it. *I* am doing this and I alone will be responsible. We will work it so that those on your staff who'll know that you've ordered steel, won't know that you've received Rearden Metal, and those who'll know that you've received Rearden Metal, won't know that you had no permit to buy it. We will tangle the bookkeeping in such a way that if the thing should ever blow up, nobody will be able to pin anything on anybody, except on me. They might suspect that I bribed someone on your staff, or they might suspect that you were in on it, but they won't be able to prove it. I want you to give me your word that you will never admit it, no matter what happens. It's *my* Metal, and if there are any chances to take, it's I who'll take them. I have been planning this from the day I received your order. I have ordered the copper for it, from a source which *will not* betray me. I did not intend to tell you about it till later, but I changed my mind. I want you to know it tonight—because I am going on trial tomorrow for the same kind of crime."

She had listened without moving. At his last sentence, he saw a faint contraction of her cheeks and lips; it was not quite a smile, but it gave him her whole answer: pain, admiration, understanding.

Then he saw her eyes becoming softer, more painfully, dangerously alive—he took her wrist, as if the tight grasp of his fingers and the severity of his glance were to give her the support she needed—and he said sternly, "Don't thank me—this is not a favor—I am doing it in order to be able to bear my work, or else I'll break like Ken Danagger."

She whispered, "All right, Hank, I won't thank you," the tone of her voice and the look of her eyes making it a lie by the time it was uttered.

He smiled. "Give me the word I asked."

She inclined her head. "I give you my word." He released her wrist. She added, not raising her head, "The only thing I'll say is that if they sentence you to jail tomorrow, I'll quit—without waiting for any destroyer to prompt me."

"You won't. And I don't think they'll sentence me to jail. I think they'll let me off very lightly. I have a hypothesis about it—I'll explain it to you afterwards, when I've put it to the test."

"What hypothesis?"

"Who is John Galt?" He smiled, and stood up. "That's all. We won't talk any further about my trial, tonight. You don't happen to have anything to drink in your office, have you?"

"No. But I think my traffic manager has some sort of a bar on one shelf of his filing closet."

"Do you think you could steal a drink for me, if he doesn't have it locked?"

"I'll try."

He stood looking at the portrait of Nat Taggart on the wall of her office—the portrait of a young man with a lifted head—until she returned, bringing a bottle of brandy and two glasses. He filled the glasses in silence.

"You know, Dagny, Thanksgiving was a holiday established by productive people to celebrate the success of their work."

The movement of his arm, as he raised his glass, went from the portrait—to her—to himself—to the buildings of the city beyond the window.

* * *

For a month in advance, the people who filled the courtroom had been told by the press that they would see the man who was a greedy enemy of society; but they had come to see the man who had invented Rearden Metal.

He stood up, when the judges called upon him to do so. He wore a gray suit, he had pale blue eyes and blond hair; it was not the colors that made his figure seem icily implacable, it was the fact that the suit had an expensive simplicity seldom flaunted these days, that it belonged in the sternly luxurious office of a rich corporation, that his bearing came from a civilized era and clashed with the place around him.

The crowd knew from the newspapers that he represented the evil of ruthless wealth; and—as they praised the virtue of chastity, then ran to see any movie that displayed a half-naked female on its posters—so they came to see him; evil, at least, did not have the stale hopelessness of a bromide which none believed and none dared to challenge. They looked at him without admiration—admiration was a feeling they had lost the capacity to experience, long ago; they looked with curiosity and with a dim sense of defiance against those who had told them that it was their duty to hate him.

A few years ago, they would have jeered at his air of self-confident wealth. But today, there was a slate-gray sky in the windows of the courtroom, which promised the first snowstorm of a long, hard winter; the last of the country's oil was vanishing, and the coal mines were not able to keep up with the hysterical scramble for winter supplies. The crowd in the courtroom remembered that this was the case which had cost them the services of Ken Danagger. There were rumors that the output of the Danagger Coal Company had fallen perceptibly within one month; the newspapers said that it was merely a matter of readjustment while Danagger's cousin was reorganizing the company he had taken over. Last week, the front pages had carried the story of a catastrophe on the site of a housing project under construction: defective steel girders had collapsed, killing four workmen; the newspapers had not mentioned, but the crowd knew, that the girders had come from Orren Boyle's Associated Steel.

They sat in the courtroom in heavy silence and they looked at the tall, gray figure, not with hope—they were losing the capacity to hope—but with an impassive neutrality spiked by a faint question mark; the question mark was placed over all the pious slogans they had heard for years.

The newspapers had snarled that the cause of the country's troubles, as this case demonstrated, was the selfish greed of rich industrialists; that it was men like Hank Rearden who were to blame for the shrinking diet, the falling temperature and the cracking roofs in the homes of the nation; that if it had not been for men who broke regulations and hampered the government's plans, prosperity would have been achieved long ago; and that a man like Hank Rearden was prompted by nothing but the profit motive. This last was stated without explanation or elaboration, as if the words "profit motive" were the self-evident brand of ultimate evil.

The crowd remembered that these same newspapers, less than two years ago, had screamed that the production of Rearden Metal should be forbidden, because its producer was endangering people's lives for the sake of his greed; they remembered that the man in gray had ridden in the cab of the first engine to run over a track of his own Metal; and that he was now on trial for the greedy crime of withholding from the public a load of the Metal which it had been his greedy crime to offer in the public market.

According to the procedure established by directives, cases of this kind were not tried by a jury, but by a panel of three judges appointed by the Bureau of Economic Planning and National Resources; the procedure, the directives had stated, was to be informal and democratic. The judge's bench had been removed from the old Philadelphia courtroom for this occasion, and replaced by a table on a wooden platform; it gave the room an atmosphere suggesting the kind of meeting where a presiding body puts something over on a mentally retarded membership.

One of the judges, acting as prosecutor, had read the charges. "You may now offer whatever plea you wish to make in your own defense," he announced.

Facing the platform, his voice inflectionless and peculiarly clear, Hank Rearden answered:

"I have no defense."

"Do you—" The judge stumbled; he had not expected it to be that easy. "Do you throw yourself upon the mercy of this court?"

"I do not recognize this court's right to try me."

"What?"

"I do not recognize this court's right to try me."

"But, Mr. Rearden, this is the legally appointed court to try this particular category of crime."

"I do not recognize my action as a crime."

"But you have admitted that you have broken our regulations controlling the sale of your Metal."

"I do not recognize your right to control the sale of my Metal."

"Is it necessary for me to point out that your recognition was not required?"

"No. I am fully aware of it and I am acting accordingly."

He noted the stillness of the room. By the rules of the complicated pretense which all those people played for one another's benefit, they should have considered his stand as incomprehensible folly; there should have been rustles of astonishment and derision; there were none; they sat still; they understood.

"Do you mean that you are refusing to obey the law?" asked the judge.

"No. I am complying with the law—to the letter. Your law holds that my life, my work and my property may be disposed of without my consent. Very well, you may now dispose of me without my participation in the matter. I will not play the part of defending myself, where no defense is possible, and I will not simulate the illusion of dealing with a tribunal of justice."

"But, Mr. Rearden, the law provides specifically that you are to be given an opportunity to present your side of the case and to defend yourself."

"A prisoner brought to trial can defend himself only if there is an objective principle of justice recognized by his judges, a principle upholding his rights, which they may not violate and which he can invoke. The law, by which you are trying me, holds that there are no principles, that I have no rights and that you may do with me whatever you please. Very well. Do it."

"Mr. Rearden, the law which you are denouncing is based on the highest principle—the principle of the public good."

"Who is the public? What does it hold as its good? There was a time when men believed that 'the good' was a concept to be defined by a code of moral values and that no man had the right to seek his good through the violation of the rights of another. If it is now believed that my fellow men may sacrifice me in any manner they please for the sake of whatever they deem to be their own good, if they believe that they may seize my property simply because they need it—well, so does any burglar. There is only this difference: the burglar does not ask me to sanction his act."

A group of seats at the side of the courtroom was reserved for the prominent visitors who had come from New York to witness the trial. Dagny sat motionless and her face showed nothing but a solemn attention, the attention of listening with the knowledge that the flow of his words would determine the course of her life. Eddie Willers sat beside her. James Taggart had not come. Paul Larkin sat hunched forward, his face thrust out, pointed like an animal's muzzle, sharpened by a look of fear now turning into malicious hatred. Mr. Mowen, who sat beside him, was a man of greater innocence and smaller understanding; his fear was of a simpler nature; he listened in bewildered indignation and he whispered to Larkin, "Good God, now he's done it! Now he'll convince the whole country that all businessmen are enemies of the public good!"

"Are we to understand," asked the judge, "that you hold your own interests above the interests of the public?"

"I hold that such a question can never arise except in a society of cannibals."

"What . . . what do you mean?"

"I hold that there is no clash of interests among men who do not demand the unearned and do not practice human sacrifices."

"Are we to understand that if the public deems it necessary to curtail your profits, you do not recognize its right to do so?"

"Why, yes, I do. The public may curtail my profits any time it wishes—by refusing to buy my product."

"We are speaking of . . . other methods."

"Any other method of curtailing profits is the method of looters —and I recognize it as such."

"Mr. Rearden, this is hardly the way to defend yourself."

"I said that I would not defend myself."

"But this is unheard of! Do you realize the gravity of the charge against you?"

"I do not care to consider it."

"Do you realize the possible consequences of your stand?"

"Fully."

"It is the opinion of this court that the facts presented by the prosecution seem to warrant no leniency. The penalty which this court has the power to impose on you is extremely severe."

"Go ahead."

"I beg your pardon?"

"Impose it."

The three judges looked at one another. Then their spokesman turned back to Rearden. "This is unprecedented," he said.

"It is completely irregular," said the second judge. "The law requires you to submit a plea in your own defense. Your only alternative is to state for the record that you throw yourself upon the mercy of the court."

"I do not."

"But you have to."

"Do you mean that what you expect from me is some sort of voluntary action?"

"Yes."

"I volunteer nothing."

"But the law demands that the defendant's side be represented on the record."

"Do you mean that you need my help to make this procedure legal?"

"Well, no . . . yes . . . that is, to complete the form."

"I will not help you."

The third and youngest judge, who had acted as prosecutor, snapped impatiently, "This is ridiculous and unfair! Do you want to let it look as if a man of your prominence had been railroaded without a—" He cut himself off short. Somebody at the back of the courtroom emitted a long whistle.

"I want," said Rearden gravely, "to let the nature of this procedure appear exactly for what it is. If you need my help to disguise it—I will not help you."

"But we are giving you a chance to defend yourself—and it is you who are rejecting it."

"I will not help you to pretend that I have a chance. I will not help you to preserve an appearance of righteousness where rights are not recognized. I will not help you to preserve an appearance of rationality by entering a debate in which a gun is the final argument. I will not help you to pretend that you are administering justice."

"But the law compels you to volunteer a defense!"

There was laughter at the back of the courtroom.

"*That* is the flaw in your theory, gentlemen," said Rearden gravely, "and I will not help you out of it. If you choose to deal with men by means of compulsion, do so. But you will discover that you need the voluntary co-operation of your victims, in many more ways than you can see at present. And your victims should discover that it is their own volition—which you cannot force—that makes you possible. I choose to be consistent and I will obey you in the manner you demand. Whatever you wish me to do, I will do it at the point of a gun. If you sentence me to jail, you will have to send armed men to carry me there—I will not volunteer to move. If you fine me, you will have to seize my property to collect the fine—I will not volunteer to pay it. If you believe that you have the right to force me—use your guns openly. I will not help you to disguise the nature of your action."

The eldest judge leaned forward across the table and his voice became suavely derisive: "You speak as if you were fighting for some sort of principle, Mr. Rearden, but what you're actually fighting for is only your property, isn't it?"

"Yes, of course. I am fighting for my property. Do you know the kind of principle *that* represents?"

"You pose as a champion of freedom, but it's only the freedom to make money that you're after."

"Yes, of course. All I want is the freedom to make money. Do you know what that freedom implies?"

"Surely, Mr. Rearden, you wouldn't want your attitude to be misunderstood. You wouldn't want to give support to the widespread impression that you are a man devoid of social conscience, who feels no concern for the welfare of his fellows and works for nothing but his own profit."

"I work for nothing but my own profit. I earn it."

There was a gasp, not of indignation, but of astonishment, in the crowd behind him and silence from the judges he faced. He went on calmly:

"No, I do not want my attitude to be misunderstood. I shall be glad to state it for the record. I am in full agreement with the facts of everything said about me in the newspapers—with the facts, but not with the evaluation. I work for nothing but my own profit—which I make by selling a product they need to men who are willing and able to buy it. I do not produce it for their benefit at the expense of mine, and they do not buy it for my benefit at the expense of theirs; I do not sacrifice my interests to them nor do they sacrifice theirs to me; we deal as equals by mutual consent to mutual advantage—and I am proud of every penny that I have earned in this manner. I am rich and I am proud of every penny I own. I have made my money by my own effort, in free exchange and through the voluntary consent of every man I dealt with—the voluntary consent of those who employed me when I started, the voluntary consent of those who work for me now, the voluntary consent of those who buy my product. I shall answer all the questions you are afraid to ask me openly. Do I wish to pay my workers more than their services are worth to me? I do not. Do I wish to sell my product for less than my customers are willing to pay me? I do not. Do I wish to sell it at a loss or give it away? I do not. If this is evil, do whatever you please about me, according to whatever standards you hold. These are mine. I am earning my own living, as every honest man must. I refuse to accept as guilt the fact of my own existence and the fact that I must work in order to support it. I refuse to accept as guilt the fact that I am able to do it and to do it well. I refuse to accept as guilt the fact that I am able to do it better than most people—the fact that my work is of greater value than the work of my neighbors and that more men are willing to pay me. I refuse to apologize for my ability—I refuse to apologize for my success—I refuse to apologize for my money. If this is evil, make the most of it. If this is what the public finds harmful to its interests, let the public destroy me. This is my code—and I will accept no other. I could say to you that I have done more good for my fellow men than you can ever hope to accomplish—but I will not say it, because

I do not seek the good of others as a sanction for my right to exist, nor do I recognize the good of others as a justification for their seizure of my property or their destruction of my life. I will not say that the good of others was the purpose of my work—my own good was my purpose, and I despise the man who surrenders his. I could say to you that you do not serve the public good—that nobody's good can be achieved at the price of human sacrifices—that when you violate the rights of one man, you have violated the rights of all, and a public of rightless creatures is doomed to destruction. I could say to you that you will and can achieve nothing but universal devastation—as any looter must, when he runs out of victims. I could say it, but I won't. It is not your particular policy that I challenge, but your moral premise. If it were true that men could achieve their good by means of turning some men into sacrificial animals, and I were asked to immolate myself for the sake of creatures who wanted to survive at the price of my blood, if I were asked to serve the interests of society apart from, above and against my own—I would refuse, I would reject it as the most contemptible evil, I would fight it with every power I possess, I would fight the whole of mankind, if one minute were all I could last before I were murdered, I would fight in the full confidence of the justice of my battle and of a living being's right to exist. Let there be no misunderstanding about me. If it is now the belief of my fellow men, who call themselves the public, that their good requires victims, then I say: The public good be damned, I will have no part of it!"

The crowd burst into applause.

Rearden whirled around, more startled than his judges. He saw faces that laughed in violent excitement, and faces that pleaded for help; he saw their silent despair breaking out into the open; he saw the same anger and indignation as his own, finding release in the wild defiance of their cheering; he saw the looks of admiration and the looks of hope. There were also the faces of loose-mouthed young men and maliciously unkempt females, the kind who led the booing in newsreel theaters at any appearance of a businessman on the screen; they did not attempt a counter-demonstration; they were silent.

As he looked at the crowd, people saw in his face what the threats of the judges had not been able to evoke: the first sign of emotion.

It was a few moments before they heard the furious beating of a gavel upon the table and one of the judges yelling:

"—or I shall have the courtroom cleared!"

As he turned back to the table, Rearden's eyes moved over the visitors' section. His glance paused on Dagny, a pause perceptible only to her, as if he were saying: It works. She would have appeared calm except that her eyes seemed to have become too large for her face. Eddie Willers was smiling the kind of smile that is a man's substitute for breaking into tears. Mr. Mowen looked stupefied. Paul Larkin was staring at the floor. There was no expression on Bertram Scudder's face

—or on Lillian's. She sat at the end of a row, her legs crossed, a mink stole slanting from her right shoulder to her left hip; she looked at Rearden, not moving.

In the complex violence of all the things he felt, he had time to recognize a touch of regret and of longing: there was a face he had hoped to see, had looked for from the start of the session, had wanted to be present more than any other face around him. But Francisco d'Anconia had not come.

"Mr. Rearden," said the eldest judge, smiling affably, reproachfully and spreading his arms, "it is regrettable that you should have misunderstood us so completely. That's the trouble—that businessmen refuse to approach us in a spirit of trust and friendship. They seem to imagine that we are their enemies. Why do you speak of human sacrifices? What made you go to such an extreme? We have no intention of seizing your property or destroying your life. We do not seek to harm your interests. We are fully aware of your distinguished achievements. Our purpose is only to balance social pressures and do justice to all. This hearing is really intended, not as a trial, but as a friendly discussion aimed at mutual understanding and co-operation."

"I do not co-operate at the point of a gun."

"Why speak of guns? This matter is not serious enough to warrant such references. We are fully aware that the guilt in this case lies chiefly with Mr. Kenneth Danagger, who instigated this infringement of the law, who exerted pressure upon you and who confessed his guilt by disappearing in order to escape trial."

"No. We did it by equal, mutual, voluntary agreement."

"Mr. Rearden," said the second judge, "you may not share some of our ideas, but when all is said and done, we're all working for the same cause. For the good of the people. We realize that you were prompted to disregard legal technicalities by the critical situation of the coal mines and the crucial importance of fuel to the public welfare."

"No. I was prompted by my own profit and my own interests. What effect it had on the coal mines and the public welfare is for you to estimate. That was not my motive."

Mr. Mowen stared dazedly about him and whispered to Paul Larkin, "Something's gone screwy here."

"Oh, shut up!" snapped Larkin.

"I am sure, Mr. Rearden," said the eldest judge, "that you do not really believe—nor does the public—that we wish to treat you as a sacrificial victim. If anyone has been laboring under such a misapprehension, we are anxious to prove that it is not true."

The judges retired to consider their verdict. They did not stay out long. They returned to an ominously silent courtroom—and announced that a fine of $5,000 was imposed on Henry Rearden, but that the sentence was suspended.

Streaks of jeering laughter ran through the applause that swept the courtroom. The applause was aimed at Rearden, the laughter—at the judges.

Rearden stood motionless, not turning to the crowd, barely hearing the applause. He stood looking at the judges. There was no triumph in his face, no elation, only the still intensity of contemplating a vision with a bitter wonder that was almost fear. He was seeing the enormity of the smallness of the enemy who was destroying the world. He felt as if, after a journey of years through a landscape of devastation, past the ruins of great factories, the wrecks of powerful engines, the bodies of invincible men, he had come upon the despoiler, expecting to find a giant—and had found a rat eager to scurry for cover at the first sound of a human step. If this is what has beaten us, he thought, the guilt is ours.

He was jolted back into the courtroom by the people pressing to surround him. He smiled in answer to their smiles, to the frantic, tragic eagerness of their faces; there was a touch of sadness in his smile.

"God bless you, Mr. Rearden!" said an old woman with a ragged shawl over her head. "Can't you save us, Mr. Rearden? They're eating us alive, and it's no use fooling anybody about how it's the rich that they're after—do you know what's happening to us?"

"Listen, Mr. Rearden," said a man who looked like a factory worker, "it's the rich who're selling us down the river. Tell those wealthy bastards, who're so anxious to give everything away, that when they give away their palaces, they're giving away the skin off our backs."

"I know it," said Rearden.

The guilt is ours, he thought. If we who were the movers, the providers, the benefactors of mankind, were willing to let the brand of evil be stamped upon us and silently to bear punishment for our virtues—what sort of "good" did we expect to triumph in the world?

He looked at the people around him. They had cheered him today; they had cheered him by the side of the track of the John Galt Line. But tomorrow they would clamor for a new directive from Wesley Mouch and a free housing project from Orren Boyle, while Boyle's girders collapsed upon their heads. They would do it, because they would be told to forget, as a sin, that which had made them cheer Hank Rearden.

Why were they ready to renounce their highest moments as a sin? Why were they willing to betray the best within them? What made them believe that this earth was a realm of evil where despair was their natural fate? He could not name the reason, but he knew that it had to be named. He felt it as a huge question mark within the courtroom, which it was now his duty to answer.

This was the real sentence imposed upon him, he thought—to discover what idea, what simple idea available to the simplest man, had made mankind accept the doctrines that led it to self-destruction.

* * *

"Hank, I'll never think that it's hopeless, not ever again," said Dagny that evening, after the trial. "I'll never be tempted to quit. You've proved that the right always works and always wins—" She stopped, then added, "—provided one knows what is the right."

Lillian said to him at dinner next day, "So you've won, have you?" Her voice was noncommittal; she said nothing else; she was watching him, as if studying a riddle.

The Wet Nurse asked him at the mills, "Mr. Rearden, what's a moral premise?" "What you're going to have a lot of trouble with." The boy frowned, then shrugged and said, laughing, "God, that was a wonderful show! What a beating you gave them, Mr. Rearden! I sat by the radio and howled." "How do you know it was a beating?" "Well, it was, wasn't it?" "Are you sure of it?" "Sure I'm sure." "The thing that makes you sure is a moral premise."

The newspapers were silent. After the exaggerated attention they had given to the case, they acted as if the trial were not worthy of notice. They printed brief accounts on unlikely pages, worded in such generalities that no reader could discover any hint of a controversial issue.

The businessmen he met seemed to wish to evade the subject of his trial. Some made no comment at all, but turned away, their faces showing a peculiar resentment under the effort to appear noncommittal, as if they feared that the mere act of looking at him would be interpreted as taking a stand. Others ventured to comment: "In my opinion, Rearden, it was extremely unwise of you. . . . It seems to me that this is hardly the time to make enemies. . . . We can't afford to arouse resentment."

"Whose resentment?" he asked.

"I don't think the government will like it."

"You saw the consequences of *that*."

"Well, I don't know . . . The public won't take it, there's bound to be a lot of indignation."

"You saw how the public took it."

"Well, I don't know . . . We've been trying hard not to give any grounds for all those accusations about selfish greed—and you've given ammunition to the enemy."

"Would you rather agree with the enemy that you have no right to your profits and your property?"

"Oh, no, no, certainly not—but why go to extremes? There's always a middle ground."

"A middle ground between you and your murderers?"

"Now why use such words?"

"What I said at the trial, was it true or not?"

"It's going to be misquoted and misunderstood."

"Was it true or not?"

"The public is too dumb to grapple with such issues."

"Was it true or not?"

"It's no time to boast about being rich—when the populace is starving. It's just goading them on to seize everything."

"But telling them that you have no right to your wealth, while *they* have—is what's going to restrain them?"

"Well, I don't know . . ."

"I don't like the things you said at your trial," said another man. "In my opinion, I don't agree with you at all. Personally, I'm proud to believe that I *am* working for the public good, not just for my own profit. I like to think that I have some goal higher than just earning my three meals a day and my Hammond limousine."

"And I don't like that idea about no directives and no controls," said another. "I grant you they're running hog-wild and overdoing it. But—no controls at all? I don't go along with that. I think *some* controls are necessary. The ones which are for the public good."

"I am sorry, gentlemen," said Rearden, "that I will be obliged to save your goddamn necks along with mine."

A group of businessmen headed by Mr. Mowen did not issue any statements about the trial. But a week later they announced, with an inordinate amount of publicity, that they were endowing the construction of a playground for the children of the unemployed.

Bertram Scudder did not mention the trial in his column. But ten days later, he wrote, among items of miscellaneous gossip: "Some idea of the public value of Mr. Hank Rearden may be gathered from the fact that of all social groups, he seems to be most unpopular with his own fellow businessmen. His old-fashioned brand of ruthlessness seems to be too much even for those predatory barons of profit."

On an evening in December—when the street beyond his window was like a congested throat coughing with the horns of pre-Christmas traffic—Rearden sat in his room at the Wayne-Falkland Hotel, fighting an enemy more dangerous than weariness or fear: revulsion against the thought of having to deal with human beings.

He sat, unwilling to venture into the streets of the city, unwilling to move, as if he were chained to his chair and to this room. He had tried for hours to ignore an emotion that felt like the pull of homesickness: his awareness that the only man whom he longed to see, was here, in this hotel, just a few floors above him.

He had caught himself, in the past few weeks, wasting time in the lobby whenever he entered the hotel or left it, loitering unnecessarily at the mail counter or the newsstand, watching the hurried currents of people, hoping to see Francisco d'Anconia among them. He had caught himself eating solitary dinners in the restaurant of the Wayne-Falkland, with his eyes on the curtains of the entrance doorway. Now he caught himself sitting in his room, thinking that the distance was only a few floors.

He rose to his feet, with a chuckle of amused indignation; he was acting, he thought, like a woman who waits for a telephone call and fights against the temptation to end the torture by making the first move. There was no reason, he thought, why he could not go to Francisco d'Anconia, if that was what he wanted. Yet when he told himself that he would, he felt some dangerous element of surrender in the intensity of his own relief.

He made a step toward the phone, to call Francisco's suite, but stopped. It was not what he wanted; what he wanted was simply to walk in, unannounced, as Francisco had walked into his office; it was this that seemed to state some unstated right between them.

On his way to the elevator, he thought: He won't be in or, if he is, you'll probably find him entertaining some floozie, which will serve you right. But the thought seemed unreal, he could not make it apply to the man he had seen at the mouth of the furnace—he stood confidently in the elevator, looking up—he walked confidently down the hall, feeling his bitterness relax into gaiety—he knocked at the door.

Francisco's voice snapped, "Come in!" It had a brusque, absent-minded sound.

Rearden opened the door and stopped on the threshold. One of the hotel's costliest satin-shaded lamps stood in the middle of the floor, throwing a circle of light on wide sheets of drafting paper. Francisco d'Anconia, in shirt sleeves, a strand of hair hanging down over his face, lay stretched on the floor, on his stomach, propped up by his elbows, biting the end of a pencil in concentration upon some point of the intricate tracing before him. He did not look up, he seemed to have forgotten the knock. Rearden tried to distinguish the drawing: it looked like the section of a smelter. He stood watching in startled wonder; had he had the power to bring into reality his own image of Francisco d'Anconia, this was the picture he would have seen: the figure of a purposeful young worker intent upon a difficult task.

In a moment, Francisco raised his head. In the next instant, he flung his body upward to a kneeling posture, looking at Rearden with a smile of incredulous pleasure. In the next, he seized the drawings and threw them aside too hastily, face down.

"What did I interrupt?" asked Rearden.

"Nothing much. Come in." He was grinning happily. Rearden felt suddenly certain that Francisco had waited, too, had waited for this as for a victory which he had not quite hoped to achieve.

"What were you doing?" asked Rearden.

"Just amusing myself."

"Let me see it."

"No." He rose and kicked the drawings aside.

Rearden noted that if he had resented as impertinence Francisco's manner of proprietorship in his office, he himself was now guilty of the same attitude—because he offered no explanation for his visit, but crossed the room and sat down in an armchair, casually, as if he were at home.

"Why didn't you come to continue what you had started?" he asked.

"You have been continuing it brilliantly without my help."

"Do you mean, my trial?"

"I mean, your trial."

"How do you know? You weren't there."

Francisco smiled, because the tone of the voice confessed an added sentence: I was looking for you. "Don't you suppose I heard every word of it on the radio?"

"You did? Well, how did you like hearing your own lines come over the air, with me as your stooge?"

"You weren't, Mr. Rearden. They weren't my lines. Weren't they the things you had always lived by?"

"Yes."

"I only helped you to see that you should have been proud to live by them."

"I am glad you heard it."

"It was great, Mr. Rearden—and about three generations too late."

"What do you mean?"

"If one single businessman had had the courage, then, to say that he worked for nothing but his own profit—and to say it proudly—he would have saved the world."

"I haven't given up the world as lost."

"It isn't. It never can be. But oh God!—what he would have spared us!"

"Well, I guess we have to fight, no matter what era we're caught in."

"Yes . . . You know, Mr. Rearden, I would suggest that you get a transcript of your trial and read what you said. Then see whether you are practicing it fully and consistently—or not."

"You mean that I'm not?"

"See for yourself."

"I know that you had a great deal to tell me, when we were interrupted, that night at the mills. Why don't you finish what you had to say?"

"No. It's too soon."

Francisco acted as if there were nothing unusual about this visit, as if he took it as a matter of natural course—as he had always acted in Rearden's presence. But Rearden noted that he was not so calm as he wished to appear; he was pacing the room, in a manner that seemed a release for an emotion he did not want to confess; he had forgotten the lamp and it still stood on the floor as the room's sole illumination.

"You've been taking an awful beating in the way of discoveries, haven't you?" said Francisco. "How did you like the behavior of your fellow businessmen?"

"I suppose it was to be expected."

His voice tense with the anger of compassion, Francisco said, "It's been twelve years and yet I'm still unable to see it indifferently!" The sentence sounded involuntary, as if, trying to suppress the sound of emotion, he had uttered suppressed words.

"Twelve years—since what?" asked Rearden.

There was an instant's pause, but Francisco answered calmly, "Since I understood what those men were doing." He added, "I know what you're going through right now . . . and what's still ahead."

"Thanks," said Rearden.

"For what?"

"For what you're trying so hard not to show. But don't worry about me. I'm still able to stand it. . . . You know, I didn't come here because I wanted to talk about myself or even about the trial."

"I'll agree to any subject you choose—in order to have you here." He said it in the tone of a courteous joke; but the tone could not disguise it; he meant it. "What did you want to talk about?"

"You."

Francisco stopped. He looked at Rearden for a moment, then answered quietly, "All right."

If that which Rearden felt could have gone directly into words, past the barrier of his will, he would have cried: Don't let me down—I need you—I am fighting all of them, I have fought to my limit and am condemned to fight beyond it—and, as sole ammunition possible to me, I need the knowledge of one single man whom I can trust, respect and admire.

Instead, he said calmly, very simply—and the only note of a personal bond between them was that tone of sincerity which comes with a direct, unqualifiedly rational statement and implies the same honesty of mind in the listener—"You know, I think that the only real moral crime that one man can commit against another is the attempt to create, by his words or actions, an impression of the contradictory, the impossible, the irrational, and thus shake the concept of rationality in his victim."

"That's true."

"If I say that that is the dilemma you've put me in, would you help me by answering a personal question?"

"I will try."

"I don't have to tell you—I think you know it—that you are the man of the highest mind I have ever met. I am coming to accept, not as right, but at least as possible, the fact that you refuse to exercise your great ability in the world of today. But what a man does out of despair, is not necessarily a key to his character. I have always thought that the real key is in that which he seeks for his enjoyment. And this is what I find inconceivable: no matter what you've given up, so long as you chose to remain alive, how can you find any pleasure in spending a life as valuable as yours on running after cheap women and on an imbecile's idea of diversions?"

Francisco looked at him with a fine smile of amusement, as if saying: No? You didn't want to talk about yourself? And what is it that you're confessing but the desperate loneliness which makes the question of my character more important to you than any other question right now?

The smile merged into a soft, good-natured chuckle, as if the question involved no problem for him, no painful secret to reveal. "There's a way to solve every dilemma of that kind, Mr. Rearden. Check your premises." He sat down on the floor, settling himself gaily, informally, for a conversation he would enjoy. "Is it your own first-hand conclusion that I am a man of high mind?"

"Yes."

"Do you know of your own first-hand knowledge that I spend my life running after women?"

"You've never denied it."

"Denied it? I've gone to a lot of trouble to create that impression."

"Do you mean to say that it isn't true?"

"Do I strike you as a man with a miserable inferiority complex?"

"Good God, no!"

"Only that kind of man spends his life running after women."

"What do you mean?"

"Do you remember what I said about money and about the men who seek to reverse the law of cause and effect? The men who try to replace the mind by seizing the products of the mind? Well, the man who despises himself tries to gain self-esteem from sexual adventures —which can't be done, because sex is not the cause, but an effect and an expression of a man's sense of his own value."

"You'd better explain that."

"Did it ever occur to you that it's the same issue? The men who think that wealth comes from material resources and has no intellectual root or meaning, are the men who think—for the same reason—that sex is a physical capacity which functions independently of one's mind, choice or code of values. They think that your body creates a desire and makes a choice for you—just about in some such way as if iron ore transformed itself into railroad rails of its own volition. Love is blind, they say; sex is impervious to reason and mocks the power of all philosophers. But, in fact, a man's sexual choice is the result and the sum of his fundamental convictions. Tell me what a man finds sexually attractive and I will tell you his entire philosophy of life. Show me the woman he sleeps with and I will tell you his valuation of himself. No matter what corruption he's taught about the virtue of selflessness, sex is the most profoundly selfish of all acts, an act which he cannot perform for any motive but his own enjoyment—just try to think of performing it in a spirit of selfless charity!—an act which is not possible in self-abasement, only in self-exaltation, only in the confidence of being desired and being worthy of desire. It is an act that forces him to stand naked in spirit, as well as in body, and to accept his real ego as his standard of value. He will always be attracted to the woman who reflects his deepest vision of himself, the woman whose surrender permits him to experience—or to fake—a sense of self-esteem. The man who is proudly certain of his own value, will want the highest type of woman he can find, the woman he admires, the strongest, the hardest to conquer—because only the possession of a heroine will give him the sense of an achievement, not the possession of a brainless slut. He does not seek to . . . What's the matter?" he asked, seeing the look on Rearden's face, a look of intensity much beyond mere interest in an abstract discussion.

"Go on," said Rearden tensely.

"He does not seek to gain his value, he seeks to express it. There is no conflict between the standards of his mind and the desires of his body. But the man who is convinced of his own worthlessness will be drawn to a woman he despises—because she will reflect his own secret self, she will release him from that objective reality in which he is a fraud, she will give him a momentary illusion of his own value and a momentary escape from the moral code that damns him. Observe the ugly mess which most men make of their sex lives—and observe the mess of contradictions which they hold as their moral philosophy. One proceeds from the other. Love is our response to our highest values—and can be nothing else. Let a man corrupt his values and his view of existence, let him profess that love is not self-enjoyment but self-denial, that virtue consists, not of pride, but of pity or pain or weakness or sacrifice, that the noblest love is born, not of admiration, but of charity, not in response to *values,* but in response to *flaws*—and he will have cut himself in two. His body will not obey him, it will not respond, it will make him impotent toward the woman he professes to love and draw him to the lowest type of whore he can find. His body will always follow the ultimate logic of his deepest convictions; if he believes that flaws are values, he has damned existence as evil and only the evil will attract him. He has damned himself and he will feel that depravity is all he is worthy of enjoying. He has equated virtue with pain and he will feel that vice is the only realm of pleasure. Then he will scream that his body has vicious desires of its own which his mind cannot conquer, that sex is sin, that true love is a pure emotion of the spirit. And then he will wonder why love brings him nothing but boredom, and sex—nothing but shame."

Rearden said slowly, looking off, not realizing that he was thinking aloud, "At least . . . I've never accepted that other tenet . . . I've never felt guilty about making money."

Francisco missed the significance of the first two words; he smiled and said eagerly, "You do see that it's the same issue? No, you'd never accept any part of their vicious creed. You wouldn't be able to force it upon yourself. If you tried to damn sex as evil, you'd still find yourself, against your will, acting on the proper moral premise. You'd be attracted to the highest woman you met. You'd always want a heroine. You'd be incapable of self-contempt. You'd be unable to believe that existence is evil and that you're a helpless creature caught in an impossible universe. You're the man who's spent his life shaping matter to the purpose of his mind. You're the man who would know that just as an idea unexpressed in physical action is contemptible hypocrisy, so is platonic love—and just as physical action unguided by an idea is a fool's self-fraud, so is sex when cut off from one's code of values. It's the same issue, and you would know it. Your inviolate sense of self-esteem would know it. You would be incapable of desire for a woman you despised. Only the man who extols the purity of a love devoid of desire, is capable of the depravity of a desire devoid of love. But observe that most people are creatures cut in half who keep swinging desperately to one side or to the other. One kind of half is the man who despises money, factories, skyscrapers and his own body. He holds undefined emotions about non-conceivable subjects as the meaning of life and as his claim to virtue. And he cries with despair, because he can feel nothing for the women he respects, but finds himself in bondage to an irresistible passion for a slut from the gutter. He is the man whom people call an idealist. The other kind of half is the man whom people call practical, the man who despises principles, abstractions, art, philosophy and his own mind. He regards the acquisition of material objects as the only goal of existence—and he laughs at the need to consider their purpose or their source. He expects them to give him pleasure—and he wonders why the more he gets, the less he feels. *He* is the man who spends his time chasing women. Observe the triple fraud which he perpetrates upon himself. He will not acknowledge his need of self-esteem, since he scoffs at such a concept as moral values; yet he feels the profound self-contempt which comes from believing that he is a piece of meat. He will not acknowledge, but he knows that sex is the physical expression of a tribute to personal values. So he tries, by going through the motions of the effect, to acquire that which should have been the cause. He tries to gain a sense of his own value from the women who surrender to him—and he forgets that the women he picks have neither character nor judgment nor standard of value. He tells himself that all he's after is physical pleasure—but observe that he tires of his women in a week or a night, that he despises professional whores and that he loves to imagine he is seducing virtuous girls who make a great exception for his sake. It is the feeling of achievement that he seeks and never finds. What glory can there be in the conquest of a mindless body? Now *that* is your woman-chaser. Does the description fit me?"

"God, no!"

"Then you can judge, without asking my word for it, how much chasing of women I've done in my life."

"But what on earth have you been doing on the front pages of newspapers for the last—isn't it twelve—years?"

"I've spent a lot of money on the most ostentatiously vulgar parties I could think of, and a miserable amount of time on being seen with the appropriate sort of women. As for the rest—" He stopped, then said, "I have some friends who know this, but you are the first person to whom I am confiding it against my own rules: I have never slept with any of those women. I have never touched one of them."

"What is more incredible than that, is that I believe you."

The lamp on the floor beside him threw broken bits of light across Francisco's face, as he leaned forward; the face had a look of guiltless amusement. "If you care to glance over those front pages, you'll see that I've never said anything. It was the women who were eager to rush into print with stories insinuating that being seen with me at a restaurant was the sign of a great romance. What do you suppose those women are after but the same thing as the chaser—the desire to gain their own value from the number and fame of the men they conquer? Only it's one step phonier, because the value they seek is not even in the actual fact, but in the impression on and the envy of other women. Well, I gave those bitches what they wanted—but what they literally wanted, without the pretense that they expected, the pretense that hides from them the nature of their wish. Do you think they wanted to sleep with me or with any man? They wouldn't be capable of so real and honest a desire. They wanted food for their vanity—and I gave it to them. I gave them the chance to boast to their friends and to see themselves in the scandal sheets in the roles of great seductresses. But do you know that it works in exactly the same way as what you did at your trial? If you want to defeat any kind of vicious fraud—comply with it literally, adding nothing of your own to disguise its nature. Those women understood. They saw whether there's any satisfaction in being envied by others for a feat one has not achieved. Instead of self-esteem, their publicized romances with me have given them a deeper sense of inferiority: each one of them knows that she's tried and failed. If dragging me into bed is supposed to be her public standard of value, she knows that she couldn't live up to it. I think those women hate me more than any other man on earth. But my secret is safe—because each one of them thinks that she was the only one who failed, while all the others succeeded, so she'll be the more vehement in swearing to our romance and will never admit the truth to anybody."

"But what have you done to your own reputation?"

Francisco shrugged. "Those whom I respect, will know the truth about me, sooner or later. The others"—his face hardened—"the others consider that which I really am as evil. Let them have what they prefer—what I appear to be on the front pages."

"But what for? Why did you do it? Just to teach them a lesson?"

"Hell, no! I wanted to be known as a playboy."

"Why?"

"A playboy is a man who just can't help letting money run through his fingers."

"Why did you want to assume such an ugly sort of role?"

"Camouflage."

"For what?"

"For a purpose of my own."

"What purpose?"

Francisco shook his head. "Don't ask me to tell you that. I've told you more than I should. You'll come to know the rest of it soon, anyway."

"If it's more than you should, why did you tell me?"

"Because . . . you've made me become impatient for the first time in years." The note of a suppressed emotion came back into his voice. "Because I've never wanted anyone to know the truth about me as I wanted you to know it. Because I knew that you'd despise a playboy more than any other sort of man—as I would, too. Playboy? I've never loved but one woman in my life and still do and always will!" It was an involuntary break, and he added, his voice low, "I've never confessed that to anyone . . . not even to her."

"Have you lost her?"

Francisco sat looking off into space; in a moment, he answered tonelessly, "I hope not."

The light of the lamp hit his face from below, and Rearden could not see his eyes, only his mouth drawn in lines of endurance and oddly solemn resignation. Rearden knew that this was a wound not to be probed any further.

With one of his swift changes of mood, Francisco said, "Oh well, it's just a little longer!" and rose to his feet, smiling.

"Since you trust me," said Rearden, "I want to tell you a secret of mine in exchange. I want you to know how much I trusted you before I came here. And I might need your help later."

"You're the only man left whom I'd like to help."

"There's a great deal that I don't understand about you, but I'm certain of one thing: that you're not a friend of the looters."

"I'm not." There was a hint of amusement in Francisco's face, as at an understatement.

"So I know that you won't betray me if I tell you that I'm going to continue selling Rearden Metal to customers of my own choice in any amount I wish, whenever I see a chance to do it. Right now, I'm getting ready to pour an order twenty times the size of the one they tried me for."

Sitting on the arm of a chair, a few feet away, Francisco leaned forward to look at him silently, frowning, for a long moment. "Do you think that you're fighting them by doing it?" he asked.

"Well, what would *you* call it? Co-operating?"

"You were willing to work and produce Rearden Metal for them at the price of losing your profits, losing your friends, enriching stray bastards who had the pull to rob you, and taking their abuse for the privilege of keeping them alive. Now you're willing to do it at the price of accepting the position of a criminal and the risk of being thrown in jail at any moment—for the sake of keeping in existence a system which can be kept going only by its victims, only by the breaking of its own laws."

"It's not for their system, but for customers whom I can't abandon to the mercy of their system—I intend to outlast that system of theirs —I don't intend to let them stop me, no matter how hard they make it for me—and I don't intend to give up the world to them, even if I am the last man left. Right now, that illegal order is more important to me than the whole of my mills."

Francisco shook his head slowly and did not answer; then he asked, "To which one of your friends in the copper industry are you going to give the valuable privilege of informing on you this time?"

Rearden smiled. "Not this time. This time, I'm dealing with a man I can trust."

"Really? Who is it?"

"You."

Francisco sat up straight. "What?" he asked, his voice so low that he almost succeeded in hiding the sound of a gasp.

Rearden was smiling. "You didn't know that I'm one of your customers now? It was done through a couple of stooges and under a phony name—but I'll need your help to prevent anyone on your staff from becoming inquisitive about it. I need that copper, I need it on time—and I don't care if they arrest me later, so long as I get this through. I know that you've lost all concern for your company, your wealth, your work, because you don't care to deal with looters like Taggart and Boyle. But if you meant all the things you taught me, if I am the last man left whom you respect, you'll help me to survive and to beat them. I've never asked for anyone's help. I'm asking for yours. I need you. I trust you. You've always professed your admiration for me. Well, there's my life in your hands—if you want it. An order of d'Anconia copper is being shipped to me right now. It left San Juan on December fifth."

"*What?!*"

It was a scream of plain shock. Francisco had shot to his feet, past any attempt to hide anything. "On December fifth?"

"Yes," said Rearden, stupefied.

Francisco leaped to the telephone. "I *told* you not to deal with d'Anconia Copper!" It was the half-moaning, half-furious cry of despair.

His hand was reaching for the telephone, but jerked back. He grasped the edge of the table, as if to stop himself from lifting the receiver, and he stood, head down, for how long a time neither he nor Rearden could tell. Rearden was held numb by the fact of watching an agonized struggle with the motionless figure of a man as its only evidence. He could not guess the nature of the struggle, he knew only that there was something which Francisco had the power to prevent in that moment and that it was a power which he would not use.

When Francisco raised his head, Rearden saw a face drawn by so great a suffering that its lines were almost an audible cry of pain, the more terrible because the face had a look of firmness, as if the decision had been made and this was the price of it.

"Francisco . . . what's the matter?"

"Hank, I . . ." He shook his head, stopped, then stood up straight. "Mr. Rearden," he said, in a voice that had the strength, the despair and the peculiar dignity of a plea he knew to be hopeless, "for the time when you're going to damn me, when you're going to doubt every word I said . . . I swear to you—by the woman I love—that I am your friend."

The memory of Francisco's face as it looked in that moment, came back to Rearden three days later, through a blinding shock of loss and hatred—it came back, even though, standing by the radio in his office, he thought that he must now keep away from the Wayne-Falkland or he would kill Francisco d'Anconia on sight—it kept coming back to him, through the words he was hearing—he was hearing that three ships of d'Anconia copper, bound from San Juan to New York, had been attacked by Ragnar Danneskjöld and sent to the bottom of the ocean—it kept coming back, even though he knew that much more than the copper had gone down for him with those ships.

ACCOUNT OVERDRAWN

It was the first failure in the history of Rearden Steel. For the first time, an order was not delivered as promised. But by February 15, when the Taggart rail was due, it made no difference to anyone any longer.

Winter had come early, in the last days of November. People said that it was the hardest winter on record and that no one could be blamed for the unusual severity of the snowstorms. They did not care to remember that there had been a time when snowstorms did not sweep, unresisted, down unlighted roads and upon the roofs of unheated houses, did not stop the movement of trains, did not leave a wake of corpses counted by the hundreds.

The first time that Danagger Coal was late in delivering fuel to Taggart Transcontinental, in the last week of December, Danagger's cousin explained that he could not help it; he had had to cut the workday down to six hours, he said, in order to raise the morale of the men who did not seem to function as they had in the days of his cousin Kenneth; the men had become listless and sloppy, he said, because they were exhausted by the harsh discipline of the former management; he could not help it if some of the superintendents and foremen had quit him without reason, men who had been with the company for ten to twenty years; he could not help it if there seemed to be some friction between his workers and his new supervisory staff, even though the new men were much more liberal than the old slave drivers; it was only a matter of readjustment, he said. He could not help it, he said, if the tonnage intended for Taggart Transcontinental had been turned over, on the eve of its scheduled delivery, to the Bureau of Global Relief for shipment to the People's State of England; it was an emergency, the people of England were starving, with all of their State factories closing down—and Miss Taggart was being unreasonable, since it was only a matter of one day's delay.

It was only one day's delay. It caused a three days' delay in the run of Freight Train Number 386, bound from California to New York with fifty-nine carloads of lettuce and oranges. Freight Train Number 386 waited on sidings, at coaling stations, for the fuel that had not arrived. When the train reached New York, the lettuce and oranges had to be dumped into the East River: they had waited their turn too long in the freight houses of California, with the train schedules cut and the engines forbidden, by directive, to pull a train of more than sixty cars. Nobody but their friends and trade associates noticed that three orange growers in California went out of business, as well as two lettuce farmers in Imperial Valley; nobody noticed the closing of a commission house in New York, of a plumbing company to which the commission house owed money, of a lead-pipe wholesaler who had supplied the plumbing company. When people were starving, said the newspapers, one did not have to feel concern over the failures of business enterprises which were only private ventures for private profit.

The coal shipped across the Atlantic by the Bureau of Global Relief did not reach the People's State of England: it was seized by Ragnar Danneskjöld.

The second time that Danagger Coal was late in delivering fuel to Taggart Transcontinental, in mid-January, Danagger's cousin snarled over the telephone that he could not help it: his mines had been shut down for three days, due to a shortage of lubricating oil for the machinery. The supply of coal to Taggart Transcontinental was four days late.

Mr. Quinn, of the Quinn Ball Bearing Company which had once moved from Connecticut to Colorado, waited a week for the freight train that carried his order of Rearden steel. When the train arrived, the doors of the Quinn Ball Bearing Company's plant were closed.

Nobody traced the closing of a motor company in Michigan, that had waited for a shipment of ball bearings, its machinery idle, its workers on full pay; or the closing of a sawmill in Oregon, that had waited for a new motor; or the closing of a lumber yard in Iowa, left without supply; or the bankruptcy of a building contractor in Illinois who, failing to get his lumber on time, found his contracts cancelled and the purchasers of his homes sent wandering off down snow-swept roads in search of that which did not exist anywhere any longer.

The snowstorm that came at the end of January blocked the passes through the Rocky Mountains, raising white walls thirty feet high across the main-line track of Taggart Transcontinental. The men who attempted to clear the track, gave up within the first few hours: the rotary plows broke down, one after another. The plows had been kept in precarious repair for two years past the span of their usefulness. The new plows had not been delivered; the manufacturer had quit, unable to obtain the steel he needed from Orren Boyle.

Three westbound trains were trapped on the sidings of Winston Station, high in the Rockies, where the main line of Taggart Transcontinental cut across the northwest corner of Colorado. For five days, they remained beyond the reach of help. Trains could not approach them through the storm. The last of the trucks made by Lawrence

Hammond broke down on the frozen grades of the mountain highways. The best of the airplanes once made by Dwight Sanders were sent out, but never reached Winston Station; they were worn past the stage of fighting a storm.

Through the driving mesh of snow, the passengers trapped aboard the trains looked out at the lights of Winston's shanties. The lights died in the night of the second day. By the evening of the third, the lights, the heat and the food had given out aboard the trains. In the brief lulls of the storm, when the white mesh vanished and left behind it the stillness of a black void merging a lightless earth with a starless sky—the passengers could see, many miles away to the south, a small tongue of flame twisting in the wind. It was Wyatt's Torch.

By the morning of the sixth day, when the trains were able to move and proceeded down the slopes of Utah, of Nevada, of California, the trainmen observed the smokeless stacks and the closed doors of small trackside factories, which had not been closed on their last run.

"Storms are an act of God," wrote Bertram Scudder, "and nobody can be held socially responsible for the weather."

The rations of coal, established by Wesley Mouch, permitted the heating of homes for three hours a day. There was no wood to burn, no metal to make new stoves, no tools to pierce the walls of the houses for new installations. In makeshift contraptions of bricks and oil cans, professors were burning the books of their libraries, and fruit-growers were burning the trees of their orchards. "Privations strengthen a people's spirit," wrote Bertram Scudder, "and forge the fine steel of social discipline. Sacrifice is the cement which unites human bricks into the great edifice of society."

"The nation which had once held the creed that greatness is achieved by production, is now told that it is achieved by squalor," said Francisco d'Anconia in a press interview. But this was not printed.

The only business boom, that winter, came to the amusement industry. People wrenched their pennies out of the quicksands of their food and heat budgets, and went without meals in order to crowd into movie theaters, in order to escape for a few hours the state of animals reduced to the single concern of terror over their crudest needs. In January, all movie theaters, night clubs and bowling alleys were closed by order of Wesley Mouch, for the purpose of conserving fuel. "Pleasure is not an essential of existence," wrote Bertram Scudder.

"You must learn to take a philosophical attitude," said Dr. Simon Pritchett to a young girl student who broke down into sudden, hysterical sobs in the middle of a lecture. She had just returned from a volunteer relief expedition to a settlement on Lake Superior; she had seen a mother holding the body of a grown son who had died of hunger. "There are no absolutes," said Dr. Pritchett. "Reality is only an illusion. How does that woman know that her son is dead? How does she know that he ever existed?"

People with pleading eyes and desperate faces crowded into tents where evangelists cried in triumphant gloating that man was unable to cope with nature, that his science was a fraud, that his mind was a failure, that he was reaping punishment for the sin of pride, for his confidence in his own intellect—and that only faith in the power of mystic secrets could protect him from the fissure of a rail or from the blowout of the last tire on his last truck. Love was the key to the mystic secrets, they cried, love and selfless sacrifice to the needs of others.

Orren Boyle made a selfless sacrifice to the needs of others. He sold to the Bureau of Global Relief, for shipment to the People's State of Germany, ten thousand tons of structural steel shapes that had been intended for the Atlantic Southern Railroad. "It was a difficult decision to make," he said, with a moist, unfocused look of righteousness, to the panic-stricken president of the Atlantic Southern, "but I weighed the fact that you're a rich corporation, while the people of Germany are in a state of unspeakable misery. So I acted on the principle that need comes first. When in doubt, it's the weak that must be considered, not the strong." The president of the Atlantic Southern had heard that Orren Boyle's most valuable friend in Washington had a friend in the Ministry of Supply of the People's State of Germany. But whether this had been Boyle's motive or whether it had been the principle of sacrifice, no one could tell and it made no difference: if Boyle had been a saint of the creed of selflessness, he would have had to do precisely what he had done. This silenced the president of the Atlantic Southern; he dared not admit that he cared for his railroad more than for the people of Germany; he dared not argue against the principle of sacrifice.

The waters of the Mississippi had been rising all through the month of January, swollen by the storms, driven by the wind into a restless grinding of current against current and against every obstruction in their way. On a night of lashing sleet, in the first week of February, the Mississippi bridge of the Atlantic Southern collapsed under a passenger train. The engine and the first five sleepers went down with the cracking girders into the twisting black spirals of water eighty feet below. The rest of the train remained on the first three spans of the bridge, which held.

"You can't have your cake and let your neighbor eat it, too," said Francisco d'Anconia. The fury of denunciations which the holders of public voices unleashed against him was greater than their concern over the horror at the river.

It was whispered that the chief engineer of the Atlantic Southern, in despair over the company's failure to obtain the steel he needed to reinforce the bridge, had resigned six months ago, telling the company that the bridge was unsafe. He had written a letter to the largest newspaper in New York, warning the public about it; the letter had not been printed. It was whispered that the first three spans of the bridge had held because they had been reinforced with structural shapes of Rearden Metal; but five hundred tons of the Metal was all that the railroad had been able to obtain under the Fair Share Law.

As the sole result of official investigations, two bridges across the Mississippi, belonging to smaller railroads, were condemned. One of the railroads went out of business; the other closed a branch line, tore up its rail and laid a track to the Mississippi bridge of Taggart Transcontinental; so did the Atlantic Southern.

The great Taggart Bridge at Bedford, Illinois, had been built by Nathaniel Taggart. He had fought the government for years, because the courts had ruled, on the complaint of river shippers, that railroads were a destructive competition to shipping and thus a threat to the public welfare, and that railroad bridges across the Mississippi were to be forbidden as a material obstruction; the courts had ordered Nathaniel Taggart to tear down his bridge and to carry his passengers across the river by means of barges. He had won that battle by a majority of one voice on the Supreme Court. His bridge was now the only major link left to hold the continent together. His last descendant had made it her strictest rule that whatever else was neglected, the Taggart Bridge would always be maintained in flawless shape.

The steel shipped across the Atlantic by the Bureau of Global Relief had not reached the People's State of Germany. It had been seized by Ragnar Danneskjöld—but nobody heard of it outside the Bureau, because the newspapers had long since stopped mentioning the activities of Ragnar Danneskjöld.

It was not until the public began to notice the growing shortage, then the disappearance from the market of electric irons, toasters, washing machines and all electrical appliances, that people began to ask questions and to hear whispers. They heard that no ship loaded with d'Anconia copper was able to reach a port of the United States; it could not get past Ragnar Danneskjöld.

In the foggy winter nights, on the waterfront, sailors whispered the story that Ragnar Danneskjöld always seized the cargoes of relief vessels, but never touched the copper: he sank the d'Anconia ships with their loads; he let the crews escape in lifeboats, but the copper went to the bottom of the ocean. They whispered it as a dark legend beyond men's power to explain; nobody could find a reason why Danneskjöld did not choose to take the copper.

In the second week of February, for the purpose of conserving copper wire and electric power, a directive forbade the running of elevators above the twenty-fifth floor. The upper floors of the buildings had to be vacated, and partitions of unpainted boards went up to cut off the stairways. By special permit, exceptions were granted—on the grounds of "essential need"—to a few of the larger business enterprises and the more fashionable hotels. The tops of the cities were cut down.

The inhabitants of New York had never had to be aware of the weather. Storms had been only a nuisance that slowed the traffic and made puddles in the doorways of brightly lighted shops. Stepping against the wind, dressed in raincoats, furs and evening slippers, people had felt that a storm was an intruder within the city. Now, facing the gusts of snow that came sweeping down the narrow streets, people felt in dim terror that they were the temporary intruders and that the wind had the right-of-way.

"It won't make any difference to us now, forget it, Hank, it doesn't matter," said Dagny when Rearden told her that he would not be able to deliver the rail; he had not been able to find a supplier of copper. "Forget it, Hank." He did not answer her. He could not forget the first failure of Rearden Steel.

On the evening of February 15, a plate cracked on a rail joint and sent an engine off the track, half a mile from Winston, Colorado, on a division which was to have been relaid with the new rail. The station agent of Winston sighed and sent for a crew with a crane; it was only one of the minor accidents that were happening in his section every other day or so, he was getting used to it.

Rearden, that evening, his coat collar raised, his hat slanted low over his eyes, the snow drifts rising to his knees, was tramping through an abandoned open-pit coal mine, in a forsaken corner of Pennsylvania, supervising the loading of pirated coal upon the trucks which he had provided. Nobody owned the mine, nobody could afford the cost of working it. But a young man with a brusque voice and dark, angry eyes, who came from a starving settlement, had organized a gang of the unemployed and made a deal with Rearden to deliver the coal. They mined it at night, they stored it in hidden culverts, they were paid in cash, with no questions asked or answered. Guilty of a fierce desire to remain alive, they and Rearden traded like savages, without rights, titles, contracts or protection, with nothing but mutual understanding and a ruthlessly absolute observance of one's given word. Rearden did not even know the name of the young leader. Watching him at the job of loading the trucks, Rearden thought that this boy, if born a generation earlier, would have become a great industrialist; now, he would probably end his brief life as a plain criminal in a few more years.

Dagny, that evening, was facing a meeting of the Taggart Board of Directors.

They sat about a polished table in a stately Board room which was inadequately heated. The men who, through the decades of their careers, had relied for their security upon keeping their faces blank, their words inconclusive and their clothes impeccable, were thrown off-key by the sweaters stretched over their stomachs, by the mufflers wound about their necks, by the sound of coughing that cut through the discussion too frequently, like the rattle of a machine gun.

She noted that Jim had lost the smoothness of his usual performance.

He sat with his head drawn into his shoulders, and his eyes kept darting too rapidly from face to face.

A man from Washington sat at the table among them. Nobody knew his exact job or title, but it was not necessary: they knew that he was the man from Washington. His name was Mr. Weatherby, he had graying temples, a long, narrow face and a mouth that looked as if he had to stretch his facial muscles in order to keep it closed; this gave a suggestion of primness to a face that displayed nothing else. The Directors did not know whether he was present as the guest, the adviser or the ruler of the Board; they preferred not to find out.

"It seems to me," said the chairman, "that the top problem for us to consider is the fact that the track of our main line appears to be in a deplorable, not to say critical, condition—" He paused, then added cautiously, "—while the only good rail we own is that of the John Galt—I mean, the Rio Norte—Line."

In the same cautious tone of waiting for someone else to pick up the intended purpose of his words, another man said, "If we consider our critical shortage of equipment, and if we consider that we are letting it wear out in the service of a branch line running at a loss—" He stopped and did not state what would occur if they considered it.

"In my opinion," said a thin, pallid man with a neat mustache, "the Rio Norte Line seems to have become a financial burden which the company might not be able to carry—that is, not unless certain re-adjustments are made, which—" He did not finish, but glanced at Mr. Weatherby. Mr. Weatherby looked as if he had not noticed it.

"Jim," said the chairman, "I think you might explain the picture to Mr. Weatherby."

Taggart's voice still retained a practiced smoothness, but it was the smoothness of a piece of cloth stretched tight over a broken glass object, and the sharp edges showed through once in a while: "I think it is generally conceded that the main factor affecting every railroad in the country is the unusual rate of business failures. While we all realize, of course, that this is only temporary, still, for the moment, it has made the railroad situation approach a stage that may well be described as desperate. Specifically, the number of factories which have closed throughout the territory of the Taggart Transcontinental system is so large that it has wrecked our entire financial structure. Districts and divisions which had always brought us our steadiest revenues, are now showing an actual operating loss. A train schedule geared to a heavy volume of freight cannot be maintained for three shippers where there had once been seven. We cannot give them the same service—at least, not at . . . our present rates." He glanced at Mr. Weatherby, but Mr. Weatherby did not seem to notice. "It seems to me," said Taggart, the sharp edges becoming sharper in his voice, "that the stand taken by our shippers is unfair. Most of them have been complaining about their competitors and have passed various local measures to eliminate competition in their particular fields. Now most of them are practically in sole possession of their markets, yet they refuse to realize that a railroad cannot give to one lone factory the freight rates which had been made possible by the production of a whole region. We are running our trains for them at a loss, yet they have taken a stand against any . . . raise in rates."

"Against any *raise?*" said Mr. Weatherby mildly, with a good imitation of astonishment. "That is not the stand they have taken."

"If certain rumors, which I refuse to credit, are true—" said the chairman, and stopped one syllable after the tone of panic had become obvious in his voice.

"Jim," said Mr. Weatherby pleasantly, "I think it would be best if we just didn't mention the subject of raising the rates."

"I wasn't suggesting an actual raise at this time," said Taggart hastily. "I merely referred to it to round out the picture."

"But, Jim," said an old man with a quavering voice, "I thought that your influence—I mean, your friendship—with Mr. Mouch would insure . . ."

He stopped, because the others were looking at him severely, in reproof for the breach of an unwritten law: one did not mention a failure of this kind, one did not discuss the mysterious ways of Jim's powerful friendships or why they had failed him.

"Fact is," said Mr. Weatherby easily, "that Mr. Mouch sent me here to discuss the demand of the railway unions for a raise in wages and the demand of the shippers for a cut in rates."

He said it in a tone of casual firmness; he knew that all these men had known it, that the demands had been discussed in the newspapers for months; he knew that the dread in these men's minds was not of the fact, but of his naming it—as if the fact had not existed, but his words held the power to make it exist; he knew that they had waited to see whether he would exercise that power; he was letting them know that he would.

Their situation warranted an outcry of protest; there was none; nobody answered him. Then James Taggart said in that biting, nervous tone which is intended to convey anger, but merely confesses uncertainty, "I wouldn't exaggerate the importance of Buzzy Watts of the National Shippers Council. He's been making a lot of noise and giving a lot of expensive dinners in Washington, but I wouldn't advise taking it too seriously."

"Oh, I don't know," said Mr. Weatherby.

"Listen, Clem, I do know that Wesley refused to see him last week."

"That's true. Wesley is a pretty busy man."

"And I know that when Gene Lawson gave that big party ten days ago, practically everybody was there, but Buzzy Watts was not invited."

"That's so," said Mr. Weatherby peaceably.

"So I wouldn't bet on Mr. Buzzy Watts, Clem. And I wouldn't let it worry me."

"Wesley's an impartial man," said Mr. Weatherby. "A man devoted to public duty. It's the interests of the country as a whole that he's got to consider above everything else." Taggart sat up; of all the danger signs he knew, this line of talk was the worst. "Nobody can deny it, Jim, that Wesley feels a high regard for you as an enlightened businessman, a valuable adviser and one of his closest personal friends." Taggart's eyes shot to him swiftly: this was still worse. "But nobody can say that Wesley would hesitate to sacrifice his personal feelings and friendships—where the welfare of the public is concerned."

Taggart's face remained blank; his terror came from things never allowed to reach expression in words or in facial muscles. The terror was his struggle against an unadmitted thought: he himself had been "the public" for so long and in so many different issues, that he knew what it would mean if that magic title, that sacred title no one dared to oppose, were transferred, along with its "welfare," to the person of Buzzy Watts.

But what he asked, and he asked it hastily, was, "You're not implying that I would place my personal interests above the public welfare, are you?"

"No, of course not," said Mr. Weatherby, with a look that was almost a smile. "Certainly not. Not you, Jim. Your public-spirited attitude—and understanding—are too well known. That's why Wesley expects you to see every side of the picture."

"Yes, of course," said Taggart, trapped.

"Well, consider the unions' side of it. Maybe you can't afford to give them a raise, but how can they afford to exist when the cost of living has shot sky-high? They've got to eat, don't they? That comes first, railroad or no railroad." Mr. Weatherby's tone had a kind of placid righteousness, as if he were reciting a formula required to convey another meaning, clear to all of them; he was looking straight at Taggart, in special emphasis of the unstated. "There are almost a million members in the railway unions. With families, dependents and poor relatives—and who hasn't got poor relatives these days?—it amounts to about five million votes. Persons, I mean. Wesley has to bear that in mind. He has to think of their psychology. And then, consider the public. The rates you're charging were established at a time when everybody was making money. But the way things are now, the cost of transportation has become a burden nobody can afford. People are screaming about it all over the country." He looked straight at Taggart; he merely looked, but his glance had the quality of a wink. "There's an awful lot of them, Jim. They're not very happy at the moment about an awful lot of things. A government that would bring the railroad rates down would make a lot of folks grateful."

The silence that answered him was like a hole so deep that no sound could be heard of the things crashing down to its bottom. Taggart knew, as they all knew, to what disinterested motive Mr. Mouch would always be ready to sacrifice his personal friendships.

It was the silence and the fact that she did not want to say it, had come here resolved not to speak, but could not resist it, that made Dagny's voice sound so vibrantly harsh:

"Got what you've been asking for, all these years, gentlemen?"

The swiftness with which their eyes moved to her was an involuntary answer to an unexpected sound, but the swiftness with which they moved away—to look down at the table, at the walls, anywhere but at her—was the conscious answer to the meaning of the sounds.

In the silence of the next moment, she felt their resentment like a starch thickening the air of the room, and she knew that it was not resentment against Mr. Weatherby, but against her. She could have borne it, if they had merely let her question go unanswered; but what made her feel a sickening tightness in her stomach, was their double fraud of pretending to ignore her and then answering in their own kind of manner.

The chairman said, not looking at her, his voice pointedly noncommittal, yet vaguely purposeful at the same time, "It would have been all right, everything would have worked out fine, if it weren't for the wrong people in positions of power, such as Buzzy Watts and Chick Morrison."

"Oh, I wouldn't worry about Chick Morrison," said the pallid man with the mustache. "He hasn't any top-level connections. Not really. It's Tinky Holloway that's poison."

"I don't see the picture as hopeless," said a portly man who wore a green muffler. "Joe Dunphy and Bud Hazleton are very close to Wesley. If their influence prevails, we'll be all right. However, Kip Chalmers and Tinky Holloway are dangerous."

"I can take care of Kip Chalmers," said Taggart.

Mr. Weatherby was the only person in the room who did not mind looking at Dagny; but whenever his glance rested upon her, it registered nothing; she was the only person in the room whom he did not see.

"I am thinking," said Mr. Weatherby casually, looking at Taggart, "that you might do Wesley a favor."

"Wesley knows that he can always count on me."

"Well, my thought is that if you granted the unions' wage raises— we might drop the question of cutting the rates, for the time being."

"I can't do that!" It was almost a cry. "The National Alliance of Railroads has taken a unanimous stand against the raises and has committed every member to refuse."

"That's just what I mean," said Mr. Weatherby softly. "Wesley needs to drive a wedge into that Alliance stand. If a railroad like Taggart Transcontinental were to give in, the rest would be easy. You would help Wesley a great deal. He would appreciate it."

"But, good God, Clem!—I'd be open to court action for it, by the Alliance rules!"

Mr. Weatherby smiled. "What court? Let Wesley take care of that."

"But listen, Clem, you know—you know just as well as I do—that we can't afford it!"

Mr. Weatherby shrugged. "That's a problem for you to work out."

"How, for Christ's sake?"

"I don't know. That's your job, not ours. You wouldn't want the government to start telling you how to run your railroad, would you?"

"No, of course not! But—"

"Our job is only to see that the people get fair wages and decent transportation. It's up to you to deliver. But, of course, if you say that you can't do the job, why then—"

"I haven't said it!" Taggart cried hastily. "I haven't said it at all!"

"Good," said Mr. Weatherby pleasantly. "We know that you have the ability to find some way to do it."

He was looking at Taggart; Taggart was looking at Dagny.

"Well, it was just a thought," said Mr. Weatherby, leaning back in his chair in a manner of modest withdrawal. "Just a thought for you to mull over. I'm only a guest here. I don't want to interfere. The purpose of the meeting was to discuss the situation of the . . . branch lines, I believe?"

"Yes," said the chairman and sighed. "Yes. Now if anyone has a constructive suggestion to offer—" He waited; no one answered. "I believe the picture is clear to all of us." He waited. "It seems to be established that we cannot continue to afford the operation of some of our branch lines . . . the Rio Norte Line in particular . . . and, therefore, some form of action seems to be indicated. . . ."

"I think," said the pallid man with the mustache, his voice unexpectedly confident, "that we should now hear from Miss Taggart." He leaned forward with a look of hopeful craftiness. As Dagny did not answer, but merely turned to him, he asked, "What do you have to say, Miss Taggart?"

"Nothing."

"I beg your pardon?"

"All I had to say was contained in the report which Jim has read to you." She spoke quietly, her voice clear and flat.

"But you did not make any recommendations."

"I have none to make."

"But, after all, as our Operating Vice-President, you have a vital interest in the policies of this railroad."

"I have no authority over the policies of this railroad."

"Oh, but we are anxious to consider your opinion."

"I have no opinions."

"Miss Taggart," he said, in the smoothly formal tone of an order, "you cannot fail to realize that our branch lines are running at a disastrous deficit—and that we expect you to make them pay."

"How?"

"I don't know. That is your job, not ours."

"I have stated in my report the reasons why that is now impossible. If there are facts which I have overlooked, please name them."

"Oh, I wouldn't know. We expect you to find some way to make it possible. Our job is only to see that the stockholders get a fair profit. It's up to you to deliver. You wouldn't want us to think that you're unable to do the job and—"

"I am unable to do it."

The man opened his mouth, but found nothing else to say; he looked at her in bewilderment, wondering why the formula had failed.

"Miss Taggart," asked the man with the green muffler, "did you imply in your report that the situation of the Rio Norte Line was critical?"

"I stated that it was hopeless."

"Then what action do you propose?"

"I propose nothing."

"Aren't you evading a responsibility?"

"What is it that you think you're doing?" She spoke evenly, addressing them all. "Are you counting on my not saying that the responsibility is yours, that it was your goddamn policies that brought us where we are? Well, I'm saying it."

"Miss Taggart, Miss Taggart," said the chairman in a tone of pleading reproach, "there shouldn't be any hard feelings among us. Does it matter now who was to blame? We don't want to quarrel over past mistakes. We must all pull together as a team to carry our railroad through this desperate emergency."

A gray-haired man of patrician bearing, who had remained silent throughout the session, with a look of the quietly bitter knowledge that the entire performance was futile, glanced at Dagny in a way which would have been sympathy had he still felt a remnant of hope. He said, raising his voice just enough to betray a note of controlled indignation, "Mr. Chairman, if it is practical solutions that we are considering, I should like to suggest that we discuss the limitation placed upon the length and speed of our trains. Of any single practice, *that* is the most disastrous one. Its repeal would not solve all of our problems, but it would be an enormous relief. With the desperate shortage of motive power and the appalling shortage of fuel, it is criminal insanity to send an engine out on the road with sixty cars when it could pull a hundred and to take four days on a run which could be made in three. I suggest that we compute the number of shippers we have ruined and the districts we have destroyed through the failures, shortages and delays of transportation, and then we—"

"Don't think of it," Mr. Weatherby cut in snappily. "Don't try dreaming about any repeals. We wouldn't consider it. We wouldn't even consider listening to any talk on the subject."

"Mr. Chairman," the gray-haired man asked quietly, "shall I continue?"

The chairman spread out his hands, with a smooth smile, indicating helplessness. "It would be impractical," he answered.

"I think we'd better confine the discussion to the status of the Rio Norte Line," snapped James Taggart.

There was a long silence.

The man with the green muffler turned to Dagny. "Miss Taggart," he asked sadly and cautiously, "would you say that if—this is just a hypothetical question—if the equipment now in use on the Rio Norte Line were made available, it would fill the needs of our transcontinental main-line traffic?"

"It would help."

"The rail of the Rio Norte Line," said the pallid man with the mustache, "is unmatched anywhere in the country and could not now be purchased at any price. We have three hundred miles of track, which means well over four hundred miles of rail of pure Rearden Metal in that Line. Would you say, Miss Taggart, that we cannot afford to waste that superlative rail on a branch that carries no major traffic any longer?"

"That is for you to judge."

"Let me put it this way: would it be of value if that rail were made available for our main-line track, which is in such urgent need of repair?"

"It would help."

"Miss Taggart," asked the man with the quavering voice, "would you say that there are any shippers of consequence left on the Rio Norte Line?"

"There's Ted Nielsen of Nielsen Motors. No one else."

"Would you say that the operating costs of the Rio Norte Line could be used to relieve the financial strain on the rest of the system?"

"It would help."

"Then, as our Operating Vice-President . . ." He stopped; she waited, looking at him; he said, "Well?"

"What was your question?"

"I meant to say . . . that is, well, as our Operating Vice-President, don't you have certain conclusions to draw?"

She stood up. She looked at the faces around the table. "Gentlemen," she said, "I do not know by what sort of self-fraud you expect to feel that if it's I who name the decision you intend to make, it will be I who'll bear the responsibility for it. Perhaps you believe that if my voice delivers the final blow, it will make me the murderer involved—since you know that this is the last act of a long-drawn-out murder. I cannot conceive what it is you think you can accomplish by a pretense of this kind, and I will not help you to stage it. The final blow will be delivered by you, as were all the others."

She turned to go. The chairman half-rose, asking helplessly, "But, Miss Taggart—"

"Please remain seated. Please continue the discussion—and take the vote in which I shall have no voice. I shall abstain from voting. I'll stand by, if you wish me to, but only as an employee. I will not pretend to be anything else."

She turned away once more, but it was the voice of the gray-haired man that stopped her. "Miss Taggart, this is not an official question, it is only my personal curiosity, but would you tell me your view of the future of the Taggart Transcontinental system?"

She answered, looking at him in understanding, her voice gentler, "I have stopped thinking of a future or of a railroad system. I intend to continue running trains so long as it is still possible to run them. I don't think that it will be much longer."

She walked away from the table, to the window, to stand aside and let them continue without her.

She looked at the city. Jim had obtained the permit which allowed them the use of electric power to the top of the Taggart Building. From the height of the room, the city looked like a flattened remnant, with but a few rare, lonely streaks of lighted glass still rising through the darkness to the sky.

She did not listen to the voices of the men behind her. She did not know for how long the broken snatches of their struggle kept rolling past her—the sounds that nudged and prodded one another, trying to edge back and leave someone pushed forward—a struggle, not to assert one's own will, but to squeeze an assertion from some unwilling victim —a battle in which the decision was to be pronounced, not by the winner, but by the loser:

"It seems to me . . . It is, I think . . . It must, in my opinion . . . If we were to suppose . . . I am merely suggesting . . . I am not implying, but . . . If we consider both sides . . . It is, in my opinion, indubitable . . . It seems to me to be an unmistakable fact . . ."

She did not know whose voice it was, but she heard it when the voice pronounced:

". . . and, therefore, I move that the John Galt Line be closed."

Something, she thought, had made him call the Line by its right name.

You had to bear it, too, generations ago—it was just as hard for you, just as bad, but you did not let it stop you—was it really as bad as this? as ugly?—never mind, it's different forms, but it's only pain, and you were not stopped by pain, not by whatever kind it was that you had to bear—you were not stopped—you did not give in to it—you faced it and this is the kind I have to face—you fought and I will have to —you did it—I will try . . . She heard, in her own mind, the quiet intensity of the words of dedication—and it was some time before she realized that she was speaking to Nat Taggart.

The next voice she heard was Mr. Weatherby's: "Wait a minute, boys. Do you happen to remember that you need to obtain permission before you can close a branch line?"

"Good God, Clem!" Taggart's cry was open panic. "Surely there's not going to be any trouble about—"

"I wouldn't be too sure of it. Don't forget that you're a public service and you're expected to provide transportation, whether you make money or not."

"But you know that it's impossible!"

"Well, that's fine for you, that solves your problem, if you close that Line—but what will it do to us? Leaving a whole state like Colorado practically without transportation—what sort of public sentiment will it arouse? Now, of course, if you gave Wesley something in return, to balance it, if you granted the unions' wage raises—"

"I can't! I gave my word to the National Alliance!"

"Your word? Well, suit yourself. We wouldn't want to force the Alliance. We much prefer to have things happen voluntarily. But these are difficult times and it's hard telling what's liable to happen. With everybody going broke and the tax receipts falling, we might—fact being that we hold well over fifty per cent of the Taggart bonds—we might be compelled to call for the payment of railroad bonds within six months."

"*What?!*" screamed Taggart.

"—or sooner."

"But you can't! Oh God, you can't! It was understood that the moratorium was for five years! It was a contract, an obligation! We were counting on it!"

"An obligation? Aren't you old-fashioned, Jim? There aren't any obligations, except the necessity of the moment. The original owners of those bonds were counting on their payments, too."

Dagny burst out laughing.

She could not stop herself, she could not resist it, she could not reject a moment's chance to avenge Ellis Wyatt, Andrew Stockton, Lawrence Hammond, all the others. She said, torn by laughter:

"Thanks, Mr. Weatherby!"

Mr. Weatherby looked at her in astonishment. "Yes?" he asked coldly.

"I knew that we would have to pay for those bonds one way or another. We're paying."

"Miss Taggart," said the chairman severely, "don't you think that I-told-you-so's are futile? To talk of what would have happened if we had acted differently is nothing but purely theoretical speculation. We cannot indulge in theory, we have to deal with the practical reality of the moment."

"Right," said Mr. Weatherby. "That's what you ought to be—practical. Now we offer you a trade. You do something for us and we'll do something for you. You give the unions their wage raises and we'll give you permission to close the Rio Norte Line."

"All right," said James Taggart, his voice choked.

Standing at the window, she heard them vote on their decision. She heard them declare that the John Galt Line would end in six weeks, on March 31.

It's only a matter of getting through the next few moments, she thought; take care of the next few moments, and then the next, a few at a time, and after a while it will be easier; you'll get over it, after a while.

The assignment she gave herself for the next few moments was to put on her coat and be first to leave the room.

Then there was the assignment of riding in an elevator down the great, silent length of the Taggart Building. Then there was the assignment of crossing the dark lobby.

Halfway through the lobby, she stopped. A man stood leaning against the wall, in a manner of purposeful waiting—and it was she who was his purpose, because he was looking straight at her. She did not recognize him at once, because she felt certain that the face she saw could not possibly be there in that lobby at this hour.

"Hi, Slug," he said softly.

She answered, groping for some great distance that had once been hers, "Hi, Frisco."

"Have they finally murdered John Galt?"

She struggled to place the moment into some orderly sequence of time. The question belonged to the present, but the solemn face came from those days on the hill by the Hudson when he would have understood all that the question meant to her.

"How did you know that they'd do it tonight?" she asked.

"It's been obvious for months that that would be the next step at their next meeting."

"Why did you come here?"

"To see how you'd take it."

"Want to laugh about it?"

"No, Dagny, I don't want to laugh about it."

She saw no hint of amusement in his face; she answered trustingly, "I don't know how I'm taking it."

"I do."

"I was expecting it, I knew they'd have to do it, so now it's only a matter of getting through"—*tonight,* she wanted to say, but said—"all the work and details."

He took her arm. "Let's go some place where we can have a drink together."

"Francisco, why don't you laugh at me? You've always laughed about that Line."

"I will—tomorrow, when I see you going on with all the work and details. Not tonight."

"Why not?"

"Come on. You're in no condition to talk about it."

"I—" She wanted to protest, but said, "No, I guess I'm not."

He led her out to the street, and she found herself walking silently in time with the steady rhythm of his steps, the grasp of his fingers on her arm unstressed and firm. He signaled a passing taxicab and held the door open for her. She obeyed him without questions; she felt relief, like a swimmer who stops struggling. The spectacle of a man acting with assurance, was a life belt thrown to her at a moment when she had forgotten the hope of its existence. The relief was not in the surrender of responsibility, but in the sight of a man able to assume it.

"Dagny," he said, looking at the city as it moved past their taxi window, "think of the first man who thought of making a steel girder. He knew what he saw, what he thought and what he wanted. He did not say, 'It seems to me,' and he did not take orders from those who say, 'In my opinion.'"

She chuckled, wondering at his accuracy: he had guessed the nature of the sickening sense that held her, the sense of a swamp which she had to escape.

"Look around you," he said. "A city is the frozen shape of human courage—the courage of those men who thought for the first time of every bolt, rivet and power generator that went to make it. The courage to say, not 'It seems to me,' but '*It is*'—and to stake one's life on one's judgment. You're not alone. Those men exist. They have always existed. There was a time when human beings crouched in caves, at the mercy of any pestilence and any storm. Could men such as those on your Board of Directors have brought them out of the cave and up to this?" He pointed at the city.

"God, no!"

"Then *there's* your proof that another kind of men do exist."

"Yes," she said avidly. "Yes."

"Think of them and forget your Board of Directors."

"Francisco, where are they now—the other kind of men?"

"Now they're not wanted."

"I want them. Oh God, how I want them!"

"When you do, you'll find them."

He did not question her about the John Galt Line and she did not speak of it, until they sat at a table in a dimly lighted booth and she saw the stem of a glass between her fingers. She had barely noticed how they had come here. It was a quiet, costly place that looked like a secret retreat; she saw a small, lustrous table under her hand, the leather of a circular seat behind her shoulders, and a niche of dark blue mirror that cut them off from the sight of whatever enjoyment or pain others had come here to hide. Francisco was leaning against the table, watching her, and she felt as if she were leaning against the steady attentiveness of his eyes.

They did not speak of the Line, but she said suddenly, looking down at the liquid in her glass:

"I'm thinking of the night when Nat Taggart was told that he had to abandon the bridge he was building. The bridge across the Mississippi. He had been desperately short of money—because people were afraid of the bridge, they called it an impractical venture. That morning, he was told that the river steamboat concerns had filed suit against him, demanding that his bridge be destroyed as a threat to the public welfare. There were three spans of the bridge built, advancing across the river. That same day, a local mob attacked the structure and set fire to the wooden scaffolding. His workers deserted him, some because they were scared, some because they were bribed by the steamboat people, and most of them because he had had no money to pay them for weeks. Throughout that day, he kept receiving word that men who had subscribed to buy the stock of the Taggart Transcontinental Railroad were cancelling their subscriptions, one after another. Toward evening, a committee, representing two banks that were his last hope of support, came to see him. It was right there, on the construction site by the river, in the old railway coach where he lived, with the door open to the view of the blackened ruin, with the wooden remnants still smoking over the twisted steel. He had negotiated a loan from those banks, but the contract had not been signed. The committee told him that he would have to give up his bridge, because he was certain to lose the suit, and the bridge would be ordered torn down by the time he completed it. If he was willing to give it up, they said, and to ferry his passengers across the river on barges, as other railroads were doing, the contract would stand and he would get the money to continue his line west on the other shore; if not, then the loan was off. What was his answer?— they asked. He did not say a word, he picked up the contract, tore it across, handed it to them and walked out. He walked to the bridge, along the spans, down to the last girder. He knelt, he picked up the tools his men had left and he started to clear the charred wreckage away from the steel structure. His chief engineer saw him there, axe in hand, alone over the wide river, with the sun setting behind him in that west where his line was to go. He worked there all night. By morning, he had thought out a plan of what he would do to find the right men, the men of independent judgment—to find them, to convince them, to raise the money, to continue the bridge."

She spoke in a low, flat voice, looking down at the spot of light that shimmered in the liquid as her fingers turned the stem of her glass once

in a while. She showed no emotion, but her voice had the intense monotone of a prayer:

"Francisco . . . if he could live through that night, what right have
I to complain? What does it matter, how I feel just now? He built that
bridge. I have to hold it for him. I can't let it go the way of the
bridge of the Atlantic Southern. I feel almost as if he'd know it, if I
let that happen, he'd know it that night when he was alone over the
river . . . no, that's nonsense, but here's what I feel: any man who
knows what Nat Taggart felt that night, any man living now and
capable of knowing it—it's him that I would betray if I let it happen
. . . and I can't."

"Dagny, if Nat Taggart were living now, what would he do?"

She answered involuntarily, with a swift, bitter chuckle, "He wouldn't
last a minute!"—then corrected herself: "No, he would. He would
find a way to fight them."

"How?"

"I don't know."

She noticed some tense, cautious quality in the attentive way he
watched her as he leaned forward and asked, "Dagny, the men of your
Board of Directors are no match for Nat Taggart, are they? There's no
form of contest in which they could beat him, there's nothing he'd have
to fear from them, there's no mind, no will, no power in the bunch of
them to equal one-thousandth of his."

"No, of course not."

"Then why is it that throughout men's history the Nat Taggarts, who
make the world, have always won—and always lost it to the men of
the Board?"

"I . . . don't know."

"How could men who're afraid to hold an unqualified opinion about
the weather, fight Nat Taggart? How could they seize his achievement,
if he chose to defend it? Dagny, he fought with every weapon he possessed, except the most important one. They could not have won, if we
—he and the rest of us—had not given the world away to them."

"Yes. You gave it away to them. Ellis Wyatt did. Ken Danagger did.
I won't."

He smiled. "Who built the John Galt Line for them?"

He saw only the faintest contraction of her mouth, but he knew that
the question was like a blow across an open wound. Yet she answered
quietly, "I did."

"For this kind of end?"

"For the men who did not hold out, would not fight and gave up."

"Don't you see that no other end was possible?"

"No."

"How much injustice are you willing to take?"

"As much as I'm able to fight."

"What will you do now? Tomorrow?"

She said calmly, looking straight at him with the faintly proud look of stressing her calm, "Start to tear it up."

"What?"

"The John Galt Line. Start to tear it up as good as with my own hands—with my own mind, by my own instructions. Get it ready to be closed, then tear it up and use its pieces to reinforce the transcontinental track. There's a lot of work to do. It will keep me busy." The calm cracked a little, in the faintest change of her voice: "You know, I'm looking forward to it. I'm glad that I'll have to do it myself. That's why Nat Taggart worked all that night—just to keep going. It's not so bad as long as there's something one can do. And I'll know, at least, that I'm saving the main line."

"Dagny," he asked very quietly—and she wondered what made her feel that he looked as if his personal fate hung on her answer, "what if it were the main line that you had to dismember?"

She answered irresistibly, "Then I'd let the last engine run over me!" —but added, "No. That's just self-pity. I wouldn't."

He said gently, "I know you wouldn't. But you'd wish you could."

"Yes."

He smiled, not looking at her; it was a mocking smile, but it was a smile of pain and the mockery was directed at himself. She wondered what made her certain of it; but she knew his face so well that she would always know what he felt, even though she could not guess his reasons any longer. She knew his face as well, she thought, as she knew every line of his body, as she could still see it, as she was suddenly aware of it under his clothes, a few feet away, in the crowding intimacy of the booth. He turned to look at her and some sudden change in his eyes made her certain that he knew what she was thinking. He looked away and picked up his glass.

"Well—" he said, "to Nat Taggart."

"And to Sebastián d'Anconia?" she asked—then regretted it, because it had sounded like mockery, which she had not intended.

But she saw a look of odd, bright clarity in his eyes and he answered firmly, with the faintly proud smile of stressing his firmness, "Yes—and to Sebastián d'Anconia."

Her hand trembled a little and she spilled a few drops on the square of paper lace that lay on the dark, shining plastic of the table. She watched him empty his glass in a single gesture; the brusque, brief movement of his hand made it look like the gesture of some solemn pledge.

She thought suddenly that this was the first time in twelve years that he had come to her of his own choice.

He had acted as if he were confidently in control, as if his confidence were a transfusion to let her recapture hers, he had given her no time to wonder that they should be here together. Now she felt, unaccountably, that the reins he had held were gone. It was only the silence of a few blank moments and the motionless outline of his forehead, cheekbone and mouth, as he sat with his face turned away from her—but she felt as if it were he who was now struggling for something he had to recapture.

She wondered what had been his purpose tonight—and noticed that he had, perhaps, accomplished it: he had carried her over the worst moment, he had given her an invaluable defense against despair—the knowledge that a living intelligence had heard her and understood. But why had he wanted to do it? Why had he cared about her hour of despair—after the years of agony he had given her? Why had it mattered to him how she would take the death of the John Galt Line? She noticed that this was the question she had not asked him in the lobby of the Taggart Building.

This was the bond between them, she thought: that she would never be astonished if he came when she needed him most, and that he would always know when to come. This was the danger: that she would trust him, even while knowing that it could be nothing but some new kind of trap, even while remembering that he would always betray those who trusted him.

He sat, leaning forward with his arms crossed on the table, looking straight ahead. He said suddenly, not turning to her:

"I am thinking of the fifteen years that Sebastián d'Anconia had to wait for the woman he loved. He did not know whether he would ever find her again, whether she would survive . . . whether she would wait for him. But he knew that she could not live through his battle and that he could not call her to him until it was won. So he waited, holding his love in the place of the hope which he had no right to hold. But when he carried her across the threshold of his house, as the first Señora d'Anconia of a new world, he knew that the battle was won, that they were free, that nothing threatened her and nothing would ever hurt her again."

In the days of their passionate happiness, he had never given her a hint that he would come to think of her as Señora d'Anconia. For one moment, she wondered whether she had known what she had meant to him. But the moment ended in an invisible shudder: she would not believe that the past twelve years could allow the things she was hearing to be possible. This was the new trap, she thought.

"Francisco," she asked, her voice hard, "what have you done to Hank Rearden?"

He looked startled that she should think of that name at that moment. "Why?" he asked.

"He told me once that you were the only man he'd ever liked. But last time I saw him, he said that he would kill you on sight."

"He did not tell you why?"

"No."

"He told you nothing about it?"

"No." She saw him smiling strangely, a smile of sadness, gratitude and longing. "I warned him that you would hurt him—when he told me that you were the only man he liked."

His words came like a sudden explosion: "He was the only man—with one exception—to whom I could have given my life!"

"Who is the exception?"

"The man to whom I have."

"What do you mean?"

He shook his head, as if he had said more than he intended, and did not answer.

"What did you do to Rearden?"

"I'll tell you some time. Not now."

"Is that what you always do to those who . . . mean a great deal to you?"

He looked at her with a smile that had the luminous sincerity of innocence and pain. "You know," he said gently, "I could say that that is what they always do to me." He added, "But I won't. The actions—and the knowledge—were mine."

He stood up. "Shall we go? I'll take you home."

She rose and he held her coat for her; it was a wide, loose garment, and his hands guided it to enfold her body. She felt his arm remain about her shoulders a moment longer than he intended her to notice.

She glanced back at him. But he was standing oddly still, staring intently down at the table. In rising, they had brushed aside the mats of paper lace and she saw an inscription cut into the plastic of the table top. Attempts had been made to erase it, but the inscription remained, as the graven voice of some unknown drunk's despair: "Who is John Galt?"

With a brusque movement of anger, she flicked the mat back to cover the words. He chuckled.

"I can answer it," he said. "I can tell you who is John Galt."

"Really? Everybody seems to know him, but they never tell the same story twice."

"They're all true, though—all the stories you've heard about him."

"Well, what's yours? Who is he?"

"John Galt is Prometheus who changed his mind. After centuries of being torn by vultures in payment for having brought to men the fire of the gods, he broke his chains and he withdrew his fire—until the day when men withdraw their vultures."

*　*　*

The band of crossties swept in wide curves around granite corners, clinging to the mountainsides of Colorado. Dagny walked down the ties, keeping her hands in her coat pockets, and her eyes on the meaningless distance ahead; only the familiar movement of straining her steps to the spacing of the ties gave her the physical sense of an action pertaining to a railroad.

A gray cotton, which was neither quite fog nor clouds, hung in sloppy wads between sky and mountains, making the sky look like an old mattress spilling its stuffing down the sides of the peaks. A crusted snow covered the ground, belonging neither to winter nor to spring. A net of moisture hung in the air, and she felt an icy pin-prick on her face once in a while, which was neither a raindrop nor a snowflake. The weather seemed afraid to take a stand and clung noncommittally to some sort of road's middle; Board of Directors' weather, she thought. The light seemed drained and she could not tell whether this was the afternoon or the evening of March 31. But she was very certain that it was March 31; that was a certainty not to be escaped.

She had come to Colorado with Hank Rearden, to buy whatever machinery could still be found in the closed factories. It had been like a hurried search through the sinking hulk of a great ship before it was to vanish out of reach. They could have given the task to employees, but they had come, both prompted by the same unconfessed motive: they could not resist the desire to attend the run of the last train, as one cannot resist the desire to give a last salute by attending a funeral, even while knowing that it is only an act of self-torture.

They had been buying machinery from doubtful owners in sales of dubious legality, since nobody could tell who had the right to dispose of the great, dead properties, and nobody would come to challenge the transactions. They had bought everything that could be moved from the gutted plant of Nielsen Motors. Ted Nielsen had quit and vanished, a week after the announcement that the Line was to be closed.

She had felt like a scavenger, but the activity of the hunt had made her able to bear these past few days. When she had found that three empty hours remained before the departure of the last train, she had gone to walk through the countryside, to escape the stillness of the town. She had walked at random through twisting mountain trails, alone among rocks and snow, trying to substitute motion for thought, knowing that she had to get through this day without thinking of the summer when she had ridden the engine of the first train. But she found herself walking back along the roadbed of the John Galt Line—and she knew that she had intended it, that she had gone out for that purpose.

It was a spur track which had already been dismembered. There were no signal lights, no switches, no telephone wires, nothing but a long band of wooden strips left on the ground—a chain of ties without rail, like the remnant of a spine—and, as its lonely guardian, at an abandoned grade crossing, a pole with slanted arms saying: "Stop. Look. Listen."

An early darkness mixed with fog was slipping down to fill the valleys, when she came upon the factory. There was an inscription high on the lustrous tile of its front wall: "Roger Marsh. Electrical Appliances." The man who had wanted to chain himself to his desk in order not to leave this, she thought. The building stood intact, like a corpse in that instant when its eyes have just closed and one still waits to see them open again. She felt that the lights would flare up at any moment behind the great sheets of windows, under the long, flat roofs. Then she saw one broken pane, pierced by a stone for some young moron's enjoyment—and she saw the tall, dry stem of a single weed rising from the steps of the main entrance. Hit by a sudden, blinding hatred, in rebellion against the weed's impertinence, knowing of what enemy this was the scout, she ran forward, she fell on her knees and jerked the weed up by its roots. Then, kneeling on the steps of a closed factory, looking at the vast silence of mountains, brush and dusk, she thought: What do you think you're doing?

It was almost dark when she reached the end of the ties that led her back to the town of Marshville. Marshville had been the end of the Line for months past; service to Wyatt Junction had been discontinued long ago; Dr. Ferris' Reclamation Project had been abandoned this winter.

The street lights were on, and they hung in mid-air at the intersections, in a long, diminishing line of yellow globes over the empty streets of Marshville. All the better homes were closed—the neat, sturdy houses of modest cost, well built and well kept; there were faded "For Sale" signs on their lawns. But she saw lights in the windows of the cheap, garish structures that had acquired, within a few years, the slovenly dilapidation of slum hovels; the homes of people who had not moved, the people who never looked beyond the span of one week. She saw a large new television set in the lighted room of a house with a sagging roof and cracking walls. She wondered how long they expected the electric power companies of Colorado to remain in existence. Then she shook her head: those people had never known that power companies existed.

The main street of Marshville was lined by the black windows of shops out of business. All the luxury stores are gone—she thought, looking at their signs; and then she shuddered, realizing what things she now called luxury, realizing to what extent and in what manner those things, once available to the poorest, had been luxuries: Dry Cleaning—Electrical Appliances—Gas Station—Drug Store—Five and Ten. The only ones left open were grocery stores and saloons.

The platform of the railroad station was crowded. The glaring arc lights seemed to pick it out of the mountains, to isolate and focus it, like a small stage on which every movement was naked to the sight of the unseen tiers rising in the vast, encircling night. People were carting luggage, bundling their children, haggling at ticket windows, the stifled panic of their manner suggesting that what they really wanted to do was to fall down on the ground and scream with terror. Their terror had the evasive quality of guilt: it was not the fear that comes from understanding, but from the refusal to understand.

The last train stood at the platform, its windows a long, lone streak of light. The steam of the locomotive, gasping tensely through the wheels, did not have its usual joyous sound of energy released for a sprint; it had the sound of a panting breath that one dreads to hear and dreads more to stop hearing. Far at the end of the lighted windows, she saw the small red dot of a lantern attached to her private car. Beyond the lantern, there was nothing but a black void.

The train was loaded to capacity, and the shrill notes of hysteria in the confusion of voices were the pleas for space in vestibules and aisles. Some people were not leaving, but stood in vapid curiosity, watching the show; they had come, as if knowing that this was the last event they would ever witness in their community and, perhaps, in their lives.

She walked hastily through the crowd, trying not to look at anyone. Some knew who she was, most of them did not. She saw an old woman with a ragged shawl on her shoulders and the graph of a lifetime's struggle on the cracked skin of her face; the woman's glance was a hopeless appeal for help. An unshaved young man with gold-rimmed glasses stood on a crate under an arc light, yelling to the faces shifting past him, "What do they mean, no business! Look at that train! It's full of passengers! There's plenty of business! It's just that there's no profits for them—that's why they're letting you perish, those greedy parasites!" A disheveled woman rushed up to Dagny, waving two tickets and screaming something about the wrong date. Dagny found herself pushing people out of the way, fighting to reach the end of the train—but an emaciated man, with the staring eyes of years of malicious futility, rushed at her, shouting, "It's all right for *you,* you've got a good overcoat and a private car, but you won't give us any trains, you and all the selfish—" He stopped abruptly, looking at someone behind her. She felt a hand grasping her elbow: it was Hank Rearden. He held her arm and led her toward her car; seeing the look on his face, she understood why people got out of their way. At the end of the platform, a pallid, plumpish man stood saying to a crying woman, "That's how it's always been in this world. There will be no chance for the poor, until the rich are destroyed." High above the town, hanging in black space like an uncooled planet, the flame of Wyatt's Torch was twisting in the wind.

Rearden went inside her car, but she remained on the steps of the vestibule, delaying the finality of turning away. She heard the "All aboard!" She looked at the people who remained on the platform as one looks at those who watch the departure of the last lifeboat.

The conductor stood below, at the foot of the steps, with his lantern in one hand and his watch in the other. He glanced at the watch, then glanced up at her face. She answered by the silent affirmation of closing her eyes and inclining her head. She saw his lantern circling through the air, as she turned away—and the first jolt of the wheels, on the rails of Rearden Metal, was made easier for her by the sight of Rearden, as she pulled the door open and went into her car.

* * *

When James Taggart telephoned Lillian Rearden from New York and said, "Why, no—no special reason, just wondered how you were and whether you ever came to the city—haven't seen you for ages and just thought we might have lunch together next time you're in New York"—she knew that he had some very special reason in mind.

When she answered lazily, "Oh, let me see—what day is this? April second?—let me look at my calendar—why, it just so happens that I have some shopping to do in New York tomorrow, so I'll be delighted to let you save me my lunch money"—he knew that she had no shopping to do and that the luncheon would be the only purpose of her trip to the city.

They met in a distinguished, high-priced restaurant, much too distinguished and high-priced ever to be mentioned in the gossip columns; not the kind of place which James Taggart, always eager for personal publicity, was in the habit of patronizing; he did not want them to be seen together, she concluded.

The half-hint of half-secret amusement remained on her face while she listened to him talking about their friends, the theater and the weather, carefully building for himself the protection of the unimportant. She sat gracefully not quite straight, as if she were leaning back, enjoying the futility of his performance and the fact that he had to stage it for her benefit. She waited with patient curiosity to discover his purpose.

"I do think that you deserve a pat on the back or a medal or something, Jim," she said, "for being remarkably cheerful in spite of all the messy trouble you're having. Didn't you just close the best branch of your railroad?"

"Oh, it's only a slight financial setback, nothing more. One has to expect retrenchments at a time like this. Considering the general state of the country, we're doing quite well. Better than the rest of them." He added, shrugging, "Besides, it's a matter of opinion whether the Rio Norte Line was our best branch. It is only my sister who thought so. It was her pet project."

She caught the tone of pleasure blurring the drawl of his syllables. She smiled and said, "I see."

Looking up at her from under his lowered forehead, as if stressing that he expected her to understand, Taggart asked, "How is *he* taking it?"

"Who?" She understood quite well.

"Your husband."

"Taking what?"

"The closing of that Line."

She smiled gaily. "Your guess is as good as mine, Jim—and mine is very good indeed."

"What do you mean?"

"You know how he would take it—just as you know how your sister is taking it. So your cloud has a double silver lining, hasn't it?"

"What has he been saying in the last few days?"

"He's been away in Colorado for over a week, so I—" She stopped; she had started answering lightly, but she noticed that Taggart's question had been too specific while his tone had been too casual, and she realized that he had struck the first note leading toward the purpose of the luncheon; she paused for the briefest instant, then finished, still more lightly, "so I wouldn't know. But he's coming back any day now."

"Would you say that his attitude is still what one might call recalcitrant?"

"Why, Jim, that would be an understatement!"

"It was to be hoped that events had, perhaps, taught him the wisdom of a mellower approach."

It amused her to keep him in doubt about her understanding. "Oh yes," she said innocently, "it would be wonderful if anything could ever make him change."

"He is making things exceedingly hard for himself."

"He always has."

"But events have a way of beating us all into a more . . . pliable frame of mind, sooner or later."

"I've heard many characteristics ascribed to him, but 'pliable' has never been one of them."

"Well, things change and people change with them. After all, it is a law of nature that animals must adapt themselves to their background. And I might add that adaptability is the one characteristic most stringently required at present by laws other than those of nature. We're in for a very difficult time, and I would hate to see you suffer the consequences of his intransigent attitude. I would hate—as your friend—to see you in the kind of danger he's headed for, unless he learns to cooperate."

"How sweet of you, Jim," she said sweetly.

He was doling his sentences out with cautious slowness, balancing himself between word and intonation to hit the right degree of semiclarity. He wanted her to understand, but he did not want her to understand fully, explicitly, down to the root—since the essence of that modern language, which he had learned to speak expertly, was never to let oneself or others understand anything down to the root.

He had not needed many words to understand Mr. Weatherby. On his last trip to Washington, he had pleaded with Mr. Weatherby that a cut in the rates of the railroads would be a deathblow; the wage raises had been granted, but the demands for the cut in rates were still heard in the press—and Taggart had known what it meant, if Mr. Mouch still permitted them to be heard; he had known that the knife was still poised at his throat. Mr. Weatherby had not answered his pleas, but had said, in a tone of idly irrelevant speculation, "Wesley has so many tough problems. If he is to give everybody a breathing spell, financially speaking, he's got to put into operation a certain emergency program of which you have some inkling. But you know what hell the unprogressive elements of the country would raise about it. A man like Rearden, for instance. We don't want any more stunts of the sort he's liable to pull. Wesley would give a lot for somebody who could keep Rearden in line. But I guess that's something nobody can deliver. Though I may be wrong. You may know better, Jim, since Rearden is a sort of friend of yours, who comes to your parties and all that."

Looking at Lillian across the table, Taggart said, "Friendship, I find, is the most valuable thing in life—and I would be amiss if I didn't give you proof of mine."

"But I've never doubted it."

He lowered his voice to the tone of an ominous warning: "I think I should tell you, as a favor to a friend, although it's confidential, that your husband's attitude is being discussed in high places—very high places. I'm sure you know what I mean."

This was why he hated Lillian Rearden, thought Taggart: she knew the game, but she played it with unexpected variations of her own. It was against all rules to look at him suddenly, to laugh in his face, and —after all those remarks showing that she understood too little—to say bluntly, showing that she understood too much, "Why, darling, of course I know what you mean. You mean that the purpose of this very excellent luncheon was not a favor you wanted to do me, but a favor you wanted to get from me. You mean that it's you who are in danger and could use that favor to great advantage for a trade in high places. And you mean that you are reminding me of my promise to deliver the goods."

"The sort of performance he put on at his trial was hardly what I'd call delivering the goods," he said angrily. "It wasn't what you had led me to expect."

"Oh my, no, it wasn't," she said placidly. "It certainly wasn't. But, darling, did you expect me not to know that after that performance of his he wouldn't be very popular in high places? Did you really think you had to tell me *that* as a confidential favor?"

"But it's true. I heard him discussed, so I thought I'd tell you."

"I'm sure it's true. I know that they would be discussing him. I know also that if there were anything they could do to him, they would have done it right after his trial. My, would they have been glad to do it! So I know that he's the only one among you who is in no danger whatever, at the moment. I know that it's they who are afraid of him. Do you see how well I understand what you mean, darling?"

"Well, if you think you do, I must say that for my part I don't understand you at all. I don't know what it is you're doing."

"Why, I'm just setting things straight—so that you'll know that I know how much you need me. And now that it's straight, I'll tell you the truth in my turn: I didn't double-cross you, I merely failed. His performance at the trial—I didn't expect it any more than you did. Less. I had good reason not to expect it. But something went wrong. I don't know what it was. I am trying to find out. When I do, I will keep my promise. Then you'll be free to take full credit for it and to tell your friends in high places that it's you who've disarmed him."

"Lillian," he said nervously, "I meant it when I said that I was anxious to give you proof of my friendship—so if there's anything I can do for—"

She laughed. "There isn't. I know you meant it. But there's nothing you can do for me. No favor of any kind. No trade. I'm a truly noncommercial person, I want nothing in return. Tough luck, Jim. You'll just have to remain at my mercy."

"But then why should you want to do it at all? What are you getting out of it?"

She leaned back, smiling. "This lunch. Just seeing you here. Just knowing that you had to come to me."

An angry spark flashed in Taggart's veiled eyes, then his eyelids narrowed slowly and he, too, leaned back in his chair, his face relaxing to a faint look of mockery and satisfaction. Even from within that unstated, unnamed, undefined muck which represented his code of values, he was able to realize which one of them was the more dependent on the other and the more contemptible.

When they parted at the door of the restaurant, she went to Rearden's suite at the Wayne-Falkland Hotel, where she stayed occasionally in his absence. She paced the room for about half an hour, in a leisurely manner of reflection. Then she picked up the telephone, with a smoothly casual gesture, but with the purposeful air of a decision reached. She called Rearden's office at the mills and asked Miss Ives when she expected him to return.

"Mr. Rearden will be in New York tomorrow, arriving on the Comet, Mrs. Rearden," said Miss Ives' clear, courteous voice.

"Tomorrow? That's wonderful. Miss Ives, would you do me a favor? Would you call Gertrude at the house and tell her not to expect me for dinner? I'm staying in New York overnight."

She hung up, glanced at her watch and called the florist of the Wayne-Falkland. "This is Mrs. Henry Rearden," she said. "I should like to have two dozen roses delivered to Mr. Rearden's drawing room aboard the Comet. . . . Yes, today, this afternoon, when the Comet reaches Chicago. . . . No, without any card—just the flowers. . . . Thank you ever so much."

She telephoned James Taggart. "Jim, will you send me a pass to your passenger platforms? I want to meet my husband at the station tomorrow."

She hesitated between Balph Eubank and Bertram Scudder, chose Balph Eubank, telephoned him and made a date for this evening's dinner and a musical show. Then she went to take a bath, and lay relaxing in a tub of warm water, reading a magazine devoted to problems of political economy.

It was late afternoon when the florist telephoned her. "Our Chicago office sent word that they were unable to deliver the flowers, Mrs. Rearden," he said, "because Mr. Rearden is not aboard the Comet."

"Are you sure?" she asked.

"Quite sure, Mrs. Rearden. Our man found at the station in Chicago that there was no compartment on the train reserved in Mr. Rearden's name. We checked with the New York office of Taggart Transcontinental, just to make certain, and were told that Mr. Rearden's name is not on the passenger list of the Comet."

"I see. . . . Then cancel the order, please. . . . Thank you."

She sat by the telephone for a moment, frowning, then called Miss Ives. "Please forgive me for being slightly scatterbrained, Miss Ives, but I was rushed and did not write it down, and now I'm not quite certain of what you said. Did you say that Mr. Rearden was coming back tomorrow? On the Comet?"

"Yes, Mrs. Rearden."

"You have not heard of any delay or change in his plans?"

"Why, no. In fact, I spoke to Mr. Rearden about an hour ago. He telephoned from the station in Chicago, and he mentioned that he had to hurry back aboard, as the Comet was about to leave."

"I see. Thank you."

She leaped to her feet as soon as the click of the instrument restored her to privacy. She started pacing the room, her steps now unrhythmically tense. Then she stopped, struck by a sudden thought. There was only one reason why a man would make a train reservation under an assumed name: if he was not traveling alone.

Her facial muscles went flowing slowly into a smile of satisfaction: this was an opportunity she had not expected.

*　*　*

Standing on the Terminal platform, at a point halfway down the length of the train, Lillian Rearden watched the passengers descending from the Comet. Her mouth held the hint of a smile; there was a spark of animation in her lifeless eyes; she glanced from one face to another, jerking her head with the awkward eagerness of a schoolgirl.

She was anticipating the look on Rearden's face when, with his mistress beside him, he would see her standing there.

Her glance darted hopefully to every flashy young female stepping off the train. It was hard to watch: within an instant after the first few figures, the train had seemed to burst at the seams, flooding the platform with a solid current that swept in one direction, as if pulled by a vacuum; she could barely distinguish separate persons. The lights were more glare than illumination, picking this one strip out of a dusty, oily darkness. She needed an effort to stand still against the invisible pressure of motion.

Her first sight of Rearden in the crowd came as a shock: she had not seen him step out of a car, but there he was, walking in her direction from somewhere far down the length of the train. He was alone. He was walking with his usual purposeful speed, his hands in the pockets of his trenchcoat. There was no woman beside him, no companion of any kind, except a porter hurrying along with a bag she recognized as his.

In a fury of incredulous disappointment, she looked frantically for any single feminine figure he could have left behind. She felt certain that she would recognize his choice. She saw none that could be possible. And then she saw that the last car of the train was a private car, and that the figure standing at its door, talking to some station official—a figure wearing, not minks and veils, but a rough sports coat that stressed the incomparable grace of a slender body in the confident posture of this station's owner and center—was Dagny Taggart. Then Lillian Rearden understood.

"Lillian! What's the matter?"

She heard Rearden's voice, she felt his hand grasping her arm, she saw him looking at her as one looks at the object of a sudden emergency. He was looking at a blank face and an unfocused glance of terror.

"What happened? What are you doing here?"

"I . . . Hello, Henry . . . I just came to meet you . . . No special reason . . . I just wanted to meet you." The terror was gone from her face, but she spoke in a strange, flat voice. "I wanted to see you, it was an impulse, a sudden impulse and I couldn't resist it, because—"

"But you look . . . looked ill."

"No . . . No, maybe I felt faint, it's stuffy here. . . . I couldn't resist coming, because it made me think of the days when you would have been glad to see me . . . it was a moment's illusion to re-create for myself. . . ." The words sounded like a memorized lesson.

She knew that she had to speak, while her mind was fighting to grasp the full meaning of her discovery. The words were part of the plan she had intended to use, if she had met him after he had found the roses in his compartment.

He did not answer, he stood watching her, frowning.

"I missed you, Henry. I know what I am confessing. But I don't expect it to mean anything to you any longer." The words did not fit the tight face, the lips that moved with effort, the eyes that kept glancing away from him down the length of the platform. "I wanted . . . I merely wanted to surprise you." A look of shrewdness and purpose was returning to her face.

He took her arm, but she drew back, a little too sharply.

"Aren't you going to say a word to me, Henry?"

"What do you wish me to say?"

"Do you hate it as much as that—having your wife come to meet you at the station?" She glanced down the platform: Dagny Taggart was walking toward them; he did not see her.

"Let's go," he said.

She would not move. "Do you?" she asked.

"What?"

"Do you hate it?"

"No, I don't hate it. I merely don't understand it."

"Tell me about your trip. I'm sure you've had a very enjoyable trip."

"Come on. We can talk at home."

"When do I ever have a chance to talk to you at home?" She was drawling her words impassively, as if she were stretching them to fill time, for some reason which he could not imagine. "I had hoped to catch a few moments of your attention—like this—between trains and business appointments and all those important matters that hold you day and night, all those great achievements of yours, such as . . . Hello, Miss Taggart!" she said sharply, her voice loud and bright.

Rearden whirled around. Dagny was walking past them, but she stopped.

"How do you do," she said to Lillian, bowing, her face expressionless.

"I am so sorry, Miss Taggart," said Lillian, smiling, "you must forgive me if I don't know the appropriate formula of condolences for the occasion." She noted that Dagny and Rearden had not greeted each other. "You're returning from what was, in effect, the funeral of your child by my husband, aren't you?"

Dagny's mouth showed a faint line of astonishment and of contempt. She inclined her head, by way of leave-taking, and walked on.

Lillian glanced sharply at Rearden's face, as if in deliberate emphasis. He looked at her indifferently, puzzled.

She said nothing. She followed him without a word when he turned to go. She remained silent in the taxicab, her face half-turned away from him, while they rode to the Wayne-Falkland Hotel. He felt certain, as he looked at the tautly twisted set of her mouth, that some uncustomary violence was raging within her. He had never known her to experience a strong emotion of any kind.

She whirled to face him, the moment they were alone in his room.

"So that's who it is?" she asked.

He had not expected it. He looked at her, not quite believing that he had understood it correctly.

"It's Dagny Taggart who's your mistress, isn't she?"

He did not answer.

"I happen to know that you had no compartment on that train. So I know where you've slept for the last four nights. Do you want to admit it or do you want me to send detectives to question her train crews and her house servants? Is it Dagny Taggart?"

"Yes," he answered calmly.

Her mouth twisted into an ugly chuckle; she was staring past him. "I should have known it. I should have guessed. That's why it didn't work!"

He asked, in blank bewilderment, "What didn't work?"

She stepped back, as if to remind herself of his presence. "Had you—when she was in our house, at the party—had you, then . . . ?"

"No. Since."

"The great businesswoman," she said, "above reproach and feminine weaknesses. The great mind detached from any concern with the body . . ." She chuckled. "The bracelet . . ." she said, with the still look that made it sound as if the words were dropped accidentally out of the torrent in her mind. "That's what she meant to you. That's the weapon she gave you."

"If you really understand what you're saying—yes."

"Do you think I'll let you get away with it?"

"Get away . . . ?" He was looking at her incredulously, in cold, astonished curiosity.

"That's why, at your trial—" She stopped.

"What about my trial?"

She was trembling. "You know, of course, that I won't allow this to continue."

"What does it have to do with my trial?"

"I won't permit you to have her. Not her. Anyone but her."

He let a moment pass, then asked evenly, "Why?"

"I won't permit it! You'll give it up!" He was looking at her without expression, but the steadiness of his eyes hit her as his most dangerous answer. "You'll give it up, you'll leave her, you'll never see her again!"

"Lillian, if you wish to discuss it, there's one thing you'd better understand: nothing on earth will make me give it up."

"But I demand it!"

"I told you that you could demand anything but that."

He saw the look of a peculiar panic growing in her eyes: it was not the look of understanding, but of a ferocious refusal to understand—as if she wanted to turn the violence of her emotion into a fog screen, as if she hoped, not that it would blind her to reality, but that her blindness would make reality cease to exist.

"But I have the right to demand it! I own your life! It's my property.

My property—by your own oath. You swore to serve my happiness. Not yours—mine! What have you done for me? You've given me nothing, you've sacrificed nothing, you've never been concerned with anything but yourself—*your* work, *your* mills, *your* talent, *your* mistress! What about me? I hold first claim! I'm presenting it for collection! You're the account I own!"

It was the look on his face that drove her up the rising steps of her voice, scream by scream, into terror. She was seeing, not anger or pain or guilt, but the one inviolate enemy: indifference.

"Have you thought of me?" she screamed, her voice breaking against his face. "Have you thought of what you're doing to me? You have no right to go on, if you know that you're putting me through hell every time you sleep with that woman! I can't stand it, I can't stand one moment of knowing it! Will you sacrifice me to your animal desire? Are you as vicious and selfish as that? Can you buy your pleasure at the price of my suffering? Can you have it, if this is what it does to me?"

Feeling nothing but the emptiness of wonder, he observed the thing which he had glimpsed briefly in the past and was now seeing in the full ugliness of its futility: the spectacle of pleas for pity delivered, in snarling hatred, as threats and as demands.

"Lillian," he said very quietly, "I would have it, even if it took your life."

She heard it. She heard more than he was ready to know and to hear in his own words. The shock, to him, was that she did not scream in answer, but that he saw her, instead, shrinking down into calm. "You have no right . . ." she said dully. It had the embarrassing helplessness of the words of a person who knows her own words to be meaningless.

"Whatever claim you may have on me," he said, "no human being can hold on another a claim demanding that he wipe himself out of existence."

"Does she mean as much as that to you?"

"Much more than that."

The look of thought was returning to her face, but in her face it had the quality of a look of cunning. She remained silent.

"Lillian, I'm glad that you know the truth. Now you can make a choice with full understanding. You may divorce me—or you may ask that we continue as we are. That is the only choice you have. It is all I can offer you. I think you know that I want you to divorce me. But I don't ask for sacrifices. I don't know what sort of comfort you can find in our marriage, but if you do, I won't ask you to give it up. I don't know why you should want to hold me now, I don't know what it is that I mean to you, I don't know what you're seeking, what form of happiness is yours or what you will obtain from a situation which I see as intolerable for both of us. By every standard of mine, you should have divorced me long ago. By every standard of mine, to maintain our marriage will be a vicious fraud. But my standards are not yours. I do not understand yours, I never have, but I will accept them. If this is the manner of your love for me, if bearing the name of my wife will give you some form of contentment, I won't take it away from you. It's I who've broken my word, so I will atone for it to the extent I can. You know, of course, that I could buy one of those modern judges and obtain a divorce any time I wished. I won't do it. I will keep my word, if you so desire, but this is the only form in which I can keep it. Now make your choice—but if you choose to hold me, you must never speak to me about her, you must never show her that you know, if you meet her in the future, you must never touch that part of my life."

She stood still, looking up at him, the posture of her body slouched and loose, as if its sloppiness were a form of defiance, as if she did not care to resume for his sake the discipline of a graceful bearing.

"Miss Dagny Taggart . . ." she said, and chuckled. "The super-woman whom common, average wives were not supposed to suspect. The woman who cared for nothing but business and dealt with men as a man. The woman of great spirit who admired you platonically, just for your genius, your mills and your Metal!" She chuckled. "I should have known that she was just a bitch who wanted you in the same way as any bitch would want you—because you are fully as expert in bed as you are at a desk, if I am a judge of such matters. But she would appreciate that better than I, since she worships expertness of any kind and since she has probably been laid by every section hand on her railroad!"

She stopped, because she saw, for the first time in her life, by what sort of look one learns that a man is capable of killing. But he was not looking at her. She was not sure whether he was seeing her at all or hearing her voice.

He was hearing his own voice saying her words—saying them to Dagny in the sun-striped bedroom of Ellis Wyatt's house. He was seeing, in the nights behind him, Dagny's face in those moments when, his body leaving hers, she lay still with a look of radiance that was more than a smile, a look of youth, of early morning, of gratitude to the fact of one's own existence. And he was seeing Lillian's face, as he had seen it in bed beside him, a lifeless face with evasive eyes, with some feeble sneer on its lips and the look of sharing some smutty guilt. He saw who was the accuser and who the accused—he saw the obscenity of letting impotence hold itself as virtue and damn the power of living as a sin—he saw, with the clarity of direct perception, in the shock of a single instant, the terrible ugliness of that which had once been his own belief.

It was only an instant, a conviction without words, a knowledge grasped as a feeling, left unsealed by his mind. The shock brought him back to the sight of Lillian and to the sound of her words. She appeared to him suddenly as some inconsequential presence that had to be dealt with at the moment.

"Lillian," he said, in an unstressed voice that did not grant her even the honor of anger, "you are not to speak of her to me. If you ever do it again, I will answer you as I would answer a hoodlum: I will beat you up. Neither you nor anyone else is to discuss her."

She glanced at him. "Really?" she said. It had an odd, casual sound —as if the word were tossed away, leaving some hook implanted in her mind. She seemed to be considering some sudden vision of her own.

He said quietly, in weary astonishment, "I thought you would be glad to discover the truth. I thought you would prefer to know—for the sake of whatever love or respect you felt for me—that if I betrayed you, it was not cheaply and casually, it was not for a chorus girl, but for the cleanest and most serious feeling of my life."

The ferocious spring with which she whirled to him was involuntary, as was the naked twist of hatred in her face. "Oh, you goddamn fool!"

He remained silent.

Her composure returned, with the faint suggestion of a smile of secret mockery. "I believe you're waiting for my answer?" she said. "No, I won't divorce you. Don't ever hope for that. We shall continue as we are—if that is what you offered and if you think it can continue. See whether you can flout all moral principles and get away with it!"

He did not listen to her while she reached for her coat, telling him that she was going back to their home. He barely noticed it when the door closed after her. He stood motionless, held by a feeling he had never experienced before. He knew that he would have to think later, to think and understand, but for the moment he wanted nothing but to observe the wonder of what he felt.

It was a sense of freedom, as if he stood alone in the midst of an endless sweep of clean air, with only the memory of some weight that had been torn off his shoulders. It was the feeling of an immense deliverance. It was the knowledge that it did not matter to him what Lillian felt, what she suffered or what became of her, and more: not only that it did not matter, but the shining, guiltless knowledge that it did not have to matter.

MIRACLE METAL

"But can we get away with it?" asked Wesley Mouch. His voice was high with anger and thin with fear.

Nobody answered him. James Taggart sat on the edge of an armchair, not moving, looking up at him from under his forehead. Orren Boyle gave a vicious tap against an ashtray, shaking the ash off his cigar. Dr. Floyd Ferris smiled. Mr. Weatherby folded his lips and hands. Fred Kinnan, head of the Amalgamated Labor of America, stopped pacing the office, sat down on the window sill and crossed his arms. Eugene Lawson, who had sat hunched downward, absent-mindedly rearranging a display of flowers on a low glass table, raised his torso resentfully and glanced up. Mouch sat at his desk, with his fist on a sheet of paper.

It was Eugene Lawson who answered. "That's not, it seems to me, the way to put it. We must not let vulgar difficulties obstruct our feeling that it's a noble plan motivated solely by the public welfare. It's for the good of the people. The people need it. Need comes first, so we don't have to consider anything else."

Nobody objected or picked it up; they looked as if Lawson had merely made it harder to continue the discussion. But a small man who sat unobtrusively in the best armchair of the room, apart from the others, content to be ignored and fully aware that none of them could be unconscious of his presence, glanced at Lawson, then at Mouch, and said with brisk cheerfulness, "That's the line, Wesley. Tone it down and dress it up and get your press boys to chant it—and you won't have to worry."

"Yes, Mr. Thompson," said Mouch glumly.

Mr. Thompson, the Head of the State, was a man who possessed the quality of never being noticed. In any group of three, his person became indistinguishable, and when seen alone it seemed to evoke a group of its own, composed of the countless persons he resembled. The country had no clear image of what he looked like: his photographs had appeared on the covers of magazines as frequently as those of his predecessors in office, but people could never be quite certain which photographs were his and which were pictures of *"a* mail clerk" or *"a* white-collar worker," accompanying articles about the daily life of the undifferentiated—except that Mr. Thompson's collars were usually wilted. He had broad shoulders and a slight body. He had stringy hair, a wide mouth and an elastic age range that made him look like a harassed forty or an unusually vigorous sixty. Holding enormous official powers, he schemed ceaselessly to expand them, because it was expected of him by those who had pushed him into office. He had the cunning of the unintelligent and the frantic energy of the lazy. The sole secret of his rise in life was the fact that he was a product of chance and knew it and aspired to nothing else.

"It's obvious that measures have to be taken. Drastic measures," said James Taggart, speaking, not to Mr. Thompson, but to Wesley Mouch. "We can't let things go the way they're going much longer." His voice was belligerent and shaky.

"Take it easy, Jim," said Orren Boyle.

"Something's got to be done and done fast!"

"Don't look at *me*," snapped Wesley Mouch. "I can't help it. I can't help it if people refuse to co-operate. I'm tied. I need wider powers."

Mouch had summoned them all to Washington, as his friends and personal advisers, for a private, unofficial conference on the national crisis. But, watching him, they were unable to decide whether his manner was overbearing or whining, whether he was threatening them or pleading for their help.

"Fact is," said Mr. Weatherby primly, in a statistical tone of voice, "that in the twelve-month period ending on the first of this year, the rate of business failures has doubled, as compared with the preceding twelve-month period. Since the first of this year, it has trebled."

"Be sure they think it's their own fault," said Dr. Ferris casually.

"Huh?" said Wesley Mouch, his eyes darting to Ferris.

"Whatever you do, don't apologize," said Dr. Ferris. "Make them feel guilty."

"I'm not apologizing!" snapped Mouch. "I'm not to blame. I need wider powers."

"But it *is* their own fault," said Eugene Lawson, turning aggressively to Dr. Ferris. "It's their lack of social spirit. They refuse to recognize that production is not a private choice, but a public duty. They have no right to fail, no matter what conditions happen to come up. They've *got* to go on producing. It's a social imperative. A man's work is not a personal matter, it's a social matter. There's no such thing as a personal matter—or a personal life. *That's* what we've got to force them to learn."

"Gene Lawson knows what I'm talking about," said Dr. Ferris, with a slight smile, "even though he hasn't the faintest idea that he does."

"What do you think you mean?" asked Lawson, his voice rising.

"Skip it," ordered Wesley Mouch.

"I don't care what you decide to do, Wesley," said Mr. Thompson, "and I don't care if the businessmen squawk about it. Just be sure you've got the press with you. Be damn sure about that."

"I've got 'em," said Mouch.

"One editor who'd open his trap at the wrong time could do us more harm than ten disgruntled millionaires."

"That's true, Mr. Thompson," said Dr. Ferris. "But can you name one editor who knows it?"

"Guess not," said Mr. Thompson; he sounded pleased.

"Whatever type of men we're counting on and planning for," said Dr. Ferris, "there's a certain old-fashioned quotation which we may safely forget: the one about counting on the wise and the honest. We don't have to consider them. They're out of date."

James Taggart glanced at the window. There were patches of blue in the sky above the spacious streets of Washington, the faint blue of mid-April, and a few beams breaking through the clouds. A monument stood shining in the distance, hit by a ray of sun: it was a tall, white obelisk, erected to the memory of the man Dr. Ferris was quoting, the man in whose honor this city had been named. James Taggart looked away.

"I don't like the professor's remarks," said Lawson loudly and sullenly.

"Keep still," said Wesley Mouch. "Dr. Ferris is not talking theory, but practice."

"Well, if you want to talk practice," said Fred Kinnan, "then let me tell you that we can't worry about businessmen at a time like this. What we've got to think about is jobs. More jobs for the people. In my unions, every man who's working is feeding five who aren't, not counting his own pack of starving relatives. If you want my advice— oh, I know you won't go for it, but it's just a thought—issue a directive making it compulsory to add, say, one-third more men to every payroll in the country."

"Good God!" yelled Taggart. "Are you crazy? We can barely meet our payrolls as it is! There's not enough work for the men we've got now! One-third more? We wouldn't have any use for them whatever!"

"Who cares whether you'd have any use for them?" said Fred Kinnan. "They need jobs. That's what comes first—*need*—doesn't it?— not your profits."

"It's not a question of profits!" yelled Taggart hastily. "I haven't said anything about profits. I haven't given you any grounds to insult me. It's just a question of where in hell we'd get the money to pay your men—when half our trains are running empty and there's not enough freight to fill a trolley car." His voice slowed down suddenly to a tone of cautious thoughtfulness: "However, we do understand the plight of the working men, and—it's just a thought —we could, perhaps, take on a certain extra number, if we were permitted to double our freight rates, which—"

"Have you lost your mind?" yelled Orren Boyle. "I'm going broke on the rates you're charging now, I shudder every time a damn boxcar pulls in or out of the mills, they're bleeding me to death, I can't afford it—and you want to *double* it?"

"It is not essential whether you can afford it or not," said Taggart coldly. "You have to be prepared to make some sacrifices. The public needs railroads. Need comes first—above your profits."

"What profits?" yelled Orren Boyle. "When did I ever make any profits? Nobody can accuse me of running a profit-making business! Just look at my balance sheet—and then look at the books of a certain competitor of mine, who's got all the customers, all the raw materials, all the technical advantages and a monopoly on secret formulas—then tell me who's the profiteer! . . . But, of course, the public does need railroads, and perhaps I could manage to absorb a certain raise in rates, if I were to get—it's just a thought—if I were to get a subsidy to carry me over the next year or two, until I catch my stride and—"

"What? Again?" yelled Mr. Weatherby, losing his primness. "How many loans have you got from us and how many extensions, suspensions and moratoriums? You haven't repaid a penny—and with all of you boys going broke and the tax receipts crashing, where do you expect us to get the money to hand you a subsidy?"

"There are people who aren't broke," said Boyle slowly. "You boys have no excuse for permitting all that need and misery to spread through the country—so long as there are people who aren't broke."

"I can't help it!" yelled Wesley Mouch. "I can't do anything about it! I need wider powers!"

They could not tell what had prompted Mr. Thompson to attend this particular conference. He had said little, but had listened with interest. It seemed as if there were something which he had wanted to learn, and now he looked as if he had learned it. He stood up and smiled cheerfully.

"Go ahead, Wesley," he said. "Go ahead with Number 10-289. You won't have any trouble at all."

They had all risen to their feet, in gloomily reluctant deference. Wesley Mouch glanced down at his sheet of paper, then said in a petulant tone of voice, "If you want me to go ahead, you'll have to declare a state of total emergency."

"I'll declare it any time you're ready."

"There are certain difficulties, which—"

"I'll leave it up to you. Work it out any way you wish. It's your job. Let me see the rough draft, tomorrow or next day, but don't bother me about the details. I've got a speech to make on the radio in half an hour."

"The chief difficulty is that I'm not sure whether the law actually grants us the power to put into effect certain provisions of Directive Number 10-289. I fear they might be open to challenge."

"Oh hell, we've passed so many emergency laws that if you hunt through them, you're sure to dig up something that will cover it."

Mr. Thompson turned to the others with a smile of good fellowship. "I'll leave you boys to iron out the wrinkles," he said. "I appreciate your coming to Washington to help us out. Glad to have seen you."

They waited until the door closed after him, then resumed their seats; they did not look at one another.

They had not heard the text of Directive No. 10-289, but they knew what it would contain. They had known it for a long time, in that special manner which consisted of keeping secrets from oneself and leaving knowledge untranslated into words. And, by the same method, they now wished it were possible for them not to hear the words of the directive. It was to avoid moments such as this that all the complex twistings of their minds had been devised.

They wished the directive to go into effect. They wished it could be put into effect without words, so that they would not have to know that what they were doing was what it was. Nobody had ever announced that Directive No. 10-289 was the final goal of his efforts. Yet, for generations past, men had worked to make it possible, and for months past, every provision of it had been prepared for by countless speeches, articles, sermons, editorials—by purposeful voices that screamed with anger if anyone named their purpose.

"The picture now is this," said Wesley Mouch. "The economic condition of the country was better the year before last than it was last year, and last year it was better than it is at present. It's obvious that we would not be able to survive another year of the same progression. Therefore, our sole objective must now be to hold the line. To stand still in order to catch our stride. To achieve total stability. Freedom has been given a chance and has failed. Therefore, more stringent controls are necessary. Since men are unable and unwilling to solve their problems voluntarily, they must be forced to do it." He paused, picked up the sheet of paper, then added in a less formal tone of voice, "Hell, what it comes down to is that we can manage to exist as and where we are, but we can't afford to move! So we've got to stand still. We've got to stand still. We've got to make those bastards stand still!"

His head drawn into his shoulders, he was looking at them with the anger of a man declaring that the country's troubles were a personal affront to him. So many men seeking favors had been afraid of him that he now acted as if his anger were a solution to everything, as if his anger were omnipotent, as if all he had to do was to get angry. Yet, facing him, the men who sat in a silent semicircle before his desk were uncertain whether the presence of fear in the room was their own emotion or whether the hunched figure behind the desk generated the panic of a cornered rat.

Wesley Mouch had a long, square face and a flat-topped skull, made more so by a brush haircut. His lower lip was a petulant bulb and the pale, brownish pupils of his eyes looked like the yolks of eggs smeared under the not fully translucent whites. His facial muscles moved abruptly, and the movement vanished, having conveyed no expression. No one had ever seen him smile.

Wesley Mouch came from a family that had known neither poverty nor wealth nor distinction for many generations; it had clung, however, to a tradition of its own: that of being college-bred and, therefore, of despising men who were in business. The family's diplomas had always hung on the wall in the manner of a reproach to the world, because the diplomas had not automatically produced the material equivalents of their attested spiritual value. Among the family's numerous relatives, there was one rich uncle. He had married his money and, in his widowed old age, he had picked Wesley as his favorite from among his many nephews and nieces, because Wesley was the least distinguished of the lot and therefore, thought Uncle Julius, the safest. Uncle Julius did not care for people who were brilliant. He did not care for the trouble of managing his money, either; so he turned the job over to Wesley. By the time Wesley graduated from college, there was no money left to manage. Uncle Julius blamed it on Wesley's cunning and cried that Wesley was an unscrupulous schemer. But there had been no scheme about it; Wesley could not have said just where the money had gone. In high school, Wesley Mouch had been one of the worst students and had passionately envied those who were the best. College taught him that he did not have to envy them at all. After graduation, he took a job in the advertising department of a company that manufactured a bogus corn-cure. The cure sold well and he rose to be the head of his department. He left it to take charge of the advertising of a hair-restorer, then of a patented brassière, then of a new soap, then of a soft drink—and then he became advertising vice-president of an automobile concern. He tried to sell automobiles as if they were a bogus corn-cure. They did not sell. He blamed it on the insufficiency of his advertising budget. It was the president of the automobile concern who recommended him to Rearden. It was Rearden who introduced him to Washington—Rearden, who knew no standard by which to judge the activities of his Washington man. It was James Taggart who gave him a start in the Bureau of Economic Planning and National Resources—in exchange for double-crossing Rearden in order to help Orren Boyle in exchange for destroying Dan Conway. From then on, people helped Wesley Mouch to advance, for the same reason as that which had prompted Uncle Julius: they were people who believed that mediocrity was safe. The men who now sat in front of his desk had been taught that the law of causality was a superstition and that one had to deal with the situation of the moment without considering its cause. By the situation of the moment, they had concluded that Wesley Mouch was a man of superlative skill and cunning, since millions aspired to power, but he was the one who had achieved it. It was not within their method of thinking to know that Wesley Mouch was the zero at the meeting point of forces unleashed in destruction against one another.

"This is just a rough draft of Directive Number 10-289," said Wesley Mouch, "which Gene, Clem and I have dashed off just to give you the general idea. We want to hear your opinions, suggestions and so forth—you being the representatives of labor, industry, transportation and the professions."

Fred Kinnan got off the window sill and sat down on the arm of a chair. Orren Boyle spit out the butt of his cigar. James Taggart looked down at his own hands. Dr. Ferris was the only one who seemed to be at ease.

"In the name of the general welfare," read Wesley Mouch, "to protect the people's security, to achieve full equality and total stability, it is decreed for the duration of the national emergency that—

"Point One. All workers, wage earners and employees of any kind whatsoever shall henceforth be attached to their jobs and shall not leave nor be dismissed nor change employment, under penalty of a term in jail. The penalty shall be determined by the Unification Board, such Board to be appointed by the Bureau of Economic Planning and National Resources. All persons reaching the age of twenty-one shall report to the Unification Board, which shall assign them to where, in its opinion, their services will best serve the interests of the nation.

"Point Two. All industrial, commercial, manufacturing and business establishments of any nature whatsoever shall henceforth remain in operation, and the owners of such establishments shall not quit nor leave nor retire, nor close, sell or transfer their business, under penalty of the nationalization of their establishment and of any and all of their property.

"Point Three. All patents and copyrights, pertaining to any devices, inventions, formulas, processes and works of any nature whatsoever, shall be turned over to the nation as a patriotic emergency gift by means of Gift Certificates to be signed voluntarily by the owners of all such patents and copyrights. The Unification Board shall then license the use of such patents and copyrights to all applicants, equally and without discrimination, for the purpose of eliminating monopolistic practices, discarding obsolete products and making the best available to the whole nation. No trademarks, brand names or copyrighted titles shall be used. Every formerly patented product shall be known by a new name and sold by all manufacturers under the same name, such name to be selected by the Unification Board. All private trademarks and brand names are hereby abolished.

"Point Four. No new devices, inventions, products, or goods of any nature whatsoever, not now on the market, shall be produced, invented, manufactured or sold after the date of this directive. The Office of Patents and Copyrights is hereby suspended.

"Point Five. Every establishment, concern, corporation or person engaged in production of any nature whatsoever shall henceforth produce the same amount of goods per year as it, they or he produced during the Basic Year, no more and no less. The year to be known as the Basic or Yardstick Year is to be the year ending on the date of this directive. Over or under production shall be fined, such fines to be determined by the Unification Board.

"Point Six. Every person of any age, sex, class or income, shall henceforth spend the same amount of money on the purchase of goods per year as he or she spent during the Basic Year, no more and no less. Over or under purchasing shall be fined, such fines to be determined by the Unification Board.

"Point Seven. All wages, prices, salaries, dividends, profits, interest rates and forms of income of any nature whatsoever, shall be frozen at their present figures, as of the date of this directive.

"Point Eight. All cases arising from and rules not specifically provided for in this directive, shall be settled and determined by the Unification Board, whose decisions will be final."

There was, even within the four men who had listened, a remnant of human dignity, which made them sit still and feel sick for the length of one minute.

James Taggart spoke first. His voice was low, but it had the trembling intensity of an involuntary scream: "Well, why not? Why should they have it, if we don't? Why should they stand above us? If we are to perish, let's make sure that we all perish together. Let's make sure that we leave them no chance to survive!"

"That's a damn funny thing to say about a very practical plan that will benefit everybody," said Orren Boyle shrilly, looking at Taggart in frightened astonishment.

Dr. Ferris chuckled.

Taggart's eyes seemed to focus, and he said, his voice louder, "Yes, of course. It's a very practical plan. It's necessary, practical and just. It will solve everybody's problems. It will give everybody a chance to feel safe. A chance to rest."

"It will give security to the people," said Eugene Lawson, his mouth slithering into a smile. "Security—that's what the people want. If they want it, why shouldn't they have it? Just because a handful of rich will object?"

"It's not the rich who'll object," said Dr. Ferris lazily. "The rich drool for security more than any other sort of animal—haven't you discovered that yet?"

"Well, who'll object?" snapped Lawson.

Dr. Ferris smiled pointedly, and did not answer.

Lawson looked away. "To hell with them! Why should we worry about *them?* We've got to run the world for the sake of the little people. It's intelligence that's caused all the troubles of humanity. Man's mind is the root of all evil. This is the day of the heart. It's the weak, the meek, the sick and the humble that must be the only objects of our concern." His lower lip was twisting in soft, lecherous motions. "Those who're big are here to serve those who aren't. If they refuse to do their moral duty, we've got to force them. There once was an Age of Reason, but we've progressed beyond it. This is the Age of Love."

"Shut up!" screamed James Taggart.

They all stared at him. "For Christ's sake, Jim, what's the matter?" said Orren Boyle, shaking.

"Nothing," said Taggart, "nothing . . . Wesley, keep him still, will you?"

Mouch said uncomfortably, "But I fail to see—"

"Just keep him still. We don't have to listen to him, do we?"

"Why, no, but—"

"Then let's go on."

"What is this?" demanded Lawson. "I resent it. I most emphatically—" But he saw no support in the faces around him and stopped, his mouth sagging into an expression of pouting hatred.

"Let's go on," said Taggart feverishly.

"What's the matter with you?" asked Orren Boyle, trying not to know what was the matter with himself and why he felt frightened.

"Genius is a superstition, Jim," said Dr. Ferris slowly, with an odd kind of emphasis, as if knowing that he was naming the unnamed in all their minds. "There's no such thing as the intellect. A man's brain is a social product. A sum of influences that he's picked up from those around him. Nobody invents anything, he merely reflects what's floating in the social atmosphere. A genius is an intellectual scavenger and a greedy hoarder of the ideas which rightfully belong to society, from which he stole them. All thought is theft. If we do away with private fortunes, we'll have a fairer distribution of wealth. If we do away with the genius, we'll have a fairer distribution of ideas."

"Are we here to talk business or are we here to kid one another?" asked Fred Kinnan.

They turned to him. He was a muscular man with large features, but his face had the astonishing property of finely drawn lines that raised the corners of his mouth into the permanent hint of a wise, sardonic grin. He sat on the arm of the chair, hands in pockets, looking at Mouch with the smiling glance of a hardened policeman at a shoplifter.

"All I've got to say is that you'd better staff that Unification Board with my men," he said. "Better make sure of it, brother—or I'll blast your Point One to hell."

"I intend, of course, to have a representative of labor on that Board," said Mouch dryly, "as well as a representative of industry, of the professions and of every cross-section of—"

"No cross-sections," said Fred Kinnan evenly. "Just representatives of labor. Period."

"What the hell!" yelled Orren Boyle. "That's stacking the cards, isn't it?"

"Sure," said Fred Kinnan.

"But that will give *you* a stranglehold on every business in the country!"

"What do you think I'm after?"

"That's unfair!" yelled Boyle. "I won't stand for it! You have no right! You—"

"Right?" said Kinnan innocently. "Are we talking about rights?"

"But, I mean, after all, there are certain fundamental property rights which—"

"Listen, pal, you want Point Three, don't you?"

"Well, I—"

"Then you'd better keep your trap shut about property rights from now on. Keep it shut tight."

"Mr. Kinnan," said Dr. Ferris, "you must not make the old-fashioned mistake of drawing wide generalizations. Our policy has to be flexible. There are no absolute principles which—"

"Save it for Jim Taggart, Doc," said Fred Kinnan. "I know what I'm talking about. That's because I never went to college."

"I object," said Boyle, "to your dictatorial method of—"

Kinnan turned his back on him and said, "Listen, Wesley, my boys won't like Point One. If I get to run things, I'll make them swallow it. If not, not. Just make up your mind."

"Well—" said Mouch, and stopped.

"For Christ's sake, Wesley, what about us?" yelled Taggart.

"You'll come to me," said Kinnan, "when you'll need a deal to fix the Board. But I'll run that Board. Me and Wesley."

"Do you think the country will stand for it?" yelled Taggart.

"Stop kidding yourself," said Kinnan. "The country? If there aren't any principles any more—and I guess the doc is right, because there sure aren't—if there aren't any rules to this game and it's only a question of who robs whom—then I've got more votes than the bunch of you, there are more workers than employers, and don't you forget it, boys!"

"That's a funny attitude to take," said Taggart haughtily, "about a measure which, after all, is not designed for the selfish benefit of workers or employers, but for the general welfare of the public."

"Okay," said Kinnan amiably, "let's talk your lingo. Who is the public? If you go by quality—then it ain't you, Jim, and it ain't Orrie Boyle. If you go by quantity—then it sure is *me,* because quantity is what I've got behind me." His smile disappeared, and with a sudden, bitter look of weariness he added, "Only I'm not going to say that I'm working for the welfare of my public, because I know I'm not. I know that I'm delivering the poor bastards into slavery, and that's all there is to it. And they know it, too. But they know that I'll have to throw them a crumb once in a while, if I want to keep my racket, while with the rest of you they wouldn't have a chance in hell. So that's why, if they've got to be under a whip, they'd rather *I* held it, not you—you drooling, tear-jerking, mealy-mouthed bastards of the public welfare! Do you think that outside of your college-bred pansies there's one village idiot whom you're fooling? I'm a racketeer—but I know it and my boys know it, and they know that I'll pay off. Not out of the kindness of my heart, either, and not a cent more than I can get away with, but at least they can count on that much. Sure, it makes me sick sometimes, it makes me sick right now, but it's not me who's built this kind of world—*you* did—so I'm playing the game as you've set it up and I'm going to play it for as long as it lasts—which isn't going to be long for any of us!"

He stood up. No one answered him. He let his eyes move slowly from face to face and stop on Wesley Mouch.

"Do I get the Board, Wesley?" he asked casually.

"The selection of the specific personnel is only a technical detail," said Mouch pleasantly. "Suppose we discuss it later, you and I?"

Everybody in the room knew that this meant the answer *Yes*.

"Okay, pal," said Kinnan. He went back to the window, sat down on the sill and lighted a cigarette.

For some unadmitted reason, the others were looking at Dr. Ferris, as if seeking guidance.

"Don't be disturbed by oratory," said Dr. Ferris smoothly. "Mr. Kinnan is a fine speaker, but he has no sense of practical reality. He is unable to think dialectically."

There was another silence, then James Taggart spoke up suddenly. "I don't care. It doesn't matter. He'll have to hold things still. Everything will have to remain as it is. Just as it is. Nobody will be permitted to change anything. Except—" He turned sharply to Wesley Mouch. "Wesley, under Point Four, we'll have to close all research departments, experimental laboratories, scientific foundations and all the rest of the institutions of that kind. They'll have to be forbidden."

"Yes, that's right," said Mouch. "I hadn't thought of that. We'll have to stick in a couple of lines about that." He hunted around for a pencil and made a few scrawls on the margin of his paper.

"It will end wasteful competition," said James Taggart. "We'll stop scrambling to beat one another to the untried and the unknown. We won't have to worry about new inventions upsetting the market. We won't have to pour money down the drain in useless experiments just to keep up with overambitious competitors."

"Yes," said Orren Boyle. "Nobody should be allowed to waste money on the new until everybody has plenty of the old. Close all those damn research laboratories—and the sooner, the better."

"Yes," said Wesley Mouch. "We'll close them. All of them."

"The State Science Institute, too?" asked Fred Kinnan.

"Oh, no!" said Mouch. "That's different. That's government. Besides, it's a non-profit institution. And it will be sufficient to take care of all scientific progress."

"Quite sufficient," said Dr. Ferris.

"And what will become of all the engineers, professors and such, when you close all those laboratories?" asked Fred Kinnan. "What are they going to do for a living, with all the other jobs and businesses frozen?"

"Oh," said Wesley Mouch. He scratched his head. He turned to Mr. Weatherby. "Do we put them on relief, Clem?"

"No," said Mr. Weatherby. "What for? There's not enough of them to raise a squawk. Not enough to matter."

"I suppose," said Mouch, turning to Dr. Ferris, "that you'll be able to absorb some of them, Floyd?"

"Some," said Dr. Ferris slowly, as if relishing every syllable of his answer. "Those who prove co-operative."

"What about the rest?" asked Fred Kinnan.

"They'll have to wait till the Unification Board finds some use for them," said Wesley Mouch.

"What will they eat while they're waiting?"

Mouch shrugged. "There's got to be some victims in times of national emergency. It can't be helped."

"We have the right to do it!" cried Taggart suddenly, in defiance to the stillness of the room. "We need it. We need it, don't we?" There was no answer. "We have the right to protect our livelihood!" Nobody opposed him, but he went on with a shrill, pleading insistence. "We'll be safe for the first time in centuries. Everybody will know his place and job, and everybody else's place and job—and we won't be at the mercy of every stray crank with a new idea. Nobody will push us out of business or steal our markets or undersell us or make us obsolete. Nobody will come to us offering some damn new gadget and putting us on the spot to decide whether we'll lose our shirt if we buy it, or whether we'll lose our shirt if we don't but somebody else does! We won't have to decide. Nobody will be permitted to decide anything. It will be decided once and for all." His glance moved pleadingly from face to face. "There's been enough invented already—enough for everybody's comfort—why should they be allowed to go on inventing? Why should we permit them to blast the ground from under our feet every few steps? Why should we be kept on the go in eternal uncertainty? Just because of a few restless, ambitious adventurers? Should we sacrifice the contentment of the whole of mankind to the greed of a few non-conformists? We don't need them. We don't need them at all. I wish we'd get rid of that hero worship! Heroes? They've done nothing but harm, all through history. They've kept mankind running a wild race, with no breathing spell, no rest, no ease, no security. Running to catch up with them . . . always, without end . . . Just as we catch up, they're years ahead. . . . They leave us no chance . . . They've never left us a chance. . . ." His eyes were moving restlessly; he glanced at the window, but looked hastily away: he did not want to see the white obelisk in the distance. "We're through with them. We've won. This is our age. Our world. We're going to have security—for the first time in centuries—for the first time since the beginning of the industrial revolution!"

"Well, this, I guess," said Fred Kinnan, "is the anti-industrial revolution."

"That's a damn funny thing for you to say!" snapped Wesley Mouch. "We can't be permitted to say that to the public."

"Don't worry, brother. I won't say it to the public."

"It's a total fallacy," said Dr. Ferris. "It's a statement prompted by ignorance. Every expert has conceded long ago that a planned economy achieves the maximum of productive efficiency and that centralization leads to super-industrialization."

"Centralization destroys the blight of monopoly," said Boyle.

"How's that again?" drawled Kinnan.

Boyle did not catch the tone of mockery, and answered earnestly, "It destroys the blight of monopoly. It leads to the democratization of industry. It makes everything available to everybody. Now, for instance, at a time like this, when there's such a desperate shortage of iron ore, is there any sense in my wasting money, labor and national resources on making old-fashioned steel, when there exists a much better metal that I could be making? A metal that everybody wants, but nobody can get. Now is that good economics or sound social efficiency or democratic justice? Why shouldn't I be allowed to manufacture that metal and why shouldn't the people get it when they need it? Just because of the private monopoly of one selfish individual? Should we sacrifice our rights to his personal interests?"

"Skip it, brother," said Fred Kinnan. "I've read it all in the same newspapers you did."

"I don't like your attitude," said Boyle, in a sudden tone of righteousness, with a look which, in a barroom, would have signified a prelude to a fist fight. He sat up straight, buttressed by the columns of paragraphs on yellow-tinged paper, which he was seeing in his mind:

> "At a time of crucial public need, are we to waste social effort on the manufacture of obsolete products? Are we to let the many remain in want while the few withhold from us the better products and methods available? Are we to be stopped by the superstition of patent rights?"

> "Is it not obvious that private industry is unable to cope with the present economic crisis? How

long, for instance, are we going to put up with the disgraceful shortage of Rearden Metal? There is a crying public demand for it, which Rearden has failed to supply."

"When are we going to put an end to economic injustice and special privileges? Why should Rearden be the only one permitted to manufacture Rearden Metal?"

"I don't like your attitude," said Orren Boyle. "So long as we respect the rights of the workers, we'll want you to respect the rights of the industrialists."

"Which rights of which industrialists?" drawled Kinnan.

"I'm inclined to think," said Dr. Ferris hastily, "that Point Two, perhaps, is the most essential one of all at present. We must put an end to that peculiar business of industrialists retiring and vanishing. We must stop them. It's playing havoc with our entire economy."

"Why are they doing it?" asked Taggart nervously. "Where are they all going?"

"Nobody knows," said Dr. Ferris. "We've been unable to find any information or explanation. But it must be stopped. In times of crisis, economic service to the nation is just as much of a duty as military service. Anyone who abandons it should be regarded as a deserter. I have recommended that we introduce the death penalty for those men, but Wesley wouldn't agree to it."

"Take it easy, boy," said Fred Kinnan in an odd, slow voice. He sat suddenly and perfectly still, his arms crossed, looking at Ferris in a manner that made it suddenly real to the room that Ferris had proposed murder. "Don't let me hear you talk about any death penalties in industry."

Dr. Ferris shrugged.

"We don't have to go to extremes," said Mouch hastily. "We don't want to frighten people. We want to have them on our side. Our top problem is, will they . . . will they accept it at all?"

"They will," said Dr. Ferris.

"I'm a little worried," said Eugene Lawson, "about Points Three and Four. Taking over the patents is fine. Nobody's going to defend industrialists. But I'm worried about taking over the copyrights. That's going to antagonize the intellectuals. It's dangerous. It's a spiritual issue. Doesn't Point Four mean that no new books are to be written or published from now on?"

"Yes," said Mouch, "it does. But we can't make an exception for the book-publishing business. It's an industry like any other. When we say 'no new products,' it's got to mean 'no new products.' "

"But this is a matter of the spirit," said Lawson; his voice had a tone, not of rational respect, but of superstitious awe.

"We're not interfering with anybody's spirit. But when you print a book on paper, it becomes a material commodity—and if we grant an exception to one commodity, we won't be able to hold the others in line and we won't be able to make anything stick."

"Yes, that's true. But—"

"Don't be a chump, Gene," said Dr. Ferris. "You don't want some recalcitrant hacks to come out with treatises that will wreck our entire program, do you? If you breathe the word 'censorship' now, they'll all scream bloody murder. They're not ready for it—as yet. But if you leave the spirit alone and make it a simple material issue—not a matter of ideas, but just a matter of paper, ink and printing presses—you accomplish your purpose much more smoothly. You'll make sure that nothing dangerous gets printed or heard—and nobody is going to fight over a material issue."

"Yes, but . . . but I don't think the writers will like it."

"Are you sure?" asked Wesley Mouch, with a glance that was almost a smile. "Don't forget that under Point Five, the publishers will have to publish as many books as they did in the Basic Year. Since there will be no new ones, they will have to reprint—and the public will have to buy—some of the old ones. There are many very worthy books that have never had a fair chance."

"Oh," said Lawson; he remembered that he had seen Mouch lunching with Balph Eubank two weeks ago. Then he shook his head and frowned. "Still, I'm worried. The intellectuals are our friends. We don't want to lose them. They can make an awful lot of trouble."

"They won't," said Fred Kinnan. "Your kind of intellectuals are the first to scream when it's safe—and the first to shut their traps at the first sign of danger. They spend years spitting at the man who feeds them—and they lick the hand of the man who slaps their drooling faces. Didn't they deliver every country of Europe, one after another, to committees of goons, just like this one here? Didn't they scream their heads off to shut out every burglar alarm and to break every padlock open for the goons? Have you heard a peep out of them since? Didn't they scream that they were the friends of labor? Do you hear them raising their voices about the chain gangs, the slave camps, the fourteen-hour workday and the mortality from scurvy in the People's States of Europe? No, but you do hear them telling the whip-beaten wretches that starvation is prosperity, that slavery is freedom, that torture chambers are brother-love and that if the wretches don't understand it, then it's their own fault that they suffer, and it's the mangled corpses in the jail cellars who're to blame for all their troubles, not the benevolent leaders! Intellectuals? You might have to worry about any other breed of men, but not about the modern intellectuals: they'll swallow anything. I don't feel so safe about the lousiest wharf rat in the longshoremen's union: he's liable to remember suddenly that he is a man—and then I won't be able to keep him in line. But the intellectuals? That's the one thing they've forgotten long ago. I guess it's the one thing that all their education was aimed to make them forget. Do anything you please to the intellectuals. They'll take it."

"For once," said Dr. Ferris, "I agree with Mr. Kinnan. I agree with his facts, if not with his feelings. You don't have to worry about the intellectuals, Wesley. Just put a few of them on the government payroll and send them out to preach precisely the sort of thing Mr. Kinnan mentioned: that the blame rests on the victims. Give them moderately comfortable salaries and extremely loud titles—and they'll forget their copyrights and do a better job for you than whole squads of enforcement officers."

"Yes," said Mouch. "I know."

"The danger that I'm worried about will come from a different quarter," said Dr. Ferris thoughtfully. "You might run into quite a bit of trouble on that 'voluntary Gift Certificate' business, Wesley."

"I know," said Mouch glumly. "That's the point I wanted Thompson to help us out on. But I guess he can't. We don't actually have the legal power to seize the patents. Oh, there's plenty of clauses in dozens of laws that can be stretched to cover it—almost, but not quite. Any tycoon who'd want to make a test case would have a very good chance to beat us. And we have to preserve a semblance of legality—or the populace won't take it."

"Precisely," said Dr. Ferris. "It's extremely important to get those patents turned over to us *voluntarily*. Even if we had a law permitting outright nationalization, it would be much better to get them as a gift. We want to leave to people the illusion that they're still preserving their private property rights. And most of them will play along. They'll sign the Gift Certificates. Just raise a lot of noise about its being a patriotic duty and that anyone who refuses is a prince of greed, and they'll sign. But—" He stopped.

"I know," said Mouch; he was growing visibly more nervous. "There will be, I think, a few old-fashioned bastards here and there who'll refuse to sign—but they won't be prominent enough to make a noise, nobody will hear about it, their own communities and friends will turn against them for their being selfish, so it won't give us any trouble. We'll just take the patents over, anyway—and those guys won't have the nerve or the money to start a test case. But—" He stopped.

James Taggart leaned back in his chair, watching them; he was beginning to enjoy the conversation.

"Yes," said Dr. Ferris, "I'm thinking of it, too. I'm thinking of a certain tycoon who is in a position to blast us to pieces. Whether we'll recover the pieces or not, is hard to tell. God knows what is liable to happen at a hysterical time like the present and in a situation as delicate as this. Anything can throw everything off balance. Blow up the whole works. And if there's anyone who wants to do it, he does. He does and can. He knows the real issue, he knows the things which must not be said—and he is not afraid to say them. He knows the one dangerous, fatally dangerous weapon. He is our deadliest adversary."

"Who?" asked Lawson.

Dr. Ferris hesitated, shrugged and answered, "The guiltless man."

Lawson stared blankly. "What do you mean and whom are you talking about?"

James Taggart smiled.

"I mean that there is no way to disarm any man," said Dr. Ferris, "except through guilt. Through that which he himself has accepted as guilt. If a man has ever stolen a dime, you can impose on him the punishment intended for a bank robber and he will take it. He'll bear any form of misery, he'll feel that he deserves no better. If there's not enough guilt in the world, we must create it. If we teach a man that it's evil to look at spring flowers and he believes us and then does it —we'll be able to do whatever we please with him. He won't defend himself. He won't feel he's worth it. He won't fight. But save us from the man who lives up to his own standards. Save us from the man of clean conscience. He's the man who'll beat us."

"Are you talking about Henry Rearden?" asked Taggart, his voice peculiarly clear.

The one name they had not wanted to pronounce struck them into an instant's silence.

"What if I were?" asked Dr. Ferris cautiously.

"Oh, nothing," said Taggart. "Only, if you were, I would tell you that I can deliver Henry Rearden. He'll sign."

By the rules of their unspoken language, they all knew—from the tone of his voice—that he was not bluffing.

"God, Jim! No!" gasped Wesley Mouch.

"Yes," said Taggart. "I was stunned, too, when I learned—what I learned. I didn't expect that. Anything but that."

"I am glad to hear it," said Mouch cautiously. "It's a constructive piece of information. It might be very valuable indeed."

"Valuable—yes," said Taggart pleasantly. "When do you plan to put the directive into effect?"

"Oh, we have to move fast. We don't want any news of it to leak out. I expect you all to keep this most strictly confidential. I'd say that we'll be ready to spring it on them in a couple of weeks."

"Don't you think that it would be advisable—before all prices are frozen—to adjust the matter of the railroad rates? I was thinking of a raise. A small but most essentially needed raise."

"We'll discuss it, you and I," said Mouch amiably. "It might be arranged." He turned to the others; Boyle's face was sagging. "There are many details still to be worked out, but I'm sure that our program won't encounter any major difficulties." He was assuming the tone and manner of a public address; he sounded brisk and almost cheerful. "Rough spots are to be expected. If one thing doesn't work, we'll try another. Trial-and-error is the only pragmatic rule of action. We'll just keep on trying. If any hardships come up, remember that it's only temporary. Only for the duration of the national emergency."

"Say," asked Kinnan, "how is the emergency to end if everything is to stand still?"

"Don't be theoretical," said Mouch impatiently. "We've got to deal with the situation of the moment. Don't bother about minor details, so long as the broad outlines of our policy are clear. We'll have the power. We'll be able to solve any problem and answer any question."

Fred Kinnan chuckled. "Who is John Galt?"

"Don't say that!" cried Taggart.

"I have a question to ask about Point Seven," said Kinnan. "It says that all wages, prices, salaries, dividends, profits and so forth will be frozen on the date of the directive. Taxes, too?"

"Oh no!" cried Mouch. "How can we tell what funds we'll need in the future?" Kinnan seemed to be smiling. "Well?" snapped Mouch. "What about it?"

"Nothing," said Kinnan. "I just asked."

Mouch leaned back in his chair. "I must say to all of you that I appreciate your coming here and giving us the benefit of your opinions. It has been very helpful." He leaned forward to look at his desk calendar and sat over it for a moment, toying with his pencil. Then the pencil came down, struck a date and drew a circle around it. "Directive 10-289 will go into effect on the morning of May first."

All nodded approval. None looked at his neighbor.

James Taggart rose, walked to the window and pulled the blind down over the white obelisk.

*　*　*

In the first moment of awakening, Dagny was astonished to find herself looking at the spires of unfamiliar buildings against a glowing, pale blue sky. Then she saw the twisted seam of the thin stocking on her own leg, she felt a wrench of discomfort in the muscles of her waistline, and she realized that she was lying on the couch in her office, with the clock on her desk saying 6:15 and the first rays of the sun giving silver edges to the silhouettes of the skyscrapers beyond the window. The last thing she remembered was that she had dropped down on the couch, intending to rest for ten minutes, when the window was black and the clock stood at 3:30.

She twisted herself to her feet, feeling an enormous exhaustion. The lighted lamp on the desk looked futile in the glow of the morning, over the piles of paper which were her cheerless, unfinished task. She tried not to think of the work for a few minutes longer, while she dragged herself past the desk to her washroom and let handfuls of cold water run over her face.

The exhaustion was gone by the time she stepped back into the office. No matter what night preceded it, she had never known a morning when she did not feel the rise of a quiet excitement that became a tightening energy in her body and a hunger for action in her mind— because this was the beginning of day and it was a day of *her* life. She looked down at the city. The streets were still empty, it made them look wider, and in the luminous cleanliness of the spring air they seemed to be waiting for the promise of all the greatness that would take form in the activity about to pour through them. The calendar in the distance said: May 1.

She sat down at her desk, smiling in defiance at the distastefulness of her job. She hated the reports that she had to finish reading, but it was her job, it was her railroad, it was morning. She lighted a cigarette, thinking that she would finish this task before breakfast; she turned off the lamp and pulled the papers forward.

There were reports from the general managers of the four Regions of the Taggart system, their pages a typewritten cry of despair over the breakdowns of equipment. There was a report about a wreck on the main line near Winston, Colorado. There was the new budget of the Operating Department, the revised budget based on the raise in rates which Jim had obtained last week. She tried to choke the exasperation of hopelessness as she went slowly over the budget's figures: all those calculations had been made on the assumption that the volume of freight would remain unchanged and that the raise would bring them added revenue by the end of the year; she knew that the freight tonnage would go on shrinking, that the raise would make little difference, that by the end of this year their losses would be greater than ever.

When she looked up from the pages, she saw with a small jolt of astonishment that the clock said 9:25. She had been dimly aware of the usual sound of movement and voices in the anteroom of her office, as her staff had arrived to begin their day; she wondered why nobody had entered her office and why her telephone had remained silent; as a daily rule, there should have been a rush of business by this hour. She glanced at her calendar; there was a note that the McNeil Car Foundry of Chicago was to phone her at nine A.M. in regard to the new freight cars which Taggart Transcontinental had been expecting for six months.

She flicked the switch of the interoffice communicator to call her secretary. The girl's voice answered with a startled little gasp: "Miss Taggart! Are you here, in your office?"

"I slept here last night, again. Didn't intend to, but did. Was there a call for me from the McNeil Car Foundry?"

"No, Miss Taggart."

"Put them through to me immediately, when they call."

"Yes, Miss Taggart."

Switching the communicator off, she wondered whether she imagined it or whether there had been something strange in the girl's voice: it had sounded unnaturally tense.

She felt the faint light-headedness of hunger and thought that she should go down to get a cup of coffee, but there was still the report of the chief engineer to finish, so she lighted one more cigarette.

The chief engineer was out on the road, supervising the reconstruction of the main track with the Rearden Metal rail taken from the corpse of the John Galt Line; she had chosen the sections most urgently in need of repair. Opening his report, she read—with a shock of incredulous anger—that he had stopped work in the mountain section of Winston, Colorado. He recommended a change of plans: he suggested that the rail intended for Winston be used, instead, to repair the track of their Washington-to-Miami branch. He gave his reasons: a derailment had occurred on that branch last week, and Mr. Tinky Holloway of Washington, traveling with a party of friends, had been delayed for three hours; it had been reported to the chief engineer that Mr. Holloway had expressed extreme displeasure. Although, from a purely technological viewpoint—said the chief engineer's report—the rail of the Miami branch was in better condition than that of the Winston section, one had to remember, from a sociological viewpoint, that the Miami branch carried a much more important class of passenger traffic; therefore, the chief engineer suggested that Winston could be kept waiting a little longer, and recommended the sacrifice of an obscure section of mountain trackage for the sake of a branch where "Taggart Transcontinental could not afford to create an unfavorable impression."

She read, slashing furious pencil marks on the margins of the pages, thinking that her first duty of the day, ahead of any other, was to stop this particular piece of insanity.

The telephone rang.

"Yes?" she asked, snatching the receiver. "McNeil Car Foundry?"

"No," said the voice of her secretary. "Señor Francisco d'Anconia."

She looked at the phone's mouthpiece for the instant of a brief shock. "All right. Put him on."

The next voice she heard was Francisco's. "I see that you're in your office just the same," he said; his voice was mocking, harsh and tense.

"Where did you expect me to be?"

"How do you like the new suspension?"

"What suspension?"

"The moratorium on brains."

"What are you talking about?"

"Haven't you seen today's newspapers?"

"No."

There was a pause; then his voice came slowly, changed and grave: "Better take a look at them, Dagny."

"All right."

"I'll call you later."

She hung up and pressed the switch of the communicator on her desk. "Get me a newspaper," she said to her secretary.

"Yes, Miss Taggart," the secretary's voice answered grimly.

It was Eddie Willers who came in and put the newspaper down on her desk. The meaning of the look on his face was the same as the tone she had caught in Francisco's voice: the advance notice of some inconceivable disaster.

"None of us wanted to be first to tell you," he said very quietly and walked out.

When she rose from her desk, a few moments later, she felt that she had full control of her body and that she was not aware of her body's existence. She felt lifted to her feet and it seemed to her that she stood straight, not touching the ground. There was an abnormal clarity about every object in the room, yet she was seeing nothing around her, but she knew that she would be able to see the thread of a cobweb if her purpose required it, just as she would be able to walk with a somnambulist's assurance along the edge of a roof. She could not know that she was looking at the room with the eyes of a person who had lost the capacity and the concept of doubt, and what remained to her was the simplicity of a single perception and of a single goal. She did not know that the thing which seemed so violent, yet felt like such a still, unfamiliar calm within her, was the power of full certainty—and that the anger shaking her body, the anger which made her ready, with the same passionate indifference, either to kill or to die, was her love of rectitude, the only love to which all the years of her life had been given.

Holding the newspaper in her hand, she walked out of her office and on toward the hall. She knew, crossing the anteroom, that the faces of her staff were turned to her, but they seemed to be many years away.

She walked down the hall, moving swiftly but without effort, with the same sensation of knowing that her feet were probably touching the ground but that she did not feel it. She did not know how many rooms she crossed to reach Jim's office, or whether there had been any people in her way, she knew the direction to take and the door to pull open to enter unannounced and walk toward his desk.

The newspaper was twisted into a roll by the time she stood before him. She threw it at his face, it struck his cheek and fell down to the carpet.

"There's my resignation, Jim," she said. "I won't work as a slave or as a slave-driver."

She did not hear the sound of his gasp; it came with the sound of the door closing after her.

She went back to her office and, crossing the anteroom, signaled Eddie to follow her inside.

She said, her voice calm and clear, "I have resigned."

He nodded silently.

"I don't know as yet what I'll do in the future. I'm going away, to think it over and to decide. If you want to follow me, I'll be at the lodge in Woodstock." It was an old hunting cabin in a forest of the Berkshire Mountains, which she had inherited from her father and had not visited for years.

"I want to follow," he whispered, "I want to quit, and . . . and I can't. I can't make myself do it."

"Then will you do me a favor?"

"Of course."

"Don't communicate with me about the railroad. I don't want to hear it. Don't tell anyone where I am, except Hank Rearden. If he asks, tell him about the cabin and how to get there. But no one else. I don't want to see anybody."

"All right."

"Promise?"

"Of course."

"When I decide what's to become of me, I'll let you know."

"I'll wait."

"That's all, Eddie."

He knew that every word was measured and that nothing else could be said between them at this moment. He inclined his head, letting it say the rest, then walked out of the office.

She saw the chief engineer's report still lying open on her desk, and thought that she had to order him at once to resume the work on the Winston section, then remembered that it was not her problem any longer. She felt no pain. She knew that the pain would come later and that it would be a tearing agony of pain, and that the numbness of this moment was a rest granted to her, not after, but before, to make her ready to bear it. But it did not matter. If that is required of me, then I'll bear it—she thought.

She sat down at her desk and telephoned Rearden at his mills in Pennsylvania.

"Hello, dearest," he said. He said it simply and clearly, as if he wanted to say it because it was real and right, and he needed to hold on to the concepts of reality and rightness.

"Hank, I've quit."

"I see." He sounded as if he had expected it.

"Nobody came to get me, no destroyer, perhaps there never was any destroyer, after all. I don't know what I'll do next, but I have to get away, so that I won't have to see any of them for a while. Then I'll decide. I know that you can't go with me right now."

"No. I have two weeks in which they expect me to sign their Gift Certificate. I want to be right here when the two weeks expire."

"Do you need me—for the two weeks?"

"No. It's worse for you than for me. You have no way to fight them. I have. I think I'm glad they did it. It's clear and final. Don't worry about me. Rest. Rest from all of it, first."

"Yes."

"Where are you going?"

"To the country. To a cabin I own in the Berkshires. If you want to see me, Eddie Willers will tell you the way to get there. I'll be back in two weeks."

"Will you do me a favor?"

"Yes."

"Don't come back until I come for you."

"But I want to be here, when it happens."

"Leave that up to me."

"Whatever they do to you, I want it done to me also."

"Leave it up to me. Dearest, don't you understand? I think that what I want most right now is what you want: not to see any of them. But I have to stay here for a while. So it will help me if I know that you, at least, are out of their reach. I want to keep one clean point in my mind, to lean against. It will be only a short while—and then I'll come for you. Do you understand?"

"Yes, my darling. So long."

It was weightlessly easy to walk out of her office and down the stretching halls of Taggart Transcontinental. She walked, looking ahead, her steps advancing with the unbroken, unhurried rhythm of finality. Her face was held level and it had a look of astonishment, of acceptance, of repose.

She walked across the concourse of the Terminal. She saw the statue of Nathaniel Taggart. But she felt no pain from it and no reproach, only the rising fullness of her love, only the feeling that she was going to join him, not in death, but in that which had been his life.

* * *

The first man to quit at Rearden Steel was Tom Colby, rolling mill foreman, head of the Rearden Steel Workers Union. For ten years, he had heard himself denounced throughout the country, because his was a "company union" and because he had never engaged in a violent conflict with the management. This was true: no conflict had ever been necessary; Rearden paid a higher wage scale than any union scale in the country, for which he demanded—and got—the best labor force to be found anywhere.

When Tom Colby told him that he was quitting, Rearden nodded, without comment or questions.

"I won't work under these conditions, myself," Colby added quietly, "and I won't help to keep the men working. They trust me. I won't be the Judas goat leading them to the stockyards."

"What are you going to do for a living?" asked Rearden.

"I've saved enough to last me for about a year."

"And after that?"

Colby shrugged.

Rearden thought of the boy with the angry eyes, who mined coal at night as a criminal. He thought of all the dark roads, the alleys, the back yards of the country, where the best of the country's men would now exchange their services in jungle barter, in chance jobs, in unrecorded transactions. He thought of the end of that road.

Tom Colby seemed to know what he was thinking. "You're on your way to end up right alongside of me, Mr. Rearden," he said. "Are you going to sign your brains over to them?"

"No."

"And after that?"

Rearden shrugged.

Colby's eyes watched him for a moment, pale, shrewd eyes in a furnace-tanned face with soot-engraved wrinkles. "They've been telling us for years that it's you against me, Mr. Rearden. But it isn't. It's Orren Boyle and Fred Kinnan against you and me."

"I know it."

The Wet Nurse had never entered Rearden's office, as if sensing that that was a place he had no right to enter. He always waited to catch a glimpse of Rearden outside. The directive had attached him to his job, as the mills' official watchdog of over-or-under-production. He stopped Rearden, a few days later, in an alley between the rows of open-hearth furnaces. There was an odd look of fierceness on the boy's face.

"Mr. Rearden," he said, "I wanted to tell you that if you want to pour ten times the quota of Rearden Metal or steel or pig iron or anything, and bootleg it all over the place to anybody at any price—I wanted to tell you to go ahead. I'll fix it up. I'll juggle the books, I'll fake the reports, I'll get phony witnesses, I'll forge affidavits, I'll commit perjury—so you don't have to worry, there won't be any trouble!"

"Now why do you want to do that?" asked Rearden, smiling, but his smile vanished when he heard the boy answer earnestly:

"Because I want, for once, to do something moral."

"That's not the way to be moral—" Rearden started, and stopped abruptly, realizing that it *was* the way, the only way left, realizing through how many twists of intellectual corruption upon corruption this boy had to struggle toward his momentous discovery.

"I guess that's not the word," the boy said sheepishly. "I know it's a stuffy, old-fashioned word. That's not what I meant. I meant—" It was a sudden, desperate cry of incredulous anger: "Mr. Rearden, they have no right to do it!"

"What?"

"Take Rearden Metal away from you."

Rearden smiled and, prompted by a desperate pity, said, "Forget it, Non-Absolute. There are no rights."

"I know there aren't. But I mean . . . what I mean is that they can't do it."

"Why not?" He could not help smiling.

"Mr. Rearden, don't sign the Gift Certificate! Don't sign it, on principle."

"I won't sign it. But there aren't any principles."

"I know there aren't." He was reciting it in full earnestness, with the honesty of a conscientious student: "I know that everything is relative and that nobody can know anything and that reason is an illusion and that there isn't any reality. But I'm just talking about Rearden Metal. Don't sign, Mr. Rearden. Morals or no morals, principles or no principles, just don't sign it—because it isn't right!"

No one else mentioned the directive in Rearden's presence. Silence was the new aspect about the mills. The men did not speak to him when he appeared in the workshops, and he noticed that they did not speak to one another. The personnel office received no formal resignations. But every other morning, one or two men failed to appear and never appeared again. Inquiries at their homes found the homes abandoned and the men gone. The personnel office did not report these desertions, as the directive required; instead, Rearden began to see unfamiliar faces among the workers, the drawn, beaten faces of the long-unemployed, and heard them addressed by the names of the men who had quit. He asked no questions.

There was silence throughout the country. He did not know how many industrialists had retired and vanished on May 1 and 2, leaving their plants to be seized. He counted ten among his own customers, including McNeil of the McNeil Car Foundry in Chicago. He had no way of learning about the others; no reports appeared in the newspapers. The front pages of the newspapers were suddenly full of stories about spring floods, traffic accidents, school picnics and golden-wedding anniversaries.

There was silence in his own home. Lillian had departed on a vacation trip to Florida, in mid-April; it had astonished him, as an inexplicable whim; it was the first trip she had taken alone since their marriage. Philip avoided him, with a look of panic. His mother stared at Rearden in reproachful bewilderment; she said nothing, but she kept bursting into tears in his presence, her manner suggesting that her tears were the most important aspect to consider in whatever disaster it was that she sensed approaching.

On the morning of May 15, he sat at the desk in his office, above the spread of the mills, and watched the colors of the smoke rising to the clear, blue sky. There were spurts of transparent smoke, like waves of heat, invisible but for the structures that shivered behind them; there were streaks of red smoke, and sluggish columns of yellow, and light, floating spirals of blue—and the thick, tight, swiftly pouring coils that looked like twisted bolts of satin tinged a mother-of-pearl pink by the summer sun.

The buzzer rang on his desk, and Miss Ives' voice said, "Dr. Floyd Ferris to see you, without appointment, Mr. Rearden." In spite of its rigid formality, her tone conveyed the question: Shall I throw him out?

There was a faint movement of astonishment in Rearden's face, barely above the line of indifference: he had not expected that particular emissary. He answered evenly, "Ask him to come in."

Dr. Ferris did not smile as he walked toward Rearden's desk; he merely wore a look suggesting that Rearden knew full well that he had good reason to smile and so he would abstain from the obvious.

He sat down in front of the desk, not waiting for an invitation; he carried a briefcase, which he placed across his knees; he acted as if words were superfluous, since his reappearance in this office had made everything clear.

Rearden sat watching him in patient silence.

"Since the deadline for the signing of the national Gift Certificates expires tonight at midnight," said Dr. Ferris, in the tone of a salesman extending a special courtesy to a customer, "I have come to obtain your signature, Mr. Rearden."

He paused, with an air of suggesting that the formula now called for an answer.

"Go on," said Rearden. "I am listening."

"Yes, I suppose I should explain," said Dr. Ferris, "that we wish to get your signature early in the day in order to announce the fact on a national news broadcast. Although the gift program has gone through quite smoothly, there are still a few stubborn individualists left, who have failed to sign—small fry, really, whose patents are of no crucial value, but we cannot let them remain unbound, as a matter of principle, you understand. They are, we believe, waiting to follow your lead. You have a great popular following, Mr. Rearden, much greater than you suspected or knew how to use. Therefore, the announcement that you have signed will remove the last hopes of resistance and, by midnight, will bring in the last signatures, thus completing the program on schedule."

Rearden knew that of all possible speeches, this was the last Dr. Ferris would make if any doubt of his surrender remained in the man's mind.

"Go on," said Rearden evenly. "You haven't finished."

"You know—as you have demonstrated at your trial—how important it is, and why, that we obtain all that property with the voluntary consent of the victims." Dr. Ferris opened his briefcase. "Here is the Gift Certificate, Mr. Rearden. We have filled it out and all you have to do is to sign your name at the bottom."

The piece of paper, which he placed in front of Rearden, looked like a small college diploma, with the text printed in old-fashioned script and the particulars inserted by typewriter. The thing stated that he, Henry Rearden, hereby transferred to the nation all rights to the metal alloy now known as "Rearden Metal," which would henceforth be manufactured by all who so desired, and which would bear the name of "Miracle Metal," chosen by the representatives of the people. Glancing at the paper, Rearden wondered whether it was a deliberate mockery of decency, or so low an estimate of their victims' intelligence, that had made the designers of this paper print the text across a faint drawing of the Statue of Liberty.

His eyes moved slowly to Dr. Ferris' face. "You would not have come here," he said, "unless you had some extraordinary kind of blackjack to use on me. What is it?"

"Of course," said Dr. Ferris. "I would expect you to understand that. That is why no lengthy explanations are necessary." He opened his briefcase. "Do you wish to see my blackjack? I have brought a few samples."

In the manner of a cardsharp whisking out a long fan of cards with one snap of the hand, he spread before Rearden a line of glossy photographic prints. They were photostats of hotel and auto court registers, bearing in Rearden's handwriting the names of Mr. and Mrs. J. Smith.

"You know, of course," said Dr. Ferris softly, "but you might wish to see whether we know it, that Mrs. J. Smith is Miss Dagny Taggart."

He found nothing to observe in Rearden's face. Rearden had not moved to bend over the prints, but sat looking down at them with grave attentiveness, as if, from the perspective of distance, he were discovering something about them which he had not known.

"We have a great deal of additional evidence," said Dr. Ferris, and tossed down on the desk a photostat of the jeweler's bill for the ruby pendant. "You wouldn't care to see the sworn statements of apartment-house doormen and night clerks—they contain nothing that would be new to you, except the number of witnesses who know where you spent your nights in New York for about the last two years. You mustn't blame those people too much. It's an interesting characteristic of epochs such as ours that people begin to be afraid of saying the things they want to say—and afraid, when questioned, to remain silent about things they'd prefer never to utter. That is to be expected. But you would be astonished if you knew who gave us the original tip."

"I know it," said Rearden; his voice conveyed no reaction. The trip to Florida was not inexplicable to him any longer.

"There is nothing in this blackjack of mine that can harm you personally," said Dr. Ferris. "We knew that no form of personal injury would ever make you give in. Therefore, I am telling you frankly that this will not hurt you at all. It will only hurt Miss Taggart."

Rearden was looking straight at him now, but Dr. Ferris wondered why it seemed to him that the calm, closed face was moving away into a greater and greater distance.

"If this affair of yours is spread from one end of the country to the other," said Dr. Ferris, "by such experts in the art of smearing as Bertram Scudder, it will do no actual damage to your reputation. Beyond a few glances of curiosity and a few raised eyebrows in a few of the stuffier drawing rooms, you will get off quite easily. Affairs of this sort are expected of a man. In fact, it will enhance your reputation. It will give you an aura of romantic glamor among the women and, among the men, it will give you a certain kind of prestige, in the nature of envy for an unusual conquest. But what it will do to Miss Taggart—with her spotless name, her reputation for being above scandal, her peculiar position of a woman in a strictly masculine business—what it will do to her, what she will see in the eyes of everyone she meets, what she will hear from every man she deals with—I will leave that up to your own mind to imagine. And to consider."

Rearden felt nothing but a great stillness and a great clarity. It was as if some voice were telling him sternly: This is the time—the scene is lighted—now look. And standing naked in the great light, he was looking quietly, solemnly, stripped of fear, of pain, of hope, with nothing left to him but the desire to know.

Dr. Ferris was astonished to hear him say slowly, in the dispassionate tone of an abstract statement that did not seem to be addressed to his listener, "But all your calculations rest on the fact that Miss Taggart is a virtuous woman, not the slut you're going to call her."

"Yes, of course," said Dr. Ferris.

"And that this means much more to me than a casual affair."

"Of course."

"If she and I were the kind of scum you're going to make us appear, your blackjack wouldn't work."

"No, it wouldn't."

"If our relationship were the depravity you're going to proclaim it to be, you'd have no way to harm us."

"No."

"We'd be outside your power."

"Actually—yes."

It was not to Dr. Ferris that Rearden was speaking. He was seeing a long line of men stretched through the centuries from Plato onward, whose heir and final product was an incompetent little professor with the appearance of a gigolo and the soul of a thug.

"I offered you, once, a chance to join us," said Dr. Ferris. "You refused. Now you can see the consequences. How a man of your intelligence thought that he could win by playing it straight, I can't imagine."

"But if I had joined you," said Rearden with the same detachment, as if he were not speaking about himself, "what would I have found worth looting from Orren Boyle?"

"Oh hell, there's always enough suckers to expropriate in the world!"

"Such as Miss Taggart? As Ken Danagger? As Ellis Wyatt? As I?"

"Such as any man who wants to be impractical."

"You mean that it is not practical to live on earth, is it?"

He did not know whether Dr. Ferris answered him. He was not listening any longer. He was seeing the pendulous face of Orren Boyle with the small slits of pig's eyes, the doughy face of Mr. Mowen with the eyes that scurried away from any speaker and any fact—he was seeing them go through the jerky motions of an ape performing a routine it had learned to copy by muscular habit, performing it in order to manufacture Rearden Metal, with no knowledge and no capacity to know what had taken place in the experimental laboratory of Rearden Steel through ten years of passionate devotion to an excruciating effort. It was proper that they should now call it "Miracle Metal"—a miracle was the only name *they* could give to those ten years and to that faculty from which Rearden Metal was born—a miracle was all that the Metal could be in their eyes, the product of an unknown, unknowable cause, an object in nature, not to be explained, but to be seized, like a stone or a weed, theirs for the seizing—"are we to let the many remain in want while the few withhold from us the better products and methods available?"

If I had not known that my life depends on my mind and my effort—he was saying soundlessly to the line of men stretched through the centuries—if I had not made it my highest moral purpose to exercise the best of my effort and the fullest capacity of my mind in order to support and expand my life, you would have found nothing to loot from me, nothing to support your own existence. It is not my sins that you're using to injure me, but my virtues—my virtues by your own acknowledgment, since your own life depends on them, since you need them, since you do not seek to destroy my achievement but to seize it.

He remembered the voice of the gigolo of science saying to him: "We're after power and we mean it. You fellows were pikers, but we know the real trick." We were not after power—he said to the gigolo's ancestors-in-spirit—and we did not live by means of that which we condemned. We regarded productive ability as virtue—and we let the degree of his virtue be the measure of a man's reward. We drew no advantage from the things we regarded as evil—we did not require the existence of bank robbers in order to operate our banks, or of burglars in order to provide for our homes, or of murderers in order to protect our lives. But you need the products of a man's ability—yet you proclaim that productive ability is a selfish evil and you turn the degree of a man's productiveness into the measure of his loss. We lived by that which we held to be good and punished that which we held to be evil. You live by that which you denounce as evil and punish that which you know to be good.

He remembered the formula of the punishment that Lillian had sought to impose on him, the formula he had considered too monstrous to believe—and he saw it now in its full application, as a system of thought, as a way of life and on a world scale. There it was: the punishment that required the victim's own virtue as the fuel to make it work—his invention of Rearden Metal being used as the cause of his expropriation—Dagny's honor and the depth of their feeling for each other being used as a tool of blackmail, a blackmail from which the depraved would be immune—and, in the People's States of Europe, millions of men being held in bondage by means of their desire to live, by means of their energy drained in forced labor, by means of their ability to feed their masters, by means of the hostage system, of their love for their children or wives or friends—by means of love, ability and pleasure as the fodder for threats and the bait for extortion, with love tied to fear, ability to punishment, ambition to confiscation, with blackmail as law, with escape from pain, not quest for pleasure, as the only incentive to effort and the only reward of achievement—men held enslaved by means of whatever living power they possessed and of whatever joy they found in life. Such was the code that the world had accepted and such was the key to the code: that it hooked man's love of existence to a circuit of torture, so that only the man who had nothing to offer would have nothing to fear, so that the virtues which made life possible and the values which gave it meaning became the agents of its destruction, so that one's best became the tool of one's agony, and man's life on earth became impractical.

"Yours was the code of life," said the voice of a man whom he could not forget. "What, then, is theirs?"

Why had the world accepted it?—he thought. How had the victims come to sanction a code that pronounced them guilty of the fact of existing? . . . And then the violence of an inner blow became the total stillness of his body as he sat looking at a sudden vision: Hadn't he done it also? Hadn't he given his sanction to the code of self-damnation? Dagny—he thought—and the depth of their feeling for each other . . . the blackmail from which the depraved would be immune . . . hadn't he, too, once called it depravity? Hadn't he been first to throw at her all the insults which the human scum was now threatening to throw at her in public? Hadn't he accepted as guilt the highest happiness he had ever found?

"You who won't allow one per cent of impurity into an alloy of metal," the unforgotten voice was saying to him, "what have you allowed into your moral code?"

"Well, Mr. Rearden?" said the voice of Dr. Ferris. "Do you understand me now? Do we get the Metal or do we make a public showplace out of Miss Taggart's bedroom?"

He was not seeing Dr. Ferris. He was seeing—in the violent clarity that was like a spotlight tearing every riddle open to him—the day he met Dagny for the first time.

It was a few months after she had become Vice-President of Taggart Transcontinental. He had been hearing skeptically, for some time, the rumors that the railroad was run by Jim Taggart's sister. That summer, when he grew exasperated at Taggart's delays and contradictions over an order of rail for a new cutoff, an order which Taggart kept placing, altering and withdrawing, somebody told him that if he wished to get any sense or action out of Taggart Transcontinental, he'd better speak to Jim's sister. He telephoned her office to make an appointment and insisted on having it that same afternoon. Her secretary told him that Miss Taggart would be at the construction site of the new cutoff, that afternoon, at Milford Station between New York and Philadelphia, but would be glad to see him there if he wished. He went to the appointment resentfully; he did not like such businesswomen as he had met, and he felt that railroads were no business for a woman to play with; he expected a spoiled heiress who used her name and sex as substitute for ability, some eyebrow-plucked, overgroomed female, like the lady executives of department stores.

He got off the last car of a long train, far beyond the platform of Milford Station. There was a clutter of sidings, freight cars, cranes and steam shovels around him, descending from the main track down the slope of a ravine where men were grading the roadbed of the new cutoff. He started walking between the sidings toward the station building. Then he stopped.

He saw a girl standing on top of a pile of machinery on a flatcar. She was looking off at the ravine, her head lifted, strands of disordered hair stirring in the wind. Her plain gray suit was like a thin coating of metal over a slender body against the spread of sun-flooded space and sky. Her posture had the lightness and unself-conscious precision of an arrogantly pure self-confidence. She was watching the work, her glance intent and purposeful, the glance of competence enjoying its own function. She looked as if this were her place, her moment and her world, she looked as if enjoyment were her natural state, her face was the living form of an active, living intelligence, a young girl's face with a woman's mouth, she seemed unaware of her body except as of a taut instrument ready to serve her purpose in any manner she wished.

Had he asked himself a moment earlier whether he carried in his mind an image of what he wanted a woman to look like, he would have answered that he did not; yet, seeing her, he knew that this was the image and that it had been for years. But he was not looking at her as at a woman. He had forgotten where he was and on what errand, he was held by a child's sensation of joy in the immediate moment, by the delight of the unexpected and undiscovered, he was held by the astonishment of realizing how seldom he came upon a sight he truly liked, liked in complete acceptance and for its own sake, he was looking up at her with a faint smile, as he would have looked at a statue or a landscape, and what he felt was the sheer pleasure of the sight, the purest esthetic pleasure he had ever experienced.

He saw a switchman going by and he asked, pointing, "Who is that?"

"Dagny Taggart," said the man, walking on.

Rearden felt as if the words struck him inside his throat. He felt the start of a current that cut his breath for a moment, then went slowly down his body, carrying in its wake a sense of weight, a drained heaviness that left him no capacity but one. He was aware—with an abnormal clarity—of the place, the woman's name, and everything it implied, but all of it had receded into some outer ring and had become a pressure that left him alone in the center, as the ring's meaning and essence—and his only reality was the desire to have this woman, now, here, on top of the flatcar in the open sun—to have her before a word was spoken between them, as the first act of their meeting, because it would say everything and because they had earned it long ago.

She turned her head. In the slow curve of the movement, her eyes came to his and stopped. He felt certain that she saw the nature of his glance, that she was held by it, yet did not name it to herself. Her eyes moved on and he saw her speak to some man who stood beside the flatcar, taking notes.

Two things struck him together: his return to his normal reality, and the shattering impact of guilt. He felt a moment's approach to that which no man may feel fully and survive: a sense of self-hatred—the more terrible because some part of him refused to accept it and made him feel guiltier. It was not a progression of words, but the instantaneous verdict of an emotion, a verdict that told him: This, then, was his nature, this was his depravity—that the shameful desire he had never been able to conquer, came to him in response to the only sight of beauty he had found, that it came with a violence he had not known to be possible, and that the only freedom now left to him was to hide it and to despise himself, but never to be rid of it so long as he and this woman were alive.

He did not know how long he stood there or what devastation that span of time left within him. All that he could preserve was the will to decide that she must never know it.

He waited until she had descended to the ground and the man with the notes had departed; then he approached her and said coldly:

"Miss Taggart? I am Henry Rearden."

"Oh!" It was just a small break, then he heard the quietly natural "How do you do, Mr. Rearden."

He knew, not admitting it to himself, that the break came from some faint equivalent of his own feeling: she was glad that a face she had liked belonged to a man she could admire. When he proceeded to speak to her about business, his manner was more harshly abrupt than it had ever been with any of his masculine customers.

Now, looking from the memory of the girl on the flatcar to the Gift Certificate lying on his desk, he felt as if the two met in a single shock, fusing all the days and doubts he had lived between them, and, by the glare of the explosion, in a moment's vision of a final sum, he saw the answer to all his questions.

He thought: Guilty?—guiltier than I had known, far guiltier than I had thought, that day—guilty of the evil of damning as guilt that which was my best. I damned the fact that my mind and body were a unit, and that my body responded to the values of my mind. I damned the fact that joy is the core of existence, the motive power of every living being, that it is the need of one's body as it is the goal of one's spirit, that my body was not a weight of inanimate muscles, but an instrument able to give me an experience of superlative joy to unite my flesh and my spirit. That capacity, which I damned as shameful, had left me indifferent to sluts, but gave me my one desire in answer to a woman's greatness. That desire, which I damned as obscene, did not come from the sight of her body, but from the knowledge that the lovely form I saw, did express the spirit I was seeing— it was not her body that I wanted, but her person—it was not the girl in gray that I had to possess, but the woman who ran a railroad.

But I damned my body's capacity to express what I felt, I damned, as an affront to her, the highest tribute I could give her—just as they damn my ability to translate the work of my mind into Rearden Metal, just as they damn me for the power to transform matter to serve my needs. I accepted their code and believed, as they taught me, that the values of one's spirit must remain as an impotent longing, unexpressed in action, untranslated into reality, while the life of one's body must be lived in misery, as a senseless, degrading performance, and those who attempt to enjoy it must be branded as inferior animals.

I broke their code, but I fell into the trap they intended, the trap of a code devised to be broken. I took no pride in my rebellion, I took it as guilt, I did not damn them, I damned myself, I did not damn their code, I damned existence—and I hid my happiness as a shameful secret. I should have lived it openly, as of our right—or made her my wife, as in truth she was. But I branded my happiness as evil and made her bear it as a disgrace. What they want to do to her now, I did it first. I made it possible.

I did it—in the name of pity for the most contemptible woman I know. That, too, was their code, and I accepted it. I believed that one person owes a duty to another with no payment for it in return. I believed that it was my duty to love a woman who gave me nothing, who betrayed everything I lived for, who demanded her happiness at the price of mine. I believed that love is some static gift which, once granted, need no longer be deserved—just as they believe that wealth is a static possession which can be seized and held without further effort. I believed that love is a gratuity, not a reward to be earned—just as they believe it is their right to demand an unearned wealth. And just as they believe that their need is a claim on my energy, so I believed that her unhappiness was a claim on my life. For the sake of pity, not justice, I endured ten years of self-torture. I placed pity above my own conscience, and *this* is the core of my guilt. My crime was committed when I said to her, "By every standard of mine, to maintain our marriage will be a vicious fraud. But my standards are not yours. I do not understand yours, I never have, but I will accept them."

Here they are, lying on my desk, those standards I accepted without understanding, here is the manner of her love for me, that love which I never believed, but tried to spare. Here is the final product of the unearned. I thought that it was proper to commit injustice, so long as I would be the only one to suffer. But nothing can justify injustice. And this is the punishment for accepting as proper that hideous evil which is self-immolation. I thought that I would be the only victim. Instead, I've sacrificed the noblest woman to the vilest. When one acts on pity against justice, it is the good whom one punishes for the sake of the evil; when one saves the guilty from suffering, it is the innocent whom one forces to suffer. There is no escape from justice, nothing can be unearned and unpaid for in the universe, neither in matter nor in spirit—and if the guilty do not pay, then the innocent have to pay it.

It was not the cheap little looters of wealth who have beaten me—it was I. They did not disarm me—I threw away my weapon. This is a battle that cannot be fought except with clean hands—because the enemy's sole power is in the sores of one's conscience—and I accepted a code that made me regard the strength of my hands as a sin and a stain.

"Do we get the Metal, Mr. Rearden?"

He looked from the Gift Certificate on his desk to the memory of the girl on the flatcar. He asked himself whether he could deliver the radiant being he had seen in that moment, to the looters of the mind and the thugs of the press. Could he continue to let the innocent bear punishment? Could he let her take the stand *he* should have taken?

Could he now defy the enemy's code, when the disgrace would be hers, not his—when the muck would be thrown at her, not at him—when she would have to fight, while he'd be spared? Could he let her existence be turned into a hell he would have no way of sharing?

He sat still, looking up at her. I love you, he said to the girl on the flatcar, silently pronouncing the words that had been the meaning of that moment four years ago, feeling the solemn happiness that belonged with the words, even though this was how he had to say it to her for the first time.

He looked down at the Gift Certificate. Dagny, he thought, you would not let me do it if you knew, you will hate me for it if you learn—but I cannot let you pay my debts. The fault was mine and I will not shift to you the punishment which is mine to take. Even if I have nothing else now left to me, I have this much: that I see the truth, that I am free of their guilt, that I can now stand guiltless in my own eyes, that I know I am right, right fully and for the first time—and that I will remain faithful to the one commandment of *my* code which I have never broken: to be a man who pays his own way.

I love you, he said to the girl on the flatcar, feeling as if the light of that summer's sun were touching his forehead, as if he, too, were standing under an open sky over an unobstructed earth, with nothing left to him except himself.

"Well, Mr. Rearden? Are you going to sign?" asked Dr. Ferris.

Rearden's eyes moved to him. He had forgotten that Ferris was there, he did not know whether Ferris had been speaking, arguing or waiting in silence.

"Oh, that?" said Rearden.

He picked up a pen and with no second glance, with the easy gesture of a millionaire signing a check, he signed his name at the foot of the Statue of Liberty and pushed the Gift Certificate across the desk.

VII

THE MORATORIUM ON BRAINS

"Where have you been all this time?" Eddie Willers asked the worker in the underground cafeteria, and added, with a smile that was an appeal, an apology and a confession of despair, "Oh, I know it's I who've stayed away from here for weeks." The smile looked like the effort of a crippled child groping for a gesture that he could not perform any longer. "I did come here once, about two weeks ago, but you weren't here that night. I was afraid you'd gone . . . so many people are vanishing without notice. I hear there's hundreds of them roving around the country. The police have been arresting them for leaving their jobs—they're called deserters—but there's too many of them and no food to feed them in jail, so nobody gives a damn any more, one way or another. I hear the deserters are just wandering about, doing odd jobs or worse—who's got any odd jobs to offer these days? . . . It's our best men that we're losing, the kind who've been with the company for twenty years or more. Why did they have to chain them to their jobs? Those men never intended to quit—but now they're quitting at the slightest disagreement, just dropping their tools and walking off, any hour of the day or night, leaving us in all sorts of jams—the men who used to leap out of bed and come running if the railroad needed them. . . . You should see the kind of human driftwood we're getting to fill the vacancies. Some of them mean well, but they're scared of their own shadows. Others are the kind of scum I didn't think existed—they get the jobs and they know that we can't throw them out once they're in, so they make it clear that they don't intend to work for their pay and never did intend. They're the kind of men who *like* it—who like the way things are now. Can you imagine that there are human beings who like it? Well, there are. . . . You know, I don't think that I really believe it—all that's happening to us these days. It's happening all right, but I don't believe it. I keep thinking that insanity is a state where a person can't tell what's real. Well, what's real now is insane—and if I accepted it as real, I'd have to lose my mind, wouldn't I? . . . I go on working and I keep telling myself that this is Taggart Transcontinental. I keep waiting for her to come back—for the door to open at any moment and—oh God, I'm not supposed to say that! . . . What? You knew it? You knew that she's gone? . . . They're keeping it secret. But I guess everybody knows it, only nobody is supposed to say it. They're telling people that she's away on a leave of absence. She's still listed as our Vice-President in Charge of Operation. I think Jim and I are the only ones who know that she has resigned for good. Jim is scared to death that his friends in Washington will take it out on him, if it becomes known that she's quit. It's supposed to be disastrous for public morale, if any prominent person quits, and Jim doesn't want them to know that he's got a deserter right in his own family. . . . But that's not all. Jim is scared that the stockholders, the employees and whoever we do business with, will lose the last of their confidence in Taggart Transcontinental if they learn that she's gone. Confidence! You'd think that it wouldn't matter now, since there's nothing any of them can do about it. And yet, Jim knows that we have to preserve some semblance of the greatness that Taggart Transcontinental once stood for. And he knows that the last of it went with her. . . . No, they don't know where she is. . . . Yes, I do, but I won't tell them. I'm the only one who knows. . . . Oh yes, they've been trying to find out. They've tried to pump me in every way they could think of, but it's no use. I won't tell anyone. . . . You should see the trained seal that we now have in her place—our new Operating Vice-President. Oh sure, we have one—that is, we have and we haven't. It's like everything they do today—it is and it ain't, at the same time. His name is Clifton Locey— he's from Jim's personal staff—a bright, progressive young man of forty-seven and a friend of Jim's. He's only supposed to be pinch-hitting for her, but he sits in her office and we all know that that's the new Operating Vice-President. He gives the orders—that is, he sees to it that he's never caught actually giving an order. He works very hard at making sure that no decision can ever be pinned down on him, so that he won't be blamed for anything. You see, his purpose is not to operate a railroad, but to hold a job. He doesn't want to run trains— he wants to please Jim. He doesn't give a damn whether there's a single train moving or not, so long as he can make a good impression on Jim and on the boys in Washington. So far, Mr. Clifton Locey has managed to frame up two men: a young third assistant, for not relaying an order which Mr. Locey had never given—and the freight manager, for issuing an order which Mr. Locey *did* give, only the freight manager couldn't prove it. Both men were fired, officially, by ruling of the Unification Board. . . . When things go well—which is never longer than half an hour—Mr. Locey makes it a point to remind us that 'these are not the days of Miss Taggart.' At the first sign of trouble, he calls me into his office and asks me—casually, in the midst of the most irrelevant drivel—what Miss Taggart used to do in such an emergency. I tell him, whenever I can. I tell myself that it's Taggart Transcontinental, and . . . and there's thousands of lives on dozens of trains that hang on our decisions. Between emergencies, Mr. Locey goes out of his way to be rude to me—that's so I wouldn't think that he needs me. He's made it a point to change everything she used to do, in every respect that doesn't matter, but he's damn cautious not to change anything that matters. The only trouble is that he can't always tell which is which. . . . On his first day in her office, he told me that it wasn't a good idea to have a picture of Nat Taggart on the wall—'Nat Taggart,' he said, 'belongs to a dark past, to the age of selfish greed, he is not exactly a symbol of our modern, progressive policies, so it could make a bad impression, people could identify me with him.' 'No, they couldn't,' I said—but I took the picture off his wall. . . . What? . . . No, she doesn't know any of it. I haven't communicated with her. Not once. She told me not to. . . . Last week, I almost quit. It was over Chick's Special. Mr. Chick Morrison of Washington, whoever the hell he is, has gone on a speaking tour of the whole country—to speak about the directive and build up the people's morale, as things are getting to be pretty wild everywhere. He demanded a special train, for himself and party—a sleeper, a parlor car and a diner with barroom and lounge. The Unification Board gave him permission to travel at a hundred miles an hour—by reason, the ruling said, of this being a non-profit journey. Well, so it is. It's just a journey to talk people into continuing to break their backs at making profits in order to support men who are superior by reason of not making any. Well, our trouble came when Mr. Chick Morrison demanded a Diesel engine for his train. We had none to give him. Every Diesel we own is out on the road, pulling the Comet and the transcontinental freights, and there wasn't a spare one anywhere on the system, except—well, that was an exception I wasn't going to mention to Mr. Clifton Locey. Mr. Locey raised the roof, screaming that come hell or high water we couldn't refuse a demand of Mr. Chick Morrison. I don't know what damn fool finally told him about the extra Diesel that was kept at Winston, Colorado, at the mouth of the tunnel. You know the way our Diesels break down nowadays, they're all breathing their last—so you can understand why that extra Diesel had to be kept at the tunnel. I explained it to Mr. Locey, I threatened him, I pleaded, I told him that she had made it our strictest rule that Winston Station was never to be left without an extra Diesel. He told me to remember that he was not Miss Taggart—as if I could ever forget it!—and that the rule was nonsense, because nothing had happened all these years, so Winston could do without a Diesel for a couple of months, and he wasn't going to worry about some theoretical disaster in the future when we were up against the very real, practical, immediate disaster of getting Mr. Chick Morrison angry at us. Well, Chick's Special got the Diesel. The superintendent of the Colorado Division quit. Mr. Locey gave that job to a friend of his own. I wanted to quit. I had never wanted to so badly. But I didn't. . . . No, I haven't heard from her. I haven't heard a word since she left. Why do you keep questioning me about her? Forget it. She won't be back. . . . I don't know what it is that I'm hoping for. Nothing, I guess. I just go day by day, and I try not to look ahead. At first, I hoped that somebody would save us. I thought maybe it would be Hank Rearden. But he gave in. I don't know what they did to him to make him sign, but I know that it must have been something terrible. Everybody thinks so. Everybody's whispering about it, wondering what sort of pressure was used on him. . . . No, nobody knows. He's made no public statements and he's refused to see anyone. . . . But, listen, I'll tell you something else that everybody's whispering about. Lean closer, will you?—I don't want to speak too loudly. They say that Orren Boyle seems to have known about that directive long ago, weeks or months in advance, because he had started, quietly and secretly, to reconstruct his furnaces for the production of Rearden Metal, in one of his lesser steel plants, an obscure little place way out on the coast of Maine. He was ready to start pouring the Metal the moment Rearden's extortion paper—I mean, Gift Certificate—was signed. But—listen—the night before they were to start, Boyle's men were heating the furnaces in that place on the coast, when they heard a voice, they didn't know whether it came from a plane or a radio or some sort of loud-speaker, but it was a man's voice and it said that he would give them ten minutes to get out of the place. They got out. They started going and they kept on going—because the man's voice had said that he was Ragnar Danneskjöld. In the next half-hour, Boyle's mills were razed to the ground. Razed, wiped out, not a brick of them left standing. They say it was done by long-range naval guns, from somewhere way out on the Atlantic. Nobody saw Danneskjöld's ship. . . . That's what people are whispering. The newspapers haven't printed a word about it. The boys in Washington say that it's only a rumor spread by panic-mongers. . . . I don't know whether the story is true. I think it is. I *hope* it is. . . . You know, when I was fifteen years old, I used to wonder how any man could become a criminal, I couldn't understand what would make it possible. Now—now I'm glad that Ragnar Danneskjöld has blown up those mills. May God bless him and never let them find him, whatever and wherever he is! . . . Yes, that's what I've come to feel. Well, how much do they think people can take? . . . It's not so bad for me in the daytime, because I can keep busy and not think, but it gets me at night. I can't sleep any more, I lie awake for hours. . . . Yes!—if you want to know it—yes, it's because I'm worried about her! I'm scared to death for her. Woodstock is just a miserable little hole of a place, miles away from everything, and the Taggart lodge is twenty miles farther, twenty miles of a twisting trail in a godforsaken forest. How do I know what might happen to her there, alone, and with the kind of gangs that are roving all through the country these nights—just through such desolate parts of the country as the Berkshires? . . . I know I shouldn't think about it. I know that she can take care of herself. Only I wish she'd drop me a line. I wish I could go there. But she told me not to. I told her I'd wait. . . . You know, I'm glad you're here tonight. It helps me—talking to you and . . . just seeing you here. You won't vanish, like all the others, will you? . . . What? Next week? . . . Oh, on your vacation. For how long? . . . How do you rate a whole month's vacation? . . . I wish I could do that, too—take a month off at my own expense. But they wouldn't let me. . . . Really? I envy you. . . . I wouldn't have envied you a few years ago. But now—now I'd like to get away. Now I envy you—if you've been able to take a month off every summer for twelve years."

* * *

It was a dark road, but it led in a new direction. Rearden walked from his mills, not toward his house, but toward the city of Philadelphia. It was a great distance to walk, but he had wanted to do it tonight, as he had done it every evening of the past week. He felt at peace in the empty darkness of the countryside, with nothing but the black shapes of trees around him, with no motion but that of his own body and of branches stirring in the wind, with no lights but the slow sparks of the fireflies flickering through the hedges. The two hours between mills and city were his span of rest.

He had moved out of his home to an apartment in Philadelphia. He had given no explanation to his mother and Philip, he had said nothing except that they could remain in the house if they wished and that Miss Ives would take care of their bills. He had asked them to tell Lillian, when she returned, that she was not to attempt to see him. They had stared at him in terrified silence.

He had handed to his attorney a signed blank check and said, "Get me a divorce. On any grounds and at any cost. I don't care what means you use, how many of their judges you purchase or whether you find it necessary to stage a frame-up of my wife. Do whatever you wish. But there is to be no alimony and no property settlement." The attorney had looked at him with the hint of a wise, sad smile, as if this were an event he had expected to happen long ago. He had answered, "Okay, Hank. It can be done. But it will take some time." "Make it as fast as you can."

No one had questioned him about his signature on the Gift Certificate. But he had noticed that the men at the mills looked at him with a kind of searching curiosity, almost as if they expected to find the scars of some physical torture on his body.

He felt nothing—nothing but the sense of an even, restful twilight, like a spread of slag over a molten metal, when it crusts and swallows the last brilliant spurt of the white glow within. He felt nothing at the thought of the looters who were now going to manufacture Rearden Metal. His desire to hold his right to it and proudly to be the only one to sell it, had been his form of respect for his fellow men, his belief that to trade with them was an act of honor. The belief, the respect and the desire were gone. He did not care what men made, what they sold, where they bought his Metal or whether any of them would know that it had been his. The human shapes moving past him in the streets of the city were physical objects without any meaning. The countryside —with the darkness washing away all traces of human activity, leaving only an untouched earth which he had once been able to handle—was real.

He carried a gun in his pocket, as advised by the policemen of the radio car that patrolled the roads; they had warned him that no road was safe after dark, these days. He felt, with a touch of mirthless amusement, that the gun had been needed at the mills, not in the peaceful safety of loneliness and night; what could some starving vagrant take from him, compared to what had been taken by men who claimed to be his protectors?

He walked with an effortless speed, feeling relaxed by a form of activity that was natural to him. This was his period of training for solitude, he thought; he had to learn to live without any awareness of people, the awareness that now paralyzed him with revulsion. He had once built his fortune, starting out with empty hands; now he had to rebuild his life, starting out with an empty spirit.

He would give himself a short span of time for the training, he thought, and then he would claim the one incomparable value still left to him, the one desire that had remained pure and whole: he would go to Dagny. Two commandments had grown in his mind; one was a duty, the other a passionate wish. The first was never to let her learn the reason of his surrender to the looters; the second was to say to her the words which he should have known at their first meeting and should have said on the gallery of Ellis Wyatt's house.

There was nothing but the strong summer starlight to guide him, as he walked, but he could distinguish the highway and the remnant of a stone fence ahead, at the corner of a country crossroad. The fence had nothing to protect any longer, only a spread of weeds, a willow tree bending over the road and, farther in the distance, the ruin of a farmhouse with the starlight showing through its roof.

He walked, thinking that even this sight still retained the power to be of value: it gave him the promise of a long stretch of space undisturbed by human intrusion.

The man who stepped suddenly out into the road must have come from behind the willow tree, but so swiftly that it seemed as if he had sprung up from the middle of the highway. Rearden's hand went to the gun in his pocket, but stopped: he knew—by the proud posture of the body standing in the open, by the straight line of the shoulders against the starlit sky—that the man was not a bandit. When he heard the voice, he knew that the man was not a beggar.

"I should like to speak to you, Mr. Rearden."

The voice had the firmness, the clarity and the special courtesy peculiar to men who are accustomed to giving orders.

"Go ahead," said Rearden, "provided you don't intend to ask me for help or money."

The man's garments were rough, but efficiently trim. He wore dark trousers and a dark blue windbreaker closed tight at his throat, prolonging the lines of his long, slender figure. He wore a dark blue cap, and all that could be seen of him in the night were his hands, his face and a patch of gold-blond hair on his temple. The hands held no weapon, only a package wrapped in burlap, the size of a carton of cigarettes.

"No, Mr. Rearden," he said, "I don't intend to ask you for money, but to return it to you."

"To return money?"

"Yes."

"What money?"

"A small refund on a very large debt."

"Owed by you?"

"No, not by me. It is only a token payment, but I want you to accept it as proof that if we live long enough, you and I, every dollar of that debt will be returned to you."

"What debt?"

"The money that was taken from you by force."

He extended the package to Rearden, flipping the burlap open. Rearden saw the starlight run like fire along a mirror-smooth surface. He knew, by its weight and texture, that what he held was a bar of solid gold.

He looked from the bar to the man's face, but the face seemed harder and less revealing than the surface of the metal.

"Who are you?" asked Rearden.

"The friend of the friendless."

"Did you come here to give this to me?"

"Yes."

"Do you mean that you had to stalk me at night, on a lonely road, in order, not to rob me, but to hand me a bar of gold?"

"Yes."

"Why?"

"When robbery is done in open daylight by sanction of the law, as it is done today, then any act of honor or restitution has to be hidden underground."

"What made you think that I'd accept a gift of this kind?"

"It is not a gift, Mr. Rearden. It is your own money. But I have one favor to ask of you. It is a request, not a condition, because there can be no such thing as conditional property. The gold is yours, so you are free to use it as you please. But I risked my life to bring it to you tonight, so I am asking, as a favor, that you save it for the future or spend it on yourself. On nothing but your own comfort and pleasure. Do not give it away and, above all, do not put it into your business."

"Why?"

"Because I don't want it to be of any benefit to anybody but you. Otherwise, I will have broken an oath taken long ago—as I am breaking every rule I had set for myself by speaking to you tonight."

"What do you mean?"

"I have been collecting this money for you for a long time. But I did not intend to see you or tell you about it or give it to you until much later."

"Then why did you?"

"Because I couldn't stand it any longer."

"Stand what?"

"I thought that I had seen everything one could see and that there was nothing I could not stand seeing. But when they took Rearden Metal away from you, it was too much, even for me. I know that you don't need this gold at present. What you need is the justice which it represents, and the knowledge that there are men who care for justice."

Struggling not to give in to an emotion which he felt rising through his bewilderment, past all his doubts, Rearden tried to study the man's face, searching for some clue to help him understand. But the face had no expression; it had not changed once while speaking; it looked as if the man had lost the capacity to feel long ago, and what remained of him were only features that seemed implacable and dead. With a shudder of astonishment, Rearden found himself thinking that it was not the face of a man, but of an avenging angel.

"Why did you care?" asked Rearden. "What do I mean to you?"

"Much more than you have reason to suspect. And I have a friend to whom you mean much more than you will ever learn. He would have given anything to stand by you today. But he can't come to you. So I came in his place."

"What friend?"

"I prefer not to name him."

"Did you say that you've spent a long time collecting this money for me?"

"I have collected much more than this." He pointed at the gold. "I am holding it in your name and I will turn it over to you when the time comes. This is only a sample, as proof that it does exist. And if you reach the day when you find yourself robbed of the last of your fortune, I want you to remember that you have a large bank account waiting for you."

"What account?"

"If you try to think of all the money that has been taken from you by force, you will know that your account represents a considerable sum."

"How did you collect it? Where did this gold come from?"

"It was taken from those who robbed you."

"Taken by whom?"

"By me."

"Who are you?"

"Ragnar Danneskjöld."

Rearden looked at him for a long, still moment, then let the gold fall out of his hands.

Danneskjöld's eyes did not follow it to the ground, but remained fixed on Rearden with no change of expression. "Would you rather I were a law-abiding citizen, Mr. Rearden? If so, which law should I abide by? Directive 10-289?"

"Ragnar Danneskjöld . . ." said Rearden, as if he were seeing the whole of the past decade, as if he were looking at the enormity of a crime spread through ten years and held within two words.

"Look more carefully, Mr. Rearden. There are only two modes of living left to us today: to be a looter who robs disarmed victims or to be a victim who works for the benefit of his own despoilers. I did not choose to be either."

"You chose to live by means of force, like the rest of them."

"Yes—openly. Honestly, if you will. I do not rob men who are tied and gagged, I do not demand that my victims help me, I do not tell them that I am acting for their own good. I stake my life in every encounter with men, and they have a chance to match their guns and their brains against mine in fair battle. Fair? It's I against the organized strength, the guns, the planes, the battleships of five continents. If it's a moral judgment that you wish to pronounce, Mr. Rearden, then who is the man of higher morality: I or Wesley Mouch?"

"I have no answer to give you," said Rearden, his voice low.

"Why should you be shocked, Mr. Rearden? I am merely complying with the system which my fellow men have established. If they believe that force is the proper means to deal with one another, I am giving them what they ask for. If they believe that the purpose of my life is to serve them, let them try to enforce their creed. If they believe that my mind is their property—let them come and get it."

"But what sort of life have you chosen? To what purpose are you giving your mind?"

"To the cause of my love."

"Which is what?"

"Justice."

"Served by being a pirate?"

"By working for the day when I won't have to be a pirate any longer."

"Which day is that?"

"The day when you'll be free to make a profit on Rearden Metal."

"Oh God!" said Rearden, laughing, his voice desperate. "Is that your ambition?"

Danneskjöld's face did not change. "It is."

"Do you expect to live to see that day?"

"Yes. Don't you?"

"No."

"Then what are you looking forward to, Mr. Rearden?"

"Nothing."

"What are you working for?"

Rearden glanced at him. "Why do you ask that?"

"To make you understand why I'm not."

"Don't expect me ever to approve of a criminal."

"I don't expect it. But there are a few things I want to help you to see."

"Even if they're true, the things you said, why did you choose to be a bandit? Why didn't you simply step out, like—" He stopped.

"Like Ellis Wyatt, Mr. Rearden? Like Andrew Stockton? Like your friend Ken Danagger?"

"Yes!"

"Would you approve of that?"

"I—" He stopped, shocked by his own words.

The shock that came next was to see Danneskjöld smile: it was like seeing the first green of spring on the sculptured planes of an iceberg. Rearden realized suddenly, for the first time, that Danneskjöld's face was more than handsome, that it had the startling beauty of physical perfection—the hard, proud features, the scornful mouth of a Viking's statue—yet he had not been aware of it, almost as if the dead sternness of the face had forbidden the impertinence of an appraisal. But the smile was brilliantly alive.

"I do approve of it, Mr. Rearden. But I've chosen a special mission of my own. I'm after a man whom I want to destroy. He died many centuries ago, but until the last trace of him is wiped out of men's minds, we will not have a decent world to live in."

"What man?"

"Robin Hood."

Rearden looked at him blankly, not understanding.

"He was the man who robbed the rich and gave to the poor. Well, I'm the man who robs the poor and gives to the rich—or, to be exact, the man who robs the thieving poor and gives back to the productive rich."

"What in blazes do you mean?"

"If you remember the stories you've read about me in the newspapers, before they stopped printing them, you know that I have never robbed a private ship and never taken any private property. Nor have I ever robbed a military vessel—because the purpose of a military fleet is to protect from violence the citizens who paid for it, which is the proper function of a government. But I have seized every loot-carrier that came within range of my guns, every government relief ship, subsidy ship, loan ship, gift ship, every vessel with a cargo of goods taken by force from some men for the unpaid, unearned benefit of others. I seized the boats that sailed under the flag of the idea which I am fighting: the idea that need is a sacred idol requiring human sacrifices—that the need of some men is the knife of a guillotine hanging over others—that all of us must live with our work, our hopes, our plans, our efforts at the mercy of the moment when that knife will descend upon us—and that the extent of our ability is the extent of our danger, so that success will bring our heads down on the block, while failure will give us the right to pull the cord. This is the horror which Robin Hood immortalized as an ideal of righteousness. It is said that he fought against the looting rulers and returned the loot to those who had been robbed, but that is not the meaning of the legend which has survived. He is remembered, not as a champion of *property,* but as a champion of *need,* not as a defender of the *robbed,* but as a provider of the *poor.* He is held to be the first man who assumed a halo of virtue by practicing charity with wealth which he did not own, by giving away goods which he had not produced, by making others pay for the luxury of his pity. He is the man who became the symbol of the idea that need, not achievement, is the source of rights, that we don't have to produce, only to want, that the earned does not belong to us, but the unearned does. He became a justification for every mediocrity who, unable to make his own living, has demanded the power to dispose of the property of his betters, by proclaiming his willingness to devote his life to his inferiors at the price of robbing his superiors. It is this foulest of creatures—the double-parasite who lives on the sores of the poor and the blood of the rich—whom men have come to regard as a moral ideal. And this has brought us to a world where the more a man produces, the closer he comes to the loss of all his rights, until, if his ability is great enough, he becomes a rightless creature delivered as prey to any claimant—while in order to be placed above rights, above principles, above morality, placed where anything is permitted to him, even plunder and murder, all a man has to do is to be in need. Do you wonder why the world is collapsing around us? That is what I am fighting, Mr. Rearden. Until men learn that of all human symbols, Robin Hood is the most immoral and the most contemptible, there will be no justice on earth and no way for mankind to survive."

Rearden listened, feeling numb. But under the numbness, like the first thrust of a seed breaking through, he felt an emotion he could not identify except that it seemed familiar and very distant, like something experienced and renounced long ago.

"What I actually am, Mr. Rearden, is a policeman. It is a policeman's duty to protect men from criminals—criminals being those who seize wealth by force. It is a policeman's duty to retrieve stolen property and return it to its owners. But when robbery becomes the purpose of the law, and the policeman's duty becomes, not the protection, but the plunder of property—then it is an outlaw who has to become a policeman. I have been selling the cargoes I retrieved to some special customers of mine in this country, who pay me in gold. Also, I have been selling my cargoes to the smugglers and the black-market traders of the People's States of Europe. Do you know the conditions of existence in those People's States? Since production and trade—not violence—were decreed to be crimes, the best men of Europe had no choice but to become criminals. The slave-drivers of those States are kept in power by the handouts from their fellow looters in countries not yet fully drained, such as this country. I do not let the handouts reach them. I sell the goods to Europe's law-breakers, at the highest prices I can get, and I make them pay me in gold. Gold is the objective value, the means of preserving one's wealth and one's future. Nobody is permitted to have gold in Europe, except the whip-wielding friends of humanity, who claim that they spend it for the welfare of their victims. That is the gold which my smuggler-customers obtain to pay me. How? By the same method I use to obtain the goods. And then I return the gold to those from whom the goods were stolen—to you, Mr. Rearden, and to other men like you."

Rearden grasped the nature of the emotion he had forgotten. It was the emotion he had felt when, at the age of fourteen, he had looked at his first pay check—when, at the age of twenty-four, he had been made superintendent of the ore mines—when, as the owner of the mines, he had placed, in his own name, his first order for new equipment from the best concern of the time, Twentieth Century Motors—an emotion of solemn, joyous excitement, the sense of winning his place in a world he respected and earning the recognition of men he admired. For almost two decades, that emotion had been buried under a mount of wreckage, as the years had added layer upon gray layer of contempt, of indignation, of his struggle not to look around him, not to see those he dealt with, not to expect anything from men and to keep, as a private vision within the four walls of his office, the sense of that world into which he had hoped to rise. Yet there it was again, breaking through from under the wreckage, that feeling of quickened interest, of listening to the luminous voice of reason, with which one could communicate and deal and live. But it was the voice of a pirate speaking about acts of violence, offering him this substitute for his world of reason and justice. He could not accept it; he could not lose whatever remnant of his vision he still retained. He listened, wishing he could escape, yet knowing that he would not miss a word of it.

"I deposit the gold in a bank—in a gold-standard bank, Mr. Rearden —to the account of men who are its rightful owners. They are the men of superlative ability who made their fortunes by personal effort, in free trade, using no compulsion, no help from the government. They are the great victims who have contributed the most and suffered the worst injustice in return. Their names are written in my book of restitution. Every load of gold which I bring back is divided among them and deposited to their accounts."

"Who are they?"

"You're one of them, Mr. Rearden. I cannot compute all the money that has been extorted from you—in hidden taxes, in regulations, in wasted time, in lost effort, in energy spent to overcome artificial obstacles. I cannot compute the sum, but if you wish to see its magnitude —look around you. The extent of the misery now spreading through this once prosperous country is the extent of the injustice which you have suffered. If men refuse to pay the debt they owe you, this is the manner in which they will pay for it. But there is one part of the debt which is computed and on record. That is the part which I have made it my purpose to collect and return to you."

"What is that?"

"Your income tax, Mr. Rearden."

"What?"

"Your income tax for the last twelve years."

"You intend to refund *that?*"

"In full and in gold, Mr. Rearden."

Rearden burst out laughing; he laughed like a young boy, in simple amusement, in enjoyment of the incredible. "Good God! You're a policeman and a collector of Internal Revenue, too?"

"Yes," said Danneskjöld gravely.

"You're not serious about this, are you?"

"Do I look as if I'm joking?"

"But this is preposterous!"

"Any more preposterous than Directive 10-289?"

"It's not real or possible!"

"Is only evil real and possible?"

"But—"

"Are you thinking that death and taxes are our only certainty, Mr. Rearden? Well, there's nothing I can do about the first, but if I lift the burden of the second, men might learn to see the connection between the two and what a longer, happier life they have the power to achieve. They might learn to hold, not death and taxes, but life and production as their two absolutes and as the base of their moral code."

Rearden looked at him, not smiling. The tall, slim figure, with the windbreaker stressing its trained muscular agility, was that of a highwayman; the stern marble face was that of a judge; the dry, clear voice was that of an efficient bookkeeper.

"The looters are not the only ones who have kept records on you, Mr. Rearden. So have I. I have, in my files, copies of all your income tax returns for the last twelve years, as well as the returns of all my other clients. I have friends in some astonishing places, who obtain the copies I need. I divide the money among my clients in proportion to the sums extorted from them. Most of my accounts have now been paid to their owners. Yours is the largest one left to settle. On the day when you will be ready to claim it—the day when I'll know that no penny of it will go back to support the looters—I will turn your account over to you. Until then—" He glanced down at the gold on the ground. "Pick it up, Mr. Rearden. It's not stolen. It's yours."

Rearden would not move or answer or look down.

"Much more than that lies in the bank, in your name."

"What bank?"

"Do you remember Midas Mulligan of Chicago?"

"Yes, of course."

"All my accounts are deposited at the Mulligan Bank."

"There is no Mulligan Bank in Chicago."

"It is not in Chicago."

Rearden let a moment pass. "Where is it?"

"I think that you will know it before long, Mr. Rearden. But I cannot tell you now." He added, "I must tell you, however, that I am the only one responsible for this undertaking. It is my own personal mission. No one is involved in it but me and the men of my ship's crew. Even my banker has no part in it, except for keeping the money I deposit. Many of my friends do not approve of the course I've chosen. But we all choose different ways to fight the same battle—and this is mine."

Rearden smiled contemptuously. "Aren't you one of those damn altruists who spends his time on a non-profit venture and risks his life merely to serve others?"

"No, Mr. Rearden. I am investing my time in my own future. When we are free and have to start rebuilding from out of the ruins, I want to see the world reborn as fast as possible. If there is, then, some working capital in the right hands—in the hands of our best, our most productive men—it will save years for the rest of us and, incidentally, centuries for the history of the country. Did you ask what you meant to me? Everything I admire, everything I want to be on the day when the earth will have a place for such state of being, everything I want to deal with—even if this is the only way I can deal with you and be of use to you at present."

"Why?" whispered Rearden.

"Because my only love, the only value I care to live for, is that which has never been loved by the world, has never won recognition or friends or defenders: human ability. That is the love I am serving—and if I should lose my life, to what better purpose could I give it?"

The man who had lost the capacity to feel?—thought Rearden, and knew that the austerity of the marble face was the form of a disciplined capacity to feel too deeply. The even voice was continuing dispassionately:

"I wanted you to know this. I wanted you to know it now, when it must seem to you that you're abandoned at the bottom of a pit among subhuman creatures who are all that's left of mankind. I wanted you to know, in your most hopeless hour, that the day of deliverance is much closer than you think. And there was one special reason why I had to speak to you and tell you my secret ahead of the proper time. Have you heard of what happened to Orren Boyle's steel mills on the coast of Maine?"

"Yes," said Rearden—and was shocked to hear that the word came as a gasp out of the sudden jolt of eagerness within him. "I didn't know whether it was true."

"It's true. I did it. Mr. Boyle is not going to manufacture Rearden Metal on the coast of Maine. He is not going to manufacture it anywhere. Neither is any other looting louse who thinks that a directive can give him a right to your brain. Whoever attempts to produce that Metal, will find his furnaces blown up, his machinery blasted, his shipments wrecked, his plant set on fire—so many things will happen to any man who tries it, that people will say there's a curse on it, and there will soon be no worker in the country willing to enter the plant of any new producer of Rearden Metal. If men like Boyle think that force is all they need to rob their betters—let them see what happens when one of their betters chooses to resort to force. I wanted you to know, Mr. Rearden, that none of them will produce your Metal nor make a penny on it."

Because he felt an exultant desire to laugh—as he had laughed at the news of Wyatt's fire, as he had laughed at the crash of d'Anconia Copper—and knew that if he did, the thing he feared would hold him, would not release him this time, and he would never see his mills again—Rearden drew back and, for a moment, kept his lips closed tight to utter no sound. When the moment was over, he said quietly, his voice firm and dead, "Take that gold of yours and get away from here. I won't accept the help of a criminal."

Danneskjöld's face showed no reaction. "I cannot force you to accept the gold, Mr. Rearden. But I will not take it back. You may leave it lying where it is, if you wish."

"I don't want your help and I don't intend to protect you. If I were within reach of a phone, I would call the police. I would and I will, if you ever attempt to approach me again. I'll do it—in self-protection."

"I understand exactly what you mean."

"You know—because I've listened to you, because you've seen me eager to hear it—that I haven't damned you as I should. I can't damn you or anyone else. There are no standards left for men to live by, so I don't care to judge anything they do today or in what manner they attempt to endure the unendurable. If this is your manner, I will let you go to hell in your own way, but I want no part of it. Neither as your inspiration nor as your accomplice. Don't expect me ever to accept your bank account, if it does exist. Spend it on some extra armor plate for yourself—because I'm going to report this to the police and give them every clue I can to set them on your trail."

Danneskjöld did not move or answer. A freight train was rolling by, somewhere in the distance and darkness; they could not see it, but they heard the pounding beat of wheels filling the silence, and it seemed close, as if a disembodied train, reduced to a long string of sound, were going past them in the night.

"You wanted to help me in my most hopeless hour?" said Rearden. "If I am brought to where my only defender is a pirate, then I don't care to be defended any longer. You speak some remnant of a human language, so in the name of that, I'll tell you that I have no hope left, but I have the knowledge that when the end comes, I will have lived by my own standards, even while I was the only one to whom they remained valid. I will have lived in the world in which I started and I will go down with the last of it. I don't think you'll want to understand me, but—"

A beam of light hit them with the violence of a physical blow. The clangor of the train had swallowed the noise of the motor and they had not heard the approach of the car that swept out of the side road, from behind the farmhouse. They were not in the car's path, yet they heard the screech of brakes behind the two headlights, pulling an invisible shape to a stop. It was Rearden who jumped back involuntarily and had time to marvel at his companion: the swiftness of Danneskjöld's self-control was that he did not move.

It was a police car and it stopped beside them.

The driver leaned out. "Oh, it's you, Mr. Rearden!" he said, touching his fingers to his cap. "Good evening, sir."

"Hello," said Rearden, fighting to control the unnatural abruptness of his voice.

There were two patrolmen in the front seat of the car and their faces had a tight look of purpose, not the look of their usual friendly intention to stop for a chat.

"Mr. Rearden, did you walk from the mills by way of Edgewood Road, past Blacksmith Cove?"

"Yes. Why?"

"Did you happen to see a man anywhere around these parts, a stranger moving along in a hurry?"

"Where?"

"He'd be either on foot or in a battered wreck of a car that's got a million-dollar motor."

"What man?"

"A tall man with blond hair."

"Who is he?"

"You wouldn't believe it if I told you, Mr. Rearden. Did you see him?"

Rearden was not aware of his own questions, only of the astonishing fact that he was able to force sounds past some beating barrier inside his throat. He was looking straight at the policeman, but he felt as if the focus of his eyes had switched to his side vision, and what he saw most clearly was Danneskjöld's face watching him with no expression, with no line's, no muscle's worth of feeling. He saw Danneskjöld's arms hanging idly by his sides, the hands relaxed, with no sign of intention to reach for a weapon, leaving the tall, straight body defenseless and open—open as to a firing squad. He saw, in the light, that the face looked younger than he had thought and that the eyes were sky-blue. He felt that his one danger would be to glance directly at Danneskjöld—and he kept his eyes on the policeman, on the brass buttons of a blue uniform, but the object filling his consciousness, more forcefully than a visual perception, was Danneskjöld's body, the naked body under the clothes, the body that would be wiped out of existence. He did not hear his own words, because he kept hearing a single sentence in his mind, without context except the feeling that it was the only thing that mattered to him in the world: "If I should lose my life, to what better purpose could I give it?"

"Did you see him, Mr. Rearden?"

"No," said Rearden. "I didn't."

The policeman shrugged regretfully and closed his hands about the steering wheel. "You didn't see any man that looked suspicious?"

"No."

"Nor any strange car passing you on the road?"

"No."

The policeman reached for the starter. "They got word that he was seen ashore in these parts tonight, and they've thrown a dragnet over five counties. We're not supposed to mention his name, not to scare the folks, but he's a man whose head is worth three million dollars in rewards from all over the world."

He had pressed the starter and the motor was churning the air with bright cracks of sound, when the second policeman leaned forward. He had been looking at the blond hair under Danneskjöld's cap.

"Who is that, Mr. Rearden?" he asked.

"My new bodyguard," said Rearden.

"Oh . . . ! A sensible precaution, Mr. Rearden, in times like these. Good night, sir."

The motor jerked forward. The red taillights of the car went shrinking down the road. Danneskjöld watched it go, then glanced pointedly at Rearden's right hand. Rearden realized that he had stood facing the policemen with his hand clutching the gun in his pocket and that he had been prepared to use it.

He opened his fingers and drew his hand out hastily. Danneskjöld smiled. It was a smile of radiant amusement, the silent laughter of a clear, young spirit greeting a moment it was glad to have lived.

And although the two did not resemble each other, the smile made Rearden think of Francisco d'Anconia.

"You haven't told a lie," said Ragnar Danneskjöld. "Your body-guard—that's what I am and what I'll deserve to be, in many more ways than you can know at present. Thanks, Mr. Rearden, and so long—we'll meet again much sooner than I had hoped."

He was gone before Rearden could answer. He vanished beyond the stone fence, as abruptly and soundlessly as he had come. When Rearden turned to look through the farm field, there was no trace of him and no sign of movement anywhere in the darkness.

Rearden stood on the edge of an empty road in a spread of loneliness vaster than it had seemed before. Then he saw, lying at his feet, an object wrapped in burlap, with one corner exposed and glistening in the moonlight, the color of the pirate's hair. He bent, picked it up and walked on.

* * *

Kip Chalmers swore as the train lurched and spilled his cocktail over the table top. He slumped forward, his elbow in the puddle, and said:

"God damn these railroads! What's the matter with their track? You'd think with all the money they've got they'd disgorge a little, so we wouldn't have to bump like farmers on a hay cart!"

His three companions did not take the trouble to answer. It was late, and they remained in the lounge merely because an effort was needed to retire to their compartments. The lights of the lounge looked like feeble portholes in a fog of cigarette smoke dank with the odor of alcohol. It was a private car, which Chalmers had demanded and obtained for his journey; it was attached to the end of the Comet and it swung like the tail of a nervous animal as the Comet coiled through the curves of the mountains.

"I'm going to campaign for the nationalization of the railroads," said Kip Chalmers, glaring defiantly at a small, gray man who looked at him without interest. "That's going to be my platform plank. I've got to have a platform plank. I don't like Jim Taggart. He looks like a soft-boiled clam. To hell with the railroads! It's time we took them over."

"Go to bed," said the man, "if you expect to look like anything human at the big rally tomorrow."

"Do you think we'll make it?"

"You've got to make it."

"I know I've got to. But I don't think we'll get there on time. This goddamn snail of a super-special is hours late."

"You've *got* to get there, Kip," said the man ominously, in that stubborn monotone of the unthinking which asserts an end without concern for the means.

"God damn you, don't you suppose I know it?"

Kip Chalmers had curly blond hair and a shapeless mouth. He came from a semi-wealthy, semi-distinguished family, but he sneered at wealth and distinction in a manner which implied that only a top-rank aristocrat could permit himself such a degree of cynical indifference. He had graduated from a college which specialized in breeding that kind of aristocracy. The college had taught him that the purpose of ideas is to fool those who are stupid enough to think. He had made his way in Washington with the grace of a cat-burglar, climbing from bureau to bureau as from ledge to ledge of a crumbling structure. He was ranked as semi-powerful, but his manner made laymen mistake him for nothing less than Wesley Mouch.

For reasons of his own particular strategy, Kip Chalmers had decided to enter popular politics and to run for election as Legislator from California, though he knew nothing about that state except the movie industry and the beach clubs. His campaign manager had done the preliminary work, and Chalmers was now on his way to face his future constituents for the first time at an overpublicized rally in San Francisco tomorrow night. The manager had wanted him to start a day earlier, but Chalmers had stayed in Washington to attend a cocktail party and had taken the last train possible. He had shown no concern about the rally until this evening, when he noticed that the Comet was running six hours late.

His three companions did not mind his mood: they liked his liquor. Lester Tuck, his campaign manager, was a small, aging man with a face that looked as if it had once been punched in and had never rebounded. He was an attorney who, some generations earlier, would have represented shoplifters and people who stage accidents on the premises of rich corporations; now he found that he could do better by representing men like Kip Chalmers.

Laura Bradford was Chalmers' current mistress; he liked her because his predecessor had been Wesley Mouch. She was a movie actress who had forced her way from competent featured player to incompetent star, not by means of sleeping with studio executives, but by taking the long-distance short cut of sleeping with bureaucrats. She talked economics, instead of glamor, for press interviews, in the belligerently righteous style of a third-rate tabloid; her economics consisted of the assertion that "we've got to help the poor."

Gilbert Keith-Worthing was Chalmers' guest, for no reason that either of them could discover. He was a British novelist of world fame, who had been popular thirty years ago; since then, nobody bothered to read what he wrote, but everybody accepted him as a walking classic. He had been considered profound for uttering such things as: "Freedom? Do let's stop talking about freedom. Freedom is impossible. Man can never be free of hunger, of cold, of disease, of physical accidents. He can never be free of the tyranny of nature. So why should he object to the tyranny of a political dictatorship?" When all of Europe put into practice the ideas which he had preached, he came to live in America. Through the years, his style of writing and his body had grown flabby. At seventy, he was an obese old man with retouched hair and a manner of scornful cynicism retouched by quotations from the yogis about the futility of all human endeavor. Kip Chalmers had invited him, because it seemed to look distinguished. Gilbert Keith-Worthing had come along, because he had no particular place to go.

"God damn these railroad people!" said Kip Chalmers. "They're doing it on purpose. They want to ruin my campaign. I can't miss that rally! For Christ's sake, Lester, do something!"

"I've tried," said Lester Tuck. At the train's last stop, he had tried, by long-distance telephone, to find air transportation to complete their journey; but there were no commercial flights scheduled for the next two days.

"If they don't get me there on time, I'll have their scalps and their railroad! Can't we tell that damn conductor to hurry?"

"You've told him three times."

"I'll get him fired. He's given me nothing but a lot of alibis about all their messy technical troubles. I expect transportation, not alibis. They can't treat me like one of their day-coach passengers. I expect them to get me where I want to go when I want it. Don't they know that I'm on this train?"

"They know it by now," said Laura Bradford. "Shut up, Kip. You bore me."

Chalmers refilled his glass. The car was rocking and the glassware tinkled faintly on the shelves of the bar. The patches of starlit sky in the windows kept swaying jerkily, and it seemed as if the stars were tinkling against one another. They could see nothing beyond the glass bay of the observation window at the end of the car, except the small halos of red and green lanterns marking the rear of the train, and a brief stretch of rail running away from them into the darkness. A wall of rock was racing the train, and the stars dipped occasionally into a sudden break that outlined, high above them, the peaks of the mountains of Colorado.

"Mountains . . ." said Gilbert Keith-Worthing, with satisfaction. "It is a spectacle of this kind that makes one feel the insignificance of man. What is this presumptuous little bit of rail, which crude materialists are so proud of building—compared to that eternal grandeur? No more than the basting thread of a seamstress on the hem of the garment of nature. If a single one of those granite giants chose to crumble, it would annihilate this train."

"Why should it choose to crumble?" asked Laura Bradford, without any particular interest.

"I think this damn train is going slower," said Kip Chalmers. "Those bastards are slowing down, in spite of what I told them!"

"Well . . . it's the mountains, you know . . ." said Lester Tuck.

"Mountains be damned! Lester, what day is this? With all those damn changes of time, I can't tell which—"

"It's May twenty-seventh," sighed Lester Tuck.

"It's May twenty-eighth," said Gilbert Keith-Worthing, glancing at his watch. "It is now twelve minutes past midnight."

"Jesus!" cried Chalmers. "Then the rally is *today?*"

"Yep," said Lester Tuck.

"We won't make it! We—"

The train gave a sharper lurch, knocking the glass out of his hand. The thin sound of its crash against the floor mixed with the screech of the wheel-flanges tearing against the rail of a sharp curve.

"I say," asked Gilbert Keith-Worthing nervously, "are your railroads safe?"

"Hell, yes!" said Kip Chalmers. "We've got so many rules, regulations and controls that those bastards wouldn't dare not to be safe! . . . Lester, how far are we now? What's the next stop?"

"There won't be any stop till Salt Lake City."

"I mean, what's the next station?"

Lester Tuck produced a soiled map, which he had been consulting every few minutes since nightfall. "Winston," he said. "Winston, Colorado."

Kip Chalmers reached for another glass.

"Tinky Holloway said that Wesley said that if you don't win this election, you're through," said Laura Bradford. She sat sprawled in her chair, looking past Chalmers, studying her own face in a mirror on the wall of the lounge; she was bored and it amused her to needle his impotent anger.

"Oh, he did, did he?"

"Uh-huh. Wesley doesn't want what's-his-name—whoever's running against you—to get into the Legislature. If you don't win, Wesley will be sore as hell. Tinky said—"

"Damn that bastard! He'd better watch his own neck!"

"Oh, I don't know. Wesley likes him very much." She added, "Tinky Holloway wouldn't allow some miserable train to make him miss an important meeting. They wouldn't dare to hold *him* up."

Kip Chalmers sat staring at his glass. "I'm going to have the government seize all the railroads," he said, his voice low.

"Really," said Gilbert Keith-Worthing, "I don't see why you haven't done it long ago. This is the only country on earth backward enough to permit private ownership of railroads."

"Well, we're catching up with you," said Kip Chalmers.

"Your country is so incredibly naïve. It's such an anachronism. All that talk about liberty and human rights—I haven't heard it since the days of my great-grandfather. It's nothing but a verbal luxury of the rich. After all, it doesn't make any difference to the poor whether their livelihood is at the mercy of an industrialist or of a bureaucrat."

"The day of the industrialists is over. This is the day of—"

The jolt felt as if the air within the car smashed them forward while the floor stopped under their feet. Kip Chalmers was flung down to the carpet, Gilbert Keith-Worthing was thrown across the table top, the lights were blasted out. Glasses crashed off the shelves, the steel of the walls screamed as if about to rip open, while a long, distant thud went like a convulsion through the wheels of the train.

When he raised his head, Chalmers saw that the car stood intact and still; he heard the moans of his companions and the first shriek of Laura Bradford's hysterics. He crawled along the floor to the doorway, wrenched it open, and tumbled down the steps. Far ahead, on the side of a curve, he saw moving flashlights and a red glow at a spot where the engine had no place to be. He stumbled through the darkness, bumping into half-clothed figures that waved the futile little flares of matches. Somewhere along the line, he saw a man with a flashlight and seized his arm. It was the conductor.

"What happened?" gasped Chalmers.

"Split rail," the conductor answered impassively. "The engine went off the track."

"Off . . . ?"

"On its side."

"Anybody . . . killed?"

"No. The engineer's all right. The fireman is hurt."

"Split rail? What do you mean, split rail?"

The conductor's face had an odd look: it was grim, accusing and closed. "Rail wears out, Mr. Chalmers," he answered with a strange kind of emphasis. "Particularly on curves."

"Didn't you know that it was worn out?"

"We knew."

"Well, why didn't you have it replaced?"

"It was going to be replaced. But Mr. Locey cancelled that."

"Who is Mr. Locey?"

"The man who is not our Operating Vice-President."

Chalmers wondered why the conductor seemed to look at him as if something about the catastrophe were his fault. "Well . . . well, aren't you going to put the engine back on the track?"

"That engine's never going to be put back on any track, from the looks of it."

"But . . . but it's got to move us!"

"It can't."

Beyond the few moving flares and the dulled sounds of screams, Chalmers sensed suddenly, not wanting to look at it, the black immensity of the mountains, the silence of hundreds of uninhabited miles, and the precarious strip of a ledge hanging between a wall of rock and an abyss. He gripped the conductor's arm tighter.

"But . . . but what are we going to do?"

"The engineer's gone to call Winston."

"Call? How?"

"There's a phone couple of miles down the track."

"Will they get us out of here?"

"They will."

"But . . ." Then his mind made a connection with the past and the future, and his voice rose to a scream for the first time: "How long will we have to wait?"

"I don't know," said the conductor. He threw Chalmers' hand off his arm, and walked away.

The night operator of Winston Station listened to the phone message, dropped the receiver and raced up the stairs to shake the station agent out of bed. The station agent was a husky, surly drifter who had been assigned to the job ten days ago, by order of the new division superintendent. He stumbled dazedly to his feet, but he was knocked awake when the operator's words reached his brain.

"What?" he gasped. "Jesus! The Comet? . . . Well, don't stand there shaking! Call Silver Springs!"

The night dispatcher of the Division Headquarters at Silver Springs listened to the message, then telephoned Dave Mitchum, the new superintendent of the Colorado Division.

"The Comet?" gasped Mitchum, his hand pressing the telephone receiver to his ear, his feet hitting the floor and throwing him upright, out of bed. "The engine done for? The *Diesel?*"

"Yes, sir."

"Oh God! Oh, God Almighty! What are we going to do?" Then, remembering his position, he added, "Well, send out the wrecking train."

"I have."

"Call the operator at Sherwood to hold all traffic."

"I have."

"What have you got on the sheet?"

"The Army Freight Special, westbound. But it's not due for about four hours. It's running late."

"I'll be right down. . . . Wait, listen, get Bill, Sandy and Clarence down by the time I get there. There's going to be hell to pay!"

Dave Mitchum had always complained about injustice, because, he said, he had always had bad luck. He explained it by speaking darkly about the conspiracy of the big fellows, who would never give him a chance, though he did not explain just whom he meant by "the big fellows." Seniority of service was his favorite topic of complaint and sole standard of value; he had been in the railroad business longer than many men who had advanced beyond him; this, he said, was proof of the social system's injustice—though he never explained just what he meant by "the social system." He had worked for many railroads, but had not stayed long with any one of them. His employers had had no specific misdeeds to charge against him, but had simply eased him out, because he said, "Nobody told me to!" too often. He did not know that he owed his present job to a deal between James Taggart and Wesley Mouch: when Taggart traded to Mouch the secret of his sister's private life, in exchange for a raise in rates, Mouch made him throw in an extra favor, by their customary rules of bargaining, which consisted of squeezing all one could out of any given trade. The extra was a job for Dave Mitchum, who was the brother-in-law of Claude Slagenhop, who was the president of the Friends of Global Progress, who were regarded by Mouch as a valuable influence on public opinion. James Taggart pushed the responsibility of finding a job for Mitchum onto Clifton Locey. Locey pushed Mitchum into the first job that came up—superintendent of the Colorado Division—when the man holding it quit without notice. The man quit when the extra Diesel engine of Winston Station was given to Chick Morrison's Special.

"What are we going to do?" cried Dave Mitchum, rushing, half-dressed and groggy with sleep, into his office, where the chief dispatcher, the trainmaster and the road foreman of engines were waiting for him.

The three men did not answer. They were middle-aged men with years of railroad service behind them. A month ago, they would have volunteered their advice in any emergency; but they were beginning to learn that things had changed and that it was dangerous to speak.

"What in hell are we going to do?"

"One thing is certain," said Bill Brent, the chief dispatcher. "We can't send a train into the tunnel with a coal-burning engine."

Dave Mitchum's eyes grew sullen: he knew that this was the one thought on all their minds; he wished Brent had not named it.

"Well, where do we get a Diesel?" he asked angrily.

"We don't," said the road foreman.

"But we can't keep the Comet waiting on a siding all night!"

"Looks like we'll have to," said the trainmaster. "What's the use of talking about it, Dave? You know that there is no Diesel anywhere on the division."

"But Christ Almighty, how do they expect us to move trains without engines?"

"Miss Taggart didn't," said the road foreman. "Mr. Locey does."

"Bill," asked Mitchum, in the tone of pleading for a favor, "isn't there anything transcontinental that's due tonight, with any sort of a Diesel?"

"The first one to come," said Bill Brent implacably, "will be Number 236, the fast freight from San Francisco, which is due at Winston at seven-eighteen A.M." He added, "That's the Diesel closest to us at this moment. I've checked."

"What about the Army Special?"

"Better not think about it, Dave. That one has superiority over everything on the line, including the Comet, by order of the Army. They're running late as it is—journal boxes caught fire twice. They're carrying munitions for the West Coast arsenals. Better pray that nothing stops them on your division. If you think we'll catch hell for holding the Comet, it's nothing to what we'll catch if we try to stop that Special."

They remained silent. The windows were open to the summer night and they could hear the ringing of the telephone in the dispatcher's office downstairs. The signal lights winked over the deserted yards that had once been a busy division point.

Mitchum looked toward the roundhouse, where the black silhouettes of a few steam engines stood outlined in a dim light.

"The tunnel—" he said and stopped.

"—is eight miles long," said the trainmaster, with a harsh emphasis.

"I was only thinking," snapped Mitchum.

"Better not think of it," said Brent softly.

"I haven't said anything!"

"What was that talk you had with Dick Horton before he quit?" the road foreman asked too innocently, as if the subject were irrelevant. "Wasn't it something about the ventilation system of the tunnel being on the bum? Didn't he say that that tunnel was hardly safe nowadays even for Diesel engines?"

"Why do you bring that up?" snapped Mitchum. "I haven't said anything!" Dick Horton, the division chief engineer, had quit three days after Mitchum's arrival.

"I thought I'd just mention it," the road foreman answered innocently.

"Look, Dave," said Bill Brent, knowing that Mitchum would stall for another hour rather than formulate a decision, "you know that there's only one thing to do: hold the Comet at Winston till morning, wait for Number 236, have her Diesel take the Comet through the tunnel, then let the Comet finish her run with the best coal-burner we can give her on the other side."

"But how late will that make her?"

Brent shrugged. "Twelve hours—eighteen hours—who knows?"

"Eighteen hours—for the Comet? Christ, that's never happened before!"

"None of what's been happening to us has ever happened before," said Brent, with an astonishing sound of weariness in his brisk, competent voice.

"But they'll blame us for it in New York! They'll put all the blame on us!"

Brent shrugged. A month ago, he would have considered such an injustice inconceivable; today, he knew better.

592

"I guess . . ." said Mitchum miserably, "I guess there's nothing else that we can do."

"There isn't, Dave."

"Oh God! Why did this have to happen to us?"

"Who is John Galt?"

It was half-past two when the Comet, pulled by an old switch engine, jerked to a stop on a siding of Winston Station. Kip Chalmers glanced out with incredulous anger at the few shanties on a desolate mountainside and at the ancient hovel of a station.

"Now what? What in hell are they stopping *here* for?" he cried, and rang for the conductor.

With the return of motion and safety, his terror had turned into rage. He felt almost as if he had been cheated by having been made to experience an unnecessary fear. His companions were still clinging to the tables of the lounge; they felt too shaken to sleep.

"How long?" the conductor said impassively, in answer to his question. "Till morning, Mr. Chalmers."

Chalmers stared at him, stupefied. "We're going to stand here till morning?"

"Yes, Mr. Chalmers."

"Here?"

"Yes."

"But I have a rally in San Francisco in the evening!"

The conductor did not answer.

"Why? Why do we have to stand? Why in hell? What happened?"

Slowly, patiently, with contemptuous politeness, the conductor gave him an exact account of the situation. But years ago, in grammar school, in high school, in college, Kip Chalmers had been taught that man does not and need not live by reason.

"Damn your tunnel!" he screamed. "Do you think I'm going to let you hold me up because of some miserable tunnel? Do you want to wreck vital national plans on account of a tunnel? Tell your engineer that I must be in San Francisco by evening and that he's got to get me there!"

"How?"

"That's *your* job, not mine!"

"There is no way to do it."

"Then find a way, God damn you!"

The conductor did not answer.

"Do you think I'll let your miserable technological problems interfere with crucial social issues? Do you know who I am? Tell that engineer to start moving, if he values his job!"

"The engineer has his orders."

"Orders be damned! *I* give the orders these days! Tell him to start at once!"

"Perhaps you'd better speak to the station agent, Mr. Chalmers. I have no authority to answer you as I'd like to," said the conductor, and walked out.

Chalmers leaped to his feet. "Say, Kip . . ." said Lester Tuck uneasily, "maybe it's true . . . maybe they can't do it."

"They can if they have to!" snapped Chalmers, marching resolutely to the door.

Years ago, in college, he had been taught that the only effective means to impel men to action was fear.

In the dilapidated office of Winston Station, he confronted a sleepy man with slack, worn features, and a frightened young boy who sat at the operator's desk. They listened, in silent stupor, to a stream of profanity such as they had never heard from any section gang.

"—and it's not *my* problem how you get the train through the tunnel, that's for *you* to figure out!" Chalmers concluded. "But if you don't get me an engine and don't start that train, you can kiss good-bye to your jobs, your work permits and this whole goddamn railroad!"

The station agent had never heard of Kip Chalmers and did not know the nature of his position. But he knew that this was the day when unknown men in undefined positions held unlimited power—the power of life or death.

"It's not up to us, Mr. Chalmers," he said pleadingly. "We don't issue the orders out here. The order came from Silver Springs. Suppose you telephone Mr. Mitchum and—"

"Who's Mr. Mitchum?"

"He's the division superintendent at Silver Springs. Suppose you send him a message to—"

"I should bother with a division superintendent! I'll send a message to Jim Taggart—that's what I'm going to do!"

Before the station agent had time to recover, Chalmers whirled to the boy, ordering, "You—take this down and send it at once!"

It was a message which, a month ago, the station agent would not have accepted from any passenger; the rules forbade it; but he was not certain about any rules any longer:

Mr. James Taggart, New York City. Am held up on the Comet at Winston, Colorado, by the incompetence of your men, who refuse to give me an engine. Have meeting in San Francisco in the evening of top-level national importance. If you don't move my train at once, I'll let you guess the consequences. Kip Chalmers.

After the boy had transmitted the words onto the wires that stretched from pole to pole across a continent as guardians of the Taggart track—after Kip Chalmers had returned to his car to wait for an answer—the station agent telephoned Dave Mitchum, who was his friend, and read to him the text of the message. He heard Mitchum groan in answer.

"I thought I'd tell you, Dave. I never heard of the guy before, but maybe he's somebody important."

"I don't know!" moaned Mitchum. "Kip Chalmers? You see his name in the newspapers all the time, right in with all the top-level boys. I don't know what he is, but if he's from Washington, we can't take any chances. Oh Christ, what are we going to do?"

We can't take any chances—thought the Taggart operator in New York, and transmitted the message by telephone to James Taggart's home. It was close to six A.M. in New York, and James Taggart was awakened out of the fitful sleep of a restless night. He listened to the telephone, his face sagging. He felt the same fear as the station agent of Winston, and for the same reason.

He called the home of Clifton Locey. All the rage which he could not pour upon Kip Chalmers, was poured over the telephone wire upon Clifton Locey. "Do something!" screamed Taggart. "I don't care what you do, it's *your* job, not mine, but see to it that that train gets through! What in hell is going on? I never heard of the Comet being held up! Is that how you run your department? It's a fine thing when important passengers have to start sending messages to *me!* At least, when my sister ran the place, I wasn't awakened in the middle of the night over every spike that broke in Iowa—Colorado, I mean!"

"I'm so sorry, Jim," said Clifton Locey smoothly, in a tone that balanced apology, reassurance and the right degree of patronizing confidence. "It's just a misunderstanding. It's somebody's stupid mistake. Don't worry, I'll take care of it. I was, as a matter of fact, in bed, but I'll attend to it at once."

Clifton Locey was not in bed; he had just returned from a round of night clubs, in the company of a young lady. He asked her to wait and hurried to the offices of Taggart Transcontinental. None of the night staff who saw him there could say why he chose to appear in person, but neither could they say that it had been unnecessary. He rushed in and out of several offices, was seen by many people and gave an impression of great activity. The only physical result of it was an order that went over the wires to Dave Mitchum, superintendent of the Colorado Division:

"Give an engine to Mr. Chalmers at once. Send the Comet through safely and without unnecessary delay. If you are unable to perform your duties, I shall hold you responsible before the Unification Board. Clifton Locey."

Then, calling his girl friend to join him, Clifton Locey drove to a country roadhouse—to make certain that no one would be able to find him in the next few hours.

The dispatcher at Silver Springs was baffled by the order that he handed to Dave Mitchum, but Dave Mitchum understood. He knew that no railroad order would ever speak in such terms as giving an engine to a passenger; he knew that the thing was a show piece, he guessed what sort of show was being staged, and he felt a cold sweat at the realization of who was being framed as the goat of the show.

"What's the matter, Dave?" asked the trainmaster.

Mitchum did not answer. He seized the telephone, his hands shaking as he begged for a conection to the Taggart operator in New York. He looked like an animal in a trap.

He begged the New York operator to get him Mr. Clifton Locey's home. The operator tried. There was no answer. He begged the operator to keep on trying and to try every number he could think of, where Mr. Locey might be found. The operator promised and Mitchum hung up, but knew that it was useless to wait or to speak to anyone in Mr. Locey's department.

"What's the matter, Dave?"

Mitchum handed him the order—and saw by the look on the trainmaster's face that the trap was as bad as he had suspected.

He called the Region Headquarters of Taggart Transcontinental at Omaha, Nebraska, and begged to speak to the general manager of the region. There was a brief silence on the wire, then the voice of the Omaha operator told him that the general manager had resigned and vanished three days ago—"over a little trouble with Mr. Locey," the voice added.

He asked to speak to the assistant general manager in charge of his particular district; but the assistant was out of town for the week end and could not be reached.

"Get me somebody else!" Mitchum screamed. "Anybody, of any district! For Christ's sake, get me somebody who'll tell me what to do!"

The man who came on the wire was the assistant general manager of the Iowa-Minnesota District.

"What?" he interrupted at Mitchum's first words. "At Winston, Colorado? Why in hell are you calling *me*? . . . No, don't tell me what happened, I don't want to know it! . . . No, I said! No! You're not going to frame me into having to explain afterwards why I did or didn't do anything about whatever it is. It's not *my* problem! . . . Speak to some region executive, don't pick on me, what do I have to do with Colorado? . . . Oh hell, I don't know, get the chief engineer, speak to him!"

The chief engineer of the Central Region answered impatiently, "Yes? What? What is it?"—and Mitchum rushed desperately to explain. When the chief engineer heard that there was no Diesel, he snapped, "Then hold the train, of course!" When he heard about Mr. Chalmers, he said, his voice suddenly subdued, "Hm . . . Kip Chalmers? Of Washington? . . . Well, I don't know. That would be a matter for Mr. Locey to decide." When Mitchum said, "Mr. Locey ordered me to arrange it, but—" the chief engineer snapped in great relief, "Then do exactly as Mr. Locey says!" and hung up.

Dave Mitchum replaced the telephone receiver cautiously. He did not scream any longer. Instead, he tiptoed to a chair, almost as if he were sneaking. He sat looking at Mr. Locey's order for a long time.

Then he snatched a glance about the room. The dispatcher was busy at his telephone. The trainmaster and the road foreman were there, but they pretended that they were not waiting. He wished Bill Brent, the chief dispatcher, would go home; Bill Brent stood in a corner, watching him.

Brent was a short, thin man with broad shoulders; he was forty, but looked younger; he had the pale face of an office worker and the hard, lean features of a cowboy. He was the best dispatcher on the system.

Mitchum rose abruptly and walked upstairs to his office, clutching Locey's order in his hand.

Dave Mitchum was not good at understanding problems of engineering and transportation, but he understood men like Clifton Locey. He understood the kind of game the New York executives were playing and what they were now doing to him. The order did not tell him to give Mr. Chalmers a coal-burning engine—just "an engine." If the time came to answer questions, wouldn't Mr. Locey gasp in shocked indignation that he had expected a division superintendent to know that only a Diesel engine could be meant in that order? The order stated that he was to send the Comet through *"safely"*—wasn't a division superintendent expected to know what was safe?—"and without unnecessary delay." What was an *unnecessary* delay? If the possibility of a major disaster was involved, wouldn't a delay of a week or a month be considered necessary?

The New York executives did not care, thought Mitchum; they did not care whether Mr. Chalmers reached his meeting on time, or whether an unprecedented catastrophe struck their rails; they cared only about making sure that they would not be blamed for either. If he held the train, they would make him the scapegoat to appease the anger of Mr. Chalmers; if he sent the train through and it did not reach the western portal of the tunnel, they would put the blame on his incompetence; they would claim that he had acted against their orders, in either case. What would he be able to prove? To whom? One could prove nothing to a tribunal that had no stated policy, no defined procedure, no rules of evidence, no binding principles—a tribunal, such as the Unification Board, that pronounced men guilty or innocent as it saw fit, with no standard of guilt or innocence.

Dave Mitchum knew nothing about the philosophy of law; but he knew that when a court is not bound by any rules, it is not bound by any facts, and then a hearing is not an issue of justice, but an issue of men, and your fate depends not on what you have or have not done, but on whom you do or do not know. He asked himself what chance he would have at such a hearing against Mr. James Taggart,

Mr. Clifton Locey, Mr. Kip Chalmers and their powerful friends.

Dave Mitchum had spent his life slipping around the necessity of ever making a decision; he had done it by waiting to be told and never being certain of anything. All that he now allowed into his brain was a long, indignant whine against injustice. Fate, he thought, had singled him out for an unfair amount of bad luck: he was being framed by his superiors on the only good job he had ever held. He had never been taught to understand that the manner in which he obtained this job, and the frame-up, were inextricable parts of a single whole.

As he looked at Locey's order, he thought that he could hold the Comet, attach Mr. Chalmers' car to an engine and send it into the tunnel, alone. But he shook his head before the thought was fully formed: he knew that this would force Mr. Chalmers to recognize the nature of the risk; Mr. Chalmers would refuse; he would continue to demand a safe and non-existent engine. And more: this would mean that he, Mitchum, would have to assume responsibility, admit full knowledge of the danger, stand in the open and identify the exact nature of the situation—the one act which the policy of his superiors was based on evading, the one key to their game.

Dave Mitchum was not the man to rebel against his background or to question the moral code of those in charge. The choice he made was not to challenge, but to follow the policy of his superiors. Bill Brent could have beaten him in any contest of technology, but here was an endeavor at which he could beat Bill Brent without effort. There had once been a society where men needed the particular talents of Bill Brent, if they wished to survive; what they needed now was the talent of Dave Mitchum.

Dave Mitchum sat down at his secretary's typewriter and, by means of two fingers, carefully typed out an order to the trainmaster and another to the road foreman. The first instructed the trainmaster to summon a locomotive crew at once, for a purpose described only as "an emergency"; the second instructed the road foreman to "send the best engine available to Winston, to stand by for emergency assistance."

He put carbon copies of the orders into his own pocket, then opened the door, yelled for the night dispatcher to come up and handed him the two orders for the two men downstairs. The night dispatcher was a conscientious young boy who trusted his superiors and knew that discipline was the first rule of the railroad business. He was astonished that Mitchum should wish to send written orders down one flight of stairs, but he asked no questions.

Mitchum waited nervously. After a while, he saw the figure of the road foreman walking across the yards toward the roundhouse. He felt relieved: the two men had not come up to confront him in person; they had understood and they would play the game as he was playing it.

The road foreman walked across the yards, looking down at the ground. He was thinking of his wife, his two children and the house which he had spent a lifetime to own. He knew what his superiors were doing and he wondered whether he should refuse to obey them. He had never been afraid of losing his job; with the confidence of a competent man, he had known that if he quarreled with one employer, he would always be able to find another. Now, he was afraid; he had no right to quit or to seek a job; if he defied an employer, he would be delivered into the unanswerable power of a single Board, and if the Board ruled against him, it would mean being sentenced to the slow death of starvation: it would mean being barred from any employment. He knew that the Board would rule against him; he knew that the key to the dark, capricious mystery of the Board's contradictory decisions was the secret power of pull. What chance would he have against Mr. Chalmers? There had been a time when the self-interest of his employers had demanded that he exercise his utmost ability. Now, ability was not wanted any longer. There had been a time when he had been required to do his best and rewarded accordingly. Now, he could expect nothing but punishment, if he tried to follow his conscience. There had been a time when he had been expected to think. Now, they did not want him to think, only to obey. They did not want him to have a conscience any longer. Then why should he raise his voice? For whose sake? He thought of the passengers—the three hundred passengers aboard the Comet. He thought of his children. He had a son in high school and a daughter, nineteen, of whom he was fiercely, painfully proud, because she was recognized as the most beautiful girl in town. He asked himself whether he could deliver his children to the fate of the children of the unemployed, as he had seen them in the blighted areas, in the settlements around closed factories and along the tracks of discontinued railroads. He saw, in astonished horror, that the choice which he now had to make was between the lives of his children and the lives of the passengers on the Comet. A conflict of this kind had never been possible before. It was by protecting the safety of the passengers that he had earned the security of his children; he had served one by serving the other; there had been no clash of interests, no call for victims. Now, if he wanted to save the passengers, he had to do it at the price of his children. He remembered dimly the sermons he had heard about the beauty of self-immolation, about the virtue of sacrificing to others that which was one's dearest. He knew nothing about the philosophy of ethics; but he knew suddenly—not in words, but in the form of a dark, angry, savage pain—that if this was virtue, then he wanted no part of it.

He walked into the roundhouse and ordered a large, ancient coal-burning locomotive to be made ready for the run to Winston.

The trainmaster reached for the telephone in the dispatcher's office, to summon an engine crew, as ordered. But his hand stopped, holding the receiver. It struck him suddenly that he was summoning men to their death, and that of the twenty lives listed on the sheet before him, two would be ended by his choice. He felt a physical sensation of cold, nothing more; he felt no concern, only a puzzled, indifferent astonishment. It had never been his job to call men out to die; his job had been to call them out to earn their living. It was strange, he thought; and it was strange that his hand had stopped; what made it stop was like something he would have felt twenty years ago—no, he thought, strange, only one month ago, not longer.

He was forty-eight years old. He had no family, no friends, no ties to any living being in the world. Whatever capacity for devotion he had possessed, the capacity which others scatter among many random concerns, he had given it whole to the person of his young brother —the brother, his junior by twenty-five years, whom he had brought up. He had sent him through a technological college, and he had known, as had all the teachers, that the boy had the mark of genius on the forehead of his grim, young face. With the same single-tracked devotion as his brother's, the boy had cared for nothing but his studies, not for sports or parties or girls, only for the vision of the things he was going to create as an inventor. He had graduated from college and had gone, on a salary unusual for his age, into the research laboratory of a great electrical concern in Massachusetts.

This was now May 28, thought the trainmaster. It was on May 1 that Directive 10-289 had been issued. It was on the evening of May 1 that he had been informed that his brother had committed suicide.

The trainmaster had heard it said that the directive was necessary to save the country. He could not know whether this was true or not; he had no way of knowing what was necessary to save a country. But driven by some feeling which he could not express, he had walked into the office of the editor of the local newspaper and demanded that they publish the story of his brother's death. "People have to know it," had been all he could give as his reason. He had been unable to explain that the bruised connections of his mind had formed the wordless conclusion that if this was done by the will of the people, then the people had to know it; he could not believe that they would do it, if they knew. The editor had refused; he had stated that it would be bad for the country's morale.

The trainmaster knew nothing about political philosophy; but he knew that that had been the moment when he lost all concern for the life or death of any human being or of the country.

He thought, holding the telephone receiver, that maybe he should warn the men whom he was about to call. They trusted him; it would never occur to them that he could knowingly send them to their death. But he shook his head: this was only an old thought, last year's thought, a remnant of the time when he had trusted them, too. It did not matter now. His brain worked slowly, as if he were dragging his thoughts through a vacuum where no emotion responded to spur them on; he thought that there would be trouble if he warned anyone, there would be some sort of fight and it was he who had to make some great effort to start it. He had forgotten what it was that one started this sort of fight for. Truth? Justice? Brother-love? He did not want to make an effort. He was very tired. If he warned all the men on his list, he thought, there would be no one to run that engine, so he would save two lives and also three hundred lives aboard the Comet. But nothing responded to the figures in his mind; "lives" was just a word, it had no meaning.

He raised the telephone receiver to his ear, he called two numbers, he summoned an engineer and a fireman to report for duty at once.

Engine Number 306 had left for Winston, when Dave Mitchum came downstairs. "Get a track motor car ready for me," he ordered, "I'm going to run up to Fairmount." Fairmount was a small station, twenty miles east on the line. The men nodded, asking no questions. Bill Brent was not among them. Mitchum walked into Brent's office. Brent was there, sitting silently at his desk; he seemed to be waiting.

"I'm going to Fairmount," said Mitchum; his voice was aggressively too casual, as if implying that no answer was necessary. "They had a Diesel there couple of weeks ago . . . you know, emergency repairs or something. . . . I'm going down to see if we could use it."

He paused, but Brent said nothing.

"The way things stack up," said Mitchum, not looking at him, "we can't hold that train till morning. We've got to take a chance, one way or another. Now I think maybe this Diesel will do it, but that's the last one we can try for. So if you don't hear from me in half an hour, sign the order and send the Comet through with Number 306 to pull her."

Whatever Brent had thought, he could not believe it when he heard it. He did not answer at once; then he said, very quietly, "No."

"What do you mean, no?"

"I won't do it."

"What do you mean, you won't? It's an order!"

"I won't do it." Brent's voice had the firmness of certainty unclouded by any emotion.

"Are you refusing to obey an order?"

"I am."

"But you have no right to refuse! And I'm not going to argue about it, either. It's what I've decided, it's my responsibility and I'm not asking for your opinion. Your job is to take my orders."

"Will you give me that order in writing?"

"Why, God damn you, are you hinting that you don't trust me? Are you . . . ?"

"Why do you have to go to Fairmount, Dave? Why can't you telephone them about that Diesel, if you think that they have one?"

"You're not going to tell me how to do my job! You're not going to sit there and question me! You're going to keep your trap shut and do as you're told or I'll give you a chance to talk—to the Unification Board!"

It was hard to decipher emotions on Brent's cowboy face, but Mitchum saw something that resembled a look of incredulous horror; only it was horror at some sight of his own, not at the words, and it had no quality of fear, not the kind of fear Mitchum had hoped for.

Brent knew that tomorrow morning the issue would be his word against Mitchum's; Mitchum would deny having given the order; Mitchum would show written proof that Engine Number 306 had been sent to Winston only "to stand by," and would produce witnesses that he had gone to Fairmount in search of a Diesel; Mitchum would claim that the fatal order had been issued by and on the sole responsibility of Bill Brent, the chief dispatcher. It would not be much of a case, not a case that could bear close study, but it would be enough for the Unification Board, whose policy was consistent only in not permitting anything to be studied closely. Brent knew that he could play the same game and pass the frame-up on to another victim, he knew that he had the brains to work it out—except that he would rather be dead than do it.

It was not the sight of Mitchum that made him sit still in horror. It was the realization that there was no one whom he could call to expose this thing and stop it—no superior anywhere on the line, from Colorado to Omaha to New York. They were in on it, all of them, they were doing the same, they had given Mitchum the lead and the method. It was Dave Mitchum who now belonged on this railroad and he, Bill Brent, who did not.

As Bill Brent had learned to see, by a single glance at a few numbers on a sheet of paper, the entire trackage of a division—so he was now able to see the whole of his own life and the full price of the decision he was making. He had not fallen in love until he was past his youth; he had been thirty-six when he had found the woman he wanted. He had been engaged to her for the last four years; he had had to wait, because he had a mother to support and a widowed sister with three children. He had never been afraid of burdens, because he had known his ability to carry them, and he had never assumed an obligation unless he was certain that he could fulfill it. He had waited, he had saved his money, and now he had reached the time when he felt himself free to be happy. He was to be married in a few weeks, this coming June. He thought of it, as he sat at his desk, looking at Dave Mitchum, but the thought aroused no hesitation, only regret and a distant sadness—distant, because he knew that he could not let it be part of this moment.

Bill Brent knew nothing about epistemology; but he knew that man must live by his own rational perception of reality, that he cannot act against it or escape it or find a substitute for it—and that there is no other way for him to live.

He rose to his feet. "It's true that so long as I hold this job, I cannot refuse to obey you," he said. "But I can, if I quit. So I'm quitting."

"You're *what?*"

"I'm quitting, as of this moment."

"But you have no right to quit, you goddamn bastard! Don't you know that? Don't you know that I'll have you thrown in jail for it?"

"If you want to send the sheriff for me in the morning, I'll be at home. I won't try to escape. There's no place to go."

Dave Mitchum was six-foot-two and had the build of a bruiser, but he stood shaking with fury and terror over the delicate figure of Bill Brent. "You can't quit! There's a law against it! I've got a law! You can't walk out on me! I won't let you out! I won't let you leave this building tonight!"

Brent walked to the door. "Will you repeat that order you gave me, in front of the others? No? Then I will."

As he pulled the door open, Mitchum's fist shot out, smashed into his face and knocked him down.

The trainmaster and the road foreman stood in the open doorway.

"He quit!" screamed Mitchum. "The yellow bastard quit at a time like this! He's a law-breaker and a coward!"

In the slow effort of rising from the floor, through the haze of blood running into his eyes, Bill Brent looked up at the two men. He saw that they understood, but he saw the closed faces of men who did not want to understand, did not want to interfere and hated him for putting them on the spot in the name of justice. He said nothing, rose to his feet and walked out of the building.

Mitchum avoided looking at the others. "Hey, you," he called, jerking his head at the night dispatcher across the room. "Come here. You've got to take over at once."

With the door closed, he repeated to the boy the story of the Diesel at Fairmount, as he had given it to Brent, and the order to send the Comet through with Engine Number 306, if the boy did not hear from him in half an hour. The boy was in no condition to think, to speak or to understand anything: he kept seeing the blood on the face of Bill Brent, who had been his idol. "Yes, sir," he answered numbly.

Dave Mitchum departed for Fairmount, announcing to every yard-man, switchman and wiper in sight, as he boarded the track motor car that he was going in search of a Diesel for the Comet.

The night dispatcher sat at his desk, watching the clock and the telephone, praying that the telephone would ring and let him hear from Mr. Mitchum. But the half-hour went by in silence, and when there were only three minutes left, the boy felt a terror he could not explain, except that he did not want to send that order.

He turned to the trainmaster and the road foreman, asking hesitantly, "Mr. Mitchum gave me an order before he left, but I wonder whether I ought to send it, because I . . . I don't think it's right. He said—"

The trainmaster turned away; he felt no pity: the boy was about the same age as his brother had been.

The road foreman snapped, "Do just as Mr. Mitchum told you. You're not supposed to think," and walked out of the room.

The responsibility that James Taggart and Clifton Locey had evaded now rested on the shoulders of a trembling, bewildered boy. He hesitated, then he buttressed his courage with the thought that one did not doubt the good faith and the competence of railroad executives. He did not know that his vision of a railroad and its executives was that of a century ago.

With the conscientious precision of a railroad man, in the moment when the hand of the clock ended the half-hour, he signed his name to the order instructing the Comet to proceed with Engine Number 306, and transmitted the order to Winston Station.

The station agent at Winston shuddered when he looked at the order, but he was not the man to defy authority. He told himself that the tunnel was not, perhaps, as dangerous as he thought. He told himself that the best policy, these days, was not to think.

When he handed their copies of the order to the conductor and the engineer of the Comet, the conductor glanced slowly about the room, from face to face, folded the slip of paper, put it into his pocket and walked out without a word.

The engineer stood looking at the paper for a moment, then threw it down and said, "I'm not going to do it. And if it's come to where this railroad hands out orders like this one, I'm not going to work for it, either. Just list me as having quit."

"But you can't quit!" cried the station agent. "They'll arrest you for it!"

"If they find me," said the engineer, and walked out of the station into the vast darkness of the mountain night.

The engineer from Silver Springs, who had brought in Number 306, was sitting in a corner of the room. He chuckled and said, "He's yellow."

The station agent turned to him. "Will *you* do it, Joe? Will you take the Comet?"

Joe Scott was drunk. There had been a time when a railroad man, reporting for duty with any sign of intoxication, would have been regarded as a doctor arriving for work with sores of smallpox on his face. But Joe Scott was a privileged person. Three months ago, he had been fired for an infraction of safety rules, which had caused a major wreck; two weeks ago, he had been reinstated in his job by order of the Unification Board. He was a friend of Fred Kinnan; he protected Kinnan's interests in his union, not against the employers, but against the membership.

"Sure," said Joe Scott. "I'll take the Comet. I'll get her through, if I go fast enough."

The fireman of Number 306 had remained in the cab of his engine. He looked up uneasily, when they came to switch his engine to the head end of the Comet; he looked up at the red and green lights of the tunnel, hanging in the distance above twenty miles of curves. But he was a placid, amicable fellow, who made a good fireman with no hope of ever rising to engineer; his husky muscles were his only asset. He felt certain that his superiors knew what they were doing, so he did not venture any questions.

The conductor stood by the rear end of the Comet. He looked at the lights of the tunnel, then at the long chain of the Comet's windows. A few windows were lighted, but most of them showed only the feeble blue glow of night lamps edging the lowered blinds. He thought that he should rouse the passengers and warn them. There had been a time when he had placed the safety of the passengers above his own, not by reason of love for his fellow men, but because that responsibility was part of his job, which he accepted and felt pride in fulfilling. Now, he felt a contemptuous indifference and no desire to save them. They had asked for and accepted Directive 10-289, he thought, they went on living and daily turning away in evasion from the kind of verdicts that the Unification Board was passing on defenseless victims—why shouldn't he now turn away from them? If he saved their lives, not one of them would come forward to defend him when the Unification Board would convict him for disobeying orders, for creating a panic, for delaying Mr. Chalmers. He had no desire to be a martyr for the sake of allowing people safely to indulge in their own irresponsible evil.

When the moment came, he raised his lantern and signaled the engineer to start.

"See?" said Kip Chalmers triumphantly to Lester Tuck, as the wheels under their feet shuddered forward. *"Fear* is the only practical means to deal with people."

The conductor stepped onto the vestibule of the last car. No one saw him as he went down the steps of the other side, slipped off the train and vanished into the darkness of the mountains.

A switchman stood ready to throw the switch that would send the Comet from the siding onto the main track. He looked at the Comet as it came slowly toward him. It was only a blazing white globe with a beam stretching high above his head, and a jerky thunder trembling through the rail under his feet. He knew that the switch should not be thrown. He thought of the night, ten years ago, when he had risked

his life in a flood to save a train from a washout. But he knew
that times had changed. In the moment when he threw the switch and
saw the headlight jerk sidewise, he knew that he would now hate his
job for the rest of his life.

The Comet uncoiled from the siding into a thin, straight line, and
went on into the mountains, with the beam of the headlight like an
extended arm pointing the way, and the lighted glass curve of the observation lounge ending it off.

Some of the passengers aboard the Comet were awake. As the train
started its coiling ascent, they saw the small cluster of Winston's lights
at the bottom of the darkness beyond their windows, then the same
darkness, but with red and green lights by the hole of a tunnel on
the upper edge of the windowpanes. The lights of Winston kept growing
smaller, each time they appeared; the black hole of the tunnel kept
growing larger. A black veil went streaking past the windows at times,
dimming the lights: it was the heavy smoke from the coal-burning
engine.

As the tunnel came closer, they saw, on the edge of the sky far
to the south, in a void of space and rock, a spot of living fire
twisting in the wind. They did not know what it was and did not care
to learn.

It is said that catastrophes are a matter of pure chance, and there
were those who would have said that the passengers of the Comet were
not guilty or responsible for the thing that happened to them.

The man in Bedroom A, Car No. 1, was a professor of sociology who
taught that individual ability is of no consequence, that individual effort is futile, that an individual conscience is a useless luxury, that there
is no individual mind or character or achievement, that everything is
achieved collectively, and that it's masses that count, not men.

The man in Roomette 7, Car No. 2, was a journalist who wrote
that it is proper and moral to use compulsion "for a good cause," who
believed that he had the right to unleash physical force upon others—
to wreck lives, throttle ambitions, strangle desires, violate convictions, to
imprison, to despoil, to murder—for the sake of whatever he chose to
consider as his own idea of "a good cause," which did not even have
to be an idea, since he had never defined what he regarded as the
good, but had merely stated that he went by "a feeling"—a feeling un-
restrained by any knowledge, since he considered emotion superior to
knowledge and relied solely on his own "good intentions" and on the
power of a gun.

The woman in Roomette 10, Car No. 3, was an elderly schoolteacher who had spent her life turning class after class of helpless
children into miserable cowards, by teaching them that the will of the
majority is the only standard of good and evil, that a majority may
do anything it pleases, that they must not assert their own personalities,
but must do as others were doing.

The man in Drawing Room B, Car No. 4, was a newspaper publisher who believed that men are evil by nature and unfit for freedom, that their basic instincts, if left unchecked, are to lie, to rob and to murder one another—and, therefore, men must be ruled by means of lies, robbery and murder, which must be made the exclusive privilege of the rulers, for the purpose of forcing men to work, teaching them to be moral and keeping them within the bounds of order and justice.

The man in Bedroom H, Car No. 5, was a businessman who had acquired his business, an ore mine, with the help of a government loan, under the Equalization of Opportunity Bill.

The man in Drawing Room A, Car No. 6, was a financier who had made a fortune by buying "frozen" railroad bonds and getting his friends in Washington to "defreeze" them.

The man in Seat 5, Car No. 7, was a worker who believed that he had "a right" to a job, whether his employer wanted him or not.

The woman in Roomette 6, Car No. 8, was a lecturer who believed that, as a consumer, she had "a right" to transportation, whether the railroad people wished to provide it or not.

The man in Roomette 2, Car No. 9, was a professor of economics who advocated the abolition of private property, explaining that intelligence plays no part in industrial production, that man's mind is conditioned by material tools, that anybody can run a factory or a railroad and it's only a matter of seizing the machinery.

The woman in Bedroom D, Car No. 10, was a mother who had put her two children to sleep in the berth above her, carefully tucking them in, protecting them from drafts and jolts; a mother whose husband held a government job enforcing directives, which she defended by saying, "I don't care, it's only the rich that they hurt. After all, I must think of my children."

The man in Roomette 3, Car No. 11, was a sniveling little neurotic who wrote cheap little plays into which, as a social message, he inserted cowardly little obscenities to the effect that all businessmen were scoundrels.

The woman in Roomette 9, Car No. 12, was a housewife who believed that she had the right to elect politicians, of whom she knew nothing, to control giant industries, of which she had no knowledge.

The man in Bedroom F, Car No. 13, was a lawyer who had said, "Me? I'll find a way to get along under any political system."

The man in Bedroom A, Car No. 14, was a professor of philosophy who taught that there is no mind—*how do you know that the tunnel is dangerous?*—no reality—*how can you prove that the tunnel exists?*—no logic—*why do you claim that trains cannot move without motive power?*—no principles—*why should you be bound by the law of cause-and-effect?*—no rights—*why shouldn't you attach men to their jobs by force?*—no morality—*what's moral about running a railroad?*—no absolutes—*what difference does it make to you whether you live or die, anyway?* He taught that we know nothing—*why oppose the orders of your superiors?*—that we can never be certain of anything—*how do you know you're right?*—that we must act on the expediency of the moment—*you don't want to risk your job, do you?*

The man in Drawing Room B, Car No. 15, was an heir who had inherited his fortune, and who had kept repeating, "Why should Rearden be the only one permitted to manufacture Rearden Metal?"

The man in Bedroom A, Car No. 16, was a humanitarian who had said, "The men of ability? I do not care what or if they are made to suffer. They must be penalized in order to support the incompetent. Frankly, I do not care whether this is just or not. I take pride in not caring to grant any justice to the able, where mercy to the needy is concerned."

These passengers were awake; there was not a man aboard the train who did not share one or more of their ideas. As the train went into the tunnel, the flame of Wyatt's Torch was the last thing they saw on earth.

BY OUR LOVE

The sun touched the tree tops on the slope of the hill, and they looked a bluish-silver, catching the color of the sky. Dagny stood at the door of the cabin, with the first sunrays on her forehead and miles of forest spread under her feet. The leaves went down from silver to green to the smoky blue of the shadows on the road below. The light trickled down through the branches and shot upward in sudden spurts when it hit a clump of ferns that became a fountain of green rays. It gave her pleasure to watch the motion of the light over a stillness where nothing else could move.

She had marked the date, as she did each morning, on the sheet of paper she had tacked to the wall of her room. The progression of the dates on that paper was the only movement in the stillness of her days, like the record kept by a prisoner on a desert island. This morning's date was May 28.

She had intended the dates to lead to a purpose, but she could not say whether she had reached it or not. She had come here with three assignments given, as orders, to herself: rest—learn to live without the railroad—get the pain out of the way. Get it out of the way, were the words she used. She felt as if she were tied to some wounded stranger who could be stricken at any moment by an attack that would drown her in his screams. She felt no pity for the stranger, only a contemptuous impatience; she had to fight him and destroy him, then her way would be clear to decide what she wished to do; but the stranger was not easy to fight.

The assignment to rest had been easier. She found that she liked the solitude; she awakened in the morning with a feeling of confident benevolence, the sense that she could venture forth and be willing to deal with whatever she found. In the city, she had lived in chronic tension to withstand the shock of anger, indignation, disgust, contempt. The only danger to threaten her here was the simple pain of some physical accident; it seemed innocent and easy by comparison.

The cabin was far from any traveled road; it had remained as her father had left it. She cooked her meals on a wood-burning stove and gathered the wood on the hillsides. She cleared the brush from under her walls, she reshingled the roof, she repainted the door and the frames of the windows. Rains, weeds and brush had swallowed the steps of what had once been a terraced path rising up the hill from the road to the cabin. She rebuilt it, clearing the terraces, re-laying the stones, bracing the banks of soft earth with walls of boulders. It gave her pleasure to devise complex systems of levers and pulleys out of old scraps of iron and rope, then to move weights of rock that were much beyond her physical power. She planted a few seeds of nasturtiums and morning glories, to see one spreading slowly over the ground and the other climbing up the tree trunks, to see them grow, to see progression and movement.

The work gave her the calm she needed; she had not noticed how she began it or why; she had started without conscious intention, but she saw it growing under her hands, pulling her forward, giving her a healing sense of peace. Then she understood that what she needed was the motion to a purpose, no matter how small or in what form, the sense of an activity going step by step to some chosen end across a span of time. The work of cooking a meal was like a closed circle, completed and gone, leading nowhere. But the work of building a path was a living sum, so that no day was left to die behind her, but each day contained all those that preceded it, each day acquired its immortality on every succeeding tomorrow. A circle, she thought, is the movement proper to physical nature, they say that there's nothing but circular motion in the inanimate universe around us, but the straight line is the badge of man, the straight line of a geometrical abstraction that makes roads, rails and bridges, the straight line that cuts the curving aimlessness of nature by a purposeful motion from a start to an end. The cooking of meals, she thought, is like the feeding of coal to an engine for the sake of a great run, but what would be the imbecile torture of coaling an engine that had no run to make? It is not proper for man's life to be a circle, she thought, or a string of circles dropping off like zeros behind him—man's life must be a straight line of motion from goal to farther goal, each leading to the next and to a single growing sum, like a journey down the track of a railroad, from station to station to—oh, stop it!

Stop it—she told herself in quiet severity, when the scream of the wounded stranger was choked off—don't think of that, don't look too far, you like building this path, build it, don't look beyond the foot of the hill.

She had driven a few times to the store in Woodstock, twenty miles away, to buy supplies and food. Woodstock was a small huddle of dying structures, built generations ago for some reason and hope long since forgotten. There was no railroad to feed it, no electric power, nothing but a county highway growing emptier year by year.

The only store was a wooden hovel, with spider-eaten corners and a rotted patch in the middle of the floor, eaten by the rains that came through the leaking roof. The storekeeper was a fat, pallid woman who moved with effort, but seemed indifferent to her own discomfort. The stock of food consisted of dusty cans with faded labels, some grain, and a few vegetables rotting in ancient bins outside the door. "Why don't you move those vegetables out of the sun?" Dagny asked once. The woman looked at her blankly, as if unable to understand the possibility of such a question. "They've always been there," she answered indifferently.

Driving back to the cabin, Dagny looked up at a mountain stream that fell with ferocious force down a sheer granite wall, its spray hanging like a mist of rainbows in the sun. She thought that one could build a hydroelectric plant, just large enough to supply the power for her cabin and for the town of Woodstock—Woodstock could be made to be productive—those wild apple trees she saw in such unusual numbers among the dense growth on the hillsides, were the remnants of orchards—suppose one were to reclaim them, then build a small spur to the nearest railroad—oh, stop it!

"No kerosene today," the storekeeper told her on her next trip to Woodstock. "It rained Thursday night, and when it rains, the trucks can't get through Fairfield gorge, the road's flooded, and the kerosene truck won't be back this way till next month." "If you know that the road gets flooded every time it rains, why don't you people repair it?" The woman answered, "The road's always been that way."

Driving back, Dagny stopped on the crest of a hill and looked down at the miles of countryside below. She looked at Fairfield gorge where the county road, twisting through marshy soil below the level of a river, got trapped in a crack between two hills. It would be simple to bypass those hills, she thought, to build a road on the other side of the river—the people of Woodstock had nothing to do, she could teach them—cut a road straight to the southwest, save miles, connect with the state highway at the freight depot of—oh, stop it!

She put her kerosene lamp aside and sat in her cabin after dark by the light of a candle, listening to the music of a small portable radio. She hunted for symphony concerts and twisted the dial rapidly past whenever she caught the raucous syllables of a news broadcast; she did not want any news from the city.

Don't think of Taggart Transcontinental—she had told herself on her first night in the cabin—don't think of it until you're able to hear the words as if they were "Atlantic Southern" or "Associated Steel." But the weeks passed and no scar would grow over the wound.

It seemed to her as if she were fighting the unpredictable cruelty of her own mind. She would lie in bed, drifting off to sleep—then find herself suddenly thinking that the conveyor belt was worn at the coaling station at Willow Bend, Indiana, she had seen it from the window of her car on her last trip, she must tell them to replace it or they—

and then she would be sitting up in bed, crying, Stop it!—and stopping it, but remaining awake for the rest of that night.

She would sit at the door of the cabin at sunset and watch the motion of the leaves growing still in the twilight—then she would see the sparks of the fireflies rising from the grass, flashing on and off in every darkening corner, flashing slowly, as if holding one moment's warning—they were like the lights of signals winking at night over the track of a—Stop it!

It was the times when she could not stop it that she dreaded, the times when, unable to stand up—as in physical pain, with no limit to divide it from the pain of her mind—she would fall down on the floor of the cabin or on the earth of the woods and sit still, with her face pressed to a chair or a rock, and fight not to let herself scream aloud, while they were suddenly as close to her and as real as the body of a lover: the two lines of rail going off to a single point in the distance—the front of an engine cutting space apart by means of the letters TT—the sound of the wheels clicking in accented rhythm under the floor of her car—the statue of Nat Taggart in the concourse of the Terminal. Fighting not to know them, not to feel them, her body rigid but for the grinding motion of her face against her arm, she would draw whatever power over her consciousness still remained to her into the soundless, toneless repetition of the words: Get it over with.

There were long stretches of calm, when she was able to face her problem with the dispassionate clarity of weighing a problem in engineering. But she could find no answer. She knew that her desperate longing for the railroad would vanish, were she to convince herself that it was impossible or improper. But the longing came from the certainty that the truth and the right were hers—that the enemy was the irrational and the unreal—that she could not set herself another goal or summon the love to achieve it, while her rightful achievement had been lost, not to some superior power, but to a loathsome evil that conquered by means of impotence.

She could renounce the railroad, she thought; she could find contentment here, in this forest; but she would build the path, then reach the road below, then rebuild the road—and then she would reach the storekeeper of Woodstock and that would be the end, and the empty white face staring at the universe in stagnant apathy would be the limit placed on her effort. Why?—she heard herself screaming aloud. There was no answer.

Then stay here until you answer it, she thought. You have no place to go, you can't move, you can't start grading a right-of-way until . . . until you know enough to choose a terminal.

There were long, silent evenings when the emotion that made her sit still and look at the unattainable distance beyond the fading light to the south, was loneliness for Hank Rearden. She wanted the sight of his unyielding face, the confident face looking at her with the hint of a smile. But she knew that she could not see him until her battle was won. His smile had to be deserved, it was intended for an adversary who traded her strength against his, not for a pain-beaten wretch who would seek relief in that smile and thus destroy its meaning. He could help her to live; he could not help her to decide for what purpose she wished to go on living.

She had felt a faint touch of anxiety since the morning when she marked "May 15" on her calendar. She had forced herself to listen to news broadcasts, once in a while; she had heard no mention of his name. Her fear for him was her last link to the city; it kept drawing her eyes to the horizon at the south and down to the road at the foot of the hill. She found herself waiting for him to come. She found herself listening for the sound of a motor. But the only sound to give her a futile start of hope at times, was the sudden crackle of some large bird's wings hurtling through the branches into the sky.

There was another link to the past, that still remained as an unsolved question: Quentin Daniels and the motor that he was trying to rebuild. By June 1, she would owe him his monthly check. Should she tell him that she had quit, that she would never need that motor and neither would the world? Should she tell him to stop and to let the remnant of the motor vanish in rust on some such junk pile as the one where she had found it? She could not force herself to do it. It seemed harder than leaving the railroad. That motor, she thought, was not a link to the past: it was her last link to the future. To kill it seemed like an act, not of murder, but of suicide: her order to stop it would be her signature under the certainty that there was no terminal for her to seek ahead.

But it is not true—she thought, as she stood at the door of her cabin, on this morning of May 28—it is not true that there is no place in the future for a superlative achievement of man's mind; it can never be true. No matter what her problem, this would always remain to her—this immovable conviction that evil was unnatural and temporary. She felt it more clearly than ever this morning: the certainty that the ugliness of the men in the city and the ugliness of her suffering were transient accidents—while the smiling sense of hope within her at the sight of a sun-flooded forest, the sense of an unlimited promise, was the permanent and the real.

She stood at the door, smoking a cigarette. In the room behind her, the sounds of a symphony of her grandfather's time were coming from the radio. She barely listened, she was conscious only of the flow of chords that seemed to play an underscoring harmony for the flow of the smoke curving slowly from her cigarette, for the curving motion of her arm moving the cigarette to her lips once in a while. She closed her eyes and stood still, feeling the rays of the sun on her body. This was the achievement, she thought—to enjoy this moment, to let no memory of pain blunt her capacity to feel as she felt right now; so long as she could preserve this feeling, she would have the fuel to go on.

She was barely aware of a faint noise that came through the music, like the scratching of an old record. The first thing to reach her consciousness was the sudden jerk of her own hand flinging the cigarette aside. It came in the same instant as the realization that the noise was growing louder and that it was the sound of a motor. Then she knew that she had not admitted to herself how much she had wanted to hear that sound, how desperately she had waited for Hank Rearden. She heard her own chuckle—it was humbly, cautiously low, as if not to disturb the drone of revolving metal which was now the unmistakable sound of a car rising up the mountain road.

She could not see the road—the small stretch under the arch of branches at the foot of the hill was her only view of it—but she watched the car's ascent by the growing, imperious strain of the motor against the grades and the screech of the tires on curves.

The car stopped under the arch of branches. She did not recognize it —it was not the black Hammond, but a long, gray convertible. She saw the driver step out: it was a man whose presence here could not be possible. It was Francisco d'Anconia.

The shock she felt was not disappointment, it was more like the sensation that disappointment would now be irrelevant. It was eagerness and an odd, solemn stillness, the sudden certainty that she was facing the approach of something unknown and of the gravest importance.

The swiftness of Francisco's movements was carrying him toward the hill while he was raising his head to glance up. He saw her above, at the door of the cabin, and stopped. She could not distinguish the expression on his face. He stood still for a long moment, his face raised to her. Then he started up the hill.

She felt—almost as if she had expected it—that this was a scene from their childhood. He was coming toward her, not running, but moving upward with a kind of triumphant, confident eagerness. No, she thought, this was not their childhood—it was the future as she would have seen it then, in the days when she waited for him as for her release from prison. It was a moment's view of a morning they would have reached, if her vision of life had been fulfilled, if they had both gone the way she had then been so certain of going. Held motionless by wonder, she stood looking at him, taking this moment, not in the name of the present, but as a salute to their past.

When he was close enough and she could distinguish his face, she saw the look of that luminous gaiety which transcends the solemn by proclaiming the great innocence of a man who has earned the right to be light-hearted. He was smiling and whistling some piece of music that seemed to flow like the long, smooth, rising flight of his steps. The melody seemed distantly familiar to her, she felt that it belonged with this moment, yet she felt also that there was something odd about it, something important to grasp, only she could not think of it now.

"Hi, Slug!"

"Hi, Frisco!"

She knew—by the way he looked at her, by an instant's drop of his eyelids closing his eyes, by the brief pull of his head striving to lean back and resist, by the faint, half-smiling, half-helpless relaxation of his lips, then by the sudden harshness of his arms as he seized her—that it was involuntary, that he had not intended it, and that it was irresistibly right for both of them.

The desperate violence of the way he held her, the hurting pressure of his mouth on hers, the exultant surrender of his body to the touch of hers, were not the form of a moment's pleasure— she knew that no physical hunger could bring a man to this—she knew that it was the statement she had never heard from him, the greatest confession of love a man could make. No matter what he had done to wreck his life, this was still the Francisco d'Anconia in whose bed she had been so proud of belonging—no matter what betrayals she had met from the world, her vision of life had been true and some indestructible part of it had remained within him—and in answer to it, her body responded to his, her arms and mouth held him, confessing her desire, confessing an acknowledgment she had always given him and always would.

Then the rest of his years came back to her, with a stab of the pain of knowing that the greater his person, the more terrible his guilt in destroying it. She pulled herself away from him, she shook her head, she said, in answer to both of them, "No."

He stood looking at her, disarmed and smiling. "Not yet. You have a great deal to forgive me, first. But I can tell you everything now."

She had never heard that low, breathless quality of helplessness in his voice. He was fighting to regain control, there was almost a touch of apology in his smile, the apology of a child pleading for indulgence, but there was also an adult's amusement, the laughing declaration that he did not have to hide his struggle, since it was happiness that he was wrestling with, not pain.

She backed away from him; she felt as if emotion had flung her ahead of her own consciousness, and questions were now catching up with her, groping toward the form of words.

"Dagny, that torture you've been going through, here, for the last month . . . answer me as honestly as you can . . . do you think you could have borne it twelve years ago?"

"No," she answered; he smiled. "Why do you ask that?"

"To redeem twelve years of my life, which I won't have to regret."

"What do you mean? And"—her questions had caught up with her—"and what do you know about my torture here?"

"Dagny, aren't you beginning to see that I would know everything about it?"

"How did you . . . Francisco! What were you whistling when you were coming up the hill?"

"Why, was I? I don't know."

"It was the Fifth Concerto by Richard Halley, wasn't it?"

"Oh . . . !" He looked startled, then smiled in amusement at himself, then answered gravely, "I'll tell you that later."

"How did you find out where I was?"

"I'll tell you that, too."

"You forced it out of Eddie."

"I haven't seen Eddie for over a year."

"He was the only one who knew it."

"It wasn't Eddie who told me."

"I didn't want anybody to find me."

He glanced slowly about him, she saw his eyes stop on the path she had built, on the planted flowers, on the fresh-shingled roof. He chuckled, as if he understood and as if it hurt him. "You shouldn't have been left here for a month," he said. "God, you shouldn't have! It's my first failure, at the one time when I didn't want to fail. But I didn't think you were ready to quit. Had I known it, I would have watched you day and night."

"Really? What for?"

"To spare you"—he pointed at her work—"all this."

"Francisco," she said, her voice low, "if you're concerned about my torture, don't you know that I don't want to hear you speak of it, because—" She stopped; she had never complained to him, not in all those years; her voice flat, she said only, "—that I don't want to hear it?"

"Because I'm the one man who has no right to speak of it? Dagny, if you think that I don't know how much I've hurt you, I'll tell you about the years when I . . . But it's over. Oh, darling, it's over!"

"Is it?"

"Forgive me, I mustn't say that. Not until you say it." He was trying to control his voice, but the look of happiness was beyond his power of control.

"Are you happy because I've lost everything I lived for? All right, I'll say it, if this is what you've come to hear: you were the first thing I lost—does it amuse you now to see that I've lost the rest?"

He glanced straight at her, his eyes drawn narrow by such an intensity of earnestness that the glance was almost a threat, and she knew that whatever the years had meant to him, "amusement" was the one word she had no right to utter.

"Do you really think that?" he asked.

She whispered, "No . . ."

"Dagny, we can never lose the things we live for. We may have to change their form at times, if we've made an error, but the purpose remains the same and the forms are ours to make."

"That is what I've been telling myself for a month. But there's no way left open toward any purpose whatever."

He did not answer. He sat down on a boulder by the door of the cabin, watching her as if he did not want to miss a single shadow of reaction on her face. "What do you think now of the men who quit and vanished?" he asked.

She shrugged, with a faint smile of helpless sadness, and sat down on the ground beside him. "You know," she said, "I used to think that there was some destroyer who came after them and made them quit. But I guess there wasn't. There have been times, this past month, when I've almost wished he would come for me, too. But nobody came."

"No?"

"No. I used to think that he gave them some inconceivable reason to make them betray everything they loved. But that wasn't necessary. I know how they felt. I can't blame them any longer. What I don't know is how they learned to exist afterward—if any of them still exist."

"Do you feel that you've betrayed Taggart Transcontinental?"

"No. I . . . I feel that I would have betrayed it by remaining at work."

"You would have."

"If I had agreed to serve the looters, it's . . . it's Nat Taggart that I would have delivered to them. I couldn't. I couldn't let his achievement, and mine, end up with the looters as our final goal."

"No, you couldn't. Do you call this indifference? Do you think that you love the railroad less than you did a month ago?"

"I think that I would give my life for just one more year on the railroad . . . But I can't go back to it."

"Then you know what they felt, all the men who quit, and what it was that they loved when they gave up."

"Francisco," she asked, not looking at him, her head bent, "why did you ask me whether I could have given it up twelve years ago?"

"Don't you know what night I am thinking of, just as you are?"

"Yes . . ." she whispered.

"That was the night I gave up d'Anconia Copper."

Slowly, with a long effort, she moved her head to glance up at him. His face had the expression she had seen then, on that next morning, twelve years ago: the look of a smile, though he was not smiling, the quiet look of victory over pain, the look of a man's pride in the price he paid and in that which made it worth paying.

"But you didn't give it up," she said. "You didn't quit. You're still the President of d'Anconia Copper, only it means nothing to you now."

"It means as much to me now as it did that night."

"Then how can you let it go to pieces?"

"Dagny, you're more fortunate than I. Taggart Transcontinental is a delicate piece of precision machinery. It will not last long without you. It cannot be run by slave labor. They will mercifully destroy it for you and you won't have to see it serving the looters. But copper-mining is a simpler job. D'Anconia Copper could have lasted for generations of looters and slaves. Crudely, miserably, ineptly—but it could have lasted and helped them to last. I had to destroy it myself."

"You—what?"

"I am destroying d'Anconia Copper, consciously, deliberately, by plan and by my own hand. I have to plan it as carefully and work as hard as if I were producing a fortune—in order not to let them notice it and stop me, in order not to let them seize the mines until it is too late. All the effort and energy I had hoped to spend on d'Anconia Copper, I'm spending them, only . . . only it's not to make it grow. I shall destroy every last bit of it and every last penny of my fortune and every ounce of copper that could feed the looters. I shall not leave it as I found it—I shall leave it as Sebastián d'Anconia found it—then let them try to exist without him or me!"

"Francisco!" she screamed. "How could you make yourself do it?"

"By the grace of the same love as yours," he answered quietly, "my love for d'Anconia Copper, for the spirit of which it was the shape. Was—and, some day, will be again."

She sat still, trying to grasp all the implications of what she now grasped only as the numbness of shock. In the silence, the music of the radio symphony went on, and the rhythm of the chords reached her like the slow, solemn pounding of steps, while she struggled to see at once the whole progression of twelve years: the tortured boy who called for help on her breasts—the man who sat on the floor of a drawing room, playing marbles and laughing at the destruction of great industries—the man who cried, "My love, I can't!" while refusing to help her—the man who drank a toast, in the dim booth of a barroom, to the years which Sebastián d'Anconia had had to wait. . . .

"Francisco . . . of all the guesses I tried to make about you . . . I never thought of it . . . I never thought that you were one of those men who had quit . . ."

"I was one of the first of them."

"I thought that they always vanished . . ."

"Well, hadn't I? Wasn't it the worst of what I did to you—that I left you looking at a cheap playboy who was not the Francisco d'Anconia you had known?"

"Yes . . ." she whispered, "only the worst was that I couldn't believe it . . . I never did . . . It was Francisco d'Anconia that I kept seeing every time I saw you. . . ."

"I know. And I know what it did to you. I tried to help you understand, but it was too soon to tell you. Dagny, if I had told you—that night or the day when you came to damn me for the San Sebastián Mines—that I was not an aimless loafer, that I was out to speed up the destruction of everything we had held sacred together, the destruction of d'Anconia Copper, of Taggart Transcontinental, of Wyatt Oil, of Rearden Steel—would you have found it easier to take?"

"Harder," she whispered. "I'm not sure I can take it, even now. Neither your kind of renunciation nor my own . . . But, Francisco"—she threw her head back suddenly to look up at him—"if this was your secret, then of all the hell you had to take, I was—"

"Oh yes, my darling, yes, *you* were the worst of it!" It was a desperate cry, its sound of laughter and of release confessing all the agony he wanted to sweep away. He seized her hand, he pressed his mouth to it, then his face, not to let her see the reflection of what his years had been like. "If it's any kind of atonement, which it isn't . . . whatever I made you suffer, that's how I paid for it . . . by knowing what I was doing to you and having to do it . . . and waiting, waiting to . . . But it's over."

He raised his head, smiling, he looked down at her and she saw a look of protective tenderness come into his face, which told her of the despair he saw in hers.

"Dagny, don't think of that. I won't claim any suffering of mine as my excuse. Whatever my reason, I knew what I was doing and I've hurt you terribly. I'll need years to make up for it. Forget what"—she knew that he meant: what his embrace had confessed—"what I haven't said. Of all the things I have to tell you, that is the one I'll say last." But his eyes, his smile, the grasp of his fingers on her wrist were saying it against his will. "You've borne too much, and there's a great deal that you have to learn to understand in order to lose every scar of the torture you never should have had to bear. All that matters now is that you're free to recover. We're free, both of us, we're free of the looters, we're out of their reach."

She said, her voice quietly desolate, "That's what I came here for—to try to understand. But I can't. It seems monstrously wrong to surrender the world to the looters, and monstrously wrong to live under their rule. I can neither give up nor go back. I can neither exist without work nor work as a serf. I had always thought that any sort of battle was proper, anything, except renunciation. I'm not sure we're right to quit, you and I, when we should have fought them. But there is no way to fight. It's surrender, if we leave—and surrender, if we remain. I don't know what is right any longer."

"Check your premises, Dagny. Contradictions don't exist."

"But I can't find any answer. I can't condemn you for what you're doing, yet it's horror that I feel—admiration and horror, at the same time. You, the heir of the d'Anconias, who could have surpassed all his ancestors of the miraculous hand that produced, you're turning your matchless ability to the job of destruction. And I—I'm playing with cobblestones and shingling a roof, while a transcontinental railroad system is collapsing in the hands of congenital ward heelers. Yet you and

I were the kind who determine the fate of the world. If this is what we let it come to, then it must have been our own guilt. But I can't see the nature of our error."

"Yes, Dagny, it *was* our own guilt."

"Because we didn't work hard enough?"

"Because we worked too hard—and charged too little."

"What do you mean?"

"We never demanded the one payment that the world owed us—and we let our best reward go to the worst of men. The error was made centuries ago, it was made by Sebastián d'Anconia, by Nat Taggart, by every man who fed the world and received no thanks in return. You don't know what is right any longer? Dagny, this is not a battle over material goods. It's a moral crisis, the greatest the world has ever faced and the last. Our age is the climax of centuries of evil. We must put an end to it, once and for all, or perish—we, the men of the mind. It was our own guilt. We produced the wealth of the world—but we let our enemies write its moral code."

"But we never accepted their code. We lived by our own standards."

"Yes—and paid ransoms for it! Ransoms in matter and in spirit—in money, which our enemies received, but did not deserve, and in honor, which we deserved, but did not receive. *That* was our guilt—that we were willing to pay. We kept mankind alive, yet we allowed men to despise us and to worship our destroyers. We allowed them to worship incompetence and brutality, the recipients and the dispensers of the unearned. By accepting punishment, not for any sins, but for our virtues, we betrayed our code and made theirs possible. Dagny, theirs is the morality of kidnappers. They use your love of virtue as a hostage. They know that you'll bear anything in order to work and produce, because you know that achievement is man's highest moral purpose, that he can't exist without it, and your love of virtue is your love of life. They count on you to assume any burden. They count on you to feel that no effort is too great in the service of your love. Dagny, your enemies are destroying you by means of your own power. Your generosity and your endurance are their only tools. Your unrequited rectitude is the only hold they have upon you. They know it. You don't. The day when you'll discover it is the only thing they dread. You must learn to understand them. You won't be free of them, until you do. But when you do, you'll reach such a stage of rightful anger that you'll blast every rail of Taggart Transcontinental, rather than let it serve them!"

"But to leave it to them!" she moaned. "To abandon it . . . To abandon Taggart Transcontinental . . . when it's . . . it's almost like a living person . . ."

"It was. It isn't any longer. Leave it to them. It won't do them any good. Let it go. We don't need it. We can rebuild it. They can't. We'll survive without it. They won't."

"But *we,* brought down to renouncing and giving up!"

"Dagny, we who've been called 'materialists' by the killers of the human spirit, we're the only ones who know how little value or meaning there is in material objects as such, because we're the ones who create their value and meaning. We can afford to give them up, for a short while, in order to redeem something much more precious. We are the soul, of which railroads, copper mines, steel mills and oil wells are the body—and they are living entities that beat day and night, like our hearts, in the sacred function of supporting human life, but only so long as they remain our body, only so long as they remain the expression, the reward and the property of achievement. Without us, they are corpses and their sole product is poison, not wealth or food, the poison of disintegration that turns men into hordes of scavengers. Dagny, learn to understand the nature of your own power and you'll understand the paradox you now see around you. *You* do not have to depend on any material possessions, they depend on you, you create them, you own the one and only tool of production. Wherever you are, you will always be able to produce. But the looters—by their own stated theory—are in desperate, permanent, congenital need and at the blind mercy of matter. Why don't you take them at their word? They need railroads, factories, mines, motors, which they cannot make or run. Of what use will your railroad be to them without you? Who held it together? Who kept it alive? Who saved it, time and time again? Was it your brother James? Who fed him? Who fed the looters? Who produced their weapons? Who gave them the means to enslave you? The impossible spectacle of shabby little incompetents holding control over the products of genius—who made it possible? Who supported your enemies, who forged your chains, who destroyed your achievement?"

The motion that threw her upright was like a silent cry. He shot to his feet with the stored abruptness of a spring uncoiling, his voice driving on in merciless triumph:

"You're beginning to see, aren't you? Dagny! Leave them the carcass of that railroad, leave them all the rusted rails and rotted ties and gutted engines—but don't leave them your mind! Don't leave them your mind! The fate of the world rests on that decision!"

"Ladies and gentlemen," said the panic-pregnant voice of a radio announcer, breaking off the chords of the symphony, "we interrupt this broadcast to bring you a special news bulletin. The greatest disaster in railroad history occurred in the early hours of the morning on the main line of Taggart Transcontinental, at Winston, Colorado, demolishing the famous Taggart Tunnel!"

Her scream sounded like the screams that had rung out in the one last moment in the darkness of the tunnel. Its sound remained with him through the rest of the broadcast—as they both ran to the radio in the cabin and stood, in equal terror, her eyes staring at the radio, his eyes watching her face.

"The details of the story were obtained from Luke Beal, fireman of the Taggart luxury main liner, the Comet, who was found unconscious at the western portal of the tunnel this morning, and who appears to be the sole survivor of the catastrophe. Through some astounding infraction of safety rules—in circumstances not yet fully established—the Comet, westbound for San Francisco, was sent into the tunnel with a coal-burning steam locomotive. The Taggart Tunnel, an eight-mile bore, cut through the summit of the Rocky Mountains and regarded as an engineering achievement not to be equaled in our time, was built by the grandson of Nathaniel Taggart, in the great age of the clean, smokeless Diesel-electric engine. The tunnel's ventilation system was not designed to provide for the heavy smoke and fumes of coal-burning locomotives—and it was known to every railroad employee in the district that to send a train into the tunnel with such a locomotive would mean death by suffocation for everyone aboard. The Comet, none the less, was so ordered to proceed. According to Fireman Beal, the effects of the fumes began to be felt when the train was about three miles inside the tunnel. Engineer Joseph Scott threw the throttle wide open, in a desperate attempt to gain speed, but the old, worn engine was inadequate for the weight of the long train and the rising grade of the track. Struggling through the thickening fumes, engineer and fireman had barely managed to force the leaking steam boilers up to a speed of forty miles per hour—when some passenger, prompted undoubtedly by the panic of choking, pulled the emergency brake cord. The sudden jolt of the stop apparently broke the engine's airhose, for the train could not be started again. There were screams coming from the cars. Passengers were breaking windows. Engineer Scott struggled frantically to make the engine start, but collapsed at the throttle, overcome by the fumes. Fireman Beal leaped from the engine and ran. He was within sight of the western portal, when he heard the blast of the explosion, which is the last thing he remembers. The rest of the story was gathered from railroad employees at Winston Station. It appears that an Army Freight Special, westbound, carrying a heavy load of explosives, had been given no warning about the presence of the Comet on the track just ahead. Both trains had encountered delays and were running off their schedules. It appears that the Freight Special had been ordered to proceed regardless of signals, because the tunnel's signal system was out of order. It is said that in spite of speed regulations and in view of the frequent breakdowns of the ventilating system, it was the tacit custom of all engineers to go full speed while in the tunnel. It appears, as far as can be established at present, that the Comet was stalled just beyond the point where the tunnel makes a sharp curve. It is believed that everyone aboard was dead by that time. It is doubted that the engineer of the Freight Special, turning a curve at eighty miles an hour, would have been able to see, in time, the observation window of the Comet's last car, which was brightly lighted when it left Winston Station. What is known is that the Freight Special crashed into the rear of the Comet. The explosion of the Special's cargo broke windows in a farmhouse five miles away and brought down such a weight of rock upon the tunnel that rescue parties have not yet been able to come within three miles of where either train had been. It is not expected that any survivors will be found—and it is not believed that the Taggart Tunnel can ever be rebuilt."

She stood still. She looked as if she were seeing, not the room around her, but the scene in Colorado. Her sudden movement had the abruptness of a convulsion. With the single-tracked rationality of a somnambulist, she whirled to find her handbag, as if it were the only object in existence, she seized it, she whirled to the door and ran.

"Dagny!" he screamed. "Don't go back!"

The scream had no more power to reach her than if he were calling to her across the miles between him and the mountains of Colorado.

He ran after her, he caught her, seizing her by both elbows, and he cried, "Don't go back! Dagny! In the name of anything sacred to you, don't go back!"

She looked as if she did not know who he was. In a contest of physical strength, he could have broken the bones of her arms without effort. But with the force of a living creature fighting for life, she tore herself loose so violently that she threw him off balance for a moment. When he regained his footing, she was running down the hill—running as he had run at the sound of the alarm siren in Rearden's mills—running to her car on the road below.

* * *

His letter of resignation lay on the desk before him—and James Taggart sat staring at it, hunched by hatred. He felt as if his enemy were this piece of paper, not the words on it, but the sheet and the ink that had given the words a material finality. He had always regarded thoughts and words as inconclusive, but a material shape was that which he had spent his life escaping: a commitment.

He had not decided to resign—not really, he thought; he had dictated the letter for a motive which he identified to himself only as "just in case." The letter, he felt, was a form of protection; but he had not signed it yet, and that was his protection against the protection. The hatred was directed at whatever had brought him to feel that he would not be able to continue extending this process much longer.

He had received word of the catastrophe at eight o'clock this morning; by noon, he had arrived at his office. An instinct that came from reasons which he knew, but spent his whole effort on not knowing, had told him that he had to be there, this time.

The men who had been his marked cards—in a game he knew how to play—were gone. Clifton Locey was barricaded behind the statement of a doctor who had announced that Mr. Locey was suffering from a heart condition which made it impossible to disturb him at present. One of Taggart's executive assistants was said to have left for Boston last night, and the other was said to have been called unexpectedly to an unnamed hospital, to the bedside of a father nobody had ever suspected him of having. There was no answer at the home of the chief engineer. The vice-president in charge of public relations could not be found.

Driving through the streets to his office, Taggart had seen the black letters of the headlines. Walking down the corridors of Taggart Transcontinental, he had heard the voice of a speaker pouring from a radio in someone's office, the kind of voice one expects to hear on unlighted street corners: it was screaming demands for the nationalization of the railroads.

He had walked through the corridors, his steps noisy, in order to be seen, and hasty, in order not to be stopped for questions. He had locked the door of his office, ordering his secretary not to admit any person or phone call and to tell all comers that Mr. Taggart was busy.

Then he sat at his desk, alone with blank terror. He felt as if he were trapped in a subterranean vault and the lock could never be broken again—and as if he were held on display in the sight of the whole city below, hoping that the lock would hold out for eternity. He had to be here, in this office, it was required of him, he had to sit idly and wait—wait for the unknown to descend upon him and to determine his actions—and the terror was both of who would come for him and of the fact that nobody came, nobody to tell him what to do.

The ringing of the telephones in the outer office sounded like screams for help. He looked at the door with a sensation of malevolent triumph at the thought of all those voices being defeated by the innocuous figure of his secretary, a young man expert at nothing but the art of evasion, which he practiced with the gray, rubber limpness of the amoral. The voices, thought Taggart, were coming from Colorado, from every center of the Taggart system, from every office of the building around him. He was safe so long as he did not have to hear them.

His emotions had clogged into a still, solid, opaque ball within him, which the thought of the men who operated the Taggart system could not pierce; those men were merely enemies to be outwitted. The sharper bites of fear came from the thought of the men on the Board of Directors; but his letter of resignation was his fire escape, which would leave them stuck with the fire. The sharpest fear came from the thought of the men in Washington. If they called, he would have to answer; his rubber secretary would know whose voices superseded his orders. But Washington did not call.

The fear went through him in spasms, once in a while, leaving his mouth dry. He did not know what he dreaded. He knew that it was not the threat of the radio speaker. What he had experienced at the sound of the snarling voice had been more like a terror which he felt because he was expected to feel it, a duty-terror, something that went with his position, like well-tailored suits and luncheon speeches. But under it, he had felt a sneaking little hope, swift and furtive like the course of a cockroach: if that threat took form, it would solve everything, save him from decision, save him from signing the letter . . . he would not be President of Taggart Transcontinental any longer, but neither would anyone else . . . neither would anyone else. . . .

He sat, looking down at his desk, keeping his eyes and his mind out of focus. It was as if he were immersed in a pool of fog, struggling not to let it reach the finality of any form. That which exists possesses identity; he could keep it out of existence by refusing to identify it.

He did not examine the events in Colorado, he did not attempt to grasp their cause, he did not consider their consequences. He did not think. The clogged ball of emotion was like a physical weight in his chest, filling his consciousness, releasing him from the responsibility of thought. The ball was hatred—hatred as his only answer, hatred as the sole reality, hatred without object, cause, beginning or end, hatred as his claim against the universe, as a justification, as a right, as an absolute.

The screaming of the telephones went on through the silence. He knew that those pleas for help were not addressed to him, but to an entity whose shape he had stolen. It was this shape that the screams were now tearing away from him; he felt as if the ringing ceased to be sounds and became a succession of slashes hitting his skull. The object of the hatred began to take form, as if summoned by the bells. The solid ball exploded within him and flung him blindly into action.

Rushing out of the room, in defiance of all the faces around him, he went running down the halls to the Operating Department and into the anteroom of the Operating Vice-President's office.

The door to the office was open: he saw the sky in the great windows beyond an empty desk. Then he saw the staff in the anteroom around him, and the blond head of Eddie Willers in the glass cubbyhole. He walked purposefully straight toward Eddie Willers, he flung the glass door open and, from the threshold, in the sight and hearing of the room, he screamed:

"Where is she?"

Eddie Willers rose slowly to his feet and stood looking at Taggart with an odd kind of dutiful curiosity, as if this were one more phenomenon to observe among all the unprecedented things he had observed. He did not answer.

"Where is she?"

"I cannot tell you."

"Listen, you stubborn little punk, this is no time for ceremony! If you're trying to make me believe that you don't know where she is, I don't believe you! You know it and you're going to tell me, or I'll report you to the Unification Board! I'll swear to them that you know it—then try and prove that you don't!"

There was a faint tone of astonishment in Eddie's voice as he answered, "I've never attempted to imply that I don't know where she is, Jim. I know it. But I won't tell you."

Taggart's scream rose to the shrill, impotent sound that confesses a miscalculation: "Do you realize what you're saying?"

"Why, yes, of course."

"Will you repeat it"—he waved at the room—"for these witnesses?"

Eddie raised his voice a little, more in precision and clarity than in volume: "I know where she is. But I will not tell you."

"You're confessing that you're an accomplice who's aiding and abetting a deserter?"

"If that's what you wish to call it."

"But it's a crime! It's a crime against the nation. Don't you know that?"

"No."

"It's against the law!"

"Yes."

"This is a national emergency! You have no right to any private secrets! You're withholding vital information! I'm the President of this railroad! I'm ordering you to tell me! You can't refuse to obey an order! It's a penitentiary offense! Do you understand?"

"Yes."

"Do you refuse?"

"I do."

Years of training had made Taggart able to watch any audience around him, without appearing to do so. He saw the tight, closed faces of the staff, faces that were not his allies. All had a look of despair, except the face of Eddie Willers. The "feudal serf" of Taggart Transcontinental was the only one who seemed untouched by the disaster. He looked at Taggart with the lifelessly conscientious glance of a scholar confronted by a field of knowledge he had never wanted to study.

"Do you realize that you're a traitor?" yelled Taggart.

Eddie asked quietly, "To whom?"

"To the people! It's treason to shield a deserter! It's economic treason! Your duty to feed the people comes first, above anything else whatever! Every public authority has said so! Don't you know it? Don't you know what they'll do to you?"

"Don't you see that I don't give a damn about that?"

"Oh, you don't? I'll quote that to the Unification Board! I have all these witnesses to prove that you said—"

"Don't bother about witnesses, Jim. Don't put them on the spot. I'll write down everything I said, I'll sign it, and you can take it to the Board."

The sudden explosion of Taggart's voice sounded as if he had been slapped: "Who are *you* to stand against the government? Who are you, you miserable little office rat, to judge national policies and hold opinions of your own? Do you think the country has time to bother about your opinions, your wishes or your precious little conscience? You're going to learn a lesson—all of you!—all of you spoiled, self-indulgent, undisciplined little two-bit clerks, who strut as if that crap about your rights was serious! You're going to learn that these are not the days of Nat Taggart!"

Eddie said nothing. For an instant, they stood looking at each other across the desk. Taggart's face was distorted by terror, Eddie's remained sternly serene. James Taggart believed the existence of an Eddie Willers too well; Eddie Willers could not believe the existence of a James Taggart.

"Do you think the nation will bother about your wishes or hers?" screamed Taggart. "It's her duty to come back! It's her duty to work! What do we care whether she wants to work or not? We *need* her!"

"Do you, Jim?"

An impulse pertaining to self-preservation made Taggart back a step away from the sound of that particular tone, a very quiet tone, in the voice of Eddie Willers. But Eddie made no move to follow. He remained standing behind his desk, in a manner suggesting the civilized tradition of a business office.

"You won't find her," he said. "She won't be back. I'm glad she won't. You can starve, you can close the railroad, you can throw me in jail, you can have me shot—what does it matter? I won't tell you where she is. If I see the whole country crashing, I won't tell you. You won't find her. You—"

They whirled at the sound of the entrance door flung open. They saw Dagny standing on the threshold.

She wore a wrinkled cotton dress, and her hair was disheveled by hours of driving. She stopped for the duration of a glance around her, as if to recapture the place, but there was no recognition of persons in her eyes, the glance merely swept through the room, as if making a swift inventory of physical objects. Her face was not the face they remembered; it had aged, not by means of lines, but by means of a still, naked look stripped of any quality save ruthlessness.

Yet their first response, ahead of shock or wonder, was a single emotion that went through the room like a gasp of relief. It was in all their faces but one: Eddie Willers, who alone had been calm a moment ago, collapsed with his face down on his desk; he made no sound, but the movements of his shoulders were sobs.

Her face gave no sign of acknowledgment to anyone, no greeting, as if her presence here were inevitable and no words were necessary. She went straight to the door of her office; passing the desk of her secretary, she said, her voice like the sound of a business machine, neither rude nor gentle, "Ask Eddie to come in."

James Taggart was the first one to move, as if dreading to let her out of his sight. He rushed in after her, he cried, "I couldn't help it!" and then, life returning to him, his own, his normal kind of life, he screamed, "It was *your* fault! You did it! You're to blame for it! Because you left!"

He wondered whether his scream had been an illusion inside his own ears. Her face remained blank; yet she had turned to him; she looked as if sounds had reached her, but not words, not the communication of a mind. What he felt for a moment was his closest approach to a sense of his own non-existence.

Then he saw the faintest change in her face, merely the indication of perceiving a human presence, but she was looking past him and he turned and saw that Eddie Willers had entered the office.

There were traces of tears in Eddie's eyes, but he made no attempt to hide them, he stood straight, as if the tears or any embarrassment or any apology for them were as irrelevant to him as to her.

She said, "Get Ryan on the telephone, tell him I'm here, then let me speak to him." Ryan had been the general manager of the railroad's Central Region.

Eddie gave her a warning by not answering at once, then said, his voice as even as hers, "Ryan's gone, Dagny. He quit last week."

They did not notice Taggart, as they did not notice the furniture around them. She had not granted him even the recognition of ordering him out of her office. Like a paralytic, uncertain of his muscles' obedience, he gathered his strength and slipped out. But he was certain of the first thing he had to do: he hurried to his office to destroy his letter of resignation.

She did not notice his exit; she was looking at Eddie. "Is Knowland here?" she asked.

"No. He's gone."

"Andrews?"

"Gone."

"McGuire?"

"Gone."

He went on quietly to recite the list of those he knew she would ask for, those most needed in this hour, who had resigned and vanished within the past month. She listened without astonishment or emotion, as one listens to the casualty list of a battle where all are doomed and it makes no difference whose names fall first.

When he finished, she made no comment, but asked, "What has been done since this morning?"

"Nothing."

"Nothing?"

"Dagny, any office boy could have issued orders here since this morning and everybody would have obeyed him. But even the office boys know that whoever makes the first move today will be held responsible for the future, the present and the past—when the buck-passing begins. He would not save the system, he would merely lose his job by the time he saved one division. Nothing has been done. It's stopped still. Whatever is moving, is moving on anyone's blind guess—out on the line where they don't know whether they're to move or to stop. Some trains are held at stations, others are going on, waiting to be stopped before they reach Colorado. It's whatever the local dispatchers decide. The Terminal manager downstairs has cancelled all transcontinental traffic for today, including tonight's Comet. I don't know what the manager in San Francisco is doing. Only the wrecking crews are working. At the tunnel. They haven't come anywhere near the wreck as yet. I don't think they will."

"Phone the Terminal manager downstairs and tell him to put all transcontinental trains back on the schedule at once, including tonight's Comet. Then come back here."

When he came back, she was bending over the maps she had spread on a table, and she spoke while he made rapid notes:

"Route all westbound trains south from Kirby, Nebraska, down the spur track to Hastings, down the track of the Kansas Western to Laurel, Kansas, then to the track of the Atlantic Southern at Jasper, Oklahoma. West on the Atlantic Southern to Flagstaff, Arizona, north on the track of the Flagstaff-Homedale to Elgin, Utah, north to Midland, northwest on the track of the Wasatch Railway to Salt Lake City. The Wasatch Railway is an abandoned narrow-gauge. Buy it. Have the gauge spread to standard. If the owners are afraid, since sales are illegal, pay them twice the money and proceed with the work. There is no rail between Laurel, Kansas, and Jasper, Oklahoma—three miles, no rail between Elgin and Midland, Utah—five and a half miles. Have the rail laid. Have construction crews start at once—recruit every local man available, pay twice the legal wages, three times, anything they ask—put three shifts on—and have the job done overnight. For rail, tear up the sidings at Winston, Colorado, at Silver Springs, Colorado, at Leeds, Utah, at Benson, Nevada. If any local stooges of the Unification Board come to stop the work—give authority to our local men, the ones you trust, to bribe them. Don't put that through the Accounting Department, charge it to me, I'll pay it. If they find some case where it doesn't work, have them tell the stooge that Directive 10-289 does not provide for local injunctions, that an injunction has to be brought against our headquarters and that they have to sue *me,* if they wish to stop us."

"Is that true?"

"How do I know? How can anybody know? But by the time they untangle it and decide whatever it is they please to decide—our track will be built."

"I see."

"I'll go over the lists and give you the names of our local men to put in charge—if they're still there. By the time tonight's Comet reaches Kirby, Nebraska, the track will be ready. It will add about thirty-six hours to the transcontinental schedule—but there will be a transcontinental schedule. Then have them get for me out of the files the old maps of our road as it was before Nat Taggart's grandson built the tunnel."

"The . . . what?" He did not raise his voice, but the catch of his breath was the break of emotion he had wanted to avoid.

Her face did not change, but a faint note in her voice acknowledged him, a note of gentleness, not reproof: "The old maps of the days before the tunnel. We're going back, Eddie. Let's hope we can. No, we won't rebuild the tunnel. There's no way to do it now. But the old grade that crossed the Rockies is still there. It can be reclaimed. Only it will be hard to get the rail for it and the men to do it. Particularly the men."

He knew, as he had known from the first, that she had seen his tears and that she had not walked past in indifference, even though her clear, toneless voice and unmoving face gave him no sign of feeling. There was some quality in her manner, which he sensed but could not translate. Yet the feeling it gave him, translated, was as if she were saying to him: I know, I understand, I would feel compassion and gratitude, if we were alive and free to feel, but we're not, are we, Eddie?—we're on a dead planet, like the moon, where we must move, but dare not stop for a breath of feeling or we'll discover that there is no air to breathe.

"We have today and tomorrow to get things started," she said. "I'll leave for Colorado tomorrow night."

"If you want to fly, I'll have to rent a plane for you somewhere. Yours is still in the shops, they can't get the parts for it."

"No, I'll go by rail. I have to see the line. I'll take tomorrow's Comet."

It was two hours later, in a brief pause between long-distance phone calls, that she asked him suddenly the first question which did not pertain to the railroad: "What have they done to Hank Rearden?"

Eddie caught himself in the small evasion of looking away, forced his glance back to meet hers, and answered, "He gave in. He signed their Gift Certificate, at the last moment."

"Oh." The sound conveyed no shock or censure, it was merely a vocal punctuation mark, denoting the acceptance of a fact. "Have you heard from Quentin Daniels?"

"No."

"He sent no letter or message for me?"

"No."

He guessed the thing she feared and it reminded him of a matter he had not reported. "Dagny, there's another problem that's been growing all over the system since you left. Since May first. It's the frozen trains."

"The what?"

"We've had trains abandoned on the line, on some passing track, in the middle of nowhere, usually at night—with the entire crew gone. They just leave the train and vanish. There's never any warning given or any special reason, it's more like an epidemic, it hits the men suddenly and they go. It's been happening on other railroads, too. Nobody can explain it. But I think that everybody understands. It's the directive that's doing it. It's our men's form of protest. They try to go on and then they suddenly reach a moment when they can't take it any longer. What can we do about it?" He shrugged. "Oh well, who is John Galt?"

She nodded thoughtfully; she did not look astonished.

The telephone rang and the voice of her secretary said, "Mr. Wesley Mouch calling from Washington, Miss Taggart."

Her lips stiffened a little, as at the unexpected touch of an insect. "It must be for my brother," she said.

"No, Miss Taggart. For you."

"All right. Put him on."

"Miss Taggart," said the voice of Wesley Mouch in the tone of a cocktail-party host, "I was so glad to hear you've regained your health that I wanted to welcome you back in person. I know that your health required a long rest and I appreciate the patriotism that made you cut your leave of absence short in this terrible emergency. I wanted to assure you that you can count on our co-operation in any step you now find it necessary to take. Our fullest co-operation, assistance and support. If there are any . . . special exceptions you might require, please feel certain that they can be granted."

She let him speak, even though he had made several small pauses inviting an answer. When his pause became long enough, she said, "I would be much obliged if you would let me speak to Mr. Weatherby."

"Why, of course, Miss Taggart, any time you wish . . . why . . . that is . . . do you mean, *now?*"

"Yes. Right now."

He understood. But he said, "Yes, Miss Taggart."

When Mr. Weatherby's voice came on the wire, it sounded cautious: "Yes, Miss Taggart? Of what service can I be to you?"

"You can tell your boss that if he doesn't want me to quit again, as he knows I did, he is never to call me or speak to me. Anything your gang has to tell me, let them send *you* to tell it. I'll speak to you, but not to him. You may tell him that my reason is what he did to Hank Rearden when he was on Rearden's payroll. If everybody else has forgotten it, I haven't."

"It is my duty to assist the nation's railroads at any time, Miss Taggart." Mr. Weatherby sounded as if he were trying to avoid the commitment of having heard what he had heard; but a sudden note of interest crept into his voice as he asked slowly, thoughtfully, with guarded shrewdness, "Am I to understand, Miss Taggart, that it is your wish to deal exclusively with *me* in all official matters? May I take this as your policy?"

She gave a brief, harsh chuckle. "Go ahead," she said. "You may list me as your exclusive property, use me as a special item of pull, and trade me all over Washington. But I don't know what good that will do you, because I'm not going to play the game, I'm not going to trade favors, I'm simply going to start breaking your laws right now—and you can arrest me when you feel that you can afford to."

"I believe that you have an old-fashioned idea about law, Miss Taggart. Why speak of rigid, unbreakable laws? Our modern laws are elastic and open to interpretation according to . . . circumstances."

"Then start being elastic right now, because I'm not and neither are railroad catastrophes."

She hung up, and said to Eddie, in the tone of an estimate passed on physical objects, "They'll leave us alone for a while."

She did not seem to notice the changes in her office: the absence of Nat Taggart's portrait, the new glass coffee table where Mr. Locey had spread, for the benefit of visitors, a display of the loudest humanitarian magazines with titles of articles headlined on their covers.

She heard—with the attentive look of a machine equipped to record, not to react—Eddie's account of what one month had done to the railroad. She heard his report on what he guessed about the causes of the catastrophe. She faced, with the same look of detachment, a succession of men who went in and out of her office with overhurried steps and hands fumbling in superfluous gestures. He thought that she had become impervious to anything. But suddenly—while pacing the office, dictating to him a list of track-laying materials and where to obtain them illegally—she stopped and looked down at the magazines on the coffee table. Their headlines said: "The New Social Conscience," "Our Duty to the Underprivileged," "Need versus Greed." With a single movement of her arm, the abrupt, explosive movement of sheer physical brutality, such as he had never seen from her before, she swept the magazines off the table and went on, her voice reciting a list of figures without a break, as if there were no connection between her mind and the violence of her body.

Late in the afternoon, finding a moment alone in her office, she telephoned Hank Rearden.

She gave her name to his secretary—and she heard, in the way he said it, the haste with which he had seized the receiver: "Dagny?"

"Hello, Hank. I'm back."

"Where?"

"In my office."

She heard the things he did not say, in the moment's silence on the wire, then he said, "I suppose I'd better start bribing people at once to get the ore to start pouring rail for you."

"Yes. As much of it as you can. It doesn't have to be Rearden Metal. It can be——" The break in her voice was almost too brief to notice, but what it held was the thought: Rearden Metal rail for going back to the time before heavy steel?—perhaps back to the time of wooden rails with strips of iron? "It can be steel, any weight, anything you can give me."

"All right. Dagny, do you know that I've surrendered Rearden Metal to them? I've signed the Gift Certificate."

"Yes, I know."

"I've given in."

"Who am I to blame you? Haven't I?" He did not answer, and she said, "Hank, I don't think they care whether there's a train or a blast furnace left on earth. We do. They're holding us by our love of it, and we'll go on paying so long as there's still one chance left to keep one single wheel alive and moving in token of human intelligence. We'll go on holding it afloat, like our drowning child, and when the flood swallows it, we'll go down with the last wheel and the last syllogism. I know what we're paying, but—price is no object any longer."

"I know."

"Don't be afraid for me, Hank. I'll be all right by tomorrow morning."

"I'll never be afraid for you, darling. I'll see you tonight."

IX

THE FACE WITHOUT PAIN OR FEAR OR GUILT

The silence of her apartment and the motionless perfection of objects that had remained just as she had left them a month before, struck her with a sense of relief and desolation together, when she entered her living room. The silence gave her an illusion of privacy and ownership; the sight of the objects reminded her that they were preserving a moment she could not recapture, as she could not undo the events that had happened since.

There was still a remnant of daylight beyond the windows. She had left the office earlier than she intended, unable to summon the effort for any task that could be postponed till morning. This was new to her —and it was new that she should now feel more at home in her apartment than in her office.

She took a shower, and stood for long, blank minutes, letting the water run over her body, but stepped out hastily when she realized that what she wanted to wash off was not the dust of the drive from the country, but the feel of the office.

She dressed, lighted a cigarette and walked into the living room, to stand at the window, looking at the city, as she had stood looking at the countryside at the start of this day.

She had said she would give her life for one more year on the railroad. She was back; but this was not the joy of working; it was only the clear, cold peace of a decision reached—and the stillness of unadmitted pain.

Clouds had wrapped the sky and had descended as fog to wrap the streets below, as if the sky were engulfing the city. She could see the whole of Manhattan Island, a long, triangular shape cutting into an invisible ocean. It looked like the prow of a sinking ship; a few tall buildings still rose above it, like funnels, but the rest was disappearing under gray-blue coils, going down slowly into vapor and space. This was how they had gone—she thought—Atlantis, the city that sank into the ocean, and all the other kingdoms that vanished, leaving the same legend in all the languages of men, and the same longing.

She felt—as she had felt it one spring night, slumped across her desk in the crumbling office of the John Galt Line, by a window facing a dark alley—the sense and vision of her own world, which she would never reach. . . . You—she thought—whoever you are, whom I have always loved and never found, you whom I expected to see at the end of the rails beyond the horizon, you whose presence I had always felt in the streets of the city and whose world I had wanted to build, it is my love for you that had kept me moving, my love and my hope to reach you and my wish to be worthy of you on the day when I would stand before you face to face. Now I know that I shall never find you— that it is not to be reached or lived—but what is left of my life is still yours, and I will go on in your name, even though it is a name I'll never learn, I will go on serving you, even though I'm never to win, I will go on, to be worthy of you on the day when I would have met you, even though I won't. . . . She had never accepted hopelessness, but she stood at the window and, addressed to the shape of a fogbound city, it was her self-dedication to unrequited love.

The doorbell rang.

She turned with indifferent astonishment to open the door—but she knew that she should have expected him, when she saw that it was Francisco d'Anconia. She felt no shock and no rebellion, only the cheerless serenity of her assurance—and she raised her head to face him, with a slow, deliberate movement, as if telling him that she had chosen her stand and that she stood in the open.

His face was grave and calm; the look of happiness was gone, but the amusement of the playboy had not returned. He looked as if all masks were down, he looked direct, tightly disciplined, intent upon a purpose, he looked like a man able to know the earnestness of action, as she had once expected him to look—he had never seemed so attractive as he did in this moment—and she noted, in astonishment, her sudden feeling that he was not a man who had deserted her, but a man whom she had deserted.

"Dagny, are you able to talk about it now?"

"Yes—if you wish. Come in."

He glanced briefly at her living room, her home which he had never entered, then his eyes came back to her. He was watching her attentively. He seemed to know that the quiet simplicity of her manner was the worst of all signs for his purpose, that it was like a spread of ashes where no flicker of pain could be revived, that even pain would have been a form of fire.

"Sit down, Francisco."

She remained standing before him, as if consciously letting him see that she had nothing to hide, not even the weariness of her posture, the price she had paid for this day and her carelessness of price.

"I don't think I can stop you now," he said, "if you've made your choice. But if there's one chance left to stop you, it's a chance I have to take."

She shook her head slowly. "There isn't. And—what for, Francisco? You've given up. What difference does it make to you whether I perish with the railroad or away from it?"

"I haven't given up the future."

"What future?"

"The day when the looters will perish, but we won't."

"If Taggart Transcontinental is to perish with the looters, then so am I."

He did not take his eyes off her face and he did not answer.

She added dispassionately, "I thought I could live without it. I can't. I'll never try it again. Francisco, do you remember?—we both believed, when we started, that the only sin on earth was to do things badly. I still believe it." The first note of life shuddered in her voice. "I can't stand by and watch what they did at that tunnel. I can't accept what they're all accepting—Francisco, it's the thing we thought so monstrous, you and I!—the belief that disasters are one's natural fate, to be borne, not fought. I can't accept submission. I can't accept helplessness. I can't accept renunciation. So long as there's a railroad left to run, I'll run it."

"In order to maintain the looters' world?"

"In order to maintain the last strip of mine."

"Dagny," he said slowly, "I know why one loves one's work. I know what it means to you, the job of running trains. But you would not run them if they were empty. Dagny, what is it you see when you think of a moving train?"

She glanced at the city. "The life of a man of ability who might have perished in that catastrophe, but will escape the next one, which I'll prevent—a man who has an intransigent mind and an unlimited ambition, and is in love with his own life . . . the kind of man who is what we were when we started, you and I. You gave him up. I can't."

He closed his eyes for an instant, and the tightening movement of his mouth was a smile, a smile substituting for a moan of understanding, amusement and pain. He asked, his voice gravely gentle, "Do you think that you can still serve him—that kind of man—by running the railroad?"

"Yes."

"All right, Dagny. I won't try to stop you. So long as you still think that, nothing can stop you, or should. You will stop on the day when you'll discover that your work has been placed in the service, not of that man's life, but of his destruction."

"Francisco!" It was a cry of astonishment and despair. "You do understand it, you know what I mean by that kind of man, you see him, too!"

"Oh yes," he said simply, casually, looking at some point in space within the room, almost as if he were seeing a real person. He added, "Why should you be astonished? You said that we were of his kind once, you and I. We still are. But one of us has betrayed him."

"Yes," she said sternly, "one of us has. We cannot serve him by renunciation."

"We cannot serve him by making terms with his destroyers."

"I'm not making terms with them. They need me. They know it. It's *my* terms that I'll make them accept."

"By playing a game in which they gain benefits in exchange for harming you?"

"If I can keep Taggart Transcontinental in existence, it's the only benefit I want. What do I care if they make me pay ransoms? Let them have what they want. I'll have the railroad."

He smiled. "Do you think so? Do you think that their need of you is your protection? Do you think that you can give them what they want? No, you won't quit until you see, of your own sight and judgment, what it is that they really want. You know, Dagny, we were taught that some things belong to God and others to Caesar. Perhaps their God would permit it. But the man you say we're serving—he does not permit it. He permits no divided allegiance, no war between your mind and your body, no gulf between your values and your actions, no tributes to Caesar. He permits no Caesars."

"For twelve years," she said softly, "I would have thought it inconceivable that there might come a day when I would have to beg your forgiveness on my knees. Now I think it's possible. If I come to see that you're right, I will. But not until then."

"You will. But not on your knees."

He was looking at her, as if he were seeing her body as she stood before him, even though his eyes were directed at her face, and his glance told her what form of atonement and surrender he was seeing in the future. She saw the effort he made to look away, his hope that she had not seen his glance or understood it, his silent struggle, betrayed by the tension of a few muscles under the skin of his face—the face she knew so well.

"Until then, Dagny, remember that we're enemies. I didn't want to tell you this, but you're the first person who almost stepped into heaven and came back to earth. You've glimpsed too much, so you have to know this clearly. It's you that I'm fighting, not your brother James or Wesley Mouch. It's you that I have to defeat. I am out to end all the things that are most precious to you right now. While you'll struggle to save Taggart Transcontinental, I will be working to destroy it. Don't ever ask me for help or money. You know my reasons. Now you may hate me—as, from your stand, you should."

She raised her head a little, there was no perceptible change in her posture, it was no more than her awareness of her own body and of its meaning to him, but for the length of one sentence she stood as a woman, the suggestion of defiance coming only from the faintly stressed spacing of her words: "And what will it do to you?"

He looked at her, in full understanding, but neither admitting nor denying the confession she wanted to tear from him. "That is no one's concern but mine," he answered.

It was she who weakened, but realized, while saying it, that this was still more cruel: "I don't hate you. I've tried to, for years, but I never will, no matter what we do, either one of us."

"I know it," he said, his voice low, so that she did not hear the pain, but felt it within herself as if by direct reflection from him.

"Francisco!" she cried, in desperate defense of him against herself. "How can you do what you're doing?"

"By the grace of my love"—for you, said his eyes—"for the man," said his voice, "who did not perish in your catastrophe and who will never perish."

She stood silently still for a moment, as if in respectful acknowledgment.

"I wish I could spare you what you're going to go through," he said, the gentleness of his voice saying: It's not me that you should pity. "But I can't. Every one of us has to travel that road by his own steps. But it's the same road."

"Where does it lead?"

He smiled, as if softly closing a door on the questions that he would not answer. "To Atlantis," he said.

"What?" she asked, startled.

"Don't you remember?—the lost city that only the spirits of heroes can enter."

The connection that struck her suddenly had been struggling in her mind since morning, like a dim anxiety she had had no time to identify. She had known it, but she had thought only of his own fate and his personal decision, she had thought of him as acting alone. Now she remembered a wider danger and sensed the vast, undefined shape of the enemy she was facing.

"You're one of them," she said slowly, "aren't you?"

"Of whom?"

"Was it *you* in Ken Danagger's office?"

He smiled. "No." But she noted that he did not ask what she meant.

"Is there—you would know it—is there actually a destroyer loose in the world?"

"Of course."

"Who is it?"

"You."

She shrugged; her face was growing hard. "The men who've quit, are they still alive or dead?"

"They're dead—as far as you're concerned. But there's to be a Second Renaissance in the world. I'll wait for it."

"No!" The sudden violence of her voice was in personal answer to him, to one of the two things he had wanted her to hear in his words. "No, don't wait for me!"

"I'll always wait for you, no matter what we do, either one of us."

The sound they heard was the turning of a key in the lock of the entrance door. The door opened and Hank Rearden came in.

He stopped briefly on the threshold, then walked slowly into the living room, his hand slipping the key into his pocket.

She knew that he had seen Francisco's face before he had seen hers. He glanced at her, but his eyes came back to Francisco, as if this were the only face he was now able to see.

It was at Francisco's face that she was afraid to look. The effort she made to pull her glance along the curve of a few steps felt as if she were pulling a weight beyond her power. Francisco had risen to his feet, as if in the unhurried, automatic manner of a d'Anconia trained to the code of courtesy. There was nothing that Rearden could see in his face. But what she saw in it was worse than she had feared.

"What are you doing here?" asked Rearden, in the tone one would use to address a menial caught in a drawing room.

"I see that I have no right to ask you the same question," said Francisco. She knew what effort was required to achieve the clear, toneless quality of his voice. His eyes kept returning to Rearden's right hand, as if he were still seeing the key between his fingers.

"Then answer it," said Rearden.

"Hank, any questions you wish to ask should be asked of me," she said.

Rearden did not seem to see or hear her. "Answer it," he repeated.

"There is only one answer which you would have the right to demand," said Francisco, "so I will answer you that that is not the reason of my presence here."

"There is only one reason for your presence in the house of any woman," said Rearden. "And I mean, any woman—as far as you're concerned. Do you think that I believe it now, that confession of yours or anything you ever said to me?"

"I have given you grounds not to trust me, but none to include Miss Taggart."

"Don't tell me that you have no chance here, never had and never will. I know it. But that I should find you here on the first—"

"Hank, if you wish to accuse me—" she began, but Rearden whirled to her.

"God, no, Dagny, I don't! But you shouldn't be seen speaking to him. You shouldn't deal with him in any way. You don't know him. I do." He turned to Francisco. "What are you after? Are you hoping to include her among your kind of conquests or—"

"No!" It was an involuntary cry and it sounded futile, with its passionate sincerity offered—to be rejected—as its only proof.

"No? Then are you here on a matter of business? Are you setting a trap, as you did for me? What sort of double-cross are you preparing for her?"

"My purpose . . . was not . . . a matter of business."

"Then what was it?"

"If you still care to believe me, I can tell you only that it involved no . . . betrayal of any kind."

"Do you think that you may still discuss betrayal, in my presence?"

"I will answer you some day. I cannot answer you now."

"You don't like to be reminded of it, do you? You've stayed away from me since, haven't you? You didn't expect to see me here? You didn't want to face me?" But he knew that Francisco was facing him as no one else did these days—he saw the eyes held straight to meet his, the features composed, without emotion, without defense or appeal, set to endure whatever was coming—he saw the open, unprotected look of courage—this was the face of the man he had loved, the man who had set him free of guilt—and he found himself fighting against the knowledge that this face still held him, above all else, above his month of impatience for the sight of Dagny. "Why don't you defend yourself, if you have nothing to hide? Why are you here? Why were you stunned to see me enter?"

"Hank, stop it!" Dagny's voice was a cry, and she drew back, knowing that violence was the most dangerous element to introduce into this moment.

Both men turned to her. "Please let me be the one to answer," Francisco said quietly.

"I told you that I hoped I'd never see him again," said Rearden. "I'm sorry if it has to be here. It doesn't concern you, but there's something he must be paid for."

"If that is . . . your purpose," Francisco said with effort, "haven't you . . . achieved it already?"

"What's the matter?" Rearden's face was frozen, his lips barely moving, but his voice had the sound of a chuckle. "Is this your way of asking for mercy?"

The instant of silence was Francisco's strain to a greater effort. "Yes . . . if you wish," he answered.

"Did you grant it when you held my future in your hands?"

"You are justified in anything you wish to think of me. But since it doesn't concern Miss Taggart . . . would you now permit me to leave?"

"No! Do you want to evade it, like all those other cowards? Do you want to escape?"

"I will come anywhere you require any time you wish. But I would rather it were not in Miss Taggart's presence."

"Why not? I want it to be in her presence, since this is the one place you had no right to come. I have nothing left to protect from you, you've taken more than the looters can ever take, you've destroyed everything you've touched, but here is one thing you're not going to touch." He knew that the rigid absence of emotion in Francisco's face was the strongest evidence of emotion, the evidence of some abnormal effort at control—he knew that this was torture and that he, Rearden, was driven blindly by a feeling which resembled a torturer's enjoyment, except that he was now unable to tell whether he was torturing Francisco or himself. "You're worse than the looters, because you betray with full understanding of that which you're betraying. I don't know what form of corruption is your motive—but I want you to learn that there are things beyond your reach, beyond your aspiration or your malice."

"You have nothing . . . to fear from me . . . now."

"I want you to learn that you are not to think of her, not to look at her, not to approach her. Of all men, it's you who're not to appear in her presence." He knew that he was driven by a desperate anger at his own feeling for this man, that the feeling still lived, that it was this feeling which he had to outrage and destroy. "Whatever your motive, it's from any contact with you that she has to be protected."

"If I gave you my word—" He stopped.

Rearden chuckled. "I know what they mean, your words, your convictions, your friendship and your oath by the only woman you ever—" He stopped. They all knew what this meant, in the same instant that Rearden knew it.

He made a step toward Francisco; he asked, pointing at Dagny, his voice low and strangely unlike his own voice, as if it neither came from nor were addressed to a living person, "Is this the woman you love?"

Francisco closed his eyes.

"Don't ask him that!" The cry was Dagny's.

"Is this the woman you love?"

Francisco answered, looking at her, "Yes."

Rearden's hand rose, swept down and slapped Francisco's face.

The scream came from Dagny. When she could see again—after an instant that felt as if the blow had struck her own cheek—Francisco's hands were the first thing she saw. The heir of the d'Anconias stood thrown back against a table, clasping the edge behind him, not to support himself, but to stop his own hands. She saw the rigid stillness of his body, a body that was pulled too straight but seemed broken, with the slight, unnatural angles of his waistline and shoulders, with his arms held stiff but slanted back—he stood as if the effort not to move were turning the force of his violence against himself, as if the motion he resisted were running through his muscles as a tearing pain. She saw his convulsed fingers struggling to grow fast to the table's edge, she wondered which would break first, the wood of the table or the bones of the man, and she knew that Rearden's life hung in the balance.

When her eyes moved up to Francisco's face, she saw no sign of struggle, only the skin of his temples pulled tight and the planes of his cheeks drawn inward, seeming faintly more hollow than usual. It made his face look naked, pure and young. She felt terror because she was seeing in his eyes the tears which were not there. His eyes were brilliant and dry. He was looking at Rearden, but it was not Rearden that he was seeing. He looked as if he were facing another presence in the room and as if his glance were saying: If this is what you demand of me, then even this is yours, yours to accept and mine to endure, there is no more than this in me to offer you, but let me be proud to know that I can offer so much. She saw—with a single artery beating under the skin of his throat, with a froth of pink in the corner of his mouth— the look of an enraptured dedication which was almost a smile, and she knew that she was witnessing Francisco d'Anconia's greatest achievement.

When she felt herself shaking and heard her own voice, it seemed to meet the last echo of her scream in the air of the room—and she realized how brief a moment had passed between. Her voice had the savage sound of rising to deliver a blow and it was crying to Rearden:

"—to protect me from *him?* Long before you ever—"

"Don't!" Francisco's head jerked to her, the brief snap of his voice held all of his unreleased violence, and she knew it was an order that had to be obeyed.

Motionless but for the slow curve of his head, Francisco turned to Rearden. She saw his hands leave the edge of the table and hang relaxed by his sides. It was Rearden that he was now seeing, and there was nothing in Francisco's face except the exhaustion of effort, but Rearden knew suddenly how much this man had loved him.

"Within the extent of your knowledge," Francisco said quietly, "you are right."

Neither expecting nor permitting an answer, he turned to leave. He bowed to Dagny, inclining his head in a manner that appeared as a simple gesture of leave-taking to Rearden, as a gesture of acceptance to her. Then he left.

Rearden stood looking after him, knowing—without context and with absolute certainty—that he would give his life for the power not to have committed the action he had committed.

When he turned to Dagny, his face looked drained, open and faintly attentive, as if he were not questioning her about the words she had cut off, but were waiting for them to come.

A shudder of pity ran through her body and ended in the movement of shaking her head: she did not know for which of the two men the pity was intended, but it made her unable to speak and she shook her head over and over again, as if trying desperately to negate some vast, impersonal suffering that had made them all its victims.

"If there's something that must be said, say it." His voice was toneless.

The sound she made was half-chuckle, half-moan—it was not a desire for vengeance, but a desperate sense of justice that drove the cutting bitterness of her voice, as she cried, consciously throwing the words at his face, "You wanted to know the name of that other man?

The man I slept with? The man who had me first? It was Francisco d'Anconia!"

She saw the force of the blow by seeing his face swept blank. She knew that if justice was her purpose, she had achieved it—because this slap was worse than the one he had dealt.

She felt suddenly calm, knowing that her words had had to be said for the sake of all three of them. The despair of a helpless victim left her, she was not a victim any longer, she was one of the contestants, willing to bear the responsibility of action. She stood facing him, waiting for any answer he would choose to give her, feeling almost as if it were her turn to be subjected to violence.

She did not know what form of torture he was enduring, or what he saw being wrecked within him and kept himself the only one to see. There was no sign of pain to give her any warning; he looked as if he were just a man who stood still in the middle of a room, making his consciousness absorb a fact that it refused to absorb. Then she noticed that he did not change his posture, that even his hands hung by his sides with the fingers half-bent as they had been for a long time, it seemed to her that she could feel the heavy numbness of the blood stopping in his fingers—and this was the only clue to his suffering she was able to find, but it told her that that which he felt left him no power to feel anything else, not even the existence of his own body. She waited, her pity vanishing and becoming respect.

Then she saw his eyes move slowly from her face down the length of her body, and she knew the sort of torture he was now choosing to experience, because it was a glance of a nature he could not hide from her. She knew that he was seeing her as she had been at seventeen, he was seeing her with the rival he hated, he was seeing them together as they would be now, a sight he could neither endure nor resist. She saw the protection of control dropping from his face, but he did not care whether he let her see his face alive and naked, because there now was nothing to read in it except an unrevealing violence, some part of which resembled hatred.

He seized her shoulders, and she felt prepared to accept that he would now kill her or beat her into unconsciousness, and in the moment when she felt certain that he had thought of it, she felt her body thrown against him and his mouth falling on hers, more brutally than the act of a beating would have permitted.

She found herself, in terror, twisting her body to resist, and, in exultation, twisting her arms around him, holding him, letting her lips bring blood to his, knowing that she had never wanted him as she did in this moment.

When he threw her down on the couch, she knew, to the rhythm of the beat of his body, that it was the act of his victory over his rival and of his surrender to him, the act of ownership brought to unendurable violence by the thought of the man whom it was defying, the act of transforming his hatred for the pleasure that man had known into the intensity of his own pleasure, his conquest of that man by means of her body—she felt Francisco's presence through Rearden's mind, she felt as if she were surrendering to both men, to that which she had worshipped in both of them, that which they held in common, that essence of character which had made of her love for each an act of loyalty to both. She knew also that this was his rebellion against the world around them, against its worship of degradation, against the long torment of his wasted days and lightless struggle—this was what he wished to assert and, alone with her in the half-darkness high in space above a city of ruins, to hold as the last of his property.

Afterwards, they lay still, his face on her shoulder. The reflection of a distant electric sign kept beating in faint flashes on the ceiling above her head.

He reached for her hand and slipped her fingers under his face to let his mouth rest against her palm for a moment, so gently that she felt his motive more than his touch.

After a while, she got up, she reached for a cigarette, lighted it, then held it out to him with a slight, questioning lift of her hand; he nodded, still sitting half-stretched on the couch; she placed the cigarette between his lips and lighted another for herself. She felt a great sense of peace between them, and the intimacy of the unimportant gestures underscored the importance of the things they were not saying to each other. Everything was said, she thought—but knew that it waited to be acknowledged.

She saw his eyes move to the entrance door once in a while and remain on it for long moments, as if he were still seeing the man who had left.

He said quietly, "He could have beaten me by letting me have the truth, any time he wished. Why didn't he?"

She shrugged, spreading her hands in a gesture of helpless sadness, because they both knew the answer. She asked, "He did mean a great deal to you, didn't he?"

"He does."

The two dots of fire at the tips of their cigarettes had moved slowly to the tips of their fingers, with the small glow of an occasional flare and the soft crumbling of ashes as sole movement in the silence, when the doorbell rang. They knew that it was not the man they wished but could not hope to see return, and she frowned with sudden anger as she went to open the door. It took her a moment to remember that the innocuously courteous figure she saw bowing to her with a standard smile of welcome was the assistant manager of the apartment house.

"Good evening, Miss Taggart. We're so glad to see you back. I just came on duty and heard that you had returned and wanted to greet you in person."

"Thank you." She stood at the door, not moving to admit him.

"I have a letter that came for you about a week ago, Miss Taggart," he said, reaching into his pocket. "It looked as if it might be important, but being marked 'personal,' it was obviously not intended to be sent to your office and, besides, they did not know your address, either—so not knowing where to forward it, I kept it in our safe and I thought I'd deliver it to you in person."

The envelope he handed to her was marked: Registered—Air Mail —Special Delivery—Personal. The return address said: Quentin Daniels, Utah Institute of Technology, Afton, Utah.

"Oh . . . Thank you."

The assistant manager noted that her voice went dropping toward a whisper, the polite disguise for a gasp, he noted that she stood looking down at the sender's name much longer than was necessary, so he repeated his good wishes and departed.

She was tearing the envelope open as she walked toward Rearden, and she stopped in the middle of the room to read the letter. It was typewritten on thin paper—he could see the black rectangles of the paragraphs through the transparent sheets—and he could see her face as she read them.

He expected it, by the time he saw her come to the end: she leaped to the telephone, he heard the violent whirl of the dial and her voice saying with trembling urgency, "Long-distance, please . . . Operator, get me the Utah Institute of Technology at Afton, Utah!"

He asked, approaching, "What is it?"

She extended the letter, not looking at him, her eyes fixed on the telephone, as if she could force it to answer.

The letter said:

Dear Miss Taggart:

I have fought it out for three weeks, I did not want to do it, I know how this will hit you and I know every argument you could offer me, because I have used them all against myself—but this is to tell you that I am quitting.

I cannot work under the terms of Directive 10-289—though not for the reason its perpetrators intended. I know that their abolition of all scientific research does not mean a damn to you or me, and that you would want me to continue. But I have to quit, because I do not wish to succeed any longer.

I do not wish to work in a world that regards me as a slave. I do not wish to be of any value to people. If I succeeded in re-building the motor, I would not let you place it in their service. I would not take it upon my conscience that anything produced by my mind should be used to bring them comfort.

I know that if we succeed, they will be only too eager to expropriate the motor. And for the sake of that prospect, we have to accept the position of criminals, you and I, and live under the threat of being arrested at any moment at their whim. And *this* is the thing that I cannot take, even were I able to take all the rest: that in order to give them an inestimable benefit, we should be made martyrs to the men who, but for us, could not have conceived of it. I might have forgiven the rest, but when I think of this, I say: May they be damned, I will see them all die of starvation, myself included, rather than forgive them for this or permit it!

To tell you the full truth, I want to succeed, to solve the secret of the motor, as much as ever. So I shall continue to work on it for my own sole pleasure and for as long as I last. But if I solve it, it will remain my private secret. I will not release it for any commercial use. Therefore, I cannot take your money any longer. Commercialism is supposed to be despicable, so all those people should truly approve of my decision, and I—I'm tired of helping those who despise me.

I don't know how long I will last or what I will do in the future. For the moment, I intend to remain in my job at this Institute. But if any of its trustees or receivers should remind me that I am now legally forbidden to cease being a janitor, I will quit.

You had given me my greatest chance and if I am now giving you a painful blow, perhaps I should ask you to forgive me. I think that you love your work as much as I loved mine, so you will know that my decision was not easy to make, but that I had to make it.

It is a strange feeling—writing this letter. I do not intend to die, but I am giving up the world and this feels like the letter of a suicide. So I want to say that of all the people I have known, you are the only person I regret leaving behind.

Sincerely yours,
Quentin Daniels

When he looked up from the letter, he heard her saying, as he had heard her through the words of the typewritten lines, her voice rising closer to despair each time:

"Keep ringing, Operator! . . . Please keep ringing!"

"What can you tell him?" he asked. "There are no arguments to offer."

"I won't have a chance to tell him! He's gone by now. It was a week ago. I'm sure he's gone. They've got him."

"Who got him?"

"Yes, Operator, I'll hold the line, keep trying!"

"What would you tell him if he answered?"

"I'd beg him to go on taking my money, with no strings attached, no conditions, just so he'll have the means to continue! I'll promise him that if we're still in a looters' world when and if he succeeds, I won't ask him to give me the motor or even to tell me its secret. But if, by that time, we're free—" She stopped.

"If we're free . . ."

"All I want from him now is that he doesn't give up and vanish, like . . . like all those others. I don't want to let them get him. If it's not too late—oh God, I don't want them to get him! . . . Yes, Operator, keep ringing!"

"What good will it do us, even if he continues to work?"

"That's all I'll beg him to do—just to continue. Maybe we'll never get a chance to use the motor in the future. But I want to know that somewhere in the world there's still a great brain at work on a great attempt—and that we still have a chance at a future. . . . If that motor is abandoned *again,* then there's nothing but Starnesville ahead of us."

"Yes. I know."

She held the receiver pressed to her ear, her arm stiff with the effort not to tremble. She waited, and he heard, in the silence, the futile clicking of the unanswered call.

"He's gone," she said. "They got him. A week is much longer than they need. I don't know how they learn when the time is right, but this" —she pointed at the letter—"this was their time and they wouldn't have missed it."

"Who?"

"The destroyer's agents."

"Are you beginning to think that they really exist?"

"Yes."

"Are you serious?"

"I am. I've met one of them."

"Who?"

"I'll tell you later. I don't know who their leader is, but I'm going to find out, one of these days. I'm going to find out. I'll be damned if I let them—"

She broke off on a gasp; he saw the change in her face the moment before he heard the click of a distant receiver being lifted and the sound of a man's voice saying, across the wire, "Hello?"

"Daniels! Is that *you?* You're alive? You're still there?"

"Why, yes. Is this you, Miss Taggart? What's the matter?"

"I . . . I thought you were gone."

"Oh, I'm sorry, I just heard the phone ringing, I was out in the back lot, gathering carrots."

"Carrots?" She was laughing with hysterical relief.

"I have my own vegetable patch out there. Used to be the Institute's parking lot. Are you calling from New York, Miss Taggart?"

"Yes. I just received your letter. Just now. I . . . I had been away."

"Oh." There was a pause, then he said quietly, "There's really nothing more to be said about it, Miss Taggart."

"Tell me, are you going away?"

"No."

"You're not planning to go?"

"No. Where?"

"Do you intend to remain at the Institute?"

"Yes."

"For how long? Indefinitely?"

"Yes—as far as I know."

"Has anyone approached you?"

"About what?"

"About leaving."

"No. Who?"

"Listen, Daniels, I won't try to discuss your letter over the phone. But I must speak to you. I'm coming to see you. I'll get there as fast as I can."

"I don't want you to do that, Miss Taggart. I don't want you to go to such an effort, when it's useless."

"Give me a chance, won't you? You don't have to promise to change your mind, you don't have to commit yourself to anything—only to give me a hearing. If I want to come, it's my risk, I'm taking it. There are things I want to say to you, I'm asking you only·for the chance to say them."

"You know that I will always give you that chance, Miss Taggart."

"I'm leaving for Utah at once. Tonight. But there's one thing I want you to promise me. Will you promise to wait for me? Will you promise to be there when I arrive?"

"Why . . . of course, Miss Taggart. Unless I die or something happens outside my power—but I don't expect it to happen."

"Unless you die, will you wait for me no matter what happens?"

"Of course."

"Do you give me your word that you'll wait?"

"Yes, Miss Taggart."

"Thank you. Good night."

"Good night, Miss Taggart."

She pressed the receiver down and picked it up again in the same sweep of her hand and rapidly dialed a number.

"Eddie? . . . Have them hold the Comet for me. . . . Yes, *tonight's* Comet. Give orders to have my car attached, then come here, to my place, at once." She glanced at her watch. "It's eight-twelve. I have an hour to make it. I don't think I'll hold them up too long. I'll talk to you while I pack."

She hung up and turned to Rearden.

"Tonight?" he said.

"I have to."

"I guess so. Don't you have to go to Colorado, anyway?"

"Yes. I intended to leave tomorrow night. But I think Eddie can manage to take care of my office, and I'd better start now. It takes three days"—she remembered—"it will now take five days to reach Utah.

I have to go by train, there are people I have to see on the line—this can't be delayed, either."

"How long will you stay in Colorado?"

"Hard to tell."

"Wire me when you get there, will you? If it looks as if it's going to be long, I'll join you there."

This was the only expression he could give to the words he had desperately wished to say to her, had waited for, had come here to say, and now wished to pronounce more than ever, but knew that it must not be said tonight.

She knew, by a faint, solemn stress in the tone of his voice, that this was his acceptance of her confession, his surrender, his forgiveness. She asked, "Can you leave the mills?"

"It will take me a few days to arrange, but I can."

He knew what her words were admitting, acknowledging and forgiving him, when she said, "Hank, why don't you meet me in Colorado in a week? If you fly your plane, we'll both get there at the same time. And then we'll come back together."

"All right . . . dearest."

* * *

She dictated a list of instructions, while pacing her bedroom, gathering her clothes, hastily packing a suitcase. Rearden had left; Eddie Willers sat at her dressing table, making notes. He seemed to work in his usual manner of unquestioning efficiency, as if he were not aware of the perfume bottles and powder boxes, as if the dressing table were a desk and the room were only an office.

"I'll phone you from Chicago, Omaha, Flagstaff and Afton," she said, tossing underwear into the suitcase. "If you need me in between, call any operator along the line, with orders to flag the train."

"The Comet?" he asked mildly.

"Hell, yes!—the Comet."

"Okay."

"Don't hesitate to call, if you have to."

"Okay. But I don't think I'll have to."

"We'll manage. We'll work by long-distance phone, just as we did when we—" She stopped.

"—when we were building the John Galt Line?" he asked quietly. They glanced at each other, but said nothing else.

"What's the latest report on the construction crews?" she asked.

"Everything's under way. I got word, just after you left the office, that the grading gangs have started—out of Laurel, Kansas, and out of Jasper, Oklahoma. The rail is on its way to them from Silver Springs. It will be all right. The hardest thing to find was—"

"The men?"

"Yes. The men to put in charge. We had trouble out West, over the Elgin to Midland stretch. All the men we were counting on are gone. I couldn't find anyone able to assume responsibility, neither on our line nor elsewhere. I even tried to get Dan Conway, but—"

"*Dan Conway?*" she asked, stopping.

"Yes. I did. I tried. Do you remember how he used to have rail laid at the rate of five miles a day, right in that part of the country? Oh, I know he'd have reason to hate our guts, but what does it matter now? I found him—he's living on a ranch out in Arizona. I phoned him myself and I begged him to save us. Just to take charge, for one night, of building five and a half miles of track. Five and a half miles, Dagny, that we're stuck with—and he's the greatest railroad builder living! I told him that I was asking him to do it as a gesture of charity to us, if he would. You know, I think he understood me. He wasn't angry. He sounded sad. But he wouldn't do it. He said one must not try to bring people back out of the grave. . . . He wished me luck. I think he meant it. . . . You know, I don't think he's one of those that the destroyer knocked out. I think he just broke by himself."

"Yes. I know he did."

Eddie saw the expression on her face and pulled himself up hastily. "Oh, we finally found a man to put in charge at Elgin," he said, forcing his voice to sound confident. "Don't worry, the track will be built long before you get there."

She glanced at him with the faint suggestion of a smile, thinking of how often she had said these words to him and of the desperate bravery with which he was now trying to tell her: Don't worry. He caught her glance, he understood, and the answering hint of his smile had a touch of embarrassed apology.

He turned back to his note pad, feeling anger at himself, sensing that he had broken his own unstated commandment: Don't make it harder for her. He should not have told her about Dan Conway, he thought; he should not have said anything to remind them both of the despair they would feel, if they felt. He wondered what was the matter with him: he thought it inexcusable that he should find his discipline slipping just because this was a room, not an office.

She went on speaking—and he listened, looking down at his pad, making a brief notation once in a while. He did not permit himself to look at her again.

She threw the door of her closet open, jerked a suit off a hanger and folded it rapidly, while her voice went on with unhurried precision. He did not look up, he was aware of her only by means of sound: the sound of the swift movements and of the measured voice. He knew what was wrong with him, he thought; he did not want her to leave, he did not want to lose her again, after so brief a moment of reunion. But to indulge any personal loneliness, at a time when he knew how desperately the railroad needed her in Colorado, was an act of disloyalty he had never committed before—and he felt a vague, desolate sense of guilt.

"Send out orders that the Comet is to stop at every division point," she said, "and that all division superintendents are to prepare for me a report on—"

He glanced up—then his glance stopped and he did not hear the rest of the words. He saw a man's dressing gown hanging on the back of the open closet door, a dark blue gown with the white initials HR on its breast pocket.

He remembered where he had seen that gown before, he remembered the man facing him across a breakfast table in the Wayne-Falkland Hotel, he remembered that man coming, unannounced, to her office late on a Thanksgiving night—and the realization that he should have known it, came to him as two subterranean jolts of a single earthquake: it came with a feeling that screamed "No!" so savagely that the scream, not the sight, brought down every girder within him. It was not the shock of the discovery, but the more terrible shock of what it made him discover about himself.

He hung on to a single thought: that he must not let her see what he had noticed or what it had done to him. He felt a sensation of embarrassment magnified to the point of physical torture; it was the dread of violating her privacy twice: by learning her secret and by revealing his own. He bent lower over the note pad and concentrated on an immediate purpose: to stop his pencil from shaking.

". . . fifty miles of mountain trackage to build, and we can count on nothing but whatever material we own."

"I beg your pardon," he said, his voice barely audible, "I didn't hear what you said."

"I said I want a report from all superintendents on every foot of rail and every piece of equipment available on their divisions."

"Okay."

"I will confer with each one of them in turn. Have them meet me in my car aboard the Comet."

"Okay."

"Send word out—unofficially—that the engineers are to make up time for the stops by going seventy, eighty, a hundred miles an hour, anything they wish as and when they need to, and that I will . . . Eddie?"

"Yes. Okay."

"Eddie, what's the matter?"

He had to look up, to face her and, desperately, to lie for the first time in his life. "I'm . . . I'm afraid of the trouble we'll get into with the law," he said.

"Forget it. Don't you see that there isn't any law left? Anything goes now, for whoever can get away with it—and, for the moment, it's we who're setting the terms."

When she was ready, he carried her suitcase to a taxicab, then down the platform of the Taggart Terminal to her office car, the last at the end of the Comet. He stood on the platform, saw the train jerk forward and watched the red markers on the back of her car slipping slowly away from him into the long darkness of the exit tunnel. When they were gone, he felt what one feels at the loss of a dream one had not known till after it was lost.

There were few people on the platform around him and they seemed to move with self-conscious strain, as if a sense of disaster clung to the rails and to the girders above their heads. He thought indifferently that after a century of safety, men were once more regarding the departure of a train as an event involving a gamble with death.

He remembered that he had had no dinner, and he felt no desire to eat, but the underground cafeteria of the Taggart Terminal was more truly his home than the empty cube of space he now thought of as his apartment—so he walked to the cafeteria, because he had no other place to go.

The cafeteria was almost deserted—but the first thing he saw, as he entered, was a thin column of smoke rising from the cigarette of the worker, who sat alone at a table in a dark corner.

Not noticing what he put on his tray, Eddie carried it to the worker's table, said, "Hello," sat down and said nothing else. He looked at the silverware spread before him, wondered about its purpose, remembered the use of a fork and attempted to perform the motions of eating, but found that it was beyond his power. After a while, he looked up and saw that the worker's eyes were studying him attentively.

"No," said Eddie, "no, there's nothing the matter with me. . . . Oh yes, a lot has happened, but what difference does it make now? . . . Yes, she's back. . . . What else do you want me to say about it? . . . How did you know she's back? Oh well, I suppose the whole company knew it within the first ten minutes. . . . No, I don't know whether I'm glad that she's back. . . . Sure, she'll save the railroad—for another year or month. . . . What do you want me to say? . . . No, she didn't. She didn't tell me what she's counting on. She didn't tell me what she thought or felt. . . . Well, how do you suppose she'd feel? It's hell for her—all right, for me, too! Only my kind of hell is my own fault. . . . No. Nothing. I can't talk about it—talk?—I mustn't even think about it, I've got to stop it, stop thinking of her and—of her, I mean."

He remained silent and he wondered why the worker's eyes—the eyes that always seemed to see everything within him—made him feel uneasy tonight. He glanced down at the table, and he noticed the butts of many cigarettes among the remnants of food on the worker's plate.

"Are you in trouble, too?" asked Eddie. "Oh, just that you've sat here for a long time tonight, haven't you? . . . For me? Why should you have wanted to wait for me? . . . You know, I never thought you cared whether you saw me or not, me or anybody, you seemed so complete in yourself, and that's why I liked to talk to you, because I felt that you always understood, but nothing could hurt you—you looked as if nothing had ever hurt you—and it made me feel free, as if . . . as if there were no pain in the world. . . . Do you know what's strange about your face? You look as if you've never known pain or fear or guilt. . . . I'm sorry I'm so late tonight. I had to see her off—she has just left, on the Comet. . . . Yes, tonight, just now. . . . Yes, she's gone. . . . Yes, it was a sudden decision—within the past hour. She intended to leave tomorrow night, but something unexpected happened and she had to go at once. . . . Yes, she's going to Colorado—afterwards. . . . To Utah—first. . . . Because she got a letter from Quentin Daniels that he's quitting—and the one thing she won't give up, couldn't stand to give up, is the motor. You remember, the motor I told you about, the remnant that she found. . . . Daniels? He's a physicist who's been working for the past year, at the Utah Institute of Technology, trying to solve the secret of the motor and to rebuild it. . . . Why do you look at me like that? . . . No, I haven't told you about him before, because it was a secret. It was a private, secret project of her own—and of what interest would it have been to you, anyway? . . . I guess I can talk about it now, because he's quit. . . . Yes, he told her his reasons. He said that he won't give anything produced by his mind to a world that regards him as a slave. He said that he won't be made a martyr to people in exchange for giving them an inestimable benefit. . . . What—what are you laughing at? . . . Stop it, will you? Why do you laugh like that? . . . The whole secret? What do you mean, the whole secret? He hasn't found the whole secret of the motor, if that's what you meant, but he seemed to be doing well, he had a good chance. Now it's lost. She's rushing to him, she wants to plead, to hold him, to make him go on—but I think it's useless. Once they stop, they don't come back again. Not one of them has. . . . No, I don't care, not any more, we've taken so many losses that I'm getting used to it. . . . Oh no! It's not Daniels that I can't take, it's—no, drop it. Don't question me about it. The whole world is going to pieces, she's still fighting to save it, and I—I sit here damning her for something I had no right to know. . . . No! She's done nothing to be damned, nothing—and, besides, it doesn't concern the railroad. . . . Don't pay any attention to me, it's not true, it's not her that I'm damning, it's myself. . . . Listen, I've always known that you loved Taggart Transcontinental as I loved it, that it meant something special to you, something personal, and that was why you liked to hear me talk about it. But this—the thing I learned today—this has nothing to do with the railroad. It would be of no importance to you.

Forget it. . . . It's something that I didn't know about her, that's all.
. . . I grew up with her. I thought I knew her. I didn't. . . . I don't
know what it was that I expected. I suppose I just thought that she
had no private life of any kind. To me, she was not a person and
not . . . not a woman. She was the railroad. And I didn't think that
anyone would ever have the audacity to look at her in any other way.
. . . Well, it serves me right. Forget it. . . . Forget it, I said! Why do
you question me like this? It's only her private life. What can it matter to you? . . . Drop it, for God's sake! Don't you see that I can't
talk about it? . . . Nothing happened, nothing's wrong with me, I just
—oh, why am I lying? I can't lie to you, you always seem to see everything, it's worse than trying to lie to myself! . . . I *have* lied to myself. I didn't know what I felt for her. The railroad? I'm a rotten
hypocrite. If the railroad was all she meant to me, it wouldn't have
hit me like this. I wouldn't have felt that I wanted to kill him! . . .
What's the matter with you tonight? Why do you look at me like that?
. . . Oh, what's the matter with all of us? Why is there nothing but
misery left for anyone? Why do we suffer so much? We weren't meant
to. I always thought that we were to be happy, all of us, as our natural
fate. What are we doing? What have we lost? A year ago, I wouldn't
have damned her for finding something she wanted. But I know that
they're doomed, both of them, and so am I, and so is everybody, and
she was all I had left. . . . It was so great, to be alive, it was such a
wonderful chance, I didn't know that I loved it and that *that* was our
love, hers and mine and yours—but the world is perishing and we
cannot stop it. Why are we destroying ourselves? Who will tell us the
truth? Who will save us? Oh, who is John Galt?! . . . No, it's no use.
It doesn't matter now. Why should I feel anything? We won't last much
longer. Why should I care what she does? Why should I care that she's
sleeping with Hank Rearden? . . . Oh God!—what's the matter with
you? Don't go! Where are you going?"

THE SIGN OF THE DOLLAR

She sat at the window of the train, her head thrown back, not moving, wishing she would never have to move again.

The telegraph poles went racing past the window, but the train seemed lost in a void, between a brown stretch of prairie and a solid spread of rusty, graying clouds. The twilight was draining the sky without the wound of a sunset; it looked more like the fading of an anemic body in the process of exhausting its last drops of blood and light. The train was going west, as if it, too, were pulled to follow the sinking rays and quietly to vanish from the earth. She sat still, feeling no desire to resist it.

She wished she would not hear the sound of the wheels. They knocked in an even rhythm, every fourth knock accented—and it seemed to her that through the rapid, running clatter of some futile stampede to escape, the beat of the accented knocks was like the steps of an enemy moving toward some inexorable purpose.

She had never experienced it before, this sense of apprehension at the sight of a prairie, this feeling that the rail was only a fragile thread stretched across an enormous emptiness, like a worn nerve ready to break. She had never expected that she, who had felt as if she were the motive power aboard a train, would now sit wishing, like a child or a savage, that this train would move, that it would not stop, that it would get her there on time—wishing it, not like an act of will, but like a plea to a dark unknown.

She thought of what a difference one month had made. She had seen it in the faces of the men at the stations. The track workers, the switchmen, the yardmen, who had always greeted her, anywhere along the line, their cheerful grins boasting that they knew who she was—had now looked at her stonily, turning away, their faces wary and closed. She had wanted to cry to them in apology, "It's not I who've done it to you!"—then had remembered that she had accepted it and that they now had the right to hate her, that she was both a slave and a driver of slaves, and so was every human being in the country, and hatred was the only thing that men could now feel for one another.

She had found reassurance, for two days, in the sight of the cities moving past her window—the factories, the bridges, the electric signs, the billboards pressing down upon the roofs of homes—the crowded, grimy, active, living conflux of the industrial East.

But the cities had been left behind. The train was now diving into the prairies of Nebraska, the rattle of its couplers sounding as if it were shivering with cold. She saw lonely shapes that had been farmhouses in the vacant stretches that had been fields. But the great burst of energy, in the East, generations ago, had splattered bright trickles to run through the emptiness; some were gone, but some still lived. She was startled when the lights of a small town swept across her car and, vanishing, left it darker than it had been before. She would not move to turn on the light. She sat still, watching the rare towns. Whenever an electric beam went flashing briefly at her face, it was like a moment's greeting.

She saw them as they went by, written on the walls of modest structures, over sooted roofs, down slender smokestacks, on the curves of tanks: Reynolds Harvesters—Macey Cement—Quinlan & Jones Pressed Alfalfa—Home of the Crawford Mattress—Benjamin Wylie Grain and Feed—words raised like flags to the empty darkness of the sky, the motionless forms of movement, of effort, of courage, of hope, the monuments to how much had been achieved on the edge of nature's void by men who had once been free to achieve—she saw the homes built in scattered privacy, the small shops, the wide streets with electric lighting, like a few luminous strokes criss-crossed on the black sheet of the wastelands—she saw the ghosts between, the remnants of towns, the skeletons of factories with crumbling smokestacks, the corpses of shops with broken panes, the slanting poles with shreds of wire—she saw a sudden blaze, the rare sight of a gas station, a glittering white island of glass and metal under the huge black weight of space and sky —she saw an ice-cream cone made of radiant tubing, hanging above the corner of a street, and a battered car being parked below, with a young boy at the wheel and a girl stepping out, her white dress blowing in the summer wind—she shuddered for the two of them, thinking: I can't look at you, I who know what it has taken to give you your youth, to give you this evening, this car and the ice-cream cone you're going to buy for a quarter—she saw, on the edge beyond a town, a building glowing with tiers of pale blue light, the industrial light she loved, with the silhouettes of machines in its windows and a billboard in the darkness above its roof—and suddenly her head fell on her arm, and she sat shaking, crying soundlessly to the night, to herself, to whatever was human in any living being: Don't let it go! . . . Don't let it go! . . .

She jumped to her feet and snapped on the light. She stood still, fighting to regain control, knowing that such moments were her greatest danger. The lights of the town were past, her window was now an empty rectangle, and she heard, in the silence, the progression of the fourth knocks, the steps of the enemy moving on, not to be hastened or stopped.

In desperate need of the sight of some living activity, she decided she would not order dinner in her car, but would go to the diner. As if stressing and mocking her loneliness, a voice came back to her mind: "But you would not run trains if they were empty." Forget it!—she told herself angrily, walking hastily to the door of her car.

She was astonished, approaching her vestibule, to hear the sound of voices close by. As she pulled the door open, she heard a shout: "Get off, God damn you!"

An aging tramp had taken refuge in the corner of her vestibule. He sat on the floor, his posture suggesting that he had no strength left to stand up or to care about being caught. He was looking at the conductor, his eyes observant, fully conscious, but devoid of any reaction. The train was slowing down for a bad stretch of track, the conductor had opened the door to a cold gust of wind, and was waving at the speeding black void, ordering, "Get going! Get off as you got on or I'll kick you off head first!"

There was no astonishment in the tramp's face, no protest, no anger, no hope; he looked as if he had long since abandoned any judgment of any human action. He moved obediently to rise, his hand groping upward along the rivets of the car's wall. She saw him glance at her and glance away, as if she were merely another inanimate fixture of the train. He did not seem to be aware of her person, any more than of his own, he was indifferently ready to comply with an order which, in his condition, meant certain death.

She glanced at the conductor. She saw nothing in his face except the blind malevolence of pain, of some long-repressed anger that broke out upon the first object available, almost without consciousness of the object's identity. The two men were not human beings to each other any longer.

The tramp's suit was a mass of careful patches on a cloth so stiff and shiny with wear that one expected it to crack like glass if bent; but she noticed the collar of his shirt: it was bone-white from repeated laundering and it still preserved a semblance of shape. He had pulled himself up to his feet, he was looking indifferently at the black hole open upon miles of uninhabited wilderness where no one would see the body or hear the voice of a mangled man, but the only gesture of concern he made was to tighten his grip on a small, dirty bundle, as if to make sure he would not lose it in leaping off the train.

It was the laundered collar and this gesture for the last of his possessions—the gesture of a sense of property—that made her feel an emotion like a sudden, burning twist within her. "Wait," she said.

The two men turned to her.

"Let him be my guest," she said to the conductor, and held her door open for the tramp, ordering, "Come in."

The tramp followed her, obeying as blankly as he had been about to obey the conductor.

He stood in the middle of her car, holding his bundle, looking around him with the same observant, unreacting glance.

"Sit down," she said.

He obeyed—and looked at her, as if waiting for further orders. There was a kind of dignity in his manner, the honesty of the open admission that he had no claim to make, no plea to offer, no questions to ask, that he now had to accept whatever was done to him and was ready to accept it.

He seemed to be in his early fifties; the structure of his bones and the looseness of his suit suggested that he had once been muscular. The lifeless indifference of his eyes did not fully hide that they had been intelligent; the wrinkles cutting his face with the record of some incredible bitterness, had not fully erased the fact that the face had once possessed the kindliness peculiar to honesty.

"When did you eat last?" she asked.

"Yesterday," he said, and added, "I think."

She rang for the porter and ordered dinner for two, to be brought to her car from the diner.

The tramp had watched her silently, but when the porter departed, he offered the only payment it was in his power to offer: "I don't want to get you in trouble, ma'am," he said.

She smiled. "What trouble?"

"You're traveling with one of those railroad tycoons, aren't you?"

"No, alone."

"Then you're the wife of one of them?"

"No."

"Oh." She saw his effort at a look of something like respect, as if to make up for having forced an improper confession, and she laughed.

"No, not that, either. I guess I'm one of the tycoons myself. My name is Dagny Taggart and I work for this railroad."

"Oh . . . I think I've heard of you, ma'am—in the old days." It was hard to tell what "the old days" meant to him, whether it was a month or a year or whatever period of time had passed since he had given up. He was looking at her with a sort of interest in the past tense, as if he were thinking that there had been a time when he would have considered her a personage worth seeing. "You were the lady who ran a railroad," he said.

"Yes," she said. "I was."

He showed no sign of astonishment at the fact that she had chosen to help him. He looked as if so much brutality had confronted him that he had given up the attempt to understand, to trust or to expect anything.

"When did you get aboard the train?" she asked.

"Back at the division point, ma'am. Your door wasn't locked." He added, "I figured maybe nobody would notice me till morning on account of it being a private car."

"Where are you going?"

"I don't know." Then, almost as if he sensed that this could sound too much like an appeal for pity, he added, "I guess I just wanted to keep moving till I saw some place that looked like there might be a chance to find work there." This was his attempt to assume the responsibility of a purpose, rather than to throw the burden of his aimlessness upon her mercy—an attempt of the same order as his shirt collar.

"What kind of work are you looking for?"

"People don't look for *kinds* of work any more, ma'am," he answered impassively. "They just look for work."

"What sort of place did you hope to find?"

"Oh . . . well . . . where there's factories, I guess."

"Aren't you going in the wrong direction for that? The factories are in the East."

"No." He said it with the firmness of knowledge. "There are too many people in the East. The factories are too well watched. I figured there might be a better chance some place where there's fewer people and less law."

"Oh, running away? A fugitive from the law, are you?"

"Not as you'd mean it in the old days, ma'am. But as things are now, I guess I am. I want to work."

"What do you mean?"

"There aren't any jobs back East. And a man couldn't give you a job, if he had one to give—he'd go to jail for it. He's watched. You can't get work except through the Unification Board. The Unification Board has a gang of its own friends waiting in line for the jobs, more friends than a millionaire's got relatives. Well, me—I haven't got either."

"Where did you work last?"

"I've been bumming around the country for six months—no, longer, I guess—I guess it's closer to about a year—I can't tell any more—mostly day work it was. Mostly on farms. But it's getting to be no use now. I know how the farmers look at you—they don't like to see a man starving, but they're only one jump ahead of starvation themselves, they haven't any work to give you, they haven't any food, and whatever they save, if the tax collectors don't get it, then the raiders do—you know, the gangs that rove all through the country—deserters, they call them."

"Do you think that it's any better in the West?"

"No. I don't."

"Then why are you going there?"

"Because I haven't tried it before. That's all there is left to try. It's somewhere to go. Just to keep moving . . . You know," he added suddenly, "I don't think it will be any use. But there's nothing to do in the East except sit under some hedge and wait to die. I don't think I'd mind it much now, the dying. I know it would be a lot easier. Only I think that it's a sin to sit down and let your life go, without making a try for it."

She thought suddenly of those modern college-infected parasites who assumed a sickening air of moral self-righteousness whenever they uttered the standard bromides about their concern for the welfare of others. The tramp's last sentence was one of the most profoundly moral statements she had ever heard; but the man did not know it; he had said it in his impassive, extinguished voice, simply, dryly, as a matter of fact.

"What part of the country do you come from?" she asked.

"Wisconsin," he answered.

The waiter came in, bringing their dinner. He set a table and courteously moved two chairs, showing no astonishment at the nature of the occasion.

She looked at the table; she thought that the magnificence of a world where men could afford the time and the effortless concern for such things as starched napkins and tinkling ice cubes, offered to travelers along with their meals for the price of a few dollars, was a remnant of the age when the sustenance of one's life had not been made a crime and a meal had not been a matter of running a race with death—a remnant which was soon to vanish, like the white filling station on the edge of the weeds of the jungle.

She noticed that the tramp, who had lost the strength to stand up, had not lost the respect for the meaning of the things spread before him. He did not pounce upon the food; he fought to keep his movements slow, to unfold his napkin, to pick up his fork in tempo with hers, his hand shaking—as if he still knew that this, no matter what indignity was ever forced upon them, was the manner proper to men.

"What was your line of work—in the old days?" she asked, when the waiter left. "Factories, wasn't it?"

"Yes, ma'am."

"What trade?"

"Skilled lathe-operator."

"Where did you work at it last?"

"In Colorado, ma'am. For the Hammond Car Company."

"Oh . . . !"

"Ma'am?"

"No, nothing. Worked there long?"

"No, ma'am. Just two weeks."

"How come?"

"Well, I'd waited a year for it, hanging around Colorado just to get that job. They had a waiting list too, the Hammond Car Company, only they didn't go by friendships and they didn't go by seniority, they went by a man's record. I had a good record. But it was just two weeks after I got the job that Lawrence Hammond quit. He quit and disappeared. They closed the plant. Afterwards, there was a citizens' committee that reopened it. I got called back. But five days was all it lasted. They started layoffs just about at once. By seniority. So I had to go. I heard they lasted for about three months, the citizens' committee. Then they had to close the plant for good."

"Where did you work before that?"

"Just about in every Eastern state, ma'am. But it was never more than a month or two. The plants kept closing."

"Did that happen on every job you've held?"

He glanced at her, as if he understood her question. "No, ma'am," he answered and, for the first time, she caught a faint echo of pride in his voice. "The first job I had, I held it for twenty years. Not the same job, but the same place, I mean—I got to be shop foreman. That was twelve years ago. Then the owner of the plant died, and the heirs who took it over, ran it into the ground. Times were bad then, but it was since then that things started going to pieces everywhere faster and faster. Since then, it seems like anywhere I turned—the place cracked and went. At first, we thought it was only one state or another. A lot of us thought that Colorado would last. But it went, too. Anything you tried, anything you touched—it fell. Anywhere you looked, work was stopping—the factories were stopping—the machines were stopping—" he added slowly, in a whisper, as if seeing some secret terror of his own, *"the motors . . . were . . . stopping."* His voice rose: "Oh God, who is—" and broke off.

"—John Galt?" she asked.

"Yes," he said, and shook his head as if to dispel some vision, "only I don't like to say that."

"I don't, either. I wish I knew why people are saying it and who started it."

"That's it, ma'am. That's what I'm afraid of. It might have been me who started it."

"What?"

"Me or about six thousand others. We might have. I think we did. I hope we're wrong."

"What do you mean?"

"Well, there was something that happened at that plant where I worked for twenty years. It was when the old man died and his heirs took over. There were three of them, two sons and a daughter, and they brought a new plan to run the factory. They let us vote on it, too, and everybody—almost everybody—voted for it. We didn't know. We thought it was good. No, that's not true, either. We thought that we were supposed to think it was good. The plan was that everybody in the factory would work according to his ability, but would be paid according to his need. We—what's the matter, ma'am? Why do you look like that?"

"What was the name of the factory?" she asked, her voice barely audible.

"The Twentieth Century Motor Company, ma'am, of Starnesville, Wisconsin."

"Go on."

"We voted for that plan at a big meeting, with all of us present, six thousand of us, everybody that worked in the factory. The Starnes heirs made long speeches about it, and it wasn't too clear, but nobody asked any questions. None of us knew just how the plan would work, but every one of us thought that the next fellow knew it. And if anybody had doubts, he felt guilty and kept his mouth shut—because they made it sound like anyone who'd oppose the plan was a child-killer at heart and less than a human being. They told us that this plan would achieve a noble ideal. Well, how were we to know otherwise? Hadn't we heard it all our lives—from our parents and our school-teachers and our ministers, and in every newspaper we ever read and every movie and every public speech? Hadn't we always been told that this was righteous and just? Well, maybe there's some excuse for what we did at that meeting. Still, we voted for the plan—and what we got, we had it coming to us. You know, ma'am, we are marked men, in a way, those of us who lived through the four years of that plan in the Twentieth Century factory. What is it that hell is supposed to be? Evil—plain, naked, smirking evil, isn't it? Well, that's what we saw and helped to make—and I think we're damned, every one of us, and maybe we'll never be forgiven. . . .

"Do you know how it worked, that plan, and what it did to people? Try pouring water into a tank where there's a pipe at the bottom draining it out faster than you pour it, and each bucket you bring breaks that pipe an inch wider, and the harder you work the more is demanded of you, and you stand slinging buckets forty hours a week, then forty-eight, then fifty-six—for your neighbor's supper—for his wife's operation—for his child's measles—for his mother's wheel chair —for his uncle's shirt—for his nephew's schooling—for the baby next door—for the baby to be born—for anyone anywhere around you— it's theirs to receive, from diapers to dentures—and yours to work, from sunup to sundown, month after month, year after year, with nothing to show for it but your sweat, with nothing in sight for you but their pleasure, for the whole of your life, without rest, without hope, without end. . . . From each according to his ability, to each according to his need. . . .

"We're all one big family, they told us, we're all in this together. But you don't all stand working an acetylene torch ten hours a day— together, and you don't all get a bellyache—together. What's whose ability and which of whose needs comes first? When it's all one pot, you can't let any man decide what his own needs are, can you? If you did, he might claim that he needs a yacht—and if his feelings is all you have to go by, he might prove it, too. Why not? If it's not right for me to own a car until I've worked myself into a hospital ward, earning a car for every loafer and every naked savage on earth—why can't he demand a yacht from me, too, if I still have the ability not to have collapsed? No? He can't? Then why can he demand that I go without cream for my coffee until he's replastered his living room? . . . Oh well . . . Well, anyway, it was decided that nobody had the right to judge his own need or ability. We *voted* on it. Yes, ma'am, we voted on it in a public meeting twice a year. How else could it be done? Do you care to think what would happen at such a meeting? It took us just one meeting to discover that we had become beggars—rotten, whining, sniveling beggars, all of us, because no man could claim his pay as his rightful earning, he had no rights and no earnings, his work didn't belong to him, it belonged to 'the family,' and they owed him nothing in return, and the only claim he had on them was his 'need' —so he had to beg in public for relief from his needs, like any lousy moocher, listing all his troubles and miseries, down to his patched drawers and his wife's head colds, hoping that 'the family' would throw him the alms. He had to claim miseries, because it's miseries, not work, that had become the coin of the realm—so it turned into a contest among six thousand panhandlers, each claiming that *his* need was worse than his brother's. How else could it be done? Do you care to guess what happened, what sort of men kept quiet, feeling shame, and what sort got away with the jackpot?

"But that wasn't all. There was something else that we discovered at the same meeting. The factory's production had fallen by forty per cent, in that first half-year, so it was decided that somebody hadn't delivered 'according to his ability.' Who? How would you tell it? 'The family' voted on that, too. They voted which men were the best, and these men were sentenced to work overtime each night for the next six months. Overtime without pay—because you weren't paid by time and you weren't paid by work, only by need.

"Do I have to tell you what happened after that—and into what sort of creatures we all started turning, we who had once been human? We began to hide whatever ability we had, to slow down and watch like hawks that we never worked any faster or better than the next fellow. What else could we do, when we knew that if we did our best for 'the family,' it's not thanks or rewards that we'd get, but punishment? We knew that for every stinker who'd ruin a batch of motors and cost the company money—either through his sloppiness, because he didn't have to care, or through plain incompetence—it's we who'd have to pay with our nights and our Sundays. So we did our best to be no good.

"There was one young boy who started out, full of fire for the noble ideal, a bright kid without any schooling, but with a wonderful head on his shoulders. The first year, he figured out a work process that saved us thousands of man-hours. He gave it to 'the family,' didn't ask anything for it, either, couldn't ask, but that was all right with him. It was for the ideal, he said. But when he found himself voted as one of our ablest and sentenced to night work, because we hadn't gotten enough from him, he shut his mouth and his brain. You can bet he didn't come up with any ideas, the second year.

"What was it they'd always told us about the vicious competition of the profit system, where men had to compete for who'd do a better job than his fellows? Vicious, wasn't it? Well, they should have seen what it was like when we all had to compete with one another for who'd do the worst job possible. There's no surer way to destroy a man than to force him into a spot where he has to aim at *not* doing his best, where he has to struggle to do a bad job, day after day. That will finish him quicker than drink or idleness or pulling stick-ups for a living. But there was nothing else for us to do except to fake unfitness. The one accusation we feared was to be suspected of ability. Ability was like a mortgage on you that you could never pay off. And what was there to work for? You knew that your basic pittance would be given to you anyway, whether you worked or not—your 'housing and feeding allowance,' it was called—and above that pittance, you had no chance to get anything, no matter how hard you tried. You couldn't count on buying a new suit of clothes next year—they might give you a 'clothing allowance' or they might not, according to whether nobody broke a leg, needed an operation or gave birth to more babies. And if there wasn't enough money for new suits for everybody, then you couldn't get yours, either.

"There was one man who'd worked hard all his life, because he'd always wanted to send his son through college. Well, the boy graduated from high school in the second year of the plan—but 'the family' wouldn't give the father any 'allowance' for the college. They said his son couldn't go to college, until we had enough to send everybody's sons to college—and that we first had to send everybody's children through high school, and we didn't even have enough for that. The father died the following year, in a knife fight with somebody in a saloon, a fight over nothing in particular—such fights were beginning to happen among us all the time.

"Then there was an old guy, a widower with no family, who had one hobby: phonograph records. I guess that was all he ever got out of life. In the old days, he used to skip meals just to buy himself some new recording of classical music. Well, they didn't give him any 'allowance' for records—'personal luxury,' they called it. But at that same meeting, Millie Bush, somebody's daughter, a mean, ugly little eight-year-old, was voted a pair of gold braces for her buck teeth—

this was 'medical need,' because the staff psychologist had said that the poor girl would get an inferiority complex if her teeth weren't straightened out. The old guy who loved music, turned to drink, instead. He got so you never saw him fully conscious any more. But it seems like there was one thing he couldn't forget. One night, he came staggering down the street, saw Millie Bush, swung his fist and knocked all her teeth out. Every one of them.

"Drink, of course, was what we all turned to, some more, some less. Don't ask how we got the money for it. When all the decent pleasures are forbidden, there's always ways to get the rotten ones. You don't break into grocery stores after dark and you don't pick your fellow's pockets to buy classical symphonies or fishing tackle, but if it's to get stinking drunk and forget—you do. Fishing tackle? Hunting guns? Snapshot cameras? Hobbies? There wasn't any 'amusement allowance' for anybody. 'Amusement' was the first thing they dropped. Aren't you always supposed to be ashamed to object when anybody asks you to give up anything, if it's something that gave you pleasure? Even our 'tobacco allowance' was cut to where we got two packs of cigarettes a month—and this, they told us, was because the money had to go into the babies' milk fund. Babies was the only item of production that didn't fall, but rose and kept on rising—because people had nothing else to do, I guess, and because they didn't have to care, the baby wasn't their burden, it was 'the family's.' In fact, the best chance you had of getting a raise and breathing easier for a while was a 'baby allowance.' Either that, or a major disease.

"It didn't take us long to see how it all worked out. Any man who tried to play straight, had to refuse himself everything. He lost his taste for any pleasure, he hated to smoke a nickel's worth of tobacco or chew a stick of gum, worrying whether somebody had more need for that nickel. He felt ashamed of every mouthful of food he swallowed, wondering whose weary nights of overtime had paid for it, knowing that his food was not his by right, miserably wishing to be cheated rather than to cheat, to be a sucker, but not a blood-sucker. He wouldn't marry, he wouldn't help his folks back home, he wouldn't put an extra burden on 'the family.' Besides, if he still had some sort of sense of responsibility, he couldn't marry or bring children into the world, when he could plan nothing, promise nothing, count on nothing. But the shiftless and the irresponsible had a field day of it. They bred babies, they got girls into trouble, they dragged in every worthless relative they had from all over the country, every unmarried pregnant sister, for an extra 'disability allowance,' they got more sicknesses than any doctor could disprove, they ruined their clothing, their furniture, their homes—what the hell, 'the family' was paying for it! They found more ways of getting in 'need' than the rest of us could ever imagine —they developed a special skill for it, which was the only ability *they* showed.

"God help us, ma'am! Do you see what we saw? We saw that we'd been given a law to live by, a *moral* law, they called it, which punished those who observed it—for observing it. The more you tried to live up to it, the more you suffered; the more you cheated it, the bigger reward you got. Your honesty was like a tool left at the mercy of the next man's dishonesty. The honest ones paid, the dishonest collected. The honest lost, the dishonest won. How long could men stay good under this sort of a law of goodness? We were a pretty decent bunch of fellows when we started. There weren't many chiselers among us. We knew our jobs and we were proud of it and we worked for the best factory in the country, where old man Starnes hired nothing but the pick of the country's labor. Within one year under the new plan, there wasn't an honest man left among us. *That* was the evil, the sort of hell-horror evil that preachers used to scare you with, but you never thought to see alive. Not that the plan encouraged a few bastards, but that it turned decent people into bastards, and there was nothing else that it could do—and it was called a moral ideal!

"What was it we were supposed to want to work for? For the love of our brothers? What brothers? For the bums, the loafers, the moochers we saw all around us? And whether they were cheating or plain incompetent, whether they were unwilling or unable—what difference did that make to us? If we were tied for life to the level of their unfitness, faked or real, how long could we care to go on? We had no way of knowing their ability, we had no way of controlling their needs—all we knew was that we were beasts of burden struggling blindly in some sort of place that was half-hospital, half-stockyards—a place geared to nothing but disability, disaster, disease—beasts put there for the relief of whatever whoever chose to say was whichever's need.

"Love of our brothers? That's when we learned to hate our brothers for the first time in our lives. We began to hate them for every meal they swallowed, for every small pleasure they enjoyed, for one man's new shirt, for another's wife's hat, for an outing with their family, for a paint job on their house—it was taken from us, it was paid for by our privations, our denials, our hunger. We began to spy on one another, each hoping to catch the others lying about their needs, so as to cut their 'allowance' at the next meeting. We began to have stool pigeons who informed on people, who reported that somebody had bootlegged a turkey to his family on some Sunday—which he'd paid for by gambling, most likely. We began to meddle into one another's lives. We provoked family quarrels, to get somebody's relatives thrown out. Any time we saw a man starting to go steady with a girl, we made life miserable for him. We broke up many engagements. We didn't want anyone to marry, we didn't want any more dependents to feed.

"In the old days, we used to celebrate if somebody had a baby, we used to chip in and help him out with the hospital bills, if he happened to be hard-pressed for the moment. Now, if a baby was born, we didn't speak to the parents for weeks. Babies, to us, had become what locusts were to farmers. In the old days, we used to help a man if he had a bad illness in the family. Now—well, I'll tell you about just one case. It was the mother of a man who had been with us for fifteen years. She was a kindly old lady, cheerful and wise, she knew us all by our first names and we all liked her—we used to like her. One day, she slipped on the cellar stairs and fell and broke her hip. We knew what that meant at her age. The staff doctor said that she'd have to be sent to a hospital in town, for expensive treatments that would take a long time. The old lady died the night before she was to leave for town. They never established the cause of death. No, I don't know whether she was murdered. Nobody said that. Nobody would talk about it at all. All I know is that I—and that's what I can't forget!—I, too, had caught myself wishing that she would die. This—may God forgive us!—was the brotherhood, the security, the abundance that the plan was supposed to achieve for us!

"Was there any reason why this sort of horror would ever be preached by anybody? Was there anybody who got any profit from it? There was. The Starnes heirs. I hope you're not going to remind me that they'd sacrificed a fortune and turned the factory over to us as a gift. We were fooled by that one, too. Yes, they gave up the factory. But profit, ma'am, depends on what it is you're after. And what the Starnes heirs were after, no money on earth could buy. Money is too clean and innocent for that.

"Eric Starnes, the youngest—he was a jellyfish that didn't have the guts to be after anything in particular. He got himself voted as Director of our Public Relations Department, which didn't do anything, except that he had a staff for the not doing of anything, so he didn't have to bother sticking around the office. The pay he got—well, I shouldn't call it 'pay,' none of us was 'paid'—the alms voted to him was fairly modest, about ten times what I got, but that wasn't riches. Eric didn't care for money—he wouldn't have known what to do with it. He spent his time hanging around among us, showing how chummy he was and democratic. He wanted to be loved, it seems. The way he went about it was to keep reminding us that he had given us the factory. We couldn't stand him.

"Gerald Starnes was our Director of Production. We never learned just what the size of his rake-off—his alms—had been. It would have taken a staff of accountants to figure that out, and a staff of engineers to trace the way it was piped, directly or indirectly, into his office. None of it was supposed to be for him—it was all for company expenses. Gerald had three cars, four secretaries, five telephones, and he used to throw champagne and caviar parties that no tax-paying tycoon in the country could have afforded. He spent more money in one year than his father had earned in profits in the last two years of his life. We saw a hundred-pound stack—a hundred pounds, we weighed them—of magazines in Gerald's office, full of stories about our factory and our noble plan, with big pictures of Gerald Starnes, calling him a great social crusader. Gerald liked to come into the shops at night, dressed in his formal clothes, flashing diamond cuff links the size of a nickel and shaking cigar ashes all over. Any cheap show-off who's got nothing to parade but his cash, is bad enough—except that he makes no bones about the cash being his, and you're free to gape at him or not, as you wish, and mostly you don't. But when a bastard like Gerald Starnes puts on an act and keeps spouting that he doesn't care for material wealth, that he's only serving 'the family,' that all the lushness is not for himself, but for our sake and for the common good, because it's necessary to keep up the prestige of the company and of the noble plan in the eyes of the public—then that's when you learn to hate the creature as you've never hated anything human.

"But his sister Ivy was worse. She really did not care for material wealth. The alms she got was no bigger than ours, and she went about in scuffed, flat-heeled shoes and shirtwaists—just to show how selfless she was. She was our Director of Distribution. She was the lady in charge of our needs. She was the one who held us by the throat. Of course, distribution was supposed to be decided by voting—by the voice of the people. But when the people are six thousand howling voices, trying to decide without yardstick, rhyme or reason, when there are no rules to the game and each can demand anything, but has a right to nothing, when everybody holds power over everybody's life except his own—then it turns out, as it did, that the voice of the people is Ivy Starnes. By the end of the second year, we dropped the pretense of the 'family meetings'—in the name of 'production efficiency and time economy,' one meeting used to take ten days—and all the petitions of need were simply sent to Miss Starnes' office. No, not sent. They had to be recited to her in person by every petitioner. Then she made up a distribution list, which she read to us for our vote of approval at a meeting that lasted three-quarters of an hour. We voted approval. There was a ten-minute period on the agenda for discussion and objections. We made no objections. We knew better by that time. Nobody can divide a factory's income among thousands of people, without some sort of a gauge to measure people's value. Her gauge was bootlicking. Selfless? In her father's time, all of his money wouldn't have given him a chance to speak to his lousiest wiper and get away with it, as she spoke to our best skilled workers and their wives. She had pale eyes that looked fishy, cold and dead. And if you ever want to see pure evil, you should have seen the way her eyes glinted when she watched some man who'd talked back to her once and who'd just heard his name on the list of those getting nothing above basic pittance. And when you saw it, you saw the real motive of any person who's ever preached the slogan: 'From each according to his ability, to each according to his need.'

"This was the whole secret of it. At first, I kept wondering how it could be possible that the educated, the cultured, the famous men of the world could make a mistake of this size and preach, as righteousness, this sort of abomination—when five minutes of thought should have told them what would happen if somebody tried to practice what they preached. Now I know that they didn't do it by any kind of mistake. Mistakes of this size are never made innocently. If men fall for some vicious piece of insanity, when they have no way to make it work and no possible reason to explain their choice—it's because they have a reason that they do not wish to tell. And we weren't so innocent either, when we voted for that plan at the first meeting. We didn't do it just because we believed that the drippy old guff they spewed was good. We had another reason, but the guff helped us to hide it from our neighbors and from ourselves. The guff gave us a chance to pass off as virtue something that we'd be ashamed to admit otherwise. There wasn't a man voting for it who didn't think that under a setup of this kind he'd muscle in on the profits of the men abler than himself. There wasn't a man rich and smart enough but that he didn't think that somebody was richer and smarter, and this plan would give him a share of his better's wealth and brain. But while he was thinking that he'd get unearned benefits from the men above, he forgot about the men below who'd get unearned benefits, too. He forgot about all his inferiors who'd rush to drain him just as he hoped to drain his superiors. The worker who liked the idea that his need entitled him to a limousine like his boss's, forgot that every bum and beggar on earth would come howling that *their* need entitled them to an icebox like his own. *That* was our real motive when we voted— that was the truth of it—but we didn't like to think it, so the less we liked it, the louder we yelled about our love for the common good.

"Well, we got what we asked for. By the time we saw what it was that we'd asked for, it was too late. We were trapped, with no place to go. The best men among us left the factory in the first week of the plan. We lost our best engineers, superintendents, foremen and highest-skilled workers. A man of self-respect doesn't turn into a milch cow for anybody. Some able fellows tried to stick it out, but they couldn't take it for long. We kept losing our men, they kept escaping from the factory like from a pesthole—till we had nothing left except the men of need, but none of the men of ability.

"And the few of us who were still any good, but stayed on, were only those who had been there too long. In the old days, nobody ever quit the Twentieth Century—and, somehow, we couldn't make ourselves believe that it was gone. After a while, we couldn't quit, because no other employer would have us—for which I can't blame him.

Nobody would deal with us in any way, no respectable person or firm. All the small shops, where we traded, started moving out of Starnesville fast—till we had nothing left but saloons, gambling joints and crooks who sold us trash at gouging prices. The alms we got kept falling, but the cost of our living went up. The list of the factory's needy kept stretching, but the list of its customers shrank. There was less and less income to divide among more and more people. In the old days, it used to be said that the Twentieth Century Motor trademark was as good as the karat mark on gold. I don't know what it was that the Starnes heirs thought, if they thought at all, but I suppose that like all social planners and like savages, they thought that this trademark was a magic stamp which did the trick by some sort of voodoo power and that it would keep them rich, as it had kept their father. Well, when our customers began to see that we never delivered an order on time and never put out a motor that didn't have something wrong with it—the magic stamp began to work the other way around: people wouldn't take a motor as a gift, if it was marked Twentieth Century. And it came to where our only customers were men who never paid and never meant to pay their bills. But Gerald Starnes, doped by his own publicity, got huffy and went around, with an air of moral superiority, demanding that businessmen place orders with us, not because our motors were good, but because we *needed* the orders so badly.

"By that time, a village half-wit could see what generations of professors had pretended not to notice. What good would our need do to a power plant when its generators stopped because of our defective engines? What good would it do to a man caught on an operating table when the electric light went out? What good would it do to the passengers of a plane when its motor failed in mid-air? And if they bought our product, not because of its merit, but because of our need, would that be the good, the right, the moral thing to do for the owner of that power plant, the surgeon in that hospital, the maker of that plane?

"Yet this was the moral law that the professors and leaders and thinkers had wanted to establish all over the earth. If this is what it did in a single small town where we all knew one another, do you care to think what it would do on a world scale? Do you care to imagine what it would be like, if you had to live and to work, when you're tied to all the disasters and all the malingering of the globe? To work—and whenever any men failed anywhere, it's you who would have to make up for it. To work—with no chance to rise, with your meals and your clothes and your home and your pleasure depending on any swindle, any famine, any pestilence anywhere on earth. To work—with no chance for an extra ration, till the Cambodians have been fed and the Patagonians have been sent through college. To work—on a blank check held by every creature born, by men whom you'll never see, whose needs you'll never know, whose ability or laziness or sloppiness or fraud you have no way to learn and no right to question —just to work and work and work—and leave it up to the Ivys and the Geralds of the world to decide whose stomach will consume the effort, the dreams and the days of your life. And *this* is the moral law to accept? *This*—a moral ideal?

"Well, we tried it—and we learned. Our agony took four years, from our first meeting to our last, and it ended the only way it could end: in bankruptcy. At our last meeting, Ivy Starnes was the one who tried to brazen it out. She made a short, nasty, snippy little speech in which she said that the plan had failed because the rest of the country had not accepted it, that a single community could not succeed in the midst of a selfish, greedy world—and that the plan was a noble ideal, but human nature was not good enough for it. A young boy—the one who had been punished for giving us a useful idea in our first year—got up, as we all sat silent, and walked straight to Ivy Starnes on the platform. He said nothing. He spat in her face. That was the end of the noble plan and of the Twentieth Century."

The man had spoken as if the burden of his years of silence had slipped suddenly out of his grasp. She knew that this was his tribute to her: he had shown no reaction to her kindness, he had seemed numbed to human value or human hope, but something within him had been reached and his response was this confession, this long, desperate cry of rebellion against injustice, held back for years, but breaking out in recognition of the first person he had met in whose hearing an appeal for justice would not be hopeless. It was as if the life he had been about to renounce were given back to him by the two essentials he needed: by his food and by the presence of a rational being.

"But what about John Galt?" she asked.

"Oh . . ." he said, remembering. "Oh, yes . . ."

"You were going to tell me why people started asking that question."

"Yes . . ." He was looking off, as if at some sight which he had studied for years, but which remained unchanged and unsolved; his face had an odd, questioning look of terror.

"You were going to tell me who was the John Galt they mean—if there ever was such a person."

"I hope there wasn't, ma'am. I mean, I hope that it's just a coincidence, just a sentence that hasn't any meaning."

"You had something in mind. What?"

"It was . . . it was something that happened at that first meeting at the Twentieth Century factory. Maybe that was the start of it, maybe not. I don't know . . . The meeting was held on a spring night, twelve years ago. The six thousand of us were crowded on bleachers built way up to the rafters of the plant's largest hangar. We had just voted for the new plan and we were in an edgy sort of mood, making too much noise, cheering the people's victory, threatening some kind of un-known enemies and spoiling for a fight, like bullies with an uneasy conscience. There were white arclights beating down on us and we felt kind of touchy and raw, and we were an ugly, dangerous mob in that moment. Gerald Starnes, who was chairman, kept hammering his gavel for order, and we quieted down some, but not much, and you could see the whole place moving restlessly from side to side, like water in a pan that's being rocked. 'This is a crucial moment in the history of mankind!' Gerald Starnes yelled through the noise. 'Re-member that none of us may now leave this place, for each of us be-longs to all the others by the moral law which we all accept!' 'I don't,' said one man and stood up. He was one of the young engineers. Nobody knew much about him. He'd always kept mostly by himself. When he stood up, we suddenly turned dead-still. It was the way he held his head. He was tall and slim—and I remember thinking that any two of us could have broken his neck without trouble—but what we all felt was fear. He stood like a man who knew that he was right. 'I will put an end to this, once and for all,' he said. His voice was clear and without any feeling. That was all he said and started to walk out. He walked down the length of the place, in the white light, not hurrying and not noticing any of us. Nobody moved to stop him. Gerald Starnes cried suddenly after him, 'How?' He turned and answered, 'I will stop the motor of the world.' Then he walked out. We never saw him again. We never heard what became of him. But years later, when we saw the lights going out, one after another, in the great factories that had stood solid like mountains for generations, when we saw the gates closing and the conveyor belts turning still, when we saw the roads growing empty and the stream of cars draining off, when it began to look as if some silent power were stopping the generators of the world and the world was crumbling quietly, like a body when its spirit is gone—then we began to wonder and to ask questions about him. We began to ask it of one another, those of us who had heard him say it. We began to think that he had kept his word, that he, who had seen and known the truth we refused to know, was the retribution we had called upon our heads, the avenger, the man of that justice which we had defied. We began to think that he had damned us and there was no escape from his verdict and we would never be able to get away from him—and this was the more terrible because he was not pursuing us, it was we who were suddenly looking for him and he had merely gone without a trace. We found no answer about him anywhere. We won-dered by what sort of impossible power he could have done what he had promised to do. There was no answer to that. We began to think of him whenever we saw another collapse in the world, which nobody could explain, whenever we took another blow, whenever we lost an-other hope, whenever we felt caught in this dead, gray fog that's descending all over the earth. Perhaps people heard us crying that question and they did not know what we meant, but they knew too well the feeling that made us cry it. They, too, felt that something had gone from the world. Perhaps this was why they began to say it, whenever they felt that there was no hope. I'd like to think that I am wrong, that those words mean nothing, that there's no conscious intention and no avenger behind the ending of the human race. But when I hear them repeating that question, I feel afraid. I think of the man who said that he would stop the motor of the world. You see, his name was John Galt."

* * *

She awakened, because the sound of the wheels had changed. It was an irregular beat, with sudden screeches and short, sharp cracks, a sound like the broken laughter of hysteria, with the fitful jerking of the car to match it. She knew, before she glanced at her watch, that this was the track of the Kansas Western and that the train had started on its long detour south from Kirby, Nebraska.

The train was half-empty; few people had ventured across the continent on the first Comet since the tunnel disaster. She had given a bedroom to the tramp, and then had remained alone with his story. She had wanted to think of it, of all the questions she intended to ask him tomorrow—but she had found her mind frozen and still, like a spectator staring at the story, unable to function, only to stare. She had felt as if she knew the meaning of that spectacle, knew it with no further questions and had to escape it. To move—had been the words beating in her mind with peculiar urgency—to move—as if movement had become an end in itself, crucial, absolute and doomed.

Through a thin layer of sleep, the sound of the wheels had kept running a race with the growth of her tension. She had kept awakening, as in a causeless start of panic, finding herself upright in the darkness, thinking blankly: What was it?—then telling herself in reassurance: We're moving . . . we're still moving. . . .

The track of the Kansas Western was worse than she had expected— she thought, listening to the wheels. The train was now carrying her hundreds of miles away from Utah. She had felt a desperate desire to get off the train on the main line, abandon all the problems of Taggart Transcontinental, find an airplane and fly straight to Quentin Daniels. It had taken a cheerless effort of will to remain in her car.

She lay in the darkness, listening to the wheels, thinking that only Daniels and his motor still remained like a point of fire ahead, pulling her forward. Of what use would the motor now be to her? She had no answer. Why did she feel so certain of the desperate need to hurry? She had no answer. To reach him in time, was the only ultimatum left in her mind. She held onto it, asking no questions. Wordlessly, she knew the real answer: the motor was needed, not to move trains, but to keep her moving.

She could not hear the beat of the fourth knocks any longer in the jumbled screeching of metal, she could not hear the steps of the enemy she was racing, only the hopeless stampede of panic. . . . I'll get there in time, she thought, I'll get there first, I'll save the motor. *There's* one motor he's not going to stop, she thought . . . he's not going to stop . . . he's not going to stop . . . He's not going to stop, she thought—awakening with a jolt, jerking her head off the pillow. The wheels had stopped.

For a moment, she remained still, trying to grasp the peculiar stillness around her. It felt like the impossible attempt to create a sensory image of non-existence. There were no attributes of reality to perceive, nothing but their absence: no sound, as if she were alone on the train—no motion, as if this were not a train, but a room in a building—no light, as if this were neither train nor room, but space without objects—no sign of violence or physical disaster, as if this were the state where disaster is no longer possible.

In the moment when she grasped the nature of the stillness, her body sprang upright with a single curve of motion, immediate and violent like a cry of rebellion. The loud screech of the window shade went like a knife-cut through the silence, as she threw the shade upward. There was nothing outside but anonymous stretches of prairie; a strong wind was breaking the clouds, and a shaft of moonlight fell through, but it fell upon plains that seemed as dead as those from which it came.

The sweep of her hand pressed the light switch and the bell to summon the porter. The electric light came on and brought her back to a rational world. She glanced at her watch: it was a few minutes past midnight. She looked out of the rear window: the track went off in a straight line and, at the prescribed distance, she saw the red lanterns left on the ground, placed conscientiously to protect the rear of the train. The sight seemed reassuring.

She pressed the porter's bell once more. She waited. She went to the vestibule, unlocked the door and leaned out to look down the line of the train. A few windows were lighted in the long, tapering band of steel, but she saw no figures, no sign of human activity. She slammed the door, came back and started to dress, her movements suddenly calm and swift.

No one came to answer her bell. When she hastened across to the next car, she felt no fear, no uncertainty, no despair, nothing but the urgency of action.

There was no porter in the cubbyhole of the next car, no porter in the car beyond. She hurried down the narrow passageways, meeting no one. But a few compartment doors were open. The passengers sat inside, dressed or half-dressed, silently, as if waiting. They watched her rush by with oddly furtive glances, as if they knew what she was after, as if they had expected someone to come and to face what they had not faced. She went on, running down the spinal cord of a dead train, noting the peculiar combination of lighted compartments, open doors and empty passages: no one had ventured to step out. No one had wanted to ask the first question.

She ran through the train's only coach, where some passengers slept in contorted poses of exhaustion, while others, awake and still, sat hunched, like animals waiting for a blow, making no move to avert it.

In the vestibule of the coach, she stopped. She saw a man, who had unlocked the door and was leaning out, looking inquiringly ahead through the darkness, ready to step off. He turned at the sound of her approach. She recognized his face: it was Owen Kellogg, the man who had rejected the future she had once offered him.

"Kellogg!" she gasped, the sound of laughter in her voice like a cry of relief at the sudden sight of a man in a desert.

"Hello, Miss Taggart," he answered, with an astonished smile that held a touch of incredulous pleasure—and of wistfulness. "I didn't know you were aboard."

"Come on," she ordered, as if he were still an employee of the railroad. "I think we're on a frozen train."

"We are," he said, and followed her with prompt, disciplined obedience.

No explanations were necessary. It was as if, in unspoken understanding, they were answering a call to duty—and it seemed natural that of the hundreds aboard, it was the two of them who should be partners-in-danger.

"Any idea how long we've been standing?" she asked, as they hurried on through the next car.

"No," he said. "We were standing when I woke up."

They went the length of the train, finding no porters, no waiters in the diner, no brakemen, no conductor. They glanced at each other once in a while, but kept silent. They knew the stories of abandoned trains, of the crews that vanished in sudden bursts of rebellion against serfdom.

They got off at the head end of the train, with no motion around them save the wind on their faces, and they climbed swiftly aboard the engine. The engine's headlight was on, stretching like an accusing arm into the void of the night. The engine's cab was empty.

Her cry of desperate triumph broke out in answer to the shock of the sight: "Good for them! They're human beings!"

She stopped, aghast, as at the cry of a stranger. She noticed that Kellogg stood watching her curiously, with the faint hint of a smile.

It was an old steam engine, the best that the railroad had been able to provide for the Comet. The fire was banked in the grates, the steam gauge was low, and in the great windshield before them the headlight fell upon a band of ties that should have been running to meet them, but lay still instead, like a ladder's steps, counted, numbered and ended.

She reached for the logbook and looked at the names of the train's last crew. The engineer had been Pat Logan.

Her head dropped slowly, and she closed her eyes. She thought of the first run on a green-blue track, that must have been in Pat Logan's mind—as it was now in hers—through the silent hours of his last run on any rail.

"Miss Taggart?" said Owen Kellogg softly.

She jerked her head up. "Yes," she said, "yes . . . Well"—her voice had no color except the metallic tinge of decision—"we'll have to get to a phone and call for another crew." She glanced at her watch. "At the rate we were running, I think we must be about eighty miles from the Oklahoma state line. I believe Bradshaw is this road's nearest division point to call. We're somewhere within thirty miles of it."

"Are there any Taggart trains following us?"

"The next one is Number 253, the transcontinental freight, but it won't get here till about seven A.M., if it's running on time, which I doubt."

"Only *one* freight in seven hours?" He said it involuntarily, with a note of outraged loyalty to the great railroad he had once been proud to serve.

Her mouth moved in the brief snap of a smile. "Our transcontinental traffic is not what it was in your day."

He nodded slowly. "I don't suppose there are any Kansas Western trains coming tonight, either?"

"I can't remember offhand, but I think not."

He glanced at the poles by the side of the track. "I hope that the Kansas Western people have kept their phones in order."

"You mean that the chances are they haven't, if we judge by the state of their track. But we'll have to try it."

"Yes."

She turned to go, but stopped. She knew it was useless to comment, but the words came involuntarily. "You know," she said, "it's those lanterns our men put behind the train to protect us that's the hardest thing to take. They . . . they felt more concern for human lives than their country had shown for theirs."

His swift glance at her was like a shot of deliberate emphasis, then he answered gravely, "Yes, Miss Taggart."

Climbing down the ladder on the side of the engine, they saw a cluster of passengers gathered by the track and more figures emerging from the train to join them. By some special instinct of their own, the men who had sat waiting knew that someone had taken charge, someone had assumed the responsibility and it was now safe to show signs of life.

They all looked at her with an air of inquiring expectation, as she approached. The unnatural pallor of the moonlight seemed to dissolve the differences of their faces and to stress the quality they all had in common: a look of cautious appraisal, part fear, part plea, part impertinence held in abeyance.

"Is there anyone here who wishes to be spokesman for the passengers?" she asked.

They looked at one another. There was no answer.

"Very well," she said. "You don't have to speak. I'm Dagny Taggart, the Operating Vice-President of this railroad, and"—there was a rustle of response from the group, half-movement, half-whisper, resembling relief—"and I'll do the speaking. We are on a train that has been abandoned by its crew. There was no physical accident. The engine is intact. But there is no one to run it. This is what the newspapers call a frozen train. You all know what it means—and you know the reasons. Perhaps you knew the reasons long before they were discovered by the men who deserted you tonight. The law forbade them to desert. But this will not help you now."

A woman shrieked suddenly, with the demanding petulance of hysteria, "What are we going to do?"

Dagny paused to look at her. The woman was pushing forward, to squeeze herself into the group, to place some human bodies between herself and the sight of the great vacuum—the plain stretching off and dissolving into moonlight, the dead phosphorescence of impotent, borrowed energy. The woman had a coat thrown over a nightgown; the coat was slipping open and her stomach protruded under the gown's thin cloth, with that loose obscenity of manner which assumes all human self-revelation to be ugliness and makes no effort to conceal it. For a moment, Dagny regretted the necessity to continue.

"I shall go down the track to a telephone," she continued, her voice clear and as cold as the moonlight. "There are emergency telephones at intervals of five miles along the right-of-way. I shall call for another crew to be sent here. This will take some time. You will please stay aboard and maintain such order as you are capable of maintaining."

"What about the gangs of raiders?" asked another woman's nervous voice.

"That's true," said Dagny. "I'd better have someone to accompany me. Who wishes to go?"

She had misunderstood the woman's motive. There was no answer. There were no glances directed at her or at one another. There were no eyes—only moist ovals glistening in the moonlight. There they were, she thought, the men of the new age, the demanders and recipients of self-sacrifice. She was struck by a quality of anger in their silence—an anger saying that she was supposed to spare them moments such as this—and, with a feeling of cruelty new to her, she remained silent by conscious intention.

She noticed that Owen Kellogg, too, was waiting; but he was not watching the passengers, he was watching her face. When he became certain that there would be no answer from the crowd, he said quietly, "I'll go with you, of course, Miss Taggart."

"Thank you."

"What about us?" snapped the nervous woman.

Dagny turned to her, answering in the formal, inflectionless monotone of a business executive, "There have been no cases of raider gang attacks upon frozen trains—unfortunately."

"Just where are we?" asked a bulky man with too expensive an overcoat and too flabby a face; his voice had a tone intended for servants by a man unfit to employ them. "In what part of what state?"

"I don't know," she answered.

"How long will we be kept here?" asked another, in the tone of a creditor who is imposed upon by a debtor.

"I don't know."

"When will we get to San Francisco?" asked a third, in the manner of a sheriff addressing a suspect.

"I don't know."

The demanding resentment was breaking loose, in small, crackling puffs, like chestnuts popping open in the dark oven of the minds who now felt certain that they were taken care of and safe.

"This is perfectly outrageous!" yelled a woman, springing forward, throwing her words at Dagny's face. "You have no right to let this happen! I don't intend to be kept waiting in the middle of nowhere! I expect transportation!"

"Keep your mouth shut," said Dagny, "or I'll lock the train doors and leave you where you are."

"You can't do that! You're a common carrier! You have no right to discriminate against me! I'll report it to the Unification Board!"

"—if I give you a train to get you within sight or hearing of your Board," said Dagny, turning away.

She saw Kellogg looking at her, his glance like a line drawn under her words, underscoring them for her own attention.

"Get a flashlight somewhere," she said, "while I go to get my handbag, then we'll start."

When they started out on their way to the track phone, walking past the silent line of cars, they saw another figure descending from the train and hurrying to meet them. She recognized the tramp.

"Trouble, ma'am?" he asked, stopping.

"The crew has deserted."

"Oh. What's to be done?"

"I'm going to a phone to call the division point."

"You can't go alone, ma'am. Not these days. I'd better go with you."

She smiled. "Thanks. But I'll be all right. Mr. Kellogg here is going with me. Say—what's your name?"

"Jeff Allen, ma'am."

"Listen, Allen, have you ever worked for a railroad?"

"No, ma'am."

"Well, you're working for one now. You're deputy-conductor and proxy-vice-president-in-charge-of-operation. Your job is to take charge of this train in my absence, to preserve order and to keep the cattle from stampeding. Tell them that I appointed you. You don't need any proof. They'll obey anybody who expects obedience."

"Yes, ma'am," he answered firmly, with a look of understanding.

She remembered that money inside a man's pocket had the power to turn into confidence inside his mind; she took a hundred-dollar bill from her bag and slipped it into his hand. "As advance on wages," she said.

"Yes, ma'am."

She had started off, when he called after her, "Miss Taggart!"

She turned. "Yes?"

"Thank you," he said.

She smiled, half-raising her hand in a parting salute, and walked on.

"Who is that?" asked Kellogg.

"A tramp who was caught stealing a ride."

"He'll do the job, I think."

"He will."

They walked silently past the engine and on in the direction of its headlight. At first, stepping from tie to tie, with the violent light beating against them from behind, they still felt as if they were at home in the normal realm of a railroad. Then she found herself watching the light on the ties under her feet, watching it ebb slowly, trying to hold it, to keep seeing its fading glow, until she knew that the hint of a glow on the wood was no longer anything but moonlight. She could not prevent the shudder that made her turn to look back. The headlight still hung behind them, like the liquid silver globe of a planet, deceptively close, but belonging to another orbit and another system.

Owen Kellogg walked silently beside her, and she felt certain that they knew each other's thoughts.

"He couldn't have. Oh God, he couldn't!" she said suddenly, not realizing that she had switched to words.

"Who?"

"Nathaniel Taggart. He couldn't have worked with people like those passengers. He couldn't have run trains for them. He couldn't have employed them. He couldn't have used them at all, neither as customers nor as workers."

Kellogg smiled. "You mean that he couldn't have grown rich by exploiting them, Miss Taggart?"

She nodded. "They . . ." she said, and he heard the faint trembling of her voice, which was love and pain and indignation, "they've said for years that he rose by thwarting the ability of others, by leaving them no chance, and that . . . that human incompetence was to his selfish interest. . . . But he . . . it wasn't obedience that he required of people."

"Miss Taggart," he said, with an odd note of sternness in his voice, "just remember that he represented a code of existence which—for a brief span in all human history—drove slavery out of the civilized world. Remember it, when you feel baffled by the nature of his enemies."

"Have you ever heard of a woman named Ivy Starnes?"

"Oh yes."

"I keep thinking that this was what she would have enjoyed—the spectacle of those passengers tonight. This was what she's after. But we—we can't live with it, you and I, can we? No one can live with it. It's not possible to live with it."

"What makes you think that Ivy Starnes's purpose is life?"

Somewhere on the edge of her mind—like the wisps she saw floating on the edges of the prairie, neither quite rays nor fog nor cloud—she felt some shape which she could not grasp, half-suggested and demanding to be grasped.

She did not speak, and—like the links of a chain unrolling through their silence—the rhythm of their steps went on, spaced to the ties, scored by the dry, swift beat of heels on wood.

She had not had time to be aware of him, except as of a providential comrade-in-competence; now she glanced at him with conscious attention. His face had the clear, hard look she remembered having liked in the past. But the face had grown calmer, as if more serenely at peace. His clothes were threadbare. He wore an old leather jacket, and even in the darkness she could distinguish the scuffed blotches streaking across the leather.

"What have you been doing since you left Taggart Transcontinental?" she asked.

"Oh, many things."

"Where are you working now?"

"On special assignments, more or less."

"Of what kind?"

"Of every kind."

"You're not working for a railroad?"

"No."

The sharp brevity of the sound seemed to expand it into an eloquent statement. She knew that he knew her motive. "Kellogg, if I told you that I don't have a single first-rate man left on the Taggart system, if I offered you any job, any terms, any money you cared to name—would you come back to us?"

"No."

"You were shocked by our loss of traffic. I don't think you have any idea of what our loss of men has done to us. I can't tell you the sort of agony I went through three days ago, trying to find somebody able to build five miles of temporary track. I have fifty miles to build through the Rockies. I see no way to do it. But it has to be done. I've combed the country for men. There aren't any. And then to run into you suddenly, to find you here, in a day coach, when I'd give half the system for one employee like you—do you understand why I can't let you go? Choose anything you wish. Want to be general manager of a region? Or assistant operating vice-president?"

"No."

"You're still working for a living, aren't you?"

"Yes."

"You don't seem to be making very much."

"I'm making enough for my needs—and for nobody else's."

"Why are you willing to work for anyone but Taggart Transcontinental?"

"Because you wouldn't give me the kind of job I'd want."

"I?" She stopped still. "Good God, Kellogg!—haven't you understood? I'd give you any job you name!"

"All right. Track walker."

"What?"

"Section hand. Engine wiper." He smiled at the look on her face. "No? You see, I said you wouldn't."

"Do you mean that you'd take a day laborer's job?"

"Any time you offered it."

"But nothing better?"

"That's right, nothing better."

"Don't you understand that I have too many men who're able to do those jobs, but nothing better?"

"I understand it, Miss Taggart. Do you?"

"What I need is your—"

"—mind, Miss Taggart? My mind is not on the market any longer."

She stood looking at him, her face growing harder. "You're one of them, aren't you?" she said at last.

"Of whom?"

She did not answer, shrugged and went on.

"Miss Taggart," he asked, "how long will you remain willing to be a common carrier?"

"I won't surrender the world to the creature you're quoting."

"The answer you gave *her* was much more realistic."

The chain of their steps had stretched through many silent minutes before she asked, "Why did you stand by me tonight? Why were you willing to help me?"

He answered easily, almost gaily, "Because there isn't a passenger on that train who needs to get where he's going more urgently than I do. If the train can be started, none will profit more than I. But when I need something, I don't sit and expect transportation, like that creature of yours."

"You don't? And what if all trains stopped running?"

"Then I wouldn't count on making a crucial journey by train."

"Where are you going?"

"West."

"On a 'special assignment'?"

"No. For a month's vacation with some friends."

"A vacation? And it's that important to you?"

"More important than anything on earth."

They had walked two miles when they came to the small gray box on a post by the trackside, which was the emergency telephone. The box hung sidewise, beaten by storms. She jerked it open. The telephone was there, a familiar, reassuring object, glinting in the beam of Kellogg's flashlight. But she knew, the moment she pressed the receiver to her ear, and he knew, when he saw her finger tapping sharply against the hook, that the telephone was dead.

She handed the receiver to him without a word. She held the flashlight, while he went swiftly over the instrument, then tore it off the wall and studied the wires.

"The wire's okay," he said. "The current's on. It's this particular instrument that's out of order. There's a chance that the next one might be working." He added, "The next one is five miles away."

"Let's go," she said.

Far behind them, the engine's headlight was still visible, not a planet any longer, but a small star winking through mists of distance. Ahead of them, the rail went off into bluish space, with nothing to mark its end.

She realized how often she had glanced back at that headlight; so long as it remained in sight, she had felt as if a life-line were holding them anchored safely; now they had to break it and dive into . . . and dive off this planet, she thought. She noticed that Kellogg, too, stood looking back at the headlight.

They glanced at each other, but said nothing. The crunch of a pebble under her shoe sole burst like a firecracker in the silence. With a coldly intentional movement, he kicked the telephone instrument and sent it rolling into a ditch: the violence of the noise shattered the vacuum.

"God damn him," he said evenly, not raising his voice, with a loathing past any display of emotion. "He probably didn't *feel* like attending to his job, and since he *needed* his pay check, nobody had the right to ask that he keep the phones in order."

"Come on," she said.

"We can rest, if you feel tired, Miss Taggart."

"I'm all right. We have no time to feel tired."

"That's our great error, Miss Taggart. We ought to take the time, some day."

She gave a brief chuckle, she stepped onto a tie of the track, stressing the step as her answer, and they went on.

It was hard, walking on ties, but when they tried to walk along the trackside, they found that it was harder. The soil, half-sand, half-dust, sank under their heels, like the soft, unresisting spread of some substance that was neither liquid nor solid. They went back to walking from tie to tie; it was almost like stepping from log to log in the midst of a river.

She thought of what an enormous distance five miles had suddenly become, and that a division point thirty miles away was now unattainable—after an era of railroads built by men who thought in thousands of transcontinental miles. That net of rails and lights, spreading from ocean to ocean, hung on the snap of a wire, on a broken connection inside a rusty phone—no, she thought, on something much more powerful and much more delicate. It hung on the connections in the minds of the men who knew that the existence of a wire, of a train, of a job, of themselves and their actions was an absolute not to be escaped. When such minds were gone, a two-thousand-ton train was left at the mercy of the muscles of her legs.

Tired?—she thought; even the strain of walking was a value, a small piece of reality in the stillness around them. The sensation of effort was a specific experience, it was pain and could be nothing else—in the midst of a space which was neither light nor dark, a soil which neither gave nor resisted, a fog which neither moved nor hung still. Their strain was the only evidence of their motion: nothing changed in the emptiness around them, nothing took form to mark their progress. She had always wondered, in incredulous contempt, about the sects that preached the annihilation of the universe as the ideal to be attained. *There,* she thought, was their world and the content of their minds made real.

When the green light of a signal appeared by the track, it gave them a point to reach and pass, but—incongruous in the midst of the floating dissolution—it brought them no sense of relief. It seemed to come from a long since extinguished world, like those stars whose light remains after they are gone. The green circle glowed in space, announcing a clear track, inviting motion where there was nothing to move. Who was that philosopher, she thought, who preached that motion exists without any moving entities? This was *his* world, too.

She found herself pushing forward with increasing effort, as if against some resistance that was, not pressure, but suction. Glancing at Kellogg, she saw that he, too, was walking like a man braced against a storm. She felt as if the two of them were the sole survivors of . . . of reality, she thought—two lonely figures fighting, not through a storm, but worse: through non-existence.

It was Kellogg who glanced back, after a while, and she followed his glance: there was no headlight behind them.

They did not stop. Looking straight ahead, he reached absently into his pocket; she felt certain that the movement was involuntary; he produced a package of cigarettes and extended it to her.

She was about to take a cigarette—then, suddenly, she seized his wrist and tore the package out of his hand. It was a plain white package that bore, as single imprint, the sign of the dollar.

"Give me the flashlight!" she ordered, stopping.

He stopped obediently and sent the beam of the flashlight at the package in her hands. She caught a glimpse of his face: he looked a little astonished and very amused.

There was no printing on the package, no trade name, no address, only the dollar sign stamped in gold. The cigarettes bore the same sign.

"Where did you get this?" she asked.

He was smiling. "If you know enough to ask that, Miss Taggart, you should know that I won't answer."

"I know that this stands for something."

"The dollar sign? For a great deal. It stands on the vest of every fat, piglike figure in every cartoon, for the purpose of denoting a crook, a grafter, a scoundrel—as the one sure-fire brand of evil. It stands—as the money of a free country—for achievement, for success, for ability, for man's creative power—and, precisely for these reasons, it is used as a brand of infamy. It stands stamped on the forehead of a man like Hank Rearden, as a mark of damnation. Incidentally, do you know where that sign comes from? It stands for the initials of the United States."

He snapped the flashlight off, but he did not move to go; she could distinguish the hint of his bitter smile.

"Do you know that the United States is the only country in history that has ever used its own monogram as a symbol of depravity? Ask yourself why. Ask yourself how long a country that did that could hope to exist, and whose moral standards have destroyed it. It was the only country in history where wealth was not acquired by looting, but by production, not by force, but by trade, the only country whose money was the symbol of man's right to his own mind, to his work, to his life, to his happiness, to himself. If this is evil, by the present standards of the world, if this is the reason for damning us, then we —we, the dollar chasers and makers—accept it and choose to be damned by that world. We choose to wear the sign of the dollar on our foreheads, proudly, as our badge of nobility—the badge we are willing to live for and, if need be, to die."

He extended his hand for the package. She held it as if her fingers would not let it go, but gave up and placed it on his palm. With deliberate slowness, as if to underscore the meaning of his gesture, he offered her a cigarette. She took it and placed it between her lips. He took one for himself, struck a match, lighted both, and they walked on.

They walked, over rotting logs that sank without resistance into the shifting ground, through a vast, uncongealed globe of moonlight and coiling mist—with two spots of living fire in their hands and the glow of two small circles to light their faces.

"Fire, a dangerous force, tamed at his fingertips . . ." she remembered the old man saying to her, the old man who had said that these cigarettes were not made anywhere on earth. "When a man thinks, there is a spot of fire alive in his mind—and it's proper that he should have the burning point of a cigarette as his one expression."

"I wish you'd tell me who makes them," she said, in the tone of a hopeless plea.

He chuckled good-naturedly. "I can tell you this much: they're made by a friend of mine, for sale, but—not being a common carrier —he sells them only to his friends."

"Sell me that package, will you?"

"I don't think you'll be able to afford it, Miss Taggart, but—all right, if you wish."

"How much is it?"

"Five cents."

"Five cents?" she repeated, bewildered.

"Five cents—" he said, and added, "in gold."

She stopped, staring at him. "In gold?"

"Yes, Miss Taggart."

"Well, what's your rate of exchange? How much is it in our normal money?"

"There is no rate of *exchange*, Miss Taggart. No amount of physical—or spiritual—currency, whose sole standard of value is the decree of Mr. Wesley Mouch, will buy these cigarettes."

"I see."

He reached into his pocket, took out the package and handed it to her. "I'll give them to you, Miss Taggart," he said, "because you've earned them many times over—and because you need them for the same purpose we do."

"What purpose?"

"To remind us—in moments of discouragement, in the loneliness of exile—of our true homeland, which has always been yours, too, Miss Taggart."

"Thank you," she said. She put the cigarettes in her pocket; he saw that her hand was trembling.

When they reached the fourth of the five mileposts, they had been silent for a long time, with no strength left for anything but the effort of moving their feet. Far ahead, they saw a dot of light, too low on the horizon and too harshly clear to be a star. They kept watching it, as they walked, and said nothing until they became certain that it was a powerful electric beacon blazing in the midst of the empty prairie.

"What is that?" she asked.

"I don't know," he said. "It looks like—"

"No," she broke in hastily, "it couldn't be. Not around here."

She did not want to hear him name the hope which she had felt for many minutes past. She could not permit herself to think of it or to know that the thought was hope.

They found the telephone box at the fifth milepost. The beacon hung like a violent spot of cold fire, less than half a mile farther south.

The telephone was working. She heard the buzz of the wire, like the breath of a living creature, when she lifted the receiver. Then a drawling voice answered, "Jessup, at Bradshaw." The voice sounded sleepy.

"This is Dagny Taggart, speaking from—"

"Who?"

"Dagny Taggart, of Taggart Transcontinental, speaking—"

"Oh . . . Oh yes . . . I see . . . Yes?"

"—speaking from your track phone Number 83. The Comet is stalled seven miles north of here. It's been abandoned. The crew has deserted."

There was a pause. "Well, what do you want me to do about it?"

She had to pause in turn, in order to believe it. "Are you the night dispatcher?"

"Yeah."

"Then send another crew out to us at once."

"A full passenger train crew?"

"Of course."

"Now?"

"Yes."

There was a pause. "The rules don't say anything about that."

"Get me the chief dispatcher," she said, choking.

"He's away on his vacation."

"Get the division superintendent."

"He's gone down to Laurel for a couple of days."

"Get me somebody who's in charge."

"I'm in charge."

"Listen," she said slowly, fighting for patience, "do you under-

stand that there's a train, a passenger limited, abandoned in the middle of the prairie?"

"Yeah, but how am I to know what I'm supposed to do about it?
The rules don't provide for it. Now if you had an accident, we'd send
out the wrecker, but if there was no accident . . . you don't need
the wrecker, do you?"

"No. We don't need the wrecker. We need men. Do you understand? Living men to run an engine."

"The rules don't say anything about a train without men. Or about
men without a train. There's no rule for calling out a full crew in the
middle of the night and sending them to hunt for a train somewhere.
I've never heard of it before."

"You're hearing it now. Don't you know what you have to do?"

"Who am I to know?"

"Do you know that your job is to keep trains moving?"

"My job is to obey the rules. If I send out a crew when I'm not
supposed to, God only knows what's going to happen! What with the
Unification Board and all the regulations they've got nowadays, who
am I to take it upon myself?"

"And what's going to happen if you leave a train stalled on the
line?"

"That's not my fault. I had nothing to do with it. They can't
blame me. I couldn't help it."

"You're to help it now."

"Nobody told me to."

"I'm telling you to!"

"How do I know whether you're supposed to tell me or not? We're
not supposed to furnish any Taggart crews. You people were to run
with your own crews. That's what we were told."

"But this is an emergency!"

"Nobody told me anything about an emergency."

She had to take a few seconds to control herself. She saw Kellogg
watching her with a bitter smile of amusement.

"Listen," she said into the phone, "do you know that the Comet
was due at Bradshaw over three hours ago?"

"Oh, sure. But nobody's going to make any trouble about that. No
train's ever on schedule these days."

"Then do you intend to leave us blocking your track forever?"

"We've got nothing due till Number 4, the northbound passenger
out of Laurel, at eight thirty-seven A.M. You can wait till then. The
day-trick dispatcher will be on then. You can speak to him."

"You blasted idiot! This is *the Comet!*"

"What's that to me? This isn't Taggart Transcontinental. You people expect a lot for your money. You've been nothing but a headache
to us, with all the extra work at no extra pay for the little fellows."
His voice was slipping into whining insolence. "You can't talk to me

that way. The time's past when you could talk to people that way."

She had never believed that there were men with whom a certain method, which she had never used, would work; such men were not hired by Taggart Transcontinental and she had never been forced to deal with them before.

"Do you know who I am?" she asked, in the cold, overbearing tone of a personal threat.

It worked. "I . . . I guess so," he answered.

"Then let me tell you that if you don't send a crew to me at once, you'll be out of a job within one hour after I reach Bradshaw, which I'll reach sooner or later. You'd better make it sooner."

"Yes, ma'am," he said.

"Call out a full passenger train crew and give them orders to run us to Laurel, where we have our own men."

"Yes, ma'am." He added, "Will you tell headquarters that it was you who told me to do it?"

"I will."

"And that it's you who're responsible for it?"

"I am."

There was a pause, then he asked helplessly, "Now how am I going to call the men? Most of them haven't got any phones."

"Do you have a call boy?"

"Yes, but he won't get here till morning."

"Is there anybody in the yards right now?"

"There's the wiper in the roundhouse."

"Send *him* out to call the men."

"Yes, ma'am. Hold the line."

She leaned against the side of the phone box, to wait. Kellogg was smiling.

"And you propose to run a railroad—a transcontinental railroad—with *that?*" he asked.

She shrugged.

She could not keep her eyes off the beacon. It seemed so close, so easily within her reach. She felt as if the unconfessed thought were struggling furiously against her, splattering bits of the struggle all over her mind: A man able to harness an untapped source of energy, a man working on a motor to make all other motors useless . . . she could be talking to him, to his kind of brain, in a few hours . . . in just a few hours. . . . What if there was no need to hurry to him? It was what she wanted to do. It was all she wanted. . . . Her work? What was her work: to move on to the fullest, most exacting use of her mind—or to spend the rest of her life doing his thinking for a man unfit to be a night dispatcher? Why had she chosen to work? Was it in order to remain where she had started—night operator of Rockdale Station—no, lower than that—she had been better than that dispatcher, even at Rockdale—was this to be the final sum: an end lower than her beginning? . . . There was no reason to hurry? *She* was the reason. . . . They needed the trains, but they did not need the motor? *She* needed the motor. . . . Her duty? To whom?

The dispatcher was gone for a long time; when he came back, his voice sounded sulky: "Well, the wiper says he can get the men all right, but it's no use, because how am I going to send them out to you? We have no engine."

"No engine?"

"No. The superintendent took one to run down to Laurel, and the other's in the shops, been there for weeks, and the switch engine jumped a rail this morning, they'll be working on her till tomorrow afternoon."

"What about the wrecker's engine that you were offering to send us?"

"Oh, she's up north. They had a wreck there yesterday. She hasn't come back yet."

"Have you a Diesel car?"

"Never had any such thing. Not around here."

"Have you a track motor car?"

"Yes. We have that."

"Send them out on the track motor car."

"Oh . . . Yes, ma'am."

"Tell your men to stop here, at track phone Number 83, to pick up Mr. Kellogg and myself." She was looking at the beacon.

"Yes, ma'am."

"Call the Taggart trainmaster at Laurel, report the Comet's delay and explain to him what happened." She put her hand into her pocket and suddenly clutched her fingers: she felt the package of cigarettes. "Say—" she asked, "what's that beacon, about half a mile from here?"

"From where you are? Oh, that must be the emergency landing field of the Flagship Airlines."

"I see . . . Well, that's all. Get your men started at once. Tell them to pick up Mr. Kellogg by track phone Number 83."

"Yes, ma'am."

She hung up. Kellogg was grinning.

"An airfield, isn't it?" he asked.

"Yes." She stood looking at the beacon, her hand still clutching the cigarettes in her pocket.

"So they're going to pick up *Mr. Kellogg,* are they?"

She whirled to him, realizing what decision her mind had been reaching without her conscious knowledge. "No," she said, "no, I didn't mean to abandon you here. It's only that I, too, have a crucial purpose out West, where I ought to hurry, so I was thinking of trying to catch a plane, but I can't do it and it's not necessary."

"Come on," he said, starting in the direction of the airfield.

"But I—"

"If there's anything you want to do more urgently than to nurse those morons—go right ahead."

"More urgently than anything in the world," she whispered.

"I'll undertake to remain in charge for you and to deliver the Comet to your man at Laurel."

"Thank you . . . But if you're hoping . . . I'm not deserting, you know."

"I know."

"Then why are you so eager to help me?"

"I just want you to see what it's like to do something *you* want, for once."

"There's not much chance that they'll have a plane at that field."

"There's a good chance that they will."

There were two planes on the edge of the airfield: one, the half-charred remnant of a wreck, not worth salvaging for scrap—the other, a Dwight Sanders monoplane, brand-new, the kind of ship that men were pleading for, in vain, all over the country.

There was one sleepy attendant at the airfield, young, pudgy and, but for a faint smell of college about his vocabulary, a brain-brother of the night dispatcher of Bradshaw. He knew nothing about the two planes: they had been there when he first took this job a year ago. He had never inquired about them and neither had anybody else. In whatever silent crumbling had gone on at the distant headquarters, in the slow dissolution of a great airline company, the Sanders monoplane had been forgotten—as assets of this nature were being forgotten everywhere . . . as the model of the motor had been forgotten on a junk pile and, left in plain sight, had conveyed nothing to the inheritors and the takers-over. . . .

There were no rules to tell the young attendant whether he was expected to keep the Sanders plane or not. The decision was made for him by the brusque, confident manner of the two strangers—by the credentials of Miss Dagny Taggart, Vice-President of a railroad—by brief hints about a secret, emergency mission, which sounded like Washington to him—by the mention of an agreement with the airline's top officials in New York, whose names he had never heard before—by a check for fifteen thousand dollars, written by Miss Taggart, as deposit against the return of the Sanders plane—and by another check, for two hundred bucks, for his own, personal courtesy.

He fueled the plane, he checked it as best he could, he found a map of the country's airports—and she saw that a landing field on the outskirts of Afton, Utah, was marked as still in existence. She had been too tensely, swiftly active to feel anything, but at the last moment, when the attendant switched on the floodlights, when she was about to climb aboard, she paused to glance at the emptiness of the sky, then at Owen Kellogg. He stood, alone in the white glare, his feet planted firmly apart, on an island of cement in a ring of blinding lights, with nothing beyond the ring but an irredeemable night—and she wondered which one of them was taking the greater chance and facing the more desolate emptiness.

"In case anything happens to me," she said, "will you tell Eddie Willers in my office to give Jeff Allen a job, as I promised?"

"I will. . . . Is this all you wish to be done . . . in case anything happens?"

She considered it and smiled sadly, in astonishment at the realization. "Yes, I guess that's all . . . Except, tell Hank Rearden what happened and that I asked you to tell him."

"I will."

She lifted her head and said firmly, "I don't expect it to happen, however. When you reach Laurel, call Winston, Colorado, and tell them that I will be there tomorrow by noon."

"Yes, Miss Taggart."

She wanted to extend her hand in parting, but it seemed inadequate, and then she remembered what he had said about times of loneliness. She took out the package and silently offered him one of his own cigarettes. His smile was a full statement of understanding, and the small flame of his match lighting their two cigarettes was their most enduring handshake.

Then she climbed aboard—and the next span of her consciousness was not separate moments and movements, but the sweep of a single motion and a single unit of time, a progression forming one entity, like the notes of a piece of music: from the touch of her hand on the starter—to the blast of the motor's sound that broke off, like a mountain rockslide, all contact with the time behind her—to the circling fall of a blade that vanished in a fragile sparkle of whirling air that cut the space ahead—to the start for the runway—to the brief pause—then to the forward thrust—to the long, perilous run, the run not to be obstructed, the straight line run that gathers power by spending it on a harder and harder and ever-accelerating effort, the straight line to a purpose—to the moment, unnoticed, when the earth drops off and the line, unbroken, goes on into space in the simple, natural act of rising.

She saw the telegraph wires of the trackside slipping past at the tip of her toes. The earth was falling downward, and she felt as if its weight were dropping off her ankles, as if the globe would go shrinking to the size of a ball, a convict's ball she had dragged and lost. Her body swayed, drunk with the shock of a discovery, and her craft rocked with her body, and it was the earth below that reeled with the rocking of her craft—the discovery that her life was now in her own hands, that there was no necessity to argue, to explain, to teach, to plead, to fight—nothing but to see and think and act. Then the earth steadied into a wide black sheet that grew wider and wider as she circled, rising. When she glanced down for the last time, the lights of the field were extinguished, there was only the single beacon left and it looked like the tip of Kellogg's cigarette, glowing as a last salute in the darkness.

Then she was left with the lights on her instrument panel and the spread of stars beyond her film of glass. There was nothing to support her but the beat of the engine and the minds of the men who had made the plane. But what else supports one anywhere?—she thought.

The line of her course went northwest, to cut a diagonal across the state of Colorado. She knew she had chosen the most dangerous route, over too long a stretch of the worst mountain barrier—but it was the shortest line, and safety lay in altitude, and no mountains seemed dangerous compared to the dispatcher of Bradshaw.

The stars were like foam and the sky seemed full of flowing motion, the motion of bubbles settling and forming, the floating of circular waves without progression. A spark of light flared up on earth once in a while, and it seemed brighter than all the static blue above. But it hung alone, between the black of ashes and the blue of a crypt, it seemed to fight for its fragile foothold, it greeted her and went.

The pale streak of a river came rising slowly from the void, and for a long stretch of time it remained in sight, gliding imperceptibly to meet her. It looked like a phosphorescent vein showing through the skin of the earth, a delicate vein without blood.

When she saw the lights of a town, like a handful of gold coins flung upon the prairie, the brightly violent lights fed by an electric current, they seemed as distant as the stars and now as unattainable. The energy that had lighted them was gone, the power that created power stations in empty prairies had vanished, and she knew of no journey to recapture it. Yet these had been her stars—she thought, looking down—these had been her goal, her beacon, the aspiration drawing her upon her upward course. That which others claimed to feel at the sight of the stars—stars safely distant by millions of years and thus imposing no obligation to act, but serving as the tinsel of futility—she had felt at the sight of electric bulbs lighting the streets of a town. It was this earth below that had been the height she had wanted to reach, and she wondered how she had come to lose it, who had made of it a convict's ball to drag through muck, who had turned its promise of greatness into a vision never to be reached. But the town was past, and she had to look ahead, to the mountains of Colorado rising in her way.

The small glass dial on her panel showed that she was now climbing. The sound of the engine, beating through the metal shell around her, trembling in the wheel against her palms, like the pounding of a heart strained to a solemn effort, told her of the power carrying her above the peaks. The earth was now a crumpled sculpture that swayed from side to side, the shape of an explosion still shooting sudden spurts to reach the plane. She saw them as dented black cuts ripping through the milky spread of stars, straight in her path and tearing wider. Her mind one with her body and her body one with the plane, she fought the invisible suction drawing her downward, she fought the sudden gusts that tipped the earth as if she were about to roll off into the sky, with half of the mountains rolling after. It was like fighting a frozen ocean where the touch of a single spray would be fatal.

There were stretches of rest when the mountains shrank down, over valleys filled with fog. Then the fog rose higher to swallow the earth and she was left suspended in space, left motionless but for the sound of the engine.

But she did not need to see the earth. The instrument panel was now her power of sight—it was the condensed sight of the best minds able to guide her on her way. Their condensed sight, she thought, offered to hers and requiring only that she be able to read it. How had they been paid for it, they, the sight-givers? From condensed milk to condensed music to the condensed sight of precision instruments—what wealth had they not given to the world and what had they received in return? Where were they now? Where was Dwight Sanders? Where was the inventor of her motor?

The fog was lifting—and in a sudden clearing, she saw a drop of fire on a spread of rock. It was not an electric light, it was a lonely flame in the darkness of the earth. She knew where she was and she knew that flame: it was Wyatt's Torch.

She was coming close to her goal. Somewhere behind her, in the northeast, stood the summits pierced by the Taggart Tunnel. The mountains were sliding in a long descent into the steadier soil of Utah. She let her plane slip closer to the earth.

The stars were vanishing, the sky was growing darker, but in the bank of clouds to the east thin cracks were beginning to appear—first as threads, then faint spots of reflection, then straight bands that were not yet pink, but no longer blue, the color of a future light, the first hints of the coming sunrise. They kept appearing and vanishing, slowly growing clearer, leaving the sky darker, then breaking it wider apart, like a promise struggling to be fulfilled. She heard a piece of music beating in her mind, one she seldom liked to recall: not Halley's Fifth Concerto, but his Fourth, the cry of a tortured struggle, with the chords of its theme breaking through, like a distant vision to be reached.

She saw the Afton airport from across a span of miles, first as a square of sparks, then as a sunburst of white rays. It was lighted for a plane about to take off, and she had to wait for her landing. Circling in the outer darkness above the field, she saw the silver body of a plane rising like a phoenix out of the white fire and—in a straight line, almost leaving an instant's trail of light to hang in space behind it—going off toward the east.

Then she swept down in its stead, to dive into the luminous funnel of beams—she saw a strip of cement flying at her face, she felt the jolt of the wheels stopping it in time, then the streak of her motion ebbing out and the plane being tamed to the safety of a car, as it taxied smoothly off the runway.

It was a small private airfield, serving the meager traffic of a few industrial concerns still remaining in Afton. She saw a lone attendant hurrying to meet her. She leaped down to the ground the moment the plane stood still, the hours of the flight swept from her mind by the impatience over the stretch of a few more minutes.

"Can I get a car somewhere to drive me to the Institute of Technology at once?" she asked.

The attendant looked at her, puzzled. "Why, yes, I guess so, ma'am. But . . . but what for? There's nobody there."

"Mr. Quentin Daniels is there."

The attendant shook his head slowly—then jerked his thumb, pointing east to the shrinking taillights of the plane. "There's Mr. Daniels going now."

"*What?*"

"He just left."

"Left? Why?"

"He went with the man who flew in for him two-three hours ago."

"What man?"

"Don't know, never saw him before, but, boy!—he's got a beauty of a ship!"

She was back at the wheel, she was speeding down the runway, she was rising into the air, her plane like a bullet aimed at two sparks of red and green light that were twinkling away into the eastern sky—while she was still repeating, "Oh no, they don't! They don't! They don't! They don't!"

Once and for all—she thought, clutching the wheel as if it were the enemy not to be relinquished, her words like separate explosions with a trail of fire in her mind to link them—once and for all . . . to meet the destroyer face to face . . . to learn who he is and where he goes to vanish . . . not the motor . . . he is not to carry the motor away into the darkness of his monstrously closed unknown . . . he is not to escape, this time. . . .

A band of light was rising in the east and it seemed to come from the earth, as a breath long-held and released. In the deep blue above it, the stranger's plane was a single spark changing color and flashing from side to side, like the tip of a pendulum swinging in the darkness, beating time.

The curve of distance made the spark drop closer to the earth, and she pushed her throttle wide open, not to let the spark out of her sight, not to let it touch the horizon and vanish. The light was flowing into the sky, as if drawn from the earth by the stranger's plane. The plane was headed southeast, and she was following it into the coming sunrise.

From the transparent green of ice, the sky melted into pale gold, and the gold spread into a lake under a fragile film of pink glass, the color of that forgotten morning which was the first she had seen on earth. The clouds were dropping away in long shreds of smoky blue. She kept her eyes on the stranger's plane, as if her glance were a towline pulling her ship. The stranger's plane was now a small black cross, like a shrinking check mark on the glowing sky.

Then she noticed that the clouds were not dropping, that they stood congealed on the edge of the earth—and she realized that the plane was headed toward the mountains of Colorado, that the struggle against the invisible storm lay ahead for her once more. She noted it without emotion; she did not wonder whether her ship or her body had the power to attempt it again. So long as she was able to move, she would move to follow the speck that was fleeing away with the last of her world. She felt nothing but the emptiness left by a fire that had been hatred and anger and the desperate impulse of a fight to the kill; these had fused into a single icy streak, the single resolve to follow the stranger, whoever he was, wherever he took her, to follow and . . . she added nothing in her mind, but, unstated, what lay at the bottom of the emptiness was: and give her life, if she could take his first.

Like an instrument set to automatic control, her body was performing the motions of driving the plane—with the mountains reeling in a bluish fog below and the dented peaks rising in her path as smoky formations of a deadlier blue. She noticed that the distance to the stranger's plane had shrunk: he had checked his speed for the dangerous crossing, while she had gone on, unconscious of the danger, with only the muscles of her arms and legs fighting to keep her plane aloft. A brief, tight movement of her lips was as close as she could come to a smile: it was he who was flying her plane for her, she thought; he had given her the power to follow him with a somnambulist's unerring skill.

As if responding of itself to his control, the needle of her altimeter was slowly moving upward. She was rising and she went on rising and she wondered when her breath and her propeller would fail. He was going southeast, toward the highest mountains that obstructed the path of the sun.

It was his plane that was struck by the first sunray. It flashed for an instant, like a burst of white fire, sending rays to shoot from its wings. The peaks of the mountains came next: she saw the sunlight reaching the snow in the crevices, then trickling down the granite sides; it cut violent shadows on the ledges and brought the mountains into the living finality of a form.

They were flying over the wildest stretch of Colorado, uninhabited, uninhabitable, inaccessible to men on foot or plane. No landing was possible within a radius of a hundred miles; she glanced at her fuel gauge: she had one half-hour left. The stranger was heading straight toward another, higher range. She wondered why he chose a course no air route did or ever would travel. She wished this range were behind her; it was the last effort she could hope to make.

The stranger's plane was suddenly slacking its speed. He was losing altitude just when she had expected him to climb. The granite barrier was rising in his path, moving to meet him, reaching for his wings—but the long, smooth line of his motion was sliding down. She could detect no break, no jolt, no sign of mechanical failure; it looked like the even movement of a controlled intention. With a sudden flash of sunlight on its wings, the plane banked into a long curve, rays dripping like water from its body—then went into the broad, smooth circles of a spiral, as if circling for a landing where no landing was conceivable.

She watched, not trying to explain it, not believing what she saw, waiting for the upward thrust that would throw him back on his course. But the easy, gliding circles went on dropping, toward a ground she could not see and dared not think of. Like remnants of broken jaws, strings of granite dentures stood between her ship and his; she could not tell what lay at the bottom of his spiral motion. She knew only that it did not look like, but was certain to be, the motion of a suicide.

She saw the sunlight glitter on his wings for an instant. Then, like the body of a man diving chest-first and arms outstretched, serenely abandoned to the sweep of the fall, the plane went down and vanished behind the ridges of rock.

She flew on, almost waiting for it to reappear, unable to believe that she had witnessed a horrible catastrophe taking place so simply and quietly. She flew on to where the plane had dropped. It seemed to be a valley in a ring of granite walls.

She reached the valley and looked down. There was no possible place for a landing. There was no sign of a plane.

The bottom of the valley looked like a stretch of the earth's crust mangled in the days when the earth was cooling, left irretrievable ever since. It was a stretch of rocks ground against one another, with boulders hanging in precarious formations, with long, dark crevices and a few contorted pine trees growing half-horizontally into the air. There was no level piece of soil the size of a handkerchief. There was no place for a plane to hide. There was no remnant of a plane's wreck.

She banked sharply, circling above the valley, dropping down a little. By some trick of light, which she could not explain, the floor of the valley seemed more clearly visible than the rest of the earth. She could distinguish it well enough to know that the plane was not there; yet this was not possible.

She circled, dropping down farther. She glanced around her—and for one frightening moment, she thought that it was a quiet summer morning, that she was alone, lost in a region of the Rocky Mountains which no plane should ever venture to approach, and, with the last of her fuel burning away, she was looking for a plane that had never existed, in quest of a destroyer who had vanished as he always vanished; perhaps it was only his vision that had led her here to be destroyed. In the next moment, she shook her head, pressed her mouth tighter and dropped farther.

She thought that she could not abandon an incalculable wealth such as the brain of Quentin Daniels on one of those rocks below, if he was still alive and within her reach to help. She had dropped inside the circle of the valley's walls. It was a dangerous job of flying, the space was much too tight, but she went on circling and dropping lower, her life hanging on her eyesight, and her eyesight flashing between two tasks: searching the floor of the valley and watching the granite walls that seemed about to rip her wings.

She knew the danger only as part of the job. It had no personal meaning any longer. The savage thing she felt was almost enjoyment. It was the last rage of a lost battle. No!—she was crying in her mind, crying it to the destroyer, to the world she had left, to the years behind her, to the long progression of defeat—No! . . . No! . . . No! . . .

Her eyes swept past the instrument panel—and then she sat still but for the sound of a gasp. Her altimeter had stood at 11,000 feet the last time she remembered seeing it. Now it stood at 10,000. But the floor of the valley had not changed. It had come no closer. It remained as distant as at her first glance down.

She knew that the figure 8,000 meant the level of the ground in this part of Colorado. She had not noticed the length of her descent. She had not noticed that the ground, which had seemed too clear and too close from the height, was now too dim and too far. She was looking at the same rocks from the same perspective, they had grown no larger, their shadows had not moved, and the oddly unnatural light still hung over the bottom of the valley.

She thought that her altimeter was off, and she went on circling downward. She saw the needle of her dial moving down, she saw the walls of granite moving up, she saw the ring of mountains growing higher, its peaks coming closer together in the sky—but the floor of the valley remained unchanged, as if she were dropping down a well with a bottom never to be reached. The needle moved to 9,500—to 9,300—to 9,000—to 8,700.

The flash of light that hit her had no source. It was as if the air within and beyond the plane became an explosion of blinding cold fire, sudden and soundless. The shock threw her back, her hands off the wheel and over her eyes. In the break of an instant, when she seized the wheel again, the light was gone, but her ship was spinning, her ears were bursting with silence and her propeller stood stiffly straight before her: her motor was dead.

She tried to pull for a rise, but the ship was going down—and what she saw flying at her face was not the spread of mangled boulders, but the green grass of a field where no field had been before.

There was no time to see the rest. There was no time to think of explanations. There was no time to come out of the spin. The earth was a green ceiling coming down upon her, a few hundred swiftly shrinking feet away.

Flung from side to side, like a battered pendulum, clinging to the wheel, half in her seat, half on her knees, she fought to pull the ship into a glide, for an attempt to make a belly-landing, while the green ground was whirling about her, sweeping above her, then below, its spiral coils coming closer. Her arms pulling at the wheel, with no chance to know whether she could succeed, with her space and time running out—she felt, in a flash of its full, violent purity, that special sense of existence which had always been hers. In a moment's consecration to her love—to her rebellious denial of disaster, to her love of life and of the matchless value that was herself—she felt the fiercely proud certainty that she would survive.

And in answer to the earth that flew to meet her, she heard in her mind, as her mockery at fate, as her cry of defiance, the words of the sentence she hated—the words of defeat, of despair and of a plea for help:

"Oh hell! Who is John Galt?"

III

A IS A

ATLANTIS

When she opened her eyes, she saw sunlight, green leaves and a man's face. She thought: I know what this is. This was the world as she had expected to see it at sixteen—and now she had reached it—and it seemed so simple, so unastonishing, that the thing she felt was like a blessing pronounced upon the universe by means of three words: But of course.

She was looking up at the face of a man who knelt by her side, and she knew that in all the years behind her, *this* was what she would have given her life to see: a face that bore no mark of pain or fear or guilt. The shape of his mouth was pride, and more: it was as if he took pride in being proud. The angular planes of his cheeks made her think of arrogance, of tension, of scorn—yet the face had none of these qualities, it had their final sum: a look of serene determination and of certainty, and the look of a ruthless innocence which would not seek forgiveness or grant it. It was a face that had nothing to hide or to escape, a face with no fear of being seen or of seeing, so that the first thing she grasped about him was the intense perceptiveness of his eyes—he looked as if his faculty of sight were his best-loved tool and its exercise were a limitless, joyous adventure, as if his eyes imparted a superlative value to himself and to the world—to himself for his ability to see, to the world for being a place so eagerly worth seeing. It seemed to her for a moment that she was in the presence of a being who was pure consciousness—yet she had never been so aware of a man's body. The light cloth of his shirt seemed to stress, rather than hide, the structure of his figure, his skin was suntanned, his body had the hardness, the gaunt, tensile strength, the clean precision of a foundry casting, he looked as if he were poured out of metal, but some dimmed, soft-lustered metal, like an aluminum-copper alloy, the color of his skin blending with the chestnut-brown of his hair, the loose strands of the hair shading from brown to gold in the sun, and his eyes completing the colors, as the one part of the casting left undimmed and harshly lustrous: his eyes were the deep, dark green of light glinting on metal. He was looking down at her with the faint trace of a smile, it was not a look of discovery, but of familiar contemplation—as if he, too, were seeing the long-expected and the never-doubted.

This was her world, she thought, this was the way men were meant to be and to face their existence—and all the rest of it, all the years of ugliness and struggle were only someone's senseless joke. She smiled at him, as at a fellow conspirator, in relief, in deliverance, in radiant mockery of all the things she would never have to consider important again. He smiled in answer, it was the same smile as her own, as if he felt what she felt and knew what she meant.

"We never had to take any of it seriously, did we?" she whispered.

"No, we never had to."

And then, her consciousness returning fully, she realized that this man was a total stranger.

She tried to draw away from him, but it was only a faint movement of her head on the grass she felt under her hair. She tried to rise. A shot of pain across her back threw her down again.

"Don't move, Miss Taggart. You're hurt."

"You know me?" Her voice was impersonal and hard.

"I've known you for many years."

"Have I known you?"

"Yes, I think so."

"What is your name?"

"John Galt."

She looked at him, not moving.

"Why are you frightened?" he asked.

"Because I believe it."

He smiled, as if grasping a full confession of the meaning she attached to his name; the smile held an adversary's acceptance of a challenge—and an adult's amusement at the self-deception of a child.

She felt as if she were returning to consciousness after a crash that had shattered more than an airplane. She could not reassemble the pieces now, she could not recall the things she had known about his name, she knew only that it stood for a dark vacuum which she would slowly have to fill. She could not do it now, this man was too blinding a presence, like a spotlight that would not let her see the shapes strewn in the outer darkness.

"Was it you that I was following?" she asked.

"Yes."

She glanced slowly around her. She was lying in the grass of a field at the foot of a granite drop that came down from thousands of feet away in the blue sky. On the other edge of the field, some crags and pines and the glittering leaves of birch trees hid the space that stretched to a distant wall of encircling mountains. Her plane was not shattered—it was there, a few feet away, flat on its belly in the grass. There was no other plane in sight, no structures, no sign of human habitation.

"What is this valley?" she asked.

He smiled. "The Taggart Terminal."

"What do you mean?"

"You'll find out."

A dim impulse, like the recoil of an antagonist, made her want to check on what strength was left to her. She could move her arms and legs; she could lift her head; she felt a stabbing pain when she breathed deeply; she saw a thin thread of blood running down her stocking.

"Can one get out of this place?" she asked.

His voice seemed earnest, but the glint of the metal-green eyes was a smile: "Actually—no. Temporarily—yes."

She made a movement to rise. He bent to lift her, but she gathered her strength in a swift, sudden jolt and slipped out of his grasp, struggling to stand up. "I think I can—" she started saying, and collapsed against him the instant her feet rested on the ground, a stab of pain shooting up from an ankle that would not hold her.

He lifted her in his arms and smiled. "No, you can't, Miss Taggart," he said, and started off across the field.

She lay still, her arms about him, her head on his shoulder, and she thought: For just a few moments—while this lasts—it is all right to surrender completely—to forget everything and just permit yourself to feel. . . . When had she experienced it before?—she wondered; there had been a moment when these had been the words in her mind, but she could not remember it now. She had known it, once—this feeling of certainty, of the final, the reached, the not-to-be-questioned. But it was new to feel protected, and to feel that it was right to accept the protection, to surrender—right, because this peculiar sense of safety was not protection against the future, but against the past, not the protection of being spared from battle, but of having won it, not a protection granted to her weakness, but to her strength. . . . Aware with abnormal intensity of the pressure of his hands against her body, of the gold and copper threads of his hair, the shadows of his lashes on the skin of his face a few inches away from hers, she wondered dimly: Protected, from what? . . . it's he who was the enemy . . . was he? . . . why? . . . She did not know, she could not think of it now. It took an effort to remember that she had had a goal and a motive a few hours ago. She forced herself to recapture it.

"Did you know that I was following you?" she asked.

"No."

"Where is your plane?"

"At the landing field."

"Where is the landing field?"

"On the other side of the valley."

"There was no landing field in this valley, when I looked down. There was no meadow, either. How did it get here?"

He glanced at the sky. "Look carefully. Do you see anything up there?"

She dropped her head back, looking straight into the sky, seeing nothing but the peaceful blue of morning. After a while she distinguished a few faint strips of shimmering air.

"Heat waves," she said.

"Refractor rays," he answered. "The valley bottom that you saw is a mountain top eight thousand feet high, five miles away from here."

"A . . . what?"

"A mountain top that no flyer would ever choose for a landing. What you saw was its reflection projected over this valley."

"How?"

"By the same method as a mirage on a desert: an image refracted from a layer of heated air."

"How?"

"By a screen of rays calculated against everything—except a courage such as yours."

"What do you mean?"

"I never thought that any plane would attempt to drop within seven hundred feet of the ground. You hit the ray screen. Some of the rays are the kind that kill magnetic motors. Well, that's the second time you beat me: I've never been followed, either."

"Why do you keep that screen?"

"Because this place is private property intended to remain as such."

"What is this place?"

"I'll show it to you, now that you're here, Miss Taggart. I'll answer questions after you've seen it."

She remained silent. She noticed that she had asked questions about every subject, but not about him. It was as if he were a single whole, grasped by her first glance at him, like some irreducible absolute, like an axiom not to be explained any further, as if she knew everything about him by direct perception, and what awaited her now was only the process of identifying her knowledge.

He was carrying her down a narrow trail that went winding to the bottom of the valley. On the slopes around them, the tall, dark pyramids of firs stood immovably straight, in masculine simplicity, like sculpture reduced to an essential form, and they clashed with the complex, feminine, overdetailed lace-work of the birch leaves trembling in the sun. The leaves let the sunrays fall through to sweep across his hair, across both their faces. She could not see what lay below, beyond the turns of the trail.

Her eyes kept coming back to his face. He glanced down at her once in a while. At first, she looked away, as if she had been caught. Then, as if learning it from him, she held his glance whenever he chose to look down—knowing that he knew what she felt and that he did not hide from her the meaning of his glance.

She knew that his silence was the same confession as her own. He did not hold her in the impersonal manner of a man carrying a wounded woman. It was an embrace, even though she felt no suggestion of it in his bearing; she felt it only by means of her certainty that his whole body was aware of holding hers.

She heard the sound of the waterfall before she saw the fragile thread that fell in broken strips of glitter down the ledges. The sound came through some dim beat in her mind, some faint rhythm that seemed no louder than a struggling memory—but they went past and the beat remained; she listened to the sound of the water, but another sound seemed to grow clearer, rising, not in her mind, but from somewhere among the leaves. The trail turned, and in a sudden clearing she saw a small house on a ledge below, with a flash of sun on the pane of an open window. In the moment when she knew what experience had once made her want to surrender to the immediate present—it had been the night in a dusty coach of the Comet, when she had heard the theme of Halley's Fifth Concerto for the first time—she knew that she was hearing it now, hearing it rise from the keyboard of a piano, in the clear, sharp chords of someone's powerful, confident touch.

She snapped the question at his face, as if hoping to catch him unprepared: "That's the Fifth Concerto by Richard Halley, isn't it?"

"Yes."

"When did he write it?"

"Why don't you ask him that in person?"

"Is he here?"

"It's he who's playing it. That's his house."

"Oh . . . !"

"You'll meet him, later. He'll be glad to speak to you. He knows that his works are the only records you like to play, in the evening, when you are alone."

"How does he know that?"

"I told him."

The look on her face was like a question that would have begun with "How in hell . . . ?"—but she saw the look of his eyes, and she laughed, her laughter giving sound to the meaning of his glance.

She could not question anything, she thought, she could not doubt, not now—not with the sound of that music rising triumphantly through the sun-drenched leaves, the music of release, of deliverance, played as it was intended to be played, as her mind had struggled to hear it in a rocking coach through the beat of wounded wheels—it was *this* that her mind had seen in the sounds, that night—this valley and the morning sun and—

And then she gasped, because the trail had turned and from the height of an open ledge she saw the town on the floor of the valley.

It was not a town, only a cluster of houses scattered at random from the bottom to the rising steps of the mountains that went on rising above their roofs, enclosing them within an abrupt, impassable circle. They were homes, small and new, with naked, angular shapes and the glitter of broad windows. Far in the distance, some structures seemed taller, and the faint coils of smoke above them suggested an industrial district. But close before her, rising on a slender granite column from a ledge below to the level of her eyes, blinding her by its glare, dimming the rest, stood a dollar sign three feet tall, made of solid gold. It hung in space above the town, as its coat-of-arms, its trademark, its beacon— and it caught the sunrays, like some transmitter of energy that sent them in shining blessing to stretch horizontally through the air above the roofs.

"What's that?" she gasped, pointing at the sign.

"Oh, that's Francisco's private joke."

"Francisco—who?" she whispered, knowing the answer.

"Francisco d'Anconia."

"Is he here, too?"

"He will be, any day now."

"What do you mean, his joke?"

"He gave that sign as an anniversary present to the owner of this place. And then we all adopted it as our particular emblem. We liked the idea."

"Aren't you the owner of this place?"

"I? No." He glanced down at the foot of the ledge and added, pointing, "There's the owner of this place, coming now."

A car had stopped at the end of a dirt road below, and two men were hurrying up the trail. She could not distinguish their faces; one of them was slender and tall, the other shorter, more muscular. She lost sight of them behind the twists of the trail, as he went on carrying her down to meet them.

She met them when they emerged suddenly from behind a rocky corner a few feet away. The sight of their faces hit her with the abruptness of a collision.

"Well, I'll be goddamned!" said the muscular man, whom she did not know, staring at her.

She was staring at the tall, distinguished figure of his companion: it was Hugh Akston.

It was Hugh Akston who spoke first, bowing to her with a courteous smile of welcome. "Miss Taggart, this is the first time anyone has ever proved me wrong. I didn't know—when I told you you'd never find him —that the next time I saw you, you would be in his arms."

"In whose arms?"

"Why, the inventor of the motor."

She gasped, closing her eyes; this was one connection she knew she should have made. When she opened her eyes, she was looking at Galt. He was smiling, faintly, derisively, as if he knew fully what this meant to her.

"It would have served you right if you'd broken your neck!" the muscular man snapped at her, with the anger of concern, almost of affection. "What a stunt to pull—for a person who'd have been admitted here so eagerly, if she'd chosen to come through the front door!"

"Miss Taggart, may I present Midas Mulligan?" said Galt.

"Oh," she said weakly, and laughed; she had no capacity for astonishment any longer. "Do you suppose I was killed in that crash—and this is some other kind of existence?"

"It *is* another kind of existence," said Galt. "But as for being killed, doesn't it seem more like the other way around?"

"Oh yes," she whispered, "yes . . ." She smiled at Mulligan. "Where is the front door?"

"Here," he said, pointing to his forehead.

"I've lost the key," she said simply, without resentment. "I've lost all keys, right now."

"You'll find them. But what in blazes were you doing in that plane?"

"Following."

"Him?" He pointed at Galt.

"Yes."

"You're lucky to be alive! Are you badly hurt?"

"I don't think so."

"You'll have a few questions to answer, after they patch you up." He turned brusquely, leading the way down to the car, then glanced at Galt. "Well, what do we do now? *There's* something we hadn't provided for: the first scab."

"The first . . . what?" she asked.

"Skip it," said Mulligan, and looked at Galt. "What do we do?"

"It will be my charge," said Galt. "I will be responsible. You take Quentin Daniels."

"Oh, *he's* no problem at all. He needs nothing but to get acquainted with the place. He seems to know all the rest."

"Yes. He had practically gone the whole way by himself." He saw her watching him in bewilderment, and said, "There's one thing I must thank you for, Miss Taggart: you did pay me a compliment when you chose Quentin Daniels as my understudy. He was a plausible one."

"Where is he?" she asked. "Will you tell me what happened?"

"Why, Midas met us at the landing field, drove me to my house and took Daniels with him. I was going to join them for breakfast, but I saw your plane spinning and plunging for that pasture. I was the closest one to the scene."

"We got here as fast as we could," said Mulligan. "I thought he deserved to get himself killed—whoever was in that plane. I never dreamed that it was one of the only two persons in the whole world whom I'd exempt."

"Who is the other one?" she asked.

"Hank Rearden."

She winced; it was like a sudden blow from another great distance. She wondered why it seemed to her that Galt was watching her face intently and that she saw an instant's change in his, too brief to define.

They had come to the car. It was a Hammond convertible, its top down, one of the costliest models, some years old, but kept in the shining trim of efficient handling. Galt placed her cautiously in the back seat and held her in the circle of his arm. She felt a stabbing pain once in a while, but she had no attention to spare for it. She watched the distant houses of the town, as Mulligan pressed the starter and the car moved forward, as they went past the sign of the dollar and a golden ray hit her eyes, sweeping over her forehead.

"Who is the owner of this place?" she asked.

"I am," said Mulligan.

"What is *he?*" She pointed to Galt.

Mulligan chuckled. "He just works here."

"And you, Dr. Akston?" she asked.

He glanced at Galt. "I'm one of his two fathers, Miss Taggart. The one who didn't betray him."

"Oh!" she said, as another connection fell into place. "Your third pupil?"

"That's right."

"The second assistant bookkeeper!" she moaned suddenly, at one more memory.

"What's that?"

"That's what Dr. Stadler called him. That's what Dr. Stadler told me he thought his third pupil had become."

"He overestimated," said Galt. "I'm much lower than that by the scale of his standards and of his world."

The car had swerved into a lane rising toward a lonely house that stood on a ridge above the valley. She saw a man walking down a path, ahead of them, hastening in the direction of the town. He wore blue denim overalls and carried a lunchbox. There was something faintly familiar in the swift abruptness of his gait. As the car went past him, she caught a glimpse of his face—and she jerked backward, her voice rising to a scream from the pain of the movement and from the shock of the sight: "Oh, stop! Stop! Don't let him go!" It was Ellis Wyatt.

The three men laughed, but Mulligan stopped the car. "Oh . . ." she said weakly, in apology, realizing she had forgotten that this was the place from which Wyatt would not vanish.

Wyatt was running toward them: he had recognized her, too. When he seized the edge of the car, to brake his speed, she saw the face and the young, triumphant smile that she had seen but once before: on the platform of Wyatt Junction.

"Dagny! You, too, at last? One of us?"

"No," said Galt. "Miss Taggart is a castaway."

"What?"

"Miss Taggart's plane crashed. Didn't you see it?"

"Crashed—*here?*"

"Yes."

"I heard a plane, but I . . ." His look of bewilderment changed to a smile, regretful, amused and friendly. "I see. Oh, hell, Dagny, it's preposterous!"

She was staring at him helplessly, unable to reconnect the past to the present. And helplessly—as one would say to a dead friend, in a dream, the words one regrets having missed the chance to say in life—she said, with the memory of a telephone ringing, unanswered, almost two years ago, the words she had hoped to say if she ever caught sight of him again, "I . . . I tried to reach you."

He smiled gently. "We've been trying to reach you ever since, Dagny. . . . I'll see you tonight. Don't worry, I won't vanish—and I don't think you will, either."

He waved to the others and went off, swinging his lunchbox. She glanced up, as Mulligan started the car, and saw Galt's eyes watching her attentively. Her face hardened, as if in open admission of pain and in defiance of the satisfaction it might give him. "All right," she said. "I see what sort of show you want to put me through the shock of witnessing."

But there was neither cruelty nor pity in his face, only the level look of justice. "Our first rule here, Miss Taggart," he answered, "is that one must always see for oneself."

The car stopped in front of the lonely house. It was built of rough granite blocks, with a sheet of glass for most of its front wall. "I'll send the doctor over," said Mulligan, driving off, while Galt carried her up the path.

"Your house?" she asked.

"Mine," he answered, kicking the door open.

He carried her across the threshold into the glistening space of his living room, where shafts of sunlight hit walls of polished pine. She saw a few pieces of furniture made by hand, a ceiling of bare rafters, an archway open upon a small kitchen with rough shelves, a bare wooden table and the astonishing sight of chromium glittering on an electric stove; the place had the primitive simplicity of a frontiersman's cabin, reduced to essential necessities, but reduced with a super-modern skill.

He carried her across the sunrays into a small guest room and placed her down on a bed. She noticed a window open upon a long slant of rocky steps and pines going off into the sky. She noticed small streaks that looked like inscriptions cut into the wood of the walls, a few scattered lines that seemed made by different handwritings; she could not distinguish the words. She noticed another door, left half-open; it led to his bedroom.

"Am I a guest here or a prisoner?" she asked.

"The choice will be yours, Miss Taggart."

"I can make no choice when I'm dealing with a stranger."

"But you're not. Didn't you name a railroad line after me?"

"Oh! . . . Yes . . ." It was the small jolt of another connection falling into place. "Yes, I—" She was looking at the tall figure with the sun-streaked hair, with the suppressed smile in the mercilessly perceptive eyes—she was seeing the struggle to build her Line and the summer day of the first train's run—she was thinking that if a human figure could be fashioned as an emblem of that Line, *this* was the figure. "Yes . . . I did . . ." Then, remembering the rest, she added, "But I named it after an enemy."

He smiled. "That's the contradiction you had to resolve sooner or later, Miss Taggart."

"It was you . . . wasn't it? . . . who destroyed my Line. . . ."

"Why, no. It was the contradiction."

She closed her eyes; in a moment, she asked, "All those stories I heard about you—which of them were true?"

"All of them."

"Was it you who spread them?"

"No. What for? I never had any wish to be talked about."

"But you do know that you've become a legend?"

"Yes."

"The young inventor of the Twentieth Century Motor Company is the one real version of the legend, isn't it?"

"The one that's concretely real—yes."

She could not say it indifferently; there was still a breathless tone and the drop of her voice toward a whisper, when she asked, "The motor . . . the motor I found . . . it was *you* who made it?"

"Yes."

She could not prevent the jolt of eagerness that threw her head up. "The secret of transforming energy—" she began, and stopped.

"I could tell it to you in fifteen minutes," he said, in answer to the desperate plea she had not uttered, "but there's no power on earth that can force me to tell it. If you understand this, you'll understand everything that's baffling you."

"That night . . . twelve years ago . . . a spring night when you walked out of a meeting of six thousand murderers—that story is true, isn't it?"

"Yes."

"You told them that you would stop the motor of the world."

"I have."

"What have you done?"

"I've done *nothing,* Miss Taggart. And that's the whole of my secret."

She looked at him silently for a long moment. He stood waiting, as if he could read her thoughts. "The destroyer—" she said in a tone of wonder and helplessness.

"—the most evil creature that's ever existed," he said in the tone of a quotation, and she recognized her own words, "the man who's draining the brains of the world."

"How thoroughly have you been watching me," she asked, "and for how long?"

It was only an instant's pause, his eyes did not move, but it seemed to her that his glance was stressed, as if in special awareness of seeing her, and she caught the sound of some particular intensity in his voice as he answered quietly, "For years."

She closed her eyes, relaxing and giving up. She felt an odd, light-hearted indifference, as if she suddenly wanted nothing but the comfort of surrendering to helplessness.

The doctor who arrived was a gray-haired man with a mild, thoughtful face and a firmly, unobtrusively confident manner.

"Miss Taggart, may I present Dr. Hendricks?" said Galt.

"Not Dr. Thomas Hendricks?" she gasped, with the involuntary rudeness of a child; the name belonged to a great surgeon, who had retired and vanished six years ago.

"Yes, of course," said Galt.

Dr. Hendricks smiled at her, in answer. "Midas told me that Miss Taggart has to be treated for shock," he said, "not for the one sustained, but for the ones to come."

"I'll leave you to do it," said Galt, "while I go to the market to get supplies for breakfast."

She watched the rapid efficiency of Dr. Hendricks' work, as he examined her injuries. He had brought an object she had never seen before: a portable X-ray machine. She learned that she had torn the cartilage of two ribs, that she had sprained an ankle, ripped patches of skin off one knee and one elbow, and acquired a few bruises spread in purple blotches over her body. By the time Dr. Hendricks' swift, competent hands had wound the bandages and the tight lacings of tape, she felt as if her body were an engine checked by an expert mechanic, and no further care was necessary.

"I would advise you to remain in bed, Miss Taggart."

"Oh no! If I'm careful and move slowly, I'll be all right."

"You ought to rest."

"Do you think I can?"

He smiled. "I guess not."

She was dressed by the time Galt came back. Dr. Hendricks gave him an account of her condition, adding, "I'll be back to check up, to-morrow."

"Thanks," said Galt. "Send the bill to me."

"Certainly not!" she said indignantly. "I will pay it myself."

The two men glanced at each other, in amusement, as at the boast of a beggar.

"We'll discuss that later," said Galt.

Dr. Hendricks left, and she tried to stand up, limping, catching at the furniture for support. Galt lifted her in his arms, carried her to the kitchen alcove and placed her on a chair by the table set for two.

She noticed that she was hungry, at the sight of the coffee pot boiling on the stove, the two glasses of orange juice, the heavy white pottery dishes sparkling in the sun on the polished table top.

"When did you sleep or eat last?" he asked.

"I don't know . . . I had dinner on the train, with—" She shook her head in helplessly bitter amusement: with the tramp, she thought, with a desperate voice pleading for escape from an avenger who would not pursue or be found—the avenger who sat facing her across the table, drinking a glass of orange juice. "I don't know . . . it seems centuries and continents away."

"How did you happen to be following me?"

"I landed at the Afton airport just as you were taking off. The man there told me that Quentin Daniels had gone with you."

"I remember your plane circling to land. But that was the one and only time when I didn't think of you. I thought you were coming by train."

She asked, looking straight at him, "How do you want me to understand that?"

"What?"

"The one and only time when you didn't think of me."

He held her glance; she saw the faint movement she had noted as typical of him: the movement of his proudly intractable mouth curving into the hint of a smile. "In any way you wish," he answered.

She let a moment pass to underscore her choice by the severity of her face, then asked coldly, in the tone of an enemy's accusation, "You knew that I was coming for Quentin Daniels?"

"Yes."

"You got him first and fast, in order not to let me reach him? In order to beat me—knowing fully what sort of beating that would mean for me?"

"Sure."

It was she who looked away and remained silent. He rose to cook the rest of their breakfast. She watched him as he stood at the stove, toasting bread, frying eggs and bacon. There was an easy, relaxed skill about the way he worked, but it was a skill that belonged to another profession; his hands moved with the rapid precision of an engineer pulling the levers of a control board. She remembered suddenly where she had seen as expert and preposterous a performance.

"Is that what you learned from Dr. Akston?" she asked, pointing at the stove.

"That, among other things."

"Did he teach you to spend your time—*your* time!—" she could not keep the shudder of indignation out of her voice—"on this sort of work?"

"I've spent time on work of much lesser importance."

When he put her plate before her, she asked, "Where did you get that food? Do they have a grocery store here?"

"The best one in the world. It's run by Lawrence Hammond."

"What?"

"Lawrence Hammond, of Hammond Cars. The bacon is from the farm of Dwight Sanders—of Sanders Aircraft. The eggs and the butter from Judge Narragansett—of the Superior Court of the State of Illinois."

She looked at her plate, bitterly, almost as if she were afraid to touch it. "It's the most expensive breakfast I'll ever eat, considering the value of the cook's time and of all those others."

"Yes—from one aspect. But from another, it's the cheapest breakfast you'll ever eat—because no part of it has gone to feed the looters who'll make you pay for it through year after year and leave you to starve in the end."

After a long silence, she asked simply, almost wistfully, "What is it that you're all doing here?"

"Living."

She had never heard that word sound so real.

"What is your job?" she asked. "Midas Mulligan said that you work here."

"I'm the handy man, I guess."

"The what?"

"I'm on call whenever anything goes wrong with any of the installations—with the power system, for instance."

She looked at him—and suddenly she tore forward, staring at the electric stove, but fell back on her chair, stopped by pain.

He chuckled. "Yes, that's true—but take it easy or Dr. Hendricks will order you back to bed."

"The power system . . ." she said, choking, "the power system here . . . it's run by means of your motor?"

"Yes."

"It's built? It's working? It's functioning?"

"It has cooked your breakfast."

"I want to see it!"

"Don't bother crippling yourself to look at that stove. It's just a plain electric stove like any other, only about a hundred times cheaper to run. And that's all you'll have a chance to see, Miss Taggart."

"You promised to show me this valley."

"I'll show it to you. But not the power generator."

"Will you take me to see the place now, as soon as we finish?"

"If you wish—and if you're able to move."

"I am."

He got up, went to the telephone and dialed a number. "Hello, Midas? . . . Yes. . . . He did? Yes, she's all right. . . . Will you rent me your car for the day? . . . Thanks. At the usual rate—twenty-five cents. . . . . Can you send it over? . . . Do you happen to have some sort of cane? She'll need it. . . . Tonight? Yes, I think so. We will. Thanks."

He hung up. She was staring at him incredulously.

"Did I understand you to say that Mr. Mulligan—who's worth about two hundred million dollars, I believe—is going to charge you twenty-five cents for the use of his car?"

"That's right."

"Good heavens, couldn't he give it to you as a courtesy?"

He sat looking at her for a moment, studying her face, as if deliberately letting her see the amusement in his. "Miss Taggart," he said, "we have no laws in this valley, no rules, no formal organization of any kind. We come here because we want to rest. But we have certain customs, which we all observe, because they pertain to the things we need to rest from. So I'll warn you now that there is one word which is forbidden in this valley: the word *'give.'* "

"I'm sorry," she said. "You're right."

He refilled her cup of coffee and extended a package of cigarettes. She smiled, as she took a cigarette: it bore the sign of the dollar.

"If you're not too tired by evening," he said, "Mulligan has invited us for dinner. He'll have some guests there whom, I think, you'll want to meet."

"Oh, of course! I won't be too tired. I don't think I'll ever feel tired again."

They were finishing breakfast when she saw Mulligan's car stopping in front of the house. The driver leaped out, raced up the path and rushed into the room, not pausing to ring or knock. It took her a moment to realize that the eager, breathless, disheveled young man was Quentin Daniels.

"Miss Taggart," he gasped, "I'm sorry!" The desperate guilt in his voice clashed with the joyous excitement in his face. "I've never broken my word before! There's no excuse for it, I can't ask you to forgive me, and I know that you won't believe it, but the truth is that I—I forgot!"

She glanced at Galt. "I believe you."

"I forgot that I promised to wait, I forgot everything—until a few minutes ago, when Mr. Mulligan told me that you'd crashed here in a plane, and then I knew it was my fault, and if anything had happened to you—oh God, are you all right?"

"Yes. Don't worry. Sit down."

"I don't know how one can forget one's word of honor. I don't know what happened to me."

"I do."

"Miss Taggart, I had been working on it for months, on that one particular hypothesis, and the more I worked, the more hopeless it seemed to become. I'd been in my laboratory for the last two days, trying to solve a mathematical equation that looked impossible. I felt I'd die at that blackboard, but wouldn't give up. It was late at night when he came in. I don't think I even noticed him, not really. He said he wanted to speak to me and I asked him to wait and went right on. I think I forgot his presence. I don't know how long he stood there, watching me, but what I remember is that suddenly his hand reached over, swept all my figures off the blackboard and wrote one brief equation. And then I noticed him! Then I screamed—because it wasn't the full answer to the motor, but it was the way to it, a way I hadn't seen, hadn't suspected, but I knew where it led! I remember I cried, 'How could you know it?'—and he answered, pointing at a photograph of your motor, 'I'm the man who made it in the first place.' And that's the last I remember, Miss Taggart—I mean, the last I remember of my own existence, because after that we talked about static electricity and the conversion of energy and the motor."

"We talked physics all the way down here," said Galt.

"Oh, I remember when you asked me whether I'd go with you," said Daniels, "whether I'd be willing to go and never come back and give up everything . . . Everything? Give up a dead Institute that's crumbling back into the jungle, give up my future as a janitor-slave-by-law, give up Wesley Mouch and Directive 10-289 and sub-animal creatures who crawl on their bellies, grunting that there is no mind! . . . Miss Taggart"—he laughed exultantly—"he was asking me whether I'd give *that* up to go with *him!* He had to ask it twice, I couldn't believe it at first, I couldn't believe that any human being would need to be asked or would think of it as a choice. To go? I would have leaped off a skyscraper just to follow him—and to hear his formula before we hit the pavement!"

"I don't blame you," she said; she looked at him with a tinge of wistfulness that was almost envy. "Besides, you've fulfilled your contract. You've led me to the secret of the motor."

"I'm going to be a janitor here, too," said Daniels, grinning happily. "Mr. Mulligan said he'd give me the job of janitor—*at the power plant.* And when I learn, I'll rise to electrician. Isn't he great—Midas Mulligan? That's what I want to be when I reach his age. I want to make money. I want to make millions. I want to make as much as he did!"

"Daniels!" She laughed, remembering the quiet self-control, the strict precision, the stern logic of the young scientist she had known. "What's the matter with you? Where are you? Do you know what you're saying?"

"I'm *here,* Miss Taggart—and there's no limit to what's possible here! I'm going to be the greatest electrician in the world and the richest! I'm going to—"

"You're going to go back to Mulligan's house," said Galt, "and sleep for twenty-four hours—or I won't let you near the power plant."

"Yes, sir," said Daniels meekly.

The sun had trickled down the peaks and drawn a circle of shining granite and glittering snow to enclose the valley—when they stepped out of the house. She felt suddenly as if nothing existed beyond that circle, and she wondered at the joyous, proud comfort to be found in a sense of the finite, in the knowledge that the field of one's concern lay within the realm of one's sight. She wanted to stretch out her arms over the roofs of the town below, feeling that her fingertips would touch the peaks across. But she could not raise her arms; leaning on a cane with one hand and on Galt's arm with the other, moving her feet by a slow, conscientious effort, she walked down to the car like a child learning to walk for the first time.

She sat by Galt's side as he drove, skirting the town, to Midas Mulligan's house. It stood on a ridge, the largest house of the valley, the only one built two stories high, an odd combination of fortress and pleasure resort, with stout granite walls and broad, open terraces. He stopped to let Daniels off, then drove on up a winding road rising slowly into the mountains.

It was the thought of Mulligan's wealth, the luxurious car and the sight of Galt's hands on the wheel that made her wonder for the first time whether Galt, too, was wealthy. She glanced at his clothes: the gray slacks and white shirt seemed of a quality intended for long wear; the leather of the narrow belt about his waistline was cracked; the watch on his wrist was a precision instrument, but made of plain stainless steel. The sole suggestion of luxury was the color of his hair—the strands stirring in the wind like liquid gold and copper.

Abruptly, behind a turn of the road, she saw the green acres of pastures stretching to a distant farmhouse. There were herds of sheep, some horses, the fenced squares of pigpens under the sprawling shapes of wooden barns and, farther away, a metal hangar of a type that did not belong on a farm.

A man in a bright cowboy shirt was hurrying toward them. Galt stopped the car and waved to him, but said nothing in answer to her questioning glance. He let her discover for herself, when the man came closer, that it was Dwight Sanders.

"Hello, Miss Taggart," he said, smiling.

She looked silently at his rolled shirt sleeves, at his heavy boots, at the herds of cattle. "So that's all that's left of Sanders Aircraft," she said.

"Why, no. There's that excellent monoplane, my best model, which you flattened up in the foothills."

"Oh, you know about that? Yes, it was one of yours. It was a wonderful ship. But I'm afraid I've damaged it pretty badly."

"You ought to have it fixed."

"I think I've ripped the bottom. Nobody can fix it."

"I can."

These were the words and the tone of confidence that she had not heard for years, this was the manner she had given up expecting—but the start of her smile ended in a bitter chuckle. "How?" she asked. "On a hog farm?"

"Why, no. At Sanders Aircraft."

"Where is it?"

"Where did you think it was? In that building in New Jersey, which Tinky Holloway's cousin bought from my bankrupt successors by means of a government loan and a tax suspension? In that building where he produced six planes that never left the ground and eight that did, but crashed with forty passengers each?"

"Where is it, then?"

"Wherever I am."

He pointed across the road. Glancing down through the tops of the pine trees, she saw the concrete rectangle of an airfield on the bottom of the valley.

"We have a few planes here and it's my job to take care of them," he said. "I'm the hog farmer and the airfield attendant. I'm doing quite well at producing ham and bacon, without the men from whom I used to buy it. But those men cannot produce airplanes without me—and, without me, they cannot even produce their ham and bacon."

"But you—you have not been designing airplanes, either."

"No, I haven't. And I haven't been manufacturing the Diesel engines I once promised you. Since the time I saw you last, I have designed and manufactured just one new tractor. I mean, *one*—I tooled it by hand—no mass production was necessary. But that tractor has cut an eight-hour workday down to four hours on"—the straight line of his arm, extended to point across the valley, moved like a royal scepter; her eyes followed it and she saw the terraced green of hanging gardens on a distant mountainside—"the chicken and dairy farm of Judge Narragansett"—his arm moved slowly to a long, flat stretch of greenish gold at the foot of a canyon, then to a band of violent green—"in the wheat fields and tobacco patch of Midas Mulligan"—his arm rose to a granite flank striped by glistening tiers of leaves—"in the orchards of Richard Halley."

Her eyes went slowly over the curve his arm had traveled, over and over again, long after the arm had dropped; but she said only, "I see."

"Now do you believe that I can fix your plane?" he asked.

"Yes. But have you seen it?"

"Sure. Midas called two doctors immediately—Hendricks for you, and me for your plane. It can be fixed. But it will be an expensive job."

"How much?"

"Two hundred dollars."

"Two hundred dollars?" she repeated incredulously; the price seemed much too low.

"In gold, Miss Taggart."

"Oh . . . ! Well, where can I buy the gold?"

"You can't," said Galt.

She jerked her head to face him defiantly. "No?"

"No. Not where you come from. Your laws forbid it."

"Yours don't?"

"No."

"Then sell it to me. Choose your own rate of exchange. Name any sum you want—in my money."

"What money? You're penniless, Miss Taggart."

"*What?*" It was a word that a Taggart heiress could not ever expect to hear.

"You're penniless in this valley. You own millions of dollars in Taggart Transcontinental stock—but it will not buy one pound of bacon from the Sanders hog farm."

"I see."

Galt smiled and turned to Sanders. "Go ahead and fix that plane. Miss Taggart will pay for it eventually."

He pressed the starter and drove on, while she sat stiffly straight, asking no questions.

A stretch of violent turquoise blue split the cliffs ahead, ending the road; it took her a second to realize that it was a lake. The motionless water seemed to condense the blue of the sky and the green of the pine-covered mountains into so brilliantly pure a color that it made the sky look a dimmed pale gray. A streak of boiling foam came from among the pines and went crashing down the rocky steps to vanish in the placid water. A small granite structure stood by the stream.

Galt stopped the car just as a husky man in overalls stepped out to the threshold of the open doorway. It was Dick McNamara, who had once been her best contractor.

"Good day, Miss Taggart!" he said happily. "I'm glad to see that you weren't hurt badly."

She inclined her head in silent greeting—it was like a greeting to the loss and the pain of the past, to a desolate evening and the desperate face of Eddie Willers telling her the news of this man's disappearance—hurt badly? she thought—I was, but not in the plane crash—on that evening, in an empty office. . . . Aloud, she asked, "What are you doing here? What was it that you betrayed me for, at the worst time possible?"

He smiled, pointing at the stone structure and down at the rocky drop where the tube of a water main went vanishing into the underbrush. "I'm the utilities man," he said. "I take care of the water lines, the power lines and the telephone service."

"Alone?"

"Used to. But we've grown so much in the past year that I've had to hire three men to help me."

"What men? From where?"

"Well, one of them is a professor of economics who couldn't get a job outside, because he taught that you can't consume more than you have produced—one is a professor of history who couldn't get a job because he taught that the inhabitants of slums were not the men who made this country—and one is a professor of psychology who couldn't get a job because he taught that men are capable of thinking."

"They work for you as plumbers and linesmen?"

"You'd be surprised how good they are at it."

"And to whom have they abandoned our colleges?"

"To those who're wanted there." He chuckled. "How long ago was it that I betrayed you, Miss Taggart? Not quite three years ago, wasn't it? It's the John Galt Line that I refused to build for you. Where is your Line now? But *my* lines have grown, in that time, from the couple of miles that Mulligan had built when I took over, to hundreds of miles of pipe and wire, all within the space of this valley."

He saw the swift, involuntary look of eagerness on her face, the look of a competent person's appreciation; he smiled, glanced at her companion and said softly, "You know, Miss Taggart, when it comes to the John Galt Line—maybe it's I who've followed it and you who're betraying it."

She glanced at Galt. He was watching her face, but she could read nothing in his.

As they drove on along the edge of the lake, she asked, "You've mapped this route deliberately, haven't you? You're showing me all the men whom"—she stopped, feeling inexplicably reluctant to say it, and said, instead—"whom I have lost?"

"I'm showing you all the men whom I have taken away from you," he answered firmly.

This was the root, she thought, of the guiltlessness of his face: he had guessed and named the words she had wanted to spare him, he had rejected a good will that was not based on his values—and in proud certainty of being right, he had made a boast of that which she had intended as an accusation.

Ahead of them, she saw a wooden pier projecting into the water of the lake. A young woman lay stretched on the sun-flooded planks, watching a battery of fishing rods. She glanced up at the sound of the car, then leaped to her feet in a single swift movement, a shade too swift, and ran to the road. She wore slacks, rolled above the knees of her bare legs, she had dark, disheveled hair and large eyes. Galt waved to her.

"Hello, John! When did you get in?" she called.

"This morning," he answered, smiling and driving on.

Dagny jerked her head to look back and saw the glance with which the young woman stood looking after Galt. And even though hopelessness, serenely accepted, was part of the worship in that glance, she experienced a feeling she had never known before: a stab of jealousy.

"Who is that?" she asked.

"Our best fishwife. She provides the fish for Hammond's grocery market."

"What else is she?"

"You've noticed that there's a 'what else' for every one of us here? She's a writer. The kind of writer who wouldn't be published outside. She believes that when one deals with words, one deals with the mind."

The car turned into a narrow path, climbing steeply into a wilderness of brush and pine trees. She knew what to expect when she saw a handmade sign nailed to a tree, with an arrow pointing the way: The Buena Esperanza Pass.

It was not a pass, it was a wall of laminated rock with a complex chain of pipes, pumps and valves climbing like a vine up its narrow ledges, but it bore, on its crest, a huge wooden sign—and the proud violence of the letters announcing their message to an impassable tangle of ferns and pine branches, was more characteristic, more familiar than the words: Wyatt Oil.

It was oil that ran in a glittering curve from the mouth of a pipe into a tank at the foot of the wall, as the only confession of the tremendous secret struggle inside the stone, as the unobtrusive purpose of all the intricate machinery—but the machinery did not resemble the installations of an oil derrick, and she knew that she was looking at the unborn secret of the Buena Esperanza Pass, she knew that this was oil drawn out of shale by some method men had considered impossible.

Ellis Wyatt stood on a ridge, watching the glass dial of a gauge imbedded in the rock. He saw the car stopping below, and called, "Hi, Dagny! Be with you in a minute!"

There were two other men working with him: a big, muscular roughneck, at a pump halfway up the wall, and a young boy, by the tank on the ground. The young boy had blond hair and a face with an unusual purity of form. She felt certain that she knew this face, but she could not recall where she had seen it. The boy caught her puzzled glance, grinned and, as if to help her, whistled softly, almost inaudibly the first notes of Halley's Fifth Concerto. It was the young brakeman of the Comet.

She laughed. "It *was* the Fifth Concerto by Richard Halley, wasn't it?"

"Sure," he answered. "But do you think I'd tell that to a scab?"

"A what?"

"What am I paying you for?" asked Ellis Wyatt, approaching; the boy chuckled, darting back to seize the lever he had abandoned for a moment. "It's Miss Taggart who couldn't fire you, if you loafed on the job. I can."

"That's one of the reasons why I quit the railroad, Miss Taggart," said the boy.

"Did you know that I stole him from you?" said Wyatt. "He used to be your best brakeman and now he's my best grease-monkey, but neither one of us is going to hold him permanently."

"Who is?"

"Richard Halley. Music. He's Halley's best pupil."

She smiled. "I know, this is a place where one employs nothing but aristocrats for the lousiest kinds of jobs."

"They're all aristocrats, that's true," said Wyatt, "because they know that there's no such thing as a lousy job—only lousy men who don't care to do it."

The roughneck was watching them from above, listening with curiosity. She glanced up at him, he looked like a truck driver, so she asked, "What were *you* outside? A professor of comparative philology, I suppose?"

"No, ma'am," he answered. "I was a truck driver." He added, "But that's not what I wanted to remain."

Ellis Wyatt was looking at the place around them with a kind of youthful pride eager for acknowledgment: it was the pride of a host at a formal reception in a drawing room, and the eagerness of an artist at the opening of his show in a gallery. She smiled and asked, pointing at the machinery, "Shale oil?"

"Uh-huh."

"That's the process which you were working to develop while you were on earth?" She said it involuntarily and she gasped a little at her own words.

He laughed. "While I was in hell—yes. I'm on earth now."

"How much do you produce?"

"Two hundred barrels a day."

A note of sadness came back into her voice: "It's the process by which you once intended to fill five tank-trains a day."

"Dagny," he said earnestly, pointing at his tank, "one gallon of it is worth more than a trainful back there in hell—because this is *mine,* all of it, every single drop of it, to be spent on nothing but myself." He raised his smudged hand, displaying the greasy stains as a treasure, and a black drop on the tip of his finger flashed like a gem in the sun. "Mine," he said. "Have you let them beat you into forgetting what that word means, what it feels like? You should give yourself a chance to relearn it."

"You're hidden in a hole in the wilderness," she said bleakly, "and you're producing two hundred barrels of oil, when you could have flooded the world with it."

"What for? To feed the looters?"

"No! To earn the fortune you deserve."

"But I'm richer now than I was in the world. What's wealth but the means of expanding one's life? There's two ways one can do it: either by producing more or by producing it faster. And that's what I'm doing: I'm manufacturing time."

"What do you mean?"

"I'm producing everything I need, I'm working to improve my methods, and every hour I save is an hour added to my life. It used to take me five hours to fill that tank. It now takes three. The two I saved are mine—as pricelessly mine as if I moved my grave two further hours away for every five I've got. It's two hours released from one task, to be invested in another—two more hours in which to work, to grow, to move forward. That's the savings account I'm hoarding. Is there any sort of safety vault that could protect this account in the outside world?"

"But what space do you have for moving forward? Where's your market?"

He chuckled. "Market? I now work for use, not for profit—*my* use, not the looters' profit. Only those who add to my life, not those who devour it, are my market. Only those who produce, not those who consume, can ever be anybody's market. I deal with the life-givers, not with the cannibals. If my oil takes less effort to produce, I ask less of the men to whom I trade it for the things I need. I add an extra span of time to their lives with every gallon of my oil that they burn. And since they're men like me, they keep inventing faster ways to make the things they make—so every one of them grants me an added minute, hour or day with the bread I buy from them, with the clothes, the lumber, the metal"—he glanced at Galt—"an added year with every month of electricity I purchase. That's our market and that's how it works for us—but that was not the way it worked in the outer world. Down what drain were they poured out there, our days, our lives and our energy? Into what bottomless, futureless sewer of the unpaid-for? Here, we trade achievements, not failures—values, not needs. We're free of one another, yet we all grow together. Wealth, Dagny? What greater wealth is there than to own your life and to spend it on growing? Every living thing must grow. It can't stand still. It must grow or perish. Look—" He pointed at a plant fighting upward from under the weight of a rock—a long, gnarled stem, contorted by an unnatural struggle, with drooping, yellow remnants of unformed leaves and a single green shoot thrust upward to the sun with the desperation of a last, spent, inadequate effort. "That's what they're doing to us back there in hell. Do you see me submitting to it?"

"No," she whispered.

"Do you see *him* submitting?" He pointed at Galt.

"God, no!"

"Then don't be astonished by anything you see in this valley."

She remained silent when they drove on. Galt said nothing.

On a distant mountainside, in the dense green of a forest, she saw a pine tree slanting down suddenly, tracing a curve, like the hand of a clock, then crashing abruptly out of sight. She knew that it was a man-made motion.

"Who's the lumberjack around here?" she asked.

"Ted Nielsen."

The road was relaxing into wider curves and gentler grades, among the softer shapes of hillsides. She saw a rust-brown slope patched by two squares of unmatching green: the dark, dusty green of potato plants, and the pale, greenish-silver of cabbages. A man in a red shirt was riding a small tractor, cutting weeds.

"Who's the cabbage tycoon?" she asked.

"Roger Marsh."

She closed her eyes. She thought of the weeds that were climbing up the steps of a closed factory, over its lustrous tile front, a few hundred miles away, beyond the mountains.

The road was descending to the bottom of the valley. She saw the roofs of the town straight below, and the small, shining spot of the dollar sign in the distance at the other end. Galt stopped the car in front of the first structure on a ledge above the roofs, a brick building with a faint tinge of red trembling over its smokestack. It almost shocked her to see so logical a sign as "Stockton Foundry" above its door.

When she walked, leaning on her cane, out of the sunlight into the dank gloom of the building, the shock she felt was part sense of anachronism, part homesickness. This was the industrial East which, in the last few hours, had seemed to be centuries behind her. This was the old, the familiar, the loved sight of reddish billows rising to steel rafters, of sparks shooting in sunbursts from invisible sources, of sudden flames streaking through a black fog, of sand molds glowing with white metal. The fog hid the walls of the structure, dissolving its size—and for a moment, this was the great, dead foundry at Stockton, Colorado, it was Nielsen Motors . . . it was Rearden Steel.

"Hi, Dagny!"

The smiling face that approached her out of the fog was Andrew Stockton's, and she saw a grimy hand extended to her with a gesture of confident pride, as if it held all of her moment's vision on its palm.

She clasped the hand. "Hello," she said softly, not knowing whether she was greeting the past or the future. Then she shook her head and added, "How come you're not planting potatoes or making shoes around here? You've actually remained in your own profession."

"Oh, Calvin Atwood of the Atwood Light and Power Company of New York City is making the shoes. Besides, my profession is one of the oldest and most immediately needed anywhere. Still, I had to fight for it. I had to ruin a competitor, first."

"What?"

He grinned and pointed to the glass door of a sun-flooded room. "There's my ruined competitor," he said.

She saw a young man bent over a long table, working on a complex model for the mold of a drill head. He had the slender, powerful hands of a concert pianist and the grim face of a surgeon concentrating on his task.

"He's a sculptor," said Stockton. "When I came here, he and his partner had a sort of combination hand-forge and repair shop. I opened a real foundry, and took all their customers away from them. The boy couldn't do the kind of job I did, it was only a part-time business for him, anyway—sculpture is his real business—so he came to work for me. He's making more money now, in shorter hours, than he used to make in his own foundry. His partner was a chemist, so he went into agriculture and he's produced a chemical fertilizer that's doubled some of the crops around here—did you mention potatoes?—potatoes, in particular."

"Then somebody could put you out of business, too?"

"Sure. Any time. I know one man who could and probably will, when he gets here. But, boy!—I'd work for him as a cinder sweeper. He'd blast through this valley like a rocket. He'd triple everybody's production."

"Who's that?"

"Hank Rearden."

"Yes . . ." she whispered. "Oh yes!"

She wondered what had made her say it with such immediate certainty. She felt, simultaneously, that Hank Rearden's presence in this valley was impossible—and that this was his place, peculiarly his, this was the place of his youth, of his start, and, together, the place he had been seeking all his life, the land he had struggled to reach, the goal of his tortured battle. . . . It seemed to her that the spirals of flame-tinged fog were drawing time into an odd circle—and while a dim thought went floating through her mind like the streamer of an unfollowed sentence: To hold an unchanging youth is to reach, at the end, the vision with which one started—she heard the voice of a tramp in a diner, saying, "John Galt found the fountain of youth which he wanted to bring down to men. Only he never came back . . . because he found that it couldn't be brought down."

A sheaf of sparks went up in the depth of the fog—and she saw the broad back of a foreman whose arm made the sweeping gesture of a signal, directing some invisible task. He jerked his head to snap an order—she caught a glimpse of his profile—and she caught her breath. Stockton saw it, chuckled and called into the fog:

"Hey, Ken! Come here! Here's an old friend of yours!"

She looked at Ken Danagger as he approached them. The great industrialist, whom she had tried so desperately to hold to his desk, was now dressed in smudged overalls.

"Hello, Miss Taggart. I told you we'd soon meet again."

Her head dropped, as if in assent and in greeting, but her hand bore down heavily upon her cane, for a moment, while she stood reliving their last encounter: the tortured hour of waiting, then the gently distant face at the desk and the tinkling of a glass-paneled door closing upon a stranger.

It was so brief a moment that two of the men before her could take it only as a greeting—but it was at Galt that she looked when she raised her head, and she saw him looking at her as if he knew what she felt—she saw him seeing in her face the realization that it was he who had walked out of Danagger's office, that day. His face gave her nothing in answer: it had that look of respectful severity with which a man stands before the fact that the truth is the truth.

"I didn't expect it," she said softly, to Danagger. "I never expected to see you again."

Danagger was watching her as if she were a promising child he had once discovered and was now affectionately amused to watch. "I know," he said. "But why are you so shocked?"

"I . . . oh, it's just that it's preposterous!" She pointed at his clothes.

"What's wrong with it?"

"Is this, then, the end of your road?"

"Hell, no! The beginning."

"What are you aiming at?"

"Mining. Not coal, though. Iron."

"Where?"

He pointed toward the mountains. "Right here. Did you ever know Midas Mulligan to make a bad investment? You'd be surprised what one can find in that stretch of rock, if one knows how to look. That's what I've been doing—looking."

"And if you don't find any iron ore?"

He shrugged. "There's other things to do. I've always been short on time in my life, never on what to use it for."

She glanced at Stockton with curiosity. "Aren't you training a man who could become your most dangerous competitor?"

"That's the only sort of men I like to hire. Dagny, have you lived too long among the looters? Have you come to think that one man's ability is a threat to another?"

"Oh no! But I thought I was almost the only one left who didn't think that."

"Any man who's afraid of hiring the best ability he can find, is a cheat who's in a business where he doesn't belong. To me—the foulest man on earth, more contemptible than a criminal, is the employer who rejects men for being too good. That's what I've always thought and— say, what are you laughing at?"

She was listening to him with an eager, incredulous smile. "It's so startling to hear," she said, "because it's so right!"

"What else can one think?"

She chuckled softly. "You know, when I was a child, I expected every businessman to think it."

"And since then?"

"Since then, I've learned not to expect it."

"But it's right, isn't it?"

"I've learned not to expect the right."

"But it stands to reason, doesn't it?"

"I've given up expecting reason."

"That's what one must never give up," said Ken Danagger.

They had returned to the car and had started down the last, descending curves of the road, when she glanced at Galt and he turned to her at once, as if he had expected it.

"It was you in Danagger's office that day, wasn't it?" she asked.

"Yes."

"Did you know, then, that I was waiting outside?"

"Yes."

"Did you know what it was like, to wait behind that closed door?"

She could not name the nature of the glance with which he looked at her. It was not pity, because she did not seem to be its object; it was the kind of glance with which one looks at suffering, but it was not *her* suffering that he seemed to be seeing.

"Oh yes," he answered quietly, almost lightly.

The first shop to rise by the side of the valley's single street was like the sudden sight of an open theater: a frame box without front wall, its stage set in the bright colors of a musical comedy—with red cubes, green circles, gold triangles, which were bins of tomatoes, barrels of lettuce, pyramids of oranges, and a spangled backdrop where the sun hit shelves of metal containers. The name on the marquee said: Hammond Grocery Market. A distinguished man in shirt sleeves, with a stern profile and gray temples, was weighing a chunk of butter for an attractive young woman who stood at the counter, her posture light as a show girl's, the skirt of her cotton dress swelling faintly in the wind, like a dance costume. Dagny smiled involuntarily, even though the man was Lawrence Hammond.

The shops were small one-story structures, and as they moved past her, she caught familiar names on their signs, like headings on the pages of a book riffled by the car's motion: Mulligan General Store—Atwood Leather Goods—Nielsen Lumber—then the sign of the dollar above the door of a small brick factory with the inscription: Mulligan Tobacco Company. "Who's the Company, besides Midas Mulligan?" she asked. "Dr. Akston," he answered.

There were few passers-by, some men, fewer women, and they walked with purposeful swiftness, as if bound on specific errands. One after another, they stopped at the sight of the car, they waved to Galt and they looked at her with the unastonished curiosity of recognition.

"Have I been expected here for a long time?" she asked. "You still are," he answered.

On the edge of the road, she saw a structure made of glass sheets held together by a wooden framework, but for one instant it seemed to her that it was only a frame for the painting of a woman—a tall, fragile woman with pale blond hair and a face of such beauty that it seemed veiled by distance, as if the artist had been merely able to suggest it, not to make it quite real. In the next instant the woman moved her head—and Dagny realized that there were people at the tables inside the structure, that it was a cafeteria, that the woman stood behind the counter, and that she was Kay Ludlow, the movie star who, once seen, could never be forgotten; the star who had retired and vanished five years ago, to be replaced by girls of indistinguishable names and interchangeable faces. But at the shock of the realization, Dagny thought of the sort of movies that were now being made—and then she felt that the glass cafeteria was a cleaner use for Kay Ludlow's beauty than a role in a picture glorifying the commonplace for possessing no glory.

The building that came next was a small, squat block of rough granite, sturdy, solid, neatly built, the lines of its rectangular bulk as severely precise as the creases of a formal garment—but she saw, like an instant's ghost, the long streak of a skyscraper rising into the coils of Chicago's fog, the skyscraper that had once borne the sign she now saw written in gold letters above a modest pine-wood door: Mulligan Bank.

Galt slowed the car while moving past the bank, as if placing the motion in some special italics.

A small brick structure came next, bearing the sign: Mulligan Mint. "A mint?" she asked. "What's Mulligan doing with a mint?" Galt reached into his pocket and dropped two small coins into the palm of her hand. They were miniature disks of shining gold, smaller than pennies, the kind that had not been in circulation since the days of Nat Taggart; they bore the head of the Statue of Liberty on one side, the words "United States of America—One Dollar" on the other, but the dates stamped upon them were of the past two years.

"That's the money we use here," he said. "It's minted by Midas Mulligan."

"But . . . on whose authority?"

"That's stated on the coin—on both sides of it."

"What do you use for small change?"

"Mulligan mints that, too, in silver. We don't accept any other currency in this valley. We accept nothing but *objective* values."

She was studying the coins. "This looks like . . . like something from the first morning in the age of my ancestors."

He pointed at the valley. "Yes, doesn't it?"

She sat looking at the two thin, delicate, almost weightless drops of gold in the palm of her hand, knowing that the whole of the Taggart Transcontinental system had rested upon them, that this had been the keystone supporting all the keystones, all the arches, all the girders of the Taggart track, the Taggart Bridge, the Taggart Building. . . . She shook her head and slipped the coins back into his hand.

"You're not making it easier for me," she said, her voice low.

"I'm making it as hard as possible."

"Why don't you say it? Why don't you tell me all the things you want me to learn?"

The gesture of his arm pointed at the town, at the road behind them. "What have I been doing?" he asked.

They drove on in silence. After a while, she asked, in the tone of a dryly statistical inquiry, "How much of a fortune has Midas Mulligan amassed in this valley?"

He pointed ahead. "Judge for yourself."

The road was winding through stretches of unleveled soil toward the homes of the valley. The homes were not lined along a street, they were spread at irregular intervals over the rises and hollows of the ground, they were small and simple, built of local materials, mostly of granite and pine, with a prodigal ingenuity of thought and a tight economy of physical effort. Every house looked as if it had been put up by the labor of one man, no two houses were alike, and the only quality they had in common was the stamp of a mind grasping a problem and solving it. Galt pointed out a house, once in a while, choosing the names she knew—and it sounded to her like a list of quotations from the richest stock exchange in the world, or like a roll call of honor: "Ken Danagger . . . Ted Nielsen . . . Lawrence Hammond . . . Roger Marsh . . . Ellis Wyatt . . . Owen Kellogg . . . Dr. Akston."

The home of Dr. Akston was the last, a small cottage with a large terrace, lifted on the crest of a wave against the rising walls of the mountains. The road went past it and climbed on into the coils of an ascending grade. The pavement shrank to a narrow path between two walls of ancient pines, their tall, straight trunks pressing against it like a grim colonnade, their branches meeting above, swallowing the path into sudden silence and twilight. There were no marks of wheels on the thin strip of earth, it looked unused and forgotten, a few minutes and a few turns seemed to take the car miles away from human habitation—and then there was nothing to break the pressure of the stillness but a rare wedge of sunlight cutting across the trunks in the depth of the forest once in a while.

The sudden sight of a house on the edge of the path struck her like the shock of an unexpected sound: built in loneliness, cut off from all ties to human existence, it looked like the secret retreat of some great defiance or sorrow. It was the humblest home of the valley, a log cabin beaten in dark streaks by the tears of many rains, only its great windows withstanding the storms with the smooth, shining, untouched serenity of glass.

"Whose house is . . . Oh!"—she caught her breath and jerked her head away. Above the door, hit by a ray of sun, its design blurred and worn, battered smooth by the winds of centuries, hung the silver coat-of-arms of Sebastián d'Anconia.

As if in deliberate answer to her involuntary movement of escape, Galt stopped the car in front of the house. For a moment, they held each other's eyes: her glance was a question, his a command, her face had a defiant frankness, his an unrevealing severity; she understood his purpose, but not his motive. She obeyed. Leaning on her cane, she stepped out of the car, then stood erect, facing the house.

She looked at the silver crest that had come from a marble palace in Spain to a shack in the Andes to a log cabin in Colorado—the crest of the men who would not submit. The door of the cabin was locked, the sun did not reach into the glazed darkness beyond the windows, and pine branches hung outstretched above the roof like arms spread in protection, in compassion, in solemn blessing. With no sound but the snap of a twig or the ring of a drop falling somewhere in the forest through long stretches of moments, the silence seemed to hold all the pain that had been hidden here, but never given voice. She stood, listening with a gentle, resigned, unlamenting respect: Let's see who'll do greater honor, you—to Nat Taggart, or I—to Sebastián d'Anconia. . . . Dagny! Help me to remain. To refuse. Even though he's right! . . .

She turned to look at Galt, knowing that *he* was the man against whom she had had no help to offer. He sat at the wheel of the car, he had not followed her or moved to assist her, as if he had wanted her to acknowledge the past and had respected the privacy of her lonely salute. She noticed that he still sat as she had left him, his forearm leaning against the wheel at the same angle, the fingers of his hand hanging down in the same sculptured position. His eyes were watching her, but that was all she could read in his face: that he had watched her intently, without moving.

When she was seated beside him once more, he said, "That was the first man I took away from you."

She asked, her face stern, open and quietly defiant, "How much do you know about that?"

"Nothing that he told me in words. Everything that the tone of his voice told me whenever he spoke of you."

She inclined her head. She had caught the sound of suffering in the faintest exaggeration of evenness in his voice.

He pressed the starter, the motor's explosion blasted the story contained in the silence, and they drove on.

The path widened a little, streaming toward a pool of sunlight ahead. She saw a brief glitter of wires among the branches, as they drove out into a clearing. An unobtrusive little structure stood against a hillside, on a rising slant of rocky ground. It was a simple cube of granite, the size of a toolshed, it had no windows, no apertures of any kind, only a door of polished steel and a complex set of wire antennae branching out from the roof. Galt was driving past, leaving it unnoticed, when she asked with a sudden start, "What's that?"

She saw the faint break of his smile. "The powerhouse."

"Oh, stop, please!"

He obeyed, backing the car to the foot of the hillside. It was her first few steps up the rocky incline that stopped her, as if there were no need to move forward, no further place to rise—and she stood as in the moment when she had opened her eyes on the earth of the valley, a moment uniting her beginning to her goal.

She stood looking up at the structure, her consciousness surrendered to a single sight and a single, wordless emotion—but she had always known that an emotion was a sum totaled by an adding machine of the mind, and what she now felt was the instantaneous total of the thoughts she did not have to name, the final sum of a long progression, like a voice telling her by means of a feeling: If she had held onto Quentin Daniels, with no hope of a chance to use the motor, for the sole sake of knowing that achievement had not died on earth—if, like a weighted diver sinking in an ocean of mediocrity, under the pressure of men with gelatin eyes, rubber voices, spiral-shaped convictions, non-committal souls and non-committing hands, she had held, as her life line and oxygen tube, the thought of a superlative achievement of the human mind—if, at the sight of the motor's remnant, in a sudden gasp of suffocation, as a last protest from his corruption-eaten lungs, Dr. Stadler had cried for something, not to look down at, but up to, and *this* had been the cry, the longing and the fuel of her life—if she had moved, drawn by the hunger of her youth for a sight of clean, hard, radiant competence—then here it was before her, reached and done, the power of an incomparable mind given shape in a net of wires sparkling peacefully under a summer sky, drawing an incalculable power out of space into the secret interior of a small stone hovel.

She thought of this structure, half the size of a boxcar, replacing the power plants of the country, the enormous conglomerations of steel, fuel and effort—she thought of the current flowing from this structure, lifting ounces, pounds, tons of strain from the shoulders of those who would make it or use it, adding hours, days and years of liberated time to their lives, be it an extra moment to lift one's head from one's task and glance at the sunlight, or an extra pack of cigarettes bought with the money saved from one's electric bill, or an hour cut from the workday of every factory using power, or a month's journey through the whole, open width of the world, on a ticket paid for by one day of one's labor, on a train pulled by the power of this motor—with all the energy of that weight, that strain, that time replaced and paid for by the energy of a single mind who had known how to make connections of wire follow the connections of his thought. But she knew that there was no meaning in motors or factories or trains, that their only meaning was in man's enjoyment of his life, which they served—and that her swelling admiration at the sight of an achievement was for the man from whom it came, for the power and the radiant vision within him which had seen the earth as a place of enjoyment and had known that the work of achieving one's happiness was the purpose, the sanction and the meaning of life.

The door of the structure was a straight, smooth sheet of stainless steel, softly lustrous and bluish in the sun. Above it, cut in the granite, as the only feature of the building's rectangular austerity, there stood an inscription:

> I SWEAR BY MY LIFE AND MY LOVE OF IT THAT I
> WILL NEVER LIVE FOR THE SAKE OF ANOTHER
> MAN, NOR ASK ANOTHER MAN TO LIVE FOR MINE.

She turned to Galt. He stood beside her; he had followed her, he had known that this salute was his. She was looking at the inventor of the motor, but what she saw was the easy, casual figure of a workman in his natural setting and function—she noted the uncommon lightness of his posture, a weightless way of standing that showed an expert control of the use of his body—a tall body in simple garments: a thin shirt, light slacks, a belt about a slender waistline—and loose hair made to glitter like metal by the current of a sluggish wind. She looked at him as she had looked at his structure.

Then she knew that the first two sentences they had said to each other still hung between them, filling the silence—that everything said since, had been said over the sound of those words, that he had known it, had held it, had not let her forget it. She was suddenly aware that they were alone; it was an awareness that stressed the fact, permitting no further implication, yet holding the full meaning of the unnamed in that special stress. They were alone in a silent forest, at the foot of a structure that looked like an ancient temple—and she knew what rite was the proper form of worship to be offered on an altar of that kind. She felt a sudden pressure at the base of her throat, her head leaned back a little, no more than to feel the faint shift of a current against her hair, but it was as if she were lying back in space, against the wind, conscious of nothing but his legs and the shape of his mouth. He stood watching her, his face still but for the faint movement of his eyelids drawing narrow as if against too strong a light. It was like the beat of three instants—this was the first—and in the next, she felt a stab of ferocious triumph at the knowledge that his effort and his struggle were harder to endure than hers—and then he moved his eyes and raised his head to look at the inscription on the temple.

She let him look at it for a moment, almost as an act of condescending mercy to an adversary struggling to refuel his strength, then she asked, with a note of imperious pride in her voice, pointing at the inscription, "What's that?"

"It's the oath that was taken by every person in this valley, but you."

She said, looking at the words, "This has always been my own rule of living."

"I know it."

"But I don't think that yours is the way to practice it."

"Then you'll have to learn which one of us is wrong."

She walked up to the steel door of the structure, with a sudden confidence faintly stressed in the movements of her body, a mere hint of stress, no more than her awareness of the power she held by means of his pain—and she tried, asking no permission, to turn the knob of the door. But the door was locked, and she felt no tremor under the pressure of her hand, as if the lock were poured and sealed to the stone with the solid steel of the sheet.

"Don't try to open that door, Miss Taggart."

He approached her, his steps a shade too slow, as if stressing his knowledge of her awareness of every step. "No amount of physical force will do it," he said. "Only a thought can open that door. If you tried to break it down by means of the best explosives in the world, the machinery inside would collapse into rubble long before the door would give way. But reach the thought which it requires—and the secret of the motor will be yours, as well as"—it was the first break she had heard in his voice—"as well as any other secret you might wish to know."

He faced her for a moment, as if leaving himself open to her full understanding, then smiled oddly, quietly at some thought of his own, and added, "I'll show you how it's done."

He stepped back. Then, standing still, his face raised to the words carved in the stone, he repeated them slowly, evenly, as if taking that oath once more. There was no emotion in his voice, nothing but the spaced clarity of the sounds he pronounced with full knowledge of their meaning—but she knew that she was witnessing the most solemn moment it would ever be given her to witness, she was seeing a man's naked soul and the cost it had paid to utter these words, she was hearing an echo of the day when he had pronounced that oath for the first time and with full knowledge of the years ahead—she knew what manner of man had stood up to face six thousand others on a dark spring night and why they had been afraid of him, she knew that this was the birth and the core of all the things that had happened to the world in the twelve years since, she knew that this was of far greater import than the motor hidden inside the structure—she knew it, to the sound of a man's voice pronouncing in self-reminder and rededication:

"I swear by my life . . . and my love of it . . . that I will never live for the sake of another man . . . nor ask another man . . . to live . . . for mine."

It did not startle her, it seemed unastonishing and almost unimportant, that at the end of the last sound, she saw the door opening slowly, without human touch, moving inward upon a growing strip of darkness. In the moment when an electric light went on inside the structure, he seized the knob and pulled the door shut, its lock clicking sealed once more.

"It's a sound lock," he said; his face was serene. "That sentence is the combination of sounds needed to open it. I don't mind telling you this secret—because I know that you won't pronounce those words until you mean them the way I intended them to be meant."

She inclined her head. "I won't."

She followed him down to the car, slowly, feeling suddenly too exhausted to move. She fell back against the seat, closing her eyes, barely hearing the sound of the starter. The accumulated strain and shock of her sleepless hours hit her at once, breaking through the barrier of the tension her nerves had held to delay it. She lay still, unable to think, to react or to struggle, drained of all emotions but one.

She did not speak. She did not open her eyes until the car stopped in front of his house.

"You'd better rest," he said, "and go to sleep right now, if you want to attend Mulligan's dinner tonight."

She nodded obediently. She staggered to the house, avoiding his help. She made an effort to tell him, "I'll be all right," then to escape to the safety of her room and last long enough to close the door.

She collapsed, face down, on the bed. It was not the mere fact of physical exhaustion. It was the sudden monomania of a sensation too complete to endure. While the strength of her body was gone, while her mind had lost the faculty of consciousness, a single emotion drew on her remnants of energy, of understanding, of judgment, of control, leaving her nothing to resist it with or to direct it, making her unable to desire, only to feel, reducing her to a mere sensation—a static sensation without start or goal. She kept seeing his figure in her mind—his figure as he had stood at the door of the structure—she felt nothing else, no wish, no hope, no estimate of her feeling, no name for it, no relation to herself—there was no entity such as herself, she was not a person, only a function, the function of seeing him, and the sight was its own meaning and purpose, with no further end to reach.

Her face buried in the pillow, she recalled dimly, as a faint sensation, the moment of her take-off from the floodlighted strip of the Kansas airfield. She felt the beat of the engine, the streak of accelerating motion gathering power in a straight-line run to a single goal—and in the moment when the wheels left the ground, she was asleep.

* * *

The floor of the valley was like a pool still reflecting the glow of the sky, but the light was thickening from gold to copper, the shores were fading and the peaks were smoke-blue—when they drove to Mulligan's house.

There was no trace of exhaustion left in her bearing and no remnant of violence. She had awakened at sundown; stepping out of her room, she had found Galt waiting, sitting idly motionless in the light of a lamp. He had glanced up at her; she had stood in the doorway, her face composed, her hair smooth, her posture relaxed and confident —she had looked as she would have looked on the threshold of her office in the Taggart Building, but for the slight angle of her body leaning on a cane. He had sat looking at her for a moment, and she had wondered why she had felt certain that this was the image he was seeing—he was seeing the doorway of her office, as if it were a sight long-imagined and long-forbidden.

She sat beside him in the car, feeling no desire to speak, knowing that neither of them could conceal the meaning of their silence. She watched a few lights come up in the distant homes of the valley, then the lighted windows of Mulligan's house on the ledge ahead. She asked, "Who will be there?"

"Some of your last friends," he answered, "and some of my first."

Midas Mulligan met them at the door. She noticed that his grim, square face was not as harshly expressionless as she had thought: he had a look of satisfaction, but satisfaction could not soften his features, it merely struck them like flint and sent sparks of humor to glitter faintly in the corners of his eyes, a humor that was shrewder, more demanding, yet warmer than a smile.

He opened the door of his house, moving his arm a shade more slowly than normal, giving an imperceptibly solemn emphasis to his gesture. Walking into the living room, she faced seven men who rose to their feet at her entrance.

"Gentlemen—Taggart Transcontinental," said Midas Mulligan.

He said it smiling, but only half-jesting; some quality in his voice made the name of the railroad sound as it would have sounded in the days of Nat Taggart, as a sonorous title of honor.

She inclined her head, slowly, in acknowledgment to the men before her, knowing that these were the men whose standards of value and honor were the same as her own, the men who recognized the glory of that title as she recognized it, knowing with a sudden stab of wistfulness how much she had longed for that recognition through all her years.

Her eyes moved slowly, in greeting, from face to face: Ellis Wyatt— Ken Danagger—Hugh Akston—Dr. Hendricks—Quentin Daniels— Mulligan's voice pronounced the names of the two others: "Richard Halley—Judge Narragansett."

The faint smile on Richard Halley's face seemed to tell her that they had known each other for years—as, in her lonely evenings by the side of her phonograph, they had. The austerity of Judge Narragansett's white-haired figure reminded her that she had once heard him described as a marble statue—a blindfolded marble statue; it was the kind of figure that had vanished from the courtrooms of the country when the gold coins had vanished from the country's hands.

"You have belonged here for a long time, Miss Taggart," said Midas Mulligan. "This was not the way we expected you to come, but—welcome home."

No!—she wanted to answer, but heard herself answering softly, "Thank you."

"Dagny, how many years is it going to take you to learn to be yourself?" It was Ellis Wyatt, grasping her elbow, leading her to a chair, grinning at her look of helplessness, at the struggle between a smile and a tightening resistance in her face. "Don't pretend that you don't understand us. You do."

"We never make assertions, Miss Taggart," said Hugh Akston. "That is the moral crime peculiar to our enemies. We do not tell—we *show*. We do not claim—we *prove*. It is not your obedience that we seek to win, but your rational conviction. You have seen all the elements of our secret. The conclusion is now yours to draw—we can help you to name it, but not to accept it—the sight, the knowledge and the acceptance must be yours."

"I feel as if I know it," she answered simply, "and more: I feel as if I've always known it, but never found it, and now I'm afraid, not afraid to hear it, just afraid that it's coming so close."

Akston smiled. "What does this look like to you, Miss Taggart?" He pointed around the room.

"This?" She laughed suddenly, looking at the faces of the men against the golden sunburst of rays filling the great windows. "This looks like . . . You know, I never hoped to see any of you again, I wondered at times how much I'd give for just one more glimpse or one more word—and now—now this is like that dream you imagine in childhood, when you think that some day, in heaven, you will see those great departed whom you had not seen on earth, and you choose, from all the past centuries, the great men you would like to meet."

"Well, that's one clue to the nature of our secret," said Akston. "Ask yourself whether the dream of heaven and greatness should be left waiting for us in our graves—or whether it should be ours here and now and on this earth."

"I know," she whispered.

"And if you met those great men in heaven," asked Ken Danagger, "what would you want to say to them?"

"Just . . . just 'hello,' I guess."

"That's not all," said Danagger. "There's something you'd want to hear from them. I didn't know it, either, until I saw him for the first time"—he pointed to Galt—"and he said it to me, and then I knew what it was that I had missed all my life. Miss Taggart, you'd want them to look at you and to say, 'Well done.'" She dropped her head and nodded silently, head down, not to let him see the sudden spurt of tears to her eyes. "All right, then: Well done, Dagny!—well done—too well—and now it's time for you to rest from that burden which none of us should ever have had to carry."

"Shut up," said Midas Mulligan, looking at her bowed head with anxious concern.

But she raised her head, smiling. "Thank you," she said to Danagger.

"If you talk about resting, then let her rest," said Mulligan. "She's had too much for one day."

"No." She smiled. "Go ahead, say it—whatever it is."

"Later," said Mulligan.

It was Mulligan and Akston who served dinner, with Quentin Daniels to help them. They served it on small silver trays, to be placed on the arms of the chairs—and they all sat about the room, with the fire of the sky fading in the windows and sparks of electric light glittering in the wine glasses. There was an air of luxury about the room, but it was the luxury of expert simplicity; she noted the costly furniture, carefully chosen for comfort, bought somewhere at a time when luxury had still been an art. There were no superfluous objects, but she noticed a small canvas by a great master of the Renaissance, worth a fortune, she noticed an Oriental rug of a texture and color that belonged under glass in a museum. This was Mulligan's concept of wealth, she thought—the wealth of selection, not of accumulation.

Quentin Daniels sat on the floor, with his tray on his lap; he seemed completely at home, and he glanced up at her once in a while, grinning like an impudent kid brother who had beaten her to a secret she had not discovered. He had preceded her into the valley by some ten minutes, she thought, but he was one of them, while she was still a stranger.

Galt sat aside, beyond the circle of lamplight, on the arm of Dr. Akston's chair. He had not said a word, he had stepped back and turned her over to the others, and he sat watching it as a spectacle in which he had no further part to play. But her eyes kept coming back to him, drawn by the certainty that the spectacle was of his choice and staging, that he had set it in motion long ago, and that all the others knew it as she knew it.

She noticed another person who was intensely aware of Galt's presence: Hugh Akston glanced up at him once in a while, involuntarily, almost surreptitiously, as if struggling not to confess the loneliness of a long separation. Akston did not speak to him, as if taking his presence for granted. But once, when Galt bent forward and a strand of hair fell down across his face, Akston reached over and brushed it back, his hand lingering for an imperceptible instant on his pupil's forehead: it was the only break of emotion he permitted himself, the only greeting; it was the gesture of a father.

She found herself talking to the men around her, relaxing in light-hearted comfort. No, she thought, what she felt was not strain, it was a dim astonishment at the strain which she should, but did not, feel; the abnormality of it was that it seemed so normal and simple.

She was barely aware of her questions, as she spoke to one man after another, but their answers were printing a record in her mind, moving sentence by sentence to a goal.

"The Fifth Concerto?" said Richard Halley, in answer to her question. "I wrote it ten years ago. We call it the Concerto of Deliverance. Thank you for recognizing it from a few notes whistled in the night. . . . Yes, I know about that. . . . Yes, since you knew my work, you would know, when you heard it, that this Concerto said everything I had been struggling to say and reach. It's dedicated to him." He pointed to Galt. "Why, no, Miss Taggart, I haven't given up music. What makes you think so? I've written more in the last ten years than in any other period of my life. I will play it for you, any of it, when you come to my house. . . . No, Miss Taggart, it will not be published outside. Not a note of it will be heard beyond these mountains."

"No, Miss Taggart, I have not given up medicine," said Dr. Hendricks, in answer to her question. "I have spent the last six years on research. I have discovered a method to protect the blood vessels of the brain from that fatal rupture which is known as a brain stroke. It will remove from human existence the terrible threat of sudden paralysis. . . . No, not a word of my method will be heard outside."

"The law, Miss Taggart?" said Judge Narragansett. "What law? I did not give it up—it has ceased to exist. But I am still working in the profession I had chosen, which was that of serving the cause of justice. . . . No, justice has not ceased to exist. How could it? It is possible for men to abandon their sight of it, and then it is justice that destroys them. But it is not possible for justice to go out of existence, because one is an attribute of the other, because justice is the act of acknowledging that which exists. . . . Yes, I am continuing in my profession. I am writing a treatise on the philosophy of law. I shall demonstrate that humanity's darkest evil, the most destructive horror machine among all the devices of men, is non-objective law. . . . No, Miss Taggart, my treatise will not be published outside."

"My business, Miss Taggart?" said Midas Mulligan. "My business is blood transfusion—and I'm still doing it. My job is to feed a life-fuel into the plants that are capable of growing. But ask Dr. Hendricks whether any amount of blood will save a body that refuses to function, a rotten hulk that expects to exist without effort. My blood bank is gold. Gold is a fuel that will perform wonders, but no fuel can work where there is no motor. . . . No, I haven't given up. I merely got fed up with the job of running a slaughter house, where one drains blood out of healthy living beings and pumps it into gutless half-corpses."

"Given up?" said Hugh Akston. "Check your premises, Miss Taggart. None of us has given up. It is the world that has. . . . What is wrong with a philosopher running a roadside diner? Or a cigarette factory, as I am doing now? All work is an act of philosophy. And when men will learn to consider productive work—and that which is its source—as the standard of their moral values, they will reach that state of perfection which is the birthright they lost. . . . The source of work? Man's mind, Miss Taggart, man's reasoning mind. I am writing a book on this subject, defining a moral philosophy that I learned from my own pupil. . . . Yes, it could save the world. . . . No, it will not be published outside."

"Why?" she cried. "Why? What are you doing, all of you?"

"We are on strike," said John Galt.

They all turned to him, as if they had been waiting for his voice and for that word. She heard the empty beat of time within her, which was the sudden silence of the room, as she looked at him across a span of lamplight. He sat slouched casually on the arm of a chair, leaning forward, his forearm across his knees, his hand hanging down idly—and it was the faint smile on his face that gave to his words the deadly sound of the irrevocable:

"Why should this seem so startling? There is only one kind of men who have never been on strike in human history. Every other kind and class have stopped, when they so wished, and have presented demands to the world, claiming to be indispensable—except the men who have carried the world on their shoulders, have kept it alive, have endured torture as sole payment, but have never walked out on the human race. Well, their turn has come. Let the world discover who they are, what they do and what happens when they refuse to function. This is the strike of the men of the mind, Miss Taggart. This is the mind on strike."

She did not move, except for the fingers of one hand that moved slowly up her cheek to her temple.

"Through all the ages," he said, "the mind has been regarded as evil, and every form of insult: from heretic to materialist to exploiter—every form of iniquity: from exile to disfranchisement to expropriation—every form of torture: from sneers to rack to firing squad—have been brought down upon those who assumed the responsibility of looking at the world through the eyes of a living consciousness and performing the crucial act of a rational connection. Yet only to the extent to which—in chains, in dungeons, in hidden corners, in the cells of philosophers, in the shops of traders—some men continued to think, only to that extent was humanity able to survive. Through all the centuries of the worship of the mindless, whatever stagnation humanity chose to endure, whatever brutality to practice—it was only by the grace of the men who perceived that wheat must have water in order to grow, that stones laid in a curve will form an arch, that two and two make four, that love is not served by torture and life is not fed by destruction—only by the grace of those men did the rest of them learn to experience moments when they caught the spark of being human, and only the sum of such moments permitted them to continue to exist. It was the man of the mind who taught them to bake their bread, to heal their wounds, to forge their weapons and to build the jails into which they threw him. He was the man of extravagant energy—and reckless generosity—who knew that stagnation is not man's fate, that impotence is not his nature, that the ingenuity of his mind is his noblest and most joyous power—and in service to that love of existence he was alone to feel, he went on working, working at any price, working for his despoilers, for his jailers, for his torturers, paying with his life for the privilege of saving theirs. This was his glory and his guilt—that he let them teach him to feel guilty of his glory, to accept the part of a sacrificial animal and, in punishment for the sin of intelligence, to perish on the altars of the brutes. The tragic joke of human history is that on any of the altars men erected, it was always man whom they immolated and the animal whom they enshrined. It was always the animal's attributes, not man's, that humanity worshipped: the idol of instinct and the idol of force—the mystics and the kings—the mystics, who longed for an irresponsible consciousness and ruled by means of the claim that their dark emotions were superior to reason, that knowledge came in blind, causeless fits, blindly to be followed, not doubted—and the kings, who ruled by means of claws and muscles, with conquest as their method and looting as their aim, with a club or a gun as sole sanction of their power. The defenders of man's soul were concerned with his feelings, and the defenders of man's body were concerned with his stomach—but both were united against his mind. Yet no one, not the lowest of humans, is ever able fully to renounce his brain. No one has ever believed in the irrational; what they do believe in is the unjust. Whenever a man denounces the mind, it is because his goal is of a nature the mind would not permit him to confess. When he preaches contradictions, he does so in the knowledge that someone will accept the burden of the impossible, someone will make it work for him at the price of his own suffering or life; destruction is the price of any contradiction. It is the victims who made injustice possible. It is the men of reason who made it possible for the rule of the brute to work. The despoiling of reason has been the motive of every anti-reason creed on earth. The despoiling of ability has been the purpose of every creed that preached self-sacrifice. The despoilers have always known it. We haven't. The time has come for us to see. What we are now asked to worship, what had once been dressed as God or king, is the naked, twisted, mindless figure of the human Incompetent. This is the new ideal, the goal to aim at, the purpose to live for, and all men are to be rewarded according to how close they approach it. This is the age of the common man, they tell us—a title which any man may claim to the extent of such distinction as he has managed not to achieve. He will rise to a rank of nobility by means of the effort he has failed to make, he will be honored for such virtue as he has not displayed, and he will be paid for the goods which he did not produce. But we—we, who must atone for the guilt of ability—we will work to support him as he orders, with his pleasure as our only reward. Since we have the most to contribute, we will have the least to say. Since we have the better capacity to think, we will not be permitted a thought of our own. Since we have the judgment to act, we will not be permitted an action of our choice. We will work under directives and controls, issued by those who are incapable of working. They will dispose of our energy, because they have none to offer, and of our product, because they can't produce. Do you say that this is impossible, that it cannot be made to work? They know it, but it is you who don't—and they are counting on you not to know it. They are counting on you to go on, to work to the limit of the inhuman and to feed them while you last—and when you collapse, there will be another victim starting out and feeding them, while struggling to survive—and the span of each succeeding victim will be shorter, and while you'll die to leave them a railroad, your last descendant-in-spirit will die to leave them a loaf of bread. This does not worry the looters of the moment. Their plan—like all the plans of all the royal looters of the past—is only that the loot shall last their lifetime. It has always lasted before, because in one generation they could not run out of victims. But this time—*it will not last*. The victims are on strike. We are on strike against martyrdom—and against the moral code that demands it. We are on strike against those who believe that one man must exist for the sake of another. We are on strike against the morality of cannibals, be it practiced in body or in spirit. We will not deal with men on any terms but ours—and our terms are a moral code which holds that man is an end in himself and not the means to any end of others. We do not seek to force our code upon them. They are free to believe what they please. But, for once, they will have to believe it and to exist—without our help. And, once and for all, they will learn the meaning of their creed. That creed has lasted for centuries solely by the sanction of the victims—by means of the victims' acceptance of punishment for breaking a code impossible to practice. But that code was intended to be broken. It is a code that thrives not on those who observe it, but on those who don't, a morality kept in existence not by virtue of its saints, but by the grace of its sinners. We have decided not to be sinners any longer. We have ceased breaking that moral code. We shall blast it out of existence forever by the one method that it can't withstand: by obeying it. We are obeying it. We are complying. In dealing with our fellow men, we are observing their code of values to the letter and sparing them all the evils they denounce. The mind is evil? We have withdrawn the works of our minds from society, and not a single idea of ours is to be known or used by men. Ability is a selfish evil that leaves no chance to those who are less able? We have withdrawn from the competition and left all chances open to incompetents. The pursuit of wealth is greed, the root of all evil? We do not seek to make fortunes any longer. It is evil to earn more than one's bare sustenance? We take nothing but the lowliest jobs and we produce, by the effort of our muscles, no more than we consume for our immediate needs—with not a penny nor an inventive thought left over to harm the world. It is evil to succeed, since success is made by the strong at the expense of the weak? We have ceased burdening the weak with our ambition and have left them free to prosper without us. It is evil to be an employer? We have no employment to offer. It is evil to own property? We own nothing. It is evil to enjoy one's existence in this world? There is no form of enjoyment that we seek from their world, and—this was hardest for us to attain—what we now feel for their world is that emotion which they preach as an ideal: indifference—the blank—the zero—the mark of death. . . . We are giving men everything they've professed to want and to seek as virtue for centuries. Now let them see whether they want it."

"It was you who started this strike?" she asked.

"I did."

He got up, he stood, hands in pockets, his face in the light—and she saw him smile with the easy, effortless, implacable amusement of certainty.

"We've heard so much about strikes," he said, "and about the dependence of the uncommon man upon the common. We've heard it shouted that the industrialist is a parasite, that his workers support him, create his wealth, make his luxury possible—and what would happen to him if they walked out? Very well. I propose to show to the world who depends on whom, who supports whom, who is the source of wealth, who makes whose livelihood possible and what happens to whom when who walks out."

The windows were now sheets of darkness, reflecting the dots of lighted cigarettes. He picked a cigarette from a table beside him, and in the flare of a match she saw the brief sparkle of gold, the dollar sign, between his fingers.

"I quit and joined him and went on strike," said Hugh Akston, "because I could not share my profession with men who claim that the qualification of an intellectual consists of denying the existence of the intellect. People would not employ a plumber who'd attempt to prove his professional excellence by asserting that there's no such thing as plumbing—but, apparently, the same standards of caution are not considered necessary in regard to philosophers. I learned from my own pupil, however, that it was I who made this possible. When thinkers accept those who deny the existence of thinking, as fellow thinkers of a different school of thought—it is they who achieve the destruction of the mind. They grant the enemy's basic premise, thus granting the sanction of reason to formal dementia. A basic premise is an absolute that permits no co-operation with its antithesis and tolerates no tolerance. In the same manner and for the same reason as a banker may not accept and pass counterfeit money, granting it the sanction, honor and prestige of his bank, just as he may not grant the counterfeiter's demand for tolerance of a mere difference of opinion—so I may not grant the title of philosopher to Dr. Simon Pritchett or compete with him for the minds of men. Dr. Pritchett has nothing to deposit to the account of philosophy, except his declared intention to destroy it. He seeks to cash in—by means of denying it—on the power of reason among men. He seeks to stamp the mint-mark of reason upon the plans of his looting masters. He seeks to use the prestige of philosophy to purchase the enslavement of thought. But that prestige is an account which can exist only so long as I am there to sign the checks. Let him do it without me. Let him—and those who entrust to him their children's minds—have exactly that which they demand: a world of intellectuals without intellect and of thinkers who proclaim that they cannot think. I am conceding it. I am complying. And when they see the absolute reality of their non-absolute world, I will not be there and it will not be I who will pay the price of their contradictions."

"Dr. Akston quit on the principle of sound banking," said Midas Mulligan. "I quit on the principle of love. Love is the ultimate form of recognition one grants to superlative values. It was the Hunsacker case that made me quit—that case when a court of law ordered that I honor, as first right to my depositors' funds, the demand of those who would offer proof that they had no right to demand it. I was ordered to hand out money earned by men, to a worthless rotter whose only claim consisted of his inability to earn it. I was born on a farm. I knew the meaning of money. I had dealt with many men in my life. I had watched them grow. I had made my fortune by being able to spot a certain kind of man. The kind who never asked you for faith, hope and charity, but offered you facts, proof and profit. Did you know that I invested in Hank Rearden's business at the time when he was rising, when he had just beaten his way out of Minnesota to buy the steel mills in Pennsylvania? Well, when I looked at that court order on my desk, I had a vision. I saw a picture, and I saw it so clearly that it changed the looks of everything for me. I saw the bright face and the eyes of young Rearden, as he'd been when I'd met him first. I saw him lying at the foot of an altar, with his blood running down into the earth—and what stood on that altar was Lee Hunsacker, with the mucus-filled eyes, whining that he'd never had a chance. . . . It's strange how simple things become, once you see them clearly. It wasn't hard for me to close the bank and go: I kept seeing, for the first time in my life, what it was that I had lived for and loved."

She looked at Judge Narragansett. "You quit over the same case, didn't you?"

"Yes," said Judge Narragansett. "I quit when the court of appeals reversed my ruling. The purpose for which I had chosen my work, was my resolve to be a guardian of justice. But the laws they asked me to enforce made me the executor of the vilest injustice conceivable. I was asked to use force to violate the rights of disarmed men, who came before me to seek my protection for their rights. Litigants obey the verdict of a tribunal solely on the premise that there is an *objective* rule of conduct, which they both accept. Now I saw that one man was to be bound by it, but the other was not, one was to obey a rule, the other was to assert an arbitrary wish—his *need*—and the law was to stand on the side of the wish. Justice was to consist of upholding the unjustifiable. I quit—because I could not have borne to hear the words 'Your Honor' addressed to me by an honest man."

Her eyes moved slowly to Richard Halley, as if she were both pleading and afraid to hear his story. He smiled.

"I would have forgiven men for my struggle," said Richard Halley. "It was their view of my success that I could not forgive. I had felt no hatred in all the years when they rejected me. If my work was new, I had to give them time to learn, if I took pride in being first to break a trail to a height of my own, I had no right to complain if others were slow to follow. That was what I had told myself through all those years —except on some nights, when I could neither wait nor believe any longer, when I cried 'why?' but found no answer. Then, on the night when they chose to cheer me, I stood before them on the stage of a theater, thinking that this was the moment I had struggled to reach, wishing to feel it, but feeling nothing. I was seeing all the other nights behind me, hearing the 'why?' which still had no answer—and their cheers seemed as empty as their snubs. If they had said, 'Sorry to be so late, thank you for waiting'—I would have asked for nothing else and they could have had anything I had to give them. But what I saw in their faces, and in the way they spoke when they crowded to praise me, was the thing I had heard being preached to artists—only I had never believed that anyone human could mean it. They seemed to say that they owed me nothing, that their deafness had provided me with a moral goal, that it had been my duty to struggle, to suffer, to bear—for their sake—whatever sneers, contempt, injustice, torture *they* chose to inflict upon me, to bear it in order to teach them to enjoy my work, that this was their rightful due and my proper purpose. And then I understood the nature of the looter-in-spirit, a thing I had never been able to conceive. I saw them reaching into my soul, just as they reach into Mulligan's pocket, reaching to expropriate the value of my person, just as they reach to expropriate his wealth—I saw the impertinent malice of mediocrity boastfully holding up its own emptiness as an abyss to be filled by the bodies of its betters—I saw them seeking, just as they seek to feed on Mulligan's money, to feed on those hours when I wrote my music and on that which made me write it, seeking to gnaw their way to self-esteem by extorting from me the admission that *they* were the goal of my music, so that precisely by reason of my achievement, it would not be they who'd acknowledge my value, but I who would bow to theirs. . . . It was that night that I took the oath never to let them hear another note of mine. The streets were empty when I left that theater, I was the last one to leave—and I saw a man whom I had never seen before, waiting for me in the light of a lamppost. He did not have to tell me much. But the concerto I dedicated to him is called the Concerto of Deliverance."

She looked at the others. "Please tell me your reasons," she said, with a faint stress of firmness in her voice, as if she were taking a beating, but wished to take it to the end.

"I quit when medicine was placed under State control, some years ago," said Dr. Hendricks. "Do you know what it takes to perform a brain operation? Do you know the kind of skill it demands, and the years of passionate, merciless, excruciating devotion that go to acquire that skill? *That* was what I would not place at the disposal of men whose sole qualification to rule me was their capacity to spout the fraudulent generalities that got them elected to the privilege of enforcing their wishes at the point of a gun. I would not let them dictate the purpose for which my years of study had been spent, or the conditions of my work, or my choice of patients, or the amount of my reward. I observed that in all the discussions that preceded the enslavement of medicine, men discussed everything—except the desires of the doctors. Men considered only the 'welfare' of the patients, with no thought for those who were to provide it. That a doctor should have any right, desire or choice in the matter, was regarded as irrelevant selfishness; his is not to choose, they said, only 'to serve.' That a man who's willing to work under compulsion is too dangerous a brute to entrust with a job in the stockyards—never occurred to those who proposed to help the sick by making life impossible for the healthy. I have often wondered at the smugness with which people assert their right to enslave me, to control my work, to force my will, to violate my conscience, to stifle my mind—yet what is it that they expect to depend on, when they lie on an operating table under my hands? Their moral code has taught them to believe that it is safe to rely on the virtue of their victims. Well, that is the virtue I have withdrawn. Let them discover the kind of doctors that their system will now produce. Let them discover, in their operating rooms and hospital wards, that it is not safe to place their lives in the hands of a man whose life they have throttled. It is not safe, if he is the sort of man who resents it—and still less safe, if he is the sort who doesn't."

"I quit," said Ellis Wyatt, "because I didn't wish to serve as the cannibals' meal and to do the cooking, besides."

"I discovered," said Ken Danagger, "that the men I was fighting were impotent. The shiftless, the purposeless, the irresponsible, the irrational—it was not I who needed them, it was not theirs to dictate terms to me, it was not mine to obey demands. I quit, to let them discover it, too."

"I quit," said Quentin Daniels, "because, if there are degrees of damnation, the scientist who places his mind in the service of brute force is the longest-range murderer on earth."

They were silent. She turned to Galt. "And you?" she asked. "You were first. What made you come to it?"

He chuckled. "My refusal to be born with any original sin."

"What do you mean?"

"I have never felt guilty of my ability. I have never felt guilty of my mind. I have never felt guilty of being a man. I accepted no unearned guilt, and thus was free to earn and to know my own value. Ever since I can remember, I had felt that I would kill the man who'd claim that I exist for the sake of his need—and I had known that *this* was the highest moral feeling. That night, at the Twentieth Century meeting, when I heard an unspeakable evil being spoken in a tone of moral righteousness, I saw the root of the world's tragedy, the key to it and the solution. I saw what had to be done. I went out to do it."

"And the motor?" she asked. "Why did you abandon it? Why did you leave it to the Starnes heirs?"

"It was their father's property. He paid me for it. It was made on his time. But I knew that it would be of no benefit to them and that no one would ever hear of it again. It was my first experimental model. Nobody but me or my equivalent could have been able to complete it or even to grasp what it was. And I knew that no equivalent of mine would come near that factory from then on."

"You knew the kind of achievement your motor represented?"

"Yes."

"And you knew you were leaving it to perish?"

"Yes." He looked off into the darkness beyond the windows and chuckled softly, but it was not a sound of amusement. "I looked at my motor for the last time, before I left. I thought of the men who claim that wealth is a matter of natural resources—and of the men who claim that wealth is a matter of seizing the factories—and of the men who claim that machines condition their brains. Well, *there* was the motor to condition them, and there it remained as just exactly what it is without man's mind—as a pile of metal scraps and wires, going to rust. You have been thinking of the great service which that motor could have rendered to mankind, if it had been put into production. I think that on the day when men understand the meaning of its fate in that factory's junk heap—it will have rendered a greater one."

"Did you expect to see that day, when you left it?"

"No."

"Did you expect a chance to rebuild it elsewhere?"

"No."

"And you were willing to let it remain in a junk heap?"

"For the sake of what that motor meant to me," he said slowly, "I had to be willing to let it crumble and vanish forever"—he looked straight at her and she heard the steady, unhesitant, uninflected ruthlessness of his voice—"just as you will have to be willing to let the rail of Taggart Transcontinental crumble and vanish."

She held his eyes, her head was lifted, and she said softly, in the tone of a proudly open plea, "Don't make me answer you now."

"I won't. We'll tell you whatever you wish to know. We won't urge you to make a decision." He added, and she was shocked by the sudden gentleness of his voice, "I said that that kind of indifference toward a world which should have been ours was the hardest thing to attain. I know. We've all gone through it."

She looked at the quiet, impregnable room, and at the light—the light that came from his motor—on the faces of men who were the most serene and confident gathering she had ever attended.

"What did you do, when you walked out of the Twentieth Century?" she asked.

"I went out to become a flame-spotter. I made it my job to watch for those bright flares in the growing night of savagery, which were the men of ability, the men of the mind—to watch their course, their struggle and their agony—and to pull them out, when I knew that they had seen enough."

"What did you tell them to make them abandon everything?"

"I told them that they were right."

In answer to the silent question of her glance, he added, "I gave them the pride they did not know they had. I gave them the words to identify it. I gave them that priceless possession which they had missed, had longed for, yet had not known they needed: a moral sanction. Did you call me the destroyer and the hunter of men? I was the walking delegate of this strike, the leader of the victims' rebellion, the defender of the oppressed, the disinherited, the exploited—and when *I* use these words, they have, for once, a literal meaning."

"Who were the first to follow you?"

He let a moment pass, in deliberate emphasis, then answered, "My two best friends. You know one of them. You know, perhaps better than anyone else, what price he paid for it. Our own teacher, Dr. Akston, was next. He joined us within one evening's conversation. William Hastings, who had been my boss in the research laboratory of Twentieth Century Motors, had a hard time, fighting it out with himself. It took him a year. But he joined. Then Richard Halley. Then Midas Mulligan."

"—who took fifteen minutes," said Mulligan.

She turned to him. "It was you who established this valley?"

"Yes," said Mulligan. "It was just my own private retreat, at first. I bought it years ago, I bought miles of these mountains, section by section, from ranchers and cattlemen who didn't know what they owned. The valley is not listed on any map. I built this house, when I decided to quit. I cut off all possible avenues of approach, except one road—and it's camouflaged beyond anyone's power to discover—and I stocked this place to be self-supporting, so that I could live here for the rest of my life and never have to see the face of a looter. When I heard that John had got Judge Narragansett, too, I invited the Judge to come here. Then we asked Richard Halley to join us. The others remained outside, at first."

"We had no rules of any kind," said Galt, "except one. When a man took our oath, it meant a single commitment: not to work in his own profession, not to give to the world the benefit of his mind. Each of us carried it out in any manner he chose. Those who had money, retired to live on their savings. Those who had to work, took the lowest jobs they could find. Some of us had been famous; others—like that young brakeman of yours, whom Halley discovered—were stopped by us before they had set out to get tortured. But we did not give up our minds or the work we loved. Each of us continued in his real profession, in whatever manner and spare time he could manage—but he did it secretly, for his own sole benefit, giving nothing to men, sharing nothing. We were scattered all over the country, as the outcasts we had always been, only now we accepted our parts with conscious intention. Our sole relief were the rare occasions when we could see one another. We found that we liked to meet—in order to be reminded that human beings still existed. So we came to set aside one month a year to spend in this valley—to rest, to live in a rational world, to bring our real work out of hiding, to trade our achievements—here, where achievements meant payment, not expropriation. Each of us built his own house here, at his own expense—for one month of life out of twelve. It made the eleven easier to bear."

"You see, Miss Taggart," said Hugh Akston, "man *is* a social being, but not in the way the looters preach."

"It's the destruction of Colorado that started the growth of this valley," said Midas Mulligan. "Ellis Wyatt and the others came to live here permanently, because they had to hide. Whatever part of their wealth they could salvage, they converted into gold or machines, as I had, and they brought it here. There were enough of us to develop the place and to create jobs for those who had had to earn their living outside. We have now reached the stage where most of us can live here full time. The valley is almost self-supporting—and as to the goods that we can't yet produce, I purchase them from the outside through a pipe line of my own. It's a special agent, a man who does not let my money reach the looters. We are not a state here, not a society of any kind— we're just a voluntary association of men held together by nothing but every man's self-interest. I own the valley and I sell the land to the others, when they want it. Judge Narragansett is to act as our arbiter, in case of disagreements. He hasn't had to be called upon, as yet. They say that it's hard for men to agree. You'd be surprised how easy it is—when both parties hold as their moral absolute that neither exists for the sake of the other and that reason is their only means of trade. The time is approaching when all of us will have to be called to live here—because the world is falling apart so fast that it will soon be starving. But we will be able to support ourselves in this valley."

"The world is crashing faster than we expected," said Hugh Akston. "Men are stopping and giving up. Your frozen trains, the gangs of raiders, the deserters, they're men who've never heard of us, and they're not part of our strike, they are acting on their own—it's the natural response of whatever rationality is still left in them—it's the same kind of protest as ours."

"We started with no time limit in view," said Galt. "We did not know whether we'd live to see the liberation of the world or whether we'd have to leave our battle and our secret to the next generations. We knew only that this was the only way we cared to live. But now we think that we will see, and soon, the day of our victory and of our return."

"When?" she whispered.

"When the code of the looters has collapsed."

He saw her looking at him, her glance half-question, half-hope, and he added, "When the creed of self-immolation has run, for once, its undisguised course—when men find no victims ready to obstruct the path of justice and to deflect the fall of retribution on themselves—when the preachers of self-sacrifice discover that those who are willing to practice it, have nothing to sacrifice, and those who have, are not willing any longer—when men see that neither their hearts nor their muscles can save them, but the mind they damned is not there to answer their screams for help—when they collapse as they must, as men without mind—when they have no pretense of authority left, no remnant of law, no trace of morality, no hope, no food and no way to obtain it—when they collapse and the road is clear—then we'll come back to rebuild the world."

The Taggart Terminal, she thought; she heard the words beating through the numbness of her mind, as the sum of a burden she had not had time to weigh. *This* was the Taggart Terminal, she thought, this room, not the giant concourse in New York—this was her goal, the end of track, the point beyond the curve of the earth where the two straight lines of rail met and vanished, drawing her forward—as they had drawn Nathaniel Taggart—this was the goal Nathaniel Taggart had seen in the distance and this was the point still holding the straight-line glance of his lifted head above the spiral motion of men in the granite concourse. It was for the sake of this that she had dedicated herself to the rail of Taggart Transcontinental, as to the body of a spirit yet to be found. She had found it, everything she had ever wanted, it was here in this room, reached and hers—but the price was that net of rail behind her, the rail that would vanish, the bridges that would crumble, the signal lights that would go out. . . . And yet . . . Everything I had ever wanted, she thought—looking away from the figure of a man with sun-colored hair and implacable eyes.

"You don't have to answer us now."

She raised her head; he was watching her as if he had followed the steps in her mind.

"We never demand agreement," he said. "We never tell anyone more than he is ready to hear. You are the first person who has learned our secret ahead of time. But you're here and you had to know. Now you know the exact nature of the choice you'll have to make. If it seems hard, it's because you still think that it does not have to be one or the other. You will learn that it does."

"Will you give me time?"

"Your time is not ours to give. Take your time. You alone can decide what you'll choose to do, and when. We know the cost of that decision. We've paid it. That you've come here might now make it easier for you—or harder."

"Harder," she whispered.

"I know."

He said it, his voice as low as hers, with the same sound of being forced past one's breath, and she missed an instant of time, as in the stillness after a blow, because she felt that this—not the moments when he had carried her in his arms down the mountainside, but this meeting of their voices—had been the closest physical contact between them.

A full moon stood in the sky above the valley, when they drove back to his house; it stood like a flat, round lantern without rays, with a haze of light hanging in space, not reaching the ground, and the illumination seemed to come from the abnormal white brightness of the soil. In the unnatural stillness of sight without color, the earth seemed veiled by a film of distance, its shapes did not merge into a landscape, but went slowly flowing past, like the print of a photograph on a cloud. She noticed suddenly that she was smiling. She was looking down at the houses of the valley. Their lighted windows were dimmed by a bluish cast, the outlines of their walls were dissolving, long bands of mist were coiling among them in torpid, unhurried waves. It looked like a city sinking under water.

"What do they call this place?" she asked.

"I call it Mulligan's Valley," he said. "The others call it Galt's Gulch."

"I'd call it—" but she did not finish.

He glanced at her. She knew what he saw in her face. He turned away.

She saw a faint movement of his lips, like the release of a breath that he was forcing to function. She dropped her glance, her arm falling against the side of the car, as if her hand were suddenly too heavy for the weakness in the crook of her elbow.

The road grew darker, as it went higher, and pine branches met over their heads. Above a slant of rock moving to meet them, she saw the moonlight on the windows of his house. Her head fell back against the seat and she lay still, losing awareness of the car, feeling only the motion that carried her forward, watching the glittering drops of water in the pine branches, which were the stars.

When the car stopped, she did not permit herself to know why she did not look at him as she stepped out. She did not know that she stood still for an instant, looking up at the dark windows. She did not hear him approach; but she felt the impact of his hands with shocking intensity, as if it were the only awareness she could now experience. He lifted her in his arms and started slowly up the path to the house.

He walked, not looking at her, holding her tight, as if trying to hold a progression of time, as if his arms were still locked over the moment when he had lifted her against his chest. She felt his steps as if they were a single span of motion to a goal and as if each step were a separate moment in which she dared not think of the next. Her head was close to his, his hair brushing her cheek, and she knew that neither of them would move his face that one breath closer. It was a sudden, stunned state of quiet drunkenness, complete in itself, their hair mingled like the rays of two bodies in space that had achieved their meeting, she saw that he walked with his eyes closed, as if even sight would now be an intrusion.

He entered the house, and as he moved across the living room, he did not look to his left and neither did she, but she knew that both of them were seeing the door on his left that led to his bedroom. He walked the length of the darkness to the wedge of moonlight that fell across the guest-room bed, he placed her down upon it, she felt an instant's pause of his hands still holding her shoulder and waistline, and when his hands left her body, she knew that the moment was over.

He stepped back and pressed a switch, surrendering the room to the harshly public glare of light. He stood still, as if demanding that she look at him, his face expectant and stern.

"Have you forgotten that you wanted to shoot me on sight?" he asked.

It was the unprotected stillness of his figure that made it real. The shudder that threw her upright was like a cry of terror and denial; but she held his glance and answered evenly, "That's true. I did."

"Then stand by it."

Her voice was low, its intensity was both a surrender and a scornful reproach: "You know better than that, don't you?"

He shook his head. "No. I want you to remember that that had been your wish. You were right, in the past. So long as you were part of the outer world, you had to seek to destroy me. And of the two courses now open to you, one will lead you to the day when you will find yourself forced to do it." She did not answer, she sat looking down, he saw the strands of her hair swing jerkily as she shook her head in desperate protest. "You are my only danger. You are the only person who could deliver me to my enemies. If you remain with them, you will. Choose that, if you wish, but choose it with full knowledge. Don't answer me now. But until you do"—the stress of severity in his voice was the sound of effort directed against himself—"remember that I know the meaning of either answer."

"As fully as I do?" she whispered.

"As fully."

He turned to go, when her eyes fell suddenly upon the inscriptions she had noticed, and forgotten, on the walls of the room.

They were cut into the polish of the wood, still showing the force of the pencil's pressure in the hands that had made them, each in his own violent writing: "You'll get over it—Ellis Wyatt" "It will be all right by morning—Ken Danagger" "It's worth it—Roger Marsh." There were others.

"What is that?" she asked.

He smiled. "This is the room where they spent their first night in the valley. The first night is the hardest. It's the last pull of the break with one's memories, and the worst. I let them stay here, so they can call for me, if they want me. I speak to them, if they can't sleep. Most of them can't. But they're free of it by morning. . . . They've all gone through this room. Now they call it the torture chamber or the anteroom—because everyone has to enter the valley through my house."

He turned to go, he stopped on the threshold and added:

"This is the room I never intended you to occupy. Good night, Miss Taggart."

THE UTOPIA OF GREED

"Good morning."

She looked at him across the living room from the threshold of her door. In the windows behind him, the mountains had that tinge of silver-pink which seems brighter than daylight, with the promise of a light to come. The sun had risen somewhere over the earth, but it had not reached the top of the barrier, and the sky was glowing in its stead, announcing its motion. She had heard the joyous greeting to the sunrise, which was not the song of birds, but the ringing of the telephone a moment ago; she saw the start of day, not in the shining green of the branches outside, but in the glitter of chromium on the stove, the sparkle of a glass ashtray on a table, and the crisp whiteness of his shirt sleeves. Irresistibly, she heard the sound of a smile in her own voice, matching his, as she answered:

"Good morning."

He was gathering notes of penciled calculations from his desk and stuffing them into his pocket. "I have to go down to the powerhouse," he said. "They've just phoned me that they're having trouble with the ray screen. Your plane seems to have knocked it off key. I'll be back in half an hour and then I'll cook our breakfast."

It was the casual simplicity of his voice, the manner of taking her presence and their domestic routine for granted, as if it were of no significance to them, that gave her the sense of an underscored significance and the feeling that he knew it.

She answered as casually, "If you'll bring me the cane I left in the car, I'll have breakfast ready for you by the time you come back."

He glanced at her with a slight astonishment; his eyes moved from her bandaged ankle to the short sleeves of the blouse that left her arms bare to display the heavy bandage on her elbow. But the transparent blouse, the open collar, the hair falling down to the shoulders that seemed innocently naked under a thin film of cloth, made her look like a schoolgirl, not an invalid, and her posture made the bandages look irrelevant.

He smiled, not quite at her, but as if in amusement at some sudden memory of his own. "If you wish," he said.

It was strange to be left alone in his house. Part of it was an emotion she had never experienced before: an awed respect that made her hesitantly conscious of her hands, as if to touch any object around her would be too great an intimacy. The other part was a reckless sense of ease, a sense of being at home in this place, as if she owned its owner.

It was strange to feel so pure a joy in the simple task of preparing a breakfast. The work seemed an end in itself, as if the motions of filling a coffee pot, squeezing oranges, slicing bread were performed for their own sake, for the sort of pleasure one expects, but seldom finds, in the motions of dancing. It startled her to realize that she had not experienced this kind of pleasure in her work since her days at the operator's desk in Rockdale Station.

She was setting the table, when she saw the figure of a man hurrying up the path to the house, a swift, agile figure that leaped over boulders with the casual ease of a flight. He threw the door open, calling, "Hey, John!"—and stopped short as he saw her. He wore a dark blue sweater and slacks, he had gold hair and a face of such shocking perfection of beauty that she stood still, staring at him, not in admiration, at first, but in simple disbelief.

He looked at her as if he had not expected to find a woman in this house. Then she saw a look of recognition melting into a different kind of astonishment, part amusement, part triumph melting into a chuckle. "Oh, have *you* joined us?" he asked.

"No," she answered dryly, "I haven't. I'm a scab."

He laughed, like an adult at a child who uses technological words beyond its understanding. "If you know what you're saying, you know that it's not possible," he said. "Not here."

"I crashed the gate. Literally."

He looked at her bandages, weighing the question, his glance almost insolent in its open curiosity. "When?"

"Yesterday."

"How?"

"In a plane."

"What were you doing in a plane in this part of the country?"

He had the direct, imperious manner of an aristocrat or a roughneck; he looked like one and was dressed like the other. She considered him for a moment, deliberately letting him wait. "I was trying to land on a prehistorical mirage," she answered. "And I have."

"You *are* a scab," he said, and chuckled, as if grasping all the implications of the problem. "Where's John?"

"Mr. Galt is at the powerhouse. He should be back any moment."

He sat down in an armchair, asking no permission, as if he were at home. She turned silently to her work. He sat watching her movements with an open grin, as if the sight of her laying out cutlery on a kitchen table were the spectacle of some special paradox.

"What did Francisco say when he saw you here?" he asked.

She turned to him with a slight jolt, but answered evenly, "He is not here yet."

"Not yet?" He seemed startled. "Are you sure?"

"So I was told."

He lighted a cigarette. She wondered, watching him, what profession he had chosen, loved and abandoned in order to join this valley. She could make no guess; none seemed to fit; she caught herself in the preposterous feeling of wishing that he had no profession at all, because any work seemed too dangerous for his incredible kind of beauty. It was an impersonal feeling, she did not look at him as at a man, but as at an animated work of art—and it seemed to be a stressed indignity of the outer world that a perfection such as his should be subjected to the shocks, the strains, the scars reserved for any man who loved his work. But the feeling seemed the more preposterous, because the lines of his face had the sort of hardness for which no danger on earth was a match.

"No, Miss Taggart," he said suddenly, catching her glance, "you've never seen me before."

She was shocked to realize that she had been studying him openly. "How do you happen to know who I am?" she asked.

"First, I've seen your pictures in the papers many times. Second, you're the only woman left in the outer world, to the best of our knowledge, who'd be allowed to enter Galt's Gulch. Third, you're the only woman who'd have the courage—and prodigality—still to remain a scab."

"What made you certain that I was a scab?"

"If you weren't, you'd know that it's not this valley, but the view of life held by men in the outer world that is a prehistorical mirage."

They heard the sound of the motor and saw the car stopping below, in front of the house. She noticed the swiftness with which he rose to his feet at the sight of Galt in the car; if it were not for the obvious personal eagerness, it would have looked like an instinctive gesture of military respect.

She noticed the way Galt stopped, when he entered and saw his visitor. She noticed that Galt smiled, but that his voice was oddly low, almost solemn, as if weighted with unconfessed relief, when he said very quietly, "Hello."

"Hi, John," said the visitor gaily.

She noticed that their handshake came an instant too late and lasted an instant too long, like the handshake of men who had not been certain that their previous meeting would not be their last.

Galt turned to her. "Have you met?" he asked, addressing them both.

"Not exactly," said the visitor.

"Miss Taggart, may I present Ragnar Danneskjöld?"

She knew what her face had looked like, when she heard Danneskjöld's voice as from a great distance: "You don't have to be frightened, Miss Taggart. I'm not dangerous to anyone in Galt's Gulch."

She could only shake her head, before she recaptured her voice to say, "It's not what you're doing to anyone . . . it's what they're doing to *you.* . . ."

His laughter swept her out of her moment's stupor. "Be careful, Miss Taggart. If that's how you're beginning to feel, you won't remain a scab for long." He added, "But you ought to start by adopting the right things from the people in Galt's Gulch, not their mistakes: they've spent twelve years worrying about me—needlessly." He glanced at Galt.

"When did you get in?" asked Galt.

"Late last night."

"Sit down. You're going to have breakfast with us."

"But where's Francisco? Why isn't he here yet?"

"I don't know," said Galt, frowning slightly. "I asked at the airport, just now. Nobody's heard from him."

As she turned to the kitchen, Galt moved to follow. "No," she said, "it's my job today."

"Let me help you."

"This is the place where one doesn't ask for help, isn't it?"

He smiled. "That's right."

She had never experienced the pleasure of motion, of walking as if her feet had no weight to carry, as if the support of the cane in her hand were merely a superfluous touch of elegance, the pleasure of feeling her steps trace swift, straight lines, of sensing the faultless, spontaneous precision of her gestures—as she experienced it while placing their food on the table in front of the two men. Her bearing told them that she knew they were watching her—she held her head like an actress on a stage, like a woman in a ballroom, like the winner of a silent contest.

"Francisco will be glad to know that it's you who were his stand-in today," said Danneskjöld, when she joined them at the table.

"His what?"

"You see, today is June first, and the three of us—John, Francisco and I—have had breakfast together on every June first for twelve years."

"Here?"

"Not when we started. But here, ever since this house was built eight years ago." He shrugged, smiling. "For a man who has more centuries of tradition behind him than I have, it's odd that Francisco should be the first to break our own tradition."

"And Mr. Galt?" she asked. "How many centuries does he have behind him?"

"John? None at all. None behind him—but all of those ahead."

"Never mind the centuries," said Galt. "Tell me what sort of year you've had behind you. Lost any men?"

"No."

"Lost any of your time?"

"You mean, was I wounded? No. I haven't had a scratch since that one time, ten years ago, when I was still an amateur, which you ought to forget by now. I wasn't in any danger whatever, this year—in fact, I was much more safe than if I were running a small-town drugstore under Directive 10-289."

"Lost any battles?"

"No. The losses were all on the other side, this year. The looters lost most of their ships to me—and most of their men to you. You've had a good year, too, haven't you? I know, I've kept track of it. Since our last breakfast together, you got everyone you wanted from the state of Colorado, and a few others besides, such as Ken Danagger, who was a great prize to get. But let me tell you about a still greater one, who is almost yours. You're going to get him soon, because he's hanging by a thin thread and is just about ready to fall at your feet. He's a man who saved my life—so you can see how far he's gone."

Galt leaned back, his eyes narrowing. "So you weren't in any danger whatever, were you?"

Danneskjöld laughed. "Oh, I took a slight risk. It was worth it. It was the most enjoyable encounter I've ever had. I've been waiting to tell you about it in person. It's a story you'll want to hear. Do you know who the man was? Hank Rearden. I—"

"No!"

It was Galt's voice; it was a command; the brief snap of sound had a tinge of violence neither of them had ever heard from him before.

"What?" asked Danneskjöld softly, incredulously.

"Don't tell me about it now."

"But you've always said that Hank Rearden was the one man you wanted to see here most."

"I still do. But you'll tell me later."

She studied Galt's face intently, but she could find no clue, only a closed, impersonal look, either of determination or of control, that tightened the skin of his cheekbones and the line of his mouth. No matter what he knew about her, she thought, the only knowledge that could explain this, was a knowledge he had had no way of acquiring.

"You've met Hank Rearden?" she asked, turning to Danneskjöld. "And he saved your life?"

"Yes."

"I want to hear about it."

"I don't," said Galt.

"Why not?"

"You're not one of us, Miss Taggart."

"I see." She smiled, with a faint touch of defiance. "Were you thinking that I might prevent you from getting Hank Rearden?"

"No, that was not what I was thinking."

She noticed that Danneskjöld was studying Galt's face, as if he, too, found the incident inexplicable. Galt held his glance, deliberately and openly, as if challenging him to find the explanation and promising that he would fail. She knew that Danneskjöld had failed, when she saw a faint crease of humor softening Galt's eyelids.

"What else," asked Galt, "have you accomplished this year?"

"I've defied the law of gravitation."

"You've always done that. In what particular form now?"

"In the form of a flight from mid-Atlantic to Colorado in a plane loaded with gold beyond the safety point of its capacity. Wait till Midas sees the amount I have to deposit. My customers, this year, will become richer by— Say, have you told Miss Taggart that she's one of my customers?"

"No, not yet. You may tell her, if you wish."

"I'm—What did you say I am?" she asked.

"Don't be shocked, Miss Taggart," said Danneskjöld. "And don't object. I'm used to objections. I'm a sort of freak here, anyway. None of them approve of my particular method of fighting our battle. John doesn't, Dr. Akston doesn't. They think that my life is too valuable for it. But, you see, my father was a bishop—and of all his teachings there was only one sentence that I accepted: 'All they that take the sword shall perish with the sword.' "

"What do you mean?"

"That violence is not practical. If my fellow men believe that the force of the combined tonnage of their muscles is a practical means to rule me—let them learn the outcome of a contest in which there's nothing but brute force on one side, and force ruled by a mind, on the other. Even John grants me that in our age I had the moral right to choose the course I've chosen. I am doing just what he is doing— only in my own way. He is withdrawing man's spirit from the looters, I'm withdrawing the products of man's spirit. He is depriving them of reason, I'm depriving them of wealth. He is draining the soul of the world, I'm draining its body. His is the lesson they have to learn, only I'm impatient and I'm hastening their scholastic progress. But, like John, I'm simply complying with their moral code and refusing to grant them a double standard at my expense. Or at Rearden's expense. Or at yours."

"What are you talking about?"

"About a method of taxing the income taxers. All methods of taxation are complex, but this one is very simple, because it's the naked essence of all the others. Let me explain it to you."

She listened. She heard a sparkling voice reciting, in the tone of a dryly meticulous bookkeeper, a report about financial transfers, bank accounts, income-tax returns, as if he were reading the dusty pages of a ledger—a ledger where every entry was made by means of offering his own blood as the collateral to be drained at any moment, at any slip of his bookkeeping pen. As she listened, she kept seeing the perfection of his face—and she kept thinking that this was the head on which the world had placed a price of millions for the purpose of delivering it to the rot of death. . . . The face she had thought too beautiful for the scars of a productive career—she kept thinking numbly, missing half his words—the face too beautiful to risk. . . . Then it struck her that his physical perfection was only a simple illustration, a childish lesson given to her in crudely obvious terms on the nature of the outer world and on the fate of any human value in a subhuman age. Whatever the justice or the evil of his course, she thought, how could they . . . no! she thought, his course *was* just, and this was the horror of it, that there was no other course for justice to select, that she could not condemn him, that she could neither approve nor utter a word of reproach.

". . . and the names of my customers, Miss Taggart, were chosen slowly, one by one. I had to be certain of the nature of their character and career. On my list of restitution, your name was one of the first."

She forced herself to keep her face expressionlessly tight, and she answered only, "I see."

"Your account is one of the last left unpaid. It is here, at the Mulligan Bank, to be claimed by you on the day when you join us."

"I see."

"Your account, however, is not as large as some of the others, even though huge sums were extorted from you by force in the past twelve years. You will find—as it is marked on the copies of your income-tax returns which Mulligan will hand over to you—that I have refunded only those taxes which you paid on the salary you earned as Operating Vice-President, but not the taxes you paid on your income from your Taggart Transcontinental stock. You deserved every penny of that stock, and in the days of your father I would have refunded every penny of your profit—but under your brother's management, Taggart Transcontinental has taken its share of the looting, it has made profits by force, by means of government favors, subsidies, moratoriums, directives. You were not responsible for it, you were, in fact, the greatest victim of that policy—but I refund only the money which was made by pure productive ability, not the money any part of which was loot taken by force."

"I see."

They had finished their breakfast. Danneskjöld lighted a cigarette and watched her for an instant through the first jet of smoke, as if he knew the violence of the conflict in her mind—then he grinned at Galt and rose to his feet.

"I'll run along," he said. "My wife is waiting for me."

"What?" she gasped.

"My wife," he repeated gaily, as if he had not understood the reason of her shock.

"Who is your wife?"

"Kay Ludlow."

The implications that struck her were more than she could bear to consider. "When . . . when were you married?"

"Four years ago."

"How could you show yourself anywhere long enough to go through a wedding ceremony?"

"We were married here, by Judge Narragansett."

"How can"—she tried to stop, but the words burst involuntarily, in helplessly indignant protest, whether against him, fate or the outer world, she could not tell—"how can she live through eleven months of thinking that you, at any moment, might be . . . ?" She did not finish.

He was smiling, but she saw the enormous solemnity of that which he and his wife had needed to earn their right to this kind of smile. "She can live through it, Miss Taggart, because we do not hold the belief that this earth is a realm of misery where man is doomed to destruction. We do not think that tragedy is our natural fate and we do not live in chronic dread of disaster. We do not expect disaster until we have specific reason to expect it—and when we encounter it, we are free to fight it. It is not happiness, but suffering that we consider unnatural. It is not success, but calamity that we regard as the abnormal exception in human life."

Galt accompanied him to the door, then came back, sat down at the table and in a leisurely manner reached for another cup of coffee.

She shot to her feet, as if flung by a jet of pressure breaking a safety valve. "Do you think that I'll ever accept his money?"

He waited until the curving streak of coffee had filled his cup, then glanced up at her and answered, "Yes, I think so."

"Well, I won't! I won't let him risk his life for it!"

"You have no choice about that."

"I have the choice never to claim it!"

"Yes, you have."

"Then it will lie in that bank till doomsday!"

"No, it won't. If you don't claim it, some part of it—a very small part—will be turned over to me in your name."

"In *my* name? Why?"

"To pay for your room and board."

She stared at him, her look of anger switching to bewilderment, then dropped slowly back on her chair.

He smiled. "How long did you think you were going to stay here, Miss Taggart?" He saw her startled look of helplessness. "You haven't thought of it? I have. You're going to stay here for a month. For the one month of our vacation, like the rest of us. I am not asking for your consent—you did not ask for ours when you came here. You broke our rules, so you'll have to take the consequences. Nobody leaves the valley during this month. I could let you go, of course, but I won't.

There's no rule demanding that I hold you, but by forcing your way here, you've given me the right to any choice I make—and I'm going to hold you simply because I want you here. If, at the end of a month, you decide that you wish to go back, you will be free to do so. Not until then."

She sat straight, the planes of her face relaxed, the shape of her mouth softened by the faint, purposeful suggestion of a smile; it was the dangerous smile of an adversary, but her eyes were coldly brilliant and veiled at once, like the eyes of an adversary who fully intends to fight, but hopes to lose.

"Very well," she said.

"I shall charge you for your room and board—it *is* against our rules to provide the unearned sustenance of another human being. Some of us have wives and children, but there is a mutual trade involved in that, and a mutual payment"—he glanced at her—"of a kind I am not entitled to collect. So I shall charge you fifty cents a day and you will pay me when you accept the account that lies in your name at the Mulligan Bank. If you don't accept the account, Mulligan will charge your debt against it and he will give me the money when I ask for it."

"I shall comply with your terms," she answered; her voice had the shrewd, confident, deliberating slowness of a trader. "But I shall not permit the use of that money for my debts."

"How else do you propose to comply?"

"I propose to earn my room and board."

"By what means?"

"By working."

"In what capacity?"

"In the capacity of your cook and housemaid."

For the first time, she saw him take the shock of the unexpected, in a manner and with a violence she had not foreseen. It was only an explosion of laughter on his part—but he laughed as if he were hit beyond his defenses, much beyond the immediate meaning of her words; she felt that she had struck his past, tearing loose some memory and meaning of his own which she could not know. He laughed as if he were seeing some distant image, as if he were laughing in its face, as if this were his victory—and hers.

"If you will hire me," she said, her face severely polite, her tone harshly clear, impersonal and businesslike, "I shall cook your meals, clean your house, do your laundry and perform such other duties as are required of a servant—in exchange for my room, board and such money as I will need for some items of clothing. I may be slightly handicapped by my injuries for the next few days, but that will not last and I will be able to do the job fully."

"Is that what you want to do?" he asked.

"That is what I want to do—" she answered, and stopped before she uttered the rest of the answer in her mind: more than anything else in the world.

He was still smiling, it was a smile of amusement, but it was as if amusement could be transmuted into some shining glory. "All right, Miss Taggart," he said, "I'll hire you."

She inclined her head in a dryly formal acknowledgment. "Thank you."

"I will pay you ten dollars a month, in addition to your room and board."

"Very well."

"I shall be the first man in this valley to hire a servant." He got up, reached into his pocket and threw a five-dollar gold piece down on the table. "As advance on your wages," he said.

She was startled to discover, as her hand reached for the gold piece, that she felt the eager, desperate, tremulous hope of a young girl on her first job: the hope that she would be able to deserve it.

"Yes, sir," she said, her eyes lowered.

*   *   *

Owen Kellogg arrived on the afternoon of her third day in the valley.

She did not know which shocked him most: the sight of her standing on the edge of the airfield as he descended from the plane—the sight of her clothes: her delicate, transparent blouse, tailored by the most expensive shop in New York, and the wide, cotton-print skirt she had bought in the valley for sixty cents—her cane, her bandages or the basket of groceries on her arm.

He descended among a group of men, he saw her, he stopped, then ran to her as if flung forward by some emotion so strong that, whatever its nature, it looked like terror.

"Miss Taggart . . ." he whispered—and said nothing else, while she laughed, trying to explain how she had come to beat him to his destination.

He listened, as if it were irrelevant, and then he uttered the thing from which he had to recover, "But we thought you were dead."

"Who thought it?"

"All of us . . . I mean, everybody in the outside world."

Then she suddenly stopped smiling, while his voice began to recapture his story and his first sound of joy.

"Miss Taggart, don't you remember? You told me to phone Winston, Colorado, and to tell them that you'd be there by noon of the next day. That was to be the day before yesterday, May thirty-first. But you did not reach Winston—and by late afternoon, the news was on all the radios that you were lost in a plane crash somewhere in the Rocky Mountains."

She nodded slowly, grasping the events she had not thought of considering.

knew the reason of her query, "Do you wish to ask for a special exception?"

"No," she answered, holding his glance.

Next morning, after breakfast, when she sat in her room, carefully placing a patch on the sleeve of Galt's shirt, with her door closed, not to let him see her fumbling effort at an unfamiliar task, she heard the sound of a car stopping in front of the house.

She heard Galt's steps hurrying across the living room, she heard him jerk the entrance door open and call out with the joyous anger of relief: "It's about time!"

She rose to her feet, but stopped: she heard his voice, its tone abruptly changed and grave, as if in answer to the shock of some sight confronting him: "What's the matter?"

"Hello, John," said a clear, quiet voice that sounded steady, but weighted with exhaustion.

She sat down on her bed, feeling suddenly drained of strength: the voice was Francisco's.

She heard Galt asking, his tone severe with concern, "What is it?"

"I'll tell you afterwards."

"Why are you so late?"

"I have to leave again in an hour."

"To *leave?*"

"John, I just came to tell you that I won't be able to stay here this year."

There was a pause, then Galt asked gravely, his voice low, "Is it as bad as that—whatever it is?"

"Yes. I . . . I might be back before the month is over. I don't know." He added, with the sound of a desperate effort, "I don't know whether to hope to be done with it quickly or . . . or not."

"Francisco, could you stand a shock right now?"

"I? Nothing could shock me now."

"There's a person, here, in my guest room, whom you have to see. It will be a shock to you, so I think I'd better warn you in advance that this person is still a scab."

"*What?* A scab? In *your* house?"

"Let me tell you how—"

"That's something I want to see for myself!"

She heard Francisco's contemptuous chuckle and the rush of his steps, she saw her door flung open, and she noticed dimly that it was Galt who closed it, leaving them alone.

She did not know how long Francisco stood looking at her, because the first moment that she grasped fully was when she saw him on his knees, holding onto her, his face pressed to her legs, the moment when she felt as if the shudder that ran through his body and left him still, had run into hers and made her able to move.

She saw, in astonishment, that her hand was moving gently over his hair, while she was thinking that she had no right to do it and feeling as if a current of serenity were flowing from her hand, enveloping them both, smoothing the past. He did not move, he made no sound, as if the act of holding her said everything he had to say.

When he raised his head, he looked as she had felt when she had opened her eyes in the valley: he looked as if no pain had ever existed in the world. He was laughing.

"Dagny, Dagny, Dagny"—his voice sounded, not as if a confession resisted for years were breaking out, but as if he were repeating the long since known, laughing at the pretense that it had ever been unsaid —"of course I love you. Were you afraid when he made me say it? I'll say it as often as you wish—I love you, darling, I love you, I always will—don't be afraid for me, I don't care if I'll never have you again, what does that matter?—you're alive and you're here and you know everything now. And it's so simple, isn't it? Do you see what it was and why I had to desert you?" His arm swept out to point at the valley. "There it is—it's *your* earth, *your* kingdom, *your* kind of world—Dagny, I've always loved you and that I deserted you, *that* was my love."

He took her hands and pressed them to his lips and held them, not moving, not as a kiss, but as a long moment of rest—as if the effort of speech were a distraction from the fact of her presence, and as if he were torn by too many things to say, by the pressure of all the words stored in the silence of years.

"The women I chased—you didn't believe that, did you? I've never touched one of them—but I think you knew it, I think you've known it all along. The playboy—it was a part that I had to play in order not to let the looters suspect me while I was destroying d'Anconia Copper in plain sight of the whole world. That's the joker in their system, they're out to fight any man of honor and ambition, but let them see a worthless rotter and they think he's a friend, they think he's safe—*safe!*—that's their view of life, but are they learning!—are they learning whether evil is safe and incompetence practical! . . . Dagny, it was the night when I knew, for the first time, that I loved you—it was then that I knew I had to go. It was when you entered my hotel room, that night, when I saw what you looked like, what you were, what you meant to me—and what awaited you in the future. Had you been less, you might have stopped me for a while. But it was you, *you* who were the final argument that made me leave you. I asked for your help, that night—against John Galt. But I knew that you were his best weapon against me, though neither you nor he could know it. You were everything that he was seeking, everything he told us to live for or die, if necessary. . . . I was ready for him, when he called me suddenly to come to New York, that spring. I had not heard from him for some time. He was fighting the same problem I was. He solved it. . . . Do you remember? It was the time when you did not hear from me for three years. Dagny, when I took over my father's business, when I began to deal with the whole industrial system of the world, it was then that I began to see the nature of the evil I had suspected, but thought too monstrous to believe. I saw the tax-collecting vermin that had grown for centuries like mildew on d'Anconia Copper, draining us by no right that anyone could name—I saw the government regulations passed to cripple me, because I was successful, and to help my competitors, because they were loafing failures—I saw the labor unions who won every claim against me, by reason of my ability to make their livelihood possible—I saw that any man's desire for money he could not earn was regarded as a righteous wish, but if he earned it, it was damned as greed—I saw the politicians who winked at me, telling me not to worry, because I could just work a little harder and outsmart them all. I looked past the profits of the moment, and I saw that the harder I worked, the more I tightened the noose around my throat, I saw that my energy was being poured down a sewer, that the parasites who fed on me were being fed upon in their turn, that they were caught in their own trap—and that there was no reason for it, no answer known to anyone, that the sewer pipes of the world, draining its productive blood, led into some dank fog nobody had dared to pierce, while people merely shrugged and said that life on earth could be nothing but evil. And then I saw that the whole industrial establishment of the world, with all of its magnificent machinery, its thousand-ton furnaces, its transatlantic cables, its mahogany offices, its stock exchanges, its blazing electric signs, its power, its wealth—all of it was run, not by bankers and boards of directors, but by any unshaved humanitarian in any basement beer joint, by any face pudgy with malice, who preached that virtue must be penalized for being virtue, that the purpose of ability is to serve incompetence, that man has no right to exist except for the sake of others. . . . I knew it. I saw no way to fight it. John found the way. There were just the two of us with him, the night when we came to New York in answer to his call, Ragnar and I. He told us what we had to do and what sort of men we had to reach. He had quit the Twentieth Century. He was living in a garret in a slum neighborhood. He stepped to the window and pointed at the skyscrapers of the city. He said that we had to extinguish the lights of the world, and when we would see the lights of New York go out, we would know that our job was done. He did not ask us to join him at once. He told us to think it over and to weigh everything it would do to our lives. I gave him my answer on the morning of the second day, and Ragnar a few hours later, in the afternoon. . . . Dagny, that was the morning after our last night together. I had seen, in a manner of vision that I couldn't escape, what it was that I had to fight for. It was for the way you looked that night, for the way you talked about your railroad—for the way you had looked when we tried to see the skyline of New York from the top of a rock over the Hudson—I had to save you, to clear the way for you, to let you find your city—not to let you stumble the years of your life away, struggling on through a poisoned fog, with your eyes still held straight ahead, still looking as they had looked in the sunlight, struggling on to find, at the end of your road, not the towers of a city, but a fat, soggy, mindless cripple performing his enjoyment of life by means of swallowing the gin *your* life had gone to pay for! *You*—to know no joy in order that *he* may know it? *You*—to serve as fodder for the pleasure of others? *You*—as the means for the subhuman as the end? Dagny, that was what I saw and that was what I couldn't let them do to you! Not to you, not to any child who had your kind of look when he faced the future, not to any man who had your spirit and was able to experience a moment of being proudly, guiltlessly, confidently, joyously alive. *That* was my love, that state of the human spirit, and I left you to fight for it, and I knew that if I were to lose you, it was still *you* that I would be winning with every year of the battle. But you see it now, don't you? You've seen this valley. It's the place we set out to reach when we were children, you and I. We've reached it. What else can I ask for now? Just to see you here—did John say you're still a scab?—oh well, it's only a matter of time, but you'll be one of us, because you've always been, if you don't see it fully, we'll wait, I don't care—so long as you're alive, so long as I don't have to go on flying over the Rockies, looking for the wreckage of your plane!"

She gasped a little, realizing why he had not come to the valley on time.

He laughed. "Don't look like that. Don't look at me as if I were a wound that you're afraid to touch."

"Francisco, I've hurt you in so many different ways—"

"No! No, you haven't hurt me—and he hasn't either, don't say anything about it, it's he who's hurt, but we'll save him and he'll come here, too, where he belongs, and he'll know, and then he, too, will be able to laugh about it. Dagny, I didn't expect you to wait, I didn't hope, I knew the chance I'd taken, and if it had to be anyone, I'm glad it's he."

She closed her eyes, pressing her lips together not to moan.

"Darling, don't! Don't you see that I've accepted it?"

But it isn't—she thought—it isn't he, and I can't tell you the truth, because it's a man who might never hear it from me and whom I might never have.

"Francisco, I did love you—" she said, and caught her breath, shocked, realizing that she had not intended to say it and, simultaneously, that this was not the tense she had wanted to use.

"But you do," he said calmly, smiling. "You still love me—even if there's one expression of it that you'll always feel and want, but will not give me any longer. I'm still what I was, and you'll always see it, and you'll always grant me the same response, even if there's a greater one that you grant to another man. No matter what you feel for him, it will not change what you feel for me, and it won't be treason to either, because it comes from the same root, it's the same payment in answer to the same values. No matter what happens in the future, we'll always be what we were to each other, you and I, because you'll always love me."

"Francisco," she whispered, "do you know that?"

"Of course. Don't you understand it now? Dagny, every form of happiness is one, every desire is driven by the same motor—by our love for a single value, for the highest potentiality of our own existence—and every achievement is an expression of it. Look around you. Do you see how much is open to us here, on an unobstructed earth? Do you see how much I am free to do, to experience, to achieve? Do you see that all of it is part of what you are to me—as I am part of it for you? And if I'll see you smile with admiration at a new copper smelter that I built, it will be another form of what I felt when I lay in bed beside you. Will I want to sleep with you? Desperately. Will I envy the man who does? Sure. But what does that matter? It's so much—just to have you here, to love you and to be alive."

Her eyes lowered, her face stern, holding her head bowed as in an act of reverence, she said slowly, as if fulfilling a solemn promise, "Will you forgive me?"

He looked astonished, then chuckled gaily, remembering, and answered, "Not yet. There's nothing to forgive, but I'll forgive it when you join us."

He rose, he drew her to her feet—and when his arms closed about her, their kiss was the summation of their past, its end and their seal of acceptance.

Galt turned to them from across the living room, when they came out. He had been standing at a window, looking at the valley—and she felt certain that he had stood there all that time. She saw his eyes studying their faces, his glance moving slowly from one to the other. His face relaxed a little at the sight of the change in Francisco's.

Francisco smiled, asking him, "Why do you stare at me?"

"Do you know what you looked like when you came in?"

"Oh, did I? That's because I hadn't slept for three nights. John, will you invite me to dinner? I want to know how this scab of yours got here, but I think that I might collapse sound asleep in the middle of a sentence—even though right now I feel as if I'll never need any sleep at all—so I think I'd better go home and stay there till evening."

Galt was watching him with a faint smile. "But aren't you going to leave the valley in an hour?"

"What? No . . ." he said mildly, in momentary astonishment. "No!" he laughed exultantly. "I don't have to! That's right, I haven't told you what it was, have I? I was searching for Dagny. For . . . for the wreck of her plane. She'd been reported lost in a crash in the Rockies."

"I see," said Galt quietly.

"I could have thought of anything, except that she would choose to crash in Galt's Gulch," Francisco said happily; he had the tone of that joyous relief which almost relishes the horror of the past, defying it by means of the present. "I kept flying over the district between Afton, Utah, and Winston, Colorado, over every peak and crevice of it, over every remnant of a car in any gully below, and whenever I saw one, I—" He stopped; it looked like a shudder. "Then at night, we went out on foot—the searching parties of railroad men from Winston—we went climbing at random, with no clues, no plan, on and on, until it was daylight again, and—" He shrugged, trying to dismiss it and to smile. "I wouldn't wish it on my worst—"

He stopped short; his smile vanished and a dim reflection of the look he had worn for three days came back to his face, as if at the sudden presence of an image he had forgotten.

After a long moment, he turned to Galt. "John," his voice sounded peculiarly solemn, "could we notify those outside that Dagny is alive . . . in case there's somebody who . . . who'd feel as I did?"

Galt was looking straight at him. "Do you wish to give any outsider any relief from the consequences of remaining outside?"

Francisco dropped his eyes, but answered firmly, "No."

"Pity, Francisco?"

"Yes. Forget it. You're right."

Galt turned away with a movement that seemed oddly out of character: it had the unrhythmical abruptness of the involuntary.

He did not turn back; Francisco watched him in astonishment, then asked softly, "What's the matter?"

Galt turned and looked at him for a moment, not answering. She could not identify the emotion that softened the lines of Galt's face: it had the quality of a smile, of gentleness, of pain, and of something greater that seemed to make these concepts superfluous.

"Whatever any of us has paid for this battle," said Galt, "you're the one who's taken the hardest beating, aren't you?"

"Who? I?" Francisco grinned with shocked, incredulous amusement. "Certainly not! What's the matter with you?" He chuckled and added, "Pity, John?"

"No," said Galt firmly.

She saw Francisco watching him with a faint, puzzled frown—because Galt had said it, looking, not at him, but at her.

* * *

The emotional sum that struck her as an immediate impression of Francisco's house, when she entered it for the first time, was not the sum she had once drawn from the sight of its silent, locked exterior. She felt, not a sense of tragic loneliness, but of invigorating brightness. The rooms were bare and crudely simple, the house seemed built with the skill, the decisiveness and the impatience typical of Francisco; it looked like a frontiersman's shanty thrown together to serve as a mere springboard for a long flight into the future—a future where so great a field of activity lay waiting that no time could be wasted on the comfort of its start. The place had the brightness, not of a home, but of a fresh wooden scaffolding erected to shelter the birth of a skyscraper.

Francisco, in shirt sleeves, stood in the middle of his twelve-foot-square living room, with the look of a host in a palace. Of all the places where she had ever seen him, this was the background that seemed most properly his. Just as the simplicity of his clothes, added to his bearing, gave him the air of a superlative aristocrat, so the crudeness of the room gave it the appearance of the most patrician retreat; a single royal touch was added to the crudeness: two ancient silver goblets stood in a small niche cut in a wall of bare logs; their ornate design had required the luxury of some craftsman's long and costly labor, more labor than had gone to build the shanty, a design dimmed by the polish of more centuries than had gone to grow the log wall's pines. In the midst of that room, Francisco's easy, natural manner had a touch of quiet pride, as if his smile were silently saying to her: This is what I am and what I have been all these years.

She looked up at the silver goblets.

"Yes," he said, in answer to her silent guess, "they belonged to Sebastián d'Anconia and his wife. That's the only thing I brought here from my palace in Buenos Aires. That, and the crest over the door. It's all I wanted to save. Everything else will go, in a very few months now." He chuckled. "They'll seize it, all of it, the last dregs of d'Anconia Copper, but they'll be surprised. They won't find much for their trouble. And as to that palace, they won't be able to afford even its heating bill."

"And then?" she asked. "Where will you go from there?"

"I? I will go to work for d'Anconia Copper."

"What do you mean?"

"Do you remember that old slogan: 'The king is dead, long live the king'? When the carcass of my ancestors' property is out of the way, then my mine will become the young new body of d'Anconia Copper, the kind of property my ancestors had wanted, had worked for, had deserved, but had never owned."

"*Your* mine? What mine? Where?"

"Here," he said, pointing toward the mountain peaks. "Didn't you know it?"

"No."

"I own a copper mine that the looters won't reach. It's here, in these mountains. I did the prospecting, I discovered it, I broke the first excavation. It was over eight years ago. I was the first man to whom Midas sold land in this valley. I bought that mine. I started it with my own hands, as Sebastián d'Anconia had started. I have a superintendent in charge of it now, who used to be my best metallurgist in Chile. The mine produces all the copper we require. My profits are deposited at the Mulligan Bank. That will be all I'll have, a few months from now. That will be all I'll need."

—to conquer the world, was the way his voice sounded on his last sentence—and she marveled at the difference between that sound and the shameful, mawkish tone, half-whine, half-threat, the tone of beggar and thug combined, which the men of their century had given to the word "need."

"Dagny," he was saying, standing at the window, as if looking out at the peaks, not of mountains, but of time, "the rebirth of d'Anconia Copper—and of the world—has to start here, in the United States. This country was the only country in history born, not of chance and blind tribal warfare, but as a rational product of man's mind. This country was built on the supremacy of reason—and, for one magnificent century, it redeemed the world. It will have to do so again. The first step of d'Anconia Copper, as of any other human value, has to come from here—because the rest of the earth has reached the consummation of the beliefs it has held through the ages: mystic faith, the supremacy of the irrational, which has but two monuments at the end of its course: the lunatic asylum and the graveyard. . . . Sebastián d'Anconia committed one error: he accepted a system which declared that the property he had earned by right, was to be his, not by right, but by permission. His descendants paid for that error. I have made the last payment. . . . I think that I will see the day when, growing out from their root in this soil, the mines, the smelters, the ore docks of d'Anconia Copper will spread again through the world and down to my native country, and I will be the first to start my country's rebuilding. I may see it, but I cannot be certain. No man can predict the time when others will choose to return to reason. It may be that at the end of my life, I shall have established nothing but this single mine—d'Anconia Copper No. 1, Galt's Gulch, Colorado, U.S.A. But, Dagny, do you remember that my ambition was to double my father's production of copper? Dagny, if at the end of my life, I produce but one pound of copper a year, I will be richer than my father, richer than all my ancestors with all their thousands of tons—because that one pound will be *mine by right* and will be used to maintain a world that knows it!"

This was the Francisco of their childhood, in bearing, in manner, in the unclouded brilliance of his eyes—and she found herself questioning him about his copper mine, as she had questioned him about his industrial projects on their walks on the shore of the Hudson, recapturing the sense of an unobstructed future.

"I'll take you to see the mine," he said, "as soon as your ankle recovers completely. We have to climb a steep trail to get there, just a mule trail, there's no truck road as yet. Let me show you the new smelter I'm designing. I've been working on it for some time, it's too complex for our present volume of production, but when the mine's output grows to justify it—just take a look at the time, labor and money that it will save!"

They were sitting together on the floor, bending over the sheets of paper he spread before her, studying the intricate sections of the smelter—with the same joyous earnestness they had once brought to the study of scraps in a junk yard.

She leaned forward just as he moved to reach for another sheet, and she found herself leaning against his shoulder. Involuntarily, she held still for one instant, no longer than for a small break in the flow of a single motion, while her eyes rose to his. He was looking down at her, neither hiding what he felt nor implying any further demand. She drew back, knowing that she had felt the same desire as his.

Then, still holding the recaptured sensation of what she had felt for him in the past, she grasped a quality that had always been part of it, now suddenly clear to her for the first time: if that desire was a celebration of one's life, then what she had felt for Francisco had always been a celebration of her future, like a moment of splendor gained in part payment of an unknown total, affirming some promise to come. In the instant when she grasped it, she knew also the only desire she had ever experienced not in token of the future but of the full and final present. She knew it by means of an image—the image of a man's figure standing at the door of a small granite structure. The final form of the promise that had kept her moving, she thought, was the man who would, perhaps, remain a promise never to be reached.

But this—she thought in consternation—was that view of human destiny which she had most passionately hated and rejected: the view that man was ever to be drawn by some vision of the unattainable shining ahead, doomed ever to aspire, but not to achieve. *Her* life and *her* values could not bring her to that, she thought; she had never found beauty in longing for the impossible and had never found the possible to be beyond her reach. But she had come to it and she could find no answer.

She could not give him up or give up the world—she thought, looking at Galt, that evening. The answer seemed harder to find in his presence. She felt that no problem existed, that nothing could stand beside the fact of seeing him and nothing would ever have the power to make her leave—and, simultaneously, that she would have no right to look at him if she were to renounce her railroad. She felt that she owned him, that the unnamed had been understood between them from the start—and, simultaneously, that he was able to vanish from her life and, on some future street of the outside world, to pass her by in unweighted indifference.

She noted that he did not question her about Francisco. When she spoke of her visit, she could find no reaction in his face, neither of approval nor of resentment. It seemed to her that she caught an imperceptible shading in his gravely attentive expression: he looked as if this were a matter about which he did not choose to feel.

Her faint apprehension grew into a question mark, and the question mark turned into a drill, cutting deeper and deeper into her mind through the evenings that followed—when Galt left the house and she remained alone. He went out every other night, after dinner, not telling her where he went, returning at midnight or later. She tried not to allow herself fully to discover with what tension and restlessness she waited for his return. She did not ask him where he spent his evenings. The reluctance that stopped her was her too urgent desire to know; she kept silent in some dimly intentional form of defiance, half in defiance of him, half of her own anxiety.

She would not acknowledge the things she feared or give them the solid shape of words, she knew them only by the ugly, nagging pull of an unadmitted emotion. Part of it was a savage resentment, of a kind she had never experienced before, which was her answer to the dread that there might be a woman in his life; yet the resentment was softened by some quality of health in the thing she feared, as if the threat could be fought and even, if need be, accepted. But there was another, uglier dread: the sordid shape of self-sacrifice, the suspicion, not to be uttered about him, that he wished to remove himself from her path and let its emptiness force her back to the man who was his best-loved friend.

Days passed before she spoke of it. Then, at dinner, on an evening when he was to leave, she became suddenly aware of the peculiar pleasure she experienced while watching him eat the food she had prepared—and suddenly, involuntarily, as if that pleasure gave her a right she dared not identify, as if enjoyment, not pain, broke her resistance, she heard herself asking him, "What is it you're doing every other evening?"

He answered simply, as if he had taken for granted that she knew it, "Lecturing."

"What?"

"Giving a course of lectures on physics, as I do every year during this month. It's my . . . What are you laughing at?" he asked, seeing the look of relief, of silent laughter that did not seem to be directed at his words—and then, before she answered, he smiled suddenly, as if he had guessed the answer, she saw some particular, intensely personal quality in his smile, which was almost a quality of insolent intimacy—in contrast to the calmly impersonal, casual manner with which he went on. "You know that this is the month when we all trade the achievements of our real professions. Richard Halley is to give concerts, Kay Ludlow is to appear in two plays written by authors who do not write for the outside world—and I give lectures, reporting on the work I've done during the year."

"Free lectures?"

"Certainly not. It's ten dollars per person for the course."

"I want to hear you."

He shook his head. "No. You'll be allowed to attend the concerts, the plays or any form of presentation for your own enjoyment, but not my lectures or any other sale of ideas which you might carry out of this valley. Besides, my customers, or students, are only those who have a practical purpose in taking my course: Dwight Sanders, Lawrence Hammond, Dick McNamara, Owen Kellogg, a few others. I've added one beginner this year: Quentin Daniels."

"Really?" she said, almost with a touch of jealousy. "How can he afford anything that expensive?"

"On credit. I've given him a time-payment plan. He's worth it."

"Where do you lecture?"

"In the hangar, on Dwight Sanders' farm."

"And where do you work during the year?"

"In my laboratory."

She asked cautiously, "Where is your laboratory? Here, in the valley?"

He held her eyes for a moment, letting her see that his glance was amused and that he knew her purpose, then answered, "No."

"You've lived in the outside world for all of these twelve years?"

"Yes."

"Do you"—the thought seemed unbearable—"do you hold some such job as the others?"

"Oh yes." The amusement in his eyes seemed stressed by some special meaning.

"Don't tell me that you're a second assistant bookkeeper!"

"No, I'm not."

"Then what do you do?"

"I hold the kind of job that the world wishes me to hold."

"Where?"

He shook his head. "No, Miss Taggart. If you decide to leave the valley, this is one of the things that you are not to know."

He smiled again with that insolently personal quality which now seemed to say that he knew the threat contained in his answer and what it meant to her, then he rose from the table.

When he had gone, she felt as if the motion of time were an oppressive weight in the stillness of the house, like a stationary, half-solid mass slithering slowly into some faint elongation by a tempo that left her no measure to know whether minutes had passed or hours. She lay half-stretched in an armchair of the living room, crumpled by that heavy, indifferent lassitude which is not the will to laziness, but the frustration of the will to a secret violence that no lesser action can satisfy.

That special pleasure she had felt in watching him eat the food she had prepared—she thought, lying still, her eyes closed, her mind moving, like time, through some realm of veiled slowness—it had been the pleasure of knowing that she had provided him with a sensual enjoyment, that one form of his body's satisfaction had come from her. . . . There is reason, she thought, why a woman would wish to cook for a man . . . oh, not as a duty, not as a chronic career, only as a rare and special rite in symbol of . . . but what have they made of it, the preachers of woman's duty? . . . The castrated performance of a sickening drudgery was held to be a woman's proper virtue—while that which gave it meaning and sanction was held as a shameful sin . . . the work of dealing with grease, steam and slimy peelings in a reeking kitchen was held to be a spiritual matter, an act of compliance with her moral duty—while the meeting of two bodies in a bedroom was held to be a physical indulgence, an act of surrender to an animal instinct, with no glory, meaning or pride of spirit to be claimed by the animals involved.

She leaped abruptly to her feet. She did not want to think of the outer world or of its moral code. But she knew that that was not the subject of her thoughts. And she did not want to think of the subject her mind was intent on pursuing, the subject to which it kept returning against her will, by some will of its own. . . .

She paced the room, hating the ugly, jerky, uncontrolled looseness of her movements—torn between the need to let her motion break the stillness, and the knowledge that this was not the form of break she wanted. She lighted cigarettes, for an instant's illusion of purposeful action—and discarded them within another instant, feeling the weary distaste of a substitute purpose. She looked at the room like a restless beggar, pleading with physical objects to give her a motive, wishing she could find something to clean, to mend, to polish—while knowing that no task was worth the effort. When nothing seems worth the effort—said some stern voice in her mind—it's a screen to hide a wish that's worth too much; what do you want? . . . She snapped a match, viciously jerking the flame to the tip of a cigarette she noticed hanging, unlighted, in the corner of her mouth. . . . What do you want?—repeated the voice that sounded severe as a judge. I want him to come back!—she answered, throwing the words, as a soundless cry, at some accuser within her, almost as one would throw a bone to a pursuing beast, in the hope of distracting it from pouncing upon the rest.

I want him back—she said softly, in answer to the accusation that there was no reason for so great an impatience. . . . I want him back —she said pleadingly, in answer to the cold reminder that her answer did not balance the judge's scale. . . . I want him back!—she cried defiantly, fighting not to drop the one superfluous, protective word in that sentence.

She felt her head drooping with exhaustion, as after a prolonged beating. The cigarette she saw between her fingers had burned the mere length of half an inch. She ground it out and fell into the armchair again.

I'm not evading it—she thought—I'm not evading it, it's just that I can see no way to any answer. . . . That which you want—said the voice, while she stumbled through a thickening fog—is yours for the taking, but anything less than your full acceptance, anything less than your full conviction, is a betrayal of everything he is. . . . Then let him damn me—she thought, as if the voice were now lost in the fog and would not hear her—let him damn me tomorrow. . . . I want him . . . back. . . . She heard no answer, because her head had fallen softly against the chair; she was asleep.

When she opened her eyes, she saw him standing three feet away, looking down at her, as if he had been watching her for some time.

She saw his face and, with the clarity of undivided perception, she saw the meaning of the expression on his face: it was the meaning she had fought for hours. She saw it without astonishment, because she had not yet regained her awareness of any reason why it should astonish her.

"This is the way you look," he said softly, "when you fall asleep in your office," and she knew that he, too, was not fully aware of letting her hear it: the way he said it told her how often he had thought of it and for what reason. "You look as if you would awaken in a world where you had nothing to hide or to fear," and she knew that the first movement of her face had been a smile, she knew it in the moment when it vanished, when she grasped that they were both awake. He added quietly, with full awareness, "But here, it's true."

Her first emotion of the realm of reality was a sense of power. She sat up with a flowing, leisurely movement of confidence, feeling the flow of the motion from muscle to muscle through her body. She asked, and it was the slowness, the sound of casual curiosity, the tone of taking the implications for granted, that gave to her voice the faintest sound of disdain, "How did you know what I look like in . . . my office?"

"I told you that I've watched you for years."

"How were you able to watch me that thoroughly? From where?"

"I will not answer you now," he said, simply, without defiance.

The slight movement of her shoulder leaning back, the pause, then the lower, huskier tone of her voice, left a hint of smiling triumph to trail behind her words: "When did you see me for the first time?"

"Ten years ago," he answered, looking straight at her, letting her see that he was answering the full, unnamed meaning of her question.

"Where?" The word was almost a command.

He hesitated, then she saw a faint smile that touched only his lips, not his eyes, the kind of smile with which one contemplates—with longing, bitterness and pride—a possession purchased at an excruciating cost; his eyes seemed directed, not at her, but at the girl of that time. "Underground, in the Taggart Terminal," he answered.

She became suddenly conscious of her posture: she had let her shoulder blades slide down against the chair, carelessly, half-lying, one leg stretched forward—and with her sternly tailored, transparent blouse, her wide peasant skirt hand-printed in violent colors, her thin stocking and high-heeled pump, she did not look like a railroad executive—the consciousness of it struck her in answer to his eyes that seemed to be seeing the unattainable—she looked like that which she was: his servant girl. She knew the moment when some faintest stress of the brilliance in his dark green eyes removed the veil of distance, replacing the vision of the past by the act of seeing her immediate person. She met his eyes with that insolent glance which is a smile without movement of facial muscles.

He turned away, but as he moved across the room his steps were as eloquent as the sound of a voice. She knew that he wanted to leave the room, as he always left it, he had never stayed for longer than a brief good night when he came home. She watched the course of his struggle, whether by means of his steps, begun in one direction and swerving in another, or by means of her certainty that her body had become an instrument for the direct perception of his, like a screen reflecting both movements and motives—she could not tell. She knew only that he who had never started or lost a battle against himself, now had no power to leave this room.

His manner seemed to show no sign of strain. He took off his coat, throwing it aside, remaining in shirt sleeves, and sat down, facing her, at the window across the room. But he sat down on the arm of a chair, as if he were neither leaving nor staying.

She felt the light-headed, the easy, the almost frivolous sensation of triumph in the knowledge that she was holding him as surely as by a physical touch; for the length of a moment, brief and dangerous to endure, it was a more satisfying form of contact.

Then she felt a sudden, blinding shock, which was half-blow, half-scream within her, and she groped, stunned, for its cause—only to realize that he had leaned a little to one side and it had been no more than the sight of an accidental posture, of the long line running from his shoulder to the angle of his waist, to his hips, down his legs. She looked away, not to let him see that she was trembling—and she dropped all thoughts of triumph and of whose was the power.

"I've seen you many times since," he said, quietly, steadily, but a little more slowly than usual, as if he could control everything except his need to speak.

"Where have you seen me?"

"Many places."

"But you made certain to remain unseen?" She knew that his was a face she could not have failed to notice.

"Yes."

"Why? Were you afraid?"

"Yes."

He said it simply, and it took her a moment to realize that he was admitting he knew what the sight of his person would have meant to her. "Did you know who I was, when you saw me for the first time?"

"Oh yes. My worst enemy but one."

"What?" She had not expected it; she added, more quietly, "Who's the worst one?"

"Dr. Robert Stadler."

"Did you have me classified with him?"

"No. He's my conscious enemy. He's the man who sold his soul. We don't intend to reclaim him. You—you were one of us. I knew it, long before I saw you. I knew also that you would be the last to join us and the hardest one to defeat."

"Who told you that?"

"Francisco."

She let a moment pass, then asked, "What did he say?"

"He said that of all the names on our list, you'd be the one most difficult to win. That was when I heard of you for the first time. It was Francisco who put your name on our list. He told me that you were the sole hope and future of Taggart Transcontinental, that you'd stand against us for a long time, that you'd fight a desperate battle for your railroad—because you had too much endurance, courage and consecration to your work." He glanced at her. "He told me nothing else. He spoke of you as if he were merely discussing one of our future strikers. I knew that you and he had been childhood friends, that was all."

"When did you see me?"

"Two years later."

"How?"

"By chance. It was late at night . . . on a passenger platform of the Taggart Terminal." She knew that this was a form of surrender, he did not want to say it, yet he had to speak, she heard both the muted intensity and the pull of resistance in his voice—he had to speak, because he had to give himself and her this one form of contact. "You wore an evening gown. You had a cape half-slipping off your body—I saw, at first, only your bare shoulders, your back and your profile—it looked for a moment as if the cape would slip further and you would stand there naked. Then I saw that you wore a long gown, the color of ice, like the tunic of a Grecian goddess, but had the short hair and the imperious profile of an American woman. You looked preposterously out of place on a railroad platform—and it was not on a railroad platform that I was seeing you, I was seeing a setting that had never haunted me before—but then, suddenly, I knew that you *did* belong among the rails, the soot and the girders, that that was the proper setting for a flowing gown and naked shoulders and a face as alive as yours—a railroad platform, not a curtained apartment—you looked like a symbol of luxury and you belonged in the place that was its source—you seemed to bring wealth, grace, extravagance and the enjoyment of life back to their rightful owners, to the men who created railroads and factories—you had a look of energy and of its reward, together, a look of competence and luxury combined—and I was the first man who had ever stated in what manner these two were inseparable—and I thought that if our age gave form to its proper gods and erected a statue to the meaning of an American railroad, yours would be that statue. . . . Then I saw what you were doing—and I knew who you were. You were giving orders to three Terminal officials, I could not hear your words, but your voice sounded swift, clear-cut and confident. I knew that you were Dagny Taggart. I came closer, close enough to hear two sentences. 'Who said so?' asked one of the men. 'I did,' you answered. That was all I heard. That was enough."

"And then?"

He raised his eyes slowly to hold hers across the room, and the submerged intensity that pulled his voice down, blurring its tone to softness, gave it a sound of self-mockery that was desperate and almost gentle: "Then I knew that abandoning my motor was not the hardest price I would have to pay for this strike."

She wondered which anonymous shadow—among the passengers who had hurried past her, as insubstantial as the steam of the engines and as ignored—which shadow and face had been his; she wondered how close she had come to him for the length of that unknown moment. "Oh, why didn't you speak to me, then or later?"

"Do you happen to remember what you were doing in the Terminal that night?"

"I remember vaguely a night when they called me from some party I was attending. My father was out of town and the new Terminal manager had made some sort of error that tied up all traffic in the tunnels. The old manager had quit unexpectedly the week before."

"It was I who made him quit."

"I see . . ."

Her voice trailed off, as if abandoning sound, as her eyelids dropped, abandoning sight. If he had not withstood it then—she thought—if he had come to claim her, then or later, what sort of tragedy would they have had to reach? . . . She remembered what she had felt when she had cried that she would shoot the destroyer on sight. . . . *I would have*—the thought was not in words, she knew it only as a trembling pressure in her stomach—*I would have shot him, afterward, if I discovered his role . . . and I would have had to discover it . . .* and yet—she shuddered, because she knew she still wished he had come to her, because the thought not to be admitted into her mind, but flowing as a dark warmth through her body, was: I would have shot him, but not before—

She raised her eyelids—and she knew that that thought was as naked to him in her eyes, as it was to her in his. She saw his veiled glance and the tautness of his mouth, she saw him reduced to agony, she felt herself drowned by the exultant wish to cause him pain, to see it, to watch it, to watch it beyond her own endurance and his, then to reduce him to the helplessness of pleasure.

He got up, he looked away, and she could not tell whether it was the slight lift of his head or the tension of his features that made his face look oddly calm and clear, as if it were stripped of emotion down to the naked purity of its structure.

"Every man that your railroad needed and lost in the past ten years," he said, "it was I who made you lose him." His voice had the single-toned flatness and the luminous simplicity of an accountant who reminds a reckless purchaser that cost is an absolute which cannot be escaped. "I have pulled every girder from under Taggart Transcontinental and, if you choose to go back, I will see it collapse upon your head."

He turned to leave the room. She stopped him. It was her voice, more than her words, that made him stop: her voice was low, it had no quality of emotion, only of a sinking weight, and its sole color was some dragging undertone, like an inner echo, resembling a threat; it was the voice of the plea of a person who still retains a concept of honor, but is long past caring for it:

"You want to hold me here, don't you?"

"More than anything else in the world."

"You could hold me."

"I know it."

His voice had said it with the same sound as hers. He waited, to regain his breath. When he spoke, his voice was low and clear, with some stressed quality of awareness, which was almost the quality of a smile of understanding:

"It's your acceptance of this place that I want. What good would it do me, to have your physical presence without any meaning? That's the kind of faked reality by which most people cheat themselves of their lives. I'm not capable of it." He turned to go. "And neither are you. Good night, Miss Taggart."

He walked out, into his bedroom, closing the door.

She was past the realm of thought—as she lay in bed in the darkness of her room, unable to think or to sleep—and the moaning violence that filled her mind seemed only a sensation of her muscles, but its tone and its twisting shades were like a pleading cry, which she knew, not as words, but as pain: Let him come here, let him break —let it be damned, all of it, my railroad and his strike and everything we've lived by!—let it be damned, everything we've been and are!—

he would, if tomorrow I were to die—then let me die, but tomorrow —let him come here, be it any price he names, I have nothing left that's not for sale to him any longer—is this what it means to be an animal?—it does and I am. . . . She lay on her back, her palms pressed to the sheet at her sides, to stop herself from rising and walking into his room, knowing that she was capable even of that. . . . It's not I, it's a body I can neither endure nor control. . . . But somewhere within her, not as words, but as a radiant point of stillness, there was the presence of the judge who seemed to observe her, not in stern condemnation any longer, but in approval and amusement, as if saying: Your body?—if he were not what you know him to be, would your body bring you to this?—why is it *his* body that you want, and no other?—do you think that you are damning them, the things you both have lived by?—are you damning that which you are honoring in this very moment, by your very desire? . . . She did not have to hear the words, she knew them, she had always known them. . . . After a while, she lost the glow of that knowledge, and there was nothing left but pain and the palms that were pressed to the sheet—and the almost indifferent wonder whether he, too, was awake and fighting the same torture.

She heard no sound in the house and saw no light from his window on the tree trunks outside. After a long while she heard, from the darkness of his room, two sounds that gave her a full answer; she knew that he was awake and that he would not come; it was the sound of a step and the click of a cigarette lighter.

* * *

Richard Halley stopped playing, turned away from the piano and glanced at Dagny. He saw her drop her face with the involuntary movement of hiding too strong an emotion, he rose, smiled and said softly, "Thank you."

"Oh no . . ." she whispered, knowing that the gratitude was hers and that it was futile to express it. She was thinking of the years when the works he had just played for her were being written, here, in his small cottage on a ledge of the valley, when all this prodigal magnificence of sound was being shaped by him as a flowing monument to a concept which equates the sense of life with the sense of beauty—while she had walked through the streets of New York in a hopeless quest for some form of enjoyment, with the screeches of a modern symphony running after her, as if spit by the infected throat of a loud-speaker coughing its malicious hatred of existence.

"But I mean it," said Richard Halley, smiling. "I'm a businessman and I never do anything without payment. You've paid me. Do you see why I wanted to play for you tonight?"

She raised her head. He stood in the middle of his living room, they were alone, with the window open to the summer night, to the dark trees on a long sweep of ledges descending toward the glitter of the valley's distant lights.

"Miss Taggart, how many people are there to whom my work means as much as it does to you?"

"Not many," she answered simply, neither as boast nor flattery, but as an impersonal tribute to the exacting values involved.

"That is the payment I demand. Not many can afford it. I don't mean your enjoyment, I don't mean your emotion—emotions be damned!—I mean your *understanding* and the fact that your enjoyment was of the same nature as mine, that it came from the same source: from your intelligence, from the conscious judgment of a mind able to judge my work by the standard of the same values that went to write it—I mean, not the fact that you *felt,* but that you felt what *I* wished you to feel, not the fact that you admire my work, but that you admire it for the things *I* wished to be admired." He chuckled. "There's only one passion in most artists more violent than their desire for admiration: their fear of identifying the nature of such admiration as they do receive. But it's a fear I've never shared. I do not fool myself about my work or the response I seek—I value both too highly. I do not care to be admired causelessly, emotionally, intuitively, instinctively—or blindly. I do not care for blindness in any form, I have too much to show—or for deafness, I have too much to say. I do not care to be admired by anyone's *heart*—only by someone's *head.* And when I find a customer with that invaluable capacity, then my performance is a mutual trade to mutual profit. An artist is a trader, Miss Taggart, the hardest and most exacting of all traders. Now do you understand me?"

"Yes," she said incredulously, "I do," incredulously because she was hearing her own symbol of moral pride, chosen by a man she had least expected to choose it.

"If you do, why did you look quite so tragic just a moment ago? What is it that you regret?"

"The years when your work has remained unheard."

"But it hasn't. I've given two or three concerts every year. Here, in Galt's Gulch. I am giving one next week. I hope you'll come. The price of admission is twenty-five cents."

She could not help laughing. He smiled, then his face slipped slowly into earnestness, as under the tide of some unspoken contemplation of his own. He looked at the darkness beyond the window, at a spot where, in a clearing of the branches, with the moonlight draining its color, leaving only its metallic luster, the sign of the dollar hung like a curve of shining steel engraved on the sky.

"Miss Taggart, do you see why I'd give three dozen modern artists for one real businessman? Why I have much more in common with Ellis Wyatt or Ken Danagger—who happens to be tone deaf—than with men like Mort Liddy and Balph Eubank? Whether it's a symphony or a coal mine, all work is an act of creating and comes from the same source: from an inviolate capacity to see through one's own eyes—which means: the capacity to perform a rational identification —which means: the capacity to see, to connect and to make what had not been seen, connected and made before. That shining vision which they talk about as belonging to the authors of symphonies and novels—what do they think is the driving faculty of men who discover how to use oil, how to run a mine, how to build an electric motor? That sacred fire which is said to burn within musicians and poets—what do they suppose moves an industrialist to defy the whole world for the sake of his new metal, as the inventors of the airplane, the builders of the railroads, the discoverers of new germs or new continents have done through all the ages? . . . An intransigent devotion to the pursuit of truth, Miss Taggart? Have you heard the moralists and the art lovers of the centuries talk about the artist's intransigent devotion to the pursuit of truth? Name me a greater example of such devotion than the act of a man who says that the earth does turn, or the act of a man who says that an alloy of steel and copper has certain properties which enable it to do certain things, that it *is* and *does*—and let the world rack him or ruin him, he will not bear false witness to the evidence of his mind! *This,* Miss Taggart, this sort of spirit, courage and love for truth—as against a sloppy bum who goes around proudly assuring you that he has almost reached the perfection of a lunatic, because he's an artist who hasn't the faintest idea what his art work is or means, he's not restrained by such crude concepts as 'being' or 'meaning,' he's the vehicle of higher mysteries, he doesn't know how he created his work or why, it just came out of him spontaneously, like vomit out of a drunkard, he did not think, he wouldn't stoop to thinking, he just *felt* it, all he has to do is feel— he *feels,* the flabby, loose-mouthed, shifty-eyed, drooling, shivering, uncongealed bastard! I, who know what discipline, what effort, what tension of mind, what unrelenting strain upon one's power of clarity are needed to produce a work of art—I, who know that it requires a labor which makes a chain gang look like rest and a severity no army-drilling sadist could impose—I'll take the operator of a coal mine over any walking vehicle of higher mysteries. The operator knows that it's not his feelings that keep the coal carts moving under the earth—and he knows what does keep them moving. Feelings? Oh yes, we do feel, he, you and I—we are, in fact, the only people capable of feeling— and we know where our feelings come from. But what we did not know and have delayed learning for too long is the nature of those who claim that they cannot account for their feelings. We did not know what it is that they feel. We are learning it now. It was a costly error. And those most guilty of it, will pay the hardest price—as, in justice, they must. Those most guilty of it were the real artists, who will now see that they are first to be exterminated and that they had prepared the triumph of their own exterminators by helping to destroy their only protectors. For if there is more tragic a fool than the businessman who doesn't know that he's an exponent of man's highest creative spirit—it's the artist who thinks that the businessman is his enemy."

It was true—she thought, when she walked through the streets of the valley, looking with a child's excitement at the shop windows sparkling in the sun—that the businesses here had the purposeful selectiveness of art—and that the art—she thought, when she sat in the darkness of a clapboard concert hall, listening to the controlled violence and the mathematical precision of Halley's music—had the stern discipline of business.

Both had the radiance of engineering—she thought, when she sat among rows of benches under the open sky, watching Kay Ludlow on the stage. It was an experience she had not known since childhood —the experience of being held for three hours by a play that told a story she had not seen before, in lines she had not heard, uttering a theme that had not been picked from the hand-me-downs of the centuries. It was the forgotten delight of being held in rapt attention by the reins of the ingenious, the unexpected, the logical, the purposeful, the new—and of seeing it embodied in a performance of superlative artistry by a woman playing a character whose beauty of spirit matched her own physical perfection.

"That's why I'm here, Miss Taggart," said Kay Ludlow, smiling in answer to her comment, after the performance. "Whatever quality of human greatness I have the talent to portray—*that* was the quality the outer world sought to degrade. They let me play nothing but symbols of depravity, nothing but harlots, dissipation-chasers and home-wreckers, always to be beaten at the end by the little girl next door, personifying the virtue of mediocrity. They used my talent—for the defamation of itself. That was why I quit."

Not since childhood, thought Dagny, had she felt that sense of exhilaration after witnessing the performance of a play—the sense that life held things worth reaching, not the sense of having studied some aspect of a sewer there had been no reason to see. As the audience filed away into the darkness from the lighted rows of benches, she noticed Ellis Wyatt, Judge Narragansett, Ken Danagger, men who had once been said to despise all forms of art.

The last image she caught, that evening, was the sight of two tall, straight, slender figures walking away together down a trail among the rocks, with the beam of a spotlight flashing once on the gold of their hair. They were Kay Ludlow and Ragnar Danneskjöld—and she wondered whether she could bear to return to a world where these were the two doomed to destruction.

The recaptured sense of her own childhood kept coming back to her whenever she met the two sons of the young woman who owned the bakery shop. She often saw them wandering down the trails of the valley—two fearless beings, aged seven and four. They seemed to face life as she had faced it. They did not have the look she had seen in the children of the outer world—a look of fear, half-secretive, half-sneering, the look of a child's defense against an adult, the look of a being in the process of discovering that he is hearing lies and of learning to feel hatred. The two boys had the open, joyous, friendly confidence of kittens who do not expect to get hurt, they had an innocently natural, non-boastful sense of their own value and as innocent a trust in any stranger's ability to recognize it, they had the eager curiosity that would venture anywhere with the certainty that life held nothing unworthy of or closed to discovery, and they looked as if, should they encounter malevolence, they would reject it contemptuously, not as dangerous, but as stupid, they would not accept it in bruised resignation as the law of existence.

"They represent my particular career, Miss Taggart," said the young mother in answer to her comment, wrapping a loaf of fresh bread and smiling at her across the counter. "They're the profession I've chosen to practice, which, in spite of all the guff about motherhood, one can't practice successfully in the outer world. I believe you've met my husband, he's the teacher of economics who works as linesman for Dick McNamara. You know, of course, that there can be no collective commitments in this valley and that families or relatives are not allowed to come here, unless each person takes the striker's oath by his own independent conviction. I came here, not merely for the sake of my husband's profession, but for the sake of my own. I came here in order to bring up my sons as human beings. I would not surrender them to the educational systems devised to stunt a child's brain, to convince him that reason is impotent, that existence is an irrational chaos with which he's unable to deal, and thus reduce him to a state of chronic terror. You marvel at the difference between my children and those outside, Miss Taggart? Yet the cause is so simple. The cause is that here, in Galt's Gulch, there's no person who would not consider it monstrous ever to confront a child with the slightest suggestion of the irrational."

She thought of the teachers whom the schools of the world had lost —when she looked at the three pupils of Dr. Akston, on the evening of their yearly reunion.

The only other guest he had invited was Kay Ludlow. The six of them sat in the back yard of his house, with the light of the sunset on their faces, and the floor of the valley condensing into a soft blue vapor far below.

She looked at his pupils, at the three pliant, agile figures half-stretched on canvas chairs in poses of relaxed contentment, dressed in slacks, windbreakers and open-collared shirts: John Galt, Francisco d'Anconia, Ragnar Danneskjöld.

"Don't be astonished, Miss Taggart," said Dr. Akston, smiling, "and don't make the mistake of thinking that these three pupils of mine are some sort of superhuman creatures. They're something much greater and more astounding than that: they're *normal men*—a thing the world has never seen—and their feat is that they managed to survive as such. It does take an exceptional mind and a still more exceptional integrity to remain untouched by the brain-destroying influences of the world's doctrines, the accumulated evil of centuries—to remain *human*, since the human is the rational."

She felt some new quality in Dr. Akston's attitude, some change in the sternness of his usual reserve; he seemed to include her in their circle, as if she were more than a guest. Francisco acted as if her presence at their reunion were natural and to be taken gaily for granted. Galt's face gave no hint of any reaction; his manner was that of a courteous escort who had brought her here at Dr. Akston's request.

She noticed that Dr. Akston's eyes kept coming back to her, as if with the quiet pride of displaying his students to an appreciative observer. His conversation kept returning to a single theme, in the manner of a father who has found a listener interested in his most cherished subject:

"You should have seen them, when they were in college, Miss Taggart. You couldn't have found three boys 'conditioned' to such different backgrounds, but—conditioners be damned!—they must have picked one another at first sight, among the thousands on that campus. Francisco, the richest heir in the world—Ragnar, the European aristocrat—and John, the self-made man, self-made in every sense, out of nowhere, penniless, parentless, tie-less. Actually, he was the son of a gas-station mechanic at some forsaken crossroads in Ohio, and he had left home at the age of twelve to make his own way—but I've always thought of him as if he had come into the world like Minerva, the goddess of wisdom, who sprang forth from Jupiter's head, fully grown and fully armed. . . . I remember the day when I saw the three of them for the first time. They were sitting at the back of the classroom—I was giving a special course for postgraduate students, so difficult a course that few outsiders ever ventured to attend these particular lectures. Those three looked too young even for freshmen—they were sixteen at the time, as I learned later. At the end of that lecture, John got up to ask me a question. It was a question which, as a teacher, I would have been proud to hear from a student who'd taken six years of philosophy. It was a question pertaining to Plato's metaphysics, which Plato hadn't had the sense to ask of himself. I answered—and I asked John to come to my office after the lecture. He came—all three of them came—I saw the two others in my anteroom and let them in. I talked to them for an hour—then I cancelled all my appointments and talked to them for the rest of the day. After which, I arranged to let them take that course and receive their credits for it. They took the course. They got the highest grades in the class. . . . They were majoring in two subjects: physics and philosophy. Their choice amazed everybody but me: modern thinkers considered it unnecessary to perceive reality, and modern physicists considered it unnecessary to think. I knew better; what amazed me was that these children knew it, too. . . . Robert Stadler was head of the Department of Physics, as I was head of the Department of Philosophy. He and I suspended all rules and restrictions for these three students, we spared them all the routine, unessential courses, we loaded them with nothing but the hardest tasks, and we cleared their way to major in our two subjects within their four years. They *worked* for it. And, during those four years, they worked for their living, besides. Francisco and Ragnar were receiving allowances from their parents, John had nothing, but all three of them held part-time jobs to earn their own experience and money. Francisco worked in a copper foundry, John worked in a railroad roundhouse, and Ragnar—no, Miss Taggart, Ragnar was not the least, but the most studiously sedate of the three— he worked as clerk in the university library. They had time for everything they wanted, but no time for people or for any communal campus activities. They . . . Ragnar!" he interrupted himself suddenly, sharply. "Don't sit on the ground!"

Danneskjöld had slipped down and was now sitting on the grass, with his head leaning against Kay Ludlow's knees. He rose obediently, chuckling. Dr. Akston smiled with a touch of apology.

"It's an old habit of mine," he explained to Dagny. "A 'conditioned' reflex, I guess. I used to tell him that in those college years, when I'd catch him sitting on the ground in my back yard, on cold, foggy evenings—he was reckless that way, he made me worry, he should have known it was dangerous and—"

He stopped abruptly; he read in Dagny's startled eyes the same thought as his own: the thought of the kind of dangers the adult Ragnar had chosen to face. Dr. Akston shrugged, spreading his hands in a gesture of helpless self-mockery. Kay Ludlow smiled at him in understanding.

"My house stood just outside the campus," he continued, sighing, "on a tall bluff over Lake Erie. We spent many evenings together, the four of us. We would sit just like this, in my back yard, on the nights of early fall or in the spring, only instead of this granite mountainside, we had the spread of the lake before us, stretching off into a peacefully unlimited distance. I had to work harder on those nights than in any classroom, answering all the questions they'd ask me, discussing the kind of issues they'd raise. About midnight, I would fix some hot chocolate and force them to drink it—the one thing I suspected was that they never took time to eat properly—and then we'd go on talking, while the lake vanished into solid darkness and the sky seemed lighter than the earth. There were a few times when we stayed there till I noticed suddenly that the sky was turning darker and the lake was growing pale and we were within a few sentences of daylight. I should have known better, I knew that they weren't getting enough sleep as it was, but I forgot it occasionally, I lost my sense of time—you see, when they were there, I always felt as if it were early morning and a long, inexhaustible day were stretching ahead before us. They never spoke of what they wished they *might* do in the future, they never wondered whether some mysterious omnipotence had favored them with some unknowable talent to achieve the things they wanted—they spoke of what they *would do*. Does affection tend to make one a coward? I know that the only times I felt fear were occasional moments when I listened to them and thought of what the world was becoming and what they would have to encounter in the future. Fear? Yes—but it was more than fear. It was the kind of emotion that makes men capable of killing—when I thought that the purpose of the world's trend was to destroy these children, that these three sons of mine were marked for immolation. Oh yes, I would have killed—but whom was there to kill? It was everyone and no one, there was no single enemy, no center and no villain, it was not the simpering social worker incapable of earning a penny or the thieving bureaucrat scared of his own shadow, it was the whole of the earth rolling into an obscenity of horror, pushed by the hand of every would-be decent man who believed that need is holier than ability, and pity is holier than justice. But these were only occasional moments. It was not my constant feeling. I listened to my children and I knew that nothing would defeat them. I looked at them, as they sat in my back yard, and beyond my house there were the tall, dark buildings of what was still a monument to unenslaved thought—the Patrick Henry University—and farther in the distance there were the lights of Cleveland, the orange glow of steel mills behind batteries of smokestacks, the twinkling red dots of radio towers, the long white rays of airports on the black edge of the sky—and I thought that in the name of any greatness that had ever existed and moved this world, the greatness of which they were the last descendants, they would win. . . . I remember one night when I noticed that John had been silent for a long time—and I saw that he had fallen asleep, stretched there on the ground. The two others confessed that he had not slept for three days. I sent the two of them home at once, but I didn't have the heart to disturb him. It was a warm spring night, I brought a blanket to cover him, and I let him sleep where he was. I sat there beside him till morning—and as I watched his face in the starlight, then the first ray of the sun on his untroubled forehead and closed eyelids, what I experienced was not a prayer, I do not pray, but that state of spirit at which a prayer is a misguided attempt: a full, confident, affirming self-dedication to my love of the right, to the certainty that the right would win and that this boy would have the kind of future he deserved." He moved his arm, pointing to the valley. "I did not expect it to be as great as this—or as hard."

It had grown dark and the mountains had blended with the sky. Hanging detached in space, there were the lights of the valley below them, the red breath of Stockton's foundry above, and the lighted string of windows of Mulligan's house, like a railroad car imbedded in the sky.

"I did have a rival," said Dr. Akston slowly. "It was Robert Stadler. . . . Don't frown, John—it's past. . . . John did love him, once. Well, so did I—no, not quite, but what one felt for a mind like Stadler's was painfully close to love, it was that rarest of pleasures: admiration. No, I did not love him, but he and I had always felt as if we were fellow survivors from some vanishing age or land, in the gibbering swamp of mediocrity around us. The mortal sin of Robert Stadler was that he never identified his proper homeland. . . . He hated stupidity. It was the only emotion I had ever seen him display toward people—a biting, bitter, weary hatred for any ineptitude that dared to oppose him. He wanted his own way, he wanted to be left alone to pursue it, he wanted to brush people out of his path—and he never identified the means to it or the nature of his path and of his enemies. He took a short cut. Are you smiling, Miss Taggart? You hate him, don't you? Yes, you know the kind of short cut he took. . . . He told you that we were rivals for these three students. That was true—or rather, that was not the way I thought of it, but I knew that he did. Well, if we were rivals, I had one advantage: I knew why they needed both our professions; he never understood their interest in mine. He never understood its importance to himself—which, incidentally, is what destroyed him. But in those years he was still alive enough to grasp at these three students. 'Grasp' was the word for it. Intelligence being the only value he worshipped, he clutched them as if they were a private treasure of his own. He had always been a very lonely man. I think that in the whole of his life, Francisco and Ragnar were his only love, and John was his only passion. It was John whom he regarded as his particular heir, as his future, as his own immortality. John intended to be an inventor, which meant that he was to be a physicist; he was to take his postgraduate course under Robert Stadler. Francisco intended to leave after graduation and go to work; he was to be the perfect blend of both of us, his two intellectual fathers: an industrialist. And Ragnar—you didn't know what profession Ragnar had chosen, Miss Taggart? No, it wasn't stunt pilot, or jungle explorer, or deep-sea diver. It was something much more courageous than these. Ragnar intended to be a philosopher. An abstract, theoretical, academic, cloistered, ivory-tower philosopher. . . . Yes, Robert Stadler loved them. And yet—I have said that I would have killed to protect them, only there was no one to kill. If that were the solution—which, of course, it isn't—the man to kill was Robert Stadler. Of any one person, of any single guilt for the evil which is now destroying the world—his was the heaviest guilt. *He* had the mind to know better. His was the only name of honor and achievement, used to sanction the rule of the looters. He was the man who delivered science into the power of the looters' guns. John did not expect it. Neither did I. . . . John came back for his postgraduate course in physics. But he did not finish it. He left, on the day when Robert Stadler endorsed the establishment of a State Science Institute. I met Stadler by chance in a corridor of the university, as he came out of his office after his last conversation with John. He looked changed. I hope that I shall never have to see again a change of that kind in a man's face. He saw me approaching—and he did not know, but I knew, what made him whirl upon me and cry, 'I'm so sick of all of you impractical idealists!' I turned away. I knew that I had heard a man pronounce a death sentence upon himself. . . . Miss Taggart, do you remember the question you asked me about my three pupils?"

"Yes," she whispered.

"I could gather, from your question, the nature of what Robert Stadler had said to you about them. Tell me, why did he speak of them at all?"

He saw the faint movement of her bitter smile. "He told me their story as a justification for his belief in the futility of human intelligence. He told it to me as an example of his disillusioned hope. 'Theirs was the kind of ability,' he said, 'one expects to see, in the future, changing the course of the world.' "

"Well, haven't they done so?"

She nodded, slowly, holding her head inclined for a long moment in acquiescence and in homage.

"What I want you to understand, Miss Taggart, is the full evil of those who claim to have become convinced that this earth, by its nature, is a realm of malevolence where the good has no chance to win. Let them check their premises. Let them check their standards of value. Let them check—before they grant themselves the unspeakable license of evil-as-necessity—whether they know what *is* the good and what are the conditions it requires. Robert Stadler now believes that intelligence is futile and that human life can be nothing but irrational. Did he expect John Galt to become a great scientist, willing to work under the orders of Dr. Floyd Ferris? Did he expect Francisco d'Anconia to become a great industrialist, willing to produce under the orders and for the benefit of Wesley Mouch? Did he expect Ragnar Danneskjöld to become a great philosopher, willing to preach, under the orders of Dr. Simon Pritchett, that there is no mind and that might is right? Would that have been a future which Robert Stadler would have considered rational? I want you to observe, Miss Taggart, that those who cry the loudest about their disillusionment, about the failure of virtue, the futility of reason, the impotence of logic—are those who have achieved the full, exact, logical result of the ideas they preached, so mercilessly logical that they dare not identify it. In a world that proclaims the non-existence of the mind, the moral righteousness of rule by brute force, the penalizing of the competent in favor of the incompetent, the sacrifice of the best to the worst—in such a world, the best have to turn against society and have to become its deadliest enemies. In such a world John Galt, the man of incalculable intellectual power, will remain an unskilled laborer—Francisco d'Anconia, the miraculous producer of wealth, will become a wastrel—and Ragnar Danneskjöld, the man of enlightenment, will become the man of violence. Society—and Dr. Robert Stadler—have achieved everything they advocated. What complaint do they now have to make? That the universe is irrational? Is it?"

He smiled; his smile had the pitiless gentleness of certainty.

"Every man builds his world in his own image," he said. "He has the power to choose, but no power to escape the necessity of choice. If he abdicates his power, he abdicates the status of man, and the grinding chaos of the irrational is what he achieves as his sphere of existence—by his own choice. Whoever preserves a single thought uncorrupted by any concession to the will of others, whoever brings into reality a matchstick or a patch of garden made in the image of his thought—*he,* and to that extent, is a man, and that extent is the sole measure of his virtue. They"—he pointed at his pupils—"made no concessions. This"—he pointed at the valley—"is the measure of what they preserved and of what they are. . . . Now I can repeat my answer to the question you asked me, knowing that you will understand it fully. You asked me whether I was proud of the way my three sons had turned out. I am more proud than I had ever hoped to be. I am proud of their every action, of their every goal—and of every *value* they've chosen. And *this,* Dagny, is my full answer."

The sudden sound of her first name was pronounced in the tone of a father; he spoke his last two sentences, looking, not at her, but at Galt. She saw Galt answering him by an open glance held steady for an instant, like a signal of affirmation. Then Galt's eyes moved to hers. She saw him looking at her as if she bore the unspoken title that hung in the silence between them, the title Dr. Akston had granted her, but had not pronounced and none of the others had caught—she saw, in Galt's eyes, a glance of amusement at her shock, of support and, incredibly, of tenderness.

*   *   *

D'Anconia Copper No. 1 was a small cut on the face of the mountain, that looked as if a knife had made a few angular slashes, leaving shelves of rock, red as a wound, on the reddish-brown flank. The sun beat down upon it. Dagny stood at the edge of a path, holding on to Galt's arm on one side and to Francisco's on the other, the wind blowing against their faces and out over the valley, two thousand feet below.

This—she thought, looking at the mine—was the story of human wealth written across the mountains: a few pine trees hung over the cut, contorted by the storms that had raged through the wilderness for centuries, six men worked on the shelves, and an inordinate amount of complex machinery traced delicate lines against the sky; the machinery did most of the work.

She noticed that Francisco was displaying his domain to Galt as much as to her, as much or more. "You haven't seen it since last year, John. . . . John, wait till you see it a year from now. I'll be through, outside, in just a few months—and then this will be my full-time job."

"Hell, no, John!" he said, laughing, in answer to a question—but she caught suddenly the particular quality of his glance whenever it rested on Galt: it was the quality she had seen in his eyes when he had stood in her room, clutching the edge of a table to outlive an unlivable moment; he had looked as if he were seeing someone before him; it was Galt, she thought; it was Galt's image that had carried him through.

Some part of her felt a dim dread: the effort which Francisco had made in that moment to accept her loss and his rival, as the payment demanded of him for his battle, had cost him so much that he was now unable to suspect the truth Dr. Akston had guessed. What will it do to him when he learns?—she wondered, and felt a bitter voice reminding her that there would, perhaps, never be any truth of this kind to learn.

Some part of her felt a dim tension as she watched the way Galt looked at Francisco: it was an open, simple, unreserved glance of surrender to an unreserved feeling. She felt the anxious wonder she had never fully named or dismissed: wonder whether this feeling would bring him down to the ugliness of renunciation.

But most of her mind seemed swept by some enormous sense of release, as if she were laughing at all doubts. Her glance kept going back over the path they had traveled to get here, over the two exhausting miles of a twisted trail that ran, like a precarious corkscrew, from the tip of her feet down to the floor of the valley. Her eyes kept studying it, her mind racing with some purpose of its own.

Brush, pines and a clinging carpet of moss went climbing from the green slopes far below, up the granite ledges. The moss and the brush vanished gradually, but the pines went on, struggling upward in thinning strands, till only a few dots of single trees were left, rising up the naked rock toward the white sunbursts of snow in the crevices at the peaks. She looked at the spectacle of the most ingenious mining machinery she had ever seen, then at the trail where the plodding hoofs and swaying shapes of mules provided the most ancient form of transportation.

"Francisco," she asked, pointing, "who designed the machines?"

"They're just adaptations of standard equipment."

"Who designed them?"

"I did. We don't have many men to spare. We had to make up for it."

"You're wasting an unconscionable amount of manpower and time, carting your ore on muleback. You ought to build a railroad down to the valley."

She was looking down and did not notice the sudden, eager shot of his glance to her face or the sound of caution in his voice: "I know it, but it's such a difficult job that the mine's output won't justify it at present."

"Nonsense! It's much simpler than it looks. There's a pass to the east where there's an easier grade and softer stone, I watched it on the way up, it wouldn't take so many curves, three miles of rail or less would do it."

She was pointing east, she did not notice the intensity with which the two men were watching her face.

"Just a narrow-gauge track is all you'll need . . . like the first railroads . . . that's where the first railroads started—at mines, only they were coal mines. . . . Look, do you see that ridge? There's plenty of clearance for a three-foot gauge, you wouldn't need to do any blasting or widening. Do you see where there's a slow rise for a stretch of almost half a mile? That would be no worse than a four per cent grade, any engine could manage it." She was speaking with a swift, bright certainty, conscious of nothing but the joy of performing her natural function in her natural world where nothing could take precedence over the act of offering a solution to a problem. "The road will pay for itself within three years. I think, at a rough glance, that the costliest part of the job will be a couple of steel trestles—and there's one spot where I might have to blast a tunnel, but it's only for a hundred feet or less. I'll need a steel trestle to throw the track across that gorge and bring it here, but it's not as hard as it looks—let me show you, have you got a piece of paper?"

She did not notice with what speed Galt produced a notebook and a pencil and thrust them into her hands—she seized them, as if she expected them to be there, as if she were giving orders on a construction site where details of this kind were not to delay her.

"Let me give you a rough idea of what I mean. If we drive diagonal piles into the rock"—she was sketching rapidly—"the actual steel span would be only six hundred feet long—it would cut off this last half-mile of your corkscrew turns—I could have the rail laid in three months and—"

She stopped. When she looked up at their faces, the fire had gone out of hers. She crumpled her sketch and flung it aside into the red dust of the gravel. "Oh, what for?" she cried, the despair breaking out for the first time. "To build three miles of railroad and abandon a transcontinental system!"

The two men were looking at her, she saw no reproach in their faces, only a look of understanding which was almost compassion.

"I'm sorry," she said quietly, dropping her eyes.

"If you change your mind," said Francisco, "I'll hire you on the spot—or Midas will give you a loan in five minutes to finance that railroad, if you want to own it yourself."

She shook her head. "I can't . . ." she whispered, "not yet . . ."

She raised her eyes, knowing that they knew the nature of her despair and that it was useless to hide her struggle. "I've tried it once," she said. "I've tried to give it up . . . I know what it will mean . . . I'll think of it with every crosstie I'll see laid here, with every spike driven . . . I'll think of that other tunnel and . . . and of Nat Taggart's bridge. . . . Oh, if only I didn't have to hear about it! If only I could stay here and never know what they're doing to the railroad, and never learn when it goes!"

"You'll have to hear about it," said Galt; it was that ruthless tone, peculiarly his, which sounded implacable by being simple, devoid of any emotional value, save the quality of respect for facts. "You'll hear the whole course of the last agony of Taggart Transcontinental. You'll hear about every wreck. You'll hear about every discontinued train. You'll hear about every abandoned line. You'll hear about the collapse of the Taggart Bridge. Nobody stays in this valley except by a full, conscious choice based on a full, conscious knowledge of every fact involved in his decision. Nobody stays here by faking reality in any manner whatever."

She looked at him, her head lifted, knowing what chance he was rejecting. She thought that no man of the outer world would have said this to her at this moment—she thought of the world's code that worshipped white lies as an act of mercy—she felt a stab of revulsion against that code, suddenly seeing its full ugliness for the first time— she felt an enormous pride for the tight, clean face of the man before her—he saw the shape of her mouth drawn firm in self-control, yet softened by some tremulous emotion, while she answered quietly, "Thank you. You're right."

"You don't have to answer me now," he said. "You'll tell me when you've decided. There's still a week left."

"Yes," she said calmly, "just one more week."

He turned, picked up her crumpled sketch, folded it neatly and slipped it into his pocket.

"Dagny," said Francisco, "when you weigh your decision, consider the first time you quit, if you wish, but consider everything about it.

In this valley, you won't have to torture yourself by shingling roofs and building paths that lead nowhere."

"Tell me," she asked suddenly, "how did you find out where I was, that time?"

He smiled. "It was John who told me. The destroyer, remember? You wondered why the destroyer had not sent anyone after you. But he had. It was he who sent me there."

"He sent you?"

"Yes."

"What did he say to you?"

"Nothing much. Why?"

"What did he say? Do you remember the exact words?"

"Yes, I do remember. He said, 'If you want your chance, take it. You've earned it.' I remember, because—" He turned to Galt with the untroubled frown of a slight, casual puzzle. "John, I never quite understood why you said it. Why that? Why—my chance?"

"Do you mind if I don't answer you now?"

"No, but—"

Someone hailed him from the ledges of the mine, and he went off swiftly, as if the subject required no further attention.

She was conscious of the long span of moments she took while turning her head to Galt. She knew that she would find him looking at her. She could read nothing in his eyes, except a hint of derision, as if he knew what answer she was seeking and that she would not find it in his face.

"You gave him a chance that *you* wanted?"

"I could have no chance till he'd had every chance possible to him."

"How did you know what he had earned?"

"I had been questioning him about you for ten years, every time I could, in every way, from every angle. No, he did not tell me—it was the way he spoke of you that did. He didn't want to speak, but he spoke too eagerly, eagerly and reluctantly together—and then I knew that it had not been just a childhood friendship. I knew how much he had given up for the strike and how desperately he hadn't given it up forever. I? I was merely questioning him about one of our most important future strikers—as I questioned him about many others."

The hint of derision remained in his eyes; he knew that she had wanted to hear this, but that this was not the answer to the one question she feared.

She looked from his face to Francisco's approaching figure, not hiding from herself any longer that her sudden, heavy, desolate anxiety was the fear that Galt might throw the three of them into the hopeless waste of self-sacrifice.

Francisco approached, looking at her thoughtfully, as if weighing some question of his own, but some question that gave a sparkle of reckless gaiety to his eyes.

"Dagny, there's only one week left," he said. "If you decide to go back, it will be the last, for a long time." There was no reproach and no sadness in his voice, only some softened quality as sole evidence of emotion. "If you leave now—oh yes, you'll still come back —but it won't be soon. And I—in a few months, I'll come to live here permanently, so if you go, I won't see you again, perhaps for years. I'd like you to spend this last week with me. I'd like you to move to my house. As my guest, nothing else, for no reason, except that I'd like you to."

He said it simply, as if nothing were or could be hidden among the three of them. She saw no sign of astonishment in Galt's face. She felt some swift tightening in her chest, something hard, reckless and almost vicious that had the quality of a dark excitement driving her blindly into action.

"But I'm an employee," she said, with an odd smile, looking at Galt, "I have a job to finish."

"I won't hold you to it," said Galt, and she felt anger at the tone of his voice, a tone that granted her no hidden significance and answered nothing but the literal meaning of her words. "You can quit the job any time you wish. It's up to you."

"No, it isn't. I'm a prisoner here. Don't you remember? I'm to take orders. I have no preferences to follow, no wishes to express, no decisions to make. I want the decision to be yours."

"You want it to be mine?"

"Yes!"

"You've expressed a wish."

The mockery of his voice was in its seriousness—and she threw at him defiantly, not smiling, as if daring him to continue pretending that he did not understand: "All right. *That's* what I wish!"

He smiled, as at a child's complex scheming which he had long since seen through. "Very well." But he did not smile, as he said, turning to Francisco, "Then—no."

The defiance toward an adversary who was the sternest of teachers, was all that Francisco had read in her face. He shrugged, regretfully, but gaily. "You're probably right. If you can't prevent her from going back—nobody can."

She was not hearing Francisco's words. She was stunned by the magnitude of the relief that hit her at the sound of Galt's answer, a relief that told her the magnitude of the fear it swept away. She knew, only after it was over, what had hung for her on his decision; she knew that had his answer been different, it would have destroyed the valley in her eyes.

She wanted to laugh, she wanted to embrace them both and laugh with them in celebration, it did not seem to matter whether she would stay here or return to the world, a week was like an endless span of time, either course seemed flooded by an unchanging sunlight—and no struggle was hard, she thought, if *this* was the nature of existence. The relief did not come from the knowledge that he would not renounce her, nor from any assurance that she would win—the relief came from the certainty that he would always remain what he was.

"I don't know whether I'll go back to the world or not," she said soberly, but her voice was trembling with a subdued violence, which was pure gaiety. "I'm sorry that I'm still unable to make a decision. I'm certain of only one thing: that I won't be afraid to decide."

Francisco took the sudden brightness of her face as proof that the incident had been of no significance. But Galt understood; he glanced at her and the glance was part amusement, part contemptuous reproach.

He said nothing, until they were alone, walking down the trail to the valley. Then he glanced at her again, the amusement sharper in his eyes, and said, "You had to put me to a test in order to learn whether I'd fall to the lowest possible stage of altruism?"

She did not answer, but looked at him in open, undefensive admission.

He chuckled and looked away, and a few steps later said slowly, in the tone of a quotation, "Nobody stays here by faking reality *in any manner whatever.*"

Part of the intensity of her relief—she thought, as she walked silently by his side—was the shock of a contrast: she had seen, with the sudden, immediate vividness of sensory perception, an exact picture of what the code of self-sacrifice would have meant, if enacted by the three of them. Galt, giving up the woman he wanted, for the sake of his friend, faking his greatest feeling out of existence and himself out of her life, no matter what the cost to him and to her, then dragging the rest of his years through the waste of the unreached and unfulfilled —she, turning for consolation to a second choice, faking a love she did not feel, being willing to fake, since her will to self-deceit was the essential required for Galt's self-sacrifice, then living out her years in hopeless longing, accepting, as relief for an unhealing wound, some moments of weary affection, plus the tenet that love is futile and happiness is not to be found on earth—Francisco, struggling in the elusive fog of a counterfeit reality, his life a fraud staged by the two who were dearest to him and most trusted, struggling to grasp what was missing from his happiness, struggling down the brittle scaffold of a lie over the abyss of the discovery that he was not the man she loved, but only a resented substitute, half-charity-patient, half-crutch, his perceptiveness becoming his danger and only his surrender to lethargic stupidity protecting the shoddy structure of his joy, struggling and giving up and settling into the dreary routine of the conviction that fulfillment is impossible to man—the three of them, who had had all the gifts of existence spread out before them, ending up as embittered hulks, who cry in despair that life is frustration—the frustration of not being able to make unreality real.

But *this*—she thought—was men's moral code in the outer world, a code that told them to act on the premise of one another's weakness, deceit and stupidity, and this was the pattern of their lives, this struggle through a fog of the pretended and unacknowledged, this belief that facts are not solid or final, this state where, denying any form to reality, men stumble through life, unreal and unformed, and die having never been born. *Here*—she thought, looking down through green branches at the glittering roofs of the valley—one dealt with men as clear and firm as sun and rocks, and the immense light-heartedness of her relief came from the knowledge that no battle was hard, no decision was dangerous where there was no soggy uncertainty, no shapeless evasion to encounter.

"Did it ever occur to you, Miss Taggart," said Galt, in the casual tone of an abstract discussion, but as if he had known her thoughts, "that there is no conflict of interests among men, neither in business nor in trade nor in their most personal desires—if they omit the irrational from their view of the possible and destruction from their view of the practical? There is no conflict, and no call for sacrifice, and no man is a threat to the aims of another—if men understand that reality is an absolute not to be faked, that lies do not work, that the unearned cannot be had, that the undeserved cannot be given, that the destruction of a value which *is,* will not bring value to that which isn't. The businessman who wishes to gain a market by throttling a superior competitor, the worker who wants a share of his employer's wealth, the artist who envies a rival's higher talent—they're all wishing facts out of existence, and destruction is the only means of their wish. If they pursue it, they will not achieve a market, a fortune or an immortal fame—they will merely destroy production, employment and art. A wish for the irrational is not to be achieved, whether the sacrificial victims are willing or not. But men will not cease to desire the impossible and will not lose their longing to destroy—so long as self-destruction and self-sacrifice are preached to them as the practical means of achieving the happiness of the recipients."

He glanced at her and added slowly, a slight emphasis as sole change in the impersonal tone of his voice, "No one's happiness but my own is in my power to achieve or to destroy. You should have had more respect for him and for me than to fear what you had feared."

She did not answer, she felt as if a word would overfill the fullness of this moment, she merely turned to him with a look of acquiescence that was disarmed, childishly humble and would have been an apology but for its shining joy.

He smiled—in amusement, in understanding, almost in comradeship of the things they shared and in sanction of the things she felt.

They went on in silence, and it seemed to her that this was a summer day out of a carefree youth she had never lived, it was just a walk through the country by two people who were free for the pleasure of motion and sunlight, with no unsolved burdens left to carry. Her sense of lightness blended with the weightless sense of walking downhill, as if she needed no effort to walk, only to restrain herself from flying, and she walked, fighting the speed of the downward pull, her body leaning back, the wind blowing her skirt like a sail to brake her motion.

They parted at the bottom of the trail; he went to keep an appointment with Midas Mulligan, while she went to Hammond's Market with a list of items for the evening's dinner as the sole concern of her world.

His wife—she thought, letting herself hear consciously the word Dr. Akston had not pronounced, the word she had long since felt, but never named—for three weeks she had been his wife in every sense but one, and that final one was still to be earned, but this much was real and today she could permit herself to know it, to feel it, to live with that one thought for this one day.

The groceries, which Lawrence Hammond was lining up at her order on the polished counter of his store, had never appeared to her as such shining objects—and, intent upon them, she was only half-conscious of some disturbing element, of something that was wrong but that her mind was too full to notice. She noticed it only when she saw Hammond pause, frown and stare upward, at the sky beyond his open store front.

In time with his words: "I think somebody's trying to repeat your stunt, Miss Taggart," she realized that it was the sound of an airplane overhead and that it had been there for some time, a sound which was not to be heard in the valley after the first of this month.

They rushed out to the street. The small silver cross of a plane was circling above the ring of mountains, like a sparkling dragonfly about to brush the peaks with its wings.

"What does he think he's doing?" said Lawrence Hammond.

There were people at the doors of the shops and standing still all down the street, looking up.

"Is . . . is anyone expected?" she asked and was astonished by the anxiety of her own voice.

"No," said Hammond. "Everyone who's got any business here is here." He did not sound disturbed, but grimly curious.

The plane was now a small dash, like a silver cigarette, streaking against the flanks of the mountains: it had dropped lower.

"Looks like a private monoplane," said Hammond, squinting against the sun. "Not an army model."

"Will the ray screen hold out?" she asked tensely, in a tone of defensive resentment against the approach of an enemy.

He chuckled. "Hold out?"

"Will he see us?"

"That screen is safer than an underground vault, Miss Taggart. As you ought to know."

The plane rose, and for a moment it was only a bright speck, like a bit of paper blown by the wind—it hovered uncertainly, then dropped down again into another circling spiral.

"What in hell is he after?" said Hammond.

Her eyes shot suddenly to his face.

"He's looking for something," said Hammond. "What?"

"Is there a telescope somewhere?"

"Why—yes, at the airfield, but—" He was about to ask what was the matter with her voice—but she was running across the road, down the path to the airfield, not knowing that she was running, driven by a reason she had no time and no courage to name.

She found Dwight Sanders at the small telescope of the control tower; he was watching the plane attentively, with a puzzled frown.

"Let me see it!" she snapped.

She clutched the metal tube, she pressed her eye to the lens, her hand guiding the tube slowly to follow the plane—then he saw that her hand had stopped, but her fingers did not open and her face remained bent over the telescope, pressed to the lens, until he looked closer and saw that the lens was pressed to her forehead.

"What's the matter, Miss Taggart?"

She raised her head slowly.

"Is it anyone you know, Miss Taggart?"

She did not answer. She hurried away, her steps rushing with the zigzagging aimlessness of uncertainty—she dared not run, but she had to escape, she had to hide, she did not know whether she was afraid to be seen by the men around her or by the plane above—the plane whose silver wings bore the number that belonged to Hank Rearden.

She stopped when she stumbled over a rock and fell and noticed that she had been running. She was on a small ledge in the cliffs above the airfield, hidden from the sight of the town, open to the view of the sky. She rose, her hands groping for support along a granite wall, feeling the warmth of the sun on the rock under her palms—she stood, her back pressed to the wall, unable to move or to take her eyes off the plane.

The plane was circling slowly, dipping down, then rising again, struggling—she thought—as she had struggled, to distinguish the sight of a wreck in a hopeless spread of crevices and boulders, an elusive spread neither clear enough to abandon nor to survey. He was searching for the wreck of her plane, he had not given up, and whatever the three weeks of it had cost him, whatever he felt, the only evidence he would give to the world and his only answer was this steady, insistent, monotonous drone of a motor carrying a fragile craft over every deadly foot of an inaccessible chain of mountains.

Through the brilliant purity of the summer air, the plane seemed intimately close, she could see it rock on precarious currents and bank under the thrusts of wind. She could see, and it seemed impossible that so clear a sight was closed to his eyes. The whole of the valley lay below him, flooded by sunlight, flaming with glass panes and green lawns, screaming to be seen—the end of his tortured quest, the fulfillment of more than his wishes, not the wreck of her plane and her body, but her living presence and his freedom—all that he was seeking or had ever sought was now spread open before him, open and waiting, his to be reached by a straight-line dive through the pure, clear air— his and asking nothing of him but the capacity to see. "Hank!" she screamed, waving her arms in desperate signal. "Hank!"

She fell back against the rock, knowing that she had no way to reach him, that she had no power to give him sight, that no power on earth could pierce that screen except his own mind and vision. Suddenly and for the first time, she felt the screen, not as the most intangible, but as the most grimly absolute barrier in the world.

Slumped against the rock, she watched, in silent resignation, the hopeless circles of the plane's struggle and its motor's uncomplaining cry for help, a cry she had no way to answer. The plane swooped down abruptly, but it was only the start of its final rise, it cut a swift diagonal across the mountains and shot into the open sky. Then, as if caught in the spread of a lake with no shores and no exit, it went sinking slowly and drowning out of sight.

She thought, in bitter compassion, of how much he had failed to see. And I?—she thought. If she left the valley, the screen would close for her as tightly, Atlantis would descend under a vault of rays more impregnable than the bottom of the ocean, and she, too, would be left to struggle for the things she had not known how to see, she, too, would be left to fight a mirage of primordial savagery, while the reality of all that she desired would never come again within her reach.

But the pull of the outer world, the pull that drew her to follow the plane, was not the image of Hank Rearden—she knew that she could not return to him, even if she returned to the world—the pull was the vision of Hank Rearden's courage and the courage of all those still fighting to stay alive. He would not give up the search for her plane, when all others had long since despaired, as he would not give up his mills, as he would not give up any goal he had chosen if a single chance was left. Was she certain that no chance remained for the world of Taggart Transcontinental? Was she certain that the terms of the battle were such that she could not care to win? They were right, the men of Atlantis, they were right to vanish if they knew that they left no value behind them—but until and unless she saw that no chance was untaken and no battle unfought, she had *no right* to remain among them. This was the question that had lashed her for weeks, but had not driven her to a glimpse of the answer.

She lay awake. through the hours of that night, quietly motionless, following—like an engineer and like Hank Rearden—a process of dispassionate, precise, almost mathematical consideration, with no regard for cost or feeling. The agony which he lived in his plane, she lived it in a soundless cube of darkness, searching, but finding no answer. She looked at the inscriptions on the walls of her room, faintly visible in patches of starlight, but the help those men had called in their darkest hour was not hers to call.

* * *

"Yes or no, Miss Taggart?"

She looked at the faces of the four men in the soft twilight of Mulligan's living room: Galt, whose face had the serene, impersonal attentiveness of a scientist—Francisco, whose face was made expressionless by the hint of a smile, the kind of smile that would fit either answer—Hugh Akston who looked compassionately gentle—Midas Mulligan, who had asked the question with no touch of rancor in his voice. Somewhere two thousand miles away, at this sunset hour, the page of a calendar was springing into light over the roofs of New York, saying: June 28—and it seemed to her suddenly that she was seeing it, as if it were hanging over the heads of these men.

"I have one more day," she said steadily. "Will you let me have it? I think I've reached my decision, but I am not fully certain of it and I'll need all the certainty possible to me."

"Of course," said Mulligan. "You have, in fact, until morning of the day after tomorrow. We'll wait."

"We'll wait after that as well," said Hugh Akston, "though in your absence, if that be necessary."

She stood by the window, facing them, and she felt a moment's satisfaction in the knowledge that she stood straight, that her hands did not tremble, that her voice sounded as controlled, uncomplaining and unpitying as theirs; it gave her a moment's feeling of a bond to them.

"If any part of your uncertainty," said Galt, "is a conflict between your heart and your mind—follow your mind."

"Consider the reasons which make us certain that we are right," said Hugh Akston, "but not the fact that we are certain. If you are not convinced, ignore our certainty. Don't be tempted to substitute our judgment for your own."

"Don't rely on our knowledge of what's best for your future," said Mulligan. "We do know, but it can't be best until *you* know it."

"Don't consider our interests or desires," said Francisco. "You have no duty to anyone but yourself."

She smiled, neither sadly nor gaily, thinking that none of it was the sort of advice she would have been given in the outer world. And knowing how desperately they wished to help her where no help was possible, she felt it was her part to give them reassurance.

"I forced my way here," she said quietly, "and I was to bear responsibility for the consequences. I'm bearing it."

Her reward was to see Galt smile: the smile was like a military decoration bestowed upon her.

Looking away, she remembered suddenly Jeff Allen, the tramp aboard the Comet, in the moment when she had admired him for attempting to tell her that he knew where he was going, to spare her the burden of his aimlessness. She smiled faintly, thinking that she had now experienced it in both roles and knew that no action could be lower or more futile than for one person to throw upon another the burden of his abdication of choice. She felt an odd calm, almost a confident repose; she knew that it was tension, but the tension of a great clarity. She caught herself thinking: She's functioning well in an emergency, I'll be all right with her—and realized that she was thinking of herself.

"Let it go till day after tomorrow, Miss Taggart," said Midas Mulligan. "Tonight you're still here."

"Thank you," she said.

She remained by the window, while they went on discussing the valley's business; it was their closing conference of the month. They had just finished dinner—and she thought of her first dinner in this house a month ago; she was wearing, as she had then worn, the gray suit that belonged in her office, not the peasant skirt that had been so easy to wear in the sun. I'm still here tonight, she thought, her hand pressed possessively to the window sill.

The sun had not yet vanished beyond the mountains, but the sky was an even, deep, deceptively clear blue that blended with the blue of invisible clouds into a single spread, hiding the sun; only the edges of the clouds were outlined by a thin thread of flame, and it looked like a glowing, twisted net of neon tubing, she thought . . . like a chart of winding rivers . . . like . . . like the map of a railroad traced in white fire on the sky.

She heard Mulligan giving Galt the names of those who were not returning to the outer world. "We have jobs for all of them," said Mulligan. "In fact, there's only ten or twelve men who're going back this year—mostly to finish off, convert whatever they own and come here permanently. I think this was our last vacation month, because before another year is over we'll all be living in this valley."

"Good," said Galt.

"We'll have to, from the way things are going outside."

"Yes."

"Francisco," said Mulligan, "you'll come back in a few months?"

"In November at the latest," said Francisco. "I'll send you word by short wave, when I'm ready to come back—will you turn the furnace on in my house?"

"I will," said Hugh Akston. "And I'll have your supper ready for you when you arrive."

"John, I take it for granted," said Mulligan, "that you're not returning to New York this time."

Galt took a moment to glance at him, then answered evenly, "I have not decided it yet."

She noticed the shocked swiftness with which Francisco and Mulligan bent forward to stare at him—and the slowness with which Hugh Akston's glance moved to his face; Akston did not seem to be astonished.

"You're not thinking of going back to that hell for another year, are you?" said Mulligan.

"I am."

"But—good God, John!—what for?"

"I'll tell you, when I've decided."

"But there's nothing left there for you to do. We got everybody we knew of or can hope to know of. Our list is completed, except for Hank Rearden—and we'll get *him* before the year is over—and Miss Taggart, if she so chooses. That's all. Your job is done. There's nothing to look for, out there—except the final crash, when the roof comes down on their heads."

"I know it."

"John, yours is the one head I don't want to be there when it happens."

"You've never had to worry about me."

"But don't you realize what stage they're coming to? They're only one step away from open violence—hell, they've taken the step and sealed and declared it long ago!—but in one more moment they'll see the full reality of what they've taken, exploding in their damned faces—plain, open, blind, arbitrary, bloodshedding violence, running amuck, hitting anything and anyone at random. That's what I don't want to see you in the midst of."

"I can take care of myself."

"John, there's no reason for you to take the risk," said Francisco.

"What risk?"

"The looters are worried about the men who've disappeared. They're suspecting something. You, of all people, shouldn't stay there any longer. There's always a chance that they might discover just who and what you are."

"There's some chance. Not much."

"But there's no reason whatever to take it. There's nothing left that Ragnar and I can't finish."

Hugh Akston was watching them silently, leaning back in his chair; his face had that look of intensity, neither quite bitterness nor quite a smile, with which a man watches a progression that interests him, but that lags a few steps behind his vision.

"If I go back," said Galt, "it won't be for our work. It will be to win the only thing I want from the world for myself, now that the work is done. I've taken nothing from the world and I've wanted nothing. But there's one thing which it's still holding and which is mine and which I won't let it have. No, I don't intend to break my oath, I won't deal with the looters, I won't be of any value or help to anyone out there, neither to looters nor neutrals—nor scabs. If I go, it won't be for anyone's sake but mine—and I don't think I'm risking my life, but if I am—well, I'm now free to risk it."

He was not looking at her, but she had to turn away and stand pressed against the window frame, because her hands were trembling.

"But, John!" cried Mulligan, waving his arm at the valley, "if anything happens to you, what would we—" He stopped abruptly and guiltily.

Galt chuckled. "What were you about to say?" Mulligan waved his hand sheepishly, in a gesture of dismissal. "Were you about to say that if anything happens to me, I'll die as the worst failure in the world?"

"All right," said Mulligan guiltily, "I won't say it. I won't say that we couldn't get along without you—we can. I won't beg you to stay here for our sake—I didn't think I'd ever revert to that rotten old plea, but, boy! —what a temptation it was, I can almost see why people do it. I know that whatever it is you want, if you wish to risk your life, that's all there is to it—but I'm thinking only that it's . . . oh God, John, it's such a valuable life!"

Galt smiled. "I know it. That's why I don't think I'm risking it—I think I'll win."

Francisco was now silent, he was watching Galt intently, with a frown of wonder, not as if he had found an answer, but as if he had suddenly glimpsed a question.

"Look, John," said Mulligan, "since you haven't decided whether you'll go—you haven't decided it yet, have you?"

"No, not yet."

"Since you haven't, would you let me remind you of a few things, just for you to consider?"

"Go ahead."

"It's the chance dangers that I'm afraid of—the senseless, unpredictable dangers of a world falling apart. Consider the physical risks of complex machinery in the hands of blind fools and fear-crazed cowards. Just think of their railroads—you'd be taking a chance on some such horror as that Winston tunnel incident every time you stepped aboard a train—and there will be more incidents of that kind, coming faster and faster. They'll reach the stage where no day will pass without a major wreck."

"I know it."

"And the same will be happening in every other industry, wherever machines are used—the machines which they thought could replace our minds. Plane crashes, oil tank explosions, blast-furnace break-outs, high-tension wire electrocutions, subway cave-ins and trestle collapses —they'll see them all. The very machines that had made their life so safe, will now make it a continuous peril."

"I know it."

"I know that you know it, but have you considered it in every specific detail? Have you allowed yourself to visualize it? I want you to see the exact picture of what it is that you propose to enter—before you decide whether anything can justify *your* entering it. You know that the cities will be hit worst of all. The cities were made by the railroads and will go with them."

"That's right."

"When the rails are cut, the city of New York will starve in two days. That's all the supply of food it's got. It's fed by a continent three thousand miles long. How will they carry food to New York? By directive and oxcart? But first, before it happens, they'll go through the whole of the agony—through the shrinking, the shortages, the hunger riots, the stampeding violence in the midst of the growing stillness."

"They will."

"They'll lose their airplanes first, then their automobiles, then their trucks, then their horsecarts."

"They will."

"Their factories will stop, then their furnaces and their radios. Then their electric light system will go."

"It will."

"There's only a worn thread holding that continent together. There will be one train a day, then one train a week—then the Taggart Bridge will collapse and—"

"No, it won't!"

It was her voice and they whirled to her. Her face was white, but calmer than it had been when she had answered them last.

Slowly, Galt rose to his feet and inclined his head, as in acceptance of a verdict. "You've made your decision," he said.

"I have."

"Dagny," said Hugh Akston, "I'm sorry." He spoke softly, with effort, as if his words were struggling and failing to fill the silence of the room. "I wish it were possible not to see this happen, I would have preferred anything—except to see you stay here by default of the courage of your convictions."

She spread her hands, palms out, her arms at her sides, in a gesture of simple frankness, and said, addressing them all, her manner so calm that she could afford to show emotion, "I want you to know this: I have wished it were possible for me to die in one more month, so that I could spend it in this valley. This is how much I've wanted to remain. But so long as I choose to go on living, I can't desert a battle which I think is mine to fight."

"Of course," said Mulligan respectfully, "if you still think it."

"If you want to know the one reason that's taking me back, I'll tell you: I cannot bring myself to abandon to destruction all the greatness of the world, all that which was mine and yours, which was made by us and is still ours by right—because I cannot believe that men can refuse to see, that they can remain blind and deaf to us forever, when the truth is ours and their lives depend on accepting it. They still love their lives—and *that* is the uncorrupted remnant of their minds. So long as men desire to live, I cannot lose my battle."

"Do they?" said Hugh Akston softly. "Do they desire it? No, don't answer me now. I know that the answer was the hardest thing for any of us to grasp and to accept. Just take that question back with you, as the last premise left for you to check."

"You're leaving as our friend," said Midas Mulligan, "and we'll be fighting everything you'll do, because we know you're wrong, but it's not you that we'll be damning."

"You'll come back," said Hugh Akston, "because yours is an error of knowledge, not a moral failure, not an act of surrender to evil, but only the last act of being victim to your own virtue. We'll wait for you—and, Dagny, when you come back, you will have discovered that there need never be any conflict among your desires, nor so tragic a clash of values as the one you've borne so well."

"Thank you," she said, closing her eyes.

"We must discuss the conditions of your departure," said Galt; he spoke in the dispassionate manner of an executive. "First, you must give us your word that you will not disclose our secret or any part of it— neither our cause nor our existence nor this valley nor your where-abouts for the past month—to anyone in the outer world, not at any time or for any purpose whatsoever."

"I give you my word."

"Second, you must never attempt to find this valley again. You are not to come here uninvited. Should you break the first condition, it will not place us in serious danger. Should you break the second—it will. It is not our policy ever to be at the arbitrary mercy of the good faith of an-other person, or at the mercy of a promise that cannot be enforced. Nor can we expect you to place our interests above your own. Since you be-lieve that your course is right, the day may come when you may find it necessary to lead our enemies to this valley. We shall, therefore, leave you no means to do it. You will be taken out of the valley by plane, blindfolded, and you will be flown a distance sufficient to make it im-possible for you ever to retrace the course."

She inclined her head. "You are right."

"Your plane has been repaired. Do you wish to reclaim it by signing a draft on your account at the Mulligan Bank?"

"No."

"Then we shall hold it, until such time as you choose to pay for it. Day after tomorrow, I will take you in my plane to a point outside the valley and leave you within reach of further transportation."

She inclined her head. "Very well."

It had grown dark, when they left Midas Mulligan's. The trail back to Galt's house led across the valley, past Francisco's cabin, and the three of them walked home together. A few squares of lighted windows hung scattered through the darkness, and the first streams of mist were weaving slowly across the panes, like shadows cast by a distant sea. They walked in silence, but the sound of their steps, blending into a single, steady beat, was like a speech to be grasped and not to be uttered in any other form.

After a while, Francisco said, "It changes nothing, it only makes the span a little longer, and the last stretch is always the hardest—but it's the last."

"I will hope so," she said. In a moment, she repeated quietly, "The last is the hardest." She turned to Galt. "May I make one request?"

"Yes."

"Will you let me go tomorrow?"

"If you wish."

When Francisco spoke again, moments later, it was as if he were addressing the unnamed wonder in her mind; his voice had the tone of answering a question: "Dagny, all three of us are in love"—she jerked her head to him—"with the same thing, no matter what its forms. Don't wonder why you feel no breach among us. You'll be one of us, so long as you'll remain in love with your rails and your engines—and they'll lead you back to us, no matter how many times you lose your way. The only man never to be redeemed is the man without passion."

"Thank you," she said softly.

"For what?"

"For . . . for the way you sound."

"How do I sound? Name it, Dagny."

"You sound . . . as if you're happy."

"I am—in exactly the same way you are. Don't tell me what you feel. I know it. But, you see, the measure of the hell you're able to endure is the measure of your love. The hell I couldn't bear to witness would be to see you being indifferent."

She nodded silently, unable to name as joy any part of the things she felt, yet feeling that he was right.

Clots of mist were drifting, like smoke, across the moon, and in the diffused glow she could not distinguish the expressions of their faces, as she walked between them: the only expressions to perceive were the straight silhouettes of their bodies, the unbroken sound of their steps and her own feeling that she wished to walk on and on, a feeling she could not define, except that it was neither doubt nor pain.

When they approached his cabin, Francisco stopped, the gesture of his hand embracing them both as he pointed to his door. "Will you come in —since it's to be our last night together for some time? Let's have a drink to that future of which all three of us are certain."

"Are we?" she asked.

"Yes," said Galt, "we are."

She looked at their faces when Francisco switched on the light in his house. She could not define their expressions, it was not happiness or any emotion pertaining to joy, their faces were taut and solemn, but it was a glowing solemnity—she thought—if this were possible, and the odd glow she felt within her, told her that her own face had the same look.

Francisco reached for three glasses from a cupboard, but stopped, as at a sudden thought. He placed one glass on the table, then reached for the two silver goblets of Sebastián d'Anconia and placed them beside it.

"Are you going straight to New York, Dagny?" he asked, in the calm, unstrained tone of a host, bringing out a bottle of old wine.

"Yes," she answered as calmly.

"I'm flying to Buenos Aires day after tomorrow," he said, uncorking the bottle. "I'm not sure whether I'll be back in New York later, but if I am, it will be dangerous for you to see me."

"I won't care about that," she said, "unless you feel that I'm not entitled to see you any longer."

"True, Dagny. You're not. Not in New York."

He was pouring the wine and he glanced up at Galt. "John, when will you decide whether you're going back or staying here?"

Galt looked straight at him, then said slowly, in the tone of a man who knows all the consequences of his words, "I *have* decided, Francisco. I'm going back."

Francisco's hand stopped. For a long moment, he was seeing nothing but Galt's face. Then his eyes moved to hers. He put the bottle down and he did not step back, but it was as if his glance drew back to a wide range, to include them both.

"But of course," he said.

He looked as if he had moved still farther and were now seeing the whole spread of their years; his voice had an even, uninflected sound, quality that matched the size of the vision.

"I knew it twelve years ago," he said. "I knew it before you could have known, and it's I who should have seen that you would see. That night, when you called us to New York, I thought of it then as"—he was speaking to Galt, but his eyes moved to Dagny—"as everything that you were seeking . . . everything you told us to live for or die, if necessary. I should have seen that you would think it, too. It could not have been otherwise. It is as it had—and ought—to be. It was set then, twelve years ago." He looked at Galt and chuckled softly. "And you say that it's *I* who've taken the hardest beating?"

He turned with too swift a movement—then, too slowly, as if in deliberate emphasis, he completed the task of pouring the wine, filling the three vessels on the table. He picked up the two silver goblets, looked down at them for the pause of an instant, then extended one to Dagny, the other to Galt.

"Take it," he said. "You've earned it—and it wasn't chance."

Galt took the goblet from his hand, but it was as if the acceptance was done by their eyes as they looked at each other.

"I would have given anything to let it be otherwise," said Galt, "except that which is beyond giving."

She held her goblet, she looked at Francisco and she let him see her eyes glance at Galt. "Yes," she said in the tone of an answer. "But I have not earned it—and what you've paid, I'm paying it now, and I don't know whether I'll ever earn enough to hold clear title, but if hell is the price—and the measure—then let me be the greediest of the three of us."

As they drank, as she stood, her eyes closed, feeling the liquid motion of the wine inside her throat, she knew that for all three of them this was the most tortured—and the most exultant—moment they had ever reached.

She did not speak to Galt, as they walked down the last stretch of the trail to his house. She did not turn her head to him, feeling that even a glance would be too dangerous. She felt, in their silence, both the calm of a total understanding and the tension of the knowledge that they were not to name the things they understood.

But she faced him, when they were in his living room, with full confidence and as if in sudden certainty of a right—the certainty that she would not break and that it was now safe to speak. She said evenly, neither as plea nor as triumph, merely as the statement of a fact, "You are going back to the outer world because I will be there."

"Yes."

"I do not want you to go."

"You have no choice about it."

"You are going for my sake."

"No, for mine."

"Will you allow me to see you there?"

"No."

"I am not to see you?"

"No."

"I am not to know where you are or what you do?"

"You're not."

"Will you be watching me, as you did before?"

"More so."

"Is your purpose to protect me?"

"No."

"What is it, then?"

"To be there on the day when you decide to join us."

She looked at him attentively, permitting herself no other reaction, but as if groping for an answer to the first point she had not fully understood.

"All the rest of us will be gone," he explained. "It will become too dangerous to remain. I will remain as your last key, before the door of this valley closes altogether."

"Oh!" She choked it off before it became a moan. Then, regaining the manner of impersonal detachment, she asked, "Suppose I were to tell you that my decision is final and that I am never to join you?"

"It would be a lie."

"Suppose I were now to decide that I wish to make it final and to stand by it, no matter what the future?"

"No matter what future evidence you observe and what convictions you form?"

"Yes."

"That would be worse than a lie."

"You are certain that I have made the wrong decision?"

"I am."

"Do you believe that one must be responsible for one's own errors?"

"I do."

"Then why aren't you letting me bear the consequences of mine?"

"I am and you will."

"If I find, when it is too late, that I want to return to this valley —why should you have to bear the risk of keeping that door open to me?"

"I don't have to. I wouldn't do it if I had no selfish end to gain."

"What selfish end?"

"I want you here."

She closed her eyes and inclined her head in open admission of defeat—defeat in the argument and in her attempt to face calmly the full meaning of that which she was leaving.

Then she raised her head and, as if she had absorbed his kind of frankness, she looked at him, hiding neither her suffering nor her longing nor her calm, knowing that all three were in her glance.

His face was as it had been in the sunlight of the moment when she had seen it for the first time: a face of merciless serenity and unflinching perceptiveness, without pain or fear or guilt. She thought that were it possible for her to stand looking at him, at the straight lines of his eyebrows over the dark green eyes, at the curve of the shadow underscoring the shape of his mouth, at the poured-metal planes of his skin in the open collar of his shirt and the casually immovable posture of his legs—she would wish to spend the rest of her life on this spot and in this manner. And in the next instant she knew that if her wish were granted, the contemplation would lose all meaning, because she would have betrayed all the things that gave it value.

Then, not as memory, but as an experience of the present, she felt herself reliving the moment when she had stood at the window of her room in New York, looking at a fogbound city, at the unattainable shape of Atlantis sinking out of reach—and she knew that she was now seeing the answer to that moment. She felt, not the words she had then addressed to the city, but that untranslated sensation from which the words had come: You, whom I have always loved and never found, you whom I expected to see at the end of the rails beyond the horizon—

Aloud, she said, "I want you to know this. I started my life with a single absolute: that the world was mine to shape in the image of my highest values and never to be given up to a lesser standard, no matter how long or hard the struggle"—you whose presence I had always felt in the streets of the city, the wordless voice within her was saying, and whose world I had wanted to build—"Now I know that I was fighting for this valley"—it is my love for you that had kept me moving—"It was this valley that I saw as possible and would exchange for nothing less and would not give up to a mindless evil"—my love and my hope to reach you and my wish to be worthy of you on the day when I would stand before you face to face—"I am going back to fight for this valley—to release it from its underground, to regain for it its full and rightful realm, to let the earth belong to you in fact, as it does in spirit—and to meet you again on the day when I'm able to deliver to you the whole of the world—or, if I fail, to remain in exile from this valley to the end of my life"—but what is left of my life will still be yours, and I will go on in your name, even though it is a name I'm never to pronounce, I will go on serving you, even though I'm never to win, I will go on, to be worthy of you on the day when I would have met you, even though I won't—"I will fight for it, even if I have to fight against you, even if you damn me as a traitor . . . even if I am never to see you again."

He had stood without moving, he had listened with no change in his face, only his eyes had looked at her as if he were hearing every word, even the words she had not pronounced. He answered, with the same look, as if the look were holding some circuit not yet to be broken, his voice catching some tone of hers, as if in signal of the same code, a voice with no sign of emotion except in the spacing of the words:

"If you fail, as men have failed in their quest for a vision that should have been possible, yet has remained forever beyond their reach—if, like them, you come to think that one's highest values are not to be attained and one's greatest vision is not to be made real—

don't damn this earth, as they did, don't damn existence. You have seen the Atlantis they were seeking, it is here, it exists—but one must enter it naked and alone, with no rags from the falsehoods of centuries, with the purest clarity of mind—not an innocent heart, but that which is much rarer: an intransigent mind—as one's only possession and key. You will not enter it until you learn that you do not need to convince or to conquer the world. When you learn it, you will see that through all the years of your struggle, nothing had barred you from Atlantis and there were no chains to hold you, except the chains you were willing to wear. Through all those years, that which you most wished to win was waiting for you"—he looked at her as if he were speaking to the unspoken words in her mind—"waiting as unremittingly as you were fighting, as passionately, as desperately—but with a greater certainty than yours. Go out to continue your struggle. Go on carrying unchosen burdens, taking undeserved punishment and believing that justice can be served by the offer of your own spirit to the most unjust of tortures. But in your worst and darkest moments, remember that you have seen another kind of world. Remember that you can reach it whenever you choose to see. Remember that it will be waiting and that it's real, it's possible—it's yours."

Then, turning his head a little, his voice as clear, but his eyes breaking the circuit, he asked, "What time do you wish to leave tomorrow?"

"Oh . . . ! As early as it will be convenient for you."

"Then have breakfast ready at seven and we'll take off at eight."

"I will."

He reached into his pocket and extended to her a small, shining disk which she could not distinguish at first. He dropped it on the palm of her hand: it was a five-dollar gold piece.

"The last of your wages for the month," he said.

Her fingers snapped closed over the coin too tightly, but she answered calmly and tonelessly, "Thank you."

"Good night, Miss Taggart."

"Good night."

She did not sleep in the hours that were still left to her. She sat on the floor of her room, her face pressed to the bed, feeling nothing but the sense of his presence beyond the wall. At times, she felt as if he were before her, as if she were sitting at his feet. She spent her last night with him in this manner.

* * *

She left the valley as she had come, carrying away nothing that belonged to it. She left the few possessions she had acquired—her peasant skirt, a blouse, an apron, a few pieces of underwear—folded neatly in a drawer of the chest in her room. She looked at them for a moment, before she closed the drawer, thinking that if she came back, she would, perhaps, still find them there. She took nothing with her but the five-dollar gold piece and the band of tape still wound about her ribs.

The sun touched the peaks of the mountains, drawing a shining circle as a frontier of the valley—when she climbed aboard the plane. She leaned back in the seat beside him and looked at Galt's face bent over her, as it had been bent when she had opened her eyes on the first morning. Then she closed her eyes and felt his hands tying the blindfold across her face.

She heard the blast of the motor, not as sound, but as the shudder of an explosion inside her body; only it felt like a distant shudder, as if the person feeling it would have been hurt if she were not so far away.

She did not know when the wheels left the ground or when the plane crossed the circle of the peaks. She lay still, with the pounding beat of the motor as her only perception of space, as if she were carried inside a current of sound that rocked once in a while. The sound came from his engine, from the control of his hands on the wheel; she held onto that; the rest was to be endured, not resisted.

She lay still, her legs stretched forward, her hands on the arms of the seat, with no sense of motion, not even her own, to give her a sense of time, with no space, no sight, no future, with the night of closed eyelids under the pressure of the cloth—and with the knowledge of his presence beside her as her single, unchanging reality.

They did not speak. Once, she said suddenly, "Mr. Galt."

"Yes?"

"No. Nothing. I just wanted to know whether you were still there."

"I will always be there."

She did not know for how many miles the memory of the sound of words seemed like a small landmark rolling away into the distance, then vanishing. Then there was nothing but the stillness of an indivisible present.

She did not know whether a day had passed or an hour, when she felt the downward, plunging motion which meant that they were about to land or to crash; the two possibilities seemed equal to her mind.

She felt the jolt of the wheels against the ground as an oddly delayed sensation: as if some fraction of time had gone to make her believe it.

She felt the running streak of jerky motion, then the jar of the stop and of silence, then the touch of his hands on her hair, removing the blindfold.

She saw a glaring sunlight, a stretch of scorched weeds going off into the sky, with no mountains to stop it, a deserted highway and the hazy outline of a town about a mile away. She glanced at her watch: forty-seven minutes ago, she had still been in the valley.

"You'll find a Taggart station there," he said, pointing at the town, "and you'll be able to take a train."

She nodded, as if she understood.

He did not follow her as she descended to the ground. He leaned across the wheel toward the open door of the plane, and they looked at each other. She stood, her face raised to him, a faint wind stirring her hair, the straight line of her shoulders sculptured by the trim suit of a business executive amidst the flat immensity of an empty prairie.

The movement of his hand pointed east, toward some invisible cities. "Don't look for me out there," he said. "You will not find me—until you want me for what I am. And when you'll want me, I'll be the easiest man to find."

She heard the sound of the door falling closed upon him; it seemed louder than the blast of the propeller that followed. She watched the run of the plane's wheels and the trail of weeds left flattened behind them. Then she saw a strip of sky between wheels and weeds.

She looked around her. A reddish haze of heat hung over the shapes of the town in the distance, and the shapes seemed to sag under a rusty tinge; above their roofs, she saw the remnant of a crumbled smokestack. She saw a dry, yellow scrap rustling faintly in the weeds beside her: it was a piece of newspaper. She looked at these objects blankly, unable to make them real.

She raised her eyes to the plane. She watched the spread of its wings grow smaller in the sky, draining away in its wake the sound of its motor. It kept rising, wings first, like a long silver cross; then the curve of its motion went following the sky, dropping slowly closer to the earth; then it seemed not to move any longer, but only to shrink. She watched it like a star in the process of extinction, while it shrank from cross to dot to a burning spark which she was no longer certain of seeing. When she saw that the spread of the sky was strewn with such sparks all over, she knew that the plane was gone.

ANTI-GREED

"What am I doing here?" asked Dr. Robert Stadler. "Why was I asked to come here? I demand an explanation. I'm not accustomed to being dragged halfway across a continent without rhyme, reason or notice."

Dr. Floyd Ferris smiled. "Which makes me appreciate it all the more that you *did* come, Dr. Stadler." It was impossible to tell whether his voice had a tone of gratitude—or of gloating.

The sun was beating down upon them and Dr. Stadler felt a streak of perspiration oozing along his temple. He could not hold an angrily, embarrassingly private discussion in the middle of a crowd streaming to fill the benches of the grandstand around them—the discussion which he had tried and failed to obtain for the last three days. It occurred to him that that was precisely the reason why his meeting with Dr. Ferris had been delayed to this moment; but he brushed the thought aside, just as he brushed some insect buzzing to reach his wet temple.

"Why was I unable to get in touch with you?" he asked. The fraudulent weapon of sarcasm now seemed to sound less effective than ever, but it was Dr. Stadler's only weapon: "Why did you find it necessary to send me messages on official stationery worded in a style proper, I'm sure, for Army"—orders, he was about to say, but didn't—"communications, but certainly not for scientific correspondence?"

"It is a *government* matter," said Dr. Ferris gently.

"Do you realize that I was much too busy and that this meant an interruption of my work?"

"Oh yes," said Dr. Ferris noncommittally.

"Do you realize that I could have refused to come?"

"But you didn't," said Dr. Ferris softly.

"Why was I given no explanation? Why didn't you come for me in person, instead of sending those incredible young hooligans with their mysterious gibberish that sounded half-science, half-pulp-magazine?"

"I was too busy," said Dr. Ferris blandly.

"Then would you mind telling me what you're doing in the middle of a plain in Iowa—and what I'm doing here, for that matter?" He waved contemptuously at the dusty horizon of an empty prairie and at the three wooden grandstands. The stands were newly erected, and the wood, too, seemed to perspire; he could see drops of resin sparkling in the sun.

"We are about to witness an historical event, Dr. Stadler. An occasion which will become a milestone on the road of science, civilization, social welfare and political adaptability." Dr. Ferris' voice had the tone of a public relations man's memorized handout. "The turning point of a new era."

"What event? What new era?"

"As you will observe, only the most distinguished citizens, the cream of our intellectual elite, have been chosen for the special privilege of witnessing this occasion. We could not omit your name, could we?—and we feel certain, of course, that we can count on your loyalty and cooperation."

He could not catch Dr. Ferris' eyes. The grandstands were rapidly filling with people, and Dr. Ferris kept interrupting himself constantly to wave to nondescript newcomers, whom Dr. Stadler had never seen before, but who were personages, as he could tell by the particular shade of gaily informal deference in Ferris' waving. They all seemed to know Dr. Ferris and to seek him out, as if he were the master of ceremonies —or the star—of the occasion.

"If you would kindly be specific for a moment," said Dr. Stadler, "and tell me what—"

"Hi, Spud!" called Dr. Ferris, waving to a portly, white-haired man who filled the full-dress uniform of a general.

Dr. Stadler raised his voice: "I said, if you would kindly concentrate long enough to explain to me what in hell is going on—"

"But it's very simple. It's the final triumph of . . . You'll have to excuse me a minute, Dr. Stadler," said Dr. Ferris hastily, tearing forward, like an overtrained lackey at the sound of a bell, in the direction of what looked like a group of aging rowdies; he turned back long enough to add two words which he seemed reverently to consider as a full explanation: *"The press!"*

Dr. Stadler sat down on the wooden bench, feeling unaccountably reluctant to brush against anything around him. The three grandstands were spaced at intervals in a semi-curve, like the tiers of a small, private circus, with room for some three hundred people; they seemed built for the viewing of some spectacle—but they faced the emptiness of a flat prairie stretching off to the horizon, with nothing in sight but the dark blotch of a farmhouse miles away.

There were radio microphones in front of one stand, which seemed reserved for the press. There was a contraption resembling a portable switchboard in front of the stand reserved for officials; a few levers of polished metal sparkled in the sun on the face of the switchboard. In an improvised parking lot behind the stands, the glitter of luxurious new cars seemed a brightly reassuring sight. But it was the building that stood on a knoll some thousand feet away that gave Dr. Stadler a vague sense of uneasiness. It was a small, squat structure of unknown purpose, with massive stone walls, no windows except a few slits protected by stout iron bars, and a large dome, grotesquely too heavy for the rest, that seemed to press the structure down into the soil. A few outlets protruded from the base of the dome, in loose, irregular shapes, resembling badly poured clay funnels; they did not seem to belong to an industrial age or to any known usage. The building had an air of silent malevolence, like a puffed, venomous mushroom; it was obviously modern, but its sloppy, rounded, ineptly unspecific lines made it look like a primitive structure unearthed in the heart of the jungle, devoted to some secret rites of savagery.

Dr. Stadler sighed with irritation; he was tired of secrets. "Confidential" and "Top Confidential" had been the words stamped on the invitation which had demanded that he travel to Iowa on a two-day notice and for an unspecified purpose. Two young men, who called themselves physicists, had appeared at the Institute to escort him; his calls to Ferris' office in Washington had remained unanswered. The young men had talked—through an exhausting trip by government plane, then a clammy ride in a government car—about science, emergencies, social equilibriums and the need of secrecy, till he knew less than he had known at the start; he noticed only that two words kept recurring in their jabber, which had also appeared in the text of the invitation, two words that had an ominous sound when involving an unknown issue: the demands for his "loyalty" and "co-operation."

The young men had deposited him on a bench in the front row of the grandstand and had vanished, like the folding gear of a mechanism, leaving him to the sudden presence of Dr. Ferris in person. Now, watching the scene around him, watching Dr. Ferris' vague, excited, loosely casual gestures in the midst of a group of newsmen, he had an impression of bewildering confusion, of senseless, chaotic inefficiency—and of a smooth machine working to produce the exact degree of that impression needed at the exact moment.

He felt a single, sudden flash of panic, in which, as in a flash of lightning, he permitted himself to know that he felt a desperate desire to escape. But he slammed his mind shut against it. He knew that the darkest secret of the occasion—more crucial, more untouchable, more deadly than whatever was hidden in the mushroom building—was that which had made him agree to come.

He would never have to learn his own motive, he thought; he thought it, not by means of words, but by means of the brief, vicious spasm of an emotion that resembled irritation and felt like acid. The words that stood in his mind, as they had stood when he had agreed to come, were like a voodoo formula which one recites when it is needed and beyond which one must not look: *What can you do when you have to deal with people?*

He noticed that the stand reserved for those whom Ferris had called the intellectual elite was larger than the stand prepared for government officials. He caught himself feeling a swift little sneak of pleasure at the thought that he had been placed in the front row. He turned to glance at the tiers behind him. The sensation he experienced was like a small, gray shock: that random, faded, shopworn assembly was not his conception of an intellectual elite. He saw defensively belligerent men and tastelessly dressed women—he saw mean, rancorous, suspicious faces that bore the one mark incompatible with a standard bearer of the intellect: the mark of uncertainty. He could find no face he knew, no face to recognize as famous and none likely ever to achieve such recognition. He wondered by what standard these people had been selected.

Then he noticed a gangling figure in the second row, the figure of an elderly man with a long, slack face that seemed faintly familiar to him, though he could recall nothing about it, except a vague memory, as of a photograph seen in some unsavory publication. He leaned toward a woman and asked, pointing, "Could you tell me. the name of that gentleman?" The woman answered in a whisper of awed respect, "That is Dr. Simon Pritchett!" Dr. Stadler turned away, wishing no one would see him, wishing no one would ever learn that he had been a member of that group.

He raised his eyes and saw that Ferris was leading the whole press gang toward him. He saw Ferris sweeping his arm at him, in the manner of a tourist guide, and declaring, when they were close enough to be heard, "But why should you waste your time on me, when *there* is the source of today's achievement, the man who made it all possible— Dr. Robert Stadler!"

It seemed to him for an instant that he saw an incongruous look on the worn, cynical faces of the newsmen, a look that was not quite respect, expectation or hope, but more like an echo of these, like a faint reflection of the look they might have worn in their youth on hearing the name of Robert Stadler. In that instant, he felt an impulse which he would not acknowledge: the impulse to tell them that he knew nothing about today's event, that his power counted for less than theirs, that he had been brought here as a pawn in some confidence game, almost as . . . as a prisoner.

Instead, he heard himself answering their questions in the smug, condescending tone of a man who shares all the secrets of the highest authorities: "Yes, the State Science Institute is proud of its record of public service. . . . The State Science Institute is not the tool of any private interests or personal greed, it is devoted to the welfare of mankind, to the good of humanity as a whole—" spouting, like a dictaphone, the sickening generalities he had heard from Dr. Ferris.

He would not permit himself to know that what he felt was self-loathing; he identified the emotion, but not its object; it was loathing for the men around him, he thought; it was they who were forcing him to go through this shameful performance. What can you do—he thought—when you have to deal with people?

The newsmen were making brief notes of his answers. Their faces now had the look of automatons acting out the routine of pretending that they were hearing news in the empty utterances of another automaton.

"Dr. Stadler," asked one of them, pointing at the building on the knoll, "is it true that you consider Project X the greatest achievement of the State Science Institute?"

There was a dead drop of silence.

"Project . . . X . . . ?" said Dr. Stadler.

He knew that something was ominously wrong in the tone of his voice, because he saw the heads of the newsmen go up, as at the sound of an alarm; he saw them waiting, their pencils poised.

For one instant, while he felt the muscles of his face cracking into the fraud of a smile, he felt a formless, an almost supernatural terror, as if he sensed again the silent working of some smooth machine, as if he were caught in it, part of it and doing its irrevocable will. "Project X?" he said softly, in the mysterious tone of a conspirator. "Well, gentlemen, the value—and the motive—of any achievement of the State Science Institute are not to be doubted, since it is a non-profit venture—need I say more?"

He raised his head and noticed that Dr. Ferris had stood on the edge of the group through the whole of the interview. He wondered whether he imagined that the look on Dr. Ferris' face now seemed less tense—and more impertinent.

Two resplendent cars came shooting at full speed into the parking lot and stopped with a flourish of screeching brakes. The newsmen deserted him in the middle of a sentence and went running to meet the group alighting from the cars.

Dr. Stadler turned to Ferris. *"What* is Project X?" he asked sternly.

Dr. Ferris smiled in a manner of innocence and insolence together. "A non-profit venture," he answered—and went running off to meet the newcomers.

From the respectful whispers of the crowd, Dr. Stadler learned that the little man in a wilted linen suit, who looked like a shyster, striding briskly in the center of the new group, was Mr. Thompson, the Head of the State. Mr. Thompson was smiling, frowning and barking answers to the newsmen. Dr. Ferris was weaving through the group, with the grace of a cat rubbing against sundry legs.

The group came closer and he saw Ferris steering them in his direction. "Mr. Thompson," said Dr. Ferris sonorously, as they approached, "may I present Dr. Robert Stadler?"

Dr. Stadler saw the little shyster's eyes studying him for the fraction of a second: the eyes had a touch of superstitious awe, as at the sight of a phenomenon from a mystical realm forever incomprehensible to Mr. Thompson—and they had the piercing, calculating shrewdness of a ward heeler who feels certain that nothing is immune from his standards, a glance like the visual equivalent of the words: What's your angle?

"It's an honor, Doctor, an honor, I'm sure," said Mr. Thompson briskly, shaking his hand.

He learned that the tall, stoop-shouldered man with a crew haircut was Mr. Wesley Mouch. He did not catch the names of the others, whose hands he shook. As the group proceeded toward the officials' grandstand, he was left with the burning sensation of a discovery he dared not face: the discovery that he had felt anxiously pleased by the little shyster's nod of approval.

A party of young attendants, who looked like movie theater ushers, appeared from somewhere with handcarts of glittering objects, which they proceeded to distribute to the assembly. The objects were field glasses. Dr. Ferris took his place at the microphone of a public-address system by the officials' stand. At a signal from Wesley Mouch, his voice boomed suddenly over the prairie, an unctuous, fraudulently solemn voice magnified by the microphone inventor's ingenuity into the sound and power of a giant:

"Ladies and gentlemen . . . !"

The crowd was struck into silence, all heads jerking unanimously toward the graceful figure of Dr. Floyd Ferris.

"Ladies and gentlemen, you have been chosen—in recognition of your distinguished public service and social loyalty—to witness the unveiling of a scientific achievement of such tremendous importance, such staggering scope, such epoch-making possibilities that up to this moment it has been known only to a very few and only as Project X."

Dr. Stadler focused his field glasses on the only thing in sight—on the blotch of the distant farm.

He saw that it was the deserted ruin of a farmhouse, which had obviously been abandoned years ago. The light of the sky showed through the naked ribs of the roof, and jagged bits of glass framed the darkness of empty windows. He saw a sagging barn, the rusted tower of a water wheel, and the remnant of a tractor lying upturned with its treads in the air.

Dr. Ferris was talking about the crusaders of science and about the years of selfless devotion, unremitting toil and persevering research that had gone into Project X.

It was odd—thought Dr. Stadler, studying the ruins of the farm—that there should be a herd of goats in the midst of such desolation. There were six or seven of them, some drowsing, some munching lethargically at whatever grass they could find among the sun-scorched weeds.

"Project X," Dr. Ferris was saying, "was devoted to some special research in the field of sound. The science of sound has astonishing aspects, which laymen would scarcely suspect. . . ."

Some fifty feet away from the farmhouse, Dr. Stadler saw a structure, obviously new and of no possible purpose whatever: it looked like a few spans of a steel trestle, rising into empty space, supporting nothing, leading nowhere.

Dr. Ferris was now talking about the nature of sound vibrations.

Dr. Stadler aimed his field glasses at the horizon beyond the farm, but there was nothing else to be seen for dozens of miles. The sudden, straining motion of one of the goats brought his eyes back to the herd. He noticed that the goats were chained to stakes driven at intervals into the ground.

". . . And it was discovered," said Dr. Ferris, "that there are certain frequencies of sound vibration which no structure, organic or inorganic, can withstand. . . ."

Dr. Stadler noticed a silvery spot bouncing over the weeds among the herd. It was a kid that had not been chained; it kept leaping and weaving about its mother.

". . . The sound ray is controlled by a panel inside the giant underground laboratory," said Dr. Ferris, pointing at the building on the knoll. "That panel is known to us affectionately as the 'Xylophone'— because one must be darn careful to strike the right keys, or, rather, to pull the right levers. For this special occasion, an extension Xylophone, connected to the one inside, has been erected here"—he pointed to the switchboard in front of the officials' stand—"so that you may witness the entire operation and see the simplicity of the whole procedure. . . ."

Dr. Stadler found pleasure in watching the kid, a soothing, reassuring kind of pleasure. The little creature seemed barely a week old, it looked like a ball of white fur with graceful long legs, it kept bounding in a manner of deliberate, gaily ferocious awkwardness, all four of its legs held stiff and straight. It seemed to be leaping at the sunrays, at the summer air, at the joy of discovering its own existence.

". . . The sound ray is invisible, inaudible and fully controllable in respect to target, direction and range. Its first public test, which you are about to witness, has been set to cover a small sector, a mere two miles, in perfect safety, with all space cleared for twenty miles beyond. The present generating equipment in our laboratory is capable of producing rays to cover—through the outlets which you may observe under the dome—the entire countryside within a radius of a hundred miles, a circle with a periphery extending from the shore of the Mississippi, roughly from the bridge of the Taggart Transcontinental Railroad, to Des Moines and Fort Dodge, Iowa, to Austin, Minnesota, to Woodman, Wisconsin, to Rock Island, Illinois. This is only a modest beginning. We possess the technical knowledge to build generators with a range of two and three hundred miles—but due to the fact that we were unable to obtain in time a sufficient quantity of a highly heat-resistant metal, such as Rearden Metal, we had to be satisfied with our present equipment and radius of control. In honor of our great executive, Mr. Thompson, under whose far-sighted administration the State Science Institute was granted the funds without which Project X would not have been possible, this great invention will henceforth be known as the Thompson Harmonizer!"

The crowd applauded. Mr. Thompson sat motionless, with his face held self-consciously stiff. Dr. Stadler felt certain that this small-time shyster had had as little to do with the Project as any of the movie-usher attendants, that he possessed neither the mind nor the initiative nor even the sufficient degree of malice to cause a new gopher trap to be brought into the world, that he, too, was only the pawn of a silent machine—a machine that had no center, no leader, no direction, a machine that had not been set in motion by Dr. Ferris or Wesley Mouch, or any of the cowed creatures in the grandstands, or any of the creatures behind the scenes—an impersonal, unthinking, unembodied machine, of which none was the driver and all were the pawns, each to the degree of his evil. Dr. Stadler gripped the edge of the bench: he felt a desire to leap to his feet and run.

". . . As to the function and the purpose of the sound ray, I shall say nothing. I shall let it speak for itself. You will now see it work. When Dr. Blodgett pulls the levers of the Xylophone, I suggest that you keep your eyes on the target—which is that farmhouse two miles away. There will be nothing else to see. The ray itself is invisible. It has long been conceded by all progressive thinkers that there are no entities, only actions—and no values, only consequences. Now, ladies and gentlemen, you will see the action and the consequences of the Thompson Harmonizer."

Dr. Ferris bowed, walked slowly away from the microphone and came to take his seat on the bench beside Dr. Stadler.

A youngish, fattish kind of man took his stand by the switchboard—and raised his eyes expectantly toward Mr. Thompson. Mr. Thompson looked blankly bewildered for an instant, as if something had slipped his mind, until Wesley Mouch leaned over and whispered some word into his ear. "Contact!" said Mr. Thompson loudly.

Dr. Stadler could not bear to watch the graceful, undulating, effeminate motion of Dr. Blodgett's hand as it pulled the first lever of the switchboard, then the next. He raised his field glasses and looked at the farmhouse.

In the instant when he focused his lens, a goat was pulling at its chain, reaching placidly for a tall, dry thistle. In the next instant, the goat rose into the air, upturned, its legs stretched upward and jerking, then fell into a gray pile made of seven goats in convulsions. By the time Dr. Stadler believed it, the pile was motionless, except for one beast's leg sticking out of the mass, stiff as a rod and shaking as in a strong wind. The farmhouse tore into strips of clapboard and went down, followed by a geyser of the bricks of its chimney. The tractor vanished into a pancake. The water tower cracked and its shreds hit the ground while its wheel was still describing a long curve through the air, as if of its own leisurely volition. The steel beams and girders of the solid new trestle collapsed like a structure of matchsticks under the breath of a sigh. It was so swift, so uncontested, so simple, that Dr. Stadler felt no horror, he felt nothing, it was not the reality he had known, it was the realm of a child's nightmare where material objects could be dissolved by means of a single malevolent wish.

He moved the field glasses from his eyes. He was looking at an empty prairie. There was no farm, there was nothing in the distance except a darkish strip that looked like the shadow of a cloud.

A single, high, thin scream rose from the tiers behind him, as some woman fainted. He wondered why she should scream so long after the fact—and then he realized that the time elapsed since the touch of the first lever was not a full minute.

He raised his field glasses again, almost as if he were suddenly hoping that the cloud shadow would be all he would see. But the material objects were still there; they were a mount of refuse. He moved his glasses over the wreckage; in a moment, he realized that he was looking for the kid. He could not find it; there was nothing but a pile of gray fur.

When he lowered the glasses and turned, he found Dr. Ferris looking at him. He felt certain that through the whole of the test, it was not the target, it was his face that Ferris had watched, as if to see whether he, Robert Stadler, could withstand the ray.

"That's all there is to it," the fattish Dr. Blodgett announced through the microphone, in the ingratiating sales tone of a department-store floorwalker. "There is no nail or rivet remaining in the frame of the structures and there is no blood vessel left unbroken in the bodies of the animals."

The crowd was rustling with jerky movements and high-pitched whispers. People were looking at one another, rising uncertainly and dropping down again, restlessly demanding anything but this pause. There was a sound of submerged hysteria in the whispers. They seemed to be waiting to be told what to think.

Dr. Stadler saw a woman being escorted down the steps from the back row, her head bent, a handkerchief pressed to her mouth: she was sick at her stomach.

He turned away and saw that Dr. Ferris was still watching him. Dr. Stadler leaned back a little, his face austere and scornful, the face of the nation's greatest scientist, and asked, "Who invented that ghastly thing?"

"You did."

Dr. Stadler looked at him, not moving.

"It is merely a practical appliance," said Dr. Ferris pleasantly, "based upon your theoretical discoveries. It was derived from your invaluable research into the nature of cosmic rays and of the spatial transmission of energy."

"Who worked on the Project?"

"A few third-raters, as you would call them. Really, there was very little difficulty. None of them could have begun to conceive of the first step toward the concept of your energy-transmission formula, but given that—the rest was easy."

"What is the practical purpose of this invention? What are the 'epoch-making possibilities'?"

"Oh, but don't you see? It is an invaluable instrument of public security. No enemy would attack the possessor of such a weapon. It will set the country free from the fear of aggression and permit it to plan its future in undisturbed safety." His voice had an odd carelessness, a tone of offhand improvisation, as if he were neither expecting nor attempting to be believed. "It will relieve social frictions. It will promote peace, stability and—as we have indicated—harmony. It will eliminate all danger of war."

"What war? What aggression? With the whole world starving and all those People's States barely subsisting on handouts from this country—where do you see any danger of war? Do you expect those ragged savages to attack you?"

Dr. Ferris looked straight into his eyes. "Internal enemies can be as great a danger to the people as external ones," he answered. "Perhaps greater." This time his voice sounded as if he expected and was certain to be understood. "Social systems are so precarious. But think of what stability could be achieved by a few scientific installations at strategic key points. It would guarantee a state of permanent peace—don't you think so?"

Dr. Stadler did not move or answer; as the seconds clicked past and his face still held an unchanged expression, it began to look paralyzed. His eyes had the stare of a man who suddenly sees that which he had known, had known from the first, had spent years trying not to see, and who is now engaged in a contest between the sight and his power to deny its existence. "I don't know what you're talking about!" he snapped at last.

Dr. Ferris smiled. "No private businessman or greedy industrialist would have financed Project X," he said softly, in the tone of an idle, informal discussion. "He couldn't have afforded it. It's an enormous investment, with no prospect of material gain. What profit could he expect from it? There are no profits henceforth to be derived from that farm." He pointed at the dark strip in the distance. "But, as you have so well observed, Project X had to be a non-profit venture. Contrary to a business firm, the State Science Institute had no trouble in obtaining funds for the Project. You have not heard of the Institute having any financial difficulties in the past two years, have you? And it used to be such a problem—getting them to vote the funds necessary for the advancement of science. They always demanded gadgets for their cash, as you used to say. Well, here was a gadget which some people in power could fully appreciate. They got the others to vote for it. It wasn't difficult. In fact, a great many of those others felt safe in voting money for a project that was secret—they felt certain it was important, since they were not considered important enough to be let in on it. There were, of course, a few skeptics and doubters. But they gave in when they were reminded that the head of the State Science Institute was Dr. Robert Stadler—whose judgment and integrity they could not doubt."

Dr. Stadler was looking down at his fingernails.

The sudden screech of the microphone jerked the crowd into an instantaneous attentiveness; people seemed to be a second's worth of self-control away from panic. An announcer, with a voice like a machine gun spitting smiles, barked cheerily that they were now to witness the radio broadcast that would break the news of the great discovery to the whole nation. Then, with a glance at his watch, his script and the signaling arm of Wesley Mouch, he yelled into the sparkling snake-head of the microphone—into the living rooms, the offices, the studies, the nurseries of the country: "Ladies and gentlemen! Project X!"

Dr. Ferris leaned toward Dr. Stadler—through the staccato hoofbeats of the announcer's voice galloping across the continent with a description of the new invention—and said in the tone of a casual remark, "It is vitally important that there be no criticism of the Project in the country at this precarious time," then added semi-accidentally, as a semi-joke, "that there be no criticism of anything at any time."

"—and the nation's political, cultural, intellectual and moral leaders," the announcer was yelling into the microphone, "who have witnessed this great event, as your representatives and in your name, will now tell you their views of it in person!"

Mr. Thompson was the first to mount the wooden steps to the platform of the microphone. He snapped his way through a brief speech, hailing a new era and declaring—in the belligerent tone of a challenge to unidentified enemies—that science belonged to the people and that every man on the face of the globe had a right to a share of the advantages created by technological progress.

Wesley Mouch came next. He spoke about social planning and the necessity of unanimous rallying in support of the planners. He spoke about discipline, unity, austerity and the patriotic duty of bearing temporary hardships. "We have mobilized the best brains of the country to work for your welfare. This great invention was the product of the genius of a man whose devotion to the cause of humanity is not to be questioned, a man acknowledged by all as the greatest mind of the century—Dr. Robert Stadler!"

"*What?*" gasped Dr. Stadler, whirling toward Ferris.

Dr. Ferris looked at him with a glance of patient mildness.

"He didn't ask my permission to say that!" Dr. Stadler half-snapped, half-whispered.

Dr. Ferris spread out his hands in a gesture of reproachful helplessness. "Now you see, Dr. Stadler, how unfortunate it is if you allow yourself to be disturbed by political matters, which you have always considered unworthy of your attention and knowledge. You see, it is not Mr. Mouch's function to ask permissions."

The figure now slouching against the sky on the speakers' platform, coiling itself about the microphone, talking in the bored, contemptuous tone of an off-color story, was Dr. Simon Pritchett. He was declaring that the new invention was an instrument of social welfare, which guaranteed general prosperity, and that anyone who doubted this self-evident fact was an enemy of society, to be treated accordingly. "This invention, the product of Dr. Robert Stadler, the pre-eminent lover of freedom—"

Dr. Ferris opened a briefcase, produced some pages of neatly typed copy and turned to Dr. Stadler. "You are to be the climax of the broadcast," he said. "You will speak last, at the end of the hour." He extended the pages. "Here's the speech you'll make." His eyes said the rest: they said that his choice of words had not been accidental.

Dr. Stadler took the pages, but held them between the tips of two straight fingers, as one might hold a scrap of waste paper about to be tossed aside. "I haven't asked you to appoint yourself as my ghost writer," he said. The sarcasm of the voice gave Ferris his clue: this was not a moment for sarcasm.

"I couldn't have allowed your invaluable time to be taken up by the writing of radio speeches," said Dr. Ferris. "I felt certain that you would appreciate it." He said it in a tone of spurious politeness intended to be recognized as spurious, the tone of tossing to a beggar the alms of face-saving.

Dr. Stadler's answer disturbed him: Dr. Stadler did not choose to answer or to glance down at the manuscript.

"Lack of faith," a beefy speaker was snarling on the platform, in the tone of a street brawl, "lack of faith is the only thing we got to fear! If we have faith in the plans of our leaders, why, the plans will work and we'll all have prosperity and ease and plenty. It's the fellows who go around doubting and destroying our morale, it's they who're keeping us in shortages and misery. But we're not going to let them do it much longer, we're here to protect the people—and if any of those doubting smarties come around, believe you me, we'll take care of them!"

"It would be unfortunate," said Dr. Ferris in a soft voice, "to arouse popular resentment against the State Science Institute at an explosive time like the present. There's a great deal of dissatisfaction and unrest in the country—and if people should misunderstand the nature of the new invention, they're liable to vent their rage on all scientists. Scientists have never been popular with the masses."

"Peace," a tall, willowy woman was sighing into the microphone, "this invention is a great, new instrument of peace. It will protect us from the aggressive designs of selfish enemies, it will allow us to breathe freely and to learn to love our fellow men." She had a bony face with a mouth embittered at cocktail parties, and wore a flowing pale blue gown, suggesting the concert garment of a harpist. "It may well be considered as that miracle which was thought impossible in history—the dream of the ages—the final synthesis of science and love!"

Dr. Stadler looked at the faces in the grandstands. They were sitting quietly now, they were listening, but their eyes had an ebbing look of twilight, a look of fear in the process of being accepted as permanent, the look of raw wounds being dimmed by the veil of infection. They knew, as he knew it, that *they* were the targets of the shapeless funnels protruding from the mushroom building's dome—and he wondered in what manner they were now extinguishing their minds and escaping that knowledge; he knew that the words they were eager to absorb and believe were the chains slipping in to hold them, like the goats, securely within the range of those funnels. They were eager to believe; he saw the tightening lines of their lips, he saw the occasional glances of suspicion they threw at their neighbors—as if the horror that threatened them was not the sound ray, but the men who would make them acknowledge it as horror. Their eyes were veiling over, but the remnant look of a wound was a cry for help.

"Why do you think they think?" said Dr. Ferris softly. "Reason is the scientist's only weapon—and reason has no power over men, has it? At a time like ours, with the country falling apart, with the mob driven by blind desperation to the edge of open riots and violence—order must be maintained by any means available. What can we do when we have to deal with people?"

Dr. Stadler did not answer.

A fat, jellied woman, with an inadequate brassière under a dark, perspiration-stained dress, was saying into the microphone—Dr. Stadler could not believe it at first—that the new invention was to be greeted with particular gratitude by the mothers of the country.

Dr. Stadler turned away; watching him, Ferris could see nothing but the noble line of the high forehead and the deep cut of bitterness at the corner of the mouth.

Suddenly, without context or warning, Robert Stadler whirled to face him. It was like a spurt of blood from a sudden crack in a wound that had almost closed: Stadler's face was open, open in pain, in horror, in sincerity, as if, for that moment, both he and Ferris were human beings, while he moaned with incredulous despair:

"In a civilized century, Ferris, in a civilized century!"

Dr. Ferris took his time to produce and prolong a soft chuckle. "I don't know what you're talking about," he answered in the tone of a quotation.

Dr. Stadler lowered his eyes.

When Ferris spoke again, his voice had the faintest edge of a tone which Stadler could not define, except that it did not belong in any civilized discussion: "It would be unfortunate if anything were to happen to jeopardize the State Science Institute. It would be most unfortunate if the Institute were to be closed—or if any one of us were to be forced to leave it. Where would we go? Scientists are an inordinate luxury these days—and there aren't many people or establishments left who're able to afford necessities, let alone luxuries. There are no doors left open to us. We wouldn't be welcome in the research department of an industrial concern, such as—let us say—Rearden Steel. Besides, if we should happen to make enemies, the same enemies would be feared by any person tempted to employ our talents. A man like Rearden would have fought for us. Would a man like Orren Boyle? But this is purely theoretical speculation, because, as a matter of practical fact, all private establishments of scientific research have been closed by law—by Directive 10-289, issued, as you might not realize, by Mr. Wesley Mouch. Are you thinking, perhaps, of universities? They are in the same position. They can't afford to make enemies. Who would speak up for us? I believe that some such man as Hugh Akston would have come to our defense—but to think of that is to be guilty of an anachronism. He belonged to a different age. The conditions set up in our social and economic reality have long since made his continued existence impossible. And I don't think that Dr. Simon Pritchett, or the generation reared under his guidance, would be able or willing to defend us. I have never believed in the efficacy of idealists—have you?—and this is no age for impractical idealism. If anyone wished to oppose a government policy, how would he make himself heard? Through these gentlemen of the press, Dr. Stadler? Through this microphone? Is there an independent newspaper left in the country? An uncontrolled radio station? A private piece of property, for that matter—or a personal opinion?" The tone of the voice was obvious now: it was the tone of a thug. "A personal opinion is the one luxury that *nobody* can afford today."

Dr. Stadler's lips moved stiffly, as stiffly as the muscles of the goats. "You are speaking to Robert Stadler."

"I have not forgotten that. It is precisely because I have not forgotten it that I am speaking. 'Robert Stadler' is an illustrious name, which I would hate to see destroyed. But what is an illustrious name nowadays? In whose eyes?" His arm swept over the grandstands. "In the eyes of people such as you see around you? If they will believe, when so told, that an instrument of death is a tool of prosperity—would they not believe it if they were told that Robert Stadler is a traitor and an enemy of the State? Would you then rely on the fact that this is not true? Are you thinking of truth, Dr. Stadler? Questions of truth do not enter into social issues. Principles have no influence on public affairs. Reason has no power over human beings. Logic is impotent. Morality is superfluous. Do not answer me now, Dr. Stadler. You will answer me over the microphone. You're the next speaker."

Looking off at the dark strip of the farm in the distance, Dr. Stadler knew that what he felt was terror, but he would not permit himself to know its nature. He, who had been able to study the particles and sub-particles of cosmic space, would not permit himself to examine his feeling and to know that it was made of three parts: one part was terror of a vision that seemed to stand before his eyes, the vision of the inscription cut, in his honor, over the door of the Institute: "To the fearless mind, to the inviolate truth"—another part was a plain, brute, animal fear of physical destruction, a humiliating fear which, in the civilized world of his youth, he had not expected ever to experience—and the third was the terror of the knowledge that by betraying the first, one delivers oneself into the realm of the second.

He walked toward the speaker's scaffold, his steps firm and slow, his head lifted, the manuscript of the speech held crumpled in his fingers. It looked like a walk to mount either a pedestal or a guillotine. As the whole of a man's life flashes before him in his dying moment, so he walked to the sound of the announcer's voice reading to the country the list of Robert Stadler's achievements and career. A faint convulsion ran over Robert Stadler's face at the words: "—former head of the Department of Physics of the Patrick Henry University." He knew, distantly, not as if the knowledge were within him, but as if it were within some person he was leaving behind, that the crowd was about to witness an act of destruction more terrible than the destruction of the farm.

He had mounted the first three steps of the scaffold, when a young newsman tore forward, ran to him and, from below, seized the railing to stop him. "Dr. Stadler!" he cried in a desperate whisper. "Tell them the truth! Tell them that you had nothing to do with it! Tell them what sort of infernal machine it is and for what purpose it's intended to be used! Tell the country what sort of people are trying to rule it! Nobody can doubt your word! Tell them the truth! Save us! You're the only one who can!"

Dr. Stadler looked down at him. He was young; his movements and voice had that swift, sharp clarity which belongs to competence; among his aged, corrupt, favor-ridden and pull-created colleagues, he had managed to achieve the rank of elite of the political press, by means and in the role of a last, irresistible spark of ability. His eyes had the look of an eager, unfrightened intelligence; they were the kind of eyes Dr. Stadler had seen looking up at him from the benches of classrooms. He noticed that this boy's eyes were hazel; they had a tinge of green.

Dr. Stadler turned his head and saw that Ferris had come rushing to his side, like a servant or a jailer. "I do not expect to be insulted by disloyal young punks with treasonable motives," said Dr. Stadler loudly.

Dr. Ferris whirled upon the young man and snapped, his face out of control, distorted by rage at the unexpected and unplanned, "Give me your press card and your work permit!"

"I am proud," Dr. Robert Stadler read into the microphone and into the attentive silence of a nation, "that my years of work in the service of science have brought me the honor of placing into the hands of our great leader, Mr. Thompson, a new instrument with an incalculable potential for a civilizing and liberating influence upon the mind of man. . . ."

* * *

The sky had the stagnant breath of a furnace and the streets of New York were like pipes running, not with air and light, but with melted dust. Dagny stood on a street corner, where the airport bus had left her, looking at the city in passive astonishment. The buildings seemed worn by weeks of summer heat, but the people seemed worn by centuries of anguish. She stood watching them, disarmed by an enormous sense of unreality.

That sense of unreality had been her only feeling since the early hours of the morning—since the moment when, at the end of an empty highway, she had walked into an unknown town and stopped the first passer-by to ask where she was.

"Watsonville," he answered. "What state, please?" she asked. The man glanced at her, said, "Nebraska," and walked hastily away. She smiled mirthlessly, knowing that he wondered where she had come from and that no explanation he could imagine would be as fantastic as the truth. Yet it was Watsonville that seemed fantastic to her, as she walked through its streets to the railroad station. She had lost the habit of observing despair as the normal and dominant aspect of human existence, so normal as to become unnoticed—and the sight of it struck her in all of its senseless futility. She was seeing the brand of pain and fear on the faces of people, and the look of evasion that refuses to know it—they seemed to be going through the motions of some enormous pretense, acting out a ritual to ward off reality, letting the earth remain unseen and their lives unlived, in dread of something namelessly forbidden—yet the forbidden was the simple act of looking at the nature of their pain and questioning their duty to bear it. She was seeing it so clearly that she kept wanting to approach strangers, to shake them, to laugh in their faces and to cry, "Snap out of it!"

There was no reason for people to be as unhappy as that, she thought, no reason whatever . . . and then she remembered that reason was the one power they had banished from their existence.

She boarded a Taggart train for the nearest airfield; she did not identify herself to anyone: it seemed irrelevant. She sat at the window of a coach, like a stranger who has to learn the incomprehensible language of those around her. She picked up a discarded newspaper; she managed, with effort, to understand what was written, but not why it should ever have been written: it all seemed so childishly senseless. She stared in astonishment at a paragraph in a syndicated column from New York, which stated overemphatically that Mr. James Taggart wished it to be known that his sister had died in an airplane crash, any unpatriotic rumors to the contrary notwithstanding. Slowly, she remembered Directive 10-289 and realized that Jim was embarrassed by the public suspicion that she had vanished as a deserter.

The wording of the paragraph suggested that her disappearance had been a prominent public issue, not yet dropped. There were other suggestions of it: a mention of Miss Taggart's tragic death, in a story about the growing number of plane crashes—and, on the back page, an ad, offering a $100,000 reward to the person who would find the wreckage of her plane, signed by Henry Rearden.

The last gave her a stab of urgency; the rest seemed meaningless. Then, slowly, she realized that her return was a public event which would be taken as big news. She felt a lethargic weariness at the prospect of a dramatic homecoming, of facing Jim and the press, of witnessing the excitement. She wished they would get it over with in her absence.

At the airfield, she saw a small-town reporter interviewing some departing officials. She waited till he had finished, then she approached him, extended her credentials and said quietly, to the gaping stare of his eyes, "I'm Dagny Taggart. Would you make it known, please, that I'm alive and that I'll be in New York this afternoon?" The plane was about to take off and she escaped the necessity of answering questions.

She watched the prairies, the rivers, the towns slipping past at an untouchable distance below—and she noted that the sense of detachment one feels when looking at the earth from a plane was the same sense she felt when looking at people: only her distance from people seemed longer.

The passengers were listening to some radio broadcast, which appeared to be important, judging by their earnest attentiveness. She caught brief snatches of fraudulent voices talking about some sort of new invention that was to bring some undefined benefits to some undefined public's welfare. The words were obviously chosen to convey no specific meaning whatever; she wondered how one could pretend that one was hearing a speech; yet that was what the passengers were doing.

They were going through the performance of a child who, not yet able to read, holds a book open and spells out anything he wishes to spell, pretending that it is contained in the incomprehensible black lines. But the child, she thought, knows that he is playing a game; these people pretend to themselves that they are not pretending; they know no other state of existence.

The sense of unreality remained as her only feeling, when she landed, when she escaped a crowd of reporters without being seen—by avoiding the taxi stands and leaping into the airport bus—when she rode on the bus, then stood on a street corner, looking at New York. She felt as if she were seeing an abandoned city.

She felt no sense of homecoming, when she entered her apartment; the place seemed to be a convenient machine that she could use for some purpose of no significance whatever.

But she felt a quickened touch of energy, like the first break in a fog —a touch of meaning—when she picked up the telephone receiver and called Rearden's office in Pennsylvania.

"Oh, Miss Taggart . . . Miss Taggart!" said, in a joyous moan, the voice of the severe, unemotional Miss Ives.

"Hello, Miss Ives. I haven't startled you, have I? You knew that I was alive?"

"Oh yes! I heard it on the radio this morning."

"Is Mr. Rearden in his office?"

"No, Miss Taggart. He . . . he's in the Rocky Mountains, searching for . . . that is . . ."

"Yes, I know. Do you know where we can reach him?"

"I expect to hear from him at any moment. He's stopping in Los Gatos, Colorado, right now. I phoned him, the moment I heard the news, but he was out and I left a message for him to call me. You see, he's out flying, most of the day . . . but he'll call me when he comes back to the hotel."

"What hotel is it?"

"The Eldorado Hotel, in Los Gatos."

"Thank you, Miss Ives." She was about to hang up.

"Oh, Miss Taggart!"

"Yes?"

"What was it that happened to you? Where were you?"

"I . . . I'll tell you when I see you. I'm in New York now. When Mr. Rearden calls, tell him please that I'll be in my office."

"Yes, Miss Taggart."

She hung up, but her hand remained on the receiver, clinging to her first contact with a matter that had importance. She looked at her apartment and at the city in the window, feeling reluctant to sink again into the dead fog of the meaningless.

She raised the receiver and called Los Gatos.

"Eldorado Hotel," said a woman's drowsily resentful voice.

"Would you take a message for Mr. Henry Rearden? Ask him, when he comes in, to—"

"Just a minute, please," drawled the voice, in the impatient tone that resents any effort as an imposition.

She heard the clicking of switches, some buzzing, some breaks of silence and then a man's clear, firm voice answering: "Hello?" It was Hank Rearden.

She stared at the receiver as at the muzzle of a gun, feeling trapped, unable to breathe.

"Hello?" he repeated.

"Hank, is that you?"

She heard a low sound, more a sigh than a gasp, and then the long, empty crackling of the wire.

"Hank!" There was no answer. "Hank!" she screamed in terror.

She thought she heard the effort of a breath—then she heard a whisper, which was not a question, but a statement saying everything: "Dagny."

"Hank, I'm sorry—oh, darling, I'm sorry!—didn't you know?"

"Where are you, Dagny?"

"Are you all right?"

"Of course."

"Didn't you know that I was back and . . . and alive?"

"No . . . I didn't know it."

"Oh God, I'm sorry I called, I—"

"What are you talking about? Dagny, where are you?"

"In New York. Didn't you hear about it on the radio?"

"No. I've just come in."

"Didn't they give you a message to call Miss Ives?"

"No."

"Are you all right?"

"Now?" She heard his soft, low chuckle. She was hearing the sound of unreleased laughter, the sound of youth, growing in his voice with every word. "When did you come back?"

"This morning."

"Dagny, where were you?"

She did not answer at once. "My plane crashed," she said. "In the Rockies. I was picked up by some people who helped me, but I could not send word to anyone."

The laughter went out of his voice. "As bad as that?"

"Oh . . . oh, the crash? No, it wasn't bad. I wasn't hurt. Not seriously."

"Then why couldn't you send word?"

"There were no . . . no means of communication."

"Why did it take you so long to get back?"

"I . . . can't answer that now."

"Dagny, were you in danger?"

The half-smiling, half-bitter tone of her voice was almost regret, as she answered, "No."

"Were you held prisoner?"

"No—not really."

"Then you could have returned sooner, but didn't?"

"That's true—but that's all I can tell you."

"Where were you, Dagny?"

"Do you mind if we don't talk about it now? Let's wait until I see you."

"Of course. I won't ask any questions. Just tell me: are you safe now?"

"Safe? Yes."

"I mean, have you suffered any permanent injuries or consequences?"

She answered, with the same sound of a cheerless smile, "Injuries—no, Hank. I don't know, as to the permanent consequences."

"Will you still be in New York tonight?"

"Why, yes. I'm . . . I'm back for good."

"Are you?"

"Why do you ask that?"

"I don't know. I guess I'm too used to what it's like when . . . when I can't find you."

"I'm back."

"Yes. I'll see you in a few hours." His voice broke off, as if the sentence were too enormous to believe. "In a few hours," he repeated firmly.

"I'll be here."

"Dagny—"

"Yes?"

He chuckled softly. "No, nothing. Just wanted to hear your voice awhile longer. Forgive me. I mean, not now. I mean, I don't want to say anything now."

"Hank, I—"

"When I see you, my darling. So long."

She stood looking at the silent receiver. For the first time since her return, she felt pain, a violent pain, but it made her alive, because it was worth feeling.

She telephoned her secretary at Taggart Transcontinental, to say briefly that she would be in the office in half an hour.

The statue of Nathaniel Taggart was real—when she stood facing it in the concourse of the Terminal. It seemed to her that they were alone in a vast, echoing temple, with fog coils of formless ghosts weaving and vanishing around them. She stood still, looking up at the statue, as for a brief moment of dedication. I'm back—were the only words she had to offer.

"Dagny Taggart" was still the inscription on the frosted glass panel of the door to her office. The look on the faces of her staff, as she entered the anteroom, was the look of drowning persons at the sight of a lifeline. She saw Eddie Willers standing at his desk in his glass enclosure, with some man before him. Eddie made a move in her direction, but stopped; he looked imprisoned. She let her glance greet every face in turn, smiling at them gently as at doomed children, then walked toward Eddie's desk.

Eddie was watching her approach as if he were seeing nothing else in the world, but his rigid posture seemed designed to pretend that he was listening to the man before him.

"Motive power?" the man was saying in a voice that had a brusque, staccato snap and a slurred, nasal drawl, together. "There's no problem about motive power. You just take—"

"Hello," said Eddie softly, with a muted smile, as to a distant vision.

The man turned to glance at her. He had a yellow complexion, curly hair, a hard face made of soft muscles, and the revolting handsomeness belonging to the esthetic standards of barroom corners; his blurred brown eyes had the empty flatness of glass.

"Miss Taggart," said Eddie, in a resonant tone of severity, the tone of slapping the man into the manners of a drawing room he had never entered, "may I present Mr. Meigs?"

"How d' do," said the man without interest, then turned to Eddie and proceeded, as if she were not present: "You just take the Comet off the schedule for tomorrow and Tuesday, and shoot the engines to Arizona for the grapefruit special, with the rolling stock from the Scranton coal run I mentioned. Send the orders out at once."

"You'll do nothing of the kind!" she gasped, too incredulous to be angry.

Eddie did not answer.

Meigs glanced at her with what would have been astonishment if his eyes were capable of registering a reaction. "Send the orders," he said to Eddie, with no emphasis, and walked out.

Eddie was jotting notations on a piece of paper.

"Are you crazy?" she asked.

He raised his eyes to her, as though exhausted by hours of beating. "We'll have to, Dagny," he said, his voice dead.

"What is that?" she asked, pointing at the outer door that had closed on Mr. Meigs.

"The Director of Unification."

"*What?*"

"The Washington representative, in charge of the Railroad Unification Plan."

"What's that?"

"It's . . . Oh, wait, Dagny, are you all right? Were you hurt? Was it a plane crash?"

She had never imagined what the face of Eddie Willers would look like in the process of aging, but she was seeing it now—aging at thirty-five and within the span of one month. It was not a matter of texture or wrinkles, it was the same face with the same muscles, but saturated by the withering look of resignation to a pain accepted as hopeless.

She smiled, gently and confidently, in understanding, in dismissal of all problems, and said, extending her hand, "All right, Eddie. Hello."

He took her hand and pressed it to his lips, a thing he had never done before, his manner neither daring nor apologetic, but simply and openly personal.

"It *was* a plane crash," she said, "and, Eddie, so that you won't worry, I'll tell you the truth: I *wasn't* hurt, not seriously. But that's not the story I'm going to give to the press and to all the others. So you're never to mention it."

"Of course."

"I had no way to communicate with anyone, but not because I was hurt. It's all I can tell you, Eddie. Don't ask me where I was or why it took me so long to return."

"I won't."

"Now tell me, what is the Railroad Unification Plan?"

"It's . . . Oh, do you mind?—let Jim tell you. He will, soon enough. I just don't have the stomach—unless you want me to," he added, with a conscientious effort at discipline.

"No, you don't have to. Just tell me whether I understood that Unificator correctly: he wants you to cancel the Comet for two days in order to give her engines to a grapefruit special in Arizona?"

"That's right."

"And he's cancelled a coal train in order to get cars to lug grapefruit?"

"Yes."

"*Grapefruit?*"

"That's right."

"Why?"

"Dagny, 'why' is a word nobody uses any longer."

After a moment, she asked, "Have you any guess about the reason?"

"Guess? I don't have to guess. I know."

"All right, what is it?"

"The grapefruit special is for the Smather brothers. The Smather brothers bought a fruit ranch in Arizona a year ago, from a man who went bankrupt under the Equalization of Opportunity Bill. He had owned the ranch for thirty years. The Smather brothers were in the punchboard business the year before. They bought the ranch by means of a loan from Washington under a project for the reclamation of distressed areas, such as Arizona. The Smather brothers have friends in Washington."

"Well?"

"Dagny, everybody knows it. Everybody knows how train schedules have been run in the past three weeks, and why some districts and some shippers get transportation, while others don't. What we're not supposed to do is say that we know it. We're supposed to pretend to believe that 'public welfare' is the only reason for any decision—and that the public welfare of the city of New York requires the immediate delivery of a large quantity of grapefruit." He paused, then added, "The Director of Unification is sole judge of the public welfare and has sole authority over the allocation of any motive power and rolling stock on any railroad anywhere in the United States."

There was a moment of silence. "I see," she said. In another moment, she asked, "What has been done about the Winston tunnel?"

"Oh, that was abandoned three weeks ago. They never unearthed the trains. The equipment gave out."

"What has been done about rebuilding the old line around the tunnel?"

"That was shelved."

"Then are we running any transcontinental traffic?"

He gave her an odd glance. "Oh yes," he said bitterly.

"Through the detour of the Kansas Western?"

"No."

"Eddie, what has been happening here in the past month?"

He smiled as if his words were an ugly confession. "We've been making money in the past month," he answered.

She saw the outer door open and James Taggart come in, accompanied by Mr. Meigs. "Eddie, do you want to be present at the conference?" she asked. "Or would you rather miss this one?"

"No. I want to be present."

Jim's face looked like a crumpled piece of paper, though its soft, puffed flesh had acquired no additional lines.

"Dagny, there's a lot of things to discuss, a lot of important changes which—" he said shrilly, his voice rushing in ahead of his person. "Oh, I'm glad to see you back, I'm happy that you're alive," he added impatiently, remembering. "Now there are some urgent—"

"Let's go to my office," she said.

Her office was like a historical reconstruction, restored and maintained by Eddie Willers. Her map, her calendar, the picture of Nat Taggart were on the walls, and no trace was left of the Clifton Locey era.

"I understand that I am still the Operating Vice-President of this railroad?" she asked, sitting down at her desk.

"You are," said Taggart hastily, accusingly, almost defiantly. "You certainly are—and don't you forget it—you haven't quit, you're still —have you?"

"No, I haven't quit."

"Now the most urgent thing to do is to tell that to the press, tell them that you're back on the job and where you were and—and, by the way, where *were* you?"

"Eddie," she said, "will you make a note on this and send it to the press? My plane developed engine trouble while I was flying over the Rocky Mountains to the Taggart Tunnel. I lost my way, looking for an emergency landing, and crashed in an uninhabited mountain section—of Wyoming. I was found by an old sheepherder and his wife, who took me to their cabin, deep in the wilderness, fifty miles away from the nearest settlement. I was badly injured and remained unconscious for most of two weeks. The old couple had no telephone, no radio, no means of communication or transportation, except an old truck that broke down when they attempted to use it. I had to remain with them until I recovered sufficient strength to walk. I walked the fifty miles to the foothills, then hitchhiked my way to a Taggart station in Nebraska."

"I see," said Taggart. "Well, that's fine. Now when you give the press interview—"

"I'm not going to give any press interviews."

"What? But they've been calling me all day! They're waiting! It's essential!" He had an air of panic. "It's most crucially essential!"

"Who's been calling you all day?"

"People in Washington and . . . and others . . . They're waiting for your statement."

She pointed at Eddie's notes. "There's my statement."

"But that's not enough! You must say that you haven't quit."

"That's obvious, isn't it? I'm back."

"You must say something about it."

"Such as what?"

"Something personal."

"To whom?"

"To the country. People were worried about you. You must reassure them."

"The story will reassure them, if anyone was worried about me."

"That's not what I mean!"

"Well, what do you mean?"

"I mean—" He stopped, his eyes avoiding hers. "I mean—" He sat, searching for words, cracking his knuckles.

Jim was going to pieces, she thought; the jerky impatience, the shrillness, the aura of panic were new; crude outbreaks of a tone of ineffectual menace had replaced his pose of cautious smoothness.

"I mean—" He was searching for words to name his meaning without naming it, she thought, to make her understand that which he did not want to be understood. "I mean, the public—"

"I know what you mean," she said. "No, Jim, I'm not going to reassure the public about the state of our industry."

"Now you're—"

"The public had better be as unreassured as it has the wits to be. Now proceed to business."

"I—"

"Proceed to business, Jim."

He glanced at Mr. Meigs. Mr. Meigs sat silently, his legs crossed, smoking a cigarette. He wore a jacket which was not, but looked like, a military uniform. The flesh of his neck bulged over the collar, and the flesh of his body strained against the narrow waistline intended to disguise it. He wore a ring with a large yellow diamond that flashed when he moved his stubby fingers.

"You've met Mr. Meigs," said Taggart. "I'm so glad that the two of you will get along well together." He made an expectant half-pause, but received no answer from either. "Mr. Meigs is the representative of the Railroad Unification Plan. You'll have many opportunities to co-operate with him."

"What is the Railroad Unification Plan?"

"It is a . . . a new national setup that went into effect three weeks ago, which you will appreciate and approve of and find extremely practical." She marveled at the futility of his method: he was acting as if, by naming her opinion in advance, he would make her unable to alter it. "It is an emergency setup which has saved the country's transportation system."

"What is the plan?"

"You realize, of course, the insurmountable difficulties of any sort of construction job during this period of emergency. It is—temporarily—impossible to lay new track. Therefore, the country's top problem is to preserve the transportation industry *as a whole,* to preserve its existing plant and all of its existing facilities. The national survival requires—"

"What is the plan?"

"As a policy of national survival, the railroads of the country have been unified into a single team, pooling their resources. All of their gross revenue is turned over to the Railroad Pool Board in Washington, which acts as trustee for the industry as a whole, and divides the total income among the various railroads, according to a . . . a more modern principle of distribution."

"What principle?"

"Now don't worry, property rights have been fully preserved and protected, they've merely been given a new form. Every railroad retains independent responsibility for its own operations, its train schedules and the maintenance of its track and equipment. As its contribution to the national pool, every railroad permits any other, when conditions so require, to use its track and facilities without charge. At the end of the year, the Pool Board distributes the total gross income, and every individual railroad is paid, not on the haphazard, old-fashioned basis of the number of trains run or the tonnage of freight carried, but on the basis of its need—that is, the preservation of its track being its main need, every individual railroad is paid according to the mileage of the track which it owns and maintains."

She heard the words; she understood the meaning; she was unable to make it real—to grant the respect of anger, concern, opposition to a nightmare piece of insanity that rested on nothing but people's willingness to pretend to believe that it was sane. She felt a numbed emptiness—and the sense of being thrown far below the realm where moral indignation is pertinent.

"Whose track are we using for our transcontinental traffic?" she asked, her voice flat and dry.

"Why, our own, of course," said Taggart hastily, "that is, from New York to Bedford, Illinois. We run our trains out of Bedford on the track of the Atlantic Southern."

"To San Francisco?"

"Well, it's much faster than that long detour you tried to establish."

"We run our trains without charge for the use of the track?"

"Besides, your detour couldn't have lasted, the Kansas Western rail was shot, and besides—"

"Without charge for the use of the Atlantic Southern track?"

"Well, we're not charging them for the use of our Mississippi bridge, either."

After a moment, she asked, "Have you looked at a map?"

"Sure," said Meigs unexpectedly. "You own the largest track mileage of any railroad in the country. So you've got nothing to worry about."

Eddie Willers burst out laughing.

Meigs glanced at him blankly. "What's the matter with you?" he asked.

"Nothing," said Eddie wearily, "nothing."

"Mr. Meigs," she said, "if you look at a map, you will see that two-thirds of the cost of maintaining a track for our transcontinental traffic is given to us free and is paid by our competitor."

"Why, sure," he said, but his eyes narrowed, watching her suspiciously, as if he were wondering what motive prompted her to so explicit a statement.

"While we're paid for owning miles of useless track which carries no traffic," she said.

Meigs understood—and leaned back as if he had lost all further interest in the discussion.

"That's not true!" snapped Taggart. "We're running a great number of local trains to serve the region of our former transcontinental line—through Iowa, Nebraska and Colorado—and, on the other side of the tunnel, through California, Nevada and Utah."

"We're running two locals a day," said Eddie Willers, in the dry, blankly innocent tone of a business report. "Fewer, some places."

"What determines the number of trains which any given railroad is obligated to run?" she asked.

"The public welfare," said Taggart.

"The Pool Board," said Eddie.

"How many trains have been discontinued in the country in the past three weeks?"

"As a matter of fact," said Taggart eagerly, "the plan has helped to harmonize the industry and to eliminate cutthroat competition."

"It has eliminated thirty per cent of the trains run in the country," said Eddie. "The only competition left is in the applications to the Board for permission to cancel trains. The railroad to survive will be the one that manages to run no trains at all."

"Has anybody calculated how long the Atlantic Southern is expected to be able to remain in business?"

"That's no skin off your—" started Meigs.

"*Please*, Cuffy!" cried Taggart.

"The president of the Atlantic Southern," said Eddie impassively, "has committed suicide."

"That had nothing to do with this!" yelled Taggart. "It was over a personal matter!"

She remained silent. She sat, looking at their faces. There was still an element of wonder in the numbed indifference of her mind: Jim had always managed to switch the weight of his failures upon the strongest plants around him and to survive by destroying them to pay for his errors, as he had done with Dan Conway, as he had done with the industries of Colorado; but *this* did not have even the rationality of a looter—this pouncing upon the drained carcass of a weaker, a half-bankrupt competitor for a moment's delay, with nothing but a cracking bone between the pouncer and the abyss.

The impulse of the habit of reason almost pushed her to speak, to argue, to demonstrate the self-evident—but she looked at their faces and she saw that they knew it. In some terms different from hers, in some inconceivable manner of consciousness, they knew all that she could tell them, it was useless to prove to them the irrational horror of their course and of its consequences, both Meigs and Taggart knew it—and the secret of their consciousness was the means by which they escaped the finality of their knowledge.

"I see," she said quietly.

"Well, what would you rather have had me do?" screamed Taggart. "Give up our transcontinental traffic? Go bankrupt? Turn the railroad into a miserable East Coast local?" Her two words seemed to have hit him worse than any indignant objection; he seemed to be shaking with terror at that which the quiet "I see" had acknowledged seeing. "I couldn't help it! We had to have a transcontinental track! There was no way to get around the tunnel! We had no money to pay for any extra costs! Something had to be done! We had to have a track!"

Meigs was looking at him with a glance of part-astonishment, part-disgust.

"I am not arguing, Jim," she said dryly.

"We couldn't permit a railroad like Taggart Transcontinental to crash! It would have been a national catastrophe! We had to think of all the cities and industries and shippers and passengers and employees and stockholders whose lives depend on us! It wasn't just for ourselves, it was for the public welfare! Everybody agrees that the Railroad Unification Plan is practical! The best-informed—"

"Jim," she said, "if you have any further business to discuss with me —discuss it."

"You've never considered the social angle of anything," he said, in a sullen, retreating voice.

She noticed that this form of pretense was as unreal to Mr. Meigs as it was to her, though for an antipodal reason. He was looking at Jim with bored contempt. Jim appeared to her suddenly as a man who had tried to find a middle course between two poles—Meigs and herself —and who was now seeing that his course was narrowing and that he was to be ground between two straight walls.

"Mr. Meigs," she asked, prompted by a touch of bitterly amused curiosity, "what is your economic plan for day after tomorrow?"

She saw his bleary brown eyes focus upon her without expression. "You're impractical," he said.

"It's perfectly useless to theorize about the future," snapped Taggart, "when we have to take care of the emergency of the moment. In the long run—"

"In the long run, we'll all be dead," said Meigs.

Then, abruptly, he shot to his feet. "I'll run along, Jim," he said. "I've got no time to waste on conversations." He added, "You talk to her about that matter of doing something to stop all those train wrecks—if she's the little girl who's such a wizard at railroading." It was said inoffensively; he was a man who would not know when he was giving offense or taking it.

"I'll see you later, Cuffy," said Taggart, as Meigs walked out with no parting glance at any of them.

Taggart looked at her, expectantly and fearfully, as if dreading her comment, yet desperately hoping to hear some word, any word.

"Well?" she asked.

"What do you mean?"

"Have you anything else to discuss?"

"Well, I . . ." He sounded disappointed. "Yes!" he cried, in the tone of a desperate plunge. "I have another matter to discuss, the most important one of all, the—"

"Your growing number of train wrecks?"

"No! Not that."

"What, then?"

"It's . . . that you're going to appear on Bertram Scudder's radio program tonight."

She leaned back. "Am I?"

"Dagny, it's imperative, it's crucial, there's nothing to be done about it, to refuse is out of the question, in times like these one has no choice, and—"

She glanced at her watch. "I'll give you three minutes to explain— if you want to be heard at all. And you'd better speak straight."

"All right!" he said desperately. "It's considered most important— on the highest levels, I mean Chick Morrison and Wesley Mouch and Mr. Thompson, as high as that—that you should make a speech to the nation, a morale-building speech, you know, saying that you haven't quit."

"Why?"

"Because everybody thought you had! . . . You don't know what's been going on lately, but . . . but it's sort of uncanny. The country is full of rumors, all sorts of rumors, about everything, all of them danger- ous. Disruptive, I mean. People seem to do nothing but whisper. They don't believe the newspapers, they don't believe the best speakers, they believe every vicious, scare-mongering piece of gossip that comes float- ing around. There's no confidence left, no faith, no order, no . . . no respect for authority. People . . . people seem to be on the verge of panic."

"Well?"

"Well, for one thing, it's that damnable business of all those big industrialists who've vanished into thin air! Nobody's been able to ex- plain it and it's giving them the jitters. There's all sorts of hysterical stuff being whispered about it, but what they whisper mostly is that 'no decent man will work for those people.' They mean the people in Washington. Now do you see? You wouldn't suspect that you were so famous, but you are, or you've become, ever since your plane crash. No- body believed the plane crash. They all thought you had broken the law, that is, Directive 10-289, and deserted. There's a lot of popular . . . misunderstanding of Directive 10-289, a lot of . . . well, unrest. Now you see how important it is that you go on the air and tell people that it isn't true that Directive 10-289 is destroying industry, that it's a sound piece of legislation devised for everybody's good, and that if they'll just be patient a little longer, things will improve and prosperity will return. They don't believe any public official any more. You . . . you're an industrialist, one of the few left of the old school, and the only one who's ever come back after they thought you'd gone. You're known as . . . as a reactionary who's opposed to Washington policies. So the people will believe you. It would have a great influence on them, it would buttress their confidence, it would help their morale. Now do you see?"

He had rushed on, encouraged by the odd look of her face, a look of contemplation that was almost a faint half-smile.

She had listened, hearing, through his words, the sound of Rearden's voice saying to her on a spring evening over a year ago: "They need some sort of sanction from us. I don't know the nature of that sanction —but, Dagny, I know that if we value our lives, we must not give it to them. If they put you on a torture rack, don't give it to them. Let them destroy your railroad and my mills, but don't give it to them."

"Now do you see?"

"Oh yes, Jim, I see!"

He could not interpret the sound of her voice, it was low, it was part-moan, part-chuckle, part-triumph—but it was the first sound of emotion to come from her, and he plunged on, with no choice but to hope. "I promised them in Washington that you'd speak! We can't fail them—not in an issue of this kind! We can't afford to be suspected of disloyalty. It's all arranged. You'll be the guest speaker on Bertram Scudder's program, tonight, at ten-thirty. He's got a radio program where he interviews prominent public figures, it's a national hookup, he has a large following, he reaches over twenty million people. The office of the Morale Conditioner has—"

"The *what?*"

"The Morale Conditioner—that's Chick Morrison—has called me three times, to make sure that nothing would go wrong. They've issued orders to all the news broadcasters, who've been announcing it all day, all over the country, telling people to listen to you tonight on Bertram Scudder's hour."

He looked at her as if he were demanding both an answer and the recognition that her answer was the element of least importance in these circumstances. She said, "You know what I think of the Washington policies and of Directive 10-289."

"At a time like this, we can't afford the luxury of thinking!"

She laughed aloud.

"But don't you see that you can't refuse them now?" he yelled. "If you don't appear after all those announcements, it will support the rumors, it will amount to an open declaration of disloyalty!"

"The trap won't work, Jim."

"What trap?"

"The one you're always setting up."

"I don't know what you mean!"

"Yes, you do. You knew—all of you knew it—that I would refuse. So you pushed me into a public trap, where my refusal would become an embarrassing scandal for you, more embarrassing than you thought I'd dare to cause. You were counting on me to save your faces and the necks you stuck out. I won't save them."

"But I promised it!"

"I didn't."

"But we can't refuse them! Don't you see that they've got us hogtied? That they're holding us by the throat? Don't you know what they can do to us through this Railroad Pool, or through the Unification Board, or through the moratorium on our bonds?"

"I knew that two years ago."

He was shaking; there was some formless, desperate, almost super-stitious quality in his terror, out of proportion to the dangers he named. She felt suddenly certain that it came from something deeper than his fear of bureaucratic reprisal, that the reprisal was the only identification of it which he would permit himself to know, a reassuring identification which had a semblance of rationality and hid his true motive. She felt certain that it was not the country's panic he wanted to stave off, but his own—that he, and Chick Morrison and Wesley Mouch and all the rest of the looting crew needed her sanction, not to reassure their victims, but to reassure themselves, though the allegedly crafty, the allegedly practical idea of deluding their victims was the only identifi-cation they gave to their own motive and their hysterical insistence. With an awed contempt—awed by the enormity of the sight—she wondered what inner degradation those men had to reach in order to arrive at a level of self-deception where they would seek the extorted approval of an unwilling victim as the moral sanction they needed, they who thought that they were merely deceiving the world.

"We have no choice!" he cried. "Nobody has any choice!"

"Get out of here," she said, her voice very quiet and low.

Some tonal quality in the sound of her voice struck the note of the unconfessed within him, as if, never allowing it into words, he knew from what knowledge that sound had come. He got out.

She glanced at Eddie; he looked like a man worn by fighting one more of the attacks of disgust which he was learning to endure as a chronic condition.

After a moment, he asked, "Dagny, what became of Quentin Daniels? You were flying after him, weren't you?"

"Yes," she said. "He's gone."

"To the destroyer?"

The word hit her like a physical blow. It was the first touch of the outer world upon that radiant presence which she had kept within her all day, as a silent, changeless vision, a private vision, not to be affected by any of the things around her, not to be thought about, only to be felt as the source of her strength. The destroyer, she realized, was the name of that vision, here, in their world.

"Yes," she said dully, with effort, "to the destroyer."

Then she closed her hands over the edge of the desk, to steady her purpose and her posture, and said, with the bitter hint of a smile, "Well, Eddie, let's see what two impractical persons, like you and me, can do about preventing the train wrecks."

It was two hours later—when she was alone at her desk, bent over sheets of paper that bore nothing but figures, yet were like a motion-picture film unrolling to tell her the whole story of the railroad in the past four weeks—that the buzzer rang and her secretary's voice said, "Mrs. Rearden to see you, Miss Taggart."

"Mr. Rearden?" she asked incredulously, unable to believe either.

"No. *Mrs.* Rearden."

She let a moment pass, then said, "Please ask her to come in."

There was some peculiar touch of emphasis in Lillian Rearden's bearing when she entered and walked toward the desk. She wore a tailored suit, with a loose, bright bow hanging casually sidewise for a note of elegant incongruity, and a small hat tilted at an angle considered smart by virtue of being considered amusing; her face was a shade too smooth, her steps a shade too slow, and she walked almost as if she were swinging her hips.

"How do you do, Miss Taggart," she said in a lazily gracious voice, a drawing-room voice which seemed to strike, in that office, the same style of incongruity as her suit and her bow.

Dagny inclined her head gravely.

Lillian glanced about the office; her glance had the same style of amusement as her hat: an amusement purporting to express maturity by the conviction that life could be nothing but ridiculous.

"Please sit down," said Dagny.

Lillian sat down, relaxing into a confident, gracefully casual posture. When she turned her face to Dagny, the amusement was still there, but its shading was now different: it seemed to suggest that they shared a secret, which would make her presence here seem preposterous to the world, but self-evidently logical to the two of them. She stressed it by remaining silent.

"What can I do for you?"

"I came to tell you," said Lillian pleasantly, "that you will appear on Bertram Scudder's broadcast tonight."

She detected no astonishment in Dagny's face, no shock, only the glance of an engineer studying a motor that makes an irregular sound. "I assume," said Dagny, "that you are fully aware of the form of your sentence."

"Oh yes!" said Lillian.

"Then proceed to support it."

"I beg your pardon?"

"Proceed to tell me."

Lillian gave a brief little laugh, its forced brevity betraying that this was not quite the attitude she had expected. "I am sure that no lengthy explanations will be necessary," she said. "You know why your appearance on that broadcast is important to those in power. I know why you have refused to appear. I know your convictions on the subject. You may have attached no importance to it, but you do know that my sympathy has always been on the side of the system now in power. Therefore, you will understand my interest in the issue and my place in it. When your brother told me that you had refused, I decided to take a hand in the matter—because, you see, I am one of the very few who know that you are not in a position to refuse."

"I am not one of those few, as yet," said Dagny.

Lillian smiled. "Well, yes, I must explain a little further. You realize that your radio appearance will have the same value for those in power as—as the action of my husband when he signed the Gift Certificate that turned Rearden Metal over to them. You know how frequently and how usefully they have been mentioning it in all of their propaganda."

"I didn't know that," said Dagny sharply.

"Oh, of course, you have been away for most of the last two months, so you might have missed the constant reminders—in the press, on the radio, in public speeches—that even Hank Rearden approves of and supports Directive 10-289, since he has voluntarily signed his Metal over to the nation. Even Hank Rearden. That discourages a great many recalcitrants and helps to keep them in line." She leaned back and asked in the tone of a casual aside, "Have you ever asked him why he signed?"

Dagny did not answer; she did not seem to hear that it was a question; she sat still and her face was expressionless, but her eyes seemed too large and they were fixed on Lillian's, as if she were now intent upon nothing but hearing Lillian to the end.

"No, I didn't think you knew it. I didn't think that he would ever tell you," said Lillian, her voice smoother, as if recognizing the signposts and sliding comfortably down the anticipated course. "Yet you must learn the reason that made him sign—because it is the same reason that will make you appear on Bertram Scudder's broadcast tonight."

She paused, wishing to be urged; Dagny waited.

"It is a reason," said Lillian, "which should please you—as far as my husband's action is concerned. Consider what that signature meant to him. Rearden Metal was his greatest achievement, the summation of the best in his life, the final symbol of his pride—and my husband, as you have reason to know, is an extremely passionate man, his pride in himself being, perhaps, his greatest passion. Rearden Metal was more than an achievement to him, it was the symbol of his ability to achieve, of his independence, of his struggle, of his rise. It was his property, his by right—and you know what rights mean to a man as strict as he, and what property means to a man as possessive. He would have gladly died to defend it, rather than surrender it to the men he despised. This is what it meant to him—and this is what he gave up. You will be glad to know that he gave it up for *your* sake, Miss Taggart. For the sake of your reputation and your honor. He signed the Gift Certificate surrendering Rearden Metal—under the threat that the adultery he was carrying on with you would be exposed to the eyes of the world. Oh yes, we had full proof of it, in every intimate detail. I believe that you hold a philosophy which disapproves of sacrifice—but in this case, you are most certainly a woman, so I'm sure that you will feel gratification at the magnitude of the sacrifice a man has made for the privilege of using your body. You have undoubtedly taken great pleasure in the nights which he spent in your bed. You may now take pleasure in the knowledge of what those nights have cost him. And since—you like bluntness, don't you, Miss Taggart?—since your chosen status is that of a whore, I take my hat off to you in regard to the price you exacted, which none of your sisters could ever have hoped to match."

Lillian's voice had kept growing reluctantly sharper, like a drillhead that kept breaking by being unable to find the line of the fault in the stone. Dagny was still looking at her, but the intensity had vanished from Dagny's eyes and posture. Lillian wondered why she felt as if Dagny's face were hit by a spotlight. She could detect no particular expression, it was simply a face in natural repose—and the clarity seemed to come from its structure, from the precision of its sharp planes, the firmness of the mouth, the steadiness of the eyes. She could not decipher the expression of the eyes, it seemed incongruous, it resembled the calm, not of a woman, but of a scholar, it had that peculiar, luminous quality which is the fearlessness of satisfied knowledge.

"It was I," said Lillian softly, "who informed the bureaucrats about my husband's adultery."

Dagny noticed the first flicker of feeling in Lillian's lifeless eyes: it resembled pleasure, but so distantly that it looked like sunlight reflected from the dead surface of the moon to the stagnant water of a swamp; it flickered for an instant and went.

"It was I," said Lillian, "who took Rearden Metal away from him." It sounded almost like a plea.

It was not within the power of Dagny's consciousness ever to understand that plea or to know what response Lillian had hoped to find; she knew only that she had not found it, when she heard the sudden shrillness of Lillian's voice: "Have you understood me?"

"Yes."

"Then you know what I demand and why you'll obey me. You thought you were invincible, you and he, didn't you?" The voice was attempting smoothness, but it was jerking unevenly. "You have always acted on no will but your own—a luxury I have not been able to afford. For once and in compensation, I will see you acting on mine. You can't fight me. You can't buy your way out of it, with those dollars which you're able to make and I'm not. There's no profit you can offer me—I'm devoid of greed. I'm not paid by the bureaucrats for doing this—I am doing it without gain. Without gain. Do you understand me?"

"Yes."

"Then no further explanations are necessary, only the reminder that all the factual evidence—hotel registers, jewelry bills and stuff like that—is still in the possession of the right persons and will be broadcast on every radio program tomorrow, unless you appear on one radio program tonight. Is this clear?"

"Yes."

"Now what is your answer?" She saw the luminous scholar-eyes looking at her, and suddenly she felt as if too much of her were seen and as if she were not seen at all.

"I am glad that you have told me," said Dagny. "I will appear on Bertram Scudder's broadcast tonight."

* * *

There was a beam of white light beating down upon the glittering metal of a microphone—in the center of a glass cage imprisoning her with Bertram Scudder. The sparks of glitter were greenish-blue; the microphone was made of Rearden Metal.

Above them, beyond a sheet of glass, she could distinguish a booth with two rows of faces looking down at her: the lax, anxious face of James Taggart, with Lillian Rearden beside him, her hand resting reassuringly on his arm—a man who had arrived by plane from Washington and had been introduced to her as Chick Morrison—and a group of young men from his staff, who talked about percentage curves of intellectual influence and acted like motorcycle cops.

Bertram Scudder seemed to be afraid of her. He clung to the microphone, spitting words into its delicate mesh, into the ears of the country, introducing the subject of his program. He was laboring to sound cynical, skeptical, superior and hysterical together, to sound like a man who sneers at the vanity of all human beliefs and thereby demands an instantaneous belief from his listeners. A small patch of moisture glistened on the back of his neck. He was describing in overcolored detail her month of convalescence in the lonely cabin of a sheepherder, then her heroic trudging down fifty miles of mountain trails for the sake of resuming her duties to the people in this grave hour of national emergency.

". . . And if any of you have been deceived by vicious rumors aimed to undermine your faith in the great social program of our leaders—you may trust the word of Miss Taggart, who—"

She stood, looking up at the white beam. Specks of dust were whirling in the beam and she noticed that one of them was alive: it was a gnat with a tiny sparkle in place of its beating wings, it was struggling for some frantic purpose of its own, and she watched it, feeling as distant from its purpose as from that of the world.

". . . Miss Taggart is an impartial observer, a brilliant businesswoman who has often been critical of the government in the past and who may be said to represent the extreme, conservative viewpoint held by such giants of industry as Hank Rearden. Yet even she—"

She wondered at how easy it felt, when one did not have to feel; she seemed to be standing naked on public display, and a beam of light was enough to support her, because there was no weight of pain in her, no hope, no regret, no concern, no future.

". . . And now, ladies and gentlemen, I will present to you the heroine of this night, our most uncommon guest, the—"

Pain came back to her in a sudden, piercing stab, like a long splinter from the glass of a protective wall shattered by the knowledge that the next words would be hers; it came back for the brief length of a name in her mind, the name of the man she had called the destroyer: she did not want him to hear what she would now have to say. If you hear it—the pain was like a voice crying it to him—you won't believe the things I have said to you—no, worse, the things which I have not said, but which you knew and believed and accepted —you will think that I was not free to offer them and that my days with you were a lie—this will destroy my one month and ten of your years— this was not the way I wanted you to learn it, not like this, not tonight —but you will, you who've watched and known my every movement, you who're watching me now, wherever you are—you will hear it—but it has to be said.

"—the last descendant of an illustrious name in our industrial history, the woman executive possible only in America, the Operating Vice-President of a great railroad—Miss Dagny Taggart!"

Then she felt the touch of Rearden Metal, as her hand closed over the stem of the microphone, and it was suddenly easy, not with the drugged ease of indifference, but with the bright, clear, living ease of action.

"I came here to tell you about the social program, the political system and the moral philosophy under which you are now living."

There was so calm, so natural, so total a certainty in the sound of her voice that the mere sound seemed to carry an immense persuasiveness.

"You have heard it said that I believe that this system has depravity as its motive, plunder as its goal, lies, fraud and force as its method, and destruction as its only result. You have also heard it said that, like Hank Rearden, I am a loyal supporter of this system and that I give my voluntary co-operation to present policies, such as Directive 10-289. I have come here to tell you the truth about it.

"It is true that I share the stand of Hank Rearden. His political convictions are mine. You have heard him denounced in the past as a reactionary who opposed every step, measure, slogan and premise of the present system. Now you hear him praised as our greatest industrialist, whose judgment on the value of economic policies may safely be trusted. It is true. You may trust his judgment. If you are now beginning to fear that you are in the power of an irresponsible evil, that the country is collapsing and that you will soon be left to starve—consider the views of our ablest industrialist, who knows what conditions are necessary to make production possible and to permit a country to survive. Consider all that you know about his views. At such times as he was able to speak, you have heard him tell you that this government's policies were leading you to enslavement and destruction. Yet he did not denounce the final climax of these policies—Directive 10-289. You have heard him fighting for his rights—his and yours—for his independence, for his property. Yet he did not fight Directive 10-289. He signed voluntarily, so you have been told, the Gift Certificate that surrendered Rearden Metal to his enemies. He signed the one paper which, by all of his previous record, you had expected him to fight to the death. What could this mean—you have constantly been told—unless it meant that even he recognized the necessity of Directive 10-289 and sacrificed his personal interests for the sake of the country? Judge his views by the motive of that action, you have constantly been told. And with this I agree unreservedly: *judge his views by the motive of that action.* And—for whatever value you attach to my opinion and to any warning I may give you—judge my views also by the motive of that action, because his convictions are mine.

"For two years, I had been Hank Rearden's mistress. Let there be no misunderstanding about it: I am saying this, not as a shameful confession, but with the highest sense of pride. I had been his mistress. I had slept with him, in his bed, in his arms. There is nothing anyone might now say to you about me, which I will not tell you first. It will be useless to defame me—I know the nature of the accusations and I will state them to you myself. Did I feel a physical desire for him? I did. Was I moved by a passion of my body? I was. Have I experienced the most violent form of sensual pleasure? I have. If this now makes me a disgraced woman in your eyes—let your estimate be your own concern. I will stand on mine."

Bertram Scudder was staring at her; this was not the speech he had expected and he felt, in dim panic, that it was not proper to let it continue, but she was the special guest whom the Washington rulers had ordered him to treat cautiously; he could not be certain whether he was now supposed to interrupt her or not; besides, he enjoyed hearing this sort of story. In the audience booth, James Taggart and Lillian Rearden sat frozen, like animals paralyzed by the headlight of a train rushing down upon them; they were the only ones present who knew the connection between the words they were hearing and the theme of the broadcast; it was too late for them to move; they dared not assume the responsibility of a movement or of whatever was to follow. In the control room, a young intellectual of Chick Morrison's staff stood ready to cut the broadcast off the air in case of trouble, but he saw no political significance in the speech he was hearing, no element he could construe as dangerous to his masters. He was accustomed to hearing speeches extorted by unknown pressure from unwilling victims, and he concluded that this was the case of a reactionary forced to confess a scandal and that, therefore, the speech had, perhaps, some political value; besides, he was curious to hear it.

"I am proud that he had chosen me to give him pleasure and that it was he who had been my choice. It was not—as it is for most of you—an act of casual indulgence and mutual contempt. It was the ultimate form of our admiration for each other, with full knowledge of the values by which we made our choice. We are those who do not disconnect the values of their minds from the actions of their bodies, those who do not leave their values to empty dreams, but bring them into existence, those who give material form to thoughts, and reality to values—those who make steel, railroads and happiness. And to such among you who hate the thought of human joy, who wish to see men's life as chronic suffering and failure, who wish men to apologize for happiness—or for success, or ability, or achievement, or wealth—to such among you, I am now saying: I wanted him, I had him, I was happy, I had known joy, a pure, full, guiltless joy, the joy you dread to hear confessed by any human being, the joy of which your only knowledge is in your hatred for those who are worthy of reaching it. Well, hate me, then—because I reached it!"

"Miss Taggart," said Bertram Scudder nervously, "aren't we departing from the subject of . . . After all, your personal relationship with Mr. Rearden has no political significance which—"

"I didn't think it had, either. And, of course, I came here to tell you about the political and moral system under which you are now living. Well, I thought that I knew everything about Hank Rearden, but there was one thing which I did not learn until today. It was the blackmail threat that our relationship would be made public that forced Hank Rearden to sign the Gift Certificate surrendering Rearden Metal. It was blackmail—blackmail by your government officials, by your rulers, by your—"

In the instant when Scudder's hand swept out to knock the microphone over, a faint click came from its throat as it crashed to the floor, signifying that the intellectual cop had cut the broadcast off the air.

She laughed—but there was no one to see her and to hear the nature of her laughter. The figures rushing into the glass enclosure were screaming at one another. Chick Morrison was yelling unprintable curses at Bertram Scudder—Bertram Scudder was shouting that he had been opposed to the whole idea, but had been ordered to do it—James Taggart looked like an animal baring its teeth, while he snarled at two of Morrison's youngest assistants and avoided the snarls of an older third. The muscles of Lillian Rearden's face had an odd slackness, like the limbs of an animal lying in the road, intact but dead. The morale conditioners were shrieking what they guessed they thought Mr. Mouch would think. "What am I to say to them?" the program announcer was crying, pointing at the microphone. "Mr. Morrison, there's an audience waiting, what am I to say?" Nobody answered him. They were not fighting over what to do, but over whom to blame.

Nobody said a word to Dagny or glanced in her direction. Nobody stopped her, when she walked out.

She stepped into the first taxicab in sight, giving the address of her apartment. As the cab started, she noticed that the dial of the radio on the driver's panel was lighted and silent, crackling with the brief, tense coughs of static: it was tuned to Bertram Scudder's program.

She lay back against the seat, feeling nothing but the desolation of the knowledge that the sweep of her action had, perhaps, swept away the man who might never wish to see her again. She felt, for the first time, the immensity of the hopelessness of finding him—if he did not choose to be found—in the streets of the city, in the towns of a continent, in the canyons of the Rocky Mountains where the goal was closed by a screen of rays. But one thing remained to her, like a log floating on a void, the log to which she had clung through the broadcast—and she knew that this was the thing she could not abandon, even were she to lose all the rest; it was the sound of his voice saying to her: "Nobody stays here by faking reality in any manner whatever."

"Ladies and gentlemen," the voice of Bertram Scudder's announcer crackled suddenly out of the static, "due to technical difficulties over which we have no control, this station will remain off the air, pending the necessary readjustments." The taxi driver gave a brief, contemptuous chuckle—and snapped the radio off.

When she stepped out and handed him a bill, he extended the change to her and, suddenly, leaned forward for a closer look at her face. She felt certain that he recognized her and she held his glance austerely for an instant. His bitter face and his overpatched shirt were worn out by a hopeless, losing struggle. As she handed him a tip, he said quietly, with too earnest, too solemn an emphasis for a mere acknowledgment of the coins, *"Thank you, ma'am."*

She turned swiftly and hurried into the building, not to let him see the emotion which was suddenly more than she could bear.

Her head was drooping, as she unlocked the door of her apartment, and the light struck her from below, from the carpet, before she jerked her head up in astonishment at finding the apartment lighted. She took a step forward—and saw Hank Rearden standing across the room.

She was held still by two shocks: one was the sight of his presence, she had not expected him to be back so soon; the other was the sight of his face. His face had so firm, so confident, so mature a look of calm, in the faint half-smile, in the clarity of the eyes, that she felt as if he had aged decades within one month, but aged in the proper sense of human growth, aged in vision, in stature, in power. She felt that he who had lived through a month of agony, he whom she had hurt so deeply and was about to hurt more deeply still, he would now be the one to give her support and consolation, his would be the strength to protect them both. She stood motionless for only an instant, but she saw his smile deepening as if he were reading her thoughts and telling her that she had nothing to fear. She heard a slight, crackling sound and saw, on a table beside him, the lighted dial of a silent radio. Her eyes moved to his as a question and he answered by the faintest nod, barely more than a lowering of his eyelids; he had heard her broadcast.

They moved toward each other in the same moment. He seized her shoulders to support her, her face was raised to his, but he did not touch her lips, he took her hand and kissed her wrist, her fingers, her palm, as the sole form of the greeting which so much of his suffering had gone to await. And suddenly, broken by the whole of this day and of that month, she was sobbing in his arms, slumped against him, sobbing as she had never done in her life, as a woman, in surrender to pain and in a last, futile protest against it.

Holding her so that she stood and moved only by means of his body, not hers, he led her to the couch and tried to make her sit down beside him, but she slipped to the floor, to sit at his feet and bury her face in his knees and sob without defense or disguise.

He did not lift her, he let her cry, with his arm tight about her. She felt his hand on her head, on her shoulder, she felt the protection of his firmness, a firmness which seemed to tell her that as her tears were for both of them, so was his knowledge, that he knew her pain and felt it and understood, yet was able to witness it calmly—and his calm seemed to lift her burden, by granting her the right to break, here, at his feet, by telling her that he was able to carry what she could not carry any longer. She knew dimly that *this* was the real Hank Rearden, and no matter what form of insulting cruelty he had once given to their first nights together, no matter how often she had seemed as the stronger of the two, this had always been within him and at the root of their bond—this strength of his which would protect her if ever hers were gone.

When she raised her head, he was smiling down at her.

"Hank . . ." she whispered guiltily, in desperate astonishment at her own break.

"Quiet, darling."

She let her face drop back on his knees; she lay still, fighting for rest, fighting against the pressure of a wordless thought: he had been able to bear and to accept her broadcast only as a confession of her love; it made the truth she now had to tell him more inhuman a blow than anyone had the right to deliver. She felt terror at the thought that she would not have the strength to do it, and terror at the thought that she would.

When she looked up at him again, he ran his hand over her forehead, brushing the hair off her face.

"It's over, darling," he said. "The worst of it is over, for both of us."

"No, Hank, it isn't."

He smiled.

He drew her to sit beside him, with her head on his shoulder. "Don't say anything now," he said. "You know that we both understand all that has to be said, and we'll speak of it, but not until it has ceased to hurt you quite so much."

His hand moved down the line of her sleeve, down a fold of her skirt, with so light a pressure that it seemed as if the hand did not feel the body inside the clothes, as if he were regaining possession, not of her body, but only of its vision.

"You've taken too much," he said. "So have I. Let them batter us. There's no reason why we should add to it. No matter what we have to face, there can be no suffering between the two of us. No added pain. Let that come from their world. It won't come from us. Don't be afraid. We won't hurt each other. Not now."

She raised her head, shaking it with a bitter smile—there was a desperate violence in her movement, but the smile was a sign of recovery: of the determination to face the despair.

"Hank, the kind of hell I let you go through in the last month—" Her voice was trembling.

"It's nothing, compared to the kind of hell I let you go through in the last hour." His voice was steady.

She got up, to pace the room, to prove her strength—her steps like words telling him that she was not to be spared any longer. When she stopped and turned to face him, he rose, as if he understood her motive.

"I know that I've made it worse for you," she said, pointing at the radio.

He shook his head. "No."

"Hank, there's something I have to tell you."

"So have I. Will you let me speak first? You see, it's something I should have said to you long ago. Will you let me speak and not answer me until I finish?"

She nodded.

He took a moment to look at her as she stood before him, as if to hold the full sight of her figure, of this moment and of everything that had led them to it.

"I love you, Dagny," he said quietly, with the simplicity of an unclouded, yet unsmiling happiness.

She was about to speak, but knew that she couldn't, even if he had permitted it, she caught her unuttered words, the movement of her lips was her only answer, then she inclined her head in acceptance.

"I love you. As the same value, as the same expression, with the same pride and the same meaning as I love my work, my mills, my Metal, my hours at a desk, at a furnace, in a laboratory, in an ore mine, as I love my ability to work, as I love the act of sight and knowledge, as I love the action of my mind when it solves a chemical equation or grasps a sunrise, as I love the things I've made and the things I've felt, as *my* product, as *my* choice, as a shape of *my* world, as my best mirror, as the wife I've never had, as that which makes all the rest of it possible: as my power to live."

She did not drop her face, but kept it level and open, to hear and accept, as he wanted her to and as he deserved.

"I loved you from the first day I saw you, on a flatcar on a siding of Milford Station. I loved you when we rode in the cab of the first engine on the John Galt Line. I loved you on the gallery of Ellis Wyatt's house. I loved you on that next morning. You knew it. But it's I who must say it to you, as I'm saying it now—if I am to redeem all those days and to let them be fully what they were for both of us. I loved you. You knew it. I didn't. And because I didn't, I had to learn it when I sat at my desk and looked at the Gift Certificate for Rearden Metal."

She closed her eyes. But there was no suffering in his face, nothing but the immense and quiet happiness of clarity.

" 'We are those who do not disconnect the values of their minds from the actions of their bodies.' You said it in your broadcast tonight. But you knew it, then, on that morning in Ellis Wyatt's house. You knew that all those insults I was throwing at you were the fullest confession of love a man could make. You knew that the physical desire I was damning as our mutual shame, is neither physical nor an expression of one's body, but the expression of one's mind's deepest values, whether one has the courage to know it or not. That was why you laughed at me as you did, wasn't it?"

"Yes," she whispered.

"You said, 'I do not want your mind, your will, your being or your soul—so long as it's to me that you will come for that lowest one of your desires.' You knew, when you said it, that it *was* my mind, my will, my being and my soul that I was giving you by means of that desire. And I want to say it now, to let that morning mean what it meant: my mind, my will, my being and my soul, Dagny—yours, for as long as I shall live."

He was looking straight at her and she saw a brief sparkle in his eyes, which was not a smile, but almost as if he had heard the cry she had not uttered.

"Let me finish, dearest. I want you to know how fully I know what I am saying. I, who thought that I was fighting them, I had accepted the worst of our enemies' creed—and *that* is what I've paid for ever since, as I am paying now and as I must. I had accepted the one tenet by which they destroy a man before he's started, the killer-tenet: the breach between his mind and body. I had accepted it, like most of their victims, not knowing it, not knowing even that the issue existed. I rebelled against their creed of human impotence and I took pride in my ability to think, to act, to work for the satisfaction of my desires. But I did not know that this was virtue, I never identified it as a moral value, as the highest of moral values, to be defended above one's life, because it's that which makes life possible. And I accepted punishment for it, punishment for virtue at the hands of an arrogant evil, made arrogant solely by my ignorance and my submission.

"I accepted their insults, their frauds, their extortions. I thought I could afford to ignore them—all those impotent mystics who prattle about their souls and are unable to build a roof over their heads. I thought that the world was mine, and that those jabbering incompetents were no threat to my strength. I could not understand why I kept losing every battle. I did not know that the force unleashed against me was my own. While I was busy conquering matter, I had surrendered to them the realm of the mind, of thought, of principle, of law, of values, of morality. I had accepted, unwittingly and by default, the tenet that ideas were of no consequence to one's existence, to one's work, to reality, to this earth—as if ideas were not the province of reason, but of that mystic faith which I despised. This was all they wanted me to concede. It was enough. I had surrendered that which all of their claptrap is designed to subvert and to destroy: man's reason. No, they were not able to deal with matter, to produce abundance, to control this earth. They did not have to. They controlled *me*.

"I, who knew that wealth is only a means to an end, created the means and let them prescribe my ends. I, who took pride in my ability to achieve the satisfaction of my desires, let them prescribe the code of values by which I judged my desires. I, who shaped matter to serve my purpose, was left with a pile of steel and gold, but with my every purpose defeated, my every desire betrayed, my every attempt at happiness frustrated.

"I had cut myself in two, as the mystics preached, and I ran my business by one code of rules, but my own life by another. I rebelled against the looters' attempt to set the price and value of my steel—but I let them set the moral values of my life. I rebelled against demands for an unearned wealth—but I thought it was my duty to grant an unearned love to a wife I despised, an unearned respect to a mother who hated me, an unearned support to a brother who plotted for my destruction. I rebelled against undeserved financial injury—but I accepted a life of undeserved pain. I rebelled against the doctrine that my productive ability was guilt—but I accepted, as guilt, my capacity for happiness. I rebelled against the creed that virtue is some disembodied unknowable of the spirit—but I damned you, *you*, my dearest one, for the desire of your body and mine. But if the body is evil, then so are those who provide the means of its survival, so is material wealth and those who produce it—and if moral values are set in contradiction to our physical existence, then it's right that rewards should be unearned, that virtue should consist of the undone, that there should be no tie between achievement and profit, that the inferior animals who're able to produce should serve those superior beings whose superiority in spirit consists of incompetence in the flesh.

"If some man like Hugh Akston had told me, when I started, that by accepting the mystics' theory of sex I was accepting the looters' theory of economics, I would have laughed in his face. I would not laugh at him now. Now I see Rearden Steel being ruled by human scum—I see the achievement of my life serving to enrich the worst of my enemies—and as to the only two persons I ever loved, I've brought a deadly insult to one and public disgrace to the other. I slapped the face of the man who was my friend, my defender, my teacher, the man who set me free by helping me to learn what I've learned. I loved him, Dagny, he was the brother, the son, the comrade I never had—but I knocked him out of my life, because he would not help me to produce for the looters. I'd give anything now to have him back, but I own nothing to offer in such repayment, and I'll never see him again, because it's I who'll know that there is no way to deserve even the right to ask forgiveness.

"But what I've done to you, my dearest, is still worse. Your speech and that you had to make it—that's what I've brought upon the only woman I loved, in payment for the only happiness I've known. Don't tell me that it was your choice from the first and that you accepted all consequences, including tonight—it does not redeem the fact that it was I who had no better choice to offer you. And that the looters forced you to speak, that you spoke to avenge me and set me free—does not redeem the fact that it was I who made their tactics possible. It was not their own convictions of sin and dishonor that they could use to disgrace you—it was mine. They merely carried out the things I believed and said in Ellis Wyatt's house. It was I who kept our love hidden as a guilty secret—they merely treated it for what it was by my own appraisal. It was I who was willing to counterfeit reality for the sake of appearance in their eyes—they merely cashed in on the right I had given them.

"People think that a liar gains a victory over his victim. What I've learned is that a lie is an act of self-abdication, because one surrenders one's reality to the person to whom one lies, making that person one's master, condemning oneself from then on to faking the sort of reality that person's view requires to be faked. And if one gains the immediate purpose of the lie—the price one pays is the destruction of that which the gain was intended to serve. The man who lies to the world, is the world's slave from then on. When I chose to hide my love for you, to disavow it in public and live it as a lie, I made it public property—and the public has claimed it in a fitting sort of manner. I had no way to avert it and no power to save you. When I gave in to the looters, when I signed their Gift Certificate, to protect you—I was still faking reality, there was nothing else left open to me—and, Dagny, I'd rather have seen us both dead than permit them to do what they threatened. But there are no white lies, there is only the blackness of destruction, and a white lie is the blackest of all. I was still faking reality, and it had the inexorable result: instead of protection, it brought you a more terrible kind of ordeal, instead of saving your name, it forced you to offer yourself for a public stoning and to throw the stones by your own hand. I know that you were proud of the things you said, and I was proud to hear you—but that was the pride we should have claimed two years ago.

"No, you did not make it worse for me, you set me free, you saved us both, you redeemed our past. I can't ask you to forgive me, we're far beyond such terms—and the only atonement I can offer you is the fact that I am happy. That I am happy, my darling, *not* that I suffer. I am happy that I have seen the truth—even if my power of sight is all that's left to me now. Were I to surrender to pain and give up in futile regret that my own error has wrecked my past—*that* would be the act of final treason, the ultimate failure toward that truth I regret having failed. But if my love of truth is left as my only possession, then the greater the loss behind me, the greater the pride I may take in the price I have paid for that love. Then the wreckage will not become a funereal mount above me, but will serve as a height I have climbed to attain a wider field of vision. My pride and my power of vision were all that I owned when I started—and whatever I achieved, was achieved by means of them. Both are greater now. Now I have the knowledge of the superlative value I had missed: of my right to be proud of my vision. The rest is mine to reach.

"And, Dagny, the one thing I wanted, as the first step of my future, was to say that I love you—as I'm saying it now. I love you, my dearest, with that blindest passion of my body which comes from the clearest perception of my mind—and my love for you is the only attainment of my past that will be left to me, unchanged, through all the years ahead. I wanted to say it to you while I still had the right to say it. And because I had not said it at our beginning, this is the way I have to say it—at the end. Now I'll tell you what it was that you wanted to tell me—because, you see, I know it and I accept: somewhere within the past month, you have met the man you love, and if love means one's final, irreplaceable choice, then he is the only man you've ever loved."

"Yes!" Her voice was half-gasp, half-scream, as under a physical blow, with shock as her only awareness. "Hank!—how did you know it?"

He smiled and pointed at the radio. "My darling, you used nothing but the past tense."

"Oh . . . !" Her voice was now half-gasp, half-moan, and she closed her eyes.

"You never pronounced the one word you would have rightfully thrown at them, were it otherwise. You said, 'I wanted him,' not, 'I love him.' You told me on the phone today that you could have returned sooner. No other reason would have made you leave me as you did. Only that one reason was valid and right."

She was leaning back a little, as if fighting for balance to stand, yet she was looking straight at him, with a smile that did not part her lips, but softened her eyes to a glance of admiration and her mouth to a shape of pain.

"It's true. I've met the man I love and will always love, I've seen him, I've spoken to him—but he's a man whom I can't have, whom I may never have and, perhaps, may never see again."

"I think I've always known that you would find him. I knew what you felt for me, I knew how much it was, but I knew that I was not your final choice. What you'll give him is not taken away from me, it's what I've never had. I can't rebel against it. What I've had means too much to me—and that I've had it, can never be changed."

"Do you want me to say it, Hank? Will you understand it, if I say that I'll always love you?"

"I think I've understood it before you did."

"I've always seen you as you are now. That greatness of yours which you are just beginning to allow yourself to know—I've always known it and I've watched your struggle to discover it. Don't speak of atonement, you have not hurt me, your mistakes came from your magnificent integrity under the torture of an impossible code—and your fight against it did not bring me suffering, it brought me the feeling I've found too seldom: admiration. If you will accept it, it will always be yours. What you meant to me can never be changed. But the man I met—he is the love I had wanted to reach long before I knew that he existed, and I think he will remain beyond my reach, but that I love him will be enough to keep me living."

He took her hand and pressed it to his lips. "Then you know what I feel," he said, "and why I am still happy."

Looking up at his face, she realized that for the first time he was what she had always thought him intended to be: a man with an immense capacity for the enjoyment of existence. The taut look of endurance, of fiercely unadmitted pain, was gone; now, in the midst of the wreckage and of his hardest hour, his face had the serenity of pure strength; it had the look she had seen in the faces of the men in the valley.

"Hank," she whispered, "I don't think I can explain it, but I feel that I have committed no treason, either to you or to him."

"You haven't."

Her eyes seemed abnormally alive in a face drained of color, as if her consciousness remained untouched in a body broken by exhaustion. He made her sit down and slipped his arm along the back of the couch, not touching her, yet holding her in a protective embrace.

"Now tell me," he asked, "where were you?"

"I can't tell you that. I've given my word never to reveal anything about it. I can say only that it's a place I found by accident, when I crashed, and I left it blindfolded—and I wouldn't be able to find it again."

"Couldn't you trace your way back to it?"

"I won't try."

"And the man?"

"I won't look for him."

"He remained there?"

"I don't know."

"Why did you leave him?"

"I can't tell you."

"Who is he?"

Her chuckle of desperate amusement was involuntary. "Who is John Galt?"

He glanced at her, astonished—but realized that she was not joking. "So there is a John Galt?" he asked slowly.

"Yes."

"That slang phrase refers to *him?*"

"Yes."

"And it has some special meaning?"

"Oh yes! . . . There's one thing I can tell you about him, because I discovered it earlier, without promise of secrecy: he is the man who invented the motor we found."

"Oh!" He smiled, as if he should have known it. Then he said softly, with a glance that was almost compassion, "He's the destroyer, isn't he?" He saw her look of shock, and added, "No, don't answer me, if you can't. I think I know where you were. It was Quentin Daniels that you wanted to save from the destroyer, and you were following Daniels when you crashed, weren't you?"

"Yes."

"Good God, Dagny!—does such a place really exist? Are they all alive? Is there . . . ? I'm sorry. Don't answer."

She smiled. "It does exist."

He remained silent for a long time.

"Hank, could you give up Rearden Steel?"

"No!" The answer was fiercely immediate, but he added, with the first sound of hopelessness in his voice, "Not yet."

Then he looked at her, as if, in the transition of his three words, he had lived the course of her agony of the past month. "I see," he said. He ran his hand over her forehead, with a gesture of understanding, of compassion, of an almost incredulous wonder. "What hell you've now undertaken to endure!" he said, his voice low.

She nodded.

She slipped down, to lie stretched, her face on his knees. He stroked her hair; he said, "We'll fight the looters as long as we can. I don't know what future is possible to us, but we'll win or we'll learn that it's hopeless. Until we do, we'll fight for our world. We're all that's left of it."

She fell asleep, lying there, her hand clasping his. Her last awareness, before she surrendered the responsibility of consciousness, was the sense of an enormous void, the void of a city and of a continent where she would never be able to find the man whom she had no right to seek.

IV

ANTI-LIFE

James Taggart reached into the pocket of his dinner jacket, pulled out the first wad of paper he found, which was a hundred-dollar bill, and dropped it into the beggar's hand.

He noticed that the beggar pocketed the money in a manner as indifferent as his own. "Thanks, bud," said the beggar contemptuously, and walked away.

James Taggart remained still in the middle of the sidewalk, wondering what gave him a sense of shock and dread. It was not the man's insolence—he had not sought any gratitude, he had not been moved by pity, his gesture had been automatic and meaningless. It was that the beggar acted as if he would have been indifferent had he received a hundred dollars or a dime or, failing to find any help whatever, had seen himself dying of starvation within this night. Taggart shuddered and walked brusquely on, the shudder serving to cut off the realization that the beggar's mood matched his own.

The walls of the street around him had the stressed, unnatural clarity of a summer twilight, while an orange haze filled the channels of intersections and veiled the tiers of roofs, leaving him on a shrinking remnant of ground. The calendar in the sky seemed to stand insistently out of the haze, yellow like a page of old parchment, saying: August 5.

No—he thought, in answer to things he had not named—it was not true, he felt fine, that's why he wanted to do something tonight. He could not admit to himself that his peculiar restlessness came from a desire to experience pleasure; he could not admit that the particular pleasure he wanted was that of celebration, because he could not admit what it was that he wanted to celebrate.

This had been a day of intense activity, spent on words floating as vaguely as cotton, yet achieving a purpose as precisely as an adding machine, summing up to his full satisfaction. But his purpose and the nature of his satisfaction had to be kept as carefully hidden from himself as they had been from others; and his sudden craving for pleasure was a dangerous breach.

The day had started with a small luncheon in the hotel suite of a visiting Argentinian legislator, where a few people of various nationalities had talked at leisurely length about the climate of Argentina, its soil, its resources, the needs of its people, the value of a dynamic, progressive attitude toward the future—and had mentioned, as the briefest topic of conversation, that Argentina would be declared a People's State within two weeks.

It had been followed by a few cocktails at the home of Orren Boyle, with only one unobtrusive gentleman from Argentina sitting silently in a corner, while two executives from Washington and a few friends of unspecified positions had talked about national resources, metallurgy, mineralogy, neighborly duties and the welfare of the globe—and had mentioned that a loan of four billion dollars would be granted within three weeks to the People's State of Argentina and the People's State of Chile.

It had been followed by a small cocktail party in a private room of the bar built like a cellar on the roof of a skyscraper, an informal party given by him, James Taggart, for the directors of a recently formed company, The Interneighborly Amity and Development Corporation, of which Orren Boyle was president and a slender, graceful, overactive man from Chile was treasurer, a man whose name was Señor Mario Martinez, but whom Taggart was tempted, by some resemblance of spirit, to call Señor Cuffy Meigs. Here they had talked about golf, horse races, boat races, automobiles and women. It had not been necessary to mention, since they all knew it, that the Interneighborly Amity and Development Corporation had an exclusive contract to operate, on a twenty-year "managerial lease," all the industrial properties of the People's States of the Southern Hemisphere.

The last event of the day had been a large dinner reception at the home of Señor Rodrigo Gonzales, a diplomatic representative of Chile. No one had heard of Señor Gonzales a year ago, but he had become famous for the parties he had given in the past six months, ever since his arrival in New York. His guests described him as a progressive businessman. He had lost his property—it was said—when Chile, becoming a People's State, had nationalized all properties, except those belonging to citizens of backward, non-People's countries, such as Argentina; but he had adopted an enlightened attitude and had joined the new regime, placing himself in the service of his country. His home in New York occupied an entire floor of an exclusive residential hotel. He had a fat, blank face and the eyes of a killer. Watching him at tonight's reception, Taggart had concluded that the man was impervious to any sort of feeling, he looked as if a knife could slash, unnoticed, through his pendulous layers of flesh—except that there was a lewd, almost sexual relish in the way he rubbed his feet against the rich pile of his Persian rugs, or patted the polished arm of his chair, or folded his lips about a cigar. His wife, the Señora Gonzales, was a small, attractive woman, not as beautiful as she assumed, but enjoying the reputation of a beauty by means of a violent nervous energy and an odd manner of loose, warm, cynical self-assertiveness that seemed to promise anything and to absolve anyone. It was known that her particular brand of trading was her husband's chief asset, in an age when one traded, not goods, but favors—and, watching her among the guests, Taggart had found amusement in wondering what deals had been made, what directives issued, what industries destroyed in exchange for a few chance nights, which most of those men had had no reason to seek and, perhaps, could no longer remember. The party had bored him, there had been only half a dozen persons for whose sake he had put in an appearance, and it had not been necessary to speak to that half-dozen, merely to be seen and to exchange a few glances. Dinner had been about to be served, when he had heard what he had come to hear: Señor Gonzales had mentioned—the smoke of his cigar weaving over the half-dozen men who had drifted toward his armchair—that by agreement with the future People's State of Argentina, the properties of d'Anconia Copper would be nationalized by the People's State of Chile, in less than a month, on September 2.

It had all gone as Taggart had expected; the unexpected had come when, on hearing those words, he had felt an irresistible urge to escape. He had felt incapable of enduring the boredom of the dinner, as if some other form of activity were needed to greet the achievement of this night. He had walked out into the summer twilight of the streets, feeling as if he were both pursuing and pursued: pursuing a pleasure which nothing could give him, in celebration of a feeling which he dared not name—pursued by the dread of discovering what motive had moved him through the planning of tonight's achievement and what aspect of it now gave him this feverish sense of gratification.

He reminded himself that he would sell his d'Anconia Copper stock, which had never rallied fully after its crash of last year, and he would purchase shares of the Interneighborly Amity and Development Corporation, as agreed with his friends, which would bring him a fortune. But the thought brought him nothing but boredom; this was not the thing he wanted to celebrate.

He tried to force himself to enjoy it: money, he thought, had been his motive, money, nothing worse. Wasn't that a normal motive? A valid one? Wasn't that what they all were after, the Wyatts, the Reardens, the d'Anconias? . . . He jerked his head to stop it: he felt as if his thoughts were slipping down a dangerous blind alley, the end of which he must never permit himself to see.

No—he thought bleakly, in reluctant admission—money meant nothing to him any longer. He had thrown dollars about by the hundreds—at that party he had given today—for unfinished drinks, for uneaten delicacies, for unprovoked tips and unexpected whims, for a long-distance phone call to Argentina because one of the guests had wanted to check the exact version of a smutty story he had started telling, for the spur of any moment, for the clammy stupor of knowing that it was easier to pay than to think.

"You've got nothing to worry about, under that Railroad Unification Plan," Orren Boyle had giggled to him drunkenly. Under the Railroad Unification Plan, a local railroad had gone bankrupt in North Dakota, abandoning the region to the fate of a blighted area, the local banker had committed suicide, first killing his wife and children—a freight train had been taken off the schedule in Tennessee, leaving a local factory without transportation at a day's notice, the factory owner's son had quit college and was now in jail, awaiting execution for a murder committed with a gang of raiders—a way station had been closed in Kansas, and the station agent, who had wanted to be a scientist, had given up his studies and become a dishwasher—that he, James Taggart, might sit in a private barroom and pay for the alcohol pouring down Orren Boyle's throat, for the waiter who sponged Boyle's garments when he spilled his drink over his chest, for the carpet burned by the cigarettes of an ex-pimp from Chile who did not want to take the trouble of reaching for an ashtray across a distance of three feet.

It was not the knowledge of his indifference to money that now gave him a shudder of dread. It was the knowledge that he would be equally indifferent, were he reduced to the state of the beggar. There had been a time when he had felt some measure of guilt—in no clearer a form than a touch of irritation—at the thought that he shared the sin of greed, which he spent his time denouncing. Now he was hit by the chill realization that, in fact, he had never been a hypocrite: in full truth, he had never cared for money. This left another hole gaping open before him, leading into another blind alley which he could not risk seeing.

I just want to do something tonight!—he cried soundlessly to someone at large, in protest and in demanding anger—in protest against whatever it was that kept forcing these thoughts into his mind—in anger at a universe where some malevolent power would not permit him to find enjoyment without the need to know what he wanted or why.

What do you want?—some enemy voice kept asking, and he walked faster, trying to escape it. It seemed to him that his brain was a maze where a blind alley opened at every turn, leading into a fog that hid an abyss. It seemed to him that he was running, while the small island of safety was shrinking and nothing but those alleys would soon be left. It was like the remnant of clarity in the street around him, with the haze rolling in to fill all exits. Why did it have to shrink?—he thought in panic. This was the way he had lived all his life—keeping his eyes stubbornly, safely on the immediate pavement before him, craftily avoiding the sight of his road, of corners, of distances, of pinnacles. He had never intended going anywhere, he had wanted to be free of progression, free of the yoke of a straight line, he had never wanted his years to add up to any sum—what had summed them up?—why had he reached some unchosen destination where one could no longer stand still or retreat? "Look where you're going, brother!" snarled some voice, while an elbow pushed him back—and he realized that he had collided with some large, ill-smelling figure and that he had been running.

He slowed his steps and admitted into his mind a recognition of the streets he had chosen in his random escape. He had not wanted to know that he was going home to his wife. That, too, was a fogbound alley, but there was no other left to him.

He knew—the moment he saw Cherryl's silent, poised figure as she rose at his entrance into her room—that this was more dangerous than he had allowed himself to know and that he would not find what he wanted. But danger, to him, was a signal to shut off his sight, suspend his judgment and pursue an unaltered course, on the unstated premise that the danger would remain unreal by the sovereign power of his wish not to see it—like a foghorn within him, blowing, not to sound a warning, but to summon the fog.

"Why, yes, I did have an important business banquet to attend, but I changed my mind, I felt like having dinner with *you* tonight," he said in the tone of a compliment—but a quiet "I see" was the only answer he obtained.

He felt irritation at her unastonished manner and her pale, unrevealing face. He felt irritation at the smooth efficiency with which she gave instructions to the servants, then at finding himself in the candlelight of the dining room, facing her across a perfectly appointed table, with two crystal cups of fruit in silver bowls of ice between them.

It was her poise that irritated him most; she was no longer an incongruous little freak, dwarfed by the luxury of the residence which a famous artist had designed; she matched it. She sat at the table as if she were the kind of hostess that room had the right to demand. She wore a tailored housecoat of russet-colored brocade that blended with the bronze of her hair, the severe simplicity of its lines serving as her only ornament. He would have preferred the jingling bracelets and rhinestone buckles of her past. Her eyes disturbed him, as they had for months: they were neither friendly nor hostile, but watchful and questioning.

"I closed a big deal today," he said, his tone part boastful, part pleading. "A deal involving this whole continent and half a dozen governments."

He realized that the awe, the admiration, the eager curiosity he had expected, belonged to the face of the little shopgirl who had ceased to exist. He saw none of it in the face of his wife; even anger or hatred would have been preferable to her level, attentive glance; the glance was worse than accusing, it was inquiring.

"What deal, Jim?"

"What do you mean, what deal? Why are you suspicious? Why do you have to start prying at once?"

"I'm sorry. I didn't know it was confidential. You don't have to answer me."

"It's not confidential." He waited, but she remained silent. "Well? Aren't you going to say anything?"

"Why, no." She said it simply, as if to please him.

"So you're not interested at all?"

"But I thought you didn't want to discuss it."

"Oh, don't be so tricky!" he snapped. "It's a big business deal. That's what you admire, isn't it, big business? Well, it's bigger than anything those boys ever dreamed of. They spend their lives grubbing for their fortunes penny by penny, while I can do it like that"—he snapped his fingers—"just like that. It's the biggest single stunt ever pulled."

"Stunt, Jim?"

"Deal!"

"And you did it? Yourself?"

"You bet I did it! That fat fool, Orren Boyle, couldn't have swung it in a million years. This took knowledge and skill and timing"—he saw a spark of interest in her eyes—"and psychology." The spark vanished, but he went rushing heedlessly on. "One had to know how to approach Wesley, and how to keep the wrong influences away from him, and how to get Mr. Thompson interested without letting him know too much, and how to cut Chick Morrison in on it, but keep Tinky Holloway out, and how to get the right people to give a few parties for Wesley at the right time, and . . . Say, Cherryl, is there any champagne in this house?"

"Champagne?"

"Can't we do something special tonight? Can't we have a sort of celebration together?"

"We can have champagne, yes, Jim, of course."

She rang the bell and gave the orders, in her odd, lifeless, uncritical manner, a manner of meticulous compliance with his wishes while volunteering none of her own.

"You don't seem to be very impressed," he said. "But what would you know about business, anyway? You wouldn't be able to understand anything on so large a scale. Wait till September second. Wait till *they* hear about it."

"They? Who?"

He glanced at her, as if he had let a dangerous word slip out involuntarily. "We've organized a setup where we—me, Orren and a few friends—are going to control every industrial property south of the border."

"Whose property?"

"Why . . . the people's. This is not an old-fashioned grab for private profit. It's a deal with a mission—a worthy, public-spirited mission—to manage the nationalized properties of the various People's States of South America, to teach their workers our modern techniques of production, to help the underprivileged who've never had a chance, to—" He broke off abruptly, though she had merely sat looking at him without shifting her glance. "You know," he said suddenly, with a cold little chuckle, "if you're so damn anxious to hide that you came from the slums, you ought to be less indifferent to the philosophy of social welfare. It's always the poor who lack humanitarian instincts. One has to be born to wealth in order to know the finer feelings of altruism."

"I've never tried to hide that I came from the slums," she said in the simple, impersonal tone of a factual correction. "And I haven't any sympathy for that welfare philosophy. I've seen enough of them to know what makes the kind of poor who want something for nothing." He did not answer, and she added suddenly, her voice astonished, but firm, as if in final confirmation of a long-standing doubt, "Jim, you don't care about it, either. You don't care about any of that welfare hogwash."

"Well, if money is all that you're interested in," he snapped, "let me tell you that that deal will bring me a fortune. That's what you've always admired, isn't it, wealth?"

"It depends."

"I think I'll end up as one of the richest men in the world," he said; he did not ask what her admiration depended upon. "There's nothing I won't be able to afford. Nothing. Just name it. I can give you anything you want. Go on, name it."

"I don't want anything, Jim."

"But I'd like to give you a present! To celebrate the occasion, see? Anything you take it into your head to ask. Anything. I can do it. I want to show you that I can do it. Any fancy you care to name."

"I haven't any fancies."

"Oh, come on! Want a yacht?"

"No."

"Want me to buy you the whole neighborhood where you lived in Buffalo?"

"No."

"Want the crown jewels of the People's State of England? They can be had, you know. That People's State has been hinting about it on the black market for a long time. But there aren't any old-fashioned tycoons left who're able to afford it. *I'm* able to afford it—or will be, after September second. Want it?"

"No."

"Then what *do* you want?"

"I don't want anything, Jim."

"But you've got to! You've got to want something, damn you!"

She looked at him, faintly startled, but otherwise indifferent.

"Oh, all right, I'm sorry," he said; he seemed astonished by his own outbreak. "I just wanted to please you," he added sullenly, "but I guess you can't understand it at all. You don't know how important it is. You don't know how big a man you're married to."

"I'm trying to find out," she said slowly.

"Do you still think, as you used to, that Hank Rearden is a great man?"

"Yes, Jim, I do."

"Well, I've got him beaten. I'm greater than any of them, greater than Rearden and greater than that other lover of my sister's, who—" He stopped, as if he had slid too far.

"Jim," she asked evenly, "what is going to happen on September second?"

He glanced up at her, from under his forehead—a cold glance, while his muscles creased into a semi-smile, as if in cynical breach of some hallowed restraint. "They're going to nationalize d'Anconia Copper," he said.

He heard the long, harsh roll of a motor, as a plane went by somewhere in the darkness above the roof, then a thin tinkle, as a piece of ice settled, melting, in the silver bowl of his fruit cup—before she answered. She said, "He was your friend, wasn't he?"

"Oh, shut up!"

He remained silent, not looking at her. When his eyes came back to her face, she was still watching him and she spoke first, her voice oddly stern: "What your sister did in her radio broadcast was great."

"Yes, I know, I know, you've been saying that for a month."

"You've never answered me."

"What is there to ans . . . ?"

"Just as your friends in Washington have never answered her." He remained silent. "Jim, I'm not dropping the subject." He did not answer. "Your friends in Washington never uttered a word about it. They did not deny the things she said, they did not explain, they did not try to justify themselves. They acted as if she had never spoken. I think they're hoping that people will forget it. Some people will. But the rest of us know what she said and that your friends were afraid to fight her."

"That's not true! The proper action was taken and the incident is closed and I don't see why you keep bringing it up."

"What action?"

"Bertram Scudder was taken off the air, as a program not in the public interest at the present time."

"Does that answer her?"

"It closes the issue and there's nothing more to be said about it."

"About a government that works by blackmail and extortion?"

"You can't say that nothing was done. It's been publicly announced that Scudder's programs were disruptive, destructive and untrustworthy."

"Jim, I want to understand this. Scudder wasn't on her side—he was on yours. He didn't even arrange that broadcast. He was acting on orders from Washington, wasn't he?"

"I thought you didn't like Bertram Scudder."

"I didn't and I don't, but—"

"Then what do you care?"

"But he was innocent, as far as your friends were concerned, wasn't he?"

"I wish you wouldn't bother with politics. You talk like a fool."

"He was innocent, wasn't he?"

"So what?"

She looked at him, her eyes incredulously wide. "Then they just made him the scapegoat, didn't they?"

"Oh, don't sit there looking like Eddie Willers!"

"Do I? I like Eddie Willers. He's honest."

"He's a damn half-wit who doesn't have the faintest idea of how to deal with practical reality!"

"But you do, don't you, Jim?"

"You bet I do!"

"Then couldn't you have helped Scudder?"

"*I?*" He burst into helpless, angry laughter. "Oh, why don't you grow up? I did my best to get Scudder thrown to the lions! Somebody had to be. Don't you know that it was *my* neck, if some other hadn't been found?"

"*Your* neck? Why not Dagny's, if she was wrong? Because she wasn't?"

"Dagny is in an entirely different category! It had to be Scudder or me."

"Why?"

"And it's much better for national policy to let it be Scudder. This way, it's not necessary to argue about what she said—and if anybody brings it up, we start howling that it was said on Scudder's program and that Scudder's programs have been discredited and that Scudder is a proven fraud and liar, etc., etc.—and do you think the public will be able to unscramble it? Nobody's ever trusted Bertram Scudder, anyway. Oh, don't stare at me like that! Would you rather they'd picked *me* to discredit?"

"Why not Dagny? Because her speech could *not* be discredited?"

"If you're so damn sorry for Bertram Scudder, you should have seen him try his damndest to make them break *my* neck! He's been doing that for years—how do you think he got to where he was, except by climbing on carcasses? He thought he was pretty powerful, too—you should have seen how the big business tycoons used to be afraid of him! But he got himself outmaneuvered, this time. This time, he belonged to the wrong faction."

Dimly, through the pleasant stupor of relaxing, of sprawling back in his chair and smiling, he knew that this was the enjoyment he wanted: to be himself. To be himself—he thought, in the drugged, precarious state of floating past the deadliest of his blind alleys, the one that led to the question of what was himself.

"You see, he belonged to the Tinky Holloway faction. It was pretty much of a seesaw for a while, between the Tinky Holloway faction and the Chick Morrison faction. But we won. Tinky made a deal and agreed to scuttle his pal Bertram in exchange for a few things he needed from us. You should have heard Bertram howl! But he was a dead duck and he knew it."

He started on a rolling chuckle, but choked it off, as the haze cleared and he saw his wife's face. "Jim," she whispered, "is that the sort of . . . victories you're winning?"

"Oh, for Christ's sake!" he screamed, smashing his fist down on the table. "Where have you been all these years? What sort of world do you think you're living in?" His blow had upset his water glass and the water went spreading in dark stains over the lace of the tablecloth.

"I'm trying to find out," she whispered. Her shoulders were sagging and her face looked suddenly worn, an odd, aged look that seemed haggard and lost.

"I couldn't help it!" he burst out in the silence. "I'm not to blame! I have to take things as I find them! It's not I who've made this world!"

He was shocked to see that she smiled—a smile of so fiercely bitter a contempt that it seemed incredible on her gently patient face; she was not looking at him, but at some image of her own. "That's what my father used to say when he got drunk at the corner saloon instead of looking for work."

"How dare you try comparing me to—" he started, but did not finish, because she was not listening.

Her words, when she looked at him again, astonished him as completely irrelevant. "The date of that nationalization, September second," she asked, her voice wistful, "was it you who picked it?"

"No. I had nothing to do with it. It's the date of some special session of their legislature. Why?"

"It's the date of our first wedding anniversary."

"Oh? Oh, that's right!" He smiled, relieved at the change to a safe subject. "We'll have been married a year. My, it doesn't seem that long!"

"It seems much longer," she said tonelessly.

She was looking off again, and he felt in sudden uneasiness that the subject was not safe at all; he wished she would not look as if she were seeing the whole course of that year and of their marriage.

. . . not to get scared, but to learn—she thought—the thing to do is not to get scared, but to learn . . . The words came from a sentence she had repeated to herself so often that it felt like a pillar polished smooth by the helpless weight of her body, the pillar that had supported her through the past year. She tried to repeat it, but she felt as if her hands were slipping on the polish, as if the sentence would not stave off terror any longer—because she was beginning to understand.

If you don't know, the thing to do is not to get scared, but to learn. . . . It was in the bewildered loneliness of the first weeks of her marriage that she said it to herself for the first time. She could not understand Jim's behavior, or his sullen anger, which looked like weakness, or his evasive, incomprehensible answers to her questions, which sounded like cowardice; such traits were not possible in the James Taggart whom she had married. She told herself that she could not condemn without understanding, that she knew nothing about his world, that the extent of her ignorance was the extent to which she misinterpreted his actions. She took the blame, she took the beating of self-reproach—against some bleakly stubborn certainty which told her that something was wrong and that the thing she felt was fear.

"I must learn everything that Mrs. James Taggart is expected to know and to be," was the way she explained her purpose to a teacher of etiquette. She set out to learn with the devotion, the discipline, the drive of a military cadet or a religious novice. It was the only way, she thought, of earning the height which her husband had granted her on trust, of living up to his vision of her, which it was now her duty to achieve. And, not wishing to confess it to herself, she felt also that at the end of the long task she would recapture her vision of him, that knowledge would bring back to her the man she had seen on the night of his railroad's triumph.

She could not understand Jim's attitude when she told him about her lessons. He burst out laughing; she was unable to believe that the laughter had a sound of malicious contempt. "Why, Jim? Why? What are you laughing at?" He would not explain—almost as if the fact of his contempt were sufficient and required no reasons.

She could not suspect him of malice: he was too patiently generous about her mistakes. He seemed eager to display her in the best drawing rooms of the city, and he never uttered a word of reproach for her ignorance, for her awkwardness, for those terrible moments when a silent exchange of glances among the guests and a burst of blood to her cheekbones told her that she had said the wrong thing again. He showed no embarrassment, he merely watched her with a faint smile. When they came home after one of those evenings, his mood seemed affectionately cheerful. He was trying to make it easier for her, she thought—and gratitude drove her to study the harder.

She expected her reward on the evening when, by some imperceptible transition, she found herself enjoying a party for the first time. She felt free to act, not by rules, but at her own pleasure, with sudden confidence that the rules had fused into a natural habit—she knew that she was attracting attention, but now, for the first time, it was not the attention of ridicule, but of admiration—she was sought after, on her own merit, she was Mrs. Taggart, she had ceased being an object of charity weighing Jim down, painfully tolerated for his sake—she was laughing gaily and seeing the smiles of response, of appreciation on the faces around her—and she kept glancing at him across the room, radiantly, like a child handing him a report card with a perfect score, begging him to be proud of her. Jim sat alone in a corner, watching her with an undecipherable glance.

He would not speak to her on their way home. "I don't know why I keep dragging myself to those parties," he snapped suddenly, tearing off his dress tie in the middle of their living room, "I've never sat through such a vulgar, boring waste of time!" "Why, Jim," she said, stunned, "I thought it was wonderful." "You would! You seemed to be quite at home—quite as if it were Coney Island. I wish you'd learn to keep your place and not to embarrass me in public." "I embarrassed you? *Tonight?*" "You did!" "How?" "If you don't understand it, I can't explain," he said in the tone of a mystic who implies that a lack of understanding is the confession of a shameful inferiority. "I don't understand it," she said firmly. He walked out of the room, slamming the door.

She felt that the inexplicable was not a mere blank, this time: it had a tinge of evil. From that night on, a small, hard point of fear remained within her, like the spot of a distant headlight advancing upon her down an invisible track.

Knowledge did not seem to bring her a clearer vision of Jim's world, but to make the mystery greater. She could not believe that she was supposed to feel respect for the dreary senselessness of the art shows which his friends attended, of the novels they read, of the political magazines they discussed—the art shows, where she saw the kind of drawings she had seen chalked on any pavement of her childhood's slums—the novels, that purported to prove the futility of science, industry, civilization and love, using language that her father would not have used in his drunkenest moments—the magazines, that propounded cowardly generalities, less clear and more stale than the sermons for which she had condemned the preacher of the slum mission as a mealy-mouthed old fraud. She could not believe that these things were the culture she had so reverently looked up to and so eagerly waited to discover. She felt as if she had climbed a mountain toward a jagged shape that had looked like a castle and had found it to be the crumbling ruin of a gutted warehouse.

"Jim," she said once, after an evening spent among the men who were called the intellectual leaders of the country, "Dr. Simon Pritchett is a phony—a mean, scared old phony." "Now, really," he answered, "do you think you're qualified to pass judgment on philosophers?" "I'm qualified to pass judgment on con men. I've seen enough of them to know one when I see him." "Now this is why I say that you'll never outgrow your background. If you had, you would have learned to appreciate Dr. Pritchett's philosophy." "What philosophy?" "If you don't understand it, I can't explain." She would not let him end the conversation on that favorite formula of his. "Jim," she said, "he's a phony, he and Balph Eubank and that whole gang of theirs—and I think you've been taken in by them." Instead of the anger she expected, she saw a brief flash of amusement in the lift of his eyelids. "That's what *you* think," he answered.

She felt an instant of terror at the first touch of a concept she had not known to be possible: What if Jim *was not* taken in by them? She could understand the phoniness of Dr. Pritchett, she thought—it was a racket that gave him an undeserved income; she could even admit the possibility, by now, that Jim might be a phony in his own business; what she could not hold inside her mind was the concept of Jim as a phony in a racket from which he gained nothing, an unpaid phony, an unvenal phony; the phoniness of a cardsharp or a con man seemed innocently wholesome by comparison. She could not conceive of his motive; she felt only that the headlight moving upon her had grown larger.

She could not remember by what steps, what accumulation of pain, first as small scratches of uneasiness, then as stabs of bewilderment, then as the chronic, nagging pull of fear, she had begun to doubt Jim's position on the railroad. It was his sudden, angry "so you don't trust me?" snapped in answer to her first, innocent questions that made her realize that she did not—when the doubt had not yet formed in her mind and she had fully expected that his answers would reassure her. She had learned, in the slums of her childhood, that honest people were never touchy about the matter of being trusted.

"I don't care to talk shop," was his answer whenever she mentioned the railroad. She tried to plead with him once. "Jim, you know what I think of your work and how much I admire you for it." "Oh, really? What is it you married, a man or a railroad president?" "I . . . I never thought of separating the two." "Well, it is not very flattering to me." She looked at him, baffled: she had thought it was. "I'd like to believe," he said, "that you love me for myself, and not for my railroad." "Oh God, Jim," she gasped, "you didn't think that I—!" "No," he said, with a sadly generous smile, "I didn't think that you married me for my money or my position. *I* have never doubted you." Realizing, in stunned confusion and in tortured fairness, that she might have given him ground to misinterpret her feeling, that she had forgotten how many bitter disappointments he must have suffered at the hands of fortune-hunting women, she could do nothing but shake her head and moan, "Oh, Jim, that's not what I meant!" He chuckled softly, as at a child, and slipped his arm around her. "Do you love me?" he asked. "Yes," she whispered. "Then you must have faith in me. Love is faith, you know. Don't you see that I need it? I don't trust anyone around me, I have nothing but enemies, I am very lonely. Don't you know that I need you?"

The thing that made her pace her room—hours later, in tortured restlessness—was that she wished desperately to believe him and did not believe a word of it, yet knew that it was true.

It was true, but not in the manner he implied, not in any manner or meaning she could ever hope to grasp. It was true that he needed her, but the nature of his need kept slipping past her every effort to define it. She did not know what he wanted of her. It was not flattery that he wanted, she had seen him listening to the obsequious compliments of liars, listening with a look of resentful inertness—almost the look of a drug addict at a dose inadequate to rouse him. But she had seen him look at her as if he were waiting for some reviving shot and, at times, as if he were begging. She had seen a flicker of life in his eyes whenever she granted him some sign of admiration—yet a burst of anger was his answer, whenever she named a reason for admiring him. He seemed to want her to consider him great, but never dare ascribe any specific content to his greatness.

She did not understand the night, in mid-April, when he returned from a trip to Washington. "Hi, kid!" he said loudly, dropping a sheaf of lilac into her arms. "Happy days are here again! Just saw those flowers and thought of you. Spring is coming, baby!"

He poured himself a drink and paced the room, talking with too light, too brash a manner of gaiety. There was a feverish sparkle in his eyes, and his voice seemed shredded by some unnatural excitement. She began to wonder whether he was elated or crushed.

"I know what it is that they're planning!" he said suddenly, without transition, and she glanced up at him swiftly: she knew the sound of one of his inner explosions. "There's not a dozen people in the whole country who know it, but I do! The top boys are keeping it secret till they're ready to spring it on the nation. Will it surprise a lot of people! Will it knock them flat! A lot of people? Hell, every single person in this country! It will affect every single person. That's how important it is."

"Affect—how, Jim?"

"It will *affect* them! And they don't know what's coming, but I do. There they sit tonight"—he waved at the lighted windows of the city—"making plans, counting their money, hugging their children or their dreams, and they don't know, but I do, that all of it will be struck, stopped, changed!"

"Changed—for the worse or the better?"

"For the better, of course," he answered impatiently, as if it were irrelevant; his voice seemed to lose its fire and to slip into the fraudulent sound of duty. "It's a plan to save the country, to stop our economic decline, to hold things still, to achieve stability and security."

"What plan?"

"I can't tell you. It's secret. Top secret. You have no idea how many people would like to know it. There's no industrialist who wouldn't give a dozen of his best furnaces for just one hint of warning, which he's not going to get! Like Hank Rearden, for instance, whom you admire so much." He chuckled, looking off into the future.

"Jim," she asked, the sound of fear in her voice telling him what the sound of his chuckle had been like, "why do you hate Hank Rearden?"

"I don't hate him!" He whirled to her, and his face, incredibly, looked anxious, almost frightened. "I never said I hated him. Don't worry, he'll approve of the plan. Everybody will. It's for everybody's good." He sounded as if he were pleading. She felt the dizzying certainty that he was lying, yet that the plea was sincere—as if he had a desperate need to reassure her, but not about the things he said.

She forced herself to smile. "Yes, Jim, of course," she answered, wondering what instinct in what impossible kind of chaos had made her say it as if it were *her* part to reassure him.

The look she saw on his face was almost a smile and almost of gratitude. "I had to tell you about it tonight. I had to tell you. I wanted you to know what tremendous issues I deal with. You always talk about my work, but you don't understand it at all, it's so much wider than you imagine. You think that running a railroad is a matter of track-laying and fancy metals and getting trains there on time. But it's not. Any underling can do that. The real heart of a railroad is in Washington. My job is politics. Politics. Decisions made on a national scale, affecting everything, controlling everybody. A few words on paper, a directive—changing the life of every person in every nook, cranny and penthouse of this country!"

"Yes, Jim," she said, wishing to believe that he was, perhaps, a man of stature in the mysterious realm of Washington.

"You'll see," he said, pacing the room. "You think they're powerful—those giants of industry who're so clever with motors and furnaces? They'll be stopped! They'll be stripped! They'll be brought down! They'll be—" He noticed the way she was staring at him. "It's not for ourselves," he snapped hastily, "it's for the people. That's the difference between business and politics—we have no selfish ends in view, no private motives, we're not after profit, we don't spend our lives scrambling for money, we don't have to! That's why we're slandered and misunderstood by all the greedy profit-chasers who can't conceive of a spiritual motive or a moral ideal or . . . We couldn't help it!" he cried suddenly, whirling to her. "We had to have that plan! With everything falling to pieces and stopping, something had to be done! We had to stop them from stopping! We couldn't help it!"

His eyes were desperate; she did not know whether he was boasting or begging for forgiveness; she did not know whether this was triumph or terror. "Jim, don't you feel well? Maybe you've worked too hard and you're worn out and—"

"I've never felt better in my life!" he snapped, resuming his pacing. "You bet I've worked hard. My work is bigger than any job you can hope to imagine. It's above anything that grubbing mechanics, like Rearden and my sister, are doing. Whatever they do, I can undo it. Let them build a track—I can come and break it, just like that!" He snapped his fingers. "Just like breaking a spine!"

"You want to break spines?" she whispered, trembling.

"I haven't said that!" he screamed. "What's the matter with you? I haven't said it!"

"I'm sorry, Jim!" she gasped, shocked by her own words and by the terror in his eyes. "It's just that I don't understand, but . . . but I know I shouldn't bother you with questions when you're so tired"— she was struggling desperately to convince herself—"when you have so many things on your mind . . . such . . . such great things . . . things I can't even begin to think of . . ."

His shoulders sagged, relaxing. He approached her and dropped wearily down on his knees, slipping his arms around her. "You poor little fool," he said affectionately.

She held onto him, moved by something that felt like tenderness and almost like pity. But he raised his head to glance up at her face, and it seemed to her that the look she saw in his eyes was part-gratification, part-contempt—almost as if, by some unknown kind of sanction, she had absolved him and damned herself.

It was useless—she found in the days that followed—to tell herself that these things were beyond her understanding, that it was her duty to believe in him, that love was faith. Her doubt kept growing—doubt of his incomprehensible work and of his relation to the railroad. She wondered why it kept growing in direct proportion to her self-admonitions that faith was the duty she owed him. Then, one sleepless night, she realized that her effort to fulfill that duty consisted of turning away whenever people discussed his job, of refusing to look at newspaper mentions of Taggart Transcontinental, of slamming her mind shut against any evidence and every contradiction. She stopped, aghast, struck by the question: What is it, then—faith versus truth? And realizing that part of her zeal to believe was her fear to know, she set out to learn the truth, with a cleaner, calmer sense of rightness than the effort at dutiful self-fraud had ever given her.

It did not take her long to learn. The evasiveness of the Taggart executives, when she asked a few casual questions, the stale generalities of their answers, the strain of their manner at the mention of their boss, and their obvious reluctance to discuss him—told her nothing concrete, but gave her a feeling equivalent to knowing the worst. The railroad workers were more specific—the switchmen, the gatemen, the ticket sellers whom she drew into chance conversations in the Taggart

Terminal and who did not know her. "Jim Taggart? That whining, sniveling, speech-making deadhead!" "Jimmy the President? Well, I'll tell you: he's the hobo on the gravy train." "The boss? Mr. Taggart? You mean *Miss* Taggart, don't you?"

It was Eddie Willers who told her the whole truth. She heard that he had known Jim since childhood, and she asked him to lunch with her. When she faced him at the table, when she saw the earnest, questioning directness of his eyes and the severely literal simplicity of his words, she dropped all attempts at casual prodding, she told him what she wanted to know and why, briefly, impersonally, not appealing for help or for pity, only for truth. He answered her in the same manner. He told her the whole story, quietly, impersonally, pronouncing no verdict, expressing no opinion, never encroaching on her emotions by any sign of concern for them, speaking with the shining austerity and the awesome power of facts. He told her who ran Taggart Transcontinental. He told her the story of the John Galt Line. She listened, and what she felt was not shock, but worse: the lack of shock, as if she had always known it. "Thank you, Mr. Willers," was all that she said when he finished.

She waited for Jim to come home, that evening, and the thing that eroded any pain or indignation, was a feeling of her own detachment, as if it did not matter to her any longer, as if some action were required of her, but it made no difference what the action would be or the consequences.

It was not anger that she felt when she saw Jim enter the room, but a murky astonishment, almost as if she wondered who he was and why it should now be necessary to speak to him. She told him what she knew, briefly, in a tired, extinguished voice. It seemed to her that he understood it from her first few sentences, as if he had expected this to come sooner or later.

"Why didn't you tell me the truth?" she asked.

"So that's your idea of gratitude?" he screamed. "So that's how you feel after everything I've done for you? Everybody told me that crudeness and selfishness was all I could expect for lifting a cheap little alley cat by the scruff of her neck!"

She looked at him as if he were making inarticulate sounds that connected to nothing inside her mind. "Why didn't you tell me the truth?"

"Is that all the love you felt for me, you sneaky little hypocrite? Is that all I get in return for my faith in you?"

"Why did you lie? Why did you let me think what I thought?"

"You should be ashamed of yourself, you should be ashamed to face me or speak to me!"

"I?" The inarticulate sounds had connected, but she could not believe the sum they made. "What are you trying to do, Jim?" she asked, her voice incredulous and distant.

"Have you thought of my feelings? Have you thought of what this would do to my feelings? You should have considered my feelings first! That's the first obligation of any wife—and of a woman in your position in particular! There's nothing lower and uglier than ingratitude!"

For the flash of one instant, she grasped the unthinkable fact of a man who was guilty and knew it and was trying to escape by inducing an emotion of guilt in his victim. But she could not hold the fact inside her brain. She felt a stab of horror, the convulsion of a mind rejecting a sight that would destroy it—a stab like a swift recoil from the edge of insanity. By the time she dropped her head, closing her eyes, she knew only that she felt disgust, a sickening disgust for a nameless reason.

When she raised her head, it seemed to her ·that she caught a glimpse of him watching her with the uncertain, retreating, calculating look of a man whose trick has not worked. But before she had time to believe it, his face was hidden again under an expression of injury and anger.

She said, as if she were naming her thoughts for the benefit of the rational being who was not present, but whose presence she had to assume, since no other could be addressed, "That night . . . those headlines . . . that glory . . . it was not you at all . . . it was Dagny."

"Shut up, you rotten little bitch!"

She looked at him blankly, without reaction. She looked as if nothing could reach her, because her dying words had been uttered.

He made the sound of a sob. "Cherryl, I'm sorry, I didn't mean it, I take it back, I didn't mean it . . ."

She remained standing, leaning against the wall, as she had stood from the first.

He dropped down on the edge of a couch, in a posture of helpless dejection. "How could I have explained it to you?" he said in the tone of abandoning hope. "It's all so big and so complex. How could I have told you anything about a transcontinental railroad, unless you knew all the details and ramifications? How could I have explained to you my years of work, my . . . Oh, what's the use? I've always been misunderstood and I should have been accustomed to it by now, only I thought that you were different and that I had a chance."

"Jim, why did you marry me?"

He chuckled sadly. "That's what everybody kept asking me. I didn't think *you'd* ever ask it. Why? Because I love you."

She wondered at how strange it was that this word—which was supposed to be the simplest in the human language, the word understood by all, the universal bond among men—conveyed to her no meaning whatever. She did not know what it was that it named in his mind.

"Nobody's ever loved me," he said. "There isn't any love in the world. People don't feel. I *feel* things. Who cares about that? All they care for is time schedules and freight loads and money. I can't live among those people. I'm very lonely. I've always longed to find understanding. Maybe I'm just a hopeless idealist, looking for the impossible. Nobody will ever understand me."

"Jim," she said, with an odd little note of severity in her voice, "what I've struggled for all this time is to understand you."

He dropped his hand in a motion of brushing her words aside, not offensively, but sadly. "I thought you could. You're all I have. But maybe understanding is just not possible between human beings."

"Why should it be impossible? Why don't you tell me what it is that you want? Why don't you help me to understand you?"

He sighed. "That's it. That's the trouble—your asking all those why's. Your constant asking of a why for everything. What I'm talking about can't be put into words. It can't be named. It has to be felt. Either you feel it or you don't. It's not a thing of the mind, but of the heart. Don't you ever feel? Just *feel*, without asking all those questions? Can't you understand me as a human being, not as if I were a scientific object in a laboratory? The great understanding that transcends our shabby words and helpless minds . . . No, I guess I shouldn't look for it. But I'll always seek and hope. You're my last hope. You're all I have."

She stood at the wall, without moving.

"I need you," he wailed softly. "I'm all alone. You're not like the others. I believe in you. I trust you. What has all that money and fame and business and struggle given me? You're all I have . . ."

She stood without moving and the direction of her glance, lowered to look down at him, was the only form of recognition she gave him. The things he said about his suffering were lies, she thought; but the suffering was real; he was a man torn by some continual anguish, which he seemed unable to tell her, but which, perhaps, she could learn to understand. She still owed him this much—she thought, with the grayness of a sense of duty—in payment for the position he had given her, which, perhaps, was all he had to give, she owed him an effort to understand him.

It was strange to feel, in the days that followed, that she had become a stranger to herself, a stranger who had nothing to want or to seek. In place of a love made by the brilliant fire of hero worship, she was left with the gnawing drabness of pity. In place of the men she had struggled to find, men who fought for their goals and refused to suffer—she was left with a man whose suffering was his only claim to value and his only offer in exchange for her life. But it made no difference to her any longer. The one who was she, had looked with eagerness at the turn of every corner ahead; the passive stranger who had taken her place, was like all the overgroomed people around her, the people who said that they were adult because they did not try to think or to desire.

But the stranger was still haunted by a ghost who was herself, and the ghost had a mission to accomplish. She had to learn to understand the things that had destroyed her. She had to know, and she lived with a sense of ceaseless waiting. She had to know, even though she felt that the headlight was closer and in the moment of knowledge she would be struck by the wheels.

What do you want of me?—was the question that kept beating in her mind as a clue. What do you want of me?—she kept crying soundlessly, at dinner tables, in drawing rooms, on sleepless nights— crying it to Jim and those who seemed to share his secret, to Balph Eubank, to Dr. Simon Pritchett—what do you want of me? She did not ask it aloud; she knew that they would not answer. What do you want of me? —she asked, feeling as if she were running, but no way were open to escape. What do you want of me?—she asked, looking at the whole long torture of her marriage that had not lasted the full span of one year.

"What do you want of me?" she asked aloud—and saw that she was sitting at the table in her dining room, looking at Jim, at his feverish face, and at a drying stain of water on the table.

She did not know how long a span of silence had stretched between them, she was startled by her own voice and by the question she had not intended to utter. She did not expect him to understand it, he had never seemed to understand much simpler queries—and she shook her head, struggling to recapture the reality of the present.

She was startled to see him looking at her with a touch of derision, as if he were mocking her estimate of his understanding.

"Love," he answered.

She felt herself sagging with hopelessness, in the face of that answer which was at once so simple and so meaningless.

"You don't love me," he said accusingly. She did not answer. "You don't love me or you wouldn't ask such a question."

"I did love you once," she said dully, "but it wasn't what you wanted. I loved you for your courage, your ambition, your ability. But it wasn't real, any of it."

His lower lip swelled a little in a faint, contemptuous thrust. "What a shabby idea of love!" he said.

"Jim, what is it that you want to be loved for?"

"What a cheap shopkeeper's attitude!"

She did not speak; she looked at him, her eyes stretched by a silent question.

"To be loved *for!*" he said, his voice grating with mockery and righteousness. "So you think that love is a matter of mathematics, of exchange, of weighing and measuring, like a pound of butter on a grocery counter? I don't want to be loved *for* anything. I want to be loved for myself—not for anything I do or have or say or think. For myself—not for my body or mind or words or works or actions."

"But then . . . what *is* yourself?"

"If you loved me, you wouldn't ask it." His voice had a shrill note of nervousness, as if he were swaying dangerously between caution and some blindly heedless impulse. "You wouldn't ask. You'd know. You'd *feel* it. Why do you always try to tag and label everything? Can't you rise above those petty materialistic definitions? Don't you ever feel— just *feel?*"

"Yes, Jim, I do," she said, her voice low. "But I am trying not to, because . . . because what I feel is fear."

"Of me?" he asked hopefully.

"No, not exactly. Not fear of what you can do to me, but of what you are."

He dropped his eyelids with the swiftness of slamming a door—but she caught a flash of his eyes and the flash, incredibly, was terror. "You're not capable of love, you cheap little gold-digger!" he cried suddenly, in a tone stripped of all color but the desire to hurt. "Yes, I said gold-digger. There are many forms of it, other than greed for money, other and worse. You're a gold-digger of the spirit. You didn't marry me for my cash—but you married me for my ability or courage or whatever value it was that you set as the price of your love!"

"Do you want . . . love . . . to be . . . causeless?"

"Love is its own cause! Love is above causes and reasons. Love is blind. But you wouldn't be capable of it. You have the mean, scheming, calculating little soul of a shopkeeper who *trades,* but never *gives!* Love is a gift—a great, free, unconditional gift that transcends and forgives everything. What's the generosity of loving a man for his virtues? What do you give him? Nothing. It's no more than cold justice. No more than he's earned."

Her eyes were dark with the dangerous intensity of glimpsing her goal. "You want it to be unearned," she said, not in the tone of a question, but of a verdict.

"Oh, you don't understand!"

"Yes, Jim, I do. That's what you want—that's what all of you really want—not money, not material benefits, not economic security, not any of the handouts you keep demanding." She spoke in a flat monotone, as if reciting her thoughts to herself, intent upon giving the solid identity of words to the torturous shreds of chaos twisting in her mind. "All of you welfare preachers—it's not unearned money that you're after. You want handouts, but of a different kind. I'm a gold-digger of the spirit, you said, because I look for value. Then you, the welfare preachers . . . it's the spirit that you want to loot. I never thought and nobody ever told us how it could be thought of and what it would mean—the unearned in spirit. But that is what you want. You want unearned love. You want unearned admiration. You want unearned greatness. You want to be a man like Hank Rearden without the necessity of being what he is. Without the necessity of being anything. Without . . . the necessity . . . of being."

"Shut up!" he screamed.

They looked at each other, both in terror, both feeling as if they were swaying on an edge which she could not and he would not name, both knowing that one more step would be fatal.

"What do you think you're saying?" he asked in a tone of petty anger, which sounded almost benevolent by bringing them back into the realm of the normal, into the near-wholesomeness of nothing worse than a family quarrel. "What sort of metaphysical subject are *you* trying to deal with?"

"I don't know . . ." she said wearily, dropping her head, as if some shape she had tried to capture had slipped once more out of her grasp. "I don't know . . . It doesn't seem possible . . ."

"You'd better not try to wade in way over your head or—" But he had to stop, because the butler entered, bringing the glittering ice bucket with the champagne ordered for celebration.

They remained silent, letting the room be filled by the sounds which centuries of men and of struggle had established as the symbol of joyous attainment: the blast of the cork, the laughing tinkle of a pale gold liquid running into two broad cups filled with the weaving reflections of candles, the whisper of bubbles rising through two crystal stems, almost demanding that everything in sight rise, too, in the same aspiration.

They remained silent, till the butler had gone. Taggart sat looking down at the bubbles, holding the stem of his glass between two limply casual fingers. Then his hand closed suddenly about the stem into an awkwardly convulsed fist and he raised it, not as one lifts a glass of champagne, but as one would lift a butcher knife.

"To Francisco d'Anconia!" he said.

She put her glass down. "No," she answered.

"Drink it!" he screamed.

"No," she answered, her voice like a drop of lead.

They held each other's glances for a moment, the light playing on the golden liquid, not reaching their faces or eyes.

"Oh, go to hell!" he cried, leaping to his feet, flinging his glass to smash on the floor and rushing out of the room.

She sat at the table, not moving, for a long time, then rose slowly and pressed the bell.

She walked to her room, her steps unnaturally even, she opened the door of a closet, she reached for a suit and a pair of shoes, she took off the housecoat, moving with cautious precision, as if her life depended on not jarring anything about or within her. She held onto a single thought: that she had to get out of this house—just get out of it for a while, if only for the next hour—and then, later, she would be able to face all that had to be faced.

* * *

The lines were blurring on the paper before her and, raising her head, Dagny realized that it had long since grown dark.

She pushed the papers aside, unwilling to turn on the lamp, permitting herself the luxury of idleness and darkness. It cut her off from the city beyond the windows of her living room. The calendar in the distance said: August 5.

The month behind her had gone, leaving nothing but the blank of dead time. It had gone into the planless, thankless work of racing from emergency to emergency, of delaying the collapse of a railroad—a month like a waste pile of disconnected days, each given to averting the disaster of the moment. It had not been a sum of achievements brought into existence, but only a sum of zeros, of that which had not happened, a sum of prevented catastrophes—not a task in the service of life, but only a race against death.

There had been times when an unsummoned vision—a sight of the valley—had seemed to rise before her, not as a sudden appearance, but as a constant, hidden presence that suddenly chose to assume an insistent reality. She had faced it, through moments of blinded stillness, in a contest between an unmoving decision and an unyielding pain, a pain to be fought by acknowledgment, by saying: All right, even this.

There had been mornings when, awakening with rays of sunlight on her face, she had thought that she must hurry to Hammond's Market to get fresh eggs for breakfast; then, recapturing full consciousness, seeing the haze of New York beyond the window of her bedroom, she had felt a tearing stab, like a touch of death, the touch of rejecting reality. You knew it—she had told herself severely—you knew what it would be like when you made your choice. And dragging her body, like an unwilling weight, out of bed to face an unwelcome day, she would whisper: All right, even this.

The worst of the torture had been the moments when, walking down the street, she had caught a sudden glimpse of chestnut-gold, a glowing streak of hair among the heads of strangers, and had felt as if the city had vanished, as if nothing but the violent stillness within her were delaying the moment when she would rush to him and seize him; but that next moment had come as the sight of some meaningless face—and she had stood, not wishing to live through the following step, not wishing to generate the energy of living. She had tried to avoid such moments; she had tried to forbid herself to look; she had walked, keeping her eyes on the pavements. She had failed: by some will of their own, her eyes had kept leaping to every streak of gold.

She had kept the blinds raised on the windows of her office, remembering his promise, thinking only: If you are watching me, wherever you are . . . There were no buildings close to the height of her office, but she had looked at the distant towers, wondering which window was his observation post, wondering whether some invention of his own, some device of rays and lenses, permitted him to observe her every movement from some skyscraper a block or a mile away. She had sat at her desk, at her uncurtained windows, thinking: Just to know that you're seeing me, even if I'm never to see you again.

And remembering it, now, in the darkness of her room, she leaped to her feet and snapped on the light.

Then she dropped her head for an instant, smiling in mirthless amusement at herself. She wondered whether her lighted windows, in the black immensity of the city, were a flare of distress, calling for his help—or a lighthouse still protecting the rest of the world.

The doorbell rang.

When she opened the door, she saw the silhouette of a girl with a faintly familiar face—and it took her a moment of startled astonishment to realize that it was Cherryl Taggart. Except for a formal exchange of greetings on a few chance encounters in the halls of the Taggart Building, they had not seen each other since the wedding.

Cherryl's face was composed and unsmiling. "Would you permit me to speak to you"—she hesitated and ended on—"Miss Taggart?"

"Of course," said Dagny gravely. "Come in."

She sensed some desperate emergency in the unnatural calm of Cherryl's manner; she became certain of it when she looked at the girl's face in the light of the living room. "Sit down," she said, but Cherryl remained standing.

"I came to pay a debt," said Cherryl, her voice solemn with the effort to permit herself no sound of emotion. "I want to apologize for the things I said to you at my wedding. There's no reason why you should forgive me, but it's my place to tell you that I know I was insulting everything I admire and defending everything I despise. I know that admitting it now, doesn't make up for it, and even coming here is only another presumption, there's no reason why you should want to hear it, so I can't even cancel the debt, I can only ask for a favor—that you let me say the things I want to say to you."

Dagny's shock of emotion, incredulous, warm and painful, was the wordless equivalent of the sentence: What a distance to travel in less than a year . . . ! She answered, the unsmiling earnestness of her voice like a hand extended in support, knowing that a smile would upset some precarious balance, "But it does make up for it, and I do want to hear it."

"I know that it was you who ran Taggart Transcontinental. It was you who built the John Galt Line. It was you who had the mind and the courage that kept all of it alive. I suppose you thought that I married Jim for his money—as what shopgirl wouldn't have? But, you see, I married Jim because I . . . I thought that he was *you*. I thought that he was Taggart Transcontinental. Now I know that he's"— she hesitated, then went on firmly, as if not to spare herself anything— "he's some sort of vicious moocher, though I can't understand of what kind or why. When I spoke to you at my wedding, I thought that I was defending greatness and attacking its enemy . . . but it was in reverse . . . it was in such horrible, unbelievable reverse! . . . So I wanted to tell you that I know the truth . . . not so much for your sake, I have no right to presume that you'd care, but . . . but for the sake of the things I loved."

Dagny said slowly, "Of course I forgive it."

"Thank you," she whispered, and turned to go.

"Sit down."

She shook her head. "That . . . that was all, Miss Taggart."

Dagny allowed herself the first touch of a smile, no more than in the look of her eyes, as she said, "Cherryl, my name is Dagny."

Cherryl's answer was no more than a faint, tremulous crease of her mouth, as if, together, they had completed a single smile. "I . . . I didn't know whether I should—"

"We're sisters, aren't we?"

"No! Not through Jim!" It was an involuntary cry.

"No, through our own choice. Sit down, Cherryl." The girl obeyed, struggling not to show the eagerness of her acceptance, not to grasp for support, not to break. "You've had a terrible time, haven't you?"

"Yes . . . but that doesn't matter . . . that's my own problem . . . and my own fault."

"I don't think it was your own fault."

Cherryl did not answer, then said suddenly, desperately, "Look . . . what I don't want is charity."

"Jim must have told you—and it's true—that I never engage in charity."

"Yes, he did ⟨ . . But what I mean is—"

"I know what you mean."

"But there's no reason why you should have to feel concern for me . . . I didn't come here to complain and . . . and load another burden on your shoulders . . . That I happen to suffer, doesn't give me a claim on you."

"No, it doesn't. But that you value all the things I value, does."

"You mean . . . if you want to talk to me, it's not alms? Not just because you feel sorry for me?"

"I feel terribly sorry for you, Cherryl, and I'd like to help you—not because you suffer, but because you haven't deserved to suffer."

"You mean, you wouldn't be kind to anything weak or whining or rotten about me? Only to whatever you see in me that's good?"

"Of course."

Cherryl did not move her head, but she looked as if it were lifted—as if some bracing current were relaxing her features into that rare look which combines pain and dignity.

"It's not alms, Cherryl. Don't be afraid to speak to me."

"It's strange . . . You're the first person I can talk to . . . and it feels so easy . . . yet I . . . I *was* afraid to speak to you. I wanted to ask your forgiveness long ago . . . ever since I learned the truth. I went as far as the door of your office, but I stopped and stood there in the hall and didn't have the courage to go in. . . . I didn't intend to come here tonight. I went out only to . . . to think something over, and then, suddenly, I knew that I wanted to see you, that in the whole of the city this was the only place for me to go and the only thing still left for me to do."

"I'm glad you did."

"You know, Miss Tag—Dagny," she said softly, in wonder, "you're not as I expected you to be at all. . . . They, Jim and his friends, they said you were hard and cold and unfeeling."

"But it's true, Cherryl. I *am,* in the sense they mean—only have they ever told you in just what sense they mean it?"

"No. They never do. They only sneer at me when I ask them what they mean by anything . . . about anything. What did they mean about you?"

"Whenever anyone accuses some person of being 'unfeeling,' he means that that person is just. He means that that person has no causeless emotions and will not grant him a feeling which he does not deserve. He means that 'to feel' is to go against reason, against moral values, against reality. He means . . . What's the matter?" she asked, seeing the abnormal intensity of the girl's face.

"It's . . . it's something I've tried so hard to understand . . . for such a long time. . . ."

"Well, observe that you never hear that accusation in defense of innocence, but always in defense of guilt. You never hear it said by a good person about those who fail to do him justice. But you always hear it said by a rotter about those who treat him as a rotter, those who don't feel any sympathy for the evil he's committed or for the pain he suffers as a consequence. Well, it's true—*that* is what I do *not* feel. But those who feel it, feel nothing for any quality of human greatness, for any person or action that deserves admiration, approval, esteem. *These* are the things *I* feel. You'll find that it's one or the other. Those who grant sympathy to guilt, grant none to innocence. Ask yourself which, of the two, are the *unfeeling* persons. And then you'll see what motive is the opposite of charity."

"What?" she whispered.

"Justice, Cherryl."

Cherryl shuddered suddenly and dropped her head. "Oh God!" she moaned. "If you knew what hell Jim has been giving me because I believed just what you said!" She raised her face in the sweep of another shudder, as if the things she had tried to control had broken through; the look in her eyes was terror. "Dagny," she whispered, "Dagny, I'm afraid of them . . . of Jim and all the others . . . not afraid of something they'll do . . . if it were that, I could escape . . . but afraid, as if there's no way out . . . afraid of what they are and . . . and that they exist."

Dagny came forward swiftly to sit on the arm of her chair and seize her shoulder in a steadying grasp. "Quiet, kid," she said. "You're wrong. You must never feel afraid of people in that way. You must never think that their existence is a reflection on yours—yet that's what you're thinking."

"Yes . . . Yes, I feel that there's no chance for me to exist, if they do . . . no chance, no room, no world I can cope with. . . . I don't want to feel it, I keep pushing it back, but it's coming closer and I know I have no place to run. . . . I can't explain what it feels like, I can't catch hold of it—and that's part of the terror, that you *can't* catch hold of anything—it's as if the whole world were suddenly destroyed, but not by an explosion—an explosion is something hard and solid—but destroyed by . . . by some horrible kind of softening . . . as if nothing were solid, nothing held any shape at all, and you could poke your finger through stone walls and the stone would give, like jelly, and mountains would slither, and buildings would switch their shapes like clouds—and that would be the end of the world, not fire and brimstone, but goo."

"Cherryl . . . Cherryl, you poor kid, there have been centuries of philosophers plotting to turn the world into just that—to destroy people's minds by making them believe that that's what they're seeing. But you don't have to accept it. You don't have to see through the eyes of others, hold onto yours, stand on your own judgment, you know that what is, *is*—say it aloud, like the holiest of prayers, and don't let anyone tell you otherwise."

"But . . . but nothing *is*, any more. Jim and his friends—they're not. I don't know what I'm looking at, when I'm among them, I don't know what I'm hearing when they speak . . . it's not real, any of it, it's some ghastly sort of act that they're all going through . . . and I don't know what they're after. . . . Dagny! We've always been told that human beings have such a great power of knowledge, so much greater than animals, but I—I feel blinder than any animal right now, blinder and more helpless. An animal knows who are its friends and who are its enemies, and when to defend itself. It doesn't expect a friend to step on it or to cut its throat. It doesn't expect to be told that love is blind, that plunder is achievement, that gangsters are statesmen and that it's great to break the spine of Hank Rearden!—oh God, what am I saying?"

"I know what you're saying."

"I mean, how am I to deal with people? I mean, if nothing held firm for the length of one hour—we couldn't go on, could we? Well, I know that things are solid—but people? Dagny! They're nothing and anything, they're not beings, they're only switches, just constant switches without any shape. But I have to live among them. How am I to do it?"

"Cherryl, what you've been struggling with is the greatest problem in history, the one that has caused all of human suffering. You've understood much more than most people, who suffer and die, never knowing what killed them. I'll help you to understand. It's a big subject and a hard battle—but first, above all, don't be afraid."

The look on Cherryl's face was an odd, wistful longing, as if, seeing Dagny from a great distance, she were straining and failing to come closer. "I wish I could wish to fight," she said softly, "but I don't. I don't even want to win any longer. There's one change that I don't seem to have the strength to make. You see, I had never expected anything like my marriage to Jim. Then when it happened, I thought that life was much more wonderful than I had expected. And now to get used to the idea that life and people are much more horrible than anything I had imagined and that my marriage was not a glorious miracle, but some unspeakable kind of evil which I'm still afraid to learn fully—*that* is what I can't force myself to take. I can't get past it." She glanced up suddenly. "Dagny, how did you do it? How did you manage to remain unmangled?"

"By holding to just one rule."

"Which?"

"To place nothing—*nothing*—above the verdict of my own mind."

"You've taken some terrible beatings . . . maybe worse than I did . . . worse than any of us. . . . What held you through it?"

"The knowledge that my life is the highest of values, too high to give up without a fight."

She saw a look of astonishment, of incredulous recognition on Cherryl's face, as if the girl were struggling to recapture some sensation across a span of years. "Dagny"—her voice was a whisper—"that's . . . that's what I felt when I was a child . . . that's what I seem to remember most about myself . . . *that* kind of feeling . . . and I never lost it, it's there, it's always been there, but as I grew up, I thought it was something that I must hide. . . . I never had any name for it, but just now, when you said it, it struck me that that's what it was. . . . Dagny, to feel that way about your own life—is that *good?*"

"Cherryl, listen to me carefully: that feeling—with everything which it requires and implies—is the highest, noblest and only good on earth."

"The reason I ask is because I . . . I wouldn't have dared to think that. Somehow, people always made me feel as if they thought it was a sin . . . as if that were the thing in me which they resented and . . . and wanted to destroy."

"It's true. Some people do want to destroy it. And when you learn to understand their motive, you'll know the darkest, ugliest and only evil in the world, but you'll be safely out of its reach."

Cherryl's smile was like a feeble flicker struggling to retain its hold upon a few drops of fuel, to catch them, to flare up. "It's the first time in months," she whispered, "that I've felt as if . . . as if there's still a chance." She saw Dagny's eyes watching her with attentive concern, and she added, "I'll be all right . . . Let me get used to it—to you, to all the things you said. I think I'll come to believe it . . . to believe that it's real . . . and that Jim doesn't matter." She rose to her feet, as if trying to retain the moment of assurance.

Prompted by a sudden, causeless certainty, Dagny said sharply, "Cherryl, I don't want you to go home tonight."

"Oh no! I'm all right. I'm not afraid, that way. Not of going home."

"Didn't something happen there tonight?"

"No . . . not really . . . nothing worse than usual. It was just that I began to see things a little more clearly, that was all. . . . I'm all right. I have to think, think harder than I ever did before . . . and then I'll decide what I must do. May I—" She hesitated.

"Yes?"

"May I come back to talk to you again?"

"Of course."

"Thank you, I . . . I'm very grateful to you."

"Will you promise me that you'll come back?"

"I promise."

Dagny saw her walking off down the hall toward the elevator, saw the slump of her shoulders, then the effort that lifted them, saw the slender figure that seemed to sway then marshal all of its strength to remain erect. She looked like a plant with a broken stem, still held together by a single fiber, struggling to heal the breach, which one more gust of wind would finish.

* * *

Through the open door of his study, James Taggart had seen Cherryl cross the anteroom and walk out of the apartment. He had slammed his door and slumped down on the davenport, with patches of spilled champagne still soaking the cloth of his trousers, as if his own discomfort were a revenge upon his wife and upon a universe that would not provide him with the celebration he had wanted.

After a while, he leaped to his feet, tore off his coat and threw it across the room. He reached for a cigarette, but snapped it in half and flung it at a painting over the fireplace.

He noticed a vase of Venetian glass—a museum piece, centuries old, with an intricate system of blue and gold arteries twisting through its transparent body. He seized it and flung it at the wall; it burst into a rain of glass as thin as a shattered light bulb.

He had bought that vase for the satisfaction of thinking of all the connoisseurs who could not afford it. Now he experienced the satisfaction of a revenge upon the centuries which had prized it—and the satisfaction of thinking that there were millions of desperate families, any one of whom could have lived for a year on the price of that vase.

He kicked off his shoes, and fell back on the davenport, letting his stocking feet dangle in mid-air.

The sound of the doorbell startled him: it seemed to match his mood. It was the kind of brusque, demanding, impatient snap of sound he would have produced if he were now jabbing his finger at someone's doorbell.

He listened to the butler's steps, promising himself the pleasure of refusing admittance to whoever was seeking it. In a moment, he heard the knock at his door and the butler entered to announce, "Mrs. Rearden to see you, sir."

"What? . . . Oh . . . Well! Have her come in!"

He swung his feet down to the floor, but made no other concession, and waited with half a smile of alerted curiosity, choosing not to rise until a moment after Lillian had entered the room.

She wore a wine-colored dinner gown, an imitation of an Empire traveling suit, with a miniature double-breasted jacket gripping her high waistline over the long sweep of the skirt, and a small hat clinging to one ear, with a feather sweeping down to curl under her chin. She entered with a brusque, unrhythmical motion, the train of her dress and the feather of her hat swirling, then flapping against her legs and throat, like pennants signaling nervousness.

"Lillian, my dear, am I to be flattered, delighted or just plain flabbergasted?"

"Oh, don't make a fuss about it! I had to see you, and it had to be immediately, that's all."

The impatient tone, the peremptory movement with which she sat down were a confession of weakness: by the rules of their unwritten language, one did not assume a demanding manner unless one were seeking a favor and had no value—no threat—to barter.

"Why didn't you stay at the Gonzales reception?" she asked, her casual smile failing to hide the tone of irritation. "I dropped in on them after dinner, just to catch hold of you—but they said you hadn't been feeling well and had gone home."

He crossed the room and picked up a cigarette, for the pleasure of padding in his stocking feet past the formal elegance of her costume. "I was bored," he answered.

"I can't stand them," she said, with a little shudder; he glanced at her in astonishment: the words sounded involuntary and sincere. "I can't stand Señor Gonzales and that whore he's got himself for a wife. It's disgusting that they've become so fashionable, they and their parties. I don't feel like going anywhere any longer. It's not the same style any more, not the same spirit. I haven't run into Balph Eubank for months, or Dr. Pritchett, or any of the boys. And all those new

894

faces that look like butcher's assistants! After all, *our* crowd were gentlemen."

"Yeah," he said reflectively. "Yeah, there's some funny kind of difference. It's like on the railroad, too: I could get along with Clem Weatherby, he was civilized, but Cuffy Meigs—that's something else again, that's . . ." He stopped abruptly.

"It's perfectly preposterous," she said, in the tone of a challenge to the space at large. "They can't get away with it."

She did not explain "who" or "with what." He knew what she meant. Through a moment of silence, they looked as if they were clinging to each other for reassurance.

In the next moment, he was thinking with pleasurable amusement that Lillian was beginning to show her age. The deep burgundy color of her gown was unbecoming, it seemed to draw a purplish tinge out of her skin, a tinge that gathered, like twilight, in the small gullies of her face, softening her flesh to a texture of tired slackness, changing her look of bright mockery into a look of stale malice.

He saw her studying him, smiling and saying crisply, with the smile as license for insult, "You *are* unwell, aren't you, Jim? You look like a disorganized stableboy."

He chuckled. "I can afford it."

"I know it, darling. You're one of the most powerful men in New York City." She added, "It's a good joke on New York City."

"It is."

"I concede that you're in a position to do anything. That's why I had to see you." She added a small, gruntlike sound of amusement, to dilute her statement's frankness.

"Good," he said, his voice comfortable and noncommittal.

"I had to come here, because I thought it best, in this particular matter, not to be seen together in public."

"That is always wise."

"I seem to remember having been useful to you in the past."

"In the past—yes."

"I am sure that I can count on you."

"Of course—only isn't that an old-fashioned, unphilosophical remark? How can we ever be sure of anything?"

"Jim," she snapped suddenly, "you've got to help me!"

"My dear, I'm at your disposal, I'd do anything to help you," he answered, the rules of their language requiring that any open statement be answered by a blatant lie. Lillian was slipping, he thought—and he experienced the pleasure of dealing with an inadequate adversary.

She was neglecting, he noted, even the perfection of her particular trademark: her grooming. A few strands were escaping from the drilled waves of her hair—her nails, matching her gown, were the deep shade of coagulated blood, which made it easy to notice the chipped polish at their tips—and against the broad, smooth, creamy expanse of her skin in the low, square cut of her gown, he observed the tiny glitter of a safety pin holding the strap of her slip.

"You've got to prevent it!" she said, in the belligerent tone of a plea disguised as a command. "You've got to stop it!"

"Really? What?"

"My divorce."

"Oh . . . !" His features dropped into sudden earnestness.

"You know that he's going to divorce me, don't you?"

"I've heard some rumors about it."

"It's set for next month. And when I say *set*, that's just what I mean. Oh, it's cost him plenty—but he's bought the judge, the clerks, the bailiffs, their backers, their backers' backers, a few legislators, half a dozen administrators—he's bought the whole legal process, like a private thoroughfare, and there's no single crossroad left for me to squeeze through to stop it!"

"I see."

"You know, of course, what made him start divorce proceedings?"

"I can guess."

"And I did it as a favor to *you!*" Her voice was growing anxiously shrill. "I told you about your sister in order to let you get that Gift Certificate for your friends, which—"

"I swear I don't know who let it out!" he cried hastily. "Only a very few at the top knew that you'd been our informer, and I'm sure nobody would dare mention—"

"Oh, I'm sure nobody did. He'd have the brains to guess it, wouldn't he?"

"Yes, I suppose so. Well, then you knew that you were taking a chance."

"I didn't think he'd go that far. I didn't think he'd ever divorce me. I didn't—"

He chuckled suddenly, with a glance of astonishing perceptiveness. "You didn't think that guilt is a rope that wears thin, did you, Lillian?"

She looked at him, startled, then answered stonily, "I don't think it does."

"It does, my dear—for men such as your husband."

"I don't want him to divorce me!" It was a sudden scream. "I don't want to let him go free! I won't permit it! I won't let the whole of my life be a total failure!" She stopped abruptly, as if she had admitted too much.

He was chuckling softly, nodding his head with a slow movement that had an air of intelligence, almost of dignity, by signifying a complete understanding.

"I mean . . . after all, he's my husband," she said defensively.

"Yes, Lillian, yes, I know."

"Do you know what he's planning? He's going to get the decree and he's going to cut me off without a penny—no settlement, no alimony, nothing! He's going to have the last word. Don't you see? If he gets away with it, then . . . then the Gift Certificate was no victory for me at all!"

"Yes, my dear, I see."

"And besides . . . It's preposterous that I should have to think of it, but what am I going to live on? The little money I had of my own is worth nothing nowadays. It's mainly stock in factories of my father's time, that have closed long ago. What am I going to do?"

"But, Lillian," he said softly, "I thought you had no concern for money or for any material rewards."

"You don't understand! I'm not talking about money—I'm talking about poverty! Real, stinking, hall-bedroom poverty! That's out of bounds for any civilized person! I—*I* to have to worry about food and rent?"

He was watching her with a faint smile; for once, his soft, aging face seemed tightened into a look of wisdom; he was discovering the pleasure of full perception—in a reality which he could permit himself to perceive.

"Jim, you've got to help me! My lawyer is powerless. I've spent the little I had, on him and on his investigators, friends and fixers—but all they could do for me was find out that they can do nothing. My lawyer gave me his final report this afternoon. He told me bluntly that I haven't a chance. I don't seem to know anyone who can help against a setup of this kind. I had counted on Bertram Scudder, but . . . well, you know what happened to Bertram. And that, too, was because I had tried to help you. You pulled yourself out of that one. Jim, you're the only person who can pull me out now. You've got your gopher-hole pipe line straight up to the top. You can reach the big boys. Slip a word to your friends to slip a word to their friends. One word from Wesley would do it. Have them order that divorce decree to be refused. Just have it be refused."

He shook his head slowly, almost compassionately, like a tired professional at an overzealous amateur. "It can't be done, Lillian," he said firmly. "I'd like to do it—for the same reasons as yours—and I think you know it. But whatever power I have is not enough in this case."

She was looking at him, her eyes dark with an odd, lifeless stillness; when she spoke, the motion of her lips was twisted by so evil a contempt that he did not dare identify it beyond knowing that it embraced them both; she said, "I know that you'd like to do it."

He felt no desire to pretend; oddly, for the first time, for this one chance, truth seemed much more pleasurable—truth, for once, serving his particular kind of enjoyment. "I think you know that it can't be done," he said. "Nobody does favors nowadays, if there's nothing to gain in return. And the stakes are getting higher and higher. The gopher holes, as you called them, are so complex, so twisted and intertwisted that everybody has something on everybody else, and nobody dares move because he can't tell who'll crack which way or when. So he'll move only when he has to, when the stakes are life or death—and that's practically the only kind of stakes we're playing for now. Well, what's your private life to any of those boys? That you'd like to hold your husband—what's in it for them, one way or another? And my personal stock-in-trade—well, there's nothing I could offer them at the moment in exchange for trying to blast a whole court clique out of a highly profitable deal. Besides, right now, the top boys wouldn't do it at any price. They have to be mighty careful of your husband—*he's* the man who's safe from them right now—ever since that radio broadcast of my sister's."

"*You* asked me to force her to speak on that broadcast!"

"I know, Lillian. We lost, both of us, that time. And we lose, both of us, now."

"Yes," she said, with the same darkness of contempt in her eyes, "both of us."

It was the contempt that pleased him; it was the strange, heedless, unfamiliar pleasure of knowing that this woman saw him as he was, yet remained held by his presence, remained and leaned back in her chair, as if declaring her bondage.

"You're a wonderful person, Jim," she said. It had the sound of damnation. Yet it was a tribute, and she meant it as such, and his pleasure came from the knowledge that they were in a realm where damnation was value.

"You know," he said suddenly, "you're wrong about those butcher's assistants, like Gonzales. They have their uses. Have you ever liked Francisco d'Anconia?"

"I can't stand him."

"Well, do you know the real purpose of that cocktail-swilling occasion staged by Señor Gonzales tonight? It was to celebrate the agreement to nationalize d'Anconia Copper in about a month."

She looked at him for a moment, the corners of her lips lifting slowly into a smile. "He was your friend, wasn't he?"

Her voice had a tone he had never earned before, the tone of an emotion which he had drawn from people only by fraud, but which now, for the first time, was granted with full awareness to the real, the actual nature of his deed: a tone of admiration.

Suddenly, he knew that this was the goal of his restless hours, this was the pleasure he had despaired of finding, *this* was the celebration he had wanted.

"Let's have a drink, Lil," he said.

Pouring the liquor, he glanced at her across the room, as she lay stretched limply in her chair. "Let him get his divorce," he said. "He won't have the last word. *They* will. The butcher's assistants. Señor Gonzales and Cuffy Meigs."

She did not answer. When he approached, she took the glass from him with a sloppily indifferent sweep of her hand. She drank, not in the manner of a social gesture, but like a lonely drinker in a saloon—for the physical sake of the liquor.

He sat down on the arm of the davenport, improperly close to her, and sipped his drink, watching her face. After a while, he asked, "What does he think of me?"

The question did not seem to astonish her. "He thinks you're a fool," she answered. "He thinks life's too short to have to notice your existence."

"He'd notice it, if—" He stopped.

"—if you bashed him over the head with a club? I'm not too sure. He'd merely blame himself for not having moved out of the club's reach. Still, that would be your only chance."

She shifted her body, sliding lower in the armchair, stomach forward, as if relaxation were ugliness, as if she were granting him the kind of intimacy that required no poise and no respect.

"That was the first thing I noticed about him," she said, "when I met him for the first time: that he was not afraid. He looked as if he felt certain that there was nothing any of us could do to him—so certain that he didn't even know the issue or the nature of what he felt."

"How long since you saw him last?"

"Three months. I haven't seen him since . . . since the Gift Certificate . . ."

"I saw him at an industrial meeting two weeks ago. He still looks that way—only more so. *Now,* he looks as if he knows it." He added, "You *have* failed, Lillian."

She did not answer. She pushed her hat off with the back of her hand; it rolled down to the carpet, its feather curling like a question mark. "I remember the first time I saw his mills," she said. *"His* mills! You can't imagine what he felt about them. You wouldn't know the kind of intellectual arrogance it takes to feel as if anything pertaining to him, anything he touched, were made sacred by the touch. *His* mills, *his* Metal, *his* money, *his* bed, *his* wife!" She glanced up at him, a small flicker piercing the lethargic emptiness of her eyes. "He never noticed your existence. He did notice mine. I'm still Mrs. Rearden—at least for another month."

"Yes . . ." he said, looking down at her with a sudden, new interest.

"Mrs. Rearden!" she chuckled. "You wouldn't know what that meant to him. No feudal lord ever felt or demanded such reverence for the title of *his* wife—or held it as such a symbol of honor. Of his unbending, untouchable, inviolate, stainless honor!" She waved her hand in a vague motion, indicating the length of her sprawled body. "Caesar's wife!" she chuckled. "Do you remember what she was supposed to be? No, you wouldn't. She was supposed to be above reproach."

He was staring down at her with the heavy, blind stare of impotent hatred—a hatred of which she was the sudden symbol, not the object. "He didn't like it when his Metal was thrown into common, public use, for any chance passer-by to make . . . did he?"

"No, he didn't."

His words were blurring a little, as if weighted with drops of the liquor he had swallowed: "Don't tell me that you helped us to get that Gift Certificate as a favor to me and that you gained nothing. . . . I know why you did it."

"You knew it at the time."

"Sure. That's why I like you, Lillian."

His eyes kept coming back to the low cut of her gown. It was not the smooth skin that attracted his glance, not the exposed rise of her breasts, but the fraud of the safety pin beyond the edge.

"I'd like to see him beaten," he said. "I'd like to hear him scream with pain, just once."

"You won't, Jimmy."

"Why does he think he's better than the rest of us—he and that sister of mine?"

She chuckled.

He rose as if she had slapped him. He went to the bar and poured himself another drink, not offering to refill her glass.

She was speaking into space, staring past him. "He did notice my existence—even though I can't lay railroad tracks for him and erect bridges to the glory of his Metal. I can't build his mills—but I can destroy them. I can't produce his Metal—but I can take it away from him. I can't bring men down to their knees in admiration—but I can bring them down to their knees."

"Shut up!" he screamed in terror, as if she were coming too close to that fogbound alley which had to remain unseen.

She glanced up at his face. "You're such a coward, Jim."

"Why don't you get drunk?" he snapped, sticking his unfinished drink at her mouth, as if he wanted to strike her.

Her fingers half-closed limply about the glass, and she drank, spilling the liquor down her chin, her breast and her gown.

"Oh hell, Lillian, you're a mess!" he said and, not troubling to reach for his handkerchief, he stretched out his hand to wipe the liquor with the flat of his palm. His fingers slipped under the gown's neckline, closing over her breast, his breath catching in a sudden gulp, like a hiccough. His eyelids were drawing closed, but he caught a glimpse of her face leaning back unresistingly, her mouth swollen with revulsion. When he reached for her mouth, her arms embraced him obediently and her mouth responded, but the response was just a pressure, not a kiss.

He raised his head to glance at her face. Her teeth were bared in a smile, but she was staring past him, as if mocking some invisible presence, her smile lifeless, yet loud with malice, like the grin of a flesh-less skull.

He jerked her closer, to stifle the sight and his own shudder. His hands were going through the automatic motions of intimacy—and she complied, but in a manner that made him feel as if the beats of her arteries under his touch were snickering giggles. They were both performing an expected routine, a routine invented by someone and imposed upon them, performing it in mockery, in hatred, in defiling parody on its inventors.

He felt a sightless, heedless fury, part-horror, part-pleasure—the horror of committing an act he would never dare confess to anyone—the pleasure of committing it in blasphemous defiance of those to whom he would not dare confess it. He was himself!—the only conscious part of his rage seemed to be screaming to him—he was, at last, himself!

They did not speak. They knew each other's motive. Only two words were pronounced between them. *"Mrs. Rearden,"* he said.

They did not look at each other when he pushed her into his bedroom and onto his bed, falling against her body, as against a soft, stuffed object. Their faces had a look of secrecy, the look of partners in guilt, the furtive, smutty look of children defiling someone's clean fence by chalking sneaky scratches intended as symbols of obscenity.

Afterward, it did not disappoint him that what he had possessed was an inanimate body without resistance or response. It was not a woman that he had wanted to possess. It was not an act in celebration of life that he had wanted to perform—but an act in celebration of the triumph of impotence.

* * *

Cherryl unlocked the door and slipped in quietly, almost surreptitiously, as if hoping not to be seen or to see the place which was her home. The sense of Dagny's presence—of Dagny's world—had supported her on her way back, but when she entered her own apartment the walls seemed to swallow her again into the suffocation of a trap.

The apartment was silent; a wedge of light cut across the anteroom from a door left half-open. She dragged herself mechanically in the direction of her room. Then she stopped.

The open band of light was the door of Jim's study, and on the illuminated strip of its carpet she saw a woman's hat with a feather stirring faintly in a draft.

She took a step forward. The room was empty, she saw two glasses, one on a table, the other on the floor, and a woman's purse lying on the seat of an armchair. She stood, in unreacting stupor, until she heard the muffled drawl of two voices behind the door of Jim's bedroom; she could not distinguish the words, only the quality of the sounds: Jim's voice had a tone of irritation, the woman's—of contempt.

Then she found herself in her own room, fumbling frantically to lock her door. She had been flung here by the blind panic of escape, as if it were she who had to hide, she who had to run from the ugliness of being seen in the act of seeing them—a panic made of revulsion, of pity, of embarrassment, of that mental chastity which recoils from confronting a man with the unanswerable proof of his evil.

She stood in the middle of her room, unable to grasp what action was now possible to her. Then her knees gave way, folding gently, she found herself sitting on the floor and she stayed there, staring at the carpet, shaking.

It was neither anger nor jealousy nor indignation, but the blank horror of dealing with the grotesquely senseless. It was the knowledge that neither their marriage nor his love for her nor his insistence on holding her nor his love for that other woman nor this gratuitous adultery had any meaning whatever, that there was no shred of sense in any of it and no use to grope for explanations. She had always thought of evil as purposeful, as a means to some end; what she was seeing now was evil for evil's sake.

She did not know how long she had sat there, when she heard their steps and voices, then the sound of the front door closing. She got up, with no purpose in mind, but impelled by some instinct from the past, as if acting in a vacuum where honesty was not relevant any longer, but knowing no other way to act.

She met Jim in the anteroom. For a moment, they looked at each other as if neither could believe the other's reality.

"When did *you* come back?" he snapped. "How long have you been home?"

"I don't know . . ."

He was looking at her face. "What's the matter with you?"

"Jim, I—" She struggled, gave up and waved her hand toward his bedroom. "Jim, I know."

"What do you know?"

"You were there . . . with a woman."

His first action was to push her into his study and slam the door, as if to hide them both, he could no longer say from whom. An unadmitted rage was boiling in his mind, struggling between escape and explosion, and it blew up into the sensation that this negligible little wife of his was depriving him of his triumph, that he would not surrender to her his new enjoyment.

"Sure!" he screamed. "So what? What are you going to do about it?"

She stared at him blankly.

"Sure! I was there with a woman! That's what I did, because that's what I felt like doing! Do you think you're going to scare me with your gasps, your stares, your whimpering virtue?" He snapped his fingers. "*That* for your opinion! I don't give a hoot in hell about your opinion! Take it and like it!" It was her white, defenseless face that drove him on, lashing him into a state of pleasure, the pleasure of feeling as if his words were blows disfiguring a human face. "Do you think you're going to make me hide? I'm sick of having to put on an act for your righteous satisfaction! Who the hell are you, you cheap little nobody? I'll do as I please, and you'll keep your mouth shut and go through the right tricks in public, like everybody else, and stop demanding that I act in my own home!—nobody is virtuous in his own home, the show is only for company!—but if you expect me to mean it—to *mean* it, you damn little fool!—you'd better grow up in a hurry!"

It was not her face that he was seeing, it was the face of the man at whom he wanted and would never be able to throw his deed of this night—but she had always stood as the worshipper, the defender, the agent of that man in his eyes, he had married her for it, so she could serve his purpose now, and he screamed, "Do you know who she was, the woman I laid? It was—"

"No!" she cried. "Jim! I don't have to know it!"

"It was Mrs. Rearden! Mrs. Hank Rearden!"

She stepped back. He felt a brief flash of terror—because she was looking at him as if she were seeing that which had to remain unadmitted to himself. She asked, in a dead voice that had the incongruous sound of common sense, "I suppose you will now want us to get divorced?"

He burst out laughing. "You goddamn fool! You still mean it! You still want it big and pure! I wouldn't think of divorcing you—and don't go imagining that I'll let you divorce me! You think it's as important as that? Listen, you fool, there isn't a husband who doesn't sleep with other women and there isn't a wife who doesn't know it, but they don't talk about it! I'll lay anybody I please, and you go and do the same, like all those bitches, and keep your mouth shut!"

He saw the sudden, startling sight of a look of hard, unclouded, unfeeling, almost inhuman intelligence in her eyes. "Jim, if I were the kind who did or would, you wouldn't have married me."

"No. I wouldn't have."

"Why did you marry me?"

He felt himself drawn as by a whirlpool, part in relief that the moment of danger was past, part in irresistible defiance of the same danger. "Because you were a cheap, helpless, preposterous little guttersnipe, who'd never have a chance at anything to equal me! Because I thought you'd love me! I thought you'd know that you had to love me!"

"As you are?"

"Without daring to ask what I am! Without reasons! Without putting me on the spot always to live up to reason after reason after reason, like being on some goddamn dress parade to the end of my days!"

"You loved me . . . because I was worthless?"

"Well, what did you think you were?"

"You loved me for being rotten?"

"What else did you have to offer? But you didn't have the humility to appreciate it. I wanted to be generous, I wanted to give you security—what security is there in being loved for one's virtues? The competition's wide open, like a jungle market place, a better person will always come along to beat you! But I—I was willing to love you for your flaws, for your faults and weaknesses, for your ignorance, your crudeness, your vulgarity—and that's safe, you'd have nothing to fear, nothing to hide, you could be yourself, your real, stinking, sinful, ugly self—everybody's self is a gutter—but you could hold my love, with nothing demanded of you!"

"You wanted me to . . . accept your love . . . as alms?"

"Did you imagine that you could *earn* it? Did you imagine that you could deserve to marry me, you poor little tramp? I used to buy the likes of you for the price of a meal! I wanted you to know, with every step you took, with every mouthful of caviar you swallowed, that you owed it all to *me,* that you had nothing and were nothing and could never hope to equal, deserve or repay!"

"I . . . tried . . . to deserve it."

"Of what use would you be to me, if you had?"

"You didn't want me to?"

"Oh, you goddamn fool!"

"You didn't want me to improve? You didn't want me to rise? You thought me rotten and you wanted me to stay rotten?"

"Of what use would you be to me, if you earned it all, and I had to work to hold you, and you could trade elsewhere if you chose?"

"You wanted it to be alms . . . for both of us and from both? You wanted us to be two beggars chained to each other?"

"Yes, you goddamn evangelist! Yes, you goddamn hero worshipper! Yes!"

"You chose me because I was worthless?"

"Yes!"

"You're lying, Jim."

His answer was only a startled glance of astonishment.

"Those girls that you used to buy for the price of a meal, they would have been glad to let their real selves become a gutter, they would have taken your alms and never tried to rise, but you would not marry one of them. You married me, because you knew that I did not accept the gutter, inside or out, that I was struggling to rise and would go on struggling—didn't you?"

"Yes!" he cried.

Then the headlight she had felt rushing upon her, hit its goal—and she screamed in the bright explosion of the impact—she screamed in physical terror, backing away from him.

"What's the matter with you?" he cried, shaking, not daring to see in her eyes the thing she had seen.

She moved her hands in groping gestures, half-waving it away, half-trying to grasp it; when she answered, her words did not quite name it, but they were the only words she could find: "You . . . you're a killer . . . for the sake of killing . . ."

It was too close to the unnamed; shaking with terror, he swung out blindly and struck her in the face.

She fell against the side of an armchair, her head striking the floor, but she raised her head in a moment and looked up at him blankly, without astonishment, as if physical reality were merely taking the form she had expected. A single pear-shaped drop of blood went slithering slowly from the corner of her mouth.

He stood motionless—and for a moment they looked at each other, as if neither dared to move.

She moved first. She sprang to her feet—and ran. She ran out of the room, out of the apartment—he heard her running down the hall, tearing open the iron door of the emergency stairway, not waiting to ring for the elevator.

She ran down the stairs, opening doors on random landings, running through the twisting hallways of the building, then down the stairs again, until she found herself in the lobby and ran to the street.

After a while, she saw that she was walking down a littered sidewalk in a dark neighborhood, with an electric bulb glaring in the cave of a subway entrance and a lighted billboard advertising soda crackers on the black roof of a laundry. She did not remember how she had come here. Her mind seemed to work in broken spurts, without connections. She knew only that she had to escape and that escape was impossible.

She had to escape from Jim, she thought. Where?—she asked, looking around her with a glance like a cry of prayer. She would have seized upon a job in a five-and-ten, or in that laundry, or in any of the dismal shops she passed. But she would work, she thought, and the harder she worked, the more malevolence she would draw from the people around her, and she would not know when truth would be expected of her and when a lie, but the stricter her honesty, the greater the fraud she would be asked to suffer at their hands. She had seen it before and had borne it, in the home of her family, in the shops of the slums, but she had thought that these were vicious exceptions, chance evils, to escape and forget. Now she knew that they were not exceptions, that theirs was the code accepted by the world, that it was a creed of living, known by all, but kept unnamed, leering at her from people's eyes in that sly, guilty look she had never been able to understand—and at the root of the creed, hidden by silence, lying in wait for her in the cellars of the city and in the cellars of their souls, there was a thing with which one could not live.

Why are you doing it to me?—she cried soundlessly to the darkness around her. Because you're good—some enormous laughter seemed to be answering from the roof tops and from the sewers. Then I won't

want to be good any longer—But you will—I don't have to—You will—
I can't bear it—You will.

She shuddered and walked faster—but ahead of her, in the foggy
distance, she saw the calendar above the roofs of the city—it was long
past midnight and the calendar said: August 6, but it seemed to her
suddenly that she saw September 2 written above the city in letters of
blood—and she thought: If she worked, if she struggled, if she rose,
she would take a harder beating with each step of her climb, until, at
the end, whatever she reached, be it a copper company or an unmort-
gaged cottage, she would see it seized by Jim on some September 2
and she would see it vanish to pay for the parties where Jim made his
deals with his friends.

Then I won't!—she screamed and whirled around and went running
back along the street—but it seemed to her that in the black sky,
grinning at her from the steam of the laundry, there weaved an enormous figure that would hold no shape, but its grin remained the same
on its changing faces, and its face was Jim's and her childhood preacher's and the woman social worker's from the personnel department of
the five-and-ten—and the grin seemed to say to her: People like you
will always stay honest, people like you will always struggle to rise, people like you will always work, so we're safe and you have no choice.

She ran. When she looked around her once more, she was walking
down a quiet street, past the glass doorways where lights were burning
in the carpeted lobbies of luxurious buildings. She noticed that she was
limping, and saw that the heel of her pump was loose; she had broken
it somewhere in her blank span of running.

From the sudden space of a broad intersection, she looked at the
great skyscrapers in the distance. They were vanishing quietly into a
veil of fog, with the faint breath of a glow behind them, with a few
lights like a smile of farewell. Once, they had been a promise, and
from the midst of the stagnant sloth around her she had looked to them
for proof that another kind of men existed. Now she knew that they
were tombstones, slender obelisks soaring in memory of the men who
had been destroyed for having created them, they were the frozen
shape of the silent cry that the reward of achievement was martyrdom.

Somewhere in one of those vanishing towers, she thought, there was
Dagny—but Dagny was a lonely victim, fighting a losing battle, to be
destroyed and to sink into fog like the others.

There is no place to go, she thought and stumbled on—I can't stand
still, nor move much longer—I can neither work nor rest—I can neither
surrender nor fight—but this . . . *this* is what they want of me, *this*
is where they want me—neither living nor dead, neither thinking nor
insane, but just a chunk of pulp that screams with fear, to be shaped
by them as they please, they who have no shape of their own.

She plunged into the darkness behind a corner, shrinking in

dread from any human figure. No, she thought, they're not evil, not all people . . . they're only their own first victims, but they all believe in Jim's creed, and I can't deal with them, once I know it . . . and if I spoke to them, they would try to grant me their good will, but I'd know what it is that they hold as the good and I would see death staring out of their eyes.

The sidewalk had shrunk to a broken strip, and splashes of garbage ran over from the cans at the stoops of crumbling houses. Beyond the dusty glow of a saloon, she saw a lighted sign "Young Women's Rest Club" above a locked door.

She knew the institutions of that kind and the women who ran them, the women who said that theirs was the job of helping sufferers. If she went in—she thought, stumbling past—if she faced them and begged them for help, "What is your guilt?" they would ask her. "Drink? Dope? Pregnancy? Shoplifting?" She would answer, "I have no guilt, I am innocent, but I'm—" "Sorry. We have no concern for the pain of the innocent."

She ran. She stopped, regaining her eyesight, on the corner of a long, wide street. The buildings and pavements merged with the sky—and two lines of green lights hung in open space, going off into an endless distance, as if stretching into other towns and oceans and foreign lands, to encircle the earth. The green glow had a look of serenity, like an inviting, unlimited path open to confident travel. Then the lights switched to red, dropping heavily lower, turning from sharp circles into foggy smears, into a warning of unlimited danger. She stood and watched a giant truck go by, its enormous wheels crushing one more layer of shiny polish into the flattened cobbles of the street.

The lights went back to the green of safety—but she stood trembling, unable to move. That's how it works for the travel of one's body, she thought, but what have they done to the traffic of the soul? They have set the signals in reverse—and the road is safe when the lights are the red of evil—but when the lights are the green of virtue, promising that yours is the right-of-way, you venture forth and are ground by the wheels. All over the world, she thought—those inverted lights go reaching into every land, they go on, encircling the earth. And the earth is littered with mangled cripples, who don't know what has hit them or why, who crawl as best they can on their crushed limbs through their lightless days, with no answer save that pain is the core of existence—and the traffic cops of morality chortle and tell them that man, by his nature, is unable to walk.

These were not words in her mind, these were the words which would have named, had she had the power to find them, what she knew only as a sudden fury that made her beat her fists in futile horror against the iron post of the traffic light beside her, against the hollow tube where the hoarse, rusty chuckle of a relentless mechanism went grating on and on.

She could not smash it with her fists, she could not batter one by one all the posts of the street stretching off beyond eyesight—as she could not smash that creed from the souls of the men she would encounter, one by one. She could not deal with people any longer, she could not take the paths they took—but what could she say to them, she who had no words to name the thing she knew and no voice that people would hear? What could she tell them? How could she reach them all? Where were the men who could have spoken?

These were not words in her mind, these were only the blows of her fists against metal—then she saw herself suddenly, battering her knuckles to blood against an immovable post, and the sight made her shudder—and she stumbled away. She went on, seeing nothing around her, feeling trapped in a maze with no exit.

No exit—her shreds of awareness were saying, beating it into the pavements in the sound of her steps—no exit . . . no refuge . . . no signals . . . no way to tell destruction from safety, or enemy from friend. . . . Like that dog she had heard about, she thought . . . somebody's dog in somebody's laboratory . . . the dog who got his signals switched on him, and saw no way to tell satisfaction from torture, saw food changed to beatings and beatings to food, saw his eyes and ears deceiving him and his judgment futile and his consciousness impotent in a shifting, swimming, shapeless world—and gave up, refusing to eat at that price or to live in a world of that kind. . . . No!—was the only conscious word in her brain—no!—no!—no!—not your way, not your world—even if this "no" is all that's to be left of mine!

It was in the darkest hour of the night, in an alley among wharfs and warehouses that the social worker saw her. The social worker was a woman whose gray face and gray coat blended with the walls of the district. She saw a young girl wearing a suit too smart and expensive for the neighborhood, with no hat, no purse, with a broken heel, disheveled hair and a bruise at the corner of her mouth, a girl staggering blindly, not knowing sidewalks from pavements. The street was only a narrow crack between the sheer, blank walls of storage structures, but a ray of light fell through a fog dank with the odor of rotting water; a stone parapet ended the street on the edge of a vast black hole merging river and sky.

The social worker approached her and asked severely, "Are you in trouble?"—and saw one wary eye, the other hidden by a lock of hair, and the face of a wild creature who has forgotten the sound of human voices, but listens as to a distant echo, with suspicion, yet almost with hope.

The social worker seized her arm. "It's a disgrace to come to such a state . . . if you society girls had something to do besides indulging your desires and chasing pleasures, you wouldn't be wandering, drunk as a tramp, at this hour of the night . . . if you stopped living for your own enjoyment, stopped thinking of yourself and found some higher—"

Then the girl screamed—and the scream went beating against the blank walls of the street as in a chamber of torture, an animal scream of terror. She tore her arm loose and sprang back, then screamed in articulate sounds:

"No! No! Not your kind of world!"

Then she ran, ran by the sudden propulsion of a burst of power, the power of a creature running for its life, she ran straight down the street that ended at the river—and in a single streak of speed, with no break, no moment of doubt, with full consciousness of acting in self-preservation, she kept running till the parapet barred her way and, not stopping, went over into space.

THEIR BROTHERS' KEEPERS

On the morning of September 2, a copper wire broke in California, between two telephone poles by the track of the Pacific branch line of Taggart Transcontinental.

A slow, thin rain had been falling since midnight, and there had been no sunrise, only a gray light seeping through a soggy sky—and the brilliant raindrops hanging on the telephone wires had been the only sparks glittering against the chalk of the clouds, the lead of the ocean and the steel of the oil derricks descending as lone bristles down a desolate hillside. The wires had been worn by more rains and years than they had been intended to carry; one of them had kept sagging, through the hours of that morning, under the fragile load of raindrops; then its one last drop had grown on the wire's curve and had hung like a crystal bead, gathering the weight of many seconds; the bead and the wire had given up together and, as soundless as the fall of tears, the wire had broken and fallen with the fall of the bead.

The men at the Division Headquarters of Taggart Transcontinental avoided looking at one another, when the break of the telephone line was discovered and reported. They made statements painfully miscalculated to seem to refer to the problem, yet to state nothing, none fooling the others. They knew that copper wire was a vanishing commodity, more precious than gold or honor; they knew that the division storekeeper had sold their stock of wire weeks ago, to unknown dealers who came by night and were not businessmen in the daytime, but only men who had friends in Sacramento and in Washington—just as the storekeeper, recently appointed to the division, had a friend in New York, named Cuffy Meigs, about whom one asked no questions. They knew that the man who would now assume the responsibility of ordering repairs and initiating the action which would lead to the discovery that the repairs could not be made, would incur retaliation from unknown enemies, that his fellow workers would become mysteriously silent and would not testify to help him, that he would prove nothing, and if he attempted to do his job, it would not be his any longer. They did not know what was safe or dangerous these days, when the guilty were not punished, but the accusers were; and, like animals, they knew that immobility was the only protection when in doubt and in danger. They remained immobile; they spoke about the appropriate procedure of sending reports to the appropriate authorities on the appropriate dates.

A young roadmaster walked out of the room and out of the headquarters building to the safety of a telephone booth in a drugstore and, at his own expense, ignoring the continent and the tiers of appropriate executives between, he telephoned Dagny Taggart in New York.

She received the call in her brother's office, interrupting an emergency conference. The young roadmaster told her only that the telephone line was broken and that there was no wire to repair it; he said nothing else and he did not explain why he had found it necessary to call her in person. She did not question him; she understood. "Thank you," was all that she answered.

An emergency file in her office kept a record of all the crucial materials still on hand, on every division of Taggart Transcontinental. Like the file of a bankrupt, it kept registering losses, while the rare additions of new supplies seemed like the malicious chuckles of some tormentor throwing crumbs at a starving continent. She looked through the file, closed it, sighed and said, "Montana, Eddie. Phone the Montana Line to ship half their stock of wire to California. Montana might be able to last without it—for another week." And as Eddie Willers was about to protest, she added, "Oil, Eddie. California is one of the last producers of oil left in the country. We don't dare lose the Pacific Line." Then she went back to the conference in her brother's office.

"Copper wire?" said James Taggart, with an odd glance that went from her face to the city beyond the window. "In a very short while, we won't have any trouble about copper."

"Why?" she asked, but he did not answer. There was nothing special to see beyond the window, only the clear sky of a sunny day, the quiet light of early afternoon on the roofs of the city and, above them, the page of the calendar, saying: September 2.

She did not know why he had insisted on holding this conference in his own office, why he had insisted on speaking to her alone, which he had always tried to avoid, or why he kept glancing at his wrist watch.

"Things are, it seems to me, going wrong," he said. "Something has to be done. There appears to exist a state of dislocation and confusion tending toward an unco-ordinated, unbalanced policy. What I mean is, there's a tremendous national demand for transportation, yet we're losing money. It seems to me—"

She sat looking at the ancestral map of Taggart Transcontinental on the wall of his office, at the red arteries winding across a yellowed continent. There had been a time when the railroad was called the blood system of the nation, and the stream of trains had been like a living circuit of blood, bringing growth and wealth to every patch of wilderness it touched. Now, it was still like a stream of blood, but like the one-way stream that runs from a wound, draining the last of a body's sustenance and life. One-way traffic—she thought indifferently—consumers' traffic.

There was Train Number 193, she thought. Six weeks ago, Train Number 193 had been sent with a load of steel, not to Faulkton, Nebraska, where the Spencer Machine Tool Company, the best machine tool concern still in existence, had been idle for two weeks, waiting for the shipment—but to Sand Creek, Illinois, where Confederated Machines had been wallowing in debt for over a year, producing unreliable goods at unpredictable times. The steel had been allocated by a directive which explained that the Spencer Machine Tool Company was a rich concern, able to wait, while Confederated Machines was bankrupt and could not be allowed to collapse, being the sole source of livelihood of the community of Sand Creek, Illinois. The Spencer Machine Tool Company had closed a month ago. Confederated Machines had closed two weeks later.

The people of Sand Creek, Illinois, had been placed on national relief, but no food could be found for them in the empty granaries of the nation at the frantic call of the moment—so the seed grain of the farmers of Nebraska had been seized by order of the Unification Board—and Train Number 194 had carried the unplanted harvest and the future of the people of Nebraska to be consumed by the people of Illinois. "In this enlightened age," Eugene Lawson had said in a radio broadcast, "we have come, at last, to realize that each one of us is his brother's keeper."

"In a precarious period of emergency, like the present," James Taggart was saying, while she looked at the map, "it is dangerous to find ourselves forced to miss pay days and accumulate wage arrears on some of our divisions, a temporary condition, of course, but—"

She chuckled. "The Railroad Unification Plan isn't working, is it, Jim?"

"I beg your pardon?"

"You're to receive a big cut of the Atlantic Southern's gross income, out of the common pool at the end of the year—only there won't be any gross income left for the pool to seize, will there?"

"That's not true! It's just that the bankers are sabotaging the Plan. Those bastards—who used to give us loans in the old days, with no security at all except our own railroad—now refuse to let me have a few measly hundred-thousands, on short term, just to take care of a few payrolls, when I have the entire plant of all the railroads of the country to offer them as security for my loan!"

She chuckled.

"We couldn't help it!" he cried. "It's not the fault of the Plan that some people refuse to carry their fair share of our burdens!"

"Jim, was this all you wanted to tell me? If it is, I'll go. I have work to do."

His eyes shot to his wrist watch. "No, no, that's not all! It's most urgent that we discuss the situation and arrive at some decision, which—"

She listened blankly to the next stream of generalities, wondering about his motive. He was marking time, yet he wasn't, not fully; she felt certain that he was holding her here for some specific purpose and, simultaneously, that he was holding her for the mere sake of her presence.

It was some new trait in him, which she had begun to notice ever since Cherryl's death. He had come running to her, rushing, unannounced, into her apartment on the evening of the day when Cherryl's body had been found and the story of her suicide had filled the newspapers, given by some social worker who had witnessed it; "an inexplicable suicide," the newspapers had called it, unable to discover any motive. "It wasn't my fault!" he had screamed to her, as if she were the only judge whom he had to placate. "I'm not to blame for it! I'm not to blame!" He had been shaking with terror—yet she had caught a few glances thrown shrewdly at her face, which had seemed, inconceivably, to convey a touch of triumph. "Get out of here, Jim," was all she had said to him.

He had never spoken to her again about Cherryl, but he had started coming to her office more often than usual, he had stopped her in the halls for snatches of pointless discussions—and such moments had grown into a sum that gave her an incomprehensible sensation: as if, while clinging to her for support and protection against some nameless terror, his arms were sliding to embrace her and to plunge a knife into her back.

"I am eager to know your views," he was saying insistently, as she looked away. "It is most urgent that we discuss the situation and . . . and you haven't said anything." She did not turn. "It's not as if there were no money to be had out of the railroad business, but—"

She glanced at him sharply; his eyes scurried away.

"What I mean is, some constructive policy has to be devised," he droned on hastily. "Something has to be done . . . by somebody. In times of emergency—"

She knew what thought he had scurried to avoid, what hint he had given her, yet did not want her to acknowledge or discuss. She knew that no train schedules could be maintained any longer, no promises kept, no contracts observed, that regular trains were cancelled at a moment's notice and transformed into emergency specials sent by unexplained orders to unexpected destinations—and that the orders came from Cuffy Meigs, sole judge of emergencies and of the public welfare. She knew that factories were closing, some with their machinery stilled for lack of supplies that had not been received, others with their warehouses full of goods that could not be delivered. She knew that the old industries—the giants who had built their power by a purposeful course projected over a span of time—were left to exist at the whim of the moment, a moment they could not foresee or control. She knew that the best among them, those of the longest range and most complex function, had long since gone—and those still struggling to produce, struggling savagely to preserve the code of an age when production had been possible, were now inserting into their contracts a line shameful to a descendant of Nat Taggart: "Transportation permitting."

And yet there were men—and she knew it—who were able to obtain transportation whenever they wished, as by a mystic secret, as by the grace of some power which one was not to question or explain. They were the men whose dealings with Cuffy Meigs were regarded by people as that unknowable of mystic creeds which smites the observer for the sin of looking, so people kept their eyes closed, dreading, not ignorance, but knowledge. She knew that deals were made whereby those men sold a commodity known as "transportation pull"—a term which all understood, but none would dare define. She knew that these were the men of the emergency specials, the men who could cancel her scheduled trains and send them to any random spot of the continent which they chose to strike with their voodoo stamp, the stamp superseding contract, property, justice, reason and lives, the stamp stating that "the public welfare" required the immediate salvation of that spot. These were the men who sent trains to the relief of the Smather Brothers and their grapefruit in Arizona—to the relief of a factory in Florida engaged in the production of pin-ball machines—to the relief of a horse farm in Kentucky—to the relief of Orren Boyle's Associated Steel.

These were the men who made deals with desperate industrialists to provide transportation for the goods stalled in their warehouses—or, failing to obtain the percentage demanded, made deals to purchase the goods, when the factory closed, at the bankruptcy sale, at ten cents on the dollar, and to speed the goods away in freight cars suddenly available, away to markets where dealers of the same kind were ready for the kill. These were the men who hovered over factories, waiting for the last breath of a furnace, to pounce upon the equipment—and over desolate sidings, to pounce upon the freight cars of undelivered goods— these were a new biological species, the hit-and-run businessmen, who did not stay in any line of business longer than the span of one deal, who had no payrolls to meet, no overhead to carry, no real estate to own, no equipment to build, whose only asset and sole investment consisted of an item known as "friendship." These were the men whom official speeches described as "the progressive businessmen of our dynamic age," but whom people called "the pull peddlers"—the species included many breeds, those of "transportation pull," and of "steel pull" and "oil pull" and "wage-raise pull" and "suspended sentence pull"—men who *were* dynamic, who kept darting all over the country while no one else could move, men who were active and mindless, active, not like animals, but like that which breeds, feeds and moves upon the stillness of a corpse.

She knew that there was money to be had out of the railroad business and she knew who was now obtaining it. Cuffy Meigs was selling trains as he was selling the last of the railroad's supplies, whenever he could rig a setup which would not let it be discovered or proved—selling rail to roads in Guatemala or to trolley companies in Canada, selling wire to manufacturers of juke boxes, selling crossties for fuel in resort hotels.

Did it matter—she thought, looking at the map—which part of the corpse had been consumed by which type of maggot, by those who gorged themselves or by those who gave the food to other maggots? So long as living flesh was prey to be devoured, did it matter whose stomachs it had gone to fill? There was no way to tell which devastation had been accomplished by the humanitarians and which by undisguised gangsters. There was no way to tell which acts of plunder had been prompted by the charity-lust of the Lawsons and which by the gluttony of Cuffy Meigs—no way to tell which communities had been immolated to feed another community one week closer to starvation and which to provide yachts for the pull-peddlers. Did it matter? Both were alike in fact as they were alike in spirit, both were in need and need was regarded as sole title to property, both were acting in strictest accordance with the same code of morality. Both held the immolation of men as proper and both were achieving it. There wasn't even any way to tell who were the cannibals and who the victims—the communities that accepted as their rightful due the confiscated clothing or fuel of a town to the east of them, found, next week, their granaries confiscated to feed a town to the west—men had achieved the ideal of the centuries, they were practicing it in unobstructed perfection, they were serving *need* as their highest ruler, need as first claim upon them, need as their standard of value, as the coin of their realm, as more sacred than right and life. Men had been pushed into a pit where, shouting that man is his brother's keeper, each was devouring his neighbor and was being devoured by his neighbor's brother, each was proclaiming the righteousness of the unearned and wondering who was stripping the skin off his back, each was devouring himself, while screaming in terror that some unknowable evil was destroying the earth.

"What complaint do they now have to make?" she heard Hugh Akston's voice in her mind. "That the universe is irrational? Is it?"

She sat looking at the map, her glance dispassionately solemn, as if no emotion save respect were permissible when observing the awesome power of logic. She was seeing—in the chaos of a perishing continent—the precise, mathematical execution of all the ideas men had held. They had not wanted to know that *this* was what they wanted, they had not wanted to see that they had the power to wish, but not the power to fake—and they had achieved their wish to the letter, to the last bloodstained comma of it.

What were they thinking now, the champions of need and the lechers of pity?—she wondered. What were they counting on? Those who had once simpered: "I don't want to destroy the rich, I only want to seize a little of their surplus to help the poor, just a *little,* they'll never miss it!"—then, later, had snapped: "The tycoons can stand being squeezed, they've amassed enough to last them for three generations"— then, later, had yelled: "Why should the people suffer while businessmen have reserves to last a year?"—*now* were screaming: "Why should we starve while some people have reserves to last a week?" What were they counting on?—she wondered.

"You must do something!" cried James Taggart.

She whirled to face him. *"I?"*

"It's *your* job, it's your province, it's your duty!"

"What is?"

"To act. To do."

"To do—what?"

"How should I know? It's *your* special talent. You're the doer."

She glanced at him: the statement was so oddly perceptive and so incongruously irrelevant. She rose to her feet.

"Is this all, Jim?"

"No! No! I want a discussion!"

"Go ahead."

"But you haven't said anything!"

"You haven't, either."

"But . . . What I mean is, there are practical problems to solve, which . . . For instance, what was that matter of our last allocation of new rail vanishing from the storehouse in Pittsburgh?"

"Cuffy Meigs stole it and sold it."

"Can you prove it?" he snapped defensively.

"Have your friends left any means, methods, rules or agencies of proof?"

"Then don't talk about it, don't be theoretical, we've got to deal with facts! We've got to deal with facts as they are today . . . I mean, we've got to be realistic and devise some practical means to protect our supplies under existing conditions, not under unprovable assumptions, which—"

She chuckled. *There* was the form of the formless, she thought, *there* was the method of his consciousness: he wanted her to protect him from Cuffy Meigs without acknowledging Meigs' existence, to fight it without admitting its reality, to defeat it without disturbing its game.

"What do you find so damn funny?" he snapped angrily.

"You know it."

"I don't know what's the matter with you! I don't know what's happened to you . . . in the last two months . . . ever since you came back. . . . You've never been so unco-operative!"

"Why, Jim, I haven't argued with you in the last two months."

"That's what I mean!" He caught himself hastily, but not fast enough to miss her smile. "I mean, I wanted to have a conference, I wanted to know your view of the situation—"

"You know it."

"But you haven't said a word!"

"I said everything I had to say, three years ago. I told you where your course would take you. It has."

"Now there you go again! What's the use of theorizing? We're *here,* we're not back three years ago. We've got to deal with the present, not the past. Maybe things would have been different, if we had followed your opinion, maybe, but the fact is that we *didn't*—and we've got to deal with facts. We've got to take reality as it is *now,* today!"

"Well, take it."

"I beg your pardon?"

"Take your reality. I'll merely take your orders."

"That's unfair! I'm asking for your opinion—"

"You're asking for reassurance, Jim. You're not going to get it."

"I beg your pardon?"

"I'm not going to help you pretend—by arguing with you—that the reality you're talking about is not what it is, that there's still a way to make it work and to save your neck. There isn't."

"Well . . ." There was no explosion, no anger—only the feebly uncertain voice of a man on the verge of abdication. "Well . . . what would *you* want me to do?"

"Give up." He looked at her blankly. "Give up—all of you, you and your Washington friends and your looting planners and the whole of your cannibal philosophy. Give up and get out of the way and let those of us who can, start from scratch out of the ruins."

"No!" The explosion came, oddly, now; it was the scream of a man who would die rather than betray his idea, and it came from a man who had spent his life evading the existence of ideas, acting with the expediency of a criminal. She wondered whether she had ever understood the essence of criminals. She wondered about the nature of the loyalty to the idea of denying ideas.

"No!" he cried, his voice lower, hoarser and more normal, sinking from the tone of a zealot to the tone of an overbearing executive. "That's impossible! That's out of the question!"

"Who said so?"

"Never mind! It's so! Why do you always think of the impractical? Why don't you accept reality as it *is* and do something about it? You're the realist, you're the doer, the mover, the producer, the Nat Taggart, you're the person who's able to achieve any goal she chooses!

You could save us now, you could find a way to make things work—if you *wanted* to!"

She burst out laughing.

There, she thought, was the ultimate goal of all that loose academic prattle which businessmen had ignored for years, the goal of all the slipshod definitions, the sloppy generalities, the soupy abstractions, all claiming that obedience to objective reality is the same as obedience to the State, that there is no difference between a law of nature and a bureaucrat's directive, that a hungry man is not free, that man must be released from the tyranny of food, shelter and clothing—all of it, for years, that the day might come when Nat Taggart, the realist, would be asked to consider the will of Cuffy Meigs as a *fact* of nature, irrevocable and absolute like steel, rails and gravitation, to accept the Meigs-made world as an objective, unchangeable reality—then to continue producing abundance in that world. *There* was the goal of all those con men of library and classroom, who sold their revelations as reason, their "instincts" as science, their cravings as knowledge, the goal of all the savages of the non-objective, the non-absolute, the relative, the tentative, the probable—the savages who, seeing a farmer gather a harvest, can consider it only as a mystic phenomenon unbound by the law of causality and created by the farmer's omnipotent whim, who then proceed to seize the farmer, to chain him, to deprive him of tools, of seeds, of water, of soil, to push him out on a barren rock and to command: *"Now* grow a harvest and feed us!"

No—she thought, expecting Jim to ask it—it would be useless to try to explain what she was laughing at, he would not be able to understand it.

But he did not ask it. Instead, she saw him slumping and heard him say—terrifyingly, because his words were so irrelevant, if he did not understand, and so monstrous, if he did, "Dagny, I'm your brother . . ."

She drew herself up, her muscles growing rigid, as if she were about to face a killer's gun.

"Dagny"—his voice was the soft, nasal, monotonous whine of a beggar—"I *want* to be president of a railroad. I *want* it. Why can't I have my wish as you always have yours? Why shouldn't I be given the fulfillment of my desires as you always fulfill any desire of your own? Why should you be happy while I suffer? Oh yes, the world is yours, you're the one who has the brains to run it. Then why do you permit suffering in your world? You proclaim the pursuit of happiness, but you doom me to frustration. Don't I have the right to demand any form of happiness I choose? Isn't that a debt which you owe me? Am I not your brother?"

His glance was like a prowler's flashlight searching her face for a shred of pity. It found nothing but a look of revulsion.

"It's *your* sin if I suffer! It's your moral failure! I'm your brother, therefore I'm your responsibility, but you've failed to supply my wants, therefore you're guilty! All of mankind's moral leaders have said so for centuries—who are you to say otherwise? You're so proud of yourself, you think that you're pure and good—but you can't be good, so long as I'm wretched. My misery is the measure of your sin. My contentment is the measure of your virtue. I *want* this kind of world, today's world, it gives me my share of authority, it allows me to feel important—make it work for me!—do something!—how do I know what?—it's *your* problem and *your* duty! You have the *privilege* of strength, but I—I have the *right* of weakness! That's a moral absolute! Don't you know it? Don't you? Don't you?"

His glance was now like the hands of a man hanging over an abyss, groping frantically for the slightest fissure of doubt, but slipping on the clean, polished rock of her face.

"You bastard," she said evenly, without emotion, since the words were not addressed to anything human.

It seemed to her that she saw him fall into the abyss—even though there was nothing to see in his face except the look of a con man whose trick has not worked.

There was no reason to feel more revulsion than usual, she thought; he had merely uttered the things which were preached, heard and accepted everywhere; but this creed was usually expounded in the third person, and Jim had had the open effrontery to expound it in the first. She wondered whether people accepted the doctrine of sacrifice provided its recipients did not identify the nature of their own claims and actions.

She turned to leave.

"No! No! Wait!" he cried, leaping to his feet, with a glance at his wrist watch. "It's time now! There's a particular news broadcast that I want you to hear!"

She stopped, held by curiosity.

He pressed the switch of the radio, watching her face openly, intently, almost insolently. His eyes had a look of fear and of oddly lecherous anticipation.

"Ladies and gentlemen!" the voice of the radio speaker leaped forth abruptly; it had a tone of panic. "News of a shocking development has just reached us from Santiago, Chile!"

She saw the jerk of Taggart's head and a sudden anxiety in his bewildered frown, as if something about the words and voice were not what he had expected.

"A special session of the legislature of the People's State of Chile had been called for ten o'clock this morning, to pass an act of utmost importance to the people of Chile, Argentina and other South American People's States. In line with the enlightened policy of Señor Ramirez, the new Head of the Chilean State—who came to power on the moral slogan that man is his brother's keeper—the legislature was to nationalize the Chilean properties of d'Anconia Copper, thus opening the way for the People's State of Argentina to nationalize the rest of the d'Anconia properties the world over. This, however, was known only to a very few of the top-level leaders of both nations. The measure had been kept secret in order to avoid debate and reactionary opposition. The seizure of the multi-billion dollar d'Anconia Copper was to come as a munificent surprise to the country.

"On the stroke of ten, in the exact moment when the chairman's gavel struck the rostrum, opening the session—almost as if the gavel's blow had set it off—the sound of a tremendous explosion rocked the hall, shattering the glass of its windows. It came from the harbor, a few streets away—and when the legislators rushed to the windows, they saw a long column of flame where once there had risen the familiar silhouettes of the ore docks of d'Anconia Copper. The ore docks had been blown to bits.

"The chairman averted panic and called the session to order. The act of nationalization was read to the assembly, to the sound of fire-alarm sirens and distant cries. It was a gray morning, dark with rain clouds, the explosion had broken an electric transmitter—so that the assembly voted on the measure by the light of candles, while the red glow of the fire kept sweeping over the great vaulted ceiling above their heads.

"But more terrible a shock came later, when the legislators called a hasty recess to announce to the nation the good news that the people now owned d'Anconia Copper. While they were voting, word had come from the closest and farthest points of the globe that there was no d'Anconia Copper left on earth. Ladies and gentlemen, not anywhere. In that same instant, on the stroke of ten, by an infernal marvel of synchronization, every property of d'Anconia Copper on the face of the globe, from Chile to Siam to Spain to Pottsville, Montana, had been blown up and swept away.

"The d'Anconia workers everywhere had been handed their last pay checks, in cash, at nine A.M., and by nine-thirty had been moved off the premises. The ore docks, the smelters, the laboratories, the office buildings were demolished. Nothing was left of the d'Anconia ore ships which had been in port—and only lifeboats carrying the crews were left of those ships which had been at sea. As to the d'Anconia mines, some were buried under tons of blasted rock, while others were found not to be worth the price of blasting. An astounding number of these mines, as reports pouring in seem to indicate, had continued to be run, even though exhausted years ago.

"Among the thousands of d'Anconia employees, the police have found no one with any knowledge of how this monstrous plot had been conceived, organized and carried out. But the cream of the d'Anconia staff are not here any longer. The most efficient of the executives, mineralogists, engineers, superintendents have vanished—all the men upon whom the People's State had been counting to carry on the work and cushion the process of readjustment. The most able—*correction:* the most selfish—of the men are gone. Reports from the various banks indicate that there are no d'Anconia accounts left anywhere; the money has been spent down to the last penny.

"Ladies and gentlemen, the d'Anconia fortune—the greatest fortune on earth, the legendary fortune of the centuries—has ceased to exist. In place of the golden dawn of a new age, the People's States of Chile and Argentina are left with a pile of rubble and hordes of unemployed on their hands.

"No clue has been found to the fate or the whereabouts of Señor Francisco d'Anconia. He has vanished, leaving nothing behind him, not even a message of farewell."

Thank you, my darling—thank you in the name of the last of us, even if you will not hear it and will not care to hear. . . . It was not a sentence, but the silent emotion of a prayer in her mind, addressed to the laughing face of a boy she had known at sixteen.

Then she noticed that she was clinging to the radio, as if the faint electric beat within it still held a tie to the only living force on earth, which it had transmitted for a few brief moments and which now filled the room where all else was dead.

As distant remnants of the explosion's wreckage, she noticed a sound that came from Jim, part-moan, part-scream, part-growl—then the sight of Jim's shoulders shaking over a telephone and his distorted voice screaming, "But, Rodrigo, you said it was safe! Rodrigo—oh God!—do you know how much I'd sunk into it?"—then the shriek of another phone on his desk, and his voice snarling into another receiver, his hand still clutching the first, "Shut your trap, Orren! What are *you* to do? What do I care, God damn you!"

There were people rushing into the office, the telephones were screaming and, alternating between pleas and curses, Jim kept yelling into one receiver, "Get me Santiago! . . . Get Washington to get me Santiago!"

Distantly, as on the margin of her mind, she could see what sort of game the men behind the shrieking phones had played and lost. They seemed far away, like tiny commas squirming on the white field under the lens of a microscope. She wondered how they could ever expect to be taken seriously when a Francisco d'Anconia was possible on earth.

She saw the glare of the explosion in every face she met through the rest of the day—and in every face she passed in the darkness of the streets, that evening. If Francisco had wanted a worthy funeral pyre for d'Anconia Copper, she thought, he had succeeded. There it was, in the streets of New York City, the only city on earth still able to understand it—in the faces of people, in their whispers, the whispers crackling tensely like small tongues of fire, the faces lighted by a look that was both solemn and frantic, the shadings of expressions appearing to sway and weave, as if cast by a distant flame, some frightened, some angry, most of them uneasy, uncertain, expectant, but all of them acknowledging a fact much beyond an industrial catastrophe, all of them knowing what it meant, though none would name its meaning, all of them carrying a touch of laughter, a laughter of amusement and defiance, the bitter laughter of perishing victims who feel that they are avenged.

She saw it in the face of Hank Rearden, when she met him for dinner that evening. As his tall, confident figure walked toward her—the only figure that seemed at home in the costly setting of a distinguished restaurant—she saw the look of eagerness fighting the sternness of his features, the look of a young boy still open to the enchantment of the unexpected. He did not speak of this day's event, but she knew that it was the only image in his mind.

They had been meeting whenever he came to the city, spending a brief, rare evening together—with their past still alive in their silent acknowledgment—with no future in their work and in their common struggle, but with the knowledge that they were allies gaining support from the fact of each other's existence.

He did not want to mention today's event, he did not want to speak of Francisco, but she noticed, as they sat at the table, that the strain of a resisted smile kept pulling at the hollows of his cheeks. She knew whom he meant, when he said suddenly, his voice soft and low with the weight of admiration, "He did keep his oath, didn't he?"

"His *oath?*" she asked, startled, thinking of the inscription on the temple of Atlantis.

"He said to me, 'I swear—by the woman I love—that I am your friend.' He was."

"He is."

He shook his head. "I have no right to think of him. I have no right to accept what he's done as an act in my defense. And yet . . ." He stopped.

"But it was, Hank. In defense of all of us—and of you, most of all."

He looked away, out at the city. They sat at the side of the room, with a sheet of glass as an invisible protection against the sweep of space and streets sixty floors below. The city seemed abnormally distant: it lay flattened down to the pool of its lowest stories. A few blocks away, its tower merging into darkness, the calendar hung at the level of their faces, not as a small, disturbing rectangle, but as an enormous screen, eerily close and large, flooded by the dead, white glow of light projected through an empty film, empty but for the letters: September 2.

"Rearden Steel is now working at capacity," he was saying indifferently. "They've lifted the production quotas off my mills—for the next five minutes, I guess. I don't know how many of their own regulations they've suspended, I don't think they know it, either, they don't bother keeping track of legality any longer, I'm sure I'm a law-breaker on five or six counts, which nobody could prove or disprove—all I know is that the gangster of the moment told me to go full steam ahead." He shrugged. "When another gangster kicks him out tomorrow, I'll probably be shut down, as penalty for illegal operation. But according to the plan of the present split-second, they've begged me to keep pouring my Metal, in any amount and by any means I choose."

She noticed the occasional, surreptitious glances that people were throwing in their direction. She had noticed it before, ever since her broadcast, ever since the two of them had begun to appear in public together. Instead of the disgrace he had dreaded, there was an air of awed uncertainty in people's manner—uncertainty of their own moral precepts, awe in the presence of two persons who dared to be certain of being right. People were looking at them with anxious curiosity, with envy, with respect, with the fear of offending an unknown, proudly rigorous standard, some almost with an air of apology that seemed to say: "Please forgive us for being married." There were some who had a look of angry malice, and a few who had a look of admiration.

"Dagny," he asked suddenly, "do you suppose he's in New York?"

"No. I've called the Wayne-Falkland. They told me that the lease on his suite had expired a month ago and he did not renew it."

"They're looking for him all over the world," he said, smiling. "They'll never find him." The smile vanished. "Neither will I." His voice slipped back to the flat, gray tone of duty: "Well, the mills are working, but I'm not. I'm doing nothing but running around the country like a scavenger, searching for illegal ways to purchase raw materials. Hiding, sneaking, lying—just to get a few tons of ore or coal or copper. They haven't lifted their regulations off my raw materials. They know that I'm pouring more Metal than the quotas they give me could produce. They don't care." He added, "They think I do."

"Tired, Hank?"

"Bored to death."

There was a time, she thought, when his mind, his energy, his inexhaustible resourcefulness had been given to the task of a producer devising better ways to deal with nature; *now,* they were switched to the task of a criminal outwitting men. She wondered how long a man could endure a change of that kind.

"It's becoming almost impossible to get iron ore," he said indifferently, then added, his voice suddenly alive, "Now it's going to be completely impossible to get copper." He was grinning.

She wondered how long a man could continue to work against himself, to work when his deepest desire was not to succeed, but to fail.

She understood the connection of his thoughts when he said, "I've never told you, but I've met Ragnar Danneskjöld."

"He told me."

"*What?* Where did you ever—" He stopped. "Of course," he said, his voice tense and low. "He would be one of them. You would have met him. Dagny, what are they like, those men who . . . No. Don't answer me." In a moment he added, "So I've met one of their agents."

"You've met two of them."

His response was a span of total stillness. "Of course," he said dully. "I knew it . . . I just wouldn't admit to myself that I knew . . . He was their recruiting agent, wasn't he?"

"One of their earliest and best."

He chuckled; it was a sound of bitterness and longing. "That night . . . when they got Ken Danagger . . . I thought that they had not sent anyone after *me*. . . ."

The effort by which he made his face grow rigid, was almost like the slow, resisted turn of a key locking a sunlit room he could not permit himself to examine. Afteì a while, he said impassively, "Dagny, that new rail we discussed last month—I don't think I'll be able to deliver it. They haven't lifted their regulations off my output, they're still controlling my sales and disposing of my Metal as they please. But the bookkeeping is in such a snarl that I'm smuggling a few thousand tons into the black market every week. I think they know it. They're pretending not to. They don't want to antagonize me, right now. But, you see, I've been shipping every ton I could snatch, to some emergency customers of mine. Dagny, I was in Minnesota last month. I've seen what's going on there. The country will starve, not next year, but *this* winter, unless a few of us act and act fast. There are no grain reserves left anywhere. With Nebraska gone, Oklahoma wrecked, North Dakota abandoned, Kansas barely subsisting—there isn't going to be any wheat this winter, not for the city of New York nor for any Eastern city. Minnesota is our last granary. They've had two bad years in succession, but they have a bumper crop this fall—and they have to be able to harvest it. Have you had a chance to take a look at the condition of the farm-equipment industry? They're not big enough, any of them, to keep a staff of efficient gangsters in Washington or to pay percentages to pull-peddlers. So they haven't been getting many allocations of materials. Two-thirds of them have shut down and the rest are about to. And farms are perishing all over the country—for lack of tools. You should have seen those farmers in Minnesota. They've been spending more time fixing old tractors that can't be fixed than plowing their fields. I don't know how they managed to survive till last spring. I don't know how they managed to plant their wheat. But they did. They did." There was a look of intensity on his face, as if he were contemplating a rare, forgotten sight: a vision of *men*—and she knew what motive was still holding him to his job. "Dagny, they had to have tools for their harvest. I've been selling all the Metal I could steal out of my own mills to the manufacturers of farm equipment. On credit. They've been sending the equipment to Minnesota as fast as they could put it out. Selling it in the same way—illegally and on credit. But they will be paid, this fall, and so will I. Charity, hell! We're helping producers— and what tenacious producers!—not lousy, mooching 'consumers.'

We're giving *loans*, not alms. We're supporting *ability,* not *need.* I'll be damned if I'll stand by and let those men be destroyed while the pull-peddlers grow rich!"

He was looking at the image of a sight he had seen in Minnesota: the silhouette of an abandoned factory, with the light of the sunset streaming, unopposed, through the holes of its windows and the cracks of its roof, with the remnant of a sign: Ward Harvester Company.

"Oh, I know," he said. "We'll save them this winter, but the looters will devour them next year. Still, we'll save them this winter. . . . Well, that's why I won't be able to smuggle any rail for you. Not in the immediate future—and there's nothing left to us but the immediate future. I don't know what is the use of feeding a country, if it loses its railroads—but what is the use of railroads where there is no food? What is the use, anyway?"

"It's all right, Hank. We'll last with such rail as we have, for—" She stopped.

"For a month?"

"For the winter—I hope."

Cutting across their silence, a shrill voice reached them from another table, and they turned to look at a man who had the jittery manner of a cornered gangster about to reach for his gun. "An act of anti-social destruction," he was snarling to a sullen companion, "at a time when there's such a desperate shortage of copper! . . . We can't permit it! We can't permit it to be true!"

Rearden turned abruptly to look off, at the city. "I'd give anything to know where he is," he said, his voice low. "Just to know where he is, right now, at this moment."

"What would you do, if you knew it?"

He dropped his hand in a gesture of futility. "I wouldn't approach him. The only homage I can still pay him is not to cry for forgiveness where no forgiveness is possible."

They remained silent. They listened to the voices around them, to the splinters of panic trickling through the luxurious room.

She had not been aware that the same presence seemed to be an invisible guest at every table, that the same subject kept breaking through the attempts at any other conversation. People sat in a manner, not quite of cringing, but as if they found the room too large and too exposed—a room of glass, blue velvet, aluminum and gentle lighting. They looked as if they had come to this room at the price of countless evasions, to let it help them pretend that theirs was still a civilized existence—but an act of primeval violence had blasted the nature of their world into the open and they were no longer able not to see.

"How could he? How could he?" a woman was demanding with petulant terror. "He had no *right* to do it!"

"It was an accident," said a young man with a staccato voice and an odor of public payroll. "It was a chain of coincidences, as any statistical curve of probabilities can easily prove. It is unpatriotic to spread rumors exaggerating the power of the people's enemies."

"Right and wrong is all very well for academic conversations," said a woman with a schoolroom voice and a barroom mouth, "but how can anybody take his own ideas seriously enough to destroy a fortune when people need it?"

"I don't understand it," an old man was saying with quavering bitterness. "After centuries of efforts to curb man's innate brutality, after centuries of teaching, training and indoctrination with the gentle and the humane!"

A woman's bewildered voice rose uncertainly and trailed off: "I thought we were living in an age of brotherhood . . ."

"I'm scared," a young girl was repeating, "I'm scared . . . oh, I don't know! . . . I'm just scared . . ."

"He couldn't have done it!" . . . "He did!" . . . "But why?" . . . "I refuse to believe it!" . . . "It's not human!" . . . "But why?" . . . "Just a worthless playboy!" . . . "But why?"

The muffled scream of a woman across the room and some half-grasped signal on the edge of Dagny's vision, came simultaneously and made her whirl to look at the city.

The calendar was run by a mechanism locked in a room behind the screen, unrolling the same film year after year, projecting the dates in steady rotation, in changeless rhythm, never moving but on the stroke of midnight. The speed of Dagny's turn gave her time to see a phenomenon as unexpected as if a planet had reversed its orbit in the sky: she saw the words "September 2" moving upward and vanishing past the edge of the screen.

Then, written across the enormous page, stopping time, as a last message to the world and to the world's motor which was New York, she saw the lines of a sharp, intransigent handwriting:

Brother, you asked for it!
Francisco Domingo Carlos Andres Sebastián d'Anconia

She did not know which shock was greater: the sight of the message or the sound of Rearden's laughter—Rearden, standing on his feet, in full sight and hearing of the room behind him, laughing above their moans of panic, laughing in greeting, in salute, in acceptance of the gift he had tried to reject, in release, in triumph, in surrender.

* * *

On the evening of September 7, a copper wire broke in Montana, stopping the motor of a loading crane on a spur track of Taggart Transcontinental, at the rim of the Stanford Copper Mine.

The mine had been working on three shifts, its days and nights blending into a single stretch of struggle to lose no minute, no drop of copper it could squeeze from the shelves of a mountain into the nation's industrial desert. The crane broke down at the task of loading a train; it stopped abruptly and hung still against the evening sky, between a string of empty cars and piles of suddenly immovable ore.

The men of the railroad and of the mine stopped in dazed bewilderment: they found that in all the complexity of their equipment, among the drills, the motors, the derricks, the delicate gauges, the ponderous floodlights beating down into the pits and ridges of a mountain—there was no wire to mend the crane. They stopped, like men on an ocean liner propelled by ten-thousand-horsepower generators, but perishing for lack of a safety pin.

The station agent, a young man with a swift body and a brusque voice, stripped the wiring from the station building and set the crane in motion again—and while the ore went clattering to fill the cars, the light of candles came trembling through the dusk from the windows of the station.

"Minnesota, Eddie," said Dagny grimly, closing the drawer of her special file. "Tell the Minnesota Division to ship half their stock of wire to Montana." "But good God, Dagny!—with the peak of the harvest rush approaching—" "They'll hold through it—I think. We don't dare lose a single supplier of copper."

"But I have!" screamed James Taggart, when she reminded him once more. "I have obtained for you the top priority on copper wire, the first claim, the uppermost ration level, I've given you all the cards, certificates, documents and requisitions—what else do you want?" "The copper wire." "I've done all I could! Nobody can blame me!"

She did not argue. The afternoon newspaper was lying on his desk—and she was staring at an item on the back page: An Emergency State Tax had been passed in California for the relief of the state's unemployed, in the amount of fifty per cent of any local corporation's gross income ahead of other taxes; the California oil companies had gone out of business.

"Don't worry, Mr. Rearden," said an unctuous voice over a long-distance telephone line from Washington, "I just wanted to assure you that you will not have to worry." "About what?" asked Rearden, baffled. "About that temporary bit of confusion in California. We'll straighten it out in no time, it was an act of illegal insurrection, their state government had no right to impose local taxes detrimental to national taxes, we'll negotiate an equitable arrangement immediately—but in the meantime, if you have been disturbed by any unpatriotic rumors about the California oil companies, I just wanted to tell you that Rearden Steel has been placed in the top category of essential need, with first claim upon any oil available anywhere in the nation, very top category, Mr. Rearden—so I just wanted you to know that you won't have to worry about the problem of fuel this winter!"

Rearden hung up the telephone receiver, with a frown of worry, not about the problem of fuel and the end of the California oil fields—

disasters of this kind had become habitual—but about the fact that the Washington planners found it necessary to placate him. This was new; he wondered what it meant. Through the years of his struggle, he had learned that an apparently causeless antagonism was not hard to deal with, but an apparently causeless solicitude was an ugly danger. The same wonder struck him again, when, walking down an alley between the mill structures, he caught sight of a slouching figure whose posture combined an air of insolence with an air of expecting to be swatted: it was his brother Philip.

Ever since he had moved to Philadelphia, Rearden had not visited his former home and had not heard a word from his family, whose bills he went on paying. Then, inexplicably, twice in the last few weeks, he had caught Philip wandering through the mills for no apparent reason. He had been unable to tell whether Philip was sneaking to avoid him or waiting to catch his attention; it had looked like both. He had been unable to discover any clue to Philip's purpose, only some incomprehensible solicitude, of a kind Philip had never displayed before.

The first time, in answer to his startled "What are you doing here?" —Philip had said vaguely, "Well, I know that you don't like me to come to your office." "What do you want?" "Oh, nothing . . . but . . . well, Mother is worried about you." "Mother can call me any time she wishes." Philip had not answered, but had proceeded to question him, in an unconvincingly casual manner, about his work, his health, his business; the questions had kept hitting oddly beside the point, not questions about business, but more about his, Rearden's, feelings toward business. Rearden had cut him short and waved him away, but had been left with the small, nagging sense of an incident that remained inexplicable.

The second time, Philip had said, as sole explanation, "We just want to know how you feel." "Who's we?" "Why . . . Mother and I. These are difficult times and . . . well, Mother wants to know how you feel about it all." "Tell her that I don't." The words had seemed to hit Philip in some peculiar manner, almost as if this were the one answer he dreaded. "Get out of here," Rearden had ordered wearily, "and the next time you want to see me, make an appointment and come to my office. But don't come unless you have something to say. This is not a place where one discusses feelings, mine or anybody else's."

Philip had not called for an appointment—but now there he was again, slouching among the giant shapes of the furnaces, with an air of guilt and snobbishness together, as if he were both snooping and slumming.

"But I do have something to say! I do!" he cried hastily, in answer to the angry frown on Rearden's face.

"Why didn't you come to my office?"

"You don't want me in your office."

"I don't want you here, either."

"But I'm only . . . I'm only trying to be considerate and not to take your time when you're so busy and . . . you *are* very busy, aren't you?"

"And?"

"And . . . well, I just wanted to catch you in a spare moment . . . to talk to you."

"About what?"

"I . . . Well, I need a job."

He said it belligerently and drew back a little. Rearden stood looking at him blankly.

"Henry, I want a job. I mean, here, at the mills. I want you to give me something to do. I need a job, I need to earn my living, I'm tired of alms." He was groping for something to say, his voice both offended and pleading, as if the necessity to justify the plea were an unfair imposition upon him. "I want a livelihood of my own, I'm not asking you for charity, I'm asking you to give me a chance!"

"This is a factory, Philip, not a gambling joint."

"Uh?"

"We don't take chances or give them."

"I'm asking you to give me a *job!*"

"Why should I?"

"Because I need it!"

Rearden pointed to the red spurts of flame shooting from the black shape of a furnace, shooting safely into space four hundred feet of steel-clay-and-steam-embodied thought above them. "I needed that furnace, Philip. It wasn't my need that gave it to me."

Philip's face assumed a look of not having heard. "You're not officially supposed to hire anybody, but that's just a technicality, if you'll put me on, my friends will okay it without any trouble and—" Something about Rearden's eyes made him stop abruptly, then ask in an angrily impatient voice, "Well, what's the matter? What have I said that's wrong?"

"What you haven't said."

"I beg your pardon?"

"What you're squirming to leave unmentioned."

"What?"

"That you'd be of no use to me whatever."

"Is that what you—" Philip started with automatic righteousness, but stopped and did not finish.

"Yes," said Rearden, smiling, *"that's* what I think of first."

Philip's eyes oozed away; when he spoke, his voice sounded as if it were darting about at random, picking stray sentences: "Everybody is entitled to a livelihood . . . How am I going to get it, if nobody gives me my chance?"

"How did I get mine?"

"I wasn't born owning a steel plant."

"Was I?"

"I can do anything you can—if you'll teach me."

"Who taught me?"

"Why do you keep saying that? I'm not talking about you!"

"I am."

In a moment, Philip muttered, "What do *you* have to worry about? It's not *your* livelihood that's in question!"

Rearden pointed to the figures of men in the steaming rays of the furnace. "Can you do what they're doing?"

"I don't see what you're—"

"What will happen if I put you there and you ruin a heat of steel for me?"

"What's more important, that your damn steel gets poured or that I eat?"

"How do you propose to eat if the steel doesn't get poured?"

Philip's face assumed a look of reproach. "I'm not in a position to argue with you right now, since you hold the upper hand."

"Then don't argue."

"Uh?"

"Keep your mouth shut and get out of here."

"But I meant—" He stopped.

Rearden chuckled. "You meant that it's I who should keep my mouth shut, because I hold the upper hand, and should give in to you, because you hold no hand at all?"

"That's a peculiarly crude way of stating a moral principle."

"But that's what your moral principle amounts to, doesn't it?"

"You can't discuss morality in materialistic terms."

"We're discussing a job in a steel plant—and, boy! is that a materialistic place!"

Philip's body drew a shade tighter together and his eyes became a shade more glazed, as if in fear of the place around him, in resentment of its sight, in an effort not to concede its reality. He said, in the soft, stubborn whine of a voodoo incantation, "It's a moral imperative, universally conceded in our day and age, that every man is entitled to a job." His voice rose: "I'm entitled to it!"

"You are? Go on, then, collect your claim."

"Uh?"

"Collect your job. Pick it off the bush where you think it grows."

"I mean—"

"You mean that it doesn't? You mean that you need it, but can't create it? You mean that you're entitled to a job which *I* must create for you?"

"Yes!"

"And if I don't?"

The silence went stretching through second after second. "I don't understand you," said Philip; his voice had the angry bewilderment of a

man who recites the formulas of a well-tested role, but keeps getting the
wrong cues in answer. "I don't understand why one can't talk to you any
more. I don't understand what sort of theory you're propounding and—"

"Oh yes, you do."

As if refusing to believe that the formulas could fail, Philip burst out
with: "Since when did *you* take to abstract philosophy? You're only a
businessman, you're not qualified to deal with questions of principle, you
ought to leave it to the experts who have conceded for centuries—"

"Cut it, Philip. What's the gimmick?"

"Gimmick?"

"Why the sudden ambition?"

"Well, at a time like this . . ."

"Like what?"

"Well, every man has the right to have some means of support and
. . . and not be left to be tossed aside . . . When things are so uncertain, a man's got to have some security . . . some foothold . . . I
mean, at a time like this, if anything happened to you, I'd have no—"

"What do you expect to happen to me?"

"Oh, I don't! I don't!" The cry was oddly, incomprehensibly genuine.
"I don't expect anything to happen! . . . Do you?"

"Such as what?"

"How do I know? . . . But I've got nothing except the pittance you
give me and . . . and you might change your mind any time."

"I might."

"And I haven't any hold on you at all."

"Why did it take you that many years to realize it and start worrying?
Why now?"

"Because . . . because you've changed. You . . . you used to have
a sense of duty and moral responsibility, but . . . you're losing it.
You're losing it, aren't you?"

Rearden stood studying him silently; there was something peculiar in
Philip's manner of sliding toward questions, as if his words were accidental, but the too casual, the faintly insistent questions were the key to his
purpose.

"Well, I'll be glad to take the burden off your shoulders, if I'm a burden to you!" Philip snapped suddenly. "Just give me a job, and your
conscience won't have to bother you about me any longer!"

"It doesn't."

"That's what I mean! You don't care. You don't care what becomes of
any of us, do you?"

"Of whom?"

"Why . . . Mother and me and . . . and mankind in general. But
I'm not going to appeal to your better self. I know that you're ready to
ditch me at a moment's notice, so—"

"You're lying, Philip. That's not what you're worried about. If it were,
you'd be angling for a chunk of cash, not for a job, not—"

"No! I want a job!" The cry was immediate and almost frantic. "Don't try to buy me off with cash! I want a job!"

"Pull yourself together, you poor louse. Do you hear what you're saying?"

Philip spit out his answer with impotent hatred: "You can't talk to me that way!"

"Can *you?*"

"I only—"

"To buy you off? Why should I try to buy you off—instead of kicking you out, as I should have, years ago?"

"Well, after all, I'm your brother!"

"What is that supposed to mean?"

"One's supposed to have some sort of feeling for one's brother."

"Do *you?*"

Philip's mouth swelled petulantly; he did not answer; he waited; Rearden let him wait. Philip muttered, "You're supposed . . . at least . . . to have some consideration for my feelings . . . but you haven't."

"Have *you* for mine?"

"Yours? Your *feelings?*" It was not malice in Philip's voice, but worse: it was a genuine, indignant astonishment. "You haven't any feelings. You've never felt anything at all. You've never *suffered!*"

It was as if a sum of years hit Rearden in the face, by means of a sensation and a sight: the exact sensation of what he had felt in the cab of the first train's engine on the John Galt Line—and the sight of Philip's eyes, the pale, half-liquid eyes presenting the uttermost of human degradation: an uncontested pain, and, with the obscene insolence of a skeleton toward a living being, demanding that this pain be held as the highest of values. You've never suffered, the eyes were saying to him accusingly—while he was seeing the night in his office when his ore mines were taken away from him—the moment when he had signed the Gift Certificate surrendering Rearden Metal—the month of days inside a plane that searched for the remains of Dagny's body. You've never suffered, the eyes were saying with self-righteous scorn—while he remembered the sensation of proud chastity with which he had fought through those moments, refusing to surrender to pain, a sensation made of his love, of his loyalty, of his knowledge that joy is the goal of existence, and joy is not to be stumbled upon, but to be achieved, and the act of treason is to let its vision drown in the swamp of the moment's torture. You've never suffered, the dead stare of the eyes was saying, you've never felt anything, because only to suffer is to feel—there's no such thing as joy, there's only pain and the absence of pain, only pain and the zero, when one feels nothing—I suffer, I'm twisted by suffering, I'm made of undiluted suffering, that's my purity, that's my virtue—and yours, you the untwisted one, you the uncomplaining, yours is to relieve me of my pain—cut your unsuffering body to patch up mine, cut your unfeeling soul to stop mine from feeling—and we'll achieve the ultimate ideal, the triumph over life, the zero! He was seeing the nature of those who, for centuries, had not recoiled from the preachers of annihilation—he was seeing the nature of the enemies he had been fighting all his life.

"Philip," he said, "get out of here." His voice was like a ray of sunlight in a morgue, it was the plain, dry, daily voice of a businessman, the sound of health, addressed to an enemy one could not honor by anger, nor even by horror. "And don't ever try to enter these mills again, because there will be orders at every gate to throw you out, if you try it."

"Well, after all," said Philip, in the angry and cautious tone of a tentative threat, "I could have my friends assign me to a job here and *compel* you to accept it!"

Rearden had started to go, but he stopped and turned to look at his brother.

Philip's moment of grasping a sudden revelation was not accomplished by means of thought, but by means of that dark sensation which was his only mode of consciousness: he felt a sensation of terror, squeezing his throat, shivering down into his stomach—he was seeing the spread of the mills, with the roving streamers of flame, with the ladles of molten metal sailing through space on delicate cables, with open pits the color of glowing coal, with cranes coming at his head, pounding past, holding tons of steel by the invisible power of magnets—and he knew that he was afraid of this place, afraid to the death, that he dared not move without the protection and guidance of the man before him—then he looked at the tall, straight figure standing casually still, the figure with the unflinching eyes whose sight had cut through rock and flame to build this place—and then he knew how easily the man he was proposing to compel could let a single bucket of metal tilt over a second ahead of its time or let a single crane drop its load a foot short of its goal, and there would be nothing left of him, of Philip the claimant—and his only protection lay in the fact that his mind would think of such actions, but the mind of Hank Rearden would not.

"But we'd better keep it on a friendly basis," said Philip.

"You'd better," said Rearden and walked away.

Men who worship pain—thought Rearden, staring at the image of the enemies he had never been able to understand—they're men who worship pain. It seemed monstrous, yet peculiarly devoid of importance. He felt nothing. It was like trying to summon emotion toward inanimate objects, toward refuse sliding down a mountainside to crush him. One could flee from the slide or build retaining walls against it or be crushed—but one could not grant any anger, indignation or moral concern to the senseless motions of the un-living; no, worse, he thought—the anti-living.

The same sense of detached unconcern remained with him while he sat in a Philadelphia courtroom and watched men perform the motions which were to grant him his divorce. He watched them utter mechanical generalities, recite vague phrases of fraudulent evidence, play an intricate game of stretching words to convey no facts and no meaning. He had paid them to do it—he whom the law permitted no other way to gain his freedom, no right to state the facts and plead the truth—the law which delivered his fate, not to objective rules objectively defined, but to the arbitrary mercy of a judge with a wizened face and a look of empty cunning.

Lillian was not present in the courtroom; her attorney made gestures once in a while, with the energy of letting water run through his fingers. They all knew the verdict in advance and they knew its reason; no other reason had existed for years, where no standards, save whim, had existed. They seemed to regard it as their rightful prerogative; they acted as if the purpose of the procedure were not to try a case, but to give them jobs, as if their jobs were to recite the appropriate formulas with no responsibility to know what the formulas accomplished, as if a courtroom were the one place where questions of right and wrong were irrelevant and they, the men in charge of dispensing justice, were safely wise enough to know that no justice existed. They acted like savages performing a ritual devised to set them free of objective reality.

But the ten years of his marriage had been real, he thought—and *these* were the men who assumed the power to dispose of it, to decide whether he would have a chance of contentment on earth or be condemned to torture for the rest of his lifetime. He remembered the austerely pitiless respect he had felt for his contract of marriage, for all his contracts and all his legal obligations—and he saw what sort of legality his scrupulous observance was expected to serve.

He noticed that the puppets of the courtroom had started by glancing at him in the sly, wise manner of fellow conspirators sharing a common guilt, mutually safe from moral condemnation. Then, when they observed that he was the only man in the room who looked steadily straight at anyone's face, he saw resentment growing in their eyes. Incredulously, he realized what it was that had been expected of him: he, the victim, chained, bound, gagged and left with no recourse save to bribery, had been expected to believe that the farce he had purchased was a process of law, that the edicts enslaving him had moral validity, that he was guilty of corrupting the integrity of the guardians of justice, and that the blame was his, not theirs. It was like blaming the victim of a holdup for corrupting the integrity of the thug. And yet—he thought—through all the generations of political extortion, it was not the looting bureaucrats who had taken the blame, but the chained industrialists, not the men who peddled legal favors, but the men who were forced to buy them; and through all those generations of crusades against corruption, the remedy had always been, not the liberating of the victims, but the granting of wider powers for extortion to the extortionists. The only guilt of the victims, he thought, had been that they accepted it as guilt.

When he walked out of the courtroom into the chilly drizzle of a gray afternoon, he felt as if he had been divorced, not only from Lillian, but from the whole of the human society that supported the procedure he had witnessed.

The face of his attorney, an elderly man of the old-fashioned school, wore an expression that made it look as if he longed to take a bath. "Say, Hank," he asked as sole comment, "is there something the looters are anxious to get from you right now?" "Not that I know of. Why?" "The thing went too smoothly. There were a few points at which I expected pressure and hints for some extras, but the boys sailed past and took no advantage of it. Looks to me as if orders had come from on high to treat you gently and let you have your way. Are they planning something new against your mills?" "Not that I know of," said Rearden —and was astonished to hear in his mind: Not that I care.

It was on the same afternoon, at the mills, that he saw the Wet Nurse hurrying toward him—a gangling, coltish figure with a peculiar mixture of brusqueness, awkwardness and decisiveness.

"Mr. Rearden, I would like to speak to you." His voice was diffident, yet oddly firm.

"Go ahead."

"There's something I want to ask you." The boy's face was solemn and taut. "I want you to know that I know you should refuse me, but I want to ask it just the same . . . and . . . and if it's presumptuous, then just tell me to go to hell."

"Okay. Try it."

"Mr. Rearden, would you give me a job?" It was the effort to sound normal that betrayed the days of struggle behind the question. "I want to quit what I'm doing and go to work. I mean, real work—in steelmaking, like I thought I'd started to, once. I want to earn my keep. I'm tired of being a bedbug."

Rearden could not resist smiling and reminding him, in the tone of a quotation, "Now why use such words, Non-Absolute? If we don't use ugly words, we won't have any ugliness and—" But he saw the desperate earnestness of the boy's face and stopped, his smile vanishing.

"I mean it, Mr. Rearden. And I know what the word means and it's the right word. I'm tired of being paid, with your money, to do nothing except make it impossible for you to make any money at all. I know that anyone who works today is only a sucker for bastards like me, but . . . well, God damn it, I'd rather be a sucker, if that's all there's left to be!" His voice had risen to a cry. "I beg your pardon, Mr. Rearden," he said stiffly, looking away. In a moment, he went on in his woodenly unemotional tone. "I want to get out of the Deputy-Director-of-Distribution racket. I don't know that I'd be of much use to you, I've got a college diploma in metallurgy, but that's not worth the paper it's printed on. But I think I've learned a little about the work in the two years I've been here—and if you could use me at all, as sweeper or scrap man or whatever you'd trust me with, I'd tell them where to put the deputy directorship and I'd go to work for you tomorrow, next week, this minute or whenever you say." He avoided looking at Rearden, not in a manner of evasion, but as if he had no right to do it.

"Why were you afraid to ask me?" said Rearden gently.

The boy glanced at him with indignant astonishment, as if the answer were self-evident. "Because after the way I started here and the way I acted and what I'm deputy of, if I come asking you for favors, you ought to kick me in the teeth!"

"You *have* learned a great deal in the two years you've been here."

"No, I—" He glanced at Rearden, understood, looked away and said woodenly, "Yeah . . . if that's what you mean."

"Listen, kid, I'd give you a job this minute and I'd trust you with more than a sweeper's job, if it were up to me. But have you forgotten the Unification Board? I'm not allowed to hire you and you're not allowed to quit. Sure, men are quitting all the time, and we're hiring others under phony names and fancy papers proving that they've worked here for years. You know it, and thanks for keeping your mouth shut. But do you think that if I hired you that way, your friends in Washington would miss it?"

The boy shook his head slowly.

"Do you think that if you quit their service to become a sweeper, they wouldn't understand your reason?"

The boy nodded.

"Would they let you go?"

The boy shook his head. After a moment, he said in a tone of forlorn astonishment, "I hadn't thought of that at all, Mr. Rearden. I forgot them. I kept thinking of whether you'd want me or not and that the only thing that counted was *your* decision."

"I know."

"And . . . it *is* the only thing that counts, in fact."

"Yes, Non-Absolute, *in fact.*"

The boy's mouth jerked suddenly into the brief, mirthless twist of a smile. "I guess I'm tied worse than any sucker . . ."

"Yes. There's nothing you can do now, except apply to the Unification Board for permission to change your job. I'll support your application, if you want to try—only I don't think they'll grant it. I don't think they'll let you work for me."

"No. They won't."

"If you maneuver enough and lie enough, they might permit you to transfer to a private job—with some other steel company."

"No! I don't want to go anywhere else! I don't want to leave this place!" He stood looking off at the invisible vapor of rain over the flame of the furnaces. After a while, he said quietly, "I'd better stay put, I guess. I'd better go on being a deputy looter. Besides, if I left, God only knows what sort of bastard they'd saddle you with in my place!" He turned. "They're up to something, Mr. Rearden. I don't know what it is, but they're getting ready to spring something on you."

"What?"

"I don't know. But they've been watching every opening here, in the last few weeks, every desertion, and slipping their own gang in. A queer sort of gang, too—real goons, some of them, that I'd swear never stepped inside a steel plant before. I've had orders to get as many of 'our boys' in as possible. They wouldn't tell me why. I don't know what it is they're planning. I've tried to pump them, but they're acting pretty cagey about it. I don't think they trust me any more. I'm losing the right touch, I guess. All I know is they're getting set to pull something here."

"Thanks for warning me."

"I'll try to get the dope on it. I'll try my damndest to get it in time." He turned brusquely and started off, but stopped. "Mr. Rearden, if it were up to you, you would have hired me?"

"I would have, gladly and at once."

"Thank you, Mr. Rearden," he said, his voice solemn and low, then walked away.

Rearden stood looking after him, seeing, with a tearing smile of pity, what it was that the ex-relativist, the ex-pragmatist, the ex-amoralist was carrying away with him for consolation.

* * *

On the afternoon of September 11, a copper wire broke in Minnesota, stopping the belts of a grain elevator at a small country station of Taggart Transcontinental.

A flood of wheat was moving down the highways, the roads, the abandoned trails of the countryside, emptying thousands of acres of farmland upon the fragile dams of the railroad's stations. It was moving day and night, the first trickles growing into streams, then rivers, then torrents—moving on palsied trucks with coughing, tubercular motors—on wagons pulled by the rusty skeletons of starving horses—on carts pulled by oxen—on the nerves and last energy of men who had lived through two years of disaster for the triumphant reward of this autumn's giant harvest, men who had patched their trucks and carts with wire, blankets, ropes and sleepless nights, to make them hold together for this one more journey, to carry the grain and collapse at destination, but to give their owners a chance at survival.

Every year, at this season, another movement had gone clicking across the country, drawing freight cars from all corners of the continent to the Minnesota Division of Taggart Transcontinental, the beat of train wheels preceding the creak of the wagons, like an advance echo rigorously planned, ordered and timed to meet the flood. The Minnesota Division drowsed through the year, to come to violent life for the weeks of the harvest; fourteen thousand freight cars had jammed its yards each year; fifteen thousand were expected this time. The first of the wheat trains had started to channel the flood into the hungry flour mills, then bakeries, then stomachs of the nation—but every train, car and storage elevator counted, and there was no minute or inch of space to spare.

Eddie Willers watched Dagny's face as she went through the cards of her emergency file; he could tell the content of the cards by her expression. "The Terminal," she said quietly, closing the file. "Phone the Terminal downstairs and have them ship half their stock of wire to Minnesota." Eddie said nothing and obeyed.

He said nothing, the morning when he put on her desk a telegram from the Taggart office in Washington, informing them of the directive which, due to the critical shortage of copper, ordered government agents to seize all copper mines and operate them as a public utility. "Well," she said, dropping the telegram into the wastebasket, "that's the end of Montana."

She said nothing when James Taggart announced to her that he was issuing an order to discontinue all dining cars on Taggart trains. "We can't afford it any longer," he explained, "we've always lost money on those goddamn diners, and when there's no food to get, when restaurants are closing because they can't grab hold of a pound of horse meat anywhere, how can railroads be expected to do it? Why in hell should we have to feed the passengers, anyway? They're lucky if we give them transportation, they'd travel in cattle cars if necessary, let 'em pack their own box lunches, what do we care?—they've got no other trains to take!"

The telephone on her desk had become, not a voice of business, but an alarm siren for the desperate appeals of disaster. "Miss Taggart, we have no copper wire!" "Nails, Miss Taggart, plain nails, could you tell somebody to send us a keg of nails?" "Can you find any paint, Miss Taggart, any sort of waterproof paint anywhere?"

But thirty million dollars of subsidy money from Washington had been plowed into Project Soybean—an enormous acreage in Louisiana, where a harvest of soybeans was ripening, as advocated and organized by Emma Chalmers, for the purpose of reconditioning the dietary habits of the nation. Emma Chalmers, better known as Kip's Ma, was an old sociologist who had hung about Washington for years, as other women of her age and type hang about barrooms. For some reason which nobody could define, the death of her son in the tunnel catastrophe had given her in Washington an aura of martyrdom, heightened by her recent conversion to Buddhism. "The soybean is a much more sturdy, nutritious and economical plant than all the extravagant foods which our wasteful, self-indulgent diet has conditioned us to expect," Kip's Ma had said over the radio; her voice always sounded as if it were falling in drops, not of water, but of mayonnaise.

"Soybeans make an excellent substitute for bread, meat, cereals and coffee—and if all of us were compelled to adopt soybeans as our staple diet, it would solve the national food crisis and make it possible to feed more people. The greatest food for the greatest number—that's my slogan. At a time of desperate public need, it's our duty to sacrifice our luxurious tastes and eat our way back to prosperity by adapting ourselves to the simple, wholesome foodstuff on which the peoples of the Orient have so nobly subsisted for centuries. There's a great deal that we could learn from the peoples of the Orient."

"Copper tubing, Miss Taggart, could you get some copper tubing for us somewhere?" the voices were pleading over her telephone. "Rail spikes, Miss Taggart!" "Screwdrivers, Miss Taggart!" "Light bulbs, Miss Taggart, there's no electric light bulbs to be had anywhere within two hundred miles of us!"

But five million dollars was being spent by the office of Morale Conditioning on the People's Opera Company, which traveled through the country, giving free performances to people who, on one meal a day, could not afford the energy to walk to the opera house. Seven million dollars had been granted to a psychologist in charge of a project to solve the world crisis by research into the nature of brother-love. Ten million dollars had been granted to the manufacturer of a new electronic cigarette lighter—but there were no cigarettes in the shops of the country. There were flashlights on the market, but no batteries; there were radios, but no tubes; there were cameras, but no film. The production of airplanes had been declared "temporarily suspended." Air travel for private purposes had been forbidden, and reserved exclusively for missions of "public need." An industrialist traveling to save his factory was not considered as publicly needed and could not get aboard a plane; an official traveling to collect taxes was and could.

"People are stealing nuts and bolts out of rail plates, Miss Taggart, stealing them at night, and our stock is running out, the division storehouse is bare, what are we to do, Miss Taggart?"

But a super-color-four-foot-screen television set was being erected for tourists in a People's Park in Washington—and a super-cyclotron for the study of cosmic rays was being erected at the State Science Institute, to be completed in ten years.

"The trouble with our modern world," Dr. Robert Stadler said over the radio, at the ceremonies launching the construction of the cyclotron, "is that too many people think too much. It is the cause of all our current fears and doubts. An enlightened citizenry should abandon the superstitious worship of logic and the outmoded reliance on reason. Just as laymen leave medicine to doctors and electronics to engineers, so people who are not qualified to think should leave all thinking to the experts and have faith in the experts' higher authority. Only experts are able to understand the discoveries of modern science, which have proved that thought is an illusion and that the mind is a myth."

"This age of misery is God's punishment to man for the sin of relying on his mind!" snarled the triumphant voices of mystics of every sect and sort, on street corners, in rain-soaked tents, in crumbling temples. "This world ordeal is the result of man's attempt to live by reason! *This* is where thinking, logic and science have brought you! And there's to be no salvation until men realize that their mortal mind is impotent to solve their problems and go back to faith, faith in God, faith in a higher authority!"

And confronting her daily there was the final product of it all, the heir and collector—Cuffy Meigs, the man impervious to thought. Cuffy Meigs strode through the offices of Taggart Transcontinental, wearing a semi-military tunic and slapping a shiny leather briefcase against his shiny leather leggings. He carried an automatic pistol in one pocket and a rabbit's foot in the other.

Cuffy Meigs tried to avoid her; his manner was part scorn, as if he considered her an impractical idealist, part superstitious awe, as if she possessed some incomprehensible power with which he preferred not to tangle. He acted as if her presence did not belong to his view of a railroad, yet as if hers were the one presence he dared not challenge. There was a touch of impatient resentment in his manner toward Jim, as if it were Jim's duty to deal with her and to protect him; just as he expected Jim to keep the railroad in running order and leave him free for activities of more practical a nature, so he expected Jim to keep her in line, as part of the equipment.

Beyond the window of her office, like a patch of adhesive plaster stuck over a wound on the sky, the page of the calendar hung blank in the distance. The calendar had never been repaired since the night of Francisco's farewell. The officials who had rushed to the tower, that night, had knocked the calendar's motor to a stop, while tearing the film out of the projector. They had found the small square of Francisco's message, pasted into the strip of numbered days, but who had pasted it there, who had entered the locked room and when and how, was never discovered by the three commissions still investigating the case. Pending the outcome of their efforts, the page hung blank and still above the city.

It was blank on the afternoon of September 14, when the telephone rang in her office. "A man from Minnesota," said the voice of her secretary.

She had told her secretary that she would accept all calls of this kind. They were the appeals for help and her only source of information. At a time when the voices of railroad officials uttered nothing but sounds designed to avoid communication, the voices of nameless men were her last link to the system, the last sparks of reason and tortured honesty flashing briefly through the miles of Taggart track.

"Miss Taggart, it is not my place to call you, but nobody else will." said the voice that came on the wire, this time; the voice sounded young and too calm. "In another day or two, a disaster's going to happen here the like of which they've never seen, and they won't be able to hide it any longer, only it will be too late by then, and maybe it's too late already."

"What is it? Who are you?"

"One of your employees of the Minnesota Division, Miss Taggart. In another day or two, the trains will stop running out of here—and you know what that means, at the height of the harvest. At the height of the biggest harvest we've ever had. They'll stop, because we have no cars. The harvest freight cars have not been sent to us this year."

"What did you say?" She felt as if minutes went by between the words of the unnatural voice that did not sound like her own.

"The cars have not been sent. Fifteen thousand should have been here by now. As far as I could learn, about eight thousand cars is all we got. I've been calling Division Headquarters for a week. They've been telling me not to worry. Last time, they told me to mind my own damn business. Every shed, silo, elevator, warehouse, garage and dance hall along the track is filled with wheat. At the Sherman elevators, there's a line of farmers' trucks and wagons two miles long, waiting on the road. At Lakewood Station, the square is packed solid and has been for three nights. They keep telling us it's only temporary, the cars are coming and we'll catch up. We won't. There aren't any cars coming. I've called everyone I could. I know, by the way they answer. They know, and not one of them wants to admit it. They're scared, scared to move or speak or ask or answer. All they're thinking of is who will be blamed when that harvest rots here around the stations—and not of who's going to move it. Maybe nobody can, now. Maybe there's nothing you can do about it, either. But I thought you're the only person left who'd want to know and that somebody had to tell you."

"I . . ." She made an effort to breathe. "I see . . . Who are you?"

"The name wouldn't matter. When I hang up, I will have become a deserter. I don't want to stay here to see it when it happens. I don't want any part of it any more. Good luck to you, Miss Taggart."

She heard the click. "Thank you," she said over a dead wire.

The next time she noticed the office around her and permitted herself to feel, it was noon of the following day. She stood in the middle of the office, running stiff, spread fingers through a strand of hair, brushing it back off her face—and for an instant, she wondered where she was and what was the unbelievable thing that had happened in the last twenty hours. What she felt was horror, and she knew that she had felt it from the first words of the man on the wire, only there had been no time to know it.

There was not much that remained in her mind of the last twenty hours, only disconnected bits, held together by the single constant that had made them possible—by the soft, loose faces of men who fought to hide from themselves that they knew the answers to the questions she asked.

From the moment when she was told that the manager of the Car Service Department had been out of town for a week and had left no address where one could reach him—she knew that the report of the man from Minnesota was true. Then came the faces of the assistants in the Car Service Department, who would neither confirm the report nor deny it, but kept showing her papers, orders, forms, file cards that bore words in the English language, but no connection to intelligible facts. "Were the freight cars sent to Minnesota?" "Form 357W is filled out in every particular, as required by the office of the Co-ordinator in conformance with the instructions of the comptroller and by Directive 11-493." "Were the freight cars sent to Minnesota?" "The entries for the months of August and September have been processed by—" "Were the freight cars sent to Minnesota?" "My files indicate the locations of freight cars by state, date, classification and—" "Do you know whether the cars were sent to Minnesota?" "As to the interstate motion of freight cars, I would have to refer you to the files of Mr. Benson and of—"

There was nothing to learn from the files. There were careful entries, each conveying four possible meanings, with references which led to references which led to a final reference which was missing from the files. It did not take her long to discover that the cars had not been sent to Minnesota and that the order had come from Cuffy Meigs—but who had carried it out, who had tangled the trail, what steps had been taken by what compliant men to preserve the appearance of a safely normal operation, without a single cry of protest to arouse some braver man's attention, who had falsified the reports, and where the cars had gone—seemed, at first, impossible to learn.

Through the hours of that night—while a small, desperate crew under the command of Eddie Willers kept calling every division point, every yard, depot, station, spur and siding of Taggart Transcontinental for every freight car in sight or reach, ordering them to unload, drop, dump, scuttle anything and proceed to Minnesota at once, while they kept calling the yards, stations and presidents of every railroad still half in existence anywhere across the map, begging for cars for Minnesota—she went through the task of tracing from face to coward's face the destination of the freight cars that had vanished.

She went from railroad executives to wealthy shippers to Washington officials and back to the railroad—by cab, by phone, by wire—pursuing a trail of half-uttered hints. The trail approached its end when she heard the pinch-lipped voice of a public relations woman in a Washington office, saying resentfully over the telephone wire, "Well, after all, it is a matter of opinion whether wheat is essential to a nation's welfare—there are those of more progressive views who feel that the soybean is, perhaps, of far greater value"—and then, by noon, she stood in the middle of her office, knowing that the freight cars intended for the wheat of Minnesota had been sent, instead, to carry the soybeans from the Louisiana swamps of Kip's Ma's project.

The first story of the Minnesota disaster appeared in the newspapers three days later. It reported that the farmers who had waited in the streets of Lakewood for six days, with no place to store their wheat and no trains to carry it, had demolished the local courthouse, the mayor's home and the railroad station. Then the stories vanished abruptly and the newspapers kept silent, then began to print admonitions urging people not to believe unpatriotic rumors.

While the flour mills and grain markets of the country were screaming over the phones and the telegraph wires, sending pleas to New York and delegations to Washington, while strings of freight cars from random corners of the continent were crawling like rusty caterpillars across the map in the direction of Minnesota—the wheat and hope of the country were waiting to perish along an empty track, under the unchanging green lights of signals that called for motion to trains that were not there.

At the communication desks of Taggart Transcontinental, a small crew kept calling for freight cars, repeating, like the crew of a sinking ship, an S.O.S. that remained unheard. There were freight cars held loaded for months in the yards of the companies owned by the friends of pull-peddlers, who ignored the frantic demands to unload the cars and release them. "You can tell that railroad to—" followed by untransmissible words, was the message of the Smather Brothers of Arizona in answer to the S.O.S. of New York.

In Minnesota, they were seizing cars from every siding, from the Mesabi Range, from the ore mines of Paul Larkin where the cars had stood waiting for a dribble of iron. They were pouring wheat into ore cars, into coal cars, into boarded stock cars that went spilling thin gold trickles along the track as they clattered off. They were pouring wheat into passenger coaches, over seats, racks and fixtures, to send it off, to get it moving, even if it went moving into track-side ditches in the sudden crash of breaking springs, in the explosions set off by burning journal boxes.

They fought for movement, for movement with no thought of destination, for movement as such, like a paralytic under a stroke, struggling in wild, stiff, incredulous jerks against the realization that movement was suddenly impossible. There were no other railroads: James Taggart had killed them; there were no boats on the Lakes: Paul Larkin had destroyed them. There was only the single line of rail and a net of neglected highways.

The trucks and wagons of waiting farmers started trickling blindly down the roads, with no maps, no gas, no feed for horses—moving south, south toward the vision of flour mills awaiting them somewhere, with no knowledge of the distances ahead, but with the knowledge of death behind them—moving, to collapse on the roads, in the gullies, in the breaks of rotted bridges. One farmer was found, half a mile south of the wreck of his truck, lying dead in a ditch, face down, still clutching a sack of wheat on his shoulders. Then rain clouds burst over the prairies of Minnesota; the rain went eating the wheat into rot at the waiting railroad stations; it went hammering the piles spilled along the roads, washing gold kernels into the soil.

The men in Washington were last to be reached by the panic. They watched, not the news from Minnesota, but the precarious balance of their friendships and commitments; they weighed, not the fate of the harvest, but the unknowable result of unpredictable emotions in unthinking men of unlimited power. They waited, they evaded all pleas, they declared, "Oh, ridiculous, there's nothing to worry about! Those Taggart people have always moved that wheat on schedule, they'll find some way to move it!"

Then, when the State Chief Executive of Minnesota sent a request to Washington for the assistance of the Army against the riots he was unable to control—three directives burst forth within two hours, stopping all trains in the country, commandeering all cars to speed to Minnesota. An order signed by Wesley Mouch demanded the immediate release of the freight cars held in the service of Kip's Ma. But by that time, it was too late. Ma's freight cars were in California, where the soybeans had been sent to a progressive concern made up of sociologists preaching the cult of Oriental austerity, and of businessmen formerly in the numbers racket.

In Minnesota, farmers were setting fire to their own farms, they were demolishing grain elevators and the homes of county officials, they were fighting along the track of the railroad, some to tear it up, some to defend it with their lives—and, with no goal to reach save violence, they were dying in the streets of gutted towns and in the silent gullies of a roadless night.

Then there was only the acrid stench of grain rotting in half-smouldering piles—a few columns of smoke rising from the plains, standing still in the air over blackened ruins—and, in an office in Pennsylvania, Hank Rearden sitting at his desk, looking at a list of men who had gone bankrupt: they were the manufacturers of farm equipment, who could not be paid and would not be able to pay him.

The harvest of soybeans did not reach the markets of the country: it had been reaped prematurely, it was moldy and unfit for consumption.

* * *

On the night of October 15, a copper wire broke in New York City, in an underground control tower of the Taggart Terminal, extinguishing the lights of the signals.

It was only the breach of one wire, but it produced a short circuit in the interlocking traffic system, and the signals of motion or danger disappeared from the panels of the control towers and from among the strands of rail. The red and green lenses remained red and green, not with the living radiance of sight, but with the dead stare of glass eyes. On the edge of the city, a cluster of trains gathered at the entrance to the Terminal tunnels and grew through the minutes of stillness, like blood dammed by a clot inside a vein, unable to rush into the chambers of the heart.

Dagny, that night, was sitting at a table in a private dining room of the Wayne-Falkland. The wax of candles was dripping down on the white camellias and laurel leaves at the base of the silver candlesticks, arithmetical calculations were penciled on the damask linen tablecloth, and a cigar butt was swimming in a finger bowl. The six men in formal dinner jackets, facing her about the table, were Wesley Mouch, Eugene Lawson, Dr. Floyd Ferris, Clem Weatherby, James Taggart and Cuffy Meigs.

"Why?" she had asked, when Jim had told her that she had to attend that dinner. "Well . . . because our Board of Directors is to meet next week." "And?" "You're interested in what's going to be decided about our Minnesota Line, aren't you?" "Is that going to be decided at the Board meeting?" "Well, not exactly." "Is it going to be decided at this dinner?" "Not exactly, but . . . oh, why do you always have to be so definite? Nothing's ever definite. Besides, they insisted that they wanted you to come." "Why?" "Isn't that sufficient?"

She did not ask why those men chose to make all their crucial decisions at parties of this kind; she knew that they did. She knew that behind the clattering, lumbering pretense of their council sessions, committee meetings and mass debates, the decisions were made in advance, in furtive informality, at luncheons, dinners and bars, the graver the issue, the more casual the method of settling it. It was the first time that they had asked her, the outsider, the enemy, to one of those secret sessions; it was, she thought, an acknowledgment of the fact that they needed her and, perhaps, the first step of their surrender; it was a chance she could not leave untaken.

But as she sat in the candlelight of the dining room, she felt certain that she had no chance; she felt restlessly unable to accept that certainty, since she could not grasp its reason, yet lethargically reluctant to pursue any inquiry.

"As, I think, you will concede, Miss Taggart, there now seems to be no economic justification for the continued existence of a railroad line in Minnesota, which . . ." "And even Miss Taggart will, I'm sure, agree that certain temporary retrenchments seem to be indicated, until . . ." "Nobody, not even Miss Taggart, will deny that there are times when it is necessary to sacrifice the parts for the sake of the whole . . ." As she listened to the mentions of her name tossed into the conversation at half-hour intervals, tossed perfunctorily, with the speaker's eyes never glancing in her direction, she wondered what motive had made them want her to be present. It was not an attempt to delude her into believing that they were consulting her, but worse: an attempt to delude themselves into believing that she had agreed. They asked her questions at times and interrupted her before she had completed the first sentence of the answer. They seemed to want her approval, without having to know whether she approved or not.

Some crudely childish form of self-deception had made them choose to give to this occasion the decorous setting of a formal dinner. They acted as if they hoped to gain, from the objects of gracious luxury, the power and the honor of which those objects had once been the product and symbol—they acted, she thought, like those savages who devour the corpse of an adversary in the hope of acquiring his strength and his virtue.

She regretted that she was dressed as she was. "It's formal," Jim had told her, "but don't overdo it . . . what I mean is, don't look too rich . . . business people should avoid any appearance of arrogance these days . . . not that you should look shabby, but if you could just seem to suggest . . . well, humility . . . it would please them, you know, it would make them feel big." "Really?" she had said, turning away.

She wore a black dress that looked as if it were no more than a piece of cloth crossed over her breasts and falling to her feet in the soft folds of a Grecian tunic; it was made of satin, a satin so light and thin that it could have served as the stuff of a nightgown. The luster of the cloth, streaming and shifting with her movements, made it look as if the light of the room she entered were her personal property, sensitively obedient to the motions of her body, wrapping her in a sheet of radiance more luxurious than the texture of brocade, underscoring the pliant fragility of her figure, giving her an air of so natural an elegance that it could afford to be scornfully casual. She wore a single piece of jewelry, a diamond clip at the edge of the black neckline, that kept flashing with the imperceptible motion of her breath, like a transformer converting a flicker into fire, making one conscious, not of the gems, but of the living beat behind them; it flashed like a military decoration, like wealth worn as a badge of honor. She wore no other ornament, only the sweep of a black velvet cape, more arrogantly, ostentatiously patrician than any spread of sables.

She regretted it now, as she looked at the men before her; she felt the embarrassing guilt of pointlessness, as if she had tried to defy the figures in a waxworks. She saw a mindless resentment in their eyes and a sneaking trace of the lifeless, sexless, smutty leer with which men look at a poster advertising burlesque.

"It's a great responsibility," said Eugene Lawson, "to hold the decision of life or death over thousands of people and to sacrifice them when necessary, but we must have the courage to do it." His soft lips seemed to twist into a smile.

"The only factors to consider are land acreage and population figures," said Dr. Ferris in a statistical voice, blowing smoke rings at the ceiling. "Since it is no longer possible to maintain both the Minnesota Line and the transcontinental traffic of this railroad, the choice is between Minnesota and those states west of the Rockies which were cut off by the failure of the Taggart Tunnel, as well as the neighboring states of Montana, Idaho, Oregon, which means, practically speaking, the whole of the Northwest. When you compute the acreage and the number of heads in both areas, it's obvious that we should scuttle Minnesota rather than give up our lines of communication over a third of a continent."

"I won't give up the continent," said Wesley Mouch, staring down at his dish of ice cream, his voice hurt and stubborn.

She was thinking of the Mesabi Range, the last of the major sources of iron ore, she was thinking of the Minnesota farmers, such as were left of them, the best producers of wheat in the country—she was thinking that the end of Minnesota would end Wisconsin, then Michigan, then Illinois—she was seeing the red breath of the factories dying out over the industrial East—as against the empty miles of western sands, of scraggly pastures and abandoned ranches.

"The figures indicate," said Mr. Weatherby primly, "that the continued maintenance of both areas seems to be impossible. The railway track and equipment of one has to be dismantled to provide the material for the maintenance of the other."

She noticed that Clem Weatherby, their technical expert on railroads, was the man of least influence among them, and Cuffy Meigs—of most. Cuffy Meigs sat sprawled in his chair, with a look of patronizing tolerance for their game of wasting time on discussions. He spoke little, but when he did, it was to snap decisively, with a contemptuous grin, "Pipe down, Jimmy!" or, "Nuts, Wes, you're talking through your hat!" She noticed that neither Jim nor Mouch resented it. They seemed to welcome the authority of his assurance; they were accepting him as their master.

"We have to be practical," Dr. Ferris kept saying. "We have to be scientific."

"I need the economy of the country as a whole," Wesley Mouch kept repeating. "I need the production of a nation."

"Is it economics that you're talking about? Is it production?" she said, whenever her cold, measured voice was able to seize a brief stretch of their time. "If it is, then give us leeway to save the Eastern states. That's all that's left of the country—and of the world. If you let us save that, we'll have a chance to rebuild the rest. If not, it's the end. Let the Atlantic Southern take care of such transcontinental traffic as still exists. Let the local railroads take care of the Northwest. But let Taggart Transcontinental drop everything else—yes, everything—and devote all our resources, equipment and rail to the traffic of the Eastern states. Let us shrink back to the start of this country, but let us hold that start. We'll run no trains west of the Missouri. We'll become a local railroad—the local of the industrial East. Let us save our industries. There's nothing left to save in the West. You can run agriculture for centuries by manual labor and oxcarts. But destroy the last of this country's industrial plant—and centuries of effort won't be able to rebuild it or to gather the economic strength to make a start. How do you expect our industries—or railroads—to survive without steel? How do you expect any steel to be produced if you cut off the supply of iron ore? Save Minnesota, whatever's left of it. The country? You have no country to save, if its industries perish. You can sacrifice a leg or an arm. You can't save a body by sacrificing its heart and brain. Save our industries. Save Minnesota. Save the Eastern Seaboard."

It was no use. She said it as many times, with as many details, statistics, figures, proofs, as she could force out of her weary mind into their evasive hearing. It was no use. They neither refuted nor agreed; they merely looked as if her arguments were beside the point. There was a sound of hidden emphasis in their answers, as if they were giving her an explanation, but in a code to which she had no key.

"There's trouble in California," said Wesley Mouch sullenly. "Their state legislature's been acting pretty huffy. There's talk of seceding from the Union."

"Oregon is overrun by gangs of deserters," said Clem Weatherby cautiously. "They murdered two tax collectors within the last three months."

"The importance of industry to a civilization has been grossly overemphasized," said Dr. Ferris dreamily. "What is now known as the People's State of India has existed for centuries without any industrial development whatever."

"People could do with fewer material gadgets and a sterner discipline of privations," said Eugene Lawson eagerly. "It would be good for them."

"Oh hell, are you going to let that dame talk you into letting the richest country on earth slip through your fingers?" said Cuffy Meigs, leaping to his feet. "It's a fine time to give up a whole continent—and in exchange for what? For a dinky little state that's milked dry, anyway! I say ditch Minnesota, but hold onto your transcontinental dragnet. With trouble and riots everywhere, you won't be able to keep people in line unless you have transportation—troop transportation—unless you hold your soldiers within a few days' journey of any point on the continent. This is no time to retrench. Don't get yellow, listening to all that talk. You've got the country in your pocket. Just keep it there."

"In the long run—" Mouch started uncertainly.

"In the long run, we'll all be dead," snapped Cuffy Meigs. He was pacing restlessly. "Retrenching, hell! There's plenty of pickings left in California and Oregon and all those places. What I've been thinking is, we ought to think of expanding—the way things are, there's nobody to stop us, it's there for the taking—Mexico, and Canada maybe—it ought to be a cinch."

Then she saw the answer; she saw the secret premise behind their words. With all of their noisy devotion to the age of science, their hysterically technological jargon, their cyclotrons, their sound rays, these men were moved forward, not by the image of an industrial skyline, but by the vision of that form of existence which the industrialists had swept away—the vision of a fat, unhygienic rajah of India, with vacant eyes staring in indolent stupor out of stagnant layers of flesh, with nothing to do but run precious gems through his fingers and, once in a while, stick a knife into the body of a starved, toil-dazed, germ-eaten creature, as a claim to a few grains of the creature's rice, then claim it from hundreds of millions of such creatures and thus let the rice grains gather into gems.

She had thought that industrial production was a value not to be questioned by anyone; she had thought that these men's urge to expropriate the factories of others was their acknowledgment of the factories' value. She, born of the industrial revolution, had not held as conceivable, had forgotten along with the tales of astrology and alchemy, what these men knew in their secret, furtive souls, knew not by means of thought, but by means of that nameless muck which they called their instincts and emotions: that so long as men struggle to stay alive, they'll never produce so little but that the man with the club won't be able to seize it and leave them still less, provided millions of them are willing to submit—that the harder their work and the less their gain, the more submissive the fiber of their spirit—that men who live by pulling levers at an electric switchboard, are not easily ruled, but men who live by digging the soil with their naked fingers, are—that the feudal baron did not need electronic factories in order to drink his brains away out of jeweled goblets, and neither did the rajahs of the People's State of India.

She saw what they wanted and to what goal their "instincts," which they called unaccountable, were leading them. She saw that Eugene Lawson, the humanitarian, took pleasure at the prospect of human starvation—and Dr. Ferris, the scientist, was dreaming of the day when men would return to the hand-plow.

Incredulity and indifference were her only reaction: incredulity, because she could not conceive of what would bring human beings to such a state—indifference, because she could not regard those who reached it, as human any longer. They went on talking, but she was unable to speak or to listen. She caught herself feeling that her only desire was now to get home and fall asleep.

"Miss Taggart," said a politely rational, faintly anxious voice—and jerking her head up, she saw the courteous figure of a waiter, "the assistant manager of the Taggart Terminal is on the telephone, requesting permission to speak to you at once. He says it's an emergency."

It was a relief to leap to her feet and get out of that room, even if in answer to the call of some new disaster. It was a relief to hear the assistant manager's voice, even though it was saying, "The interlocker system is out, Miss Taggart. The signals are dead. There are eight incoming trains held up and six outgoing. We can't move them in or out of the tunnels, we can't find the chief engineer, we can't locate the breach of the circuit, we have no copper wire for repairs, we don't know what to do, we—" "I'll be right down," she said, dropping the receiver.

Hurrying to the elevator, then half-running through the stately lobby of the Wayne-Falkland, she felt herself returning to life at the summons of the possibility of action.

Taxicabs were rare, these days, and none came in answer to the doorman's whistle. She started rapidly down the street, forgetting what she wore, wondering why the touch of the wind seemed too cold and too intimately close.

Her mind on the Terminal ahead, she was startled by the loveliness of a sudden sight: she saw the slender figure of a woman hurrying toward her, the ray of a lamppost sweeping over lustrous hair, naked arms, the swirl of a black cape and the flame of a diamond on her breast, with the long, empty corridor of a city street behind her and skyscrapers drawn by lonely dots of light. The knowledge that she was seeing her own reflection in the side mirror of a florist's window, came an instant too late: she had felt the enchantment of the full context to which that image and city belonged. Then she felt a stab of desolate loneliness, much wider a loneliness than the span of an empty street—and a stab of anger at herself, at the preposterous contrast between her appearance and the context of this night and age.

She saw a taxi turn a corner, she waved to it and leaped in, slamming the door against a feeling which she hoped to leave behind her, on the empty pavement by a florist's window. But she knew—in self-mockery, in bitterness, in longing—that this feeling was the sense of expectation she had felt at her first ball and at those rare times when she had wanted the outward beauty of existence to match its inner splendor. What a time to think of it! she told herself in mockery—not now! she cried to herself in anger—but a desolate voice kept asking her quietly to the rattle of the taxi's wheels: You who believed you must live for your happiness, what do you now have left of it?—what are you gaining from your struggle?—yes! say it honestly: what's in it for you?—or are you becoming one of those abject altruists who has no answer to that question any longer? . . . Not now!—she ordered, as the glowing entrance to the Taggart Terminal flared up in the rectangle of the taxi's windshield.

The men in the Terminal manager's office were like extinguished signals, as if here, too, a circuit were broken and there were no living current to make them move. They looked at her with a kind of inanimate passivity, as if it made no difference whether she let them stay still or threw a switch to set them in motion.

The Terminal manager was absent. The chief engineer could not be found; he had been seen at the Terminal two hours ago, not since. The assistant manager had exhausted his power of initiative by volunteering to call her. The others volunteered nothing. The signal engineer was a college-boyish man in his thirties, who kept saying aggressively, "But this has never happened before, Miss Taggart! The interlocker has never failed. It's not supposed to fail. We know our jobs, we can take care of it as well as anybody can—but not if it breaks down when it's not supposed to!" She could not tell whether the dispatcher, an elderly man with years of railroad work behind him, still retained his intelligence but chose to hide it, or whether months of suppressing it had choked it for good, granting him the safety of stagnation.

"We don't know what to do, Miss Taggart." "We don't know whom to call for what sort of permission." "There are no rules to cover an emergency of this kind." "There aren't even any rules about who's to lay down the rules for it!"

She listened, she reached for the telephone without a word of explanation, she ordered the operator to get her the operating vice-president of the Atlantic Southern in Chicago, to get him at his home and out of bed, if necessary.

"George? Dagny Taggart," she said, when the voice of her competitor came on the wire. "Will you lend me the signal engineer of your Chicago terminal, Charles Murray, for twenty-four hours? . . . Yes. . . . Right. . . . Put him aboard a plane and get him here as fast as you can. Tell him we'll pay three thousand dollars. . . . Yes, for the one day. . . . Yes, as bad as that. . . . Yes, I'll pay him in cash, out of my own pocket, if necessary. I'll pay whatever it takes to bribe his way aboard a plane, but get him on the first plane out of Chicago. . . . No, George, not one—not a single mind left on Taggart Transcontinental. . . . Yes, I'll get all the papers, exemptions, exceptions and emergency permissions. . . . Thanks, George. So long."

She hung up and spoke rapidly to the men before her, not to hear the stillness of the room and of the Terminal, where no sound of wheels was beating any longer, not to hear the bitter words which the stillness seemed to repeat: Not a single mind left on Taggart Transcontinental. . . .

"Get a wrecking train and crew ready at once," she said. "Send them out on the Hudson Line, with orders to tear down every foot of copper wire, any copper wire, lights, signals, telephone, everything that's company property. Have it here by morning." "But, Miss Taggart! Our service on the Hudson Line is only temporarily suspended and the Unification Board has refused us permission to dismantle the line!" "I'll be responsible." "But how are we going to get the wrecking train out of here, when there aren't any signals?" "There will be signals in half an hour." "How?" "Come on," she said, rising to her feet.

They followed her as she hurried down the passenger platforms, past the huddling, shifting groups of travelers by the motionless trains. She hurried down a narrow catwalk, through a maze of rail, past blinded signals and frozen switches, with nothing but the beat of her satin sandals to fill the great vaults of the underground tunnels of Taggart Transcontinental, with the hollow creaking of planks under the slower steps of men trailing her like a reluctant echo—she hurried to the lighted glass cube of Tower A, that hung in the darkness like a crown without a body, the crown of a deposed ruler above a realm of empty tracks.

The tower director was too expert a man at too exacting a job to be able wholly to conceal the dangerous burden of intelligence. He understood what she wanted him to do from her first few words and answered only with an abrupt "Yes, ma'am," but he was bent over his charts by the time the others came following her up the iron stairway, he was grimly at work on the most humiliating job of calculation he had ever had to perform in his long career. She knew how fully he understood it, from a single glance he threw at her, a glance of indignation and endurance that matched some emotion he had caught in her face. "We'll do it first and feel about it afterwards," she said, even though he had made no comment. "Yes, ma'am," he answered woodenly.

His room, on the top of an underground tower, was like a glass verandah overlooking what had once been the swiftest, richest and most orderly stream in the world. He had been trained to chart the course of over ninety trains an hour and to watch them roll safely through a maze of tracks and switches in and out of the Terminal, under his glass walls and his fingertips. Now, for the first time, he was looking out at the empty darkness of a dried channel.

Through the open door of the relay room, she saw the tower men standing grimly idle—the men whose jobs had never permitted a moment's relaxation—standing by the long rows that looked like vertical copper pleats, like shelves of books and as much of a monument to human intelligence. The pull of one of the small levers, which protruded like bookmarks from the shelves, threw thousands of electric circuits into motion, made thousands of contacts and broke as many others, set dozens of switches to clear a chosen course and dozens of signals to light it, with no error left possible, no chance, no contradiction —an enormous complexity of thought condensed into one movement of a human hand to set and insure the course of a train, that hundreds of trains might safely rush by, that thousands of tons of metal and lives might pass in speeding streaks a breath away from one another, protected by nothing but a thought, the thought of the man who devised the levers. But they—she looked at the face of her signal engineer

—they believed that that muscular contraction of a hand was the only
thing required to move the traffic—and now the tower men stood idle—
and on the great panels in front of the tower director, the red and green
lights, which had flashed announcing the progress of trains at a distance
of miles, were now so many glass beads—like the glass beads for which
another breed of savages had once sold the Island of Manhattan.

"Call all of your unskilled laborers," she said to the assistant manager, "the section hands, trackwalkers, engine wipers, whoever's in
the Terminal right now, and have them come here at once."

"Here?"

"Here," she said, pointing at the tracks outside the tower. "Call all
your switchmen, too. Phone your storehouse and have them bring here
every lantern they can lay their hands on, any sort of lantern, conductors' lanterns, storm lanterns, anything."

"Lanterns, Miss Taggart?"

"Get going."

"Yes, ma'am."

"What is it we're doing, Miss Taggart?" asked the dispatcher.

"We're going to move trains and we're going to move them manually."

"Manually?" said the signal engineer.

"Yes, brother! Now why should *you* be shocked?" She could not
resist it. "Man is only muscles, isn't he? We're going back—back to
where there were no interlocking systems, no semaphores, no electricity
—back to the time when train signals were not steel and wire, but men
holding lanterns. Physical men, serving as lampposts. You've advocated
it long enough—you got what you wanted. Oh, you thought that your
tools would determine your ideas? But it happens to be the other way
around—and now you're going to see the kind of tools your ideas have
determined!"

But even to go back took an act of intelligence—she thought, feeling
the paradox of her own position, as she looked at the lethargy of the
faces around her.

"How will we work the switches, Miss Taggart?"

"By hand."

"And the signals?"

"By hand."

"How?"

"By placing a man with a lantern at every signal post."

"How? There's not enough clearance."

"We'll use alternate tracks."

"How will the men know which way to throw the switches?"

"By written orders."

"Uh?"

"By written orders—just as in the old days." She pointed to the tower
director. "He's working out a schedule of how to move the trains and

which tracks to use. He'll write out an order for every signal and switch, he'll pick some men as runners and they'll keep delivering the orders to every post—and it will take hours to do what used to take minutes, but we'll get those waiting trains into the Terminal and out on the road."

"We're to work it that way all night?"

"And all day tomorrow—until the engineer who's got the brains for it, shows you how to repair the interlocker."

"There's nothing in the union contracts about men standing with lanterns. There's going to be trouble. The union will object."

"Let them come to me."

"The Unification Board will object."

"I'll be responsible."

"Well, I wouldn't want to be held for giving the orders—"

"I'll give the orders."

She stepped out on the landing of the iron stairway that hung on the side of the tower; she was fighting for self-control. It seemed to her for a moment as if she, too, were a precision instrument of high technology, left without electric current, trying to run a transcontinental railroad by means of her two hands. She looked out at the great, silent darkness of the Taggart underground—and she felt a stab of burning humiliation that she should now see it brought down to the level where human lampposts would stand in its tunnels as its last memorial statues.

She could barely distinguish the faces of the men when they gathered at the foot of the tower. They came streaming silently through the darkness and stood without moving in the bluish murk, with blue bulbs on the walls behind them and patches of light falling on their shoulders from the tower's windows. She could see the greasy garments, the slack, muscular bodies, the limply hanging arms of men drained by the unrewarding exhaustion of a labor that required no thought. These were the dregs of the railroad, the younger men who could now seek no chance to rise and the older men who had never wanted to seek it. They stood in silence, not with the apprehensive curiosity of workmen, but with the heavy indifference of convicts.

"The orders which you are about to receive have come from me," she said, standing above them on the iron stairs, speaking with resonant clarity. "The men who'll issue them are acting under my instructions. The interlocking control system has broken down. It will now be replaced by human labor. Train service will be resumed at once."

She noticed some faces in the crowd staring at her with a peculiar look: with a veiled resentment and the kind of insolent curiosity that made her suddenly conscious of being a woman. Then she remembered what she wore, and thought that it did look preposterous—and then, at the sudden stab of some violent impulse that felt like defiance and like loyalty to the full, real meaning of the moment, she threw her cape back and stood in the raw glare of light, under the sooted columns, like a figure at a formal reception, sternly erect, flaunting the luxury of naked arms, of glowing black satin, of a diamond flashing like a military cross.

"The tower director will assign switchmen to their posts. He will select men for the job of signaling trains by means of lanterns and for the task of transmitting his orders. Trains will—"

She was fighting to drown a bitter voice that seemed to be saying: That's all they're fit for, these men, if even that . . . there's not a single mind left anywhere on Taggart Transcontinental. . . .

"Trains will continue to be moved in and out of the Terminal. You will remain at your posts until—"

Then she stopped. It was his eyes and hair that she saw first—the ruthlessly perceptive eyes, the streaks of hair shaded from gold to copper that seemed to reflect the glow of sunlight in the murk of the underground—she saw John Galt among the chain gang of the mindless, John Galt in greasy overalls and rolled shirt sleeves, she saw his weightless way of standing, his face held lifted, his eyes looking at her as if he had seen this moment many moments ago.

"What's the matter, Miss Taggart?"

It was the soft voice of the tower director, who stood by her side, with some sort of paper in his hand—and she thought it was strange to emerge from a span of unconsciousness which had been the span of the sharpest awareness she had ever experienced, only she did not know how long it had lasted or where she was or why. She had been aware of Galt's face, she had been seeing, in the shape of his mouth, in the planes of his cheeks, the crackup of that implacable serenity which had always been his, but he still retained it in his look of acknowledging the breach, of admitting that this moment was too much even for him.

She knew that she went on speaking, because those around her looked as if they were listening, though she could not hear a sound, she went on speaking as if carrying out a hypnotic order given to herself some endless time ago, knowing only that the completion of that order was a form of defiance against him, neither knowing nor hearing her own words.

She felt as if she were standing in a radiant silence where sight was her only capacity and his face was its only object, and the sight of his face was like a speech in the form of a pressure at the base of her throat. It seemed so natural that he should be here, it seemed so unendurably simple—she felt as if the shock were not his presence, but the presence of others on the tracks of her railroad, where he belonged and they did not. She was seeing those moments aboard a train when, at its plunge into the tunnels, she had felt a sudden, solemn tension, as if this place were showing her in naked simplicity the essence of her railroad and of her life, the union of consciousness and matter, the frozen form of a mind's ingenuity giving physical existence to its purpose; she had felt a sense of sudden hope, as if this place held the meaning of all of her values, and a sense of secret excitement, as if a nameless promise were awaiting her under the ground—it was right that she should now meet him here, *he* had been the meaning and the promise—she was not seeing his clothing any longer, nor to what level her railroad had reduced him—she was seeing only the vanishing torture of the months when he had been outside her reach—she was seeing in his face the confession of what those months had cost him —the only speech she heard was as if she were saying to him: This is the reward for all my days—and as if he were answering: For all of mine.

She knew that she had finished speaking to the strangers when she saw that the tower director had stepped forward and was saying something to them, glancing at a list in his hand. Then, drawn by a sense of irresistible certainty, she found herself descending the stairs, slipping away from the crowd, not toward the platforms and the exit, but into the darkness of the abandoned tunnels. You will follow me, she thought —and felt as if the thought were not in words, but in the tension of her muscles, the tension of her will to accomplish a thing she knew to be outside her power, yet she knew with certainty that it would be accomplished and by her wish . . . no, she thought, not by her wish, but by its total rightness. You will follow me—it was neither plea nor prayer nor demand, but the quiet statement of a fact, it contained the whole of her power of knowledge and the whole of the knowledge she had earned through the years. You will follow me, if we are what we are, you and I, if we live, if the world exists, if you know the meaning of this moment and can't let it slip by, as others let it slip, into the senselessness of the unwilled and unreached. You will follow me—she felt an exultant assurance, which was neither hope nor faith, but an act of worship for the logic of existence.

She was hurrying down the remnants of abandoned rails, down the long, dark corridors twisting through granite. She lost the sound of the director's voice behind her. Then she felt the beat of her arteries and heard, in answering rhythm, the beat of the city above her head, but she felt as if she heard the motion of her blood as a sound filling the silence, and the motion of the city as the beat inside her body—and, far behind her, she heard the sound of steps. She did not glance back. She went faster.

She went past the locked iron door where the remnant of his motor was still hidden, she did not stop, but a faint shudder was her answer to the sudden glimpse of the unity and logic in the events of the last two years. A string of blue lights went on into the darkness, over patches of glistening granite, over broken sandbags spilling drifts on the rails, over rusty piles of scrap metal. When she heard the steps coming closer, she stopped and turned to look back.

She saw a sweep of blue light flash briefly on the shining strands of

Galt's hair, she caught the pale outline of his face and the dark hollows of his eyes. The face disappeared, but the sound of his steps served as the link to the next blue light that swept across the line of his eyes, the eyes that remained held level, directed ahead—and she felt certain that she had stayed in his sight from the moment he had seen her at the tower.

She heard the beat of the city above them—these tunnels, she had once thought, were the roots of the city and of all the motion reaching to the sky—but they, she thought, John Galt and she, were the living power within these roots, they were the start and aim and meaning—he, too, she thought, heard the beat of the city as the beat of his body.

She threw her cape back, she stood defiantly straight, as he had seen her stand on the steps of the tower—as he had seen her for the first time, ten years ago, here, under the ground—she was hearing the words of his confession, not as words, but by means of that beating which made it so difficult to breathe: You looked like a symbol of luxury and you belonged in the place that was its source . . . you seemed to bring the enjoyment of life back to its rightful owners . . . you had a look of energy and of its reward, together . . . and I was the first man who had ever stated in what manner these two were inseparable. . . .

The next span of moments was like flashes of light in stretches of blinded unconsciousness—the moment when she saw his face, as he stopped beside her, when she saw the unastonished calm, the leashed intensity, the laughter of understanding in the dark green eyes—the moment when she knew what he saw in her face, by the tight, drawn harshness of his lips—the moment when she felt his mouth on hers, when she felt the shape of his mouth both as an absolute shape and as a liquid filling her body—then the motion of his lips down the line of her throat, a drinking motion that left a trail of bruises—then the sparkle of her diamond clip against the trembling copper of his hair.

Then she was conscious of nothing but the sensations of her body, because her body acquired the sudden power to let her know her most complex values by direct perception. Just as her eyes had the power to translate wave lengths of energy into sight, just as her ears had the power to translate vibrations into sound, so her body now had the power to translate the energy that had moved all the choices of her life, into immediate sensory perception. It was not the pressure of a hand that made her tremble, but the instantaneous sum of its meaning, the knowledge that it was *his* hand, that it moved as if her flesh were his possession, that its movement was his signature of acceptance under the whole of that achievement which was herself—it was only a sensation of physical pleasure, but it contained her worship of him, of everything that was his person and his life—from the night of the mass meeting in a factory in Wisconsin, to the Atlantis of a valley hidden in the Rocky Mountains, to the triumphant mockery of the green eyes of the superlative intelligence above a worker's figure at the foot of the tower—it contained her pride in herself and that it should be she whom he had chosen as his mirror, that it should be her body which was now giving him the sum of his existence, as his body was giving her the sum of hers. These were the things it contained—but what she knew was only the sensation of the movement of his hand on her breasts.

He tore off her cape and she felt the slenderness of her own body by means of the circle of his arms, as if his person were only a tool for her triumphant awareness of herself, but that self were only a tool for her awareness of him. It was as if she were reaching the limit of her capacity to feel, yet what she felt was like a cry of impatient demand, which she was now incapable of naming, except that it had the same quality of ambition as the course of her life, the same inexhaustible quality of radiant greed.

He pulled her head back for a moment, to look straight into her eyes, to let her see his, to let her know the full meaning of their actions, as if throwing the spotlight of consciousness upon them for the meeting of their eyes in a moment of intimacy greater than the one to come.

Then she felt the mesh of burlap striking the skin of her shoulders, she found herself lying on the broken sandbags, she saw the long, tight gleam of her stockings, she felt his mouth pressed to her ankle, then rising in a tortured motion up the line of her leg, as if he wished to own its shape by means of his lips, then she felt her teeth sinking into the flesh of his arm, she felt the sweep of his elbow knocking her head aside and his mouth seizing her lips with a pressure more viciously painful than hers—then she felt, when it hit her throat, that which she knew only as an upward streak of motion that released and united her body into a single shock of pleasure—then she knew nothing but the motion of his body and the driving greed that went reaching on and on, as if she were not a person any longer, only a sensation of endless reaching for the impossible—then she knew that it was possible, and she gasped and lay still, knowing that nothing more could be desired, ever.

He lay beside her, on his back, looking up at the darkness of the granite vault above them, she saw him stretched on the jagged slant of sandbags as if his body were fluid in relaxation, she saw the black wedge of her cape flung across the rails at their feet, there were beads of moisture twinkling on the vault, shifting slowly, running into invisible cracks, like the lights of a distant traffic. When he spoke, his voice sounded as if he were quietly continuing a sentence in answer to the questions in her mind, as if he had nothing to hide from her any longer and what he owed her now was only the act of undressing his soul, as simply as he would have undressed his body:

". . . this is how I've watched you for ten years . . . from here, from under the ground under your feet . . . knowing every move you made in your office at the top of the building, but never seeing you, never enough . . . ten years of nights, spent waiting to catch a glimpse of you, here, on the platforms, when you boarded a train. . . . Whenever the order came down to couple your car, I'd know of it and wait and see you come down the ramp, and wish you didn't walk so fast . . . it was so much like you, that walk, I'd know it anywhere . . . your walk and those legs of yours . . . it was always your legs that I'd see first, hurrying down the ramp, going past me as I looked up at you from a dark side track below. . . . I think I could have molded a sculpture of your legs, I knew them, not with my eyes, but with the palms of my hands when I watched you go by . . . when I turned back to my work . . . when I went home just before sunrise for the three hours of sleep which I didn't get . . ."

"I love you," she said, her voice quiet and almost toneless except for a fragile sound of youth.

He closed his eyes, as if letting the sound travel through the years behind them. "Ten years, Dagny . . . except that once there were a few weeks when I had you before me, in plain sight, within reach, not hurrying away, but held still, as on a lighted stage, a private stage for me to watch . . . and I watched you for hours through many evenings . . . in the lighted window of an office that was called the John Galt Line. . . . And one night—"

Her breath was a faint gasp. "Was it you, that night?"

"Did you see me?"

"I saw your shadow . . . on the pavement . . . pacing back and forth . . . it looked like a struggle . . . it looked like—" She stopped; she did not want to say "torture."

"It was," he said quietly. "That night, I wanted to walk in, to face you, to speak, to . . . That was the night I came closest to breaking my oath, when I saw you slumped across your desk, when I saw you broken by the burden you were carrying—"

"John, that night, it was *you* that I was thinking of . . . only I didn't know it . . ."

"But, you see, *I* knew it."

". . . it was you, all my life, through everything I did and everything I wanted . . ."

"I know it."

"John, the hardest was not when I left you in the valley . . . it was—"

"Your radio speech, the day you returned?"

"Yes! Were you listening?"

"Of course. I'm glad you did it. It was a magnificent thing to do. And I—I knew it, anyway."

"You knew . . . about Hank Rearden?"

"Before I saw you in the valley."

"Was it . . . when you learned about him, had you expected it?"

"No."

"Was it . . . ?" she stopped.

"Hard? Yes. But only for the first few days. That next night . . . Do you want me to tell you what I did the night after I learned it?"

"Yes."

"I had never seen Hank Rearden, only pictures of him in the newspapers. I knew that he was in New York, that night, at some conference of big industrialists. I wanted to have just one look at him. I went to wait at the entrance of the hotel where that conference was held. There were bright lights under the marquee of the entrance, but it was dark beyond, on the pavement, so I could see without being seen, there were a few loafers and vagrants hanging around, there was a drizzle of rain and we clung to the walls of the building. One could tell the members of the conference when they began filing out, by their clothes and their manner—ostentatiously prosperous clothes and a manner of overbearing timidity, as if they were guiltily trying to pretend that they were what they appeared to be for that moment. There were chauffeurs driving up their cars, there were a few reporters delaying them for questions and hangers-on trying to catch a word from them. They were worn men, those industrialists, aging, flabby, frantic with the effort to disguise uncertainty. And then I saw him. He wore an expensive trenchcoat and a hat slanting across his eyes. He walked swiftly, with the kind of assurance that has to be earned, as he'd earned it. Some of his fellow industrialists pounced on him with questions, and those tycoons were acting like hangers-on around him. I caught a glimpse of him as he stood with his hand on the door of his car, his head lifted, I saw the brief flare of a smile under the slanting brim, a confident smile, impatient and a little amused. And then, for one instant, I did what I had never done before, what most men wreck their lives on doing—I saw that moment out of context, I saw the world as he made it look, as if it matched him, as if he were its symbol—I saw a world of achievement, of unenslaved energy, of unobstructed drive through purposeful years to the enjoyment of one's reward—I saw, as I stood in the rain in a crowd of vagrants, what my years would have brought me, if that world had existed, and I felt a desperate longing—he was the image of everything I should have been . . . and he had everything that should have been mine. . . . But it was only a moment. Then I saw the scene in full context again and in all of its actual meaning—I saw what price he was paying for his brilliant ability, what torture he was enduring in silent bewilderment, struggling to understand what *I* had understood—I saw that the world he suggested, did not exist and was yet to be made, I saw him again for what he was, the symbol of my battle, the unrewarded hero whom *I* was to avenge and to release—and then . . . then I accepted what I had learned about you and him. I saw that it changed nothing, that I should have expected it—that it was right."

He heard the faint sound of her moan and he chuckled softly.

"Dagny, it's not that I don't suffer, it's that I know the unimportance of suffering, I know that pain is to be fought and thrown aside, not to be accepted as part of one's soul and as a permanent scar across one's view of existence. Don't feel sorry for me. It was gone right then."

She turned her head to look at him in silence, and he smiled, lifting himself on an elbow to look down at her face as she lay helplessly still. She whispered, "You've been a track laborer, here—here!—for twelve years . . ."

"Yes."

"Ever since—"

"Ever since I quit the Twentieth Century."

"The night when you saw me for the first time . . . you were working here, then?"

"Yes. And the morning when you offered to work for me as my cook, I was only your track laborer on leave of absence. Do you see why I laughed as I did?"

She was looking up at his face; hers was a smile of pain, his—of pure gaiety. "John . . ."

"Say it. But say it all."

"You were here . . . all those years . . ."

"Yes."

". . . all those years . . . while the railroad was perishing . . . while I was searching for men of intelligence . . . while I was struggling to hold onto any scrap of it I could find . . ."

". . . while you were combing the country for the inventor of my motor, while you were feeding James Taggart and Wesley Mouch, while you were naming your best achievement after the enemy whom you wanted to destroy."

She closed her eyes.

"I was here all those years," he said, "within your reach, inside your own realm, watching your struggle, your loneliness, your longing, watching you in a battle you thought you were fighting for me, a battle in which you were supporting my enemies and taking an endless defeat—I was here, hidden by nothing but an error of your sight, as Atlantis is hidden from men by nothing but an optical illusion—I was here, waiting for the day when you would see, when you would know that by the code of the world you were supporting, it's to the darkest bottom of the underground that all the things you valued would have to be consigned and that it's there that you would have to look. I was here. I was waiting for you. I love you, Dagny. I love you more than my life, I who have taught men how life is to be loved. I've taught them also never to expect the unpaid for—and what I did tonight, I did it with full knowledge that I would pay for it and that my life might have to be the price."

"No!"

He smiled, nodding. "Oh yes. You know that you've broken me for once, that I broke the decision I had set for myself—but I did it consciously, knowing what it meant, I did it, not in blind surrender to the moment, but with full sight of the consequences and full willingness to bear them. I could not let this kind of moment pass us by, it was ours, my love, we had earned it. But you're not ready to quit and join me—you don't have to tell me, I know—and since I chose to take what I wanted before it was fully mine, I'll have to pay for it, I have no way of knowing how or when, I know only that if I give in to an enemy, I'll take the consequences." He smiled in answer to the look on her face. "No, Dagny, you're not my enemy in mind—and *that* is what brought me to this—but you *are* in fact, in the course you're pursuing, though you don't see it yet, but I do. My actual enemies are of no danger to me. *You* are. You're the only one who can lead them to find me. They would never have the capacity to know what I am, but with your help —they will."

"No!"

"No, not by your intention. And you're free to change your course, but so long as you follow it, you're not free to escape its logic. Don't frown, the choice was mine and it's a danger I chose to accept. I am a trader, Dagny, in all things. I wanted you, I had no power to change your decision, I had only the power to consider the price and decide whether I could afford it. I could. My life is mine to spend or to invest —and you, you're"—as if his gesture were continuing his sentence, he raised her across his arm and kissed her mouth, while her body hung limply in surrender, her hair streaming down, her head falling back, held only by the pressure of his lips—"you're the one reward I had to have and chose to buy. I wanted you, and if my life is the price, I'll give it. My life—but not my mind."

There was a sudden glint of hardness in his eyes, as he sat up and smiled and asked, "Would you want me to join you and go to work? Would you like me to repair that interlocking signal system of yours within an hour?"

"No!" The cry was immediate—in answer to the flash of a sudden image, the image of the men in the private dining room of the Wayne-Falkland.

He laughed. "Why not?"

"I don't want to see *you* working as their serf!"

"And yourself?"

"I think that they're crumbling and that I'll win. I can stand it just a little longer."

"True, it's just a little longer—not till you win, but till you learn."

"I can't let it go!" It was a cry of despair.

"Not yet," he said quietly.

He got up, and she rose obediently, unable to speak.

"I will remain here, on my job," he said. "But don't try to see me. You'll have to endure what I've endured and wanted to spare you—you'll have to go on, knowing where I am, wanting me as I'll want you, but never permitting yourself to approach me. Don't seek me here. Don't come to my home. Don't ever let them see us together. And when you reach the end, when you're ready to quit, don't tell them, just chalk a dollar sign on the pedestal of Nat Taggart's statue—where it belongs —then go home and wait. I'll come for you in twenty-four hours."

She inclined her head in silent promise.

But when he turned to go, a sudden shudder ran through her body, like a first jolt of awakening or a last convulsion of life, and it ended in an involuntary cry: "Where are you going?"

"To be a lamppost and stand holding a lantern till dawn—which is the only work your world relegates me to and the only work it's going to get."

She seized his arm, to hold him, to follow, to follow him blindly, abandoning everything but the sight of his face. "John!"

He gripped her wrist, twisted her hand and threw it off. "No," he said.

Then he took her hand and raised it to his lips and the pressure of his mouth was more passionate a statement than any he had chosen to confess. Then he walked away, down the vanishing line of rail, and it seemed to her that both the rail and the figure were abandoning her at the same time.

When she staggered out into the concourse of the Terminal, the first blast of rolling wheels went shuddering through the walls of the building, like the sudden beat of a heart that had stopped. The temple of Nathaniel Taggart was silent and empty, its changeless light beating down on a deserted stretch of marble. Some shabby figures shuffled across it, as if lost in its shining expanse. On the steps of the pedestal, under the statue of the austere, exultant figure, a ragged bum sat slumped in passive resignation, like a wing-plucked bird with no place to go, resting on any chance cornice.

She fell down on the steps of the pedestal, like another derelict, her dust-smeared cape wrapped tightly about her, she sat still, her head on her arm, past crying or feeling or moving.

It seemed to her only that she kept seeing a figure with a raised arm holding a light, and it looked at times like the Statue of Liberty and then it looked like a man with sun-streaked hair, holding a lantern against a midnight sky, a red lantern that stopped the movement of the world.

"Don't take it to heart, lady, whatever it is," said the bum, in a tone of exhausted compassion. "Nothing's to be done about it, anyway. . . . What's the use, lady? Who is John Galt?"

THE CONCERTO OF DELIVERANCE

On October 20, the steel workers' union of Rearden Steel demanded a raise in wages.

Hank Rearden learned it from the newspapers; no demand had been presented to him and it had not been considered necessary to inform him. The demand was made to the Unification Board; it was not explained why no other steel company was presented with a similar claim. He was unable to tell whether the demanders did or did not represent his workers, the Board's rules on union elections having made it a matter impossible to define. He learned only that the group consisted of those newcomers whom the Board had slipped into his mills in the past few months.

On October 23, the Unification Board rejected the union's petition, refusing to grant the raise. If any hearings had been held on the matter, Rearden had not known about it. He had not been consulted, informed or notified. He had waited, volunteering no questions.

On October 25, the newspapers of the country, controlled by the same men who controlled the Board, began a campaign of commiseration with the workers of Rearden Steel. They printed stories about the refusal of the wage raise, omitting any mention of who had refused it or who held the exclusive legal power to refuse, as if counting on the public to forget legal technicalities under a barrage of stories implying that an employer was the natural cause of all miseries suffered by employees. They printed a story describing the hardships of the workers of Rearden Steel under the present rise in the cost of their living—next to a story describing Hank Rearden's profits, of five years ago. They printed a story on the plight of a Rearden worker's wife trudging from store to store in a hopeless quest for food—next to a story about a champagne bottle broken over somebody's head at a drunken party given by an unnamed steel tycoon at a fashionable hotel; the steel tycoon had been Orren Boyle, but the story mentioned no names. "Inequalities still exist among us," the newspapers were saying, "and cheat us of the benefits of our enlightened age." "Privations have worn the nerves and temper of the people. The situation is reaching the danger point. We fear an outbreak of violence." "We fear an outbreak of violence," the newspapers kept repeating.

On October 28, a group of the new workers at Rearden Steel attacked a foreman and knocked the tuyères off a blast furnace. Two days later, a similar group broke the ground-floor windows of the administration building. A new worker smashed the gears of a crane, upsetting a ladle of molten metal within a yard of five bystanders. "Guess I went nuts, worrying about my hungry kids," he said, when arrested. "This is no time to theorize about who's right or wrong," the newspapers commented. "Our sole concern is the fact that an inflammatory situation is endangering the steel output of the country."

Rearden watched, asking no questions. He waited, as if some final knowledge were in the process of unraveling before him, a process not to be hastened or stopped. No—he thought through the early dusk of autumn evenings, looking out the window of his office—no, he was not indifferent to his mills; but the feeling which had once been passion for a living entity was now like the wistful tenderness one feels for the memory of the loved and dead. The special quality of what one feels for the dead, he thought, is that no action is possible any longer.

On the morning of October 31, he received a notice informing him that all of his property, including his bank accounts and safety deposit boxes, had been attached to satisfy a delinquent judgment obtained against him in a trial involving a deficiency in his personal income tax of three years ago. It was a formal notice, complying with every requirement of the law—except that no such deficiency had ever existed and no such trial had ever taken place.

"No," he said to his indignation-choked attorney, "don't question them, don't answer, don't object." "But this is fantastic!" "Any more fantastic than the rest?" "Hank, do you want me to do nothing? To take it lying down?" "No, standing up. And I mean, *standing*. Don't move. Don't act." "But they've left you helpless." "Have they?" he asked softly, smiling.

He had a few hundred dollars in cash, left in his wallet, nothing else. But the odd, glowing warmth in his mind, like the feel of a distant handshake, was the thought that in a secret safe of his bedroom there lay a bar of solid gold, given to him by a gold-haired pirate.

Next day, on November 1, he received a telephone call from Washington, from a bureaucrat whose voice seemed to come sliding down the wire on its knees in protestations of apology. "A mistake, Mr. Rearden! It was nothing but an unfortunate mistake! That attachment was not intended for you. You know how it is nowadays, with the inefficiency of all office help and with the amount of red tape we're tangled in, some bungling fool mixed the records and processed the attachment order against you—when it wasn't your case at all, it was, in fact, the case of a soap manufacturer! Please accept our apologies, Mr. Rearden, our deepest personal apologies at the top level." The voice slid to a slight, expectant pause. "Mr. Rearden . . . ?" "I'm listening." "I can't tell you how sorry we are to have caused you any embarrassment or inconvenience. And with all those damn formalities that we have to go through—you know how it is, red tape!—it will take a few days, perhaps a week, to de-process that order and to lift the attachment. . . . Mr. Rearden?" "I heard you." "We're desperately sorry and ready to make any amends within our power. You will, of course, be entitled to claim damages for any inconvenience this might cause you, and we are prepared to pay. We won't contest it. You will, of course, file such a claim and—" "I have not said that." "Uh? No, you haven't . . . that is . . . well, what *have* you said, Mr. Rearden?" "I have said nothing."

Late on the next afternoon, another voice came pleading from Washington. This one did not seem to slide, but to bounce on the telephone wire with the gay virtuosity of a tight-rope walker. It introduced itself as Tinky Holloway and pleaded that Rearden attend a conference, "an informal little conference, just a few of us, the top-level few," to be held in New York, at the Wayne-Falkland Hotel, day after next.

"There have been so many misunderstandings in the past few weeks!" said Tinky Holloway. "Such unfortunate misunderstandings—and so unnecessary! We could straighten everything out in a jiffy, Mr. Rearden, if we had a chance to have a little talk with you. We're extremely anxious to see you."

"You can issue a subpoena for me any time you wish."

"Oh, no! no! no!" The voice sounded frightened. "No, Mr. Rearden—why think of such things? You don't understand us, we're anxious to meet you on a friendly basis, we're seeking nothing but your voluntary co-operation." Holloway paused tensely, wondering whether he had heard the faint sound of a distant chuckle; he waited, but heard nothing else. "Mr. Rearden?"

"Yes?"

"Surely, Mr. Rearden, at a time like this, a conference with us could be to your great advantage."

"A conference—about what?"

"You've encountered so many difficulties—and we're anxious to help you in any way we can."

"I have not asked for help."

"These are precarious times, Mr. Rearden, the public mood is so uncertain and inflammatory, so . . . so dangerous . . . and we want to be able to protect you."

"I have not asked for protection."

"But surely you realize that we're in a position to be of value to you, and if there's anything you want from us, any . . ."

"There isn't."

"But you must have problems you'd like to discuss with us."

"I haven't."

"Then . . . well, then" —giving up the attempt at the play of granting a favor, Holloway switched to an open plea—"then won't you just give us a hearing?"

"If you have anything to say to me."

"We have, Mr. Rearden, we certainly have! That's all we're asking for—a hearing. Just give us a chance. Just come to this conference. You wouldn't be committing yourself to anything—" He said it involuntarily, and stopped, hearing a bright, mocking stab of life in Rearden's voice, an unpromising sound, as Rearden answered:

"I know it."

"Well, I mean . . . that is . . . well, then, will you come?"

"All right," said Rearden. "I'll come."

He did not listen to Holloway's assurances of gratitude, he noted only that Holloway kept repeating, "At seven P.M., November fourth, Mr. Rearden . . . November fourth . . ." as if the date had some special significance.

Rearden dropped the receiver and lay back in his chair, looking at the glow of furnace flames on the ceiling of his office. He knew that the conference was a trap; he knew also that he was walking into it with nothing for any trappers to gain.

Tinky Holloway dropped the receiver, in his Washington office, and sat up tensely, frowning. Claude Slagenhop, president of Friends of Global Progress, who had sat in an armchair, nervously chewing a matchstick, glanced up at him and asked, "Not so good?"

Holloway shook his head. "He'll come, but . . . no, not so good." He added, "I don't think he'll take it."

"That's what my punk told me."

"I know."

"The punk said we'd better not try it."

"God damn your punk! We've got to! We'll have to risk it!"

The punk was Philip Rearden who, weeks ago, had reported to Claude Slagenhop: "No, he won't let me in, he won't give me a job, I've tried, as you wanted me to, I've tried my best, but it's no use, he won't let me set foot inside his mills. And as to his frame of mind—listen, it's bad. It's worse than anything I expected. I know him and I can tell you that you won't have a chance. He's pretty much at the end of his rope. One more squeeze will snap it. You said the big boys wanted to know. Tell them not to do it. Tell them he . . . Claude, God help us, if they do it, they'll lose him!" "Well, you're not of much help," Slagenhop had said dryly, turning away. Philip had seized his sleeve and asked, his voice shrinking suddenly into open anxiety, "Say, Claude . . . according to . . . to Directive 10-289 . . . if he goes, there's . . . there's to be no heirs?" "That's right." "They'd seize the mills and . . . and everything?" "That's the law." "But . . . Claude, they wouldn't do that to *me*, would they?" "They don't want him to go. You know that. Hold him, if you can." "But I can't! You know I can't! Because of my political ideas and . . . and everything I've done for you,

you know what he thinks of me! I have no hold on him at all!" "Well, that's *your* tough luck." "Claude!" Philip had cried in panic. "Claude, they won't leave me out in the cold, will they? I belong, don't I? They've always said I belonged, they've always said they needed me . . . they said they needed men like me, not like him, men with my . . . my sort of spirit, remember? And after all I've done for them, after all my faith and service and loyalty to the cause—" "You damn fool," Slagenhop had snapped, "of what use are you to us without *him?*"

On the morning of November 4, Hank Rearden was awakened by the ringing of the telephone. He opened his eyes to the sight of a clear, pale sky, the sky of early dawn, in the window of his bedroom, a sky the delicate color of aquamarine, with the first rays of an invisible sun giving a shade of porcelain pink to Philadelphia's ancient roof tops. For a moment, while his consciousness had a purity to equal the sky's, while he was aware of nothing but himself and had not yet reharnessed his soul to the burden of alien memories, he lay still, held by the sight and by the enchantment of a world to match it, a world where the style of existence would be a continuous morning.

The telephone threw him back into exile: it was screaming at spaced intervals, like a nagging, chronic cry for help, the kind of cry that did not belong in his world. He lifted the receiver, frowning. "Hello?"

"Good morning, Henry," said a quavering voice; it was his mother.

"Mother—at this hour?" he asked dryly.

"Oh, you're always up at dawn, and I wanted to catch you before you went to the office."

"Yes? What is it?"

"I've got to see you, Henry. I've got to speak to you. Today. Sometime today. It's important."

"Has anything happened?"

"No . . . yes . . . that is . . . I've got to have a talk with you in person. Will you come?"

"I'm sorry, I can't. I have an appointment in New York tonight. If you want me to come tomorrow—"

"No! No, not tomorrow. It's got to be today. It's got to." There was a dim tone of panic in her voice, but it was the stale panic of chronic helplessness, not the sound of an emergency—except for an odd echo of fear in her mechanical insistence.

"What is it, Mother?"

"I can't talk about it over the telephone. I've got to see you."

"Then if you wish to come to the office—"

"No! Not at the office! I've got to see you alone, where we can talk. Can't you come here today, as a favor? It's your mother who's asking you a favor. You've never come to see us at all. And maybe you're not the one to blame for it, either. But can't you do it for me this once, if I beg you to?"

"All right, Mother. I'll be there at four o'clock this afternoon."

"That will be fine, Henry. Thank you, Henry. That will be fine."

It seemed to him that there was a touch of tension in the air of the mills, that day. It was a touch too slight to define—but the mills, to him, were like the face of a loved wife where he could catch shades of feeling almost ahead of expression. He noticed small clusters of the new workers, just three or four of them huddling together in conversation —once or twice too often. He noticed their manner, a manner suggesting a poolroom corner, not a factory. He noticed a few glances thrown at him as he went by, glances a shade too pointed and lingering. He dismissed it; it was not quite enough to wonder about—and he had no time to wonder.

When he drove up to his former home, that afternoon, he stopped his car abruptly at the foot of the hill. He had not seen the house since that May 15, six months ago, when he had walked out of it— and the sight brought back to him the sum of all he had felt in ten years of daily home-coming: the strain, the bewilderment, the gray weight of unconfessed unhappiness, the stern endurance that forbade him to confess it, the desperate innocence of the effort to understand his family . . . the effort to be just.

He walked slowly up the path toward the door. He felt no emotion, only the sense of a great, solemn clarity. He knew that this house was a monument of guilt—of his guilt toward himself.

He had expected to see his mother and Philip; he had not expected the third person who rose, as they did, at his entrance into the living room: it was Lillian.

He stopped on the threshold. They stood looking at his face and at the open door behind him. Their faces had a look of fear and cunning, the look of that blackmail-through-virtue which he had learned to understand, as if they hoped to get away with it by means of nothing but his pity, to hold him trapped, when a single step back could take him out of their reach.

They had counted on his pity and dreaded his anger; they had not dared consider the third alternative: his indifference.

"What is she doing here?" he asked, turning to his mother, his voice dispassionately flat.

"Lillian's been living here ever since your divorce," she answered defensively. "I couldn't let her starve on the city pavements, could I?"

The look in his mother's eyes was half-plea, as if she were begging him not to slap her face, half-triumph, as if she had slapped his. He knew her motive: it was not compassion, there had never been much love between Lillian and her, it was their common revenge against him, it was the secret satisfaction of spending his money on the ex-wife he had refused to support.

Lillian's head was poised to bow in greeting, with the tentative hint of a smile on her lips, half-timid, half-brash. He did not pretend to ignore her; he looked at her, as if he were seeing her fully, yet as if no presence were being registered in his mind. He said nothing, closed the door and stepped into the room.

His mother gave a small sigh of uneasy relief and dropped hastily into the nearest chair, watching him, nervously uncertain of whether he would follow her example.

"What was it you wanted?" he asked, sitting down.

His mother sat erect and oddly hunched, her shoulders raised, her head half-lowered. "Mercy, Henry," she whispered.

"What do you mean?"

"Don't you understand me?"

"No."

"Well"—she spread her hands in an untidily fluttering gesture of helplessness—"well . . . " Her eyes darted about, struggling to escape his attentive glance. "Well, there are so many things to say and . . . and I don't know how to say them, but . . . well, there's one practical matter, but it's not important by itself . . . it's not why I called you here . . ."

"What is it?"

"The practical matter? Our allowance checks—Philip's and mine. It's the first of the month, but on account of that attachment order, the checks couldn't come through. You know that, don't you?"

"I know it."

"Well, what are we going to do?"

"I don't know."

"I mean, what are *you* going to do about it?"

"Nothing."

His mother sat staring at him, as if counting the seconds of silence. "Nothing, Henry?"

"I have no power to do anything."

They were watching his face with a kind of searching intensity; he felt certain that his mother had told him the truth, that immediate financial worry was not their purpose, that it was only the symbol of a much wider issue.

"But, Henry, we're caught short."

"So was I."

"But can't you send us some cash or something?"

"They gave me no warning, no time to get any cash."

"Then . . . Look, Henry, the thing was so unexpected, it scared people, I guess—the grocery store refuses to give us credit, unless *you* ask for it. I think they want you to sign a credit card or something. So will you speak to them and arrange it?"

"I will not."

"You won't?" She choked on a small gasp. "Why?"

"I will not assume obligations that I can't fulfill."

"What do you mean?"

"I will not assume debts I have no way of repaying."

"What do you mean, no way? That attachment is only some sort of technicality, it's only temporary, everybody knows that!"

"Do they? I don't."

"But, Henry—a grocery bill! You're not sure you'll be able to pay a grocery bill, *you,* with all the millions you own?"

"I'm not going to defraud the grocer by pretending that I own those millions."

"What are you talking about? Who owns them?"

"Nobody."

"What do you mean?"

"Mother, I think you understand me fully. I think you understood it before I did. There isn't any ownership left in existence or any property. It's what you've approved of and believed in for years. You wanted me tied. I'm tied. Now it's too late to play any games about it."

"Are you going to let some political ideas of yours—" She saw the look on his face and stopped abruptly.

Lillian sat looking down at the floor, as if afraid to glance up at this moment. Philip sat cracking his knuckles.

His mother dragged her eyes into focus again and whispered, "Don't abandon us, Henry." Some faint stab of life in her voice told him that the lid of her real purpose was cracking open. "These are terrible times, and we're scared. That's the truth of it, Henry, we're scared, because you're turning away from us. Oh, I don't mean just that grocery bill, but that's a sign—a year ago you wouldn't have let that happen to us. Now . . . now you don't care." She made an expectant pause. "Do you?"

"No."

"Well . . . well, I guess the blame is ours. That's what I wanted to tell you—that we know we're to blame. We haven't treated you right, all these years. We've been unfair to you, we've made you suffer, we've used you and given you no thanks in return. We're guilty, Henry, we've sinned against you, and we confess it. What more can we say to you now? Will you find it in your heart to forgive us?"

"What is it you want me to do?" he asked, in the clear, flat tone of a business conference.

"I don't know! Who am I to know? But that's not what I'm talking of right now. Not of *doing,* only of *feeling.* It's your feeling that I'm begging you for, Henry—just your feeling—even if we don't deserve it. You're generous and strong. Will you cancel the past, Henry? Will you forgive us?"

The look of terror in her eyes was real. A year ago, he would have told himself that this was her way of making amends; he would have choked his revulsion against her words, words which conveyed nothing to him but the fog of the meaningless; he would have violated his mind to give them meaning, even if he did not understand; he would have ascribed to her the virtue of sincerity in her own terms, even if they were not his. But he was through with granting respect to any terms other than his own.

"Will you forgive us?"

"Mother, it would be best not to speak of that. Don't press me to tell you why. I think you know it as well as I do. If there's anything you want done, tell me what it is. There's nothing else to discuss."

"But I *don't* understand you! I don't! That's what I called you here for—to ask your forgiveness! Are you going to refuse to answer me?"

"Very well. What would it mean, my forgiveness?"

"Uh?"

"I said, what would it mean?"

She spread her hands out in an astonished gesture to indicate the self-evident. "Why, it . . . it would make us feel better."

"Will it change the past?"

"It would make us feel better to know that you've forgiven it."

"Do you wish me to pretend that the past has not existed?"

"Oh God, Henry, can't you see? All we want is only to know that you . . . that you feel some concern for us."

"I don't feel it. Do you wish me to fake it?"

"But that's what I'm begging you for—to *feel* it!"

"On what ground?"

"Ground?"

"In exchange for what?"

"Henry, Henry, it's not business we're talking about, not steel tonnages and bank balances, it's *feelings*—and you talk like a trader!"

"I am one."

What he saw in her eyes was terror—not the helpless terror of struggling and failing to understand, but the terror of being pushed toward the edge where to avoid understanding would no longer be possible.

"Look, Henry," said Philip hastily, "Mother can't understand those things. We don't know how to approach you. We can't speak your language."

"I don't speak yours."

"What she's trying to say is that we're sorry. We're terribly sorry that we've hurt you. You think we're not paying for it, but we are. We're suffering remorse."

The pain in Philip's face was real. A year ago, Rearden would have felt pity. Now, he knew that they had held him through nothing but his reluctance to hurt them, his fear of *their* pain. He was not afraid of it any longer.

"We're sorry, Henry. We know we've harmed you. We wish we could atone for it. But what can we do? The past is past. We can't undo it."

"Neither can I."

"You can accept our repentance," said Lillian, in a voice glassy with caution. "I have nothing to gain from you now. I only want you to know that whatever I've done, I've done it because I loved you."

He turned away, without answering.

"Henry!" cried his mother. "What's happened to you? What's changed you like that? You don't seem to be human any more! You keep pressing us for answers, when we haven't any answers to give. You keep beating us with logic—what's logic at a time like this?—what's logic when people are suffering?"

"We can't help it!" cried Philip.

"We're at your mercy," said Lillian.

They were throwing their pleas at a face that could not be reached. They did not know—and their panic was the last of their struggle to escape the knowledge—that his merciless sense of justice, which had been their only hold on him, which had made him take any punishment and give them the benefit of every doubt, was now turned against them—that the same force that had made him tolerant, was now the force that made him ruthless—that the justice which would forgive miles of innocent errors of knowledge, would not forgive a single step taken in conscious evil.

"Henry, don't you understand us?" his mother was pleading.

"I do," he said quietly.

She looked away, avoiding the clarity of his eyes. "Don't you care what becomes of us?"

"I don't."

"Aren't you human?" Her voice grew shrill with anger. "Aren't you capable of any love at all? It's your heart I'm trying to reach, not your mind! Love is not something to argue and reason and bargain about! It's something to give! To feel! Oh God, Henry, can't you feel without thinking?"

"I never have."

In a moment, her voice came back, low and droning: "We're not as smart as you are, not as strong. If we've sinned and blundered, it's because we're helpless. We need you, you're all we've got—and we're losing you—and we're afraid. These are terrible times, and getting worse, people are scared to death, scared and blind and not knowing what to do. How are we to cope with it, if you leave us? We're small and weak and we'll be swept like driftwood in that terror that's running loose in the world. Maybe we had our share of guilt for it, maybe we helped to bring it about, not knowing any better, but what's done is done—and we can't stop it now. If you abandon us, we're lost. If you give up and vanish, like all those men who—"

It was not a sound that stopped her, it was only a movement of his eyebrows, the brief, swift movement of a check mark. Then they saw him smile; the nature of the smile was the most terrifying of answers.

"So that's what you're afraid of," he said slowly.

"You can't quit!" his mother screamed in blind panic. "You can't quit now! You could have, last year, but not now! Not today! You can't turn deserter, because now they take it out on your family! They'll leave us penniless, they'll seize everything, they'll leave us to starve, they'll—"

"Keep still!" cried Lillian, more adept than the others at reading danger signs in Rearden's face.

His face held the remnant of a smile, and they knew that he was not seeing them any longer, but it was not in their power to know why his smile now seemed to hold pain and an almost wistful longing, or why he was looking across the room, at the niche of the farthest window.

He was seeing a finely sculptured face held composed under the lashing of his insults, he was hearing a voice that had said to him quietly, here, in this room: "It is against the sin of forgiveness that I wanted to warn you." You who had known it then, he thought . . . but he did not finish the sentence in his mind, he let it end in the bitter twist of his smile, because he knew what he had been about to think: You who had known it then—forgive me.

There it was—he thought, looking at his family—the nature of their pleas for mercy, the logic of those feelings they so righteously proclaimed as non-logical—*there* was the simple, brutal essence of all men who speak of being able to feel without thought and of placing mercy over justice.

They had known what to fear; they had grasped and named, before he had, the only way of deliverance left open to him; they had understood the hopelessness of his industrial position, the futility of his struggle, the impossible burdens descending to crush him; they had known that in reason, in justice, in self-preservation, his only course was to drop it all and run—yet they wanted to hold him, to keep him in the sacrificial furnace, to make him let them devour the last of him in the name of mercy, forgiveness and brother-cannibal love.

"If you still want me to explain it, Mother," he said very quietly, "if you're still hoping that I won't be cruel enough to name what you're pretending not to know, then *here's* what's wrong with your idea of forgiveness: You regret that you've hurt me and, as your atonement for it, you ask that I offer myself to total immolation."

"Logic!" she screamed. "There you go again with your damn logic! It's pity that we need, pity, not logic!"

He rose to his feet.

"Wait! Don't go! Henry, don't abandon us! Don't sentence us to perish! Whatever we are, we're human! We want to live!"

"Why, no—" he started in quiet astonishment and ended in quiet horror, as the thought struck him fully, "I don't think you do. If you did, you would have known how to value me."

As if in silent proof and answer, Philip's face went slowly into an expression intended as a smile of amusement, yet holding nothing but fear and malice. "You won't be able to quit and run away," said Philip. "You can't run away without money."

It seemed to strike its goal; Rearden stopped short, then chuckled. "Thanks, Philip," he said.

"Uh?" Philip gave a nervous jerk of bewilderment.

"So that's the purpose of the attachment order. That's what your friends are afraid of. I knew they were getting set to spring something on me today. I didn't know that the attachment was their idea of cutting off escape." He turned incredulously to look at his mother. "And that's why you had to see me *today*, before the conference in New York."

"Mother didn't know it!" cried Philip, then caught himself and cried louder, "I don't know what you're talking about! I haven't said anything! I haven't said it!" His fear now seemed to have some much less mystic and much more practical quality.

"Don't worry, you poor little louse, I won't tell them that you've told me anything. And if you were trying—"

He did not finish; he looked at the three faces before him, and a sudden smile ended his sentence, a smile of weariness, of pity, of incredulous revulsion. He was seeing the final contradiction, the grotesque absurdity at the end of the irrationalists' game: the men in Washington had hoped to hold him by prompting *these* three to try for the role of hostages.

"You think you're so good, don't you?" It was a sudden cry and it came from Lillian; she had leaped to her feet to bar his exit; her face was distorted, as he had seen it once before, on that morning when she had learned the name of his mistress. "You're so good! You're so proud of yourself! Well, *I* have something to tell you!"

She looked as if she had not believed until this moment that her game was lost. The sight of her face struck him like a last shred completing a circuit, and in sudden clarity he knew what her game had been and why she had married him.

If to choose a person as the constant center of one's concern, as the focus of one's view of life, was to love—he thought—then it was true that she loved him; but if, to him, love was a celebration of one's self and of existence—then, to the self-haters and life-haters, the pursuit of destruction was the only form and equivalent of love. It was for the best of his virtues that Lillian had chosen him, for his strength, his confidence, his pride—she had chosen him as one chooses an object of love, as the symbol of man's living power, but the destruction of that power had been her goal.

He saw them as they had been at their first meeting: he, the man of violent energy and passionate ambition, the man of achievement, lighted by the flame of his success and flung into the midst of those pretentious ashes who called themselves an intellectual elite, the burned-out remnants of undigested culture, feeding on the afterglow of the minds of others, offering their denial of the mind as their only claim to distinction, and a craving to control the world as their only lust—she, the woman hanger-on of that elite, wearing their shopworn sneer as her answer to the universe, holding impotence as superiority and emptiness as virtue—he, unaware of their hatred, innocently scornful of their posturing fraud—she, seeing him as the danger to their world, as a threat, as a challenge, as a reproach.

The lust that drives others to enslave an empire, had become, in her limits, a passion for power over *him*. She had set out to break him, as if, unable to equal his value, she could surpass it by destroying it, as if the measure of his greatness would thus become the measure of hers, as if—he thought with a shudder—as if the vandal who smashed a statue were greater than the artist who had made it, as if the murderer who killed a child were greater than the mother who had given it birth.

He remembered her hammering derision of his work, his mills, his Metal, his success, he remembered her desire to see him drunk, just once, her attempts to push him into infidelity, her pleasure at the thought that he had fallen to the level of some sordid romance, her terror on discovering that that romance had been an attainment, not a degradation. Her line of attack, which he had found so baffling, had been constant and clear—it was his self-esteem she had sought to destroy, knowing that a man who surrenders his value is at the mercy of anyone's will; it was his moral purity she had struggled to breach, it was his confident rectitude she had wanted to shatter by means of the poison of guilt—as if, were he to collapse, his depravity would give her a right to hers.

For the same purpose and motive, for the same satisfaction, as others weave complex systems of philosophy to destroy generations, or establish dictatorships to destroy a country, so she, possessing no weapons except femininity, had made it her goal to destroy one man.

Yours was the code of life—he remembered the voice of his lost young teacher—*what, then, is theirs?*

"I have something to tell you!" cried Lillian, with the sound of that impotent rage which wishes that words were brass knuckles. "You're so proud of yourself, aren't you? You're so proud of your name! Rearden Steel, Rearden Metal, Rearden Wife! That's what I was, wasn't I? Mrs. Rearden! Mrs. Henry Rearden!" The sounds she was making were now a string of cackling gasps, an unrecognizable corruption of laughter. "Well, I think you'd like to know that your wife's been laid by another man! I've been unfaithful to you, do you hear me? I've been unfaithful, not with some great, noble lover, but with the scummiest louse, with Jim Taggart! Three months ago! Before your divorce! While I was your wife! While I was still your wife!"

He stood listening like a scientist studying a subject of no personal relevance whatever. There, he thought, was the final abortion of the creed of collective interdependence, the creed of non-identity, non-property, non-fact: the belief that the moral stature of one is at the mercy of the action of another.

"I've been unfaithful to you! Don't you hear me, you stainless Puritan? I've slept with Jim Taggart, you incorruptible hero! Don't you hear me? . . . Don't you hear me? . . . Don't you . . . ?"

He was looking at her as he would have looked if a strange woman had approached him on the street with a personal confession—a look like the equivalent of the words: Why tell it to me?

Her voice trailed off. He had not known what the destruction of a person would be like; but he knew that he was seeing the destruction of Lillian. He saw it in the collapse of her face, in the sudden slackening of features, as if there were nothing to hold them together, in the eyes, blind, yet staring, staring inward, filled with that terror which no outer threat can equal. It was not the look of a person losing her mind, but the look of a mind seeing total defeat and, in the same instant, seeing her own nature for the first time—the look of a person seeing that after years of preaching non-existence, she had achieved it.

He turned to go. His mother stopped him at the door, seizing his arm. With a look of stubborn bewilderment, with the last of her effort at self-deceit, she moaned in a voice of tearfully petulant reproach, "Are you really incapable of forgiveness?"

"No, Mother," he answered, "I'm not. I would have forgiven the past—if, today, you had urged me to quit and disappear."

There was a cold wind outside, tightening his overcoat about him like an embrace, there was the great, fresh sweep of country stretching at the foot of the hill, and the clear, receding sky of twilight. Like two sunsets ending the day, the red glow of the sun was a straight, still band in the west, and the breathing red band in the east was the glow of his mills.

The feel of the steering wheel under his hands and of the smooth highway streaming past, as he sped to New York, had an oddly bracing quality. It was a sense of extreme precision and of relaxation, together, a sense of action without strain, which seemed inexplicably youthful—until he realized that this was the way he had acted and had expected always to act, in his youth—and what he now felt was like the simple, astonished question: Why should one ever have to act in any other manner?

It seemed to him that the skyline of New York, when it rose before him, had a strangely luminous clarity, though its shapes were veiled by distance, a clarity that did not seem to rest in the object, but felt as if the illumination came from him. He looked at the great city, with no tie to any view or usage others had made of it, it was not a city of gangsters or panhandlers or derelicts or whores, it was the greatest industrial achievement in the history of man, its only meaning was that which it meant to him, there was a personal quality in his sight of it, a quality of possessiveness and of unhesitant perception, as if he were seeing it for the first time—or the last.

He paused in the silent corridor of the Wayne-Falkland, at the door of the suite he was to enter; it took him a long moment's effort to lift his hand and knock: it was the suite that had belonged to Francisco d'Anconia.

There were coils of cigarette smoke weaving through the air of the drawing room, among the velvet drapes and bare, polished tables. With its costly furniture and the absence of all personal belongings, the room had that air of dreary luxury which pertains to transient occupancy, as dismal as the air of a flophouse. Five figures rose in the fog at his entrance: Wesley Mouch, Eugene Lawson, James Taggart, Dr. Floyd Ferris and a slim, slouching man who looked like a rat-faced tennis player and was introduced to him as Tinky Holloway.

"All right," said Rearden, cutting off the greetings, the smiles, the offers of drinks and the comments on the national emergency, "what did you want?"

"We're here as your friends, Mr. Rearden," said Tinky Holloway, "purely as your friends, for an informal conversation with a view to closer mutual teamwork."

"We're anxious to avail ourselves of your outstanding ability," said Lawson, "and your expert advice on the country's industrial problems."

"It's men like you that we need in Washington," said Dr. Ferris. "There's no reason why you should have remained an outsider for so long, when your voice is needed at the top level of national leadership."

The sickening thing about it, thought Rearden, was that the speeches were only half-lies; the other half, in their tone of hysterical urgency, was the unstated wish to have it somehow be true. "What did you want?" he asked.

"Why . . . to listen to *you*, Mr. Rearden," said Wesley Mouch, the jerk of his features imitating a frightened smile; the smile was faked, the fear was real. "We . . . we want the benefit of your opinion on the nation's industrial crisis."

"I have nothing to say."

"But, Mr. Rearden," said Dr. Ferris, "all we want is a chance to co-operate with you."

"I've told you once, publicly, that I don't co-operate at the point of a gun."

"Can't we bury the hatchet at a time like this?" said Lawson beseechingly.

"The gun? Go ahead."

"Uh?"

"It's you who're holding it. Bury it, if you think you can."

"That . . . that was just a figure of speech," Lawson explained, blinking. "I was speaking metaphorically."

"I wasn't."

"Can't we all stand together for the sake of the country in this hour of emergency?" said Dr. Ferris. "Can't we disregard our differences of opinion? We're willing to meet you halfway. If there's any aspect of our policy which you oppose, just tell us and we'll issue a directive to—"

"Cut it, boys. I didn't come here to help you pretend that I'm not in the position I'm in and that any halfway is possible between us. Now come to the point. You've prepared some new gimmick to spring on the steel industry. What is it?"

"As a matter of fact," said Mouch, "we do have a vital question to discuss in regard to the steel industry, but . . . but your language, Mr. Rearden!"

"We don't want to *spring* anything on you," said Holloway. "We asked you here to *discuss* it with you."

"I came here to take orders. Give them."

"But, Mr. Rearden, we don't want to look at it that way. We don't want to give you *orders*. We want your *voluntary* consent."

Rearden smiled. "I know it."

"You do?" Holloway started eagerly, but something about Rearden's smile made him slide into uncertainty. "Well, then—"

"And you, brother," said Rearden, "know that *that* is the flaw in your game, the fatal flaw that will blast it sky-high. Now do you tell me what clout on my head you're working so hard not to let me notice—or do I go home?"

"Oh no, Mr. Rearden!" cried Lawson, with a sudden dart of his eyes to his wrist watch. "You can't go now!—That is, I mean, you wouldn't want to go without hearing what we have to say."

"Then let me hear it."

He saw them glancing at one another. Wesley Mouch seemed afraid to address him; Mouch's face assumed an expression of petulant stubbornness, like a signal of command pushing the others forward; whatever their qualifications to dispose of the fate of the steel industry, they had been brought here to act as Mouch's conversational bodyguards. Rearden wondered about the reason for the presence of James Taggart; Taggart sat in gloomy silence, sullenly sipping a drink, never glancing in his direction.

"We have worked out a plan," said Dr. Ferris too cheerfully, "which will solve the problems of the steel industry and which will meet with your full approval, as a measure providing for the general welfare, while protecting your interests and insuring your safety in a—"

"Don't try to tell me what I'm going to think. Give me the facts."

"It is a plan which is fair, sound, equitable and—"

"Don't tell me your evaluation. Give me the facts."

"It is a plan which—" Dr. Ferris stopped; he had lost the habit of naming facts.

"Under this plan," said Wesley Mouch, "we will grant the industry a five per cent increase in the price of steel." He paused triumphantly.

Rearden said nothing.

"Of course, some minor adjustments will be necessary," said Holloway airily, leaping into the silence as onto a vacant tennis court. "A certain increase in prices will have to be granted to the producers of iron ore—oh, three per cent at most—in view of the added hardships which some of them, Mr. Larkin of Minnesota, for instance, will now encounter, inasmuch as they'll have to ship their ore by the costly means of trucks, since Mr. James Taggart has had to sacrifice his Minnesota branch line to the public welfare. And, of course, an increase in freight rates will have to be granted to the country's railroads—let's say, seven per cent, roughly speaking—in view of the absolutely essential need for—"

Holloway stopped, like a player emerging from a whirlwind activity to notice suddenly that no opponent was answering his shots.

"But there will be no increase in wages," said Dr. Ferris hastily. "An essential point of the plan is that we will grant no increase in wages to the steel workers, in spite of their insistent demands. We do wish to be fair to you, Mr. Rearden, and to protect your interests—even at the risk of popular resentment and indignation."

"Of course, if we expect labor to make a sacrifice," said Lawson, "we must show them that management, too, is making certain sacrifices for the sake of the country. The mood of labor in the steel industry is extremely tense at present, Mr. Rearden, it is dangerously explosive and . . . and in order to protect you from . . . from . . ." He stopped.

"Yes?" said Rearden. "From?"

"From possible . . . violence, certain measures are necessary, which . . . Look, Jim"—he turned suddenly to James Taggart—"why don't you explain it to Mr. Rearden, as a fellow industrialist?"

"Well, somebody's got to support the railroads," said Taggart sullenly, not looking at him. "The country needs railroads and somebody's got to help us carry the load, and if we don't get an increase in freight rates—"

"No, no, no!" snapped Wesley Mouch. "Tell Mr. Rearden about the working of the Railroad Unification Plan."

"Well, the Plan is a full success," said Taggart lethargically, "except for the not fully controllable element of time. It is only a question of time before our unified teamwork puts every railroad in the country back on its feet. The Plan, I'm in a position to assure you, would work as successfully for any other industry."

"No doubt about that," said Rearden, and turned to Mouch. "Why do you ask the stooge to waste my time? What has the Railroad Unification Plan to do with me?"

"But, Mr. Rearden," cried Mouch with desperate cheerfulness, "that's the pattern we're to follow! *That's* what we called you here to discuss!"

"What?"

"The *Steel* Unification Plan!"

There was an instant of silence, as of breaths drawn after a plunge. Rearden sat looking at them with a glance that seemed to be a glance of interest.

"In view of the critical plight of the steel industry," said Mouch with a sudden rush, as if not to give himself time to know what made him uneasy about the nature of Rearden's glance, "and since steel is the most vitally, crucially basic commodity, the foundation of our entire industrial structure, drastic measures must be taken to preserve the country's steel-making facilities, equipment and plant." The tone and impetus of public speaking carried him that far and no farther. "With this objective in view, our Plan is . . . our Plan is . . ."

"Our Plan is really very simple," said Tinky Holloway, striving to prove it by the gaily bouncing simplicity of his voice. "We'll lift all restrictions from the production of steel and every company will produce all it can, according to its ability. But to avoid the waste and danger of dog-eat-dog competition, all the companies will deposit their gross earnings into a common pool, to be known as the Steel Unification Pool, in charge of a special Board. At the end of the year, the Board will distribute these earnings by totaling the nation's steel output and dividing it by the number of open-hearth furnaces in existence, thus arriving at an average which will be fair to all—and every company will be paid according to its need. The preservation of its furnaces being its basic need, every company will be paid according to the number of furnaces it owns."

He stopped, waited, then added, "That's it, Mr. Rearden," and getting no answer, said, "Oh, there's a lot of wrinkles to be ironed out, but . . . but that's it."

Whatever reaction they had expected, it was not the one they saw. Rearden leaned back in his chair, his eyes attentive, but fixed on space, as if looking at a not too distant distance, then he asked, with an odd note of quietly impersonal amusement, "Will you tell me just one thing, boys: what is it you're counting on?"

He knew that they understood. He saw, on their faces, that stubbornly evasive look which he had once thought to be the look of a liar cheating a victim, but which he now knew to be worse: the look of a man cheating himself of his own consciousness. They did not answer. They remained silent, as if struggling, not to make him forget his question, but to make themselves forget that they had heard it.

"It's a sound, practical Plan!" snapped James Taggart unexpectedly, with an angry edge of sudden animation in his voice. "It will work! It has to work! We *want* it to work!"

No one answered him.

"Mr. Rearden . . . ?" said Holloway timidly.

"Well, let me see," said Rearden. "Orren Boyle's Associated Steel owns 60 open-hearth furnaces, one-third of them standing idle and the rest producing an average of 300 tons of steel per furnace per day. I own 20 open-hearth furnaces, working at capacity, producing 750 tons of Rearden Metal per furnace per day. So we own 80 'pooled' furnaces with a 'pooled' output of 27,000 tons, which makes an average of 337.5 tons per furnace. Each day of the year, I, producing 15,000 tons, will be paid for 6,750 tons. Boyle, producing 12,000 tons, will be paid for 20,250 tons. Never mind the other members of the pool, they won't change the scale, except to bring the average still lower, most of them doing worse than Boyle, none of them producing as much as I. Now how long do you expect me to last under your Plan?"

There was no answer, then Lawson cried suddenly, blindly, righteously, "In time of national peril, it is your duty to serve, suffer and work for the salvation of the country!"

"I don't see why pumping my earnings into Orren Boyle's pocket is going to save the country."

"You have to make certain sacrifices to the public welfare!"

"I don't see why Orren Boyle is more 'the public' than I am."

"Oh, it's not a question of Mr. Boyle at all! It's much wider than any one person. It's a matter of preserving the country's natural resources—such as factories—and saving the whole of the nation's industrial plant. We cannot permit the ruin of an establishment as vast as Mr. Boyle's. The country needs it."

"I think," said Rearden slowly, "that the country needs me much more than it needs Orren Boyle."

"But of course!" cried Lawson with startled enthusiasm. "The country needs you, Mr. Rearden! You do realize that, don't you?"

But Lawson's avid pleasure at the familiar formula of self-immolation, vanished abruptly at the sound of Rearden's voice, a cold, trader's voice answering: "I do."

"It's not Boyle alone who's involved," said Holloway pleadingly. "The country's economy would not be able to stand a major dislocation at the present moment. There are thousands of Boyle's workers, suppliers and customers. What would happen to them if Associated Steel went bankrupt?"

"What will happen to the thousands of my workers, suppliers and customers when *I* go bankrupt?"

"*You*, Mr. Rearden?" said Holloway incredulously. "But you're the richest, safest and strongest industrialist in the country at this moment!"

"What about the moment after next?"

"Uh?"

"How long do you expect me to be able to produce at a loss?"

"Oh, Mr. Rearden, I have complete faith in you!"

"To hell with your faith! How do you expect me to do it?"

"You'll manage!"

"How?"

There was no answer.

"We can't theorize about the future," cried Wesley Mouch, "when there's an immediate national collapse to avoid! We've got to save the country's economy! We've got to do something!" Rearden's imperturbable glance of curiosity drove him to heedlessness. "If you don't like it, do you have a better solution to offer?"

"Sure," said Rearden easily. "If it's production that you want, then get out of the way, junk all of your damn regulations, let Orren Boyle go broke, let me buy the plant of Associated Steel—and it will be pouring a thousand tons a day from every one of its sixty furnaces."

"Oh, but . . . but we couldn't!" gasped Mouch. "That would be monopoly!"

Rearden chuckled. "Okay," he said indifferently, "then let my mills superintendent buy it. He'll do a better job than Boyle."

"Oh, but that would be letting the strong have an advantage over the weak! We couldn't do that!"

"Then don't talk about saving the country's economy."

"All we want is—" He stopped.

"All you want is production without men who're able to produce, isn't it?"

"That . . . that's theory. That's just a theoretical extreme. All we want is a temporary adjustment."

"You've been making those temporary adjustments for years. Don't you see that you've run out of time?"

"That's just theo . . ." His voice trailed off and stopped.

"Well, now, look here," said Holloway cautiously, "it's not as if Mr. Boyle were actually . . . weak. Mr. Boyle is an extremely able man. It's just that he's suffered some unfortunate reverses, quite beyond his control. He had invested large sums in a public-spirited project to assist the undeveloped peoples of South America, and that copper crash of theirs has dealt him a severe financial blow. So it's only a matter of giving him a chance to recover, a helping hand to bridge the gap, a bit of temporary assistance, nothing more. All we have to do is just equalize the sacrifice—then everybody will recover and prosper."

"You've been equalizing sacrifice for over a hundred"—he stopped —"for thousands of years," said Rearden slowly. "Don't you see that you're at the end of the road?"

"That's just theory!" snapped Wesley Mouch.

Rearden smiled. "I know your practice," he said softly. "It's your theory that I'm trying to understand."

He knew that the specific reason behind the Plan was Orren Boyle; he knew that the working of an intricate mechanism, operated by pull, threat, pressure, blackmail—a mechanism like an irrational adding machine run amuck and throwing up any chance sum at the whim of any moment—had happened to add up to Boyle's pressure upon these men to extort for him this last piece of plunder. He knew also that Boyle was not the cause of it or the essential to consider, that Boyle was only a chance rider, not the builder, of the infernal machine that had destroyed the world, that it was not Boyle who had made it possible, nor any of the men in this room. They, too, were only riders on a machine without a driver, they were trembling hitchhikers who knew that their vehicle was about to crash into its final abyss—and it was not love or fear of Boyle that made them cling to their course and press on toward their end, it was something else, it was some one nameless element which they knew and evaded knowing, something which was neither thought nor hope, something he identified only as a certain look in their faces, a furtive look saying: I can get away with it. Why? —he thought. Why do they think they can?

"We can't afford any theories!" cried Wesley Mouch. "We've got to act!"

"Well, then, I'll offer you another solution. Why don't you take over my mills and be done with it?"

The jolt that shook them was genuine terror.

"Oh no!" gasped Mouch.

"We wouldn't think of it!" cried Holloway.

"We stand for free enterprise!" cried Dr. Ferris.

"We don't want to harm you!" cried Lawson. "We're your friends, Mr. Rearden. Can't we all work together? We're your friends."

There, across the room, stood a table with a telephone, the same table, most likely, and the same instrument—and suddenly Rearden felt as if he were seeing the convulsed figure of a man bent over that telephone, a man who had then known what he, Rearden, was now beginning to learn, a man fighting to refuse him the same request which he was now refusing to the present tenants of this room—he saw the finish of that fight, a man's tortured face lifted to confront him and a desperate voice saying steadily: "Mr. Rearden, I swear to you . . . by the woman I love . . . that I am your friend."

This was the act he had then called treason, and this was the man he had rejected in order to go on serving the men confronting him now. Who, then, had been the traitor?—he thought; he thought it almost without feeling, without right to feel, conscious of nothing but a solemnly reverent clarity. Who had chosen to give its present tenants the means to acquire this room? Whom had he sacrificed and to whose profit?

"Mr. Rearden!" moaned Lawson. "What's the matter?"

He turned his head, saw Lawson's eyes watching him fearfully and guessed what look Lawson had caught in his face.

"We don't *want* to seize your mills!" cried Mouch.

"We don't want to deprive you of your property!" cried Dr. Ferris. "You don't understand us!"

"I'm beginning to."

A year ago, he thought, they would have shot him; two years ago, they would have confiscated his property; generations ago, men of their kind had been able to afford the luxury of murder and expropriation, the safety of pretending to themselves and their victims that material loot was their only objective. But their time was running out and his fellow victims had gone, gone sooner than any historical schedule had promised, and they, the looters, were now left to face the undisguised reality of their own goal.

"Look, boys," he said wearily. "I know what you want. You want to eat my mills and have them, too. And all I want to know is this: what makes you think it's possible?"

"I don't know what you mean," said Mouch in an injured tone of voice. "We said we didn't want your mills."

"All right, I'll say it more precisely: You want to eat *me* and have me, too. How do you propose to do it?"

"I don't know how you can say that, after we've given you every assurance that we consider you of invaluable importance to the country, to the steel industry, to—"

"I believe you. That's what makes the riddle harder. You consider me of invaluable importance to the country? Hell, you consider me of invaluable importance even to your own necks. You sit there trembling, because you know that I'm the last one left to save your lives—and you know that time is as short as that. Yet you propose a plan to destroy me, a plan which demands, with an idiot's crudeness, without loopholes, detours or escape, that I work *at a loss*—that I work, with every ton I pour costing me more than I'll get for it—that I feed the last of my wealth away until we all starve together. That much irrationality is not possible to any man or any looter. For your own sake—never mind the country's or mine—you must be counting on something. What?"

He saw the getting-away-with-it look on their faces, a peculiar look that seemed secretive, yet resentful, as if, incredibly, it were *he* who was hiding some secret from them.

"I don't see why you should choose to take such a defeatist view of the situation," said Mouch sullenly.

"Defeatist? Do you really expect me to be able to remain in business under your Plan?"

"But it's only temporary!"

"There's no such thing as a temporary suicide."

"But it's only for the duration of the emergency! Only until the country recovers!"

"How do you expect it to recover?"

There was no answer.

"How do you expect me to produce after I go bankrupt?"

"You won't go bankrupt. You'll always produce," said Dr. Ferris indifferently, neither in praise nor in blame, merely in the tone of stating a fact of nature, as he would have said to another man: You'll always be a bum. "You can't help it. It's in your blood. Or, to be more scientific: you're conditioned that way."

Rearden sat up: it was as if he had been struggling to find the secret combination of a lock and felt, at those words, a faint click within, as of the first tumbril falling into place.

"It's only a matter of weathering this crisis," said Mouch, "of giving people a reprieve, a chance to catch up."

"And then?"

"Then things will improve."

"How?"

There was no answer.

"What will improve them?"

There was no answer.

"Who will improve them?"

"Christ, Mr. Rearden, people don't just stand still!" cried Holloway. "They do things, they grow, they move forward!"

"What people?"

Holloway waved his hand vaguely. "People," he said.

"What people? The people to whom you're going to feed the last of Rearden Steel, without getting anything in return? The people who'll go on consuming more than they produce?"

"Conditions will change."

"Who'll change them?"

There was no answer.

"Have you anything left to loot? If you didn't see the nature of your policy before—it's not possible that you don't see it now. Look around you. All those damned People's States all over the earth have been existing only on the handouts which you squeezed for them out of this country. But you—you have no place left to sponge on or mooch from. No country on the face of the globe. This was the greatest and last. You've drained it. You've milked it dry. Of all that irretrievable splendor, I'm only one remnant, the last. What will you do, you and your People's Globe, after you've finished me? What are you hoping for? What do you see ahead—except plain, stark, animal starvation?"

They did not answer. They did not look at him. Their faces wore expressions of stubborn resentment, as if *his* were the plea of a liar.

Then Lawson said softly, half in reproach, half in scorn, "Well, after all, you businessmen have kept predicting disasters for years, you've cried catastrophe at every progressive measure and told us that we'll perish—but we haven't." He started a smile, but drew back from the sudden intensity of Rearden's eyes.

Rearden had felt another click in his mind, the sharper click of the second tumbril connecting the circuits of the lock. He leaned forward. "What are you counting on?" he asked; his tone had changed, it was low, it had the steady, pressing, droning sound of a drill.

"It's only a matter of gaining time!" cried Mouch.

"There isn't any time left to gain."

"All we need is a chance!" cried Lawson.

"There are no chances left."

"It's only until we recover!" cried Holloway.

"There is no way to recover."

"Only until our policies begin to work!" cried Dr. Ferris.

"There's no way to make the irrational work." There was no answer.
"What can save you now?"

"Oh, you'll do something!" cried James Taggart.

Then—even though it was only a sentence he had heard all his life—he felt a deafening crash within him, as of a steel door dropping open at the touch of the final tumbril, the one small number completing the sum and releasing the intricate lock, the answer uniting all the pieces, the questions and the unsolved wounds of his life.

In the moment of silence after the crash, it seemed to him that he heard Francisco's voice, asking him quietly in the ballroom of this building, yet asking it also here and now: "Who is the guiltiest man in this room?" He heard his own answer of the past: "I suppose— James Taggart?" and Francisco's voice saying without reproach: "No, Mr. Rearden, it's not James Taggart,"—but here, in this room and this moment, his mind answered: "I am."

He had cursed these looters for their stubborn blindness? It was he who had made it possible. From the first extortion he had accepted, from the first directive he had obeyed, he had given them cause to believe that reality was a thing to be cheated, that one could demand the irrational and someone somehow would provide it. If he had accepted the Equalization of Opportunity Bill, if he had accepted Directive 10-289, if he had accepted the law that those who could not equal his ability had the right to dispose of it, that those who had not earned were to profit, but he who had was to lose, that those who could not think were to command, but he who could was to obey them—then were they illogical in believing that they existed in an irrational universe? He had made it for them, he had provided it. Were they illogical in believing that theirs was only *to wish,* to wish with no concern for the possible—and that *his* was to fulfill their wishes, by means they did not have to know or name? They, the impotent mystics, struggling to escape the responsibility of reason, had known that he, the rationalist, had undertaken to serve their whims. They had known that he had given them a blank check on reality— his was not to ask *why?*—theirs was not to ask *how?*—let them demand that he give them a share of his wealth, then all that he owns, then more than he owns—impossible?—no, *he'll do something!*

He did not know that he had leaped to his feet, that he stood staring down at James Taggart, seeing in the unbridled shapelessness of

Taggart's features the answer to all the devastation he had witnessed through the years of his life.

"What's the matter, Mr. Rearden? What have I said?" Taggart was asking with rising anxiety—but he was out of the reach of Taggart's voice.

He was seeing the progression of the years, the monstrous extortions, the impossible demands, the inexplicable victories of evil, the preposterous plans and unintelligible goals proclaimed in volumes of muddy philosophy, the desperate wonder of the victims who thought that some complex, malevolent wisdom was moving the powers destroying the world—and all of it had rested on one tenet behind the shifty eyes of the victors: *he'll do something!* . . . We'll get away with it—he'll let us—*he'll do something!* . . .

You businessmen kept predicting that we'd perish, but we haven't. . . . It was true, he thought. They had not been blind to reality, *he* had—blind to the reality he himself had created. No, they had not perished, but who had? Who had perished to pay for their manner of survival? Ellis Wyatt . . . Ken Danagger . . . Francisco d'Anconia.

He was reaching for his hat and coat, when he noticed that the men in the room were trying to stop him, that their faces had a look of panic and their voices were crying in bewilderment: "What's the matter, Mr. Rearden? . . . Why? . . . But why? . . . What have we said? . . . You're not going! . . . You can't go! . . . It's too early! . . . Not yet! Oh, not yet!"

He felt as if he were seeing them from the rear window of a speeding express, as if they stood on the track behind him, waving their arms in futile gestures and screaming indistinguishable sounds, their figures growing smaller in the distance, their voices fading.

One of them tried to stop him as he turned to the door. He pushed him out of his way, not roughly, but with a simple, smooth sweep of his arm, as one brushes aside an obstructing curtain, then walked out.

Silence was his only sensation, as he sat at the wheel of his car, speeding back down the road to Philadelphia. It was the silence of immobility within him, as if, possessing knowledge, he could now afford to rest, with no further activity of soul. He felt nothing, neither anguish nor elation. It was as if, by an effort of years, he had climbed a mountain to gain a distant view and, having reached the top, had fallen to lie still, to rest before he looked, free to spare himself for the first time.

He was aware of the long, empty road streaming, then curving, then streaming straight before him, of the effortless pressure of his hands on the wheel and the screech of the tires on the curves. But he felt as if he were speeding down a skyway suspended and coiling in empty space.

The passers-by at the factories, the bridges, the power plants along his road saw a sight that had once been natural among them: a trim, expensively powerful car driven by a confident man, with the concept of success proclaimed more loudly than by any electric sign, proclaimed by the driver's garments, by his expert steering, by his purposeful speed. They watched him go past and vanish into the haze equating earth with night.

He saw his mills rising in the darkness, as a black silhouette against a breathing glow. The glow was the color of burning gold, and "Rearden Steel" stood written across the sky in the cool, white fire of crystal.

He looked at the long silhouette, the curves of blast furnaces standing like triumphal arches, the smokestacks rising like a solemn colonnade along an avenue of honor in an imperial city, the bridges hanging like garlands, the cranes saluting like lances, the smoke waving slowly like flags. The sight broke the stillness within him and he smiled in greeting. It was a smile of happiness, of love, of dedication. He had never loved his mills as he did in that moment, for—seeing them by an act of his own vision, cleared of all but his own code of values, in a luminous reality that held no contradictions—he was seeing the reason of his love: the mills were an achievement of his mind, devoted to his enjoyment of existence, erected in a rational world to deal with rational men. If those men had vanished, if that world was gone, if his mills had ceased to serve his values—then the mills were only a pile of dead scrap, to be left to crumble, the sooner the better—to be left, not as an act of treason, but as an act of loyalty to their actual meaning.

The mills were still a mile ahead when a small spurt of flame caught his sudden attention. Among all the shades of fire in the vast spread of structures, he could tell the abnormal and the out-of-place: this one was too raw a shade of yellow and it was darting from a spot where no fire had reason to be, from a structure by the gate of the main entrance.

In the next instant, he heard the dry crack of a gunshot, then three answering cracks in swift succession, like an angry hand slapping a sudden assailant.

Then the black mass barring the road in the distance took shape, it was not mere darkness and it did not recede as he came closer—it was a mob squirming at the main gate, trying to storm the mills.

He had time to distinguish waving arms, some with clubs, some with crowbars, some with rifles—the yellow flames of burning wood gushing from the window of the gatekeeper's office—the blue cracks of gunfire darting out of the mob and the answers spitting from the roofs of the structures—he had time to see a human figure twisting backward and falling from the top of a car—then he sent his wheels into a shrieking curve, turning into the darkness of a side road.

He was going at the rate of sixty miles an hour down the ruts of an unpaved soil, toward the eastern gate of the mills—and the gate was in sight when the impact of tires on a gully threw the car off the road, to the edge of a ravine where an ancient slag heap lay at the bottom. With the weight of his chest and elbow on the wheel, pitted against two tons of speeding metal, the curve of his body forced the curve of the car to complete its screaming half-circle, sweeping it back onto the road and into the control of his hands. It had taken one instant, but in the next his foot went down on the brake, tearing the engine to a stop: for in the moment when his headlights had swept the ravine, he had glimpsed an oblong shape, darker than the gray of the weeds on the slope, and it had seemed to him that a brief white blur had been a human hand waving for help.

Throwing off his overcoat, he went hurrying down the side of the ravine, lumps of earth giving way under his feet, he went catching at the dried coils of brush, half-running, half-sliding toward the long black form which he could now distinguish to be a human body. A scum of cotton was swimming against the moon, he could see the white of a hand and the shape of an arm lying stretched in the weeds, but the body lay still, with no sign of motion.

"Mr. Rearden . . ."

It was a whisper struggling to be a cry, it was the terrible sound of eagerness fighting against a voice that could be nothing but a moan of pain.

He did not know which came first, it felt like a single shock: his thought that the voice was familiar, a ray of moonlight breaking through the cotton, the movement of falling down on his knees by the white oval of a face, and the recognition. It was the Wet Nurse.

He felt the boy's hand clutching his with the abnormal strength of agony, while he was noticing the tortured lines of the face, the drained lips, the glazing eyes and the thin, dark trickle from a small, black hole in too wrong, too close a spot on the left side of the boy's chest.

"Mr. Rearden . . . I wanted to stop them . . . I wanted to save you . . ."

"What happened to you, kid?"

"They shot me, so I wouldn't talk . . . I wanted to prevent"—his hand fumbled toward the red glare in the sky—"what they're doing . . . I was too late, but I've tried to . . . I've tried . . . And . . . and I'm still able . . . to talk . . . Listen, they—"

"You need help. Let's get you to a hospital and—"

"No! Wait! I . . . I don't think I have much time left to me and . . . and I've got to tell you . . . Listen, that riot . . . it's staged . . . on orders from Washington . . . It's not workers . . . not *your* workers . . . it's those new boys of theirs and . . . and a lot of goons hired on the outside . . . Don't believe a word they'll tell you about it . . . It's a frame-up . . . it's *their* rotten kind of frame-up . . ."

There was a desperate intensity in the boy's face, the intensity of a crusader's battle, his voice seemed to gain a sound of life from some fuel burning in broken spurts within him—and Rearden knew that the greatest assistance he could now render was to listen.

"They . . . they've got a Steel Unification Plan ready . . . and they need an excuse for it . . . because they know that the country won't take it . . . and you won't stand for it . . . They're afraid this one's going to be too much for everybody . . . it's just a plan to skin you alive, that's all . . . So they want to make it look like you're starving your workers . . . and the workers are running amuck and you're unable to control them . . . and the government's got to step in for your own protection and for public safety . . . That's going to be their pitch, Mr. Rearden . . ."

Rearden was noticing the torn flesh of the boy's hands, the drying mud of blood and dust on his palms and his clothing, gray patches of dust on knees and stomach, scrambled with the needles of burs. In the intermittent fits of moonlight, he could see the trail of flattened weeds and glistening smears going off into the darkness below. He dreaded to think how far the boy had crawled and for how long.

"They didn't want you to be here tonight, Mr. Rearden . . . They didn't want you to see their 'People's rebellion' . . . Afterwards . . . you know how they screw up the evidence . . . there won't be a straight story to get anywhere . . . and they hope to fool the country . . . and you . . . that they're acting to protect you from violence . . . Don't let them get away with it, Mr. Rearden! . . . Tell the country . . . tell the people . . . tell the newspapers . . . Tell them that I told you . . . it's under oath . . . I swear it . . . that makes it legal, doesn't it? . . . doesn't it? . . . that gives you a chance?"

Rearden pressed the boy's hand in his. "Thank you, kid."

"I . . . I'm sorry I'm late, Mr. Rearden, but . . . but they didn't let me in on it till the last minute . . . till just before it started . . . They called me in on a . . . a strategy conference . . . there was a man there by the name of Peters . . . from the Unification Board . . . he's a stooge of Tinky Holloway . . . who's a stooge of Orren Boyle . . . What they wanted from me was . . . they wanted me to sign a lot of passes . . . to let some of the goons in . . . so they'd start trouble from the inside and the outside together . . . to make it look like they really were your workers . . . I refused to sign the passes."

"You did? After they'd let you in on their game?"

"But . . . but, of course, Mr. Rearden . . . Did you think I'd play *that kind* of game?"

"No, kid, no, I guess not. Only—"

"What?"

"Only that's when you stuck your neck out."

"But I had to! . . . I couldn't help them wreck the mills, could I? . . . How long was I to keep from sticking my neck out? Till they broke yours? . . . And what would I do with my neck, if that's how I had to keep it? . . . You . . . you understand it, don't you, Mr. Rearden?"

"Yes. I do."

"I refused them . . . I ran out of the office . . . I ran to look for the superintendent . . . to tell him everything . . . but I couldn't find him . . . and then I heard shots at the main gate and I knew it had started . . . I tried to phone your home . . . the phone wires were cut . . . I ran to get my car, I wanted to reach you or a policeman or a newspaper or somebody . . . but they must have been following me . . . that's when they shot me . . . in the parking lot . . . from behind . . . all I remember is falling and . . . and then, when I opened my eyes, they had dumped me here . . . on the slag heap . . ."

"On the slag heap?" said Rearden slowly, knowing that the heap was a hundred feet below.

The boy nodded, pointing vaguely down into the darkness. "Yeah . . . down there . . . And then I . . . I started crawling . . . crawling up . . . I wanted . . . I wanted to last till I told somebody who'd tell you." The pain-twisted lines of his face smoothed suddenly into a smile; his voice had the sound of a lifetime's triumph as he added, "I have." Then he jerked his head up and asked, in the tone of a child's astonishment at a sudden discovery, "Mr. Rearden, is this how it feels to . . . to want something very much . . . very desperately much . . . and to make it?"

"Yes, kid, that's how it feels." The boy's head dropped back against Rearden's arm, the eyes closing, the mouth relaxing, as if to hold a moment's profound contentment. "But you can't stop there. You're not through. You've got to hang on till I get you to a doctor and—" He was lifting the boy cautiously, but a convulsion of pain ran through the boy's face, his mouth twisting to stop a cry—and Rearden had to lower him gently back to the ground.

The boy shook his head with a glance that was almost apology. "I won't make it, Mr. Rearden . . . No use fooling myself . . . I know I'm through."

Then, as if by some dim recoil against self-pity, he added, reciting a memorized lesson, his voice a desperate attempt at his old, cynical, intellectual tone, "What does it matter, Mr. Rearden? . . . Man is only a collection of . . . conditioned chemicals . . . and a man's dying doesn't make . . . any more difference than an animal's."

"You know better than that."

"Yes," he whispered. "Yes, I guess I do."

His eyes wandered over the vast darkness, then rose to Rearden's face; the eyes were helpless, longing, childishly bewildered. "I know . . . it's crap, all those things they taught us . . . all of it, everything they said . . . about living or . . . or dying . . . Dying . . . it wouldn't make any difference to chemicals, but—" he stopped, and all of his desperate protest was only in the intensity of his voice dropping lower to say, "—but it does, to me . . . And . . . and, I guess, it makes a difference to an animal, too . . . But they said there are no values . . . only social customs . . . No values!" His hand clutched blindly at the hole in his chest, as if trying to hold that which he was losing. "No . . . values . . ."

Then his eyes opened wider, with the sudden calm of full frankness. "I'd like to live, Mr. Rearden. God, how I'd like to!" His voice was passionately quiet. "Not because I'm dying . . . but because I've just discovered it tonight, what it means, really to be alive . . . And . . . it's funny . . . do you know when I discovered it? . . . In the office . . . when I stuck my neck out . . . when I told the bastards to go to hell . . . There's . . . there's so many things I wish I'd known sooner . . . But . . . well, it's no use crying over spilled milk." He saw Rearden's involuntary glance at the flattened trail below and added, "Over spilled anything, Mr. Rearden."

"Listen, kid," said Rearden sternly, "I want you to do me a favor."

"*Now*, Mr. Rearden?"

"Yes. Now."

"Why, of course, Mr. Rearden . . . if I can."

"You've done me a big favor tonight, but I want you to do a still bigger one. You've done a great job, climbing out of that slag heap. Now will you try for something still harder? You were willing to die to save my mills. Will you try to live for me?"

"For *you*, Mr. Rearden?"

"For me. Because I'm asking you to. Because I want you to. Because we still have a great distance to climb together, you and I."

"Does it . . . does it make a difference to *you*, Mr. Rearden?"

"It does. Will you make up your mind that you want to live—just as you did down there on the slag heap? That you want to last and live? Will you fight for it? You wanted to fight my battle. Will you fight this one with me, as our first?"

He felt the clutching of the boy's hand; it conveyed the violent eagerness of the answer; the voice was only a whisper: "I'll try, Mr. Rearden."

"Now help me to get you to a doctor. Just relax, take it easy and let me lift you."

"Yes, Mr. Rearden." With the jerk of a sudden effort, the boy pulled himself up to lean on an elbow.

"Take it easy, Tony."

He saw a sudden flicker in the boy's face, an attempt at his old, bright, impudent grin. "Not 'Non-Absolute' any more?"

"No, not any more. You're a full absolute now, and you know it."

"Yes. I know several of them, now. There's one"—he pointed at the wound in his chest—"that's an absolute, isn't it? And"—he went on speaking while Rearden was lifting him from the ground by imperceptible seconds and inches, speaking as if the trembling intensity of his words were serving as an anesthetic against the pain—"and men can't live . . . if rotten bastards . . . like the ones in Washington

. . . get away with things like . . . like the one they're doing tonight . . . if everything becomes a stinking fake . . . and nothing is
real . . . and nobody is anybody . . . men can't live that way . . .
that's an absolute, isn't it?"

"Yes, Tony, that's an absolute."

Rearden rose to his feet by a long, cautious effort; he saw the tortured spasm of the boy's features, as he settled him slowly against his
chest, like a baby held tight in his arms—but the spasm twisted into
another echo of the impudent grin, and the boy asked, "Who's the
Wet Nurse now?"

"I guess I am."

He took the first steps up the slant of crumbling soil, his body tensed
to the task of shock absorber for his fragile burden, to the task of maintaining a steady progression where there was no foothold to find.

The boy's head dropped on Rearden's shoulder, hesitantly, almost
as if this were a presumption. Rearden bent down and pressed his lips
to the dust-streaked forehead.

The boy jerked back, raising his head with a shock of incredulous,
indignant astonishment. "Do you know what you did?" he whispered, as
if unable to believe that it was meant for him.

"Put your head down," said Rearden, "and I'll do it again."

The boy's head dropped and Rearden kissed his forehead; it was
like a father's recognition granted to a son's battle.

The boy lay still, his face hidden, his hands clutching Rearden's
shoulders. Then, with no hint of sound, with only the sudden beat of
faint, spaced, rhythmic shudders to show it, Rearden knew that the
boy was crying—crying in surrender, in admission of all the things
which he could not put into the words he had never found.

Rearden went on moving slowly upward, step by groping step, fighting for firmness of motion against the weeds, the drifts of dust, the
chunks of scrap metal, the refuse of a distant age. He went on, toward
the line where the red glow of his mills marked the edge of the pit
above him, his movement a fierce struggle that had to take the form of
a gentle, unhurried flow.

He heard no sobs, but he felt the rhythmic shudders, and, through
the cloth of his shirt, in place of tears, he felt the small, warm,
liquid spurts flung from the wound by the shudders. He knew that the
tight pressure of his arms was the only answer which the boy was now
able to hear and understand—and he held the trembling body as if
the strength of his arms could transfuse some part of his living power
into the arteries beating ever fainter against him.

Then the sobbing stopped and the boy raised his head. His face
seemed thinner and paler, but the eyes were lustrous, and he looked up
at Rearden, straining for the strength to speak.

"Mr. Rearden . . . I . . . I liked you very much."

"I know it."

The boy's features had no power to form a smile, but it was a smile that spoke in his glance, as he looked at Rearden's face—as he looked at that which he had not known he had been seeking through the brief span of his life, seeking as the image of that which he had not known to be his values.

Then his head fell back, and there was no convulsion in his face, only his mouth relaxing to a shape of serenity—but there was a brief stab of convulsion in his body, like a last cry of protest—and Rearden went on slowly, not altering his pace, even though he knew that no caution was necessary any longer because what he was carrying in his arms was *now* that which had been the boy's teachers' idea of man—a collection of chemicals.

He walked, as if this were his form of last tribute and funeral procession for the young life that had ended in his arms. He felt an anger too intense to identify except as a pressure within him: it was a desire to kill.

The desire was not directed at the unknown thug who had sent a bullet through the boy's body, or at the looting bureaucrats who had hired the thug to do it, but at the boy's teachers who had delivered him, disarmed, to the thug's gun—at the soft, safe assassins of college classrooms who, incompetent to answer the queries of a quest for reason, took pleasure in crippling the young minds entrusted to their care.

Somewhere, he thought, there was this boy's mother, who had trembled with protective concern over his groping steps, while teaching him to walk, who had measured his baby formulas with a jeweler's caution, who had obeyed with a zealot's fervor the latest words of science on his diet and hygiene, protecting his unhardened body from germs—then had sent him to be turned into a tortured neurotic by the men who taught him that he had no mind and must never attempt to think. Had she fed him tainted refuse, he thought, had she mixed poison into his food, it would have been more kind and less fatal.

He thought of all the living species that train their young in the art of survival, the cats who teach their kittens to hunt, the birds who spend such strident effort on teaching their fledglings to fly—yet man, whose tool of survival is the mind, does not merely fail to teach a child to think, but devotes the child's education to the purpose of destroying his brain, of convincing him that thought is futile and evil, before he has started to think.

From the first catch-phrases flung at a child to the last, it is like a series of shocks to freeze his motor, to undercut the power of his consciousness. "Don't ask so many questions, children should be seen and not heard!"—"Who are you to think? It's so, because I say so!"—"Don't argue, obey!"—"Don't try to understand, believe!"—"Don't rebel, adjust!"—"Don't stand out, belong!"—"Don't struggle, compromise!" —"Your heart is more important than your mind!"—"Who are you to know? Your parents know best!"—"Who are you to know? Society knows best!"—"Who are you to know? The bureaucrats know best!"—"Who are you to object? All values are relative!"—"Who are you to want to escape a thug's bullet? That's only a personal prejudice!"

Men would shudder, he thought, if they saw a mother bird plucking the feathers from the wings of her young, then pushing him out of the nest to struggle for survival—yet *that* was what they did to their children.

Armed with nothing but meaningless phrases, this boy had been thrown to fight for existence, he had hobbled and groped through a brief, doomed effort, he had screamed his indignant, bewildered protest —and had perished in his first attempt to soar on his mangled wings.

But a different breed of teachers had once existed, he thought, and had reared the men who created this country; he thought that mothers should set out on their knees to look for men like Hugh Akston, to find them and beg them to return.

He went through the gate of the mills, barely noticing the guards who let him enter, who stared at his face and his burden; he did not pause to listen to their words, as they pointed to the fighting in the distance; he went on walking slowly toward the wedge of light which was the open door of the hospital building.

He stepped into a lighted room full of men, bloody bandages and the odor of antiseptics; he deposited his burden on a bench, with no word of explanation to anyone, and walked out, not glancing behind him.

He walked in the direction of the front gate, toward the glare of fire and the bursts of guns. He saw, once in a while, a few figures running through the cracks between structures or darting behind black corners, pursued by groups of guards and workers; he was astonished to notice that his workers were well armed. They seemed to have subdued the hoodlums inside the mills, and only the siege at the front gate remained to be beaten. He saw a lout scurrying across a patch of lamplight, swinging a length of pipe at a wall of glass panes, battering them down with an animal relish, dancing like a gorilla to the sound of crashing glass, until three husky human figures descended upon him, carrying him writhing to the ground.

The siege of the gate appeared to be ebbing, as if the spine of the mob had been broken. He heard the distant screeches of their cries— but the shots from the road were growing rarer, the fire set to the gate-keeper's office was put out, there were armed men on the ledges and at windows, posted in well-planned defense.

On the roof of a structure above the gate, he saw, as he came closer, the slim silhouette of a man who held a gun in each hand and, from behind the protection of a chimney, kept firing at intervals down into the mob, firing swiftly and, it seemed, in two directions at once, like a sentinel protecting the approaches to the gate. The confident skill of his movements, his manner of firing, with no time wasted to take aim, but with the kind of casual abruptness that never misses a target, made him look like a hero of Western legend—and Rearden watched him with detached, impersonal pleasure, as if the battle of the mills were not his any longer, but he could still enjoy the sight of the competence and certainty with which men of that distant age had once combatted evil.

The beam of a roving searchlight struck Rearden's face, and when the light swept past he saw the man on the roof leaning down, as if peering in his direction. The man waved to someone to replace him, then vanished abruptly from his post.

Rearden hurried on through the short stretch of darkness ahead —but then, from the side, from the crack of an alley, he heard a drunken voice yell, "There he is!" and whirled to see two beefy figures advancing upon him. He saw a leering, mindless face with a mouth hung loose in a joyless chuckle, and a club in a rising fist—he heard the sound of running steps approaching from another direction, he attempted to turn his head, then the club crashed down on his skull from behind—and in the moment of splitting darkness, when he wavered, refusing to believe it, then felt himself going down, he felt a strong, protective arm seizing him and breaking his fall, he heard a gun exploding an inch above his ear, then another explosion from the same gun in the same second, but it seemed faint and distant, as if he had fallen down a shaft.

His first awareness, when he opened his eyes, was a sense of profound serenity. Then he saw that he was lying on a couch in a modern, sternly gracious room—then he realized that it was his office and that the two men standing beside him were the mills' doctor and the superintendent. He felt a distant pain in his head, which would have been violent had he cared to notice it, and he felt a strip of tape across his hair, on the side of his head. The sense of serenity was the knowledge that he was free.

The meaning of his bandage and the meaning of his office were not to be accepted or to exist, together—it was not a combination for men to live with—this was not his battle any longer, nor his job, nor his business.

"I think I'll be all right, Doctor," he said, raising his head.

"Yes, Mr. Rearden, fortunately." The doctor was looking at him as if still unable to believe that this had happened to Hank Rearden inside his own mills; the doctor's voice was tense with angry loyalty and indignation. "Nothing serious, just a scalp wound and a slight concussion. But you must take it easy and allow yourself to rest."

"I will," said Rearden firmly.

"It's all over," said the superintendent, waving at the mills beyond the window. "We've got the bastards beaten and on the run. You don't have to worry, Mr. Rearden. It's all over."

"It is," said Rearden. "There must be a lot of work left for you to do, Doctor."

"Oh yes! I never thought I'd live to see the day when—"

"I know. Go ahead, take care of it. I'll be all right."

"Yes, Mr. Rearden."

"I'll take care of the place," said the superintendent, as the doctor hurried out. "Everything's under control, Mr. Rearden. But it was the dirtiest—"

"I know," said Rearden. "Who was it that saved my life? Somebody grabbed me as I fell, and fired at the thugs."

"Did he! Straight at their faces. Blew their heads off. That was that new furnace foreman of ours. Been here two months. Best man I've ever had. He's the one who got wise to what the gravy boys were planning and warned me, this afternoon. Told me to arm our men, as many as we could. We got no help from the police or the state troopers, they dodged all over the place with the fanciest delays and excuses I ever heard of, it was all fixed in advance, the goons weren't expecting any armed resistance. It was that furnace foreman—Frank Adams is his name—who organized our defense, ran the whole battle, and stood on a roof, picking off the scum that came too close to the gate. Boy, what a marksman! I shudder to think how many of our lives he saved tonight. Those bastards were out for blood, Mr. Rearden."

"I'd like to see him."

"He's waiting somewhere outside. It's he who brought you here, and he asked permission to speak to you, when possible."

"Send him in. Then go back out there, take charge, finish the job."

"Is there anything else I can do for you, Mr. Rearden?"

"No, nothing else."

He lay still, alone in the silence of his office. He knew that the meaning of his mills had ceased to exist, and the fullness of the knowledge left no room for the pain of regretting an illusion. He had seen, in a final image, the soul and essence of his enemies: the mindless face of the thug with the club. It was not the face itself that made him draw back in horror, but the professors, the philosophers, the moralists, the mystics who had released that face upon the world.

He felt a peculiar cleanliness. It was made of pride and of love for this earth, this earth which was his, not theirs. It was the feeling which had moved him through his life, the feeling which some among men know in their youth, then betray, but which *he* had never betrayed and had carried within him as a battered, attacked, unidentified, but living motor—the feeling which he could now experience in its full, uncontested purity: the sense of his own superlative value and the superlative value of his life. It was the final certainty that his life was his, to be lived with no bondage to evil, and that that bondage had never been necessary. It was the radiant serenity of knowing that he was free of fear, of pain, of guilt.

If it's true, he thought, that there are avengers who are working for the deliverance of men like me, let them see me now, let them tell me their secret, let them claim me, let them—"Come in!" he said aloud, in answer to the knock on his door.

The door opened and he lay still. The man standing on the threshold, with disheveled hair, a soot-streaked face and furnace-smudged arms, dressed in scorched overalls and bloodstained shirt, standing as if he wore a cape waving behind him in the wind, was Francisco d'Anconia.

It seemed to Rearden that his consciousness shot forward ahead of his body, it was his body that refused to move, stunned by shock, while his mind was laughing, telling him that this was the most natural, the most-to-have-been-expected event in the world.

Francisco smiled, a smile of greeting to a childhood friend on a summer morning, as if nothing else had ever been possible between them—and Rearden found himself smiling in answer, some part of him feeling an incredulous wonder, yet knowing that it was irresistibly right.

"You've been torturing yourself for months," said Francisco, approaching him, "wondering what words you'd use to ask my forgiveness and whether you had the right to ask it, if you ever saw me again—but now you see that it isn't necessary, that there's nothing to ask or to forgive."

"Yes," said Rearden, the word coming as an astonished whisper, but by the time he finished his sentence he knew that this was the greatest tribute he could offer, "yes, I know it."

Francisco sat down on the couch beside him, and slowly moved his hand over Rearden's forehead. It was like a healing touch that closed the past.

"There's only one thing I want to tell you," said Rearden. "I want you to hear it from me: you kept your oath, you *were* my friend."

"I knew that you knew it. You knew it from the first. You knew it, no matter what you thought of my actions. You slapped me because you could not force yourself to doubt it."

"That . . ." whispered Rearden, staring at him, *"that* was the thing I had no right to tell you . . . no right to claim as my excuse . . ."

"Didn't you suppose I'd understand it?"

"I wanted to find you . . . I had no right to look for you . . . And all that time, you were—" He pointed at Francisco's clothes, then his hand dropped helplessly and he closed his eyes.

"I was your furnace foreman," said Francisco, grinning. "I didn't think you'd mind that. You offered me the job yourself."

"You've been here, as my bodyguard, for two months?"

"Yes."

"You've been here, ever since—" He stopped.

"That's right. On the morning of the day when you were reading my farewell message over the roofs of New York, I was reporting here for my first shift as your furnace foreman."

"Tell me," said Rearden slowly, "that night, at James Taggart's wedding, when you said that you were after your greatest conquest . . . you meant me, didn't you?"

"Of course."

Francisco drew himself up a little, as if for a solemn task, his face earnest, the smile remaining only in his eyes. "I have a great deal to tell you," he said. "But first, will you repeat a word you once offered me and I . . . I had to reject, because I knew that I was not free to accept it?"

Rearden smiled. "What word, *Francisco?*"

Francisco inclined his head in acceptance, and answered, "Thank you, *Hank.*" Then he raised his head. "Now I'll tell you the things I had come to say, but did not finish, that night when I came here for the first time. I think you're ready to hear it."

"I am."

The glare of steel being poured from a furnace shot to the sky beyond the window. A red glow went sweeping slowly over the walls of the office, over the empty desk, over Rearden's face, as if in salute and farewell.

"THIS IS JOHN GALT SPEAKING"

The doorbell was ringing like an alarm, in a long, demanding scream, broken by the impatient stabs of someone's frantic finger.

Leaping out of bed, Dagny noticed the cold, pale sunlight of late morning and a clock on a distant spire marking the hour of ten. She had worked at the office till four A.M. and had left word not to expect her till noon.

The white face ungroomed by panic, that confronted her when she threw the door open, was James Taggart.

"He's gone!" he cried.

"Who?"

"Hank Rearden! He's gone, quit, vanished, disappeared!"

She stood still for a moment, holding the belt of the dressing gown she had been tying; then, as the full knowledge reached her, her hands jerked the belt tight—as if snapping her body in two at the waistline—while she burst out laughing. It was a sound of triumph.

He stared at her in bewilderment. "What's the matter with you?" he gasped. "Haven't you understood?"

"Come in, Jim," she said, turning contemptuously, walking into the living room. "Oh yes, I've understood."

"He's quit! Gone! Gone like all the others! Left his mills, his bank accounts, his property, everything! Just vanished! Took some clothing and whatever he had in the safe in his apartment—they found a safe left open in his bedroom, open and empty—that's all! No word, no note, no explanation! They called me from Washington, but it's all over town! The news, I mean, the story! They can't keep it quiet! They've tried to, but . . . Nobody knows how it got out, but it went through the mills like one of those furnace break-outs, the word that he'd gone, and then . . . before anyone could stop it, a whole bunch of them vanished! The superintendent, the chief metallurgist, the chief engineer, Rearden's secretary, even the hospital doctor! And God knows how many others! Deserting, the bastards! Deserting us, in spite of all the penalties we've set up! He's quit and the rest are quitting and those mills are just left there, standing still! Do you understand what that means?"

"Do *you?*" she asked.

He had thrown his story at her, sentence by sentence, as if trying to knock the smile off her face, an odd, unmoving smile of bitterness and triumph; he had failed. "It's a national catastrophe! What's the matter with you? Don't you see that it's a fatal blow? It will break the last of the country's morale and economy! We can't let him vanish! You've got to bring him back!"

Her smile disappeared.

"*You* can!" he cried. "You're the only one who can! He's your lover, isn't he? . . . Oh, don't look like that! It's no time for squeamishness! It's no time for anything except that we've got to have him! You must know where he is! You can find him! You must reach him and bring him back!"

The way she now looked at him was worse than her smile—she looked as if she were seeing him naked and would not endure the sight much longer. "I can't bring him back," she said, not raising her voice. "And I wouldn't, if I could. Now get out of here."

"But the national catastrophe—"

"Get out."

She did not notice his exit. She stood alone in the middle of her living room, her head dropping, her shoulders sagging, while she was smiling, a smile of pain, of tenderness, of greeting to Hank Rearden. She wondered dimly why she should feel so glad that he had found liberation, so certain that he was right, and yet refuse herself the same deliverance. Two sentences were beating in her mind; one was the triumphant sweep of: He's free, he's out of their reach!—the other was like a prayer of dedication: There's still a chance to win, but let me be the only victim. . . .

It was strange—she thought, in the days that followed, looking at the men around her—that catastrophe had made them aware of Hank Rearden with an intensity that his achievements had not aroused, as if the paths of their consciousness were open to disaster, but not to value. Some spoke of him in shrill curses—others whispered, with a look of guilt and terror, as if a nameless retribution were now to descend upon them—some tried, with hysterical evasiveness, to act as if nothing had happened.

The newspapers, like puppets on tangled strings, were shouting with the same belligerence and on the same dates: "It is social treason to ascribe too much importance to Hank Rearden's desertion and to undermine public morale by the old-fashioned belief that an individual can be of any significance to society." "It is social treason to spread rumors about the disappearance of Hank Rearden. Mr. Rearden has not disappeared, he is in his office, running his mills, as usual, and there has been no trouble at Rearden Steel, except a minor disturbance, a private scuffle among some workers." "It is social treason to cast an unpatriotic light upon the tragic loss of Hank Rearden. Mr. Rearden has not deserted, he was killed in an automobile accident on his way to work, and his grief-stricken family has insisted on a private funeral."

It was strange, she thought, to obtain news by means of nothing but denials, as if existence had ceased, facts had vanished and only the frantic negatives uttered by officials and columnists gave any clue to the reality they were denying. "It is not true that the Miller Steel Foundry of New Jersey has gone out of business." "It is not true that the Jansen Motor Company of Michigan has closed its doors." "It is a vicious, anti-social lie that manufacturers of steel products are collapsing under the threat of a steel shortage. There is no reason to expect a steel shortage." "It is a slanderous, unfounded rumor that a Steel Unification Plan had been in the making and that it had been favored by Mr. Orren Boyle. Mr. Boyle's attorney has issued an emphatic denial and has assured the press that Mr. Boyle is now vehemently opposed to any such plan. Mr. Boyle, at the moment, is suffering from a nervous breakdown."

But some news could be witnessed in the streets of New York, in the cold, dank twilight of autumn evenings: a crowd gathered in front of a hardware store, where the owner had thrown the doors open, inviting people to help themselves to the last of his meager stock, while he laughed in shrieking sobs and went smashing his plate-glass windows—a crowd gathered at the door of a run-down apartment house, where a police ambulance stood waiting, while the bodies of a man, his wife and their three children were being removed from a gas-filled room; the man had been a small manufacturer of steel castings.

If they see Hank Rearden's value now—she thought—why didn't they see it sooner? Why hadn't they averted their own doom and spared him his years of thankless torture? She found no answer.

In the silence of sleepless nights, she thought that Hank Rearden and she had now changed places: he was in Atlantis and she was locked out by a screen of light—he was, perhaps, calling to her as she had called to his struggling airplane, but no signal could reach her through that screen.

Yet the screen split open for one brief break—for the length of a letter she received a week after he vanished. The envelope bore no return address, only the postmark of some hamlet in Colorado. The letter contained two sentences:

> I have met him. I don't blame you.
>
> H.R.

She sat still for a long time, looking at the letter, as if unable to move or to feel. She felt nothing, she thought, then noticed that her shoulders were trembling in a faint, continuous shudder, then grasped that the tearing violence within her was made of an exultant tribute, of gratitude and of despair—her tribute to the victory that the meeting of these two men implied, the final victory of both—her gratitude that those in Atlantis still regarded her as one of them and had granted her the exception of receiving a message—the despair of the knowledge that her blankness was a struggle not to hear the questions she was now hearing. Had Galt abandoned her? Had he gone to the valley to meet his greatest conquest? Would he come back? Had he given her up? The unendurable was not that these questions had no answer, but that the answer was so simply, so easily within her reach and that she had no right to take a step to reach it.

She had made no attempt to see him. Every morning, for a month, on entering her office, she had been conscious, not of the room around her, but of the tunnels below, under the floors of the building—and she had worked, feeling as if some marginal part of her brain was computing figures, reading reports, making decisions in a rush of lifeless activity, while her living mind was inactive and still, frozen in contemplation, forbidden to move beyond the sentence: He's down there. The only inquiry she had permitted herself had been a glance at the payroll list of the Terminal workers. She had seen the name: Galt, John. The list had carried it, openly, for over twelve years. She had seen an address next to the name—and, for a month, had struggled to forget it.

It had seemed hard to live through that month—yet now, as she looked at the letter, the thought that Galt had gone was still harder to bear. Even the struggle of resisting his proximity had been a link to him, a price to pay, a victory achieved in his name. Now there was nothing, except a question that was not to be asked. His presence in the tunnels had been her motor through those days—just as his presence in the city had been her motor through the months of that summer—just as his presence somewhere in the world had been her motor through the years before she ever heard his name. Now she felt as if her motor, too, had stopped.

She went on, with the bright, pure glitter of a five-dollar gold piece, which she kept in her pocket, as her last drop of fuel. She went on, protected from the world around her by a last armor: indifference.

The newspapers did not mention the outbreaks of violence that had begun to burst across the country—but she watched them through the reports of train conductors about bullet-riddled cars, dismantled tracks, attacked trains, besieged stations, in Nebraska, in Oregon, in Texas, in Montana—the futile, doomed outbreaks, prompted by nothing but despair, ending in nothing but destruction. Some were the explosions of local gangs; some spread wider. There were districts that rose in blind rebellion, arrested the local officials, expelled the agents of Washington, killed the tax collectors—then, announcing their secession from the country, went on to the final extreme of the very evil that had destroyed them, as if fighting murder with suicide: went on to seize all property within their reach, to declare community bondage of all to all, and to perish within a week, their meager loot consumed, in the bloody hatred of all for all, in the chaos of no rule save that of the gun, to perish under the lethargic thrust of a few worn soldiers sent out from Washington to bring order to the ruins.

The newspapers did not mention it. The editorials went on speaking of self-denial as the road to future progress, of self-sacrifice as the moral imperative, of greed as the enemy, of love as the solution—their threadbare phrases as sickeningly sweet as the odor of ether in a hospital.

Rumors went spreading through the country in whispers of cynical terror—yet people read the newspapers and acted as if they believed what they read, each competing with the others on who would keep most blindly silent, each pretending that he did not know what he knew, each striving to believe that the unnamed was the unreal. It was as if a volcano were cracking open, yet the people at the foot of the mountain ignored the sudden fissures, the black fumes, the boiling trickles, and went on believing that their only danger was to acknowledge the reality of these signs.

"Listen to Mr. Thompson's report on the world crisis, November 22!"

It was the first acknowledgment of the unacknowledged. The announcements began to appear a week in advance and went ringing across the country. "Mr. Thompson will give the people a report on the world crisis! Listen to Mr. Thompson on every radio station and television channel at 8 P.M., on November 22!"

First, the front pages of the newspapers and the shouts of the radio voices had explained it: "To counteract the fears and rumors spread by the enemies of the people, Mr. Thompson will address the country on November 22 and will give us a full report on the state of the world in this solemn moment of global crisis. Mr. Thompson will put an end to those sinister forces whose purpose is to keep us in terror and despair. He will bring light into the darkness of the world and will show us the way out of our tragic problems—a stern way, as befits the gravity of this hour, but a way of glory, as granted by the rebirth of light. Mr. Thompson's address will be carried by every radio station in this country and in all countries throughout the world, wherever radio waves may still be heard."

Then the chorus broke loose and went growing day by day. "Listen to Mr. Thompson on November 22!" said daily headlines. "Don't forget Mr. Thompson on November 22!" cried radio stations at the end of every program. "Mr. Thompson will tell you the truth!" said placards in subways and buses—then posters on the walls of buildings —then billboards on deserted highways.

"Don't despair! Listen to Mr. Thompson!" said pennants on government cars. "Don't give up! Listen to Mr. Thompson!" said banners in offices and shops. "Have faith! Listen to Mr. Thompson!" said voices in churches. "Mr. Thompson will give you the answer!" wrote army airplanes across the sky, the letters dissolving in space, and only the last two words remaining by the time the sentence was completed.

Public loud-speakers were built in the squares of New York for the day of the speech, and came to rasping life once an hour, in time with the ringing of distant clocks, to send over the worn rattle of the traffic, over the heads of the shabby crowds, the sonorous, mechanical cry of an alarm-toned voice: "Listen to Mr. Thompson's report on the world crisis, November 22!"—a cry rolling through the frosted air and vanishing among the foggy roof tops, under the blank page of a calendar that bore no date.

On the afternoon of November 22, James Taggart told Dagny that Mr. Thompson wished to meet her for a conference before the broadcast.

"In Washington?" she asked incredulously, glancing at her watch.

"Well, I must say that you haven't been reading the newspapers or keeping track of important events. Don't you know that Mr. Thompson is to broadcast from New York? He has come here to confer with the leaders of industry, as well as of labor, science, the professions, and the best of the country's leadership in general. He has requested that I bring you to the conference."

"Where is it to be held?"

"At the broadcasting studio."

"They don't expect me to speak on the air in support of their policies, do they?"

"Don't worry, they wouldn't let *you* near a microphone! They just want to hear your opinion, and you can't refuse, not in a national emergency, not when it's an invitation from Mr. Thompson in person!" He spoke impatiently, avoiding her eyes.

"When is that conference to be held?"

"At seven-thirty."

"Not much time to give to a conference about a national emergency, is it?"

"Mr. Thompson is a very busy man. Now please don't argue, don't start being difficult, I don't see what you're—"

"All right," she said indifferently, "I'll come," and added, prompted by the kind of feeling that would have made her reluctant to venture without a witness into a conference of gangsters, "but I'll bring Eddie Willers along with me."

He frowned, considering it for a moment, with a look of annoyance more than anxiety. "Oh, all right, if you wish," he snapped, shrugging.

She came to the broadcasting studio with James Taggart as a policeman at one side of her and Eddie Willers as a bodyguard at the other. Taggart's face was resentful and tense, Eddie's—resigned, yet wondering and curious. A stage set of pasteboard walls had been erected in a corner of the vast, dim space, representing a stiffly traditional suggestion of a cross between a stately drawing room and a modest study. A semicircle of empty armchairs filled the set, suggesting a grouping from a family album, with microphones dangling like bait at the end of long poles extended for fishing among the chairs.

The best leadership of the country, that stood about in nervous clusters, had the look of a remnant sale in a bankrupt store: she saw Wesley Mouch, Eugene Lawson, Chick Morrison, Tinky Holloway, Dr. Floyd Ferris, Dr. Simon Pritchett, Ma Chalmers, Fred Kinnan, and a seedy handful of businessmen among whom the half-scared, half-flattered figure of Mr. Mowen of the Amalgamated Switch and Signal Company was, incredibly, intended to represent an industrial tycoon.

But the figure that gave her an instant's shock was Dr. Robert Stadler. She had not known that a face could age so greatly within the brief space of one year: the look of timeless energy, of boyish eagerness, was gone, and nothing remained of the face except the lines of contemptuous bitterness. He stood alone, apart from the others, and she saw the moment when his eyes saw her enter; he looked like a man in a whorehouse who had accepted the nature of his surroundings until suddenly caught there by his wife: it was a look of guilt in the process of becoming hatred. Then she saw Robert Stadler, the scientist, turn away as if he had not seen her—as if his refusal to see could wipe a fact out of existence.

Mr. Thompson was pacing among the groups, snapping at random bystanders, in the restless manner of a man of action who feels contempt for the duty of making speeches. He was clutching a sheaf of typewritten pages, as if it were a bundle of old clothing about to be discarded.

James Taggart caught him in mid-step, to say uncertainly and loudly, "Mr. Thompson, may I present my sister, Miss Dagny Taggart?"

"So nice of you to come, Miss Taggart," said Mr. Thompson, shaking her hand as if she were another voter from back home whose name he had never heard before; then he marched briskly off.

"Where's the conference, Jim?" she asked, and glanced at the clock: it was a huge white dial with a black hand slicing the minutes, like a knife moving toward the hour of eight.

"I can't help it! I don't run this show!" he snapped.

Eddie Willers glanced at her with a look of bitterly patient astonishment, and stepped closer to her side.

A radio receiver was playing a program of military marches broadcast from another studio, half-drowning the fragments of nervous voices, of hastily aimless steps, of screeching machinery being pulled to focus upon the drawing-room set.

"Stay tuned to hear Mr. Thompson's report on the world crisis at eight P.M.!" cried the martial voice of an announcer, from the radio receiver—when the hand on the dial reached the hour of 7:45.

"Step on it, boys, step on it!" snapped Mr. Thompson, while the radio burst into another march.

It was 7:50 when Chick Morrison, the Morale Conditioner, who seemed to be in charge, cried, "All right, boys and girls, all right, let's take our places!" waving a bunch of notepaper, like a baton, toward the light-flooded circle of armchairs.

Mr. Thompson thudded down upon the central chair, in the manner of grabbing a vacant seat in a subway.

Chick Morrison's assistants were herding the crowd toward the circle of light.

"A happy family," Chick Morrison explained, "the country must see us as a big, united, happy—What's the matter with that thing?" The radio music had gone off abruptly, choking on an odd little gasp of static, cut in the middle of a ringing phrase. It was 7:51. He shrugged and went on: "—happy family. Hurry up, boys. Take close-ups of Mr. Thompson, first."

The hand of the clock went slicing off the minutes, while press photographers clicked their cameras at Mr. Thompson's sourly impatient face.

"Mr. Thompson will sit between science and industry!" Chick Morrison announced. "Dr. Stadler, please—the chair on Mr. Thompson's left. Miss Taggart—this way, please—on Mr. Thompson's right."

Dr. Stadler obeyed. She did not move.

"It's not just for the press, it's for the television audiences," Chick Morrison explained to her, in the tone of an inducement.

She made a step forward. "I will not take part in this program," she said evenly, addressing Mr. Thompson.

"You won't?" he asked blankly, with the kind of look he would have worn if one of the flower vases had suddenly refused to perform its part.

"Dagny, for Christ's sake!" cried James Taggart in panic.

"What's the matter with her?" asked Mr. Thompson.

"But, Miss Taggart! Why?" cried Chick Morrison.

"You all know why," she said to the faces around her. "You should have known better than to try that again."

"Miss Taggart!" yelled Chick Morrison, as she turned to go. "It's a national emer—"

Then a man came rushing toward Mr. Thompson, and she stopped, as did everyone else—and the look on the man's face swept the crowd into an abruptly total silence. He was the station's chief engineer, and it was odd to see a look of primitive terror struggling against his remnant of civilized control.

"Mr. Thompson," he said, "we . . . we might have to delay the broadcast."

"*What?*" cried Mr. Thompson.

The hand of the dial stood at 7:58.

"We're trying to fix it, Mr. Thompson, we're trying to find out what it is . . . but we might not be on time and—"

"What are you talking about? What happened?"

"We're trying to locate the—"

"What happened?"

"I don't know! But . . . We . . we can't get on the air, Mr. Thompson."

There was a moment of silence, then Mr. Thompson asked, his voice unnaturally low, "Are you crazy?"

"I must be. I wish I were. I can't make it out. The station is dead."

"Mechanical trouble?" yelled Mr. Thompson, leaping to his feet. "Mechanical trouble, God damn you, at a time like this? If that's how you run this station—"

The chief engineer shook his head slowly, in the manner of an adult who is reluctant to frighten a child. "It's not this station, Mr. Thompson," he said softly. "It's every station in the country, as far as we've been able to check. And there is no mechanical trouble. Neither here nor elsewhere. The equipment is in order, in perfect order, and they all report the same, but . . . but all radio stations went off the air at seven-fifty-one, and . . . and nobody can discover why."

"But—" cried Mr. Thompson, stopped, glanced about him and screamed, "Not tonight! You can't let it happen tonight! You've got to get me on the air!"

"Mr. Thompson," the man said slowly, "we've called the electronic laboratory of the State Science Institute. They . . . they've never seen anything like it. They said it might be a natural phenomenon, some sort of cosmic disturbance of an unprecedented kind, only—"

"Well?"

"Only they don't think it is. We don't, either. They said it looks like radio waves, but of a frequency never produced before, never observed anywhere, never discovered by anybody."

No one answered him. In a moment, he went on, his voice oddly solemn: "It looks like a wall of radio waves jamming the air, and we can't get through it, we can't touch it, we can't break it. . . . What's more, we can't locate its source, not by any of our usual methods. . . . Those waves seem to come from a transmitter that . . . that makes any known to us look like a child's toy!"

"But that's not possible!" The cry came from behind Mr. Thompson and they all whirled in its direction, startled by its note of peculiar terror; it came from Dr. Stadler. "There's no such thing! There's nobody on earth to make it!"

The chief engineer spread his hands out. "That's it, Dr. Stadler," he said wearily. "It can't be possible. It shouldn't be possible. But there it is."

"Well, do something about it!" cried Mr. Thompson to the crowd at large.

No one answered or moved.

"I won't permit this!" cried Mr. Thompson. "I won't permit it! Tonight of all nights! I've got to make that speech! Do something! Solve it, whatever it is! I order you to solve it!"

The chief engineer was looking at him blankly.

"I'll fire the lot of you for this! I'll fire every electronic engineer in the country! I'll put the whole profession on trial for sabotage, desertion and treason! Do you hear me? Now do something, God damn you! Do something!"

The chief engineer was looking at him impassively, as if words were not conveying anything any longer.

"Isn't there anybody around to obey an order?" cried Mr. Thompson. "Isn't there a brain left in this country?"

The hand of the clock reached the dot of 8:00.

"Ladies and gentlemen," said a voice that came from the radio receiver—a man's clear, calm, implacable voice, the kind of voice that had not been heard on the airwaves for years—"Mr. Thompson will not speak to you tonight. His time is up. I have taken it over. You were to hear a report on the world crisis. That is what you are going to hear."

Three gasps of recognition greeted the voice, but nobody had the power to notice them among the sounds of the crowd, which were beyond the stage of cries. One was a gasp of triumph, another—of terror, the third—of bewilderment. Three persons had recognized the speaker: Dagny, Dr. Stadler, Eddie Willers. Nobody glanced at Eddie Willers; but Dagny and Dr. Stadler glanced at each other. She saw that his face was distorted by as evil a terror as one could ever bear to see; he saw that she knew and that the way she looked at him was as if the speaker had slapped his face.

"For twelve years, you have been asking: Who is John Galt? This is John Galt speaking. I am the man who loves his life. I am the man who does not sacrifice his love or his values. I am the man who has deprived you of victims and thus has destroyed your world, and if you wish to know why you are perishing—you who dread knowledge—I am the man who will now tell you."

The chief engineer was the only one able to move; he ran to a television set and struggled frantically with its dials. But the screen remained empty; the speaker had not chosen to be seen. Only his voice filled the airways of the country—of the world, thought the chief engineer—sounding as if he were speaking here, in this room, not to a group, but to one man; it was not the tone of addressing a meeting, but the tone of addressing a mind.

"You have heard it said that this is an age of moral crisis. You have said it yourself, half in fear, half in hope that the words had no meaning.

You have cried that man's sins are destroying the world and you have cursed human nature for its unwillingness to practice the virtues you demanded. Since virtue, to you, consists of sacrifice, you have demanded more sacrifices at every successive disaster. In the name of a return to morality, you have sacrificed all those evils which you held as the cause of your plight. You have sacrificed justice to mercy. You have sacrificed independence to unity. You have sacrificed reason to faith. You have sacrificed wealth to need. You have sacrificed self-esteem to self-denial. You have sacrificed happiness to duty.

"You have destroyed all that which you held to be evil and achieved all that which you held to be good. Why, then, do you shrink in horror from the sight of the world around you? That world is not the product of your sins, it is the product and the image of your virtues. It is your moral ideal brought into reality in its full and final perfection. You have fought for it, you have dreamed of it, you have wished it, and I —I am the man who has granted you your wish.

"Your ideal had an implacable enemy, which your code of morality was designed to destroy. I have withdrawn that enemy. I have taken it out of your way and out of your reach. I have removed the source of all those evils you were sacrificing one by one. I have ended your battle. I have stopped your motor. I have deprived your world of man's mind.

"Men do not live by the mind, you say? I have withdrawn those who do. The mind is impotent, you say? I have withdrawn those whose mind isn't. There are values higher than the mind, you say? I have withdrawn those for whom there aren't.

"While you were dragging to your sacrificial altars the men of justice, of independence, of reason, of wealth, of self-esteem—I beat you to it, I reached them first. I told them the nature of the game you were playing and the nature of that moral code of yours, which they had been too innocently generous to grasp. I showed them the way to live by another morality—mine. It is mine that they chose to follow.

"All the men who have vanished, the men you hated, yet dreaded to lose, it is I who have taken them away from you. Do not attempt to find us. We do not choose to be found. Do not cry that it is our duty to serve you. We do not recognize such duty. Do not cry that you need us. We do not consider need a claim. Do not cry that you own us. You don't. Do not beg us to return. We are on strike, we, the men of the mind.

"We are on strike against self-immolation. We are on strike against the creed of unearned rewards and unrewarded duties. We are on strike against the dogma that the pursuit of one's happiness is evil. We are on strike against the doctrine that life is guilt.

"There is a difference between our strike and all those you've practiced for centuries: our strike consists, not of making demands, but of granting them. We are evil, according to your morality. We have chosen not to harm you any longer. We are useless, according to your economics. We have chosen not to exploit you any longer. We are dangerous and to be shackled, according to your politics. We have chosen not to endanger you, nor to wear the shackles any longer. We are only an illusion, according to your philosophy. We have chosen not to blind you any longer and have left you free to face reality—the reality you wanted, the world as you see it now, a world without mind.

"We have granted you everything you demanded of us, we who had always been the givers, but have only now understood it. We have no demands to present to you, no terms to bargain about, no compromise to reach. You have nothing to offer us. *We do not need you.*

"Are you now crying: No, this was not what you wanted? A mindless world of ruins was not your goal? You did not want us to leave you? You moral cannibals, I know that you've always known what it was that you wanted. But your game is up, because *now* we know it, too.

"Through centuries of scourges and disasters, brought about by your code of morality, you have cried that your code had been broken, that the scourges were punishment for breaking it, that men were too weak and too selfish to spill all the blood it required. You damned man, you damned existence, you damned this earth, but never dared to question your code. Your victims took the blame and struggled on, with your curses as reward for their martyrdom—while you went on crying that your code was noble, but human nature was not good enough to practice it. And no one rose to ask the question: Good?—by what standard?

"You wanted to know John Galt's identity. I am the man who has asked that question.

"Yes, this *is* an age of moral crisis. Yes, you *are* bearing punishment for your evil. But it is not man who is now on trial and it is not human nature that will take the blame. It is your moral code that's through, this time. Your moral code has reached its climax, the blind alley at the end of its course. And if you wish to go on living, what you now need is not to *return* to morality—you who have never known any—but to *discover* it.

"You have heard no concepts of morality but the mystical or the social. You have been taught that morality is a code of behavior imposed on you by whim, the whim of a supernatural power or the whim of society, to serve God's purpose or your neighbor's welfare, to please an authority beyond the grave or else next door—but not to serve *your* life or pleasure. Your pleasure, you have been taught, is to be found in immorality, your interests would best be served by evil, and any moral code must be designed not *for* you, but *against* you, not to further your life, but to drain it.

"For centuries, the battle of morality was fought between those who claimed that your life belongs to God and those who claimed that it belongs to your neighbors—between those who preached that the good is self-sacrifice for the sake of ghosts in heaven and those who preached that the good is self-sacrifice for the sake of incompetents on earth. And no one came to say that your life belongs to you and that the good is to live it.

"Both sides agreed that morality demands the surrender of your self-interest and of your mind, that the moral and the practical are opposites, that morality is not the province of reason, but the province of faith and force. Both sides agreed that no rational morality is possible, that there is no right or wrong in reason—that in reason there's no reason to be moral.

"Whatever else they fought about, it was against man's mind that all your moralists have stood united. It was man's mind that all their schemes and systems were intended to despoil and destroy. Now choose to perish or to learn that the anti-mind is the anti-life.

"Man's mind is his basic tool of survival. Life is given to him, survival is not. His body is given to him, its sustenance is not. His mind is given to him, its content is not. To remain alive, he must act, and before he can act he must know the nature and purpose of his action. He cannot obtain his food without a knowledge of food and of the way to obtain it. He cannot dig a ditch—or build a cyclotron—without a knowledge of his aim and of the means to achieve it. To remain alive, he must think.

"But to think is an act of choice. The key to what you so recklessly call 'human nature,' the open secret you live with, yet dread to name, is the fact that *man is a being of volitional consciousness.* Reason does not work automatically; thinking is not a mechanical process; the connections of logic are not made by instinct. The function of your stomach, lungs or heart is automatic; the function of your mind is not. In any hour and issue of your life, you are free to think or to evade that effort. But you are not free to escape from your nature, from the fact that *reason* is your means of survival—so that for *you,* who are a human being, the question 'to be or not to be' is the question 'to think or not to think.'

"A being of volitional consciousness has no automatic course of behavior. He needs a code of values to guide his actions. 'Value' is that which one acts to gain and keep, 'virtue' is the action by which one gains and keeps it. 'Value' presupposes an answer to the question: of value to whom and for what? 'Value' presupposes a standard, a purpose and the necessity of action in the face of an alternative. Where there are no alternatives, no values are possible.

"There is only one fundamental alternative in the universe: existence or non-existence—and it pertains to a single class of entities: to living organisms. The existence of inanimate matter is unconditional, the existence of life is not: it depends on a specific course of action. Matter is indestructible, it changes its forms, but it cannot cease to exist. It is only a living organism that faces a constant alternative: the issue of life or death. Life is a process of self-sustaining and self-generated action. If an organism fails in that action, it dies; its chemical elements remain, but its life goes out of existence. It is only the concept of 'Life' that makes the concept of 'Value' possible. It is only to a living entity that things can be good or evil.

"A plant must feed itself in order to live; the sunlight, the water, the chemicals it needs are the values its nature has set it to pursue; its life is the standard of value directing its actions. But a plant has no choice of action; there are alternatives in the conditions it encounters, but there is no alternative in its function: it acts automatically to further its life, it cannot act for its own destruction.

"An animal is equipped for sustaining its life; its senses provide it with an automatic code of action, an automatic knowledge of what is good for it or evil. It has no power to extend its knowledge or to evade it. In conditions where its knowledge proves inadequate, it dies. But so long as it lives, it acts on its knowledge, with automatic safety and no power of choice, it is unable to ignore its own good, unable to decide to choose the evil and act as its own destroyer.

"Man has no automatic code of survival. His particular distinction from all other living species is the necessity to act in the face of alternatives by means of *volitional choice*. He has no automatic knowledge of what is good for him or evil, what values his life depends on, what course of action it requires. Are you prattling about an instinct of self-preservation? An *instinct* of self-preservation is precisely what man does not possess. An 'instinct' is an unerring and automatic form of knowledge. A desire is not an instinct. A desire to live does not give you the knowledge required for living. And even man's desire to live is not automatic: your secret evil today is that *that* is the desire you do not hold. Your fear of death is not a love for life and will not give you the knowledge needed to keep it. Man must obtain his knowledge and choose his actions by a process of thinking, which nature will not force him to perform. Man has the power to act as his own destroyer—and that is the way he has acted through most of his history.

"A living entity that regarded its means of survival as evil, would not survive. A plant that struggled to mangle its roots, a bird that fought to break its wings would not remain for long in the existence they affronted. But the history of man has been a struggle to deny and to destroy his mind.

"Man has been called a rational being, but rationality is a matter of choice—and the alternative his nature offers him is: rational being or suicidal animal. Man has to be man—by choice; he has to hold his life as a value—by choice; he has to learn to sustain it—by choice; he has to discover the values it requires and practice his virtues—by choice.

"A code of values accepted by choice is a code of morality.

"Whoever you are, you who are hearing me now, I am speaking to whatever living remnant is left uncorrupted within you, to the remnant of the human, to your *mind,* and I say: There *is* a morality of reason, a morality proper to man, and *Man's Life* is its standard of value.

"All that which is proper to the life of a rational being is the good; all that which destroys it is the evil.

"Man's life, as required by his nature, is not the life of a mindless brute, of a looting thug or a mooching mystic, but the life of a thinking being—not life by means of force or fraud, but life by means of achievement—not survival at any price, since there's only one price that pays for man's survival: reason.

"Man's life is the *standard* of morality, but your own life is its *purpose.* If existence on earth is your goal, you must choose your actions and values by the standard of that which is proper to man—for the purpose of preserving, fulfilling and enjoying the irreplaceable value which is your life.

"Since life requires a specific course of action, any other course will destroy it. A being who does not hold his own life as the motive and goal of his actions, is acting on the motive and standard of *death.* Such a being is a metaphysical monstrosity, struggling to oppose, negate and contradict the fact of his own existence, running blindly amuck on a trail of destruction, capable of nothing but pain.

"Happiness is the successful state of life, pain is an agent of death. Happiness is that state of consciousness which proceeds from the achievement of one's values. A morality that dares to tell you to find happiness in the renunciation of your happiness—to value the failure of your values—is an insolent negation of morality. A doctrine that gives you, as an ideal, the role of a sacrificial animal seeking slaughter on the altars of others, is giving you *death* as your standard. By the grace of reality and the nature of life, man—every man—is an end in himself, he exists for his own sake, and the achievement of his own happiness is his highest moral purpose.

"But neither life nor happiness can be achieved by the pursuit of irrational whims. Just as man is free to attempt to survive in any random manner, but will perish unless he lives as his nature requires, so he is free to seek his happiness in any mindless fraud, but the torture of frustration is all he will find, unless he seeks the happiness proper to man. The purpose of morality is to teach you, not to suffer and die, but to enjoy yourself and live.

"Sweep aside those parasites of subsidized classrooms, who live on the profits of the mind of others and proclaim that man needs no morality, no values, no code of behavior. They, who pose as scientists and claim that man is only an animal, do not grant him inclusion in the law of existence they have granted to the lowest of insects. They recognize that every living species has a way of survival demanded by its nature, they do not claim that a fish can live out of water or that a dog can live without its sense of smell—but man, they claim, the most complex of beings, man can survive in any way whatever, man has no identity, no nature, and there's no practical reason why he cannot live with his means of survival destroyed, with his mind throttled and placed at the disposal of any orders *they* might care to issue.

"Sweep aside those hatred-eaten mystics, who pose as friends of humanity and preach that the highest virtue man can practice is to hold his own life as of no value. Do they tell you that the purpose of morality is to curb man's instinct of self-preservation? It is for the purpose of self-preservation that man needs a code of morality. The only man who desires to be moral is the man who desires to live.

"No, you do not have to live; it is your basic act of choice; but if you choose to live, you must live as a man—by the work and the judgment of your mind.

"No, you do not have to live as a man; it is an act of moral choice. But you cannot live as anything else—and the alternative is that state of living death which you now see within you and around you, the state of a thing unfit for existence, no longer human and less than animal, a thing that knows nothing but pain and drags itself through its span of years in the agony of unthinking self-destruction.

"No, you do not have to think; it is an act of moral choice. But someone had to think to keep you alive; if you choose to default, you default on existence and you pass the deficit to some moral man, expecting him to sacrifice his good for the sake of letting you survive by your evil.

"No, you do not have to be a man; but today those who are, are not there any longer. I have removed your means of survival—your victims.

"If you wish to know how I have done it and what I told them to make them quit, you are hearing it now. I told them, in essence, the statement I am making tonight. They were men who had lived by my code, but had not known how great a virtue it represented. I made them see it. I brought them, not a re-evaluation, but only an identification of their values.

"We, the men of the mind, are now on strike against you in the name of a single axiom, which is the root of our moral code, just as the root of yours is the wish to escape it: the axiom that *existence exists*.

"Existence exists—and the act of grasping that statement implies two corollary axioms: that something exists which one perceives and that one exists possessing consciousness, consciousness being the faculty of perceiving that which exists.

"If nothing exists, there can be no consciousness: a consciousness with nothing to be conscious of is a contradiction in terms. A consciousness conscious of nothing but itself is a contradiction in terms: before it could identify itself as consciousness, it had to be conscious of something. If that which you claim to perceive does not exist, what you possess is not consciousness.

"Whatever the degree of your knowledge, these two—existence and consciousness—are axioms you cannot escape, these two are the ir-reducible primaries implied in any action you undertake, in any part of your knowledge and in its sum, from the first ray of light you perceive at the start of your life to the widest erudition you might acquire at its end. Whether you know the shape of a pebble or the structure of a solar system, the axioms remain the same: that *it* exists and that you *know* it.

"To exist is to be something, as distinguished from the nothing of non-existence, it is to be an entity of a specific nature made of specific attributes. Centuries ago, the man who was—no matter what his errors—the greatest of your philosophers, has stated the formula defining the concept of existence and the rule of all knowledge: *A is A*. A thing is itself. You have never grasped the meaning of his statement. I am here to complete it: Existence is Identity, Consciousness is Identification.

"Whatever you choose to consider, be it an object, an attribute or an action, the law of identity remains the same. A leaf cannot be a stone at the same time, it cannot be all red and all green at the same time, it cannot freeze and burn at the same time. A is A. Or, if you wish it stated in simpler language: You cannot have your cake and eat it, too.

"Are you seeking to know what is wrong with the world? All the disasters that have wrecked your world, came from your leaders' attempt to evade the fact that A is A. All the secret evil you dread to face within you and all the pain you have ever endured, came from your own attempt to evade the fact that A is A. The purpose of those who taught you to evade it, was to make you forget that Man is Man.

"Man cannot survive except by gaining knowledge, and reason is his only means to gain it. Reason is the faculty that perceives, identifies and integrates the material provided by his senses. The task of his senses is to give him the evidence of existence, but the task of identifying it belongs to his reason, his senses tell him only that something *is*, but *what* it is must be learned by his mind.

"All thinking is a process of identification and integration. Man perceives a blob of color; by integrating the evidence of his sight and his touch, he learns to identify it as a solid object; he learns to identify the object as a table; he learns that the table is made of wood; he learns that the wood consists of cells, that the cells consist of molecules, that the molecules consist of atoms. All through this process, the work of his mind consists of answers to a single question: *What* is it? His means to establish the truth of his answers is logic, and logic rests on the axiom that existence exists. Logic is the art of *non-contradictory identification*. A contradiction cannot exist. An atom is itself, and so is the universe; neither can contradict its own identity; nor can a part contradict the whole. No concept man forms is valid unless he integrates it without contradiction into the total sum of his knowledge. To arrive at a contradiction is to confess an error in one's thinking; to maintain a contradiction is to abdicate one's mind and to evict oneself from the realm of reality.

"Reality is that which exists; the unreal does not exist; the unreal is merely that negation of existence which is the content of a human consciousness when it attempts to abandon reason. Truth is the recognition of reality; reason, man's only means of knowledge, is his only standard of truth.

"The most depraved sentence you can now utter is to ask: *Whose* reason? The answer is: *Yours*. No matter how vast your knowledge or how modest, it is your own mind that has to acquire it. It is only with your own knowledge that you can deal. It is only your own knowledge that you can claim to possess or ask others to consider. Your mind is your only judge of truth—and if others dissent from your verdict, reality is the court of final appeal. Nothing but a man's mind can perform that complex, delicate, crucial process of identification which is thinking. Nothing can direct the process but his own judgment. Nothing can direct his judgment but his moral integrity.

"You who speak of a 'moral instinct' as if it were some separate endowment opposed to reason—man's reason *is* his moral faculty. A process of reason is a process of constant choice in answer to the question: True or False?—*Right or Wrong?* Is a seed to be planted in soil in order to grow—right or wrong? Is a man's wound to be disinfected in order to save his life—right or wrong? Does the nature of atmospheric electricity permit it to be converted into kinetic power—right or wrong? It is the answers to such questions that gave you everything you have—and the answers came from a man's mind, a mind of intransigent devotion to that which is *right*.

"A rational process is a *moral* process. You may make an error at any step of it, with nothing to protect you but your own severity, or you may try to cheat, to fake the evidence and evade the effort of the quest—but if devotion to truth is the hallmark of morality, then there is no greater, nobler, more heroic form of devotion than the act of a man who assumes the responsibility of thinking.

"That which you call your soul or spirit is your consciousness, and that which you call 'free will' is your mind's freedom to think or not, the only will you have, your only freedom, the choice that controls all the choices you make and determines your life and your character.

"Thinking is man's only basic virtue, from which all the others proceed. And his basic vice, the source of all his evils, is that nameless act which all of you practice, but struggle never to admit: the act of blanking out, the willful suspension of one's consciousness, the refusal to think—not blindness, but the refusal to see; not ignorance, but the refusal to know. It is the act of unfocusing your mind and inducing an inner fog to escape the responsibility of judgment—on the unstated premise that a thing will not exist if only you refuse to identify it, that A will not be A so long as you do not pronounce the verdict 'It *is*.'

Non-thinking is an act of annihilation, a wish to negate existence, an attempt to wipe out reality. But existence exists; reality is not to be wiped out, it will merely wipe out the wiper. By refusing to say 'It is,' you are refusing to say 'I am.' By suspending your judgment, you are negating your person. When a man declares: 'Who am I to know?'—he is declaring: 'Who am I to live?'

"This, in every hour and every issue, is your basic moral choice: thinking or non-thinking, existence or non-existence, A or non-A, entity or zero.

"To the extent to which a man is rational, life is the premise directing his actions. To the extent to which he is irrational, the premise directing his actions is death.

"You who prattle that morality is social and that man would need no morality on a desert island—it is on a desert island that he would need it most. Let him try to claim, when there are no victims to pay for it, that a rock is a house, that sand is clothing, that food will drop into his mouth without cause or effort, that he will collect a harvest tomorrow by devouring his stock seed today—and reality will wipe him out, as he deserves; reality will show him that life is a value to be bought and that thinking is the only coin noble enough to buy it.

"If I were to speak your kind of language, I would say that man's only moral commandment is: Thou shalt think. But a 'moral commandment' is a contradiction in terms. The moral is the chosen, not the forced; the understood, not the obeyed. The moral is the rational, and reason accepts no commandments.

"My morality, the morality of reason, is contained in a single axiom: existence exists—and in a single choice: to live. The rest proceeds from these. To live, man must hold three things as the supreme and ruling values of his life: Reason—Purpose—Self-esteem. Reason, as his only tool of knowledge—Purpose, as his choice of the happiness which that tool must proceed to achieve—Self-esteem, as his inviolate certainty that his mind is competent to think and his person is worthy of happiness, which means: is worthy of living. These three values imply and require all of man's virtues, and all his virtues pertain to the relation of existence and consciousness: rationality, independence, integrity, honesty, justice, productiveness, pride.

"Rationality is the recognition of the fact that existence exists, that nothing can alter the truth and nothing can take precedence over that act of perceiving it, which is thinking—that the mind is one's only judge of values and one's only guide of action—that reason is an absolute that permits no compromise—that a concession to the irrational invalidates one's consciousness and turns it from the task of perceiving to the task of faking reality—that the alleged short-cut to knowledge, which is faith, is only a short-circuit destroying the mind—that the acceptance of a mystical invention is a wish for the annihilation of existence and, properly, annihilates one's consciousness.

"Independence is the recognition of the fact that yours is the responsibility of judgment and nothing can help you escape it—that no substitute can do your thinking, as no pinch-hitter can live your life—that the vilest form of self-abasement and self-destruction is the subordination of your mind to the mind of another, the acceptance of an authority over your brain, the acceptance of his assertions as facts, his say-so as truth, his edicts as middle-man between your consciousness and your existence.

"Integrity is the recognition of the fact that you cannot fake your consciousness, just as honesty is the recognition of the fact that you cannot fake existence—that man is an indivisible entity, an integrated unit of two attributes: of matter and consciousness, and that he may permit no breach between body and mind, between action and thought, between his life and his convictions—that, like a judge impervious to public opinion, he may not sacrifice his convictions to the wishes of others, be it the whole of mankind shouting pleas or threats against him—that courage and confidence are practical necessities, that courage is the practical form of being true to existence, of being true to truth, and confidence is the practical form of being true to one's own consciousness.

"Honesty is the recognition of the fact that the unreal is unreal and can have no value, that neither love nor fame nor cash is a value if obtained by fraud—that an attempt to gain a value by deceiving the mind of others is an act of raising your victims to a position higher than reality, where you become a pawn of their blindness, a slave of their non-thinking and their evasions, while their intelligence, their rationality, their perceptiveness become the enemies you have to dread and flee—that you do not care to live as a dependent, least of all a dependent on the stupidity of others, or as a fool whose source of values is the fools he succeeds in fooling—that honesty is not a social duty, not a sacrifice for the sake of others, but the most profoundly selfish virtue man can practice: his refusal to sacrifice the reality of his own existence to the deluded consciousness of others.

"Justice is the recognition of the fact that you cannot fake the character of men as you cannot fake the character of nature, that you must judge all men as conscientiously as you judge inanimate objects, with the same respect for truth, with the same incorruptible vision, by as pure and as *rational* a process of identification—that every man must be judged for what he *is* and treated accordingly, that just as you do not pay a higher price for a rusty chunk of scrap than for a piece of shining metal, so you do not value a rotter above a hero—that your moral appraisal is the coin paying men for their virtues or vices, and this payment demands of you as scrupulous an honor as you bring to financial transactions—that to withhold your contempt from men's vices is an act of moral counterfeiting, and to withhold your admiration from their virtues is an act of moral embezzlement—that to place any other con-

cern higher than justice is to devaluate your moral currency and defraud the good in favor of the evil, since only the good can lose by a
default of justice and only the evil can profit—and that the bottom of
the pit at the end of that road, the act of moral bankruptcy, is to punish
men for their virtues and reward them for their vices, that that is the
collapse to full depravity, the Black Mass of the worship of death, the
dedication of your consciousness to the destruction of existence.

"Productiveness is your acceptance of morality, your recognition of
the fact that you choose to live—that productive work is the process by
which man's consciousness controls his existence, a constant process of
acquiring knowledge and shaping matter to fit one's purpose, of translating an idea into physical form, of remaking the earth in the image
of one's values—that all work is creative work if done by a thinking
mind, and no work is creative if done by a blank who repeats in uncritical stupor a routine he has learned from others—that your work is
yours to choose, and the choice is as wide as your mind, that nothing
more is possible to you and nothing less is human—that to cheat your
way into a job bigger than your mind can handle is to become a fear-
corroded ape on borrowed motions and borrowed time, and to settle
down into a job that requires less than your mind's full capacity is to
cut your motor and sentence yourself to another kind of motion: decay—that your work is the process of achieving your values, and to lose
your ambition for values is to lose your ambition to live—that your
body is a machine, but your mind is its driver, and you must drive as
far as your mind will take you, with achievement as the goal of your
road—that the man who has no purpose is a machine that coasts downhill at the mercy of any boulder to crash in the first chance ditch, that
the man who stifles his mind is a stalled machine slowly going to rust,
that the man who lets a leader prescribe his course is a wreck being
towed to the scrap heap, and the man who makes another man his
goal is a hitchhiker no driver should ever pick up—that your work is
the purpose of your life, and you must speed past any killer who assumes the right to stop you, that any value you might find outside your
work, any other loyalty or love, can be only travelers you choose to
share your journey and must be travelers going on their own power in
the same direction.

"Pride is the recognition of the fact that you are your own highest
value and, like all of man's values, it has to be earned—that of any
achievements open to you, the one that makes all others possible
is the creation of your own character—that your character, your actions, your desires, your emotions are the products of the premises held
by your mind—that as man must produce the physical values he needs
to sustain his life, so he must acquire the values of character that
make his life worth sustaining—that as man is a being of self-made
wealth, so he is a being of self-made soul—that to live requires a sense
of self-value, but man, who has no automatic values, has no automatic

sense of self-esteem and must earn it by shaping his soul in the image of his moral ideal, in the image of Man, the rational being he is born able to create, but must create by choice—that the first precondition of self-esteem is that radiant selfishness of soul which desires the best in all things, in values of matter and spirit, a soul that seeks above all else to achieve its own moral perfection, valuing nothing higher than itself—and that the proof of an achieved self-esteem is your soul's shudder of contempt and rebellion against the role of a sacrificial animal, against the vile impertinence of any creed that proposes to immolate the irreplaceable value which is your consciousness and the incomparable glory which is your existence to the blind evasions and the stagnant decay of others.

"Are you beginning to see who is John Galt? I am the man who has earned the thing you did not fight for, the thing you have renounced, betrayed, corrupted, yet were unable fully to destroy and are now hiding as your guilty secret, spending your life in apologies to every professional cannibal, lest it be discovered that somewhere within you, you still long to say what I am now saying to the hearing of the whole of mankind: I am proud of my own value and of the fact that I wish to live.

"This wish—which you share, yet submerge as an evil—is the only remnant of the good within you, but it is a wish one must learn to deserve. His own happiness is man's only moral purpose, but only his own virtue can achieve it. Virtue is not an end in itself. Virtue is not its own reward or sacrificial fodder for the reward of evil. *Life* is the reward of virtue—and happiness is the goal and the reward of life.

"Just as your body has two fundamental sensations, pleasure and pain, as signs of its welfare or injury, as a barometer of its basic alternative, life or death, so your consciousness has two fundamental emotions, joy and suffering, in answer to the same alternative. Your emotions are estimates of that which furthers your life or threatens it, lightning calculators giving you a sum of your profit or loss. You have no choice about your capacity to feel that something is good for you or evil, but *what* you will consider good or evil, what will give you joy or pain, what you will love or hate, desire or fear, depends on your standard of value. Emotions are inherent in your nature, but their content is dictated by your mind. Your emotional capacity is an empty motor, and your values are the fuel with which your mind fills it. If you choose a mix of contradictions, it will clog your motor, corrode your transmission and wreck you on your first attempt to move with a machine which you, the driver, have corrupted.

"If you hold the irrational as your standard of value and the impossible as your concept of the good, if you long for rewards you have not earned, for a fortune or a love you don't deserve, for a loophole in the law of causality, for an A that becomes non-A at your whim, if you desire the opposite of existence—you will reach it. Do not cry, when you reach it, that life is frustration and that happiness is impossible to man; check your fuel: it brought you where you wanted to go.

"Happiness is not to be achieved at the command of emotional whims. Happiness is not the satisfaction of whatever irrational wishes you might blindly attempt to indulge. Happiness is a state of non-contradictory joy—a joy without penalty or guilt, a joy that does not clash with any of your values and does not work for your own destruction, not the joy of escaping from your mind, but of using your mind's fullest power, not the joy of faking reality, but of achieving values that are real, not the joy of a drunkard, but of a producer. Happiness is possible only to a rational man, the man who desires nothing but rational goals, seeks nothing but rational values and finds his joy in nothing but rational actions.

"Just as I support my life, neither by robbery nor alms, but by my own effort, so I do not seek to derive my happiness from the injury or the favor of others, but earn it by my own achievement. Just as I do not consider the pleasure of others as the goal of my life, so I do not consider my pleasure as the goal of the lives of others. Just as there are no contradictions in my values and no conflicts among my desires—so there are no victims and no conflicts of interest among rational men, men who do not desire the unearned and do not view one another with a cannibal's lust, men who neither make sacrifices nor accept them.

"The symbol of all relationships among such men, the moral symbol of respect for human beings, is *the trader*. We, who live by values, not by loot, are traders, both in matter and in spirit. A trader is a man who earns what he gets and does not give or take the undeserved. A trader does not ask to be paid for his failures, nor does he ask to be loved for his flaws. A trader does not squander his body as fodder or his soul as alms. Just as he does not give his work except in trade for material values, so he does not give the values of his spirit—his love, his friendship, his esteem—except in payment and in trade for human virtues, in payment for his own selfish pleasure, which he receives from men he can respect. The mystic parasites who have, throughout the ages, reviled the traders and held them in contempt, while honoring the beggars and the looters, have known the secret motive of their sneers: a trader is the entity they dread—a man of justice.

"Do you ask what moral obligation I owe to my fellow men? None—except the obligation I owe to myself, to material objects and to all of existence: rationality. I deal with men as my nature and theirs demands: by means of reason. I seek or desire nothing from them except such relations as they care to enter of their own voluntary choice. It is only with their mind that I can deal and only for my own self-interest, when they see that my interest coincides with theirs. When they don't, I enter no relationship; I let dissenters go their way and I do not swerve from mine. I win by means of nothing but logic and I surrender to nothing but logic. I do not surrender my reason or deal with men who surrender theirs. I have nothing to gain from fools or cowards; I have no benefits to seek from human vices: from stupidity, dishonesty or fear. The only value men can offer me is the work of their mind. When I disagree with a rational man, I let reality be our final arbiter; if I am right, he will learn; if I am wrong, I will; one of us will win, but both will profit.

"Whatever may be open to disagreement, there is one act of evil that may not, the act that no man may commit against others and no man may sanction or forgive. So long as men desire to live together, no man may *initiate*—do you hear me? no man may *start*—the use of physical force against others.

"To interpose the threat of physical destruction between a man and his perception of reality, is to negate and paralyze his means of survival; to force him to act against his own judgment, is like forcing him to act against his own sight. Whoever, to whatever purpose or extent, initiates the use of force, is a killer acting on the premise of death in a manner wider than murder: the premise of destroying man's capacity to live.

"Do not open your mouth to tell me that your mind has convinced you of your right to force my mind. Force and mind are opposites; morality ends where a gun begins. When you declare that men are irrational animals and propose to treat them as such, you define thereby your own character and can no longer claim the sanction of reason—as no advocate of contradictions can claim it. There can be no 'right' to destroy the source of rights, the only means of judging right and wrong: the mind.

"To force a man to drop his own mind and to accept your will as a substitute, with a gun in place of a syllogism, with terror in place of proof, and death as the final argument—is to attempt to exist in defiance of reality. Reality demands of man that he act for his own rational interest; your gun demands of him that he act against it. Reality threatens man with death if he does not act on his rational judgment; you threaten him with death if he does. You place him into a world where the price of his life is the surrender of all the virtues required by life—and death by a process of gradual destruction is all that you and your system will achieve, when death is made to be the ruling power, the winning argument in a society of men.

"Be it a highwayman who confronts a traveler with the ultimatum: 'Your money or your life,' or a politician who confronts a country with the ultimatum: 'Your children's education or your life,' the meaning of that ultimatum is: 'Your mind or your life'—and neither is possible to man without the other.

"If there are degrees of evil, it is hard to say who is the more contemptible: the brute who assumes the right to force the mind of others or the moral degenerate who grants to others the right to force his mind. *That* is the moral absolute one does not leave open to debate. I do not grant the terms of reason to men who propose to deprive me of reason. I do not enter discussions with neighbors who think they can forbid me to think. I do not place my moral sanction upon a murderer's wish to kill me. When a man attempts to deal with me by force, I answer him—by force.

"It is only as retaliation that force may be used and only against the man who starts its use. No, I do not share his evil or sink to his concept of morality: I merely grant him his choice, destruction, the only destruction he had the right to choose: his own. He uses force to seize a value; I use it only to destroy destruction. A holdup man seeks to gain wealth by killing me; I do not grow richer by killing a holdup man. I seek no values by means of evil, nor do I surrender my values to evil.

"In the name of all the producers who had kept you alive and received your death ultimatums in payment, I now answer you with a single ultimatum of our own: Our work or your guns. You can choose either; you can't have both. We do not initiate the use of force against others or submit to force at their hands. If you desire ever again to live in an industrial society, it will be on *our* moral terms. Our terms and our motive power are the antithesis of yours. You have been using fear as your weapon and have been bringing death to man as his punishment for rejecting your morality. We offer him life as his reward for accepting ours.

"You who are worshippers of the zero—you have never discovered that achieving life is not the equivalent of avoiding death. Joy is not 'the absence of pain,' intelligence is not 'the absence of stupidity,' light is not 'the absence of darkness,' an entity is not 'the absence of a nonentity.' Building is not done by abstaining from demolition; centuries of sitting and waiting in such abstinence will not raise one single girder for you to abstain from demolishing—and now you can no longer say to me, the builder: 'Produce, and feed us in exchange for our *not* destroying your production.' I am answering in the name of all your victims: Perish with and in your own void. Existence is not a negation of negatives. Evil, not value, is an absence and a negation, evil is impotent and has no power but that which we let it extort from us. Perish, because we have learned that a zero cannot hold a mortgage over life.

"You seek escape from pain. We seek the achievement of happiness. You exist for the sake of avoiding punishment. We exist for the sake of earning rewards. Threats will not make us function; fear is not our incentive. It is not death that we wish to avoid, but life that we wish to live.

"You, who have lost the concept of the difference, you who claim that fear and joy are incentives of equal power—and secretly add that fear is the more 'practical'—you do not wish to live, and only fear of death still holds you to the existence you have damned. You dart in panic through the trap of your days, looking for the exit you have closed, running from a pursuer you dare not name to a terror you dare not acknowledge, and the greater your terror the greater your dread of the only act that could save you: thinking. The purpose of your struggle is not to know, not to grasp or name or hear the thing I shall now state to your hearing: that yours is the Morality of Death.

"Death is the standard of your values, death is your chosen goal, and you have to keep running, since there is no escape from the pursuer who is out to destroy you or from the knowledge that that pursuer is yourself. Stop running, for once—there is no place to run—stand naked, as you dread to stand, but as I see you, and take a look at what you dared to call a moral code.

"Damnation is the start of your morality, destruction is its purpose, means and end. Your code begins by damning man as evil, then demands that he practice a good which it defines as impossible for him to practice. It demands, as his first proof of virtue, that he accept his own depravity without proof. It demands that he start, not with a standard of value, but with a standard of evil, which is himself, by means of which he is then to define the good: the good is that which he is not.

"It does not matter who then becomes the profiteer on his renounced glory and tormented soul, a mystic God with some incomprehensible design or any passer-by whose rotting sores are held as some inexplicable claim upon him—it does not matter, the good is not for him to understand, his duty is to crawl through years of penance, atoning for the guilt of his existence to any stray collector of unintelligible debts, his only concept of a value is a zero: the good is that which is non-man.

"The name of this monstrous absurdity is Original Sin.

"A sin without volition is a slap at morality and an insolent contradiction in terms: that which is outside the possibility of choice is outside the province of morality. If man is evil by birth, he has no will, no power to change it; if he has no will, he can be neither good nor evil; a robot is amoral. To hold, as man's sin, a fact not open to his choice is a mockery of morality. To hold man's nature as his sin is a mockery of nature. To punish him for a crime he committed before he was born is a mockery of justice. To hold him guilty in a matter where no innocence exists is a mockery of reason. To destroy morality, nature, justice and reason by means of a single concept is a feat of evil hardly to be matched. Yet *that* is the root of your code.

"Do not hide behind the cowardly evasion that man is born with free will, but with a 'tendency' to evil. A free will saddled with a tendency is like a game with loaded dice. It forces man to struggle through the effort of playing, to bear responsibility and pay for the game, but the decision is weighted in favor of a tendency that he had no power to escape. If the tendency is of his choice, he cannot possess it at birth; if it is not of his choice, his will is not free.

"What is the nature of the guilt that your teachers call his Original

Sin? What are the evils man acquired when he fell from a state they consider perfection? Their myth declares that he ate the fruit of the tree of knowledge—he acquired a mind and became a rational being. It was the knowledge of good and evil—he became a moral being. He was sentenced to earn his bread by his labor—he became a productive being. He was sentenced to experience desire—he acquired the capacity of sexual enjoyment. The evils for which they damn him are reason, morality, creativeness, joy—all the cardinal values of his existence. It is not his vices that their myth of man's fall is designed to explain and condemn, it is not his errors that they hold as his guilt, but the essence of his nature as man. Whatever he was—that robot in the Garden of Eden, who existed without mind, without values, without labor, without love—he was not man.

"Man's fall, according to your teachers, was that he gained the virtues required to live. These virtues, by their standard, are his Sin. His evil, they charge, is that he's man. His guilt, they charge, is that he lives.

"They call it a morality of mercy and a doctrine of love for man.

"No, they say, they do not preach that man is evil, the evil is only that alien object: his body. No, they say, they do not wish to kill him, they only wish to make him lose his body. They seek to help him, they say, against his pain—and they point at the torture rack to which they've tied him, the rack with two wheels that pull him in opposite directions, the rack of the doctrine that splits his soul and body.

"They have cut man in two, setting one half against the other. They have taught him that his body and his consciousness are two enemies engaged in deadly conflict, two antagonists of opposite natures, contradictory claims, incompatible needs, that to benefit one is to injure the other, that his soul belongs to a supernatural realm, but his body is an evil prison holding it in bondage to this earth—and that the good is to defeat his body, to undermine it by years of patient struggle, digging his way to that glorious jail-break which leads into the freedom of the grave.

"They have taught man that he is a hopeless misfit made of two elements, both symbols of death. A body without a soul is a corpse, a soul without a body is a ghost—yet such is their image of man's nature: the battleground of a struggle between a corpse and a ghost, a corpse endowed with some evil volition of its own and a ghost endowed with the knowledge that everything known to man is non-existent, that only the unknowable exists.

"Do you observe what human faculty that doctrine was designed to ignore? It was man's mind that had to be negated in order to make him fall apart. Once he surrendered reason, he was left at the mercy of two monsters whom he could not fathom or control: of a body moved by unaccountable instincts and of a soul moved by mystic revelations—

he was left as the passively ravaged victim of a battle between a robot and a dictaphone.

"And as he now crawls through the wreckage, groping blindly for a way to live, your teachers offer him the help of a morality that proclaims that he'll find no solution and must seek no fulfillment on earth. Real existence, they tell him, is that which he cannot perceive, true consciousness is the faculty of perceiving the non-existent—and if he is unable to understand it, *that* is the proof that his existence is evil and his consciousness impotent.

"As products of the split between man's soul and body, there are two kinds of teachers of the Morality of Death: the mystics of spirit and the mystics of muscle, whom you call the spiritualists and the materialists, those who believe in consciousness without existence and those who believe in existence without consciousness. Both demand the surrender of your mind, one to their revelations, the other to their reflexes. No matter how loudly they posture in the roles of irreconcilable antagonists, their moral codes are alike, and so are their aims: in matter—the enslavement of man's body, in spirit—the destruction of his mind.

"The good, say the mystics of spirit, is God, a being whose only definition is that he is beyond man's power to conceive—a definition that invalidates man's consciousness and nullifies his concepts of existence. The good, say the mystics of muscle, is Society—a thing which they define as an organism that possesses no physical form, a super-being embodied in no one in particular and everyone in general except yourself. Man's mind, say the mystics of spirit, must be subordinated to the will of God. Man's mind, say the mystics of muscle, must be subordinated to the will of Society. Man's standard of value, say the mystics of spirit, is the pleasure of God, whose standards are beyond man's power of comprehension and must be accepted on faith. Man's standard of value, say the mystics of muscle, is the pleasure of Society, whose standards are beyond man's right of judgment and must be obeyed as a primary absolute. The purpose of man's life, say both, is to become an abject zombie who serves a purpose he does not know, for reasons he is not to question. His reward, say the mystics of spirit, will be given to him beyond the grave. His reward, say the mystics of muscle, will be given on earth—to his great-grandchildren.

"*Selfishness*—say both—is man's evil. Man's good—say both—is to give up his personal desires, to deny himself, renounce himself, surrender; man's good is to negate the life he lives. *Sacrifice*—cry both—is the essence of morality, the highest virtue within man's reach.

"Whoever is now within reach of my voice, whoever is man the victim, not man the killer, I am speaking at the deathbed of your mind, at the brink of that darkness in which you're drowning, and if there still remains within you the power to struggle to hold on to those fading sparks which had been yourself—use it now. The word that has destroyed you is 'sacrifice.' Use the last of your strength to understand its meaning. You're still alive. You have a chance.

" 'Sacrifice' does not mean the rejection of the worthless, but of the precious. 'Sacrifice' does not mean the rejection of the evil for the sake of the good, but of the good for the sake of the evil. 'Sacrifice' is the surrender of that which you value in favor of that which you don't.

"If you exchange a penny for a dollar, it is *not* a sacrifice; if you exchange a dollar for a penny, it *is*. If you achieve the career you wanted, after years of struggle, it is *not* a sacrifice; if you then renounce it for the sake of a rival, it *is*. If you own a bottle of milk and give it to your starving child, it is *not* a sacrifice; if you give it to your neighbor's child and let your own die, it *is*.

"If you give money to help a friend, it is *not* a sacrifice; if you give it to a worthless stranger, it *is*. If you give your friend a sum you can afford, it is *not* a sacrifice; if you give him money at the cost of your own discomfort, it is only a partial virtue, according to this sort of moral standard; if you give him money at the cost of disaster to yourself—*that* is the virtue of sacrifice in full.

"If you renounce all personal desires and dedicate your life to those you love, you do not achieve full virtue: you still retain a value of your own, which is your love. If you devote your life to random strangers, it is an act of greater virtue. If you devote your life to serving men you hate—*that* is the greatest of the virtues you can practice.

"A sacrifice is the surrender of a value. Full sacrifice is full surrender of all values. If you wish to achieve full virtue, you must seek no gratitude in return for your sacrifice, no praise, no love, no admiration, no self-esteem, not even the pride of being virtuous; the faintest trace of any gain dilutes your virtue. If you pursue a course of action that does not taint your life by any joy, that brings you no value in matter, no value in spirit, no gain, no profit, no reward—if you achieve this state of total zero, you have achieved the ideal of moral perfection.

"You are told that moral perfection is impossible to man—and, by this standard, it is. You cannot achieve it so long as you live, but the value of your life and of your person is gauged by how closely you succeed in approaching that ideal zero which is *death*.

"If you start, however, as a passionless blank, as a vegetable seeking to be eaten, with no values to reject and no wishes to renounce, you will not win the crown of sacrifice. It is not a sacrifice to renounce the unwanted. It is not a sacrifice to give your life for others, if death is your personal desire. To achieve the virtue of sacrifice, you must want to live, you must love it, you must burn with passion for this earth and for all the splendor it can give you—you must feel the twist of every knife as it slashes your desires away from your reach and drains your love out of your body. It is not mere death that the morality of sacrifice holds out to you as an ideal, but death by slow torture.

"Do not remind me that it pertains only to this life on earth. I am concerned with no other. Neither are you.

"If you wish to save the last of your dignity, do not call your best actions a 'sacrifice': that term brands you as immoral. If a mother buys food for her hungry child rather than a hat for herself, it is *not* a sacrifice: she values the child higher than the hat; but it *is* a sacrifice to the kind of mother whose higher value is the hat, who would prefer her child to starve and feeds him only from a sense of duty. If a man dies fighting for his own freedom, it is *not* a sacrifice: he is not willing to live as a slave; but it *is* a sacrifice to the kind of man who's willing. If a man refuses to sell his convictions, it is *not* a sacrifice, unless he is the sort of man who has no convictions.

"Sacrifice could be proper only for those who have nothing to sacrifice—no values, no standards, no judgment—those whose desires are irrational whims, blindly conceived and lightly surrendered. For a man of moral stature, whose desires are born of rational values, sacrifice is the surrender of the right to the wrong, of the good to the evil.

"The creed of sacrifice is a morality for the immoral—a morality that declares its own bankruptcy by confessing that it can't impart to men any personal stake in virtues or values, and that their souls are sewers of depravity, which they must be taught to sacrifice. By its own confession, it is impotent to teach men to be good and can only subject them to constant punishment.

"Are you thinking, in some foggy stupor, that it's only *material* values that your morality requires you to sacrifice? And *what* do you think are material values? Matter has no value except as a means for the satisfaction of human desires. Matter is only a tool of human values. To what service are you asked to give the material tools your virtue has produced? To the service of that which *you* regard as evil: to a principle you do not share, to a person you do not respect, to the achievement of a purpose opposed to your own—else your gift is *not* a sacrifice.

"Your morality tells you to renounce the material world and to divorce your values from matter. A man whose values are given no expression in material form, whose existence is unrelated to his ideals, whose actions contradict his convictions, is a cheap little hypocrite— yet *that* is the man who obeys your morality and divorces his values from matter. The man who loves one woman, but sleeps with another— the man who admires the talent of a worker, but hires another—the man who considers one cause to be just, but donates his money to the support of another—the man who holds high standards of craftsmanship, but devotes his effort to the production of trash—*these* are the men who have renounced matter, the men who believe that the values of their spirit cannot be brought into material reality.

"Do you say it is the spirit that such men have renounced? Yes, of course. You cannot have one without the other. You are an indivisible entity of matter and consciousness. Renounce your consciousness and you become a brute. Renounce your body and you become a fake. Renounce the material world and you surrender it to evil.

"And *that* is precisely the goal of your morality, the duty that your code demands of you. Give to that which you do not enjoy, serve that which you do not admire, submit to that which you consider evil— surrender the world to the values of others, deny, reject, renounce your *self*. Your self is your *mind;* renounce it and you become a chunk of meat ready for any cannibal to swallow.

"It is your *mind* that they want you to surrender—all those who preach the creed of sacrifice, whatever their tags or their motives, whether they demand it for the sake of your soul or of your body, whether they promise you another life in heaven or a full stomach on this earth. Those who start by saying: 'It is selfish to pursue your own wishes, you must sacrifice them to the wishes of others'—end up by saying: 'It is selfish to uphold your convictions, you must sacrifice them to the convictions of others.'

"This much is true: the most *selfish* of all things is the independent mind that recognizes no authority higher than its own and no value higher than its judgment of truth. You are asked to sacrifice your intellectual integrity, your logic, your reason, your standard of truth— in favor of becoming a prostitute whose standard is the greatest good for the greatest number.

"If you search your code for guidance, for an answer to the question: 'What *is* the good?'—the only answer you will find is *'The good of others.'* The good is whatever others wish, whatever you feel they feel they wish, or whatever you feel they ought to feel. 'The good of others' is a magic formula that transforms anything into gold, a formula to be recited as a guarantee of moral glory and as a fumigator for any action, even the slaughter of a continent. Your standard of virtue is not an object, not an act, not a principle, but an *intention*. You need no proof, no reasons, no success, you need not achieve *in fact* the good of others —all you need to know is that your motive was the good of others, *not* your own. Your only definition of the good is a negation: the good is the 'non-good for me.'

"Your code—which boasts that it upholds eternal, absolute, objective moral values and scorns the conditional, the relative and the subjective —your code hands out, as its version of the absolute, the following rule of moral conduct: If *you* wish it, it's evil; if others wish it, it's good; if the motive of your action is *your* welfare, don't do it; if the motive is the welfare of others, then anything goes.

"As this double-jointed, double-standard morality splits you in half, so it splits mankind into two enemy camps: one is *you,* the other is all the rest of humanity. *You* are the only outcast who has no right to wish or live. *You* are the only servant, the rest are the masters, *you* are the only giver, the rest are the takers, *you* are the eternal debtor, the rest are the creditors never to be paid off. You must not question their right to your sacrifice, or the nature of their wishes and their needs: their right is conferred upon them by a negative, by the fact that they are 'non-you.'

"For those of you who might ask questions, your code provides a consolation prize and booby-trap: it is for your own happiness, it says, that you must serve the happiness of others, the only way to achieve your joy is to give it up to others, the only way to achieve your prosperity is to surrender your wealth to others, the only way to protect your life is to protect all men except yourself—and if you find no joy in this procedure, it is your own fault and the proof of your evil; if you were good, you would find your happiness in providing a banquet for others, and your dignity in existing on such crumbs as *they* might care to toss you.

"You who have no standard of self-esteem, accept the guilt and dare not ask the questions. But you know the unadmitted answer, refusing to acknowledge what you see, what hidden premise moves your world. You know it, not in honest statement, but as a dark uneasiness within you, while you flounder between guiltily cheating and grudgingly practicing a principle too vicious to name.

"I, who do not accept the unearned, neither in values nor in *guilt*, am here to ask the questions you evaded. Why is it moral to serve the happiness of others, but not your own? If enjoyment is a value, why is it moral when experienced by others, but immoral when experienced by you? If the sensation of eating a cake is a value, why is it an immoral indulgence in your stomach, but a moral goal for you to achieve in the stomach of others? Why is it immoral for you to desire, but moral for others to do so? Why is it immoral to produce a value and keep it, but moral to give it away? And if it is not moral for you to keep a value, why is it moral for others to accept it? If you are selfless and virtuous when you give it, are they not selfish and vicious when they take it? Does virtue consist of serving vice? Is the moral purpose of those who are good, self-immolation for the sake of those who are evil?

"The answer you evade, the monstrous answer is: No, the takers are not evil, provided they did not *earn* the value you gave them. It is not immoral for them to accept it, provided they are unable to produce it, unable to deserve it, unable to give you any value in return. It is not immoral for them to enjoy it, provided they do not obtain it *by right*.

"Such is the secret core of your creed, the other half of your double standard: it is immoral to live by your own effort, but moral to live by the effort of others—it is immoral to consume your own product, but moral to consume the products of others—it is immoral to earn, but moral to mooch—it is the parasites who are the moral justification for the existence of the producers, but the existence of the parasites is an end in itself—it is evil to profit by achievement, but good to profit by sacrifice—it is evil to create your own happiness, but good to enjoy it at the price of the blood of others.

"Your code divides mankind into two castes and commands them to live by opposite rules: those who may desire anything and those who may desire nothing, the chosen and the damned, the riders and the carriers, the eaters and the eaten. What standard determines your caste? What passkey admits you to the moral elite? The passkey is *lack of value.*

"Whatever the value involved, it is your lack of it that gives you a claim upon those who don't lack it. It is your *need* that gives you a claim to rewards. If you are able to satisfy your need, your ability annuls your right to satisfy it. But a need you are *unable* to satisfy gives you first right to the lives of mankind.

"If you succeed, any man who fails is your master; if you fail, any man who succeeds is your serf. Whether your failure is just or not, whether your wishes are rational or not, whether your misfortune is undeserved or the result of your vices, it is *misfortune* that gives you a right to rewards. It is *pain,* regardless of its nature or cause, pain as a primary absolute, that gives you a mortgage on all of existence.

"If you heal your pain by your own effort, you receive no moral credit: your code regards it scornfully as an act of self-interest. Whatever value you seek to acquire, be it wealth or food or love or rights, if you acquire it by means of your virtue, your code does not regard it as a moral acquisition: you occasion no loss to anyone, it is a trade, not alms; a payment, not a sacrifice. The *deserved* belongs in the selfish, commercial realm of mutual profit; it is only the *undeserved* that calls for that moral transaction which consists of profit to one at the price of disaster to the other. To demand rewards for your virtue is selfish and immoral; it is your *lack of virtue* that transforms your demand into a moral right.

"A morality that holds *need* as a claim, holds emptiness—non-existence—as its standard of value; it rewards an *absence,* a defect: weakness, inability, incompetence, suffering, disease, disaster, the lack, the fault, the flaw—the *zero.*

"Who provides the account to pay these claims? Those who are cursed for being non-zeros, each to the extent of his distance from that ideal. Since all values are the product of virtues, the degree of your virtue is used as the measure of your penalty; the degree of your faults is used as the measure of your gain. Your code declares that the rational man must sacrifice himself to the irrational, the independent man to parasites, the honest man to the dishonest, the man of justice to the unjust, the productive man to thieving loafers, the man of integrity to compromising knaves, the man of self-esteem to sniveling neurotics. Do you wonder at the meanness of soul in those you see around you? The man who achieves these virtues will not accept your moral code; the man who accepts your moral code will not achieve these virtues.

"Under a morality of sacrifice, the first value you sacrifice is morality;

the next is self-esteem. When need is the standard, every man is both victim and parasite. As a victim, he must labor to fill the needs of others, leaving himself in the position of a parasite whose needs must be filled by others. He cannot approach his fellow men except in one of two disgraceful roles: he is both a beggar and a sucker.

"You fear the man who has a dollar less than you, that dollar is rightfully his, he makes you feel like a moral defrauder. You hate the man who has a dollar more than you, that dollar is rightfully yours, he makes you feel that you are morally defrauded. The man below is a source of your guilt, the man above is a source of your frustration. You do not know what to surrender or demand, when to give and when to grab, what pleasure in life is rightfully yours and what debt is still unpaid to others—you struggle to evade, as 'theory,' the knowledge that by the moral standard you've accepted you are guilty every moment of your life, there is no mouthful of food you swallow that is not *needed* by someone somewhere on earth—and you give up the problem in blind resentment, you conclude that moral perfection is not to be achieved *or desired,* that you will muddle through by snatching as snatch can and by avoiding the eyes of the young, of those who look at you as if self-esteem were possible and they expected you to have it. Guilt is all that you retain within your soul—and so does every other man, as he goes past, avoiding *your* eyes. Do you wonder why your morality has not achieved brotherhood on earth or the good will of man to man?

"The justification of sacrifice, that your morality propounds, is more corrupt than the corruption it purports to justify. The motive of your sacrifice, it tells you, should be *love*—the love you ought to feel for every man. A morality that professes the belief that the values of the spirit are more precious than matter, a morality that teaches you to scorn a whore who gives her body indiscriminately to all men—this same morality demands that you surrender your soul to promiscuous love for all comers.

"As there can be no causeless wealth, so there can be no causeless love or any sort of causeless emotion. An emotion is a response to a fact of reality, an estimate dictated by your standards. To love is to *value.* The man who tells you that it is possible to value without values, to love those whom you appraise as worthless, is the man who tells you that it is possible to grow rich by consuming without producing and that paper money is as valuable as gold.

"Observe that he does not expect you to feel a causeless fear. When his kind get into power, they are expert at contriving means of terror, at giving you ample cause to feel the fear by which they desire to rule you. But when it comes to love, the highest of emotions, you permit them to shriek at you accusingly that you are a moral delinquent if you're incapable of feeling causeless love. When a man feels fear without reason, you call him to the attention of a psychiatrist; you are not so careful to protect the meaning, the nature and the dignity of love.

"Love is the expression of one's values, the greatest reward you can earn for the moral qualities you have achieved in your character and person, the emotional price paid by one man for the joy he receives from the virtues of another. Your morality demands that you divorce your love from values and hand it down to any vagrant, not as response to his worth, but as response to his *need,* not as reward, but as alms, not as a payment for virtues, but as a blank check on vices. Your morality tells you that the purpose of love is to set you free of the bonds of morality, that love is superior to moral judgment, that true love transcends, forgives and survives every manner of evil in its object, and the greater the love the greater the depravity it permits to the loved. To love a man for his virtues is paltry and human, it tells you; to love him for his flaws is divine. To love those who are worthy of it is self-interest; to love the unworthy is sacrifice. You owe your love to those who don't deserve it, and the less they deserve it, the more love you owe them—the more loathsome the object, the nobler your love—the more unfastidious your love, the greater your virtue—and if you can bring your soul to the state of a dump heap that welcomes anything on equal terms, if you can cease to value moral values, you have achieved the state of moral perfection.

"Such is your morality of sacrifice and such are the twin ideals it offers: to refashion the life of your body in the image of a human stockyards, and the life of your spirit in the image of a dump.

"Such was your goal—and you've reached it. Why do you now moan complaints about man's impotence and the futility of human aspirations? Because you were unable to prosper by seeking destruction? Because you were unable to find joy by worshipping pain? Because you were unable to live by holding death as your standard of value?

"The degree of your ability to live was the degree to which you broke your moral code, yet you believe that those who preach it are friends of humanity, you damn yourself and dare not question their motives or their goals. Take a look at them now, when you face your last choice—and if you choose to perish, do so with full knowledge of how cheaply how small an enemy has claimed your life.

"The mystics of both schools, who preach the creed of sacrifice, are germs that attack you through a single sore: your fear of relying on your mind. They tell you that they possess a means of knowledge higher than the mind, a mode of consciousness superior to reason—like a special pull with some bureaucrat of the universe who gives them secret tips withheld from others. The mystics of spirit declare that they possess an extra sense you lack: this special sixth sense consists of contradicting the whole of the knowledge of your five. The mystics of muscle do not bother to assert any claim to extrasensory perception; they merely declare that your senses are not valid, and that their wisdom consists of perceiving your blindness by some manner of un-specified means. Both kinds demand that you invalidate your own consciousness and surrender yourself into their power. They offer you, as proof of their superior knowledge, the fact that they assert the opposite of everything you know, and as proof of their superior ability to deal with existence, the fact that they lead you to misery, self-sacrifice, starvation, destruction.

"They claim that they perceive a mode of being superior to your existence on this earth. The mystics of spirit call it 'another dimension,' which consists of denying dimensions. The mystics of muscle call it 'the future,' which consists of denying the present. To exist is to possess identity. What identity are they able to give to their superior realm? They keep telling you what it is *not,* but never tell you what it *is*. All their identifications consist of negating: God is that which no human mind can know, they say—and proceed to demand that you consider it knowledge—God is non-man, heaven is non-earth, soul is non-body, virtue is non-profit, A is non-A, perception is non-sensory, knowledge is non-reason. Their definitions are not acts of defining, but of wiping out.

"It is only the metaphysics of a leech that would cling to the idea of a universe where a zero is a standard of identification. A leech would want to seek escape from the necessity to name its own nature—escape from the necessity to know that the substance on which it builds its private universe is blood.

"What is the nature of that superior world to which they sacrifice the world that exists? The mystics of spirit curse matter, the mystics of muscle curse profit. The first wish men to profit by renouncing the earth, the second wish men to inherit the earth by renouncing all profit. Their non-material, non-profit worlds are realms where rivers run with milk and coffee, where wine spurts from rocks at their command, where pastry drops on them from clouds at the price of opening their mouth. On this material, profit-chasing earth, an enormous investment of virtue—of intelligence, integrity, energy, skill—is required to construct a railroad to carry them the distance of one mile; in their non-material, non-profit world, they travel from planet to planet at the cost of a wish. If an honest person asks them: 'How?'—they answer with righteous scorn that a 'how' is the concept of vulgar realists; the concept of superior spirits is 'Somehow.' On this earth restricted by matter and profit, rewards are achieved by thought; in a world set free of such restrictions, rewards are achieved by wishing.

"And *that* is the whole of their shabby secret. The secret of all their esoteric philosophies, of all their dialectics and super-senses, of their evasive eyes and snarling words, the secret for which they destroy civilization, language, industries and lives, the secret for which they pierce their own eyes and eardrums, grind out their senses, blank out their minds, the purpose for which they dissolve the absolutes of reason, logic, matter, existence, reality—is to erect upon that plastic fog a single holy absolute: their *Wish*.

"The restriction they seek to escape is the law of identity. The freedom they seek is freedom from the fact that an A will remain an A, no matter what their tears or tantrums—that a river will not bring them milk, no matter what their hunger—that water will not run uphill, no matter what comforts they could gain if it did, and if they want to lift it to the roof of a skyscraper, they must do it by a process of thought and labor, in which the nature of an inch of pipe line counts, but their feelings do not—that their feelings are impotent to alter the course of a single speck of dust in space or the nature of any action they have committed.

"Those who tell you that man is unable to perceive a reality undistorted by his senses, mean that they are unwilling to perceive a reality undistorted by their feelings. 'Things as they are' are things as perceived by your mind; divorce them from reason and they become 'things as perceived by your wishes.'

"There is no honest revolt against reason—and when you accept any part of their creed, your motive is to get away with something your reason would not permit you to attempt. The freedom you seek is freedom from the fact that if you stole your wealth, you are a scoundrel, no matter how much you give to charity or how many prayers you recite—that if you sleep with sluts, you're not a worthy husband, no matter how anxiously you feel that you love your wife next morning—that you are an entity, not a series of random pieces scattered through a universe where nothing sticks and nothing commits you to anything, the universe of a child's nightmare where identities switch and swim, where the rotter and the hero are interchangeable parts arbitrarily assumed at will—that you are a man—that you are an entity—that you *are*.

"No matter how eagerly you claim that the goal of your mystic wishing is a higher mode of life, the rebellion against identity is the wish for non-existence. The desire not to be anything is the desire not to be.

"Your teachers, the mystics of both schools, have reversed causality in their consciousness, then strive to reverse it in existence. They take their emotions as a cause, and their mind as a passive effect. They make their emotions their tool for perceiving reality. They hold their desires as an irreducible primary, as a fact superseding all facts. An honest man does not desire until he has identified the object of his desire. He says: 'It is, therefore I want it.' They say: 'I want it, therefore it is.'

"They want to cheat the axiom of existence and consciousness, they want their consciousness to be an instrument not of *perceiving* but of *creating* existence, and existence to be not the *object* but the *subject* of their consciousness—they want to be that God they created in their image and likeness, who creates a universe out of a void by means of an arbitrary whim. But reality is not to be cheated. What they achieve is the opposite of their desire. They want an omnipotent power over existence; instead, they lose the power of their consciousness. By refusing to know, they condemn themselves to the horror of a perpetual unknown.

"Those irrational wishes that draw you to their creed, those emotions you worship as an idol, on whose altar you sacrifice the earth, that dark, incoherent passion within you, which you take as the voice of God or of your glands, is nothing more than the corpse of your mind. An emotion that clashes with your reason, an emotion that you cannot explain or control, is only the carcass of that stale thinking which you forbade your mind to revise.

"Whenever you committed the evil of refusing to think and to see, of exempting from the absolute of reality some one small wish of yours, whenever you chose to say: Let me withdraw from the judgment of reason the cookies I stole, or the existence of God, let me have my one irrational whim and I will be a man of reason about all else—*that* was the act of subverting your consciousness, the act of corrupting your mind. Your mind then became a fixed jury who takes orders from a secret underworld, whose verdict distorts the evidence to fit an absolute it dares not touch—and a censored reality is the result, a splintered reality where the bits you chose to see are floating among the chasms of those you didn't, held together by that embalming fluid of the mind which is an emotion exempted from thought.

"The links you strive to drown are causal connections. The enemy you seek to defeat is the law of causality: it permits you no miracles. The law of causality is the law of identity applied to action. All actions are caused by entities. The nature of an action is caused and determined by the nature of the entities that act; a thing cannot act in contradiction to its nature. An action not caused by an entity would be caused by a zero, which would mean a *zero* controlling a *thing,* a nonentity controlling an entity, the non-existent ruling the existent—which is the universe of your teachers' desire, the *cause* of their doctrines of causeless action, the *reason* of their revolt against reason, the goal of their morality, their politics, their economics, the ideal they strive for: the reign of the zero.

"The law of identity does not permit you to have your cake and eat it, too. The law of causality does not permit you to eat your cake *before* you have it. But if you drown both laws in the blanks of your mind, if you pretend to yourself and to others that you don't see—then you can try to proclaim your right to eat your cake today and mine tomorrow, you can preach that the way to have a cake is to eat it first, before you bake it, that the way to produce is to start by consuming, that all wishers have an equal claim to all things, since nothing is caused by anything. The corollary of the *causeless* in matter is the *unearned* in spirit.

"Whenever you rebel against causality, your motive is the fraudulent desire, not to escape it, but worse: to reverse it. You want unearned love, as if love, the effect, could give you personal value, the cause—you want unearned admiration, as if admiration, the effect, could give you virtue, the cause—you want unearned wealth, as if wealth, the effect, could give you ability, the cause—you plead for mercy, *mercy,* not justice, as if an unearned forgiveness could wipe out the *cause* of your plea. And to indulge your ugly little shams, you support the doctrines of your teachers, while they run hog-wild proclaiming that spending, the effect, creates riches, the cause, that machinery, the effect, creates intelligence, the cause, that your sexual desires, the effect, create your philosophical values, the cause.

"Who pays for the orgy? Who causes the causeless? Who are the victims, condemned to remain unacknowledged and to perish in silence, lest their agony disturb your pretense that they do not exist? *We* are, we, the men of the mind.

"We are the *cause* of all the values that you covet, we who perform the process of *thinking,* which is the process of defining *identity* and discovering *causal connections.* We taught you to know, to speak, to produce, to desire, to love. You who abandon reason—were it not for us who preserve it, you would not be able to fulfill or even to conceive your wishes. You would not be able to desire the clothes that had not been made, the automobile that had not been invented, the money that had not been devised, as exchange for goods that did not exist, the admiration that had not been experienced for men who had achieved nothing, the love that belongs and pertains only to those who preserve their capacity to think, to choose, *to value.*

"You—who leap like a savage out of the jungle of your feelings into the Fifth Avenue of *our* New York and proclaim that you want to keep the electric lights, but to destroy the generators—it is *our* wealth that you use while destroying us, it is *our* values that you use while damning us, it is *our* language that you use while denying the mind.

"Just as your mystics of spirit invented their heaven in the image of our earth, omitting our existence, and promised you rewards created by miracle out of non-matter—so your modern mystics of muscle omit our existence and promise you a heaven where matter shapes itself of its own causeless will into all the rewards desired by your non-mind.

"For centuries, the mystics of spirit had existed by running a protection racket—by making life on earth unbearable, then charging you for consolation and relief, by forbidding all the virtues that make existence possible, then riding on the shoulders of your guilt, by declaring production and joy to be sins, then collecting blackmail from the sinners. We, the men of the mind, were the unnamed victims of their creed, we who were willing to break their moral code and to bear damnation for the sin of reason—we who thought and acted, while they wished and prayed—we who were moral outcasts, we who were bootleggers of life when life was held to be a crime—while they basked in moral glory for the virtue of surpassing material greed and of distributing in selfless charity the material goods produced by—blank-out.

"*Now* we are chained and commanded to produce by savages who do not grant us even the identification of sinners—by savages who proclaim that we do not exist, then threaten to deprive us of the life we don't possess, if we fail to provide them with the goods we don't produce. Now we are expected to continue running railroads and to know the minute when a train will arrive after crossing the span of a continent, we are expected to continue running steel mills and to know the molecular structure of every drop of metal in the cables of your bridges and in the body of the airplanes that support you in mid-air—while the tribes of your grotesque little mystics of muscle fight over the carcass of our world, gibbering in sounds of non-language that there are no principles, no absolutes, no knowledge, no mind.

"Dropping below the level of a savage, who believes that the magic words he utters have the power to alter reality, they believe that reality can be altered by the power of the words they do *not* utter—and their magic tool is the blank-out, the pretense that nothing can come into existence past the voodoo of their refusal to identify it.

"As they feed on stolen wealth in body, so they feed on stolen concepts in mind, and proclaim that honesty consists of refusing to know that one is stealing. As they use effects while denying causes, so they use our concepts while denying the roots and the existence of the concepts they are using. As they seek, not to build, but to *take over* industrial plants, so they seek, not to think, but to *take over* human thinking.

"As they proclaim that the only requirement for running a factory is the ability to turn the cranks of the machines, and blank out the question of who created the factory—so they proclaim that there are no entities, that nothing exists but motion, and blank out the fact that *motion* presupposes the thing which moves, that without the concept of entity, there can be no such concept as 'motion.' As they proclaim their right to consume the unearned, and blank out the question of who's to produce it—so they proclaim that there is no law of identity, that nothing exists but change, and blank out the fact that *change* presupposes the concepts of what changes, from what and to what, that without the law of identity no such concept as 'change' is possible. As they rob an industrialist while denying his value, so they seek to seize power over all of existence while denying that existence exists.

" 'We know that we know nothing,' they chatter, blanking out the fact that they are claiming knowledge—'There are no absolutes,' they chatter, blanking out the fact that they are uttering an absolute—'You cannot *prove* that you exist or that you're conscious,' they chatter, blanking out the fact that *proof* presupposes existence, consciousness and a complex chain of knowledge: the existence of something to know, of a consciousness able to know it, and of a knowledge that has learned to distinguish between such concepts as the proved and the unproved.

"When a savage who has not learned to speak declares that existence must be proved, he is asking you to prove it by means of non-existence—when he declares that your consciousness must be proved, he is asking you to prove it by means of unconsciousness—he is asking you to step into a void outside of existence and consciousness to give him proof of both—he is asking you to become a zero gaining knowledge about a zero.

"When he declares that an axiom is a matter of arbitrary choice and he doesn't choose to accept the axiom that he exists, he blanks out the fact that he has accepted it by uttering that sentence, that the only way to reject it is to shut one's mouth, expound no theories and die.

"An axiom is a statement that identifies the base of knowledge and of any further statement pertaining to that knowledge, a statement necessarily contained in all others, whether any particular speaker chooses to identify it or not. An axiom is a proposition that defeats its opponents by the fact that they have to accept it and use it in the process of any attempt to deny it. Let the caveman who does not choose to accept the axiom of identity, try to present his theory without using the concept of identity or any concept derived from it—let the anthropoid who does not choose to accept the existence of nouns, try to devise a language without nouns, adjectives or verbs—let the witch-doctor who does not choose to accept the validity of sensory perception, try to prove it without using the data he obtained by sensory perception—let the head-hunter who does not choose to accept the validity of logic, try to prove it without using logic—let the pigmy who proclaims that a skyscraper needs no foundation after it reaches its fiftieth story, yank the base from under *his* building, not yours—let the cannibal who snarls that the freedom of man's mind was needed to *create* an industrial civilization, but is not needed to *maintain* it, be given an arrowhead and bearskin, not a university chair of economics.

"Do you think they are taking you back to dark ages? They are taking you back to darker ages than any your history has known. Their goal is not the era of pre-science, but the era of pre-language. Their purpose is to deprive you of the concept on which man's mind, his life and his culture depend: the concept of an *objective* reality. Identify the development of a human consciousness—and you will know the purpose of their creed.

"A savage is a being who has not grasped that A is A and that reality is real. He has arrested his mind at the level of a baby's, at the stage when a consciousness acquires its initial sensory perceptions and has not learned to distinguish solid objects. It is to a baby that the world appears as a blur of motion, without things that move—and the birth of his mind is the day when he grasps that the streak that keeps flickering past him is his mother and the whirl beyond her is a curtain, that the two are solid entities and neither can turn into the other, that they *are* what they are, that they *exist*. The day when he grasps that matter has no volition is the day when he grasps that *he* has—and this is his birth as a *human* being. The day when he grasps that the reflection he sees in a mirror is not a delusion, that it is real, but it is not himself, that the mirage he sees in a desert is not a delusion, that the air and the light rays that cause it are real, but it is not a city, it is a city's reflection—the day when he grasps that he is not a passive recipient of the sensations of any given moment, that his senses do not provide him with automatic knowledge in separate snatches independent of context, but only with the material of knowledge, which his mind must learn to integrate—the day when he grasps that his senses cannot deceive him, that physical objects cannot act without causes, that his organs of perception are physical and have no volition, no power to invent or to distort, that the evidence they give him is an absolute, but his mind must learn to understand it, his mind must discover the nature, the causes, the full context of his sensory material, his mind must identify the things that he perceives—*that* is the day of his birth as a thinker and scientist.

"*We* are the men who reach that day; you are the men who choose to reach it partly; a savage is a man who never does.

"To a savage, the world is a place of unintelligible miracles where anything is possible to inanimate matter and nothing is possible to *him*. His world is not the unknown, but that irrational horror: the unknowable. He believes that physical objects are endowed with a mysterious volition, moved by *causeless,* unpredictable whims, while *he* is a helpless pawn at the mercy of forces beyond his control. He believes that nature is ruled by demons who possess an omnipotent power and that reality is their fluid plaything, where they can turn his bowl of meal into a snake and his wife into a beetle at any moment, where the A he has never discovered can be any non-A they choose, where the only knowledge he possesses is that he must not attempt to know. He can count on nothing, he can only *wish,* and he spends his life on wishing, on begging his demons to grant him his wishes by the arbitrary power of their will, giving them credit when they do, taking the blame when they don't, offering them sacrifices in token of his gratitude and sacrifices in token of his guilt, crawling on his belly in fear and worship of sun and moon and wind and rain and of any thug who announces himself as their spokesman, provided his words are unintelligible and his mask sufficiently frightening—he wishes, begs and crawls, and dies, leaving you, as a record of his view of existence, the distorted monstrosities of his idols, part-man, part-animal, part-spider, the embodiments of the world of non-A.

"*His* is the intellectual state of your modern teachers and *his* is the world to which they want to bring you.

"If you wonder by what means they propose to do it, walk into any college classroom and you will hear your professors teaching your children that man can be certain of nothing, that his consciousness has no validity whatever, that he can learn no facts and no laws of existence, that he's incapable of knowing an objective reality. What, then, is his standard of knowledge and truth? Whatever others *believe,* is their answer. There is no knowledge, they teach, there's only *faith:* your belief that you exist is an act of faith, no more valid than another's faith in his right to kill you; the axioms of science are an act of faith, no more valid than a mystic's faith in revelations; the belief that electric light can be produced by a generator is an act of faith, no more valid than the belief that it can be produced by a rabbit's foot kissed under a stepladder on the first of the moon—truth is whatever people want it to be, and *people* are everyone except yourself; reality is whatever people choose to say it is, there are no objective facts, there are only people's arbitrary wishes—a man who seeks knowledge in a laboratory by means of test tubes and logic is an old-fashioned, superstitious fool; a true scientist is a man who goes around taking public polls—and if it weren't for the selfish greed of the manufacturers of steel girders, who have a vested interest in obstructing the progress of science, you would learn that New York City does not exist, because a poll of the entire population of the world would tell you by a landslide majority that their *beliefs* forbid its existence.

"For centuries, the mystics of spirit have proclaimed that faith is superior to reason, but have not dared deny the existence of reason. Their heirs and product, the mystics of muscle, have completed their job and achieved their dream: they proclaim that everything is faith, and call it a revolt against believing. As revolt against unproved assertions, they proclaim that nothing can be proved; as revolt against supernatural knowledge, they proclaim that no knowledge is possible; as revolt against the enemies of science, they proclaim that science is superstition; as revolt against the enslavement of the mind, they proclaim that there is no mind.

"If you surrender your power to perceive, if you accept the switch of your standard from the *objective* to the *collective* and wait for mankind to tell you what to think, you will find another switch taking place before the eyes you have renounced: you will find that your teachers become the rulers of the collective, and if you then refuse to obey them, protesting that they are not the whole of mankind, they will answer: 'By what means do you know that we are not? *Are,* brother? Where did you get that old-fashioned term?'

"If you doubt that such is their purpose, observe with what passionate consistency the mystics of muscle are striving to make you forget that a concept such as '*mind*' has ever existed. Observe the twists of undefined verbiage, the words with rubber meanings, the terms left floating in midstream, by means of which they try to get around the recognition of the concept of *'thinking.'* Your consciousness, they tell you, consists of 'reflexes,' 'reactions,' 'experiences,' 'urges,' and 'drives' —and refuse to identify the means by which they acquired that knowledge, to identify the act they are performing when they tell it or the act you are performing when you listen. Words have the power to 'condition' you, they say and refuse to identify the reason why words have the power to change your—blank-out. A student reading a book understands it through a process of—blank-out. A scientist working on an invention is engaged in the activity of—blank-out. A psychologist helping a neurotic to solve a problem and untangle a conflict, does it by means of—blank-out. An industrialist—blank-out—there is no such person. A factory is a 'natural resource,' like a tree, a rock or a mud puddle.

"The problem of production, they tell you, has been solved and deserves no study or concern; the only problem left for your 'reflexes' to solve is now the problem of distribution. Who solved the problem of production? Humanity, they answer. What was the solution? The goods are here. How did they get here? Somehow. What caused it? Nothing has causes.

"They proclaim that every man born is entitled to exist without labor and, the laws of reality to the contrary notwithstanding, is entitled to receive his 'minimum sustenance'—his food, his clothes, his shelter—with no effort on his part, as his due and his birthright. To receive it—from whom? Blank-out. Every man, they announce, owns an equal share of the technological benefits created in the world. Created—by whom? Blank-out. Frantic cowards who posture as defenders of industrialists now define the purpose of economics as 'an adjustment between the unlimited *desires* of men and the goods supplied in limited quantity.' Supplied—by whom? Blank-out. Intellectual hoodlums who pose as professors, shrug away the thinkers of the past by declaring that their social theories were based on the impractical assumption that man was a rational being—but since men are not rational, they declare, there ought to be established a system that will make it possible for them to exist while being *irrational*, which means: while defying reality. Who will make it possible? Blank-out. Any stray mediocrity rushes into print with plans to control the production of mankind—and whoever agrees or disagrees with his statistics, no one questions his right to enforce his plans by means of a gun. Enforce—on whom? Blank-out. Random females with causeless incomes flitter on trips around the globe and return to deliver the message that the backward peoples of the world *demand* a higher standard of living. Demand—of whom? Blank-out.

"And to forestall any inquiry into the cause of the difference between a jungle village and New York City, they resort to the ultimate obscenity of explaining man's industrial progress—skyscrapers, cable bridges, power motors, railroad trains—by declaring that man is an animal who possesses an *'instinct of tool-making.'*

"Did you wonder what is wrong with the world? You are now seeing the climax of the creed of the uncaused and unearned. All your gangs of mystics, of spirit or muscle, are fighting one another for power to rule you, snarling that love is the solution for all the problems of your spirit and that a whip is the solution for all the problems of your body— you who have agreed to have no mind. Granting man less dignity than they grant to cattle, ignoring what an animal trainer could tell them—that no animal can be trained by fear, that a tortured elephant will trample its torturer, but will not work for him or carry his burdens —they expect man to continue to produce electronic tubes, supersonic airplanes, atom-smashing engines and interstellar telescopes, with his ration of meat for reward and a lash on his back for incentive.

"Make no mistake about the character of mystics. To undercut your consciousness has always been their only purpose throughout the ages —and *power,* the power to rule you by force, has always been their only lust.

"From the rites of the jungle witch-doctors, which distorted reality into grotesque absurdities, stunted the minds of their victims and kept them in terror of the supernatural for stagnant stretches of centuries— to the supernatural doctrines of the Middle Ages, which kept men huddling on the mud floors of their hovels, in terror that the devil might steal the soup they had worked eighteen hours to earn—to the seedy little smiling professor who assures you that your brain has no capacity to think, that you have no means of perception and must blindly obey the omnipotent will of that supernatural force: Society—all of it is the same performance for the same and only purpose: to reduce you to the kind of pulp that has surrendered the validity of its consciousness.

"But it cannot be done to you without your consent. If you permit it to be done, you deserve it.

"When you listen to a mystic's harangue on the impotence of the human mind and begin to doubt *your* consciousness, not his, when you permit your precariously semi-rational state to be shaken by any assertion and decide it is safer to trust his superior certainty and knowledge, the joke is on both of you: your sanction is the only source of certainty he has. The supernatural power that a mystic dreads, the unknowable spirit he worships, the consciousness he considers omnipotent is—*yours.*

"A mystic is a man who surrendered his mind at its first encounter with the minds of others. Somewhere in the distant reaches of his childhood, when his own understanding of reality clashed with the assertions of others, with their arbitrary orders and contradictory demands, he gave in to so craven a fear of independence that he renounced his rational faculty. At the crossroads of the choice between

'I know' and 'They say,' he chose the authority of others, he chose to submit rather than to understand, to *believe* rather than to think. Faith in the supernatural begins as faith in the superiority of others. His surrender took the form of the feeling that he must hide his lack of understanding, that others possess some mysterious knowledge of which he alone is deprived, that reality is whatever they want it to be, through some means forever denied to him.

"From then on, afraid to think, he is left at the mercy of unidentified feelings. His feelings become his only guide, his only remnant of personal identity, he clings to them with ferocious possessiveness—and whatever thinking he does is devoted to the struggle of hiding from himself that the nature of his feelings is terror.

"When a mystic declares that he *feels* the existence of a power superior to reason, he feels it all right, but that power is not an omniscient super-spirit of the universe, it is the consciousness of any passer-by to whom he has surrendered his own. A mystic is driven by the urge to impress, to cheat, to flatter, to deceive, *to force* that omnipotent consciousness of others. 'They' are his only key to reality, he feels that he cannot exist save by harnessing their mysterious power and extorting their unaccountable consent. 'They' are his only means of perception and, like a blind man who depends on the sight of a dog, he feels he must leash them in order to live. To control the consciousness of others becomes his only passion; power-lust is a weed that grows only in the vacant lots of an abandoned mind.

"Every dictator is a mystic, and every mystic is a potential dictator. A mystic craves obedience from men, not their agreement. He wants them to surrender their consciousness to his assertions, his edicts, his wishes, his whims—as *his* consciousness is surrendered to theirs. He wants to deal with men by means of faith and force—he finds no satisfaction in their consent if he must earn it by means of facts and reason. Reason is the enemy he dreads and, simultaneously, considers precarious; reason, to him, is a means of deception; he *feels* that men possess some power more potent than reason—and only their causeless belief or their forced obedience can give him a sense of security, a proof that he has gained control of the mystic endowment he lacked. His lust is to command, not to convince: conviction requires an act of independence and rests on the absolute of an objective reality. What he seeks is power over reality and over men's means of perceiving it, their mind, the power to interpose his will between existence and consciousness, as if, by agreeing to fake the reality he orders them to fake, men would, in fact, create it.

"Just as the mystic is a parasite in matter, who expropriates the wealth created by others—just as he is a parasite in spirit, who plunders the ideas created by others—so he falls below the level of a lunatic who creates his own distortion of reality, to the level of a parasite of lunacy who seeks a distortion created by others.

"There is only one state that fulfills the mystic's longing for infinity, non-causality, non-identity: *death*. No matter what unintelligible causes he ascribes to his incommunicable feelings, whoever rejects reality rejects existence—and the feelings that move him from then on are hatred for all the values of man's life, and lust for all the evils that destroy it. A mystic relishes the spectacle of suffering, of poverty, subservience and terror; these give him a feeling of triumph, a proof of the defeat of rational reality. But no other reality exists.

"No matter whose welfare he professes to serve, be it the welfare of God or of that disembodied gargoyle he describes as 'The People,' no matter what ideal he proclaims in terms of some supernatural dimension—*in fact, in reality, on earth,* his ideal is *death,* his craving is to kill, his only satisfaction is to torture.

"Destruction is the only end that the mystics' creed has ever achieved, as it is the only end that you see them achieving today, and if the ravages wrought by their acts have not made them question their doctrines, if they profess to be moved by love, yet are not deterred by piles of human corpses, it is because the truth about their souls is worse than the obscene excuse you have allowed them, the excuse that the end justifies the means and that the horrors they practice are means to nobler ends. The truth is that those horrors are their ends.

"You who're depraved enough to believe that you could adjust yourself to a mystic's dictatorship and could please him by obeying his orders—there is no way to please him; when you obey, he will reverse his orders; he seeks obedience for the sake of obedience and destruction for the sake of destruction. You who are craven enough to believe that you can make terms with a mystic by giving in to his extortions—there is no way to buy him off, the bribe he wants is your life, as slowly or as fast as you are willing to give it in—and the monster he seeks to bribe is the hidden blank-out in his mind, which drives him to kill in order not to learn that the death he desires is his own.

"You who are innocent enough to believe that the forces let loose in your world today are moved by greed for material plunder—the mystics' scramble for spoils is only a screen to conceal from their mind the nature of their motive. Wealth is a means of human life, and they clamor for wealth in imitation of living beings, to pretend to themselves that they desire to live. But their swinish indulgence in plundered luxury is not enjoyment, it is escape. They do not want to own your fortune, they want you to lose it; they do not want to succeed, they want you to fail; they do not want to live, they want you to die; they desire nothing, they hate existence, and they keep running, each trying not to learn that the object of his hatred is himself.

"You who've never grasped the nature of evil, you who describe them as 'misguided idealists'—may the God you invented forgive you!—*they* are the essence of evil, they, those anti-living objects who seek, by devouring the world, to fill the *selfless* zero of their soul. It is not your wealth that they're after. Theirs is a conspiracy against the mind, which means: against life and man.

"It is a conspiracy without leader or direction, and the random little thugs of the moment who cash in on the agony of one land or another are chance scum riding the torrent from the broken dam of the sewer of centuries, from the reservoir of hatred for reason, for logic, for ability, for achievement, for joy, stored by every whining anti-human who ever preached the superiority of the 'heart' over the mind.

"It is a conspiracy of all those who seek, not to live, but to *get away with living,* those who seek to cut just one small corner of reality and are drawn, by feeling, to all the others who are busy cutting other corners—a conspiracy that unites by links of evasion all those who pursue a *zero* as a value: the professor who, unable to think, takes pleasure in crippling the mind of his students, the businessman who, to protect his stagnation, takes pleasure in chaining the ability of competitors, the neurotic who, to defend his self-loathing, takes pleasure in breaking men of self-esteem, the incompetent who takes pleasure in defeating achievement, the mediocrity who takes pleasure in demolishing greatness, the eunuch who takes pleasure in the castration of all pleasure—and all their intellectual munition-makers, all those who preach that the immolation of virtue will transform vices into virtue. *Death* is the premise at the root of their theories, *death* is the goal of their actions in practice—and *you* are the last of their victims.

"We, who were the living buffers between you and the nature of your creed, are no longer there to save you from the effects of your chosen beliefs. We are no longer willing to pay with our lives the debts you incurred in yours or the moral deficit piled up by all the generations behind you. You had been living on borrowed time—and I am the man who has called in the loan.

"I am the man whose existence your blank-outs were intended to permit you to ignore. I am the man whom you did not want either to live or to die. You did not want me to live, because you were afraid of knowing that I carried the responsibility you dropped and that your lives depended upon me; you did not want me to die, because you knew it.

"Twelve years ago, when I worked in your world, I was an inventor. I was one of a profession that came last in human history and will be first to vanish on the way back to the sub-human. An inventor is a man who asks 'Why?' of the universe and lets nothing stand between the answer and his mind.

"Like the man who discovered the use of steam or the man who discovered the use of oil, I discovered a source of energy which was available since the birth of the globe, but which men had not known how to use except as an object of worship, of terror and of legends about a thundering god. I completed the experimental model of a motor that would have made a fortune for me and for those who had hired me, a motor that would have raised the efficiency of every human installation using power and would have added the gift of higher productivity to every hour you spend at earning your living.

"Then, one night at a factory meeting, I heard myself sentenced to death by reason of my achievement. I heard three parasites assert that my brain and my life were their property, that my right to exist was conditional and depended on the satisfaction of their desires. The purpose of my ability, they said, was to serve the needs of those who were less able. I had no right to live, they said, by reason of my competence for living; their right to live was unconditional, by reason of their incompetence.

"Then I saw what was wrong with the world, I saw what destroyed men and nations, and where the battle for life had to be fought. I saw that the enemy was an inverted morality—and that my sanction was its only power. I saw that evil was impotent—that evil was the irrational, the blind, the anti-real—and that the only weapon of its triumph was the willingness of the good to serve it. Just as the parasites around me were proclaiming their helpless dependence on my mind and were expecting me voluntarily to accept a slavery they had no power to enforce, just as they were counting on my self-immolation to provide them with the means of their plan—so throughout the world and throughout men's history, in every version and form, from the extortions of loafing relatives to the atrocities of collectivized countries, it is the good, the able, the men of reason, who act as their own destroyers, who transfuse to evil the blood of their virtue and let evil transmit to them the poison of destruction, thus gaining for evil the power of survival, and for their own values—the impotence of death. I saw that there comes a point, in the defeat of any man of virtue, when his own consent is needed for evil to win—and that no manner of injury done to him by others can succeed if he chooses to withhold his consent. I saw that I could put an end to your outrages by pronouncing a single word in my mind. I pronounced it. The word was 'No.'

"I quit that factory. I quit your world. I made it my job to warn your victims and to give them the method and the weapon to fight you. The method was to refuse to deflect retribution. The weapon was justice.

"If you want to know what you lost when I quit and when my strikers deserted your world—stand on an empty stretch of soil in a wilderness unexplored by men and ask yourself what manner of survival you would achieve and how long you would last if you refused to think, with no one around to teach you the motions, or, if you chose to think, how much your mind would be able to discover—ask yourself how many independent conclusions you have reached in the course of your life and how much of your time was spent on performing the actions you learned from others—ask yourself whether you would be able to discover how to till the soil and grow your food, whether you would be able to invent a wheel, a lever, an induction coil, a generator, an electronic tube—then decide whether men of ability are exploiters who live by the fruit of *your* labor and rob you of the wealth that *you* produce, and whether you dare to believe that you possess the power to enslave them. Let your women take a look at a jungle female with her shriveled face and pendulous breasts, as she sits grinding meal in a bowl, hour after hour, century by century—then let them ask themselves whether their 'instinct of tool-making' will provide them with their electric refrigerators, their washing machines and vacuum cleaners, and, if not, whether they care to destroy those who provided it all, but not 'by instinct.'

"Take a look around you, you savages who stutter that ideas are created by men's means of production, that a machine is not the product of human thought, but a mystical power that produces human thinking. You have never discovered the industrial age—and you cling to the morality of the barbarian eras when a miserable form of human subsistence was produced by the muscular labor of slaves. Every mystic had always longed for slaves, to protect him from the material reality he dreaded. But *you,* you grotesque little atavists, stare blindly at the skyscrapers and smokestacks around you and dream of enslaving the material providers who are scientists, inventors, industrialists. When you clamor for public ownership of the means of production, you are clamoring for public ownership of the mind. I have taught my strikers that the answer you deserve is only: 'Try and get it.'

"You proclaim yourself unable to harness the forces of inanimate matter, yet propose to harness the minds of men who are able to achieve the feats you cannot equal. You proclaim that you cannot survive without us, yet propose to dictate the terms of our survival. You proclaim that you need us, yet indulge the impertinence of asserting your right to rule us by force—and expect that we, who are not afraid of that physical nature which fills you with terror, will cower at the sight of any lout who has talked you into voting him a chance to command us.

"You propose to establish a social order based on the following tenets: that you're incompetent to run your own life, but competent to run the lives of others—that you're unfit to exist in freedom, but fit to become an omnipotent ruler—that you're unable to earn your living by the use of your own intelligence, but able to judge politicians and to vote them into jobs of total power over arts you have never seen, over sciences you have never studied, over achievements of which you have no knowledge, over the gigantic industries where you, by your own definition of your capacity, would be unable successfully to fill the job of assistant greaser.

"This idol of your cult of zero-worship, this symbol of impotence—the congenital dependent—is your image of man and your standard of value, in whose likeness you strive to refashion your soul. 'It's only human,' you cry in defense of any depravity, reaching the stage of self-abasement where you seek to make the concept *'human'* mean the weakling, the fool, the rotter, the liar, the failure, the coward, the fraud, and to exile from the human race the hero, the thinker, the producer, the inventor, the strong, the purposeful, the pure—as if 'to feel' were human, but to think were not, as if to fail were human, but to succeed were not, as if corruption were human, but virtue were not —as if the premise of *death* were proper to man, but the premise of *life* were not.

"In order to deprive us of honor, that you may then deprive us of our wealth, you have always regarded us as slaves who deserve no moral recognition. You praise any venture that claims to be non-profit, and damn the men who made the profits that make the venture possible. You regard as 'in the public interest' any project serving those who do not pay; it is not in the public interest to provide any services for those who do the paying. 'Public benefit' is anything given as alms; to engage in trade is to injure the public. 'Public welfare' is the welfare of those who do not earn it; those who do, are entitled to no welfare. *'The public,'* to you, is whoever has failed to achieve any virtue or value; whoever achieves it, whoever provides the goods you require for survival, ceases to be regarded as part of the public or as part of the human race.

"What blank-out permitted you to hope that you could get away with this muck of contradictions and to plan it as an ideal society, when the 'No' of your victims was sufficient to demolish the whole of your structure? What permits any insolent beggar to wave his sores in the face of his betters and to plead for help in the tone of a threat? You cry, as he does, that you are counting on our pity, but your secret hope is the moral code that has taught you to count on our *guilt.* You expect us to feel guilty of our virtues in the presence of your vices, wounds and failures—guilty of succeeding at existence, guilty of enjoying the life that you damn, yet beg us to help you to live.

"Did you want to know who is John Galt? I am the first man of ability who refused to regard it as guilt. I am the first man who would not do penance for my virtues or let them be used as the tools of my destruction. I am the first man who would not suffer martyrdom at the hands of those who wished me to perish for the privilege of keeping them alive. I am the first man who told them that I did not need them, and until they learned to deal with me as traders, giving value for value, they would have to exist without me, as I would exist without them; then I would let them learn whose is the need and whose the ability—and if human survival is the standard, whose terms would set the way to survive.

"I have done by plan and intention what had been done throughout history by silent default. There have always been men of intelligence who went on strike, in protest and despair, but they did not know the meaning of their action. The man who retires from public life, to think, but not to share his thoughts—the man who chooses to spend his years in the obscurity of menial employment, keeping to himself the fire of his mind, never giving it form, expression or reality, refusing to bring it into a world he despises—the man who is defeated by revulsion, the man who renounces before he has started, the man who gives up rather than give in, the man who functions at a fraction of his capacity, disarmed by his longing for an ideal he has not found—they are on strike, on strike against unreason, on strike against your world and your values. But not knowing any values of their own, they abandon the quest to know—in the darkness of their hopeless indignation, which is righteous without knowledge of the right, and passionate without knowledge of desire, they concede to you the power of reality and surrender the incentives of their mind—and they perish in bitter futility, as rebels who never learned the object of their rebellion, as lovers who never discovered their love.

"The infamous times you call the Dark Ages were an era of intelligence on strike, when men of ability went underground and lived undiscovered, studying in secret, and died, destroying the works of their mind, when only a few of the bravest of martyrs remained to keep the human race alive. Every period ruled by mystics was an era of stagnation and want, when most men were on strike against existence, working for less than their barest survival, leaving nothing but scraps for their rulers to loot, refusing to think, to venture, to produce, when the ultimate collector of their profits and the final authority on truth or error was the whim of some gilded degenerate sanctioned as superior to reason by divine right and by grace of a club. The road of human history was a string of blank-outs over sterile stretches eroded by faith and force, with only a few brief bursts of sunlight, when the released energy of the men of the mind performed the wonders you gaped at, admired and promptly extinguished again.

"But there will be no extinction, this time. The game of the mystics is up. You will perish in and by your own unreality. We, the men of reason, will survive.

"I have called out on strike the kind of martyrs who had never deserted you before. I have given them the weapon they had lacked: the knowledge of their own moral value. I have taught them that the world is ours, whenever we choose to claim it, by virtue and grace of the fact that ours is the Morality of Life. They, the great victims who had produced all the wonders of humanity's brief summer, they, the industrialists, the conquerors of matter, had not discovered the nature of their right. They had known that theirs was the power. I taught them that theirs was the glory.

"You, who dare to regard us as the moral inferiors of any mystic who claims supernatural visions—you, who scramble like vultures for plundered pennies, yet honor a fortune-teller above a fortune-maker—you, who scorn a businessman as ignoble, but esteem any posturing artist as exalted—the root of your standards is that mystic miasma which comes from primordial swamps, that cult of death, which pronounces a businessman immoral by reason of the fact that he keeps you alive. You, who claim that you long to rise above the crude concerns of the body, above the drudgery of serving mere physical needs—*who* is enslaved by physical needs: the Hindu who labors from sunrise to sunset at the shafts of a hand-plow for a bowl of rice, or the American who is driving a tractor? *Who* is the conqueror of physical reality: the man who sleeps on a bed of nails or the man who sleeps on an inner-spring mattress? *Which* is the monument to the triumph of the human spirit over matter: the germ-eaten hovels on the shorelines of the Ganges or the Atlantic skyline of New York?

"Unless you learn the answers to these questions—and learn to stand at reverent attention when you face the achievements of man's mind—you will not stay much longer on this earth, which we love and will not permit you to damn. You will not sneak by with the rest of your lifespan. I have foreshortened the usual course of history and have let you discover the nature of the payment you had hoped to switch to the shoulders of others. It is the last of your own living power that will now be drained to provide the unearned for the worshippers and carriers of Death. Do not pretend that a malevolent reality defeated you—you were defeated by your own evasions. Do not pretend that you will perish for a noble ideal—you will perish as fodder for the haters of man.

"But to those of you who still retain a remnant of the dignity and will to love one's life, I am offering the chance to make a choice. Choose whether you wish to perish for a morality you have never believed or practiced. Pause on the brink of self-destruction and examine your values and your life. You had known how to take an inventory of your wealth. Now take an inventory of your mind.

"Since childhood, you have been hiding the guilty secret that you feel no desire to be moral, no desire to seek self-immolation, that you dread and hate your code, but dare not say it even to yourself, that you're devoid of those moral 'instincts' which others profess to feel. The less you felt, the louder you proclaimed your selfless love and servitude to others, in dread of ever letting them discover your own self, the self that you betrayed, the self that you kept in concealment, like a skeleton in the closet of your body. And they, who were at once your dupes and your deceivers, they listened and voiced their loud approval, in dread of ever letting you discover that they were harboring the same unspoken secret. Existence among you is a giant pretense, an act you all perform for one another, each feeling that he is the only guilty freak, each placing his moral authority in the unknowable known only to others, each faking the reality he feels they expect him to fake, none having the courage to break the vicious circle.

"No matter what dishonorable compromise you've made with your impracticable creed, no matter what miserable balance, half-cynicism, half-superstition, you now manage to maintain, you still preserve the root, the lethal tenet: the belief that the moral and the practical are opposites. Since childhood, you have been running from the terror of a choice you have never dared fully to identify: If the *practical,* whatever you must practice to exist, whatever works, succeeds, achieves your purpose, whatever brings you food and joy, whatever profits you, is evil—and if the good, the moral, is the *impractical,* whatever fails, destroys, frustrates, whatever injures you and brings you loss or pain—then your choice is to be moral or to live.

"The sole result of that murderous doctrine was to remove morality from life. You grew up to believe that moral laws bear no relation to the job of living, except as an impediment and threat, that man's existence is an amoral jungle where anything goes and anything works. And in that fog of switching definitions which descends upon a frozen mind, you have forgotten that the evils damned by your creed were the virtues required for living, and you have come to believe that actual evils are the *practical* means of existence. Forgetting that the impractical 'good' was self-sacrifice, you believe that self-esteem is impractical; forgetting that the practical 'evil' was production, you believe that robbery is practical.

"Swinging like a helpless branch in the wind of an uncharted moral wilderness, you dare not fully to be evil or fully to live. When you are honest, you feel the resentment of a sucker; when you cheat, you feel terror and shame. When you are happy, your joy is diluted by guilt; when you suffer, your pain is augmented by the feeling that pain is your natural state. You pity the men you admire, you believe they are doomed to fail; you envy the men you hate, you believe they are the masters of existence. You feel disarmed when you come up against a scoundrel: you believe that evil is bound to win, since the moral is the impotent, the *impractical.*

"Morality, to you, is a phantom scarecrow made of duty, of boredom, of punishment, of pain, a cross-breed between the first schoolteacher of your past and the tax collector of your present, a scarecrow standing in a barren field, waving a stick to chase away your pleasures —and *pleasure,* to you, is a liquor-soggy brain, a mindless slut, the stupor of a moron who stakes his cash on some animal's race, since pleasure cannot be moral.

"If you identify your actual belief, you will find a triple damnation —of yourself, of life, of virtue—in the grotesque conclusion you have reached: you believe that morality is a necessary evil.

"Do you wonder why you live without dignity, love without fire and die without resistance? Do you wonder why, wherever you look, you see nothing but unanswerable questions, why your life is torn by impossible conflicts, why you spend it straddling irrational fences to evade artificial choices, such as soul or body, mind or heart, security or freedom, private profit or public good?

"Do you cry that you find no answers? By what means did you hope to find them? You reject your tool of perception—your mind—then complain that the universe is a mystery. You discard your key, then wail that all doors are locked against you. You start out in pursuit of the irrational, then damn existence for making no sense.

"The fence you have been straddling for two hours—while hearing my words and seeking to escape them—is the coward's formula contained in the sentence: 'But we don't have to go to extremes!' The extreme you have always struggled to avoid is the recognition that reality is final, that A is A and that the truth is true. A moral code impossible to practice, a code that demands imperfection or death, has taught you to dissolve all ideas in fog, to permit no firm definitions, to regard any concept as approximate and any rule of conduct as elastic, to hedge on any principle, to compromise on any value, to take the middle of any road. By extorting your acceptance of supernatural absolutes, it has forced you to reject the absolute of nature. By making moral judgments impossible, it has made you incapable of rational judgment. A code that forbids you to cast the first stone, has forbidden you to admit the identity of stones and to know when or if you're being stoned.

"The man who refuses to judge, who neither agrees nor disagrees, who declares that there are no absolutes and believes that he escapes responsibility, is the man responsible for all the blood that is now spilled in the world. Reality is an absolute, existence is an absolute, a speck of dust is an absolute and so is a human life. Whether you live or die is an absolute. Whether you have a piece of bread or not, is an absolute. Whether you eat your bread or see it vanish into a looter's stomach, is an absolute.

"There are two sides to every issue: one side is right and the other is wrong, but the middle is always evil. The man who is wrong still retains some respect for truth, if only by accepting the responsibility of choice. But the man in the middle is the knave who blanks out the truth in order to pretend that no choice or values exist, who is willing to sit out the course of any battle, willing to cash in on the blood of the innocent or to crawl on his belly to the guilty, who dispenses justice by condemning both the robber and the robbed to jail, who solves conflicts by ordering the thinker and the fool to meet each other halfway. In any compromise between food and poison, it is only death that can win. In any compromise between good and evil, it is only evil that can profit. In that transfusion of blood which drains the good to feed the evil, the compromiser is the transmitting rubber tube.

"You, who are half-rational, half-coward, have been playing a con game with reality, but the victim you have conned is yourself. When men reduce their virtues to the approximate, then evil acquires the force of an absolute, when loyalty to an unyielding purpose is dropped by the virtuous, it's picked up by scoundrels—and you get the indecent spectacle of a cringing, bargaining, traitorous good and a self-righteously uncompromising evil. As you surrendered to the mystics of muscle when they told you that ignorance consists of claiming knowledge, so now you surrender to them when they shriek that immorality consists of pronouncing moral judgment. When they yell that it is selfish to be certain that you are right, you hasten to assure them that you're certain of nothing. When they shout that it's immoral to stand on your convictions, you assure them that you have no convictions whatever. When the thugs of Europe's People's States snarl that you are guilty of intolerance, because you don't treat your desire to live and their desire to kill you as a difference of opinion—you cringe and hasten to assure them that you are not intolerant of any horror. When some barefoot bum in some pesthole of Asia yells at you: How dare you be rich—you apologize and beg him to be patient and promise him you'll give it all away.

"You have reached the blind alley of the treason you committed when you agreed that you had no right to exist. Once, you believed it was 'only a compromise': you conceded it was evil to live for yourself, but moral to live for the sake of your children. Then you conceded that it was selfish to live for your children, but moral to live for your community. Then you conceded that it was selfish to live for your community, but moral to live for your country. *Now,* you are letting this greatest of countries be devoured by any scum from any corner of the earth, while you concede that it is selfish to live for your country and that your moral duty is to live for the globe. A man who has no right to life, has no right to values and will not keep them.

"At the end of your road of successive betrayals, stripped of weapons, of certainty, of honor, you commit your final act of treason and sign your petition of intellectual bankruptcy: while the muscle-mystics of the People's States proclaim that they're the champions of reason and science, you agree and hasten to proclaim that *faith* is your cardinal principle, that reason is on the side of your destroyers, but yours is the side of faith. To the struggling remnants of rational honesty in the twisted, bewildered minds of your children, you declare that you can offer no rational argument to support the ideas that created this country, that there is no rational justification for freedom, for property, for justice, for rights, that they rest on a mystical insight and can be accepted only on faith, that in reason and logic the enemy is right, but faith is superior to reason. You declare to your children that it is rational to loot, to torture, to enslave, to expropriate, to murder, but that they must resist the temptations of logic and stick to the discipline of remaining irrational—that skyscrapers, factories, radios, airplanes were the products of faith and mystic intuition, while famines, concentration camps and firing squads are the products of a reasonable manner of existence—that the industrial revolution was the revolt of the men of faith against that era of reason and logic which is known as the Middle Ages. Simultaneously, in the same breath, to the same child, you declare that the looters who rule the People's States will surpass this country in material production, since they are the representatives of science, but that it's evil to be concerned with physical wealth and that one must renounce material prosperity—you declare that the looters' ideals are noble, but they do not mean them, while you do; that your purpose in fighting the looters is only to accomplish their aims, which they cannot accomplish, but you can; and that the way to fight them is to beat them to it and give one's wealth away. Then you wonder why your children join the People's thugs or become half-crazed delinquents, you wonder why the looters' conquests keep creeping closer to your doors—and you blame it on human stupidity, declaring that the masses are impervious to reason.

"You blank out the open, public spectacle of the looters' fight against the mind, and the fact that their bloodiest horrors are unleashed to punish the crime of thinking. You blank out the fact that most mystics of muscle started out as mystics of spirit, that they keep switching from one to the other, that the men you call materialists and spiritualists are only two halves of the same dissected human, forever seeking completion, but seeking it by swinging from the destruction of the flesh to the destruction of the soul and vice versa—that they keep running from your colleges to the slave pens of Europe to an open collapse into the mystic muck of India, seeking any refuge against reality, any form of escape from the mind.

"You blank it out and cling to your hypocrisy of 'faith' in order to blank out the knowledge that the looters have a stranglehold upon you, which consists of your moral code—that the looters are the final and consistent practitioners of the morality you're half-obeying, half-evading—that they practice it the only way it can be practiced: by turning the earth into a sacrificial furnace—that your morality forbids you to oppose them in the only way they can be opposed: by refusing to become a sacrificial animal and proudly asserting your right to exist—that in order to fight them to the finish and with full rectitude, *it is your morality that you have to reject.*

"You blank it out, because your self-esteem is tied to that mystic 'unselfishness' which you've never possessed or practiced, but spent so many years pretending to possess that the thought of denouncing it fills you with terror. No value is higher than self-esteem, but you've invested it in counterfeit securities—and now your morality has caught you in a trap where you are forced to protect your self-esteem by fighting for the creed of self-destruction. The grim joke is on you: that need of self-esteem, which you're unable to explain or to define, belongs to *my* morality, not yours; it's the objective token of my code, it is my proof within your own soul.

"By a feeling he has not learned to identify, but has derived from his first awareness of existence, from his discovery that he has to make choices, man knows that his desperate need of self-esteem is a matter of life or death. As a being of volitional consciousness, he knows that he must know his own value in order to maintain his own life. He knows that he has to be *right;* to be wrong in action means danger to his life; to be wrong in person, to be *evil,* means to be unfit for existence.

"Every act of man's life has to be willed; the mere act of obtaining or eating his food implies that the person he preserves is worthy of being preserved; every pleasure he seeks to enjoy implies that the person who seeks it is worthy of finding enjoyment. He has no choice about his need of self-esteem, his only choice is the standard by which to gauge it. And he makes his fatal error when he switches this gauge protecting his life into the service of his own destruction, when he chooses a standard contradicting existence and sets his self-esteem against reality.

"Every form of causeless self-doubt, every feeling of inferiority and secret unworthiness is, in fact, man's hidden dread of his inability to deal with existence. But the greater his terror, the more fiercely he clings to the murderous doctrines that choke him. No man can survive the moment of pronouncing himself irredeemably evil; should he do it, his next moment is insanity or suicide. To escape it—if he's chosen an irrational standard—he will fake, evade, blank out; he will cheat himself of reality, of existence, of happiness, of mind; and he will ultimately cheat himself of self-esteem by struggling to preserve its illusion rather than to risk discovering its lack. To fear to face an issue is to believe that the worst is true.

"It is not any crime you have ever committed that infects your soul with permanent guilt, it is none of your failures, errors or flaws, but the *blank-out* by which you attempt to evade them—it is not any sort of Original Sin or unknown prenatal deficiency, but the knowledge and fact of your basic default, of suspending your mind, of refusing to think. Fear and guilt are your chronic emotions, they are real and you do deserve them, but they don't come from the superficial reasons you invent to disguise their cause, not from your 'selfishness,' weakness or ignorance, but from a real and basic threat to your existence: *fear,* because you have abandoned your weapon of survival, *guilt,* because you know you have done it volitionally.

"The *self* you have betrayed is your mind; *self-esteem* is reliance on one's power to think. The ego you seek, that essential '*you*' which you cannot express or define, is not your emotions or inarticulate dreams, but your *intellect,* that judge of your supreme tribunal whom you've impeached in order to drift at the mercy of any stray shyster you describe as your 'feeling.' Then you drag yourself through a self-made night, in a desperate quest for a nameless fire, moved by some fading vision of a dawn you had seen and lost.

"Observe the persistence, in mankind's mythologies, of the legend about a paradise that men had once possessed, the city of Atlantis or the Garden of Eden or some kingdom of perfection, always behind us. The root of that legend exists, not in the past of the race, but in the past of every man. You still retain a sense—not as firm as a memory, but diffused like the pain of hopeless longing—that somewhere in the starting years of your childhood, before you had learned to submit, to absorb the terror of unreason and to doubt the value of your mind, you had known a radiant state of existence, you had known the independence of a rational consciousness facing an open universe. *That* is the paradise which you have lost, which you seek—which is yours for the taking.

"Some of you will never know who is John Galt. But those of you who have known a single moment of love for existence and of pride in being its worthy lover, a moment of looking at this earth and letting your glance be its sanction, have known the state of being a man, and I —I am only the man who knew that that state is not to be betrayed. I am the man who knew what made it possible and who chose consistently to practice and to be what you had practiced and been in that one moment.

"That choice is yours to make. That choice—the dedication to one's highest potential—is made by accepting the fact that the noblest act you have ever performed is the act of your mind in the process of grasping that two and two make four.

"Whoever you are—you who are alone with my words in this moment, with nothing but your honesty to help you understand—the choice is still open to be a human being, but the price is to start from scratch, to stand naked in the face of reality and, reversing a costly historical error, to declare: 'I am, therefore I'll think.'

"Accept the irrevocable fact that your life depends upon your mind. Admit that the whole of your struggle, your doubts, your fakes, your evasions, was a desperate quest for escape from the responsibility of a volitional consciousness—a quest for automatic knowledge, for instinctive action, for intuitive certainty—and while you called it a longing for the state of an angel, what you were seeking was the state of an animal. Accept, as your moral ideal, the task of becoming a man.

"Do not say that you're afraid to trust your mind because you know so little. Are you safer in surrendering to mystics and discarding the little that you know? Live and act within the limit of your knowledge and keep expanding it to the limit of your life. Redeem your mind from the hockshops of authority. Accept the fact that you are not omniscient, but playing a zombie will not give you omniscience—that your mind is fallible, but becoming mindless will not make you infallible—that an error made on your own is safer than ten truths accepted on faith, because the first leaves you the means to correct it, but the second destroys your capacity to distinguish truth from error. In place of your dream of an omniscient automaton, accept the fact that any knowledge man acquires is acquired by his own will and effort, and that *that* is his distinction in the universe, *that* is his nature, his morality, his glory.

"Discard that unlimited license to evil which consists of claiming that man is imperfect. By what standard do you damn him when you claim it? Accept the fact that in the realm of morality nothing less than perfection will do. But perfection is not to be gauged by mystic commandments to practice the impossible, and your moral stature is not to be gauged by matters not open to your choice. Man has a single basic choice: to think or not, and *that* is the gauge of his virtue. Moral perfection is an *unbreached rationality*—not the degree of your intelligence, but the full and relentless use of your mind, not the extent of your knowledge, but the acceptance of reason as an absolute.

"Learn to distinguish the difference between errors of knowledge and breaches of morality. An error of knowledge is not a moral flaw, provided you are willing to correct it; only a mystic would judge human beings by the standard of an impossible, automatic omniscience. But a breach of morality is the conscious choice of an action you know to be evil, or a willful evasion of knowledge, a suspension of sight and of thought. That which you do not know, is not a moral charge against you; but that which you refuse to know, is an account of infamy growing in your soul. Make every allowance for errors of knowledge; do not forgive or accept any breach of morality. Give the benefit of the doubt to those who seek to know; but treat as potential killers those specimens of insolent depravity who make demands upon you, announcing that they have and seek no reasons, proclaiming, as a license, that they 'just feel it' —or those who reject an irrefutable argument by saying: 'It's only logic,' which means: 'It's only reality.' The only realm opposed to reality is the realm and premise of death.

"Accept the fact that the achievement of your happiness is the only *moral* purpose of your life, and that *happiness*—not pain or mindless self-indulgence—is the proof of your moral integrity, since it is the proof and the result of your loyalty to the achievement of your values. Happiness was the responsibility you dreaded, it required the kind of rational discipline you did not value yourself enough to assume—and the anxious staleness of your days is the monument to your evasion of the knowledge that there is no moral substitute for happiness, that there is no more despicable coward than the man who deserted the battle for his joy, fearing to assert his right to existence, lacking the courage and the loyalty to life of a bird or a flower reaching for the sun. Discard the protective rags of that vice which you called a virtue: humility—learn to value yourself, which means: to fight for your happiness—and when you learn that *pride* is the sum of all virtues, you will learn to live like a man.

"As a basic step of self-esteem, learn to treat as the mark of a cannibal any man's *demand* for your help. To demand it is to claim that your life is *his* property—and loathsome as such claim might be, there's something still more loathsome: your agreement. Do you ask if it's ever proper to help another man? No—if he claims it as his right or as a moral duty that you owe him. Yes—if such is your own desire based on your own selfish pleasure in the value of his person and his struggle. Suffering as such is not a value; only man's fight against suffering, is. If you choose to help a man who suffers, do it only on the ground of his virtues, of his fight to recover, of his rational record, or of the fact that he suffers unjustly; then your action is still a trade, and his virtue is the payment for your help. But to help a man who has no virtues, to help him on the ground of his suffering as such, to accept his faults, his *need,* as a claim —is to accept the mortgage of a zero on your values. A man who has no virtues is a hater of existence who acts on the premise of death; to help him is to sanction his evil and to support his career of destruction. Be it only a penny you will not miss or a kindly smile he has not earned, a tribute to a zero is treason to life and to all those who struggle to maintain it. It is of such pennies and smiles that the desolation of your world was made.

"Do not say that my morality is too hard for you to practice and that you fear it as you fear the unknown. Whatever living moments you have known, were lived by the values of *my* code. But you stifled, negated, betrayed it. You kept sacrificing your virtues to your vices, and the best among men to the worst. Look around you: what you have done to society, you had done it first within your soul; one is the image of the other. This dismal wreckage, which is now your world, is the physical form of the treason you committed to your values, to your friends, to your defenders, to your future, to your country, to yourself.

"We—whom you are now calling, but who will not answer any longer—we had lived among you, but you failed to know us, you refused to think and to see what we were. You failed to recognize the motor I invented—and it became, in *your* world, a pile of dead scrap. You failed to recognize the hero in your soul—and you failed to know me when I passed you in the street. When you cried in despair for the unattainable spirit which you felt had deserted your world, you gave it my name, but what you were calling was your own betrayed self-esteem. You will not recover one without the other.

"When you failed to give recognition to man's mind and attempted to rule human beings by force—those who submitted had no mind to surrender; those who had, were men who don't submit. Thus the man of productive genius assumed in *your* world the disguise of a playboy and became a destroyer of wealth, choosing to annihilate his fortune rather than surrender it to guns. Thus the thinker, the man of reason, assumed in *your* world the role of a pirate, to defend his values by force against your force, rather than submit to the rule of brutality. Do you hear me, Francisco d'Anconia and Ragnar Danneskjöld, my first friends, my fellow fighters, my fellow outcasts, in whose name and honor I speak?

"It was the three of us who started what I am now completing. It was the three of us who resolved to avenge this country and to release its imprisoned soul. This greatest of countries was built on *my* morality—on the inviolate supremacy of man's right to exist—but you dreaded to admit it and live up to it. You stared at an achievement unequaled in history, you looted its effects and blanked out its cause. In the presence of that monument to human morality, which is a factory, a highway or a bridge—you kept damning this country as immoral and its progress as 'material greed,' you kept offering apologies for this country's greatness to the idol of primordial starvation, to decaying Europe's idol of a leprous, mystic bum.

"This country—the product of *reason*—could not survive on the morality of sacrifice. It was not built by men who sought self-immolation or by men who sought handouts. It could not stand on the mystic split that divorced man's soul from his body. It could not live by the mystic doctrine that damned this earth as evil and those who succeeded on earth as depraved. From its start, this country was a threat to the ancient rule of mystics. In the brilliant rocket-explosion of its youth, this country displayed to an incredulous world what greatness was possible to man, what happiness was possible on earth. It was one or the other: America or mystics. The mystics knew it; you didn't. You let them infect you with the worship of *need*—and this country became a giant in body with a mooching midget in place of its soul, while its living soul was driven underground to labor and feed you in silence, unnamed, unhonored, negated, its soul and hero: the industrialist. Do you hear me now, Hank Rearden, the greatest of the victims I have avenged?

"Neither he nor the rest of us will return until the road is clear to rebuild this country—until the wreckage of the morality of sacrifice has been wiped out of our way. A country's political system is based on its code of morality. We will rebuild America's system on the moral premise which had been its foundation, but which you treated as a guilty underground, in your frantic evasion of the conflict between that premise and your mystic morality: the premise that man is an end in himself, not the means to the ends of others, that man's life, his freedom, his happiness are *his* by inalienable right.

"You who've lost the concept of a right, you who swing in impotent evasiveness between the claim that rights are a gift of God, a supernatural gift to be taken on faith, or the claim that rights are a gift of society, to be broken at its arbitrary whim—the source of man's rights is not divine law or congressional law, but the law of identity. A is A—and Man is Man. *Rights* are conditions of existence required by man's nature for his proper survival. If man is to live on earth, it is *right* for him to use his mind, it is *right* to act on his own free judgment, it is *right* to work for his values and to keep the product of his work. If life on earth is his purpose, he has a *right* to live as a rational being: nature forbids him the irrational. Any group, any gang, any nation that attempts to negate man's rights, is *wrong*, which means: is evil, which means: is anti-life.

"*Rights* are a moral concept—and morality is a matter of choice. Men are free not to choose man's survival as the standard of their morals and their laws, but not free to escape from the fact that the alternative is a cannibal society, which exists for a while by devouring its best and collapses like a cancerous body, when the healthy have been eaten by the diseased, when the rational have been consumed by the irrational. Such has been the fate of your societies in history, but you've evaded the knowledge of the cause. I am here to state it: the agent of retribution was the law of identity, which you cannot escape. Just as man cannot live by means of the irrational, so two men cannot, or two thousand, or two billion. Just as man can't succeed by defying reality, so a nation can't, or a country, or a globe. A is A. The rest is a matter of time, provided by the generosity of victims.

"Just as man can't exist without his body, so no rights can exist without the right to translate one's rights into reality—to think, to work and to keep the results—which means: the right of property. The modern mystics of muscle who offer you the fraudulent alternative of 'human rights' versus 'property rights,' as if one could exist without the other, are making a last, grotesque attempt to revive the doctrine of soul versus body. Only a ghost can exist without material property; only a slave can work with no right to the product of his effort. The doctrine that 'human rights' are superior to 'property rights' simply means that some human beings have the right to make property out of others; since the competent have nothing to gain from the incompetent, it means the right of the incompetent to own their betters and to use them as productive cattle. Whoever regards this as human and right, has no right to the title of 'human.'

"The source of property rights is the law of causality. All property and all forms of wealth are produced by man's mind and labor. As you cannot have effects without causes, so you cannot have wealth without its source: without intelligence. You cannot force intelligence to work: those who're able to think, will not work under compulsion; those who will, won't produce much more than the price of the whip needed to keep them enslaved. You cannot obtain the products of a mind except on the owner's terms, by trade and by volitional consent. Any other policy of men toward man's property is the policy of criminals, no matter what their numbers. Criminals are savages who play it short-range and starve when their prey runs out—just as you're starving today, you who believed that crime could be 'practical' if your government decreed that robbery was legal and resistance to robbery illegal.

"The only proper purpose of a government is to protect man's rights, which means: to protect him from physical violence. A proper government is only a policeman, acting as an agent of man's self-defense, and, as such, may resort to force *only* against those who *start* the use of force. The only proper functions of a government are: the police, to protect you from criminals; the army, to protect you from foreign invaders; and the courts, to protect your property and contracts from breach or fraud by others, to settle disputes by rational rules, according to *objective* law. But a government that *initiates* the employment of force against men who had forced no one, the employment of armed compulsion against disarmed victims, is a nightmare infernal machine designed to annihilate morality: such a government reverses its only moral purpose and switches from the role of protector to the role of man's deadliest enemy, from the role of policeman to the role of a criminal vested with the right to the wielding of violence against victims deprived of the right of self-defense. Such a government substitutes for morality the following rule of social conduct: you may do whatever you please to your neighbor, provided your gang is bigger than his.

"Only a brute, a fool or an evader can agree to exist on such terms or agree to give his fellow men a blank check on his life and his mind, to accept the belief that others have the right to dispose of his person at their whim, that the will of the majority is omnipotent, that the physical force of muscles and numbers is a substitute for justice, reality and truth. We, the men of the mind, we who are traders, not masters or slaves, do not deal in blank checks or grant them. We do not live or work with any form of the non-objective.

"So long as men, in the era of savagery, had no concept of objective reality and believed that physical nature was ruled by the whim of unknowable demons—no thought, no science, no production were possible. Only when men discovered that nature was a firm, predictable absolute were they able to rely on their knowledge, to choose their course, to plan their future and, slowly, to rise from the cave. *Now* you have placed modern industry, with its immense complexity of scientific precision, back into the power of unknowable demons—the unpredictable power of the arbitrary whims of hidden, ugly little bureaucrats. A farmer will not invest the effort of one summer if he's unable to calculate his chances of a harvest. But you expect industrial giants—who plan in terms of decades, invest in terms of generations and undertake ninety-nine-year contracts—to continue to function and produce, not knowing what random caprice in the skull of what random official will descend upon them at what moment to demolish the whole of their effort. Drifters and physical laborers live and plan by the range of a day. The better the mind, the longer the range. A man whose vision extends to a shanty, might continue to build on your quicksands, to grab a fast profit and run. A man who envisions skyscrapers, will not. Nor will he give ten years of unswerving devotion to the task of inventing a new product, when he knows that gangs of entrenched mediocrity are juggling the laws against him, to tie him, restrict him and force him to fail, but should he fight them and struggle and succeed, they will seize his rewards and his invention.

"Look past the range of the moment, you who cry that you fear to compete with men of superior intelligence, that their mind is a threat to your livelihood, that the strong leave no chance to the weak in a market of voluntary trade. What determines the material value of your work? Nothing but the productive effort of your mind—if you lived on a desert island. The less efficient the thinking of your brain, the less your physical labor would bring you—and you could spend your life on a single routine, collecting a precarious harvest or hunting with bow and arrows, unable to think any further. But when you live in a rational society, where men are free to trade, you receive an incalculable bonus: the material value of your work is determined not only by your effort, but by the effort of the best productive minds who exist in the world around you.

"When you work in a modern factory, you are paid, not only for your labor, but for all the productive genius which has made that factory possible: for the work of the industrialist who built it, for the work of the investor who saved the money to risk on the untried and the new, for the work of the engineer who designed the machines of which you are pushing the levers, for the work of the inventor who created the product which you spend your time on making, for the work of the scientist who discovered the laws that went into the making of that product, for the work of the philosopher who taught men how to think and whom you spend your time denouncing.

"The machine, the frozen form of a living intelligence, is the power that expands the potential of your life by raising the productivity of your time. If you worked as a blacksmith in the mystics' Middle Ages, the whole of your earning capacity would consist of an iron bar produced by your hands in days and days of effort. How many tons of rail do you produce per day if you work for Hank Rearden? Would you dare to claim that the size of your pay check was created solely by your physical labor and that those rails were the product of your muscles? The standard of living of that blacksmith is all that your muscles are worth; the rest is a gift from Hank Rearden.

"Every man is free to rise as far as he's able or willing, but it's only the degree to which he thinks that determines the degree to which he'll rise. Physical labor as such can extend no further than the range of the moment. The man who does no more than physical labor, consumes the material value-equivalent of his own contribution to the process of production, and leaves no further value, neither for himself nor others. But the man who produces an idea in any field of rational endeavor—the man who discovers new knowledge—is the permanent benefactor of humanity. Material products can't be shared, they belong to some ultimate consumer; it is only the value of an idea that can be shared with unlimited numbers of men, making all sharers richer at no one's sacrifice or loss, raising the productive capacity of whatever labor they perform. It is the value of his own time that the strong of the intellect transfers to the weak, letting them work on the jobs he discovered, while devoting his time to further discoveries. This is mutual trade to mutual advantage; the interests of the mind are one, no matter what the degree of intelligence, among men who desire to work and don't seek or expect the unearned.

"In proportion to the mental energy he spent, the man who creates a new invention receives but a small percentage of his value in terms of material payment, no matter what fortune he makes, no matter what millions he earns. But the man who works as a janitor in the factory producing that invention, receives an enormous payment in proportion to the mental effort that his job requires of *him*. And the same is true of all men between, on all levels of ambition and ability. The man at the top of the intellectual pyramid contributes the most to all those below him, but gets nothing except his material payment, receiving no intellectual bonus from others to add to the value of his time. The man at the bottom who, left to himself, would starve in his hopeless ineptitude, contributes nothing to those above him, but receives the bonus of all of their brains. Such is the nature of the 'competition' between the strong and the weak of the intellect. Such is the pattern of 'exploitation' for which you have damned the strong.

"Such was the service we had given you and were glad and willing to give. What did we ask in return? Nothing but freedom. We required that you leave us free to function—free to think and to work as we choose—free to take our own risks and to bear our own losses—free to earn our own profits and to make our own fortunes—free to gamble on *your* rationality, to submit our products to your judgment for the purpose of a voluntary trade, to rely on the objective value of our work and on your mind's ability to see it—free to count on your intelligence and honesty, and to deal with nothing but your mind. Such was the price we asked, which you chose to reject as too high. You decided to call it unfair that we, who had dragged you out of your hovels and provided you with modern apartments, with radios, movies and cars, should own our palaces and yachts—you decided that *you* had a right to your wages, but *we* had no right to our profits, that you did not want us to deal with your mind, but to deal, instead, with your gun. Our answer to *that*, was: 'May you be damned!' Our answer came true. You are.

"You did not care to compete in terms of intelligence—you are now competing in terms of brutality. You did not care to allow rewards to be won by successful production—you are now running a race in which rewards are won by successful plunder. You called it selfish and cruel that men should trade value for value—you have now established an unselfish society where they trade extortion for extortion. Your system is a legal civil war, where men gang up on one another and struggle for possession of the law, which they use as a club over rivals, till another gang wrests it from their clutch and clubs them with it in their turn, all of them clamoring protestations of service to an unnamed public's unspecified good. You had said that you saw no difference between economic and political power, between the power of money and the power of guns—no difference between reward and punishment, no difference between purchase and plunder, no difference between pleasure and fear, no difference between life and death. You are learning the difference now.

"Some of you might plead the excuse of your ignorance, of a limited mind and a limited range. But the damned and the guiltiest among you are the men who *had* the capacity to know, yet chose to blank out reality, the men who were willing to sell their intelligence into cynical servitude to force: the contemptible breed of those mystics of science who profess a devotion to some sort of 'pure knowledge'— the purity consisting of their claim that such knowledge has no practical purpose on this earth—who reserve their logic for inanimate matter, but believe that the subject of dealing with men requires and deserves no rationality, who scorn money and sell their souls in exchange for a laboratory supplied by loot. And since there is no such thing as 'non-practical knowledge' or any sort of 'disinterested' action, since they scorn the use of their science for the purpose and profit of life, they deliver their science to the service of death, to the only practical purpose it can ever have for looters: to inventing weapons of coercion and destruction. They, the intellects who seek escape from moral values, *they* are the damned on this earth, *theirs* is the guilt beyond forgiveness. Do you hear me, Dr. Robert Stadler?

"But it is not to him that I wish to speak. I am speaking to those among you who have retained some sovereign shred of their soul, unsold and unstamped: '—to the order of others.' If, in the chaos of the motives that have made you listen to the radio tonight, there was an honest, *rational* desire to learn what is wrong with the world, you are the man whom I wished to address. By the rules and terms of my code, one owes a rational statement to those whom it does concern and who're making an effort to know. Those who're making an effort to fail to understand me, are not a concern of mine.

"I am speaking to those who desire to live and to recapture the honor of their soul. Now that you know the truth about your world, *stop supporting your own destroyers.* The evil of the world is made possible by nothing but the sanction you give it. Withdraw your sanction. Withdraw your support. Do not try to live on your enemies' terms or to win at a game where they're setting the rules. Do not seek the favor of those who enslaved you, do not beg for alms from those who have robbed you, be it subsidies, loans or jobs, do not join their team to recoup what they've taken by helping them rob your neighbors. One cannot hope to maintain one's life by accepting bribes to condone one's destruction. Do not struggle for profit, success or security at the price of a lien on your right to exist. Such a lien is not to be paid off; the more you pay them, the more they will demand; the greater the values you seek or achieve, the more vulnerably helpless you become. Theirs is a system of *white blackmail* devised to bleed you, not by means of your sins, but by means of your love for existence.

"Do not attempt to rise on the looters' terms or to climb a ladder while they're holding the ropes. Do not allow their hands to touch the only power that keeps them in power: your living ambition. Go on strike—in the manner I did. Use your mind and skill in private, extend your knowledge, develop your ability, but do not share your achievements with others. Do not try to produce a fortune, with a looter riding on your back. Stay on the lowest rung of their ladder, earn no more than your barest survival, do not make an extra penny to support the looters' state. Since you're captive, act as a captive, do not help them pretend that you're free. Be the silent, incorruptible enemy they dread. When they force you, obey—but *do not volunteer.* Never volunteer a step in their direction, or a wish, or a plea, or a purpose. Do not help a holdup man to claim that he acts as your friend and benefactor. Do not help your jailers to pretend that their jail is your natural state of existence. Do not help them to fake reality. That fake is the only dam holding off their secret terror, the terror of knowing they're unfit to exist; remove it and let them drown; your sanction is their only life belt.

"If you find a chance to vanish into some wilderness out of their reach, do so, but not to exist as a bandit or to create a gang competing with their racket; build a productive life of your own with those who accept your moral code and are willing to struggle for a human existence. You have no chance to win on the Morality of Death or by the code of faith and force; raise a standard to which the honest *will* repair: the standard of Life and Reason.

"Act as a rational being and aim at becoming a rallying point for all those who are starved for a voice of integrity—act on your rational values, whether alone in the midst of your enemies, or with a few of your chosen friends, or as the founder of a modest community on the frontier of mankind's rebirth.

"When the looters' state collapses, deprived of the best of its slaves, when it falls to a level of impotent chaos, like the mystic-ridden nations of the Orient, and dissolves into starving robber gangs fighting to rob one another—when the advocates of the morality of sacrifice perish with their final ideal—then and on that day we will return.

"We will open the gates of our city to those who deserve to enter, a city of smokestacks, pipe lines, orchards, markets and inviolate homes. We will act as the rallying center for such hidden outposts as you'll build. With the sign of the dollar as our symbol—the sign of free trade and free minds—we will move to reclaim this country once more from the impotent savages who never discovered its nature, its meaning, its splendor. Those who choose to join us, will join us; those who don't, will not have the power to stop us; hordes of savages have never been an obstacle to men who carried the banner of the mind.

"Then this country will once more become a sanctuary for a vanishing species: the rational being. The political system we will build is contained in a single moral premise: no man may obtain any values from others by resorting to physical force. Every man will stand or fall, live or die by his rational judgment. If he fails to use it and falls, he will be his only victim. If he fears that his judgment is inadequate, he will not be given a gun to improve it. If he chooses to correct his errors in time, he will have the unobstructed example of his betters, for guidance in learning to think; but an end will be put to the infamy of paying with one life for the errors of another.

"In that world, you'll be able to rise in the morning with the spirit you had known in your childhood: that spirit of eagerness, adventure and certainty which comes from dealing with a rational universe. No child is afraid of nature; it is your fear of men that will vanish, the fear that has stunted your soul, the fear you acquired in your early encounters with the incomprehensible, the unpredictable, the contradictory, the arbitrary, the hidden, the faked, *the irrational* in men. You will live in a world of responsible beings, who will be as consistent and reliable as facts; the guarantee of their character will be a system of existence where objective reality is the standard and the judge. Your virtues will be given protection, your vices and weaknesses will not. Every chance will be open to your good, none will be provided for your evil. What you'll receive from men will not be alms, or pity, or mercy, or forgiveness of sins, but a single value: *justice*. And when you'll look at men or at yourself, you will feel, not disgust, suspicion and guilt, but a single constant: *respect*.

"Such is the future you are capable of winning. It requires a struggle; so does any human value. All life is a purposeful struggle, and your only choice is the choice of a goal. Do you wish to continue the battle of your present or do you wish to fight for my world? Do you wish to continue a struggle that consists of clinging to precarious ledges in a sliding descent to the abyss, a struggle where the hardships you endure are irreversible and the victories you win bring you closer to destruction? Or do you wish to undertake a struggle that consists of rising from ledge to ledge in a steady ascent to the top, a struggle where the hardships are investments in your future, and the victories bring you irreversibly closer to the world of your moral ideal, and should you die without reaching full sunlight, you will die on a level touched by its rays? Such is the choice before you. Let your mind and your love of existence decide.

"The last of my words will be addressed to those heroes who might still be hidden in the world, those who are held prisoner, not by their evasions, but by their virtues and their desperate courage. My brothers in spirit, check on your virtues and on the nature of the enemies you're serving. Your destroyers hold you by means of your endurance, your generosity, your innocence, your love—the endurance that carries their burdens—the generosity that responds to their cries of despair—the innocence that is unable to conceive of their evil and gives them the benefit of every doubt, refusing to condemn them without understanding and incapable of understanding such motives as theirs—the love, your love of life, which makes you believe that they are men and that they love it, too. But the world of today is the world they wanted; life is the object of their hatred. Leave them to the death they worship. In the name of your magnificent devotion to this earth, leave them, don't exhaust the greatness of your soul on achieving the triumph of the evil of theirs. Do you hear me . . . my love?

"In the name of the best within you, do not sacrifice this world to those who are its worst. In the name of the values that keep you alive, do not let your vision of man be distorted by the ugly, the cowardly, the mindless in those who have never achieved his title. Do not lose your knowledge that man's proper estate is an upright posture, an intransigent mind and a step that travels unlimited roads. Do not let your fire go out, spark by irreplaceable spark, in the hopeless swamps of the approximate, the not-quite, the not-yet, the not-at-all. Do not let the hero in your soul perish, in lonely frustration for the life you deserved, but have never been able to reach. Check your road and the nature of your battle. The world you desired can be won, it exists, it is real, it is possible, it's yours.

"But to win it requires your total dedication and a total break with the world of your past, with the doctrine that man is a sacrificial animal who exists for the pleasure of others. Fight for the value of your person. Fight for the virtue of your pride. Fight for the essence of that which is man: for his sovereign rational mind. Fight with the radiant certainty and the absolute rectitude of knowing that yours is the Morality of Life and that yours is the battle for any achievement, any value, any grandeur, any goodness, any joy that has ever existed on this earth.

"You will win when you are ready to pronounce the oath I have taken at the start of my battle—and for those who wish to know the day of my return, I shall now repeat it to the hearing of the world:

"I swear—by my life and my love of it—that I will never live for the sake of another man, nor ask another man to live for mine."

VIII

THE EGOIST

"It wasn't real, was it?" said Mr. Thompson.

They stood in front of the radio, as the last sound of Galt's voice had left them. No one had moved through the span of silence; they had stood, looking at the radio, as if waiting. But the radio was now only a wooden box with some knobs and a circle of cloth stretched over an empty loud-speaker.

"We seem to have heard it," said Tinky Holloway.

"We couldn't help it," said Chick Morrison.

Mr. Thompson was sitting on a crate. The pale, oblong smear at the level of his elbow was the face of Wesley Mouch, who was seated on the floor. Far behind them, like an island in the vast semi-darkness of the studio space, the drawing room prepared for their broadcast stood deserted and fully lighted, a semicircle of empty armchairs under a cobweb of dead microphones in the glare of the floodlights which no one had taken the initiative to turn off.

Mr. Thompson's eyes were darting over the faces around him, as if in search of some special vibrations known only to him. The rest of them were trying to do it surreptitiously, each attempting to catch a glimpse of the others without letting them catch his own glance.

"Let me out of here!" screamed a young third-rate assistant, suddenly and to no one in particular.

"Stay put!" snapped Mr. Thompson.

The sound of his own order and the hiccough-moan of the figure immobilized somewhere in the darkness, seemed to help him recapture a familiar version of reality. His head emerged an inch higher from his shoulders.

"Who permitted it to hap—" he began in a rising voice, but stopped; the vibrations he caught were the dangerous panic of the cornered. "What do you make of it?" he asked, instead. There was no answer. "Well?" He waited. "Well, say something, somebody!"

"We don't have to believe it, do we?" cried James Taggart, thrusting his face toward Mr. Thompson, in a manner that was almost a threat. "Do we?" Taggart's face was distorted; his features seemed shapeless; a mustache of small beads sparkled between his nose and mouth.

"Pipe down," said Mr. Thompson uncertainly, drawing a little away from him.

"We don't have to believe it!" Taggart's voice had the flat, insistent sound of an effort to maintain a trance. "Nobody's ever said it before! It's just one man! We don't have to believe it!"

"Take it easy," said Mr. Thompson.

"Why is he so sure he's right? Who is he to go against the whole world, against everything ever said for centuries and centuries? Who is he to know? Nobody can be sure! Nobody can know what's right! There isn't any right!"

"Shut up!" yelled Mr. Thompson. "What are you trying to—"

The blast that stopped him was a military march leaping suddenly forth from the radio receiver—the military march interrupted three hours ago, played by the familiar screeches of a studio record. It took them a few stunned seconds to grasp it, while the cheerful, thumping chords went goose-stepping through the silence, sounding grotesquely irrelevant, like the mirth of a half-wit. The station's program director was blindly obeying the absolute that no radio time was ever to be left blank.

"Tell them to cut it off!" screamed Wesley Mouch, leaping to his feet. "It will make the public think that we authorized that speech!"

"You damn fool!" cried Mr. Thompson. "Would you rather have the public think that we didn't?"

Mouch stopped short and his eyes shot to Mr. Thompson with the appreciative glance of an amateur at a master.

"Broadcasts as usual!" ordered Mr. Thompson. "Tell them to go on with whatever programs they'd scheduled for this hour! No special announcements, no explanations! Tell them to go on as if nothing had happened!"

Half a dozen of Chick Morrison's morale conditioners went scurrying off toward telephones.

"Muzzle the commentators! Don't allow them to comment! Send word to every station in the country! Let the public wonder! Don't let them think that we're worried! Don't let them think that it's important!"

"No!" screamed Eugene Lawson. "No, no, no! We can't give people the impression that we're endorsing that speech! It's horrible, horrible, horrible!" Lawson was not in tears, but his voice had the undignified sound of an adult sobbing with helpless rage.

"Who's said anything about endorsing it?" snapped Mr. Thompson.

"It's horrible! It's immoral! It's selfish, heartless, ruthless! It's the most vicious speech ever made! It . . . it will make people demand to be happy!"

"It's only a speech," said Mr. Thompson, not too firmly.

"It seems to me," said Chick Morrison, his voice tentatively helpful, "that people of nobler spiritual nature, you know what I mean, people of . . . of . . . well, of mystical insight"—he paused, as if waiting to be slapped, but no one moved, so he repeated firmly—"yes, of mystical insight, won't go for that speech. Logic isn't everything, after all."

"The workingmen won't go for it," said Tinky Holloway, a bit more helpfully. "He didn't sound like a friend of labor."

"The women of the country won't go for it," declared Ma Chalmers. "It is, I believe, an established fact that women don't go for that stuff about the mind. Women have finer feelings. You can count on the women."

"You can count on the scientists," said Dr. Simon Pritchett. They were all pressing forward, suddenly eager to speak, as if they had found a subject they could handle with assurance. "Scientists know better than to believe in reason. He's no friend of the scientists."

"He's no friend of anybody," said Wesley Mouch, recapturing a shade of confidence at the sudden realization, "except maybe of big business."

"No!" cried Mr. Mowen in terror. "No! Don't accuse us! Don't say it! I won't have you say it!"

"What?"

"That . . . that . . . that anybody is a friend of business!"

"Don't let's make a fuss about that speech," said Dr. Floyd Ferris. "It was too intellectual. Much too intellectual for the common man. It will have no effect. People are too dumb to understand it."

"Yeah," said Mouch hopefully, "that's so."

"In the first place," said Dr. Ferris, encouraged, "people can't think. In the second place, they don't want to."

"In the third place," said Fred Kinnan, "they don't want to starve. And what do you propose to do about that?"

It was as if he had pronounced the question which all of the preceding utterances had been intended to stave off. No one answered him, but heads drew faintly deeper into shoulders, and figures drew faintly closer to one another, like a small cluster under the weight of the studio's empty space. The military march boomed through the silence with the inflexible gaiety of a grinning skull.

"Turn it off!" yelled Mr. Thompson, waving at the radio. "Turn that damn thing off!"

Someone obeyed him. But the sudden silence was worse.

"Well?" said Mr. Thompson at last, raising his eyes reluctantly to Fred Kinnan. "What do you think we ought to do?"

"Who, me?" chuckled Kinnan. "I don't run this show."

Mr. Thompson slammed his fist down on his knee. "Say something —" he ordered, but seeing Kinnan turn away, added, "somebody!" There were no volunteers. "What are we to do?" he yelled, knowing that the man who answered would, thereafter, be the man in power. "What are we to do? Can't somebody tell us what to do?"

"I can!"

It was a woman's voice, but it had the quality of the voice they had heard on the radio. They whirled to Dagny before she had time to step forward from the darkness beyond the group. As she stepped forward, her face frightened them—because it was devoid of fear.

"I can," she said, addressing Mr. Thompson. "You're to give up."

"Give up?" he repeated blankly.

"You're through. Don't you see that you're through? What else do you need, after what you've heard? Give up and get out of the way. Leave men free to exist." He was looking at her, neither objecting nor moving. "You're still alive, you're using a human language, you're asking for answers, you're counting on reason—you're still counting on reason, God damn you! You're able to understand. It isn't possible that you haven't understood. There's nothing you can now pretend to hope, to want or gain or grab or reach. There's nothing but destruction ahead, the world's and your own. Give up and get out."

They were listening intently, but as if they did not hear her words, as if they were clinging blindly to a quality she was alone among them to possess: the quality of being alive. There was a sound of exultant laughter under the angry violence of her voice, her face was lifted, her eyes seemed to be greeting some spectacle at an incalculable distance, so that the glowing patch on her forehead did not look like the reflection of a studio spotlight, but of a sunrise.

"You wish to live, don't you? Get out of the way, if you want a chance. Let those who can, take over. *He* knows what to do. You don't. *He* is able to create the means of human survival. You aren't."

"Don't listen to her!"

It was so savage a cry of hatred that they drew away from Dr. Robert Stadler, as if he had given voice to the unconfessed within them. His face looked as they feared theirs would look in the privacy of darkness.

"Don't listen to her!" he cried, his eyes avoiding hers, while hers paused on him for a brief, level glance that began as a shock of astonishment and ended as an obituary. "It's your life or his!"

"Keep quiet, Professor," said Mr. Thompson, brushing him off with the jerk of one hand. Mr. Thompson's eyes were watching Dagny, as if some thought were struggling to take shape inside his skull.

"You know the truth, all of you," she said, "and so do I, and so does every man who's heard John Galt! What else are you waiting for? For proof? He's given it to you. For facts? They're all around you. How many corpses do you intend to pile up before you renounce it—your guns, your power, your controls and the whole of your miserable altruistic creed? Give it up, if you want to live. Give it up, if there's anything left in your mind that's still able to want human beings to remain alive on this earth!"

"But it's treason!" cried Eugene Lawson. "She's talking pure treason!"

"Now, now," said Mr. Thompson. "You don't have to go to extremes."

"Huh?" asked Tinky Holloway.

"But . . . but surely it's outrageous?" asked Chick Morrison.

"You're not agreeing with her, are you?" asked Wesley Mouch.

"Who's said anything about agreeing?" said Mr. Thompson, his tone surprisingly placid. "Don't be premature. Just don't you be premature, any of you. There's no harm in listening to any argument, is there?"

"That kind of argument?" asked Wesley Mouch, his finger stabbing again and again in Dagny's direction.

"Any kind," said Mr. Thompson placidly. "We mustn't be intolerant."

"But it's treason, ruin, disloyalty, selfishness and big-business propaganda!"

"Oh, I don't know," said Mr. Thompson. "We've got to keep an open mind. We've got to give consideration to every one's viewpoint. She might have something there. *He knows what to do.* We've got to be flexible."

"Do you mean that you're willing to quit?" gasped Mouch.

"Now don't jump to conclusions," snapped Mr. Thompson angrily. "If there's one thing I can't stand, it's people who jump to conclusions. And another thing is ivory-tower intellectuals who stick to some pet theory and haven't any sense of practical reality. At a time like this, we've got to be flexible above all."

He saw a look of bewilderment on all the faces around him, on Dagny's and on the others, though not for the same reasons. He smiled, rose to his feet and turned to Dagny.

"Thank you, Miss Taggart," he said. "Thank you for speaking your mind. That's what I want you to know—that you can trust me and speak to me with full frankness. We're not your enemies, Miss Taggart. Don't pay any attention to the boys—they're upset, but they'll come down to earth. We're not your enemies, nor the country's. Sure, we've made mistakes, we're only human, but we're trying to do our best for the people—that is, I mean, for everybody—in these difficult times. We can't make snap judgments and reach momentous decisions on the spur of the moment, can we? We've got to consider it, and mull it over, and weigh it carefully. I just want you to remember that we're not *anybody's* enemies—you realize that, don't you?"

"I've said everything I had to say," she answered, turning away from him, with no clue to the meaning of his words and no strength to attempt to find it.

She turned to Eddie Willers, who had watched the men around them with a look of so great an indignation that he seemed paralyzed —as if his brain were crying, "It's evil!" and could not move to any further thought. She jerked her head, indicating the door; he followed her obediently.

Dr. Robert Stadler waited until the door had closed after them, then whirled on Mr. Thompson. "You bloody fool! Do you know what you're playing with? Don't you understand that it's life or death? That it's you or him?"

The thin tremor that ran along Mr. Thompson's lips was a smile of contempt. "It's a funny way for a professor to behave. I didn't think professors ever went to pieces."

"Don't you understand? Don't you see that it's one or the other?"

"And what is it that you want me to do?"

"You must kill him."

It was the fact that Dr. Stadler had not cried it, but had said it in a flat, cold, suddenly and fully conscious voice, that brought a chill moment of silence as the whole room's answer.

"You must find him," said Dr. Stadler, his voice cracking and rising once more. "You must leave no stone unturned till you find him and destroy him! If he lives, he'll destroy all of us! If he lives, we can't!"

"How am I to find him?" asked Mr. Thompson, speaking slowly and carefully.

"I . . . I can tell you. I can give you a lead. Watch that Taggart woman. Set your men to watch every move she makes. She'll lead you to him, sooner or later."

"How do you know that?"

"Isn't it obvious? Isn't it sheer chance that she hasn't deserted you long ago? Don't you have the wits to see that she's one of *his* kind?" He did not state what kind.

"Yeah," said Mr. Thompson thoughtfully, "yeah, that's true." He jerked his head up with a smile of satisfaction. "The professor's got something there. Put a tail on Miss Taggart," he ordered, snapping his fingers at Mouch. "Have her tailed day and night. We've got to find him."

"Yes, sir," said Mouch blankly.

"And when you find him," Dr. Stadler asked tensely, "you'll kill him?"

"Kill him, you damn fool? We *need* him!" cried Mr. Thompson.

Mouch waited, but no one ventured the question that was on everyone's mind, so he made the effort to utter stiffly, "I don't understand you, Mr. Thompson."

"Oh, you theoretical intellectuals!" said Mr. Thompson with exasperation. "What are you all gaping at? It's simple. Whoever he is, he's a man of action. Besides, he's got a pressure group: he's cornered all the men of brains. He knows what to do. We'll find him and he'll tell us. He'll tell us what to do. He'll make things work. He'll pull us out of the hole."

"*Us*, Mr. Thompson?"

"Sure. Never mind your theories. We'll make a deal with him."

"With *him?*"

"Sure. Oh, we'll have to compromise, we'll have to make a few concessions to big business, and the welfare boys won't like it, but what the hell!—do you know any other way out?"

"But his ideas—"

"Who cares about ideas?"

"Mr. Thompson," said Mouch, choking, "I . . . I'm afraid he's a man who's not open to a deal."

"There's no such thing," said Mr. Thompson.

* * *

A cold wind rattled the broken signs over the windows of abandoned shops, in the street outside the radio station. The city seemed abnormally quiet. The distant rumble of the traffic sounded lower than usual and made the wind sound louder. Empty sidewalks stretched off into the darkness; a few lone figures stood in whispering clusters under the rare lights.

Eddie Willers did not speak until they were many blocks away from the station. He stopped abruptly, when they reached a deserted square where the public loud-speakers, which no one had thought of turning off, were now broadcasting a domestic comedy—the shrill voices of a husband and wife quarreling over Junior's dates—to an empty stretch of pavement enclosed by unlighted house fronts. Beyond the square, a few dots of light, scattered vertically above the twenty-fifth-floor limit of the city, suggested a distant, rising form, which was the Taggart Building.

Eddie stopped and pointed at the building, his finger shaking. "Dagny!" he cried, then lowered his voice involuntarily. "Dagny," he whispered, "I know him. He . . . he works there . . . there . . ." He kept pointing at the building with incredulous helplessness. "He works for Taggart Transcontinental . . ."

"I know," she answered; her voice was a lifeless monotone.

"As a track laborer . . . as the lowest of track laborers . . ."

"I know."

"I've talked to him . . . I've been talking to him for years . . . in the Terminal cafeteria. . . . He used to ask questions . . . all sorts of questions about the railroad, and I—God, Dagny! was I protecting the railroad or was I helping to destroy it?"

"Both. Neither. It doesn't matter now."

"I could have staked my life that he loved the railroad!"

"He does."

"But he's destroyed it."

"Yes."

She tightened the collar of her coat and walked on, against a gust of wind.

"I used to talk to him," he said, after a while. "His face . . . Dagny, it didn't look like any of the others, it . . . it showed that he understood so much. . . . I was glad, whenever I saw him there, in the cafeteria . . . I just talked . . . I don't think I knew that he was asking questions . . . but he was . . . so many questions about the railroad and . . . and about you."

"Did he ever ask you what I look like, when I'm asleep?"

"Yes . . . Yes, he did . . . I'd found you once, asleep in the office, and when I mentioned it, he—" He stopped, as a sudden connection crashed into place in his mind.

She turned to him, in the ray of a street lamp, raising and holding her face in full light for a silent, deliberate moment, as if in answer and confirmation of his thought.

He closed his eyes. "Oh God, Dagny!" he whispered.

They walked on in silence.

"He's gone by now, isn't he?" he asked. "From the Taggart Terminal, I mean."

"Eddie," she said, her voice suddenly grim, "if you value his life, don't ever ask that question. You don't want them to find him, do you? Don't give them any leads. Don't ever breathe a word to anyone about having known him. Don't try to find out whether he's still working in the Terminal."

"You don't mean that he's still there?"

"I don't know. I know only that he might be."

"*Now?*"

"Yes."

"*Still?*"

"Yes. Keep quiet about it, if you don't want to destroy him."

"I think he's gone. He won't be back. I haven't seen him since . . . since . . ."

"Since when?" she asked sharply.

"The end of May. The night when you left for Utah, remember?" He paused, as the memory of that night's encounter and the full understanding of its meaning struck him together. He said with effort, "I saw him that night. Not since . . . I've waited for him, in the cafeteria . . . He never came back."

"I don't think he'll let you see him now, he'll keep out of your way. But don't look for him. Don't inquire."

"It's funny. I don't even know what name he used. It was Johnny something or—"

"It was John Galt," she said, with a faint, mirthless chuckle. "Don't look at the Terminal payroll. The name is still there."

"Just like that? All these years?"

"For twelve years. Just like that."

"And it's still there now?"

"Yes."

After a moment, he said, "It proves nothing, I know. The personnel office hasn't taken a single name off the payroll list since Directive 10-289. If a man quits, they give his name and job to a starving friend of their own, rather than report it to the Unification Board."

"Don't question the personnel office or anyone. Don't call attention to his name. If you or I make any inquiries about him, somebody might begin to wonder. Don't look for him. Don't make any move in his direction. And if you ever catch sight of him by chance, act as if you didn't know him."

He nodded. After a while, he said, his voice tense and low, "I wouldn't turn him over to them, not even to save the railroad."

"Eddie—"

"Yes?"

"If you ever catch sight of him, tell me."

He nodded.

Two blocks later, he asked quietly, "You're going to quit, one of these days, and vanish, aren't you?"

"Why do you say that?" It was almost a cry.

"Aren't you?"

She did not answer at once; when she did, the sound of despair was present in her voice only in the form of too tight a monotone: "Eddie, if I quit, what would happen to the Taggart trains?"

"There would be no Taggart trains within a week. Maybe less."

"There will be no looters' government within ten days. Then men like Cuffy Meigs will devour the last of our rails and engines. Should I lose the battle by failing to wait one more moment? How can I let it go—Taggart Transcontinental, Eddie—go forever, when one last effort can still keep it in existence? If I've stood things this long, I can stand them a little longer. Just a little longer. I'm not helping the looters. Nothing can help them now."

"What are they going to do?"

"I don't know. What can they do? They're finished."

"I suppose so."

"Didn't you see them? They're miserable, panic-stricken rats, running for their lives."

"Does it mean anything to them?"

"What?"

"Their lives."

"They're still struggling, aren't they? But they're through and they know it."

"Have they ever acted on what they know?"

"They'll have to. They'll give up. It won't be long. And we'll be here to save whatever's left."

* * *

"Mr. Thompson wishes it to be known," said official broadcasts on the morning of November 23, "that there is no cause for alarm. He urges the public not to draw any hasty conclusions. We must preserve our discipline, our morale, our unity and our sense of broad-minded tolerance. The unconventional speech, which some of you might have heard on the radio last night, was a thought-provoking contribution to our pool of ideas on world problems. We must consider it soberly, avoiding the extremes of total condemnation or of reckless agreement. We must regard it as one viewpoint out of many in our democratic forum of public opinion, which, as last night has proved, is open to all. The truth, says Mr. Thompson, has many facets. We must remain impartial."

"They're silent," wrote Chick Morrison, as a summary of its content, across the report from one of the field agents he had sent out on a mission entitled Public Pulse Taking. "They're silent," he wrote across the next report, then across another and another. "Silence," he wrote, with a frown of uneasiness, summing up his report to Mr. Thompson. "People seem to be silent."

The flames that went up to the sky of a winter night and devoured a home in Wyoming were not seen by the people of Kansas, who watched a trembling red glow on the prairie horizon, made by the flames that went up to devour a farm, and the glow was not reflected by the windows of a street in Pennsylvania, where the twisting red tongues were reflections of the flames that went up to devour a factory. Nobody mentioned, next morning, that those flames had not been set off by chance and that the owners of the three places had vanished. Neighbors observed it without comment—and without astonishment. A few homes were found abandoned in random corners across the nation, some left locked, shuttered and empty, others open and gutted of all movable goods—but people watched it in silence and, through the snowdrifts of untended streets in the haze of pre-morning darkness, went on trudging to their jobs, a little slower than usual.

Then, on November 27, a speaker at a political meeting in Cleveland was beaten up and had to escape by scurrying down dark alleys. His silent audience had come to sudden life when he had shouted that the cause of all their troubles was their selfish concern with their own troubles.

On the morning of November 29, the workers of a shoe factory in Massachusetts were astonished, on entering their workshop, to find that the foreman was late. But they went to their usual posts and went on with their habitual routine, pulling levers, pressing buttons, feeding leather into automatic cutters, piling boxes on a moving belt, wondering, as the hours went by, why they did not catch sight of the foreman, or the superintendent, or the general manager, or the company president. It was noon before they discovered that the front offices of the plant were empty.

"You goddamn cannibals!" screamed a woman in the midst of a crowded movie theater, breaking into sudden, hysterical sobs—and the audience showed no sign of astonishment, as if she were screaming for them all.

"There is no cause for alarm," said official broadcasts on December 5. "Mr. Thompson wishes it to be known that he is willing to negotiate with John Galt for the purpose of devising ways and means to achieve a speedy solution of our problems. Mr. Thompson urges the people to be patient. We must not worry, we must not doubt, we must not lose heart."

The attendants of a hospital in Illinois showed no astonishment when a man was brought in, beaten up by his elder brother, who had supported him all his life: the younger man had screamed at the elder, accusing him of selfishness and greed—just as the attendants of a hospital in New York City showed no astonishment at the case of a woman who came in with a fractured jaw: she had been slapped in the face by a total stranger, who had heard her ordering her five-year-old son to give his best toy to the children of neighbors.

Chick Morrison attempted a whistle-stop tour to buttress the country's morale by speeches on self-sacrifice for the general welfare. He was stoned at the first of his stops and had to return to Washington.

Nobody had ever granted them the title of "the better men" or, granting it, had paused to grasp that title's meaning, but everybody knew, each in his own community, neighborhood, office or shop and in his own unidentified terms, who would be the men that would now fail to appear at their posts on some coming morning and would silently vanish in search of unknown frontiers—the men whose faces were tighter than the faces around them, whose eyes were more direct, whose energy was more conscientiously enduring—the men who were now slipping away, one by one, from every corner of the country—of the country which was now like the descendant of what had once been regal glory, prostrated by the scourge of hemophilia, losing the best of its blood from a wound not to be healed.

"But we're willing to negotiate!" yelled Mr. Thompson to his assistants, ordering the special announcement to be repeated by all radio stations three times a day. "We're willing to negotiate! He'll hear it! He'll answer!"

Special listeners were ordered to keep watch, day and night, at radio receivers tuned to every known frequency of sound, waiting for an answer from an unknown transmitter. There was no answer.

Empty, hopeless, unfocused faces were becoming more apparent in the streets of the cities, but no one could read their meaning. As some men were escaping with their bodies into the underground of uninhabited regions, so others could only save their souls and were escaping into the underground of their minds—and no power on earth could tell whether their blankly indifferent eyes were shutters protecting hidden treasures at the bottom of shafts no longer to be mined, or were merely gaping holes of the parasite's emptiness never to be filled.

"I don't know what to do," said the assistant superintendent of an oil refinery, refusing to accept the job of the superintendent who had vanished—and the agents of the Unification Board were unable to tell whether he lied or not. It was only an edge of precision in the tone of his voice, an absence of apology or shame, that made them wonder whether he was a rebel or a fool. It was dangerous to force the job on either.

"Give us men!" The plea began to hammer progressively louder upon the desk of the Unification Board, from all parts of a country ravaged by unemployment, and neither the pleaders nor the Board dared to add the dangerous words which the cry was implying: "Give us men of ability!" There were waiting lines years' long for the jobs of janitors, greasers, porters and bus boys; there was no one to apply for the jobs of executives, managers, superintendents, engineers.

The explosions of oil refineries, the crashes of defective airplanes, the break-outs of blast furnaces, the wrecks of colliding trains, and the rumors of drunken orgies in the offices of newly created executives, made the members of the Board fear the kind of men who did apply for the positions of responsibility.

"Don't despair! Don't give up!" said official broadcasts on December 15, and on every day thereafter. "We will reach an agreement with John Galt. We will get him to lead us. He will solve all our problems. He will make things work. Don't give up! We will get John Galt!"

Rewards and honors were offered to applicants for managerial jobs —then to foremen—then to skilled mechanics—then to any man who would make an effort to deserve a promotion in rank: wage raises, bonuses, tax exemptions and a medal devised by Wesley Mouch, to be known as "The Order of Public Benefactors." It brought no results. Ragged people listened to the offers of material comforts and turned away with lethargic indifference, as if they had lost the concept of "Value." *These,* thought the public-pulse-takers with terror, were men who did not care to live—or men who did not care to live on present terms.

"Don't despair! Don't give up! John Galt will solve our problems!" said the radio voices of official broadcasts, traveling through the silence of falling snow into the silence of unheated homes.

"Don't tell them that we haven't got him!" cried Mr. Thompson to his assistants. "But for God's sake tell them to find him!" Squads of Chick Morrison's boys were assigned to the task of manufacturing rumors: half of them went spreading the story that John Galt was in Washington and in conference with government officials—while the other half went spreading the story that the government would give five hundred thousand dollars as reward for information that would help to find John Galt.

"No, not a clue," said Wesley Mouch to Mr. Thompson, summing up the reports of the special agents who had been sent to check on every man by the name of John Galt throughout the country. "They're a shabby lot. There's a John Galt who's a professor of ornithology, eighty years old —there's a retired greengrocer with a wife and nine children—there's an unskilled railroad laborer who's held the same job for twelve years— and other such trash."

"Don't despair! We will get John Galt!" said official broadcasts in the daytime—but at night, every hour on the hour, by a secret, official order, an appeal was sent from short-wave transmitters into the empty reaches of space: "Calling John Galt! . . . Calling John Galt! . . . Are you listening, John Galt? . . . We wish to negotiate. We wish to confer with you. Give us word on where you can be reached. . . . Do you hear us, John Galt?" There was no answer.

The wads of worthless paper money were growing heavier in the pockets of the nation, but there was less and less for that money to buy. In September, a bushel of wheat had cost eleven dollars; it had cost thirty dollars in November; it had cost one hundred in December; it was now approaching the price of two hundred—while the printing presses of the government treasury were running a race with starvation, and losing.

When the workers of a factory beat up their foreman and wrecked the machinery in a fit of despair— no action could be taken against them. Arrests were futile, the jails were full, the arresting officers winked at their prisoners and let them escape on their way to prison— men were going through the motions prescribed for the moment, with no thought of the moment to follow. No action could be taken when mobs of starving people attacked warehouses on the outskirts of cities. No action could be taken when punitive squadrons joined the people they had been sent to punish.

"Are you listening, John Galt? . . . We wish to negotiate. We might meet your terms. . . . Are you listening?"

There were whispered rumors of covered wagons traveling by night through abandoned trails, and of secret settlements armed to resist the attacks of those whom they called the "Indians"—the attacks of any looting savages, be they homeless mobs or government agents. Lights were seen, once in a while, on the distant horizon of a prairie, in the hills, on the ledges of mountains, where no buildings had been known to exist. But no soldiers could be persuaded to investigate the sources of those lights.

On the doors of abandoned houses, on the gates of crumbling factories, on the walls of government buildings, there appeared, once in a while, traced in chalk, in paint, in blood, the curving mark which was the sign of the dollar.

"Can you hear us, John Galt? . . . Send us word. Name your terms. We will meet any terms you set. Can you hear us?"

There was no answer.

The shaft of red smoke that shot to the sky on the night of January

22 and stood abnormally still for a while, like a solemn memorial obelisk, then wavered and swept back and forth across the sky, like a searchlight sending some undecipherable message, then went out as abruptly as it had come, marked the end of Rearden Steel—but the inhabitants of the area did not know it. They learned it only on subsequent nights, when they—who had cursed the mills for the smoke, the fumes, the soot and the noise—looked out and, instead of the glow pulsating with life on their familiar horizon, they saw a black void.

The mills had been nationalized, as the property of a deserter. The first bearer of the title of "People's Manager," appointed to run the mills, had been a man of the Orren Boyle faction, a pudgy hanger-on of the metallurgical industry, who had wanted nothing but to follow his employees while going through the motions of leading. But at the end of a month, after too many clashes with the workers, too many occasions when his only answer had been that he couldn't help it, too many undelivered orders, too many telephonic pressures from his buddies, he had begged to be transferred to some other position. The Orren Boyle faction had been falling apart, since Mr. Boyle had been confined to a rest home, where his doctor had forbidden him any contact with business and had put him to the job of weaving baskets, as a means of occupational therapy. The second "People's Manager" sent to Rearden Steel had belonged to the faction of Cuffy Meigs. He had worn leather leggings and perfumed hair lotions, he had come to work with a gun on his hip, he had kept snapping that discipline was his primary goal and that by God he'd get it or else. The only discernible rule of the discipline had been his order forbidding all questions. After weeks of frantic activity on the part of insurance companies, of firemen, of ambulances and of first-aid units, attending to a series of inexplicable accidents—the "People's Manager" had vanished one morning, having sold and shipped to sundry racketeers of Europe and Latin America most of the cranes, the automatic conveyors, the supplies of refractory brick, the emergency power generator, and the carpet from what had once been Rearden's office.

No one had been able to untangle the issues in the violent chaos of the next few days—the issues had never been named, the sides had remained unacknowledged, but everyone had known that the bloody encounters between the older workers and the newer had not been driven to such ferocious intensity by the trivial causes that kept setting them off—neither guards nor policemen nor state troopers had been able to keep order for the length of a day—nor could any faction muster a candidate willing to accept the post of "People's Manager." On January 22, the operations of Rearden Steel had been ordered temporarily suspended.

The shaft of red smoke, that night, had been caused by a sixty-year-old worker, who had set fire to one of the structures and had been caught in the act, laughing dazedly and staring at the flames. "To avenge Hank Rearden!" he had cried defiantly, tears running down his furnace-tanned face.

Don't let it hurt you like this—thought Dagny, slumped across her desk, over the page of the newspaper where a single brief paragraph announced the "temporary" end of Rearden Steel—don't let it hurt you so much. . . . She kept seeing the face of Hank Rearden, as he had stood at the window of his office, watching a crane move against the sky with a load of green-blue rail. . . . Don't let it hurt him like this—was the plea in her mind, addressed to no one—don't let him hear of it, don't let him know. . . . Then she saw another face, a face with unflinching green eyes, saying to her, in a voice made implacable by the quality of respect for facts: "You'll have to hear about it. . . . You'll hear about every wreck. You'll hear about every discontinued train. . . . Nobody stays in this valley by faking reality in any manner whatever. . . ." Then she sat still, with no sight and no sound in her mind, with nothing but that enormous presence which was pain —until she heard the familiar cry that had become a drug killing all sensations except the capacity to act: "Miss Taggart, we don't know what to do!"—and she shot to her feet to answer.

"The People's State of Guatemala," said the newspapers on January 26, "declines the request of the United States for the loan of a thousand tons of steel."

On the night of February 3, a young pilot was flying his usual route, a weekly flight from Dallas to New York City. When he reached the empty darkness beyond Philadelphia—in the place where the flames of Rearden Steel had for years been his favorite landmark, his greeting in the loneliness of night, the beacon of a living earth—he saw a snow-covered spread, dead-white and phosphorescent in the starlight, a spread of peaks and craters that looked like the surface of the moon. He quit his job, next morning.

Through the frozen nights, over dying cities, knocking in vain at unanswering windows, beating on unechoing walls, rising above the roofs of lightless buildings and the skeletal girders of ruins, the plea went on crying through space, crying to the stationary motion of the stars, to the heatless fire of their twinkling: "Can you hear us, John Galt? Can you hear us?"

"Miss Taggart, we don't know what to do," said Mr. Thompson; he had summoned her to a personal conference on one of his scurrying trips to New York. "We're ready to give in, to meet his terms, to let him take over—but where is he?"

"For the third time," she said, her face and voice shut tight against any fissure of emotion, "I do not know where he is. What made you think I did?"

"Well, I didn't know, I had to try . . . I thought, just in case . . . I thought, maybe if you had a way to reach him—"

"I haven't."

"You see, we can't announce, not even by short-wave radio, that we're willing to surrender altogether. People might hear it. But if you had some way to reach him, to let him know that we're ready to give in, to scrap our policies, to do anything he tells us to—"

"I said I haven't."

"If he'd only agree to a conference, just a conference, it wouldn't commit him to anything, would it? We're willing to turn the whole economy over to him—if he'd only tell us when, where, how. If he'd give us some word or sign . . . if he'd answer us . . . Why doesn't he answer?"

"You've heard his speech."

"But what are we to do? We can't just quit and leave the country without any government at all. I shudder to think what would happen. With the kind of social elements now on the loose—why, Miss Taggart, it's all I can do to keep them in line or we'd have plunder and bloody murder in broad daylight. I don't know what's got into people, but they just don't seem to be civilized any more. We can't quit at a time like this. We can neither quit nor run things any longer. What are we to do, Miss Taggart?"

"Start decontrolling."

"Huh?"

"Start lifting taxes and removing controls."

"Oh, no, no, no! That's out of the question!"

"Out of whose question?"

"I mean, not at this time, Miss Taggart, not at this time. The country isn't ready for it. Personally, I'd agree with you, I'm a freedom-loving man, Miss Taggart, I'm not after power—but this is an emergency. People aren't ready for freedom. We've got to keep a strong hand. We can't adopt an idealistic theory, which—"

"Then don't ask me what to do," she said, and rose to her feet.

"But, Miss Taggart—"

"I didn't come here to argue."

She was at the door when he sighed and said, "I hope he's still alive." She stopped. "I hope they haven't done anything rash."

A moment passed before she was able to ask, "Who?" and to make it a word, not a scream.

He shrugged, spreading his arms and letting them drop helplessly. "I can't hold my own boys in line any longer. I can't tell what they might attempt to do. There's one clique—the Ferris-Lawson-Meigs faction—that's been after me for over a year to adopt stronger measures. A tougher policy, they mean. Frankly, what they mean is: to resort to terror. Introduce the death penalty for civilian crimes, for critics, dissenters and the like. Their argument is that since people won't co-operate, won't act for the public interest voluntarily, we've got to force them to. Nothing will make our system work, they say, but terror.

And they may be right, from the look of things nowadays. But Wesley won't go for strong-arm methods; Wesley is a peaceful man, a liberal, and so am I. We're trying to keep the Ferris boys in check, but . . . You see, they're set against any surrender to John Galt. They don't want us to deal with him. They don't want us to find him. I wouldn't put anything past them. If they found him first, they'd—there's no telling what they might do. . . . That's what worries me. Why doesn't he answer? Why hasn't he answered us at all? What if they've found him and killed him? I wouldn't know. . . . So I hoped that perhaps you had some way . . . some means of knowing that he's still alive . . ." His voice trailed off into a question mark.

The whole of her resistance against a rush of liquefying terror went into the effort to keep her voice as stiff as her knees, long enough to say, "I do not know," and her knees stiff enough to carry her out of the room.

* * *

From behind the rotted posts of what had once been a corner vegetable stand, Dagny glanced furtively back at the street: the rare lamp posts broke the street into separate islands, she could see a pawnshop in the first patch of light, a saloon in the next, a church in the farthest, and black gaps between them; the sidewalks were deserted; it was hard to tell, but the street seemed empty.

She turned the corner, with deliberately resonant steps, then stopped abruptly to listen: it was hard to tell whether the abnormal tightness inside her chest was the sound of her own heartbeats, and hard to distinguish it from the sound of distant wheels and from the glassy rustle which was the East River somewhere close by; but she heard no sound of human steps behind her. She jerked her shoulders, it was part-shrug, part-shudder, and she walked faster. A rusty clock in some unlighted cavern coughed out the hour of four A.M.

The fear of being followed did not seem fully real, as no fear could be real to her now. She wondered whether the unnatural lightness of her body was a state of tension or relaxation; her body seemed drawn so tightly that she felt as if it were reduced to a single attribute: to the power of motion; her mind seemed inaccessibly relaxed, like a motor set to the automatic control of an absolute no longer to be questioned. If a naked bullet could feel in mid-flight, this is what it would feel, she thought; just the motion and the goal, nothing else. She thought it vaguely, distantly, as if her own person were unreal; only the word "naked" seemed to reach her: naked . . . stripped of all concern but for the target . . . for the number "367," the number of a house on the East River, which her mind kept repeating, the number it had so long been forbidden to consider.

Three-sixty-seven—she thought, looking for an invisible shape ahead, among the angular forms of tenements—three-sixty-seven . . .

that is where he lives . . . if he lives at all. . . . Her calm, her detachment and the confidence of her steps came from the certainty that this was an "if" with which she could not exist any longer.

She had existed with it for ten days—and the nights behind her were a single progression that had brought her to this night, as if the momentum now driving her steps were the sound of her own steps still ringing, unanswered, in the tunnels of the Terminal. She had searched for him through the tunnels, she had walked for hours, night after night—the hours of the shift he had once worked—through the underground passages and platforms and shops and every twist of abandoned tracks, asking no questions of anyone, offering no explanations of her presence. She had walked, with no sense of fear or hope, moved by a feeling of desperate loyalty that was almost a feeling of pride. The root of that feeling was the moments when she had stopped in sudden astonishment in some dark subterranean corner and had heard the words half-stated in her mind: This is my railroad—as she looked at a vault vibrating to the sound of distant wheels; this is my life—as she felt the clot of tension, which was the stopped and the suspended within herself; this is my love—as she thought of the man who, perhaps, was somewhere in those tunnels. There can be no conflict among these three . . . what am I doubting? . . . what can keep us apart, *here*, where only he and I belong? . . . Then, recapturing the context of the present, she had walked steadily on, with the sense of the same unbroken loyalty, but the sound of different words: You have forbidden me to look for you, you may damn me, you may choose to discard me . . . but by the right of the fact that *I* am alive, I must know that *you* are . . . I must see you this once . . . not to stop, not to speak, not to touch you, only to see. . . . She had not seen him. She had abandoned her search, when she had noticed the curious, wondering glances of the underground workers, following her steps.

She had called a meeting of the Terminal track laborers for the alleged purpose of boosting their morale, she had held the meeting twice, to face all the men in turn—she had repeated the same unintelligible speech, feeling a stab of shame at the empty generalities she uttered and, together, a stab of pride that it did not matter to her any longer—she had looked at the exhausted, brutalized faces of men who did not care whether they were ordered to work or to listen to meaningless sounds. She had not seen his face among them. "Was everyone present?" she had asked the foreman. "Yeah, I guess so," he had answered indifferently.

She had loitered at the Terminal entrances, watching the men as they came to work. But there were too many entrances to cover and no place where she could watch while remaining unseen—she had stood in the soggy twilight on a sidewalk glittering with rain, pressed to the wall of a warehouse, her coat collar raised to her cheekbones, raindrops falling off the brim of her hat—she had stood exposed to the sight of the street, knowing that the glances of the men who passed her were glances of recognition and astonishment, knowing that her vigil was too dangerously obvious. If there was a John Galt among them, someone could guess the nature of her quest . . . if there was no John Galt among them . . . if there was no John Galt in the world, she thought, then no danger existed—and no world.

No danger and no world, she thought—as she walked through the streets of the slums toward a house with the number "367," which was or was not his home. She wondered whether this was what one felt while awaiting a verdict of death: no fear, no anger, no concern, nothing but the icy detachment of light without heat or of cognition without values.

A tin can clattered from under her toes, and the sound went beating too loudly and too long, as if against the walls of an abandoned city. The streets seemed razed by exhaustion, not by rest, as if the men inside the walls were not asleep, but had collapsed. He would be home from work at this hour, she thought . . . if he worked . . . if he still had a home. . . . She looked at the shapes of the slums, at the crumbling plaster, the peeling paint, the fading signboards of failing shops with unwanted goods in unwashed windows, the sagging steps unsafe to climb, the clotheslines of garments unfit to wear, the undone, the unattended, the given up, the incomplete, all the twisted monuments of a losing race against two enemies: "no time" and "no strength" —and she thought that this was the place where *he* had lived for twelve years, he who possessed such extravagant power to lighten the job of human existence.

Some memory kept struggling to reach her, then came back: its name was Starnesville. She felt the sensation of a shudder. But this is New York City!—she cried to herself in defense of the greatness she had loved; then she faced with unmoving austerity the verdict pronounced by her mind: a city that had left him in these slums for twelve years was damned and doomed to the future of Starnesville.

Then, abruptly, it ceased to matter; she felt a peculiar shock, like the shock of sudden silence, a sense of stillness within her, which she took for a sense of calm: she saw the number "367" above the door of an ancient tenement.

She was calm, she thought, it was only time that had suddenly lost its continuity and had broken her perception into separate snatches: she knew the moment when she saw the number—then the moment when she looked at a list on a board in the moldy half-light of a doorway and saw the words "John Galt, 5th, rear" scrawled in pencil by some illiterate hand—then the moment when she stopped at the foot of a stairway, glanced up at the vanishing angles of the railing and suddenly leaned against the wall, trembling with terror, preferring not to know—then the moment when she felt the movement of her foot coming to rest on the first of the steps—then a single, unbroken progression of lightness, of rising without effort or doubt or fear, of feeling the twisting installments of stairway dropping down beneath her unhesitant feet, as if the momentum of her irresistible rise were coming from the straightness of her body, the poise of her shoulders, the lift of her head and the solemnly exultant certainty that in the moment of ultimate decision, it was not disaster she expected of her life, at the end of a rising stairway she had needed thirty-seven years to climb.

At the top, she saw a narrow hallway, its walls converging to an unlighted door. She heard the floorboards creaking in the silence, under her steps. She felt the pressure of her finger on a doorbell and heard the sound of ringing in the unknown space beyond. She waited. She heard the brief crack of a board, but it came from the floor below. She heard the sliding wail of a tugboat somewhere on the river. Then she knew that she had missed some span of time, because her next awareness was not like a moment of awakening, but like a moment of birth: as if two sounds were pulling her out of a void, the sound of a step behind the door and the sound of a lock being turned—but she was not present until the moment when suddenly there was no door before her and the figure standing on the threshold was John Galt, standing casually in his own doorway, dressed in slacks and shirt, the angle of his waistline slanting faintly against the light behind him.

She knew that his eyes were grasping this moment, then sweeping over its past and its future, that a lightning process of calculation was bringing it into his conscious control—and by the time a fold of his shirt moved with the motion of his breath, he knew the sum—and the sum was a smile of radiant greeting.

She was now unable to move. He seized her arm, he jerked her inside the room, she felt the clinging pressure of his mouth, she felt the slenderness of his body through the suddenly alien stiffness of her coat. She saw the laughter in his eyes, she felt the touch of his mouth again and again, she was sagging in his arms, she was breathing in gasps, as if she had not breathed for five flights of stairs, her face was pressed to the angle between his neck and shoulder, to hold him, to hold him with her arms, her hands and the skin of her cheek.

"John . . . you're alive . . ." was all she could say.

He nodded, as if he knew what the words were intended to explain.

Then he picked up her hat that had fallen to the floor, he took off her coat and put it aside, he looked at her slender, trembling figure, a sparkle of approval in his eyes, his hand moving over the tight, high-collared, dark blue sweater that gave to her body the fragility of a schoolgirl and the tension of a fighter.

"The next time I see you," he said, "wear a white one. It will look wonderful, too."

She realized that she was dressed as she never appeared in public,

as she had been dressed at home through the sleepless hours of that
night. She laughed, rediscovering the ability to laugh: she had expected
his first words to be anything but that.

"If there is a next time," he added calmly.

"What . . . do you mean?"

He went to the door and locked it. "Sit down," he said.

She remained standing, but she took the time to glance at the room
she had not noticed: a long, bare garret with a bed in one corner and
a gas stove in another, a few pieces of wooden furniture, naked
boards stressing the length of the floor, a single lamp burning on a
desk, a closed door in the shadows beyond the lamp's circle—and New
York City beyond an enormous window, the spread of angular structures and scattered lights, and the shaft of the Taggart Building far in
the distance.

"Now listen carefully," he said. "We have about half an hour, I
think. I know why you came here. I told you that it would be hard
to stand and that you would be likely to break. Don't regret it. You
see?—I can't regret it, either. But now, we have to know how to act,
from here on. In about half an hour, the looters' agents, who followed
you, will be here to arrest me."

"Oh no!" she gasped.

"Dagny, whoever among them had any remnant of human perceptiveness would know that you're not one of them, that you're their
last link to me, and would not let you out of his sight—or the sight
of his spies."

"I wasn't followed! I watched, I—"

"You wouldn't know how to notice it. Sneaking is one art they're
expert at. Whoever followed you is reporting to his bosses right now.
Your presence in this district, at this hour, my name on the board
downstairs, the fact that I work for your railroad—it's enough even
for them to connect."

"Then let's get out of here!"

He shook his head. "They've surrounded the block by now. Your
follower would have every policeman in the district at his immediate
call. Now I want you to know what you'll have to do when they come
here. Dagny, you have only one chance to save me. If you did not
quite understand what I said on the radio about the man in the middle,
you'll understand it now. There is no middle for you to take. And you
cannot take my side, not so long as we're in their hands. Now you
must take *their* side."

"*What?*"

"You must take their side, as fully, consistently and loudly as your
capacity for deception will permit. You must act as one of them. You
must act as my worst enemy. If you do, I'll have a chance to come
out of it alive. They need me too much, they'll go to any extreme before

they bring themselves to kill me. Whatever they extort from people, they can extort it only through their victims' values—and they have no value of mine to hold over my head, nothing to threaten me with. But if they get the slightest suspicion of what we are to each other, they will have you on a torture rack—I mean, physical torture—before my eyes, in less than a week. I am not going to wait for that. At the first mention of a threat to you, I will kill myself and stop them right there."

He said it without emphasis, in the same impersonal tone of practical calculation as the rest. She knew that he meant it and that he was right to mean it: she saw in what manner she alone had the power to succeed at destroying him, where all the power of his enemies would fail. He saw the look of stillness in her eyes, a look of understanding and of horror. He nodded, with a faint smile.

"I don't have to tell you," he said, "that if I do it, it won't be an act of self-sacrifice. I do not care to live on their terms, I do not care to obey them and I do not care to see you enduring a drawn-out murder. There will be no values for me to seek after that—and I do not care to exist without values. I don't have to tell you that we owe no morality to those who hold us under a gun. So use every power of deceit you can command, but convince them that you hate me. Then we'll have a chance to remain alive and to escape—I don't know when or how, but I'll know that I'm free to act. Is this understood?"

She forced herself to lift her head, to look straight at him and to nod.

"When they come," he said, "tell them that you had been trying to find me for them, that you became suspicious when you saw my name on your payroll list and that you came here to investigate."

She nodded.

"I will stall about admitting my identity—they might recognize my voice, but I'll attempt to deny it—so that it will be *you* who'll tell them that I am the John Galt they're seeking."

It took her a few seconds longer, but she nodded.

"Afterwards, you'll claim—and accept—that five-hundred-thousand-dollar reward they've offered for my capture."

She closed her eyes, then nodded.

"Dagny," he said slowly, "there is no way to serve your own values under their system. Sooner or later, whether you intended it or not, they had to bring you to the point where the only thing you can do for me is to turn against me. Gather your strength and do it—then we'll earn this one half-hour and, perhaps, the future."

"I'll do it," she said firmly, and added, "if that is what happens, if they—"

"It will happen. Don't regret it. I won't. You haven't seen the nature of our enemies. You'll see it now. If I have to be the pawn in the demonstration that will convince you, I'm willing to be—and to win you from them, once and for all. You didn't want to wait any longer? Oh, Dagny, Dagny, neither did I!"

It was the way he held her, the way he kissed her mouth that made her feel as if every step she had taken, every danger, every doubt, even her treason against him, if it was treason, all of it were giving her an exultant right to this moment. He saw the struggle in her face, the tension of an incredulous protest against herself—and she heard the sound of his voice through the strands of her hair pressed to his lips: "Don't think of them now. Never think of pain or danger or enemies a moment longer than is necessary to fight them. You're here. It's our time and our life, not theirs. Don't struggle not to be happy. You are."

"At the risk of destroying you?" she whispered.

"You won't. But—yes, even that. You don't think it's indifference, do you? Was it indifference that broke you and brought you here?"

"I—" And then the violence of the truth made her pull his mouth down to hers, then throw the words at his face: "I didn't care whether either one of us lived afterwards, just to see you this once!"

"I would have been disappointed if you hadn't come."

"Do you know what it was like, waiting, fighting it, delaying it one more day, then one more, then—"

He chuckled. "Do I?" he said softly.

Her hand dropped in a helpless gesture: she thought of his ten years. "When I heard your voice on the radio," she said, "when I heard the greatest statement I ever . . . No, I have no right to tell you what I thought of it."

"Why not?"

"You think that I haven't accepted it."

"You will."

"Were you speaking from here?"

"No, from the valley."

"And then you returned to New York?"

"The next morning."

"And you've been here ever since?"

"Yes."

"Have you heard the kind of appeals they're sending out to you every night?"

"Sure."

She glanced slowly about the room, her eyes moving from the towers of the city in the window to the wooden rafters of his ceiling, to the cracked plaster of his walls, to the iron posts of his bed. "You've been here all that time," she said. "You've lived here for twelve years . . . here . . . like this . . ."

"Like this," he said, throwing open the door at the end of the room.

She gasped: the long, light-flooded, windowless space beyond the threshold, enclosed in a shell of softly lustrous metal, like a small ball-room aboard a submarine, was the most efficiently modern laboratory she had ever seen.

"Come in," he said, grinning. "I don't have to keep secrets from you any longer."

It was like crossing the border into a different universe. She looked at the complex equipment sparkling in a bright, diffused glow, at the mesh of glittering wires, at the blackboard chalked with mathematical formulas, at the long counters of objects shaped by the ruthless disci-pline of a purpose—then at the sagging boards and crumbling plaster of the garret. Either-or, she thought; this was the choice confronting the world: a human soul in the image of one or of the other.

"You wanted to know where I worked for eleven months out of the year," he said.

"All this," she asked, pointing at the laboratory, "on the salary of"—she pointed at the garret—"of an unskilled laborer?"

"Oh, no! On the royalties Midas Mulligan pays me for his power-house, for the ray screen, for the radio transmitter and a few other jobs of that kind."

"Then . . . then why did you have to work as a track laborer?"

"Because no money earned in the valley is ever to be spent out-side."

"Where did you get this equipment?"

"I designed it. Andrew Stockton's foundry made it." He pointed to an unobtrusive object the size of a radio cabinet in a corner of the room: "There's the motor you wanted," and chuckled at her gasp, at the involuntary jolt that threw her forward. "Don't bother studying it, you won't give it away to them now."

She was staring at the shining metal cylinders and the glistening coils of wire that suggested the rusted shape resting, like a sacred relic, in a glass coffin in a vault of the Taggart Terminal.

"It supplies my own electric power for the laboratory," he said. "No one has had to wonder why a track laborer is using such exorbitant amounts of electricity."

"But if they ever found this place—"

He gave an odd, brief chuckle. "They won't."

"How long have you been—?"

She stopped; this time, she did not gasp; the sight confronting her could not be greeted by anything except a moment of total inner still-ness: on the wall, behind a row of machinery, she saw a picture cut out of a newspaper—a picture of her, in slacks and shirt, standing by the side of the engine at the opening of the John Galt Line, her head lifted, her smile holding the context, the meaning and the sun-light of that day.

A moan was her only answer, as she turned to him, but the look on his face matched hers in the picture.

"I was the symbol of what you wanted to destroy in the world," he said. "But you were my symbol of what I wanted to achieve." He pointed at the picture. "This is how men expect to feel about their life once or twice, as an exception, in the course of their lifetime. But I—*this* is what I chose as the constant and normal."

The look on his face, the serene intensity of his eyes and of his mind made it real to her, now, in this moment, in this moment's full context, in this city.

When he kissed her, she knew that their arms, holding each other, were holding their greatest triumph, that this was the reality untouched by pain or fear, the reality of Halley's Fifth Concerto, this was the reward they had wanted, fought for and won.

The doorbell rang.

Her first reaction was to draw back, his—to hold her closer and longer.

When he raised his head, he was smiling. He said only, "Now is the time not to be afraid."

She followed him back to the garret. She heard the door of the laboratory clicking locked behind them.

He held her coat for her silently, he waited until she had tied its belt and had put on her hat—then he walked to the entrance door and opened it.

Three of the four men who entered were muscular figures in military uniforms, each with two guns on his hips, with broad faces devoid of shape and eyes untouched by perception. The fourth, their leader, was a frail civilian with an expensive overcoat, a neat mustache, pale blue eyes and the manner of an intellectual of the public-relations species.

He blinked at Galt, at the room, made a step forward, stopped, made another step and stopped.

"Yes?" said Galt.

"Are . . . are you John Galt?" he asked too loudly.

"That's my name."

"Are you *the* John Galt?"

"Which one?"

"Did you speak on the radio?"

"When?"

"Don't let him fool you." The metallic voice was Dagny's and it was addressed to the leader. "He—is—John—Galt. I shall report the proof to headquarters. You may proceed."

Galt turned to her as to a stranger. "Will you tell me *now* just who you are and what it was that you wanted here?"

Her face was as blank as the faces of the soldiers. "My name is Dagny Taggart. I wanted to convince myself that you are the man whom the country is seeking."

He turned to the leader. "All right," he said. "I *am* John Galt—but if you want me to answer you at all, keep your stool pigeon"—he pointed at Dagny—"away from me."

"Mr. Galt!" cried the leader with the sound of an enormous joviality. "It is an honor to meet you, an honor and a privilege! Please, Mr. Galt, don't misunderstand us—we're ready to grant you your wishes—no, of course, you don't have to deal with Miss Taggart, if you prefer not to —Miss Taggart was only trying to do her patriotic duty, but—"

"I said keep her away from me."

"We're not your enemies, Mr. Galt, I assure you we're not your enemies." He turned to Dagny. "Miss Taggart, you have performed an invaluable service to the people. You have earned the highest form of public gratitude. Permit us to take over from here on." The soothing motions of his hands were urging her to stand back, to keep out of Galt's sight.

"Now what do you want?" asked Galt.

"The nation is waiting for you, Mr. Galt. All we want is a chance to dispel misapprehensions. Just a chance to co-operate with you." His gloved hand was waving a signal to his three men; the floorboards creaked, as the men proceeded silently to the task of opening drawers and closets; they were searching the room. "The spirit of the nation will revive tomorrow morning, Mr. Galt, when they hear that you have been found."

"What do you want?"

"Just to greet you in the name of the people."

"Am I under arrest?"

"Why think in such old-fashioned terms? Our job is only to escort you safely to the top councils of the national leadership, where your presence is urgently needed." He paused, but got no answer. "The country's top leaders desire to confer with you—just to confer and to reach a friendly understanding."

The soldiers were finding nothing but garments and kitchen utensils; there were no letters, no books, not even a newspaper, as if the room were the habitation of an illiterate.

"Our objective is only to assist you to assume your rightful place in society, Mr. Galt. You do not seem to realize your own public value."

"I do."

"We are here only to protect you."

"Locked!" declared a soldier, banging his fist against the laboratory door.

The leader assumed an ingratiating smile. "What is behind that door, Mr. Galt?"

"Private property."

"Would you open it, please?"

"No."

The leader spread his hands out in a gesture of pained helplessness.

"Unfortunately, my hands are tied. Orders, you know. We have to enter that room."

"Enter it."

"It's only a formality, a mere formality. There's no reason why things should not be handled amicably. Won't you please co-operate?"

"I said, no."

"I'm sure you wouldn't want us to resort to any . . . unnecessary means." He got no answer. "We have the authority to break that door down, you know—but, of course, we wouldn't want to do it." He waited, but got no answer. "Force that lock!" he snapped to the soldier.

Dagny glanced at Galt's face. He stood impassively, his head held level, she saw the undisturbed lines of his profile, his eyes directed at the door. The lock was a small, square plate of polished copper, without keyhole or fixtures.

The silence and the sudden immobility of the three brutes were involuntary, while the burglar's tools in the hands of the fourth went grating cautiously against the wood of the door.

The wood gave way easily, and small chips fell down, their thuds magnified by the silence into the rattle of a distant gun. When the burglar's jimmy attacked the copper plate, they heard a faint rustle behind the door, no louder than the sigh of a weary mind. In another minute, the lock fell out and the door shuddered forward the width of an inch.

The soldier jumped back. The leader approached, his steps irregular like hiccoughs, and threw the door open. They faced a black hole of unknown content and unrelieved darkness.

They glanced at one another and at Galt; he did not move; he stood looking at the darkness.

Dagny followed them, when they stepped over the threshold, preceded by the beams of their flashlights. The space beyond was a long shell of metal, empty but for heavy drifts of dust on the floor, an odd, grayish-white dust that seemed to belong among ruins undisturbed for centuries. The room looked dead like an empty skull.

She turned away, not to let them see in her face the scream of the knowledge of what that dust had been a few minutes ago. Don't try to open that door, he had said to her at the entrance to the powerhouse of Atlantis . . . if you tried to break it down, the machinery inside would collapse into rubble long before the door would give way. . . . Don't try to open that door—she was thinking, but knew that what she was now seeing was the visual form of the statement: Don't try to force a mind.

The men backed out in silence and went on backing toward the exit door, then stopped uncertainly, one after another, at random points of the garret, as if abandoned by a receding tide.

"Well," said Galt, reaching for his overcoat and turning to the leader, "let's go."

* * *

Three floors of the Wayne-Falkland Hotel had been evacuated and transformed into an armed camp. Guards with machine guns stood at every turn of the long, velvet-carpeted corridors. Sentinels with bayonets stood on the landings of the fire-stairways. The elevator doors of the fifty-ninth, sixtieth and sixty-first floors were padlocked; a single door and one elevator were left as sole means of access, guarded by soldiers in full battle regalia. Peculiar-looking men loitered in the lobbies, restaurants and shops of the ground floor: their clothes were too new and too expensive, in unsuccessful imitation of the hotel's usual patrons, a camouflage impaired by the fact that the clothes were badly fitted to their wearers' husky figures and were further distorted by bulges in places where the garments of businessmen have no cause to bulge, but the garments of gunmen have. Groups of guards with Tommy guns were posted at every entrance and exit of the hotel, as well as at strategic windows of the adjoining streets.

In the center of this camp, on the sixtieth floor, in what was known as the royal suite of the Wayne-Falkland Hotel, amidst satin drapes, crystal candelabra and sculptured garlands of flowers, John Galt, dressed in slacks and shirt, sat in a brocaded armchair, one leg stretched out on a velvet hassock, his hands crossed behind his head, looking at the ceiling.

This was the posture in which Mr. Thompson found him, when the four guards, who had stood outside the door of the royal suite since five A.M., opened it at eleven A.M. to admit Mr. Thompson, and locked it again.

Mr. Thompson experienced a brief flash of uneasiness when the click of the lock cut off his escape and left him alone with the prisoner. But he remembered the newspaper headlines and the radio voices, which had been announcing to the country since dawn: "John Galt is found!—John Galt is in New York!—John Galt has joined the people's cause!—John Galt is in conference with the country's leaders, working for a speedy solution of all our problems!"—and he made himself feel that he believed it.

"Well, well, well!" he said brightly, marching up to the armchair. "So you're the young fellow who's started all the trouble—Oh," he said suddenly, as he got a closer look at the dark green eyes watching him. "Well, I . . . I'm tickled pink to meet you, Mr. Galt, just tickled pink." He added, "I'm Mr. Thompson, you know."

"How do you do," said Galt.

Mr. Thompson thudded down on a chair, the brusqueness of the movement suggesting a cheerily businesslike attitude. "Now don't go imagining that you're under arrest or some such nonsense." He pointed at the room. "This is no jail, as you can see. You can see that we'll treat you right. You're a big person, a very big person—and we know it. Just make yourself at home. Ask for anything you please. Fire any flunky that doesn't obey you. And if you take a dislike to any of the army boys outside, just breathe the word—and we'll send another one to replace him."

He paused expectantly. He received no answer.

"The only reason we brought you here is just that we wanted to talk to you. We wouldn't have done it this way, but you left us no choice. You kept hiding. And all we wanted was a chance to tell you that you got us all wrong."

He spread his hands out, palms up, with a disarming smile. Galt's eyes were watching him, without answer.

"That was some speech you made. Boy, are you an orator! You've done something to the country—I don't know what or why, but you have. People seem to want something you've got. But you thought we'd be dead set against it? That's where you're wrong. We're not. Personally, I think there was plenty in that speech that made sense. Yes, sir, I do. Of course, I don't agree with every word you said—but what the hell, you don't expect us to agree with everything, do you? Differences of opinion—that's what makes horse racing. Me, I'm always willing to change my mind. I'm open to any argument."

He leaned forward invitingly. He obtained no answer.

"The world is in a hell of a mess. Just as you said. There, I agree with you. We have a point in common. We can start from that. Something's got to be done about it. All I wanted was—Look," he cried suddenly, "why don't you let me talk to you?"

"You are talking to me."

"I . . . well, that is . . . well, you know what I mean."

"Fully."

"Well? . . . Well, what have *you* got to say?"

"Nothing."

"Huh?!"

"Nothing."

"Oh, come now!"

"I didn't seek to talk to you."

"But . . . but look! . . . we have things to discuss!"

"I haven't."

"Look," said Mr. Thompson, after a pause, "you're a man of action. A practical man. Boy, are you a practical man! Whatever else I don't quite get about you, I'm sure of that. Now aren't you?"

"Practical? Yes."

"Well, so am I. We can talk straight. We can put our cards on the table. Whatever it is you're after, I'm offering you a deal."

"I'm always open to a deal."

"I knew it!" cried Mr. Thompson triumphantly, slamming his fist down on his own knee. "I told them so—all those fool intellectual theorizers, like Wesley!"

"I'm always open to a deal—with anyone who has a value to offer me."

Mr. Thompson could not tell what made him miss a beat before he answered, "Well, write your own ticket, brother! Write your own ticket!"

"What have you got to offer me?"

"Why—anything."

"Such as?"

"Anything you name. Have you heard our short-wave broadcasts to you?"

"Yes."

"We said we'll meet your terms, any terms. We meant it."

"Have you heard me say on the radio that I have no terms to bargain about? I meant it."

"Oh, but look, you misunderstood us! You thought we'd fight you. But we won't. We're not that rigid. We're willing to consider any idea. Why didn't you answer our calls and come to a conference?"

"Why should I?"

"Because . . . because we wanted to speak to you in the name of the country."

"I don't recognize your right to speak in the name of the country."

"Now look here, I'm not used to . . . Well, okay, won't you just give me a hearing? Won't you listen?"

"I'm listening."

"The country is in a terrible state. People are starving and giving up, the economy is falling to pieces, nobody is producing any longer. We don't know what to do about it. You do. You know how to make things work. Okay, we're ready to give in. We want you to tell us what to do."

"I told you what to do."

"What?"

"Get out of the way."

"That's impossible! That's fantastic! That's out of the question!"

"You see? I told you we had nothing to discuss."

"Now, wait! Wait! Don't go to extremes! There's always a middle ground. You can't have everything. We aren't . . . people aren't ready for it. You can't expect us to ditch the machinery of State. We've got to preserve the system. But we're willing to amend it. We'll modify it any way you wish. We're not stubborn, theoretical dogmatists—we're flexible. We'll do anything you say. We'll give you a free hand. We'll co-operate. We'll compromise. We'll split fifty-fifty. We'll keep the sphere of politics and give you total power over the sphere of economics. We'll turn the production of the country over to you, we'll make you a present of the entire economy. You'll run it any way you wish, you'll give the orders, you'll issue the directives—and you'll have the organized power of the State at your command to enforce your decisions. We'll stand ready to obey you, all of us, from me on down. In the field of production, we'll do whatever you say. You'll be—you'll be the Economic Dictator of the nation!"

Galt burst out laughing.

It was the simple amusement of the laughter that shocked Mr. Thompson. "What's the matter with you?"

"So that's your idea of a compromise, is it?"

"What's the . . . ? Don't sit there grinning like that! . . . I don't think you understood me. I'm offering you *Wesley Mouch's* job—and there's nothing bigger that anyone could offer you! . . . You'll be free to do anything you wish. If you don't like controls—repeal them. If you want higher profits and lower wages—decree them. If you want special privileges for the big tycoons—grant them. If you don't like labor unions—dissolve them. If you want a free economy—order people to be free! Play it any way you please. But get things going. Get the country organized. Make people work again. Make them produce. Bring back your own men—the men of brains. Lead us to a peaceful, scientific, industrial age and to prosperity."

"At the point of a gun?"

"Now look, I . . . Now what's so damn funny about it?"

"Will you tell me just one thing: if you're able to pretend that you haven't heard a word I said on the radio, what makes you think I'd be willing to pretend that I haven't said it?"

"I don't know what you mean! I—"

"Skip it. It was just a rhetorical question. The first part of it answers the second."

"Huh?"

"I don't play your kind of games, brother—if you want a translation."

"Do you mean that you're refusing my offer?"

"I am."

"But why?"

"It took me three hours on the radio to tell you why."

"Oh, that's just theory! I'm talking business. I'm offering you the greatest job in the world. Will you tell me what's wrong with it?"

"What I told you, in three hours, was that it won't work."

"*You* can make it work."

"How?"

Mr. Thompson spread his hands out. "I don't know. If I did, I wouldn't come to you. It's for you to figure out. You're the industrial genius. You can solve anything."

"I said it can't be done."

"*You* could do it."

"How?"

"Somehow." He heard Galt's chuckle, and added, "Why not? Just tell me why not?"

"Okay, I'll tell you. You want me to be the Economic Dictator?"

"Yes!"

"And you'll obey any order I give?"

"Implicitly!"

"Then start by abolishing all income taxes."

"Oh, no!" screamed Mr. Thompson, leaping to his feet. "We couldn't do that! That's . . . that's not the field of production. That's the field of distribution. How would we pay government employees?"

"Fire your government employees."

"Oh, no! *That's* politics! That's not economics! You can't interfere with politics! You can't have everything!"

Galt crossed his legs on the hassock, stretching himself more comfortably in the brocaded armchair. "Want to continue the discussion? Or do you get the point?"

"I only—" He stopped.

"Are you satisfied that *I* got the point?"

"Look," said Mr. Thompson placatingly, resuming the edge of his seat. "I don't want to argue. I'm no good at debates. I'm a man of action. Time is short. All I know is that you've got a mind. Just the sort of mind we need. You can do anything. You could make things work if you *wanted* to."

"All right, put it your own way: I don't want to. I don't want to be an Economic Dictator, not even long enough to issue that order for people to be free—which any rational human being would throw back in my face, because he'd know that his rights are not to be held, given or received by your permission or mine."

"Tell me," said Mr. Thompson, looking at him reflectively, "what is it you're after?"

"I told you on the radio."

"I don't get it. You said that you're out for your own selfish interest—and *that*, I can understand. But what can you possibly want in the future that you couldn't get right now, from us, handed down to you on a platter? I thought you were an egoist—and a practical man. I offer you a blank check on anything you wish—and you tell me that you don't want it. Why?"

"Because there are no funds behind your blank check."

"*What?*"

"Because you have no value to offer me."

"I can offer you anything you can ask. Just name it."

"You name it."

"Well, you talked a lot about wealth. If it's money that you want—you couldn't make in three lifetimes what I can hand over to you in a minute, this minute, cash on the barrel. Want a billion dollars—a cool, neat billion dollars?"

"Which *I'll* have to produce, for you to give me?"

"No, I mean straight out of the public treasury, in fresh, new bills . . . or . . . or even in gold, if you prefer."

"What will it buy me?"

"Oh, look, when the country gets back on its feet—"

"When *I* put it back on its feet?"

"Well, if what you want is to run things your own way, if it's power that you're after, I'll guarantee you that every man, woman and child in this country will obey your orders and do whatever you wish."

"After *I* teach them to do it?"

"If you want anything for your own gang—for all those men who've disappeared—jobs, positions, authority, tax exemptions, any special favor at all—just name it and they'll get it."

"After *I* bring them back?"

"Well, what on earth *do* you want?"

"What on earth do I need *you* for?"

"Huh?"

"What have you got to offer me that I couldn't get without you?"

There was a different look in Mr. Thompson's eyes when he drew back, as if cornered, yet looked straight at Galt for the first time and said slowly, "Without me, you couldn't get out of this room, right now."

Galt smiled. "True."

"You wouldn't be able to produce anything. You could be left here to starve."

"True."

"Well, don't you see?" The loudness of homey joviality came back into Mr. Thompson's voice, as if the hint given and received were now to be safely evaded by means of humor. "What I've got to offer you is your life."

"It's not yours to offer, Mr. Thompson," said Galt softly.

Something about his voice made Mr. Thompson jerk to glance at him, then jerk faster to look away: Galt's smile seemed almost gentle.

"Now," said Galt, "do you see what I meant when I said that a zero can't hold a mortgage over life? It's I who'd have to grant you that kind of mortgage—and I don't. The removal of a threat is not a payment, the negation of a negative is not a reward, the withdrawal of your armed hoodlums is not an incentive, the offer not to murder me is not a value."

"Who . . . who's said anything about murdering you?"

"Who's said anything about anything else? If you weren't holding me here at the point of a gun, under threat of death, you wouldn't have a chance to speak to me at all. And *that* is as much as your guns can accomplish. I don't pay for the removal of threats. I don't buy my life from anyone."

"That's not true," said Mr. Thompson brightly. "If you had a broken leg, you'd pay a doctor to set it."

"Not if he was the one who broke it." He smiled at Mr. Thompson's silence. "I'm a practical man, Mr. Thompson. I don't think it's practical to establish a person whose sole means of livelihood is the breaking of my bones. I don't think it's practical to support a protection racket."

Mr. Thompson looked thoughtful, then shook his head. "I don't think you're practical," he said. "A practical man doesn't ignore the facts of reality. He doesn't waste his time wishing things to be different or trying to change them. He takes things as they are. We're holding you. It's a fact. Whether you like it or not, it's a fact. You should act accordingly."

"I am."

"What I mean is, you should co-operate. You should recognize an existing situation, accept it and adjust to it."

"If you had blood poisoning, would you adjust to it or act to change it?"

"Oh, that's different! That's physical!"

"You mean, physical facts are open to correction, but your whims are not?"

"Huh?"

"You mean, physical nature can be adjusted to men, but your whims are above the laws of nature, and men must adjust to *you?*"

"I mean that I hold the upper hand!"

"With a gun in it?"

"Oh, forget about guns! I—"

"I can't forget a fact of reality, Mr. Thompson. That would be impractical."

"All right, then: I hold a gun. What are you going to do about it?"

"I'll act accordingly. I'll obey you."

"What?"

"I'll do whatever you *tell* me to."

"Do you mean it?"

"I mean it. *Literally.*" He saw the eagerness of Mr. Thompson's face ebb slowly under a look of bewilderment. "I will perform any motion you order me to perform. If you order me to move into the office of an Economic Dictator, I'll move into it. If you order me to sit at a desk, I will sit at it. If you order me to issue a directive, I will issue the directive you order me to issue."

"Oh, but I don't know what directives to issue!"

"I don't, either."

There was a long pause.

"Well?" said Galt. "What are your orders?"

"I want you to save the economy of the country!"

"I don't know how to save it."

"I want you to find a way!"

"I don't know how to find it."

"I want you to think!"

"How will your gun make me do that, Mr. Thompson?"

Mr. Thompson looked at him silently—and Galt saw, in the tightened lips, in the jutting chin, in the narrowed eyes, the look of an adolescent bully about to utter that philosophical argument which is expressed by the sentence: I'll bash your teeth in. Galt smiled, looking straight at him, as if hearing the unspoken sentence and underscoring it. Mr. Thompson looked away.

"No," said Galt, "you don't want me to think. When you force a man to act against his own choice and judgment, it's his thinking that you want him to suspend. You want him to become a robot. I shall comply."

Mr. Thompson sighed. "I don't get it," he said in a tone of genuine helplessness. "Something's off and I can't figure it out. Why should you ask for trouble? With a brain like yours—you can beat anybody. I'm no match for you, and you know it. Why don't you pretend to join us, then gain control and outsmart me?"

"For the same reason that makes you offer it: because you'd win."

"Huh?"

"Because it's the attempt of your betters to beat you on *your* terms that has allowed your kind to get away with it for centuries. Which one of us would succeed, if I were to compete with you for control over your musclemen? Sure, I could pretend—and I wouldn't save your economy or your system, nothing will save them now—but I'd perish and what you'd win would be what you've always won in the past: a postponement, one more stay of execution, for another year—or month—bought at the price of whatever hope and effort might still be squeezed out of the best of the human remnants left around you, including me. That's all you're after and *that* is the length of your range. A month? You'd settle for a week—on the unchallenged absolute that there will always be another victim to find. But you've found your last victim—the one who refuses to play his historical part. The game is up, brother."

"Oh, that's just theory!" snapped Mr. Thompson, a little too sharply; his eyes were roving about the room, in the manner of a substitute for pacing; he glanced at the door, as if longing to escape. "You say that if we don't give up the system, we'll perish?" he asked.

"Yes."

"Then, since we're holding you, you will perish with us?"

"Possibly."

"Don't you want to live?"

"Passionately." He saw the snap of a spark in Mr. Thompson's eyes and smiled. "I'll tell you more: I know that I want to live much more intensely than you do. I know that that's what you're counting on. I know that you, in fact, do not want to live at all. I want it. And because I want it so much, I will accept no substitute."

Mr. Thompson jumped to his feet. "That's not true!" he cried. "My not wanting to live—it's not true! Why do you talk like that?" He stood, his limbs drawn faintly together, as if against a sudden chill.

"Why do you say such things? I don't know what you mean." He backed a few steps away. "And it's not true that I'm a gunman. I'm not. I don't intend to harm you. I never intended to harm anybody. I want people to like me. I want to be your friend . . . I want to be your friend!" he cried to the space at large.

Galt's eyes were watching him, without expression, giving him no clue to what they were seeing, except that they were seeing it.

Mr. Thompson jerked suddenly into bustling, unnecessary motions, as if he were in a hurry. "I've got to run along," he said. "I . . . I have so many appointments. We'll talk about it some more. Think it over. Take your time. I'm not trying to high-pressure you. Just relax, take it easy and make yourself at home. Ask for anything you like—food, drinks, cigarettes, the best of anything." He waved his hand at Galt's garments. "I'm going to order the most expensive tailor in the city to make some decent clothes for you. I want you to get used to the best. I want you to be comfortable and . . . Say," he asked, a little too casually, "have you got any family? Any relatives you'd like to see?"

"No."

"Any friends?"

"No."

"Have you got a sweetheart?"

"No."

"It's just that I wouldn't want you to get lonesome. We can let you have visitors, any visitor you name, if there's anyone you care for."

"There isn't."

Mr. Thompson paused at the door, turned to look at Galt for a moment and shook his head. "I can't figure you out," he said. "I just can't figure you out."

Galt smiled, shrugged and answered, "Who is John Galt?"

*　*　*

A whirling mesh of sleet hung over the entrance of the Wayne-Falkland Hotel, and the armed guards looked oddly, desolately helpless in the circle of light: they stood hunched, heads down, hugging their guns for warmth—as if, were they to release all the spitting violence of their bullets at the storm, it would not bring comfort to their bodies.

From across the street, Chick Morrison, the Morale Conditioner—on his way to a conference on the fifty-ninth floor—noted that the rare, lethargic passers-by were not taking the trouble to glance at the guards, as they did not take the trouble to glance at the soggy headlines of a pile of unsold newspapers on the stand of a ragged, shivering vendor: "John Galt Promises Prosperity."

Chick Morrison shook his head uneasily: six days of front-page stories—about the united efforts of the country's leaders working with John Galt to shape new policies—had brought no results. People were moving, he observed, as if they did not care to see anything around them. No one took any notice of his existence, except a ragged old woman who stretched out her hand to him silently, as he approached the lights of the entrance; he hurried past, and only drops of sleet fell on the gnarled, naked palm.

It was his memory of the streets that gave a jagged sound to Chick Morrison's voice, when he spoke to a circle of faces in Mr. Thompson's room on the fifty-ninth floor. The look of the faces matched the sound of his voice.

"It doesn't seem to work," he said, pointing to a pile of reports from his public-pulse-takers. "All the press releases about our collaborating with John Galt don't seem to make any difference. People don't care. They don't believe a word of it. Some of them say that he'll never collaborate with us. Most of them don't even believe that we've got him. I don't know what's happened to people. They don't believe anything any more." He sighed. "Three factories went out of business in Cleveland, day before yesterday. Five factories closed in Chicago yesterday. In San Francisco—"

"I know, I know," snapped Mr. Thompson, tightening the muffler around his throat: the building's furnace had gone out of order. "There's no choice about it: he's *got* to give in and take over. He's got to!"

Wesley Mouch glanced at the ceiling. "Don't ask me to talk to him again," he said, and shuddered. "I've tried. One can't talk to that man."

"I . . . I can't, Mr. Thompson!" cried Chick Morrison, in answer to the stop of Mr. Thompson's roving glance. "I'll resign, if you want me to! I can't talk to him again! Don't make me!"

"Nobody can talk to him," said Dr. Floyd Ferris. "It's a waste of time. He doesn't hear a word you say."

Fred Kinnan chuckled. "You mean, he hears too much, don't you? And what's worse, he answers it."

"Well, why don't *you* try it again?" snapped Mouch. "You seem to have enjoyed it. Why don't *you* try to persuade him?"

"I know better," said Kinnan. "Don't fool yourself, brother. Nobody's going to persuade him. I won't try it twice. . . . Enjoyed it?" he added, with a look of astonishment. "Yeah . . . yeah, I guess I did."

"What's the matter with you? Are you falling for him? Are you letting him win you over?"

"Me?" Kinnan chuckled mirthlessly. "What use would he have for me? I'll be the first one to go down the drain when he wins. . . . It's only"—he glanced wistfully up at the ceiling—"it's only that he's a man who talks straight."

"He won't win!" snapped Mr. Thompson. "It's out of the question!"

There was a long pause.

"There are hunger riots in West Virginia," said Wesley Mouch. "And the farmers in Texas have—"

"Mr. Thompson!" said Chick Morrison desperately. "Maybe . . . maybe we could let the public see him . . . at a mass rally . . . or maybe on TV . . . just see him, just so they'd believe that we've really got him. . . . It would give people hope, for a while . . . it would give us a little time. . . ."

"Too dangerous," snapped Dr. Ferris. "Don't let him come anywhere near the public. There's no limit to what he'll permit himself to do."

"He's got to give in," said Mr. Thompson stubbornly. "He's got to join us. One of you must—"

"No!" screamed Eugene Lawson. "Not me! I don't want to see him at all! Not once! I don't want to have to believe it!"

"What?" asked James Taggart; his voice had a note of dangerously reckless mockery; Lawson did not answer. "What are you scared of?" The contempt in Taggart's voice sounded abnormally stressed, as if the sight of someone's greater fear were tempting him to defy his own. "What is it you're scared to believe, Gene?"

"I won't believe it! I won't!" Lawson's voice was half-snarl, half-whimper. "You can't make me lose my faith in humanity! You shouldn't permit such a man to be possible! A ruthless egoist who—"

"You're a fine bunch of intellectuals, you are," said Mr. Thompson scornfully. "I thought you could talk to him in his own lingo—but he's scared the lot of you. Ideas? Where are your ideas now? Do something! Make him join us! Win him over!"

"Trouble is, he doesn't want anything," said Mouch. "What can we offer a man who doesn't want anything?"

"You mean," said Kinnan, "what can we offer a man who wants to live?"

"Shut up!" screamed James Taggart. "Why did you say that? What made you say it?"

"What made you scream?" asked Kinnan.

"Keep quiet, all of you!" ordered Mr. Thompson. "You're fine at fighting one another, but when it comes to fighting a real man—"

"So he's got you, too?" yelled Lawson.

"Aw, pipe down," said Mr. Thompson wearily. "He's the toughest bastard I've ever been up against. You wouldn't understand that. He's as hard as they come . . ." The faintest tinge of admiration crept into his voice. "As hard as they come . . ."

"There are ways to persuade tough bastards," drawled Dr. Ferris casually, "as I've explained to you."

"No!" cried Mr. Thompson. "No! Shut up! I won't listen to you! I won't hear of it!" His hands moved frantically, as if struggling to dispel something he would not name. "I told him . . . that that's not true . . . that we're not . . . that I'm not a . . ." He shook his head violently, as if his own words were some unprecedented form of danger. "No, look, boys, what I mean is, we've got to be practical . . . and cautious. Damn cautious. We've got to handle it peacefully. We can't afford to antagonize him or . . . or harm him. We don't dare take any chances on . . . anything happening to him. Because . . . because, if he goes, we go. He's our last hope. Make no mistake about it. If he goes, we perish. You all know it." His eyes swept over the faces around him: they knew it.

The sleet of the following morning fell down on front-page stories announcing that a constructive, harmonious conference between John Galt and the country's leaders, on the previous afternoon, had produced "The John Galt Plan," soon to be announced. The snowflakes of the evening fell down upon the furniture of an apartment house whose front wall had collapsed—and upon a crowd of men waiting silently at the closed cashier's window of a plant whose owner had vanished.

"The farmers of South Dakota," Wesley Mouch reported to Mr. Thompson, next morning, "are marching on the state capital, burning every government building on their way, and every home worth more than ten thousand dollars."

"California's blown to pieces," he reported in the evening. "There's a civil war going on there—if that's what it is, which nobody seems to be sure of. They've declared that they're seceding from the Union, but nobody knows who's now in power. There's armed fighting all over the state, between a 'People's Party,' led by Ma Chalmers and her soybean cult of Orient-admirers—and something called 'Back to God,' led by some former oil-field owners."

"Miss Taggart!" moaned Mr. Thompson, when she entered his hotel room next morning, in answer to his summons. "What are we going to do?"

He wondered why he had once felt that she possessed some reassuring kind of energy. He was looking at a blank face that seemed composed, but the composure became disquieting when one noticed that it lasted for minute after minute, with no change of expression, no sign of feeling. Her face had the same look as all the others, he thought, except for something in the set of the mouth that suggested endurance.

"I trust you, Miss Taggart. You've got more brains than all my boys," he pleaded. "You've done more for the country than any of them—it's you who found him for us. What are we to do? With everything falling to pieces, he's the only one who can lead us out of this mess—but he won't. He refuses to lead. He simply refuses to lead. I've never seen anything like it: a man who has no desire to command. We beg him to give orders—and he answers that he wants to obey them! It's preposterous!"

"It is."

"What do you make of it? Can you figure him out?"

"He's an arrogant egoist," she said. "He's an ambitious adventurer. He's a man of unlimited audacity who's playing for the biggest stakes in the world."

It was easy, she thought. It would have been difficult in that distant time when she had regarded language as a tool of honor, always to be used as if one were under oath—an oath of allegiance to reality and to respect for human beings. Now it was only a matter of making sounds, inarticulate sounds addressed to inanimate objects unrelated to such concepts as reality, human or honor.

It had been easy, that first morning, to report to Mr. Thompson how she had traced John Galt to his home. It had been easy to watch Mr. Thompson's gulping smiles and his repeated cries of *"That's my girl!"* uttered with glances of triumph at his assistants, the triumph of a man whose judgment in trusting her had been vindicated. It had been easy to express an angry hatred for Galt—"I used to agree with his ideas, but I won't let him destroy my railroad!"—and to hear Mr. Thompson say, "Don't you worry, Miss Taggart! We'll protect you from him!"

It had been easy to assume a look of cold shrewdness and to remind Mr. Thompson of the five-hundred-thousand-dollar reward, her voice clear and cutting, like the sound of an adding machine punching out the sum of a bill. She had seen an instant's pause in Mr. Thompson's facial muscles, then a brighter, broader smile—like a silent speech declaring that he had not expected it, but was delighted to know what made her tick and that it was the kind of ticking he understood. "Of course, Miss Taggart! Certainly! That reward is yours—all yours! The check will be sent to you, in full!"

It had been easy, because she had felt as if she were in some dreary non-world, where her words and actions were not facts any longer—not reflections of reality, but only distorted postures in one of those side-show mirrors that project deformity for the perception of beings whose consciousness is not to be treated as consciousness. Thin, single and hot, like the burning pressure of a wire within her, like a needle selecting her course, was her only concern: the thought of his safety. The rest was a blur of shapeless dissolution, half-acid, half-fog.

But this—she thought with a shudder—was the state in which they lived, all those people whom she had never understood, this was the state they desired, this rubber reality, this task of pretending, distorting, deceiving, with the credulous stare of some Mr. Thompson's panic-bleary eyes as one's only purpose and reward. Those who desired this state—she wondered—did they want to live?

"The biggest stakes in the world, Miss Taggart?" Mr. Thompson was asking her anxiously. "What is it? What does he want?"

"Reality. This earth."

"I don't know quite what you mean, but . . . Look, Miss Taggart, if you think you can understand him, would you . . . would you try to speak to him once more?"

She felt as if she heard her own voice, many light-years away, crying that she would give her life to see him—but in this room, she heard the voice of a meaningless stranger saying coldly, "No, Mr. Thompson, I wouldn't. I hope I'll never have to see him again."

"I know that you can't stand him, and I can't say I blame you, but couldn't you just try to—"

"I tried to reason with him, the night I found him. I heard nothing but insults in return. I think he resents me more than he'd resent anyone else. He won't forgive me the fact that it was I who trapped him. I'd be the last person to whom he would surrender."

"Yeah . . . yeah, that's true. . . . Do you think he will ever surrender?"

The needle within her wavered for a moment, burning its oscillating way between two courses: should she say that he would not, and see them kill him?—should she say that he would, and see them hold onto their power till they destroyed the world?

"He will," she said firmly. "He'll give in, if you treat him right. He's too ambitious to refuse power. Don't let him escape, but don't threaten him—or harm him. Fear won't work. He's impervious to fear."

"But what if . . . I mean, with the way things are collapsing . . . what if he holds out too long?"

"He won't. He's too practical for that. By the way, are you letting him hear any news about the state of the country?"

"Why . . . no."

"I would suggest that you let him have copies of your confidential reports. He'll see that it won't be long now."

"That's a good idea! A very good idea! . . . You know, Miss Taggart," he said suddenly, with the sound of some desperate clinging in his voice, "I feel better whenever I talk to you. It's because I trust you. I don't trust anybody around me. But you—you're different. You're solid."

She was looking unflinchingly straight at him. "Thank you, Mr. Thompson," she said.

It had been easy, she thought—until she walked out into the street and noticed that under her coat, her blouse was sticking damply to her shoulder blades.

Were she able to feel—she thought as she walked through the concourse of the Terminal—she would know that the heavy indifference she now felt for her railroad was hatred. She could not get rid of the feeling that she was running nothing but freight trains: the passengers, to her, were not living or human. It seemed senseless to waste such enormous effort on preventing catastrophes, on protecting the safety of trains carrying nothing but inanimate objects. She looked at the faces in the Terminal: if he were to die, she thought, to be murdered by the rulers of their system, that *these* might continue to eat, sleep and travel—would she work to provide them with trains? If she were to scream for their help, would one of them rise to his defense? Did they want him to live, they who had heard him?

The check for five hundred thousand dollars was delivered to her office, that afternoon; it was delivered with a bouquet of flowers from Mr. Thompson. She looked at the check and let it flutter down to her desk: it meant nothing and made her feel nothing, not even a suggestion of guilt. It was a scrap of paper, of no greater significance than the ones in the office wastebasket. Whether it could buy a diamond necklace or the city dump or the last of her food, made no difference. It would never be spent. It was not a token of value and nothing it purchased could be a value. But this—she thought—this inanimate indifference was the permanent state of the people around her, of men who had no purpose and no passion. *This* was the state of a non-valuing soul; those who chose it—she wondered—did they want to live?

The lights were out of order in the hall of the apartment house, when she came home that evening, numb with exhaustion—and she did not notice the envelope at her feet until she switched on the light in her foyer. It was a blank, sealed envelope that had been slipped under her door. She picked it up—and then, within a moment, she was laughing soundlessly, half-kneeling, half-sitting on the floor, not to move off that spot, not to do anything but stare at the note written by a hand she knew, the hand that had written its last message on the calendar above the city. The note said:

Dagny:
Sit tight. Watch them. When he'll need our help, call me at OR 6-5693.

F.

The newspapers of the following morning admonished the public not to believe the rumors that there was any trouble in the Southern states. The confidential reports, sent to Mr. Thompson, stated that armed fighting had broken out between Georgia and Alabama, for the possession of a factory manufacturing electrical equipment—a factory cut off by the fighting and by blasted railroad tracks from any source of raw materials.

"Have you read the confidential reports I sent you?" moaned Mr. Thompson, that evening, facing Galt once more. He was accompanied by James Taggart, who had volunteered to meet the prisoner for the first time.

Galt sat on a straight-backed chair, his legs crossed, smoking a cigarette. He seemed erect and relaxed, together. They could not decipher the expression on his face, except that it showed no sign of apprehension.

"I have," he answered.

"There's not much time left," said Mr. Thompson.

"There isn't."

"Are you going to let such things go on?"

"Are *you?*"

"How can you be so sure you're right?" cried James Taggart; his voice was not loud, but it had the intensity of a cry. "How can you take it upon yourself, at a terrible time like this, to stick to your own ideas at the risk of destroying the whole world?"

"Whose ideas should I consider safer to follow?"

"How can you be sure you're right? How can you *know?* Nobody can be sure of his knowledge! Nobody! You're no better than anyone else!"

"Then why do you want me?"

"How can you gamble with other people's lives? How can you permit yourself such a *selfish* luxury as to hold out, when people need you?"

"You mean: when they need *my* ideas?"

"Nobody is fully right or wrong! There isn't any black or white! You don't have a monopoly on truth!"

There was something wrong in Taggart's manner—thought Mr. Thompson, frowning—some odd, too personal resentment, as if it were not a political issue that he had come here to solve.

"If you had any sense of responsibility," Taggart was saying, "you wouldn't dare take such a chance on nothing but your own judgment! You would join us and consider some ideas other than your own and admit that we might be right, too! You would help us with our plans! You would—"

Taggart went on speaking with feverish insistence, but Mr. Thompson could not tell whether Galt was listening: Galt had risen and was pacing the room, not in a manner of restlessness, but in the casual manner of a man enjoying the motion of his own body. Mr. Thompson noted the lightness of the steps, the straight spine, the flat stomach, the relaxed shoulders. Galt walked as if he were both unconscious of his body and tremendously conscious of his pride in it. Mr. Thompson glanced at James Taggart, at the sloppy posture of a tall figure slumped in ungainly self-distortion, and caught him watching Galt's movements with such hatred that Mr. Thompson sat up, fearing it would become audible in the room. But Galt was not looking at Taggart.

". . . your conscience!" Taggart was saying. "I came here to appeal to your conscience! How can you value your mind above thousands of human lives? People are perishing and—Oh, for Christ's sake," he snapped, "stop pacing!"

Galt stopped. "Is this an order?"

"No, no!" said Mr. Thompson hastily. "It's not an order. We don't want to give you orders. . . . Take it easy, Jim."

Galt resumed his pacing. "The world is collapsing," said Taggart, his eyes following Galt irresistibly. "People are perishing—and it's you who could save them! Does it matter who's right or wrong? You should join us, even if you think we're wrong, you should sacrifice your mind to save them!"

"By what means will I then save them?"

"Who do you think you are?" cried Taggart.

Galt stopped. "You know it."

"You're an egoist!"

"I am."

"Do you realize what sort of egoist you are?"

"Do *you?*" asked Galt, looking straight at him.

It was the slow withdrawal of Taggart's body into the depth of his armchair, while his eyes were holding Galt's, that made Mr. Thompson unaccountably afraid of the next moment.

"Say," Mr. Thompson interrupted in a brightly casual voice, "what sort of cigarette are you smoking?"

Galt turned to him and smiled. "I don't know."

"Where did you get it?"

"One of your guards brought me a package of them. He said some man asked him to give it to me as a present. . . . Don't worry," he added, "your boys have put it through every kind of test. There were no hidden messages. It was just a present from an anonymous admirer."

The cigarette between Galt's fingers bore the sign of the dollar.

James Taggart was no good at the job of persuasion, Mr. Thompson concluded. But Chick Morrison, whom he brought the next day, did no better.

"I . . . I'll just throw myself on your mercy, Mr. Galt," said Chick Morrison with a frantic smile. "You're right. I'll concede that you're right—and all I can appeal to is your pity. Deep down in my heart, I can't believe that you're a total egoist who feels no pity for the people." He pointed to a pile of papers he had spread on a table. "Here's a plea signed by ten thousand schoolchildren, begging you to join us and save them. Here's a plea from a home for the crippled. Here's a petition sent by the ministers of two hundred different faiths. Here's an appeal from the mothers of the country. Read them."

"Is this an order?"

"No!" cried Mr. Thompson. "It's not an order!"

Galt remained motionless, not extending his hand for the papers.

"These are just plain, ordinary people, Mr. Galt," said Chick Morrison in a tone intended to project their abject humility. "They can't tell you what to do. They wouldn't know. They're merely begging you. They may be weak, helpless, blind, ignorant. But you, who are so intelligent and strong, can't you take pity on them? Can't you help them?"

"By dropping my intelligence and following their blindness?"

"They may be wrong, but they don't know any better!"

"But I, who do, should obey them?"

"I can't argue, Mr. Galt. I'm just begging for your pity. They're suffering. I'm begging you to pity those who suffer. I'm . . . Mr. Galt," he asked, noticing that Galt was looking off at the distance beyond the window and that his eyes were suddenly implacable, "what's the matter? What are you thinking of?"

"Hank Rearden."

"Uh . . . why?"

"Did they feel any pity for Hank Rearden?"

"Oh, but that's different! He—"

"Shut up," said Galt evenly.

"I only—"

"Shut up!" snapped Mr. Thompson. "Don't mind him, Mr. Galt. He hasn't slept for two nights. He's scared out of his wits."

Dr. Floyd Ferris, next day, did not seem to be scared—but it was worse, thought Mr. Thompson. He observed that Galt remained silent and would not answer Ferris at all.

"It's the question of moral responsibility that you might not have studied sufficiently, Mr. Galt," Dr. Ferris was drawling in too airy, too forced a tone of casual informality. "You seem to have talked on the radio about nothing but sins of commission. But there are .also the sins of omission to consider. To fail to save a life is as immoral as to murder. The consequences are the same—and since we must judge actions by their consequences, the moral responsibility is the same. . . . For instance, in view of the desperate shortage of food, it has been suggested that it might become necessary to issue a directive ordering that every third one of all children under the age of ten and of all adults over the age of sixty be put to death, to secure the survival of the rest. You wouldn't want this to happen, would you? You can prevent it. One word from you would prevent it. If you refuse and all those people are executed—it will be *your* fault and *your* moral responsibility!"

"You're crazy!" screamed Mr. Thompson, recovering from shock and leaping to his feet. "Nobody's ever suggested any such thing! Nobody's ever considered it! Please, Mr. Galt! Don't believe him! He doesn't mean it!"

"Oh yes, he does," said Galt. "Tell the bastard to look at me, then look in the mirror, then ask himself whether I would ever think that *my* moral stature is at the mercy of *his* actions."

"Get out of here!" cried Mr. Thompson, yanking Ferris to his feet. "Get out! Don't let me hear another squeak out of you!" He flung the door open and pushed Ferris at the startled face of a guard outside.

Turning to Galt, he spread his arms and let them drop with a gesture of drained helplessness. Galt's face was expressionless.

"Look," said Mr. Thompson pleadingly, "isn't there anybody who can talk to you?"

"There's nothing to talk about."

"We've got to. We've got to convince you. Is there anyone you'd *want* to talk to?"

"No."

"I thought maybe . . . it's because she talks—used to talk—like you, at times . . . maybe if I sent Miss Dagny Taggart to tell you—"

"That one? Sure, she used to talk like me. She's my only failure. I thought she was the kind who belonged on my side. But she double-crossed me, to keep her railroad. She'd sell her soul for her railroad. Send her in, if you want me to slap her face."

"No, no, no! You don't have to see her, if that's how you feel. I don't want to waste more time on people who rub you the wrong way. . . . Only . . . only if it's not Miss Taggart, I don't know whom to pick. . . . If . . . if I could find somebody you'd be willing to consider or . . ."

"I've changed my mind," said Galt. "There *is* somebody I'd like to speak to."

"Who?" cried Mr. Thompson eagerly.

"Dr. Robert Stadler."

Mr. Thompson emitted a long whistle and shook his head apprehensively. "That one is no friend of yours," he said in a tone of honest warning.

"He's the one I want to see."

"Okay, if you wish. If you say so. Anything you wish. I'll have him here tomorrow morning."

That evening, dining with Wesley Mouch in his own suite, Mr. Thompson glared angrily at a glass of tomato juice placed before him. "What? No grapefruit juice?" he snapped; his doctor had prescribed grapefruit juice as protection against an epidemic of colds.

"No grapefruit juice," said the waiter, with an odd kind of emphasis.

"Fact is," said Mouch bleakly, "that a gang of raiders attacked a train at the Taggart Bridge on the Mississippi. They blew up the track and damaged the bridge. Nothing serious. It's being repaired—but all traffic is held up and the trains from Arizona can't get through."

"That's ridiculous! Aren't there any other—?" Mr. Thompson stopped; he knew that there were no other railroad bridges across the Mississippi. After a moment, he spoke up in a staccato voice. "Order army detachments to guard the bridge. Day and night. Tell them to pick their best men for it. If anything happened to that bridge—"

He did not finish; he sat hunched, staring down at the costly china plates and the delicate hors d'oeuvres before him. The absence of so prosaic a commodity as grapefruit juice had suddenly made real to him, for the first time, what it was that would happen to the city of New York if anything happened to the Taggart Bridge.

"Dagny," said Eddie Willers, that evening, "the bridge is not the only problem." He snapped on her desk lamp which, in forced concentration on her work, she had neglected to turn on at the approach of dusk. "No transcontinental trains can leave San Francisco. One of the fighting factions out there—I don't know which one—has seized our terminal and imposed a 'departure tax' on trains. Meaning that they're holding trains for ransom. Our terminal manager has quit. Nobody knows what to do there now."

"I can't leave New York," she answered stonily.

"I know," he said softly. "That's why it's *I* who'll go there to straighten things out. At least, to find a man to put in charge."

"No! I don't want you to. It's too dangerous. And what for? It doesn't matter now. There's nothing to save."

"It's still Taggart Transcontinental. I'll stand by it. Dagny, wherever you go, you'll always be able to build a railroad. I couldn't. I don't even want to make a new start. Not any more. Not after what I've seen. You should. I can't. Let me do what I can."

"Eddie! Don't you want—" She stopped, knowing that it was useless. "All right, Eddie. If you wish."

"I'm flying to California tonight. I've arranged for space on an army plane. . . . I know that you will quit as soon as . . . as soon as you can leave New York. You might be gone by the time I return. When you're ready, just go. Don't worry about me. Don't wait to tell me. Go as fast as you can. I . . . I'll say good-bye to you, now."

She rose to her feet. They stood facing each other; in the dim half-light of the office, the picture of Nathaniel Taggart hung on the wall between them. They were both seeing the years since that distant day when they had first learned to walk down the track of a railroad. He inclined his head and held it lowered for a long moment.

She extended her hand. "Good-bye, Eddie."

He clasped her hand firmly, not looking down at his fingers; he was looking at her face.

He started to go, but stopped, turned to her and asked, his voice low, but steady, neither as plea nor as despair, but as a last gesture of conscientious clarity to close a long ledger, "Dagny . . . did you know . . . how I felt about you?"

"Yes," she said softly, realizing in this moment that she had known it wordlessly for years, "I knew it."

"Good-bye, Dagny."

The faint rumble of an underground train went through the walls of the building and swallowed the sound of the door closing after him.

It was snowing, next morning, and melting drops were like an icy, cutting touch on the temples of Dr. Robert Stadler, as he walked down the long corridor of the Wayne-Falkland Hotel, toward the door of the royal suite. Two husky men walked by his sides; they were from the department of Morale Conditioning, but did not trouble to hide what method of conditioning they would welcome a chance to employ.

"Just remember Mr. Thompson's orders," one of them told him contemptuously. "One wrong squawk out of you—and you'll regret it, brother."

It was not the snow on his temples—thought Dr. Stadler—it was a burning pressure, it had been there since that scene, last night, when he had screamed to Mr. Thompson that he could not see John Galt. He had screamed in blind terror, begging a circle of impassive faces not to make him do it, sobbing that he would do anything but that. The faces had not condescended to argue or even to threaten him; they had merely given him orders. He had spent a sleepless night, telling himself that he would not obey; but he was walking toward that door. The burning pressure on his temples and the faint, dizzying nausea of unreality came from the fact that he could not recapture the sense of being Dr. Robert Stadler.

He noticed the metallic gleam of the bayonets held by the guards at the door, and the sound of a key being turned in a lock. He found himself walking forward and heard the door being locked behind him.

Across the long room, he saw John Galt sitting on the window sill, a tall, slender figure in slacks and shirt, one leg slanting down to the floor, the other bent, his hands clasping his knee, his head of sun-streaked hair raised against a spread of gray sky—and suddenly Dr. Stadler saw the figure of a young boy sitting on the porch-railing of his home, near the campus of the Patrick Henry University, with the sun on the chestnut hair of a head lifted against a spread of summer blue, and he heard the passionate intensity of his own voice saying twenty-two years ago: "The only sacred value in the world, John, is the human mind, the inviolate human mind . . ." —and he cried to that boy's figure, across the room and across the years:

"I couldn't help it, John! I couldn't help it!"

He gripped the edge of a table between them, for support and as a protective barrier, even though the figure on the window sill had not moved.

"I didn't bring you to this!" he cried. "I didn't mean to! I couldn't help it! It's not what I intended! . . . John! I'm not to blame for it! I'm not! I never had a chance against them! They own the world! They left me no place in it! . . . What's reason to them? What's science? You don't know how deadly they are! You don't understand them! They don't think! They're mindless animals moved by irrational feelings—by their greedy, grasping, blind, unaccountable feelings! They seize whatever they want, that's all they know: that they want it, regardless of cause, effect or logic—they *want* it, the bloody, grubbing pigs! . . . The mind? Don't you know how futile it is, the mind, against those mindless hordes? Our weapons are so helplessly, laughably childish: truth, knowledge, reason, values, rights! Force is all *they* know, force, fraud and plunder! . . . John! Don't look at me like that! What could I do against their fists? I had to live, didn't I? It wasn't for myself—it was for the future of science! I had to be left alone, I had to be protected, I had to make terms with them—there's no way to live except on their terms—there isn't!—do you hear me?—there isn't! . . . What did you want me to do? Spend my life begging for jobs? Begging my inferiors for funds and endowments? Did you want my work to depend on the mercy of the ruffians who have a knack for making money? I had no time to compete with them for money or markets or any of their miserable material pursuits! Was that your idea of justice—that they should spend their money on liquor, yachts and women, while the priceless hours of *my* life were wasted for lack of scientific equipment? Persuasion? How could I persuade them? What language could I speak to men who don't think? . . . You don't know how lonely I was, how starved for some spark of intelligence! How lonely and tired and helpless! Why should a mind like mine have to bargain with ignorant fools? They'd never contribute a penny to science! Why shouldn't they be forced? It wasn't you that I wanted to force! That gun was not aimed at the intellect! It wasn't aimed at men like you and me, only at mindless materialists! . . . Why do you look at me that way? I had no choice! There isn't any choice except to beat them at their own game! Oh yes, it is *their* game, *they* set the rules! What do we count, the few who can think? We can only hope to get by, unnoticed—and to trick them into serving our aims! . . . Don't you know how noble a purpose it was— my vision of the future of science? Human knowledge set free of material bonds! An unlimited end unrestricted by means! I am not a traitor, John! I'm not! I was serving the cause of the mind! What I saw ahead, what I wanted, what I *felt,* was not to be measured in their miserable dollars! I wanted a laboratory! I needed it! What do I care where it came from or how? I could do so much! I could reach such heights! Don't you have any pity? I *wanted* it! . . . What if they had to be forced? Who are they to think, anyway? Why did you teach them to rebel? It would have worked, if you hadn't withdrawn them! It would have worked, I tell you! It wouldn't be—like this! . . . Don't accuse me! We can't be guilty . . . all of us . . . for centuries. . . . We can't be so totally wrong! . . . We're not to be damned! We had no choice! There is no other way to live on earth! . . . Why don't you answer me? What are you seeing? Are you thinking of that speech you made? I don't *want* to think of it! It was only logic! One can't live by logic! Do you hear me? . . . Don't look at me! You're asking the impossible! Men can't exist your way! You permit no moments of weakness, you don't allow for human frailties or human feelings! What do you want of us? Rationality twenty-four hours a day, with no loophole, no rest, no escape? . . . Don't look at me, God damn you! I'm not afraid of you any longer! Do you hear me? I am not afraid! Who are you to blame me, you miserable failure? Here's where *your* road has brought you! Here you are, caught, helpless, under guard, to be killed by those brutes at any moment—and you dare to accuse me of being impractical! Oh yes, you're going to be killed! You won't win! You can't be allowed to win! *You* are the man who has to be destroyed!"

Dr. Stadler's gasp was a muffled scream, as if the immobility of the figure on the window sill had served as a silent reflector and had suddenly made him see the full meaning of his own words.

"No!" moaned Dr. Stadler, moving his head from side to side, to escape the unmoving green eyes. "No! . . . No! . . . No!"

Galt's voice had the same unbending austerity as his eyes: "You have said everything I wanted to say to you."

Dr. Stadler banged his fists against the door; when it was opened, he ran out of the room.

* * *

For three days, no one entered Galt's suite except the guards who brought his meals. Early on the evening of the fourth day, the door opened to admit Chick Morrison with two companions. Chick Morrison was dressed in dinner clothes, and his smile was nervous, but a shade more confident than usual. One of his companions was a valet. The other was a muscular man whose face seemed to clash with his tuxedo: it was a stony face with sleepy eyelids, pale, darting eyes and a prizefighter's broken nose; his skull was shaved except for a patch of faded blond curls on top; he kept his right hand in the pocket of his trousers.

"You will please dress, Mr. Galt," said Chick Morrison persuasively, pointing to the door of the bedroom, where a closet had been filled with expensive garments which Galt had not chosen to wear. "You will please put on your dinner clothes." He added, "This *is* an order, Mr. Galt."

Galt walked silently into the bedroom. The three men followed. Chick Morrison sat on the edge of a chair, starting and discarding one cigarette after another. The valet went through too many too courteous motions, helping Galt to dress, handing him his shirt studs, holding his coat. The muscular man stood in a corner, his hand in his pocket. No one said a word.

"You will please co-operate, Mr. Galt," said Chick Morrison, when Galt was ready, and indicated the door with a courtly gesture of invitation to proceed.

So swiftly that no one could catch the motion of his hand, the muscular man was holding Galt's arm and pressing an invisible gun against his ribs. "Don't make any false moves," he said in an expressionless voice.

"I never do," said Galt.

Chick Morrison opened the door. The valet stayed behind. The three figures in dinner clothes walked silently down the hall to the elevator.

They remained silent in the elevator, the clicks of the flashing numbers above the door marking their downward progress.

The elevator stopped on the mezzanine floor. Two armed soldiers preceded them and two others followed, as they walked through the long, dim corridors. The corridors were deserted except for armed sentinels posted at the turns. The muscular man's right arm was linked to Galt's left; the gun remained invisible to any possible observer. Galt felt the small pressure of the muzzle against his side; the pressure was expertly maintained: not to be felt as an impediment and not to be forgotten for a moment.

The corridor led to a wide, closed doorway. The soldiers seemed to melt away into the shadows, when Chick Morrison's hand touched the doorknob. It was his hand that opened the door, but the sudden contrast of light and sound made it seem as if the door were flung open by an explosion: the light came from three hundred bulbs in the blazing chandeliers of the grand ballroom of the Wayne-Falkland Hotel; the sound was the applause of five hundred people.

Chick Morrison led the way to the speakers' table raised on a platform above the tables filling the room. The people seemed to know, without announcement, that of the two figures following him, it was the tall, slender man with the gold-copper hair that they were applauding. His face had the same quality as the voice they had heard on the radio: calm, confident—and out of reach.

The seat reserved for Galt was the place of honor in the center of the long table, with Mr. Thompson waiting for him at his right and the muscular man slipping skillfully into the seat at his left, not relinquishing his arm or the pressure of the muzzle. The jewels on the naked shoulders of women carried the glitter of the chandeliers to the shadows of the tables crowded against the distant walls; the severe black-and-white of the men's figures rescued the room's style of solemnly regal luxury from the discordant slashes made by news cameras, microphones and a dormant array of television equipment. The crowd was on its feet, applauding. Mr. Thompson was smiling and watching Galt's face, with the eager, anxious look of an adult waiting for a child's reaction to a spectacularly generous gift. Galt sat facing the ovation, neither ignoring it nor responding.

"The applause you are hearing," a radio announcer was yelling into a microphone in a corner of the room, "is in greeting to John Galt, who has just taken his place at the speakers' table! Yes, my friends, John Galt *in person*—as those of you who can find a television set will have a chance to see for yourself in a short while!"

I must remember where I am—thought Dagny, clenching her fists under the tablecloth, in the obscurity of a side table. It was hard to maintain a sense of double reality in the presence of Galt, thirty feet away from her. She felt that no danger or pain could exist in the world so long as she could see his face—and, simultaneously, an icy terror, when she looked at those who held him in their power, when she remembered the blind irrationality of the event they were staging. She fought to keep her facial muscles rigid, not to betray herself by a smile of happiness or by a scream of panic.

She wondered how his eyes had been able to find her in that crowd. She had seen the brief pause of his glance, which no one else could notice; the glance had been more than a kiss, it had been a handshake of approval and support.

He did not glance again in her direction. She could not force herself to look away. It was startling to see him in evening clothes and more startling still that he wore them so naturally; he made them look like a work uniform of honor; his figure suggested the kind of banquet, in the days of a distant past, where he would have been receiving an industrial award. Celebrations—she remembered her own words, with a stab of longing—should be only for those who have something to celebrate.

She turned away. She struggled not to look at him too often, not to attract the attention of her companions. She had been placed at a table prominent enough to display her to the assembly, but obscure enough to keep her out of the line of Galt's sight, along with those who had incurred Galt's disfavor: with Dr. Ferris and Eugene Lawson.

Her brother Jim, she noted, had been placed closer to the platform; she could see his sullen face among the nervous figures of Tinky Holloway, Fred Kinnan, Dr. Simon Pritchett. The tortured faces strung out above the speakers' table were not succeeding in their efforts to hide that they looked like men enduring an ordeal; the calm of Galt's face seemed radiant among them; she wondered who was prisoner here and who was master. Her glance moved slowly down the line-up of his table: Mr. Thompson, Wesley Mouch, Chick Morrison, some generals, some members of the Legislature and, preposterously, Mr. Mowen, chosen as a bribe to Galt, as a symbol of big business. She glanced about the room, looking for the face of Dr. Stadler; he was not present.

The voices filling the room were like a fever chart, she thought; they kept darting too high and collapsing into patches of silence; the occasional spurts of someone's laughter broke off, incompleted, and attracted the shuddering turn of the heads at the neighboring tables. The faces were drawn and twisted by the most obvious and least dignified form of tension: by forced smiles. These people—she thought—knew, not by means of their reason, but by means of their panic, that this banquet was the ultimate climax and the naked essence of their world. They knew that neither their God nor their guns could make this celebration mean what they were struggling to pretend it meant.

She could not swallow the food that was placed before her; her throat seemed closed by a rigid convulsion. She noticed that the others at her table were also merely pretending to eat. Dr. Ferris was the only one whose appetite seemed unaffected.

When she saw a slush of ice cream in a crystal bowl before her, she noticed the sudden silence of the room and heard the screeching of the television machinery being dragged forward for action. *Now*—she thought, with a sinking sense of expectation, and knew that the same question mark was on every mind in the room. They were all staring at Galt. His face did not move or change.

No one had to call for silence, when Mr. Thompson waved to an announcer: the room did not seem to breathe.

"Fellow citizens," the announcer cried into a microphone, "of this country and of any other that's able to listen—from the grand ballroom of the Wayne-Falkland Hotel in New York City, we are bringing you the inauguration of the John Galt Plan!"

A rectangle of tensely bluish light appeared on the wall behind the speakers' table—a television screen to project for the guests the images which the country was now to see.

"The John Galt Plan for Peace, Prosperity and Profit!" cried the announcer, while a shivering picture of the ballroom sprang into view on the screen. "The dawn of a new age! The product of a harmonious collaboration between the humanitarian spirit of our leaders and the scientific genius of John Galt! If your faith in the future has been undermined by vicious rumors, you may now see for yourself our happily united family of leadership! . . . Ladies and gentlemen"—as the television camera swooped down to the speakers' table, and the stupefied face of Mr. Mowen filled the screen—"Mr. Horace Bussby Mowen, the American Industrialist!" The camera moved to an aged collection of facial muscles shaped in imitation of a smile. "General of the Army Whittington S. Thorpe!" The camera, like an eye at a police line-up, moved from face to scarred face—scarred by the ravages of fear, of evasion, of despair, of uncertainty, of self-loathing, of guilt. "Majority Leader of the National Legislature, Mr. Lucian Phelps! . . . Mr. Wesley Mouch! . . . Mr. Thompson!" The camera paused on Mr. Thompson; he gave a big grin to the nation, then turned and looked off-screen, to his left, with an air of triumphant expectancy. "Ladies and gentlemen," the announcer said solemnly, "John Galt!"

Good God!—thought Dagny—what are they doing? From the screen, the face of John Galt was looking at the nation, the face without pain or fear or guilt, implacable by virtue of serenity, invulnerable by virtue of self-esteem. *This* face—she thought—among those others? Whatever it is that they're planning, she thought, it's undone—nothing more can or has to be said—*there's* the product of one code and of the other, there's the choice, and whoever is human will know it.

"Mr. Galt's personal secretary," said the announcer, while the camera blurred hastily past the next face and went on. "Mr. Clarence 'Chick' Morrison . . . Admiral Homer Dawley . . . Mr.—"

She looked at the faces around her, wondering: Did they see the contrast? Did they know it? Did they see him? Did they want him to be real?

"This banquet," said Chick Morrison, who had taken over as master of ceremonies, "is in honor of the greatest figure of our time, the ablest producer, the man of the 'know-how,' the new leader of our economy—John Galt! If you have heard his extraordinary radio speech, you can have no doubt that *he* can make things work. Now he is here to tell you that he will make them work for *you*. If you have been misled by those old-fashioned extremists who claimed that he would never join us, that no merger is possible between his way of life and ours, that it's either one or the other—tonight's event will prove to you that anything can be reconciled and united!"

Once they have seen him—thought Dagny—can they wish to look at anybody else? Once they know that *he* is possible, that this is what man can be, what else can they want to seek? Can they now feel any desire except to achieve in their souls what *he* has achieved in his? Or are they going to be stopped by the fact that the Mouches, the Morrisons, the Thompsons of the world had not chosen to achieve it? Are they going to regard the Mouches as the human and *him* as the impossible?

The camera was roving over the ballroom, flashing to the screen and to the country the faces of the prominent guests, the faces of the tensely watchful leaders and—once in a while—the face of John Galt. He looked as if his perceptive eyes were studying the men outside this room, the men who were seeing him across the country; one could not tell whether he was listening: no reaction altered the composure of his face.

"I am proud to pay tribute tonight," said the leader of the Legislature, the next speaker, "to the greatest economic organizer the world has ever discovered, the most gifted administrator, the most brilliant planner—John Galt, the man who will save us! I am here to thank him in the name of the people!"

This—thought Dagny, with a sickened amusement—was the spectacle of the sincerity of the dishonest. The most fraudulent part of the fraud was that they meant it. They were offering Galt the best that their view of existence could offer, they were trying to tempt him with that which was their dream of life's highest fulfillment: this spread of mindless adulation, the unreality of this enormous pretense—approval without standards, tribute without content, honor without causes, admiration without reasons, love without a code of values.

"We have discarded all our petty differences," Wesley Mouch was now saying into the microphone, "all partisan opinions, all personal interests and selfish views—in order to serve under the selfless leadership of John Galt!"

Why are they listening?—thought Dagny. Don't they see the hallmark of death in those faces, and the hallmark of life in his? Which state do they wish to choose? Which state do they seek for mankind? . . . She looked at the faces in the ballroom. They were nervously blank; they showed nothing but the sagging weight of lethargy and the staleness of a chronic fear. They were looking at Galt and at Mouch, as if unable to perceive any difference between them or to feel concern if a difference existed, their empty, uncritical, unvaluing stare declaring: "Who am I to know?" She shuddered, remembering his sentence: "The man who declares, 'Who am I to know?' is declaring, 'Who am I to live?'" Did they care to live?—she thought. They did not seem to care even for the effort of raising that question. . . . She saw a few faces who seemed to care. They were looking at Galt with a desperate plea, with a wistfully tragic admiration—and with hands lying limply on the tables before them. These were the men who saw what he was, who lived in frustrated longing for his world—but tomorrow, if they saw him being murdered before them, their hands would hang as limply and their eyes would look away, saying, "Who am I to act?"

"Unity of action and purpose," said Mouch, "will bring us to a happier world. . . ."

Mr. Thompson leaned toward Galt and whispered with an amiable smile, "You'll have to say a few words to the country, later on, after me. No, no, not a long speech, just a sentence or two, no more. Just 'hello, folks' or something like that, so they'll recognize your voice." The faintly stressed pressure of the "secretary's" muzzle against Galt's side added a silent paragraph. Galt did not answer.

"The John Galt Plan," Wesley Mouch was saying, "will reconcile all conflicts. It will protect the property of the rich and give a greater share to the poor. It will cut down the burden of your taxes and provide you with more government benefits. It will lower prices and raise wages. It will give more freedom to the individual and strengthen the bonds of collective obligations. It will combine the efficiency of free enterprise with the generosity of a planned economy."

Dagny observed some faces—it took her an effort fully to believe it—who were looking at Galt with hatred. Jim was one of them, she noted. When the image of Mouch held the screen, these faces were relaxed in bored contentment, which was not pleasure, but the comfort of license, of knowing that nothing was demanded of them and nothing was firm or certain. When the camera flashed the image of Galt, their lips grew tight and their features were sharpened by a look of peculiar caution. She felt with sudden certainty that they feared the precision of his face, the unyielding clarity of his features, the look of being an entity, a look of asserting existence. They hate him for being himself—she thought, feeling a touch of cold horror, as the nature of their souls became real to her—they hate him for his capacity to live. Do *they* want to live?—she thought in self-mockery. Through the stunned numbness of her mind, she remembered the sound of his sentence: "The desire not to be anything, is the desire not to be."

It was now Mr. Thompson who was yelling into the microphone in his briskest and folksiest manner: "And I say to you: kick them in the teeth, all those doubters who're spreading disunity and fear! They told you that John Galt would never join us, didn't they? Well, here he is, in person, of his own free choice, at this table and at the head

of our State! Ready, willing and able to serve the people's cause!
Don't you ever again, any of you, start doubting or running or
giving up! Tomorrow is here today—and what a tomorrow! With three
meals a day for everyone on earth, with a car in every garage, and
with electric power given *free,* produced by some sort of a motor the
like of which we've never seen! And all you have to do is just be patient
a little while longer! Patience, faith and unity—*that's* the recipe for
progress! We must stand united among ourselves and united with the
rest of the world, as a great big happy family, all working for the
good of all! We have found a leader who will beat the record of our
richest and busiest past! It's his love for mankind that has made him
come here—to serve you, protect you and take care of you! He has
heard your pleas and has answered the call of our common human
duty! Every man is his brother's keeper! No man is an island unto
himself! And now you will hear his voice—now you will hear his
own message! . . . Ladies and gentlemen," he said solemnly, "John
Galt—to the collective family of mankind!"

The camera moved to Galt. He remained still for a moment. Then,
with so swift and expert a movement that his secretary's hand was
unable to match it, he rose to his feet, leaning sidewise, leaving the
pointed gun momentarily exposed to the sight of the world—then,
standing straight, facing the cameras, looking at all his invisible
viewers, he said:

"Get the hell out of my way!"

"Get the hell out of my way!"

Dr. Robert Stadler heard it on the radio in his car. He did not know whether the next sound, part-gasp, part-scream, part-laughter, started rising from him or from the radio—but he heard the click that cut them both off. The radio went dead. No further sounds came from the Wayne-Falkland Hotel.

He jerked his hand from knob to knob under the lighted dial. Nothing came through, no explanations, no pleas of technical trouble, no silence-hiding music. All stations were off the air.

He shuddered, he gripped the wheel, leaning forward across it, like a jockey at the close of a race, and his foot pressed down on the accelerator. The small stretch of highway before him bounced with the leaping of his headlights. There was nothing beyond the lighted strip but the emptiness of the prairies of Iowa.

He did not know why he had been listening to the broadcast; he did not know what made him tremble now. He chuckled abruptly—it sounded like a malevolent growl—either at the radio, or at those in the city, or at the sky.

He was watching the rare posts of highway numbers. He did not need to consult a map: for four days, that map had been printed on his brain, like a net of lines traced in acid. They could not take it away from him, he thought; they could not stop him. He felt as if he were being pursued; but there was nothing for miles behind him, except the two red lights on the rear of his car—like two small signals of danger, fleeing through the darkness of the Iowa plains.

The motive directing his hands and feet was four days behind him. It was the face of the man on the window sill, and the faces he had confronted when he had escaped from that room. He had cried to them that he could not deal with Galt and neither could they, that Galt would destroy them all, unless they destroyed him first. "Don't get smart, Professor," Mr. Thompson had answered coldly. "You've done an awful lot of yelling about hating his guts, but when it comes to action, you haven't helped us at all. I don't know which side you're on. If he doesn't give in to us peaceably, we might have to resort to pressure—such as hostages whom he wouldn't want to see hurt—and you're first on the list, Professor." *"I?"* he had screamed, shaking with terror and with bitterly desperate laughter. "I? But he damns me more than anyone on earth!" "How do I know?" Mr. Thompson had answered. "I hear that you used to be his teacher. And, don't forget, you're the only one he asked for."

His mind liquid with terror, he had felt as if he were about to be crushed between two walls advancing upon him: he had no chance, if Galt refused to surrender—and less chance, if Galt joined these men. It was then that a distant shape had come swimming forward in his mind: the image of a mushroom-domed structure in the middle of an Iowa plain.

All images had begun to fuse in his mind thereafter. Project X—he had thought, not knowing whether it was the vision of that structure or of a feudal castle commanding the countryside, that gave him the sense of an age and a world to which he belonged. . . . I'm Robert Stadler —he had thought—it's *my* property, it came from my discoveries, they said it was I who invented it. . . . I'll show them!—he had thought, not knowing whether he meant the man on the window sill or the others or the whole of mankind. . . . His thoughts had become like chips floating in a liquid, without connections: To seize control . . . I'll show them! . . . To seize control, to rule . . . There is no other way to live on earth. . . .

These had been the only words that named the plan in his mind. He had felt that the rest was clear to him—clear in the form of a savage emotion crying defiantly that he did not have to make it clear. He would seize control of Project X and he would rule a part of the country as his private feudal domain. The means? His emotion had answered: Somehow. The motive? His mind had repeated insistently that his motive was terror of Mr. Thompson's gang, that he was not safe among them any longer, that his plan was a practical necessity. In the depth of his liquid brain, his emotion had held another kind of terror, drowned along with the connections between his broken chips of words.

These chips had been the only compass directing his course through four days and nights—while he drove down deserted highways, across a country collapsing into chaos, while he developed a monomaniac's cunning for obtaining illegal purchases of gas, while he snatched random hours of restless sleep, in obscure motels, under assumed names. . . . I'm Robert Stadler—he had thought, his mind repeating it as a formula of omnipotence. . . . To seize control—he had thought, speeding against the futile traffic lights of half-abandoned towns—speeding on the vibrating steel of the Taggart Bridge across the Mississippi—speeding past the occasional ruins of farms in the empty stretches of Iowa. . . . I'll show them—he had thought—let them pursue, they won't stop me this time. . . . He had thought it, even though no one had pursued him—as no one was pursuing him now, but the taillights of his own car and the motive drowned in his mind.

He looked at his silent radio and chuckled; the chuckle had the emotional quality of a fist being shaken at space. It's I who am practical—he thought—I have no choice . . . I have no other way . . . I'll show all those insolent gangsters, who forget that I am Robert Stadler . . . They will all collapse, but I won't! . . . I'll survive! . . . I'll win! . . . I'll show them!

The words were like chunks of solid ground in his mind, in the midst of a fiercely silent swamp; the connections lay submerged at the bottom. If connected, his words would have formed the sentence: I'll show *him* that there is no other way to live on earth! . . .

The scattered lights in the distance ahead were the barracks erected on the site of Project X, now known as Harmony City. He observed, as he came closer, that something out of the ordinary was going on at Project X. The barbed-wire fence was broken, and no sentinels met him at the gate. But some sort of abnormal activity was churning in the patches of darkness and in the glare of some wavering spotlights: there were armored trucks and running figures and shouted orders and the gleam of bayonets. No one stopped his car. At the corner of a shanty, he saw the motionless body of a soldier sprawled on the ground. Drunk—he thought, preferring to think it, wondering why he felt unsure of it.

The mushroom structure crouched on a knoll before him; there were lights in the narrow slits of its windows—and the shapeless funnels protruded from under its dome, aimed at the darkness of the country. A soldier barred his way, when he alighted from his car at the entrance. The soldier was properly armed, but hatless, and his uniform seemed too sloppy. "Where are you going, bud?" he asked.

"Let me in!" Dr. Stadler ordered contemptuously.

"What's your business here?"

"I'm Dr. Robert Stadler."

"I'm Joe Blow. I said, What's your business? Are you one of the new or one of the old?"

"Let me in, you idiot! I'm Dr. Robert Stadler!"

It was not the name, but the tone of voice and the form of address that seemed to convince the soldier. "One of the new," he said and, opening the door, shouted to somebody inside, "Hey, Mac, take care of Grandpaw here, see what he wants!"

In the bare, dim hall of reinforced concrete, he was met by a man who might have been an officer, except that his tunic was open at the throat and a cigarette hung insolently in the corner of his mouth.

"Who are *you?*" he snapped, his hand jerking too swiftly to the holster on his hip.

"I'm Dr. Robert Stadler."

The name had no effect. "Who gave you permission to come here?"

"I need no permission."

This seemed to have an effect; the man removed the cigarette from his mouth. "Who sent for you?" he asked, a shade uncertainly.

"Will you please let me speak to the commandant?" Dr. Stadler demanded impatiently.

"The commandant? You're too late, brother."

"The chief engineer, then!"

"The chief-who? Oh, Willie? Willie's okay, he's one of us, but he's out on an errand just now."

There were other figures in the hall, listening with an apprehensive curiosity. The officer's hand summoned one of them to approach—an unshaved civilian with a shabby overcoat thrown over his shoulders. "What do you want?" he snapped at Stadler.

"Would someone please tell me where are the gentlemen of the scientific staff?" Dr. Stadler asked in the courteously peremptory tone of an order.

The two men glanced at each other, as if such a question were irrelevant in this place. "Do you come from Washington?" the civilian asked suspiciously.

"I do not. I will have you understand that I'm through with that Washington gang."

"Oh?" The man seemed pleased. "Are you a Friend of the People, then?"

"I would say that I'm the best friend the people ever had. I'm the man who gave them all this." He pointed around him.

"You did?" said the man, impressed. "Are you one of those who made a deal with the Boss?"

"*I'm* the boss here, from now on."

The men looked at each other, retreating a few steps. The officer asked, "Did you say the name was Stadler?"

"*Robert Stadler.* And if you don't know what that means, you'll find out!"

"Will you please follow me, sir?" said the officer, with shaky politeness.

What happened next was not clear to Dr. Stadler, because his mind refused to admit the reality of the things he was seeing. There were shifting figures in half-lighted, disordered offices, there were too many firearms on everybody's hips, there were senseless questions asked of him by jerky voices that alternated between impertinence and fear. He did not know whether any of them tried to give him an explanation; he would not listen; he could not permit this to be true. He kept stating in the tone of a feudal sovereign, "*I'm* the boss here, from now on . . . I give the orders . . . I came to take over . . . I own this place. . . . I am Dr. Robert Stadler—and if you don't know *that* name in *this* place, you have no business being here, you infernal idiots! You'll blow yourselves to pieces, if that's the state of your knowledge! Have you had a high-school course in physics? You don't look to me as if you've ever been allowed inside a high school, any of you! What are you doing here? Who are you?"

It took him a long time to grasp—when his mind could not block it any longer—that somebody had beaten him to his plan: somebody had held the same view of existence as his own and had set out to achieve the same future. He grasped that these men, who called themselves the Friends of the People, had seized possession of Project X, tonight, a few hours ago, intending to establish a reign of their own. He laughed in their faces, with bitterly incredulous contempt.

"You don't know what you're doing, you miserable juvenile delinquents! Do you think that you—you!—can handle a high-precision instrument of science? Who is your leader? I demand to see your leader!"

It was his tone of overbearing authority, his contempt and their own panic—the blind panic of men of unbridled violence, who have no standards of safety or danger—that made them waver and wonder whether he was, perhaps, some secret top-level member of their leadership; they were equally ready to defy or to obey any authority. After being shunted from one jittery commander to another, he found himself at last being led down iron stairways and down long, echoing, underground corridors of reinforced concrete to an audience with "The Boss" in person.

The Boss had taken refuge in the underground control room. Among the complex spirals of the delicate scientific machinery that produced the sound ray, against the wall panel of glittering levers, dials and gauges, known as the Xylophone, Robert Stadler faced the new ruler of Project X. It was Cuffy Meigs.

He wore a tight, semi-military tunic and leather leggings; the flesh of his neck bulged over the edge of his collar; his black curls were matted with sweat. He was pacing restlessly, unsteadily in front of the Xylophone, shouting orders to men who kept rushing in and out of the room:

"Send couriers to every county seat within our reach! Tell 'em that the Friends of the People have won! Tell 'em they're not to take orders from Washington any longer! The new capital of the People's Commonwealth is Harmony City, henceforth to be known as Meigsville! Tell 'em that I'll expect five hundred thousand dollars per every five thousand heads of population, by tomorrow morning—or else!"

It took some time before Cuffy Meigs' attention and bleary brown eyes could be drawn to focus on the person of Dr. Stadler. "Well, what is it? What is it?" he snapped.

"I am Dr. Robert Stadler."

"Huh?— Oh, yeah! Yeah! You're the big guy from outer spaces, aren't you? You're the fellow who catches atoms or something. Well, what on earth are you doing here?"

"It is I who should ask you that question."

"Huh? Look, Professor, I'm in no mood for jokes."

"I have come here to take control."

"Control? Of what?"

"Of this equipment. Of this place. Of the countryside within its radius of operation."

Meigs stared at him blankly for a moment, then asked softly, "How did you get here?"

"By car."

"I mean, whom did you bring with you?"

"Nobody."

"What weapons did you bring?"

"None. My name is sufficient."

"You came here alone, with your name and your car?"

"I did."

Cuffy Meigs burst out laughing in his face.

"Do you think," asked Dr. Stadler, "that *you* can operate an installation of this kind?"

"Run along, Professor, run along! Beat it, before I have you shot! We've got no use for intellectuals around here!"

"How much do you know about *this?*" Dr. Stadler pointed at the Xylophone.

"Who cares? Technicians are a dime a dozen these days! Beat it! This ain't Washington! I'm through with those impractical dreamers in Washington! They won't get anywhere, bargaining with that radio ghost and making speeches! Action—that's what's needed! Direct action! Beat it, Doc! Your day is over!" He was weaving unsteadily back and forth, catching at a lever of the Xylophone once in a while. Dr. Stadler realized that Meigs was drunk.

"Don't touch those levers, you fool!"

Meigs jerked his hand back involuntarily, then waved it defiantly at the panel. "I'll touch anything I please! Don't *you* tell me what to do!"

"Get away from that panel! Get out of here! This is mine! Do you understand? It's *my* property!"

"Property? Huh!" Meigs gave a brief bark that was a chuckle.

"I invented it! I created it! I made it possible!"

"You did? Well, many thanks, Doc. Many thanks, but we don't need you any longer. We've got our own mechanics."

"Have you any idea what I had to know in order to make it possible? You couldn't think of a single tube of it! Not a single bolt!"

Meigs shrugged. "Maybe not."

"Then how dare you think that you can own it? How dare you come here? What claim do you have to it?"

Meigs patted his holster. *"This."*

"Listen, you drunken lout!" cried Dr. Stadler. "Do you know what you're playing with?"

"Don't you talk to me like that, you old fool! Who are *you* to talk to me like that? I can break your neck with my bare hands! Don't you know who I am?"

"You're a scared thug way out of his depth!"

"Oh, I am, am I? I'm the Boss! I'm the Boss and I'm not going to be stopped by an old scarecrow like you! Get out of here!"

They stood staring at each other for a moment, by the panel of the Xylophone, both cornered by terror. The unadmitted root of Dr. Stadler's terror was his frantic struggle not to acknowledge that he was looking at his final product, that *this* was his spiritual son. Cuffy Meigs' terror had wider roots, it embraced all of existence; he had lived in chronic terror all his life, but now he was struggling not to acknowledge what it was that he had dreaded: in the moment of his triumph, when he expected to be safe, that mysterious, occult breed—the intellectual —was refusing to fear him and defying his power.

"Get out of here!" snarled Cuffy Meigs. "I'll call my men! I'll have you shot!"

"Get out of here, you lousy, brainless, swaggering moron!" snarled Dr. Stadler. "Do you think I'll let you cash in on *my* life? Do you think it's for *you* that I . . . that I sold—" He did not finish. "Stop touching those levers, God damn you!"

"Don't you give me orders! I don't need you to tell me what to do! You're not going to scare me with your classy mumbo-jumbo! I'll do as I please! What did I fight for, if I can't do as I please?" He chuckled and reached for a lever.

"Hey, Cuffy, take it easy!" yelled some figure in the back of the room, darting forward.

"Stand back!" roared Cuffy Meigs. "Stand back, all of you! Scared, am I? I'll show you who's boss!"

Dr. Stadler leaped to stop him—but Meigs shoved him aside with one arm, gave a gulp of laughter at the sight of Stadler falling to the floor, and, with the other arm, yanked a lever of the Xylophone.

The crash of sound—the screeching crash of ripped metal and of pressures colliding on conflicting circuits, the sound of a monster turning upon itself—was heard only inside the structure. No sound was heard outside. Outside, the structure merely rose into the air, suddenly and silently, cracked open into a few large pieces, shot some hissing streaks of blue light to the sky and came down as a pile of rubble. Within the circle of a radius of a hundred miles, enclosing parts of four states, telegraph poles fell like matchsticks, farmhouses collapsed into chips, city buildings went down as if slashed and minced by a single second's blow, with no time for a sound to be heard by the twisted bodies of the victims—and, on the circle's periphery, halfway across the Mississippi, the engine and the first six cars of a passenger train flew as a shower of metal into the water of the river, along with the western spans of the Taggart Bridge, cut in half.

On the site of what had once been Project X, nothing remained alive among the ruins—except, for some endless minutes longer, a huddle of torn flesh and screaming pain that had once been a great mind.

* * *

There was a sense of weightless freedom—thought Dagny—in the feeling that a telephone booth was her only immediate, absolute goal, with no concern for any of the goals of the passers-by in the streets around her. It did not make her feel estranged from the city: it made her feel, for the first time, that she owned the city and that she loved it, that she had never loved it before as she did in this moment, with so personal, solemn and confident a sense of possession. The night was still and clear; she looked at the sky; as her feeling was more solemn than joyous, but held the sense of a future joy—so the air was more windless than warm, but held the hint of a distant spring.

Get the hell out of my way—she thought, not with resentment, but almost with amusement, with a sense of detachment and deliverance, addressing it to the passers-by, to the traffic when it impeded her hurried progress, and to any fear she had known in the past. It was less than an hour ago that she had heard him utter that sentence, and his voice still seemed to ring in the air of the streets, merging into a distant hint of laughter.

She had laughed exultantly, in the ballroom of the Wayne-Falkland, when she had heard him say it; she had laughed, her hand pressed to her mouth, so that the laughter was only in her eyes—and in his, when he had looked straight at her and she had known that he heard it. They had looked at each other for the span of a second, above the heads of the gasping, screaming crowd—above the crash of the microphones being shattered, though all stations had been instantly cut off—above the bursts of breaking glass on falling tables, as some people went stampeding to the doors.

Then she had heard Mr. Thompson cry, waving his arm at Galt, "Take him back to his room, but guard him with your lives!"—and the crowd had parted as three men led him out. Mr. Thompson seemed to collapse for a moment, dropping his forehead on his arm, but he rallied, jumped to his feet, waved vaguely at his henchmen to follow and rushed out, through a private side exit. No one addressed or instructed the guests: some were running blindly to escape, others sat still, not daring to move. The ballroom was like a ship without captain. She cut through the crowd and followed the clique. No one tried to stop her.

She found them huddled in a small, private study: Mr. Thompson was slumped in an armchair, clutching his head with both hands, Wesley Mouch was moaning, Eugene Lawson was sobbing with the sound of a nasty child's rage, Jim was watching the others with an oddly expectant intensity. "I told you so!" Dr. Ferris was shouting. "I told you so, didn't I? *That's* where you get with your 'peaceful persuasion'!"

She remained standing by the door. They seemed to notice her presence, but they did not seem to care.

"I resign!" yelled Chick Morrison. "I resign! I'm through! I don't know what to say to the country! I can't think! I won't try! It's no use! I couldn't help it! You're not going to blame me! I've resigned!" He waved his arms in some shapeless gesture of futility or farewell, and ran out of the room.

"He has a hide-out all stocked for himself in Tennessee," said Tinky Holloway reflectively, as if he, too, had taken a similar precaution and were now wondering whether the time had come.

"He won't keep it for long, if he gets there at all," said Mouch. "With the gangs of raiders and the state of transportation—" He spread his hands and did not finish.

She knew what thoughts were filling the pause; she knew that no matter what private escapes these men had once provided for themselves, they were now grasping the fact that all of them were trapped.

She observed that there was no terror in their faces; she saw hints of it, but it looked like a perfunctory terror. Their expressions ranged from blank apathy to the relieved look of cheats who had believed that the game could end no other way and were making no effort to contest it or regret it—to the petulant blindness of Lawson, who refused to be conscious of anything—to the peculiar intensity of Jim, whose face suggested a secret smile.

"Well? Well?" Dr. Ferris was asking impatiently, with the crackling energy of a man who feels at home in a world of hysteria. "What are you *now* going to do with him? Argue? Debate? Make speeches?"

No one answered.

"He . . . has . . . to . . . save . . . us," said Mouch slowly, as if straining the last of his mind into blankness and delivering an ultimatum to reality. "He has to . . . take over . . . and save the system."

"Why don't you write him a love letter about it?" said Ferris.

"We've got to . . . *make him* . . . take over . . . We've got to force him to rule," said Mouch in the tone of a sleepwalker.

"Now," said Ferris, suddenly dropping his voice, "do you see what a valuable establishment the State Science Institute really is?"

Mouch did not answer him, but she observed that they all seemed to know what he meant.

"You objected to that private research project of mine as 'impractical,'" said Ferris softly. "But what did I tell you?"

Mouch did not answer; he was cracking his knuckles.

"This is no time for squeamishness," James Taggart spoke up with unexpected vigor, but his voice, too, was oddly low. "We don't have to be sissies about it."

"It seems to me . . ." said Mouch dully, "that . . . that the end justifies the means . . ."

"It's too late for any scruples or any principles," said Ferris. "Only direct action can work now."

No one answered; they were acting as if they wished that their pauses, not their words, would state what they were discussing.

"It won't work," said Tinky Holloway. "He won't give in."

"That's what *you* think!" said Ferris, and chuckled. "You haven't seen our experimental model in action. Last month, we got three confessions in three unsolved murder cases."

"If . . ." started Mr. Thompson, and his voice cracked suddenly into a moan, "if he dies, we all perish!"

"Don't worry," said Ferris. "He won't. The Ferris Persuader is safely calculated against that possibility."

Mr. Thompson did not answer.

"It seems to me . . . that we have no other choice . . ." said Mouch; it was almost a whisper.

They remained silent; Mr. Thompson was struggling not to see that they were all looking at him. Then he cried suddenly, "Oh, do anything you want! I couldn't help it! Do anything you want!"

Dr. Ferris turned to Lawson. "Gene," he said tensely, still whispering, "run to the radio-control office. Order all stations to stand by. Tell them that I'll have Mr. Galt on the air within three hours."

Lawson leaped to his feet, with a sudden, mirthful grin, and ran out of the room.

She knew. She knew what they intended doing and what it was within them that made it possible. They did not think that this would succeed. They did not think that Galt would give in; they did not want him to give in. They did not think that anything could save them now; they did not want to be saved. Moved by the panic of their nameless emotions, they had fought against reality all their lives—and now they had reached a moment when at last they felt at home. They did not have to know why they felt it, they who had chosen never to know what they felt—they merely experienced a sense of recognition, since *this* was what they had been seeking, *this* was the kind of reality that had been implied in all of their feelings, their actions, their desires, their choices, their dreams. This was the nature and the method of the rebellion against existence and of the undefined quest for an unnamed Nirvana. They did not want to live; they wanted *him* to die.

The horror she felt was only a brief stab, like the wrench of a switching perspective: she grasped that the objects she had thought to be human were not. She was left with a sense of clarity, of a final answer and of the need to act. He was in danger; there was no time and no room in her consciousness to waste emotion on the actions of the subhuman.

"We must make sure," Wesley Mouch was whispering, "that nobody ever learns about it . . ."

"Nobody will," said Ferris; their voices had the cautious drone of conspirators. "It's a secret, separate unit on the Institute grounds . . . Sound-proofed and safely distant from the rest . . . Only a very few of our staff have ever entered it. . . ."

"If we were to fly—" said Mouch, and stopped abruptly, as if he had caught some warning in Ferris' face.

She saw Ferris' eyes move to her, as if he had suddenly remembered her presence. She held his glance, letting him see the untroubled indifference of hers, as if she had neither cared nor understood. Then, as if merely grasping the signal of a private discussion, she turned slowly, with the suggestion of a shrug, and left the room. She knew that they were now past the stage of worrying about her.

She walked with the same unhurried indifference through the halls and through the exit of the hotel. But a block away, when she had turned a corner, her head flew up and the folds of her evening gown slammed like a sail against her legs with the sudden violence of the speed of her steps.

And now, as she rushed through the darkness, thinking only of finding a telephone booth, she felt a new sensation rising irresistibly within her, past the immediate tension of danger and concern: it was the sense of freedom of a world that had never had to be obstructed.

She saw the wedge of light on the sidewalk, that came from the window of a bar. No one gave her a second glance, as she crossed the half-deserted room: the few customers were still waiting and whispering tensely in front of the crackling blue void of an empty television screen.

Standing in the tight space of the telephone booth, as in the cabin of a ship about to take off for a different planet, she dialed the number OR 6-5693.

The voice that answered at once was Francisco's. "Hello?"

"Francisco?"

"Hello, Dagny. I was expecting you to call."

"Did you hear the broadcast?"

"I did."

"They are now planning to force him to give in." She kept her voice to the tone of a factual report. "They intend to torture him. They have some machine called the Ferris Persuader, in an isolated unit on the grounds of the State Science Institute. It's in New Hampshire. They mentioned flying. They mentioned that they would have him on the radio within three hours."

"I see. Are you calling from a public phone booth?"

"Yes."

"You're still in evening clothes, aren't you?"

"Yes."

"Now listen carefully. Go home, change your clothes, pack a few things you'll need, take your jewelry and any valuables that you can carry, take some warm clothing. We won't have time to do it later.

Meet me in forty minutes, on the northwest corner, two blocks east of the main entrance of the Taggart Terminal."

"Right."

"So long, Slug."

"So long, Frisco."

She was in the bedroom of her apartment, in less than five minutes, tearing off her evening gown. She left it lying in the middle of the floor, like the discarded uniform of an army she was not serving any longer. She put on a dark blue suit and—remembering Galt's words—a white, high-collared sweater. She packed a suitcase and a bag with a strap that she could carry swung over her shoulder. She put her jewelry in a corner of the bag, including the bracelet of Rearden Metal she had earned in the outside world, and the five-dollar gold piece she had earned in the valley.

It was easy to leave the apartment and to lock the door, even though she knew she would probably never open it again. It seemed harder, for a moment, when she came to her office. No one had seen her come in; the anteroom of her office was empty; the great Taggart Building seemed unusually quiet. She stood looking for a moment at this room and at all the years it had contained. Then she smiled—no, it was not too hard, she thought; she opened her safe and took the documents she had come here to get. There was nothing else that she wanted to take from her office—except the picture of Nathaniel Taggart and the map of Taggart Transcontinental. She broke the two frames, folded the picture and the map, and slipped them into her suitcase.

She was locking the suitcase, when she heard the sound of hurrying steps. The door flew open and the chief engineer rushed in; he was shaking; his face was distorted.

"Miss Taggart!" he cried. "Oh, thank God, Miss Taggart, you're here! We've been calling for you all over!"

She did not answer; she looked at him inquiringly.

"Miss Taggart, have you heard?"

"What?"

"Then you haven't! Oh God, Miss Taggart, it's . . . I can't believe it, I still can't believe it, but . . . Oh God, what are we going to do? The . . . the Taggart Bridge is gone!"

She stared at him, unable to move.

"It's gone! Blown up! Blown up, apparently, in one second! Nobody knows for certain what happened—but it looks like . . . they think that something went wrong at Project X and . . . it looks like those sound rays, Miss Taggart! We can't get through to any point within a radius of a hundred miles! It's not possible, it can't be possible, but it looks as if everything in that circle has been wiped out! . . . We can't get any answers! Nobody can get an answer—the newspapers, the radio stations, the police! We're still checking, but the stories that are coming from the rim of that circle are—" He shuddered. "Only one thing is certain: the bridge is gone! Miss Taggart! We don't know what to do!"

She leaped to her desk and seized the telephone receiver. Her hand stopped in mid-air. Then, slowly, twistedly, with the greatest effort ever demanded of her, she began to move her arm down to place the receiver back. It seemed to her that it took a long time, as if her arm had to move against some atmospheric pressure that no human body could combat—and in the span of these few brief moments, in the stillness of a blinding pain, she knew what Francisco had felt, that night, twelve years ago—and what a boy of twenty-six had felt when he had looked at his motor for the last time.

"Miss Taggart!" cried the chief engineer. "We don't know what to do!"

The receiver clicked softly back into its cradle. "I don't, either," she answered.

In a moment, she knew it was over. She heard her voice telling the man to check further and report to her later—and she waited for the sound of his steps to vanish in the echoing silence of the hall.

Crossing the concourse of the Terminal for the last time, she glanced at the statue of Nathaniel Taggart—and remembered a promise she had made. It would be only a symbol now, she thought, but it would be the kind of farewell that Nathaniel Taggart deserved. She had no other writing instrument, so she took the lipstick from her bag and, smiling up at the marble face of the man who would have understood, she drew a large sign of the dollar on the pedestal under his feet.

She was first to reach the corner, two blocks east of the Terminal entrance. As she waited, she observed the first trickles of the panic that was soon to engulf the city: there were automobiles driving too fast, some of them loaded with household effects, there were too many police cars speeding by, and too many sirens bursting in the distance. The news of the destruction of the Bridge was apparently spreading through the city; they would know that the city was doomed and they would start a stampede to escape—but they had no place to go, and it was not her concern any longer.

She saw Francisco's figure approaching from some distance away; she recognized the swiftness of his walk, before she could distinguish the face under the cap pulled low over his eyes. She caught the moment when he saw her, as he came closer. He waved his arm, with a smile of greeting. Some conscious stress in the sweep of his arm made it the gesture of a d'Anconia, welcoming the arrival of a long-awaited traveler at the gates of his own domain.

When he approached, she stood solemnly straight and, looking at his face and at the buildings of the greatest city in the world, as at the kind of witnesses she wanted, she said slowly, her voice confident and steady:

"I swear—by my life and my love of it—that I will never live for the sake of another man, nor ask another man to live for mine."

He inclined his head, as if in sign of admittance. His smile was now a salute.

Then he took her suitcase with one hand, her arm with the other, and said, "Come on."

* * *

The unit known as "Project F"—in honor of its originator, Dr. Ferris—was a small structure of reinforced concrete, low on the slope of the hill that supported the State Science Institute on a higher, more public level. Only the small gray patch of the unit's roof could be seen from the Institute's windows, hidden in a jungle of ancient trees; it looked no bigger than the cover of a manhole.

The unit consisted of two stories in the shape of a small cube placed asymmetrically on top of a larger one. The first story had no windows, only a door studded with iron spikes; the second story had but one window, as if in reluctant concession to daylight, like a face with a single eye. The men on the staff of the Institute felt no curiosity about that structure and avoided the paths that led down to its door; nobody had ever suggested it, but they had the impression that the structure housed a project devoted to experiments with the germs of deadly diseases.

The two floors were occupied by laboratories that contained a great many cages with guinea pigs, dogs and rats. But the heart and meaning of the structure was a room in its cellar, deep under the ground; the room had been incompetently lined with the porous sheets of soundproofing material; the sheets had begun to crack and the naked rock of a cave showed through.

The unit was always protected by a squad of four special guards. Tonight, the squad had been augmented to sixteen, summoned for emergency duty by a long-distance telephone call from New York. The guards, as well as all other employees of "Project F," had been carefully chosen on the basis of a single qualification: an unlimited capacity for obedience.

The sixteen were stationed for the night outside the structure and in the deserted laboratories above the ground, where they remained uncritically on duty, with no curiosity about anything that might be taking place below.

In the cellar room, under the ground, Dr. Ferris, Wesley Mouch and James Taggart sat in armchairs lined up against one wall. A machine that looked like a small cabinet of irregular shape stood in a corner across from them. Its face bore rows of glass dials, each dial marked by a segment of red, a square screen that looked like an amplifier, rows of numbers, rows of wooden knobs and plastic buttons, a single lever controlling a switch at one side and a single red glass button at the other. The face of the machine seemed to have more expression than the face of the mechanic in charge of it; he was a husky young man in a sweat-stained shirt with sleeves rolled above the elbows; his pale blue eyes were glazed by an enormously conscientious concentration on his task; he moved his lips once in a while, as if reciting a memorized lesson.

A short wire led from the machine to an electric storage battery behind it. Long coils of wire, like the twisted arms of an octopus, stretched forward across the stone floor, from the machine to a leather mattress spread under a cone of violent light. John Galt lay strapped to the mattress. He was naked; the small metal disks of electrodes at the ends of the wires were attached to his wrists, his shoulders, his hips and his ankles; a device resembling a stethoscope was attached to his chest and connected to the amplifier.

"Get this straight," said Dr. Ferris, addressing him for the first time. "We want you to take full power over the economy of the country. We want you to become a dictator. We want you to rule. Understand? We want you to give orders and to figure out the right orders to give. What we want, we mean to get. Speeches, logic, arguments or passive obedience won't save you now. We want ideas—or else. We won't let you out of here until you tell us the exact measures you'll take to save our system. Then we'll have you tell it to the country over the radio." He raised his wrist, displaying a stop-watch. "I'll give you thirty seconds to decide whether you want to start talking right now. If not, then *we'll* start. Do you understand?"

Galt was looking straight at them, his face expressionless, as if he understood too much. He did not answer.

They heard the sound of the stop-watch in the silence, counting off the seconds, and the sound of Mouch's choked, irregular breathing as he gripped the arms of his chair.

Ferris waved a signal to the mechanic at the machine. The mechanic threw the switch; it lighted the red glass button and set off two sounds: one was the low, humming drone of an electric generator, the other was a peculiar beat, as regular as the ticking of a clock, but with an oddly muffled resonance. It took them a moment to realize that it came from the amplifier and that they were hearing the beat of Galt's heart.

"Number three," said Ferris, raising a finger in signal.

The mechanic pressed a button under one of the dials. A long shudder ran through Galt's body; his left arm shook in jerking spasms, convulsed by the electric current that circled between his wrist and shoulder. His head fell back, his eyes closed, his lips drawn tight. He made no sound.

When the mechanic lifted his finger off the button, Galt's arm stopped shaking. He did not move.

The three men glanced about them with an instant's look of groping. Ferris' eyes were blank, Mouch's terrified, Taggart's disappointed. The sound of the thumping beat went on through the silence.

"Number two," said Ferris.

It was Galt's right leg that twisted in convulsions, with the current now circling between his hip and ankle. His hands gripped the edges of the mattress. His head jerked once, from side to side, then lay still. The beating of the heart grew faintly faster.

Mouch was drawing away, pressing against the back of his armchair. Taggart was sitting on the edge of his, leaning forward.

"Number one, gradual," said Ferris.

Galt's torso jerked upward and fell back and twisted in long shudders, straining against his strapped wrists—as the current was now running from his one wrist to the other, across his lungs. The mechanic was slowly turning a knob, increasing the voltage of the current; the needle on the dial was moving toward the red segment that marked danger. Galt's breath was coming in broken, panting sounds out of convulsed lungs.

"Had enough?" snarled Ferris, when the current went off.

Galt did not answer. His lips moved faintly, opening for air. The beat from the stethoscope was racing. But his breath was falling to an even rhythm, by a controlled effort at relaxation.

"You're too easy on him!" yelled Taggart, staring at the naked body on the mattress.

Galt opened his eyes and glanced at them for a moment. They could tell nothing, except that his glance was steady and fully conscious. Then he dropped his head again and lay still, as if he had forgotten them.

His naked body looked strangely out of place in this cellar. They knew it, though none of them would identify that knowledge. The long lines of his body, running from his ankles to the flat hips, to the angle of the waist, to the straight shoulders, looked like a statue of ancient Greece, sharing that statue's meaning, but stylized to a longer, lighter, more active form and a gaunter strength, suggesting more restless an energy—the body, not of a chariot driver, but of a builder of airplanes. And as the meaning of a statue of ancient Greece—the statue of man as a god—clashed with the spirit of this century's halls, so his body clashed with a cellar devoted to prehistorical activities. The clash was the greater, because he seemed to belong with electric wires, with stainless steel, with precision instruments, with the levers of a control board. Perhaps—this was the thought most fiercely resisted and most deeply buried at the bottom of his watchers' sensations, the thought they knew only as a diffused hatred and an unfocused terror—perhaps it was the absence of such statues from the modern world that had transformed a generator into an octopus and brought a body such as his into its tentacles.

"I understand you're some sort of electrical expert," said Ferris, and chuckled. "So are we—don't you think so?"

Two sounds answered him in the silence: the drone of the generator and the beating of Galt's heart.

"The mixed series!" ordered Ferris, waving one finger at the mechanic.

The shocks now came at irregular, unpredictable intervals, one after another or minutes apart. Only the shuddering convulsions of Galt's legs, arms, torso or entire body showed whether the current was racing between two particular electrodes or through all of them at once. The needles on the dials kept coming close to the red marks, then receding: the machine was calculated to inflict the maximum intensity of pain without damaging the body of the victim.

It was the watchers who found it unbearable to wait through the minutes of the pauses filled with the sound of the heartbeat: the heart was now racing in an irregular rhythm. The pauses were calculated to let that beat slow down, but allow no relief to the victim, who had to wait for a shock at any moment.

Galt lay relaxed, as if not attempting to fight the pain, but surrendering to it, not attempting to negate it, but to bear it. When his lips parted for breath and a sudden jolt slammed them tight again, he did not resist the shaking rigidity of his body, but he let it vanish the instant the current left him. Only the skin of his face was pulled tight, and the sealed line of his lips twisted sidewise once in a while. When a shock raced through his chest, the gold-copper strands of his hair flew with the jerking of his head, as if waving in a gust of wind, beating against his face, across his eyes. The watchers wondered why his hair seemed to be growing darker, until they realized that it was drenched in sweat.

The terror of hearing one's own heart struggling as if about to burst at any moment, had been intended to be felt by the victim. It was the torturers who were trembling with terror, as they listened to the jagged, broken rhythm and missed a breath with every missing beat. It sounded now as if the heart were leaping, beating frantically against its cage of ribs, in agony and in a desperate anger. The heart was protesting; the man would not. He lay still, his eyes closed, his hands relaxed, hearing his heart as it fought for his life.

Wesley Mouch was first to break. "Oh God, Floyd!" he screamed. "Don't kill him! Don't dare kill him! If he dies, we die!"

"He won't," snarled Ferris. "He'll wish he did, but he won't! The machine won't let him! It's mathematically computed! It's safe!"

"Oh, isn't it enough? He'll obey us now! I'm sure he'll obey!"

"No! It's not enough! I don't want him to obey! I want him to *believe!* To accept! To *want* to accept! We've got to have him work for us *voluntarily!*"

"Go ahead!" cried Taggart. "What are you waiting for? Can't you make the current stronger? He hasn't even screamed yet!"

"What's the matter with you?" gasped Mouch, catching a glimpse of Taggart's face while a current was twisting Galt's body: Taggart was staring at it intently, yet his eyes seemed glazed and dead, but around that inanimate stare the muscles of his face were pulled into an obscene caricature of enjoyment.

"Had enough?" Ferris kept yelling to Galt. "Are you ready to want what *we* want?"

They heard no answer. Galt raised his head once in a while and looked at them. There were dark rings under his eyes, but the eyes were clear and conscious.

In mounting panic, the watchers lost their sense of context and language—and their three voices blended into a progression of indiscriminate shrieks: "We want you to take over! . . . We want you to rule! . . . We order you to give orders! . . . We demand that you dictate! . . . We order you to save us! . . . We order you to think! . . ."

They heard no answer but the beating of the heart on which their own lives depended.

The current was shooting through Galt's chest and the beating was coming in irregular spurts, as if it were racing and stumbling—when suddenly his body fell still, relaxing: the beating had stopped.

The silence was like a stunning blow, and before they had time to scream, their horror was topped by another: by the fact that Galt opened his eyes and raised his head.

Then they realized that the drone of the motor had ceased, too, and that the red light had gone out on the control panel: the current had stopped; the generator was dead.

The mechanic was jabbing his finger at the button, to no avail. He yanked the lever of the switch again and again. He kicked the side of the machine. The red light would not go on; the sound did not return.

"Well?" snapped Ferris. "Well? What's the matter?"

"The generator's on the blink," said the mechanic helplessly.

"What's the matter with it?"

"I don't know."

"Well, find out and fix it!"

The man was not a trained electrician; he had been chosen, not for his knowledge, but for his uncritical capacity for pushing any buttons; the effort he needed to learn his task was such that his consciousness could be relied upon to have no room for anything else. He opened the rear panel of the machine and stared in bewilderment at the intricate coils: he could find nothing visibly out of order. He put on his rubber gloves, picked up a pair of pliers, tightened a few bolts at random, and scratched his head.

"I don't know," he said; his voice had a sound of helpless docility. "Who am I to know?"

The three men were on their feet, crowding behind the machine to stare at its recalcitrant organs. They were acting merely by reflex: they knew that they did not know.

"But you've *got* to fix it!" yelled Ferris. "It's *got* to work! We've *got* to have electricity!"

"We must continue!" cried Taggart; he was shaking. "It's ridiculous! I won't have it! I won't be interrupted! I won't let *him* off!" He pointed in the direction of the mattress.

"Do something!" Ferris was crying to the mechanic. "Don't just stand there! Do something! Fix it! I order you to fix it!"

"But I don't know what's wrong with it," said the man, blinking.

"Then find out!"

"How am I to find out?"

"I order you to fix it! Do you hear me? Make it work—or I'll fire you and throw you in jail!"

"But I don't know what's wrong with it." The man sighed, bewildered. "I don't know what to do."

"It's the vibrator that's out of order," said a voice behind them; they whirled around; Galt was struggling for breath, but he was speaking in the brusque, competent tone of an engineer. "Take it out and pry off the aluminum cover. You'll find a pair of contacts fused together. Force them apart, take a small file and clean up the pitted surfaces. Then replace the cover, plug it back into the machine—and your generator will work."

There was a long moment of total silence.

The mechanic was staring at Galt; he was holding Galt's glance—and even he was able to recognize the nature of the sparkle in the dark green eyes: it was a sparkle of contemptuous mockery.

He made a step back. In the incoherent dimness of his consciousness, in some wordless, shapeless, unintelligible manner, even he suddenly grasped the meaning of what was occurring in that cellar.

He looked at Galt—he looked at the three men—he looked at the machine. He shuddered, he dropped his pliers and ran out of the room.

Galt burst out laughing.

The three men were backing slowly away from the machine. They were struggling not to allow themselves to understand what the mechanic had understood.

"No!" cried Taggart suddenly, glancing at Galt and leaping forward. "No! I won't let him get away with it!" He fell down on his knees, groping frantically to find the aluminum cylinder of the vibrator. "*I'll* fix it! I'll work it myself! We've got to go on! We've got to break him!"

"Take it easy, Jim," said Ferris uneasily, jerking him up to his feet.

"Hadn't we . . . hadn't we better lay off for the night?" said Mouch pleadingly; he was looking at the door through which the mechanic had escaped, his glance part-envy, part-terror.

"No!" cried Taggart.

"Jim, hasn't he had enough? Don't forget, we have to be careful."

"No! He hasn't had enough! He hasn't even screamed yet!"

"Jim!" cried Mouch suddenly, terrified by something in Taggart's face. "We can't afford to kill him! You know it!"

"I don't care! I want to break him! I want to hear him scream! I want—"

And then it was Taggart who screamed. It was a long, sudden, piercing scream, as if at some sudden sight, though his eyes were staring at space and seemed blankly sightless. The sight he was confronting was within him. The protective walls of emotion, of evasion, of pretense, of semi-thinking and pseudo-words, built up by him through all of his years, had crashed in the span of one moment—the moment when he knew that he wanted Galt to die, knowing fully that his own death would follow.

He was suddenly seeing the motive that had directed all the actions of his life. It was not his incommunicable soul or his love for others or his social duty or any of the fraudulent sounds by which he had maintained his self-esteem: it was the lust to destroy whatever was living, for the sake of whatever was not. It was the urge to defy reality by the destruction of every living value, for the sake of proving to himself that *he* could exist in defiance of reality and would never have to be bound by any solid, immutable facts. A moment ago, he had been able to feel that he hated Galt above all men, that the hatred was proof of Galt's evil, which he need define no further, that he wanted Galt to be destroyed for the sake of his own survival. Now he knew that he had wanted Galt's destruction at the price of his own destruction to follow, he knew that he had never wanted to survive, he knew that it was Galt's *greatness* he had wanted to torture and destroy—he was seeing it as greatness by his own admission, greatness by the only standard that existed, whether anyone chose to admit it or not: the greatness of a man who was master of reality in a manner no other had equaled. In the moment when he, James Taggart, had found himself facing the ultimatum: to accept reality or die, it was death his emotions had chosen, death, rather than surrender to that realm of which Galt was so radiant a son. In the person of Galt—he knew—he had sought the destruction of all existence.

It was not by means of words that this knowledge confronted his consciousness: as all his knowledge had consisted of emotions, so now he was held by an emotion and a vision that he had no power to dispel. He was no longer able to summon the fog to conceal the sight of all those blind alleys he had struggled never to be forced to see: now, at the end of every alley, he was seeing his hatred of existence—he was seeing the face of Cherryl Taggart with her joyous eagerness to live and that it was this particular eagerness he had always wanted to defeat—he was seeing his face as the face of a killer whom all men should rightfully loathe, who destroyed values for being values, who killed in order not to discover his own irredeemable evil.

"No . . ." he moaned, staring at that vision, shaking his head to escape it. "No . . . No . . ."

"Yes," said Galt.

He saw Galt's eyes looking straight at his, as if Galt were seeing the things he was seeing.

"I told you that on the radio, didn't I?" said Galt.

This was the stamp James Taggart had dreaded, from which there was no escape: the stamp and proof of objectivity. "No . . ." he said feebly once more, but it was no longer the voice of a living consciousness.

He stood for a moment, staring blindly at space, then his legs gave way, folding limply, and he sat on the floor, still staring, unaware of his action or surroundings.

"Jim . . . !" called Mouch. There was no answer.

Mouch and Ferris did not ask themselves or wonder what it was that had happened to Taggart: they knew that they must never attempt to discover it, under peril of sharing his fate. They knew who it was that had been broken tonight. They knew that *this* was the end of James Taggart, whether his physical body survived or not.

"Let's . . . let's get Jim out of here," said Ferris shakily. "Let's get him to a doctor . . . or somewhere . . ."

They pulled Taggart to his feet; he did not resist, he obeyed lethargically, and he moved his feet when pushed. It was he who had reached the state to which he had wanted Galt to be reduced. Holding his arms at both sides, his two friends led him out of the room.

He saved them from the necessity of admitting to themselves that they wanted to escape Galt's eyes. Galt was watching them; his glance was too austerely perceptive.

"We'll be back," snapped Ferris to the chief of the guards. "Stay here and don't let anyone in. Understand? No one."

They pushed Taggart into their car, parked by the trees at the entrance. "We'll be back," said Ferris to no one in particular, to the trees and the darkness of the sky.

For the moment, their only certainty was that they had to escape from that cellar—the cellar where the living generator was left tied by the side of the dead one.

IN THE NAME OF THE BEST WITHIN US

Dagny walked straight toward the guard who stood at the door of "Project F." Her steps sounded purposeful, even and open, ringing in the silence of the path among the trees. She raised her head to a ray of moonlight, to let him recognize her face.

"Let me in," she said.

"No admittance," he answered in the voice of a robot. "By order of Dr. Ferris."

"I am here by order of Mr. Thompson."

"Huh? . . . I . . . I don't know about that."

"I do."

"I mean, Dr. Ferris hasn't told me . . . ma'am."

"*I* am telling you."

"But I'm not supposed to take any orders from anyone excepting Dr. Ferris."

"Do you wish to disobey Mr. Thompson?"

"Oh, no, ma'am! But . . . but if Dr. Ferris said to let nobody in, that means nobody—" He added uncertainly and pleadingly, "—doesn't it?"

"Do you know that I am Dagny Taggart and that you've seen my pictures in the papers with Mr. Thompson and all the top leaders of the country?"

"Yes, ma'am."

"Then decide whether you wish to disobey their orders."

"Oh, no, ma'am! I don't!"

"Then let me in."

"But I can't disobey Dr. Ferris, either!"

"Then choose."

"But I can't choose, ma'am! Who am I to choose?"

"You'll have to."

"Look," he said hastily, pulling a key from his pocket and turning to the door, "I'll ask the chief. He—"

"No," she said.

Some quality in the tone of her voice made him whirl back to her: she was holding a gun pointed levelly at his heart.

"Listen carefully," she said. "Either you let me in or I shoot you. You may try to shoot me first, if you can. You have that choice—and no other. Now decide."

His mouth fell open and the key dropped from his hand.

"Get out of my way," she said.

He shook his head frantically, pressing his back against the door. "Oh Christ, ma'am!" he gulped in the whine of a desperate plea. "I can't shoot at you, seeing as you come from Mr. Thompson! And I can't let you in against the word of Dr. Ferris! What am I to do? I'm only a little fellow! I'm only obeying orders! It's not up to me!"

"It's your life," she said.

"If you let me ask the chief, he'll tell me, he'll—"

"I won't let you ask anyone."

"But how do I know that you *really* have an order from Mr. Thompson?"

"You don't. Maybe I haven't. Maybe I'm acting on my own—and you'll be punished for obeying me. Maybe I have—and you'll be thrown in jail for disobeying. Maybe Dr. Ferris and Mr. Thompson agree about this. Maybe they don't—and you have to defy one or the other. These are the things you have to decide. There is no one to ask, no one to call, no one to tell you. You will have to decide them yourself."

"But I *can't* decide! Why me?"

"Because it's *your* body that's barring my way."

"But I can't decide! I'm not *supposed* to decide!"

"I'll count to three," she said. "Then I'll shoot."

"Wait! Wait! I haven't said yes or no!" he cried, cringing tighter against the door, as if immobility of mind and body were his best protection.

"One—" she counted; she could see his eyes staring at her in terror —"Two—" she could see that the gun held less terror for him than the alternative she offered—"Three."

Calmly and impersonally, she, who would have hesitated to fire at an animal, pulled the trigger and fired straight at the heart of a man who had wanted to exist without the responsibility of consciousness.

Her gun was equipped with a silencer; there was no sound to attract anyone's attention, only the thud of a body falling at her feet.

She picked up the key from the ground—then waited for a few brief moments, as had been agreed upon.

Francisco was first to join her, coming from behind a corner of the building, then Hank Rearden, then Ragnar Danneskjöld. There had been four guards posted at intervals among the trees, around the building. They were now disposed of: one was dead, three were left in the brush, bound and gagged.

She handed the key to Francisco without a word. He unlocked the door and went in, alone, leaving the door open to the width of an inch. The three others waited outside, by that opening.

The hall was lighted by a single naked bulb stuck in the middle of the ceiling. A guard stood at the foot of the stairs leading to the second floor.

"Who are you?" he cried at the sight of Francisco entering as if he owned the place. "Nobody's supposed to come in here tonight!"

"I did," said Francisco.

"Why did Rusty let you in?"

"He must have had his reasons."

"He wasn't supposed to!"

"Somebody has changed your suppositions." Francisco's eyes were taking a lightning inventory of the place. A second guard stood on the landing at the turn of the stairs, looking down at them and listening.

"What's your business?"

"Copper-mining."

"Huh? I mean, who are you?"

"The name's too long to tell you. I'll tell it to your chief. Where is he?"

"*I'm* asking the questions!" But he backed a step away. "Don't . . . don't you act like a big shot or I'll—"

"Hey, Pete, he *is!*" cried the second guard, paralyzed by Francisco's manner.

The first one was struggling to ignore it; his voice grew louder with the growth of his fear, as he snapped at Francisco, "What are you after?"

"I said I'll tell it to your chief. Where is he?"

"I'm asking the questions!"

"I'm not answering them."

"Oh, you're not, are you?" snarled Pete, who had but one recourse when in doubt: his hand jerked to the gun on his hip.

Francisco's hand was too fast for the two men to see its motion, and his gun was too silent. What they saw and heard next was the gun flying out of Pete's hand, along with a splatter of blood from his shattered fingers, and his muffled howl of pain. He collapsed, groaning. In the instant when the second guard grasped it, he saw that Francisco's gun was aimed at him.

"Don't shoot, mister!" he cried.

"Come down here with your hands up," ordered Francisco, holding his gun aimed with one hand and waving a signal to the crack of the door with the other.

By the time the guard descended the stairs, Rearden was there to disarm him, and Danneskjöld to tie his hands and feet. The sight of Dagny seemed to frighten him more than the rest; he could not understand it: the three men wore caps and windbreakers, and, but for their manner, could be taken for a gang of highwaymen; the presence of a lady was inexplicable.

"Now," said Francisco, "where is your chief?"

The guard jerked his head in the direction of the stairs. "Up there."

"How many guards are there in the building?"

"Nine."

"Where are they?"

"One's on the cellar stairs. The others are all up there."

"Where?"

"In the big laboratory. The one with the window."

"All of them?"

"Yes."

"What are these rooms?" He pointed at the doors leading off the hall.

"They're labs, too. They're locked for the night."

"Who's got the key?"

"Him." He jerked his head at Pete.

Rearden and Danneskjöld took the key from Pete's pocket and hurried soundlessly to check the rooms, while Francisco continued, "Are there any other men in the building?"

"No."

"Isn't there a prisoner here?"

"Oh . . . yeah, I guess so. There must be, or they wouldn't've kept us all on duty."

"Is he still here?"

"That, I don't know. They'd never tell us."

"Is Dr. Ferris here?"

"No. He left ten-fifteen minutes ago."

"Now, that laboratory upstairs—does it open right on the stair landing?"

"Yes."

"How many doors are there?"

"Three. It's the one in the middle."

"What are the other rooms?"

"There's the small laboratory on one side and Dr. Ferris' office on the other."

"Are there connecting doors between them?"

"Yes."

Francisco was turning to his companions, when the guard said pleadingly, "Mister, can I ask you a question?"

"Go ahead."

"Who are you?"

He answered in the solemn tone of a drawing-room introduction, "Francisco Domingo Carlos Andres Sebastián d'Anconia."

He left the guard gaping at him and turned to a brief, whispered consultation with his companions.

In a moment, it was Rearden who went up the stairs—swiftly, soundlessly and alone.

Cages containing rats and guinea pigs were stacked against the walls of the laboratory; they had been put there by the guards who were playing poker on the long laboratory table in the center. Six of them were playing; two were standing in opposite corners, watching the entrance door, guns in hand. It was Rearden's face that saved him from being shot on sight when he entered: his face was too well known to them and too unexpected. He saw eight heads staring at him with recognition and with inability to believe what they were recognizing.

He stood at the door, his hands in the pockets of his trousers, with the casual, confident manner of a business executive.

"Who is in charge here?" he asked in the politely abrupt voice of a man who does not waste time.

"You . . . you're not . . ." stammered a lanky, surly individual at the card table.

"I'm Hank Rearden. Are you the chief?"

"Yeah! But where in blazes do *you* come from?"

"From New York."

"What are you doing here?"

"Then, I take it, you have not been notified."

"Should I have . . . I mean, about *what?*" The swift, touchy, resentful suspicion that his superiors had slighted his authority, was obvious in the chief's voice. He was a tall, emaciated man, with jerky movements, a sallow face and the restless, unfocused eyes of a drug addict.

"About my business here."

"You . . . you can't have any business here," he snapped, torn between the fear of a bluff and the fear of having been left out of some important, top-level decision. "Aren't you a traitor and a deserter and a—"

"I see that you're behind the times, my good man."

The seven others in the room were staring at Rearden with an awed, superstitious uncertainty. The two who held guns still held them aimed at him in the impassive manner of automatons. He did not seem to take notice of them.

"What is it *you* say is your business here?" snapped the chief.

"I am here to take charge of the prisoner whom you are to deliver to me."

"If you came from headquarters, you'd know that I'm not supposed to know anything about any prisoner—and that nobody is to touch him!"

"Except me."

The chief leaped to his feet, darted to a telephone and seized the receiver. He had not raised it halfway to his ear when he dropped it abruptly with a gesture that sent a vibration of panic through the room:

he had had time to hear that the telephone was dead and to know that the wires were cut.

His look of accusation, as he whirled to Rearden, broke against the faintly contemptuous reproof of Rearden's voice: "That's no way to guard a building—if *this* is what you allowed to happen. Better let me have the prisoner, before anything happens to him—if you don't want me to report you for negligence, as well as insubordination."

The chief dropped heavily back on his chair, slumped forward across the table and looked up at Rearden with a glance that made his emaciated face resemble the animals that were beginning to stir in the cages.

"*Who* is the prisoner?" he asked.

"My good man," said Rearden, "if your immediate superiors did not see fit to tell you, I certainly will not."

"They didn't see fit to tell me about your coming here, either!" yelled the chief, his voice confessing the helplessness of anger and broadcasting the vibrations of impotence to his men. "How do I know you're on the level? With the phone out of order, who's going to tell me? How am I to know what to do?"

"That's *your* problem, not mine."

"I don't believe you!" His cry was too shrill to project conviction. "I don't believe that the government would send you on a mission, when you're one of those vanishing traitors and friends of John Galt who—"

"But haven't you heard?"

"What?"

"John Galt has made a deal with the government and has brought us all back."

"Oh, thank God!" cried one of the guards, the youngest.

"Shut your mouth! You're not to have any political opinions!" snapped the chief, and jerked back to Rearden. "Why hasn't it been announced on the radio?"

"Do *you* presume to hold opinions on when and how the government should choose to announce its policies?"

In the long moment of silence, they could hear the rustle of the animals clawing at the bars of their cages.

"I think I should remind you," said Rearden, "that your job is not to question orders, but to obey them, that you are not to *know* or understand the policies of your superiors, that you are not to judge, to choose or to doubt."

"But I don't know whether I'm supposed to obey *you!*"

"If you refuse, you'll take the consequences."

Crouching against the table, the chief moved his glance slowly, appraisingly, from Rearden's face to the two gunmen in the corners. The gunmen steadied their aim by an almost imperceptible movement. A nervous rustle went through the room. An animal squeaked shrilly in one of the cages.

"I think I should also tell you," said Rearden, his voice faintly harder, "that I am not alone. My friends are waiting outside."

"Where?"

"All around this room."

"How many?"

"You'll find out—one way or the other."

"Say, Chief," moaned a shaky voice from among the guards, "we don't want to tangle with *those* people, they're—"

"Shut up!" roared the chief, leaping to his feet and brandishing his gun in the direction of the speaker. "You're not going to turn yellow on me, any of you bastards!" He was screaming to ward off the knowledge that they had. He was swaying on the edge of panic, fighting against the realization that something somehow had disarmed his men. "There's nothing to be scared of!" He was screaming it to himself, struggling to recapture the safety of his only sphere: the sphere of violence. "Nothing and nobody! I'll show you!" He whirled around, his hand shaking at the end of his sweeping arm, and fired at Rearden.

Some of them saw Rearden sway, his right hand gripping his left shoulder. Others, in the same instant, saw the gun drop out of the chief's hand and hit the floor in time with his scream and with the spurt of blood from his wrist. Then all of them saw Francisco d'Anconia standing at the door on the left, his soundless gun still aimed at the chief.

All of them were on their feet and had drawn their guns, but they lost that first moment, not daring to fire.

"I wouldn't, if I were you," said Francisco.

"Jesus!" gasped one of the guards, struggling for the memory of a name he could not recapture. "That's . . . that's the guy who blew up all the copper mines in the world!"

"It is," said Rearden.

They had been backing involuntarily away from Francisco—and turned to see that Rearden still stood at the entrance door, with a pointed gun in his right hand and a dark stain spreading on his left shoulder.

"Shoot, you bastards!" screamed the chief to the wavering men. "What are you waiting for? Shoot them down!" He was leaning with one arm against the table, blood running out of the other. "I'll report any man who doesn't fight! I'll have him sentenced to death for it!"

"Drop your guns," said Rearden.

The seven guards stood frozen for an instant, obeying neither.

"Let me out of here!" screamed the youngest, dashing for the door on the right.

He threw the door open and sprang back: Dagny Taggart stood on the threshold, gun in hand.

The guards were drawing slowly to the center of the room, fighting an invisible battle in the fog of their minds, disarmed by a sense of unreality in the presence of the legendary figures they had never expected to see, feeling almost as if they were ordered to fire at ghosts.

"Drop your guns," said Rearden. "You don't know why you're here. We do. You don't know who your prisoner is. We do. You don't know why your bosses want you to guard him. We know why we want to get him out. You don't know the purpose of your fight. We know the purpose of ours. If you die, you won't know what you're dying for. If we do, we will."

"Don't . . . don't listen to him!" snarled the chief. "Shoot! I order you to shoot!"

One of the guards looked at the chief, dropped his gun and, raising his arms, backed away from the group toward Rearden.

"God damn you!" yelled the chief, seized a gun with his left hand and fired at the deserter.

In time with the fall of the man's body, the window burst into a shower of glass—and from the limb of a tree, as from a catapult, the tall, slender figure of a man flew into the room, landed on its feet and fired at the first guard in reach.

"Who are *you?*" screamed some terror-blinded voice.

"Ragnar Danneskjöld."

Three sounds answered him: a long, swelling moan of panic—the clatter of four guns dropped to the floor—and the bark of the fifth, fired by a guard at the forehead of the chief.

By the time the four survivors of the garrison began to reassemble the pieces of their consciousness, their figures were stretched on the floor, bound and gagged; the fifth one was left standing, his hands tied behind his back.

"Where is the prisoner?" Francisco asked him.

"In the cellar . . . I guess."

"Who has the key?"

"Dr. Ferris."

"Where are the stairs to the cellar?"

"Behind a door in Dr. Ferris' office."

"Lead the way."

As they started, Francisco turned to Rearden. "Are you all right, Hank?"

"Sure."

"Need to rest?"

"Hell, no!"

From the threshold of a door in Ferris' office, they looked down a steep flight of stone stairs and saw a guard on the landing below.

"Come here with your hands up!" ordered Francisco.

The guard saw the silhouette of a resolute stranger and the glint of a gun: it was enough. He obeyed immediately; he seemed relieved to escape from the damp stone crypt. He was left tied on the floor of the office, along with the guard who had led them.

Then the four rescuers were free to fly down the stairs to the locked steel door at the bottom. They had acted and moved with the precision of a controlled discipline. Now, it was as if their inner reins had broken.

Danneskjöld had the tools to smash the lock. Francisco was first to enter the cellar, and his arm barred Dagny's way for the fraction of a second—for the length of a look to make certain that the sight was bearable—then he let her rush past him: beyond the tangle of electric wires, he had seen Galt's lifted head and glance of greeting.

She fell down on her knees by the side of the mattress. Galt looked up at her, as he had looked on their first morning in the valley, his smile was like the sound of a laughter that had never been touched by pain, his voice was soft and low:

"We never had to take any of it seriously, did we?"

Tears running down her face, but her smile declaring a full, confident, radiant certainty, she answered, "No, we never had to."

Rearden and Danneskjöld were cutting his bonds. Francisco held a flask of brandy to Galt's lips. Galt drank, and raised himself to lean on an elbow when his arms were free. "Give me a cigarette," he said.

Francisco produced a package of dollar-sign cigarettes. Galt's hand shook a little, as he held a cigarette to the flame of a lighter, but Francisco's hand shook much more.

Glancing at his eyes over the flame, Galt smiled and said in the tone of an answer to the questions Francisco was not asking, "Yes, it was pretty bad, but bearable—and the kind of voltage they used leaves no damage."

"I'll find them some day, whoever they were . . ." said Francisco; the tone of his voice, flat, dead and barely audible, said the rest.

"If you do, you'll find that there's nothing left of them to kill."

Galt glanced at the faces around him; he saw the intensity of the relief in their eyes and the violence of the anger in the grimness of their features; he knew in what manner they were now reliving his torture.

"It's over," he said. "Don't make it worse for yourself than it was for me."

Francisco turned his face away. "It's only that it was you . . ." he whispered, *"you* . . . if it were anyone but you . . ."

"But it had to be me, if they were to try their last, and they've tried, and"—he moved his hand, sweeping the room—and the meaning of those who had made it—into the wastelands of the past—"and that's that."

Francisco nodded, his face still turned away; the violent grip of his fingers clutching Galt's wrist for a moment was his answer.

Galt lifted himself to a sitting posture, slowly regaining control of his muscles. He glanced up at Dagny's face, as her arm shot forward to help him; he saw the struggle of her smile against the tension of her resisted tears; it was the struggle of her knowledge that nothing could matter beside the sight of his naked body and that this body was living —against her knowledge of what it had endured. Holding her glance, he raised his hand and touched the collar of her white sweater with his fingertips, in acknowledgment and in reminder of the only things that were to matter from now on. The faint tremor of her lips, relaxing into a smile, told him that she understood.

Danneskjöld found Galt's shirt, slacks and the rest of his clothing, which had been thrown on the floor in a corner of the room. "Do you think you can walk, John?" he asked.

"Sure."

While Francisco and Rearden were helping Galt to dress, Danneskjöld proceeded calmly, systematically, with no visible emotion, to demolish the torture machine into splinters.

Galt was not fully steady on his feet, but he could stand, leaning on Francisco's shoulder. The first few steps were hard, but by the time they reached the door, he was able to resume the motions of walking. His one arm encircled Francisco's shoulders for support; his other arm held Dagny's shoulders, both to gain support and to give it.

They did not speak as they walked down the hill, with the darkness of the trees closing in about them for protection, cutting off the dead glow of the moon and the deader glow in the distance behind them, in the windows of the State Science Institute.

Francisco's airplane was hidden in the brush, on the edge of a meadow beyond the next hill. There were no human habitations for miles around them. There were no eyes to notice or to question the sudden streaks of the airplane's headlights shooting across the desolation of dead weeds, and the violent burst of the motor brought to life by Danneskjöld, who took the wheel.

With the sound of the door slamming shut behind them and the forward thrust of the wheels under their feet, Francisco smiled for the first time.

"This is my one and only chance to give you orders," he said, helping Galt to stretch out in a reclining chair. "Now lie still, relax and take it easy . . . You, too," he added, turning to Dagny and pointing at the seat by Galt's side.

The wheels were running faster, as if gaining speed and purpose and lightness, ignoring the impotent obstacles of small jolts from the ruts of the ground. When the motion turned to a long, smooth streak, when they saw the dark shapes of the trees sweeping down and dropping past their windows, Galt leaned silently over and pressed his lips to Dagny's hand: he was leaving the outer world with the one value he had wanted to win from it.

Francisco had produced a first-aid kit and was removing Rearden's shirt to bandage his wound. Galt saw the thin red trickle running from Rearden's shoulder down his chest.

"Thank you, Hank," he said.

Rearden smiled. "I will repeat what you said when I thanked you, on our first meeting: 'If you understand that I acted for my own sake, you know that no gratitude is required.' "

"I will repeat," said Galt, "the answer you gave me: '*That* is why I thank you.' "

Dagny noticed that they looked at each other as if their glance were the handshake of a bond too firm to require any statement. Rearden saw her watching them—and the faintest contraction of his eyes was like a smile of sanction, as if his glance were repeating to her the message he had sent her from the valley.

They heard the sudden sound of Danneskjöld's voice raised cheerfully in conversation with empty space, and they realized that he was speaking over the plane's radio: "Yes, safe and sound, all of us. . . . Yes, he's unhurt, just shaken a little, and resting. . . . No, no permanent injury. . . . Yes, we're all here. Hank Rearden got a flesh wound, but"—he glanced over his shoulder—"but he's grinning at me right now. . . . Losses? I think we lost our temper for a few minutes back there, but we're recovering. . . . Don't try to beat me to Galt's Gulch, I'll land first—and I'll help Kay in the restaurant to fix your breakfast."

"Can any outsiders hear him?" asked Dagny.

"No," said Francisco. "It's a frequency they're not equipped to get."

"Whom is he talking to?" asked Galt.

"To about half the male population of the valley," said Francisco, "or as many as we had space for on every plane available. They are flying behind us right now. Did you think any of them would stay home and leave you in the hands of the looters? We were prepared to get you by open, armed assault on that Institute or on the Wayne-Falkland, if necessary. But we knew that in such case we would run the risk of their killing you when they saw that they were beaten. That's why we decided that the four of us would first try it alone. Had we failed, the others would have proceeded with an open attack. They were waiting, half a mile away. We had men posted among the trees on the hill, who saw us get out and relayed the word to the others. Ellis Wyatt was in charge. Incidentally, he's flying your plane. The reason we couldn't get to New Hampshire as fast as Dr. Ferris, is that we had to get our planes from distant, hidden landing places, while he had the advantage of open airports. Which, incidentally, he won't have much longer."

"No," said Galt, "not much longer."

"That was our only obstacle. The rest was easy. I'll tell you the whole story later. Anyway, the four of us were all that was necessary to beat their garrison."

"One of these centuries," said Danneskjöld, turning to them for a moment, "the brutes, private or public, who believe that they can rule their betters by force, will learn the lesson of what happens when brute force encounters mind and force."

"They've learned it," said Galt. "Isn't that the particular lesson you have been teaching them for twelve years?"

"I? Yes. But the semester is over. Tonight was the last act of violence that I'll ever have to perform. It was my reward for the twelve years. My men have now started to build their homes in the valley. My ship is hidden where no one will find her, until I'm able to sell her for a much more civilized use. She'll be converted into a transatlantic passenger liner—an excellent one, even if of modest size. As for me, I will start getting ready to give a different course of lessons. I think I'll have to brush up on the works of our teacher's first teacher."

Rearden chuckled. "I'd like to be present at your first lecture on philosophy in a university classroom," he said. "I'd like to see how your students will be able to keep their mind on the subject and how you'll answer the sort of irrelevant questions I won't blame them for wanting to ask you."

"I will tell them that they'll find the answers in the subject."

There were not many lights on the earth below. The countryside was an empty black sheet, with a few occasional flickers in the windows of some government structures, and the trembling glow of candles in the windows of thriftless homes. Most of the rural population had long since been reduced to the life of those ages when artificial light was an exorbitant luxury, and a sunset put an end to human activity. The towns were like scattered puddles, left behind by a receding tide, still holding some precious drops of electricity, but drying out in a desert of rations, quotas, controls and power-conservation rules.

But when the place that had once been the source of the tide—New York City—rose in the distance before them, it was still extending its lights to the sky, still defying the primordial darkness, almost as if, in an ultimate effort, in a final appeal for help, it were now stretching its arms to the plane that was crossing its sky. Involuntarily, they sat up, as if at respectful attention at the deathbed of what had been greatness.

Looking down, they could see the last convulsions: the lights of the cars were darting through the streets, like animals trapped in a maze, frantically seeking an exit, the bridges were jammed with cars, the approaches to the bridges were veins of massed headlights, glittering bottlenecks stopping all motion, and the desperate screaming of sirens reached faintly to the height of the plane. The news of the continent's severed artery had now engulfed the city, men were deserting their posts, trying, in panic, to abandon New York, seeking escape where all roads were cut off and escape was no longer possible.

The plane was above the peaks of the skyscrapers when suddenly, with the abruptness of a shudder, as if the ground had parted to engulf it, the city disappeared from the face of the earth. It took them a moment to realize that the panic had reached the power stations—and that the lights of New York had gone out.

Dagny gasped. "Don't look down!" Galt ordered sharply.

She raised her eyes to his face. His face had that look of austerity with which she had always seen him meet facts.

She remembered the story Francisco had told her: "He had quit the Twentieth Century. He was living in a garret in a slum neighborhood. He stepped to the window and pointed at the skyscrapers of the city. He said that we had to extinguish the lights of the world, and when we would see the lights of New York go out, we would know that our job was done."

She thought of it when she saw the three of them—John Galt, Francisco d'Anconia, Ragnar Danneskjöld—look silently at one another for a moment.

She glanced at Rearden; he was not looking down, he was looking ahead, as she had seen him look at an untouched countryside: with a glance appraising the possibilities of action.

When she looked at the darkness ahead, another memory rose in her mind—the moment when, circling above the Afton airport, she had seen the silver body of a plane rise like a phoenix from the darkness of the earth. She knew that now, at this hour, their plane was carrying all that was left of New York City.

She looked ahead. The earth would be as empty as the space where their propeller was cutting an unobstructed path—as empty and as free. She knew what Nat Taggart had felt at his start and why now, for the first time, she was following him in full loyalty: the confident sense of facing a void and of knowing that one has a continent to build.

She felt the whole struggle of her past rising before her and dropping away, leaving her here, on the height of this moment. She smiled—and the words in her mind, appraising and sealing the past, were the words of courage, pride and dedication, which most men had never understood, the words of a businessman's language: "Price no object."

She did not gasp and she felt no tremor when, in the darkness below, she saw a small string of lighted dots struggling slowly westward through the void, with the long, bright dash of a headlight groping to protect the safety of its way; she felt nothing, even though it was a train and she knew that it had no destination but the void.

She turned to Galt. He was watching her face, as if he had been following her thoughts. She saw the reflection of her smile in his. "It's the end," she said. "It's the beginning," he answered.

Then they lay still, leaning back in their chairs, silently looking at each other. Then their persons filled each other's awareness, as the sum and meaning of the future—but the sum included the knowledge of all that had had to be earned, before the person of another being could come to embody the value of one's existence.

New York was far behind them, when they heard Danneskjöld answer a call from the radio: "Yes, he's awake. I don't think he'll sleep tonight. . . . Yes, I think he can." He turned to glance over his shoulder. "John, Dr. Akston would like to speak to you."

"What? Is *he* on one of those planes behind us?"

"Certainly."

Galt leaped forward to seize the microphone. "Hello, Dr. Akston," he said; the quiet, low tone of his voice was the audible image of a smile transmitted through space.

"Hello, John." The too-conscious steadiness of Hugh Akston's voice confessed at what cost he had waited to learn whether he would ever pronounce these two words again. "I just wanted to hear your voice . . . just to know that you're all right."

Galt chuckled and—in the tone of a student proudly presenting a completed task of homework as proof of a lesson well learned—he answered, "Of course I am all right, Professor. I had to be. A is A."

* * *

The locomotive of the eastbound Comet broke down in the middle of a desert in Arizona. It stopped abruptly, for no visible reason, like a man who had not permitted himself to know that he was bearing too much: some overstrained connection snapped for good.

When Eddie Willers called for the conductor, he waited a long time before the man came in, and he sensed the answer to his question by the look of resignation on the man's face.

"The engineer is trying to find out what's wrong, Mr. Willers," he answered softly, in a tone implying that it was his duty to hope, but that he had held no hope for years.

"He doesn't know?"

"He's working on it." The conductor waited for a polite half-minute and turned to go, but stopped to volunteer an explanation, as if some dim, rational habit told him that any attempt to explain made any unadmitted terror easier to bear. "Those Diesels of ours aren't fit to be sent out on the road, Mr. Willers. They weren't worth repairing long ago."

"I know," said Eddie Willers quietly.

The conductor sensed that his explanation was worse than none: it led to questions that men did not ask these days. He shook his head and went out.

Eddie Willers sat looking at the empty darkness beyond the window. This was the first eastbound Comet out of San Francisco in many days: she was the child of his tortured effort to re-establish transcontinental service. He could not tell what the past few days had cost him or what he had done to save the San Francisco terminal from the blind chaos of a civil war that men were fighting with no concept of their goals; there was no way to remember the deals he had made on the basis of the range of every shifting moment. He knew only that he had obtained immunity for the terminal from the leaders of three different warring factions; that he had found a man for the post of terminal manager who did not seem to have given up altogether; that he had started one more Taggart Comet on her eastward run, with the best Diesel engine and the best crew available; and that he had boarded her for his return journey to New York, with no knowledge of how long his achievement would last.

He had never had to work so hard; he had done his job as conscientiously well as he had always done any assignment; but it was as if he had worked in a vacuum, as if his energy had found no transmitters and had run into the sands of . . . of some such desert as the one beyond the window of the Comet. He shuddered: he felt a moment's kinship with the stalled engine of the train.

After a while, he summoned the conductor once more. "How is it going?" he asked.

The conductor shrugged and shook his head.

"Send the fireman to a track phone. Have him tell the Division Headquarters to send us the best mechanic available."

"Yes, sir."

There was nothing to see beyond the window; turning off the light, Eddie Willers could distinguish a gray spread dotted by the black spots of cacti, with no start to it and no end. He wondered how men had ever ventured to cross it, and at what price, in the days when there were no trains. He jerked his head away and snapped on the light.

It was only the fact that the Comet was in exile, he thought, that gave him this sense of pressing anxiety. She was stalled on an alien rail—on the borrowed track of the Atlantic Southern that ran through Arizona, the track they were using without payment. He had to get her out of here, he thought; he would not feel like this once they returned to their own rail. But the junction suddenly seemed an insurmountable distance away: on the shore of the Mississippi, at the Taggart Bridge.

No, he thought, that was not all. He had to admit to himself what images were nagging him with a sense of uneasiness he could neither grasp nor dispel; they were too meaningless to define and too inexplicable to dismiss. One was the image of a way station they had passed without stopping, more than two hours ago: he had noticed the empty platform and the brightly lighted windows of the small station building; the lights came from empty rooms; he had seen no single human figure, neither in the building nor on the tracks outside. The other image was of the next way station they had passed: its platform was jammed with an agitated mob. Now they were far beyond the reach of the light or sound of any station.

He had to get the Comet out of here, he thought. He wondered why he felt it with such urgency and why it had seemed so crucially important to re-establish the Comet's run. A mere handful of passengers was rattling in her empty cars; men had no place to go and no goals to reach. It was not for their sake that he had struggled; he could not say for whose. Two phrases stood as the answer in his mind, driving him with the vagueness of a prayer and the scalding force of an absolute.

One was: From Ocean to Ocean, forever—the other was: Don't let it go! . . .

The conductor returned an hour later, with the fireman, whose face looked oddly grim.

"Mr. Willers," said the fireman slowly, "Division Headquarters does not answer."

Eddie Willers sat up, his mind refusing to believe it, yet knowing suddenly that for some inexplicable reason *this* was what he had expected. "It's impossible!" he said, his voice low; the fireman was looking at him, not moving. "The track phone must have been out of order."

"No, Mr. Willers. It was not out of order. The line was alive all right. The Division Headquarters wasn't. I mean, there was no one there to answer, or else no one who cared to."

"But you know that that's impossible!"

The fireman shrugged; men did not consider any disaster impossible these days.

Eddie Willers leaped to his feet. "Go down the length of the train," he ordered the conductor. "Knock on all the doors—the occupied ones, that is—and see whether there's an electrical engineer aboard."

"Yes, sir."

Eddie knew that they felt, as he felt it, that they would find no such man; not among the lethargic, extinguished faces of the passengers they had seen. "Come on," he ordered, turning to the fireman.

They climbed together aboard the locomotive. The gray-haired engineer was sitting in his chair, staring out at the cacti. The engine's headlight had stayed on and it stretched out into the night, motionless and straight, reaching nothing but the dissolving blur of crossties.

"Let's try to find what's wrong," said Eddie, removing his coat, his voice half-order, half-plea. "Let's try some more."

"Yes, sir," said the engineer, without resentment or hope.

The engineer had exhausted his meager store of knowledge; he had checked every source of trouble he could think of. He went crawling over and under the machinery, unscrewing its parts and screwing them back again, taking out pieces and replacing them, dismembering the motors at random, like a child taking a clock apart, but without the child's conviction that knowledge is possible.

The fireman kept leaning out of the cab's window, glancing at the black stillness and shivering, as if from the night air that was growing colder.

"Don't worry," said Eddie Willers, assuming a tone of confidence. "We've got to do our best, but if we fail, they'll send us help sooner or later. They don't abandon trains in the middle of nowhere."

"They didn't used to," said the fireman.

Once in a while, the engineer raised his grease-smeared face to look at the grease-smeared face and shirt of Eddie Willers. "What's the use, Mr. Willers?" he asked.

"We can't let it go!" Eddie answered fiercely; he knew dimly that what he meant was more than the Comet . . . and more than the railroad.

Moving from the cab through the three motor units and back to the cab again, his hands bleeding, his shirt sticking to his back, Eddie Willers was struggling to remember everything he had ever known about engines, anything he had learned in college, and earlier: anything he had picked up in those days when the station agents at Rockdale Station used to chase him off the rungs of their lumbering switch engines. The pieces connected to nothing; his brain seemed jammed and tight; he knew that motors were not his profession, he knew that he did not know and that it was now a matter of life or death for him to discover the knowledge. He was looking at the cylinders, the blades, the wires, the control panels still winking with lights. He was struggling not to allow into his mind the thought that was pressing against its periphery: What were the chances and how long would it take—according to the mathematical theory of probability—for primitive men, working by rule-of-thumb, to hit the right combination of parts and re-create the motor of this engine?

"What's the use, Mr. Willers?" moaned the engineer.

"We can't let it go!" he cried.

He did not know how many hours had passed when he heard the fireman shout suddenly, "Mr. Willers! Look!"

The fireman was leaning out the window, pointing into the darkness behind them.

Eddie Willers looked. An odd little light was swinging jerkily far in the distance; it seemed to be advancing at an imperceptible rate; it did not look like any sort of light he could identify.

After a while, it seemed to him that he distinguished some large black shapes advancing slowly; they were moving in a line parallel with the track; the spot of light hung low over the ground, swinging; he strained his ears, but heard nothing.

Then he caught a feeble, muffled beat that sounded like the hoofs of horses. The two men beside him were watching the black shapes with a look of growing terror, as if some supernatural apparition were advancing upon them out of the desert night. In the moment when they chuckled suddenly, joyously, recognizing the shapes, it was Eddie's face that froze into a look of terror at the sight of a ghost more frightening than any they could have expected: it was a train of covered wagons.

The swinging lantern jerked to a stop by the side of the engine. "Hey, bud, can I give you a lift?" called a man who seemed to be the leader; he was chuckling. "Stuck, aren't you?"

The passengers of the Comet were peering out of the windows; some were descending the steps and approaching. Women's faces peeked from the wagons, from among the piles of household goods; a baby wailed somewhere at the rear of the caravan.

"Are you crazy?" asked Eddie Willers.

"No, I mean it, brother. We got plenty of room. We'll give you folks a lift—for a price—if you want to get out of here." He was a lanky, nervous man, with loose gestures and an insolent voice, who looked like a side-show barker.

"This is the Taggart Comet," said Eddie Willers, choking.

"The Comet, eh? Looks more like a dead caterpillar to me. What's the matter, brother? You're not going anywhere—and you can't get there any more, even if you tried."

"What do you mean?"

"You don't think you're going to New York, do you?"

"We *are* going to New York."

"Then . . . then you haven't heard?"

"What?"

"Say, when was the last time you spoke to any of your stations?"

"I don't know! . . . Heard *what?"*

"That your Taggart Bridge is gone. Gone. Blasted to bits. Sound-ray explosion or something. Nobody knows exactly. Only there ain't any bridge any more to cross the Mississippi. There ain't any New York any more—leastways, not for folks like you and me to reach."

Eddie Willers did not know what happened next; he had fallen back against the side of the engineer's chair, staring at the open door of the motor unit; he did not know how long he stayed there, but when, at last, he turned his head, he saw that he was alone. The engineer and the fireman had left the cab. There was a scramble of voices outside, screams, sobs, shouted questions and the sound of the side-show barker's laughter.

Eddie pulled himself to the window of the cab: the Comet's passengers and crew were crowding around the leader of the caravan and his semi-ragged companions; he was waving his loose arms in gestures of command. Some of the better-dressed ladies from the Comet—whose husbands had apparently been first to make a deal—were climbing aboard the covered wagons, sobbing and clutching their delicate make-up cases.

"Step right up, folks, step right up!" the barker was yelling cheerfully. "We'll make room for everybody! A bit crowded, but moving—better than being left here for coyote fodder! The day of the iron horse is past! All we got is plain, old-fashioned horse! Slow, but sure!"

Eddie Willers climbed halfway down the ladder on the side of the engine, to see the crowd and to be heard. He waved one arm, hanging onto the rungs with the other. "You're not going, are you?" he cried to his passengers. "You're not abandoning the Comet?"

They drew a little away from him, as if they did not want to look at him or answer. They did not want to hear questions their minds were incapable of weighing. He saw the blind faces of panic.

"What's the matter with the grease-monkey?" asked the barker, pointing at Eddie.

"Mr. Willers," said the conductor softly, "it's no use . . ."

"Don't abandon the Comet!" cried Eddie Willers. "Don't let it go! Oh God, don't let it go!"

"Are *you* crazy?" cried the barker. "You've no idea what's going on at your railroad stations and headquarters! They're running around like a pack of chickens with their heads cut off! I don't think there's going to be a railroad left in business this side of the Mississippi, by tomorrow morning!"

"Better come along, Mr. Willers," said the conductor.

"No!" cried Eddie, clutching the metal rung as if he wanted his hand to grow fast to it.

The barker shrugged. "Well, it's *your* funeral!"

"Which way are you going?" asked the engineer, not looking at Eddie.

"Just going, brother! Just looking for some place to stop . . . somewhere. We're from Imperial Valley, California. The 'People's Party' crowd grabbed the crops and any food we had in the cellars. Hoarding, they called it. So we just picked up and went. Got to travel by night, on account of the Washington crowd. . . . We're just looking for some place to live. . . . You're welcome to come along, buddy, if you've got no home—or else we can drop you off closer to some town or another."

The men of that caravan—thought Eddie indifferently—looked too mean-minded to become the founders of a secret, free settlement, and not mean-minded enough to become a gang of raiders; they had no more destination to find than the motionless beam of the headlight; and, like that beam, they would dissolve somewhere in the empty stretches of the country.

He stayed on the ladder, looking up at the beam. He did not watch while the last men ever to ride the Taggart Comet were transferred to the covered wagons.

The conductor went last. "Mr. Willers!" he called desperately. "Come along!"

"No," said Eddie.

The side-show barker waved his arm in an upward sweep at Eddie's figure on the side of the engine above their heads. "I hope you know what you're doing!" he cried, his voice half-threat, half-plea. "Maybe somebody will come this way to pick you up—next week or next month! Maybe! Who's going to, these days?"

"Get away from here," said Eddie Willers.

He climbed back into the cab—when the wagons jerked forward and went swaying and creaking off into the night. He sat in the engineer's chair of a motionless engine, his forehead pressed to the useless throttle.

He felt like the captain of an ocean liner in distress, who preferred to go down with his ship rather than be saved by the canoe of savages taunting him with the superiority of their craft.

Then, suddenly, he felt the blinding surge of a desperate, righteous anger. He leaped to his feet, seizing the throttle. He had to start this train; in the name of some victory that he could not name, he had to start the engine moving.

Past the stage of thinking, calculation or fear, moved by some righteous defiance, he was pulling levers at random, he was jerking the throttle back and forth, he was stepping on the dead man's pedal, which was dead, he was groping to distinguish the form of some vision that seemed both distant and close, knowing only that his desperate battle was fed by that vision and was fought for its sake.

Don't let it go! his mind was crying—while he was seeing the streets of New York—Don't let it go!—while he was seeing the lights of railroad signals—Don't let it go!—while he was seeing the smoke rising proudly from factory chimneys, while he was struggling to cut through the smoke and reach the vision at the root of these visions.

He was pulling at coils of wire, he was linking them and tearing them apart—while the sudden sense of sunrays and pine trees kept pulling at the corners of his mind. Dagny!—he heard himself crying soundlessly— Dagny, in the name of the best within us! . . . He was jerking at futile levers and at a throttle that had nothing to move. . . . Dagny!—he was crying to a twelve-year-old girl in a sunlit clearing of the woods— in the name of the best within us, I must now start this train! . . . Dagny, *that* is what it was . . . and you knew it, then, but I didn't . . . you knew it when you turned to look at the rails. . . . I said, "not business or earning a living" . . . but, Dagny, business and earning a living and that in man which makes it possible—*that* is the best within us, *that* was the thing to defend . . . in the name of saving it, Dagny, I must now start this train. . . .

When he found that he had collapsed on the floor of the cab and knew that there was nothing he could do here any longer, he rose and he climbed down the ladder, thinking dimly of the engine's wheels, even though he knew that the engineer had checked them. He felt the crunch of the desert dust under his feet when he let himself drop to the ground. He stood still and, in the enormous silence, he heard the rustle of tumbleweeds stirring in the darkness, like the chuckle of an invisible army made free to move when the Comet was not. He heard a sharper rustle close by—and he saw the small gray shape of a rabbit rise on its *haunches to sniff at the steps of a car of the Taggart Comet. With a jolt* of murderous fury, he lunged in the direction of the rabbit, as if he could defeat the advance of the enemy in the person of that tiny gray form. The rabbit darted off into the darkness—but he knew that the advance was not to be defeated.

He stepped to the front of the engine and looked up at the letters TT.

Then he collapsed across the rail and lay sobbing at the foot of the engine, with the beam of a motionless headlight above him going off into a limitless night.

* * *

The music of Richard Halley's Fifth Concerto streamed from his keyboard, past the glass of the window, and spread through the air, over the lights of the valley. It was a symphony of triumph. The notes flowed up, they spoke of rising and they were the rising itself, they were the essence and the form of upward motion, they seemed to embody every human act and thought that had ascent as its motive. It was a sunburst of sound, breaking out of hiding and spreading open. It had the freedom of release and the tension of purpose. It swept space clean and left nothing but the joy of an unobstructed effort. Only a faint echo within the sounds spoke of that from which the music had escaped, but spoke in laughing astonishment at the discovery that there was no ugliness or pain, and there never had had to be. It was the song of an immense deliverance.

The lights of the valley fell in glowing patches on the snow still covering the ground. There were shelves of snow on the granite ledges and on the heavy limbs of the pines. But the naked branches of the birch trees had a faintly upward thrust, as if in confident promise of the coming leaves of spring.

The rectangle of light on the side of a mountain was the window of Mulligan's study. Midas Mulligan sat at his desk, with a map and a column of figures before him. He was listing the assets of his bank and working on a plan of projected investments. He was noting down the locations he was choosing: "New York—Cleveland—Chicago . . . New York—Philadelphia . . . New York . . . New York . . . New York . . ."

The rectangle of light at the bottom of the valley was the window of Danneskjöld's home. Kay Ludlow sat before a mirror, thoughtfully studying the shades of film make-up, spread open in a battered case. Ragnar Danneskjöld lay stretched on a couch, reading a volume of the works of Aristotle: ". . . for these truths hold good for everything that is, and not for some special genus apart from others. And all men use them, because they are true of being *qua* being. . . . For a principle which every one must have who understands anything that is, is not a hypothesis. . . . Evidently then such a principle is the most certain of all; which principle this is, let us proceed to say. It is, that the same attribute cannot at the same time belong and not belong to the same subject in the same respect. . . ."

The rectangle of light in the acres of a farm was the window of the library of Judge Narragansett. He sat at a table, and the light of his lamp fell on the copy of an ancient document. He had marked and crossed out the contradictions in its statements that had once been the cause of its destruction. He was now adding a new clause to its pages: "Congress shall make no law abridging the freedom of production and trade . . ."

The rectangle of light in the midst of a forest was the window of the cabin of Francisco d'Anconia. Francisco lay stretched on the floor, by the dancing tongues of a fire, bent over sheets of paper, completing the drawing of his smelter. Hank Rearden and Ellis Wyatt sat by the fireplace. "John will design the new locomotives," Rearden was saying, "and Dagny will run the first railroad between New York and Philadelphia. She——" And, suddenly, on hearing the next sentence, Francisco threw his head up and burst out laughing, a laughter of greeting, triumph and release. They could not hear the music of Halley's Fifth Concerto now flowing somewhere high above the roof, but Francisco's laughter matched its sounds. Contained in the sentence he had heard, Francisco was seeing the sunlight of spring on the open lawns of homes across the country, he was seeing the sparkle of motors, he was seeing the glow of the steel in the rising frames of new skyscrapers, he was seeing the eyes of youth looking at the future with no uncertainty or fear.

The sentence Rearden had uttered was: "She will probably try to take the shirt off my back with the freight rates she's going to charge, but—I'll be able to meet them."

The faint glitter of light weaving slowly through space, on the highest accessible ledge of a mountain, was the starlight on the strands of Galt's hair. He stood looking, not at the valley below, but at the darkness of the world beyond its walls. Dagny's hand rested on his shoulder, and the wind blew her hair to blend with his. She knew why he had wanted to walk through the mountains tonight and what he had stopped to consider. She knew what words were his to speak and that she would be first to hear them.

They could not see the world beyond the mountains, there was only a void of darkness and rock, but the darkness was hiding the ruins of a continent: the roofless homes, the rusting tractors, the lightless streets, the abandoned rail. But far in the distance, on the edge of the earth, a small flame was waving in the wind, the defiantly stubborn flame of Wyatt's Torch, twisting, being torn and regaining its hold, not to be uprooted or extinguished. It seemed to be calling and waiting for the words John Galt was now to pronounce.

"The road is cleared," said Galt. "We are going back to the world."

He raised his hand and over the desolate earth he traced in space the sign of the dollar.

THE END

ABOUT THE AUTHOR

"My personal life," says Ayn Rand, "is a postscript to my novels; it consists of the sentence: '*And I mean it.*' I have always lived by the philosophy I present in my books—and it has worked for me, as it works for my characters. The concretes differ, the abstractions are the same.

"I decided to be a writer at the age of nine, and everything I have done was integrated to that purpose. I am an American by choice and conviction. I was born in Europe, but I came to America because this was the country based on my moral premises and the only country where one could be fully free to write. I came here alone, after graduating from a European college. I had a difficult struggle, earning my living at odd jobs, until I could make a financial success of my writing. No one helped me, nor did I think at any time that it was anyone's duty to help me.

"In college, I had taken history as my major subject, and philosophy as my special interest; the first—in order to have a factual knowledge of men's past, for my future writing; the second—in order to achieve an objective definition of my values. I found that the first could be learned, but the second had to be done by me.

"I have held the same philosophy I now hold, for as far back as I can remember. I have learned a great deal through the years and expanded my knowledge of details, of specific issues, of definitions, of applications—and I intend to continue expanding it—but I have never had to change any of my fundamentals. My philosophy, in essence, is the concept of man as a heroic being, with his own happiness as the moral purpose of his life. with productive achievement as his noblest activity, and reason as his only absolute.

"The only philosophical debt I can acknowledge is to Aristotle. I most emphatically disagree with a great many parts of his philosophy—but his definition of the laws of logic and of the means of human knowledge is so great an achievement that his errors are irrelevant by comparison. You will find my tribute to him in the titles of the three parts of ATLAS SHRUGGED.

"My other acknowledgment is on the dedication page of this novel. I knew what values of character I wanted to find in a man. I met such a man—and we have been married for twenty-eight years. His name is Frank O'Connor.

"To all the readers who discovered *The Fountainhead* and asked me many questions about the wider application of its ideas, I want to say that I am answering these questions in the present novel and that *The Fountainhead* was only an overture to ATLAS SHRUGGED.

"I trust that no one will tell me that men such as I write about don't exist. That this book has been written—and published—is my proof that they do."

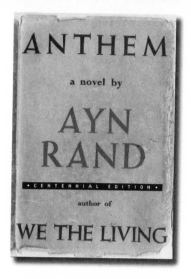